a perfect
moment

Mary Hosty

POOLBEG

This novel is entirely a work of fiction. The names, characters and incidents portrayed in it are the work of the author's imagination. Any resemblance to actual persons, living or dead, events or localities is entirely coincidental.

Published 2005
by Poolbeg Press Ltd
123 Grange Hill, Baldoyle
Dublin 13, Ireland
E-mail: poolbeg@poolbeg.com

1 3 5 7 9 10 8 6 4 2

A catalogue record for this book is available from the British Library.

ISBN 1-84223-206-1

Typeset by Patricia Hope in Palatino 9.6/13
Printed by Litografia Rosés, S.A, Spain

About the Author

Mary Hosty has published extensively in newspapers, magazines and in the field of education. She is the author of two best-selling novels *The Men in Her Life* and *Learning to Fly*. She lives in Dublin with her husband and two sons.

Also by Mary Hosty

The Men in Her Life
Learning to Fly

Acknowledgements

I am once again indebted to a whole load of people for ongoing friendship and support. Scribbling yarns is solitary work and when a person emerges from weeks of keyboard bashing, it's a truly great pleasure to be with family, friends and colleagues.

So a very big thank-you to the following:

Friends in Ireland and abroad.

Colleagues and fellow writers.

My extended family and the wonderful in-laws. A special thank-you this year to Maureen Kelleher, Maura Maloy and Denine.

Thanks also once again to the Magnificent Maciarhos Productions – where is that damned screenplay though?

Paula Campbell and all the team at Poolbeg.

Gaye Shortland – my editor who has taught me so much about the process of weaving a seamless story, not to mention the finer points of thong flipping.

Ger Nicholl, agent, for looking after my interests so well.

I'm indebted to the following people who gave freely of their time, knowledge and expertise in helping me to research various aspects of the story:

Audrey Gunne of Gunne Auctioneers and
www.myhome.ie
Karen O'Grady, Sherry Fitzgerald
Solicitors Beverley Turner & Mary Hayes Manning

Dr Claire McNicholas GP
Andy Ruane, Like it Love it Productions
Michael Lucey, Greenhills College, Computer Department

Thanks to everyone who read *The Men in Her Life* and *Learning to Fly*. I hope you also enjoy *A Perfect Moment*.

Finally, thanks to Macdara and Seán (two great sons) for information on cars, sport, computers, music, fashion and especially the banter, and thanks to Pádhraic for everything.

Apology

It has been brought to my attention that I may have inadvertently offended redheads with a comment made by Sophie, a character in my last book. There has been talk of going to court – but I think this can all be sorted out by a dignified statement of regret from me – so here it is: Oh. My. God. I. Am. So. Truly. Madly. Deeply. Sorry . . . Redheads! I love redheads! My mother was a redhead! My first boyfriend was a redhead! My best friend at school was a redhead! My fabulous nieces are redheads. That ought to do it. Oh and the central character in this book is Aoife whose hair tumbles about her face in a mane of coppery red curls.

To Macdara,
Seán & Pádhraic

CHAPTER 1

Aoife tiptoed carefully across the wooden floor of the landing. It wouldn't do at all to wake Berry up. Berry could make life quite miserable for a full morning at least if she didn't get her full eight hours' sleep. And, mind you, Aoife was quite a big fan of the eight-hour night herself. At weekends and after late nights, she had often been known to languish in the feather-pillowed pits of balmy slumber for eleven or even twelve hours at a stretch.

But it was six a.m. now and if she didn't get cracking she'd miss the only early train from Larkhaven into town where she worked as a junior negotiator in Kevin Vernon's Estate Agency.

The wooden floor felt bumpy and draughty on her feet. She cursed herself for neglecting to don raggy old slippers and prayed that today of all days she would avoid the affliction of yet another splinter in her toe.

"Whose bloody bright idea was it to lift that perfectly

1

decent carpet?" she mumbled as she hobbled along the landing towards the bathroom. Then she remembered it had been her very own bright idea.

She'd scarcely been back in the house ten minutes when she'd cast her doleful eye up the stairs and along the landing, then told Berry bluntly: "That carpet has to go – it's a health hazard."

"What do you mean?" Berry had asked. For the past few months, carpets hadn't been that high on her agenda.

"I mean all that swirling crimson – it's disturbing – it can't be psychologically healthy. If I'm to stay – it has to go."

"But we can't afford to replace it – and the wooden floor underneath isn't in good condition," said Berry, her long, angular face calm and reasonable.

At that, the rounded, plump features of her younger sister's face lit up and her voice rippled excitedly. "Wooden floor, Berry? But that's wonderful! It's much better than carpet. You should see the amount of money people will pay for houses with genuine old wooden floors. Do you think it's old pine or maybe even oak? Let's lift the carpet now – it won't take long. We can sand and polish the boards and then it will be what we in the trade call an architectural feature."

Berry had shrugged and given her younger sister the benefit of one of her older-wiser-pursed-lipped smiles – but the swirling crimson carpet had been removed. That had been two months ago and neither one of them had had the time or felt the inclination to do anything in the line of sanding or polishing the floor since. Though they had managed to figure out that the boards were made of the finest oak, well seasoned with age. But as a direct result of throwing out the swirling crimson carpet, twice since returning home Aoife had been the victim of a rogue splinter incident. Once her middle toe had even got infected and she'd had to hobble down to the doctor's on the main street where he gave her an injection and a long droning lecture on young girls waltzing about the house in their bare feet asking for trouble and people stripping their floorboards bare like there was no tomorrow. If floorboards were meant to be bare, then why had God invented carpets, he'd asked malevolently as he shoved the large needle roughly into her well-padded left buttock.

But thankfully this morning she made it to the bathroom without incident. She squeezed the door handle as gently as she could, hoping that just this once the door would open with a well-behaved silent pop, rather than its more usual long-drawn-out haunted-house type of creaky squeak. That would most certainly disturb Berry whose room was right next to the bathroom.

"Damn!" hissed Aoife as the door did its usual audition for *Nightmare on Elm Street*, sounding like a moany old cat with a septic throat.

"What time is it?" Berry groaned from beyond her door and beneath a duvet.

"Shhhh! Go back to sleep – sorry!" Aoife said and slipped into the bathroom, closing the door firmly behind her.

Beneath the sullen drizzle of water that sulked from the ancient shower, Aoife attempted to shampoo her hair vigorously as she contemplated the day ahead. The new branch manager was arriving – and it was important for her to make a good impression. If Flann Slevin liked her, she might quickly be promoted to senior negotiator – giving her loads of experience in selling the larger houses and also the opportunity for much bigger commissions.

Downstairs in the kitchen she sat at the table eating a bowl of value-pack cereal while trying to knock some shape into the tumble of coppery auburn tresses that framed her freckled round face. In the end she gave up, scraped it back and twisted it all into a crinkled knot that she fastened with a stout butterfly clip at the nape of her neck. The cereal wasn't quite Kellogg's Crunchy Nut Cornflakes but there was nothing else in the cupboard, so she finished the last of it and guiltily placed the bowl at the top of a large pile of dishes in the sink. She found a battered notepad, ripped out an almost empty page and hastily scribbled a note to Berry.

Really sorry for waking you – must oil the hinges of that damn bathroom door. Didn't get time to do the wash-up after all. Won't be home tonight – summer barbeque in Kevin Vernon's new place out in Dalkey – hear it's a mansion and that Stella has exquisite taste so will have full report for you when I get home tomorrow.

Suppose I'll stay in Dermot's – handy for the train in the morning and he's been getting on to me lately about not spending more time with him.

Hope business is brisk today.

Lots of love Aoife XX

PS: Will definitely be back in time to give cottage mega-clean-over before new tenant arrives tomorrow. I promise!

She still couldn't believe they'd got someone who wanted to stay in the cottage, and was convinced he must be really desperate or nuts. Granted, the rent was tiny – just about manageable for someone on a pension – but she had honestly thought they were going to have to pay someone to stay there.

Let's hope Ben Searson isn't a potty old psychopath or anything anti-social like that, she thought, as she stood on the front doorstep of Bloomfield House and pulled on a light jacket. A cool early-morning mist hung low in the air and she could barely make out the gateway a scant fifty yards away, and the tattered old cottage beside it. With overnight bag in hand, she made her way quickly along the gravelled driveway to the main road.

She walked briskly through the village, past the neat row of cottages, past High Court Judge Patricia de Vere's house and perfectly lovely front garden. Then she skirted the small harbour with the tiny arc of a beach beside it, passed the Bayview Hotel and the little steepled church close by it, this year painted a cheerful duck-egg blue, in contrast to the warm Tuscan rose wash of previous years.

At last she reached the tiny Larkhaven train station.

Breathless and now quite warm from the early-morning exertion, she barely made it onto the train before it pulled away from the platform. Since Larkhaven was only the second stop, there was almost always plenty of room and she sat with her back to the driver, sleepily watching the hilly landscape roll away from her. The sun was well up now and over the brow of the hills the sea glinted and shimmered in the morning light.

She retrieved a book from her bag and tried to read – but she found it hard to concentrate. For a while she speculated on what the new boss might be like and then her thoughts shifted to Bloomfield House and how she'd found herself back there at twenty-seven when she'd always sworn she'd be over the hills and far away. She'd planned to be a rich property investor, dividing her time between a stylish loft in Manhattan and a sleek yacht in Puerto Banus by the time she was twenty-four. But her sister was more important to her than anything and Aoife could not have turned her back on Berry or their old home for all the money in the world. Even so, she'd had to work hard at ignoring all the well-meant warnings of friends and relatives.

"Village life is not for the faint-hearted," Kevin Vernon, her boss and sometimes surrogate father, had warned. "It's one thing being a little girl fishing for tadpoles and larking about on the farm or in the sand dunes for a few weeks in summer – but it's quite another going back there as an adult. In the city you can lose yourself – be whoever you want to be. You have to tailor yourself more carefully in a village. It takes moral courage and emotional stamina. Not that you are, but if you *were* any kind of fake or fraud, it wouldn't stay hidden for long in a village. Why do you think all the criminals and lowlifes congregate in cities? It's because they find it much easier to hide there. I lived in a village once for a year and it frightened the living daylights out of me."

Though she wasn't quite sure what Kevin had meant, Aoife had a strong suspicion all the same that he was right. The prospect of returning to village life scared the hell out of her too.

And Auntie Yvonne hadn't been all that encouraging either. "Are you sure you want to go back to that place? I mean, it's a big decision. You know you're welcome to stay on with us," she had told Aoife for the hundredth time as she'd loaded her suitcases into the back of husband Liam's car. "We'd love you to stay on. The house will be so lonely without you."

Yvonne had sounded oddly forlorn and the offer to stay on with the Kellys was very tempting. Aoife had lodged with her Aunty Yvonne, her husband Liam and their daughter Nathalie for the previous three years and it really had become a home from home. She'd grown to love Yvonne, and Nathalie had become like a second sister.

She even adored grumpy Liam. She remembered how surprised she'd been when he stuck his craggy, close-shaven Bruce-Willis-type head into the kitchen one morning on his way to work, smiled a rare deep blue-eyed smile and told her: "No sense in you going back to Larkhaven. Aren't you grand here?"

"I have to go home – for Berry's sake," she told them all. "She can't manage that old house on her own – it's too much – and she won't sell it. So just until she gets the business up and running – I can stick it out till then."

Almost every morning since that day she'd spent a good part of the daily train journey into the city wondering if she'd done the right thing by moving home.

Bloomfield House had been left to both sisters equally with thirty acres of land and a little ramshackle cottage at the gates. Berry, eight years older than Aoife, had quickly realised that she hardly knew the difference between a cow and a bull and she soon rented out the land to a canny local farmer. The income just about paid for running repairs and now Berry was working her threadbare socks off trying to make ends meet.

If it hadn't been allowed to fall into its current state of raggedy, slightly overgrown neglect, Bloomfield House could have been a perfectly lovely home. It was small enough and double-fronted, a Georgian Glebe house painted in a pale rose-washed colour, with three low granite steps leading up to a delightful fanlighted door and perfectly proportioned sashed windows on either side. It was the sort of house that estate agents got very excited about. Even in its current neglected state, it would have fetched a fine price at auction – a place that might appeal to a successful author or film producer or a professional couple relocating to the country with their children. But it needed big money spent on it and neither of the Joyce sisters had much in the way of cash. And though Aoife had gently hinted at selling once or twice, Berry wouldn't hear of it.

"No way! This is our home, our childhood, and our past history. It stays with us."

There was no more to be said on the subject.

Once the decision had been made to move home, Aoife made several attempts to find suitable work in the village but in the end she'd kept her job in Vernon's Estate Agents in the city centre. Kevin had been very accommodating, even offering the option of finishing early on Fridays if she worked through a couple of lunch-times. Aoife knew that she was unusually lucky in having a boss like him. She vowed on an almost daily basis to be worthy of his trust and approval. Somehow it seemed vitally important.

Now she commuted, and lived at home in Bloomfield House to help Berry pay the bills. It was an uphill struggle. The old house just gobbled up money and when friends made envious noises about Aoife living in a grand country home in one of the prettiest villages in the country, she just bit her lip and mumbled something about things not always being what that they seemed.

The train was more crowded as it gathered up speed

for the last leg of the journey. Aoife felt a mild knot of anxiety as she thought of the working day that lay ahead of her. She wondered about the new boss. Would he be easy to work with? Would he encourage and value her as Kevin had always done? Then she wondered a little enviously if Kevin planned to give him the sale of the house on Talavera Road – probably the best property to come onto their books this season. Still there was no sense in worrying about it and she forced her thoughts on to the busy day that lay ahead. She had to show a prospective American buyer around a couple of old properties near the canal. Three new houses had also come on the market the previous day and it was her job to make a realistic valuation, assemble the details, get the 'for sale' signs organised and the advertisements in the papers, then deal with any potential buyers. She enjoyed the work, loved looking over houses and helping people to find the home of their dreams. She'd been doing the work for two years now and up until recently she'd looked forward to each working day with enthusiasm.

But lately it felt as though her career was in the doldrums. Kevin kept promising to move her to a larger section with a broader range of properties for sale, but in spite of his constant stated interest in her welfare, the promotion never seemed to materialise. When Flann Slevin's predecessor retired, Aoife was bursting to apply for his job, but Kevin had warned her against it.

"You're not ready. It's as simple as that," he'd said when she'd expressed an interest in going forward.

Now she arrived at Vernon's earlier than usual and she bustled through the plate-glass front door, thrilled to have an extra half hour to organise things before the new boss arrived. There was even time to chat with Joe, the night porter. He was sitting at the desk, leafing through a book of criminal law.

"Coffee, Joe?" she called from within as she cranked up the machine.

"Don't mind if I do!" he called back to her.

It was their regular morning routine before he left for home and the others in the office arrived.

She returned minutes later with two steaming mugs of coffee.

"Thanks," he said, taking his mug before shoving a large black book in her direction. *"Prima facie?"*

"What?"

"I was at *prima facie*."

Aoife sighed and took the book reluctantly in her hand. "OK. *Prima facie*?"

"On first appearance!"

"Good. *Pro forma*?"

"As a matter of form."

"Nolle prosequi?"

Joe took a loud sip of coffee, shut his eyes tightly and clenched a fist.

"I'll have to hurry you!" Aoife said like she was chairing University Challenge.

"Wait – don't tell me! For the time? No? Temporarily?"

"Just as I thought," she said, sliding the book back in his direction. "You've gone and learnt the list off by heart from start to finish. *Nolle prosequi* is when the prosecutor says 'I do not wish to pursue'."

Joe hung his head despondently. He didn't really want to have anything to do with Law at all. He'd spent a year in college doing philosophy to please his parents. But he couldn't stick it and he'd dropped out. That was over five years ago and now here he was again half-heartedly going through the motions, working as a porter and paying his way to do an evening course in Law – just to please his mother whose dearest wish was that she could boast of having a lawyer in the family.

"Why don't you give it up?" Aoife said to him. "I mean, you don't really want to be poncing round in wigs and frocks anyway, do you?"

"I can't give it up! My mother would eat me alive! Life's too short. I'll get through it – the exams are not for a couple of months yet. I just need time."

Aoife gave him a vague encouraging smile. She quite liked Joe though she knew very little about him.

He glanced suddenly over her shoulder and quickly adopted a more formal stance. He murmured through his teeth without moving his lips just like a ventriloquist: "Better look sharp – at a guess I'd say new boss behind you at ten o'clock!"

Aoife swung round, her curiosity getting the better of her.

"Ah, coffee – just the ticket! I'll have some of that," the newcomer said before breezing into his office on a bright and cheery "Thank you!", closing the door softly behind him. She'd barely managed to catch sight of him. She was exchanging looks with Joe when the door opened once more and Flann Slevin's head reappeared briefly.

"A teaspoon of slimline milk? No sugar. Great. Thanks."

She hoped he wouldn't make a habit of that sort of thing but, since it was his first day, in less time that it would take to say '*Nowaygetityourselfyoulazylumpwhatsortofaneejitdo-youthinkIam?*' Aoife had very quietly placed a mug of coffee on his desk, accompanied by two borrowed best dark-chocolate orange-crunch biscuits belonging to Claire.

"Great," he mumbled, his hand reaching out towards the mug while his head remained studiously bent over a pile of documents, thick jet-black hair falling forward and hiding his broad high-cheekboned face from view.

"You're welcome," Aoife said.

She turned to leave but hesitated for a moment. Might he say something else? Would it be bad manners to go? In spite of his brusqueness, should she offer to show him round the office, introduce him to the coffee machine, explain the complex biscuit-cupboard situation? Perhaps she should run through her day's business with him – the American coming to look at the house in Portobello? It wasn't strictly in her patch – but Kevin had insisted she take it onto her list. Then there were the other three properties in Dolphin's Barn that looked set to fetch a good price. It was an up-and-coming area. Her routine in the past was to set the valuation, based on a complicated series of comparisons and permutations and combinations, and then to show it to Kevin for approval. But the growth of the business meant that Kevin wouldn't be in the office so much any more and now Flann would be the person approving her valuations. She would go to Flann if she had a problem. She would be with Flann for a good portion of her working day. She prayed that they would get on and, as she looked down at his thick jet-black hair, she decided that they would. Kevin simply wouldn't hire anybody who wasn't nice to Aoife.

"I've left the list of properties for my section on your desk," she said. "Kevin usually takes a quick glance over them. So see you later when you've had a chance to look them over. Say nine thirty?"

"Thanks, that's fine," he said, without looking up.

"Call through to me when you're ready," she said before leaving the room.

She bumped into Claire in the corridor.

"Morning," said Claire from beneath a starburst of dead straight funereal black hair and a ton of white Goth-style make-up.

"Good weekend?" Aoife asked.

"Never even got home to change until this morning – that's how good it was. You missed probably the best gig of the year. I wish I could play guitar like Blood McAlinden – he's a genius."

"Oh?" said Aoife, suppressing a yawn.

Her interest in Claire's Gothic lifestyle was strictly limited, though she and Claire got on very well and Claire was the lynchpin of the office in some respects. Only, with all that white pan make-up and kohl-rimmed eyes and deadly-nightshade nail varnish, she wasn't really the sort of person you could release on an unsuspecting public too often. Claire had hobbies that were different – like playing bass guitar with her local heavy metal band, Coffin Silk. When she wasn't tormenting the neighbours with screaming guitar riffs, she was out in all weathers restoring old graveyards. So life round Claire was always a bit weird – and the funny thing was that beneath all the make-up and heavily darkened hair – Claire was fantastically good-looking. Aoife's boyfriend, Dermot, had often remarked on how fantastically lovely she was.

"Anyway – the new boss has arrived – don't know what he's going to make of you in all that black gear."

"Like I care?" Claire said, pulling at a long and very straight strand of deep purple fringe. "It doesn't interfere with how I do my job. Kevin never bothers me about it – so why should anyone else?"

And that was another thing about Claire that was hard to figure. She really did not give a damn about what anyone thought about her. It must be a wonderfully liberating way to be, thought Aoife, as she headed back to her office.

"*Pro tempore*?" Claire breezed as she whizzed past Joe's desk.

"Easy! For the time being!" he called after her.

Back in her office Aoife sent her cousin Nathalie a quick email as she waited for the American client to arrive.

Then she remembered just in time that it would be only good manners to fill Dermot in on the night's plans. After all, he would be providing a bed for the night.

Hey Dermot

Sorry I haven't answered your last few mails – it's just that I've been so busy settling back into Larkhaven. Fancy going to a movie next week? Not Thursday though, I'm busy. Did I mention office barbeque tonight in Dalkey? Thing is, I need a bed and hope I can stay in yours.

Best love

Aoife XXXX

She then gathered details on the three new properties, checking for errors before printing them off. The glossy photos had arrived and one of the houses in particular, an old redbrick converted meeting hall, looked especially good. It was coming up for auction in a couple of weeks but she wouldn't be at all surprised if it sold out before getting to auction at all. Just as she had armed herself with the files and was bracing up for a foray into Flann's office, she noticed Dermot had replied to her mail.

Hi Aoife

Would love to go to a movie next week. And no problem with the bed!!! Also very happy to accompany you to the barbeque – unless you've had a better offer????

Dermot

She pulled a face at the screen, then, with the files clutched tightly under her arm, she typed in hastily with two fingers:

Dermot sweets

Thanks a million – you're a complete star – but didn't I mention the barbeque is not a partners thing? Otherwise of course I'd bring you along in a shot. See you later.

Hugs and kisses

Aoife

She sent the reply and then as usual deleted all personal mails. She had blanched as she typed the lie – not a lie exactly, but an untruth – but she just didn't want to attend the most exciting night of her working year with Dermot in tow. Somewhere in the back of Aoife Joyce's mind was the still strong belief that, out there in the big wide open beyond, was a wonderfully dashing, horrendously charming, unbearably handsome and unbelievably considerate man, who would simply walk into the offices of Vernon's Estate Agents some day and sweep her off her feet. All of life had prepared her for that moment – those childhood fairy stories, those girlie magazines, those wonderful movies like *Pretty Woman*. If you couldn't have the man of your dreams, then what on earth was the point of settling for anything less? And, alas, Dermot fell into the 'anything less' bracket. She thought of him in mostly negative terms. He wasn't ugly. He wasn't bad-tempered. He didn't dress like a cross between Ozzie Osbourne and that scruffy-looking man who did Patricia de Vere's garden. He didn't lust after other women. He wasn't a heavy drinker. He never criticised her. He didn't make her sit through Match of the Day. He never forgot her birthday. The problem was . . . there was little positive she could say about him.

"He's gorgeous," Nathalie was constantly telling her.

But Aoife couldn't see anything gorgeous about him.

"He's just gorgeous and if you don't stop stringing him along, some other girl will snatch him up and you'll have the rest of your life to regret that you let Dermot Kavanagh slip through your fingers!"

Nathalie might be right – but Aoife just couldn't see it that way. Where was the spark? Where were the explosive, dazzling, sky-splashing, heart-stopping fireworks? Where was the dizzying, earth-moving, gut-wrenching, room-swirling, stomach-churning sensation that she'd read about so often? The most exciting thing she'd ever done with Dermot was to go and see Fungi the Dolphin in Dingle on Whit Weekend last year. Her stomach had churned all right but that had been the lurching movement of the boat. No – she was not in love and any day now she was going to have to regrettably point this out to him. It was just important to get the timing right.

Moments later, having pushed guilty thoughts about Dermot to one side, she stood poised outside Flann Slevin's door. It was almost ten o'clock and he'd probably forgotten all about their meeting. Well – it was his first day – he most likely had too much other stuff on his mind.

She really ought to have reminded him. She felt mildly expectant – not nervous but anxious to make a good impression, hopeful of getting off to a positive start. He certainly couldn't find any fault with her valuations. She'd worked on them for ages – but all the same she felt apprehensive and worried suddenly that she mightn't measure up in some way. Kevin had always showered her with bucketloads of positive feedback and encouragement – almost like a father encouraging his child. Flann was hardly likely to go on like that. For starters he didn't look more than a few years older than her. She straightened up and sucked in a deep breath before rapping softly on the door with her knuckles.

There was no response from within so she rapped again, this time more loudly. After a few moments, to her surprise, the door opened rather suddenly and Flann's head appeared.

"Yes?" Steely grey eyes fixed onto hers.

"We were to meet. It's almost ten o'clock."

"Sorry – I lost track of time. Come on in. By the way – don't think we were introduced. Flann Slevin." He held out his hand and she shook it.

"Aoife – Aoife Joyce. I'm a junior negotiator – I look after some of the smaller properties. Did you get a chance to look over my valuations?"

She was sitting stiffly into the chair, tweaking at an unruly tendril of hair. He had eased his long angular frame back into the swivel-chair, and now smiled easily at her. He looked like the sort who could take anything in his stride. Aoife marvelled at how comfortable he seemed already even though he'd only been in Vernon's for less than three hours. It must have something to do with confidence, she decided, remembering how it had taken her the best part of a year to find her way round the office.

"Ah yes – the valuations," he said, holding a document aloft and slapping it down on the desk in front of her. "I hope you don't take this the wrong way but I'm increasing the guide price on this house in Portobello."

"What?"

He smiled as if to reassure her. "You would have been spot on with this valuation two, maybe even three months ago, believe you me," he said evenly, holding up a sheet of paper and pointing to her valuation of the house. "But the market's changing all the time – as you no doubt know. There have also been complaints about estate agents setting their guide prices too low . . . the government is cracking down. This little gem here – it's charming, oozes style, location, location, location, delightful garden etc etc etc." He tilted his jet-black head back, swivelled very slightly in his chair and smiled mildly at her.

Aoife swallowed. Kevin Vernon never spoke to her like that or questioned her judgement. She felt sure she'd set the correct valuation. It was part of her job and she rarely, if ever, got it wrong. Besides Kevin got very cross if properties were over or undervalued.

"But I –"

He continued. "Lived in Portobello myself briefly – as a student – wild and wonderful times – all night parties, wacky tobaccy – but where do the years go?" He stared off into the middle distance for a moment, apparently recalling the distant days of his wild and decadent youth all of seven years earlier. Then he continued: "Thing is – Aoife – I know the market in that particular neck of the woods. Buckets of atmospheric appeal – especially on the overseas market – and with the arty set – Yanks in particular – buckets of cash, if you follow me. Can't disappoint the vendor – and we certainly don't want to attract hordes of people not in the appropriate price league." He sucked in a long breath through wide thin lips and let it out in low staccato whistles as he continued to stare at her.

"I'm not for a moment questioning your judgement –" she began, the palms of her hands sweaty now.

"Good!" he said, skewering her with a cool smile.

She opened her mouth to speak again. But before she could say another word, he had leapt to his feet and was holding the door open for her.

"Though I have to say you did real well on those Dolphin's Barn Evaluations. Well done, you! I just haven't got a clue when it comes to that part of town. Still, I suppose that's what Kevin meant in the interview when he said we all help each other out in Vernon's. I'm looking forward to being on the team with you, Aoife."

"Yes, me too," she said, feeling quite annoyed yet not wanting to say anything that might get them off to a bad start. "Well, must go. Showing the house in Portobello to an American artist."

"Brilliant! Then I'm glad we've sorted out that valuation. Will I see you at the barbeque? We can have a dance. I'm a pretty mean dancer." He chuckled and did a brief little shimmy.

Aoife wasn't sure how to react so she gave him a brief wide-eyed stare. It was her special look of mild disapproval.

"Yes, well . . . see you then," he said easily as she left him standing in the doorway and made her way down the corridor to her office.

Aoife was kept busier than usual that morning because Kevin Vernon was scrupulous about Internet security and today he had ordered a random scan of all computers in the office. He breezed round the office – all thick spectacles, and thin straggling ginger hair, trousers hitched up around his chest and a jacket that looked as if it had seen action in the First World War. As usual, it was a big lot of fuss over nothing and it took ages for all the computers to be checked. There was practically a Code Red Alert when it was discovered that Claire had been downloading properties from another agency. But it turned out that she was only trying to find out what Blood McAlinden's house was like.

They were just finished in Aoife's office when the American arrived in the foyer and, though she had been looking forward to showing him round the house in Portobello, now her heart sank. She would have to tell him that the reserve price had been increased – very steeply.

She tried raising the subject before they set out on the short walk from the office, but he simply cut her short with a shake of his head and a pleasant smile.

"Hush – not a word – let me just see the house first."

He was an artist, much older than her, late forties she guessed, with floppy faded blond hair and crinkly blue eyes, slightly camp she figured – but nicely mannered. His name was Clement. Flann was right – as soon as Clement saw the house he was charmed beyond words and he trawled through it delightedly, even identifying the room he would set aside as a studio.

"I love it – I want it – I aim to have it," he said, eyes bright with excitement.

Aoife bit her lip. She felt like a complete fraud now. Her only hope was that he was terribly rich and wouldn't mind about the huge hike in the price. She hesitated for a moment and said: "I'm really sorry but the reserve price on this one has gone up considerably." She looked at him steadily with her blue-green eyes, feeling even guiltier when she saw the childish delight drain from his face.

She was worried he might become angry and take it out on her – but he didn't and that was almost worse because he just sank into a chair in the hallway and let his shoulders slump dejectedly. He was on the verge of tears.

"I'm sorry. I only found out just before you arrived at the office," she said, not knowing what else to say.

"But I thought . . . oh dear, I simply couldn't afford . . . it was going to be a struggle even at the first figure you mentioned . . . and I just know my partner would have loved it. He's an interior designer . . ."

Aoife bowed her head in embarrassment, feeling horribly responsible for his disappointment.

CHAPTER 2

Nathalie Kelly, Aoife's cousin, sat at her desk in the offices of Nutopia Telesales. The phones purred insistently along banks of monitors in the insanely dull, orange-painted, breeze-blocked offices. They sounded like a hundred baby crows all calling feebly for attention. Interspersed with the crow-like sounds, were the voices of telesales assistants, ploughing their way through a designated seventy cold calls a day, forced to repeat the same carefully worded conversation from morning to night.

Nathalie had recently been demoted from a job she'd quite enjoyed in the Salaries Office and given a special place along the cold-selling line – on account of the accident. But she tried to be thankful for small mercies. At least she had a wider desk in a quieter corner. And above all she didn't have the X Client List, which was whisperingly referred to as The Price List, after Gretta Price, Nathalie's boss.

Every day Nathalie tried valiantly to blot out the fact

that she was deeply unhappy in Nutopia and that management was watching out for any excuse to be rid of her.

She scrolled down through the list of client accounts and made her thirtieth call of the day. "Good morning, madam. I'm calling from Nutopia Telesales and Marketing. Will you be travelling to Europe at all in the next six months? We are currently offering a special insurance deal with all car rentals on the continent of Europe for the summer months . . ."

The thought of going through the same rigmarole another forty times before she left the office was something she couldn't afford to think about right now. She pulled herself up, made a doomed attempt to tidy her unruly light brown hair and smiled into the mouthpiece as Gretta Price moved relentlessly forward, like a Sherman tank.

Gretta Price had definitely missed her vocation. She would have been perfect as one of those guards in a Southern States prison, waving a truncheon and saying "y'all" to her charges. Gretta made little speeches to her troops with one-liners that only she could see the humour in. A favourite was "What we have here is a failure to communicate" which she always said in a fake American accent as a knowing smile played at the corners of her wide tight-lipped mouth. Nathalie was sure that Miss Price (as she liked to be called) had stolen the line from a film.

At home, later that evening, Nathalie helped her mother clear the table after tea while her father sat in his own personal armchair and disappeared behind the evening newspaper.

Yvonne tried a little conversation with her husband. "Wouldn't you miss Aoife round the place?"

"I suppose," he said, settling his broad, muscular frame more comfortably into the chair.

"I hope she's settling back into Larkhaven. Maybe we should pay her a visit at the weekend."

"Don't worry about her. She'll be grand," he said, running a hand absently through his close-cropped flaxen hair as he settled into an in-depth analysis of Ireland's chances in the next Olympics.

She gave up trying to make conversation with him and curled up on the sofa with Nathalie to watch *The Holiday Show*. Yvonne loved *The Holiday Show* and together she and her daughter would dream about luxurious holidays in far-off happy places.

"You're a pair of eejits going on like that," Liam Kelly mumbled from behind his paper.

Yvonne had perfected a way of raising her eyebrows and rolling her eyes to heaven, which her husband took to be an expression of absolute agreement, and warm, tolerant affection. In actual fact, her raised eyebrows meant: "What in God's name did I ever see in that crabby old sack of misery slouched over there behind the newspaper?"

It was Nathalie's father who had insisted that she should sue Nutopia when she'd had the accident. She really didn't want to cause any trouble and the thought of having to deal with lawyers and company bosses frightened the wits out of her. Besides, Gretta Price had assured her that the accident was entirely her own fault and only a whingeing compo cheat would take the company to court about it. But Liam Kelly knew his rights and he knew his daughter's rights as well. She'd suffered permanent damage to her hand. She'd lost earnings, undergone two expensive and unsuccessful operations, suffered pain and embarrassment. Someone was going to pay for it.

The Tailgating Incident, as it was referred to now at high-level Human Resource Management meetings, had occurred about eighteen months earlier when Nathalie was clocking in through the security gate inside the front doors of Nutopia. Above her on the wall, beside the Company Mission Statement, was a large laminated sign that said in big bold black letters: NO TAILGATING! It meant that no one should rush in through security on the tail of someone else's pass. She waited patiently as her friend Johanne swiped through her card and stood beneath the metal frame to be cleared for entry. Nathalie often wondered as she stood there why a telesales company needed such an elaborate security system. There was hardly anything to steal except the computer mice and mouse pads. But Gretta Price regularly gave them lectures about industrial espionage and about not discussing company business outside the office.

"Makes her feel all-important – like she's head of the CIA or something," Johanne always said. Johanne was Nathalie's closest and dearest friend since childhood. They'd even started working in Nutopia on the same day.

Johanne regularly gave cheek to Miss Price and was on her last warning.

"It's important to be a good team player, Johanne," Price frequently told her with cool management reserve. "You must develop the right positive attitudes, shed all that negative thinking. It's holding you back."

"What she really means," Joanne would say, "is 'You cheeky little cow, how dare you think you can contradict someone as important as me and get away with it!'."

But Nathalie was made of more patient stuff than Johanne. Passing through company security procedures was tedious but not the end of the world.

On that morning she stepped forward after Johanne, to swipe her card through the machine. She stood patiently under the metal arc as usual. But just as she stepped forward, Clinton Waters, a new bloke in Accounts, pushed in alongside her, doing exactly what the sign on the wall said he shouldn't – he tailgated her. Nathalie got such a surprise that she jumped and caught the third and little finger on her right hand in the machine that swiped the cards. Ordinarily she might have come away with nothing more damaging than a bruise but that day the machine seemed to take on a life of its own and severed a bunch of nerves. Despite two operations, several weeks off work without pay and lots of consultations with doctors, Nathalie was now condemned to life with two useless fingers.

More upsetting, when she'd finally returned to work, she found that Gretta Price had demoted her. "We're happy to have you back on the team, Nathalie," Gretta had told her. "Glad we can accommodate you – only not in Salaries – we want you in Telesales from here on."

But now it looked like Nathalie had a case. At least that was how Felicity Norton, the solicitor, saw it. She'd consulted a barrister and he said that Nutopia were liable – even though it was technically Clinton Waters' fault. Nathalie had been forced to run up sizeable medical bills. The damage to the fingers on her right hand was permanent. She'd been out of work for three months and endured enough pain and suffering to warrant some level of financial compensation. Nathalie had been asked to do an action replay of what exactly had happened at the security check that morning. Then an engineer had been called in to check the machine and take a close look at the Service and Maintenance Log. His report had indicated that the card-swiping machine was faulty and hadn't been serviced for months prior to the accident. That showed negligence on the part of Nutopia. So Nathalie's legal team had made a Statement of Claim and the hearing was coming up very soon.

Nathalie was in a bit of a state this evening and not much in the mood for *The Holiday Show* or anything else. Felicity had arranged a meeting with Mark Tierney, the barrister, for Monday of the following week. Nathalie had never met a barrister before and, though she wasn't the sort to be easily intimidated by anyone, she just knew he would be full of his own importance and regard her as a silly little thing with no education past the Junior Cert – which, as Gretta Price constantly reminded her, was all she was.

Why, oh why, had she let her dad talk her into suing Nutopia?

When Aoife finally escaped the office that evening, Dermot was waiting outside for her. Leaning languidly against a lamppost, he waved at her from across the street, like someone from an old movie.

"Lucky you," said Claire, casting an envious glance in Dermot's direction from beneath her thick spiky fringe.

His warm brown eyes glinted in the evening sunshine and his lean athletic frame seemed to ripple with laidback energy as he ambled easily towards them.

"Hi," Aoife said, offering her cheek as he bent to kiss her.

He went to wrap his arms about her in a big hug, but she slipped from his embrace to say goodbye to Claire.

"See you at the barbeque!" she said as they air-kissed one another.

"See you, Dermot," Claire cooed in a most unGoth-like way as she set off towards the bus stop.

"Come on – it's a fine evening – let's have a drink somewhere nice," Dermot said, once they were alone.

Aoife pulled a face. "I'd just love to – but it's going to take me two hours at least to get ready – so maybe some other time?" She bit her lip and smiled winningly at him.

He looked down at her for a moment, seemed about to agree, and then grabbed her forcefully by the hand. "Nope! It's Friday evening and I can't begin to tell you what a tough week I've had. And you and I haven't been alone together in weeks. We're going to put your things in my car, then have a stroll in the sunshine to my favourite bar and you're going to tell me all about work and living in Larkhaven and I'm going to tell you all about my new office." Then he stopped and frowned as if confused about something, or like he wanted to say something else.

"What is it?" Aoife said, wondering if he might have some interesting snippet of gossip to pass on to her.

"Nothing," he said quickly. "Then I'll drive you back to the apartment with plenty of time to get ready for the party."

She felt a fleeting dart of exasperation and then told herself not to be silly.

If nothing else, Dermot was a really good friend. Since they'd met two years ago, they had fallen easily into the habit of telling each other almost everything that was happening in their lives. If anything big or important was ever happening to Aoife, it was invariably Dermot who got to hear about it first. When things were getting her down, it was Dermot she turned to for advice and comfort. Of course, she loved him – it was just that she didn't *Love* him. Which was where the big difficulty lay. Because he was clearly in love with her. Once or twice she'd even suspected that he was building up to proposing marriage or if not marriage then at least something awesomely serious like moving in together – but luckily she'd been able to divert his attention.

"OK," she said relenting at last. "But I can't stay too long."

Berry Joyce surveyed the few remaining customers in her shop. It was almost closing time. She was tired. She hadn't slept after Aoife had left the house earlier that morning, and now she guiltily longed for the stragglers to leave. She was very grateful for their custom and all, but they hadn't exactly spent a whole pile of money. Soon she would be shutting up shop for the evening and she dreaded going through the till to count the day's takings. Not that she was in any sense grabby or anything, but where was the sense in running a business if it didn't bring in enough money to pay the bills? The whole point of setting up the shop had been to bring in a good income, which in turn would help her get Bloomfield House in order. And she felt sure she'd done her market research properly. She'd figured correctly that Larkhaven needed two businesses badly – a laundrette to cater for the bigger laundry jobs, the holiday homes and cottage rental market – and an Internet café. So she had provided both. The Surf Line she'd called it. But it was open six months now and she was barely breaking even. She'd put up posters everywhere she could think of, advertised on the local radio station, got someone to design a website, started out with some very good introductory offers: *Get All Your Curtains Laundered With Free Online Access For A Day*. But still, old Jim who ran the second-hand bookshop next door was doing better business than her.

This evening The Surf Line had three clients: Patricia de Vere, High Court Judge and Chairperson of the Larkhaven Ladies' Association, sending out emails while overseeing the washing of her guestroom duvets; Agnes Ndogo, a newly arrived seamstress from Kenya who was having some handstitched tablecloths laundered while she emailed her family back home; and lastly Harry Robson – thirty-something landowner.

Harry was proud of his rolling farm of rich pastureland and though he had a slightly rakish reputation in the neighbourhood, he was also well liked because he was friendly and he worked hard. Recently though, he had got an unexpected windfall from the sale of a few acres of stony soil and he had hired a temporary manager to look after the farm while he completed an online course in agri-business. So he was using Berry's Internet café on an almost daily basis. Now he sat at a monitor in his loose-fitting jeans and hiking boots – catching up on an assignment and sipping from a large mug of complimentary frothy cappuccino.

Berry felt sure that Patricia de Vere had state-of-the-art

broadband Internet technology at home in her imposing split-level bungalow overlooking the beach, and suspected that she was merely using the online facilities in The Surf Line as a spying operation for the Larkhaven Ladies' Association. Berry suppressed a dart of gnawing anxiety. The Larkhaven Ladies' Association wielded the sort of secret power in the village that was normally more associated with the Freemasons or Opus Dei or the CIA. Dan Brown could get a great novel out of the covert, clandestine, cloak and dagger, semi-sinister machinations of the society – and call it *The De Vere Code*. Patricia had an aura of breezy overbearing menace about her, and there wasn't a person in the village that didn't cower a little bit in her presence. If Patricia de Vere didn't approve of you, it was said, you wouldn't last a week in Larkhaven.

"We're closing soon," Berry said, approaching the judge with mild trepidation.

Patricia quickly closed the screen and logged off. "My home connection is down," she said quickly. "Damn nuisance – but this is very slow. Not satisfactory at all."

"Perhaps I can help," said Berry evenly. "What was it you were trying to access?"

"It's fine – nothing that can't wait," Patricia said breezily as she rose and unfolded her tall Chanel-suited frame with intimidating grace. Before Berry could even think of replying, the judge had swept out regally onto the main street.

Harry glanced after the judge for a brief moment.

"Scary lady!" he murmured before returning to his work.

Kevin Vernon's barbeque was in full swing. His back garden, newly landscaped in gentle terraces and flanked by rows of billowing pink rhododendron bushes, swept down to a rocky shore. Trestle tables groaned beneath the weight of salads and breads and cold meats. Two chefs presided over a massive barbeque grill. The succulent aroma of grilling meat filled the air. A four-piece band was positioned on a decked area and they were playing a lively mix of Latin American music. A few couples danced and swayed in the evening sunshine. Stella Vernon drifted among the guests and quietly went about the business of making each person feel at ease. She had a knack for it. No one ever came away from Stella's house feeling inadequate or envious. She didn't go in for that sort of cut-throat socialising. She recognised her good fortune on a daily basis and took a girlish delight in sharing it about whenever possible. Their only child, Thomas, lived abroad and Stella was the first to admit that a huge loneliness for him was a major driving force behind many of the social and charity events that she organised. She simply enjoyed the company of others.

Stella had just left the garden, entering the house through the French windows that opened on to the terrace, when she heard Aoife's sweet light voice in the hallway. Stella was especially fond of Aoife and she hurried to welcome her.

Aoife, Claire at her side, greeted Stella with a warm affectionate kiss. "Your house is beautiful," she gasped as she took in the grand marble pillars and wide-open expanse of marbled floor.

Stella grinned at her crookedly. "Never mind all that beautiful-house rubbish. The party's in full swing out in the garden." She gestured through the French windows at the lively mixed crowd of guests.

"Any rockers?" Claire asked through plump, plum-glossed lips, sweeping her glittering dark eyes across the crowd. She wore a black-leather jacket over a deep purple lace dress and she had coloured her hair with temporary matching purple highlights and spiked and gelled it up into what looked like a Transylvanian sunburst.

"I thought you two might have brought your own," Stella said – and Aoife noticed a flicker of disappointment in her hostess's eyes. Stella was particularly fond of Dermot.

"May we look around the house?" asked Aoife eagerly.

"Of course – go ahead," said Stella. "But I must get back to mingling." And with a smile she left them.

"So this is what it's like to be rich," said Claire to Aoife as they drifted wide-eyed through the massive Victorian house. "You could fit four of my shoebox apartments into the kitchen alone. Do you know what? It's not fair."

"Maybe it's not fair but it's just beautiful," said Aoife, her professional eye admiring every perfect detail of the house, noticing how each piece of furniture seemed to sit perfectly in its chosen space. The rooms were vast and high-ceilinged with exquisite oriental rugs on the floors, and the walls hung here and there with fine original paintings.

"I might meet a heavy-metal millionaire here tonight," Claire drawled sardonically, as they finally moved out into the garden.

"We both might," said Aoife.

"You've already got a man. Don't be greedy," Claire said, darting off in the direction of the food and drink and the people and the music.

Aoife followed. "Oh God, help!" she murmured as she

saw the throng of people, briefly regretting that she'd left Dermot at home.

Claire had disappeared and Stella was deep in conversation with a group of ladies standing in a worshipful circle around one of her rare plants. Aoife didn't recognise even one face in the crowd. She swallowed and forced herself onward, hoping that she would soon see someone familiar. A passing waiter stopped and offered her a glass of champagne, which she took eagerly. At least it would give her something to do while she went about the business of finding someone to talk to. The garden was full of glamorous women dressed up to the nines and men in tuxedos and she felt horribly out of place in last year's pale pink Monsoon chiffon and lace dress.

She drifted towards the musicians as she recognised a piece of music she'd heard in salsa classes.

"Spice it up – *Echade Salsita!*" the dark-haired vocalist rasped breathily into the microphone, as though he might make forbidden love behind the rhododendron bushes to a number of women any minute now. He trapped Aoife in his licentious gaze for a few moments but she looked away and stared out to sea.

Might this be the night? Would darkness fall on the magnificent terraces of Kevin and Stella's new garden? Would the Latin minstrels conjure up a mood of giddy possibility? And would the crowd part in a moment, to reveal some cloudy vision of a high romance – a tall and imposing figure whose smouldering eyes would lock onto hers and who would turn out to be the love of her life?

Aoife began to tap the floor with the ball of her foot. Her hips swayed to the infectious rhythm of the music. She wished desperately that she had a partner, and that she could at least float off into a giddy mindless dancing joy – well, just until the love of her life arrived. She looked around, eyes searching the crowd for a familiar face. But there was only Kevin, her boss, and he was deep in conversation with a business colleague so she couldn't very well ask him to dance. And what with the champagne and all, she began to feel that if she didn't get out to dance soon, she might just burst on the spot.

Then she saw Flann Slevin standing in a small group of guests and without even meaning to, her eyes met his. She regretted it and looked away instantly but before she could even protest or think of an excuse, he had broken away from the group, grabbed her hand and pulled her onto the floor.

"Come on, dance!" he said and her whole body was now so consumed by the rhythm that she couldn't refuse.

Once Aoife hit the dance floor, in her mind she was in Havana, in Colombia, in Puerto Rico. She was in the arms of some dark and potent lover, the one who was going to come along some day and overpower her with love, their bodies moving and swaying in perfect harmony. She was utterly possessed.

It was only when the music stopped that she came back to reality with a jolt. No lover, no Havana, definitely no harmony – just Flann Slevin.

"Thank you, I enjoyed that," he said after a brief uneasy silence.

She stared at him half-wildly, the infectious rhythm of the music still playing tricks with her. With the cool breeze blowing in from the bay and ruffling his blue-black hair, he looked attractive, and the germ of a rather alarming idea began to form in the back of Aoife's mind.

"You like dancing?" she asked, surprised that he'd managed quite well *not* to look like a completely unhinged stick-insect on Ecstasy, as blokes she danced with usually did. So now it occurred to Aoife, that behind his cool and slightly off-putting exterior, Flann Slevin was a man with hidden depths, probably even hot-blooded and romantic depths.

He stepped closer to her, took her hand in his, looked down at her earnestly. "I like dancing with you."

Aoife was suddenly at a loss for words. She even blushed – and hoped he wouldn't notice it. The very last thing she wanted was to end up feeling all uncomfortable and teenage-crushy around her new boss. She'd never once formed even the slightest little post-beneath-the-mistletoe-kiss-attachment to any of her colleagues. Having seen Claire teetering on the brink of bunny-boiling madness once from a soured affair with a colleague, Aoife had always given her workmates a clear berth in the lust and love department.

She brushed a corkscrewed copper tendril from her flushed face. "Excuse me, I need to get a glass of water," she stammered and stumbled away from him through the crowd.

CHAPTER 3

Each first Saturday of the month, at ten a.m., the Larkhaven Ladies' Association convened in the Community Hall, their meetings presided over by Patricia de Vere. Around the table in various stages and ages of womanhood were Sheila Hendron, a nursery-school teacher, Charlotte Pobjoy who owned the candle and potpourri shop, Gloria Brabazon who specialised in the art of being beautiful and Berry Joyce. The good women of Larkhaven could not simply apply to join the association. Membership was very strictly by invitation only. Which was how Berry came to be there. She had been the last member to be invited to join and her presence at the table was entirely half-hearted – as in, she didn't really want to be there at all. The only reason she still attended meetings was on the off-chance that she might figure out why she'd been invited along to become a member in the first place.

In the past few years this little band of steadfast women had been the driving force behind many initiatives in the village – some more successful than others: stylish new street lights along the main Larkhaven boulevard, the ruthless Citizens against Chewing Gum Programme, a Christmas Tinsel to The Third World Initiative. They had organised the selection of paintings and sculptures on display around the village, most notably a bronze statue on the village green of a little girl with a lark resting in her hand. The husbands and men of the village might have been under the illusion that they had brought all these changes into being. But the whole village knew otherwise. Larkhaven stayed the place it was because of the Ladies. They had steered the village through the chaos of a new water scheme and the uncertainty of recent land-rezoning matters. They had stood firm against threats of pool halls, and doner kebaberies and lap-dancing clubs. So that Larkhaven remained much as it had been in the nineteen-seventies – a haven of nostalgic tranquillity, a sanctuary of common sense and decency, safe from the wicked excesses of the New Ireland.

But now suddenly after years of peace and harmony they were in turmoil again because Patricia de Vere had just proposed a new member. They sat around the fine beech board-table, sipping still mineral water and trying to come to terms with her proposal.

"It's against the rules of membership," said Gloria Brabazon, beautiful blonde Gloria, who was very occasionally the subject of idle gossip in the village.

Patricia was quick to respond, as always an intimidating aura of courtroom authority about her. She had the look of a woman who actually kept her own personally sharpened sword of truth and particularly merciless scales of justice in the back of her closet. Today, being Saturday, she was dressed in less formal cream trousers and a loose pale blue striped shirt – but she still cut an imposing figure.

"There is nothing in the rules about it. I've checked." She held up a leaflet and began to read coolly: *"The Larkhaven Ladies' Association will convene la la la . . . membership will be open to those who are proposed by an existing association member only blab la bla . . . loyalty and honesty is the motto of the group . . . anyone failing to abide by these rules will be asked to account for themselves and may, if found guilty, be voted out by existing members of the association . . ."*

"Yes, but it's understood – no need for it to be spelt out – look at our name for heaven's sake!" It was Sheila Hendron talking now, the colour in her face heightening with annoyance.

Only last year Sheila had proposed her sister-in-law for membership and had been rejected. Patricia had been the most outspoken on the matter and Sheila had never quite forgiven her.

Now Patricia looked down along the line of her fine aquiline nose and eyed Sheila steadily across the table with large candid grey eyes, then addressed the group once more. "It's time to move on – time for change . . ." Her eyes swept around the table, quickly noting those who might be wavering in their support. She knew she could count on most of them. It was just Sheila – being a damn nuisance, nitpicking as always, never quite singing from the same hymn sheet as the rest of them. Sometimes Patricia wondered, very privately of course, how Sheila had come to be a member of the association in the first place.

Berry sat quietly at the end of the table. She didn't feel there was anything useful she could say to contribute to the arguments on either side. As always she got the feeling she was there only on sufferance or because she might be useful in some way.

"Personally I'm in favour," she said, measuring her words carefully and hoping the meeting would be over soon so that she could rush home and clean the cottage before the new tenant arrived.

"This is all very well," interjected Charlotte Pobjoy, "but shouldn't we be addressing the real reason this meeting was called?"

"Later!" said Patricia and then softened her voice slightly for she quite liked Charlotte. "There will be plenty of time for all that later. First let's deal with the issue of new members."

Dermot had been fast in a very deep sleep when Aoife slipped in beside him, having finally made it home in a taxi from Kevin Vernon's at some unearthly hour. She'd curled up beside him, comfortably savouring his smooth, hard, tanned body as she drifted away to sleep.

But now, late the following morning, Dermot was uncoiling in that panther-like stretch – the one he always did before he reached across and tugged her gently into his arms.

"*Mmmmm*," he mumbled raspily into her tumbled hair. "Had a good night without me?"

"Great! It was just fantastic!" she breezed airily and then added quickly: "But it was all work people – you wouldn't have enjoyed it. And you – what did you get up to?"

"Nothing much. I had a bad headache. Went to bed early."

"Why didn't you take two paracetamol and go clubbing like everyone else?"

"Like I said – it was a really bad headache. But it's well and truly gone now," he whispered into her ear, unfurling and uncurling his body some more as she felt his warm breath on her cheek.

"God, look at the time," she said, catapulting her naked body quickly towards the shower. "Berry will kill me! I'm supposed to be helping her clean up the cottage for the new tenant!"

He growled softly beneath the blankets and she was almost tempted to climb back in beside him as she felt a warm ripple of desire flood through her. But no – it wouldn't be fair. It would be leading him on. She didn't love him so there was no point in having sex with him any more. He threw the sheet back and lay naked before her, rubbing a hand idly across his chest. Aoife swallowed hard and dived into the shower.

Ben Searson, formerly Ben Pearse, bumped and coaxed his battered old Renault 4 along the winding country road towards Larkhaven. He showed little interest in the pretty hilly countryside, barely noticing the sea gleaming in the mid-morning sun between the edge of the green fields and the low indigo horizon.

He had come to a crossroads in his life, a time and place when all the things he had once thought mattered no longer seemed important. He had travelled far from the arrogant and high-principled man of his youth and now bore himself with an air of dignified but weary disappointment.

Life had not been overly kind to Ben in recent years. He had stepped into the adult world with all the confidence and certainty of a young man born into privilege. He had grown to maturity cosseted in the warmth of a loving family, buttressed from the humdrum perils of the world by money, status and security. Now at thirty-three, he was without hope, without money, without friends. The world, once a broad and exciting sweep of possibilities had shrunk to a barren wasteland, his life a mere existence, his heart a dead thing. He no longer reflected on his bad fortune but endured it.

"Endure and Renounce," his old Classics teacher was fond of saying. He'd never understood what it meant until now – now that life had spewed out some of its nastier bile onto him. But it had taught him to endure his pain and renounce as much of the world as a man reasonably could in the twenty-first century. At the prime of life, when other men were busy scrambling up the greasy treacherous pole of their own ambitions, Ben was walking away from it all, casting aside his old life and even his old name, Pearse, without as much as a backward glance, his past carefully erased, his future hopefully a clean slate.

He was at another crossroads too – this one about two miles from Larkhaven. The estate agent's directions had been confusing, the map not nearly detailed enough. He applied the brakes on the old car and pulled up onto the dense green verge. Then he unfolded the map that lay on the empty seat next to him, hoping to make sense of the directions. He didn't have a mobile phone. In any case, who would he have called? It was Saturday and the letting agency was closed. There was no one else he could or would contact.

He ran a hand through the thick mess of black hair that fell in unkempt waves about his rugged face. He traced the lines of the map with his index finger. "Bloomfield Cottage . . . Bloomfield Cottage . . . ah – got it!" He stabbed at the map with his finger and allowed himself a small smile.

Then he started the car once more and drove off in the direction of Berry and Aoife Joyce's house.

Berry poured herself another cup of tea and fingered the small bundle of papers that lay untidily on her kitchen table. There were emails and faxes, handwritten notes – some on the backs of envelopes, one or two carefully penned notes on tasteful little greeting cards and some rather more formal typed letters on grand headed notepaper. They would form the basis of her weekly *Larkhaven Notes* column in the local newspaper, *The County Sentinel*, and she really ought to get to work on them straight away but the sheer effort of scrubbing down the little cottage had exhausted her. Plus, as she sometimes had to remind herself, she'd already done more than most people's full working week in the Internet café. Not that she minded – the very thought of being idle sent a vague shiver of unease down her spine. Still she suppressed a sigh of annoyance when she was forced to admit that Aoife had once again managed to wriggle out of the hardest work. Now only the kitchen cupboards remained to be cleared and scrubbed. But hopefully Aoife would at least get back to do that. If not, then Berry supposed she would end up doing that too. Maybe soon she'd challenge her little sister about not pulling her weight. But she couldn't do it now. In fact, Aoife's laid-back attitude to most aspects of home life was the least of her worries at this moment.

There was another pile of envelopes and papers in a little secret stash in a kitchen drawer – a more sinister and menacing little stash – and she tried to pretend for hours on end, and sometimes even succeeded in convincing herself, that they didn't exist. She forced them from her mind and concentrated on this comforting little stack of notes for the newspaper. They would take less than an hour to work through and, most importantly of all, they had the very distinct advantage of posing Berry Joyce no sort of personal anguish or worry at all. Besides, they yielded a weekly income of thirty valuable euro.

She heaved a weary sigh and hauled out her laptop from its sleek leather casing, setting it up on the kitchen table where the light was best. The laptop had been a cast-off present from an old friend in Dublin.

She clicked on the Desktop icon marked *Larkhaven and County Sentinel*, created a new file and then picked up the scrappy little bundle of papers once more. There wasn't anything much exciting this week – just the everyday humdrum events of village life.

An email proclaimed the headline: *Respected Larkhaven Family Almost Wins Lotto* – it was a story about the Byrnes who had got as far as having five numbers in the previous week's draw. A rare plant had been discovered growing in a sand-dune close to the shore and a botanist was travelling from New York to take photographs and make notes. A note from the Yacht Club announced that Kathleen O'Hegarty, the village poet, had been commissioned to write a lengthy poem commemorating the one hundredth anniversary of the building of the new pier. A gala dinner would be held in the winter to raise funds for the new marina. A tersely typed page informed her that Colin Farrell had most definitely been spotted driving through Larkhaven on his way to a film director's party in an exclusive village a few miles down the road. A pretty greeting card with roses on the front had the headline: *A Revered Village Pensioner Recalls The Day She Saw John F Kennedy In Dublin,* and beneath it a brief description of the momentous occasion written in a neat but shaky hand by Nancy Lemon. She'd been sending the same note to Berry every week for the past year and each time, though Berry vowed to include it, Nancy Lemon's thrilling glimpse of the dashing president ended up at the bottom of next week's pile. This time though there were such slim pickings that Nancy and her president would surely make it into print.

Ever since she'd come back to live in Larkhaven four years ago, Berry had written the *Larkhaven Notes.* She'd inherited the column from her mother who'd been the gentle and affectionate chronicler of village life for almost thirty years. Berry's mother, Nora, had often cheekily described herself as both a glitzy gossip columnist and a highly influential political commentator, to people who used to enquire snootily if she worked for a living. But in reality the little column in *The Sentinel* earned barely enough egg-money to pay for her daughters' schoolbooks and probably the seagulls had a more powerful political influence in the village than she had. They certainly made more noise and mess. Still, Nora had loved her job as the Teller of Larkhaven Tales and the recorder of events. Simple though her news stories were, she always wrote them with kindness and sensitivity and with an eye to the future. There was never gossip or cruelty – no tales of murder or bankruptcy, no rattling of village skeletons, no bitter feuds or faithless wives or violent men. Instead she wrote of births and weddings, epic battles on the football pitch, hard-won victories on the golf course, beauty queens and bonny babies, fantastic events like the giant squid that had washed up on the shore one blustery winter's day or the huge mushroom that had been found in the wooded area behind the church. She wrote about the simple and exquisite loveliness of each passing season.

Having often watched her mother patiently stitching and patching together the weekly column, it had come quite naturally to Berry to follow on in the tradition. She worked away now, putting together a flowing piece about the weekly events of the parish, and a gentle but pointed reminder of the mammoth changes that were even now lumbering inexorably towards the village. Then she wrote a nice little paragraph about Nancy Lemon and the president and surrounded it with a neat box to set it apart from the rest of the text. There would even be room for the small photo that had been included, which would please Nancy no end.

She leaned back in the chair and surveyed her work on screen. It looked fine and Berry suspected her mother would have been quite pleased.

She saved the document, then emailed a copy of it to the editor of *The County Sentinel*. She could drop the photo by tomorrow. She got up and was about to throw the raggedy bundle of notes and letters in the bin when a plain sheet of lined blue notepaper caught her attention. Beneath a neatly printed address and telephone number, there were only three lines of handwriting on the page in a distinctive tall angular style of writing, the letters leaning forward like regiments of tilting little soldiers. There was no mistaking the writer though. She'd never forget the handwriting, not if she were to live for a thousand years. How had she missed it earlier? She held the note in her hand and sank into a chair. She tried to focus on the writing but the words danced in front of her eyes.

'*My Dear Berry,*' she tried to read the words aloud, as if by reading them, she could somehow diminish their effect. But it was no use. Tears streaked down her face and before she knew what she was doing, she'd crumpled up the page and thrown it onto the blazing fire in the range.

"Right," she said, sweeping the salty tears from her face. She kicked off her light indoor shoes. Then she picked up the mud-encrusted hiking boots that she always kept at the back door and rammed her feet into them. "Weeding – cures all but the most lethal doses of self-pity," she told herself as she strode down the front garden path wielding a hoe and a bucket. She hacked at the thick roots of dock weeds as if they were her worst enemies. She dug down several inches to pull the fine but deep-set roots of nettles from the rich black soil. She blanked out the emotional wave that had threatened to engulf her earlier in the kitchen and thought only of her good earth and the things she intended to plant there the following spring.

So when Aoife went scurrying by some time later with barely a wave of her hand, it took several moments before Berry noticed her.

"Aoife!"

"Sorry, Berry!" Aoife called over her shoulder. "I'm really sorry – but the train was late and now I'm late."

The sight of Aoife scuttling into the house brought Berry back to her senses. She called crossly after her sister: "You're just in time to do the kitchen cupboards. I've left bleach, a mop and a bucket. And better get your skates on. Ben Searson is due in less than an hour."

"Don't worry. I'll sort it," Aoife called back breathlessly. "I'll do a really good job – I promise."

Minutes later, Berry watched in exasperated amusement as Aoife dashed back down the avenue, her arms awkwardly brandishing a selection of mops, buckets and containers, and bolted into the little cottage.

Inside the cottage, Aoife set down her collection of washing utensils, peeled off her hoodie and rolled up her sleeves. Then she worked busily at clearing out the contents of each kitchen press into a large black refuse sack. When the cupboards were empty, she filled up a bucket with lots of hot water and a generous helping of bleach. She'd forgotten to bring rubber gloves, which meant that her hands would smell like a public swimming baths for the rest of the evening but it couldn't be helped. The most important thing now was to get the job finished before the new tenant got here.

In her garden, Berry continued to grapple with weeds. Now she was feeling her way along an elaborate underground network of roots that spread over several feet. It was couch grass and she knew that if she didn't get every last bit of weed and root no matter how fine – the damn thing would be back thicker than ever in a few weeks' time. She teased at it gently with her little twisting fork, loosening the roots and watching the soil crumbling away in rich dark granules. She knew all the weeds by name: dock, colt's foot, bindweed, stinging nettle, plantain and hundreds more. They were like worthy enemies – to be tamed and defeated. But in a way their presence in her garden meant that her soil was rich and well fed. With one final tug the large network of fine roots came clear of the soil and she placed it in a bucket for burning later. She sat back on her heels. It was a small victory but she enjoyed it. She raked the little fork idly through the clear soil. Good earth – no chemicals.

What would she plant there in that little corner? A clump of delicate irises maybe, or pale pink hellebores to brighten up the winter months?

Whatever it turned out to be would be new and lovely and delightful to look at each morning as she set out to work and she would lavish the same low-key love and attention on it as she did on almost every other aspect of her life.

She forked a little grit and fertiliser through the soil and turned her attention to the next weed-infested patch. The work was hard and soon she'd worked up quite a sweat. She pulled her old fleecy jacket off and wiped away beads of perspiration from her forehead with a clay-encrusted hand.

She heard footsteps on the gravelled path. Aoife, no doubt – coming to apologise yet again and to declare that at least the cupboards were clean. But Berry didn't plan to let her off that lightly.

"You really are something else," she said, bending forward to work the soil away from a thick dock-root with her fork. "You still think the world exists for your pleasure!"

She expected Aoife to stumble through yet another truly abject apology and she was not prepared for the sound of a low dismissive snort. It didn't sound like Aoife at all and Berry turned quickly – to see a stranger. He towered over her and she couldn't quite make out his face as she squinted up at him in the afternoon sunshine. She stood up quickly and saw he was dark-haired, unkempt-looking, almost like he'd crawled out of a coalmine. He had several days' beard and was wearing a tattered old navy crewneck sweater and faded corduroy jeans. He looked to be in his early thirties. A grubby-looking rucksack was slung at his feet.

"Oh sorry, I thought you were . . . I mean, you must be Ben Searson." She did her best to wipe the clay from one of her hands, then held it out to him. "Berry! Berry Joyce – your landlady, I suppose."

He looked at her suspiciously for a moment, and then shook her hand firmly. "Ben."

"Welcome to Larkhaven," she said brightly after a pause.

"Thanks," he mumbled and stood there, hands jammed in frayed pockets. He didn't seem to want to make conversation at all and Berry found herself quite suddenly at a loss for words.

"I parked at the gate," he finally said. "I wasn't sure where to . . ."

She pointed down the little avenue to the tiny house at the gate and felt quite mean suddenly. "You're in the gate lodge. It's not much, I'm afraid. I'm sorry, I thought you'd be . . ." She couldn't finish the sentence. What could she say – older, smaller, less bulky?

"Yes?"

"I thought you'd be – well, the rooms are very small and, look, if you change your mind – no worries." What was she saying? She was hardly in a position to turn down a welcome bit of rent now.

"All I want is a roof over my head."

She paused, tempted for a moment to say something witty, something that might bring a smile to his bleak face – but she resisted. "Then you are welcome. I'll walk back with you – show you the ropes."

"Cool," he said. He lifted up the dingy old rucksack and slung it over his shoulder and they set off down the avenue together.

Berry led the way through the door of the little house and quickly introduced him to her sister. "Aoife – this is the new tenant – Ben Searson."

"Hi," said Aoife looking him up and down. "Sorry, can't shake hands – covered in bleach. Anyway, I'll just get on – finish the cupboards, I mean."

"Leave it. I won't notice, I promise."

"But –"

"Look, I'm tired – thank you for all the cleaning, but right now I'd really like the place to myself."

"Of course," said Aoife, and she set about gathering up her things.

They'd tried to make the house as clean and comfortable as possible for him. Berry had left a pile of their old sheets and pillowcases and a duvet in the bedroom. They'd left a few antique electric fires in place for him. They'd left a packet of tea and sugar and a pint of milk, a loaf of bread and some butter and jam. Berry had set down a vase of wild garden flowers on the kitchen table –

bluebells and dog rose. Maybe Bloomfield Cottage wasn't exactly the Taj Mahal – but they had done their best to make it comfortable and homely for him.

Somewhat offended by his abruptness, Aoife now felt they shouldn't have bothered.

On the way out, she glimpsed a Rolex watch on his wrist and she shot Berry a quick pointed glance.

Later in the evening the sisters sat together in the kitchen, sipping tea and wondering about their new tenant.

"Odd!" said Aoife, biting half-heartedly into a value-pack Rich Tea biscuit. It was horrid but there was nothing else sweet in the house and so she munched onwards valiantly.

Berry nodded absently. She was thinking about the letter that she'd burned, wondering if she'd been over-hasty. She now regretted not keeping the phone number at least. She'd only glanced at the address and seen that it was Dublin and here she was now – wondering all over again about what might have been. She drew in her breath sharply and reminded herself that the very last thing she needed right now was to leave herself open to the sort of emotional bungee-jumping that she'd worked so hard to distance herself from. No – she was right to burn the letter – she could see already how it had upset her – a letter now after all this time, when she'd thought the entire heart-cleaving and shameful event was well and truly buried in the deepest, darkest corner of her heart. It felt as if someone had taken hold of her and was shaking her to the verge of disintegration.

"Very odd!" said Aoife, reaching for her fourth value-pack biscuit. Actually they weren't so bad – not when she dunked them in the hot sweet tea.

"What? What do you mean?" said Berry.

"God, you're miles away. Ben Searson is what I mean. I think he's odd – rushing us out of the house like that, wanting to be alone. Don't you? Who does he think he is? Greta Garbo?"

"He seems OK," said Berry. "It will be good to have someone staying in the cottage and, as long as he pays the rent and doesn't frighten the animals, isn't that all that matters?"

"I mean," Aoife continued, completely disregarding her sister's cool appraisal of the new neighbour, "I was expecting an old man – you know, retiring to a little country cottage – living out the twilight years of his life fishing off the rocks and making sloe gin and writing his memoirs of working in the Civil Service. But he's young. You don't suppose he's out of prison for murdering his wife or something?"

Berry grinned broadly. "Like I said – right now I don't really care as long as he pays the rent."

"And don't you think it's funny," Aoife continued, "that he has a Rolex watch but his last address is a corporation flat in the city?"

Berry shrugged uninterestedly.

"Maybe I'll just do a Google search on him all the same," Aoife said, before heading off to bed.

Chapter 4

It was Monday morning and, while her mother rustled up the full Irish breakfast that Liam Kelly demanded every morning come hell or high water, Nathalie tried to have a nice conversation with him. She liked things to be nice. She liked everyone to get on. Her mother said she was wasting her time expecting Liam Kelly to have a nice conversation with anyone. He no longer knew the meaning of the word 'conversation' – let alone the word 'nice' – as if he had been brought up on some planet where the whole language was made up of about ten different types of grunts. Maybe he was a throwback to the apes. As to what, if anything, was going on inside her husband's head, Yvonne Kelly had not one clue any more. In her lighter moments, she called him The Riddle of the Sphinx or The Armchair Oracle. Sometimes in particularly withering mood, she would refer to him as The Guru of Glennstown. If it weren't for her part-time job in the local bank, and her daughter's company, she felt that she might go quietly mad.

But Nathalie was devoted to both her parents and she still kept up her attempts to have nice chats with her dad, though it was even harder these days since Aoife had gone home to Larkhaven. She poured him a cup of tea and kissed him lightly on the crown of his head. Though he flinched slightly, and kept his eyes firmly fixed on the sports page, she ignored that. She patted his broad shoulders and rubbed the fingers of her good hand lightly through the ends of his cropped fair hair.

"Time for a haircut, Dad."

"What? Oh, right."

"Want me to do it for you?"

"Ah, no, you're all right."

"I can trim it for you this evening. How's that?"

"I'll be grand."

Behind him, Yvonne rolled her eyes to heaven and shook her head. Was ever a man more rude and distant to such a sweet-natured daughter? She often had visions of herself like some cartoon character clobbering him with a rolling pin or a frying-pan, something that would knock some sense and manners into him.

"I'm meeting the barrister today."

"Oh, right. Take no nonsense from the likes of them."

"Dad, his job is to help me."

"Help you and line his own pocket."

Nathalie suppressed a little sigh of frustration. It was the only thing about her dad that she would change, given the chance: his division of the world into two classes – the likes of them and the likes of us. She wondered at times if something had happened to make him bitter in this respect – because in almost every other way he was about as far from bitter as a man could be. She reached across the table and rested her hand on his, rough and calloused from years on the buildings.

"Don't worry,"she said. "I'll be fine."

Though Yvonne couldn't really understand why Nathalie was always at great pains to be nice to such a miserable old grouch, Nathalie herself could see nothing strange in it. Grumpy and all as he was now, she still had vivid memories of being carried proudly to school on his shoulders, of being paraded up and down the street to be shown off to the neighbours, with him clutching her tiny fingers gently in his big spade of a plaster-and-paint-encrusted hand. She remembered how he would always slip her a few pence to buy an ice cream, how if he was ever away on a job he would return with some silly gift for her – a pink brush and comb set, a My Little Pony Rainbow pencil case, or a Care Bears patchwork quilt to put over her dolls.

The Kellys lived in a neatly tended tree-lined cul-de-sac in Glennstown. Yvonne said it was the best little road in Dublin. The neighbours were mostly wonderful – except for Darren Walker and his six Dobermans who didn't exactly court popularity. All the other neighbours kept their brick-fronted houses neat and well maintained. The front gardens were full of colourful flowers and shrubs. If they were giving out prizes for the best, though, Yvonne's house would certainly win. She loved her home – every single aspect of it. There was not a flower in the garden that she hadn't thought about carefully before planting, not a lovingly filled terracotta pot that wasn't fussed over and almost talked to on a daily basis. Her patio brimmed with pots of shiny healthy bamboo, fig, camellia, begonia, and exotic tree ferns, plants that others couldn't coax into life at all. In one corner she even had a large shallow terracotta bowl done out like a miniature rockery with tiny rocks and delicate alpines.

Over the years she'd cajoled, coaxed and bullied Liam into improving their house. He was, after all, a builder. In those days, which seemed a lifetime away now, Yvonne hadn't minded the energy and skill and tact required to manoeuvre her husband into extending or renovating. These days she dreaded asking him to change a light bulb. But back then she was unfailingly cheerful, ever hopeful. As a result, Liam had built a large extension to the rear of the house, incorporating a spacious kitchen and conservatory downstairs and upstairs a bedroom and bathroom and dressing-room – fit for his princess, his only child.

They'd wanted more children. "I'll give you a half a dozen easy," he used to whisper with tender roughness to her under the sheets at night – but somehow, after Nathalie, it had never happened. Yvonne watched her biological clock ticking away with relentless regularity, every twenty-eight days a mini-heartbreak. And at last she'd been forced to accept that there would be no other children. Liam had never been willing to discuss the problem. She suspected he thought it was his fault and she had not pressed him, fearful that, if he discovered it was, it would destroy his pride and possibly their marriage. Now she was sorry. Their marriage had withered away anyway.

But no child was ever more loved or more indulged than Nathalie. Of all the jobs he'd ever done on any house, large or small, Liam lavished the most work and attention on Nathalie's room. It had the best timbers, the most expensive paint, the most glamorous gold bathroom fittings and a dressing-room with the finest built-in maple units, glass-fronted drawers, pull-out units for shoes, a special stand for belts and scarves, a rich stained-glass window at the far end, featuring the figure of a little girl chasing butterflies. The bedroom itself was furnished with a fine wrought-iron bed, an antique pine dressing-table, a desk, a television and stereo system and a large comfortable leather sofa to lounge on. One wall housed nothing but bookshelves and a desk where she kept her computer. There was even a tiny little unit that housed a coffee-maker and mini-fridge.

Nathalie knew she was unusually lucky to have so much space, what amounted almost to an apartment of her own at home that she didn't have to pay for. Johanne came from a family of five and, though twenty-two, she was still sharing a room with her teenage sister. Sometimes Joanne would talk longingly of getting a place of her own, even a little one-room bed-sitter. But Nathalie had no such desire. Besides, despite the strangeness of her parents' relationship, nothing would make her leave them – at least until she met the man of her dreams. And she'd quite given up on that.

Sometimes she felt there might be something wrong with her, that she wasn't out clubbing and pubbing, on constant man-alert. Wasn't that human nature? To find a mate and propagate? But currently Nathalie had very little interest in sex. She wasn't a virgin. That particular status had been lost on her nineteenth birthday to her then-boyfriend, Warren Logan. Warren had insisted that he was just the man to bring her to the heights of sexual ecstasy, that he was experienced, that he would be gentle and considerate. Nathalie wasn't entirely convinced but she wanted to be rid of her virginity, have it safely out of the way so no one could tease her about it. So, with a coolness that surprised her, she'd let Warren take her to his bedroom while his parents were out, and been highly disappointed to discover that Warren's finely honed and polished technique had merely consisted of half-removing her bra and panties, kneading her breasts clumsily before tugging his jeans awkwardly down his thighs, sliding his penis into her, jigging around while talking a lot about the peaks that he planned to bring her to, shuddering and letting out a little snort on reaching what she concluded must be an orgasm.

She hadn't felt in the slightest bit aroused or even interested in the proceedings, was glad she'd insisted he use a condom, smiled kindly when he said, "Brilliant, wasn't it?" and gracefully rejected his offer of a repeat experience.

Currently Nathalie was boyfriendless.

Nathalie waited nervously outside the door of Gretta Price's office. She'd knocked lightly on the door and heard Gretta's voice saying with chilly superiority: "One moment, please."

After what seemed like an age, but was probably only two minutes and enough time for Nathalie, despite her earlier shower, to break out in a mild sweat, the door opened and Gretta Price appeared, dressed in her customary navy blue skirt and jacket.

"Nathalie. Shouldn't you be at your station?"

Nathalie swallowed and picked her words carefully. "I-I need to have a brief word, Miss Price."

"Very well."

Sitting in the low chair facing Gretta's desk, Nathalie tried not to feel like a five-year-old But Gretta Price did not go out of her way to put people at their ease. While Gretta answered a pressing email, Nathalie amused herself by reading the company mission statement emblazoned on the wall behind Gretta's head.

Our first responsibility is to our customers, those who avail of our services every day.

Our second responsibility is to our Nutopia Team, those who provide the heroic commitment, the remarkable intelligence, the superlative competence and the passionate heart that sustains the very lifeblood of our company. We believe in fostering a collaborative team environment that yields creativity, quality, innovation, and success – every hour, every day, every week, and every year.

All team members will be treated in a manner consistent with this company policy . . .

"Well?" said Gretta suddenly.

Nathalie began. "I need to – that is – I was wondering if it were at all possible, I mean I know that you have a roster to organise and of course I will make up the time . . . so I'm asking to –"

"Do stop babbling, Nathalie. I haven't the time. Say what you have to say and get back to work."

"I'm asking to . . . to take a couple of hours off . . ."

Gretta stared for a long moment, then pointed to the mission statement – to the word 'team'. "See that word there, Nathalie? Spell it out for me, would you?"

"T–E–A–M," said Nathalie in a series of squeaks, inwardly cursing that she sounded like such a timid mouse.

"No 'I' in team, is there?" said Gretta, smiling grimly at her.

Nathalie didn't point out what she and Johanne and some of the other girls often giggled about in private when Gretta did her "no 'I' in team" bit. It was the fact that the word 'team' did actually contain within it the word 'me'.

"No, Miss Price. There is no 'I' in team. But this is an appointment I have to keep." She didn't want to blurt out that the appointment was with a barrister.

"Can't you reschedule? This is very short notice."

"I only found out about it yesterday afternoon."

"Very well. While you're here, I notice your sales haven't been so good for the past few weeks."

"Yes – I'm sorry. Just the time of year, I suppose. I will try harder. I promise."

"Show me the money!" Gretta said in her fake American accent. "Show me the money, Nathalie! Don't forget – we did you a favour taking you back. The company was under no legal obligation, you understand. And I did you a personal favour in giving you our best client list. I don't need to tell you that some of the other client lists are . . . well, how shall I put this?" Gretta gazed into the distance as she struggled to find a movie quotation that would convey the sheer awfulness of the X Client List aka The Price List.

Nathalie forced herself to look calm and unfazed.

"Oh, the horror – the horror, Nathalie," Gretta intoned sadly as she drew her gaze back from the middle distance and examined a sliver of stray cuticle. "So let's not go there," she added with sudden brightness.

"Yes, Miss Price." And before she could think of

anything else to add, Gretta had swooped to the door and shown her out.

The plush waiting-room of Norton ffrench Solicitors was empty except for Nathalie, who sat up as straight as she could in one of the very low, very soft red-leather chairs.

She had arrived early for her appointment and spent a while in the rest room trying to tease her wavy light-brown hair into some kind of shape and dashing on a coating of lip-gloss – more for something to do than anything else. She would have liked to have worn the smart new denim jacket and printed pale-lilac skirt that she'd bought in Karen Millen and a cute pair of matching pumps, but Gretta Price insisted on everyone wearing conventional black suits to work. (Johanne reckoned it was because Gretta couldn't bear the sight of younger, slimmer and prettier girls in Nutopia looking even younger, slimmer and prettier in brighter colours and more fashionable styles. Making all the girls wear shapeless black suits was a way to even things up in the beauty stakes.) So since she had come to the solicitor's directly from work, Nathalie had no option but to wear her usual black trouser suit. She felt it made her look pale and washed out. And even at her best, she was no beauty. But still, she thought, as she looked in the mirror, better count her blessings – her complexion was clear, her skin fresh and her soft grey eyes flecked with brown looked warm and friendly.

Felicity showed her into a small office. Over tea and biscuits they went back over the story of the tailgating incident once more, for what must have been the tenth time.

"I feel I'm making a big fuss over nothing," Nathalie sighed.

But Felicity smiled reassuringly at her. "A finger isn't 'nothing'."

"Yes, I know – I only mean in comparison to the awful things that happen to other people – like being stuck in a wheelchair . . . or being brain-damaged or even dead."

"It makes no sense to compare. And besides, if you were a violinist or a surgeon, the damage to your hand might cause the loss of your whole livelihood."

"Yes, but I'm not a violinist and I'm not a surgeon, so this barrister will probably think I'm only on the make – you know, like that man who drank twenty-seven pints and then sued the pub because he fell over and fractured his skull."

Felicity smiled. It was refreshing to deal with someone so honest.

"I mean when all those really awful things happen to people, a lot of the time they just have to put up with it – without any compensation. Of course, I'm unhappy that it happened and I do feel conscious of it and I wish my hand was in full working order. You'd be surprised how hard it is to do up buttons first thing in the morning with two fingers missing – not to mention the typing. But there's nothing I can do about it now – all the specialists have said the same thing – so I have to move on. It would make less sense to sit around moaning about it. I'm just not that kind of person."

"Yes, I know what you mean. And it shows what an honest and sensible person you are to think that way. But the fact remains that it wasn't your fault Clinton Waters pushed into you and caused the accident and therefore you are entitled to seek compensation. Isn't that why you were demoted to cold-calling – because you couldn't type as fast at the keyboard? What about writing? It can't be easy to hold a pen properly if half of your hand isn't functioning."

"I suppose the whole idea of going to court scares me and people will be bound to make comments about it."

Felicity shook her head and flashed a brief warm smile at her client. "People will always be more than happy to pass comment – so that shouldn't influence you either way. Now Mark Tierney should be here soon – so you can talk all these issues over with him." And she smiled reassuringly at Nathalie, then left to see another client.

Nathalie sat alone in the room. She was deep in thought, her head bent low, when the door opened and one of the young office lads appeared.

"You all right?" he enquired.

She nodded but barely looked up. She hoped he would leave soon so that she could compose herself for Mr Tierney.

But he didn't. He stepped forward and lowered himself at the knees so that his eyes were level with hers, a bit like someone doing a mime of going down an escalator. She had no option but to look up.

"Sure?" he asked.

She nodded and bent her head again.

"Sure you're sure?" he said, lowering himself further.

"Listen!" she said, looking directly into his eyes. "Thank you but I'm . . ."

She stopped. He had smiling green eyes, something like a mischievous glint in them and a slightly crooked, boyish grin – he looked like the sort of chancer that would charm the birds off the trees, would be her mother's verdict. She couldn't help smiling back.

"That's better," he said, getting up and standing back, winking cheekily at her.

He was very casually dressed for an office boy – jeans and a black T-shirt. And she was surprised to see that they allowed him to wear an earring. He also had a small tattoo of a bird on his forearm, which Nathalie also noticed was a nice, strong, tanned forearm. Instantly she sat up rigidly straight and tore her eyes away from the tanned forearm.

"Thank you, I'm fine," she said, trying not to make contact with the mischievous green eyes. "As a matter of fact, I'm waiting for Mr Tierney, my barrister." She said it with a certain degree of haughtiness, because in a way having a barrister did make her sound more important.

"Is that so?"

He sat on the side of the desk and folded his arms with no end of cheek. He'd surely get the sack if he continued carrying on like that. In Nutopia Telesales and Marketing, fellas were not allowed to wear earrings and tattoos were never to be visible and they certainly never sat on bosses' desks with their arms folded. Gretta Price would probably spontaneously combust if anyone had the nerve to park himself on her desk.

And the way he was staring at her – as if he were amused by her! She began to feel most uncomfortable. In the end she had to say something, anything, to break the silence.

"Won't Mr Tierney mind you sitting on his desk?" As soon as she had said it, she could have bitten her tongue, it sounded so silly.

He shrugged lazily but didn't move. "What's he like, do you know?"

She was surprised at this. Must be a new employee.

Well, it looked like he wouldn't last long in this job! "I haven't met him yet," she said, as she eyed him curiously.

"So how do you know he'd mind me sitting on his desk?"

"Well, he's a barrister."

"So?"

"So . . . so he's probably quite formal."

Office Boy was still looking quizzical.

"So he probably talks like he has a pound of grapes in his mouth," she went on, "and sounds like he's swallowed a dictionary for breakfast."

"Hmmm!" he said mildly and then nodded as if she might be right.

She felt encouraged to continue. "I'd say he drinks a lot of wine and he has two big dinners every day. So he's probably as fat as a fool with a big red nose as well."

Office Boy nodded with interest. "So tell me all about this hand then," he said.

Nathalie froze, not liking at all the idea that such a cheeky bloke should know her business. Not very professional of the firm, was it? She should complain. "How do you know about my hand?"

"It's my business to know these things."

"Your business! How could it be your business?"

"If I'm to represent you . . ."

What? "I don't understand . . ."

He grinned. "I'm sorry to disappoint you about the big belly and the big nose but I'm Mark Tierney, summoned here by Felicity to represent you – whether you like it or not."

"Yeah, right! And I'm Ally McBeal!" she retorted.

It was the oldest trick in the book, pretending to be

someone really important to impress a girl – but she was no silly little bimbo. She might only have a Junior Cert from school but she was well qualified in the school of life, having plenty of unofficial certificates and diplomas which specialised in the smarmy, charmy, devious, conniving, cheeky, gutless ploys that men would use just to impress girls.

"I can prove it to you if you like," he said.

"OK then, prove it."

Very gently he retrieved an ID card from his wallet. On the card was his photo, the name *Mark Tierney* and the words *Barrister at Law, Junior Counsel* beneath.

Nathalie eyed it sceptically for a moment, but she was feeling increasingly unsure of herself. "Anyone can have a fake ID made up. I had one done when I was sixteen to get me into all the nightclubs."

"Tut tut, Nathalie – better not mention that in court. They might think you're the sort of person who doesn't tell the truth."

"Well, if you're a barrister – where's your wig?" It was another silly question. She knew it.

He slapped his forehead in mock annoyance. "Knew I'd forgotten something. Thing is – the mother put it in the wash by mistake and it shrunk. Then, of course, she made matters worse by trying to iron it!" He sat at the desk and produced a number of documents. "Anyway – down to business."

Nathalie felt her face reddening horribly. But thankfully he didn't seem to notice as he began to outline her details.

Nathalie was happy to let him talk.

CHAPTER 5

Ben found he quite liked the cottage. That surprised him. It felt safe and contained – like he was in a manageable place – like he might after all begin to recover. And if he didn't – what would it matter? The world would never notice that he'd left it.

He had quickly settled in, an easy task considering the fact he hadn't brought anything much with him – some clothes and a pair of working boots, a book or two, a razor and some soap. It was funny, he thought, to have been born with so much and now to have his entire life packed into one rucksack.

The landladies had done their best to make the cottage comfortable but it needed a lot of fixing up. One of the windows was cracked. The plumbing was faulty and the kitchen table was close to collapse.

On Monday evening he decided to light a fire, in order to create a cosy cottage ambience, but then wondered whether the chimney needed sweeping. He didn't particularly want to go up to the house and ask – the less contact he had with his new landladies, the better he'd like it.

He went outside, gathered some kindling and lit a small fire in the grate, which quickly filled up the tiny room with dank and sooty clouds of smoke.

He cursed and quickly extinguished the fire, then pulled on an old jacket and rambled up the potholed avenue to the house. He planned to knock at the front door and ask for brushes to sweep the chimney. He stood on the granite step for a few moments, was on the point of knocking but then changed his mind and turned to leave. He didn't want to have to make conversation; in fact the very thought of having to make conversation made his whole chest seize up and contract into a horrible knot of anxiety. He kicked at the gravel and smiled ruefully at his own foolishness. How the old Ben would have scoffed at his wimpishness.

"You're such a loser!" the old Ben would have said. The old Ben would have stridden up that avenue as if he was some kind of Greek hero, Hollywood sex symbol, as if he planned to ravish both Berry and Aoife Joyce together in the same bed at the same time with champagne and oysters and the Kama Sutra on DVD. And he would have! Several times over!

"Damn!" said Ben now as, too late, he saw Berry Joyce appearing from the side of the house.

A navy sweater hung loosely on her long bony frame and she wore faded corduroy jeans tucked into scuffed brown-leather boots. Her straight dark-brown hair was twisted into an untidy bun at the nape of her neck. She smiled easily at him.

"Settling in OK?" she asked.

"Yes, thanks. Everything's fine."

"Cup of tea? I'm just back from my shop. Could murder a cup myself." She pushed through the front door and held it open for him. He wanted to make his excuses and get away but it wouldn't do to be rude either so he followed her meekly into the house and down the dark narrow corridor to the kitchen.

He sat into a chair at the table and shifted about uncomfortably, racking his brains to think of something to say. It's amazing, he thought, how quickly he'd slipped the safe anchor of small and meaningless talk. Once upon a time Ben was the king of small talk and slick meaningless babble. He could sell ice to the Eskimos – sand to the Arabs – cocaine to the Colombian drug barons. Now the thought of even being in the same room as a bunch of movers and shakers, wheelers and dealers, brought him out in a cold sweat. The kitchen was quiet except for the sound of bubbling simmering water in the kettle.

Berry set a mug of tea on the table in front of him, leaving her own mug standing on the counter. She set about emptying the dishwasher.

"You own a shop?" he said at last.

"I think the bank manager might take issue with your use of the word 'own'. And I suppose 'shop' isn't accurate either. It's an Internet café and laundrette. No, don't laugh – everyone else does and it's beginning to get tedious."

"I wasn't going to laugh. I was just going to say that's good, because I suppose I'll need to use the laundry."

"Here's a tip. Mondays are always busy – it's when all the bachelor farmers and divorced fishermen come into town to do their washing and their surfing. And the Internet is always very slow on Fridays for some reason."

"Thanks for the tip but I don't think I'll have much use for the Internet. I've left all that behind me."

Berry suppressed a mild flicker of curiosity about what he had left behind him. She clattered an assortment of chipped and unmatched dinner plates onto a scrubbed wooden shelf, wondering what she might say next. She didn't think he'd be much interested in the weather.

"So you're settling in OK?" she said at last.

"Yes, fine, thanks."

"I hope everything's OK . . . I mean warm enough and clean and so forth? I intended to paint the kitchen but it's so difficult to find the time – and I know the table's a little bit bockety – I'll need to get someone to fix it."

"Don't worry," he said, draining the last of his tea and getting up – obviously about to leave already. "Thanks. I was thirsty."

Berry shrugged and smiled amiably at him. If she thought he was just the slightest bit eccentric, she was careful not to show it.

"I was going to clean the chimney in the cottage," he added, on his way out the door.

"Great! I mean, are you sure you wouldn't mind? My dad used to do all that sort of thing. I meant to get it done – but somehow I've been so busy. I'm afraid I haven't got any of those new-fangled vacuum things. But there's a set of brushes in one of the outhouses – oh, and an axe for chopping logs as well if you fancy a bit of vigorous exercise. There are a few old trunks of trees thrown in your back garden – you can chop them up and use them for fuel if you like."

The chimney was a tougher job than he'd expected. It probably hadn't been swept in years and various birds had nested in it, which was the cause of the dank billowing smoke. When it was at last clear he cleaned up the room as best he could, set a fire in the grate once more and made a sandwich. Then he sat by the fire and tried to concentrate on his book. It was *The Alchemist* by Paulo Coelho, given to him by his sister Paula many years ago, and unopened until this very evening. He had never even noticed the dedication on the front page before. *To my dear little brother Ben on your eighteenth birthday – I hope some day that you find your treasure too. With much love, Paula.*

"A bit late for that now," he said, chuckling grimly to himself.

Nathalie was sitting at the kitchen table, drinking tea and telling her mother about work and Mark Tierney.

"He's not at all like I was expecting. For a barrister, I mean."

"Even barristers are human."

"Well, he was real nice. I didn't even believe that he was a barrister at first. It was so embarrassing . . ."

As Nathalie talked on, Yvonne bustled around the kitchen, methodically preparing a dinner of lamb, carrots, potatoes, and fresh peas. She'd had years of practice, could almost make the meal in her sleep, felt that soon she would be making it in her sleep. For Liam Kelly would allow himself to be served only two dishes: roast lamb and roast beef. It was a costly menu to have to stick to and Yvonne often felt frustrated that she couldn't show her imaginative flair with fish or the cheaper cuts of meat – or, God forbid, chicken, which you couldn't even mention.

"Chicken!" he'd say in a rare moment of animation. "That's not real meat."

The women in his life survived Liam's totalitarian beef and mutton regime with shared conspiratorial smiles, Yvonne occasionally clenching a fist in apparent good humour behind his back.

Today it was mutton. Yvonne had prepared the leg of lamb as always, sprinkling it with a few knobs of butter and some sprigs of rosemary. She had shelled the peas, peeled as little skin as possible from the potatoes, as per instructions, and cut the carrots into little circles.

Sometimes she thought she might just die from the boredom of it all. She knew that the day was fast approaching when she would be unable to refrain from doing something drastic. Perhaps she'd reached a stage in her life when she could no longer control her emotions. She'd even talked to her doctor about it . . .

"Doctor, do you think there might be some pill somewhere which would be guaranteed to stop me from murdering my husband?"

The doctor, a kindly northerner with a beard, nodded sympathetically. "Would it surprise you to know that lots of women fantasise about killing their husbands – or at least losing them permanently? Particularly at this stage in life. Indeed, my own wife confesses to a great fury at me sometimes."

"Yes, but why has my husband become so unbearable at this point?"

Yvonne wondered, if there were so many women who felt like that, why there wasn't a support group: MWA – Murderous Wives Anonymous. Truthfully, she'd felt guilty in recent years for not loving her husband more, for being so mean-minded. It had never occurred to her that other women would feel the same thing.

"Why now?" replied Doctor O'Flaherty. "It's no excuse of course – but men – some men, find this stage in life difficult."

Yvonne was not impressed. Her eyebrows said so. "Don't give me any of that mid-life crisis crap, Doctor – Liam Kelly's been in crisis for four years. I don't know how much more I can take. Maybe I would be doing him a favour by bumping him off and putting him out of his misery – you know, like a poor mad old dog!"

"Some of us are all mangled up inside – in our hearts – in our souls – and it's hard for us to find the words to explain. That's how it is for Liam. If he lives to old age, he may get over it with remarkable grace and tranquillity."

Yvonne's eyebrows were now somewhere near the top of her forehead. The idea that Liam Kelly would be all mangled up inside was just too preposterous. The suggestion that he had a heart or a soul, or any potential for grace and tranquillity, was verging on the ridiculous. The thought that he might live to old age just plain scared the hell out of her.

"Like I said, Doctor," she replied finally. "If you ever do hear of a pill . . ."

Yvonne made an effort to stop brooding and pay attention to what her daughter was telling her. "And what did this barrister say about the tailgating incident?"

"First of all that I wasn't to feel a bit bad about suing the company, that I had suffered clear loss of earnings, that they were well covered against any insurance claims and that anyway they were technically at fault."

"You don't have to go through with this, you know. Your father –"

"I know. But Mark – I mean Mr Tierney – was talking about things I could do with the money – good things . . . and there are things I'd like to do."

"What sort of things?"

Nathalie had a good relationship with her mother, apart from the few usual spats of her teenage years, and she could confide in Yvonne about almost anything. On this occasion though, she didn't want to say. What if things didn't work out? She didn't want her mother worrying, trying to smooth the way with her dad. Best to say nothing – because none of it might even happen.

"Nothing much. Start saving, I suppose."

Yvonne smiled affectionately. She knew her daughter had plans and they didn't necessarily include saving. But she never pushed things. Sometimes she thought that Nathalie might be destined for a very different career. Though she didn't dare to hope. She had only one child and it was enough that she should be healthy and happy.

All the rest was gravy.

Speaking of gravy, Liam was most particular about his: the juices of the lamb, mixed with a spoonful or two of wine, a sprig of fresh herbs, a sprinkling of cornflour for thickening and some stock. Lately he'd begun insisting that she put a spoonful of redcurrant jelly in as well. Where, she wondered, did he get such notions? Though she had to admit, his recipe for gravy, especially with the redcurrant jelly, was surprisingly tasty. She wondered vaguely where it had come from, but had more sense than to ask.

Lately she was afraid to ask him even the most simple

of questions. How was work? Was the traffic bad? Are you hungry? Would you like dessert? Any one of these seemingly harmless questions could push him into a state of acute grumpiness.

Just then she heard his car pulling into the driveway. "Here he is!" She exchanged resigned smiles with Nathalie, sighed and smoothed down her silk blouse.

They heard his key in the front door, then his measured steps across the hall into the kitchen. He always insisted on going to work in a suit and proper shoes. He changed into overalls on the site. It had been something that Yvonne found quite intriguing in the early days of their marriage – that he would never 'insult' her by coming into the house in muddy boots or cement-spattered working clothes. Life with Liam Kelly was quite romantic in those days – as far as she could remember anyway.

"Hello, Dad!"

"Hello, love." Liam dropped a kiss on Nathalie's cheek as she passed him on her way upstairs.

"Dinner's ready, Nathalie! Don't disappear!" called Yvonne.

"Just a minute, Mum!"

Liam sat into his armchair and opened his newspaper.

"How was work?" asked Yvonne.

"Grand."

"Traffic bad?"

"I've seen worse."

"Are you hungry?"

"You could say that." He began to study the sports page.

Yvonne would not be put off. Every evening it was the same and every evening she gave him a damn good run for his money. If he wanted to sit and glower in his chair, then he'd have to do some talking first. Fair was fair.

Yvonne made a great show of stirring the spoonful of redcurrant jelly into the gravy. "What about that big house? Did you find out who bought it?"

"Does it matter? Some flash bloke."

"But who?"

"That fella – the one who sold his company for millions."

Yvonne cast a brief look of weary resentment at her husband – or, rather, at the back of his newspaper. "I do so enjoy our little chats," she mumbled and set about carving the meat.

Yvonne Grogan had been just nineteen when she first met Liam Kelly in the early seventies.

She was working as a typist in one of the building societies in the city centre. She earned twenty pounds a week and was able to put most of it into a savings account because she lived at home with her parents, two brothers and a sister in a nice bungalow down a quiet cul-de-sac in Killester. She didn't have a boyfriend. In the seventies there weren't so many nightclubs or bars as there are now. Besides she wasn't all that keen on pubs and though she'd been to one or two nightclubs, she didn't really like them and thought that most of the men who frequented them were either married or a bit creepy. And she was only nineteen with plenty of time yet to meet a nice man. There was one young man, Guy Bushell, who she had gone out with for some time. His parents were quite well off and quite friendly with her mam and dad. Yvonne's dad often said that he'd love to see his daughter set up for life with a rich young man like Guy. But, after dating him for a while, she found she had no interest in him. He was dull and arrogant and showed no real interest in anything she had to say. In any case, she then met Liam Kelly.

It was the year of the Oil Crisis. Suddenly petrol was the only thing anyone seemed concerned about. There were stories of people siphoning off petrol from their neighbours' cars. Petrol vouchers became more valuable than money. Everybody stopped going on long journeys and loads of people in her neighbourhood in Killester joined car pools or took to riding bikes. For those who absolutely needed their cars to get to work, there was the new weekly chore of queuing for a few gallons of the liquid gold. Yvonne's father, a travelling salesman whose work took him all around North Leinster, needed a regular supply of petrol and sometimes, as a favour to him, she would take his place in the long queue of cars and sit for hours on end waiting for the weekly ration.

One Friday evening as usual she sat in line, her foot switching between brake and accelerator as the car inched forward slowly. She was tired. It had been a tough day at work and in the drowsy warmth of the car, she began to nod off, her head listing sideways against the window. Then she awoke to the sound of a loud crumpling bang and the sensation of the car shuddering. Confused for a few moments, she then realised that she'd driven into the back of the black Ford Cortina in front of her.

She climbed out apprehensively to inspect the damage, fearful of how the Cortina driver would react. The man was climbing out of his car, a youngish fair-haired man. Perhaps she could try apologising first. It wouldn't do any harm. Though if he was like most car owners he would probably completely overreact.

"Are you all right?" he asked quietly as he inspected the damage. His bumper was badly dinged and one of his rear lights was shattered.

The damage to her father's car was much worse with quite a sizeable dinge to the front wing and the grill panel completely crumpled in. As she looked at it, she felt like crumpling in herself. Her father would be furious. He always took special care of his car.

The man stood with hands shoved idly in his pockets.

"Could be worse," he said as he pulled a piece of shattered glass from one of the lights.

"I suppose you'll need to get my insurance details so you can make a claim," she said, her voice shaking. She got out a notebook and pen.

He shook his head. "There's no need for all that insurance malarkey. I'll have this fixed myself in no time. It won't cost more than a few pounds."

"Won't it?"

"Honestly, no."

"But . . . wait . . ." She scribbled down her name and number, tore out the page and handed it to him. "Take this anyway, in case you change your mind."

"Well . . . OK so." He pointed to her dad's car. "That will cost a few bob though."

"Will it?" she said, horribly close to tears.

"But no one's hurt. It's only tin. You'll be grand," he tried to reassure her.

"I suppose," she said, the tears brimming up now. He was being so nice it just made her want to cry even more.

"I know a good mechanic down in Fairview – one of

those little back-lane garages. But he's good and he won't cost too much."

He took the notebook from her and wrote the name and number down.

Then she couldn't fight the tears for one moment longer. "Thanks – you're being so nice about this," she sobbed, "but my dad will kill me – I know he will!"

He shifted about uneasily, clearly uncomfortable with this deluge of female emotion.

She felt woefully embarrassed. She ought to just climb back into the car but somehow she felt rooted to the spot.

"Ah now – here – you'll be grand. Don't cry. There's no need to cry. God, I'm hopeless when women cry." He fished out a clean white hankie and held it out to her.

Just then, people in the cars behind started hooting their horns and Yvonne bolted back into her dad's car.

"Thanks!" she shouted out to him as he moved up to get his few gallons of petrol.

A few days later, she was curled up on the couch watching *The Good Life* with her mother, when the phone rang.

It was Liam Kelly.

"I was just calling to see if you got the car sorted out?" Maybe he was going to make a claim on the insurance after all.

"My dad's taking care of it."

"Well, that's grand."

"Thanks for asking though."

"That's all really . . . except I hope you're not still upset."

"I feel so silly. It was all my fault."

"Like I said, no one was hurt."

There was an awkward silence.

"Thanks again for being so nice," she said.

"Ah, not at all."

"OK. Bye so."

She leaned forward to replace the receiver.

"Wait!" she heard him say. "Don't hang up. I have to go to a dinner dance. A GAA thing. It's our local club. Would you like to come?"

She was so surprised she didn't know what to say.

"I'm sorry," he went on hastily. "I shouldn't have asked you over the phone like that. I mean you hardly know me and . . . well, it's just that I'm really desperate for a partner – I don't mean desperate – but I've been busy and I've left it very late – and you seem like a nice person and well . . . look, forget I ever mentioned it. It was pure thick of me to ask a nice girl like you out at the last minute. I'm awful sorry."

Yvonne tried to remember what he looked like. But apart from the fact that he was tall and fair and broad-shouldered, she could recall nothing else about him. Though he had a nice deep voice. And he had been very nice to her about the dinge. And it was pure comical listening to him trying to explain himself over the phone. But wasn't it a bit strange that he'd invited her to a dance when they'd only met for a few moments? She was under no illusions about her looks. Men did not as a rule drop jaws when they saw her. Maybe he was just a bit of a chancer.

"You've been so kind that I don't want to say no straight out," she said. "Leave me your number and I'll think about it. Even if I do say no, thanks for asking me."

Her mother said he sounded real nice – and what harm could it do? Even if he turned out to be a bit of a lad, she was safe enough going to a dinner dance with him, where there would be loads of other people.

"Who knows!" said her mother. "He could turn out to be the love of your life."

Her father was less enthusiastic and reminded her yet again that Guy Bushell was a much more suitable boy.

When Liam Kelly landed on her doorstep a few evenings later dressed in a smart tuxedo and a simple black bow-tie, Yvonne was stunned. She felt a strange little flutter at the pit of her stomach. He was golden-haired, with strong set features and honest, blue-green eyes. He had a nice friendly smile and he handed her a box of Black Magic chocolates and a pale pink orchid to pin on her dress and told her she looked lovely.

Yvonne's mother was very impressed.

"Hang on to that one!" she had whispered in her daughter's ear.

CHAPTER 6

Ben awoke early on Tuesday morning and made a simple toast and tea breakfast. Then he drove to the village, bought some groceries and visited the little hardware store. He bought some paint and a hammer and nails and some glue. He was hard at work scrubbing down the walls before most people had even begun their day's work. Then he painted the walls a simple white.

After a late lunch, with slow and careful diligence he removed the two loose legs from the kitchen table, and stripped off the old glue with steel wool and a mixture of vinegar and warm water. Then he wiped the surfaces clean with a damp cloth. When everything was dry he applied a new coating of glue and set the joints once more. In the morning the table would be as good as new.

Then he began to chop logs. He grabbed a quick bite to eat around seven and then went back outside to his chopping. Finding a slow steady rhythm, he cut each circle of timber into wedges and stacked them in a neat pile in a small shed to the side of the cottage. He worked until the sun was low on the horizon. Even then he would have kept going if he hadn't been interrupted.

"You need to stop before it gets dark!" It was Aoife, passing by on her way home. "You might injure yourself." Then she added playfully: "And we're not insured for accidents after nightfall."

He set the axe down carefully and wiped his newly calloused hands on the seat of his jeans. "I've done enough for one day," he said non-committally.

"You've chopped a lot of logs!" Aoife said, unable to keep the surprised and searching note from her voice. The more she saw of Ben Searson, the more curious she felt about him. He was far too scruffy and uncouth-looking to be attractive, hard to tell what he even really looked like with the thickening beard. But there was definitely something mysterious about him, puzzling things that just didn't add up. She really must remember to Google him tomorrow.

For starters he didn't speak like a man who'd had to spend the formative years of his life chopping logs or sweeping chimneys. And she could see from the way he'd laid the axe down that his hands hurt like mad.

And then she felt guilty for being so nosey and just a tiny bit sorry for him and before she knew it she'd blurted out: "I've got calamine lotion in the house. It's the very best thing for blisters. It won't take me a second to find it."

"Thanks, but I'll be fine. Goodnight," he said and disappeared into the tiny cottage.

It was an awkward week at the office for Aoife. Every time she bumped into Flann Slevin, each time business threw them together, each time she found herself alone with him – she remembered how their eyes had met briefly but disquietingly after she'd danced with him, beneath the evening sky, the light breeze tossing his blue-black hair across his cheeks.

On Monday he had sidled into her office wearing a knowing conspiratorial smile.

"Hey, Aoife – my dancing partner!"

"Hi," she'd said, rather stuck for words. There was something incredibly unsettling about the way he said the words 'dancing partner'.

She was almost sorry she had danced with him. She would never get involved with someone at work – but, after all, it was just a bit of light-hearted salsa. Only now there was this funny atmosphere between them. She tried to ignore it and get on with her work. Hopefully, they would both have forgotten all about it in a few days.

But she hadn't. And neither, it seemed, had he. As the week wore on, he found more and more reasons to be alone with her, either in her office or his. There were several sets of house details that he needed to show her – which involved standing close and looking at the pages over her shoulder. When she went to the little café round the corner for a quick coffee on her way back from a house viewing, Flann just happened to be there.

Then on Thursday afternoon he appeared in her office.

"Got a moment, Aoife?" he said in a tone of easy intimacy as he shut the door behind him. "There's an important matter I need to discuss with you."

On Friday evening after work, Nathalie and Aoife met up

in the Light Fandango for a plate of spicy chicken wings, a glass of beer and a catch-up gossip.

"It sounds lovely," Nathalie said when Aoife had finished telling her about life in Larkhaven. "Don't be surprised if I land on your doorstep one of these days."

"Why?" asked Aoife, then added tactfully: "Of course you'd be very welcome – but why?"

Nathalie tried to explain about her parents – her father's gloominess and her mother's increasing frustration.

"I just don't understand it. They always seemed to get on well when I was growing up – but now in the past few months, if feels like they almost hate one another. They can hardly say a civil word to each other and sometimes I dread going home. I don't know what to do."

"But they seemed to be getting on fine when I stayed with you."

"That's just it. I think it might have been all a front . . . or maybe it's my fault . . . I don't know."

Aoife pulled a face. Nathalie's theory just didn't make sense. Liam and Yvonne never exactly went around joined at the hip – but they'd always seemed to have a comfortable liking and respect for one another.

"Anyway, that's enough about me," Nathalie said. "How's the new boss working out?"

At the mention of his name, Aoife flushed. "I don't want to talk about that!" she said and tried to change the subject. "Let me tell you about our new tenant! Not an old retired, senile person at all – but a rather young and dishevelled, but kind of dishy-in-an-indescribably-scruffy-gipsy-sort-of-way guy! But definitely something mysterious about him – not quite right. I Googled him yesterday in the office, but found nothing and –"

"Stop!" said Nathalie. "You're babbling and I don't want to hear about your new tenant. He sounds like a grand man who's just trying to mind his own business and you shouldn't be so nosey. I want to know about Flann Slevin. What's happened? Come on, out with it!"

Aoife blushed again at the mention of his name. She'd left the office the evening before, wishing she could blot out the whole embarrassing afternoon incident and make believe it never happened . . .

It had been a busy morning. She'd been dashing about showing the house in Portobello to another interested buyer and then taking a preliminary look at a little backstreet cottage that had just come on the market. But the afternoon was mercifully quiet and she caught up with phone calls and updating the database. Aoife always felt a little sleepy in the late afternoon, so she saved the mind-numbing work until then. First she updated the client database. Then, she was midway through proofreading a new brochure, when she remembered her idea about Googling Ben Searson. It would hardly take more than a moment and it might be just the little diversion she needed to keep awake.

Quickly she typed in his name and a few sites came up mentioning a young Canadian Celtic-rock music group, Searsons' pub on Baggot Street, then the poet Ben Jonson. There was no Ben Searson to be found. She then tried Benjamin and finally Benedict Searson – a few links to genealogy sites came up, but the dates were wrong by about a century. Then she typed in just 'Searson' and added in the words 'criminal record' – more for a laugh than anything else. She wasn't really surprised that nothing about Ben's past surfaced. The only vaguely related hit was the Director of Public Prosecutions website informing her that records concerning criminal case files were not available under the Freedom of Information Act. When she removed the word 'Searson' from the search the very same website popped up. So there was nothing to be discovered about him from the Internet at least.

Still, the bit of cyber excitement had woken her up and she turned back to proofreading the brochure with renewed energy. When she next looked at her watch she was surprised to see it was ten minutes to closing time.

Then there was a soft rap of a knuckle on her door. It was Flann.

"Got a moment, Aoife? There's an important matter I need to discuss with you," he said, shutting the door quietly behind him.

"Sure!" she said, indicating the chair on the other side of the desk, trying to inject an air of breezy cool efficiency into her voice. She still felt embarrassed about the whole salsa-dancing-disquieting-eye-contact thing.

He settled into the chair and smiled oddly at her. She couldn't quite figure out whether she should smile back warmly at him – or just bolt from the room. For some reason it occurred to her to buzz Claire on the intercom.

"Hiya!" Claire's light cheerful voice answered almost instantly.

"Oops! Pressed the buzzer by mistake. Don't know why I did that. Sorry!" Aoife said and turned off the intercom. She felt glued to her swivel-chair.

"I like the brochure you put together for those two houses in Rialto. Well done."

"Thanks."

"I mean it," he added, tapping out a rhythm on the edge of her desk with his index finger.

"I'm not exactly new to the job," she said. "I have been putting valuations on properties and assembling brochures for a couple of years now."

He stopped drumming his index finger and grinned at her. "Stupid of me. Of course, you've been doing it for ages. I just wanted you to know how much I appreciate your support since I came to Vernon's. Sorry if it came out awkwardly."

Aoife shrugged. Technically he was her boss – though now he was talking to her like an equal. She made circles on the desk with a pink mouse.

"Listen," he said, leaning forward casually onto her desk, "I'd like to pick your brain about a tricky valuation in Rathmines. Fancy a drink? I'm parched."

"Oh, I don't know. If I miss the train . . . and my sister is expecting me home."

He straightened up quickly. "Of course. It's no big deal. We can discuss the valuation tomorrow."

Aoife felt bad that she had refused him and he seemed vaguely disappointed. "But I'd love to go for a drink – another time – really I would," she said impetuously, and her eyes met his across the desk.

"You would?"

"Yes!" she said, horrified to find that she was blushing. "I mean – to discuss valuations!"

"Of course!" he said.

Then he reached across the table and rested his hand lightly on hers for a fleeting moment. Aoife's throat was suddenly dry, her heart drumming loudly in her chest. She stood up quickly and began to fold her laptop away in its case, aware that his grey eyes were boring into her.

"You can feel it – can't you?" he said, suddenly at her side.

"What?"

"It's something between us. The night of the barbeque you felt it – I know you did. A feeling like this . . . it only lingers for a reason."

Aoife felt sort of dizzy, sort of not quite in control. Somehow she felt the sensation of his breath on her neck and it made her wonder what it would be like to kiss him.

"So?" he said, hands now shoved in his pockets as he smiled down at her.

"So?" she replied, feeling like she was on a ship about to capsize. She tugged a maroon corduroy jacket from the back of her chair and made a big show of pulling it on and buttoning it up.

"You do feel it," he said. "I know you do." Then before she could do a thing about it, he bent and rested the lightest of kisses on her cheek.

Aoife had barely slept a wink that night – not to mention the fact that she'd spent every moment in the office on Friday slinking around trying to avoid him . . .

"Sounds like trouble to me," Nathalie said.

"Well, I'm not so sure. I mean he's very professional – knows his stuff and gets the work done. I get the feeling I can learn so much from him."

Nathalie observed her cousin with fond disapproval. "He doesn't sound all that professional to me. He's your boss. He shouldn't be coming on to you like that – end of story!"

"Nonsense! I mean if everybody in the world observed that rule then doctors wouldn't marry nurses. Film directors wouldn't date actresses. Record producers wouldn't ever marry musicians and artists wouldn't fall head over heels in love with their models. Sometimes, Nathalie, you can be incredibly naïve."

Nathalie was not to be put off. "I mean he's hardly in the place a wet week, and he's chatting you up and making inappropriate advances."

"What inappropriate advances?"

"Inviting you for a drink!"

"That was to discuss valuations."

Nathalie pulled a disbelieving face. "Touching your hand across the desk!"

"Hardly a hanging offence."

"And then – kissing you on the cheek!"

"Ah, come on! It was hardly rape! And Kevin often kisses me on the cheek – when I come back from holidays – or at Christmas for instance."

"It's entirely different and you know it. Aoife, you surely wouldn't think of letting this go any further? Besides, it may have escaped your attention, but you already have a boyfriend. A really handsome, sexy, and considerate boyfriend."

"But Flann is really nice. And he's definitely going places. Quite honestly, I sometimes think Dermot has completely missed the boat. He just doesn't get the whole ambition thing."

"Maybe Flann is really nice. But that's not the point. It all sounds wrong and if I were you I'd put it out of my head this instant."

"God, you sound like an old granny! But you're

probably right," Aoife said with a little sigh. "Please don't tell Dermot – he'd be so hurt. You know he's nuts about me."

"Lucky you," said Nathalie, an uncharacteristic dejected note in her voice.

Ben had been working hard on the cottage. Outside he'd swept and cleaned, painted and whitewashed, until the little place looked quite pretty. He found a few old chipped terracotta pots in one of the sheds and he filled them with rich garden soil. Then he planted summer bulbs and cuttings and set them at the front door in a little semi-circle. It hadn't taken long to chop the rest of the logs and now a neat display of fragrant timber was stacked against an old stone wall.

He looked down at his hands that were blistered and calloused, the skin around his thumbnails cracked and bleeding. Yet it didn't bother him and that was a surprise.

Time to eat. He'd made a nice little stew – some rib roast and chunks of bacon, a few mushrooms, a mug of cheap red wine and a bunch of herbs he'd borrowed from Berry's kitchen garden. The sweet warm aroma of it filled the kitchen. He put a match to the fire, set a place at the table, opened out a favourite old history book. Then he ladled a generous portion of the stew onto a plate and broke off a hefty lump of bread from a fresh baguette he'd bought that morning.

He was knee-deep in the decline and fall of the Roman Empire when he heard a light knock.

"Damn!" he murmured, reluctantly getting up to open the door.

It was Aoife Joyce.

"Mmm! Smells good," she said, beaming warmly at him as she stood on the doorstep.

"Thanks," he muttered.

"What is it?"

"Beef stew," he said. "Come on in."

"Sorry – didn't mean to barge in like this – just coming home and remembered that I forgot to drop some post in to you this morning – it came to the house for you."

Ben stiffened as she held out an envelope.

"Looks like junk mail," she said.

He quickly examined the address and the stamp and then set it aside with what sounded like a faint sigh of relief. "Thanks," he said, giving her a dismissive look.

But Aoife couldn't help lingering for a moment. Apart from the fact that she'd wanted to deliver his post, she'd been drawn towards the delicious smell. Though Berry would have a meal ready, Berry wasn't exactly Nigella Lawson in the kitchen. In fact, Aoife hadn't had a really decent home-cooked meal since she'd left Yvonne and Nathalie's house some months earlier. She often longed for Yvonne's roast lamb dinner and Liam's delicious gravy recipe. Now she stood awkwardly in Ben Searson's kitchen and tried to stop herself from drooling. Not that she expected him to feed her or anything – but it all just smelt too mouth-watering. And she would just *love* him to offer her some . . .

But he was clearly waiting for her to remove herself.

"Well, *bon appetit* so," she said.

"Thank you," he replied and ushered her to the door.

And so she trudged reluctantly up the drive to Berry's value-pack tinned tuna casserole for two.

Back in the cottage, Ben poured a glass of red wine and tucked into his dinner. He examined the letter once more. Aoife had been right. It was simply a piece of junk mail – offering a loyalty card in the new supermarket. His eye was drawn to his name: Searson. He said it out loud as if trying it out for size. He supposed he'd get used to it eventually. It wasn't such a bad name and besides – he was well and truly stuck with it now.

After dinner Berry and Aoife cleared away the things and laid out their bills on the big old kitchen table. There were a lot to be paid – house insurance, electricity, heating, phone bill, TV licence – all the boring humdrum stuff attached to running a house – and then, of course, there were the business overheads as well. Berry ran a hand through her chestnut-brown hair and frowned with uncharacteristic anxiety.

"Business still quiet?" Aoife probed gently.

"Disastrous. What was I thinking of? I really feel like throwing in the towel – like the whole thing was a big mistake and I should just shut up shop and try to get my old job back."

Aoife glanced across the table at her older, much wiser, completely sorted and ultra-sensible and capable sister and saw a single massive tear plop down onto the phone bill.

"Oh, Aoife – it's a complete disaster. I'm close to ruin. I feel so foolish thinking I could just set up a business like that and make a go of it. Everyone must think I'm such an idiot. I have one or two good customers – Harry, Judge Patricia and Mrs Ndogo and her family – but if it wasn't for them I wouldn't last till the weekend. Some people grumble and complain about the cost of everything and Sheila Hendron tries to get out of paying altogether – even though she's probably got more money than the rest of the village put together. Anyway, if it was such a good business idea I'd be turning good customers away . . ."

Berry rambled on. Aoife had never seen her so distraught.

"I don't know how we're going to get out of this mess," she said finally, coming to the end of her long litany of despair.

"I didn't realise things were this bad."

Berry rubbed a hand roughly across her eyes and forced a weak smile. "I didn't want to worry you and anyway you were so good leaving Nathalie's and coming home that I didn't want to make it any harder for you. But we've reached a crisis point now. I'll make an appointment to see the bank manager – then we're completely at his mercy . . ."

CHAPTER 7

Patricia de Vere cast a cold eye around the room. Her aristocratic brow was raised and furrowed with anxiety. Charlotte Pobjoy smiled comfortingly at her while Gloria fixed a straying thread around a button. Sheila Hendron leafed through *The County Sentinel*. Three or four others watched Patricia anxiously. They didn't want to make a fuss but really it was time to be getting on home.

"I just don't know where she could have got to!" said Patricia, staring at Berry Joyce's empty chair and willing her to appear. How could they vote on the new name or the new member without Berry being present and making a note of it for the following week's *Sentinel*? The whole point of co-opting Berry onto the Ladies' Association was to make sure they had an instant and sympathetic line into the local media.

"It's been almost an hour now since the meeting convened. She's not coming," said Sheila briskly. "And I don't know about the rest of you ladies, but I personally have more to be doing with my time than hanging round in a cold draughty room on the off-chance that Berry Joyce of all people might turn up. We can vote perfectly well on this matter without her. And that's exactly what we should do. Besides, we need to discuss more pressing matters." She looked across the table, eyeing Patricia directly, the growing glint of a challenge in her eye.

"Fine," said Patricia coolly. The last thing she needed now was for Sheila to go off on one of her long-winded and unsubtle leadership challenges. "Let's vote without Berry if you like. Though it's hardly good manners. So all those in favour of changing the name of this organisation to the Larkhaven Association raise their right hand . . ." Patricia allowed herself a self-satisfied smile as she counted the raised hands. "Motion carried! Now all those in favour of admitting men into the Larkhaven Association raise their hands."

A ghastly silence hung in the air – hovering like a poisonous wraith.

"If you really think it's the right thing," Charlotte broke the silence at last, her voice trembling anxiously.

"No great objections," said Gloria coolly, sweeping a hand through her mane of glorious golden hair.

Some of the others mumbled their assent.

"Sheila?"

"Whatever gets us out of here quickly," said Sheila and raised her hand. She had an appointment at the beauty salon and it was certainly more important than what went on at the Larkhaven Ladies' Association or the Larkhaven Association as it was now to be called. And why all this fuss about bringing men into the association? Perhaps Patricia had some idiotic notion that she could ensnare some man by getting him to join them. Which was a plan that was doomed to failure when the plain truth of the matter was that Patricia de Vere would scare the Louis Copeland pants off any man brave or daft enough to come within an ass's roar of her.

"Now that we have decided to allow men in our group, won't you tell us what or who this is all about?" said Charlotte hesitantly.

"Yes, of course," said Patricia. "I propose Harry Robson for membership."

"What?" said Sheila and Gloria together. Harry would not have been high on their list of influential new members. Admittedly he owned a lot of land in the village hinterland – but he'd never bothered to get involved in village business before.

"I'll second the motion," said Charlotte, her pale blue eyes twinkling with excitement.

"All those in favour?" Patricia said and began counting raised hands.

Sheila rolled her eyes heavenwards and raised a reluctant hand.

"Motion carried. Harry Robson is now a fully-fledged member of the Larkhaven Association. The next item of business concerns HyperShop. HyperShop, you will remember, bought land from Harry some time back. I propose we discuss this matter at an extraordinary meeting of the association next week. You will understand then why it is so important that Harry Robson is on our side."

"I can't wait," Sheila said acidly before picking up her pink Lulu Guinness bag and evaporating from the room in a slightly too young Juicy Couture tracksuit.

As soon as they had all left, Patricia heaved a sigh of relief, then slipped on a jacket and sat into her car to drive the short distance to Berry's house. She parked crookedly on the gravel driveway and unfolded her tall voluptuous frame from the car. She knocked on the door loudly, then rang the bell for good measure. There didn't appear to be anybody at home. She rapped loudly on the front window, and then marched round to the rear of the house to try the back door. It was open. Inside, everything appeared to be normal. The kettle was warm. A rather stately, plump cat called Mulligan was curled up contentedly on a soft old cushion in a corner by the range. There was a half empty mug of tea on the table next to a pile of news items for next week's *Sentinel*. Patricia resisted a strong urge to rummage through them for gossip.

"Berry!" she called out firmly. She moved along the hall and shouted up the stairs, "Berry, are you there?"

Not a sound.

"You missed the meeting – not good form!" she called loudly while making her way up the stairs.

She was becoming mildly concerned. Although the two women didn't know one another all that well, Patricia knew it wasn't like Berry not to turn up for a meeting without phoning or sending a message. She peered round one or two doors but found nothing. At the end of the landing, just beside the bathroom, she noticed one of the doors was shut. No, of course it was none of her business. Yes, indeed, it was snooping of the worst kind – but what if Berry had been taken ill suddenly? What if some ghastly burglar had broken into the house and tied the unfortunate Berry to the bed with a view to illegal matters of a carnal kind? Patricia rapped loudly on the door and when there was no response she opened it gingerly.

"Berry?" she called out as she looked round the room. At first she could see nothing. Berry Joyce, it seemed, didn't tend to keep a whole lot of order on her knickers or her seemingly endless collection of frayed and faded low-hipped jeans. But just as she was about to turn and leave, Patricia heard a groan coming from the area of a massive old mahogany wardrobe in the corner.

Then some of the faded jeans began to move and groan and Patricia quickly realised that she was looking at the rear end of Berry Joyce.

"Berry? What on earth are you doing?"

"Hhhumnnngh?" Berry's muffled voice replied from inside the wardrobe. Then slowly her head and the rest of her body appeared. "*Patricia!* You gave me a fright. What are you doing here?"

"I might ask you the same question. You missed the meeting. Otherwise I can assure you I would hardly be snooping round your house."

Berry's face fell. "But the meeting isn't until . . ."

Patricia pursed her lips as if she was about to reluctantly sentence Berry to penal servitude for life.

"Sorry, I lost track of time," said Berry timidly.

"Not to worry – the motion was carried anyway. But what are you doing half-buried in the bottom of a wardrobe?"

"Just looking for something. Can't find it though. Never mind."

"Was it important?"

"No – not at all." She stood up. "What happened at the meeting anyway?"

"We're no longer a ladies' association. Which should help us to attract a broader range of members."

"Is that all?"

"Oh yes – and Harry Robson has been elected as our first male member." Patricia stopped and smiled stiffly. "Oh dear! That came out all wrong."

"Why Harry? He's a nice guy and all – but he's never bothered to involve himself much in village life up to now. We could have asked the bank manager or the man who owns the hotel."

Patricia's aquiline face spread into a rare smile. "Oh, but that's where you're wrong. Harry Robson is, shall we say, the Harry Potter of Larkhaven?"

"What?"

"He has secret powers – but like Harry Potter he doesn't know he has them just yet."

"Patricia, what are you on about? Or perhaps I should be asking what are you on?"

"Stop gaping and make me a cup of tea. Then I'll tell you all about it."

CHAPTER 8

Nathalie showered and dried her light brown hair with more than usual care. She'd talked her mother into buying her a blue silk and lace blouse with a rounded collar and tiny lemon and grey rosebuds stitched into the fabric. It had cost quite a lot of money but Yvonne had been quite happy to splash out if it meant her daughter felt more confident and relaxed going into court. The blouse looked well with her black trousers and jacket. She polished a pair of black slingback shoes and borrowed her mother's best black leather handbag. She applied a light tinted moisturiser and a lipgloss. Then a splash of her favourite perfume, Light Blue, a birthday gift from Aoife.

"All set, love?" said her mother as she appeared in the kitchen.

"Yes, I think so."

"You look grand anyway."

"Thanks."

"Doesn't she look grand, Liam?"

"I suppose so," he said, casting a brief appreciative eye over his daughter before returning to his food.

Yvonne was determined that she would not add to the pressures of her daughter's day and so she didn't on this occasion reach for the rolling pin and clout her husband with it. Though she couldn't quite control one of her eyebrows, which seemed to have taken on a life of its own and was now arching so highly that it was in danger of breaking through the ozone layer.

"Now what would you like to eat?"

Breakfasts were one of Yvonne's many home-making talents. Friends often told her she should be running a bed and breakfast. And sometimes the idea did appeal to her – but not with Liam. Lately she'd been contemplating life without Liam quite a bit – and it looked very attractive. She might just divorce him, buy a little place in Wexford and run it as a B & B. After all, she'd given him the best years of her life – and for what?

So this morning she tried to tempt Nathalie with puddings, rashers, sausages and eggs, or savoury scrambled egg, or French toast, or creamy porridge with maple syrup, or omelette, or home-made buttermilk brown bread.

"Nothing thanks, Mam. Just a cup of tea. I'm not all that hungry."

"Nerves – that's all. It will be over and forgotten about before you know it."

Nathalie wasn't so sure. Mark Tierney kept saying the same thing but now that the day of her court case had arrived, she would have given anything to avoid it. She would be standing up in court, answering a load of questions in front of strangers and then the judge would probably laugh and call her a scheming compo parasite.

Her only chance was if Nutopia decided at the last minute to settle out of court. Then she wouldn't have to give evidence in front of anyone.

"No need to be nervous," said her father.

"Thanks, Dad."

Nathalie thought of asking her dad to drive her to the offices of Norton ffrench in Fitzwilliam Square. But it would bring him in the opposite direction from his work and she hated to inconvenience him. He worked hard and was a good provider. It was more than many of her friends could say. He might not be as jolly as Johanne's dad who was always joking and good-humoured – but then Johanne's dad never seemed to be able to hold down a job for longer than a couple of months. And sometimes when she was coming home from work in the evenings, she might see him walking unsteadily, or leaning drunkenly against a wall to get his bearings. Nathalie's dad might not say much, might not be the warmest most affectionate dad in the world, but in his daughter's mind at least, he was steady as a rock.

So she was very surprised when she heard the following words issuing from behind the newspaper.

"I'll run you to the solicitor's office if you like."

"I'll be fine. I'll get the bus."

"No! What if the bus is late? What if it doesn't come at all? What if you miss the stop? You'll need all your wits about you with the likes of them."

"Are you sure, Dad?"

"Be ready in five minutes."

The traffic was mercifully light and on the journey into Fitzwilliam Square, Liam pointed out all the grand houses he'd worked on. His face lit up when he described skilfully carved banisters, elaborate stucco-work, fine old oak doors and panels.

"Finest job I ever worked on," he said, pointing to a large old three-storey house in Leeson Street. "No expense spared, of course."

Listening to him helped to take her mind off the looming court case.

Mark had prepared her well, going through all the questions they might ask and offering advice on how to give straightforward answers. Even though she had now met him several times, she still couldn't believe that he was a fully qualified barrister. He seemed too young, too nice and far too normal. But yet it was obvious that he was highly competent at his job. Even though it was a very small case, he'd researched it thoroughly and explained each stage of the case, treating her as an equal – not as silly little Nathalie Kelly with nothing more than a Junior Cert.

Mark and Felicity were waiting for her in the office. It was the first time she'd ever seen him in a suit and it made him look much older and more serious. It was a dark navy pin-striped suit and beneath it he wore a plain white cotton shirt and a simple maroon silk tie. His black shoes were polished to perfection.

She was overcome with nerves suddenly and couldn't think of a thing to say.

"What do you think of the tie?" he asked.

"It's OK."

They were sitting in the foyer waiting for the taxi.

"Only OK?" He smiled warmly at her.

"No – it's lovely. I mean it looks very well."

He was always so relaxed and friendly with her and

sometimes she longed to be relaxed and friendly right back at him. But she knew it would be pointless. He was just being nice, putting her at her ease. It wouldn't do at all to start getting familiar with Mark Tierney – she would only end up looking very foolish. So she was always on her guard with him, watchful of what she said, careful to be polite and pleasant but always a little formal.

"Good," he said. "Would you like me to go over anything with you?"

"No, thanks. I'm a bit nervous though. I hope I don't mess things up."

He rested his hand on hers for a brief moment and the fleeting sensation made her feel quite peculiar inside. There was a sudden awkward silence and Nathalie forced her eyes to meet his.

"You'll be fine," he said quickly. "Stop worrying. You've more brains than half the people that will be in that courtroom."

"Thanks," she said.

"You don't believe me, do you?"

"You're only trying to build up my confidence before I take the stand. That's your job."

He smiled his warm, crooked smile and winked at her, just like he'd done on the first day.

"It's true. Now, let's go."

What was true – that she had more brains than half the courtroom or that he was only trying to build up her confidence? It must be the latter. And it did make her feel better in one way. But in another way it made her feel worse because it made her realise that to him she *was* just a silly girl who needed to be flattered and humoured and coaxed with sugar lumps like a dumb mule. And resting his hand on hers like that was simply a patronising gesture of comfort. On the way to the Circuit Court she kept her distance from him, pointedly talking to Felicity in a way that excluded him. Not that he noticed. He was completely engrossed in his notes. Outside the Courts, Nathalie drank from a chilled bottle of water and psyched herself up for the ordeal ahead.

He disappeared into the building.

Felicity smiled at her. "You'll be fine. I know it. I wish all my clients were as sharp as you. What will you do with the money if you get it?"

"Well, I'm not going to buy a new pair of fingers and that's for sure! I want to go to college and get a degree. Maybe become a teacher."

"Or why not even a lawyer?" said Felicity as she beamed fondly at her client. She'd seen people drinking themselves through hundreds of thousands worth of compensation, or blowing it all on flashy cars and expensive holidays. She wasn't all that keen on doing compensation cases, though they paid the bills, but she fervently hoped that Nathalie Kelly would win. Better still that Nutopia would settle out of court and Nathalie would be saved the ordeal of a court hearing.

Nathalie's mobile flashed. It was a good luck message from her mum. Then a message from Aoife arrived. When she turned back Felicity was talking quietly to someone in a black gown and wig. She looked a bit cross, annoyed about something. Then she beckoned to Nathalie.

"A bit of a setback, Nathalie, I'm afraid."

"What is it?"

"Mark says they refuse to settle. They want their day in court."

It had been her only hope of avoiding the courtroom. But she was puzzled. "When did Mark tell you this?"

"Just now," said the man in the wig.

She looked up at him and realised that beneath the flowing black gown and thick grey wig that showed no signs of his mother's machine-washing and ironing – was Mark Tierney. She held a hand up to her mouth to suppress a giggle and was glad she did because he looked down at her very solemnly.

"It's time to go. Remember everything I told you and you'll be fine."

"OK," she said, trying to smooth out her unruly hair.

"Good luck, Nathalie," he said sternly.

In spite of being nervous, she began to find the whole experience quite exciting – all the barristers in wigs, the solicitors, people in the gallery, the judge sitting at his high bench, Johanne who had been called as a witness all dolled up in her best pink bouclé suit and pink mules with the feathers on – it was all a bit *Legally Blonde* or *Judge Judy*.

When Johanne was called to the witness box, she gave an Oscar-winning performance describing dramatically the moment when Nathalie's hand came into contact with the swiping machine.

"It is a moment that will remain engraved on my heart forever and I hope, Your Excellency and Members of the Jury, that today we can divert a serious miscarriage," she said passionately.

"Have you anything further to add?" asked Mark.

"No, thank you. I rest my case," she replied haughtily.

Then it was Nathalie's turn.

Mark asked her a whole load of questions that she answered quite easily, the nerves settling down as she got into her stride. She was glad that he wasn't being friendly to her. Quite the opposite – he questioned her coldly, weighing up her answers, talking to her without expression or intonation of any kind. It made her feel quite at ease. She had been terrified that he would wink at her or ask her what she thought of his cuff links or something – and that would have only confused and embarrassed her.

The barrister for Nutopia, James Comiskey, was a tall beak-nosed man. He tried to catch her out a few times. But Mark had prepared her well and she looked steadily at Comiskey and answered his questions simply and honestly.

He made a very long-winded speech about people like Nathalie and how irresponsible young people were and how sometimes compensation wasn't the answer, because unfortunately some people just didn't have the maturity or the education to invest their money wisely. Nathalie flushed angrily when he said this and was about to stand up and shout "Objection, Your Honour!" when she remembered that it wasn't her place to object at all. She glanced over at Mark who shook his head briefly and raised his hand in a gesture of caution.

Then the judge asked her a few questions, wanted to see the famous hand, which Nathalie showed him.

"You mean to say you have completely lost the use of two fingers? Can't anything be done to restore them?"

Nathalie shook her head.

"Even after two operations?"

"No, Your Honour."

"And may I ask – what would you do with thirty thousand euro?"

Nathalie paused, blushed, and looked around. She was reluctant to say. People might laugh. Mark Tierney might laugh. She caught Felicity's eye and Felicity nodded reassuringly to her.

"Go to college and get a degree," she stammered, "maybe become a teacher or – if I was to work really hard – a lawyer."

The judge looked her up and down searchingly for several moments. James Comiskey scrutinised her superciliously.

"Very well," The judge intoned gravely as if about to pronounce the death penalty. "Court will resume in five minutes."

Then he disappeared into his rooms.

Nathalie was sitting quietly between Mark and Felicity when the judge returned.

Felicity squeezed her hand. She looked across at Johanne who gave her the thumbs-up sign. Mark sat back in his chair and said nothing. He was looking intently at the judge.

"I find Nutopia to be negligent and entirely at fault. I order Nutopia to pay thirty-five thousand euro in compensation to Nathalie Kelly for loss of earnings, future loss of earnings, pain and suffering, medical costs, and to compensate for the permanency of the injury. Nutopia is to pay all costs in relation to this case."

"Holy shit!" said Johanne.

Nathalie threw her arms around Felicity and gave her a big hug.

"Well done!" said Felicity.

"Thanks, Felicity."

She turned to Mark; he was tidying up his papers and looked stern and preoccupied.

"Thank you, Mark." She held out her hand to him.

He shook hands with her, his mind clearly elsewhere.

"It was a very good result," he said, smiling stiffly.

There was a sudden awkward silence and then Felicity spoke. "Nathalie and I are going for a drink to celebrate. How about you, Mark?"

"Sorry – can't. I'm tied up with another case. Have one for me though."

He had already moved on to his next client, Nathalie Kelly and her funny little case forgotten. She'd enjoyed her few weeks with him but now they would say their goodbyes and not meet again. What was it Yvonne would say – ships that pass in the night? Mark Tierney was destined for great things – that was obvious. She felt sure that beyond payment of his fees, not a single thought about Nathalie Kelly would ever enter his head again. The chances of anyone like her bumping into anyone like him again were verging on the non-existent. She tried to force all thought of him from her mind

Nathalie ought to have been in a great mood for celebrating. Johanne had planned some sort of night out on the town – dinner in a nice little Chinese place down by the river, followed by clubbing in Johanne's latest favourite pulling joint – The Burgundy Cathouse which was, as Johanne described it: "Absolutely jam-packed on a Thursday night with the kind of blokes you'd not half mind waking up beside late on a Saturday morning!"

Nathalie was dreading it. Now that the excitement of

the court case was over she longed for her life to get back to normal as swiftly as possible. There would be time enough in the months ahead to plan how she would spend the money. But for now she wanted more than anything to simply go home and sit with her mam and plan a holiday somewhere exotic – something that might take her mind off the strange and sudden emptiness she felt.

CHAPTER 9

Although she would love to have stayed in town to celebrate with Nathalie, Aoife had promised Berry that she would be home that evening to clear out the spare room. Besides, it had been a most peculiar and in some respects a very disturbing day and she was quite exhausted. She made her way hurriedly up the broad street of Larkhaven now and sighed deeply as she reflected back over the day's events.

"Shit!" she muttered to herself as she strode purposefully past Ben Searson's little cottage and up the avenue to Bloomfield House. "What am I going to do?"

Early that morning Aoife had taken the train from Larkhaven as usual. It had been an uneventful journey, except for having to sit next to Patricia de Vere who looked like she might be passing death sentences in her head. But thankfully Patricia didn't seem in the mood for any sort of conversation, intimidating or otherwise, and Aoife spent the journey gazing out the window and dreaming of the man of her dreams. He wasn't Dermot. He was like a cross between George Clooney, Johnny Depp and Colin Farrell – with the merest hint of Dylan Moran for a touch of subversion. No, of course he didn't exist.

Aoife arrived in the office before anyone else that morning and since she had a little time in hand, she set about trying to get to grips with an increasingly long list of greetings cards. Aoife spread the huge array of cards in front of her. They'd cost her the bones of fifty euro in the village newsagent's a few days before but there was no avoiding the mountain of well wishes that she had to send out this month. Every day it seemed as though some occasion needed to be marked and Aoife hated to miss any of them. Old Mrs Murphy's husband had died and that meant a Mass card. Then there was Aoife's cousin's little girl who had just turned five and was very big into birthdays. Claire at work had just passed her driving test, Dermot had recently been made permanent in his new job and Maggie, a girl she used to work with, was moving into her first new apartment in Ringsend. Ordinarily she was very happy to send out cards full of well wishes – but money was quite tight at the moment and it was a question of knowing where to draw the line. She had agonised for a full twenty minutes over whether to buy Berry a Congratulations card for having bravely and fearlessly given up the fags after years of being the country's most dedicated smoker. But in the end she decided that Berry could do without. Although if things kept going this way in the whole greeting card business she'd be sending out *'Congratulations On Your New Replacement Windows'* to several of the neighbours in Larkhaven and *'Good Luck With your Extra-Marital Affair'* to a number of the company clients in Dublin 4. But still she prepared a carefully thought-out message on each card, penned each one in her best handwriting and sealed the envelopes for posting later. She looked at her watch. It was still only 8.15. Strictly speaking she wasn't obliged to start work until nine o'clock. But usually she was deeply engrossed in updating clients' files or checking details on the www.myhome.ie website by 8.30. She scanned down through Kevin's weekly memo and noted that he hadn't yet assigned anyone to the house in Talavera Road. Though she felt almost sure that Flann would get the sale of it now since he had settled in so well as senior negotiator. She suppressed a dart of envy. There would be other houses – and other commissions.

There was no sign of Claire for their usual early-morning gossip and Joe the porter wasn't in evidence either. So Aoife popped out to the tiny kitchen and made up a quick mug of instant coffee – strong and black to give her that early-morning jolt of alertness. When she returned to her desk she set the coffee mug down on an old mousepad and was about to set to work on the clients' files, when, almost as if by some strange supernatural intervention or quirk of fate, a little flyer popped up on the top right-hand corner of the screen. It flashed in neon colours and shimmied provocatively on the screen.

It read:

'Discreet and professional private investigations. All your enquiries served quickly and thoroughly . . .'

She wondered why it had popped up and realised that she hadn't updated her spam software since typing in Ben Searson's name and – she blushed to think of it now – the words 'Criminal Record' in a Google search. Aoife's curiosity was quickly aroused. Wasn't it really amazing the sort of sordid, sleazy lives some people led? It was hard to imagine anyone she knew having to get involved in any of the following grubby sorts of carry-on . . .

> *Surveillance and Counter Surveillance*
> *DNA Testing*
> *Discreet Marital and Domestic Surveillance*
> *Sweeps and Searches*
> *Video and Photographic evidence*
> *State of the Art Electronic Equipment*

FREE INTRODUCTORY OFFER!

The most sophisticated bit of surveillance she'd ever come across up to now was when the biscuit tin in the tiny office canteen had suddenly begun to empty almost on a daily basis even before anyone had got to it for the morning coffee break. It had been Claire who took it upon herself to lie in wait one morning, lurking stealthily behind the door for almost an hour, only to discover that it was Kevin stealing the biscuits all the time – because his wife had put him on a low cholesterol diet that he just couldn't hack.

Aoife looked at the screen once more.

FREE INTRODUCTORY OFFER!

Without even thinking, she clicked on the website to find out more. It was one of those sites where you could subscribe for nothing and avail of their free introductory offer, presumably on the assumption that once hooked she would become yet another satisfied customer. The website asked her for a brief summary of her query.

What query?

She had no query. Though perhaps for the sake of curiosity and the free offer she ought to write down something.

Her fingers hovered over the keyboard for a moment. What should she type?

Then the little germ of an idea formed in her mind. Her friends and family might all be above board, but there was the question of the free offer and it wasn't exactly as if she was in a position to turn up her nose at free offers at the moment. In fact, Aoife was becoming one of www.Pigsback.com's most regular visitors these days. This week she'd acquired a complimentary dessert voucher for Tasty Thursday's restaurant, two complimentary Cosmopolitans in the Purple Pepper, ten per cent off all travel insurance to anywhere in Africa or South America, twenty-five complimentary texts to Hungary and Austria, and a DVD to help improve her soccer skills, a ring-tone that sounded like a cat purring and the offer of a six-month supply of natural breast-enhancing pills. Still you never knew when they might all come in useful. So perhaps she ought to avail of the free private investigation offer.

She suppressed any niggling little pangs of guilt and began to type.

Dear Sir

I wish to take advantage of your excellent introductory offer. We have recently rented a small property to a new tenant and as we were anxious at the time to let the house, we didn't insist on references. However, there seems to be something a little bit . . .

A little bit what? Sinister? Mysterious? Not quite right? Secretive? That was it.

. . . secretive about him. He does not mention his past and he

has gone to great pains to avoid any mention of the subject when in conversation with us. He has no family or visitors to speak of. Yet he seems to be well educated and his clothes, though few, are well made – for instance, the Ralph Lauren cords and sweater. And those nice Savile Row shirts. Oh and of course the slightly battered Rolex watch. He also got very anxious one day when I delivered his mail. His name is Ben Searson. When renting the cottage, he gave 19 St Patrick's Mansions (a corporation flat in the inner city) as his most recent address. He is tall and lean with wavy dark hair and very brown eyes. I am guessing that he is in his early thirties. I'm not trying to pry into his private life or anything – obviously – but if you should find that Ben Searson has any kind of a criminal record or anything that might make him the sort of man we shouldn't have as a tenant, I would be grateful if you could let me know at your earliest convenience as part of your introductory free offer.

Yours sincerely

Aoife Joyce.

She was still agonising over whether to send it or not when there was a knock at the door. Quickly, without thinking, she clicked on the *Send* button.

"Shit!" she muttered under her breath as Kevin Vernon stuck his head round the door, thick spectacles perched on the end of his nose, and his straggling ginger hair forming a wispy halo about his head.

"A quick word, Aoife?" he said, closing the door firmly behind him and parking himself on a chair facing her across the desk.

She quickly closed the screen – but not quickly enough.

"Checking out fellas on the Internet – ah now, Aoife – I thought you'd have more sense," he said, smiling paternally at her.

"No – honestly. It's just our new tenant Ben Searson. There's something odd about him – thought it best to check him out."

"Ben Searson? Name rings a bell. Searson?" he took off his glasses and stared blindly into the middle distance as he always did when he was thinking hard. "No! Can't remember. Damn brain is packing in. Anyway, to business." He brushed down a wisp of ginger hair and smiled broadly at her. "I'm very pleased with your work, Aoife. I tell Stella every day how proud your parents would be of you."

She blushed and wondered what he was leading up to.

"Flann has been settling in well, I'm glad to say," he went on.

Aoife figured he wanted to tell her about assigning the house in Talavera Road to Flann. She pasted a breezy smile on her face and prepared to hide her disappointment.

"Any buyers for that little place in Portobello?" he asked.

Aoife shook her head. With Flann's new higher valuation, interest in the house had faded to nothing.

Kevin pulled a face. "I noticed you put up the guide price."

"Yes – we thought . . ." she stopped. She didn't want to sound critical of her new boss.

"Not like you to get it wrong. We'll have to leave it for a few weeks and then maybe change it back."

Well, she could definitely say goodbye to any chance of selling Talavera Road now, having made a blunder like that.

"Now, to bigger business," Kevin said. "I'd like you to take over that place in Talavera Road."

Had she misheard? She stared at him for a moment.

"I'm assigning you to negotiate the sale of the house," Kevin said, observing her incredulity.

"But I . . . but . . ."

"No buts. I've given it a lot of thought and it's time you got the chance of a solid commission. Besides, you will love this house. It's been made over by the best interior designer in town and – I haven't seen it yet – but I hear it's the last word in chic and style. It's going to be a high profile sale. You'll be dealing exclusively with the vendor's solicitor. I know it's not in your district, but Flann's books are chock-a-block at the moment so I want you to put everything else on hold and look after this for me. This is a particularly important property – very special – in my view the most important sale we'll make this year. I want to make sure that it gets the best possible price."

"But I don't think –" she began.

"Nonsense! I've been a bit worried about you lately, Aoife. You started off so well and now for some reason your work seems to have fallen back. It's all to do with confidence, you know! I'm sure of it and Stella agrees. We need to build up your confidence – and this job is just the ticket. I'm expecting you to do well with us. I'm hoping that in a few months you will be ready for promotion. I know you have great ability, so don't let me down." He stood up and frowned, before then beaming broadly at her. "Sorry to give you such short notice – there will be some buyers there this afternoon."

Aoife swallowed, not knowing whether to be overwhelmed and flattered by the faith Kevin was putting in her, or scared witless of the very real possibility that she might end up getting it utterly and completely wrong. Being given sole charge of a large house on Talavera Road was a giant step for her. She took a deep breath, beamed her brightest smile at the boss and said, without gushing, though she was fit to fly with excitement: "Thanks, I'll do my best."

And she did. She put everything else aside and for the rest of the morning she worked on familiarising herself with the house – the history of it, the style, its unique features and selling points, the state of maintenance – plumbing, heating, roofing, windows and doors, plasterwork, floors and ceilings, maintenance and restoration records. She spent a long time poring over photocopies of the original house plans and layout, the most recent renovation plans drawn up and carried out some six years ago. She double-checked floor measurements and scaled drawings. She studied the sale of similar houses in the neighbourhood. She even spoke to the architect who'd done the delightful orangerie extension to the rear of the house. By lunch-time, Aoife was about as up to scratch as it was possible to be with any house without actually seeing it. She would have a chance to look over the house itself in the afternoon before the buyers arrived.

Now her stomach was rumbling and she suddenly longed for one of those massive cream and smoky bacon bagels they sold round the corner. Outside in the corridor she could hear the low murmur of Claire chatting to Joe. Joe had miraculously passed his Introductory Law Module and was now faced with a whole new legal mountain to climb. Aoife stood in the doorway watching the unlikely couple: Joe, the privately educated porter, always immaculately turned out in that Abercrombie & Fitch rich casual look – and Claire, dressed in a black shroudlike garment – looking like she'd just rocked in from a heavy-metal Black Mass somewhere deep underground.

". . . so now I have to study Serious Offences against the Person and Property Offences . . ." Joe said wearily.

Claire reached out her long pale fingers and examined the top sheet of a pile of notes.

"Right then – let's start with this one – Aggravated Burglary . . ."

Joe stared at her blankly.

"A person is guilty of aggravated burglary if he or she commits . . ." she prompted.

He shook his head and frowned anxiously. "Oh – I don't know – it's got firearms or imitation firearms and weapons of offence in it – that's all I know."

"You better know it by tomorrow." Her dark kohl-rimmed eyes flashed at him.

At that moment Aoife realised that in recent days, Claire seemed to have a new spring in her cool, gliding Gothic step. Was it perhaps something to do with Joe?

"You two make an interesting couple," Aoife teased as they tucked into big bagels a while later.

Claire threw her a most scornful look. "Don't be daft! He's a mammy's boy and way too conventional for me. Anyway – no time for men right now – too busy with the job, the music and the graveyards."

Aoife suppressed a sigh. Sometimes she wished Claire was just a little bit less weird.

Back in the office, she checked her messages and mail and that was when she discovered that Nathalie had won her courtcase.

Celebrations tonight? She texted to her cousin.

Probably – hope you can come, Nathalie responded.

Can't! Have just been asked to do one of our biggest sales of

*the season!!! Am fit to burst with excitement! Plus promised
Berry I'd help her clean out the spare room. I've ducked out of it
so many times – I just can't let her down again. Really sorry –
but we'll catch up soon.*

She also noticed an email from Dermot. It was strange
that she hadn't heard from him since the party. He was
usually in touch almost every other day. Maybe he was
just very busy in his new job. It was quite a long email and
she began to glance through it quickly.

*Hi Aoife, Sorry haven't been in touch – incredibly busy with
new job.*

There – she was right. Dermot was about as dependable
as a guy could be. He was the sort you could trust with
you life, generally speaking. Good old Dermot – what a
complete pity she just didn't love him. She read on, quickly
skimming through the words – a hasty run through his
week's work, then a few words about a fortnightly tennis
game with his younger brother, a mention of a new heavy-
metal album he'd bought in HMV, his heavy-metal jamming
sessions with his best friend Steve – yeah – it was all the
usual Dermot stuff. She hurried quickly to the end,
wishing that he didn't always feel the need to tell her
absolutely everything that he'd been doing that week. She
decided to skip the next few lines – it was probably more
of the same heavy-metal-tennis jamming – and then she
got to the last line.

*So that is why I think we should meet up this weekend.
Early evening drink in The Purple Pepper on Saturday?? Lots
of love, Dermot.*

She sent him back a quick reply.

*Sounds like you're being kept busy. Really busy here. Just
got landed with biggest house on the books this month. So*

probably no point in emailing me for the next few days. Drink in the PP sounds good.

Kisses

Aoife

Then, as usual, she deleted both Dermot's mail and her reply to it. That had been something Kevin had insisted on when she'd joined the firm. "It stops the personal stuff getting mixed up with work – and believe me it can happen. April 2003 – our Galway branch – bunch of raunchy emails from the manager to his married girlfriend somehow ended up in a client's mailbox. Best to delete them – that sort of thing isn't good for an old man's heart, you know."

It was at that point of the day that things took a decidedly funny turn with the arrival of an email from the online detective agency.

Aoife was on her way out the door to the house in Talavera Road when she noticed it. Of course, she ought to have left it – but curiosity got the better of her. And perhaps if her mind hadn't been distracted by thoughts of Ben Searson, then she mightn't have found herself in a subsequently disastrous situation later that afternoon.

She was now running late for her arrival at the house in Talavera Road, so she printed off a copy of the detective agency email – signed by someone called Mike Mordaunt – and dashed out through the swish glass doors of Vernon's Estate Agents. She read through the tightly printed document with a growing sense of alarm as she cantered less than elegantly along the two blocks to Talavera Road.

"I would strongly urge that you contact us immediately with a view to putting in place strategies and procedures involving customised electronic solutions that will meet with your specific needs. We can assure you of our utmost discretion

in all matters relating to any further investigations that you might wish to instigate in view of the information that we now place at your disposal – free of charge as outlined in our online advertisement. This information would normally cost you in the region of three hundred euro (VAT not included) . . .

She read on through the mire of dense wording – hoping to make sense of it. And then a sentence in the middle of it jumped – or rather leapt out and did a provocative war dance in front of her: *No record of Ben Searson previously of 19 St Patrick's Mansions . . .*

Of course not. What was she thinking of snooping into someone else's life like some little Famous Five teenage detective? Then she read on.

We have scrutinised names of all recent occupants at that address . . . including one Bernard Pearse resident in 19 St Patrick's Mansions on the dates given . . . criminal record . . . robbery with violence . . . assault causing actual bodily harm . . .

Aoife skidded to a halt, eyes popping, heart pounding.

Bernard Pearse – Ben Searson? She rolled the two names round in her mind. There was hardly likely to be any connection, she told herself reassuringly. Yes, of course Ben could possibly be short for Bernard but that was as far as it went. Pearse and Searson were two completely different names. Weren't they? God, but they were similar though!

And the name Bernard Pearse did ring a slight bell of sorts . . .

Still there was no time to think about Ben Searson or Bernard Pearse or anyone else right now.

Aoife took a deep breath and resumed her flight towards Talavera Road. Reaching it, she hurtled along the long narrow path, to the house she was supposed to be presenting to prospective buyers. She recognised instantly. It was a broad elegant double-fronted building with a wide sweep of steps leading up to a grand pillared door. She was dead late and it wasn't a good start.

On the doorstep of the house, standing in the shelter of the berrington blue, fanlighted door, she quickly sent a text to Berry: *Ben Searson came up clear in my Internet search – so it looks like he's maybe not dangerous after all. But he could be, on the other hand. Explain later, XXA*

Then she fished out the key of the house, stuck it apprehensively in the brass keyhole and pushed the door open gently.

"Hallo?" she called out, in case any of the owners were about. But the house was silent. She gasped in admiration at the magnificent polished oak floors, the rich deep raspberry brocade drapes, meticulously restored late Georgian plasterwork, the walls painted a pale dimity shade, a series of Persian rugs that she could tell by their colour and detail were worth a small fortune in themselves. A broad oak staircase swept elegantly up to the first-floor landing. She set down her handbag and mobile phone on a chair in the long expansive hallway and began to make her way hesitantly through the grand rooms. When the present owners had bought the house, they had immediately enlisted the help of one of the best period restoration firms in the country. It had taken three long years to get the house in order, stripping away decades of bad taste and poor workmanship to return to the masterful and understated craftsmanship of the Georgian era. Now it was just like the home of Aoife's dreams, her other favourite daydream on the train when she wasn't dreaming about the man of her dreams.

She drifted into the gigantic drawing-room and then

she just couldn't help herself. She sank down into a vast ivory-coloured sofa in the splendid room and gazed in wonder at each carefully chosen painting on the walls, at the grand pillared Italian marble fireplace with its large cast-iron basket grate, at elegant bow-fronted tables with tapered legs, satinwood break-fronted cabinets, and a highly polished escritoire in rich deep walnut. There was a sense of bright airy space about the rooms, all emphasised by the pale parchment-shaded walls.

Aoife felt as if she had landed in her own daydreamed vision of heaven. She half-expected George Clooney to appear, bearing a glass of champagne in one hand and a ludicrously enormous diamond in the other.

Aoife was glad to see that the owners had wisely removed any smaller items of value that might have the misfortune to accidentally fall into some viewer's cavernous handbag. But one piece of porcelain on the mantelpiece caught her eye and she wondered if the owners had overlooked it. When she had lived with Nathalie, Aoife had done an evening course in Chinese porcelain and she recognised this immediately as Imperial work and dating from the Ming dynasty, Jiajing period. It was a smallish piece, decorated with four flying horses beneath ochre and red clouds, on a base of crashing waves and lotus flowers. With its bright red, green and yellow enamelled colours it was a bit garish for her taste – but still worth about several times her monthly salary. Vernon's always advised their clients not to leave anything too valuable in the house when it was open for viewing. She longed to pick it up and inspect the markings underneath. She remembered from her classes the individual signatures that porcelain craftsmen put on their work, their signature stamps recorded for all time. But she didn't dare touch the vase. Besides, she didn't have time.

She took out her notes on the house and concentrated on pulling her thoughts together and preparing a tour of the property. The prospective buyer would be arriving in less than half an hour and this was her big chance to make an impression on Kevin. If she got this right, then a big commission and promotion would certainly come her way. He'd as much as said so. It was simply a question now of going round the house and looking over each individual room. That would take up most of the half-hour.

"Right! I can't spend the whole day admiring this house. To work!" she said, forcing herself up out of the deep plump sofa.

She took her clipboard in hand and set out to inspect the rest of the house. Each new room was more beautifully decorated than the last and, though Aoife strove hard to keep her mind on the task in hand, she found it difficult not to gasp out loud at the harmony and proportion of the grand old house.

"If I owned this house, I'd never sell it – not in a million years!" she declared as she descended the grand stairs at last. She glanced at her watch. It was almost three o'clock, time for the prospective buyers to arrive. She ducked into the little white tiled bathroom to the rear of the study and freshened up her hair and lipstick. Then in the kitchen she poured a glass of water from the dispenser and sipped from it as she set out her papers and brochures along the polished granite top of the island counter.

There was still no sign of the buyers and she strolled round the house again, idly inspecting paintings, smiling at old family photos of babies and small gap-toothed children, and one photo of two men taken by the looks of things back in the eighties – probably brothers, standing in bright sunshine and grinning warmly at the cameras. Everyone in the photos looked happy and content.

She looked out at the garden for a while and it too had been landscaped to perfection, incorporating some old trees and providing an oasis of privacy for the owners. Time wore on and she found herself back in the large elegant drawing-room, again staring at the piece of Imperial Ming porcelain. It wasn't that large – about the size of a big teapot. Yes, it really ought to be stored somewhere safe. It was hardly likely that any viewer was going to steal it – but perhaps it would be better not to take any chances. She'd noticed a cupboard in the kitchen that could be locked. She'd store the vase there and then let the owners know about their oversight.

"I wonder are you early or late sixteenth century?" she asked the vase as she leaned forward to the grand mantel to retrieve it. Six tidy markings on the base would confirm her guess. She reached out carefully for the priceless piece of porcelain.

Berry's café was not busy. In one corner Harry Robson sipped a frothy cappuccino as he waited for his brother in New Zealand to reply to an email. Harry had recently ended a long-standing relationship with an interior designer, so to pass the time he was browsing through a few Internet dating sites, more for a laugh than anything else.

A number of websites promised to match him to the

bride of his dreams. Was he perhaps destined to bring an exquisitely beautiful and lightly framed Thai girl home to his one-hundred-and-fifty-acre estate? Or might a sturdier lady from the Russian Steppes be more suitable for his needs and might she feel more at home in his kitchen? Then he found a marvellous site that offered only Latino girls – from Colombia and Argentina and Peru.

Berry tried to suppress a laugh when Harry let out a low whistle and murmured: "Oh baby – you could be the one!"

"Harry Robson – just what *are* you playing at?" she said, scolding him gently.

He beckoned her excitedly to his desk, so she went and sat down beside him.

"Look, Berry," he said, grinning mischievously at her. "It says here Maria is fun-loving but would love to settle down with a kind and loving man. And then look at Sofia – she's hungry for love and will make any man happy beyond his wildest expectations . . ." He ran calloused hands through his wavy coppery hair. "Which would you go for?"

She smiled easily at him, ignoring his attempt at a wind-up.

Just then Patricia de Vere came striding through the door. She placed a large plastic bag on the counter.

Berry got up and went to serve her.

"Did you ever find what you were looking for at the back of the wardrobe?" asked Patricia abruptly after Berry had unpacked the bag.

Berry shook her head and quickly steered the conversation on to Patricia's bag of laundry. "Nice tablecloths. I'll give them the special laundering and starching."

"Perfect. There's no rush. I don't expect to have any VIP guests for a week or two. How's business?" Patricia cast a cold eye about the half-empty Surf Line.

Berry shrugged and struggled to wear her most philosophical smile. "Not exactly booming – but ticking over."

"What about HyperShop?"

"What about them?" Berry said, struggling to hide her growing anxiety about the new supermarket. "They won't have an Internet café, that's for sure. So I guess that's one thing I don't have to worry about."

"You're probably right," Patricia said. Then she folded her tall statuesque frame into a chair and immediately immersed herself in business.

Berry had been embarrassed when Patricia found her rummaging through the bottom of the big old mahogany wardrobe in her bedroom. Patricia would probably be consumed with withering derision if she were to discover the cause of Berry's frantic search. Regretting as she did that she had thrown Conor's letter into the fire, she had brooded on her mistake a lot, and eventually a memory had surfaced: at the time in question, she had owned a little maroon gold-embossed address book. And she had no memory of ever having thrown that out.

A strenuous search had ended in the bottom of the mahogany wardrobe in a wicker basket full of old letters and mementoes. Patricia had arrived just as Berry had at last laid her hand on the little address book.

After the judge had left, Berry had sat by the range in the kitchen leafing through it – until she came to a page near the end. A little scrap of paper – a slightly faded restaurant receipt – fell out. It was a souvenir of the last lunch they'd had – and he'd scribbled his email address on the back. "Just in case you ever want to talk," he'd said. She was grateful for the offer – the acknowledgement that something deep enough had happened between them, something that mightn't just be shut off by a simple 'Bye and take care'. But she'd never taken up his offer all the same. It had been enough that he recognised the great and largely unspoken earthquake of desire and affection that had somehow shuddered beneath them. His denial would have been the final straw.

Patricia and Harry and the one or two other customers were deeply engrossed in their own business and so Berry sat at a screen and typed in an email address.

To: renaissanceman@mainmail.com

From: bjoyce@eircom.net

Subject: Your letter

Dear Conor

I am so surprised to hear from you –. I want you to know that I am well and happy and I hope that you are too. I try not to think about you – or that episode in my life. It is past and I am so much older, sadder and hopefully wiser because of it. So there – every cloud has a silver lining – doesn't it?

Love always

Berry

Her eyes moistened with the beginnings of a tear but she squeezed her lids shut for a moment and the urge to cry passed. The cursor hovered over the *Send* button and she was on the point of mailing it when she changed her mind. Instead she deleted the email and tore the scrap of paper into tiny pieces. She would not, could not have even a single moment of Conor Lynch in her life again. A moment of supreme foolishness – brought on by strange vanity and crippling desire – that had led her to the point of destroying several lives . . .

Berry pushed thoughts of Conor Lynch aside and when she checked her mobile phone messages, she found the text from Aoife, telling her that Ben Searson had come up clear in her childish investigations and that he probably wasn't dangerous after all, or *"he could be, on the other hand"*. Well, that was helpful! Aoife might be twenty-seven, but she still had the over-active imagination of a little girl in some respects and she'd always enjoyed a bit of drama. This one would be right up there with the time Aoife was convinced that Colin Farrell was hiding out in the Bayview Hotel, disguised as a Hindu Sikh salesman, in his efforts to evade the paparazzi. Even if Aoife had discovered something awful about Ben Searson, it could mean anything from finding out he hadn't paid his car tax to hearing that he'd once been thrown out of the Shelbourne Hotel for smoking.

As if on cue, the door opened and there stood the dangerous man himself, dark hair tousled and flattened from the wind and the rain, large frame bending to get through the door.

"Ben! Thought you weren't into using the Internet."

"I was in town anyway and I thought I'd pop in and say hello – try to be sociable and all that."

She could see that it was an ordeal for him. He smiled but it was a forced smile and he kept his eyes guarded.

Yes, dangerous! Very dangerous! But not at all in the way Aoife meant. Berry swallowed and suppressed a half-forgotten memory – a silly old painful remembrance of things past. No – she wouldn't be going there again. She didn't have the stomach for it.

"Then it's good to see you," she said pleasantly.

"While I'm here I suppose I may as well send a few emails," he said and pulled out a chair at one of the monitors.

"How about a nice coffee?"

"Sounds good," he said and folded his lean frame into a chair. "Business is very quiet today?"

"Business is very quiet every day. Like I told you. Anyway I mustn't complain. I've got three customers now – so that's three more than I had earlier."

"A place like this – it ought to be heaving with customers. Have you advertised it enough?"

And not that it's any of your business, she felt like saying. And not like you're in a position to give advice on anything – you renting a tumbledown old cottage and chopping logs all day – what the hell would you know about it? She sucked in her breath and smiled a little less warmly at him this time.

"Yes – I did all my homework – advertised it, free offers, grand opening with free access for the day. I did write to Colin Farrell asking him to come and launch it – but he's too busy just now. I wrote to Bono as well. Then someone suggested that Bono might be too busy as well and that I should write to The Edge instead. So I did – I wrote to The Edge."

"And?"

"He sent me back a postcard."

"A postcard?"

"Yeah – a postcard. Geddit?"

"No. No, I'm afraid I don't."

"*Postcard From The Edge* – I got a postcard from The Edge. Ah forget it – it was a bad joke to begin with. Anyway, the point is – I think I'm the greatest businesswoman in the whole history of women setting up business on their own. I have a background in computers. I have come up with an idea that no other woman has ever dreamt of. It's a sure-fire winner in my view. But, well, here we are – and the people of Larkhaven just haven't twigged yet what a magnificent service is on their doorstep."

"Well, there's your problem."

"What?"

"You're being arrogant about it. It's the wrong approach. People don't want to be told that their lives are lacking in something."

"Arrogant? Well, thanks. That's really helpful. Have you any other insights based on your ten seconds' acquaintance with my character? It may surprise you to know that most people round here consider me down-to-earth and just plain nice."

He raised his hands in a gesture of peace. "Just an observation. Clearly wrong – on reflection."

"Clearly!" sniped Berry

He turned away from her and began picking out single letters on the keyboard with his index finger.

CHAPTER 10

It was just as Aoife suspected. When she carefully tipped it over, the unusual vase was marked with six elegant Chinese markings on its base.

She clasped the vase carefully between her two hands with the intention of carrying it to the safety of a secure kitchen cupboard. Then just as she had it firmly in her grip a voice boomed loudly and suddenly behind her.

"Just what the hell do you think you're doing?"

It must have been the sudden shock of the loud voice from nowhere or the fright or the odd position she was standing in – because ordinarily Aoife was not a clumsy person. It was partly why dancing came so easily to her. She always seemed to be able to control her limbs elegantly, in a way that Berry in particular envied. Aoife had been born graceful – not quite the most beautiful or the slimmest girl in the world but she had a delicate gracefulness that more than made up for it. But now all her poise deserted her. She started and jumped at the sudden booming voice behind her and, before she knew it, the vase was flying through the air and heading inexorably to the marble hearth beneath her. Then everything went into a horrible slow motion as she lunged to try to grab the precious vase.

It was a moment that she was to replay constantly in her head in the coming weeks – the blue and white of the little vase as it arced through the air and began its downward fall, then the moment of impact as it hit the marble with a harsh jangling sound and burst in a strange kind of beauty into a thousand little shards. When it was all over, she stared at the scattered pieces on the floor, willing them to somehow replay the last few moments and all join back together again, like a backwards video.

"Oh dear!" said the same booming voice and Aoife turned around, speechless with shock. "Just as well I came down here to keep an eye on you. Lord knows what you would have got up to next!"

She stared at Flann Slevin, unable to frame even one single logical thought in her head.

"I'd better get the dustpan and sweep up this little lot," he said casually before disappearing into the broom cupboard beneath the stairs.

When he returned Aoife was still in shock, though she had managed to sit herself down on the vast ivory sofa. The awfulness of the situation was beginning to dawn on her. Kevin had trusted her with the biggest house on the books, had given her full responsibility, spoken of his great trust in her. Now what would he think? And for Flann Slevin of all people to find her in such an awful situation was just about the last straw. He would surely feel obliged to tell Kevin exactly what had happened.

Then if Kevin didn't actually sack Aoife, well, he'd probably be demoting her to coffee duties and docking her salary for the next seventy-five years – and Flann would probably get an even bigger promotion than the last – all because of her silly curiosity. It wasn't even as if she'd been that curious about the vase in the first place. It was just that the people coming to view the house were late and she'd found herself briefly, fatefully, and catastrophically at a loose end. One horrible tiny inconsequential little moment and her whole life had changed forever. Oh God, she couldn't even bear to think about it!

Great big dollops of tears cascaded suddenly down her cheeks and hung in horrid salty globules on the base of her chin as her body was seized with a ghastly bout of shivers and uncontrollable gasps.

"Here – you'd better have this." Flann was holding out a glass of water to her and smiling – smiling?

"Thmkps," she said thickly, unable suddenly to form even the simplest words in her mouth.

He sat down on the sofa beside her and then, without even trying to make a pass at her, he offered her a nice clean tissue as well.

"Thmkps," she said again, then took the tissue and began dabbing at her eyes.

"That's it. You have a good cry," he said, with surprising gentleness in his voice.

Aoife was in no state to argue and so she took his advice and sobbed and snuffled away quietly for a few moments.

"I think I hear the buyers arriving," he said, standing up and looking out the large mullioned window.

"*Ooooohhhhhgggggooooddddd!*" she wailed and began a new bout of sobbing.

"Now listen," he said, adopting a firm but kindly tone, "you can't possibly show anyone round in this state. And you can't go back to work. Kevin would only ask too many questions. So I suggest you take the afternoon off and go home. Meanwhile I'll think of a way out of this."

"But what about the vase? I have to tell the owners – it's very valuable – they're bound to miss it straight away."

He laughed. "Are you kidding? The sort of people who own a house like this – they won't even notice that vase is missing until the removal men empty the packing cases in their next home sometime next spring. My advice is to say nothing."

Then another dreadful thought occurred to her. "Now I'll lose the sale and the commission!"

"Don't worry," said Flann, patting her hand reassuringly. "It will be all right."

The numbness of the shock was beginning to wear off now and she could hear footsteps on the long path outside and voices coming closer. She was in an acute state of panic, not able to think straight. Still, she didn't think that Flann was right in the advice he was giving her, although she had to admit he was being incredibly sweet and kind to her now and so very understanding. Wasn't it strange that it was often only in a crisis that people showed their true goodness?

"I can't do that. It would be wrong – like stealing. I'll just have to tell the truth and face the consequences."

"Look, we can sort it out tomorrow – there's no rush," he said, his voice soft and calming. "But you need to get on home now – to that lovely old house in Larkhaven – you've had a nasty shock and you're not in any fit state to tell anybody about anything."

Yes, he was right. She was in a terrible state. Even if

she did try to tell Kevin about what had happened, she would probably only make a mess of it. Better to wait until tomorrow when she could at least suffer whatever punishment awaited her with some measure of dignity.

"OK then. I don't suppose it will make any difference if we leave telling Kevin till tomorrow."

"No, it won't. And I'll go with you when you tell him – for moral support. I insist. I'm sure he'll let you keep the sale."

She felt her heart lighten slightly. Things might come right after all. And he was being nice – even when there was no reason for him to be nice. Aoife sighed loudly and even managed a tight brave smile.

"That's better!" he said, grinning widely back at her. "Now you just hide yourself in the study across the hall and, when I lead the buyers into the kitchen, you can make a quick getaway. Then they won't have to see you've been crying."

"I wouldn't have thought of that. Thanks."

"No need to thank me. Off you go! See you tomorrow."

All the way home on the train, Aoife couldn't stop replaying the entire incident in her head – the sudden loud boom of Flann's voice, the vase flying through the air, shattering into a thousand blue and white pieces on the marble, then Flann being so kind, making sure he cleaned every last scrap of the broken china away, bringing her water, offering to take over the house showing from her. She sighed loudly several times as she stared out the window and she was glad when the train at last rattled into the tiny Larkhaven station.

"What the hell's the matter with you?" said Berry as her sister tumbled through the kitchen door and made for the range where she curled herself up into a battered old armchair and began to sob her heart out.

"Nothing!" wailed Aoife plaintively.

In many respects Berry Joyce had assumed the role and duties of mother to Aoife when their own mother had died some ten years earlier. Aoife had only been seventeen and it had fallen to Berry, then aged twenty-five, to fill the horrible gaping emotional hole in her younger sister's life.

"But I've lost my mother too," she used to complain to her father. "It's not fair."

"It's different for you, Berry – Aoife's still only a child. And it's a terrible thing to lose a mother when you're still so young." That had been her father's assessment and so Aoife had always been humoured and protected and cosseted from the harsher realities of life.

It was Berry who'd had to sit down and learn all about balancing the books and paying the bills and worrying about filling the oil tank for the winter and bleeding the radiators and lagging the water pipes and having the gutters cleaned and doing all those dull but necessary tasks of adulthood. Whenever Aoife had a crisis, there was always Berry to turn to, always Berry to break her fall, always Berry to pat her hand maternally and say: "There, there, things will look better in the morning." But who was there for Berry to turn to? No one!

Now she stood in the kitchen bemused and a little annoyed by her younger sister's histrionics. "So what's up?"

"Nothing!"

"Ah, nothing! That old nothing! Making trouble again.

If I had a fiver for all the times I've been told that a problem has been caused by 'nothing' . . . come on, out with it!"

"I can't! It's just too truly awful."

Berry rolled her eyes to heaven. Aoife was spoilt rotten and had no idea of what 'truly awful' could really be. She had a lovely job and a lovely boyfriend. She had a great social life. She had no trouble in doing herself up and looking nice. She had no real money worries, no creditors looming malevolently in the background.

Berry tried again. "Is it something to do with that weird text you sent me about Ben Searson?"

At the mention of Ben, Aoife descended into a new bout of wailing.

Twenty Questions time.

"Is it Dermot?"

Aoife stopped snuffling for a moment then shook her head.

That was it. She'd call Dermot. He'd know what to do. She pulled out her mobile and pressed his number. Her spirits began to lift as she thought about how she would outline the problems of the day to him and he would put his wonderful problem-solving brain to work and they would come up with a solution in no time at all. If the vase were worth two or maybe three thousand euro, he'd find the most cost-effective way of paying the money back as quickly as possible.

But most unusually for Dermot, he didn't answer his phone and Aoife was forced to leave a forlorn little message in his mailbox: "*Hiya – it's me. Just calling to say hi. Bye.*"

Then she spilled out the whole story about Kevin giving her the sale of the house in Talavera Road and then the vase shattering.

"Why the hell didn't you leave the stupid vase alone? I mean it's one of those unwritten rules of physics, isn't it? Expensive vase – not mine – I pick it up – it breaks!" Berry chastised her.

Aoife shook her head. "I've asked myself the same question a thousand times since it happened."

"So what happens now?"

"Flann says not to say anything to Kevin until the morning, until I'm less upset."

"Wait a minute – would that be Flann the new boss – that you can't quite make out?"

"Well, that's just the thing. I mean he was really nice and kind and everything. Quite honestly I don't know how I would have got myself out of that house in one piece if it hadn't been for him. Anyway, I don't suppose there's a whole pile I can do about it now until tomorrow." She sighed hugely. "So . . . how about you? Did you have a busy day?"

Berry shook her head. "This morning I had Patricia de Vere briefly, Harry Robson for his usual lunch-hour and Ben Searson. This afternoon, just a few passing stragglers."

"What did Ben Searson want? I'm still not a hundred per cent sure about him."

"Oh," said Berry indifferently as she stirred something steaming in a pot.

Aoife told the story about the free offer from the online detective agency and how the name Bernard Pearse with a string of criminal convictions attached had come up under the same address.

Berry nodded her head sceptically.

"Well, didn't you hear what I said?" said Aoife. "Ben

Searson – Bernard Pearse – he might be living under an alias – I mean, it's almost the same name –"

"No, it's not."

"Yes, it is! He could be a criminal – robbery with violence! I don't think I'll sleep easily in my bed wondering every night if he's going to come up here and take an axe to me." The day's events made Aoife sound more distraught than usual. "I'm sure he's perfectly innocent – but why take the risk?" she added trying to sound more reasonable.

Berry nodded distractedly. "Why don't I talk to him about it in the morning?"

"Do you think that's wise?"

"Oh, don't worry. I'll ask him to come to the Internet café – where it will all be safe and in the open. He's hardly likely to whip out his machete in full view of the village, now is he?"

"You're mocking me but you'll see – there's something not quite right about him – a kind of sinister secretiveness – I'd tread very carefully round Ben Searson if I were you."

Berry sighed, and began setting out today's dinner of stewed chicken dumplings and value-pack noodles.

"Oh God," Aoife murmured under her breath as she glanced down at the greyish sticky lumps that formed a sad lunar landscape on her dinner plate. "I've just lost my appetite."

Chapter 11

The following morning, Aoife awoke from a restless sleep and by the time she reached the bathroom, she was in a complete panic. What if Kevin had already found out about the disaster with the vase in Talavera Road? There was no doubt that she would lose the commission but what if she got the sack as well – thrown out without a reference? And then if all the others at work heard that she had slunk home sneakily instead of going back to work and facing the music, none of them would ever speak to her again. She took a cold shower and dressed quickly. She donned her most sober black suit. Then, because she couldn't face breakfast, she set out immediately on the long trudge to the station.

All the way to the station, she racked her brains for an excuse not to go to work. She gave serious consideration to phoning in sick but that was only postponing the awful moment with Kevin. She could pretend that she had an urgent medical or dental appointment but what if he decided to check up on her?

No, she told herself, taking her seat ever so reluctantly on the train, time to face the music!

Then Patricia de Vere appeared and sat opposite her, seeming to fix her with an accusing eye as the train sped onwards.

Aoife tried to read her book but the words swam and danced in front of her. Then she closed her eyes, leaned her head against the window and, in an effort to escape the looming catastrophe that awaited her in the office, tried to summon up one of her favourite daydreams: her dream home – the beautifully restored Georgian house with the perfect little fanlight above the door, the cosy cream and blue Aga kitchen, the small batch of impossibly cute little boys and girls, dressed in brightly coloured designer clothes, arranged artistically on the Italian tiled floor, drawing colourful Picasso-style masterpieces as they slurped happily, without dribbling, on sugar-free juice and raw carrot sticks. She summoned up images of entertaining a wide circle of wonderfully happy, successful, good-looking and discerning friends – serving them champagne cocktails and superb canapés, as they stood around making staggeringly intelligent conversation while admiring her richly polished wooden floors, her antique furniture, her carefully chosen Impressionist paintings and exquisite antique ornaments spanning the centuries and brought back from delightful little backstreets in exotic far-flung cities on her many romantic trips abroad!

Ornaments!

"Oh God!" she groaned out loud and banged her head against the glass, trying to banish the accident with the vase from memory.

She must have looked quite distraught because Patricia

de Vere leaned forward, tapped her on the knee and said: "Is everything OK? You look a little bit upset."

A Little Bit Upset – well, that hardly began to describe it.

"It's nothing," she said, a tiny bit sharply.

Like she would ever tell some batty battle-axe judge like Patricia de Vere her ghastly problems anyway. A woman like that couldn't begin to understand how less than twenty-four hours ago, Aoife had been riding on the crest of a wave, her boss giving her the best project on the books, her bank account almost in the black, no dodgy impostors living at close quarters to keep her awake at night. Now things were spiralling out of control. Unless Flann was able to come up with a solution as he'd promised. Was she wrong to put her trust in him? No, she really didn't think so. She'd slept on it, and now in the cold light of day, she realised that Flann Slevin was set to be her knight in shining armour. The odd moment between them at the barbeque, the strange little incident in the office the other week, well, it was all adding up – wasn't it? When the chips were down, and in this case thousands of tiny little china chips, Flann had ridden in to her rescue like any decent knight in shining armour. In fact, in this instance he'd been far more helpful than Dermot – who had been absolutely no help at all.

She turned her face to the window and racked her brains to think of some solution to her problem. Perhaps she ought to try Dermot again. It was strange how he hadn't replied to her message. But he would surely be awake by now. He always kept to a very regular routine. He'd jump out of the bed just after the seven o'clock news. Then he'd do twenty press-ups in his bare ripply chest and skintight boxers, and then eat a bowl of Weetabix followed by one slice of wholemeal toast and a strong black coffee. Then he would shower and dress and catch up on his emails for half an hour before setting out to the office at eight o'clock. It was quarter to eight now. He would surely have his phone turned on. She pressed his number but it rang out, this time not even giving her the option of leaving a message. Well, he'd probably just forgotten to turn it on. She'd send him a nice text and then he'd call her just as soon as it reached him.

She speed-texted: *Please call. Need your help. Lots of love X XAoife*

Then she slipped her mobile back into her bag and waited for him to reply.

You could never accuse Aoife Joyce of being a coward. On the few occasions in her life to date when bravery and heroism were called for, she'd not flinched – unless there was physical pain involved, as in dentist – or perhaps a mouse – or some of the more bizarre sexual practices – or, God forbid, one of those big hairy black spiders. Once in school, she'd even fearlessly owned up to robbing a bar of chocolate that she knew for a fact had been nicked by a boy in the back row of the classroom. But she remembered the day clearly, the awful suspense as the teacher glared round menacingly at each pupil in the class, the guilty boy sitting there calmly like butter wouldn't melt in his mouth – the horrible stodgy silence as though the air had solidified into cold porridge and she hadn't been able to stop herself. "I stole the Macaroon Bar, Miss!" she'd blurted out, even managing to inject a bit of pride into her voice, as she lied innocently through her teeth. It had certainly done away with the awful stodgy atmosphere of suspense but, in her heroism, Aoife had become the first student under the age of seven to be suspended from The Sacred Heart School. Still, she had faced the music then and here she was now walking purposefully down Dame Street towards the office, preparing to face the music once again – this time with Kevin.

What was the worst that could happen? Really? Surely the very worst he could do was sack her and order her to replace the value of the vase?

She could live with that. It was a small price to pay for her foolishness. Yes, it would be hard – but she could go to her credit union and explain the situation and they would lend her money no bother. By the time it had to be paid back, she would undoubtedly have a new job – maybe even a better one. Perhaps this was going to be one of those turning points – where one small incident would alter the whole course of her life forever. This might be a major golden opportunity, disguised as a minor catastrophe, to take her life in a whole new direction. And, after all, the person who never made a mistake never made anything.

By the time she reached the entrance to Vernon's, Aoife had decided that breaking the Imperial Ming vase was probably the best thing that had ever happened to her.

In she swept through the door, smiling cheerfully and humming "I Will Survive" quietly to herself.

But did she imagine the funny look Joe at the desk gave her?

"Define 'weapon'!" she chirped as cheerfully as she could as she passed him.

"Claire covered all that with me yesterday," he said dismissively. "Today I'm doing Intellectual Property."

Aoife shrugged and looked around for Claire who was usually bustling round the office by this stage. But now she was nowhere to be seen. What was going on?

Aoife decided she was being paranoid and set to organising her working day. Kevin wouldn't be in until after nine so it gave her plenty of time to compose and prepare herself for the meeting.

There were a few emails to be answered and one or two letters to be drafted and sent out so she set to work on those, noticing as she read through the emails that there was another mail from the online detective agency.

Once again we urge you to contact us as a matter of extreme urgency . . .

Aoife binned it. She was hardly going to be in a position now to go paying out hundreds of euro for checking out Ben Searson or Bernard Pearse or whoever he was. She was about to pop out to the loo one last time to make sure her hair was neat and her lipstick unsmudged and her tights unladdered when she heard the unmistakable sound of Kevin's voice in the foyer.

"Is Aoife in yet? I need to have a word with her." He sounded terribly serious, not his usual booming jocular self at all.

Oh God! He knew already.

She slipped out of her office quietly and tapped gently on Kevin's door.

"Yes. Come on in – whoever it is."

"It's me," she squeaked, sticking her head round the door fearfully.

"Ah, there you are. Now sit down. I need to talk to you about what happened yesterday in Talavera Road."

Her heart plunged down to somewhere near New Zealand – or maybe even the Antarctic. Possibly it shot out of the bottom of the universe altogether. She sucked in her breath and closed her eyes, waiting for the worst. A strange damp coldness slithered down her spine.

"I think you did the right thing," Kevin said, then added, "Well done!"

Aoife was rigid with fright and she stared at him wide-eyed for several moments, not really understanding what he was saying.

"Yes," he continued, when she didn't respond, "We'll inform the bank that are handling the sale and no doubt they will let the owners know. Just how the little rascal got in there in the first place I'd like to know – I mean you must have got an awful fright, and keeping your head like that – well done, you! I have to say I'm not one bit surprised – and awfully proud, Aoife. This is certainly an indicator that your career is on the up. Oh and don't worry about the vase – they're well covered by insurance – I've checked. I mean if you hadn't arrived when you did, the little brat might have made off with far more valuable stuff . . . so they'll be more than grateful."

"I'm sorry?" she managed at last. "Little brat?"

"Yes – and brat is too kind a word – but I'm an old-fashioned gentleman and I won't use strong language in front of a lady. Anyway Flann's explained the whole thing."

"He has?"

Aoife was beginning to feel a strange sense of guilty relief flooding through her – although she didn't dare hope that she was off the hook just yet. And besides – what was all that about some little rascal making off with the vase? It sounded to her like Flann had told Kevin some cock-and-bull story about a burglar to cover up for her. She glanced across anxiously at him knowing that it was only right and decent to put him straight.

Here goes, she told herself and sucked in her breath. Tell the truth and shame the devil.

"I think there must be some mistake."

"How do you mean?"

"I mean, Kevin . . ." Oh God, why was she finding this so hard? "I mean, Kevin – the thing is that – well, about what happened with the vase – there was no – I mean it was me that . . ."

Kevin handed her a list of people who were coming to look over the house in the afternoon. "List of potential buyers – one or two extremely big hitters . . . you'll be dealing with them. I'm sorry, you were saying – it was you that what?"

Aoife looked down at the list in her hands, thought of the commission she would earn from the sale of the house, whizzed quickly through all the things she could do with the money – put in a new kitchen at home, pay off bills, even take Berry away on a holiday to Sicily –

"Nothing," she said brightly to Kevin. "Don't worry – I won't let you down. I promise."

"I know," he said smiling paternally and holding the door open for her. "Like I said, it's very important that we get the best price possible for this house. And I know you can do it."

The sense of relief Aoife felt was indescribable. Her job was safe. Her reputation was safe. Most of all Kevin still trusted her. She felt like doing a giddy samba or a wild wild hip-rolling rhumba down the corridor back to her office. The best thing to do now was to move on and forget about the whole silly episode. After all, no one was out of pocket. The owners would probably get more than the value of the vase on insurance and then they could go out and buy something much nicer. Because, Aoife reasoned, it hadn't even really been a very nice vase – certainly not worth losing her job over. She texted Nathalie to meet for lunch – she wanted to share her relief with someone.

But before that there was one more thing she had to do. She straightened herself up and strode purposefully down the corridor to Flann's office at the far end. Then she knocked lightly, almost airily, certainly less formally than she would ever have done before.

"Come in!" she heard his voice say from within.

She stuck her head round the door and smiled warmly at him.

"Aoife," he said, grinning broadly at her and leaning back in his swivel-chair. "What can I do for you?"

"Are you busy – only I was wondering if I could have a word?"

"Never too busy to talk to you – take a seat."

She faced him squarely across the desk, composed herself and began her little speech.

"I want to thank you for what you did. Though I wished you hadn't lied on my behalf. I have tried to explain to Kevin what really happened yesterday with the vase – but now I'm afraid I'll upset him and he's given me sole responsibility of the house and it's such a big step-up for me that – anyway you've really averted a big catastrophe for me and I'm really really grateful."

"Aoife," he said her name softly, "forget about it. You've

got a big house to sell – a huge commission to make. Go for it."

"Then – all I can say is – thanks. You really saved my skin and I really appreciate it."

"Hey, stop saying 'really' and as for the rest – we're colleagues – we look out for each other – that's all. That's how it is in Vernon's. I know you'd probably do the same for me if the situation was reversed."

God, the relief she felt as she glided along Stephen's Green through the crowds, as if she was walking on a kind of drug-induced cloud of good will and happiness. She hadn't felt such relief since she'd thought she was pregnant with Dermot's baby six months earlier and done the little test in the loo on the train on her way into work from Larkhaven. That had been a mildly embarrassing moment – emerging from the cramped little space and coming face to face with Harry Robson – then kissing him passionately on the cheek in her state of pure unpregnant joy.

Today she had arranged to meet Nathalie in Kinshasa – a new African Fusion Café bar down a quiet lane near the Iveagh Gardens where the music was all Lady Smith Black Mombasa and the food was all mild Swahili curries and seafood cooked with cloves and cinnamon.

Nathalie would be a few minutes late because she had to take the Luas in from the dreary industrial estate where Nutopia had their offices. So while waiting, Aoife checked her phone messages. Oddly she noted Dermot's message hadn't delivered. At least she hadn't got a message-delivered report back. That meant that either his phone was broken or he hadn't switched it on. It surprised her until she remembered that he was most probably very busy with the new job. Anyway the crisis was over now – so she didn't feel the urgent need to talk to him any more. She picked up the menu and waited for Nathalie.

CHAPTER 12

Nathalie's court-case celebrations were short-lived. When she'd logged onto her station at work this morning, there had been an internal email from Gretta.

Please come to my office at 9.30 promptly to discuss your current status within the company. G Price.

Nathalie's heart sank when she saw the message. This was why she hadn't wanted to go to court in the first place. She knew Gretta would be gunning for her big time now. It wasn't just the matter of the money she'd won. That would be peanuts to a big multinational corporation like Nutopia. No – it was the fact that she, a mere telesales assistant, had taken on the High And Mighty Corporation and won. She wasn't going to be allowed to forget that in a hurry.

Outside Gretta's office she drew in her breath and tried to compose herself. Then she knocked tentatively on the door.

"One moment please," said the icy cold voice of Gretta from within.

Nathalie breathed deeply in an effort to remain calm.

The door opened at last and Gretta loomed menacingly. She indicated to Nathalie to come in and then she shut the door with a slow ominous click.

"You must be feeling pretty pleased with yourself," she said sneeringly, lowering herself with regal importance into the large red-leather swivel-chair.

Nathalie stared at her wide-eyed. "How do you mean?" she stammered at last.

"I suppose you think you're someone now – winning this ridiculous little case against your employers – trying to destroy our good name and reputation." Gretta sucked in her breath and snorted derisively. "Well, think again! It would take someone with far greater talent than you, Nathalie Kelly, to even put a tiny dint in our reputation. Do you know what this proves more than anything?"

"What?" said Nathalie who was beginning to wonder if she shouldn't just hand in her notice there and then and be done with it.

"Oh, come now! Don't play the innocent with me! It means that you are not a team player – and I have to say it saddens me, Nathalie." Gretta lowered her head and tucked in her chin in a display of benevolent corporate disappointment. She followed all that up with a sad tight little smile before resuming her more normal expression of chin-jutting efficiency. "Of course, as you know, Nutopia is bigger than any one little Ego or Agenda. We do not let the selfish self-centred actions of any one individual eat into the noble fabric of our corporate family. If this were any other company, your desk would have been cleared yesterday afternoon. But we are prepared to keep you on. It's what makes us a truly great organisation – that we can allow for the tiresome little problems caused by people like you."

Gretta swivelled the mouse around on her desk in tight little circles, then drummed her perfectly manicured magenta-shaded nails on its smooth plastic surface, as if waiting for Nathalie to make some gesture of gratitude. Then she shook her head with measured weariness. "You could have been a contender, Nathalie – you could have been someone . . . so disappointing." She paused, still waiting for some response.

"Yes, Miss Price," said Nathalie evenly, and wearing a blank smile which gave nothing away.

"So – to move on and get some closure from this unfortunate situation, we are happy to draw a line under the matter and we look forward to the pleasure of your continued employment with us."

This last bit was rattled off in tinny parrot fashion, and Nathalie realised Gretta was only saying the words as a guard against any possible charges of discrimination or bullying or unfair dismissal. But still and all Nathalie was confused. At first, she'd thought Gretta was all gearing up to sack her or at least put her on the graveyard shift. Now it seemed like nothing was going to change at all. Was it possible that, behind it all, Gretta was a decent and fair-minded person?

Gretta stood up and held out a large brown envelope to Nathalie. "Your client list for the next month," she said, holding the door open and practically sweeping Nathalie out into the corridor.

Nathalie's heart plummeted when she saw that Gretta had handed her The Price List.

"The cow!" said Johanne when she looked over it. "No

one can get any sales on that list. It's all the customers who are either just out of prison or sick in the head or just plain mean and nasty. You'll have to tell her you can't do it – refuse. Magda Lynch had a nervous breakdown after only three months with that list."

"I can't."

"You will go mad with this calling list – I promise you."

"It can't be that bad," said Nathalie, determined to put a brave face on things.

"No? You don't believe me? Here – let's have a go. Number one: Mr Norbert James." She quickly punched in the phone number and pulled the mouthpiece up to her mouth.

"Good morning, Mr James. How are you this morning?"

Nathalie could hear a sharp raspy voice on the other end saying what sounded awfully like: *"None of your fuckin' business!"*

"My name is Johanne and I'm calling from . . ."

"Johanne? Johanne who? I don't know any Johanne."

". . . Nutopia Telesales and we were wondering would you be travelling to Mainland Europe at all this year, sir?"

". . . bunch of fuckin' wankers – haven't I told you lot a hundred times – leave me alone – I don't want anything to do with . . ."

"We're sorry for disturbing you, sir," said Johanne before hanging up and turning to Nathalie. "See? Now I happen to know that they get worse as you go down the list."

"Oh God!" said Nathalie. "What am I going to do?"

Nathalie had intended talking through her future options with Aoife in Kinshasa but instead she'd got completely caught up in Aoife's story about the house in Talavera Road and the vase.

"But anyway, all's well that ends well," said Aoife, her appetite now completely restored as she tucked eagerly into a Zanzibar fish curry.

Nathalie had listened to Aoife very carefully, measuring up every little detail of the story. She'd learned quite a lot about listening to stories from Mark and particularly about finding inconsistencies and contradictions. But now, although she loved her cousin dearly, she had to address some very major inconsistencies in her story.

"So Flann covered up for you by making up some story about a kid breaking into the house while you were there?"

"Yeah – I didn't ask him to do that – and I did try to tell Kevin the truth. But I have to ask now – where's the harm? Owning up to the real truth now – it would only cause a lot of people a lot of unnecessary bother."

"So Flann is the only other person who knows the real truth."

"Yes, luckily for me."

"Is it?"

"Yes. You should have seen how kind he was to me yesterday – I was in such a terrible state – and he just took over and managed everything. I look forward to a whole new relationship with Flann Slevin from now on."

"What's that supposed to mean?" Nathalie asked, eyeing her sharply.

"Oh nothing," Aoife said and smiled enigmatically.

Nathalie was on the point of saying that she wasn't sure if she quite liked the sound of Flann Slevin but Aoife cut her short.

"So what about our night on the town this Saturday – let's push the boat out – we'll start off in Paradise, then move on to Snow and then we'll meet up with the others before hitting The Burgundy Cathouse and –"

"Wait. Stop! I can't keep up. Before you hit the Burgundy Cathouse and everywhere else – just remember one thing."

"What's that?"

"Flann Slevin has a hold over you now – unless and until you decide to tell your boss the truth."

"Don't be ridiculous!" Aoife snorted derisively at her cousin. "Flann and me – we're sorted – the best of mates now. And if you really want a bit of sizzling drama – let me tell you more about the very dramatic discovery I made yesterday about our new tenant. I'm not a hundred per cent certain but . . ."

CHAPTER 13

Sitting in the bar of the Bayview Hotel, overlooking the choppy metally grey waters of the harbour, savouring his very own harbour in the tempest, Ben Searson was quite unaware that he had become the unwitting subject of Aoife Joyce's Free Introductory On-line Investigations Offer.

He ought to have been feeling quite gloomy. It had been his default mode for the past eighteen months. But somehow now for the first time in over two years, he felt almost close to being content. It was quite fine, he decided, to have so much time on his hands. Nothing had to be rushed. He could deal with a day's unfolding possibilities in a calm orderly fashion. Or he could just ignore the day completely and stay in bed if he wanted to. He was only in the village today because he needed to stock up on essentials.

He sipped coffee and browsed idly through a complimentary copy of *The County Sentinel* that lay half-crumpled on the table in front of him, whilst at the same time keeping an eye on events or rather non-events in the harbour. The little boats all bobbed and nudged at the pier. It was blustery – not a day for fishermen and so the pier was almost deserted. It was quite soothing to observe the emptiness of the scene. He realised why artists were so often drawn to seascapes and pretty little fishing harbours and he gazed out at it quite happily. There was nothing much of interest in the *Sentinel* in any case – not until he came to page seven and a routine photograph of a group of people at some glitzy media event in the city. Reluctantly he felt his full attention focus on the photo and the memory it evoked. He shook his head in exasperation and cast the local rag aside. Why was it that just when he thought he'd wiped the memory of the entire sorry business from his head, some insignificant little thing would crop up to remind him of it? His mind turned back now to his days as the emperor of glitzy media events, the pretty scene in front of him receding to nothing more than a blur of sea and pier and sky, as the past flooded in to haunt him . . .

"Pearse, you're some jammy bastard," a passing friend murmured enviously to him at the bar.

Ben was dressed in a tuxedo, and he looked mighty fine in it. There was no sense in denying the truth. Where was the point in false modesty? He was leaning against the bar, trapped in a delicious little honeypot of blondes. Were they models or wannabee pop stars? Perhaps they were just the marketing people. Did it matter? Not in the slightest! They were all over him, knew he was the man who could make their dreams of stardom come true. They might need to sleep with him. But what did that matter? After all, apart from being the most powerful man in the room, he was certainly the most interesting looking, handsome in a dark, scruffy, tousled-haired, just-climbed-out-of-the-coalhole, clouded-brow sort of way. Who wouldn't want to fall into bed with Ben Pearse?

He was cool. No one else did cool like Ben. He gave off an air of what one woman had called 'understated sexual menace'.

Not that he intended to. No, he hadn't set out to be a sexual menace at all – understated or otherwise. But that was the way it had turned out, the women throwing themselves at him, the blondes gushing around him. He'd have one or two of them before the night ended. But he wouldn't linger for more than a couple of days. Ben Pearse didn't do relationships – nothing beyond the most superficial level of social or sexual engagement.

He hadn't intended to be like that. In school he'd been a rather lean and earnest captain of the debating team and even House Prefect. He didn't play for the school rugby team, which made him quite invisible to large quantities of girls. His classmates regarded him as a dozy wimp. His teachers described him as a pleasant but lacklustre student. Not destined for anything much academically.

In those days, girls hadn't much noticed his gangling frame, his hollow adolescent cheekbones and his floppy chestnut-brown hair. Though he'd been regarded as quite a decent person, spearheading for instance the largest single schools donation to a Homeless Hostel for Christmas, and once to his classmates' amusement being cited in a TV news story for rescuing a small child from the path of an oncoming bus.

Then somehow or other he'd ended up as quite a mover and a shaker in the TV and film industry. He'd made a bit of money devising some Reality TV show that he'd sold at a profit and set up a nice little production company of his own. Oh, he wasn't rich – far from it! But he was terribly powerful. He could make or break a TV career by a simple curl of his lip or a moment's eye contact. Every man in the Ice Bar that night knew it and regarded him with a mixture of admiration, fear and raw resentment. Every woman knew it too – wannabee starlets with childish starry dreams of super stardom, earnest college girls who dreamed of cleaning up politics and wiping out famine in Africa, aspiring capricious actresses who longed for Hollywood and all its works, and the ones he couldn't fathom at all – the ones he made all his money from – the ones who dreamed of being on Reality TV. Reality, he'd read once in some book was 'the dream of a mad philosopher, the nucleus of a vacuum'. He often recalled the definition with a twisted sardonic grin.

"It's a dull way to make a living – but someone's got to do it," he would reply glibly to envious friends while casting his casting eye around the room. At first, he'd been uncomfortable with the power – like an oversized coat, he felt swamped by it. It was something that had come as a by-product of his success. He'd been horrified at first when girls he barely knew began flinging themselves at him. He'd even tried to reason with them, explain that he was just a regular sort of bloke who had happened to hit on a winning formula for a programme. It didn't mean he was any better or more interesting than anybody else. But they'd just kept on coming at him anyway in virtual waves of seduction and temptation. What was a guy to do?

"I'm yours, Ben honey," blonde girls with impossibly

large breasts would whisper to him in passing at large media events, while slipping their room number into his pocket. Who could resist such temptation? What began as an embarrassing source of amusement became in time an easy pleasure and at last an insidious form of narcissism and a further means of wielding power. Sex and power became quite inseparable.

He was the master of media savvy, aloof from the unsuccessful, disdainful of those who sought to benefit through his power. He did not reflect on his life or his actions. Nor did he trust to love or any other emotion that might require him to engage with those around him.

"I love you, Ben," a woman had told him once. They'd been sleeping over in one another's apartments for several weekends on the trot.

"Don't be ridiculous! You don't even know me," he'd said and grinned his rare, most winning smile at her, before striding out of her apartment and never clapping eyes on her again.

There were frustrations. The most exasperating of all being that no sooner had he got the measure of a woman's pleasure in bed, than he would become quite sick to the teeth of her. It was a bizarre sort of erotic Catch 22 situation. But apart from that it had all been quite perfect and even now, some three years later, staring out at the pretty little safe harbour of Larkhaven, it was a puzzle to figure out how it had all gone so quickly and so disastrously wrong.

Although Ben still couldn't figure how life had changed so suddenly and violently in the space of less than a year, he could remember now with alarming clarity the moment when things began to fall apart, although it didn't seem like a 'momentous moment' at the time. In fact it was a rather humdrum little moment over two large lattes in his accountant's office as they scratched their heads over the latest profits.

"Quadrupled on last year!" said Maurice the accountant, casually slinging the document into the centre of the desk like it was a Royal Flush.

"Unbelievable!" said Ben, scarcely glancing at the sheet of paper. He continued to stare out the large window. He couldn't think of anything better to say. There just weren't the words in his vocabulary. It was like winning the lottery without ever even having bought a ticket. His idea for celebrity *'What's In Your Attic?'* had been mentioned one day at a meeting as the joke of a desperate man. They'd all laughed their heads off and then gone out and done it.

"Fuck it, Maurice – we're rich and powerful! We could make *Celebrity Eyebrow-Plucking* now and they'd buy it."

Maurice laughed happily. He loved books that balanced and his had balanced with a kind of fiscal artistry that most accountants only dreamed of.

"Or *Celebrity Root Canal Work*, or *Celebrity What's In Your Bathroom Cabinet?* – or *Celebrity Brazilian Wax* . . ." Ben continued to joke. But there was a sudden and unexpected hard edge to his laughter.

They went out on the town to celebrate: dinner in Solange, vintage champagne, and then their usual trawl through the Burgundy Cathouse for some passing lovelies. In the end though, despite plenty of champagne, Ben felt deeply uninterested in any of the beautiful women who paraded past him in their magnificent clubbing finery. He couldn't see the beauty in any of them. He knew, of course, that they must be beautiful. They wouldn't have got past the bouncers otherwise. But he just couldn't see it. He felt gloomy suddenly, and terribly angry.

"What's up with you?" Maurice was well into his second bottle of Bollinger – and quite up for anything with any number of anyones in any place.

Ben glowered into his glass. "Half of these staggeringly beautiful women are only coming onto us because we're rich or because we might just get them a role in the next big Hollywood movie."

"Brilliant, isn't it!" grinned Maurice a touch vacantly. "I mean, is this heaven or what? And we've barely had to lift a finger – like that Carlsberg ad: *Carlsberg don't do rags-to-riches stories but if we did . . .*"

Ben glared at him. "I think I'll head home."

"But what about the babes?" said Maurice to no one in particular as his boss disappeared out the heavy art-deco doors of the Burgundy Cathouse.

Ben dropped into the Surf Line on his way home and spent over an hour doing his banking online, paying his car tax and insurance online, checking his hotmail account (empty – and how else would it be?).

There was just Berry at the laundry counter ironing clothes and he was glad to have the place to himself. He logged onto www.epicurious.com for a seafood risotto recipe, then printed off the result which looked quite appetising.

"I wasn't planning to have much to do with the Internet – but I find it all too easy and useful, I'm afraid," he said to Berry with a note of self-mockery.

She had been watching him intermittently since his arrival as she carefully pressed Patricia de Vere's linen tablecloths.

"I'm glad of the business," she said pleasantly but he felt her eyes lingering on him – as though there was something she wanted to say – or ask, or as though she was looking at him in a new way. He knew it was only a matter of time before the truth came out and then he would have to hurry away to some new point of refuge. Perhaps he should just tell her now and get it over and done with.

But how should he begin? Should he begin by telling her his real name? She was bound to find it out soon anyway. And then what would he say that wouldn't have him instantly shunned by the close-knit village? Since his arrival, he'd felt a few faltering moments of peace and hope that made him want to stay on in his little cottage. He'd especially felt the calm and unflappable presence of Berry Joyce and he liked the idea of being near her for a while longer.

He felt her cool, perceptive gaze on him now. She looked into his eyes – a wise and searching look.

"Berry – I owe it to you to be honest . . ." he began hesitantly then stopped.

She swept the iron across the folded cloth one last time as though waiting for him to continue. Then she carefully rested the iron in its stand and raised her eyes to him once more.

"To tell you about . . ." his voice strangled the words.

"I know," she answered, cutting him off dismissively. "The coffee's cold." Then she added with a sardonic smile: "It won't happen again, Mr Searson – my apologies."

He smiled gratefully at her and turned his attention to two other bits of business that needed sorting, painful little residues from his old life – one a brief thank-you note that he felt compelled to send, the other a more pressing matter – payment of an undertaker's bill. He would have liked to ignore them altogether but instead he attended to them with quick and cold efficiency. As a reward to himself, he ordered some books – a history and two volumes of travel writing. In the end he felt quite pleased. The whole Internet thing had all gone so swimmingly that for a brief moment he gave serious consideration to installing a PC in the cottage. Then he'd never have to go out again – the world could come to his door and simply deposit its little necessities on his doorstep. There he'd be like some modern-day Silas Marner – younger of course and without the money hidden under the floor – well, not as eccentric obviously and with much better dress sense – but he knew what the old weaver must have felt like, wanting to hide his sad old broken heart away from the world forever. And wouldn't it be so deliciously easy to snuggle up in the warm and cosy duck-down duvet of self-pity that beckoned to him on a daily basis?

"Boys – what is the most destructive emotion in the world?" his old games master would demand of his shivering young charges as he sent them trudging round the pitch another five times for poor passing and messing up the calls in the line-out on a cold November's evening.

"Self-pity," they would intone mournfully through chattering teeth and muck-encrusted lips, carefully hiding their resentment and massive self-pity in case they got another five laps.

No – self-pity was not an option for Ben. It had never been allowed in the Pearse household.

Back home, he'd prepared and cooked the seafood

risotto with requisite Arborio rice, shrimps and scallops, garlic and white wine. He'd been quite pleased with the result and had polished off two hearty bowlfuls. In the space of a few weeks he had become quite a serviceable cook. Who'd have believed it?

It had begun to rain. Ben hugged the little fire in his kitchen to keep warm. He was tired. Today had been a break from his routine but, on any given day, it amazed him how the simple day-to-day chores of living could fill up his time so easily. There was an endless stream of things to do: next he needed to mend some broken slates on the roof and replace a cracked pane of glass in the tiny bathroom. He didn't have to do those things but that was how he'd been brought up – never to pass a problem without trying to do something useful about it. (In a sense it was that very approach to life that had got him into this peculiar mess. All in the past now – but, boy, was he living with the consequences!)

He sat back almost contentedly in his chair, half-listening to the nearly comforting sounds of wind and rain and resin-scented logs sparking and crackling in the grate. He lowered his head to his book once more but found he couldn't concentrate. He felt an odd emptiness inside, not a feeling he recognised or was used to but maybe like an old cigarette craving – and at first he couldn't identify what it was. He poked at the fire, leafed restlessly through his book, poured himself a glass of wine, took one sip then set it aside impatiently.

"Company. That's what it is. Dammit – I want company."

He dragged on an old green waxed jacket and huddled in the doorway, squinting out at the downpour. He was tempted for a brief moment to hurtle through the wind and rain towards the village, maybe to the hotel, maybe to that cosy-looking little bar at the far end of the village, pick up a pretty redhead – or two . . .

"You sad bastard," he muttered to himself, then stepped inside, and fastened his door against the stormy night, his thoughts slipping back to the past once more . . .

"Mr Pearse – that young fella from *The Daily Post* has been on . . . wanting to do another interview with you . . ." Grace Fitzgerald fluttered a lightly mascaraed set of eyelashes at her rather handsome young boss while a faintly maternal and ironic smile hovered about the corners of her mouth.

"Ah – and what would they like me to tell them about this time?"

She paused for a moment. "Anything under the sun it seems. Absolutely anything in the world you might like to talk about, he says. He's got a page to fill. He's wondering what your next big programme venture will be. He suggests he could do an interview with you about your favourite restaurant, dish, newspaper, keep fit regime, flower, sexual position, mountain, beach, childhood memory, colour, share, book, aftershave, film star, rock album – the person you'd most like to punch, kiss, have dinner or oral sex with . . . anything. He says he's completely desperate. He says he's interested in knowing absolutely everything about you – at least the readers of his column are. You've captured the imagination of his readers, he says."

"You don't seem all that impressed yourself."

"No – I'm not! It's a disgrace the way you make your money. You ought to be completely ashamed of yourself. I don't know what your mother would say if she were still alive. The poor woman is probably turning in her grave. And as for all those people wanting to know everything about you – have they nothing better to be doing with their time than listening to you spouting any old nonsense that comes into your head?"

"If you don't like it there's the door," he said, grinning at her.

She raised a scornful eyebrow and pursed her lips.

"Who'd keep any kind of manners on you if I left? I'd better stay put."

"Where would I be without you?"

"In jail probably," Grace breezed cheerfully at Ben as she turned away to tackle a mound of correspondence.

A horrible sharp draught pierced the hard-won warmth of his cottage, slunk along the floor and shot up through him. He was wearing two fine cashmere sweaters and thick cords (warm and soft against the skin – the very best designer stuff). Still the cold speared through him. He put a rolled-up rug against the door to block out the draught and stacked up the fire with logs and the last of some coal he'd found in the shed. He stared into the grate as the flames licked into life, then refusing to let his mind drift into the past again, he sat back to read his book once more.

CHAPTER 14

A few days had passed and in Nutopia, wedged between Johanne and sun-bleached Mitch from Melbourne, Nathalie began to plan her future in earnest as she struggled to come to grips with her new list of customers.

Things at work were deteriorating very rapidly now. Apart altogether from the horror of calling what sounded like every looper in the country, Gretta Price was making her life hell almost on an hourly basis. Gretta made a point of asking every day how her hand was and if her desk in the corner of the room was safe and comfortable. Gretta sent around hazard report forms, which staff was supposed to fill in with stuff like *"The rubber mats in the foyer are worn and might cause a slippage"* or *"The ventilation in Accounts is poor and might facilitate the spread of contagious diseases"*. She paid particular attention to the comments Nathalie put on her form. Or rather didn't put.

"I thought you of all people would have plenty to put on a hazard sheet," Gretta said, holding up the empty sheet – just high enough for all fifty people in the office to see.

"The scabby old bitch," murmured Johanne from the next desk.

"I just couldn't think of anything, Miss Price." Nathalie forced herself to remain polite. It was obvious that Gretta was trying to provoke her into some display of unprofessional conduct that would give Nutopia the perfect excuse for sacking her. But though Nathalie was sweet and gentle by nature she also had her father's steeliness and her mother's determination. Gretta Price was nothing but a bully and Nathalie would not allow herself to be intimidated by her.

"Oh, come now, Nathalie – it's bread and butter to someone like you."

"Bread and butter?"

"I mean, you being a clever girl who can hold her own in court and everything."

"She's not getting it – not getting it at all these nights, I'd say," whispered Johanne.

"Shush, Johanne – you'll only get me in trouble," Nathalie said, quickly suppressing a giggle.

"Well, if you do think of anything, Nathalie, I earnestly hope you point it out to us. We can't afford to have people getting injured at work now, can we?"

"No, Miss Price."

"Bully!" muttered Johanne under her breath.

Gretta turned to Johanne. "As for you," she said acidly, "do you think you're the only person working in this company?"

Johanne eyed her squarely, her lip and eyebrow curling up in a fine display of insolence.

"What's the problem? I filled in your list."

Gretta read aloud. *"My chair is rickety. The screen protector on my monitor is damaged. I have to roll my mouse's ball with my fingers . . ."*

Some of the lads across the aisle sniggered.

"I have to walk all the way to the end of the telesales centre to get a glass of water . . ."

"So! It's the truth."

Gretta smiled patiently. "Me! Me! Me! Johanne, what am I always saying? There's no 'I' in team!"

"Aye, aye, Miss Price!" Johanne retorted brazenly.

When Gretta stormed off in disgust, Nathalie warned Johanne yet again. "You'll get the sack – talking to her like that. She won't renew your contract. Anyway, what's the point? Save your energy for something important."

"It's worth it just to see that pinched look on her face. It's about the only bit of excitement I get around here. Fancy going clubbing at the weekend?"

"OK, why not? Aoife's staying over so we can all go out together."

"It's payday tomorrow. Why don't we blag our way into The Burgundy Cathouse. I'm going to buy a new top to go with my green silk skirt and I've seen this deadly pair of mules in Dundrum . . ."

Johanne chattered on, planning their night out, but Nathalie was only half-listening. This evening she had to go to the university. She'd sent off the application and they'd written back calling her to interview after work on Thursday. There was no time to go home and change or even do much preparation. Anyway, she couldn't think who to ask for help.

She took the bus from the dreary Beechfield Industrial

Estate to the gates of the university. The bus was packed to bursting with people on their way home from work. A woman on the bus reminded her of Felicity Norton and then she realised that she'd been foolish not to think of calling the solicitor, who was just the sort of person who might have given her loads of helpful advice for the interview. There was Mark, of course – but she didn't think she'd ever call Mark – even though she still had his number. "In case you ever need to get in touch," he'd said.

The university campus was huge – miles and miles of buildings and car parks and fields and sports pitches. It even had its own shopping centre and bank and lots of little restaurants dotted around the place. The Arts building was about half a mile walk from the bus stop at the gates and she walked along feeling very out of place in her navy-blue office skirt and jacket, plain black court shoes and shoulder bag.

She arrived at the door of the interview room on the fifth floor twenty minutes early. To pass the time she examined the notice-boards which were covered with tutorial lists and notices about assignments and posters advertising lectures on worrying subjects like

"Is Morality Dead?" and *"Death, Then What?"*

Yet another declared in bold italics:

"NELLIE, I AM HEATHCLIFF!" WAS CATHERINE EARNSHAW REALLY A MAN? THE MYSTERY AT THE CORE OF WUTHERING HEIGHTS*!*

Nathalie grew increasingly nervous and worried. She'd never heard of any of the famous names on the notice-boards, except for *Wuthering Heights*, which she had studied in school – and which now, to her horror, she could only remember very vaguely. Her body broke out in a cold sweat and she suddenly wanted to turn and run. Maybe she was just too stupid to go to college.

A stylish poster featured the photo of a striking dark-haired woman and beneath it the caption: *Reading English Literature? Then come and hear 'The Tortured Journey of a Profound Literary Soul' – a talk by eminent writer Marina de Burgo.*

The words screamed out at her accusingly. She was neither tortured nor profound. And that could only mean one thing. She was plain thick. Her heart thumped in her chest. Why had she set herself up for such a humiliation? Wouldn't it be better by far to stay at Nutopia and maybe eventually get promoted to supervisor like Gretta Price? Couldn't she still spend her compensation money on something sensible like a car or put it down as a deposit on a little apartment somewhere close to her parents in Glennstown? The more she paced up and down past the bewildering notice-boards, the more she concluded that she was really in the wrong place, had silly ideas above her station, that her own foolish pride and obsession about becoming a teacher or a lawyer had led her here to this spot outside an interview room on the fifth floor – just so that she could make a total eejit of herself in front of a bunch of professors.

She quickly gathered up her things, intending to bolt for the door at the end of the corridor.

"Miss Kelly?" a voice called behind her and she froze, like a schoolgirl caught in some act of boldness.

She turned around sheepishly and came face-to-face with an olive-skinned man who looked as if he was in his thirties.

"We are ready to see you, Miss Kelly."

His accent was Italian or Spanish. She wasn't quite sure.

"I've changed my mind," she blurted out.

He smiled kindly at her from behind stylish black-rimmed glasses and beckoned with his hand. "Come now. We are not people who are biting you."

The funny way he said it made her smile and relax slightly and before she knew it, she was in the interview room facing three people across a long desk. The Italian man introduced himself as Doctor Romeo Dettori, from the Admissions Department. To his right was a studious-looking woman, wearing a very battered old tweed suit. Flyaway strands of crinkly grey hair stuck out at odd angles from her face. She was Professor Daphne Joyce from the Law Faculty. To his left sat a lean, sharply groomed, very dark-haired woman who introduced herself as Doctor Lucinda Tarpey from the English Department. Doctor Dettori and Professor Joyce smiled warmly at her but Doctor Tarpey merely raised a carefully plucked eyebrow and looked Nathalie over with the briefest of glances.

Doctor Dettori began a little speech. He told her not to think of their meeting as an interview – but more of an informal chat where they could get to know each other a little. He said she should feel free to ask as many questions as she liked. Professor Joyce added that universities could be scary places at first when you weren't used to them, but they were really just like schools – only bigger and with fewer rules, which Nathalie guessed was said to put her at her ease.

Lucinda Tarpey cut in sharply. "More precisely, Miss Kelly, universities are very special places, the highest seats of learning, repositories of noble ideas and aspirations, if you follow . . ."

Nathalie didn't follow at all. She didn't even understand half the words and it made her feel like a complete fool. She swallowed and shifted about in her chair.

"We liked your application," Professor Joyce said. "It was honest and forthright and I'm glad to say written in plain English."

Nathalie thought the professor glanced briefly across at her smartly groomed colleague as she spoke.

"So tell us again, Nathalie," said Doctor Dettori, "why you want to study at university."

"I don't know . . . maybe it's because I like . . . I mean . . ." Her brain was a blank. She could not think of one sensible thing to say.

"You don't know!" said Lucinda Tarpey, pouncing and twiddling a pen with casual menace.

Doctor Dettori hurried in to rescue her. "You wrote on the application that you like to read. That's good because reading is a big part of university. We have here a library the size of a department store – only no assistants trying to sell you perfume." His eyes twinkled with amusement at his own little joke.

Nathalie wanted to laugh but she felt far too nervous.

"What books do you like to read?" Daphne Joyce asked.

Nathalie racked her brains under the increasingly withering glare of Lucinda Tarpey with her twiddling pen. Doctor Dettori and Professor Joyce were doing their best to be nice – but they didn't really understand how terribly small she felt at that moment.

"So what have you been reading?" Doctor Tarpey enquired with bored disinterest.

Then Nathalie remembered the notice-board in the corridor and she got a brainwave.

"I've been reading *Wuthering Heights*," she said.

Lucinda Tarpey stopped twiddling her pen. "Oh. And what is your critical assessment of the novel's central dilemma?"

Oh shit! She didn't even understand the question. She thought hard, trying to remember what else was on the notice-board. "I think it asks 'Death, then what?'"

Doctor Tarpey nodded in surprise. The professor and Daphne Joyce smiled in agreement and urged her to continue.

"Well, when Catherine says to Nellie 'I am Heathcliff'– what does it mean? And who is Nellie? Why is she so important?"

Lucinda Tarpey looked like she might have to eat her words about Nathalie Kelly not being suitable university material. But she fired one last question. "Much has been made of the symbolism of the window in *Wuthering Heights*, Miss Kelly. What is your view?"

Doctor Dettori cut in half-jokingly, "Lucinda, this is a tough question. Miss Kelly should have the opportunity to attend some lectures before answering!"

"If Miss Kelly has read her *Wuthering Heights* as she claims, it is not a difficult question. Indeed the window is considered by many to be the central leitmotif of the work."

Nathalie felt annoyed with herself for lying so foolishly. She was bound to be caught out in the end. "I don't know," she said, now perched on the edge of her seat, poised to escape.

"I see," responded Doctor Tarpey with a cold triumphant tilt of the head.

"Maybe you and I don't read the same kind of books,"

Nathalie said, surprising herself, "but what does that prove? Nothing much! Maybe I don't know the first thing about literature just yet! But the only thing I have to prove right now is that I'm smart enough and interested enough to get through three years of study."

"Well said, Nathalie!" beamed Daphne Joyce who seemed to have taken a liking to her.

After that, Nathalie felt quite at ease and talked away about what she was looking forward to most if she got a place in the university, about her interest in law and her plans for the future.

"One last question?" Professor Joyce said. "You have applied to study either Law or The Arts. If you had your choice – which would you choose?"

Nathalie thought for a moment – she hardly knew the answer herself. "I like them both," she said, "but I think I like the certainty and discipline of the Law."

Daphne Joyce pursed her lips and lowered her head. "Law is very difficult – difficult to get into – difficult to stay in. I hate saying this – but people sometimes have a very romantic idea of law. They think of Ally MacBeal or the novels of John Grisham – but no profession is as it appears on TV."

"Yes, I know that," Nathalie said calmly.

"I don't want to dampen your thirst for learning or your desire to build a new career for yourself – but I would be concerned about you overreaching yourself."

Doctor Joyce spoke kindly but Nathalie knew then that there was no question of her getting on the Law course. Still, she wasn't too disappointed. She'd be very pleased to get into an Arts course. And they seemed very satisfied with her otherwise and, by the time the interview ended, she was almost disappointed to be leaving. Both Professor Joyce and Doctor Dettori wished her good luck with her studies and even Doctor Tarpey smiled fleetingly at her.

"When will I know if I've got a place?"

"In a week or two. And thank you for coming in today," Doctor Dettori said as he held the door open for her.

At home, in the kitchen that was her powerhouse, centre of strategic planning and theatre of operations, Yvonne Kelly was having a fit of stove rage. Something had gone wrong with the thermostat in the cooker and she couldn't get the temperature above one hundred and sixty. It meant that although the joint of lamb was cooked, it wouldn't get that nice crispy brown crust that Liam insisted on. And his roast potatoes wouldn't be crisp either.

But what was really bothering her was her anxiety about Nathalie. She was worried that her daughter might be pushing herself too far by trying to get into university. Nathalie would be home from her interview soon and Yvonne was determined to be supportive and encouraging. The very last thing she needed was Liam Kelly sitting in the corner, glowering behind his newspaper like Daddy Bear because his dinner wasn't cooked to his liking.

She heard his key in the door, and felt her stomach churn mildly. Dear God, did all marriages end up like this – the man a bad-tempered lump of sullenness in the corner and the woman a nervous wreck living in daily dread of her husband's bad humour? Yvonne felt she was approaching something like breaking-point. These days with Liam barely a civil word passed between them. More and more she speculated on what life would be like without him – how peaceful it would be, how calm. Standing over the stove stirring the redcurrant jelly into his special gravy, she suppressed her rage and gave herself up to daydreaming like a lovestruck teenager. Only she wasn't dreaming about meeting Prince Charming but ditching Prince Grumpy. If she won the lotto, she might buy a nice red-brick terraced house down by the sea in Clontarf. She'd have it gutted and decorated simply. She'd paint the walls in soothing pale colours and decorate it with a few nice paintings and she'd spend five hundred euro on a gnarled old olive-tree, specially transplanted from an olive grove in North Africa, which she would stand in a giant terracotta pot in the hall. And she'd have a neat little back garden with borders of tall flowers and pots and pots of shrubs and colourful plants. She'd have a cat for company and every day she'd go for walks on the strand with Nathalie who would be married to a wonderful, kind, sensitive, loving, good-humoured husband and who would take his adored young bride – and sometimes her mother – out to dinner at the weekend.

She listened to Liam pounding about upstairs, showering, and changing into the clean sweatshirt and jeans she'd laid out on the bed for him.

Then he appeared at the door of the kitchen. "What's for dinner?"

Pan-fried slivers of *pâté de foie gras* with a sprinkling of basil, a drizzle of *jus* and the merest hint of Parmesan scrapings all served on a bed of spicy rocket salad with truffle shavings, she said in her head.

"Roast lamb," she said out loud.

"Did you put the redcurrant jelly into the gravy?"

"Yes. Two teaspoonfuls."

"Grand."

He sat into the big old armchair and instantly buried himself behind the newspaper. Yvonne wondered if the paper would burst into spontaneous flames some day from the amount of times she glared at it. It was hard to imagine now, but long ago in the early days of their marriage, when Liam came through the front door, they would fall into each other's arms and tumble up the stairs, hungrily tearing off their clothes. In those days, dinner might be a hastily thrown-together omelette or a toasted sandwich when the hunger finally drove them back downstairs to the kitchen.

These days, if the word sex was even mentioned on the telly, Liam Kelly would suddenly remember that the radiator pipe in the bathroom was leaking or that the gutters needed cleaning. Yvonne wondered about all those women whose husbands pestered them constantly for sex. She would quite like to be pestered occasionally. She was married to the most handsome man on the road, still broad-shouldered and muscular and strong, with a firm square jaw, neat cropped flaxen hair and distant blue eyes. If she let it, her heart would still skip a beat to see him coming. But what good was it? What good was any of it when he was so cold and distant and angry all the time? What other choice had she but to return his coldness in kind?

But Yvonne would have been astonished, even incredulous, if she had but known the thoughts running through her husband's head as he sheltered behind his newspaper.

For Liam had a secret – something that had haunted him since the early days of his marriage – something he'd tried with mixed success to bury in the deep recesses of his mind. For a very long time, after Nathalie was born, he'd hardly thought about it. But somehow, in the middle years, it came back to haunt him. Often he'd braced himself to confide the whole grubby story to his wife. But the time was never right. Besides, he knew that she would hate and despise him for it. Many times, she'd asked him about what it was that troubled him and the more she'd probed, the more deeply he guarded the secret. So that in time his love became swathed in a thick blanket of reserve, becoming at last what seemed like mere sullenness and indifference.

Now with his daughter fully grown, straining gently to be freed of her parents' protective love, this secret came back to haunt Liam. What if Nathalie ever found out? Wouldn't she also judge him harshly? Wouldn't she despise him? He thought about these things all the time, when he seemed to be reading the newspaper, when he appeared to be watching telly, when he pretended to sleep at night.

Could you go back and change the past? Liam didn't think so. But these days he thought often about trying.

Nathalie breezed into the kitchen. She kicked off her shoes and kissed each of her parents fondly before grabbing a slice of cheese from the fridge.

"You'll ruin your appetite, pet," said Yvonne. "How did it go at the university?"

"I don't know. It was scary – and I nearly chickened out of the interview. But two of them were really nice."

"I'm sure you'll get a place, love. We've every faith in you," Yvonne said and hugged her daughter.

Ten minutes later, Liam was eating the carrots, dipped in his special gravy, but only picking at the meat and soggy roast potatoes.

"I'll cook you a bit of steak if you like," Yvonne said, hurt that he couldn't even force a few mouthfuls down so as not to offend her.

"Ah, no, you're grand."

Shortly afterwards he rose and cleaned off his plate into the bin, then rinsed it and put it in the dishwasher.

"I'm off out for a walk," he said, pulling on a light jacket.

Yvonne's eyebrow shot up towards the ozone layer as she watched him disappear through the door. Then she turned to her daughter.

"Honestly, Nathalie, that man is driving me mad!"

Later, alone in the kitchen, Yvonne baked an apple tart and reviewed her life with Liam Kelly.

Since her marriage, she had worn out four cookers, three refrigerators, five irons, five washing-machines, three vacuum-cleaners, several kettles and toasters, three food-mixers, and several sets of crockery. She had redecorated the house from top to bottom five times and redesigned the garden three times. She had baked twenty-four Christmas cakes, forty-eight Christmas puddings, about a thousand apple tarts, several hundred sponge cakes and around four hundred rounds of Yorkshire pudding. As for roast lamb – the inventory ran into thousands. She had washed and ironed over eight thousand shirts, sorted sixteen thousand odd socks, polished several hundred pairs of shoes – all for Liam Kelly.

And what thanks had she got? None.

CHAPTER 15

Thank God for her part-time job in the bank, thought Yvonne. It was a lifeline. There were twenty people in the office and they all got on well. People laughed and had interesting conversations and remembered one another's birthdays and noticed when someone was upset or under pressure. Sometimes they all went out for drinks on Friday evening and then on to the nice little Italian restaurant round the corner.

Yvonne didn't often join them but this Friday she was so annoyed at Liam that when Alan Halvey, the manager, suggested drinks after work in the Shangri La, Yvonne didn't refuse outright as she usually did.

"Go on," said Treasa who worked alongside her at the Customer Care Desk. "It will do you good."

"OK," said Yvonne. Nathalie would be out for the evening and anything was better than sitting at home with Grumpy Liam.

And so, after work, Yvonne found herself sitting with Treasa in the upstairs lounge of the Shangri La with Alan Halvey and some of the others.

"I think he fancies you," Treasa said to Yvonne when Alan went to the bar to buy his round.

"Don't be daft. I've a good ten years on him. Anyway he's married and I'm married, so that's that."

"But you should see the way he looks at you sometimes. I'd say he has it real bad."

While it was quite a nice feeling to have an admirer, even a married younger one, Yvonne felt uncomfortable with the idea that any man might be throwing lustful looks at her and especially that other people in the office might notice. Besides, living with Liam Kelly might be a bit like living with an exceptionally sullen rock, but she still cared enough never to make a fool of him behind his back.

But when Alan Halvey returned from the bar, she found herself examining him with new interest. He had a pleasant face, she thought, not strikingly handsome but warm, with intelligent light-brown eyes. Most of the others drifted away and for an hour the three of them sat exchanging office gossip, discussing the traffic and the roadworks at the end of the street. They talked about holiday plans and nice new restaurants and films they wanted to see. There was no problem at all knocking talk out of Alan Halvey and midway into her third drink, Yvonne began to really enjoy herself.

Then Treasa pulled on her jacket. "I've just remembered. I've a man coming to look at my washing-machine. Gotta go. I'm sorry."

"I should go too," Yvonne said, anxious not to be left in a compromising position.

"Nonsense," said Treasa. "Sit there and finish your drink. Where's your rush?" She winked knowingly at Yvonne who now shifted uneasily in her seat.

"We'll just finish this drink and then I'll drive you home. How's that?" said Alan, sensing her discomfort.

When Treasa left, Alan moved from his chair across the table and slid in along the red leather seat beside Yvonne. She felt vaguely uncomfortable, as if he might expect something. Determined not to give any misleading signals, she talked enthusiastically about Liam and how wonderful he was about the house, all the extensions, Nathalie's apartment, how she never had to spend a penny on plumbers or electricians.

"Good for him! I'm pure useless when it comes to DIY."

"Yes, I suppose I'm very lucky," she said as chirpily as she could and they fell into an awkward silence.

"I guess that's why you always look so lovely," he said then. "Because you don't have a care in the world."

Now that was flirting! And she was having none of it! Besides it was entirely wrong to say that she hadn't a care in the world. She had plenty of cares. She was married to the stubbornest, sullenest, moodiest, fussiest man in the world for instance. That was a fairly stressful state of affairs. And her husband no longer found her sexually attractive. That didn't make her feel one bit lovely. It had never crossed her mind before, but now sitting here with a man – not her husband – she wondered if Liam had ever strayed. Was that it? Was he so in love with someone else that he couldn't bring himself to be even half-civil to the wife who'd cared for him since nineteen seventy-five?

She hastily gathered up her things. "Thanks for the drink, Alan. I'd better go now."

"Was it something I said?" He smiled at her mischievously.

"Not at all! Liam and I always go for a meal on Friday nights. That's all."

"What a devoted couple you are," he said with just a hint of irony. "Well, let's go then."

If only you knew the half of it, Yvonne mused.

He dropped her at her front door and told her he looked forward to seeing her on Monday.

After dinner, eaten in the kitchen as usual, Liam retired to the dining-room to sort out his tax and Yvonne decided to take a long, soaking hot bath. She lit scented candles, poured some concoction that promised to make her feel like a teenager into the bath, tied her hair back and put on a rejuvenating face mask before sliding into the hot scented water.

After a long luxurious soak, she donned her towelling robe and moved into the bedroom. Her figure was still good. She carried a bit more weight than in her thirties, but it suited her and she was blessed with a smooth and unlined complexion. If Alan Halvey found her attractive, then why didn't her husband? She longed for affection, for tender words, for sweet caresses. Perhaps, if she prepared herself really well, perhaps if she wore the special black silk negligee that Nathalie had innocently bought her for Christmas, he might be coaxed into reaching out and touching her. Even an embrace would be nice. It didn't have to be full-blown sex. She wasn't going to expect miracles. Yes, a nice warm cuddle and an affectionate peck on the cheek would be just perfect.

She smoothed body lotion all over her skin to give it a silken feel, put on make-up – just a very light dusting of powder, a touch of lipstick and a hint of blue eye shadow. She sprayed herself with Private Collection then slipped into the black lace negligee before climbing between freshly laundered sheets. He was in the bathroom brushing his teeth. He wouldn't be long. She heard his measured steps on the landing and turned the light down so that the room was bathed in a warm, relaxing glow.

He appeared. "Is there something wrong with the bulb?"

"I just turned it down – more relaxing."

"I was thinking of reading."

She wouldn't be put off. "What are you reading?"

"Just that old thing about how they built the Empire State Building."

"Is it good? I mean are you enjoying it?"

"It's grand," he said, climbing in beside her and turning on his own bedside light, before instantly immersing himself in the book.

"Liam?"

"What?"

"Will you turn off the light? Let's just chat and have a cuddle. It's ages since we had a cuddle."

"Ah, you're grand! Go to sleep."

She tumbled from the bed in a hot flood of anger. "I will! I will go to sleep! But not with you! Never again with you!"

He set the book down carefully on the duvet and looked at her intently for a brief moment. It was impossible to read the expression on his face.

"Yvonne, what's wrong?"

"What's wrong? *You're* what's wrong. Well, I've had enough!"

Then she did something that she hadn't done since the early days when they'd had lovers' tiffs. She took herself off to the spare room, vowing never to speak to him again. The only difference was – this time he didn't follow her. This time she didn't want him to follow her. And this time she didn't sneak back to snuggle up warmly beside him in the middle of the night.

CHAPTER 16

It was Saturday and Aoife sat in the Purple Pepper, popping peppered black olives into her mouth and waiting for Dermot to show up. He was unusually late. Never before in the entire history of their relationship – eighteen months of Aoife going 'I'm not sure that I want to get into a heavy relationship scene just now – love you to bits though – mwagh mwagh!'– and Dermot going 'Whatever you like, sweet thing' – had he ever once been late. It made her feel kind of annoyed or restless somehow. It was her job to be late and her job to cancel a date at the last moment. That was something she seemed to be forced to do quite often – which Dermot had never done. If only he was less available, more mysterious, a little bit dangerous even!

She thought of Flann Slevin and she reflected that in some respects he was a bit mysterious with even that requisite hint of danger. And he certainly couldn't be described as dull or predictable. But he was also kind enough to watch out for her. Hhmmm! There was still no sign of Dermot, so availing of one of her her Pigsback vouchers, she ordered a Purple Pepper speciality – their Cosmopolitan – lemon vodka, cointreau, cranberry juice and a dash of lime with some crushed ice. It slid down the throat with a luscious ease, coursing warmly through her body in delicious little jolts of pleasure. She hadn't meant to finish it quite so quickly but it was so nice she just couldn't stop.

Dermot was now half an hour late. What the hell did he think he was playing at?

She had splashed out and bought a magazine for the train journey home to Larkhaven – but now she pulled it from the bag and leafed through it irritably, looking for something that might hold her attention. But apart from a ludicrous horiscope warning her that she was in for a few nasty shocks, it was all fashions and house makeovers she couldn't afford.

"Another Cosmopolitan, please!" she told the friendly Ukranian waiter.

He returned promptly and set the cocktail glass down in front of her with a flourish. Time passed and she began to get a little anxious. Where was Dermot?

She leafed through the magazine a second time, filled in the crossword on the back page and before she knew it her glass was empty. She had one last voucher in her bag. It was clear Dermot wasn't going to show. She felt let down, abandoned and quite annoyed. Aoife was not the sort of girl to sit alone in a bar drinking – but examining her options now she realised that with over an hour to go before the next train it was either sit in the cold draughty station or sit here in the cosy warmth of the Purple Pepper.

She held out the voucher to the waiter and ordered one last Cosmopolitan. They weren't costing anything and they were Just So Nice. And besides, nobody on the last train would notice if she was a little bit tipsy.

She tried Dermot's mobile one last time, then left a message: *"Hi – I've waited over an hour – you never showed. Don't know what you're playing at – but it's really not very nice. How would you feel if I treated you like that?"*

Although, as she sat blearily in the taxi on her way to the station, Aoife realised that she maybe had treated Dermot like that once or twice, well, all right – three or four – or maybe even a few more times – but never deliberately. And perhaps he was simply trying to teach her a lesson.

As she mused on these points, the taxi made its way slowly down Gordon Street through the late-evening traffic. They were stuck outside the pink-clad Gordon Bar – a popular gay venue. Aoife amused herself by admiring the men as they gathered round the entrance to the night-club. Even the older men were paragons of style and elegance. There were tables and chairs on the sidewalk alongside the building. One man in particular looked very stylish in a broad brown fedora and a stone-coloured linen suit. She noticed that he wore spats. He was all over some younger man whose back was to her, holding his hand and everything. Some men have interesting necks and Aoife found that she was quite fascinated by the neck of this younger guy. It had a nice sturdy set to it – solid-looking, something almost familiar about it, and she craned her neck in the back of the taxi to get a better look.

"Ah, no sense in looking at any of them lads, sweetheart – them pig's-ears don't have the same rules of the road in any way. It does wreck me buzz just lookin' at them," the cab driver said. He jerked the car into gear and shot off down the street.

Ben Searson had also been in town that day – tying up some of the tiresome loose ends of his ex-life, trying not to notice when ex-friends stopped and stared at him in Grafton Street – and didn't say hello. By the end of the day, he'd felt an odd mixture of despair and relief and he'd spent a few hours wandering about the city aimlessly, half-tempted to look up one or two old friends – but eventually resisting the urge. What would they have to talk about? He imagined the conversation – their forced bonhomie, the offer of a drink somewhere discreet and not quite at the hub of things, empty chatter about the weather and the traffic, some fancy conversational footwork as they sidestepped the rather awkward and truly spectacularly appalling circumstances of Ben's downfall. "So sad," their wives would murmur pityingly – "Tragic," the men would add, "but sure it was all his own fault" – so they would all chant reassuringly to each other once he was out of earshot.

No! To hell with them all! Home to my little cottage! He smiled for the first time that day, reminded of his old grandmother who used to sing "My Little Grey Home in The West" after three stiff Scotch whiskies.

He drank a pint of Guinness and ate a plain ham sandwich in a little old hotel on Merrion Square and he read a book – *Seabiscuit*. Then he strolled at his leisure to the station. He sat into the train and quickly became immersed in his book once more. He barely noticed the journey, was completely enthralled by the story of the broken-down millionaire, the half-crippled jockey and the completely banjaxed horse. At this precise moment he could identify with all three of them.

At last the train chugged and rattled into the quiet little Larkhaven station, coming to a slow and stately halt at the platform. It was late but he was fully awake and feeling oddly happy with himself. He gathered up his things and stepped down onto the platform, then began to make his way towards the little picket-fenced exit. He walked quickly past the carriages. And it wasn't until he was almost at the gate that he realised something.

There was a shadow in one of the carriages he had passed, an unevenness along one of the seats that had caught the corner of his eye. He ought to check it out – tell the station master. It looked like someone had left a bag behind by mistake. He went back and peered through the window to get a better look and realised that it wasn't a bag – it was a person. He tapped on the window but got no response. He had no other option than to get back on the train and that was how a few short moments later Aoife Joyce woke up in very strange surroundings and found herself face to face with a man known to her as possibly a violent criminal.

"Ghhhhrrrlllllahhh!" she said thickly in strangled tones with a tongue that now felt like it had been licking sand off the rougher dunes of the Sahara Desert.

"Sorry – I didn't mean to frighten you – but I thought you might like to be woken up," Ben told her softly.

"What?" she said, staring at him wild-eyed. It was the middle of the night. Where was she? Was it perhaps some kind of nightmare? And what was Ben Searson doing in it anyway? She shut her eyes tightly, frantically trying to remember how she came to be here in an empty train carriage. Gradually the memory of the evening came back to her. She'd arranged to meet Dermot in the Purple Pepper only he hadn't turned up and then she remembered the four Cosmopolitans, and finally getting a taxi to the station and tipping herself unsteadily into the train carriage. She sat up quickly, straightened out her legs and hitched down her perfectly lovely box-pleated mini, tugging the hem futilely towards her knees with great resolve. She regretted wearing the little skirt now and wished she'd gone for something with a bit more fabric.

"Thank you but I'm fine now," she said, pulling on her coat and standing up in a valiant attempt to look completely sober.

"Sure?" he said, towering over her in the cramped gloom of the carriage.

"Yes," she replied, shuffling past him towards the door.

She'd made it to the platform but the world began to turn a bit funnily at that point and from the distance she heard his voice calling. "Wait!"

Some time later she was propped against the door of Bloomfield House, Ben Searson's arm holding her tightly round the waist, his other hand pressed firmly on the front-door bell.

The noise of the bell ringing made a horrible drilling echo in her head and she leaned on the door and begged him to stop.

"Don't suppose you have a key?" he said.

Aoife shook her head blearily. She didn't feel at all well – quite peculiar in fact, considering she'd only had four

Cosmopolitans. All she could think of was getting away from Ben Searson's vicelike grip and falling into bed.

She was delighted at last to hear Berry's reassuring footsteps in the hall.

"Well, goodnight then," she said.

"Yes, goodnight," he said, not making any move.

"I'll be fine now. There's really no . . ."

Just then, the door opened and Berry stood framed in the door, her hair up in a towel, an old blue cotton dressing-gown hanging loosely on her slender frame.

"Oh, sorry – I thought it was just Aoife," she said, flustered, shooting Aoife a fleeting alarmed look.

"No . . . it's just that Dermot never showed up and then Vladimir gave me an extra Cosmopolitan and then Ben here woke me up on the train and –"

"It was lucky that I spotted her," he said.

"Well, I'm home now – safe and sound," Aoife said, swaying into the house behind her sister and promptly collapsing on the floor.

Berry eyed Aoife's crumpled frame with barely concealed annoyance. "Get up! You can't sleep there!" She shook her sister's shoulder a little more sharply than necessary but there was no response.

They made an odd tableau – Ben's large melancholy frame filling the door in the moonlight, Berry in her flimsy cotton dressing-gown with her hair turbaned up in a towel and Aoife a drunken crumpled mess on the floor.

"Any thoughts?" Berry said to Ben.

"Just the one," he answered and stepped into the hall. In one swift movement he scooped Aoife up into his arms and headed up the old oak staircase.

Berry followed.

"Any particular bedroom?" he said as he reached the landing.

"First door on the left."

They lay Aoife down on the bed and Berry pulled a quilt up over her. Then she bent and kissed her sister goodnight.

"Thanks," she said to Ben as they stood next to each other on the landing outside Aoife's room.

He shrugged and smiled dismissively. Then his eyes were drawn to the only other open door on the landing. Beyond was Berry's big old double bed with the saggy mattress, the mahogany wardrobe, a heavy Victorian dressing-table and matching chair. The room was scattered with the comfortable clutter of her single life.

"Yours, I take it?" he said, looking like he might take a step in that direction.

"Yes."

He brushed a strand of hair from her face and then bent his lips to her forehead as though he might kiss her there. But in a moment his lips were on hers – the briefest, most fleeting contact. Scarcely a kiss – more of a featherlight touching of mouths. A warm little shock of pleasure!

Then he bounded across the landing and took the stairs two at a time.

"She'll be as right as rain in the morning!" he called up. "Goodnight!"

Berry stood at the top of the stairs and watched him slip out the front door into the night.

CHAPTER 17

Aoife's head was fairly thumping the next morning and it didn't help matters that Berry had decided to do her distinctive version of the Full Irish Breakfast. It's not an easy dish to make a mess of. After all, you simply melt a little oil and butter in a pan until it sizzles, fry the sausages and the black and white pudding until they are a crisp succulent golden brown. Grill the bacon at a medium temperature – until it is also just crisp. Sprinkle some mushrooms with salt and pepper and sauté them lightly in butter with a tiny dash of balsamic vinegar. Remove the sausages and pudding from the pan, then fry the eggs and some brown soda bread. Make a huge pot of Barry's Classic Blend tea – and *voilà!* – the Full Irish Breakfast. There are optional embellishments – potato cakes, baked beans, fried potatoes. But the main secret is simply good basic ingredients and getting the timing and the order of cooking right.

Aoife came downstairs in her dressing-gown and pink

fluffy slippers and opened the kitchen door gingerly. She was met with a blast of smoke and the acrid smell of burning fat.

"Almost ready," chirped Berry waving her arms in the air to dispel another puff of smoke that was wafting up from the grill.

"Is something burning?"

"No! Everything's all in order," she said cheerfully, piling Aoife's plate high with a selection of burnt and greasy objects. Her good humour was irritating enough but Aoife's stomach was also churning nauseatingly at the mere sight of the food. She didn't want to hurt her sister's feelings – but, even if she wasn't horribly hung over, this was Berry's worst offering yet. She poured two mugs of tea and poked wretchedly at a charred sausage with her fork.

"*Bon appetit!*" said Berry, oblivious to the horrors of her own cooking and shovelling a large slippery sliver of blackened egg into her mouth. "How's Dermot?"

"He never showed up. I just don't understand it. He didn't even leave a message. I mean, we've been going out on and off for almost eighteen months and all of a sudden he's beginning to act like the worst kind of love rat."

"And you're surprised?"

"What do you mean by that?"

"I mean you've treated him like a doormat. Using him when you want someone to go out with or you need a bed in town for the night – and then not bothering to return his calls when it doesn't suit you or when you see someone more interesting on the horizon. If you want my opinion – he should have ditched you long ago."

"Stop! You're being really mean and you've got it all wrong. Dermot and I – well, we just have an open relationship."

"Oh, is that what you call it? Do you want to know what I think?"

"No, actually I don't. And this food's disgusting by the way!" Aoife shoved her plate brusquely to one side and eyed it disapprovingly. "I mean – it's burnt and it's greasy and even the cat could cook a better breakfast than you!"

Aoife and Berry didn't really fight much any more – but when hostilities did break out – they didn't hold back.

Berry stood up coolly from the table and began to clear away the things. "You're hardly in a position to complain – falling through the front door drunk to the horrors last night. Making a show of yourself in front of Ben Searson." She stopped, remembering the kiss on the landing. Just as well Aoife hadn't seen the blush of longing that had swept across Berry's face, or the blaze of desire that had flashed in her eyes as his lips grazed lightly on hers. She took a deep breath and continued to scold her sister. "Anyway, I didn't hear you jumping out of bed and offering to cook anything much lately. If I'm such a bad cook, then why don't you take over in the kitchen? Let's see if you can do any better!"

"Don't be ridiculous! I'm out of the house before you've even turned over for your second sleep. I work really really hard in my job and then I get home much later than you – completely crocked with the tiredness. It wouldn't be fair to expect me to cook all the meals as well. I thought we had agreed about that."

"I don't remember us agreeing anything like that. In fact I don't remember us drawing up any agreements of any kind – except I get to do all the work around here – cleaning, washing, cooking, fixing!"

"I can't see why you're getting so worked up," said Aoife defensively, as she poured herself another cup of tea. "I do my fair share of work – and I pay over most of my salary to help with the bills. I'm so broke that I don't even know when I last bought a new outfit."

"New outfit! Oh please!"

Aoife was amazed at how cross Berry was. It wasn't usually her style to get too worked up about anything.

"Do you want to know what I think?" said Berry. "I think Dermot's finally found someone genuinely nice who appreciates him for the dishy, intelligent and considerate guy he really is – only he's trying to build up the courage to tell you. He didn't turn up yesterday because he simply didn't have the nerve. And I don't blame him."

"That's ridiculous!" Aoife stood up, angry herself now, sickened by the fry and deeply hungover. "Dermot loves me! He would never look at another woman!"

"Oh, you have much to learn!" said Berry.

"Oh, I have, have I?" Aoife said. She reached into a drawer, pulled out a comb and began tugging it crossly through her hair. "Well, if you're so smart – how come you've done nothing about Ben Searson? You were supposed to ask him straight up if that was his real name."

Berry didn't say anything for a few moments. She rammed dishes into the dishwasher and then she drew in her breath sharply. "Because . . ." she said weakly.

Aoife was standing now, hands on hips, knowing she was gaining the upper hand in the argument. "Because why?" she asked coolly.

"Because . . . because . . . I was going to. But I didn't have the heart. Anyway I think it's all nonsense about that not being his real name."

Aoife sighed and once again went patiently and carefully through the information she had received from Mike Mordaunt's Detective Agency.

"That means nothing," Berry said dismissively. "Where's your proof? It's probably some scam the agency operates to suck in customers. I mean, think about it, Aoife – think sensibly for once in your life. If Ben Searson had a criminal record and his real name was Bernard Pearse, wouldn't the gardai have to be informed about it? He'd be on their records, wouldn't he? And if he was any real sort of threat – well, they'd be on his case from the minute he landed in Larkhaven, wouldn't they?"

"Not necessarily," retorted Aoife. "And anyway – why are you so quick to jump to his defence? Maybe you're getting a bit of a soft spot for him? Maybe you *fancy* Ben Searson!"

The words were out before she could stop them – and as soon as they had zinged callously and spitefully from her mouth, Aoife wished she hadn't said them. She looked across at her sister and saw the glint of a tiny tear in the corner of her eye. "Oh God, Berry, I'm really sorry! That was a completely mean thing to say."

Berry said nothing and then Aoife went and put her arms tightly round her sister. "Berry, I love you more than anyone else in the world and you are right. I don't pull my weight around the house and I haven't been nice to Dermot. And the gardai probably know all about Ben Searson or Pearse or whatever his name is – and I'm mean and selfish and I'm really sorry, Berry. Please forgive me.

If you want me to leave – I will. I can go back to Nathalie's if you like – I mean I wouldn't blame you one bit for throwing me out . . ."

Berry pushed her away and forced back the tears with a dry smile. "Stop! Stop! It's just a Sunday morning spat between sisters. Everybody has little tiffs – it's perfectly normal – and nobody's moving out anywhere. And stop pussyfooting around me as if I can never ever be teased again about having a man in my life because of . . . because of Conor . . ."

She'd met him when working in one of the big IT companies. As senior systems analyst, she headed up the division and Conor had joined only recently. Not exactly straight from college – but in some respects still wet behind the ears. He'd also married very young, a family tradition it appeared, and by the time he arrived at SoftSkills Solutions, he had become a doting father of two children – a girl aged four and a boy scarcely a year younger. Two days after his arrival, he proudly propped a family photo on his desk – it was probably meant as a very unsubtle sign to one of the office girls who had made a big play for him on the first day.

Berry had absently admired the photo. She was seven years his senior and quite amused by his earnest untested virtue. Sometimes now she wondered if she hadn't taken on Conor Lynch as some sort of challenge – to prove to him that untested virtues are not really virtues at all.

One evening, he had to stay late to finish off a project. They were both late and when the work was done, they went for a drink – just two colleagues sharing their thoughts on a routine project. She smiled fondly at his boyish enthusiasm. He was totally fired up with ambition.

"I want to give my wife and children the best quality of life possible. We live in a small house now – but as I get on, we'll move. I own a site in Stepaside. We're going to build our dream home there."

"You have it all worked out," she said, teasing him.

"Yup!" He grinned broadly at her as he emptied his pint glass.

"Then may it all work out as you plan!" she said, raising her glass to him.

"You sound just like my mum. I didn't think someone as smart as you would be cynical."

She shook her head and beamed a warm smile at him, ignoring the tactless comparison with his mother. "No – not cynical at all. But life has this habit of throwing up nasty surprises – when you least expect. The Greeks spent centuries writing tragedies about it – so it must be true. I really do hope you get on and build that wonderful life with your family – you're a nice guy and you work hard and you definitely deserve it."

"But?"

"But nothing," she said, patting his hand lightly as a big sister would. "My granny used always say to me – be prepared for the surprises of this life – not all of them are wonderful."

"Thanks, Ma," he said, pecking her on the cheek like a wayward, affectionate son. "You're so wise."

Somehow a relationship developed – where he would consult her as some sort of much older, wiser and fiercely dependable sister. He was good company – quite witty without being goofy and terribly terribly proper and courteous. Berry began to envy his pretty young wife. The world was full of less than wholesome men and, boy, did she know all about that! At thirty-two, she was beginning to lose faith in ever finding a man she could share her life with. Conor's wife, Sarah, at twenty-five, seemed to have it all – dream husband, two adorable children, and the prospect of a dream home on the horizon as well.

"Tell me about your wife," she said to him one evening. "She looks very lovely in the photo."

"Best decision of my life," he chirruped and leaned back proudly. "We met in college. Actually Sarah was pregnant when we got married – but our folks were amazed we decided to wed at all. No one does any more, my mother says. You don't have to tie yourself down, they kept saying; it was different for our generation. But Sarah and I knew we were right for each other – so where was the point in waiting? Sarah works in the home and she's a genius with money. Maybe you'll come and have lunch with us some day. Sarah is a brilliant cook. I just don't know how she does it all – the house, the children, the food. I'm a lucky man and I know it! I pity my friends – the ones that don't have girlfriends – they're missing out on so much."

"Maybe they pity you? Maybe they think you're missing out on stuff? Have you ever wondered about that?"

He laughed – a little tetchily, she noticed.

And then she was afraid she'd gone too far. "Sorry – that was out of order. Shouldn't have said that. I just like to burst your smug little bubble sometimes."

"It's OK. My mum talks to me like that all the time."

Now it was her turn to be tetchy. "Conor – just so as

you know – I'm not actually quite old enough to be your mum – by a factor of about ten years – and it slightly annoys me that every time I say something you put it in the same category as something your mum would say." Berry was becoming quite heated, anger bubbling up out of nowhere. She didn't understand it.

"I didn't mean anything like that. You're not at all like my mum. For starters you're really good-looking for an older woman."

Berry realised at that moment that there was simply no common ground between them, and that the delicate little friendship she'd foolishly imagined blossoming was nothing more than a bit of light-hearted office banter. She was livid with herself for having any expectations at all in the matter. After all, she had lots of valued friends already, people whose company she loved and even Jim – a very occasional if uninspiring boyfriend. So why did it suddenly feel as though Conor Lynch was somebody important in her life – somebody with the rare capacity to ignite Berry Joyce's temper?

"I'd better be going," she said. "Give my best regards to Sarah. I look forward to meeting her sometime."

Relations, if you could call them that, were a bit strained for the next few weeks. She was very busy with quarterly reports and didn't have the time or feel inclined to seek out his company. He, in any case, seemed to have become totally immersed in his work. They would greet one another with a wary smile or a hand held in the air for the skimpiest moment. He would sit at his desk for hours, scarcely coming up for a quick ten-minute sandwich at lunch-time. Often he was still at his desk when she was leaving. Once on a bright Sunday morning, she saw him in the distance on Sandymount Strand, holding hands with his wife, both windswept, their two little children toddling along happily behind them, a dog cavorting in the sand.

In her very kind and generous heart, Berry Joyce wished them well at that moment and said a little prayer that Conor Lynch and his lovely family would remain that close and happy always. She vowed to rekindle their friendship, to act as his mentor – encouraging him up the ladder of success.

She never for a moment imagined that they might fall in love. But now five years later she still blushed at her foolishness and his recklessness, at her one and only mad lapse of common sense. Since then, she'd only dated terrifically sensible men – and even then rarely and with a slightly wooden heart. Berry's heart would never burn so brightly again. Sometimes, as she reflected on the situation in the cold, clear light of reason, she concluded that she'd been possessed with a sort of beautiful madness.

A few weeks after they'd had their little disagreement, he appeared in the door of her office. He looked unusually despondent.

"Mind if I come in?" he said.

"Be my guest."

She was glad of the opportunity to rescue the situation between them, to get their relationship back on a companionable footing. "How's the work going? I've been so busy with quarterly reports – but I hope you're settling in well."

"Yes – things couldn't be better for me here. But there's more to the work than I thought."

"Meaning?"

"I think my weak spot is that I tend not to see how a particular project is multi-layered. This software package for the engineering firm, for instance. Anyway – I'm learning."

"I have every faith in you," she said. "And don't forget – there's always a bit of leeway with deadlines, so you don't need to feel under too much pressure."

"Thanks, I appreciate that," he said, sliding into a chair and letting out a faint sigh. "So how are things with you anyway?"

She grinned crookedly at him across the desk. "Now – why do I get the impression that you're not really interested in hearing the answer to that question?"

He shrugged and made a scowly teenage smile and then wagged a scolding finger at her.

"Smart lady! You're too smart for me."

Then there followed one of those fleeting silences – when the world seems to tumble slightly out of kilter for a brief moment. Was that it? Was that the moment?

"I'm not that smart," she said "but I'm not denying I like the compliment either. So what's up?"

"How do you mean?"

"I'm not sure. We don't know each other that well but you seem a bit – well, subdued – maybe something like that."

He ducked his head and ran a knuckle lightly across his chin. "I have no idea why I'm telling you this – but here goes. Remember when you said about life throwing up all sorts of surprises – not all of them nice?"

Berry nodded, feeling slightly embarrassed. Looking back now, she realised she must have sounded quite condescending and superior.

"Something's happened – there's no one else I can talk to . . ." His cool blue eyes clouded over with confusion.

Berry wanted to reach across the desk and rest her hand on his for a moment – just to comfort him – but instead she sat like some kindly mother figure and urged him gently:

"Whatever it is, you can tell me. And it won't pass these walls – I promise you that."

He smiled gratefully at her and leaned forward in his chair. "I knew you were someone very special – the very first day we met," he said.

If you only knew the half of it, Berry thought wryly to herself as he settled back to begin his tale.

A short time later, she was looking at him incredulously. "Conor Lynch! That is the daftest thing I have ever heard. You're imagining things."

He ran a knuckle lightly across his chin. It was his habit, she noticed, when he was worried about something.

"I don't think so."

Berry drew leaf shapes on a page and spoke in even, measured tones. It was the end of a very long day and she was tired. Instinct told her to back away. Quickly. "Well, even if there's the slightest chance of it being true, I'm not the one you should be talking to. What about your mother? What about Sarah? Don't you have a sister or a brother or something?"

He shook his head. "No one I'd feel comfortable talking to about this. Besides, Sarah would kill me if she thought I was talking to family about our personal stuff. I just can't believe what she's done."

"But how can you be sure you haven't just got the wrong end of the stick?"

"I found a whole stash of bills – hidden in the back of a drawer. I asked her about it and she said that things had got a bit out of hand over the Christmas. She was storing up the bills until she got a chance to pay them."

"But you said she was great with money." Berry could feel herself being drawn in spite of her instincts.

"I don't understand it. She says that having a little bet here and there is about the only fun she has and apart from that she won't talk about it – just clams up and says I don't understand what it's like to be stuck in the house all day with kids."

"I'm with her on that. I don't know how anybody can spend longer than five minutes with small kids. And she probably wants to protect you from the worry as well."

"She says other mums in our road do a whole lot worse and that it's only money."

There was a new hardness in his voice that she'd never noticed before. Berry knew that there wasn't much she could do except to listen carefully and try to be supportive. She knew especially that she couldn't take sides. She was only hearing Conor's side of things.

"Then we had a big row last night and she locked me out of the bedroom. I couldn't sleep and I started browsing on the Internet – that's when I discovered where the money's gone. She's been gambling in the online casinos – a little bit here and there. But it all adds up. I tried to talk to her about it in the morning before the kids were up and she threw me out."

At that moment, Berry might have reflected that really none of this was her business and that Conor Lynch was a grown man who was well capable of solving his own problems. But she found it hard to shut her heart against the look of surprised anguish on his face.

"Maybe she's calmed down now. Try calling. I'll bet she's feeling bad and just wondering when you're going to be home."

"I've been trying all day. She just hangs up."

"Is there anywhere you can stay tonight?" she asked him.

He shook his head.

"Then take the spare room in my place. Things won't look so bad after a good night's sleep."

"I couldn't do that," he said.

"What are you going to do? Sleep behind the photocopier? I promise I won't sneak into your bed in the middle of the night and get you in a compromising position. You look like you could do with a good night's sleep."

"You don't mind?"

"Not at all. As long as you don't say anything round the office. You'd be surprised how rumours get started round this place."

He gave a grateful shrug and came home with her. They ate a ready-made pasta dish for two and drank a glass of Pinot Grigio as they watched an old episode of *Friends*.

"I'll leave you to it," she said when the credits began to roll. "Hope you sleep well."

She went to wake him the next morning – but he'd already gone. He'd made the bed though and left a note on the pillow.

"Slept really well. Thanks a million. See you later."

And there it should all have ended.

CHAPTER 18

Vernon's Estate Agents was fairly buzzing with business and busyness on Monday morning as Aoife sailed in, determined to put all thoughts of Dermot's disappearance and Ben Searson's true identity behind her.

She snatched the top sheet from Joe's pile and read out the prompt to him. *"Criminal Justice Theft & Fraud Act 2001 . . . exceptions to theft?"*

Joe closed his eyes and bit his lip. "Wait – got it. A person cannot steal land or things forming part of . . ."

Aoife barely listened to him. She needed to get into her office to collect her thoughts for the busy day ahead and looking after potential buyers for the house in Talavera Road. It wasn't just any potential buyer, but one of the richest men in the country. Kevin had once again reminded her about the particular importance of getting a good price for this house. She'd dressed especially smartly for the occasion, her best Quin & Donnelly working suit with a pale pink silk and lace blouse and a pair of smart heeled court shoes. She'd even found time to manicure her nails and paint them a nice shade of ivory. She'd made a special effort with her hair and tied it up into a neatish little chignon knot at the nape of her neck. Though she wasn't able to do much about the gleaming but unruly auburn curls that fell about her forehead and cheeks.

"Hey, great suit," said Claire, appearing from nowhere. Her eyes positively sparkled with life. "Fabulous shade of black," she added.

"Have a good weekend?" Aoife enquired.

"Oh yes! One of the best!" Claire smiled her smouldering enigmatic smile before quickly slipping into Flann's office.

In her office Aoife assembled the relevant documentation into a neat pile on her desk. She was just about to put it into her briefcase and take a taxi to the house in Talavera Road, when Flann Slevin walked in. She'd hardly seen him since the day after the vase incident.

"Looks like you've got everything under control," he said, glancing at her pile of documents.

"Hopefully," she said, opening her briefcase and setting the documents neatly inside.

"Very impressive," he said.

"Thanks."

"Look – best of luck with the house. I hear you have a big buyer coming along today. At least that's what Claire said. Anyone we know?"

Aoife paused for a split second. She wasn't really sure if she was supposed to give out that sort of information – but what the heck – weren't she and Flann on the same side?

"It's that billionaire philanthropist – you know,

Andrew McRory – the one who's put so much funding into the universities. He lives in Florida for most of the year – but apparently he wants a base in Dublin. Kevin says that even having him or his agent present at the auction next month will beef up the price."

"Kevin seems awfully keen on beefing up the price on this particular house," he said, with one eye on her briefcase.

Aoife shook her head and smiled. "That's Kevin. He makes every sale seem like the most important sale in the world. Even those one-bedroom apartments I sold last year – remember? He told me they were crucial sales – I mean, we've only like sold two hundred apartments since last year – and Kevin says every single one of them is crucial or critical or essential. I don't think this is any different."

"Yeah – you're probably right," said Flann. "I'll stick my head in this afternoon, see how you're getting on – if that's OK?"

She wanted to ask him not to, to tell him that this was her big chance and that she really wanted to handle it on her own – but for some reason, she couldn't. It would be rude, she concluded, and ungrateful, especially as he'd been so helpful.

"Sure," she said and forced a smile.

She took a taxi from the office and asked the driver to stop off for a moment at the newsagent's. Then she darted inside and quickly bought a Mars Bar, reasoning that she hadn't actually had a proper breakfast and the bar would give her the little energy fix that she needed to be on her best form for Andrew McRory. Then the taxi dropped her off at the house and she made her way up the long narrow garden pathway once more and let herself into the house. She broke into a kind of a cold sweat when she glanced into the drawing-room and saw the space on the mantelpiece where the vase had been – but she forced the incident from her mind and made her way to the kitchen to set up her laptop and brochures. She'd also brought along a flask of coffee in case it was needed.

Aoife had well learned her lesson. Never again would she touch anything valuable in a client's house, unless she absolutely had to. It was the one good thing to be said for the whole experience – that it had taught her such a valuable lesson. And so she had made that one terrible mistake of her career – but hadn't she got a whole bunch of wisdom out of it?

For instance: never pick up a Ming Vase that's on a high mantelpiece and expect it not to shatter into a million tiny shards. Wasn't there a saying that deep pain brings with it profound wisdom? And that was certainly true in this case. I am a much older, much wiser woman, she told herself. And hasn't the deep pain and anxiety of it all led me to a deeper understanding of the human condition and thus to the profound realisation that Flann Slevin really is someone special – a truly kind and decent man who is a friend in a very real sense?

The doorbell rang insistently and she took a deep breath. This was it. The start of a whole new phase in her career – Aoife Joyce was about to become an incredibly successful, fantastically brilliant, dazzlingly sophisticated and sensationally glamorous estate agent. She straightened up and raised her chin, feeling like she'd just grown six inches. She touched a hand to her hair – reflecting that after all it wasn't a tangled mess of curls – but a rich auburn crown of gleaming tresses. She smoothed down the navy jacket over her hips – reminding herself that she wasn't so much slightly plump as slightly voluptuous. She ran a quick extra slick of crimson bordello lipstick over her full young lips and, with a new and somehow more confident swagger in her step, went to answer the front door.

She recognised his face instantly from the newspapers. The interesting thing about Andrew McRory from a woman's point of view was that, despite being the owner of a vast betting empire that made him probably one of the richest and eligible men in Dublin, somehow he'd never married. This, of course, had led to plenty of gossip and speculation in certain female circles. It was not right, they protested. He was gay, of course, they insisted. The fact that he didn't even play the field of the beautiful leggy blonde women who paraded in front of him on a daily basis was all the proof needed. How could you have a billion-euro fortune and reach forty-eight without having married at least twice, with mistresses and several casual affairs included? Like – it wasn't as if he was ugly. He mightn't be described as incredibly handsome but he had nice smooth sallow skin, dreamy brown eyes and a winning smile. He had a wide circle of friends, sponsored several charities, drank and ate in moderation, smoked a very occasional Cuban cigar and drove around in a selection of Ferraris and Beamers. He simply had to be gay. And if more proof were needed, it was a commonly known fact that by far the most striking thing about Andrew McRory, the quality that almost everyone who met him remarked upon, was what a genuinely nice and unassuming man he was.

"I'm Andrew," he said, smiling warmly and holding out his hand.

"Hi," she said, overcome by a sudden bout of shyness and a terrible anxiety that she would mess up the viewing of the house. She continued to grin at him in a frozen sort of way until she remembered that she was blocking his way into the house. "Come in," she stammered and led him through the grand wide hall into the large kitchen to the rear.

She was surprised that he didn't have an army of hangers-on with him – solicitors, concerned lady friends, interior designers, architects – and it felt quite uncomfortable being alone with him, having to make conversation. Still – it was her job to be here and she'd just have to get over her childish awkwardness. If she was to make a success of this new phase in her career, she'd just have to get used to making small talk with billionaires.

She offered him a mug of coffee.

"Love one."

Then, as she handed him the steaming mug, he said, "Don't suppose you brought a biscuit or anything with you? I'm starving – no time for breakfast – back-to-back meetings all morning, then bringing my mother to the doctor for a check-up – she's just had her hip replaced. And I have to rush to the airport after this – I'm off to Prague this afternoon for another meeting."

"Wow, that's busy!" said Aoife. "The only travelling I have to do today is to take the train home this evening."

"I love trains. My big dream is to travel around the world by train."

"Why don't you do it? I mean if you can afford it. Sorry – oh dear – that sounds really rude!"

He laughed out loud. "If you think that's rude then you've lived a very sheltered life. And to answer your question, it's that I don't have time – too busy making money – maybe some day . . . God, I'm so hungry!" He looked forlornly about the kitchen.

"Wait a sec!" Aoife said, suddenly rummaging into the bottom of her bag and producing the Mars bar. "There you are! Sorry – if I'd known I'd have brought along some croissants – but this might just tide you over till you get to the airport."

He poured another cup of coffee and bit into the bar hungrily. "That's better! Thank you, Aoife – you've probably saved my life." He grinned at her broadly and she began to feel relaxed and comfortable with him.

"Shall we?" she said, indicating that they should begin the tour.

"Yes, better get a move on, I suppose," he said, dispatching the last of the Mars bar.

After that – it was plain sailing. She led him through the house as he explained that he simply wanted a nice city base. He owned a large estate in Meath – but somewhere in Ballsbridge would be useful for the occasional night in town. It had been suggested to him that he ought to buy a grand penthouse with acres and acres of space – but an old house was much more to his liking.

"And, besides all that, there's too much of the bachelor pad about a penthouse apartment – it's not for me. I like this house – it has a feeling of home about it."

The whole viewing had taken about an hour and Aoife was feeling quite pleased with herself. He seemed very taken by the house and she'd managed to draw his attention to its very best features, leaving out nothing.

They stood in the hall now and he shook her hand in a very old-fashioned formal way.

"Thank you for showing me round. And thanks especially for the Mars bar."

"Think nothing of it," she said. "All part of the Vernon service."

"Well, thanks anyway. I'll be in touch. I may be away on business for the auction but I will certainly be sending someone along to bid on my behalf."

Aoife tried to hide her satisfaction. It had turned out exactly as Kevin wished. Having Andrew McRory at the auction, whether he bought or not, would bring up the price of the property. Just as she was about to retrieve his coat from the cloakroom, the doorbell rang again and she went to answer it, thinking it might be another prospective buyer. But it was Flann, coming along as he had promised, to see how she was getting on.

"Hi – I'm Flann. I work with Aoife," he said, holding out his hand to Andrew.

"Nice house," said Andrew, shaking hands. "Aoife's just given me the grand tour. I'm impressed."

"Impressed enough to buy?" Flann asked.

Andrew smiled enigmatically at him and Aoife sensed some sort of protective barrier coming down, like he wanted to bring the conversation to a swift end. But it was strange – she hadn't felt anything like that during the hour that she had been alone with him.

"Right," Andrew said, checking his phone. "My driver's outside. I'm off. Thanks again, Aoife!" He breezed down the steps and disappeared swiftly down the narrow garden path.

"Funny sort of bloke," said Flann after he'd left.

"How do you mean?"

"A bit of an oddball, I've heard. Gay, between you and me – and don't get me wrong – nothing wrong with being gay – but he can be a bit 'unreliable', I've heard."

"Unreliable? I didn't get that impression."

"When you've been around a while as I have, Aoife, you get a gut feeling for people like that. Anyway, there's all the talk about him – holidays in Morocco and Thailand, patron of the Arts, slightly unpredictable, no woman in his life – unless you count his mother!"

She wanted to jump to Andrew's defence – say how very nice he was, how comfortable he made her feel – but for some reason she couldn't think of anything to say that wouldn't make her sound foolish. "What does his private life matter anyway," she stammered at last. "As long as he's interested in the house – that's all that counts as far as I'm concerned."

Flann looked at her sharply for a moment. "Yes – well – I'm not trying to burst your bubble or anything – but don't be too disappointed if you never hear from Andrew McRory again. He has that sort of reputation."

"Thanks for the tip, but I think you're wrong," she said. But she knew Flann only had her best interests at heart.

Back at the office, Kevin told Aoife how pleased he was with her. Andrew McRory had emailed, thanking him for sending someone so down-to-earth and capable to show him round the house.

"Take the rest of the afternoon off," said Kevin. "There's nothing much happening here and you deserve it."

"Thanks," she said. She couldn't stop herself grinning

from ear to ear. He only ever gave people time off when he was particularly pleased with them. Yes – the newest, most dazzlingly wonderful, spectacularly successful age of Aoife Joyce's life was just dawning. She could feel it in her fingers. She could feel it in her toes.

But first there was the little matter of a disappearing boyfriend. Where the hell had Dermot got to? She'd taken the rather unusual step of phoning his office earlier in the morning to be told that he was out on sick leave.

"But he can't be! Not without telling me! Since when? For how long? What's wrong with him?"

"I'm sorry," said the girl in his office. "That's all I know. I can take a message if you like."

It was most unlike Dermot to pull a sickie. In the eighteen months that she'd known him, she couldn't remember him being sick even once. Even if he was badly hung over –which, now that she thought of it, didn't really happen much either – he still went to work with dogged punctuality and determination.

But now that Kevin had given her the bit of extra free time, she decided that instead of going home early to Larkhaven, she would take the opportunity to call round to Dermot's apartment and find out once and for all what he was playing at. The whole disappearance business was beginning to annoy her intensely. After all, it wasn't as if she even cared very much about him but for him to disappear like that without as much as a word of explanation, well, it was just plain inconsiderate.

CHAPTER 19

"Nathalie," said Yvonne as breezily as she could, while feeling distinctly nervous, "a letter came from the university."

Nathalie gasped. She took the letter and held it in her hands, fearful of opening it. What if it was a rejection? She slid the single sheet of paper from the envelope and tried to read it. The words danced on the page in front of her eyes.

"Dear Miss Kelly,

We regret to inform you that you have been unsuccessful in your application to secure a place on our Arts Degree Programme . . ."

She felt her whole body choking up with disappointment and she couldn't read any further.

"I didn't get a place," she said, not bothering to read any more, but crumpling up the sheet of paper and flinging it on the table.

"What do you mean?" said Yvonne, grabbing the letter and quickly reading through it.

Nathalie wrestled with her tears. "Never mind," she said, wiping them away roughly. "It's not important. No one's ill or been in an accident or anything."

"They haven't said anything about your application for Law," Yvonne said, trying to give her daughter some hope.

Nathalie sat up straight and forced herself to look at the situation realistically. "If they don't want me for Arts – they'll definitely not take me for Law. Professor Joyce as good as said so at the interview."

"I'm really sorry," Yvonne said, hugging her daughter tightly.

"What's all this?" Liam had appeared in the doorway.

"Nathalie didn't get her college place."

Liam's large frame filled the doorway. He looked from his wife to his daughter. "Is that all?" he said going to his daughter and patting her gently on the shoulder.

"Is that all?" Yvonne hissed at her husband.

"Could be a lot worse," he said. "No one's been in an accident or anything. Have you seen the three-in-one oil? The back door is squeaking badly."

If there was a single nerve left inside her that Liam Kelly hadn't got on, Yvonne couldn't find it. Her entire body was ready now to explode with a furious rage, a rage that had been gathering like a particularly destructive approaching storm over the past ten years. She knew this was the moment that she was finally going to flip. She could no longer hold in the violent torrent of anger about to spew forth.

Nothing could stop her.

"I hope I'm not interrupting anything." It was Geraldine Flynn, her next-door neighbour. And when

Geraldine heard that Liam Kelly was more inclined to oil his creaking doors than console his disappointed daughter, she grabbed him by the scruff of the neck and sat him down at the kitchen table.

"Typical! Harry's just the same. Now tell us all about it, Nathalie."

So, as is sometimes the case, a gruesome domestic murder was once again averted by the timely arrival of a friendly neighbour.

Now, as she struggled through the Call List from Hell, Nathalie waited for further news from the university. But, she knew, if they didn't want her for an Arts degree it was hardly likely they'd consider her for Law. Still, she longed to have the certainty of a letter confirming it. Only then could she begin to think about other options for her future. And she needed to think about them because she didn't know how much longer she could stick her job in Nutopia.

She longed to talk to someone about it – but who? She didn't want to worry her parents who seemed to have enough problems of their own at the moment. It crossed her mind that she really ought to discuss her future with someone smart who could look at her situation with a cool and intelligent eye – and instantly, against all her most specific wishes, Mark Tierney's face sprang into mind. What would he think about her even applying to do Law? He might laugh at her – but somehow she doubted it. She still had his phone number. He'd told her that if ever she needed his help she was to get in touch with him. But had he really meant it? She tried hard to imagine his reaction and the look on his face if she walked into his office, and she quickly realised that he would simply regard her as a very minor and insignificant ex-client. He would most probably pass on her query to some lesser person in his office and she wouldn't even get the chance to talk to him.

And then Nathalie had to examine her conscience very hard and consider whether she was really thinking of calling up Mark Tierney because he might be able to help her – or because night after night it was becoming increasingly clear that she couldn't stop thinking about him. Each night when she tumbled into bed, tired after a long day, she wondered if he too was tumbling into bed after a hard day's work. She wondered if he took his earring out at night. She wondered what his bedroom was like. Did he have posters on the wall? Were the walls lined with books? Was there a TV, sound system, personal computer? Did he sleep on his left or his right side or did his body sprawl across the sheets, as he lay naked on his back, arms outstretched, head tossed languidly to one side. Sometimes thinking about him like that made her very hot and she could feel her heart thumping loudly in her chest. And she was only able to calm down by reminding herself that he was probably in bed with his perfectly beautiful, slim, elegant, blonde-haired, china-blue-eyed barrister girlfriend who had been brought up with similar wealth to himself in some splendid mansion somewhere like Ailesbury Road. She, the girlfriend, was probably called something like Portia and they almost certainly spent their evenings having highly intelligent conversation about poetry or philosophy over lobster dinners and bottles of the finest wine. At the weekends they most probably played golf in somewhere horribly exclusive and dined out with similar friends in suffocatingly fashionable restaurants. Portia almost certainly spent an hour each morning working out in the Athena Health and Fitness Club and Saturday mornings were put aside for hair and nails and skin and all that high-maintenance personal grooming that rich and successful ladies seemed to go in for. But by far the most annoying thing about Portia, as far as Nathalie was concerned, was the fact that she was almost certainly a really nice person and head over heels in love with Mark and wanting nothing but his eternal happiness. Of course, she did. Mark wouldn't go out with anyone who wasn't nice.

And, of course, the other thing to remember was that Mark had seemed kind and gentle and really quite considerate – but it would only be a matter of time before he turned into just another pompous, arrogant and highly opinionated man of the Law.

Nathalie sighed crossly with herself. Where was the point in longing for someone that she could never possibly have? Why couldn't she just fancy one of the other blokes in the call centre since it looked like she was going to be stuck there forever now anyway? Mitch from Melbourne was very handsome and no end of fun and Johanne had a big crush on him – but Nathalie just couldn't work up the enthusiasm. For better or worse, Mark Tierney had stirred up her heart and soul, and every other man she had ever met and was ever likely to meet would simply be a pale reflection of him. Slowly but surely she was coming to the most alarming conclusion – a conclusion that was so terrifying she could barely form the thought in her head, let alone shape the words or put them into some kind of fateful sentence.

"Oh God," she moaned with an uncharacteristic note of despair, burying her head miserably in her hands, "please, please let me stop being a total eejit and make me forget about Mark Tierney once and for all so that I can get on with whatever else life has in store for me! Amen."

"Feeling unwell, are we, Nathalie?" said the unmistakable barbed-wire and curdled-vinegar voice of Gretta Price.

Nathalie sat bolt upright and wiped away a tiny tear that had trickled down her cheek. She looked up and saw Gretta Price glaring down at her like she was some sort of low-life, subhuman species of bug. "What? No, Miss Price, it's just that –"

"Nutopia is no place for slackers. We're going for new sales records this month." She smiled as a person would smile at a child they didn't really like – just to be polite. "You gotta to work it, baby – work it!" She clicked her fingers a few times in rapid succession and moved on up the line.

Nathalie turned back to her list of clients from hell, and pushed thoughts of Mark Tierney from her mind.

"Good morning, Mrs O'Brien – this is Nathalie in Nutopia here. How are you today?"

"What do you want?" said a small crackly voice at the other end of the line.

"Will you be travelling to Europe at all this year, Mrs O'Brien?"

"What if I am? What business is it of yours?"

"We can arrange comprehensive travel insurance for you – in case you got sick or anything –"

"Sick? Who told you I was sick? Did my nephew tell you that? Well, I'm not and if he thinks he's going to dump me in a home and get his grubby little meat-hooks –"

232

"No! No one did. Look, I'm sorry, I think I've called a wrong number. I'm very sorry for disturbing you, Mrs O'Brien. Have a nice day."

Nathalie hung up, took a deep breath and dialled the next number.

After work she met Aoife for a drink, intending to confide in her about Mark – but as always Aoife was having far more drama to deal with than she herself had.

In a quiet corner of the ultra-trendy Kinshasa, Aoife began to recount the latest events to her cousin.

"You'll never guess what's happened to Dermot!"

"What?"

"I'll tell you in a minute – but first I just have to tell you about me and that lovely house in Talavera Road that I was telling you about – and guess who?"

"Who?"

"Andrew McRory! He came round to look at the house and he's really nice."

"Lucky you. Hey, maybe you'll be the woman he falls for – I can see it all in the Sunday papers: *Dizzy Young Estate Agent Worker Weds Billionaire Bookie!*"

"Don't be daft. He's nearly old enough to be my dad. But we got on really well and he's a genuinely nice bloke. And if he does buy the house I'll maybe get a good commission and then I could spend some of the money paying off our debts on the house – and maybe even have enough left over for a holiday!"

"Sounds great," said Nathalie, forcing herself to sound enthusiastic.

"Why don't you come along to the auction in the

Merrion Hotel in a few weeks? It's not every day you get to meet an obscenely rich man."

"I don't know . . ."

"He's really nice – honestly – and anyway you might find it interesting. There are a few big houses up for auction – could be a pop star or two – who knows, Colin Farrell might even put in an appearance."

Nathalie pulled a face. "Colin's really hot and everything – but I'm not all that into him any more," she said with a trace of sadness, half-hoping that Aoife would pick up on it.

But she didn't.

"Oh, but the really odd thing is about Dermot," said Aoife, "I called his office and they told me he was off sick and then this afternoon I went round to his apartment."

"Is he OK?"

"Well, that's the thing – he's not there either. Macdara, his flatmate, hasn't seen him for days and his bed hasn't been slept in and his electric guitar's gone."

"Maybe he's gone home to his parents for a break – you know what men are like when they get sick – needing their mammies all over again."

"His folks are away in Spain. They spend half the year there – so he's not likely to be at home and I'm beginning to get really worried." She bit her lip anxiously.

Nathalie smiled doubtfully. It was an entirely new experience to see Aoife being worried about anyone.

"The thing is that he did email me last week and to be honest the email was so long that I didn't read the half of it – except the bit that said we should meet up in the Purple Pepper. Then I deleted the mail and now I'm beginning to think there was something really important in it – something that he was trying to tell me."

"Has he been behaving strangely lately or anything that might give you a clue?"

Aoife racked her brains but could think of nothing. "No! Same old reliable Dermot – you could set your watch by him. Except – there was that one tiny little thing . . ." Her voice trailed away as the germ of a rather startling idea formed in her head.

"What?"

"He's been complaining of headaches – and it's not like him because he never complains and he's not a big drinker and he's always out and about. And now I'm beginning to think maybe he's not well and maybe there's something awful wrong with him – and I've been too stupid to see it." She was suddenly becoming quite worked up about it all.

"Do you want to know what I think?" said Nathalie.

"What?"

Nathalie picked her words carefully, anxious not to hurt her cousin. "I think perhaps he's just decided to go away for a while on his own – maybe start a new job and a new life abroad."

"He wouldn't do that without telling me!"

"Maybe – but don't forget you haven't exactly bathed him in love and affection lately. He doesn't really owe you anything. He might think there was no real reason to tell you – because he might have the impression that possibly – I mean very possibly – I mean maybe – he thinks – and you couldn't blame him for getting the impression – even if it isn't true –"

"Nathalie – get to the point – what are you trying to say?"

"Maybe he thinks you don't care about him at all."

Aoife stared at her cousin for a moment in pure amazement and began to feel quite annoyed. "Don't be ridiculous. Of course, I care about him. He's a really good mate. I can't believe you would even think such a thing – let alone say it to me!"

"Then I'm glad I'm wrong," Nathalie said gently, not wanting to cause her cousin any further grief.

"Though, now that I come to think of it . . . Berry said almost exactly the same thing to me . . . but I thought *you* at least would understand. Anyway," she abruptly changed the subject, "thanks for listening. Have you heard anything back from the university?"

Nathalie shook her head and forced a brave smile. "They don't want me for an Arts degree – so that means they definitely won't look at me for Law. The Law professor said as much at the interview. So it probably wasn't meant to be. That's all. Silly of me to think it was ever even possible. Oh well – I'm a lot luckier than most. I have money in the bank, a lovely home, great friends, nice cousins and really life is fine."

So why was she tormenting herself with chasing after dreams that hadn't the slightest chance of coming true? Yvonne had always encouraged Nathalie to follow her dreams – and now here she was, dreaming about following her dreams and feeling what she could only conclude must be miserable unhappiness. It was a new and unwelcome sensation, and absolutely horrible, and all because she'd been foolish enough to entertain a pair of silly dreams that didn't have the slightest chance of coming true.

"What's wrong?" said Aoife, only realising now that she'd been babbling on selfishly about her own stuff for the past half-hour without noticing that her cousin was uncharacteristically out of sorts. "It's not just waiting for the letter from college, is it?"

"It's nothing," Nathalie answered, forcing a tight smile and finishing the last of her white wine. "Really – life couldn't be better!"

She only wished it was true.

CHAPTER 20

In recent months, Berry hadn't found much reason to don her only good suit – but today was the day. She was glad the house was empty. She could gather her thoughts, prepare her case, find and maintain some kind of composure and dignity. She showered and shampooed her shoulder-length dark-brown hair. Ordinarily she pinned it up in an untidy knot, but today she took great care in drying it straight and brushing a serum through it, which added to its healthy shine. Berry hadn't had occasion to wear make-up in six months but today was definitely a day for slapping on the war paint. She couldn't see that it made her look any better – it was just that it gave her an extra glowy layer of confidence. And she didn't hold back – foundation, concealer – loads of it, eyeliner, shadow, blusher, lip pencil, several layers of lipstick and a good dusting of powder. A simple string of pearls inherited from her mother and matching pearl earrings added the finishing touches. Then she slipped into a pair of elegant high heels and stood back to observe herself in the mirror.

"Berry Joyce – I'd hardly know you," she said, quite pleased with the result and feeling sorry that life these days didn't throw up many opportunities for glamming it up. "Mr Aidan McCarthy will be so dazzled that he'll be paying you to take money from him."

Aidan McCarthy was the bank manager in the local town and though he was no pushover he was known to have not only a good heart but also an eye for a pretty woman – especially one with nice pins. And though Berry was no great classical beauty, she had an exceptionally elegant pair of long slender legs. Lately they had mostly been used for legging it into town on foot when her old banger broke down, or digging in the garden or clambering up rickety ladders in search of blocked gutters. In fact she hadn't even really looked at them closely for a while and was worried that all the rough and manual work might have destroyed them. But she needn't have worried. There they were now – clad in her best and only pair of sheer Wolford tights (the packet hidden at the back of the wardrobe for several months in case Aoife got hold of them), and she realised that all the hard work had made them even firmer and shapelier. She simply knew they would work wonders in the bank.

She sat into her battered old Toyota and not for the first time wondered if she could get the *Pimp My Ride* team to come to Ireland and do a free makeover job on it. She wouldn't ask for much – she could live without a hair and beauty salon in the back seat or even a sunbed. She'd manage quite well without a mini drinks cabinet, a foot spa, a home cinema or a GPS navigation system. She could even cope without heating, or properly sealed windows and covered upholstery. But an engine would be nice.

She turned the key in the ignition, did some magic manoeuvring with the clutch and gear-stick and somehow coaxed the engine to stutter to life.

When she arrived in town she parked in a sidestreet and glanced in the mirror one last time as she applied a fourth and completely unnecessary layer of lipstick. Yes, she looked – all right. Aidan McCarthy would be so mesmerised by her legs and her long dark hair that he would simply beg her to take the money in the end. *Thirty thousand euro, Miss Joyce? Are you sure you don't want more?* She fixed a stray wisp of hair and stepped out onto the pavement.

"I've an appointment with the manager," she told the bank assistant at the counter and smiled her sweetest smile.

"Take a seat. He'll be with you in a moment."

Berry spent the time going over her prepared speech yet again.

"Hi, Mr McCarthy," cross one leg over the other, "thanks so much for seeing me – I know you're a busy man," discreetly smooth hem of skirt to edge of knee. "Now – I know that from a bank manager's point of view my current situation mightn't look all that promising . . ." smile and twirl ankle very slightly, "but let me just run through a few projected figures with you and . . ." flutter eyelashes and then reach into bag for document case and papers. Difficult to avoid bending over slightly and uncrossing and recrossing knees in this terribly obvious but highly necessary manoeuvre. "Perhaps you might like to have a look at these . . ." Lean forward gracefully and with a sweep of perfectly manicured hand set the documents down on the desk in front of him. "So you see, Mr McCarthy – I am sort of at your mercy." Then look directly into his eyes with an expression of helpless warmth and appealing vulnerability.

It might just work!

Although Berry hadn't ever actually bothered much with eyelash-fluttering and leg-crossing in the past, this was an increasingly desperate situation and desperate situations required desperate remedies. You've got the legs – she reminded herself – just use them!

What could possibly go wrong?

"The manager will see you now," the assistant told her and led her into a spacious office where, across a wide expanse of desk that she didn't remember from before, sat someone who definitely wasn't Aidan McCarthy.

"I'm sorry," she said, "I think there's some mistake. I had an appointment with the manager."

"It is I," said the baby-faced young fella who sat in the large swivel-chair, looking as if his mammy might just pop out from behind at any moment, pop a plastic bib across his tiny chest and start feeding him baby rice from a nice blue plastic spoon.

Berry's face fell a few kilometres. She knew she wasn't exactly fresh out of the cradle or anything – but thirty-seven wasn't all that old. But this bloke looked like he could easily be her son. One thing was for sure. It was definitely time to rethink the whole knee-crossing, ankle-twirling, eyelash-fluttering strategy very quickly – or she might be arrested for some kind of attempted sexual perversion with a minor. A quick tabloid headline flashed in her head. *Middle-aged Shop-owner in Attempt to Bonk Boy Bank Manager Shock!!!*

On quick reflection, it was a relief not to have to resort to feminine wiles to sort out such an important personal and business matter. And, she thought charitably as she lowered herself into the chair, this young fella was probably a complete financial whiz kid. Surely he wouldn't be a bank manager otherwise.

"I am Toby Looby, the new manager," he said.

She tried hard to ignore the light boyish crack in his voice.

He held out a hand across the table and smiled blankly at her like he'd just had his entire face frozen with a dodgy Botox needle.

Berry sucked in her breath and, deciding it was best to get straight to the point, she plunged in. "I'm having a short-term cashflow slowdown experience. I need to optimise my credit situation by taking advantage of bank resources – on a temporary-scenario basis of course . . ." Berry figured that if she used enough jargon, it would make her financial problems seem less appalling. In any case, she was hardly going to blurt out that she was completely broke and that even if she did sell the family home, she'd still owe more money than she'd ever be able to repay in a lifetime. Could she tell him that lately she lay awake most nights imagining herself sleeping in a doorway and working eighteen-hour days just to pay back the interest on loans she'd been foolish enough to take out? Should she confide that in the past week she'd only had fifteen customers and that in total they'd spent a staggering forty euro?

"Hmmm!" he said, frowning without any furrows appearing in his brow. He made a steeple of his hands and leaned forward in his swivel-chair.

She was desperately afraid he might fall off. She tried

to peek under the desk to see if his feet were actually resting on the ground but then realised that she was being silly. Just because he looked only six months old didn't mean he wasn't highly successful in his chosen field. He probably had an MBA from the Harvard Business School. He might be just the man to sort out the whole sorry business of Berry Joyce's business.

She took the papers from her document case and placed them on the table in front of him.

"Ah!" he said, fingering them delicately and shoving them about on the desk. "Mmmm!" he added as he perused them more closely and sucked in a loud breath through surprisingly wide nasal passages. "March? Oh dear! Bills outstanding? September? *Nnnnngggrrrhhh!*"

Berry didn't want to be unkind or anything – but it sounded like he was trying to relieve himself of the body's natural waste.

"Is everything all right?" she asked.

"All right?" He stared across at her, wide-eyed. "It's terrible. These figures are terrible. The whole thing's a complete mess."

Berry's heart sank.

"I mean – nothing adds up. Nothing balances. You're spending more on rent and heating and lighting in a week than you're earning in a month."

"Yes, I know," she said, trying not to sound too desperate. "But even the most successful companies in the world have had tough start-up periods. I mean Megasoft nearly went to the wall three times before becoming the biggest multinational corporation in the world. Mickey O'Byrne went bankrupt twice before finally getting it right with all that property development and now he owns half of Budapest. So Toby – I mean, Mr Looby – I'm trying to keep my eye on the bigger picture here and not get too bogged down in short-term cashflow challenges."

He closed his eyes, frowned some more, let out a big sigh and took to staring out the window. Then he turned back to her quite suddenly. "Let me tell you a little story about my mam."

"I'm sorry?"

"You see – you and my mam have lots in common."

"We do?"

"Yes!" he said sounding half-strangled now like he was straining in earnest to get a knot out of his lower intestine. "Both older women – you see, that's the key economic factor here. Mam – I'll call her Rosaleen – because she likes it when I call her Rosaleen – anyway, Ma – Rosaleen – started up a little florist's business for herself there a while back – and of course, having the Masters Degree in Economics, I was able to be a great help to her. You can see now where I'm going with this, can't you? The big rental overheads, problems with the suppliers, a delivery van, orders, a shop assistant – sure she hadn't thought it out properly at all. Now don't get me wrong – Rosaleen's the mam and I love her to bits – but in economic terms she's not a good risk – not a good investment if you see what I mean. Like – yourself and Rosaleen – well, let's face it – you're not getting any younger, are you? And there comes a time in a woman's life when. . ." he stopped suddenly for a brief moment. "Sorry about that. I hope you don't think I'm being ageist or anything – only Rosaleen herself admitted as much in the end. 'At this stage of my life, I'm just not up to it, Toby son, and you were right all along.' Those were her exact words . . ."

Berry was beginning to realise why Toby Looby had been sent to preside over the tiny bank of Larkhaven rather than straight to the directors' floor in banking HQ in the IFSC. And though she didn't know the first thing about Rosaleen Looby, she felt a nagging sympathy for the poor woman. But most of all her heart sank because she could see that Toby Looby would rather eat his own laptop than part with any money or help in any practical way to dig her out of her difficulties.

"With all due respect," she began, trying to find some reasonable argument that might appeal to his better nature – when what she most wanted was to do something extremely nasty and painful to him with one of her stilettos, "Mr McCarthy thought I was a good risk. He said I might have to give it two years before I began to even break even. And I haven't fallen behind in my loan repayments to the bank – it's just that I need a bit of time now to get over this little hiccup – a few months' grace and a bit more cash to keep me afloat – that's all I ask. Business is building slowly – it just takes time."

"I'm sorry," he said, smiling weakly at her. "I really am. If there was any way at all I could give you the bit of cash, you know I would. I mean, I've been through it all with my m– Rosaleen. The disappointment! The heartbreak! The disillusionment! But it's for the best. No sense in living in a fool's paradise now, is there?" At this point he even had the cheek to wink at her – like he'd just done her the favour of a lifetime. "I'll tell you what I'll do though – because you really do remind me of Mam – and that's a compliment, believe me – I'll give you a month's grace with the repayments. How's that?" And he beamed broadly like he'd just handed her the winning lotto ticket.

Or maybe it was just time for his bottle.

She was so furious she couldn't even reply.

Berry hardly remembered the drive back to Larkhaven. She didn't often get angry – but she could scarcely see the road for temper. It was just as well she was driving the old banger because if she'd been at the controls of anything that could go faster than five point seven miles an hour, she might have caused a serious accident.

Back in Larkhaven, and still simmering with rage, she parked the car, pulled off the heels, wrestled herself awkwardly out of the Wolford tights, threw them unceremoniously on what was left of the back seat of the car, jammed her feet into a pair of trainers that she kept for emergencies and headed for the beach.

Larkhaven beach was one of the scenic treasures of the locality. There was the little crescent-shaped beach beside the harbour. But the main strand stretched for four miles – a wide flat expanse of sand. People did their yoga and their Pilates on the beach. They jogged, walked their dogs, and exercised their horses. Couples who were deeply in love walked there hand in hand, in their little bubble of love, no doubt passing close by other couples who were deeply out of love and planning their divorce. Sometimes teachers from the local school took their charges to the shore for nature trips or simply just to let off steam. Today though, the strand was mercifully empty and Berry walked close to the shoreline, hoping that the creamy jade sea and the mild breeze and the clear air and the softly rippling waves would all work together to soothe and restore her. It usually did the trick. There was nothing in the world that couldn't be put in its place by a long walk on Larkhaven Strand.

She set off briskly and pretty soon she was kicking up a cloud of sand in her wake. In the distance she could just make out a small outcrop of rock. She would walk that far and then turn back. Surely in that time, something would occur to her – some little light would shine in her head and lead her out of this terrible mess and into a world where she had money in the bank and all the bills were paid and she had a business that was thriving and a house that didn't have holes in the roof and cracks in the window-panes. A warm breeze blustered gently and blew her hair in thick strands across her face. She could hear nothing but the wind and the soft sighing waves. She tried to blot Toby Looby and his preposterous arrogance from her mind but it wouldn't go away. And instead of her anger abating, she found herself growing more furious with each pounding stride. Berry worked hard, allowed herself no luxuries – unless you counted the Wolford tights and they were a one-off moment of careless rapture several months ago. She'd put every penny into the kitting out of the café and laundrette and worked endlessly without any backup, to build up business. She'd sacrificed her social life, given up on romance, convinced herself that Grafton Street and its classiest shops no longer existed in the same galaxy or dimension as her. She hadn't been at a theatre, cinema or even the local cheap and cheerful pizzeria for over a year. She'd put every ounce of energy – physical, emotional, spiritual, mental and financial – into this business venture. And all for what? She might as well be gathering mussels on the beach and selling them in the streets for all the money she was making. How was it that other people who set up in business seemed to be able to make a go of things? And it was bad enough being in such dire financial straits – but the worst thing of all was to have to humiliate herself before a wisp of a lad like Toby Looby.

Yes – she'd been a complete and utter fool – and Ben Searson was probably right – there must have been a hint of arrogance in her heart as she'd set up the business, an idea that she might really be enhancing people's lives – a feeling even that they might be grateful to her for improving the whole ambience of the village so much.

"Fool! Fool!" she muttered to herself as she reached the little outcrop of rock. But instead of turning back she flopped down on a rock in a disconsolate heap. She kicked at the hard grey stone and stared out vacantly to sea. Tears streaked down her face – but she didn't even bother to wipe them away. She probably looked a complete fright – but what did streaks of mascara and smudged lipstick matter? What did anything matter? And perhaps Toby Looby was right. She would soon be old and irrelevant anyway. Why not just accept the fact and take up crazy golf and bingo and gossiping about the neighbours? A month's grace was all she had. It was hardly going to make any difference. She was staring failure and humiliation in the face. But more importantly – she was facing ruin. Bloomfield House would have to be put up for sale to pay her debts and then she and Aoife would be homeless.

She turned a sickly green at the thought of it all and, fighting back a new wave of tears, she looked up to find Ben Searson standing beside her.

"May I join you?" he said. "Or is this a private weeping and gnashing of teeth and general staring into the black hellish pit of despair?"

Berry shrugged. She didn't have the energy to smile.

He fished in his pocket and pulled out a crumpled hanky. "Here – it's not starched or anything – but it's clean."

"Thanks."

"Only – there's a lot of black stuff on your face – you might want to wipe it off before you get back to the village."

"Mascara," she said, rubbing at her cheeks with the hanky. "Don't know why I bothered. I was never cut out for heavy-duty make-up."

He sat beside her and gazed out to sea and said nothing. She was grateful to him for not asking what was wrong – for not saying 'Want to talk about it?' or 'Cheer up' or any of that. She didn't think she could even begin to explain how awful she felt without making a complete fool of herself. A year ago she'd been bursting with confidence and brimming with girlish enthusiasm and energy for this new venture into the business world. Now she scarcely recognised herself. She felt melancholy, angry and even slightly bitter. She could barely admit those things to herself, let alone try to explain them to a stranger.

"OK?" he said at last.

"Yes, fine," she said, feeling calmer.

"That's good," he said, resting his hand lightly on hers for a moment. The light touch reminded her of the way he'd kissed her on the landing. She became aware of his shoulder pressed lightly against hers, his long sturdy leg glancing gently against her knee. She could hear his steady low breathing and longed for a moment to feel his breath on her skin, to have that warm flicker of a kiss on her lips again.

She tried to steady her own breathing and to suppress the desire to reach out and touch him. Then she sighed impatiently at her own foolishness. Who was Ben Searson really? What had really brought a man like him to a ramshackle cottage in the middle of nowhere? She knew he'd tried to tell her something important that day in the café but she'd seen the anguish in his face and pitied him. Would she live to regret not listening to him?

"I wouldn't mind a coffee. Will you join me?" he said, standing up and brushing sand from his faded chords.

Berry slid off the rock, and stood up, anxious now to get away from him.

"Thanks – but I have to get back to work – no rest for the wicked." She managed a bleak smile and turned to go.

"Please," he said, touching her shoulder lightly with his hand.

It was a gesture of – of what? She couldn't fathom it – but it felt awfully like a plea.

"I could do with the company," he added.

Why? Why could you do with the company? she wanted to ask. What have you done that keeps you here in some kind of self-imposed isolation?

"I don't really think . . ." she began.

"If it's because I kissed you the other night . . . I'm sorry. A moment of madness. I guess it's a while since I've been alone with a beautiful woman outside a bedroom door. But it won't happen again – I promise."

"OK," she said. "You're forgiven. And I suppose I could do with a cup of coffee and the bit of company too."

"Great."

They walked in silence for a while. Berry found she liked being in the company of someone who didn't feel the need to talk and didn't feel uncomfortable in the silence. Besides, it wasn't silence really because of the sighing of the sea and the blustering wind.

"Is everything in the cottage OK for you?"

"Perfect. It's everything I need."

"Only it's a bit cramped and the cooker and everything's a bit ancient. You know, if you ever need to use anything at the house – use the washing-machine or store something in the freezer – you're welcome." She smiled to herself, thinking how horrified Aoife would be by that last invitation, thinking how her sister was determined to find out something dramatic about Ben Searson. Or was it Bernard Pearse? She stole a glance at him now as they strolled along the last few hundred yards of beach. His eyes squinted against the bright sunlight. His hair blustered untidily about his face. But it was difficult to read that face. Was it the face of a violent man? Berry didn't think so. And even if he had changed his name, sometimes people take on new identities for private but lawful reasons. But in the past she hadn't exactly shown herself to be a particularly good judge of men. So under the circumstances it was probably wise to reserve judgement on Ben Searson.

In the hotel they sat at the bar and sipped two frothy coffees. They remained in companionable silence for a while, warming themselves with the hot aromatic brew.

"I really like the cottage," he said again after a while. "Right now – I couldn't wish for anything more."

She looked across at him, not knowing quite what to

say that wouldn't sound nosey or pass-remarkable. "That's good," she said, chancing a little smile.

"Oh – and of course," he smiled warmly, "the landlady's a real – " He stopped suddenly.

"A real what?"

"I was going to say 'a real stunner' – but that's a kind of out-of-order flirting again, isn't it? Especially with the landlady."

Berry blushed – to her further embarrassment. She felt a fleeting moment of childish pleasure. "Thank you," she said, poking at the last of the froth on her coffee. "It's nice to get a compliment – flirting or not."

"It's also true."

The barman stacked bottles of lager on a shelf, working in a slow, steady clinking rhythm. Berry observed him idly for a few moments, then turned to Ben.

"What are you doing here?" she asked gently.

"I don't understand."

"Why are you in Larkhaven?"

"Just taking stock of my life for a few months," he said evenly.

Yes, but why, she longed to ask but an invisible barrier had descended between them and she was far too tactful to pursue the matter.

He drained the last of his coffee. "Look, I'm sure you've got a busy day ahead in the Internet café," he said. A distant formality had crept back into his speech and he stood up quickly. "I enjoyed the coffee."

"Yes, very busy," she lied and glanced at her watch. "Oh dear – I lost track of time. Must rush! So much to do! Goodbye, then!"

She strode to the door and into the foyer before he could even say goodbye.

It's possible to repair damaged arteries, replace malfunctioning kidneys, even in some cases restore sight – but a broken heart is notoriously difficult to mend. Any doctor will tell you that. A doctor did tell Berry that.

"Tightness in the chest, churning in the stomach, insomnia, incurable melancholy, a crisis of confidence? It sounds like the work of a man to me!" he'd said, probing gently.

Of course, he was right and even now, some three years later, the very thought of forming any sort of romantic attachment with a man was enough to send her hurtling swiftly for cover.

Conor Lynch's wife had not wanted him back the next day. He was cruel and unreasonable, she said, and she wanted time alone to think about her options. In the office, the shiny happy photo that Conor had planted on his desk with such smug pride some months earlier disappeared quietly into the back of a desk drawer. He was working twelve-hour days – struggling to pay off his wife's debts, cover the cost of his mortgage and keep up repayments on the site in Stepaside.

So Berry didn't have the heart to throw him out of her apartment. In fairness, he paid his way – equal halves on the groceries, equal halves on the cleaning and a nominal contribution to the rent.

He continued to sleep in the spare room.

There were no awkward moments alone as the lights went down. Berry made well sure of that. She kept a friendly distance between them and looked forward to the day when Conor Lynch finally went home to his wife and kids, when she could have the apartment all to herself once more. And when she wouldn't have to wrestle with her feelings for him any more.

One evening, he came home in a terrible state. Berry tried to keep her distance, but in the end the sight of him in such turmoil upset her.

"She wants a divorce," he said. He appeared totally confused.

"But why?"

He shrugged. "Who knows? It's like she's just lost all sense of proportion, like she can't hold the reins of her own life any more. In spite of the gambling she'll get custody of the kids . . ."

Berry saw tears form in his eyes. She sat beside him on the sofa and held his hand and tried to comfort him.

"God, I've been so wrong about her," he said. "A complete fool! And now this!" He eyed a crumpled brown envelope in his hands.

"I'm really sorry," Berry said, not knowing how else to comfort him.

"It's not your fault. You've been so good to me. You're more of a woman than she'll ever be."

Berry suppressed a little smile.

"I mean it. It's easy to talk to you. You're so sensible . . . so much fun. I shouldn't even say this – but so incredibly sexy."

"Steady on!" she said, jumping up. "Conor, this is hardly the time to be talking about that sort of thing."

"You are," he said, following her. "Anyway, it's been all over between me and Sarah for months."

She went and stood at the window, looking out over the city, wishing he would just go away and yet longing for him to touch her.

He stood just behind her, his breath on her neck, his hand brushing her shoulder lightly.

"Conor – please, don't. It wouldn't be right."

"I want you, Berry – have wanted you for months. Don't tell me you haven't noticed."

"Well, I haven't."

She felt his lips brush softly against the nape of her neck and shivered. Now – now was the moment to stop and turn away. She would slip from his arms and smile coolly and send him packing and never see him again. That would put an end to it. She could see the alternative unfolding in her mind – even as his hand slid around her waist and gently tugged her body towards his. She saw the intensity of it, some few brief happy moments, before pain and despair set in. She knew exactly how it would end – could almost write the script in her head.

"We were made for each other," he mumbled into her ear.

"Maybe – just maybe we were," she said, knowing that it was all nonsense.

If Berry thought that Ben Searson's delicious kiss on the landing, then a bit of mild flirting followed by iceberg-style brush-off over a coffee had been a bit peculiar, she didn't really get much time to reflect on it. When she'd finally made it into the Internet café that afternoon, another nasty surprise was waiting for her – in the shape of a brash expensively produced flyer.

"Hey, Berry," Harry Robson had said, breezing into the café some minutes later, "I think I might just continue with my quest for an online bride!"

But she'd scarcely heard him. Instead she'd sunk down into her chair and tried to contemplate her imminent downfall.

CHAPTER 21

Yvonne Kelly had decided to take a few days' break from her husband. It was, she felt, the opening shot in what was bound to be a long and bitter divorce. But it couldn't be helped. Since the night she'd gone to sleep in the spare room, nothing had improved between her and Liam. Her marriage was over – there was no escaping that fact. It was a dead, lifeless thing – a beached old carcass, picked dry and lying empty and forlorn in the horribly bare landscape of her life. Now she needed a few days away – to gather her thoughts and find a way of breaking the news to Nathalie. She packed a little suitcase and stuck a couple of Post-its in the centre of the kitchen table, beside the vase of scented roses that she'd picked from the garden that morning.

Work is very quiet at the moment so gone to stay with Mum and keep her company. Back in a couple of days. Don't forget the man is coming to do the patio tomorrow. I've ordered new curtains for the sitting-room and they're to be delivered this afternoon. I'll hang them when I get back. We ought to get someone to look at that chimney – it's smoking a lot and making the upholstery smell. You have my mobile number if you need me.

Yvonne.

She hung two newly cleaned and pressed jackets in Liam's wardrobe. Beside them she placed a neatly folded pile of shirts in one deep pullout drawer and some jeans in another. She set down three polished sets of shoes in the shoerack beneath. In the little en-suite bathroom that gleamed and sparkled with cleanness, she laid out fresh razor, shaving cream, soap, toothbrush and toothpaste. She arranged them all in a fan shape over a freshly laundered white cotton hand-towel. On the shelf above the bath she arranged a neatly folded pile of bath towels. Then she carried her little wheelie bag downstairs and while waiting for the taxi took one last scout round the kitchen – making sure she'd left everything in order. The fridge was packed with prepared dishes – peeled and sliced vegetables, three foil dishes with lamb shanks – just ready to go into the oven. She'd also baked one rhubarb crumble and an apple sponge. Nathalie would of course be able to manage fine in the kitchen – but she worked a long day and lately, since the court case, she often didn't get home from Nutopia until seven or eight o'clock in the evenings. For that reason, Yvonne had pinned little Post-its on each dish – giving Liam precise cooking instructions.

She looked around the kitchen!

Spotless!

Fit for a *House & Home* magazine.

If a bus runs me down, she thought grimly to herself, at least my kitchen will be in order. Sitting in the taxi on her way to the station, Yvonne wondered where and how her marriage had all gone so awfully and disastrously wrong when it had begun with such great promise of happiness.

When Nathalie arrived home that evening, she didn't at first notice the yellow Post-its in the centre of the kitchen table. She was far too busy rummaging through the post. And there it was – at last – a long brown envelope with the university stamp on it. She ripped it open quickly, terrified to read the contents but longing to put an end to the uncertainty once and for all.

Still, she felt weak and giddy when she read through the letter. It was a long letter – very formal and signed by Professor Daphne Joyce.

Dear Miss Kelly, it began.

We have considered your application to be taken into the Faculty of Law very carefully. As I believe I outlined in our last meeting, the careful study of Law places many heavy demands on the learner. Consequently your application had to be reviewed by . . .

Nathalie wished they had written a shorter letter for it was taking her ages to get to the point of it.

Then in the third paragraph – she could scarcely believe her eyes. She reread the paragraph in case she'd made a mistake.

Yes! They wanted her! Nathalie Kelly who only had a Junior Cert, who didn't really know why the window was such an important symbol in *Wuthering Heights* – they wanted her and thought that she might just be clever and hard-working enough to get a Law degree and do something other than cold-calling from the Price List for the rest of her life!

When her father came trudging through the door minutes later, she threw her arms around his neck and danced around the room.

"I'm in! They want me! I'm going to get a proper degree! Oh, Dad! This is just brilliant!"

"I suppose you expect me to be proud of you now as well as everything else?" said Liam, beaming at her before extracting himself from her embrace.

"You suppose!"

"And I suppose you expect me to take yourself and your mother out for a meal to celebrate?"

She beamed fondly at him. She understood his gruff affectionate ways.

Liam looked around the kitchen he'd built and kitted out with the finest cherrywood cabinets and tiled with the best Italian tiles and he noticed immediately that something was different.

"That's funny," he said, opening the fridge door and examining the contents. "Your mam's forgotten to take the leg of lamb out of the fridge. It's not like her. She's usually so organised."

It was only then that Nathalie noticed the two yellow Post-its in the centre of the table and she felt a horrible cold shiver ripple down her spine. She picked them up gingerly, read them, then handed them to her father.

"She never said she was going anywhere," said Liam, bewildered. "She never goes anywhere without telling me. Do you think she's all right? It's not like her to go off suddenly like that."

"She probably just needs a break from us two,"

Nathalie said, trying to reassure him. "We sometimes take her completely for granted. I know – I'll call her – tell her my good news."

When she heard the news, in spite of never really wanting to see her husband again, Yvonne declared she would come home right away. She knew how much it meant, how happy Nathalie would be to leave her job in Nutopia and start a new life doing something she really loved.

"No, Mam – enjoy your break. Dad and me, we'll be fine. And Dad sends you his love by the way – says he misses you too."

"Misses having his dinner cooked and his shirts ironed, more like. Well, all that's going to change – change forever." Nathalie heard her mother's strangled sob at the other end of the line.

"Mam – are you OK?"

"I'm fine. I'll be home in a couple of days."

CHAPTER 22

In the plush offices of Vernon's Estate Agents, Aoife felt that life was slipping up a few notches for her and she reflected that it was nothing more than she deserved. It was as if she'd grown a few inches or suddenly lost a stone, become as fit as Sonia O'Sullivan and as beautiful as Charlise Theron with the business-like authority of Condoleeza Rice.

And, damn, it felt good!

Since Kevin had given her sole responsibility for the sale of the house in Talavera Road, she'd shown several clients around and overseen two open viewings on the property. She discussed top-class architectural restoration firms and interior decorators with some very high-profile clients over the phone. People in the office seemed to be seeking out her opinion more often, asking her views on different properties that were coming on the market. Kevin was always very busy – away at meetings or dealing with the larger corporate clients and the commercial sector – so she didn't see all that much of him. But her new-found status in the company meant that she had to spend a lot of time with Flann. It wasn't hard. Somehow they just gelled together. Despite technically being her boss, he treated her as an equal, showing a respectful regard for her opinion and often including her at meetings where before she would have been excluded. And, of course, there was that bit of chemistry – hovering in the background all the time. Both of them were too professional ever to draw it down, but she just knew from occasional brief awkward silences and occasional glances at odd moments, that something exciting was brewing between them.

"You must be getting very excited about your first big auction," he said to her over lunch in Café Bar Deli.

"Can't wait," she said, shovelling a large clump of dry rocket leaves into her mouth. She was determined to have lost a few pounds for the auction. Not only was this going to be the sale of the season but she was going to be the negotiator of the season as well. Even just eating the lettuce made it feel as though her tummy was shrinking.

"Yes, it's a big day," he agreed. "I well remember my first big sale. I managed three times the guide price and I was so thrilled that I took the entire office out to dinner. Champagne all round – it was a great buzz."

"But it's kind of nerve-racking as well. I couldn't sleep for ages last night just thinking about all the things that could go wrong."

He had paid the bill in spite of her protestations and now they were strolling along the banks of the canal. There was warm sunshine and ducks nudging each other in the water.

"It will be fine. Don't worry about it," he said.

He was very interested in hearing about Bloomfield House and so she told him all about inheriting it and the high cost of maintaining it.

"So if I get a good commission on the sale – I can pay off some of our bills. Between you and me, if we don't get some money in quickly to cover expenses, I don't know what might happen."

She then asked about his family.

His parents lived in the midlands. He had a brother in New Zealand and a sister in Capetown. He had been living with a girl for three years – but things hadn't worked out and they had split up.

"I'm sorry," Aoife said.

He shrugged. "Just one of those things. And isn't that the marvellous thing about life these days? If something doesn't work out, then you just needn't stick with it any more. I had an aunt and uncle who absolutely detested each other and still they stuck together because there was no other option in those days. Poor sods."

Aoife nodded sympathetically.

"So how about you?" he asked.

"How do you mean?"

"Have you got someone? I mean – a relationship? Boyfriend sort of thing? Of course, you do. Not my business anyway. Sorry for asking."

"No – it's OK! I don't mind you asking at all. And I haven't got a boyfriend – well, not really – not any more. As you say – things just haven't worked out."

"Poor little Aoife," he said, making sympathetic eye contact with her.

She grinned at him broadly. "On the contrary, life

couldn't be better for Aoife just now." Her eyes sparkled with delight. A flirtatious smile hovered about her lips.

Back in the office she put all her energies into finishing the auction brochure. Somehow, because it was her first big project, she felt a strong personal attachment to this beautiful house, and a wish that all would go well, that the person selling the house would get a good price and that the buyer would be someone nice like Andrew McRory who would look after the house in the way that it deserved. She'd almost forgotten about the Ming vase by now and Kevin had told her that the insurance company had covered the cost of the loss without any questions asked. It was something she still felt uneasy about – but there was no point in going back over it now. She knew that she ought to have owned up at the time – but then she had left several messages with the owner's solicitor, advising that anything valuable be put away. So it wasn't entirely her fault that she'd been put in the position of trying to find a less conspicuous place for the vase. And what would owning up and telling the truth achieve now after all that time? She forced niggling doubts to the back of her mind and leafed through the glossy gold-embossed booklet that showed photos of the house in all its glory. She thought that someday she might end up living in a house like that – if she met the man of her dreams – if he was rich – if he had style and taste – if he truly loved her and wanted to grow old contentedly with her. It was a lot of ifs – and for some odd reason it reminded her that she still hadn't done anything about Dermot. She was about to pick up the phone and try his mobile yet again when Claire put a call through from reception.

"Someone on the line about that house in Talavera Road," said Claire. She sounded oddly excited. "I offered to look after him – but he says he wants to talk to the negotiator in charge of the sale."

"Put him through."

"Hi, I'm enquiring about that gaff in Talavera Road . . ." It was a man's voice – sort of slow and drawly.

Gaff? The cheek – that beautiful house couldn't by any stretch of the imagination be termed a gaff! "Yes – how may I help you?"

"I was just chillin' over the weekend and saw the house in the paper – man, it's hot – but it's like – old school – needs a bit of work to be a rocker's gaff – know what I mean? But hey – I got the bread – see what I'm saying?"

"Erm . . ." God, he sounded like someone who had divided their formative years between the more vicious criminal gangs of Dublin and New York.

"So how about you send me out the gaff deeeetails . . ."

"Certainly, sir – I'll just take a name and address."

"I'm at The Four Seasons right now – you can mail the stuff here – The Presidential Suite should get me."

At this point, Aoife couldn't help the very tiny giggle that escaped. The Presidential Suite of The Four Seasons Hotel indeed! This was just another prank call. What a chancer! "And that would be Mr who?"

"That would be Mr Smith."

"OK then – I'll just pop a set of details in the post to a Mr Smith, The Presidential Suite, Four Seasons Hotel, Dublin 4. Correct?"

"That's mighty fine of you – oh, and I didn't catch your name . . .?"

"Aoife Joyce," she said, wondering if it was wise to give her name.

As she put down the phone, Claire appeared at the door.

Her spiky black hair seemed spikier than usual. Her kohl-rimmed eyes were sparkling. And, yes, there was definitely an unusual and most un-Goth-like spring in her step – almost like she was a woman in love. No, but that would be ridiculous. Goths went in for drinking one another's blood – like Angelina Jolie and Billy Bob. She'd never heard a Goth talking about love or romance or getting engaged, getting a mortgage and a three-year-old Ford Fiesta with third party, fire and theft insurance.

"Well – how did you make out with Mr Smith?" Claire asked.

"Aren't people gas though?" Aoife said. "It's funny how some of them get their kicks. Weird!"

"Yeah! Yeah, well – I suppose when you're raking in that sort of money – you can afford to be as weird as you like."

"How do you mean? What kind of money?"

Claire stared at her. "My God, don't you know who you were talking to?"

"Should I?"

"That was Rufus Smith speaking to you!" Claire said it like Aoife had just been on a hot line to someone very important like God or Bono.

"Never heard of him. Who is he? And why does he talk like a doped-up teenager?"

Claire ran a finger lightly over some of the glorious purple-black spikes of her hair. She smiled mysteriously – like she'd just got a hot date with Dracula. "Who is he?

He's about the biggest heavy-metal act to come out of the States in the past five years. He's the front man for Cradle of Slime. He's probably richer than all of U2 put together and he talks like a doped-up teenager because – well, because – that's the way rock stars are expected to talk. It would sound very peculiar if he started talking like a barrister or a news presenter, now wouldn't it?"

"I suppose so," said Aoife, feeling a bit of a fool, and trying to remember where she had come across Cradle of Slime before. Then it came to her. She felt almost sure she'd seen Cradle of Slime in Dermot's iPod. One of the reasons that Claire liked Dermot so much was because they had similar tastes in music – all of which annoyed Aoife whenever they got together because she felt quite left out of the conversation.

"But why would Rufus Smith want a house in Talavera Road?"

"Who knows? I wouldn't worry about it too much. He's probably only passing the time. It can be very boring being a rock star. It all looks really exciting but they spend hours just holed up in hotel rooms reading the papers, and talking to their accountants and getting their hair dyed and their nails painted black. Anyway Rufus Smith and the Cradle of Slime are playing a small gig on Thursday night."

"That's the same day as the auction."

"Well, there you are – he probably won't even turn up – but send him the details anyway."

On her way to meet Nathalie, Aoife tried several times to call Dermot but got no reply.

"You'll have to go to the guards," Nathalie said to her later over a drink in Kinshasa.

"But what will I say? I mean he's packed a bag and taken his guitar. So he's not exactly missing and they might think I was only wasting their time – when there are so many really awful cases of people going missing and never being found."

"You said yourself that he might be sick – all those headaches . . ."

"Maybe," she said doubtfully. "I'll leave it for another few days. I'm sure he'll turn up."

She fingered her drink, idly running her index finger along the rim. She didn't want Nathalie to see that she was actually becoming quite concerned about Dermot. In fact, she was beginning to worry quite seriously about him.

But at the same time she was becoming quite interested in Flann Slevin and thinking about him more than was strictly necessary for a colleague.

It was a very welcome distraction to hear Nathalie's good news about the place in college.

"But it's brilliant! We have to celebrate."

"Oh, I don't know. . ." Nathalie said, not sure if she was in the mood for going out on the town. She certainly didn't feel in the mood for clubbing and pulling and all the dizzying games of eye contact and body language that clubbing and pulling involved. But Aoife knew that with a little bit of coaxing, her cousin would be more than happy to dance the night away in the Burgundy Cathouse.

Johanne arrived, then Mitch from Melbourne and a lively gang from Nutopia. Then Claire turned up in a mesmerising outfit of black lace and tulle, quickly followed by Joe and Flann Slevin who looked very smart in a preppy Ralph Lauren way. Pretty soon a small gathering of Nathalie and Aoife's friends was spread out over two alcoves in Kinshasa. The drink flowed and the night glowed and Aoife decided to stay over with Nathalie. At about midnight she remembered to send Berry a text explaining that she wouldn't be home. She wasn't really surprised not to get a reply. Berry wasn't a great believer in texting.

Getting into the Burgundy Cathouse wasn't easy but Mitch knew one of the bouncers and they quickly found themselves inside in the flashing darkness, easing forwards through a heaving crowd. The place was jammed with impossibly beautiful and implausibly thin girls, who had fabulously glistening tumbling cascades of hair and slender shapely legs that went on for miles. All the dark-haired girls looked like Keira Knightley and all the blondes looked like Sienna Miller.

"I feel completely ugly," said Nathalie, fighting a sudden urge to run when she saw how beautiful everyone was.

But Aoife propelled her forward to a corner at the far end of the room. "Come on! Interesting-looking men at ten o'clock! Shoulders back! Nose in the air. Look cool and terribly bored!"

Nathalie tried her best to head on a neat diagonal trajectory to the far corner as Aoife had directed, but found herself pushed sideways, eventually colliding with a couple on the dance floor.

The girl glared at her haughtily.

"Sorry," Nathalie mumbled, trying to edge her way in

the other direction and only then catching sight of the girl's partner.

It was Mark Tierney.

"Nathalie! What are you doing here?"

As in – Nathalie, what's a stupid girl from a call centre doing in the sort of night club where important people like me and fabulously glamorous people like my girlfriend hang out?

She longed to tell him that she was celebrating getting a place in college to study Law just like him, that she was celebrating discovering that she wasn't stupid after all, that if she set her mind to it she might even decide to become a barrister just like him. But his partner linked her arm through his and drew her slender sheathed frame up against him.

"Mark – won't you introduce us?"

"What? Sorry – Zoe – Nathalie – Nathalie – Zoe."

So – she wasn't called Portia after all. She was Zoe – but in every other way, she was exactly as Nathalie had imagined – slim, tall, blonde, elegant, looking like she spent one half of the day reading Russian novels and the other half having her toenails painted.

Zoe said hi quite coolly but Nathalie could see that she didn't mean 'hi' so much as 'fuck off' in a totally posh way.

"My friends are waiting," said Nathalie, finding her voice at last. "I'd better go."

"Yes – OK – well, good to see you again, Nathalie – cheers," he said, turning away and melting into the arms of Zoe.

After that, all Nathalie really wanted to do was go home. But she was in company and forced to stay there and endure the painful sight of Mark Tierney being deeply in love with his girlfriend. So she pasted on her best most cheerful, nicest, warmest, homeliest Nathalie Kelly smile and propelled herself out onto the dance floor with Mitch and Johanne. She tried to make sure she danced with her back to Mark, but somehow in the crowded dance floor they kept ending up in one another's line of vision. Zoe danced like someone who'd done a PhD in seduction. She writhed and slithered and bumped and rubbed herself against him. She flicked her hair and tossed her head.

"Would you look at the state of her?" said Johanne waspishly as she caught sight of Zoe. "You'd think an intelligent man like that would have better taste."

"What do you mean?" said Nathalie. "She's beautiful – look at her – and what a dancer! She looks to me like every man's dream."

Johanne snorted dismissively. "Yeah, and I know what kind of dreams. Do you think she learned to dance like that in Law School?"

Nathalie forced a tight smile.

"Hey – I know you're soft on him," Joanne went on, "but, look, if that's the sort of woman he likes – then you're better off without him. Anyway – you're going off to college now and you'll meet fellas that are ten times smarter than Mark Tierney – fellas that don't want to have some Paris Hilton wannabee hanging off their elbows all the time."

"I didn't think it was so obvious that I liked him," Nathalie said forlornly, quickly calculating that if it had been so easy for Johanne to figure out, then it must have been plain obvious to him too and he probably got some sort of silly puffed-up barrister ego-kick out of it. She had a quick image of him boasting to pals over port and big fat Cuban cigars that one of his silly little clients had developed a silly little crush on him during her silly little court case.

"Don't look now but he's peeled Paris – I mean Zoe – off his chest and he's heading this way," Johanne said out of the side of her mouth.

"Oh God," Nathalie groaned before she dived past Johanne and plunged into the crowd, struggling to reach the door. She felt a terrible strong urge to avoid coming face to face with Mark Tierney again.

In a far dark and crowded corner of the Burgundy Cathouse, as Nathalie struggled to avoid Mark, Aoife found herself dancing with Flann. He mouthed something at her over the loud music but she wasn't a great lip-reader so he leaned forward, his lips close to her ear.

"You're one hot babe," he said.

"Why, thank you, Mr Slevin," she replied and abandoned herself to the music.

Then the slow music began and there was a brief flicker of eye contact. She simply knew he was going to slide his arm around her waist and draw her close to him. And she realised that she was quite looking forward to it.

But just then Nathalie appeared out of nowhere, looking pale and miserable. "Aoife, I have to go home."

"What's wrong? You look like you've seen a ghost."

"Just a headache."

"Is Johanne going home with you?"

"She's getting on really well with Mitch – so I don't want to drag her away."

Aoife shot Flann an apologetic look. "Right – you're not going home alone," she said. "I'm coming with you."

Flann was looking downright disappointed now. So

while Nathalie went to get the coats, Aoife tried to explain.

"Sorry – but I can't let her go home alone. She's a bit upset about something."

"No worries," he said easily. "We'll finish that dance some other time."

At home in Kellys', Nathalie and Aoife found Liam sitting in his favourite armchair. He was fast asleep, a book fallen on the floor beside him.

"Dad!" Nathalie said softly as she tapped him gently on the shoulder.

He groaned and opened his eyes.

"You should be in bed, Dad. It's almost two o'clock."

"Didn't know if you had your key."

"Thanks, Dad. You're the best."

On his way up the stairs, he noticed Aoife. "Don't stay up nattering all night, you two."

"We won't."

In the kitchen Aoife made tea and they sat huddled over the breakfast bar sipping the hot comforting brew as Nathalie unfolded her romantic tale of woe.

"And that's the real reason I wanted to leave the nightclub. Don't be mad at me. I just couldn't stomach looking at Mark with that Zoe all over him. I know I have no right to feel like that – no right in the world – but that's just how it is. And all I want to say is – if this is what's commonly referred to as *being in love* it is the most painful, miserable, disgusting, empty and frustrating feeling in the world!"

"Well, thank God for that," Aoife said brightly.

"What do you mean?"

"I mean – I was beginning to think you had no interest in men. But it's just a little crush, that's all, and perfectly natural under the circumstances. You'll get over it. It's probably just your heart limbering up for the real thing."

"The real thing?"

"Yes – any day now you'll probably really fall in love with someone."

"Probably," Nathalie said, not entirely convinced by her cousin's neat assessment of the situation. She longed to talk to her mother about it and wished that Yvonne would come home quickly and sort out her differences with Liam so that life could return to normal.

But as she struggled to get to sleep, Nathalie's head filled up with a new and alarming thought. What if her mother didn't come home?

She was just drifting off when she heard a soft whisper.

"So what did you think of Flann Slevin anyway?" Aoife said sleepily as she didn't bother to stifle a contented yawn.

"Hard to say from the bit I saw of him," Nathalie said, hoping that this wasn't the start of another long conversation. "Nice trousers," she added diplomatically.

"Mmmm!" Aoife murmured happily.

CHAPTER 23

While Aoife was partying the evening away in town, Berry lit a fire in the sitting-room of Bloomfield House and prayed that the chimney wouldn't smoke. Ben had stacked a pile of chopped logs in a shed and she went outside and filled up a basket. She lit a small flame beneath a neat pyramid of twigs and, pretty soon, the room was cosy with the blazing fire and the homely scent of burning wood. She tugged the shutters across the window and closed out the late evening light. She rummaged in the freezer and found a gourmet seafood supper for two that she'd been saving for a special occasion. Well, this was special, wasn't it? The day her life finally went down the tubes! The night of total ruin? The painful messy spluttering-out last-gasp death-rattle of all her hopes and dreams! Yes, this was a night for enjoying what was left of the small pleasures in her life.

In another cupboard, in a storeroom off the kitchen, she remembered storing a bottle of quite nice vintage champagne. She put it in the fridge to chill. There were some grapes and a nice cheese she'd bought at market the previous Saturday. She set it all up on a tray, grabbed a book from the bookcase, put Ray Charles on the CD player and for once allowed Mulligan the cat to join her in the best room. She looked around her – at the bookcase filled with her parents' books, photos of family on the walls, the mantelpiece groaning with mementoes and trophies that she and Aoife had won as children, on the floor a fine old Chinese rug bought at auction by her mother. Even the big old plum-coloured sofa had been one of her mother's purchases and it had been bought for just such a night as this. It was large and deep and the cushions were plump and soft. She curled up at one end and stared into the fire, listening to the crackle and flickering, the sound of Mulligan purring quietly as he stared out regally from his large tapestried cushion, definitely looking like he believed he was not Mulligan – a fairly overfed slouchy lazy lump – but Mulligan, The Lion King – fast, graceful, regal, born to lead and destined to rule. Even animals have their delusions of grandeur, she thought. She took the colourful flyer in her hand and examined it once more, feeling herself engulfed in a leaden torrent of misery and despair.

"*HyperShop – coming soon to Larkhaven,*" she read aloud woodenly, not for the first time. "*Not just a supermarket – a whole shopping experience – banking, healthcare, beauty parlour, online café and meeting area.*"

She had thought Toby Looby was the last straw – but she hadn't bargained on HyperShop having an Internet café. There was simply no way that Berry could compete with HyperShop. HyperShop had a marketing machine that closely resembled the saturation-bombing campaign of a world superpower. She could predict with awful clarity what was coming next. It was just a few leaflets today – but tomorrow and next week there would be complete and utter saturation of the media, huge advertisements in the local and national papers and magazines – tie-ins with neighbourhood businesses and charities. *HyperShop Donates Ten Thousand Euro to Local National School for IT. HyperShop Fish Counter Sponsors Village Trawler.* Some glamorous local resident such as Hollywood actress Vienna Clayton would appear in every magazine and on every chat show in the country, looking sinfully beautiful and talking breathlessly about how HyperShop had brought joy and beauty and deep spiritual fulfilment to her life. Little gold tulips on a red background, the international HyperShop logo would soon be sprouting up everywhere – in hotels, restaurants, the cinema, car stickers, petrol stations, agricultural co-operatives. Then quietly and without any fuss all the perfectly nice and wonderfully helpful little shops in Larkhaven would close up and become estate agents or mortgage brokers. HyperShop would keep going until it had sucked every good thing out of the village, until it was the only shop left standing and until everyone who needed a job melded into the gigantically bland corporate family of HyperShop, and everyone who needed to shop just went there because it really did have everything they needed and because they really were too busy or too tired to think of going anywhere else.

It was the fate of modern life and Berry would have to accept it. There was simply no sense in being bitter and playing the hard-done-by victim. She would just have to sell off what she could and get out quickly before any more damage was done. Then she would have to get a job of some kind.

"Maybe I'll end up working in HyperShop – just like everyone else," she murmured grimly to herself as she popped the luxury seafood dinner for two into the oven of the range. Back in the sitting-room, she poured a generous glass of champagne.

"Cheers, Mulligan!" she said to the cat. "Let's go down in style!" She took a large gulp of champagne. It was delicious. "Now that reminds me – if we're going to go out in style, I need just one more thing."

She reached into the back of the large old oak cabinet and pulled out a walnut box. Inside it was one very large and fat Cuban cigar. She held it up to her nose, savouring its sweet peppery smell. She read the intricately decorated little paper label – *Rafael Gonzales Lonsdale*. She'd splashed out on it one day in town – gone into the finest cigar shop and asked for something extra special – something to smoke on a very big occasion. Now she lit a match and watched as elegant plumes of heady smoke curled up towards the ceiling. It was a very symbolic action – the cigar she knew had cost twice as much as the very expensive vintage champagne – completely decadent – she lay back on the couch like some exotic lady from a Turkish harem in her sloppiest purple cotton jogpants, inhaling the cool burning smoke, savouring the rich texture and the spicy, earthy, honeyed perfume – and raised two fingers in the air to HyperShop!!

She had managed to fill the room with a dense cloud of Havana smoke when she heard the doorbell ring. It was frustrating to be disturbed in her symbolic moment of solitary defiance and she was tempted to ignore it. It rang again. Sighing, she stood up and shuffled along the hall in her bare feet, the fat cigar still in her hand. She hoped it was just someone looking for directions or distributing leaflets.

It was Ben Searson.

"Sorry," he said quickly. "You're obviously entertaining. It will do some other time."

"What will do?" she said, making a half-hearted attempt to hide the cigar.

"It's nothing. Sorry for disturbing you."

"Look – it's just me, here all alone. I know – terribly sad – drinking alone and puffing on this big fat thing – you'd think I should know better. But why don't you come in anyway – I can offer you a glass of vintage champagne."

"OK," he said. "If you're sure I'm not bothering you."

She led him down the hallway and into the sitting-room where she filled a glass of champagne for him and topped up her own glass.

"Cheers! Here's to life!" she said defiantly. She settled herself back into the corner of the large sofa and stared glumly into the flames of the fire.

"Ray Charles . . . 'Georgia on My Mind' . . . sad," he said, sitting at the other end of the sofa and examining the CD cover.

"It's the sort of mood I'm in." She forced a determined smile.

When he didn't say anything she thought he might not have heard and she was glad. It was really better if he didn't know what a pathetic and miserable failure she was. She watched him in the half-light of the fire. She hadn't really noticed before but he was handsome –

something troubled but warm about his eyes, a kind of severe dignity about his face.

"I'm sorry I was a bit odd the other day," he said, leaning forward and resting his elbows on his knees.

"Odd?"

"First, I kissed you that night on the landing – then in the hotel I paid you a compliment, said that you were stunning – and then I went a bit funny – stupid and rude of me – I'm sorry."

"I'm still grateful for the compliment and let's just leave it at that. I'm sure you had your reasons – but I don't really need to know them."

"But I'd like to explain."

"Hey – I can hardly remember the rest of the conversation – really. And I've got other stuff on my mind right now – hence the champagne and the cigar."

He didn't seem to hear her. "You see, for a minute there on the beach and over the coffee, I was ready to say whatever it took to get you into bed."

"What!" Berry was stunned. "Look – I really don't –"

"I've done all that stuff – in another life. I have lied, cheated, doled out the lowest cheapest flattery, made the most nauseating promises. But that life is over and I have this chance to start over – and I don't want to spoil it all."

Berry looked at him quizzically.

"I'm not explaining this very well," he went on. "I can see you're not impressed."

"It takes a lot to impress me these days."

"It sounds like you're talking from bitter experience."

"On the contrary! Sweet experience! Bitter ending!"

"Sorry."

"Don't be. It's a few years ago now. And don't they say

if you haven't had your heart broken once, then you haven't really lived?" She sighed dismissively and glanced across at him. "Have you ever been in love?"

"Nope!" He didn't seem at all put out by her question.

"Lucky you! I wouldn't really recommend it. It's a form of horrible insanity and, once it grips you, it seems there isn't a cure. You become like a complete vegetable – limp spinach or soggy broccoli – and then you start doing embarrassing things in public!"

Ben laughed and smiled across at her. It was a nice smile – guarded but like there was some faint thread of a bond between them all the same.

"Then it sounds like I've been spared a terrible affliction," he said.

"It sounds like you have. I thought at first you might have come to Larkhaven to get over a failed marriage or something – but now I see that's not likely." She leaned forward and topped up his glass. "Aoife's got a silly notion that you were in some kind of trouble with the law. She has this idea that your real name is Bernard Pearse – or something like that. I keep telling her to mind her own business and not to be silly – she doesn't mean any harm – but I think secretly she'd be quite pleased and excited if it turned out you had some kind of *interesting* secret in your past!"

There was a sudden silence in the room.

"There are a few things that may need explaining at some point," he said easily though she noticed he was watching her face carefully.

"I'm sorry," she said. "That was prying really, wasn't it? Who cares if Ben Searson isn't your real name? And to be honest, Ben, right now as long as you pay the rent and you're not a rapist or a serial killer, that's all I care about. Why don't you stay for dinner – such as it is? I'm ashamed to say I don't think I can cope with being alone this evening after all. And there's a luxury fish pie for two and a bottle of OK white wine in the fridge There's no need for you to go explaining your life to me – or vice versa. I just really need the company."

She was wondering where the torrent of words had come from. She certainly hadn't planned to say anything like that. After all, she hardly knew him.

"Please!" she said, resting her hand lightly on his chest.

"If that's what you want . . ."

"Oh God, I don't know what I'm going to do!" she heard herself gasping out as somehow her head ended up being half-buried in his chest. But the words were all so strangled and knotted up that he probably hadn't understood. She'd made a complete fool of herself now – there was no turning back. And he was a shoulder to cry on, literally, and they didn't seem to come along too often these days. So she carried right on sobbing, pausing only to mop up with a tissue.

To give him his due, he barely moved – a very important feature of any half-decent shoulder that is being cried upon. The sobbing and weeping seemed to go on for ages and once he even patted her head with his large hand and then when she felt there were no more tears or sobs left, she gave him some kind of awkward hug and pulled back. No way was she telling him about the extent of her financial devastation.

"God, the dinner will be completely burnt!" she said, sticking her nose up in the air and leaping to her feet, then bolting for the kitchen where she was overcome with a horrid dose of embarrassment.

When Ben appeared in the kitchen she breezed about in bustling businesslike mood. She laid the luxury fish supper for two out on the kitchen table and served it up with a tossed salad. Then she poured a large glass of cheap Lidl Pinot Grigio for him and a large glass of tap water for herself.

"*Bon appetit!*" she said briskly. "Tuck in."

For the next while she managed to steer the conversation into calm waters – the weather, and jobs to be done on the house, her little column in *The County Sentinel*, Aoife and the Kellys. She even managed to convince herself that the odd sobbing on the shoulder moment in the sitting-room hadn't happened at all. Ben was politeness itself. He went along with the pretence that nothing even slightly embarrassing had happened between them, complimenting the food and the wine, talking about some of his own cooking efforts and offering to help with the wash-up.

"Oh no – that's fine. I'll leave it till the morning – it's not as if . . ." She was about to say, as if she would have much else to do. She was about to say that soon she might be out of house and home and that a time might come when she would relish the memory of simple things like washing up and sweeping a floor space that was actually her own. "Anyway, it's late and I'm sure you want to get home."

"Or we could go back to that lovely fire in the sitting-room and maybe finish the wine."

"Eh?" was about all she could manage.

"You're not the only one who could do with the company. I'm quite happy to just sit and listen to Ray

Charles – if you don't want to make small talk. But if you want to talk – I'm not a bad listener. And then there are things that perhaps I should tell you . . ."

It was a tempting offer – a shoulder to cry on, someone to listen coolly to her problems and maybe offer some kind of rational advice. Perhaps she ought to tell Ben Searson all about her money problems, her visit to tiny Toby Looby in his massive swivel-chair in the bank and the mega-monster that was slowly and casually winding its way towards her with its promise of total annihilation – HyperShop. But if she told him, she would look a complete fool – and it was bad enough being a complete fool without the whole world knowing about it as well. While she was deciding what to do or say, they somehow ended up beside the log fire once more.

"Things you should tell me?" she said, carefully steering the conversation away from her own problems as she settled into the big old sofa once more.

"Well, the truth is that I'd like to tell you and in fairness maybe should tell you . . . Aoife . . . she's not too far off the mark . . ."

"About . . .?"

"About my real name not being Ben Searson."

"Now you have got my attention," she said, her heartbeat quickening.

He rubbed a hand roughly across his jaw, like he was trying to figure out how best to explain himself. For a long time he just stared into space.

Berry didn't know whether she was apprehensive or just plain curious.

He didn't seem inclined to continue.

"Go on," she said at last.

"I suppose I should have told you . . . I'm trying to rebuild some sort of life . . . and I have paid my debt . . . so, in a sense . . ."

"Paid your debt – how do you mean?" She was sitting up straight now.

"Prison," he said simply. "You know – the place where they send criminals to make them pay their debt to society . . ."

"But what did you do?" she asked, quickly reassuring herself by making a mental list of all the relatively harmless and undangerous things that a man could do that might result in him being sent to prison – not paying his TV licence, minor tax evasion, protesting against globalisation, smoking a few joints too many, saying mean things about Bono very loudly outside the Clarence Hotel, handling stolen goods – all very wrong of course – but in the whole grand scheme of things – hardly hanging offences and easy to forgive.

"Breaking and entering . . ." he said quietly.

"Oh!"

"And robbery . . ."

"Ah . . ."

"And . . ."

"And?" Berry was quite on the edge of the sofa now.

He took a deep gulp of his wine and looked across at her, dark eyes boring into hers.

"Aggravated assault, assault with a deadly weapon, assault causing actual bodily harm . . ."

She took a deep breath and forced herself to look him straight in the eye. "It's quite a list."

He nodded. He sat perfectly still, his breath hardly audible.

Berry watched him, scanning his face for a telltale crease at the corner of his mouth, or a sparkle in his eye that would indicate he was just winding her up, or trying to impress her in some odd way.

"Well – you've got me there then," she said at last. "I really haven't a clue what to say or do now."

"I can't say I blame you."

"I don't suppose you want to tell me more?"

"What more do you want to know?"

She shrugged impatiently. "Maybe something like you were only trying to rob a dope peddlar to get enough money to buy life-saving drugs for your dear old gran . . ." She smiled grimly at him.

He shook his head. "Nothing so noble, I'm afraid." He stood up and placed his glass carefully on the marble mantelpiece. He opened his mouth to say something and then appeared to think better of it.

"I probably should have told you before," he said, his voice hovering over a vaguely apologetic note.

Berry said nothing for a few moments, mostly because she couldn't think of a single sensible thing to say.

"Well, as I said at the start, you've certainly got my attention," she said at last.

He ducked his head and rubbed the back of his neck. "I can either sit here for the next couple of hours and tell you now or leave it until some other more appropriate time."

"Now seems as good a time as any, Ben," Berry said. "If that's OK with you? If you are still Ben? Or Bernard even?"

But she never got to hear his answer. Just as it looked like he was about to sink down into the sofa once more, her phone bleeped loudly.

It was a text message from Aoife, explaining that she was staying over at Nathalie's. It was only a short message but, by the time she'd retrieved it, the moment had passed. Before she had even switched off her phone, he had slipped off down the hallway.

"Thanks for dinner!" she heard him call as he opened the big old door. "And by the way – it's still Ben." And he closed the door quietly behind him.

CHAPTER 24

Aoife was glad she'd stayed over with Nathalie because there was an important weekly meeting the following day in the boardroom of Vernon's. It was an early morning meeting and she was in the office for eight o'clock. It meant that she hadn't time for breakfast and now, sitting at her desk waiting for Kevin and all the others to arrive, she tucked into an enormous chocolate muffin and a big frothy cappuccino that she'd bought in the deli round the corner. She finished it off and disposed of any crumbs before assembling an up-dated report on the house sale – a summary of the three-week advertising campaign on www.myhome.ie and in the property magazines and supplements, her meeting with the vendor's solicitor, the finalisation of the auction date and a list of potential bidders expected to attend. Head Office had requested an updated database of clients, sales and properties so she spent a while entering any new details for sending later. There was an email from Nathalie headed *Catch-up in*

Purple Pepper and she typed in a hasty reply. It was still only 8.15. She checked to see if any new properties had come up for sale in her district, then she scanned through some of the other agencies to see what they were selling in the same area. They had nothing to rival the beautiful house in Talavera Road and once again she felt a sense of personal pride, almost a protective feeling towards the house. If Kevin's valuation was correct, the house would probably go for several millions and that would mean a substantial commission for Aoife. Of course, she had all sorts of wild dreams about going on exotic holidays – but she knew in her heart that most of the money should and would go to Berry.

With all of that in mind, and feeling awash with good will and affection for her older sister, she emailed Berry.

Hope you enjoyed having the house to yourself last night. Busy day today – but see you this evening. Fancy going out to dinner at the weekend? My treat – please say yes!! We both deserve a bit of spoiling and pampering.

Lol

Aoife

With five minutes still in hand before the meeting she checked through her mailbox – the usual queries from potential vendors and buyers, a few jokes from Amy, the customary spam, yet another mail from Mike Mordaunt urging her as a matter of extreme urgency to get in touch about the violent criminal Bernard Pearse. Yes . . . yes! she muttered to herself. Just as soon as this auction is out of the way! It's not as if he's going to take an axe to us all between now and Thursday – is he?

She noticed one email from an address she didn't recognise: <u>d-bochery@forfree.ie</u>. It sounded like someone's idea of a joke – debauchery: d-bochery. She clicked to open it – praying that it wasn't some awful virus that had somehow broken through Vernon's iron curtain of internet security.

Guess you're wondering what's happened to me? Sorry for checking out and not telling you – but something came up and you'd been so cool lately I didn't fancy telling you about it. I'll explain all later – but I just wanted you to know I'm OK. I was afraid you might be worried – only then I thought about it and I realised you couldn't care less if you never saw me again. Still, my dad always told me to be straight and fair with people – especially girls – so I'm writing to let you know I'm safe and well. White slave-traders haven't kidnapped me. I'm not languishing in the Bangkok Hilton. I am not stretched in a hospital ward somewhere in Africa suffering from poisonous snakebite. Some appalling older Mrs Robinson type has not got me chained and bound to her sleighbed, spread out all day on her leopardskin-print duvet, lathered in baby oil and wearing nothing but black leather boxer shorts and pink feathery handcuffs.

I just thought you ought to know all that.

Anyway   I have to go now – people to meet – stuff to do. I'll explain later.

Regards

Dermot

Aoife stared at the screen of her computer as if it had just sprouted a big red nose, waved a pair of sticky-out ears and poked out a slimy spiteful tongue at her. She was relieved – of course. And she was rather surprised to hear the words 'Oh, thank God!' zinging softly from her mouth when she realised that Dermot was fine – safe and well in fact. But once the sense of relief abated, she began to feel oddly troubled and unsteady, as if the ground was shifting menacingly beneath her feet, as if she was in a very small boat and now found herself quite suddenly being pitched about in huge swelling waves that she had no control over. It was a truly horrible feeling and her first reaction was to blame the gigantic chocolate-chip muffin.

But she really didn't have a whole pile of time to think about it because she was due in the meeting. So she made her way gingerly down the corridor. Outside the boardroom she bumped into Claire who today was sporting a purple and black lace kaftan and sequinned harem slippers. Usually Claire looked like she might be prepared to coolly devour any number of non-Goths for breakfast, but today, Aoife noticed, she looked oddly sheepish.

"Nice shade of purple," Aoife offered tactfully.

"Thanks. It's bluebottle mauve actually," Claire said, tugging uneasily at a black satin neck choker.

Aoife couldn't think of anything else to say back so they both stood in awkward silence for a few moments. Claire seemed to be blushing and under the white make-up it gave her skin an eerie lilac tinge.

"The thing is . . ." she said to Aoife at last.

"What?"

"What do you mean 'what'?"

"The thing is – what?"

"I mean . . . the thing is . . . oh, dear . . . well, I'd better just spit it out. Aoife, there's something I'd like to tell you. No, scrap that. There's something I *must* tell you."

From inside Kevin and some of the senior partners were eyeing them disapprovingly.

"You'll have to tell me later."

"But it can't wait – I'll lose my nerve again." Claire was looking quite agitated now.

"You know how Kevin hates it when we're late," Aoife hissed and ushered Claire into the room. She smiled apologetically to Kevin and lowered herself carefully into an empty seat facing Flann.

"Are you OK?" he mouthed across at her and she nodded back gratefully to him, settling into her chair and taking a few sips of water. She was just about coming to her senses when she realised that she'd left the all-important file at her desk. Aoife's brain was now trying to function on three different levels. She had a very uneasy feeling about Claire and her head was quickly getting into a knot trying to figure out what it was she might need to tell her. And she was genuinely anxious about Dermot. But mostly she was trying to think of a way to cover up for the fact that she'd left the Talavera Road file at her desk.

"Aoife – just in time to bring us up to date on the auction this Thursday," Kevin said and smiled anxiously at her. "Perhaps you'd pass round the relevant documents and run through a quick update."

"Yes, of course," she stammered, looking around the table. "Well, I – I mean . . . everything is in order and . . . I just need to get the file." Her mouth suddenly felt like it was full of dusty bubble-wrap.

Kevin observed her curiously. She could see disappointment flicker across his face. She hated to think that he might regard her as unprofessional or not up to the job.

As she rose to her feet, she heard Flann cut in quickly, "Time is pressing on and there are two big commercial sales coming up in my area next month – I think we should look at those in the meantime . . ."

"Very well," said Kevin.

Aoife smiled gratefully. "Thanks," she mouthed before darting down the corridor to retrieve the file.

After the meeting, Kevin insisted that Claire accompany him to a meeting with one of his larger commercial clients and so there was no chance for Aoife to find out what it was that Claire so desperately needed to tell her. But there was a little niggling nerve of premonition in the back of her brain and she speculated about Claire's news with increasing unease.

The rest of the day was taken up with showing clients around a new development of apartments between Sandymount Strand and Ringsend. All day there was a constant stream of potential buyers – parents buying first homes for their children, married men with their mistresses, single girls who had scrimped and saved every penny to get on the property ladder and finally a young couple, handsome and pretty, happy and full of hopes, longing to set up their first home together.

It made Aoife feel strange just standing in the same room as them. They seemed so content, so relaxed in each other's company. They teased and joked and when their eyes met there was no denying the huge amount of love and pure desire they had for each other. Yet it was all half-hidden and unspoken and it seemed so simple and uncomplicated. And for some reason it made her think about Dermot. She felt deeply annoyed with him – angry in a way that usually felt like too much effort – but now seemed like a perfectly understandable dose of righteous indignation.

It was a pleasant sunny evening and she walked back from Ringsend to Ballsbridge – muttering to herself as she made her way past pretty little terraces of red-brick houses, along the canal, and along some of the lusher and leafier roads.

"Hmmph!" she said a few times.

"The nerve!" she mumbled.

"Who does he think he is?"

Back in the office she penned a quick reply to him. She resisted a strong urge to give a long lecture about thoughtlessness and taking other people's feelings into consideration – and instead opted for a cooler approach.

Glad that you are OK. Some of us were actually worried about you. Can you let me know where exactly you are – only you never said and just in case I have to get in touch with you urgently for any reason. Also – I hope you don't think I'm being nosey but what stuff do you have to do exactly?

Aoife.

She checked her watch. If she left in ten minutes, there would be just enough time to make it to the station for the late evening train. She quickly mailed off a few property details to buyers and then she sent Nathalie a thank-you note for the night before. She was about to switch off her computer when a reply came back from Dermot.

In Spain – catch up later.

It was unusually brief for him but at least she had some idea where he was now. Then she noticed that the database she'd updated earlier in the day had not returned to Head Office. It sometimes happened with the bigger files.

"Damn – now I'm going to have to wait for the late train," she hissed as she pressed send once more. She knew it would take ages for the file to deliver because it was so large and she had no option but to sit there until it was finished.

Flann Slevin seemed to be working late too and, just as she was about to leave, he stuck his head round the door.

"I'm impressed," he said. "You'll go places." He smiled broadly at her.

"Yeah, right!" she pulled a face. "I forgot to send the updated client list back to Head Office and now I'm going to miss my train. And there isn't another one for two hours." She glared at the screen as if she could somehow make it go faster.

"How long will it take?"

"About another twenty minutes," she said.

"Let me take care of it," he said.

Aoife was about to refuse when she realised how very tired she was. It had been a long day. But it wouldn't be fair or professional to dump her work on him.

"No – that's very kind of you – but I couldn't possibly . . ." She thought of the long journey home.

"Look – I only live round the corner," he said as if reading her mind. "I have a few last-minute things to do so I'll see that the file goes through to Head Office. There's really no sense in you losing your entire evening over one tiresome file."

"It makes a certain amount of sense when you put it like that . . ." she said, biting her lip and thinking of the dreary train journey and the long walk through the village at the other end. .

He smiled warmly at her.

"Thanks a million," she said. "I'm so tired – so I graciously accept your offer."

"What did Kevin say on my first day with Vernon's? We all help each other out here? I like it that way. See you tomorrow."

"I owe you," she said. There would be just enough time to make it to the station now. She pulled on her jacket hastily and thanked him again.

"See you tomorrow," he said as she slipped out of the office.

Aoife was tired when she bundled onto the train. The previous night's clubbing was beginning to catch up on her now and also the longer-than-usual working day. She made a pillow of her corduroy jacket and placed it between her head and the window. The carriage was warm and the slow rocking rhythm was soothing and relaxing. She wondered again what Claire was so anxious to tell her. Maybe she was planning to give it all up and become a rock star. She certainly spent enough time banging about loudly on that old bass guitar of hers. Then she thought about Dermot's letter for a while, regretted for a moment that she hadn't written a nicer reply. Still, at least he was safe and well. She began to drift into a strange slumber. Little snatches and patches of odd mismatched and very lifelike dreams began to fill her head and she sank into an uneven restless sleep.

She dreamed of Dermot – lying semi-naked on a leopardskin spread, his smooth hard chest rippling, his long muscular thighs angled languidly on the bed. He smiled and stirred sensuously, and then, eyeing her hungrily, he beckoned to her. She rushed towards him, tearing off her blouse and whispering his name softly. But before she could reach him another woman barged in and pushed Aoife aside and Dermot looked at Aoife apologetically and said, 'As you can see I've moved on – I suggest you do the same.' Then he turned adoringly to the other woman.

Aoife sat up bolt upright in the carriage.

She recognised the other woman.

It was Claire – no longer a Goth with jet-black everything – but still recognisable.

Aoife cried out in shock. She looked around, disorientated for a moment by her surroundings and saw Patricia de Vere observing her oddly from across the aisle. Maybe the judge could read minds or see the dreams of others. Aoife blushed hotly and sat up straight. She was glad to see that the train was approaching Larkhaven station. She gathered up her things and thought about the dream and suddenly everything clicked into place. Dermot and Claire had always got on, liked all that rock music, even jammed together on occasion. Claire had been looking so smug and glowy lately – it had to be a man. Aoife had occasionally wondered about it but thought it might be Joe. But no! Behind her back, sneakily, slimily, underhandedly – Claire and Dermot must have got together. Her best office friend, her boyfriend – and it must have been going on for weeks, perhaps even months. No wonder Dermot had disappeared. He never did have the backbone to face anything head on. And all the while Aoife was worrying and fretting about him, Dermot was cosying up to Gothic Claire and her white pan make-up. Anger and rage bubbled up through her. She didn't know what felt worse – Dermot's betrayal or the fact that she'd been left out of the loop completely. She yanked out her mobile phone.

"*Traitor!*" she texted Claire.

Then she sat glaring as she waited for Claire's reply. She didn't have to wait long.

"*How did you find out? I knew you'd be mad as hell – that's why I put off telling you.*"

You don't know the meaning of the word *mad*, Aoife hissed under her breath and turned off her mobile. She would deal with Claire in the morning.

But as the train rattled through the darkness towards Larkhaven, Aoife began to consider the situation more calmly. Maybe it really was time to move on – time to let Dermot go – and focus on a new relationship. She didn't love Dermot – and now it would seem that he didn't love her either – so that it would be entirely right for each of them to go their separate ways. Dermot and Claire were probably made for one another anyway.

Meanwhile she would write Dermot a really nice email to make up for the horribly narky one she'd sent earlier. She wouldn't demand to know why he had gone and fallen for Claire behind her back. But she would simply tell him how much fun he had always been, how handsome he was, how thinking about him would always make her feel hot and horny all over, how she would probably spend the rest of her life telling friends about the fun times she'd had with Dermot. She'd thank him for all that – for the compliments he'd paid her, the surprise gifts he'd brought her, the signed photo of Colin Farrell he'd bullied his best friend into getting for her, the long weekend away in Venice that he'd gone into debt for, the lazy walks along the beach at weekends . . . She'd wish him all the very best in his future life with Claire. Then she'd sign off with cool affection . . . something like . . .

You'll always be in my thoughts – have a good life – fondest love – Aoife. Then she'd give Claire a good strong tongue-lashing and Claire would be prostrate with guilt and Aoife would forgive her and they would make up and be friends forever.

Yes, it would be the perfect way to close that romantic chapter of her life. And though it was painful right now to think of Claire and Dermot getting together behind her back, no doubt in years to come she would look back on it as a blessing in disguise.

CHAPTER 25

Things in the Internet café had been very slow in the afternoon and Berry closed early and went home to work on her weekly news column for *The County Sentinel*. She read through about ten emails concerning local events and worked steadily, editing them down so that they would fit in the news page. She was so engrossed in her work that she almost missed seeing an email from <u>renaissanceman@mainmail.com</u>. She felt suddenly excited and deeply weary at the same time. It was a short note.

My dear Berry

I hope that you are keeping well. I think of you often. Things are working out for me at last. The divorce is through and we have agreed joint custody of the children. I have managed to pay off most of the debts and it looks like I might be in line for a good promotion soon. So – there you are – in spite of everything, it all worked out in the end. I would really like for us to meet up again – maybe now that my life is more stable we could make a go of things. It wasn't just a fling as far as I'm concerned.

Think about it.

Love

Conor.

She clicked on *reply* and wrote a quick response:

Conor – I'm glad that things have finally worked out for you. OK – let's meet and see what happens – why not?

Love

Berry

She pressed *send* and almost instantly regretted it. There could be no future with Conor Lynch. Too much water had passed under the bridge. Too much emotional history lurked in the shadows between them . . .

. . . and there he was one dark Friday evening when she came home from the office, his long lean frame stretched out along the sofa, his feet on the arm rest. She was about to chastise him gently when she noticed that the dining-table had been set with candles and her best china. A bottle of expensive champagne was cooling in an ice bucket and there were fresh flowers in the centre of the table. A warm savory aroma of something vaguely Italian was wafting from the kitchen.

Conor jumped up and took her coat, then led her to the table and sat her down.

"What's all this?" she said, laughing with delight.

"Payback time," he said simply before disappearing into the kitchen.

There was wine and food and candlelight and soft music. There was long intimate conversation and eye contact and flirting. And even as he took her by the hand and led her into the bedroom Berry knew that she was making the biggest mistake of her life. And though the next few weeks were probably the happiest she'd ever experienced, she felt like someone waiting on Death Row.

It was six weeks before anyone in the office rumbled it but then in a matter of days it had spread right round every department in the building. After all, there is nothing like a juicy sex scandal to justify other people's own choices in life. She could imagine their tittle-tattle over the water dispenser. *Sleeping with a married man who's nearly ten years younger than her! How sad is that? I may have bullied my elderly mother into a miserable nursing home where she is deeply unhappy – but at least I've never seduced a junior colleague and broken up his marriage. Taking complete advantage of her position as division leader!!* One morning she was summoned to the managing director's office. Someone had lodged an official complaint against her for passing on the month's more lucrative assignments to Conor. She was guilty – no doubt about it. But on the other hand, his wife's gambling problem was spiralling out of control. He was trying to protect his children by keeping things at home as stable as possible. In the past Berry had often divvied out assignments with lucrative overtime to people who she knew needed the money – couples planning weddings, singletons struggling to get on the mortgage ladder. Helping Conor out in a tight spot was no different.

But that wasn't how the management had seen it in the end. She was given a month's pay in lieu of notice and told to vacate her office by the end of the week. Not long after that her father took ill and became in need of constant care. She left the apartment and went home to Bloomfield House, glad of the chance to look after her father and to get away from her ill-judged romance and her shattered career. One day she took the train into town from Larkhaven, met Conor for lunch and told him they couldn't see each other any more. It was a painful meeting for both of them and she hadn't seen him since.

Aoife arrived home and was trying hard to hide her upset about Claire and Dermot carrying on behind her back.

"What's up?" asked Berry, always willing to engross herself in other people's problems as an antidote to her own. She was putting the finishing touches to a Chicken Caesar salad. Some essential ingredients were missing, including the chicken and the Caesar salad dressing. But she tossed the lettuce leaves, chunks of onion and tomato and some slices of value-pack chicken roll in a bowl with some mayonnaise and set it down on the table between them.

"Nothing much," Aoife said despondently as she speared a clump of wilted leaves and a sliver of chicken roll. "What's for dessert?"

"Made up a bit of a treat this evening." Berry produced a covered dish from the fridge.

Aoife reached towards it.

"Ah, ah! Eat your main course first," said Berry. "And tell me why you're looking so glum. I thought everything at work was going wonderfully. Huge commission in the pipeline . . . brilliant new boss who thinks you're wonderful . . ."

"Nothing much. I'm just beginning to feel that Dermot has been less than honest with me." She couldn't bring herself to tell Berry about the latest development between Dermot and Claire.

Berry speared her with a raised eyebrow. "Time to move on. Best to put the whole Dermot situation in the past. Learn from your mistake and move on. Nothing's going to come of it now anyway."

Aoife poked around at the salad, said that it was really lovely but she wanted to leave some room for dessert.

Berry raised the lid with a flourish and set the dish down on the table.

Aoife studied it carefully for a few moments. "Mmmm! Looks yummy. What is it by the way?"

Berry smiled triumphantly. "I found a tin of prunes in the cupboard, some caraway seed and a packet of pineapple-flavoured jelly. So I made a prune and caraway trifle and topped it off with some whipped cream and stale biscuit crumbs. *Bon appetit!*"

"It's great," Aoife said, forcing a spoonful of the poisonous concoction down.

"We're invited to the Kellys' for Sunday lunch," Berry said. "Yvonne called earlier. She says she's been very lonely since you left them and they would all love the company. Maybe I was just imagining things but she sounded lonely and even sad. I mean, Aoife, when have you ever heard Yvonne being sad? She's the most cheerful person I know – always keeping the bright side out. I've always sort of envied the Kellys – so close and happy and all. And as for Liam – if he wasn't married to our aunt – don't you think he's gorgeous?"

Aoife gave her a doubtful look.

"I mean, he's sort of like Bruce Willis," Berry continued, "all craggy and tough-looking. When Nathalie was little, he and Yvonne were always holding hands and going out for romantic evenings. I suppose even the truest romances settle into middle-aged boredom in the end. You don't think . . .?"

"Think what?"

"Well, that Liam – you know – him being like Bruce Willis and all . . . ?"

"What! That's the maddest thing I've ever heard."

"Stranger things have happened," Berry said, taking a spoonful of the prune and pineapple-jelly dessert and pulling a face. "Must remember the sugar next time."

The news that they were invited to Kellys' for Sunday lunch perked Aoife up. She didn't know how much longer her stomach could tolerate the ghastly array of dishes that Berry set down in front of her each evening. But home-made vegetable soup, roast spring lamb with a rich burgundy and redcurrant jelly gravy followed by a big juicy rhubarb tart – now that would be a meal worth waiting for.

"By the way," Aoife said, forcing down another mouthful of the revolting pineapple, caraway and prune concoction, "did you ever find out anything more about Ben Searson?"

Berry shook her head, remembering how he'd been on the point of telling her when a message from Aoife had shattered the moment.

"Nothing," she said. "Your on-line detective agency probably got it wrong."

"Probably," Aoife concurred as she slid the remains of her dessert into the bin.

CHAPTER 26

Ben had gone for a run. Five miles along the beach – it was nothing. One of the ironies of his life over the past couple of years was that his body had never been in better shape. When he was Emperor of Reality TV – long hours sitting at a desk or entertaining clients had left his flesh tending towards the flabby. There was a lot of alcohol, suffocating bouts of chain-smoking that had left him with a ravaging cough – and the occasional night of cocaine insanity. But now he savoured the easy stretch in his legs as his feet struck the closely packed sand in a regular rhythm, the effortless stamina as he powered his body forward. He felt more like a racehorse or some wild creature of the forest – fast and unthinking and not entirely ungraceful.

He had mixed feelings about telling some of his story to Berry Joyce. Now that he'd started, he almost longed to tell her the whole thing and had been disappointed when Aoife's phone-call had interrupted them. But now he wondered if it might not be better all round to keep the matter to himself. If the subject came up for discussion again he could simply dismiss it as just a drunken fracas outside a nightclub and an unsympathetic judge. After all, it's not that easy to find out if someone has a criminal record, not even on the Internet. People can hire private detectives – but he of all people knew about human nature and while most people were curious about their neighbours, they didn't feel at all comfortable with actively nosing about in their business. Besides, the counsellor at the prison pre-release program had advised him to say nothing and hinted that the gardai probably wouldn't get round to keeping tabs on him – unless he did something to get their attention.

He had no intention of coming to their attention.

"I was thinking about making a few different programmes," he said to Maurice, his accountant and now partner of six months. Business was going from strength to strength. They were ensconced in a quiet corner of a new dockland restaurant, tucking into two very fresh lobsters. A young waitress hovered with a little too much eagerness.

"Great," Maurice said, grinning at him and grappling with the pink-marbled shell of the lobster. Noisily, he slurped down some very fine white burgundy. "What did you have in mind? I loved *Celebrity What's in Your Attic*? And more to the point – the punters loved it. We've sold it to about fifty different TV stations now. Come up with a few more ideas like that and we'll never have to work again."

"No – it was nothing like that. I'm fed up with all that shit, Maurice."

Maurice made a face, shoved a large lump of lobster in his mouth and began chewing industriously.

"Just for once I'd like to do something real," said Ben.

"Nothing more real than Reality TV!" Maurice said, scoffing slightly.

"But that's just it!" Ben said growing more heated. "That's where you're wrong. There's nothing less real than Reality TV. Reality TV is the most fake thing in the world!"

"Would you listen to yourself? You're not making any sense at all. How could something real be fake?"

"Maybe not all of it – there are some really brilliant Reality TV shows – but none of them are made by this company – I've never come up with an idea for a brilliant reality show. I'm Mr Sleaze – Mr Lowest Common Denominator. My old school friends – the ones in the legal profession and the ones who save people's lives every day in hospital – regard me with a mixture of pity and scorn. Oh, they invite me along to their parties – sometimes they are even kind enough to mention my 'work' – but the truth of it is, behind my back they talk about 'poor Ben Pearse who was the most promising pupil in his year at school, who was destined to leave the world a much better place, who had the finest women in the city wanting to bear his children – who threw it all away to make cheap and tacky TV shows for a few dollars more'. In their eyes – I'm a complete loser, Maurice."

"Is that so important to you – what a few old school friends think?"

Ben shoved the lobster around on his plate. He ought to have been a very happy man. Parked outside was his top-of-the-range Mercedes Maybach. He would drive home to his penthouse apartment overlooking the river, with panoramic views across the city. At the weekend he would race or sail or play golf with a close and probably even closed circle of friends – new friends that had come along somewhere along the line and somehow supplanted the old friends, the ones from school and college, the ones he'd vowed always to cherish come what may.

No – life wasn't turning out at all like he'd expected and the living proof of all of this was wafting towards him now on a pair of long slender legs.

"Ben, darling," she said, leaning slightly towards him as he stood up to greet her with the customary two-cheeked kiss. She swept back a long, lustrous lock of glistening blonde hair.

"Lillian! I wasn't expecting you to join us."

"Well, don't sound so surprised, my love. Why shouldn't I join you?" She folded herself elegantly into a chair and smiled with heavy-lidded eyes at Maurice. "You don't mind, Maurice, do you? I like to keep close to my darling." She leaned over and tweaked a thick wavy lock of hair away from Ben's forehead. "I hope he hasn't been going on about giving it all up – it's too silly for words. Maurice, you must talk sense into him – I'm relying on you." She smiled charmingly, flashing a mouth of perfect white teeth.

Maurice flirted back – just enough to flatter her, not enough to cause trouble.

Ben felt his stomach churn. The awful truth was he could barely remember Lillian's second name. What was it? Something like Lane! No, not Lane – Crane! Not that either. Bane – that was it! Lillian Bane. Somehow – he wasn't quite sure how – Lillian Bane had attached herself to him over the past few months – in that wonderfully charming, seamless and faux-beguiling way of hers. She seemed to have taken complete control of his diary. Events he'd never have dreamed of going to had suddenly become *'we absolutely must-do, sweetheart'* and *'darling, we simply can't miss'*. He was being sucked into what was sometimes referred to as 'Society', his name featuring routinely in the social columns, his photo with glamorous model Lillian Bane an almost weekly event in the Sunday newspapers. In the past three months he'd been sailing in the Med, horse-racing in France, clubbing in London and Madrid, attending house parties at chateaux in the Dordogne and castles in the Highlands. There were the usual rumours of impending marriage between Ben and Lillian, which were always quickly countered by rumours of a break-up. Lillian gave lots of interviews where she spoke of love and hinted with carefully practised smiles that there was something truly deep and profound between them.

She had that unquantifiable look of a woman who was sizzling hot in bed – like contained within her were bucketsful of barely suppressed lust, like she would happily trawl through the most esoteric of sex positions and fetishes for days on end. A sort of middle-class Irish Belle-de-Jour. Alas for Ben, despite appearances Lillian was quite lukewarm in the lust department and she tended to the occasional pained and briefest of surrenders rather than passionate nights of mutual pleasure. She liked doing it with mirrors but only because it gave her a chance to admire her own magnificently toned body. Sometimes Ben reckoned that the pillow on which she rested her beautiful head responded better than Lillian.

Maurice declined to stay with them for dessert. "Two's company," he said. "But thanks all the same."

Ben's spirits began to flag. He would be alone with Lillian now for the rest of the evening. She would drag him along to some terribly exclusive nightclub, orchestrate a couple of photo opportunities, flutter around making meaningless conversation with some other society types. She would beam her vacuous smile at the entire clientele but, if he so much as hinted that he was bored and wanted to go home, she had a way of hissing out of the side of her mouth while still smiling that could pulverise any man.

"*The Sunday Irish News* wants to do a feature on us," she trilled as they sat into the deep leather-upholstered seats of his Maybach.

"Great," he mumbled.

"Well, it is great. That's like eight weeks in a row we've been in the news and every week there's been a story or a feature on us – the public likes us, Ben – we make a good couple. We're like the Posh and Becks of the Irish TV world."

Ben pulled a face.

"Oh, come on!" she said. "Don't be such a pain. It's helping my career and not doing your business any harm either. People see you in the papers – they know who you are – they watch your programmes – buy your programmes. Where's the problem?"

"Lillian, I don't want to argue. I'm tired. I've had a long and busy week."

"Who's arguing? Anyway, I've had a long busy week too. But you don't hear me whingeing about it. We only get one shot at this life, Ben. Life is not a dress rehearsal – as I constantly remind you – and where's the point in sitting at home on a Friday night when we can be out clubbing? I tend to the view that we can sleep all we want when we're dead."

There was no arguing with that sort of logic and he went along with her plans for the evening.

In the end though, a few weeks later, Ben sort of got his way.

One afternoon he sat down with Maurice and explained that he was taking six months off to do voluntary work with teenage street boys in Brazil.

Maurice was suitably unimpressed. "Go and patronise the underclasses if it gives you a thrill – but don't you see – nothing you can do will ever make a real difference to their lives. It will make *you* feel better – that's all."

"I have to try all the same."

"Why?"

He couldn't form any coherent answers beyond saying that he felt like he was living in a goldfish bowl in a fairground, so he didn't bother to try. Maurice could keep things ticking over till he came back and for all he knew – the break away might revitalise his interest in the TV business. Lillian would probably waste no time in finding a flashier, richer boyfriend – someone who enjoyed the media spotlight. And that would be perfectly fine with Ben.

"Ya big eejit," Grace Fitzgerald, his secretary, said to him when he informed her of his plans. "Do you honestly think them young fellas out there in Brazil won't see through your egotistical posturing?"

"Egotistical posturing, Mrs Fitzgerald?" He always called her Mrs Fitzgerald when he felt she was criticising him unfairly.

"You know what I mean – doing this to bring some meaning to your own life – not some real benefit to theirs. Only because you're rich enough to take time out of your successful life – so that you can play at being a superhero! Slipping into your Superman outfit for a few months – just to be able to tell yourself that you have done it! What real sacrifices will you be making? None! What real suffering will you have? None! And when it all gets too much after a few months – when the cold harsh reality of their tough lives begins to really encroach on yours – what will you do?"

Ben shrugged like a fractious teenager.

"You'll come bolting home like you have a red-hot rocket stuck up your arse and resume your empty aimless life, and maybe you'll make a nice little TV documentary about the whole experience – just to salve your conscience."

"That's a bit harsh," he said, knowing that she wasn't too far off the truth.

"Yes, it is," she said, silence hovering in the air, waiting to swoop and whip up a storm of anger.

He stared her down for several moments. "No, I'll never get anything past you," he said at last. Since his mother's premature death Grace had stood like a sentinel between him and any delusions he might have. And he loved her dearly for it. Besides, she ran his office with terrifying efficiency. He did not think that there was another woman in the world even half as organised and capable as Grace Fitzgerald.

"I know your heart is in the right place," she said more kindly. "And of course you will be doing something good. I just don't want you having any illusions about it."

"I know," he said. "But I'll go mad if I stick at what I'm doing much longer. I feel I'm in some sort of horrible sticky trap. Lillian has me plastered all over the papers like some soccer-playing, pop-star sex symbol. Maurice only thinks in numbers and balance sheets – he's dreaming about buying out the BBC and ITV and he's just the man to do it. Maurice wants to conquer Europe, then maybe Asia and America. It's all getting out of control. I have to try and do something a bit useful. And you're probably right – my motives are just as mixed up as everyone else's when they decide they want to help people. But if we all thought that way – nothing good would ever be done and no one would ever help anyone. So I'm going anyway and I'm relying on you to keep Maurice in his place while I'm gone."

"I'll do my best," Grace said coolly. She never felt the need to say that she would probably be prepared to stake her life for Ben Pearse if the situation ever called for it.

Six weeks later he was in the city of Salvador in Brazil. He had a contact out there from school, John, who in a matter of days had chipped away at some of Ben's soft, woolly, cosseted outlook. Ben was assigned a room in an old converted monastery – a hard bed, a chair and table. Meals were taken with several other men and women in a sparsely furnished dining-room. They took turns in cooking the food and cleaning and shopping. They rose early and went out to work – teaching, nursing, rescuing, coaching, bricklaying, plastering, wiring, counselling, feeding, tending to the dying – whatever was needed.

They were building a hostel in the grounds of the old

monastery. A wealthy builder had donated the bricks and mortar. One of the men had been an engineer and he drew up the plans. They dug foundations and set to work. Ben was roped into the bricklaying and very soon he became accomplished at it. He learned to get the right consistency in the mortar, not to let it stiffen too much and to get the bricks level. At first he used a spirit level and the others laughed at him – but as the days and weeks went by it began to feel as if he had been a bricklayer all his life.

The boys John worked with were a peculiar mixture of toughness and vulnerability and Ben made slow progress with them. His job was to teach English to them for one hour every day – but it was a tough hour. They were suspicious of him and huddled in corners, ignoring him and talking quietly to each other in Portuguese. It was quite a change to be ignored and dismissed in this way. It even hurt a bit. The language was a problem too because his Portuguese was only very basic. One day he brought in a football and they played a game. Then he made them play in English – which they all laughed at – but it broke the ice. And gradually they came to trust him a little bit.

He emailed home to Maurice and to Grace and they kept him informed about the business. It was all going on quite well without him. A new young whiz kid Maurice had taken on had come up with a brilliant idea for reality shows aimed at the younger audience – and there was lots of interest from buyers. He'd explained as delicately as he could that he couldn't possibly expect Lillian to put her life on hold for him, but very much to his surprise she also kept in regular touch. Her idea seemed to be that, once he'd got this daft notion out of his head, he would be more than happy to slip back into the glitzy, glamorous world that she seemed to crave so much. He repeated again and again that it really wasn't fair to keep her hanging on like that – but Lillian was adamant. They had something too precious and much too special to leave behind. All the newspaper articles said so.

The months passed quickly and Ben became increasingly immersed in the lives of the boys. He wanted to do more for them – broaden their education – perhaps encourage and finance one or two to go on to university. He felt completely alive for the first time in many years. Every night he slept like a child, worn out from physical work, contented in his mind. Gradually the production company receded in his mind. Maurice mailed with regular financial updates and he would check them carefully before sending back the briefest of replies.

Grace wanted to know when he was coming home. He told her was planning to extend his stay by another few months. "Don't leave it too much longer," Grace said. "It's not wise for a man to be away from his business too long."

He was very torn – but then he reckoned that if he were to sponsor the education of some of these boys, his business would also have to be in good shape. And, being realistic, he could probably do more good at home by making one documentary than he could in Brazil even if he spent the rest of his life laying bricks and giving English lessons. In the end and with great reluctance he told John and the boys that he would have to go home. Then he went to the phone booth outside the school to call Grace and tell her the good news. He knew she would gloat in her own matronly way and as he dialled the number he smiled to himself, imagining how she would try to hide her relief by being cross with him. The booth was stuffy and it seemed to take her forever to answer the phone. He drummed his fingers impatiently on the glass as he waited. At last he heard a voice at the other end.

"Hi, Grace – it's Ben."

"Grace is on her annual leave. How may I help you, sir?"

"But this is July. Grace never goes on holidays in July. She hates the crowds and always waits till September. Are you sure we're talking about Grace Fitzgerald?"

"Yes, sir. Quite sure."

CHAPTER 27

Nathalie Kelly travelled to the offices of Nutopia one last time, taking one bus to the city centre and another to Beechfield Industrial Estate. The bus was filled with Nutopia workers and she sat in the middle next to Johanne who was texting a new boyfriend.

"Hey, Nathalie – suppose you won't talk to us at all when you go to the college?" said Dylan who worked in the stores.

Nathalie smiled and told him he was being silly.

"What makes you think she'd want to talk to you anyway?" Johanne sniped without even bothering to look back at Dylan McKeown. "Nathalie has more taste."

Nathalie poked her in the ribs and told her to shush – but Johanne loved the cut and thrust of slagging just as much as Nathalie hated it.

The bus stop was a good half-mile walk from Utopia's telesales empire and Nathalie and Johannes strolled in the warm sunshine, in T-shirts with bare arms, hoodies wrapped around their waists, closely pursued by the still slagging Dylan McKeown.

"Hey, Johanne – are you wearing that skirt for a bet?"

"Yeah – I bet someone fifty quid you'd try and make a stupid joke about it."

So it continued until they reached the entrance and Nathalie stood in line one last time to swipe her identity card through the security machine. She was feeling sad and quite nostalgic. Of course, she wouldn't miss Nutopia and most of all she wouldn't miss Gretta Price who'd made her life absolute hell since she'd finally handed in her notice. But she'd miss Johanne, Mitch from Melbourne, Dylan and the rest of the lads. She'd miss the conversations over lunch, the nights out clubbing in a gang, their constant solidarity in the face of the enemy – or Gretta Price as she was better known. To someone with a more glamorous job in the city centre or a rich person who didn't need to work at all – the kind who spent mornings in the gym and afternoons in the beauty salon – Nutopia might seem a bit like a grim open prison. But Nathalie knew that all human life was quietly happening there amongst the few hundred workers. She'd enjoyed watching love affairs blossom and agonised with workmates as romance gripped their lives and lovers sometimes broke their hearts. She'd sympathised with couples struggling to make a home and start a family, sparkled with joy when colleagues brought new babies to be shown off and passed around in warm admiring embraces. She'd laughed at men who could tumble in a moment from elation to despair as their soccer team faced relegation – but who were too tongue-tied to ask a girl out on a date. She'd been shocked by their jokes, amused by their wit, unsettled by their flirtiness, annoyed by their occasional denseness, often comforted by their simplicity and lack of bitchiness. When she'd confided this, Johanne laughed scornfully.

"Are you mad in the head? You have the chance of a lifetime. I'll probably be stuck here forever more saying 'Are you travelling to fucking Europe at all this year, madam/sir?' You'll meet loads of interesting people and some nice bloke who'll want to marry you and take care of you and then you'll get a big job and earn loads of money."

"Even if I do, it won't be the same. I know I should be happy and excited but it's the opposite. I'm terrified and I think I'll never again make friends like you and the rest of the girls."

"Don't be daft," said Johanne – which was pretty much her stock reply to anything she didn't really want to think about. "Anyway, never mind all that. I knew it would be pure stupid to arrange a surprise party for you because you'd only find out about it – so I'm telling you now. A few of us girls are taking you to Stefano's this evening for a meal. We'd like to have done something really special for you but I left it a bit late to organise and anyway it's Wednesday and everyone's broke till the weekend. But we're treating you to a meal at Stefano's and that's final."

Gretta Price made no allowances for the fact that it was her last day and Nathalie was forced to work her way through at least seventy calls on a list that Gretta had compiled. Gretta had even changed her to a temporary desk beside the supervisor and blocked off her Internet access so that for the last week of her employment with Nutopia, Nathalie only had access to internal mail. But she didn't really mind. It wasn't as if she was expecting any important emails from anyone.

"It's a security matter," Gretta said. "Just in case you had the bright idea of mailing our client lists to anyone else."

"As if anyone would want their scabby client lists," Johanne muttered behind her back. But now it was her last day and Nathalie sat at the temporary desk with good-humoured resignation. By the tenth call she began to wonder if Gretta had somehow got hold of the numbers of the seventy rudest, crankiest people in the country because every single one of them snapped at her and slammed down the phone. It meant she was getting through the calls a bit faster than usual, though. But if Gretta saw her twiddling her thumbs, another list of numbers might appear. At last Nathalie got onto a soft-spoken man with a country accent. He sounded really old.

"Good morning, sir. Will you be travelling to Europe at all this year?"

He laughed at the very idea. "I've never been outside Kerry – except to go to Croke Park for the All Ireland. I'd love to go to Europe, mind you, because the wife and I always planned to go to Paris for a nice weekend – but she passed away a few years ago and I don't think I'd like to go without her."

"Oh dear. I'm sorry. You must miss her terribly."

"Yes, I do. The world just isn't the same without her."

There were strict guidelines for dealing with customers who attempted to make idle chit-chat, a list of ways to end a conversation without damaging the all-important image of the company . . . thank you for taking our call . . . we'll send you a brochure in the post . . . we'll call you in the spring. And there were even stricter guidelines about getting familiar with customers over the phone. Nathalie could vividly remember Gretta Price giving a Powerpoint presentation on that very subject quite soon after she'd arrived at Nutopia.

"No flirting, no small talk, no familiarity, no listening to sob stories. Just remember there are a lot of sad and lonely people out there. It is not our function to keep them company or listen to their grim little life stories. If they want a counselling service, let them pay for it."

The man was still on the line, telling her about how he'd first met his wife, about their courting days, their life together, their children.

"What was her name?" Nathalie asked.

"Kathleen. Kathleen O'Sullivan. I loved her all my life. Isn't that something great to be able to say?"

"Yes, it is," she replied, thinking of her own parents who lately seemed to have lost touch with each other completely.

"Well, you sound like a grand girl and thanks for listening. Sorry for holding you up and pity I don't have any business for you."

"Oh, that's OK. It's my last day anyway. Bye."

She hadn't noticed that Gretta Price was standing right behind her. "Keep going like that and you won't get out of here until nine o'clock tonight, Missie."

"I couldn't hang up. He was talking about his wife who's dead."

"That's not my problem. Now get on with your work."

"Her vibrator is probably banjaxed," said Johanne under her breath, which sent a wave of sniggers down the line.

In between calls, every time Nathalie looked at her computer screen, there seemed to be another good-luck message in her mailbox.

At lunch-time in the canteen, Eileen made up her favourite chicken, lettuce and mayonnaise sandwich even though it wasn't on the menu any more. Mr O'Flaherty, who was the senior manager, came in carrying a card and a small package wrapped in pink paper and called for silence from the hundred or so people who were finishing off the last of their lunch. Gretta Price stood woodenly at his side while he made a short speech thanking Nathalie for all her good work, her unfailing cheerfulness and her nearly unblemished work record. He didn't even mention the tailgating incident. He said the people in Nutopia would all miss her and he wished her the best of luck at her studies. Then he presented her with the card and package and kissed her shyly on the cheek, at which point Dylan and some of the other lads whistled. Then Mr O'Flaherty rushed off because he had to attend a board meeting.

Gretta Price looked at her watch and sharply reminded the assembled workers that while Nathalie might be able to spend the next couple of years swanning around and living off the taxpayers' money, the rest of them still had jobs to do.

At last Nathalie made the final call on her list. The person wasn't going to Europe this year for their holidays. They did not want travel insurance. She thanked them for their time and hung up for the very last time. She went to the cloakroom, gathered up her things from the locker and stood for a final moment at her desk. A few people came up and wished her luck and then she slipped out through the security gate.

"Hurry up! We'll miss the bus!" Johanne called impatiently as Nathalie turned to give Nutopia one last lingering look.

At home, the atmosphere in Yvonne Kelly's kitchen was thick with something nasty. Nathalie felt it the moment she walked in. Her father ate his roast lamb dinner in silence.

"How did your last day go, love?"

"It was lovely really. They gave me a present."

In all the excitement of goodbyes, she'd forgotten to open it and now she quickly unwrapped it to find – a pink radio-alarm clock in the shape of a teddy bear.

Liam glanced at it dismissively.

"It's nice really – I might put it in my bathroom," said Nathalie. "We're going out to Stefano's for dinner later on. So I might be a bit late coming home."

"Don't worry about rushing home. I'm going out later as well," Yvonne said, radiating enough rage at her husband to power a nuclear energy plant.

Liam Kelly rattled his paper and engrossed himself in the sports page.

"You'll be all right on your own, won't you, Liam?"

"What? I'll be grand."

"There you are. Nothing to worry about! Loves his own company, your father."

Nathalie could hear a new spiteful anger in her mother's voice and wondered what could be the cause of it. But she was afraid to ask, afraid she might only stir things up and make them worse. And she was worried. Could she somehow be the cause of their misery?

She showered and changed into a pair of jeans and a spaghetti-strap lace-trimmed cotton top. She slipped her dainty feet into a new pair of jewel-encrusted mules. Then she put on a tiny bit of make-up, more to please Johanne than anything.

Johanne was waiting at the top of the steps leading down to Stefano's Restaurant in a quiet lane near Temple Bar. Inside, the restaurant was dark and practically empty. Some awful wallpaper music was playing tinnily in the background. Stefano welcomed them glumly and led them to the best table in the room.

"Business is very bad tonight," he said woefully. "Some silly waitress made mistake with the bookings. Lucky for me, you ladies are here or I'd have to close altogether." He was close to tears.

Nathalie and Johanne exchanged glances, spent a few moments wondering if they could ever show their faces in Stefano's again if they walked out now and decided quickly that they would have to stay, at least until Niamh and Lisa from Accounts arrived. They ordered some wine and tried to force a bit of jollity into the dead atmosphere. Business was so bad that Stefano had cleared away the tables in the inner section altogether – and the place had a haunted, half-abandoned look about it. But then Niamh and Lisa swept in, bubbling with good humour and general excitement about life. They dismissed the emptiness of the restaurant as not important and more wine was ordered with antipasti.

"Well, this is great," said Niamh, obviously trying to inject some fun into the evening. "A genuine girlie night."

Nathalie's heart sank.

"Fabulous! A girlie night! It'll be like a hen night – only

no one will have to get married in the morning," said Lisa.

"Yeah – a girlie night. *Brilliant!* We can drink all we want and talk about men and cover all the gossip and swap make-up secrets. Then we can get a hilarious taxi-ride back to Lisa's place and drink vodka and watch *When Harry Met Sally*, and talk about our love lives!" said Johanne, grinning with anticipation.

Nathalie grinned back with grim determination. If there was one thing she hated with a passion, it was girlie nights – well, at least the sort of girlie nights which began with the phrase "Let's have a girlie night!", nights which ended up awash, adrift and eventually capsized in a turbulent sea of forced laughter, spilt wine, tears and arguments – in that order. Listening to the girls chattering with manufactured glee, she wondered if it might be possible to leave early without hurting their feelings. She doubted it.

Then just as Lisa was about to launch enthusiastically into her "Ten Most Shaggable Men Of All Time" list, the door at the top of the stairs leading into the restaurant opened suddenly and in marched Mr O'Flaherty and a few people from his department.

"Look who it is," said Nathalie, desperate to get away from shaggable men. She waved over at Mr O'Flaherty. "Small world, isn't it? Thanks for the clock by the way!" She thought it might be possible to get him to join them.

He smiled but then nodded dismissively and turned away, probably embarrassed to be in the same restaurant as his staff.

Amid squeals of delight, eager nods of agreement for George Clooney and violent groans of rejection for nerdy Ian from the IT department, Lisa reached the end of her list of shaggable men. Nathalie tried to get a bit excited over whether George Clooney should be at Number 1 instead of Colin Farrell but her heart wasn't in it at all.

She tucked into lasagne and rocket salad, her mouth brimming over with greenery. Then she looked up and noticed her solicitor Felicity Norton coming through the door with a couple of friends. Felicity waved casually but went to a corner at the far end of the room. Soon afterwards, Nathalie's heart took an unexpected detour down to the soles of her feet, when Mark Tierney strolled in with Zoe from the nightclub and joined Felicity. He didn't even notice Nathalie.

But it was when Gretta Price made a grand entrance in a stunning red dress with a surprisingly handsome beefy type on her arm that Nathalie began to get a strange feeling about the evening.

"It's weird."

"What is?" asked Johanne who was now wrestling with a plate of Dublin Bay prawns and losing.

"I know everyone in the restaurant."

"Mmmm," said Johanne.

"Well, don't you think it's strange?"

"Not really. Six degrees of separation and all that – you're never more than six people away from knowing anyone else in the world. Here's an example – me and George Clooney – my brother's best friend lives in Blanchardstown. His next-door neighbour's son used to sit next to Colin Farrell's next-door neighbour's son in English class. Colin Farrell's next door neighbour used to see Colin Farrell regularly. Colin Farrell works in Hollywood. George Clooney works in Hollywood. There you are!" said Johanne like she had just successfully explained

Einstein's theory of Relativity to a class of five-year-olds.

"Here – more wine," said Niamh. "Never mind that lot! It's going to be a Great Girlie Night!" And she filled up everyone's glass.

Shortly after that, the door leading into the restaurant opened once more and Nathalie watched in dazed confusion as one by one Dylan, Bob, Gerry and Dave from Stores rambled in, Colm and Eoin from Accounts and nerdy Ian from the IT department, quickly followed by about thirty people from the telesales department. Suddenly the restaurant was jammed with people.

But it wasn't until Berry and Aoife arrived immediately after, that it finally dawned on Nathalie.

"But . . . I thought you'd arranged a girlie night." She looked around at Johanne, Niamh, and Lisa who were now giggling ferociously into their glasses.

"Oh come on, Nathalie Kelly! The whole world knows that you are totally allergic to girlie nights!"

"You mean – you've been winding me up – all that stuff about getting drunk and slagging the taxi driver and watching *Harry Met Sally* –"

"As if!" said Niamh horrified.

"No way am I sharing my make-up secrets with anyone!" added Lisa.

The wallpaper music gave way to lively thumping dance music. Nathalie glanced over at the gloomy vacant space beyond the arch and it was now bathed in bright disco lights. Through the flashing light, she could just about make out Mitch from Melbourne propped up on a stool with his entire DJ sound system.

"*So, Nathalie!*" he roared. "*This one's especially for you!*"

The sound of music and laughter and a load of people

generally having a good time filled the little restaurant. Stefano and a team of waitresses bustled about the place serving food and wine.

Then Johanne banged a spoon on her glass and called for silence. She had a few words to say.

"I'd first of all like to thank Stefano for putting on such a brilliant act earlier. He nearly had me in tears. Thanks to everyone who's had a part in our little secret and thanks to you all for coming along tonight. Nathalie, I know that sitting on your bathroom window right now is a pink alarm-clock in the shape of a teddy bear and I'd like you to know we went to quite a lot of trouble to find it for you!"

Everyone laughed and Nathalie blushed to be addressed in front of so many people. She smiled and mumbled a thank-you, suddenly aware that Mark Tierney must have been involved in this entire set-up of Johanne's and, of all the people in the room, she could feel his eyes on her.

"But, Nathalie, you didn't really think we'd just let you off with a pink alarm-clock and a chicken lettuce and mayonnaise sandwich at lunch-time? We might be cheap but we're not that cheap! We're going to give you a proper send-off. On behalf of all of us in Nutopia – and a few other hangers-on – I'd like to wish you the very best in your new life! And don't forget about us."

Then Johanne, never one for open affection or kissing, gave Nathalie a big hug and handed her a massive card.

Nathalie stared at it, overcome.

"Well, open it!" hissed Johanne.

Nathalie fumbled with the gigantic envelope and finally pulled a card from it signed by loads of people from Nutopia. Stuck on the inside was a small envelope and inside the envelope was a cheque for five hundred euro.

"It's from all of us – so you can afford the occasional night out!" said Johanne.

Nathalie was generally quite good at containing her emotions. But now she couldn't stop herself. And a whole torrent of tears splashed down on the remains of the rocket salad. Johanne passed a tissue to her and told her to pull herself together because she'd have to get up and make a little speech.

"No way!" babbled Nathalie.

"Yes way! It will be good practice for when you're in the Four Courts." Johanne poked her painfully in the ribs. "And be quick about it. That Mark Tierney is giving you awful queer looks. Are you sure he's a barrister? He looks more like a barman. Come on! Hurry up!"

Nathalie shuffled to her feet and turned around to face the gathered crowd. They were all there to give her a good send off. Even Gretta Price – who was probably delighted to see the back of her. They'd pooled their money and given her a going-away present beyond her wildest dreams. They'd given up their night – to spend it with her – and she realised at that moment that she would never ever again come across a grander set of people.

"*Speech!*" Dylan shouted and everyone laughed.

"You're next!" Johanne shouted down to him.

Nathalie glanced around the room, from Mr O'Flaherty in his casual gear to Gretta in her red siren's dress, from rowdy Dylan to Niamh and Lisa. At the end of the room Felicity was smiling up at her, nodding encouragingly. Then her eyes came to rest on Mark Tierney sitting next to his girlfriend. He was leaning back lazily in his chair and their eyes met for the briefest of moments. She swallowed and opened her mouth to speak but for a moment she could make no sound. Mark shifted in his chair, took a sip of wine from his glass, then leaned forward and winked at her – just as he had done the very first day she'd met him. Then he gave her the thumbs-up sign and she smiled nervously at him.

"I don't know what to say – this is just about the nicest thing that's ever happened to me. I really don't deserve it and all I can say is thank you all very much. I will put the money to good use. I promise. And I really will miss everyone at Nutopia. I'm not going to say anything else because I'm no good at speeches. But have a great evening and thanks a million again."

Everyone clapped and cheered and Dylan and his gang whistled and Mark Tierney winked cheekily at her again. She wished he wouldn't, because it was having quite an odd effect on her. And if she was the sort to waste her time drawing up her own list of the Ten Most Shaggable Men, a strange and deliciously warm knot at the pit of her stomach made her suddenly realise that Mark Tierney would most probably be very near the top of that list. But as she watched him disappear into the night with Zoe, she realised she would never have the courage to tell him.

CHAPTER 28

Yvonne stood in front of the mirror in the sitting-room putting the finishing touches to her make-up. She'd had her hair restyled, highlights touched up – for the price of a few legs of spring lamb. She was wearing black jersey-silk trousers and an ivory and coral-pink silk top. The trousers fitted well and in recent weeks she'd managed to lose a few pounds. She felt she had recaptured some of the sassy swagger of her twenties and thirties. She sprayed herself with a dash of Nathalie's Hugo Boss perfume and applied a final coating of new crimson lipstick to her lips. The lipstick had set her back the price of another leg of lamb and, when she thought about that, she smiled wickedly.

Liam was sitting in his favourite armchair, clutching the remote control like a life-support system. What would happen, she wondered, if he accidentally let it fall? Would it bring on some kind of cardiac arrest or neurological collapse? He even brought it with him to the toilet. She'd watched him many times – the routine was always the same. He'd stand up, press the mute button and then take the remote control with him – leaving Yvonne and Nathalie staring at a silent screen – like they just didn't exist when he was out of the room.

Well, he could have it permanently welded to his chest now for all she cared. She would never sit in the same room with him again – except when Nathalie was around. Where Nathalie was concerned, no sacrifice was too great for Yvonne Kelly.

She smoothed down her blouse, fixed two pearl studs into her ears and picked up her handbag – which matched the new pair of black suede slingbacks that she had bought in Arnotts for six legs of lamb.

He was hopping manically from channel to channel, never staying at the same channel for longer than thirty seconds. He'd been doing it for the past hour. Thank God she didn't have to put up with it.

"I'm going out," she said.

"Grand."

"Don't wait up for me."

"Fair enough."

She stopped briefly at the door. "See you so."

"Grand."

As she slammed the door, she thought she heard him say something, but dismissed the thought. What could he possibly have to say? What did it matter now anyway?

Yvonne was on her way to Sheehy's Shack, a restaurant cum hotel just a few miles out in the suburbs.

She was planning to commit adultery.

Adultery! She said the word over and over in her head, hoping that the sheer awfulness of it would sink in and that she would turn back for home, safe from her inner sinner. But it sounded quite a harmless little word – adultery – more like an inoffensive sort of embroidery or a very routine chemical process. It sounded like some initiation rite you underwent before becoming a real adult. It did not sound at all like going to meet a married man in a hotel with the sole purpose of having mad abandoned sex with him. She thought of Alan Halvey and wondered quite clinically what he would look like in the naked state. It occurred to her that he might not have the same broad chunkiness of her husband, but she pushed the thought aside. What did her husband's chunkiness matter now? Was she doing him wrong? No, she wasn't! It might say 'husband' on the marriage certificate but he'd long ago ceased to fulfil that function. Husband! Now there was another word with a peculiar ring to it.

She drove along in the semi-darkness, feeling more like someone about to attend a mildly interesting sales conference than a woman about to betray her husband. In the car park of Sheehy's Shack, she checked her make-up in the mirror. Then she crunched across the gravelled forecourt in her black suede slingbacks and passed through the revolving doors. Alan Halvey sat on a sofa in the foyer nursing a drink. He was dressed in impeccable casuals. His thinning light-brown hair was neatly cropped and his hands were clean and well manicured. He was wearing quite a lot of aftershave.

He stood to welcome her. "I didn't think you'd come."

"Yes, well – here I am. As promised."

"How about a drink before we eat?"

Yvonne ordered a large gin and tonic and sipped first, then gulped, as they made awkward stilted conversation about the traffic, the decor of the hotel and the impressiveness of the menu. After a while, a waitress came and led them to a secluded table in a shadowy corner of the dining-room. A bottle of champagne instantly arrived.

"How nice!"

"I thought a glass of champagne would get us in the party mood."

"Yes, of course."

She knocked back a glass very quickly, the bubbles doing their best to effervesce up her nose. She ordered sole and he ordered beef. She couldn't help noticing that he had a funny exaggerated way of chewing as if his food was too hot. Sometimes he chewed so hard his jaw clicked.

But apart from that, he was good company. He had an endless store of funny little stories from his early years in the bank. He laughed a lot and teased the waitress in a nice, harmless sort of way. He asked Yvonne loads of questions about herself – not too personal. What did she think of Italian food? Had she really not been to The United States? He was interested in hearing about Nathalie, especially about her decision to study for a Law degree.

Between his easy company and the heady wine atmosphere, Yvonne found herself rambling on more than she should.

"Sorry. I'm probably boring you," she said eventually.

"Not at all! You would never bore me!" he said and brushed the palm of his hand over hers.

Instantly the atmosphere shifted. They both fell silent.

"God, I fancy you so much!" he murmured.

His voice sounded like hungry gravel, she thought – of which of course there was no such thing. Hungry gravel!

Yvonne straightened up, then stiffened. This was it then! Adultery! She tried to grasp the terrifying enormity of it all but instead found herself wondering if she ought to slip into the bathroom to reapply her lipstick. It might have set her back the price of a decent leg of lamb but she was sure it hadn't survived the meal.

While she was agonising about her lipstick, Alan reached beneath the table and slid his hand deftly along her thigh. His light brown eyes bored into hers now, transmitting all his lustful longings across the table at her. She tried to gaze back at him – to transmit all her own lustful longings right back at him. Surely the smouldering eruption of lust was only a matter of pupil-dilating psychic telepathy now. In a moment, they would both rise from the table in a whirling storm of base animal hunger and somehow find themselves in a darkened room ripping the clothes from one another with ease.

Perhaps she really ought to fix that lipstick first. If he saw her without the lipstick he might take flight – and she didn't want that to happen. Or perhaps she should wait for the whirling storm of animal hunger first. She deliberated on these weighty matters while still trying to transmit looks of lustful longing.

"Come on! Let's go!" he rasped.

"OK." She had intended to rasp huskily right back but instead her "OK!" sounded more like the squeak of a mouse.

He took her by the hand and led her upstairs.

In the executive-size room, he sat on the edge of the bed and pulled her towards him, sliding his hands skilfully beneath her cream and coral-pink blouse. Yvonne stood obediently while he quickly set to work on the little buttons. Perhaps she in return ought to be doing something sexy with her hands. She'd quite forgotten what to do. Should she kneel and kiss him or pull his face to her breasts? Maybe she ought to start undoing the buckle of his belt. That would be a clear statement of intent. But where was the whirling storm of lust that was supposed to have engulfed her by now? She felt nothing other than a mild sense of impatience. And a need to use the loo. Then she remembered the lipstick. There was also the matter of perfume. If she wanted to seriously get in the mood for adultery, perhaps she should pop into the bathroom and splash on some more scent? Not to mention the problem of the red lace and satin Agent Provocateur thong (three legs of lamb – boned and stuffed) she'd bought specially for the occasion. She hadn't really got the hang of wearing it properly and the damn thing had been cutting into her all evening.

Alan's experienced fingers had finally undone the twenty or so tiny buttons on her blouse and loosened the straps of her bra. Now amid some whispered murmurings which she couldn't quite make sense of, he turned his very focussed attention to the zip of her black jersey-silk trousers.

"Just a moment," she said and dived into the bathroom before he could progress any further.

She had a quick pee, then fixed up her hair, reapplied the crimson lipstick yet again and splashed on some more Hugo Boss. She eyed herself steadily in the mirror. There was no question of turning back. Alan Halvey fancied the thong off her. He was an attentive, interesting and reasonably handsome man. He was bound to be a fantastic lover. And a fantastic lover was just what she wanted, what she needed, and what she so desperately lacked. To be honest she also desperately lacked an attentive and interesting companion. Life is short, she told herself. Seize the moment! Remember all those women on the *Titanic* who turned down the dessert trolley.

She hadn't quite expected to find him stark naked when she returned to the room. But there he was spread-eagled across the bedspread, an erection pointing slightly heavenwards.

He stretched out his arms. "Undress for me!"

Yvonne slipped out of her blouse and bra and loosened her trousers, letting them fall to the floor. Then she stood uneasily in front of him, trying to tug discreetly at the thong that was now threatening to slice her most delicate parts in two.

"Let me remove that for you," he said, pulling her to him once more and expertly flipping the thong off her.

She lay down beside him on the bed, eagerly waiting for the whirling storm of lust – which must be only moments away now. She let him kiss her hotly on the lips. She didn't resist when his hands shot off busily in all directions. She closed her eyes, caressed his shoulders, nibbled his ear, and trailed her lips on his neck. She bent over him to plant little butterfly kisses on his chest – like she used to do to Liam.

But just at that moment she saw a little black shiny thing peeping out from beneath the *Gideon Bible* and the *Koran*. In an instant and before she even realised fully what she was doing herself, Yvonne was backing away from a desperately confused and deeply dismayed Alan Halvey.

"What's up? What's wrong?"

"Nothing," she panted as she began to struggle with the blasted thong, ending up with the thing on back to front. "You're very nice – but I have to go."

"I don't get it."

Mercifully her bra didn't get twisted as she put it on. "Thanks for the dinner and the champagne and everything. Sorry. I just can't do this." She wriggled clumsily into her trousers, and pulled on the silk blouse quickly tugging it across her breast – to hell with all those buttons.

He had pulled the sheet up over himself and was scowling slightly. "You could have timed it better. I mean, leading a bloke on like that!"

She slipped into the six-lamb-leg slingbacks. "Yes, I know. I am really, really sorry. We can still be friends, can't we?"

Strangely that didn't seem to placate him but there seemed no point in prolonging the conversation and she backed out of the room as quickly as she could.

She drove home slowly, her mind racing with a tangle of unpleasant thoughts. She was annoyed with herself for chickening out of what could have been a sizzling night of pleasure, embarrassed for having gone as far as getting all her clothes off in front of an equally naked colleague, confused at her own complete lack of sexual feeling of any kind. Finally – and there was no easy way of telling herself this – she was deeply ashamed. Her cheeks, her whole body burnt with it. Yvonne Kelly – who had never done anything more shameful than forgetting to put her newspapers in the green recycling bin – had stood willingly on the brink of wanton wickedness.

What stopped her? What brought her to her senses?

The remote control – that's what! When she spied it, shiny and black, peeping out from beneath the *Gideon Bible*, it reminded her of the sullen, bad-tempered man she'd left sitting at home, zapping from channel to channel. And just at the moment when she should have been getting down and dirty with Alan Halvey, she had an image of Liam Kelly innocently propped in his armchair like an abandoned sprouting potato zapping constantly from one channel to the next. And though she still felt murderous fury at him, though she might still bury her best meat cleaver in him sometime very soon, she felt horribly ashamed – and a faint twinge of something else as well. It took her the entire journey to identify the feeling, not even a feeling – little more than a fleeting sensation. But by the time she turned the car into the cul-de-sac where they lived, she'd figured it out.

Yvonne pitied her poor uncommunicative spud of a husband.

CHAPTER 29

Aoife sat facing Claire in a tiny wooden alcove of the pub. Her chin was tucked in, her mouth pursed and her eyebrows raised. She didn't quite have her arms folded but her whole expression and body language conveyed disappointment and disapproval. She was glad to note that Claire was squirming. "So. . . how did you find out?" Claire muttered, making slow circles on the table with a beermat.

"Let's just say I guessed."

"You mean . . . you didn't actually *see* anything?"

"Didn't have to."

"Oh. So I suppose you want to hear the details then?" The nerve of the woman!

"It would probably be best."

"Well, OK. Right. Dermot and I . . ." Claire stopped and glanced at her friend anxiously.

"Yes?" Aoife said coldly, determined not to make it easy for her. Despite the fact that she didn't really care about Dermot, treachery was still treachery – especially where boyfriends were concerned.

"Well, we've always got on well together. There's the whole rock music thing and guitar jamming and all that . . ."

"Just get to the point!"

"I'll be honest with you, Aoife –"

Aoife snorted dismissively. Honest! Huh! She sipped from a glass of Cidona.

"Dermot's been your boyfriend for over a year and you've treated him like shit! I mean, keeping him hanging on all that time – just until someone better comes along. You've cancelled dates at a moment's notice and sometimes even not turned up. I've even seen you out with Dermot and flirting with other men – right under his nose. Is it any wonder that you've lost him?"

Aoife raised an eyebrow. She hadn't quite envisaged the conversation taking this turn. Gothic Claire who thought *Interview with a Vampire* was the most romantic movie she'd ever seen, Gothic Claire who liked to clean up old graveyards at the weekend *and who stole people's boyfriends* – having the nerve to give Aoife Joyce lectures on morality.

"I'm pure sick of everyone telling me how badly I've treated Dermot. And how dare you! I've never flirted with another man in front of Dermot!"

Claire gave her a funny look and instantly Aoife realised that she'd walked right into a rather unpleasant admission about herself.

Claire examined raven-black varnished nails, twirled her silver ring with the antique bone-resin hooded skull of the Grim Reaper and observed her colleague with frank blue eyes. "So we spent quite a few evenings together a few months back – Dermot and I."

"Tell me something I haven't guessed already."

Claire slid the Grim Reaper ring up and down her finger distractedly.

"But then, I sort of lost touch with him. There was this rare old headstone out in an old graveyard near Enfield that was in danger of collapsing if someone didn't do something about it – and I got all caught up in trying to rescue that."

"Has anyone ever told you how truly, madly weird you are!" Aoife said by way of a cutting remark.

Claire shrugged. "This is me – I can't really be anyone else. I don't want to be anyone else. Anyway – I didn't see much of Dermot for a while. Then one evening a few weeks ago, I was on my way to a concert in Smithfield when I saw him."

"And that was when you pounced?"

"What? I was going to see Haunted Hearse when I saw him sitting outside a bar, sipping from a glass of wine. I was just about to wave across to him when I noticed his companion. It was an older man – very well dressed – a bit flamboyant – you know the sort of thing – wide-brimmed fedora hat, cream linen suit and spats – some sort of pink patterned tie."

"So?" Aoife said, a vague uneasy memory stirring at the back of her mind.

"So – the man took Dermot's hand in his and kissed it and then leaned across and kissed Dermot and they were both smiling and gazing into one another's eyes." Claire looked at Aoife anxiously. "I'm really sorry to be the one to tell you this. I've put off telling you – but it's best you should know."

Aoife pushed at the cuticles on her nails as she struggled to comprehend this new information and strained to recall the memory that was niggling at the back of her mind. There was a long silence between them.

Then finally Aoife cleared her throat and spoke. "So – you and Dermot – you haven't been carrying on behind my back . . ."

Now it was Claire's turn to look gobsmacked. "What?"

"Um, you and Dermot . . . I thought . . ."

Claire glared at Aoife. "Is *that* what you thought? How could you! I would never do a thing like that! Not on a friend! Even one who isn't nice to her boyfriend! I thought you knew that!"

Claire's brilliant blue eyes blazed indignantly at her and Aoife suddenly felt quite small.

"I'm sorry," Aoife said shamefacedly. "I just got hold of the wrong end of the stick. But maybe this all explains why Dermot's gone missing. I've often seen gay men admiring him – he has that kind of lean and interesting appeal. I just never got the faintest hint that he might be that way. I mean – in bed and – Claire, he was absolute dynamite in bed – even though I didn't fancy him all that much . . ." She trailed off as she remembered the little thing that was niggling at her. On the night that Dermot had stood her up in the Purple Pepper when she'd got drunk on Cosmopolitans and taken a taxi to the station – she had seen a man in a fedora sitting with someone vaguely familiar, holding his hand, sitting close together and gazing in each other's eyes, just as Claire was describing now. Now she realised it was the back of Dermot's neck she'd been looking at. And then a new thought occurred to her. "But this means he was deceiving me all along. All along he was at least bisexual and he never told me. Then I don't feel so bad about how I've treated him and maybe in the back of my mind there was something stopping me from getting too involved."

Claire laughed. "You always manage to turn things round to justify your own behaviour!"

Aoife shrugged. She was still struggling to take in the news about Dermot. And she wasn't at all happy with the way he'd lied to her.

CHAPTER 30

Yvonne donned an overall and rubber gloves and spent longer than usual cleaning the kitchen. She wiped down the counters carefully and spent ages working on a stubborn tea-stain near the toaster. Then she started on the oven. She filled a basin with hot soapy water and set to work on a couple of stubborn stains inside. She was glad that the visit had gone well but she was harbouring some negative feelings too.

The girls had arrived a little late, giggling and squabbling about how they had got lost on the way.

They had told the story over lunch much to everyone's amusement . . .

Berry's battered Toyota had scuttled and juddered round the Walkinstown Roundabout like a decrepit old tin crab. She couldn't quite remember which one of the seven hundred and eighty-four exits she should take for

Glennstown. And Aoife was less than useless – parked on the passenger seat, her head thrown back, her mouth wide open letting out the occasional truncated snore.

When they passed the Windhover Pub for what seemed like the tenth time Berry noticed that a crowd in the lounge were standing at the window and laughing at them.

"Here goes," she said, swerving quickly into the outside lane and making a hasty exit onto a busy road that she hoped would lead her in the general direction of Glennstown. It brought her directly into an old industrial estate.

Berry nudged her sister.

"Whasup?" Aoife said sleepily.

"We're lost!"

Aoife sat up straight and looked around her. "Have you no sense of direction? How could you get lost? I showed you exactly how to get here on the map."

"Well – you didn't have to fall asleep. I mean you must be the only person in the world who falls asleep in a car before the engine even starts running. It's ridiculous."

Aoife glared at her sister and tutted loudly. "I can't help falling asleep. You could have woken me. Here – go up to the end of that road there and take a sharp left."

Quite a while later, Yvonne was welcoming them warmly while they babbled their excuses for being so late. She beamed proudly when they admired her front garden, which although it was autumn was still bright with splashes of pink and white and purple dahlias and chrysanthemums.

In the large extended kitchen, Liam Kelly welcomed the guests and Nathalie poured drinks. They all sat around the big old oak table that Liam had salvaged from a semi-derelict house and restored, and tucked into delicious roast lamb. Yvonne had produced her best china, the linen cloth Nathalie had brought home from a trip to France, and her canteen of best Newbridge cutlery. Aoife tucked into the food hungrily and smiled gratefully at Yvonne.

Surprisingly Liam rose to the occasion and was in almost cheerful humour. He chatted away to Berry about Bloomfield House and his builder's knowledge of it. He even offered to travel to Larkhaven and do some roof repairs at the end of the season when he wasn't so busy. Then he talked about some of the houses he'd worked on, and the strange things people asked him to do to their homes. He told them about the owner who had insisted he knock down every interior wall of an old Victorian house so that what remained was one massive room with a huge balcony. And about the minor film star who wanted the entire back garden of his Sandymount home covered over in glass.

Yvonne couldn't ignore the youthful glint in his normally steely blue eyes as he lapped up the attention of her two nieces. She felt an odd emotion and couldn't quite identify it at first – a strange unpleasant knot in her stomach, a sense that the ground wasn't quite firm beneath her feet. But as she carefully cut slices in a newly baked rhubarb tart, it came to her. She was jealous. Looking across the room at her husband, she recognised how very handsome he was still, noticed how Berry chatted easily to him, saw how their presence seemed to shake years off him. And after all he was only fifty-two, not much older than Bruce Willis and in her opinion –

though she wouldn't normally admit it – a lot better-looking.

But she'd lost him. Somewhere in the middle of all the carefully laundered shirts, the perfectly executed roast-lamb dinners, the melt-in-the-mouth apple-pies, the lovingly maintained house, she'd lost her husband. It was clear he didn't love her any more. And even if he still had a scrap of affection left for her, it wouldn't be for long. Not when she'd tell him about her sordid little thong-twisting adventure in Sheehy's Shack with Alan Halvey. What devil had driven her to even think about such a grubby escapade – let alone embark on it? In the weeks since it had happened, she'd barely slept a wink, going over and over her own foolishness every night as she lay in bed. Liam Kelly might go down in the *Guinness Book of Records* as the world's most murderable husband, but that didn't give her the right to betray him with another man, a man who when the chips were down and the Y-fronts were off didn't measure up in any way to her own husband. So she'd made up her mind to tell him this very evening – after the guests had left, when Nathalie was out with Johanne. Come what may, she'd tell him the truth. There was no question of not telling him. She would simply not be able to live with the guilt. Of course it would mean the complete end of their marriage and it would be entirely her own fault. Why couldn't she have muddled on in sullen silence with him – for Nathalie's sake if nothing else? Now the person who would really suffer was the one person who was entirely blameless, their daughter.

Now that the girls had left and Nathalie had gone along

to stay with Johanne overnight, and the kitchen was almost clean and everything tidied neatly away, Yvonne carried on with cleaning the oven and sighed deeply.

Liam pottered about mending a door handle and then sorting through a few bills. He even made one or two attempts at normal conversation.

"Nice girls. They've turned out very well. A credit to your sister."

Even though they were his nieces, Yvonne was shocked by her own jealousy at the attention he'd paid the younger women. So she said nothing and carried on scouring.

"I'm glad she's going to college after all. She's doing the right thing. You can see her confidence growing already," he continued.

It was a revolutionary statement coming from him and under normal circumstances she might have paid it more attention – but she had too much else on her mind. "I suppose."

"And the dinner was lovely. You did a grand job."

"It was just lamb and a rhubarb tart."

"But it was grand all the same."

She put down the steel-wool pad and gave one last careful wipe to the inside of the oven. Then she washed her hands at the sink and dried them and rubbed in some handcream.

"Well, if that's everything, I think I'll go for a walk," he said, reaching for his coat.

She turned around to face him.

"There's something we need to talk about," she said, removing her apron and straightening her hair needlessly.

"We can talk about it when I get back. But if I don't go for a walk now, I might be too tired to bother later."

"We need to talk now. We need to sit down together at this table and talk right now."

Her voice wobbled fearfully. She thought about postponing the awful moment but knew she couldn't. This thing had been festering away for too long. For the past couple of years it had rotted and corrupted their marriage. The only solution was to have it out and go their separate ways and pick up what was left of their individual lives.

He seemed to recognise the desperation in her voice because he hung his coat back on the rack and sat down awkwardly at the table.

She sat facing him. "There's something I have to tell you." Well, it wasn't a very original line – more like something out of a soap opera. But then wasn't their marriage a soap opera lately anyway?

"This sounds serious," he said, a vague hint of apprehension in his voice. His handsome features were set grimly.

Where to begin? She struggled to find the right place to start and regretted not having thought out what she was going to say more carefully. Should she go on the attack and tell him that his cold sullenness had driven her to the brink of adultery? Or should she just tell him their marriage was over because they might as well admit they didn't love each other any more and because she'd been unfaithful.

"You . . . that is, I . . . we don't seem to be able to . . . I mean, it seems to me that you don't care any more . . . and I feel so lonely and that's why I . . ." She took a deep breath and plunged in. "You never show me any affection . . . or talk to me . . . I heard more out of you today at the dinner table with Berry and Aoife and Nathalie than you've said to me over the last six months . . . so is it any wonder that I . . ."

She stopped. He was looking across at her with a pained expression. Did he already know what was coming? But how could he know? His usually expressionless eyes were wide with concern and even – could it be? – sadness? Well, yes – the end of any marriage is sad. Of course he would be sad. After all, he wasn't a completely heartless monster.

"Go on," he said expressionlessly. "I'm listening."

"I've had an involvement with another man."

He barely flinched, just the slightest tensing of his hand. "When?"

"Just recently. In Sheehy's Shack."

"How long did it last?"

"Well, there was a few drinks, then dinner, then . . ." She swallowed. "Then we went up to the bedroom . . . we got undressed . . ."

"Did you have sex with him?"

"I was going to – but when I was lying beside him on the bed – I –" She stopped suddenly.

She wanted to tell him how awful he was to live with, how cold he was, how completely lacking in sympathy or affection, how she dreamed about leaving him, sometimes even shamefully wished him dead or at least far away in another galaxy. She wanted to list out exactly how many shirts she'd laundered, how many roast lamb dinners she'd sweated over, how many times she'd painted and decorated the house, the hours she'd spent tending the garden so that it was the finest plot in the road, the nights in bed when she'd lain awake longing for him to show that he still needed her. But his face was dark and clouded, his shoulders tense with emotion. He studied his hands and would not look up at her. After all the years of being rejected and taken for granted she ought to have felt quite pleased at this moment – now that she'd finally hurt him back. But instead she felt horribly cheap and petty. She'd planned to say that she didn't love him any more and that there was no sense in staying together just for Nathalie's sake, that she would pack her things and be gone in the morning, that she could stay with her mother in Killester until she found a place of her own. But, suddenly, she couldn't find the words.

Silence hung in the air, threatening to descend and suffocate them like a cloud of poisonous anthrax. Here they were, two people who'd travelled the biggest part of their lives together, now hovering fearfully on the brink of separation.

Yvonne was suddenly frozen with horror for what she'd almost done.

"Then I suppose it's time I told you something too," he said.

"What?" she asked, startled.

"Something I should have told you long ago."

He was not a drinking man. He liked a glass of wine with Sunday lunch and an occasional pint of stout in the pub on a Friday evening. Now he got up and poured two stiff brandies into her best crystal and slid one glass slowly across the table to her. They sat together sipping the brandy in silence. He didn't look at her.

She'd never seen a man in such anguish and it distressed her more deeply than she could have imagined. It was obvious what was coming next. He would tell her about some woman he'd loved from way back and how he was sorry but he still loved this woman and still saw her and made love to her, and got gravy recipes from her. He would apologise for his coldness and he would agree that the best thing for them to do now was to separate.

She took a large gulp of brandy.

"I knew I never deserved your love," he said quietly. "I don't know why or how you were stupid enough to marry me."

She had to admit it was an unusual approach and answered without thinking. "I thought you were the finest man I'd ever met. Until lately I've never even looked at another man."

"But this house, a tiny garden you can hardly swing a cat in, cheap holidays in tacky Spanish resorts, I've given you nothing for Christ's sake!" Now the emotion was forcing its way through his voice. "You could fit three of these houses into your parent's bungalow." His voice was harsh and bitter. "I hate the front garden – I hate everything you've done to it because it makes me feel guilty. And I hate the back garden even more."

Yvonne knocked back the last of her brandy. The conversation was taking an odd turn. She wasn't quite sure where it was leading, not at all sure how she should react, except to be deeply hurt by his comments about the garden. Perhaps he was building up to saying how he hated her most of all and how that had driven him back into the arms of his one true love.

"I detest this house," he continued. "I'm ashamed of it."

"What?"

That was going a bit far surely! And where was the

halting confession about a mistress, where was the strangled plea to be allowed to leave, the declaration that he could not do his duty without the help and support of the woman he loved? The woman who had clearly given him the recipe for redcurrent-jelly gravy and crispy roast potatoes!

"Ashamed! Why?"

"Because it's all I've ever been able to give you and Nathalie. I've been a complete let-down to you, Yvonne – I know that. If you'd married Guy Bushell like your father wanted, you'd probably be living in a grand house in Malahide now. You'd be in the tennis club and the golf club and the yacht club. You'd have posh friends and your children would be in the best schools. You'd have a villa in Portugal and you'd spend your weekends going to dinner parties and charity balls. And what have I dragged you both down to? This miserable little box!"

He flung the glass on the floor he'd tiled with some Liscannor slate that had been left over from a big restoration job.

Yvonne was stunned into silence by these revelations but the sound of her best crystal glass shattering on the slate floor brought her to her senses.

"I haven't a clue what's going on with you," she said crossly. "And not that it makes any difference now – since the marriage is as good as over – but for your information, I love this 'little box' as you call it. I love my front garden and I love my back garden even more. And if I lived in the biggest mansion on Howth Head, I'd never have neighbours like these. And some of the best times we've had were on holidays in Spain. I don't like tennis and I absolutely hate golf. As for sailing – crossing the

Ha'penny Bridge gives me motion sickness. And why would I want to live in a bigger house? It's hard enough keeping order on the one I have. As for a villa in Portugal – yeah, well, I'll grant you, I wouldn't say no to that. It's not the house or the life I'm unhappy with – it's you! You and your coldness, your indifference, your complete lack of affection, the way you sometimes even try to avoid me – how the last nice thing you said to me was 'Did you get your hair done?' three years ago before your mother's funeral!"

"That's not true!" he said, aggrieved. "You were all dressed up a few weeks ago and as you were going I called after you that you looked real sexy."

Yvonne could feel herself turning a nauseating shade of green. It was the night she'd gone to commit adultery with Alan Halvey, dressed in a slinky killer top, hip-skimming jersey pants and brothel underwear. It shamed her now to be reminded of her grubby vanity. Because that's all it was – a sordid little ego trip – something to make her feel good about herself – only it had ended up having exactly the opposite effect. And now she felt like the cheapest old slapper in town.

"Anyway, you don't seem to care one scrap about me. So is there someone else or not?" she said, going half-heartedly on the attack.

He stared, then reached over and touched her hand – briefly, a fleeting gesture, so quick she thought she'd dreamt it. "Don't be daft. Who else would put up with a contrary bastard like me?"

It was true. She wasn't about to contradict him. She probably deserved a medal for endurance.

"So," she said at last, "is that it then? Is that the

'something' you should have told me long ago? That you hate our house? That you hate our garden? That you hate our life together?"

"Of course not! I'm sorry . . . I'm telling it all back to front . . . but then I never was a talker."

"So there's something else?"

"Yes," he answered heavily.

While he poured two more brandies, she began to imagine all sorts of dreadful possibilities. And she remembered with a shudder some of the stories she'd heard over the years. Petite Kathleen Sheelin's six-foot-four husband owned up to being a transvestite after fifteen years of seemingly perfect wedded bliss, and only when she found a pair of extra ginormous sequinned Wolford stockings in the laundry basket. Josie McKenna first learned that her husband was a compulsive gambler when the debtors came round one morning and cleaned out her house. Yvonne didn't think Liam would be that interested in dressing up as a woman. He had no interest in dressing up full stop. As for gambling, every penny he earned was put into a joint account. Every penny he spent was carefully accounted for. He was the type that still believed in saving for a rainy day.

She watched him anxiously, fearful of the revelations to come. By tomorrow she would be gone and they could begin the slow and painful process of dismantling their marriage. And in a sense it didn't matter what he told her now. But all the same, it would only add to the hurt if she discovered he'd been living some kind of sordid lie throughout their married life.

"Something happened a long time ago . . ." he began, then stopped, struggling to say the words.

Then, and she really thought the brandy was causing

her to hallucinate now, a huge tear rolled down his cheek, splashing onto the oak table. He brushed at it roughly with his hand and then his entire body began to shudder and he buried his face in his hands.

She leapt to his side, wrapped her arms about his broad shoulders, and kissed the top of his close-cropped blond hair.

"I'm so sorry," she said. "I feel cheap and horrible. If it makes you feel any better – it was a truly humiliating experience and honestly nothing happened. He wasn't anything like you and in the end I couldn't do it to you. But I don't blame you for being hurt and angry."

It was becoming almost unbearable. She longed for their old life of sullen monosyllabic conversation back. She longed for him to just stop weeping and do a few unnecessary jobs around the house or even hide behind his newspaper.

He put her hand to his mouth and kissed it. "How can I get it into that head of yours that this is nothing at all to do with your night in Sheehy's Shack? And no, it doesn't make me feel better to think of any man humiliating you or making you feel bad. This is something else altogether and I'm trying to tell you but I just can't find the words right now."

What happened next was a bit fuzzy, probably because of the two brandies, but in what seemed like nothing more than a second, Liam was holding her tightly in his arms and kissing her with more tenderness than she could have imagined possible. He stroked her hair, caressed her cheeks, then with an intense gentleness that took her breath away, he kissed her softly on the lips.

"God, I love you so much, Yvonne," he murmured

huskily in her ears. "I've never stopped loving you, never wanted to be with anyone else, will never want to be with anyone else – and I don't want to lose you – ever!"

Yvonne was experiencing a tidal wave of conflicting emotions, feelings that had been half-buried with time – confusion, suspicion, sympathy, warmth, affection – love.

Love!

What the hell was that about?

She'd been about to announce their imminent divorce.

Could it be that she did still love him after all? And what was this oddly familiar warm sensation that was flooding through her body and driving all conscious thought from her mind? Might it be a hot flush? She was deeply unsure and confused, especially when she found her hands sliding up beneath her husband's freshly laundered cotton shirt and caressing his smooth hard chest. Then the years of frustrated longing melted away as he carried her up the stairs and laid her gently on the bed. She remembered now why she had longed so deeply for him even after years of marriage. He'd always loved her with a mixture of rough impatience and tender coaxing. It made her feel beautiful and deeply loved.

Afterwards she lay in the crook of his arm and told him that she could never love anyone else. She apologised again for having any involvement with another man.

"Hardly an involvement," he said dismissively. "And there's nothing to forgive. I know I drove you to it."

"Will we survive, do you think? Or is this just a parting gesture?"

He didn't answer for a long while. "There's something I have to do. And perhaps then, when you know the full truth, you'll be more than happy to see the back of me."

"Why can't you tell me now?"

His face clouded over. "I need to go somewhere and find out something once and for all first."

"Well, what is it?" she asked stupidly. "Can't you tell me? I am your wife."

He sighed deeply and his steely blue eyes bored into hers. "No," he said quickly. "I don't want to involve you. When I come back I'll tell you everything. And whatever the outcome, I promise to put it out of my mind forever."

Did he think she was a complete fool – with all this mystery baloney? Yes, of course he was leaving. He'd made love to her with such tenderness it had to be just for old times' sake. He would go away and never come back. Cora Fennessy's husband had popped out for a bag of Maltesers and the next she'd heard was a postcard from Brazil two years later asking her to post out his old Italia 90 jersey and his collection of Phil Collins CDs.

"Can't you just tell me what it is now? Why do you have to go away anywhere?"

He shook his head.

"How long will you be gone?" She regretted even asking. It sounded needy somehow. But after all she was his wife and if he was going to slip off to South America or someplace she had the right to know. Nathalie had the right to know.

"I don't know," he said.

CHAPTER 31

"Berry – I'm expecting a whole crop of stuff, offers of marriage from here, there and everywhere next week," Harry Robson teased as he slurped loudly through the froth on his cappuccino.

"More fool them," Berry said. She wasn't really paying him much attention. She was bent over the desk calculating the extent of her debts. She didn't go in for hair-pulling and gnashing of teeth – but if she had she'd have been utterly bald and toothless by now.

Patricia de Vere made a grand entrance in the afternoon and huddled over a screen for almost an hour before paying her bill and progressing grandly out onto the street.

Then Ben put in a brief appearance, drank a cup of coffee and sent a few emails.

Berry eyed him curiously. She'd been so busy over the past week that she had been forced to put his garbled tale of robbery and assault and prison to the back of her mind.

Ought she to raise it with him now? *Oh, by the way, Ben –
or is it Bernard/ – I was just wondering about that old actual
bodily harm thing – I mean, any chance you explain it all to me
over a coffee in the Bayview later?* No – it wasn't a topic of
conversation that could be broached that casually. And
then there was that most fleeting of kisses on the landing
the night he'd brought Aoife home. Berry had done her
best to forget about it – but found herself thinking about
it more than was wise.

One or two other stragglers came and went. But by
five o'clock it was just Berry and Harry again and the
background hum of computers.

"Any on-line brides today?" she said, forcing a joke as
Harry stood at the counter to pay his bill.

"As if!" he said, grinning rakishly at her. "Harry
Robson doesn't go looking for women – the women come
looking for me."

"Yes, I've noticed a steady stream of admirers."

"Nothing more than a temporary lull while I finish my
online horticulture course. You'll see," a huge wink, "the
hottest babe in Larkhaven will be trembling with desire
for me before long."

Berry blinked in surprise. Did he mean her? A sudden
alarming thought came to her: did Harry have a secret
ulterior motive for frequenting the Surf Line? She pushed
the thought away. "No flirting with the staff," she told
him as she handed back some change.

"It's worth a try," he said easily. "By the way – that
Searson bloke?"

Berry's ears pricked up.

"Something familiar about him. I've seen him before,
I'm sure of it."

"Yeah – he was in here last week," she said, quickly trying to hide her interest.

Harry shook his head and narrowed his eyes pensively. "No – I've seen him somewhere else. It'll come to me," he said as he slipped out the door.

When he'd gone, she tidied up and cleaned down the counters. Then she considered the day's takings – a few notes and coins in the half-empty till. She set the notes in a neat pile and arranged the coins in little stacks. There it was – the entire reward for her efforts, long hours of work, abandoned social life, the numerous small but precious sacrifices she'd been making every day for the past eighteen months – all for twenty-two euro and forty-seven cents!

She felt angry with herself for having been so arrogant and proud in the face of harsh commercial realities. But above all else, she felt a suffocating sense of shame that she had squandered the little money their parents had left, funds to be used for the rainy day, or the upkeep of the house. Yet here it was – all gone – wasted on a foolish dream that had come to nothing but twenty-two euro and forty-seven cents. She would have been better off going out and blowing it all on one big Chanel ball-gown or a nice little string of diamonds. At least she'd have had the pleasure of wearing them.

She pulled the shutters down and locked up for the night.

Aoife had decided to stay in town because the big auction was to be held the following morning so Berry didn't even have the distraction of having to cook dinner. At home in the kitchen, she put the day's meagre takings away in a cupboard and sank down at the kitchen table, feeling as if some sinister force was tugging her heart down into the bowels of the earth. It would have been a relief to cry but she felt too oppressed with strain and worry to find the release of shedding a few tears. Besides, tomorrow was the weekly deadline for submitting the week's events to *The County Sentinel* and she still hadn't even begun to work through the pile of notes and emails that she had received over the past few days.

She read through the relevant emails on her laptop, relieved to see that Conor hadn't replied to her note. The more she reflected, the more she regretted having responded to him at all.

Then in the middle of a pile of spam she noticed a mail informing her that there was a problem with the server his end and there would be a delay in delivering her mail. Good, she reflected. Perhaps by the time he got her mail, he'd have gone off the whole idea of them meeting up again. If he did reply now – she'd just have to explain that after all there was simply no point in them meeting again.

She dragged out the little bundle of notes for the *Sentinel*, forcing herself to look through them. Harry Robson's sister Paula had just given birth to her second child. He was to be called Henry after his uncle. Harry would be pleased about that. A meeting of the Larkhaven Association would take place the following Saturday to protest about the granting of planning permission to global corporation HyperShop. For all the good that will do, she grumbled, as she typed the article into her laptop. There had been yet another sighting of Colin Farrell – this time with two super-models and a starlet – all scouting for a summer holiday home on the coast. John de Vere, Patricia's nephew, was named outstanding player of the year by Larkhaven GAA club. The annual parish barbeque would take place as usual on the beach and the committee was gearing up for its biggest event yet. Iris Lemon had sent in a little thank-you note on behalf of her Aunt Nancy who had been so thrilled to see her meeting with President John F Kennedy chronicled at last in the local paper.

Who cares? Berry grumbled, unable, for the first time that she could ever remember, to summon up even the slightest flicker of interest in the lives of her neighbours. Who cares about any of it? In a hundred years from now we'll all be dead and there won't be a word about us, she thought. What's the point of compiling all these silly and inconsequential stories week after week when nothing that ever happened in Larkhaven was of the slightest importance anywhere else? Even this time next year it would all be forgotten about – of interest only to future Transition Year students doing their Local History projects. She leaned on the table, burying her head in her hands.

That was the image Ben Searson saw as he passed by Berry's kitchen window. He had just been fixing a bit of loose fencing at the end of the garden and now he was heading back to the little cottage to eat a dish of pork and chillies and onions in a rich sauce of wine and tomatoes. It had been slow-cooking in the oven for the best part of three hours and the fresh air had whipped up his appetite. Now he could almost smell the aromas wafting up the avenue – like waves in a cartoon. He would stir in a few tablespoons of sour cream and chop up a few spring onions and crisp lettuce leaves– then set it all out on the kitchen table with some simple white bread and a glass or two of full-bodied Chilean wine.

But the sight of Berry with her head buried forlornly in her hands stopped him in his tracks. He felt uncomfortable in the role of secret onlooker yet he stood looking through the kitchen window for several moments, unwilling to tear himself away. He could see she was in distress, her face strained and drawn – her usual expression of cool amusement quite disappeared. He leaned forward to tap on the window but thought better of it. Embarrassment would only add to her distress.

Yet he felt compelled to do something. He made his way carefully away from the window, then walked briskly down the little avenue. The tiny cottage kitchen was warm with the smell of pork and chillies. He reached into the oven, pulled out the casserole dish and placed it on the table. Then he hurriedly chopped a few spring onions and some fresh green lettuce leaves and put them in a plastic tub. Next he took a tub of sour cream from the cramped fridge and a bottle of Chilean wine from his little home-made cellar just inside the back door. Finally he added a fresh crusty baguette to the collection.

Outside in the deepening darkness, he set everything neatly onto the front seat of the battered old Renault 4 and drove the short distance to the front door of Bloomfield House. As soon as he rang the doorbell he realised that he would have to come up with a convincing story very quickly. Berry Joyce would probably see through the most plausible and convincing of yarns.

Think! Think, for God's sake! Anyone who can come up with *'Celebrity Brazilian Wax'* and *'Celebrity What's in Your*

Attic?' would surely be able to come up with a convincing reason for landing on a woman's doorstep with an entire dinner for two just ready to be served.

He heard her footsteps along the polished wooden floor of the hall.

"Hi," he said, pasting on an apologetic smile as the door opened and he came face to face with Berry.

"Ben!" she said, struggling to look cheerful and businesslike. He could see it was a huge strain and he realised he would have to do some pretty smart lying.

"I'm really sorry about this, Berry – but I was hoping you'd be up for a little company."

"It's not really a good night, Ben. I've got stuff to do."

"Please! It doesn't happen often but I'm having a lonely moment – you know – when you just can't bear the thought of being alone. I mean I'd cooked a whole dinner and everything – but for some reason I just can't endure the thought of sitting down and eating it alone! Does that sound weird?"

"Yes – quite weird!" she said, cutting him short. "Look, if this is some sort of prelude to you and me ending up in bed – like I said earlier, it's not a good time."

"No, nothing like that," he said, reaching into the car and producing the casserole dish. "This just needs a few minutes in the oven. I'll carry it through to the kitchen and maybe you could grab the bread and wine and stuff?"

She seemed to hesitate. Aha! He'd got her.

"No, really, Ben, I –"

"And, Berry, besides . . . I want to tell you everything about me."

"Who says I want to know? Look, I'll grant you I'm

curious about your criminal record and why you had to change your name and all – but, to be honest, I've more to worry about right now."

"No – it's only right and proper that you should know," he said as he sailed past her and headed for the kitchen as if there was no question of a refusal.

Berry stared after him. Then she fetched the things from the car and shut the door. It seemed she didn't really have much choice.

"I have to keep busy," he said by way of explanation as he bustled about the kitchen, setting out places at the big old pine table, slicing the bread, uncorking the wine and pouring her a hefty glass. "I've been advised it's the best way to put the past behind me."

Temporarily distracted from her woes, Berry watched in fascination as an entire dinner appeared on the table.

"I hope you don't think I'm being rude," she said, "but I'm not really hungry."

"You don't have to eat anything. Just take a little on the plate to humour me," he said, spooning some of the succulent meat and chilli sauce onto her plate.

It did smell delicious and without even realising she'd reached for a thick wedge of bread and was dipping it in the sauce.

He held up his glass. "Cheers! Here's to the future!" he said.

"The future!" she said, meeting his dark eyes across the table, suddenly feeling drawn to him, a wild reckless hunger sweeping through her body – like a condemned prisoner calling for the last and most scrumptious meal of her life. She wanted at least one nice perfect thing to happen before life was snatched away from her and she plunged into grotesque poverty and sleeping in doorways. So what if he was a violent criminal?

But oddly enough for a man who had mentioned only a few days ago how he'd been thinking of talking her into bed, now he seemed quite cool and distant in that respect. He met the sudden and hungry invitation in her eyes with a cool, reserved smile.

"How's the food?" he asked.

"Good," she said.

There was a sudden, heavy silence – strange chemistry hanging in the air.

"Are you ready to hear the full truth about me now?" he said at last.

Berry examined his face across the table – quite candidly. His hair had grown since his arrival and it fell now in thick unruly waves about his face. He was clean-shaven but there was a dark shadow of beard on his face. It all made an impression of hidden turmoil somehow and, yes, she was deeply, madly curious. Besides it would be a welcome distraction from her own woes.

"OK, go ahead," she said, fingering her glass.

"I need to talk about it," he said, taking a large gulp of wine. "I haven't talked to anyone about it. But here I am – and here you are – so let's just say, I'm getting it off my chest."

He took a deep breath, his eyes clouded over.

Berry tried to smile at him encouragingly but he barely seemed to notice.

"Where do I begin? OK – I'll start with Grace."

"Who's Grace?" Berry asked him.

"A woman I loved," he said simply.

"And lost?"

"Yes, but it wasn't that sort of love." He turned his chair sideways from the table, stretched out his legs and examined the scuffed toes of his Timberland boots. "Grace was one tough lady. Grace Fitzgerald was her name. She was a friend of my mother's who fell on hard times. Her husband ran off with another woman – left her with three children and big debts."

"Let me guess – she seduced you and left you a broken man – your whole life ruined because of her?"

"I wish! No such luck. Grace was the sort of woman who'd chew you up and spit you out in little pieces." He stopped for a moment and smiled at the memory of her, and then he went on. "My main connection with Grace was that I used to own a business."

"What kind of business?"

"A TV production company. We made Reality TV shows. Remember *Celebrity What's in Your Attic?*"

Berry shook her head vaguely. She was not a TV watcher.

"And while we're at it – my name's Pearse – not Searson."

"So Aoife was right?"

He nodded contritely.

"I'll get back to the name change. But about *Celebrity What's in Your Attic* – you had a lucky escape," he said. "Anyway – that was my brilliant idea – I made quite a lot of money from it. You'd be amazed at the amount of money people will pay for that kind of programme."

Berry nodded politely. She wasn't really keen on hearing successful business stories just now.

"I hired Grace to be my right-hand woman – my office administrator. She worked ridiculously hard, criminally long hours and put up with no end of shit from me – and a lot of other people. In return, I paid her well and dealt with her debts. And she was worth every penny. More important than any of that, she was a really good friend."

"You talk about the past like it's a hundred years ago."

"In my head it is – the life I'm trying to live now is a million light years away from what I was."

"So I gather," she said, unable to keep a note of mild mockery from her voice. But yet she was quite caught up in his story now and she liked the sound of Grace very much. "Anyway, go on."

He hesitated, then continued. "I got fed up with it all – the Reality TV business. Some of it's good – but I just didn't want to spend the rest of my life rummaging through celebrities' attics and watching celebrities trying to make out as postmen, teachers, wedding planners. I had a rock-solid business partner – Maurice – an accountant who had magic bookkeeping fingers. I took a career break and left him in charge."

"What did you do on the break?"

His face spread into a weary smile of self-mockery. "I went to Brazil – to help build a centre for homeless boys. Yes, I know – it sounds so awfully tacky – so vain – thinking I was off to save the world like an earnest undergraduate – not a successful businessman with a nice little production company under his belt. So feel free to laugh – everyone else did – including my girlfriend of the time."

"I wasn't going to laugh."

"The plan was that I would get the Superman complex out of the way and on my return we would expand the business – buy other production companies – broaden the base of our programmes – go into more serious documentaries, sport – maybe even at some stage buy our own TV station."

"So what happened?"

"Grace was to keep an eye on things. When she discovered that Maurice my partner was dipping into company funds, she spoke to him about it. He reacted by trying to sack her. When that didn't work he made daily working life so miserable that in the end she had no choice but to go on extended leave until I came home. She tried to warn me and pleaded with me to come home – but I guess I was so far up my own ass with doing my little bit to better mankind that I wasn't really listening."

"You're very hard on yourself," Berry said.

He shrugged again – that self-mocking, world-weary shrug. "Just so as you don't jump to any wrong conclusions about me – I'm a self-serving, arrogant prick. I deserved most of what I got."

"You mentioned a girlfriend. What happened to her?"

"Lillian! Lillian Bane – she *decided* she was my girlfriend – even though I was sleeping with lots of other girls at the time. But that didn't stop Lillian. She had it in her head that she was destined to be the wife of someone very rich and Big in the Media World and that she was well able to blast away any competition. She was totally in love with the idea of dating the owner of a production company. Though in financial terms I wasn't even slightly rich – not compared to big property developers or software people, big fish that Lillian couldn't land. But I was doing nicely thank you and Lillian just loved the idea of that. She was completely hooked into the whole celebrity thing – she used to fall into a major depression if her face didn't appear in at least two publications every week. They even did a feature on us in *Celeb Magazine*."

"I don't read it. I regret to say I've never even heard of Lillian Bane."

"It was lots of cheesy photos and Lillian talking about having met the love of her life and how much she would miss me while I was in Salvador saving the world. It was all nonsense. She was what you might call a gold-digger. Though even I was mildly surprised when somehow Lillian and Maurice got together while I was away. Maurice must have managed to persuade Lillian that he was a much better bet – celebrity wise."

"That must have hurt?"

"Not so much – but it's never nice to be betrayed. What really hurt is that my own stupid vanity left the way so open for him to virtually take over the company. Grace warned me not to go away – but I wouldn't listen. I was hell-bent on making the world a better place."

"I think we both need more wine," said Berry, filling up their two empty glasses. She was finding Ben's story oddly comforting – because he was telling it to her at all and because he told it with such fierce honesty. She also knew from his hinting that there was a lot worse to come. But it made her reflect on her own situation. If he could haul himself back from the precipice of such catastrophes – surely she could keep her head through the disintegration of a small business and emerge the other end with something like his wounded dignity.

"Anyway, at last I came home from Brazil and that's when the trouble really began. I wasn't at all surprised or even disappointed when I discovered Lillian was now shacked up with Maurice. My first task was to sort out the business. I kept Maurice on but with much less responsibility than before. That was punishment enough for him. I worked day and night putting together a portfolio of new programmes. I enlisted some of the hottest new presenters in town, worked on scripts and made demo tapes with them. We had the best graphics, sound engineers and locations. My head brimmed with ideas for programmes. My laptop could scarcely contain the number of demos and samples it held. Pretty soon I was the toast of Dublin Media circles once more. I knew this because Lillian began making hints at reconciliation. I ignored her. The company was only treading water financially but I figured that with this new portfolio of programmes and ideas I would have no bother attracting serious funding."

"What about Grace?"

"I'm coming to that. She'd been away on holidays when I'd got back from Brazil and so it had been a long time since I'd seen her. I decided I wanted her with me when I went looking for funding. I called her up and we met in the Merrion Hotel for lunch . . ." he stopped suddenly as if wrestling with a painful memory.

"What happened?"

"I barely recognised her. The Grace I knew was tall – imposing – what you might call handsome. But she'd shrunk to nothing . . ."

She looked like she might collapse like a flimsy balsa-wood doll. Still, a warm smile crept across her face when she saw Ben making his way across the dining-room to her. She'd spent an hour that morning trying to coax some life into her face with make-up. But it was all a wasted effort. Her skin was the colour of faded ivory, her lips thinned and bloodless. Lipstick and rouge only emphasised how life was ebbing from her body. She could feel it seeping out of her in waves, she who had always been so bursting with life.

"Ben," she said and stood up. Her whole body ached, each joint a hinge of agony. She forced a smile and did her best to ignore the shock in his face as he saw her.

Being Ben, he didn't beat around the bush.

"Why didn't you tell me you were ill? I would have made it my business to get home sooner!"

She shrugged bony shoulders. "You had enough on your plate."

He scowled at her and then took her hand in his. "What have the doctors said?"

She suppressed a little whimper. "The usual – weeks rather than months – prepare to meet thy doom – you're teetering on the brink of the great abyss and any day now you'll just topple over into it . . . or words to that effect." She smiled bleakly at him. "Still – mustn't dwell on the dark side. My kids are reared and settled and you're back from that daft trip to Brazil and Lillian has failed to get her grubby little meat-hooks into you."

"Sharp as ever, Mrs Fitzgerald," he said, trying to enter into the mood of sardonic banter.

She raised an eyebrow. "How will you survive without me? You're pure useless."

He told her about his plans – the new programmes, the funding he would have to raise.

"I wouldn't be much use to you now with fund-raising," she said. "But you'll manage fine without me. A word of warning though – Maurice may look like he's learned his lesson and that he's more than happy to give you full backing – but don't trust him."

"He made a big mistake. He's paying for it. I can't go on punishing him forever."

"Please, Ben – don't trust him."

"Something you haven't told me?"

She sighed and shoved a prawn around her plate. "I don't have to tell you everything. Just be wary of him. Now drink up your wine and tell me all about Brazil."

A few days after he'd had lunch with Grace, Ben prepared for his final meeting with the financial backers in their dockland headquarters. They were very keen to invest in his company, could see without even looking at a sample of his wares how talented he was. But when he arrived for the meeting – he got a cool reception.

"We've changed our mind – it's a simple as that," one of them said. "We've decided to invest somewhere else.

Backing out of the boardroom, he heard someone muttering about a really brilliant new production company called Bane. It didn't take a genius to figure out that Lillian and Maurice had stolen the portfolio from under his nose.

"You are *sooo* clever but so incredibly naïve," Grace said when he told her the news.

"You did try to warn me," he said.

She nodded, hating to see him so despondent, hoping that her last glimpse of Ben Pearse would be a happy one – Ben with all that amazing, swaggering, intelligent energy about him.

She lay in the bed – a thin strip of crumpled parchment. "I should have told you earlier that I was ill. But I didn't want to sound all whiney and miserable. I've always believed in taking life on the chin and there's nothing you can do about death but take it on the chin as well."

"You're so . . ."

"Brave? I've learned to hate the word 'brave'. For someone in my position it has a peculiarly menacing ring to it."

Ben smiled and sponged her forehead with a cool flannel. "Not brave, just – sensible, I suppose."

"When I got ill – it was the perfect excuse for him to get rid of me."

"Maurice knew that you were ill when he forced you from your job?"

"I didn't want to worry you when you were away. Doctors thought I might be OK – and, boy, were they wrong . . . but when Maurice heard I was poorly I think his exact words were 'There's enough dead weight around this company' . . . which when you think of it was an ironic thing to say . . ." She smiled weakly at Ben.

He bent and kissed her on the forehead and left the room quietly. Outside in the hospital grounds, he was overcome with a guilty smothering rage, like the air was being squeezed out of his body. . .

". . . I don't much remember the next few hours. Somehow I ended up at Maurice's place. The therapist at the prison told me later that I was in the grip of a temporary sort of madness. I knew Maurice was out with Lillian at some flashy charity ball. My intention was to break in and retrieve my portfolio of ideas. Maybe I planned to do a bit of damage to his tediously minimalist apartment – you know – pour a bottle of his vintage wine over his best white rug – something like that. But I thought better of it. I had found the portfolio and was about to leave when I heard a key in the front door. It appeared that Lillian had not received the sort of media-flashbulb attention that she'd expected and so they'd left early. I could hear her shrill voice in the corridor as I nipped into a closet and listened to Lillian give vent to her disappointment.

"I mean, they were absolutely all over that ghastly model Amandine – and has anyone ever even heard of her?" Lillian was furious. "I mean, Maurice – I don't think you fully understand how important it is to keep my profile up!"

I almost felt sorry for the bastard – until I thought of Grace. I think at that point I realised how absurd it was to be hiding in a closet and I stepped out in front of Lillian who let out an affected little scream. Anyway, to cut a very long story short – they asked me to leave and I said not until we'd straightened out a few things. Maurice took a golf club in his hand and threatened me with it and then I tried to wrestle it from him. He ended up getting clobbered with the club and I knocked him unconscious. I pleaded self-defence."

Berry was practically cheering him on now. She'd have clobbered Maurice herself by the sound of things.

"Who could blame you?" she said.

His jaw tightened and he scowled. "If only life were that simple. The truth is I wanted to thrash him from here to eternity. My own rage terrified me. Lord knows what stopped me. Then it was my word against Lillian's. She's from a long line of accomplished liars. Maurice had good legal connections and my plea of self-defence was thrown out. I spent a year in prison. My reputation was destroyed.

My life was destroyed – losing Grace was like losing a second mother. I felt this awful guilt – that if I hadn't abandoned her she might have lived. When I was released from prison – I could hardly function. It was the prison counsellor who advised me to rent a place by the sea for a while till I got my head sorted out. So I ended up here."

"As Ben Searson not Bernard Pearse?"

"Bernard? I was never Bernard. Bernard on the birth cert but always Ben. Ben Pearse. BP Productions."

"I've seen BP Productions written at the end of programmes and now I realise I've heard of that Ben Pearse. But I've been under such strain recently – so focused on my own problems, my brain has hardly been functioning – I just didn't make the connection."

He sat quietly, wondering if he'd said too much.

Berry reached across the table and touched his hand lightly. "Thank you for telling me all this," she said softly. "I'll let you know someday how comforting it is."

He took her hand in his, held it firmly, almost like he'd crush it. "I needed to tell you."

There was a sudden suffocating silence – like the vast empty airless silence of space. It felt for a moment as if she was suspended in a gigantic vacuum with only Ben for company. He looked across the table, black brooding eyes boring into her and she could see now why women would have flocked to his bed. She tried to wrestle her hand from his but he held it too tight.

"Berry – I would love . . ."

"You would love what?"

"To kiss you," he said, his voice low – almost a whisper. "Again."

Berry observed him with her cool green eyes, took in

the strong outline of his features – a jaw cut like granite, a firm full-lipped mouth. She felt her body tumble quickly into some strange sort of liquid stupor as a long-forgotten flood of longing swept through it. She wanted to remain in control, but the feeling of longing was too sweet and much too powerful to quench. She welcomed it and rejoiced in it. In her mind, she was already upstairs, undressing for him, her body hot for him, feeling his hands slide gently along her thighs, pulling her towards him. God, she was in her very own imagined porn movie. Erotic images thronged in her head and her mouth filled with all those lovely smutty things that lovers say to each other. Oh yes! Yes! Ben – fuck me every way you can! I'm dying for it! I want to lick you all over – to drench you in my juice – we'll just lock the door and fuck each other senseless all night long!

She was rigid with lust. There was enough electricity in the air to light up the whole island.

He released her hand and bounded quickly from the chair. "Sorry! Out of order! Old habits die harder than you think, I guess."

"What?" she croaked, jumping out of her chair with the shock. "What do you mean?"

"Bad form – coming on to you like that. I hope you believe me when I say that I certainly didn't come up here to soft-talk you into bed. It's time I went home."

Berry stared at him. She knew her face was flushed and she felt sure her pupils were dilating horribly, making her look like a nymphomaniac wildcat. Her entire body was throbbing and she seemed to have passed into some kind of feral state where her mind had shut down and only her body was in control. She found herself drifting towards him in the glow of the candlelight, like she was in a classy Edward Hopper painting that had somehow also morphed into a cinematically tasteful porn movie. She took his hand and held it to her breast. Then she pressed her slight body against his, felt the delicious all-over hardness of him, smelt the musky man-chopping-logs-and-plain-soap scent of him.

Then out of her usually quite refined mouth Berry heard herself rasp the following words into his ear: "Take me upstairs now, Ben Searson, and fuck me senseless – or I'll never speak to you again!"

Afterwards they lay on her bed, she crooked in his arm, her head resting on his shoulder, his body was splayed out on the bed with a rough kind of gracefulness. She ran a finger idly across his chest, took in the broadness of him, his long muscular legs. She hadn't realised that behind all those loose Tricot Marine sweaters and shapeless jeans, Ben was very well built – in all quarters.

He scrunched up his eyes and peered at his watch. "It's midnight."

"So? Do you, like, turn into a mouse or a pumpkin or something?"

"No, but I should probably go home."

"You should probably *not* go home," said Berry, climbing on top of him and smiling down at him crookedly, before planting a long moist kiss on his mouth. This was the best fun she'd had in ages. Well, it was almost the only fun she'd had in ages. And Aoife had texted to say she was staying in town. "Anyway, what's the point in leaving now? If we're going to regret this in the morning – we might as well make it a night that we can feel *really* embarrassed about."

She tightened her legs on him and pinned her hands to his shoulders.

He stirred slightly beneath her and she could feel him hardening once more.

"If you try to resist – I will simply have to tie you to the bed," she said, stirring herself against his hardened penis.

"If you put it like that . . ." he said like he was yielding to her. "But I'll make any tying decisions – if it's all the same to you!" and he quickly tumbled her over so that now his body lay across hers and she was pinned to the bed.

Berry fretted briefly – after all she still didn't know everything about him. What if he was some sort of kinky sex fiend? She didn't mind a bit of inventiveness in the bedroom but what if he was the sort to take things too far? Maybe he'd tie her to the bed and leave her there until Aoife arrived home the following day? Maybe she shouldn't have mentioned the whole tying thing at all – and actually she wasn't really into it – she was only fooling around.

"When I said tie you to the bed – what I actually meant was –" she squeaked weakly.

"It's too late now . . ." he answered roughly but he was looking down at her with an unfathomable sort of gentleness.

God, he was beautiful.

It was really pointless to resist.

"I see these nipples are being very disobedient," he growled softly and bent to take each one in his mouth. "A hard nipple must be tamed and subdued with lots of sucking and licking."

Berry thought she'd come on the spot. But he kept going at her like that for ages, teasing her nipples and then sliding his fingers into her and stopping just when she was on the point of explosion. In the end she had to beg.

"Please! Please! Ben Searson or Pearse or whoever you are! Don't make me wait any longer. You're being really mean. It's cruel!"

"There's no end to my cruelty," he murmured as he slid his mouth away from her breasts and moved his way down to her groin, working his way gently inwards with his tongue.

She thought she'd just die on the spot. She found herself pounding the bed with her fists.

"OK, I give in! Do whatever you want with me! I'll be your sex-slave fantasy-woman forever! Whatever you want!"

Well, he must have felt sorry for her then because at last he seemed to get the point. He moved up and began to kiss her passionately on the lips, his tongue flickering gently in her mouth. Then he was on top, sliding in and then plunging deep into her.

"Oh my God!" she heard herself shout with unseemly astonishment as they both exploded at the very same moment. It felt like they were tumbling in a spinning room, hurtling through space. She closed her eyes, savouring the pure joyful pleasure of it.

"Oh my!" she yelped when her heart finally stopped thumping loudly.

He put his arm about her and kissed her tenderly on the forehead. "There now," he said smiling. "We've given it our best shot."

They lay quietly for a while and Berry even fell into a lovely warm sleepy daze.

"Feeling better?" he said after a while.

"How do you mean?"

"I shouldn't say – but earlier – I passed by the window – you were in the kitchen and I . . ."

Berry froze.

"You what?" she asked.

"I felt sorry for you and helpless and I suppose I wanted to make things better for you. You looked so lonely . . . hence the dinner . . . but I wasn't expecting to . . ."

Berry sat bold upright in the bed – the warm post-coital glow completely evaporated now. "So this is what you might call a sympathy fuck – is that it?" she said, her voice sharp.

"No – it's not like that!" He sounded genuinely shocked, his eyes dilated. "For starters – you were the one who –"

"I was the one who what? Yes, I invited you to bed – but only because – only because . . . It's rude to spy on people through their windows – did you know that? But you came over here with your smarmy pork and chilli casserole and your bottle of Chilean wine and spinning me some big long yarn about your mother's best friend – and I fell for it. I think you'd better leave."

She was amazed at how cool she sounded now. Inside she was burning up with shame and anger. And this definitely was the last straw. She'd thought Toby Looby was the last straw. And then she'd thought HyperShop was the last straw. But this was definitely it! It wasn't the ending up in bed and having sex bit. That was quite wonderful and had so far exceeded her expectations that she didn't think she'd want to have sex again for at least ten years. It was the pity bit she was angry about. That all evening she'd thought she was listening to him and his problems, and that he'd really wanted her, when in reality he had come to her on some sort of misguided mercy mission.

"Sure," he said, cool now, gathering up his things. "Look, I blurted that out the wrong way. The fact is, Berry, that we both needed each other this evening and if it makes any difference – I have never had sex like that before – you are beautiful and –"

"Save it!"

"I'll see myself out so," he said sheepishly as he loped down the stairs. "Thanks for . . ." Berry didn't hear the end of the sentence. She had already closed her bedroom door quietly.

CHAPTER 32

Aoife had slept over with Nathalie because she wanted to be ready in time for the big auction. She'd got her best suit cleaned and bought a new pair of black stilettos that emphasised the shape of her legs. A hairdresser had trimmed her tumbling auburn hair and given her a light serum to hold her unruly curls in place. Examining herself in the mirror the following morning, Aoife felt that for the first time in her life she looked truly grown up. What would Dermot make of her now, she wondered vaguely, as she put the final touches to her make-up. He'd always said she was beautiful – but Aoife had always assumed that he was merely banking a few compliments on deposit just to keep him in credit in the mad, passionate, hot and horny-sex account department. Perhaps, she mused, as she ran smartly manicured fingers along the smooth lycra of her legs, perhaps he was telling the truth all along.

"You look beautiful," Nathalie told her. "I bet the house is going to go for a big price and you'll get a huge commission. Then you'll start to get all the big houses for sale and who knows – maybe you'll end up opening your own Estate Agency in Larkhaven."

"Thanks. I just hope everything goes well," Aoife said. She glanced across at her cousin who was looking oddly forlorn – not at all her usual bright and cheerful self. "What's wrong? You've hardly spoken two words since I arrived yesterday evening. Are you having second thoughts about going to college?"

Nathalie shook her head vehemently. "No! I can't wait to begin. I've been out buying books and I've used some of the claim money to get a little car."

"You kept that quiet!"

Nathalie shrugged.

"So what's up? I know you too well, Nathalie Kelly. And you're never in bad humour without a very specific reason. The rest of the world hurtles from happiness to despair and backwards on a daily and sometimes even an hourly basis – but never you. Is it Mark Tierney?" She stopped and examined her cousin's face closely for telltale signs of guilt, then continued. "Because, guys like him, they're two a penny."

"It's nothing to do with Mark. There's no sense me being in bad humour about Mark."

"Good, that's the sensible approach."

"After all, there was nothing between us in the first place. I just have to stop thinking about him. That's all. It's that simple. You can be sure that he's not sitting in court right now, chewing on his pencil and saying to himself between cross-examining witnesses 'I wonder what Nathalie Kelly is doing now and has she started lectures yet?' I bet you anything he's never once had a dream about me and woken up all upset about it, or that he's ever imagined seeing me a thousand times in a crowd or spotted me driving the opposite way in the traffic!"

Aoife stared at her cousin and saw the beginnings of two glistening tears form on the rims of her eyes. "Oh my God, Nathalie – I'm sorry." She crossed the bedroom and gave her cousin a big warm hug. "There, there," she said as Nathalie gave in to a rare and violent bout of sobbing.

"I don't know what I'm going to do. I feel like a complete eejit."

"You're not an eejit. Not at all! It would be a very dull world if we were able to pick who we fall in love with . . . I mean, imagine it . . . 'Yes – he's nice and sensible and has a good job and I know we mix in the same circles, my dad plays golf with his dad and his mum really likes me and I know he's nuts about me and that he'll look after me really well. I'll just forget altogether about that other completely unsuitable, unreliable and unworthy one with the motorbike and horrible friends and fall in love with this paragon of virtue – thank you very much.' If only that was how it worked!"

Nathalie snuffled quietly into her hanky.

"However . . ." Aoife continued.

"However – what?"

Aoife shook her head and gave her cousin an extra-big tight and sympathetic squeeze.

"However – it's just not going to happen for you and Mark. I'm sorry – but that's the reality of it."

"I know that! But –"

"No buts! You've got to stop wasting valuable time thinking about him. Move onwards and upwards!"

Aoife was amazed at how sensible she sounded. She

thought Nathalie might make some pointed reference to Dermot and how Aoife wasn't really in a position to be doling out advice on how to be sensible in romance – but thankfully she didn't.

"Now be a love and help me run through my introduction to the auction one last time," Aoife said, then promptly began in a clear formal voice: "Ladies and gentlemen, welcome to this, the finest auction at Vernon's this season. I know you will all agree with me that this house is one of the jewels in our sales crown this year. Built in the nineteenth . . ."

Nathalie tried hard to listen actively to her cousin's speech rehearsal – but she was finding it hard to concentrate. It wasn't just her feelings for Mark that were making her sad. There was something else she longed to confide in Aoife – something she felt ashamed and confused and deeply anxious about. But she couldn't even bring herself to talk about her dad. She still couldn't quite believe that he had disappeared and that her mother was lying so blatantly to her about it. But people would be bound to notice he was gone eventually.

For the first time in her life, Nathalie felt deeply angry with her mother. It had to be her fault. Why else would Liam Kelly leave the family home? And if proof were needed that it was her mother's fault, Nathalie had been sorting through the laundry basket one day when she'd come across a red and black lace and satin thong. It was clear from the label that it had cost a fortune. When she'd teased her mother about it, Yvonne had been uncharacteristically sharp. "It's none of your business – just throw it in the bin and don't mention it to your father," she'd snapped. Which had led Nathalie to the inescapable conclusion that her mother was having some sort of gross and steamy love affair. The thought sickened her and especially when it dawned on her that her mother's unfaithfulness was most probably the cause of her father's sudden departure.

She was struggling hard to cope with his disappearance. But to date it was the worst thing she had ever experienced. She realised quickly what a sheltered life she'd led, how shielded she'd been from the painful troubles that seemed to beset other people. Johanne's father went absent without leave almost on a monthly basis, disappearing for anything up to a week, and then turning up full of the joys of spring and with tremendous welcome for himself. Up to now the most traumatic thing that had happened in Nathalie's life was losing the power of her fingers and standing up in a courtroom in front of Mark Tierney to give evidence about it. And, of course, losing Mark Tierney without ever having had him in the first place.

Now she had difficulty sleeping and could barely eat. Her stomach was in a constant knot and it was difficult to keep food down. As for her long-cherished dream of going to college – the good was gone out of it somehow. Instead of looking forward to the start of her student days, she was dreading them.

She'd often heard stories of men who walked out on their families and weren't seen until years later when they turned up living rough on the streets and drinking meths from bottles in brown paper bags. What if that was to happen to her dad? What if he became confused or depressed and someone took advantage of him, or he got into a fight and was arrested and thrown in jail? A hundred and one horrible scenarios raced through her head constantly, in spite of the fact that Liam Kelly was broad and strong and well able to take care of himself.

"Look, like I asked you before, why don't you come along to the auction today?" Aoife asked, thinking that her cousin's mind was still on Mark Tierney. "You've nothing else on. It will be fun."

"I don't know. I'm not really in the mood."

"Come on! You'll love it! Who knows, you might even meet a nice millionaire. Andrew McRory is single . . ."

"I suppose," said Nathalie half-heartedly.

"Right – no time to waste. Get your best gear on."

She pointed Nathalie in the direction of the big wardrobe and while her cousin dithered between jeans and a little pink cord jacket or a pretty floral skirt and denim jacket, Aoife checked her phone for messages.

There were two voice-mail messages. The first was from Berry wondering if she would be home for dinner this evening or if she would be staying in town to celebrate the success of the big auction.

Will keep you posted! Wish me luck! She texted to her sister.

The second was from Kevin Vernon and Aoife guessed it would be a reminder of their final pre-auction meeting at 8.30 in one of the little negotiation rooms beside the auction chamber.

While she listened to the message, she quickly applied one last coating of lipstick and examined her face in the mirror.

Aoife – please call me as soon as you get this message. We need to talk urgently.

She was mildly surprised at the uncharacteristically

abrupt tone in Kevin's voice but she put it down to his natural anxiety over the most important sale of the season. Maybe there had been a sudden and sharp change of plan. Perhaps Andrew McRory had offered a massive amount of money up front just to cut out the bother of having to sit through an auction. Rich people sometimes did that. They made such a ginormous offer that the vendors couldn't refuse and the rich buyer didn't have to suffer the angst and tension of worrying about keeping up with the bidding. Gosh – maybe the vendors had decided not to sell at all – which would be disastrous for Aoife. She'd put in a lot of hard work and long hours preparing for the sale. She would feel very let down now to be denied the opportunity of closing the deal and bringing the full extent of her negotiating skills to bear in concluding the sale. Not to mention the commission! She'd already booked dinner for two with Berry in the spine-chillingly expensive Maison de Faux a mile out the road from Larkhaven. It was going to cost four arms and several legs – but she owed it to Berry and she loved Berry and she was going to make up to Berry for all the times she'd been mean and thoughtless and just plain silly.

She keyed in Kevin's number, scarcely able to contain her excitement and anxiety.

"Hi, Kevin. It's Aoife. I just got your message."

"I need to talk to you."

"I'm on my way. I should be there in twenty minutes."

"Fine," he said and hung up.

Aoife began to feel unusually odd almost immediately. It was something to do with Kevin's tone of voice over the phone – or rather lack of tone of voice. He sounded like a talking lump of granite suddenly. Kevin was always really nice to her, and he constantly used that funny fatherly tone when he spoke – like he was fond of her, like he had somehow taken over the role of father figure in her life. But now he sounded all cold and distant as though he was being forced to make small talk with a rather disagreeable serial killer instead of his surrogate daughter. Maybe he was just having a bad day.

"Come on," she said, grabbing Nathalie. "No time for breakfast. You can grab a coffee round the corner from Vernon's."

Luckily the LUAS came straight away and they were at Vernon's with minutes to spare. Aoife steered Nathalie to the little coffee shop round the corner and they arranged to meet up in the auction room later. Once Nathalie was sorted, Aoife bounded through the entrance of Vernon's.

"You look gorgeous," exclaimed Joe at the desk when he looked up from a huge book of legal judgements and caught sight of her in new high heels, her smart black suit, full make-up and the hair swept up in a chic crinkly bun.

"Don't sound so surprised," she said, grinning broadly at him.

Yes – this was the start of a new phase in Aoife's life – the glamorous, sophisticated, coolly elegant, successful, woman-about-town phase. From here on in, it would be all snappy suits and killer leg action, buckets of make-up and magnificent manicures.

"*Phoargh!*" said Eddie, one of the other really cute negotiators who'd never even noticed her before, as he passed her by in the corridor. God, it felt good to be noticed! She made her way to Kevin's office and tapped lightly on the door. She thought she heard him tell her to come in so she opened the door quietly and stepped inside.

Kevin was sitting at his desk, engrossed in a set of documents. They were so important that he didn't even have the time to look up and acknowledge her presence.

Aoife lowered herself into the chair facing him and sat silently for a few moments.

"I hope I'm not late," she said, by way of a reminder in case he'd forgotten she was there.

"No," he said, taking a pen in his hands and making a few notes in the margin of a document.

Aoife was beginning to feel quite uncomfortable. She shifted about in the chair, sneaked a glance at her watch and tried to read Kevin's inscrutable face. At last she couldn't stay quiet. People would be arriving for the auction and she ought to be there to welcome them and put them at their ease – in particular Andrew McRory – after all, it was her duty to look after him. Brochures had to be handed out and she needed to have a quiet word with Ivor the auctioneer about potential bidders. Examining Kevin's face now, he looked grey and stony – and she wondered suddenly if he was ill. He was sixty-one and Aoife's own dad had died suddenly a week after his sixtieth birthday – so it was a distinct possibility. Peering at him more closely now, she could see unhealthy red patches in his cheeks and his mouth seemed to have tightened into the shape and colour of an ancient dried apricot. No, he didn't look one bit well.

"You don't look well at all, Kevin," she said finally, unable to stop herself. "If you don't feel well you should go home, you know – we've got everything in hand for the auction."

He looked up then as if he'd only just realised she was

there. Intense clouded grey eyes stared at her. God, he was in an awful state altogether.

"Why, Aoife, why?" he said quietly.

"Why? Because you don't look at all well," she repeated in that kind but firm tone of a daughter finally forced to take control of an ailing parent. She added an encouraging smile.

"I trusted you," he said, straightening up and suddenly not looking at all sick.

Aoife struggled to find a word to describe his expression. He was looking at her coldly but also kind of glowering at the same time. He wasn't sick – he was angry – fuming. She shifted uneasily in her chair, wondering what he might be referring to. She racked her brains about anything to do with the auction. But no – she'd kept a careful record of all her expenses and she'd displayed consistent professionalism throughout – with the vendor's solicitor and with any potential buyers – even batty old Mrs O'Brien who'd managed to wangle a private viewing even though her annual pension would hardly cover the cost of heating the place for a week. No, Aoife could not fault herself on anything. She now felt confident and equipped to negotiate the sale of any bigger houses that might come up. Having dealt with a mega-trillionaire like Andrew McRory, and a rock god like Rufus Smith, she no longer felt intimidated by people of wealth and power. She defied Kevin Vernon to find fault with her performance.

"I don't follow you," she said uneasily.

"I'd never have thought you were that sort of girl, Aoife – but you can stop the performing now. It saddens me to say that you're a far better actress than I would have given you credit for – but the game's up."

Aoife gaped at him dumbly. "Actress? Sort of girl? Game?" she stammered woodenly.

Kevin eyed her with arctic iciness – like she was a particularly nasty species of cockroach. He began tidying up the papers on his desk, to indicate that their meeting was over already.

Aoife was completely lost. Clearly there had been some sort of misunderstanding – but now was not the time to talk about it. She looked at her watch again and realised there was only half an hour to go before Ivor stood at the podium and began the auction for her house.

"Look, Kevin," she said quickly when she found her voice, "there's been a mistake – or a misunderstanding – I don't know what you think I've done . . ."

"Aoife, don't make things worse by denying it. I know what you did."

"But I don't know what you're talking about! I haven't done anything –" But then, just as the words hurtled from her mouth, Aoife remembered the little vase and how she'd broken it. Was that it? Had Flann let it slip in the end? Not that she'd blame him when he'd been so wonderfully kind to her. She knew very well that it was a holy terror trying to keep a secret – especially someone else's. Usually people were very careful about keeping it quiet for the first few days but then after a week or two they sometimes forgot that it was a secret in the first place and blurted it out without thinking. Was that how it happened?

But she'd only been trying to tidy the vase away and it was well covered by insurance. Surely Kevin wouldn't be *this* angry over something that was an accident?

But there was no time to talk about it now.

"The auction! I'm supposed to be down there – greeting everybody and keeping an eye on things."

"That's all been taken care of."

"Taken care of?" she said now, her voice wobbling horribly.

"I've handed over the sale to Flann. I should have given it to him in the first place. He is the senior negotiator. There are quite a few issues to be cleared up before you leave us, Aoife – but now is not the time. I just wanted you to know how disappointed I am on a personal level that you could operate so slyly. I cannot begin to tell you how unprofessional your behaviour has been."

Aoife stared at him.

She could feel the bounce going out of her hair, the sparkle in her eyes fading and flickering out, her body suddenly losing its newly found grace and elegance. Even the smart suit seemed to sag and lose its sharpness suddenly. Every bone in her body ached and her head thrummed. Her legs began to wobble like a pair of spineless jellied stalks. It felt as if she'd been sat on by a bunch of angry Sumo wrestlers and battered to pieces by a herd of oncoming trains. Kevin was continuing to talk and through the thundering rumble of blood stampeding through her head, she strained to hear what he was saying.

". . . to the auction room now. The buyers will be expecting to see you there."

A while later, Aoife found herself sitting in a stupor at the back of the Ballsbridge auction room with Nathalie while Flann Slevin took the podium and made the speech that she had rehearsed so carefully with Nathalie. She felt as if she was in some sort of horrible nightmare and that any moment now she would wake up and everything would be fine. Flann would look down at her, wink and smile broadly and say something like: *'Ha – got you there, Aoife – just my little joke!'* But he didn't. He welcomed everybody with a warm smile and went through a description of the property one last time. Then he ran the video film and the assembled crowd were taken on one final virtual tour of the property.

"It's just lovely!" Nathalie whispered. "But I thought you were supposed to be doing all that?"

"Change of plan!" Aoife said quickly and summoning up a huge effort, she managed to paste a mask of reasonable indifference onto her face. Inside however, she was in a state of complete turmoil. She felt that the entire room could see her hands and legs trembling. Her heart was thumping so violently that she thought it might just hop out and start zinging around the room like a Tasmanian devil. Her stomach churned with nasty sinister spasms. She prayed that she wouldn't be sick. It was just as well that she was sitting next to Nathalie in the back row because she wasn't fit to stand. She tried to concentrate hard on the room full of buyers. She could identify most of them and had a good idea of who the serious bidders would turn out to be. The solicitor selling the house had said that the owners would be there in the little room to the rear of the auction chamber and, until Kevin had dropped his bombshell, Aoife had been looking forward to meeting them and finding out if they were pleased with her work on their behalf.

The room was crowded. Claire had arrived, dressed in

her best purple-trimmed black suit, her hair an elaborate multi-tinted confection of spikes and feathers. She sat at the back of the room and craned her neck for a glimpse of Rufus Smith from Cradle of Slime. Everybody else in the room was in good spirits. There was plenty of good-humoured banter and smiles all round as Ivor took to the podium. He was the top auctioneer in town and he conducted his sales with wit and a great sense of drama. In a sense he was a one-man show.

Aoife had been so looking forward to introducing him, to standing alongside and watching the drama unfold, looking down and trying to read the faces of bidders, second-guessing on whose behalf the anonymous solicitors might be bidding. But here she was crammed into the back row like a sad old sardine – a woman of absolutely no importance at all. She looked directly at Flann, wondering if he might make some apologetic nod in her direction but he kept his eyes studiously averted from her corner of the room.

The auction was in full swing now – Ivor cracking jokes and coaxing higher and higher bids from about six potential buyers. One solicitor was bidding on behalf of a mystery client.

Aoife ought to have been delighted with the soaring bids – but each new offer only emphasised the fact that apart from losing the sale and the experience and the prestige and even just the sheer excitement of presiding over the sale, she was also now watching a sizeable commission drain away. She felt angry with Flann – though she knew it really wasn't his fault. After all, he was only doing what Kevin had directed. Aoife had never felt so wretched in her life. The worst of it was having to pretend to be completely enthralled with the whole auction process, having to smile and look supremely professional while all the time she wanted to bolt from the room and throw up in some dark alleyway. She couldn't even tell Nathalie.

Ivor must have been born with an auctioneer's hammer in his hand. When you met him off the podium, he was quiet and didn't really have much to say for himself at all. But up on the stand with the hammer in his hand and a room full of house-hunters with plenty of money in their pockets, Ivor was clearly in his natural habitat.

Three bidders had dropped out and it was down to Andrew McRory, the mystery solicitor and an embassy buyer. The embassy buyer kept going to three and a half million but then dropped out. Now came the climax of the auction – that final few minutes when the two remaining bidders battled it out with subtle nods and gestures. In spite of all her woes, Aoife couldn't help being sucked into the tense excitement of it all. Who would end up being the owner of this house that she had become so surprisingly attached to? Her eyes shot from one bidder to the other and up to Ivor who now had the entire room in the palm of his hand.

Andrew McRory's rival had just bid three million, seven hundred and fifty thousand euro.

"Oh my God!" whispered Nathalie from behind her programme.

"What?"

"Andrew McRory!"

"Yeah," said Aoife dully.

"His solicitor!"

"Yeah."

"It's Mark!"

"What?"

Sure enough when they both tipped forward in their chairs to make sure, there was Mark Tierney, minus his earring, scribbling notes on the back of the brochure and whispering the odd word into Andrew McRory's ear.

"I have a bid for three million, seven hundred and fifty thousand euro, ladies and gentlemen . . . for this fine property . . . three million, seven hundred and –"

Andrew McRory raised a hand.

"Four million, ladies and gentlemen. Four million euro for this magnificent home . . ."

Everyone in the room gasped. Surely that would be the end of it. No one could go higher than four million. Any sensible person would call it a day now. They would pin their hopes on other houses and other auctions. Aoife's heart lurched when she thought about the commission that was about to tumble so effortlessly into Flann's lap.

Ivor's eyes sparkled with exhilaration. He looked about the room, holding the hammer aloft in his hand. "Four million, ladies and gentlemen. I'm giving four million once, four million twice, four million three –"

He stopped – his hammer held aloft with Shakespearean theatricality.

"Four and a quarter million . . ."

Ivor's eye rested for the briefest of moments on the head of the mystery buyer's solicitor. Only Aoife and those who knew him well could see how surprised he was. It took him a moment or two to get back into his stride.

During this brief lull in the proceedings, all eyes in the room swivelled discreetly in the direction of the mystery buyer's solicitor. Flann took the opportunity to catch Aoife's eye and flash a brief apologetic smile at her. She responded with a helpless shrug. Mark Tierney whispered to Andrew McRory who caught Ivor's eye and shook his head firmly.

"I'm giving four and a quarter million once, four and a quarter million twice . . ."

So this was it – the final bid – and from an unknown bidder. It would make a good story in the property supplement the next week and bring good publicity to Vernon's. More people with grand houses to sell would bring their business to Kevin. She glanced across at her soon-to-be-ex-boss and saw that he was pleased. Sometimes estate agents had a reputation for being opportunist and crooked but Kevin wasn't like that. He was as hard-nosed as the next businessman for sure – but he was first and foremost a gentleman. And it upset Aoife more than anything now to think that she had lost his friendship and his respect so suddenly and so completely. And though she knew that much of the success of this sale could be put down to her own hard work, she felt deeply ashamed at her own foolishness in not telling Kevin the truth about the vase in the first place. But who would have thought he would be so angry, so *disgusted*?

Ivor brought his hammer down with gusto. "*Sold* to the client of Mr Clive Chapman for four and a quarter million euro! Thank you, ladies and gentlemen."

The room began to empty out quickly and a few journalists clustered around Flann and Clive Chapman. Aoife would have to go behind now and congratulate the vendors. Her name was on all the correspondence, even though it wasn't even her sale any more. She took a deep breath and started to make her way through the crowd.

"Wait," Nathalie said, grabbing her by the sleeve, "don't leave me! He's coming this way with Andrew McRory. Please, Aoife – just one minute!"

Aoife could see Kevin eyeing her coldly across the room. There was nothing she could do now to get his approval back in any case. So where was the point in rushing into the little negotiating room to shake hands and smile with complete strangers just for the sake of it – when she wasn't even going to see a single cent of the commission? It was company practice to break open a bottle of champagne with the vendors when an auction had gone particularly well – and so there would be plenty of time to simply put her head round the door and say quick and breezy congratulations.

Andrew McRory arrived beside her, beamed warmly and gave her a fond hug.

"I'm sorry," Aoife said. "I was really hoping you'd get the house."

"Ah – no worries – plenty more houses in the sea," he said.

Aoife turned to introduce Nathalie to Andrew but found that Mark Tierney had drawn her aside and clearly Nathalie had eyes only for him.

"We meet again, Miss Kelly," Mark was saying to Nathalie. "Do you think it's fate?" Then his mischievous green eyes met hers for a moment.

"Who knows?" she said, forcing a cool and disinterested smile. She knew he was just teasing her.

Aoife turned back to Andrew with an apologetic shrug.

"Well, Aoife, thanks for everything," said Andrew. "Now I've got a meeting somewhere or other – erm – Frankfurt or is it Madrid? – damned if I can remember. You take care of yourself, Miss Aoife Joyce. I predict you'll go far in the Estate Agency business – and if you're ever looking for a backer – don't hesitate to give me a shout. I mean that."

Aoife turned pale. If he only knew the half of it he wouldn't even be talking to her now.

"Mark! I'll speak to you on the phone. Thanks!" And he began to edge his way through the thinning crowd.

"Thanks!" Aoife called after him, struggling not to sound woeful.

Claire appeared out of nowhere, her purple and black clad figure drawing odd glances. "Rufus Smith," she whispered in Aoife's ear.

"What?"

"Mystery solicitor – four and a quarter million – he told me – Rufus bought the house," she said. "He'll probably want to paint it all black," she added mischievously.

"Like I even care," Aoife said, though the idea horrified her.

"But what happened to you?" said Claire. "Why didn't you –"

"Oh God!" Aoife wailed, remembering she had to go and congratulate the vendors, and she bolted towards the negotiating room.

Nathalie was not much used to auction rooms or mixing with the sort of people who could throw around a few million euro without even batting an eyelid. She felt sort of frozen and fascinated at the same time. And in spite of her dad's disappearance and the complete and utter foolishness of her feelings for Mark Tierney, she had thoroughly enjoyed the auction.

But here she was now – back to reality with an ear-splitting bang, standing right next to the man she had so foolishly given her heart to – and why? She could make no sense of it at all. Contrary to all her girlish dreams and expectations, being in love was turning out to be a dreadful state of affairs entirely – like some awful biblical affliction for which there was no real cure. The important thing for now though was to be nice and polite and to get out of the room quickly without looking like a total fool. Though she might just let him know that she would soon be a Law student.

"I didn't think I'd see you here," she began, trying to force a smile.

"Well, I wasn't exactly expecting to see you here either."

Nathalie blushed. No, of course! What would a silly young one like her be doing at a fabulous auction in Ballsbridge? She was out of her league in absolutely every respect. She eyed the exit door longingly.

"I mean I thought you'd be at lectures," he added, trying to catch her eye.

"Lectures don't start until next week."

"What course did you get by the way?"

"Law," she said quickly.

"But that's great news!" he said instantly.

She saw how his green eyes lit up and then to her dismay she felt his arms about her and his body pressed against hers for a brief moment.

"Congratulations!" he said, planting a big smacker of

a kiss on her face. The touch of his lips sent shock waves of longing through her body. "Well done you!" he added and stood back from her. And then there was just a horrible sticky silence as Nathalie reminded herself once more that he was just being friendly. She felt like she was swimming in a vat of tepid treacle. She kept her eyes on the door, not daring to look at him in case he might see the outrageous amount of love she had for him.

"Good luck with it anyway," he said, moving around, still trying to catch her eye.

"Thanks. Look, I have to go," she said. "See you around."

She made quickly for the door. She thought her heart was probably somewhere around Tasmania now – a heavy sodden mess of hopeless longing. She got as far as the door, turned and managed a quick wave and a breezy smile.

"Bye," she mouthed.

He waved after her and she just had time to catch his peculiar mischievous grin before she made a swift exit onto the street.

Outside in the bright sunshine she squinted up her eyes and plastered on a determined smile as she stood on the kerb waiting for the lights to change. She would walk down Ailesbury Road past the fine houses and cross over to Sydney Parade Dart station. Then she would sit into the train and stare out at the houses and office blocks until she reached the city centre, where she would transfer to a tram that would take her out through the suburbs to Glennstown.

She set off down the road, forcing her mind to concentrate on the beautiful houses that towered over her on each side of the road. She crossed over the busy road and walked briskly towards Sydney Parade. She was almost at the little railway crossing when she realised that tears were streaming down her cheeks. She wiped them away roughly with the cuff of her jacket. She had a return ticket and, since there wouldn't be another train for five minutes, she flopped down onto an empty bench and stared along the two gleaming rail tracks.

"Did anyone ever tell you you're a terrible fast walker?" a voice said.

It was Mark.

For a moment she wondered what he might be doing at the station – but then she remembered he'd probably travelled to the auction on the DART.

"I didn't want to miss the train," she said, feeling foolish.

"I'm glad I caught up with you," he said, sitting down beside her on the bench.

"Yes?" She couldn't quite keep the note of curiosity out of her voice.

"Yes – I just wanted to know how you're getting on – I mean, if you're all set for college – that sort of thing. Call it after-sales service if you like!"

"After-sales service? You make me sound like a car."

"If you were a car – you'd be a Mercedes Benz," he said, completely straight-faced.

"I'm not sure I like the sound of that at all."

"Oh but it's very good. Strong and reliable – but sophisticated and . . ." He stopped.

"And?"

"And good acceleration – handles well on city roads!" he finished off with a lame grin.

Nathalie shifted uneasily on the bench. She had never felt so uncomfortable in her life and yet she dreaded the arrival of the train when they would go their separate ways.

"I didn't know barristers did property work for their clients," she said after a brief silence.

"They don't usually," he answered. "But Andrew McRory is an old friend of my dad's. So you know how it is. I was just doing him a favour."

Yes, she knew exactly how it was and the fact that his dad was a friend of Andrew McRory simply catapulted him further out of her league. She examined the toes of her black suede boots with great concentration.

"My dad and I are good mates," he added unnecessarily.

She could picture the Tierney family at home on a Sunday – Mrs Tierney supervising her Filippino kitchen staff as they cooked the traditional Sunday roast and set out a grand mahogany table that seated twelve people at least. Their regular guests would be the McRorys and other people in their small but perfectly rich and wonderfully happy circle. Mark and his father would keep the party buzzing with plenty of good-natured banter. And Zoe would be there, making up to Mrs Tierney – because that's what future daughters-in-law do. And it all emphasised how horribly fractured her own family was suddenly – her father missing, her mother behaving oddly and she herself floundering for the first time in her life, instead of being on top of the world for winning her court case and getting the place in college. Instead of all that here she was, feeling low and confused.

She tapped the toe of one boot against the other, beating out the rhythm of a song – "Accidentally in Love". The words definitely suited her predicament.

"Listen – this is going to sound like a really daft idea," she heard Mark say, "but I'm finished in the office for the day and the sun is shining – fancy a walk on the beach?"

"What?"

"Yeah! Let's go for a walk. I mean maybe you're busy. So obviously if you're busy then there'd be no point. I mean, I've got plenty on this afternoon as well as it happens – in fact I was on my way back to the office – only I thought – us being near Sandymount Strand and all. Personally, I find that a half-hour walk on the beach does wonders for my brain – so in a sense it's an essential element of my working day . . ."

Nathalie looked down at her black suede boots and cursed inwardly.

Mark also glanced down at her boots. "Well, maybe not – I didn't think of the boots. And, you know, when I come to think of it – I really should be getting back to the office."

"What would Zoe think if she saw you walking along the strand with another girl?" Oh God, what a stupid thing to say!

"I've no idea. Zoe is a cross I have to bear."

What did he mean? "That's not a very nice thing to say."

"She's from Belfast. She shares a flat with my sister. And any time my sister and Zoe want to go on the town and they need to be seen with a man in tow – I'm roped in. They pay, mind. I can't afford nightclubs just yet. Maybe she'd like to take things further – but I'm not interested. But I don't want to hurt her feelings either. Yes, I can hear you thinking 'What sort of bloke allows his sister and her mate to push him around like that?' – but hey – life's too short already – that's my view."

He wasn't really interested in Zoe? Had she heard right? Then perhaps he was available after all. Then perhaps he was really pleased to see her and it would be fine to walk the beach with him. Then perhaps . . . but no – best not to think beyond that.

"As a matter of fact – I'm not seeing anyone just now. I wanted you to know that," he added and looked at her very pointedly.

Was he teasing her? Was he letting her know that he didn't want to get into any sort of relationship?

"But I'm open to attractive offers," he said and leaned towards her so that she could feel his shoulder pressing against hers.

She could not suppress a smile and suddenly she noticed the warm rays of sunshine and the lovely little breeze that was fluttering up from the strand. And she pictured the pair of them, strolling hand in hand along the shore. She hesitated fatally.

"Right!" he said. "Let's go."

Pretty soon they were on the strand and Nathalie was struggling to keep up as the heels of her boots sank into the sand. In the end she kicked them off and hoped he wouldn't notice that she hadn't had a fabulously expensive pedicure any time in the last ten years. And besides – what did it matter? He was hardly going to look her over. He was just being friendly and light-hearted, she reminded herself, and maybe she could learn to settle for that. She couldn't ever imagine falling in love with anyone else. It was just too indescribably painful. But friendship was worth something. Friendship with Mark Tierney, however fleeting, was nothing to be sneered at.

Freed from the restricting boots, she couldn't stop

herself skipping along the beach, darting off in short spurts occasionally to dab her toes in the water and then squealing delightedly like a little girl when the water splashed up around her ankles and shins. Mark followed behind, not really paying much heed to her sudden reversion to childhood. He picked up shells and skimmed flat, black stones along the water. He found pieces of driftwood, smooth round discs of glass, strange fronds of seaweed. He examined each specimen carefully before discarding it.

"Picnic?" he said when they finally came to a halt along the grassy headland.

"Oh, yeah, sure," she said laughing, having images of wicker hampers and pink champagne and caviar sandwiches and knowing full well that even the nearest service station was now two miles away.

He led her out onto a large flat rock that sloped out to sea. They could see great big tankers and sailing boats and chugging maintenance craft and one or two trawlers. Nathalie enjoyed the scene for a while but then she began to feel hungry.

"I wish you hadn't mentioned food," she said. "I could murder a ham sandwich – a big thick one with loads of mustard."

He laughed and reached into his pocket. "I bought these in the station," he said and on the flat rock between them he set down two sandwich packs, two bottles of chilled water and two walnut whips.

Nathalie stared hungrily at the little feast, resisting the urge to just grab a sandwich there and then.

"It's not much, I know," he said mistaking her silence for disapproval.

"It's just lovely," said Nathalie.

"But I wish it was something a bit fancier!"

"Can we just eat? The sea air has made me ravenous."

They tucked in, sitting on their big flat rock, staring out to sea and munching contentedly through the bread and ham.

"I know all about you and yet you know nothing much about me," he said after a while – biting into the walnut whip.

Nathalie shrugged and smiled pleasantly. She didn't want to spoil the moment by saying anything meaningful. Sitting out here on the rock with the man she loved to distraction, munching on railway station sandwiches and sipping bottled water was probably the closest thing to a perfect moment she'd ever experienced in her life. She wanted to savour every second, to bottle it up in her heart so that she could return to it day after day, year after year – the sort of memory that would linger in her heart like a warm glow forever.

"So here's a potted history," he said before shoving the last of the whip into his mouth. "I hlighve wirhmtgh nmyrgy phrangentgs . . ."

"Sorry?"

He swallowed the last of the whip and repeated: "I live with my parents. My dad works in the Blackrock Clinic."

Not a barrister then – but a consultant – probably one of those blokes that did heart replacements or hip transplants. "Nice," she said, determined not to spoil the moment by dwelling on the enormous social chasm between them.

"My mother runs the home – she's nice – she'd like you."

Nathalie suppressed a dry smile, knowing full well that the sort of mother who would have Mark Tierney as a son would most probably regard her as some kind of tiresome household pest.

"Tell you what? Come round for dinner some evening. See for yourself."

She stared at him across the little expanse of smooth rock, wishing she could just simply press a replay button to double-check his words.

"How about the weekend?" he added, looking at her expectantly.

"OK," she said with a quick nervous laugh, thinking that would be the end of the conversation.

"Good. Actually great!" he said, smiling broadly at her, and lightly brushing a strand of hair from her face.

Nathalie froze beneath the soft warm touch of his fingers, willing him against all common sense to lean over and kiss her long and hard.

But he didn't.

He glanced quickly at his watch and frowned.

"Time to go, I'm afraid," he said, jumping up quickly. "Here . . ." He pulled a scrap of paper from his pocket and scribbled a number down. "It's my mobile. Come to dinner with the family on Saturday evening. Call me on Saturday afternoon for directions."

"Sure," she said, shoving the scrap of paper in her pocket.

The walk back to the station was quick and she filled the many awkward silences that fell between them with a virtual ocean of small talk. In the end she felt quite pleased with how cool she was.

"Well, see you Saturday," he said, as she stood on the

platform, ready to board the train. She was terrified that he might kiss her again and yet she longed for it.

She darted quickly into the train, rolled down the window and called out to him: "See you Saturday!"

Travelling home to Glennstown on the LUAS, Nathalie's heart was thumping so loudly that she felt sure everyone in the carriage could see and hear it. She took a deep breath and tried to remain calm. She tried to trace back over the events of the morning but her mind kept darting off in all directions.

All she knew was that she had spent a perfect morning with Mark Tierney who was not seeing anyone else – and that he'd invited her out – not on a date exactly – but to meet his family. She sighed deeply and wondered how she would last the next few days without seeing him.

CHAPTER 33

By the time Aoife reached the little negotiating room to the rear of the auction chamber, the vendors had left. But scattered round the table were the remnants of a happy sale – a cluster of half-empty champagne flutes and a couple of empty bottles, a few lonely black olives huddled in a canapé dish, crunched-up bits of paper and brochures strewn across the table. Across one of the brochures someone had printed out YES!!!!! in big black capitals.

Lucky them! She thought grumpily. They only got to leave Vernon's Auction Rooms with four and a quarter million in their pocket! She on the other hand would be leaving Vernon's in a different sense, under a big black cloud of shame and infamy, her reputation in tatters, her good name lost forever. Soon all of Dublin would know about the shameful incident of the Ming vase. She knew there was little point in appealing to Kevin, in trying to present her version of the facts.

Unless!

Unless Flann were to come to her rescue! If he were to go to Kevin and somehow straighten out the story – then maybe Aoife would at least get some sort of reference when she left. She sat down at the table, feeling like she had the entire universe resting on her shoulders. The hair she had pinned up with such confidence only a few hours before had come tumbling down in a tangled mess about her face.

There was a knock at the door and, almost as if he'd heard what she was thinking, Flann appeared at the door.

"Aoife, I can't begin to tell you how awful I feel about all this."

She could feel big splodges of stinging tears threatening to burst forth. She straightened up, trying to fend them off.

Flann sat beside her and wrung his hands in anguish and sighed painfully before continuing. "I don't know. I think Kevin's lost it. I tried to explain about how distraught you were when you broke the vase, and now somehow he's got it into his head that you were trying to steal it and that you deliberately came on to me – just so that I would help you cover it up. I was in his office for an hour last night and he just kept on and on about trust and loyalty. Then he mumbled something about how it wasn't really about the vase but something much more serious. Quite honestly, Aoife, I think he may be having some sort of breakdown."

"Something more serious? Well, I suppose he means his trust in me," she said, her voice trembling.

"But to see you sitting there in the auction room today, knowing that this should have been your big moment, your commission, your ticket to certain promotion – I

417

can't tell you how uncomfortable I feel about the whole business."

"There's no sense in the pair of us feeling bad," Aoife snuffled, not trying to hide the tears any more.

"Oh God, Aoife, don't – please don't cry." He put his arm about her shoulders and tugged her gently towards him, pressing her head to his wide chest in a protective gesture.

"I can't help it!" she wailed. "I just feel terrible! What's to become of me?"

"Sssssshhhhh! Sssshhhh!" he whispered soothingly as he patted her head lightly. He even planted a few light kisses in her hair – ever so gently. "My sweet Aoife, I wish I could stop the hurting for you. You deserve so much more than this."

He was probably right there.

He rubbed and patted her back like she was a colicky baby and then he took her chin in his hand and tilted her face up to his. It felt like he was taking charge and she was grateful – she knew that right now she couldn't manage on her own. She was in such a state of shock and despair that she could scarcely remember her own name.

"It's like I'm feeling your pain," he said gently "and . . . I want to make it go away." Then he bent his head and kissed her softly on the lips.

She felt a sense of great surprise.

"Let me comfort you," he mumbled as his hand slid round her waist and his lips found her mouth once more.

This wasn't right. She wasn't able to think straight but she tried to push him gently away. "No, Flann. Don't. I just want to go home."

"In a minute," he breathed into her ear as he began to tug at her silk top.

"Please, Flann, no!" she said, now having to use more effort to stop him.

He didn't seem to heed her pleas but held her tighter while he continued to nuzzle her neck.

"Get off, Flann!" she said, trying to squirm out of his arms. "Now is a really bad time for me!"

Now his hand was sliding up her thigh under her skirt.

"What's wrong with you?" she cried, continuing to wrestle with him.

Now he did stop but still held her close. "Come on, Aoife," he said breathlessly. "It's not like you have anything left to lose. Your career with Vernon's is at an end. So's mine by the way. I'm planning to set up on my own. I've been out checking over premises already. I'm thinking somewhere along the coast – Wicklow maybe. Somewhere like Larkhaven – it's a grand spot, Aoife, for those who can afford it. And like I said – Kevin's going a bit gaga anyway. Maybe I'll ask you to come and work for me and if you're nice – hey – I'll splash out some of that generous commission on you – we could have a week away together in the sun – or I've no objections to coughing up for the bit of bling for a woman who pleases me. I could spend hours just telling you about the sort of thing that really pleases me . . ."

She managed to wriggle out of his clutches and darted to the door where she stood, poised for flight. She could scarcely believe what she was hearing. She stared at him as if she was seeing him for the first time. It was a truly horrible sight – like she'd finally come face to face with some previously insubstantial monster of childhood nightmares.

He sat in the chair leering at her, his eyelids drooping with lust.

"Go on! Off you go!" He chuckled horribly. "You're well and truly fucked now anyway. You just wait. In another few weeks you'll be begging me for help."

"What do you mean?"

"In this line of work, the best man is always the best informed."

"Does Kevin know you're going to take the commission from him and slither off just like that?"

"Kevin's ancient history. A man like that – there's no room for him in this line of business any more."

"That's really horrible. He doesn't deserve to be treated like that."

"Oh – my darling Aoife – how incredibly naïve you are!"

She stared at him for a moment, too furious to speak. But then she realised something.

He was right!

She was the most terrifyingly naïve person she knew. It felt like she'd been drifting through a virtual version of life on a bed of rose petals wearing nothing but a huge pair of rose-tinted glasses. Now, though, the real world with all is slimy, horrible sludge-green bile was rearing up in front of her like a multi-headed reptile from outer space.

And here it was flashing before her eyes like a series of grim snapshots – the barefaced truth!

Flann Slevin had gone through the whole pretence of trying to help her, that day she had broken the vase – just so that he would have a hold over her. Was it too far-fetched to think he might even have shouted at her deliberately to frighten her and make her lose her grip on the priceless piece of china? Whatever about that, he had then let her do all the work on preparing for the sale, bringing in the big buyers. Then he simply went to Kevin and told a very embroidered version of the truth – knowing full well that Kevin would then hand over the sale to him. In Kevin's eyes she was now a thief willing to sleep with a colleague just to cover up her behaviour. No wonder he wanted her out of the company. She wondered what other poisonous lies Flann had told Kevin about her?

She wanted desperately to bolt from the room and get away but there were still a few unanswered questions.

"What do you mean I will soon be begging you to help me?"

Again that horrible leer as he sat slumped in the chair, his legs spread out in front of her in some horrid gesture that she didn't even want to think about.

"I heard your sister was forced to pay a visit to the bank manager. Her business is going to the wall. But I assume you already knew that."

Aoife leaned against the door to steady herself. It couldn't be true! She would know! Berry would have told her.

"She's planning to sell Bloomfield House to cover the debts. Nice bit of property – will do well when done up by professionals. Much too big and demanding for two women on their own . . ."

"You bastard!" she choked, before stumbling blindly from the room.

Outside in the street, she stood shivering and staring vacantly at the passing traffic. She could not frame one coherent thought in her head.

Where was she to go?

What was she to do?

She ought to go home to Larkhaven to poor Berry who needed her support but she felt too horribly ashamed. Whoever said that if you never made a mistake you never made anything was wrong. She'd made just about as many mistakes as a girl could make – blind to her sister's troubles, putting her trust in the wrong man, and casting aside with casual arrogance Dermot who loved her and treated her like an empress, who had gone off in despair and become some old queen's toy boy. She'd betrayed Kevin and if she thought long and hard about it – she'd probably find that she'd let down a lot of other people as well.

She set off down the broad busy road, walking in no particular direction. A light drizzle began to fall. She couldn't stop thinking about Berry. How had she been so blind to her sister's plight? Sadly she knew the answer very well. Because she was wrapped up in a silly world of fantasy men and on-line detective agents, and a fantasy sales commission that was never going to be hers either.

Too late now to make amends!

Aoife trudged along until she came to a little bar. Once inside, she sat up at the counter and ordered a Cosmopolitan. She knocked it back in one go – then drank three more in quick succession. She had never sat at a bar alone before, never sat in a pub getting drunk alone before. Well, except for the night Dermot had stood her up . . .

She figured she must look truly awful because none of the men at the bar approached her. Even the barman kept the conversation to a minimum. She went out to the loo and made her way back unsteadily to the barstool. The world seemed to have tilted on its axis and the walls and the bottles on the bar seemed to be moving somehow. But it all appeared to settle down once she was firmly reseated on the stool.

Too numb to think, she just stared at the bar and the barman and the comings and goings of other customers and wondered vaguely if she could call a cab and stay with Nathalie for the night. The only alternative was to stay here and drink to oblivion. She ordered another drink as she fished out her mobile and tried to call Nathalie. There was no reply and she left a garbled message.

"Ingr a bar shumwheare. Sringlightly pisshed – d'n't shay earlier buth 'ave had the worsht day of nmy life. Pleaase can I shtay with yew? Thrnpks."

Nathalie didn't call back and two hours later, as Aoife's head slumped on the counter in a state of extreme unconsciousness, the barman was forced to pick up her mobile and try to get in touch with someone who might collect her. He figured that whoever was on speed dial would be the 'significant other' of this poor girl at the counter and so it was that shortly afterwards, Dermot arrived at the little pub and picking up the ex-love of his life – literally – carted her off in his car to his newly acquired apartment.

A warm burst of appetising heat filled the kitchen as Yvonne opened the door of the oven to check on dinner. She'd selected Marks & Spencer seafood pasta for two. Yes, it looked quite fine. It smelt appetising. It would be perfect with the carrot and courgette salad she'd made according to the Avoca Handweavers' Cookbook. Nathalie would be home from town soon, tired and hungry. The past few weeks hadn't been easy on her, what with college starting in a matter of days and Liam disappearing. Yvonne had tried to make it sound as if he was gone away on account of his work – but her daughter wasn't stupid.

He'd left early in the morning without saying a word, was well gone by the time she'd woken.

And when she confided in Geraldine next door, Geraldine had said ominously: "That is how men leave."

"What do you mean?"

"They leave quietly – in the middle of the night or when the house is empty. They leave and they move on."

"But he didn't sneak off – he told me he had to go away for a while," she protested feebly.

Why couldn't he even ring Nathalie? She could not believe that someone who had been a part of their lives for so long could just vanish into thin air and effectively cease to exist. She found herself roaming around Glennstown, hoping against hope that she might catch sight of him. Sometimes in the evenings, she sat into her car and travelled the neighbourhood in darkness, feeling utterly desolate and abandoned. Once or twice she even ventured into places she knew he liked to go for an occasional drink. She never asked if anyone had seen him. It would have been too humiliating.

It took tremendous willpower to keep a smile on her face at home and act as if nothing was wrong. She'd even made a joke with Nathalie about how they could have a whole week without even the smell of a roast lamb dinner. And Nathalie was fooled until she'd come across her mother in the bedroom, sobbing quietly. It was probably one of the most awful moments in Yvonne's life. She struggled to find words of comfort, desperate to ease her daughter's pain.

"He's a man, love. Something's gone wrong and he can't talk about it so he's gone away."

"Where has he gone?"

"I don't know."

"Will he come back?"

"I don't know that either."

That had been three days ago and, since then, Nathalie had barely spoken two words to her. It was clear she blamed her for driving him away. Why else would he have gone? Why else would he leave the daughter who loved him more than anything?

In an effort to improve matters, Yvonne had driven into town and gone into Marks & Spencer's Food Hall and filled a trolley with exotic foods – Chinese duck, Italian sauces, primavera and carbonara, seafood in filo pastry, asparagus, rocket leaves, Stilton cheese, lemon syllabubs, onion and roast pepper breads, sweet Italian panettone cake, sparkling wine, and warm red clarets. It had long been a fantasy – to sweep carelessly through the aisles of Marks & Spencer and buy whatever she fancied, regardless of the cost. But now she felt an odd sense of anticlimax, and standing at the fish counter selecting succulent pink queen scallops, she was startled to find herself looking longingly at the legs of lamb at the next counter.

Nathalie came home, peered through the glass door of the oven at the seafood pasta and announced that she wasn't hungry before disappearing up to her room. Feeling doubly abandoned, feeling as though she barely existed any more, Yvonne did something she'd never before done in her life. She sat down on the sofa and drank her way through an entire bottle of wine, before collapsing into a dishevelled mess on the sofa.

CHAPTER 34

The suburbs of London felt alien to Liam. He emerged from the District Line station and stood for a moment to find his bearings. To his right was Wimbledon Hill, one of the finest Edwardian roads in South London. It rose gently and gracefully and followed an elegant straight line between rows of mature beech and lime trees. Liam Kelly knew exactly where Larchfield Gardens was and now he left the station grounds and strode purposefully up the hill along the raised footpath.

A cool breeze was blowing and occasional drops of rain spattered on his coat as he walked. As he turned his collar up, it crossed his mind that he was on a fool's errand, that he should go home and tell Yvonne the whole stupid story, maybe even confront her about it. Explain how somehow, since Nathalie had turned twenty-one and was slowly but surely slipping away from them, it had all flooded back to haunt him, how he lay awake at night thinking about it, how he could do nothing with his life until he knew the complete truth.

The High Street bustled. Smart ladies dipped in and out of forbiddingly elegant boutiques. Portly men in pin-striped suits strode confidently to fulsome lunches in exquisite little restaurants. He ducked into a pub called the Rose and Crown and sat at the bar nursing a glass of beer and a ploughman's lunch, planning his confrontation of Bushell.

Then he set out again.

The house was impossible to miss. It was an imposing Queen Anne structure, red-brick detached, double-fronted with mullioned windows, in its own small but secluded grounds. A long way from Glennstown and a very long way from Kennedy's Builders and Suppliers on the Long Mile Road in Dublin which was where Liam had first met Guy Bushell.

They'd started work on the same day, straight from school, sat at desks beside one another, doing all the menial jobs and hating every moment. But whereas Liam needed every penny he earned, every bit of extra training he could coax from the company – to Guy it was nothing much more than an expensive hobby, a means of learning the building trade and keeping his father happy.

Liam knocked loudly on the door and from within he could hear the sound of light footsteps across the hall. For long years he'd wondered how he would react if he ever came face to face with Guy again. Mostly he'd never gone beyond imagining punching him hard in the face.

It was a big heavy door and it opened slowly, revealing a woman about his age, expensively dressed, carefully groomed. He felt suddenly awkward, gauche, clumsy – a fool on a fool's errand.

"Can I help you?" Her voice was light, English.

"I've come to see Guy Bushell. I'm an old acquaintance of his."

"Is he expecting you?" She seemed surprised.

"No. He isn't."

"May I ask what it's in connection with?"

"It's all right," he said, suddenly just anxious to get away. "If he's busy – I'll call another time."

She smiled at him. She had a nice smile – warm and sunny. "You may as well see him now – no sense in going away and coming back, is there? Besides, it's such a ghastly day."

She led the way into a palatial hall, tastefully furnished with antiques and old darkened oil paintings, and took his coat.

"Just one thing. He's in bed."

"Is he ill?"

She nodded and excused herself to hang his damp coat in an airing cupboard. She returned moments later and gestured towards a door. "Go ahead."

Surprised, having expected Guy to be upstairs, Liam stepped forward into a room that was in semi-darkness. By the looks of the wallpaper, the grand fireplace and the furniture, it was a drawing-room or a morning-room – but in the corner was a bed, beside it a table dense with pill bottles.

In the bed, propped up on voluminous pillows, a man.

"Hello, Guy."

Guy studied him for a few moments, then recognition came. "Liam! It's been a long time. He held out his hand in a vague gesture of welcome.

"What's wrong with you?" Liam said, ignoring his hand.

Guy stirred on the pillows and winced. "Everything you could think of. I'm not a well man, as they say." His accent was polished and clipped, scarcely a trace of Dublin in it now. He made a great show of clearing his throat.

Ordinarily Liam might have been moved to pity, but all he could think of was the anger and disappointment and suspicion that he'd carried around with him for so long and the way it had eventually destroyed his marriage. He looked around the room, taking in the rich furnishings, the tasteful paintings, the rare ornaments.

"Your wife seems like a nice lady."

"Philippa? Yes, I suppose she is. We've been married a long time. I can't remember whether she's nice or not."

Liam had long anticipated this moment but he hadn't expected to find his old adversary at death's door. It seemed churlish now to dig up the past.

"What do you do now? Workwise, I mean?" Guy's tone was condescending and for a brief moment Liam contemplated telling a string of lies – a mansion in Wicklow, several cars, a villa in Bermuda, three sons doing law.

"I'm a foreman now, Guy."

"It's a damn shame," Guy continued. "I always thought you were smart. Still married? More children?"

Liam clenched his fists. "Only my daughter."

"Strange," Guy said, his voice thin and reedy. "Weren't you going to have half a dozen at least? Funny how I remember you saying that."

Anger swept over Liam and he struggled to control it. He strode to the window and stared out blindly at the lavish garden. He became conscious of the fact that his hands were still clenched and he flexed them – straining to relax. He took a few deep breaths and tried to focus on the reason for his visit.

"Why did you really come here?" came Guy's voice from behind him.

Liam turned away from the window and slowly approached the bed. Guy's eyes met his.

"I have a question to ask you," said Liam.

The room was silent except for a soft wheeze coming from Guy's throat.

"I need the truth – or so help me . . ."

"I can scarcely contain my alarm," Guy said, rolling his eyes to heaven mockingly.

Liam continued to stare coldly at him.

"Why lie about ancient history?" Guy said at last in a low easy murmur.

Ancient history! Liam's hands curled into fists again. But he would not allow his anger to deflect him from his purpose now.

"Was it true?" he asked. "When you told me you had slept with Yvonne just weeks before our wedding?" His eyes bored into the other man, willing him to speak the truth. "That our daughter . . ."

Guy stared at him with wide watery eyes and gurgled a horrible wispy laugh. "What a sad loser you are, Liam Kelly. So leadenly predictable! Even still after all those years. Didn't your wife ever tell you? No – I don't suppose she did. Of course it was a lie – a jealous lie. I wanted her – and you got her – even though you had nothing. And I regret to say, old man, that from my point of view your lovely young fiancée was amusingly virtuous. Oh dear – did you really think you were a cuckold all those years? That your daughter was in fact my daughter? How incredibly old-fashioned and conventional of you! Sweet in a pathetic sort of way." Guy paused for a moment, sipped water from a plastic beaker, then resumed. "And I see now the true purpose of your visit – some sort of noble revenge, I'd imagine. Some sort of Bruce Willis *Die Hard* Revenge of the Common Man." Guy's face twisted into a provocative smirk.

Liam looked down at him for a moment, pictured his fists landing a couple of good bruising belts into Bushell's peevish face.

"Get well soon," he said dryly instead and, turning, left the room, closing the door quietly behind him.

Philippa was in the hall. She'd dried most of the rain from his coat and now she led him into a cosy kitchen where she poured him tea. He would have preferred to leave but felt it would be discourteous.

"Are you OK?" she asked tentatively. "You seem upset somehow?"

"No, I'm grand."

Very grand now, he thought to himself. Couldn't be grander. It felt as if someone had lifted a sack of rocks from his shoulders, as if his heart, tightened by years of resentment, was about to burst free and be a living thing again. All those years thinking Yvonne had tricked him, nights of looking at Nathalie in her cradle and wondering if she might truly be Guy Bushell's after all.

He drank the tea and it warmed him. Philippa had made sandwiches and kept pressing them on him until it would have been plain rude to refuse and he tucked in, more hungry than he realised. God! How had a lovely woman like this ended up with a total bastard like Guy Bushell?

"If it's his illness that's bothering you – don't fret yourself."

"How do you mean?"

She ignored his question. "Are you good friends? I didn't know he had any friends. Well, there was one guy he used to play tennis with – but they had a falling out. Even our boys can't really stand the sight of him."

"No. We were never friends."

"Then I don't understand. Why did you come to see him?"

She had lovely blue eyes, a sad face, but one full of warmth.

"It seems kind of petty now and it's not easy to talk about. I've never talked about it to anyone. I'm not the sort to talk about my business. I suppose, to answer your question, I came because I wanted to find out the truth about something once and for all."

"My husband seems to have the rare knack of making enemies from all walks of life. What did he do to you? Oh, go ahead and say! You won't hurt my feelings. I loathe him."

He didn't want to tell her about Yvonne and Nathalie and that festering suspicion that had all but ruined his marriage. He couldn't tell her how, when Yvonne had failed to get pregnant again, he had taken it as proof positive that Nathalie was not his child but Guy's. He groaned inwardly when he thought of how he had shied away from any suggestion that they should seek medical aid. He feared that if it was proved he was infertile, the whole sham would be brought to light and he and Yvonne would have to acknowledge that Nathalie was not his daughter.

Instead, he told Philippa the other half of the story. He told her about the university scholarship which Mr Kennedy had set up to encourage his brighter employees to better themselves. How he, talented and hard-working, was tipped to get it – how Guy, to whom life had already given so much, wanted it for himself and blackened his good name.

"He hated me. It wasn't simply that he wanted the scholarship. He wanted to destroy me. He . . . he had previously been going out with the girl I married . . . it wasn't that he loved her . . . but, when she chose me, his pride couldn't take it. "

"That's my Guy," said Philippa dryly. "Not capable of loving *anyone*, and full of malice."

Liam nodded. "So Guy got the prestigious scholarship and the college education – I got the sack."

"But what did he say about you?"

"That I had stolen money from the company and that he had covered up for me. In fact, it was the other way round. He was a gambler and he needed the money to pay his debts. It doesn't sound much now in the telling – but I left the job under a cloud that never quite shifted and it shook my confidence. He, on the other hand, has clearly never looked back."

He looked around again – a vast brand-new kitchen, every gadget you could think of, the sort of kitchen Yvonne had always dreamed of, the sort of place he would love to have given her.

Philippa threw her head back and laughed, a sexy throaty laugh. "He doesn't own this. It's mine. He married me for my money. As for being ill, there isn't a thing wrong with him. He just does that every time I threaten to throw him out."

"But I thought that he –"

"He's a bum. Hasn't a penny to his name. Hasn't

worked in ten years. Fond of the good life though, is our Guy – as you seem to know. I met him at Ascot and he can do the charming Irishman routine when it suits him. Long ago when I was young and foolish . . . Then our boys came along. Anyway, this time, I really do mean to get rid of him."

"My God, I've spent all these years thinking he'd done well and I was the failure . . . it's almost wrecked my marriage . . . in fact, it probably has wrecked my marriage. My wife will never forgive . . ." He stopped. He really mustn't be tempted to burden Philippa Bushell with the full extent of his problems.

"I wish I'd known – I could have told you. The only life he's lived is the life of a scrounger."

"Why have you stuck it for so long?"

"For years it was just for the children. Then habit, I'm ashamed to say! I just didn't have the strength of mind to throw him out. Does that sound awful?"

On the way out, Liam passed by Guy's room, paused and briefly reconsidered thrashing the man to within an inch of his life. But he realised with a sharp leap in his chest that he no longer cared. And besides, Guy Bushell was not to blame for all his mistakes.

He said goodbye to Philippa and wished her well.

CHAPTER 35

Aoife woke and quickly figured she was in the hands of a spiteful brain surgeon. It seemed he was drilling holes in her skull with a big jackhammer and without even the benefit of an aspirin. Her entire head rattled and thrummed. Her mouth was dry as the afternoon desert but also coated in slimy wet foul-smelling mucus. She opened one eye apprehensively and saw nothing but white – white walls, white billowing things that might be curtains and glimpses of glaring white in the distance. Dazzling white sheets and throws even!

She tried to sit up but her body seemed paralysed, legs numbed and somehow glued to the bed.

She moaned and called out weakly.

For a while there was no response. She stared at the billowing white curtains and the glaring white beyond and wondered if she was in some sort of post-life existence. Any minute now the Archangel Gabriel would flutter out from behind those frothy curtains on a beam of celestial light and call out her name in a strange echoing voice. She watched the curtains intently for what seemed like ages but no heavenly being materialised. At last she heard a voice and she turned to see a blurry figure standing at the end of the bed.

"You're alive then?"

It wasn't the Archangel Gabriel.

She nodded weakly.

"Big breakfast?"

But maybe it was his short-order cook.

"No," she said quickly.

"Tea and toast? Solpadeine?"

It had taken her a moment or two to identify the voice but now she was in no doubt.

"Dermot?"

"Yeah!" he said, retreating from the bed and getting even blurrier.

"Wait. Don't go," she whimpered.

He stopped and seemed to shimmer and hover before her eyes.

"Am I dead or something?"

He shook his head. "No."

"But it feels like I'm dead. And why are you hovering in mid-air and making yourself all blurry like that if I'm not in the afterlife?"

"Dunno! Maybe you've got alcoholic poisoning. And I'm not hovering in mid-air. Look!" he said, stamping on the wooden floor so loudly that the sound echoed thunderously in Aoife's head.

"Stop!" she wailed and pulled a big soft pillow up round her ears. "Well, how did I get here so? And as a matter of fact – where exactly is here? I don't remember your flat being like this."

"I got fed up of renting. So I got this place."

"You never told me."

"Didn't think you'd be interested. Back in a minute," he said, leaving the room.

While she waited for his return, Aoife slid up onto the pile of deep soft pillows. Sure enough in the corner of the room there was a stack of packing cases that hadn't even been opened and some of Dermot's things – his electric guitar, his golf clubs, some old prints and a few little piles of books, CDs and magazines. She thought back on how he had disappeared without explanation, the strange email she'd got from him, Claire's story about how she'd seen Dermot hanging out with some flamboyant old queen, and her own sighting of him outside the Gordon Bar. And now this! An apartment decorated almost exclusively in white, massive big soft pillows on the bed, white waffle-weave throw and even a white rug. It was an obviously expensive apartment far beyond Dermot's means.

He reappeared at the door carrying a breakfast tray.

"So this is the old queen's apartment? Or did he buy it for you?" she said.

He threw her a strange look but didn't respond. Instead he set the tray up for her on the bed – a pot of tea, a glass of fresh orange juice, two slices of fresh toast and butter, two Solpadeine. He filled up a white porcelain mug with the piping hot tea and added some milk. Then he spread a large napkin across her lap.

"In case of crumbs," he said simply.

"You *are* gay!"

He shrugged as if to say that she was merely stating something terribly obvious.

"Have your tea before it gets cold," he said before disappearing once more.

Aoife was wide-awake now. She knocked back the pills with a shot of orange juice. Then she munched through half a slice of toast and quickly drained the mug of tea. Soon she was in the shower and trying valiantly to wash away her terrible hangover and to clear her head and to understand the awful sharp pain that had suddenly shot across her chest. Dermot – her Dermot – with somebody else! Man or woman, it didn't matter. The point was he clearly didn't think much of her any more – and who could blame him? All round her now, she could see evidence of gayness – the generous array of bathroom accessories, the little glass dish with the exquisite shells in it, soaps in the shape of flowers. In the bedroom, she noticed how neat and tidy everything was – apart from the little cluster of packing cases and those other things. Most likely the old queen was an old fusspot.

She needed to find Dermot – to hear it from his own mouth. Somehow that was important. It would mean she hadn't made such a mistake in neglecting him. It would mean her instincts were good and she'd been right not to give her heart to him.

The apartment was quite large, she quickly discovered once she'd left the bedroom. She was in a long corridor and down at the far end she could hear dishes rattling. She followed the noise and came to a large bright kitchen. It even had its own little balcony looking out over the river.

"It's a nice place," she said, wondering how either Dermot or the old queen could afford it. She knew only too well from working in Vernon's that these days a spacious apartment generally meant somewhere that had six inches of unused space between the sofa and the kitchen area, somewhere that actually involved taking more than one step from the bed to the en suite shower. But this was huge. Through a wide archway she could see into a vast marble-tiled lounge area. This room also led onto an even larger balcony.

"It's OK," he said noncommittally as he wiped down the kitchen counter.

"You were in a bad state when I found you last night," he said, his voice mildly questioning as he stacked a few dishes in the dishwasher.

Aoife bowed her head, not even wanting to think of the mistakes she'd made in recent months, not the least of them being how she had trusted a slimy reptile like Flann Slevin.

"But I won't ask," he added. "And in a way it's not even my business any more." He closed up the dishwasher and set it on a rinse cycle. Then he quickly wiped over the sink.

She stood awkwardly in the middle of the room observing him going about routine domestic tasks. But he couldn't be gay. He looked too – too what? Oh God – too *hot* was the answer! Even if he was cleaning the sink, he wasn't doing it in a gay way. It looked more like he was flexing his muscles or getting ready to go into battle or something. So he was most likely one of the macho gays – the sort that hangs out in black leather and chains and sports a military look. She had a sudden image of him standing in a gay bar looking mean, dressed in leather hot pants and a leather Nazi peaked hat and cracking a whip. She forced it from her mind.

Quickly reflecting on the tattered and shredded remains of her life, Aoife knew that in the grand catastrophic scheme of things – Dermot's gayness and his newfound happiness with an older man was hardly worth bothering about. Except that glancing across at him now as he shoved things into cupboards she couldn't help feeling a hot stab of longing for his broad strong shoulders, a yearning to be held in those big rough arms and to rest her head on that magnificent expanse of chest.

But that time in her life was well and truly over. She had seen the moment of her greatness flicker – and splutter out in a flash.

Now she would spend what was left of her life wondering about what might have been. If she'd only realised sooner, recognised the true nature of her feelings for Dermot! She'd always expected love to come as a bolt of lightning – some big dramatic glance-across-a-crowded-room earth-shifting moment. But it had all sort of crept up on her stealthily – in spite of herself.

And there he was now in a raggedy-looking T-shirt that had seen better days, in a pair of threadbare old jeans and leather flip-flops, looking sinfully un-gay, unshaven and with his hair all ruffled up, and his warm brown eyes smiling coolly at her.

"I've been a complete bitch to you, and I'm so sorry," she said finally.

"It's not important now," he said and strolled past her into the large living area.

He flopped down into a big white leather armchair

and began shuffling through a pile of documents on the glass coffee table. She registered that one or two of them looked vaguely familiar – though she could scarcely be less interested in bundles of papers right now.

"It is to me," she said following him. "Important, I mean. We were such good friends – and I just used you. And I've only just realised now that . . ."

"That what?" he said absently as he worked his way through the papers.

"That . . . well, that . . . I mean . . . you know, I'm just glad, Dermot, that you've found happiness and this place – it's just lovely – and I hope you both have very many happy days here. And I am truly sorry from the bottom of my completely stupid heart that I was so mean to you."

He looked at her askance, and seemed to be about to tell her something – but then thought better of it.

Extremely large volumes of tears began to gather in her eyes and the struggle to stop them bursting forth was becoming quite painful. "Anyway, listen, thanks for bringing me home and taking care of me last night. I didn't deserve it. Now I have to go – Berry needs me."

She stood up and prepared to leave.

"No worries," he said and continued to take notes.

"Please don't think badly of me – I've been a complete fool and now of course I'm paying for it."

"Sure," he said, tutting softly as he came to a particularly detailed-looking sheet of paper.

God, he must hate her! The very thought made a whole new wave of tears gather ominously. A large lump of play dough seemed to have lodged in her neck and before she could even get herself out of the room, tears ruptured forth and the large lump in her throat constricted and tightened so that she felt she was about to choke.

"Aoife? What's wrong? Aoife?"

"I've just had the worst week of my life!" she wailed. Then the whole list of catastrophes came tumbling out: the shattered Ming vase months ago, Flann Slevin and his malicious whisperings to Kevin and assault on her, Berry's business going wallop, a dodgy character lodging in the cottage and then getting the sack from Vernon's. She wondered how he could even understand since her account sounded so strangled and garbled. But he seemed to be able to make sense of most of it.

She wrung a sodden tissue in her hands. "Oh, I feel terrible dumping all this on you – when you have so much to cope with – coming out, setting up in your new home," she glanced at the pile of paperwork and added, "and all the work in your new job. I don't know what I'm going to do."

Dermot said nothing for a few moments and then he slapped his thighs loudly in some sort of macho 'I'm not really gay' sort of gesture. "OK – some quick solutions! The first thing you have to do is to tell Kevin the truth. He's a good man. I know he'll believe you when you tell the truth to him – which is what you should have done in the first place."

"I don't know . . ." She didn't think Kevin Vernon would ever want to see her again. She was fixed in his mind as a sly little thief and maybe something else equally awful and she figured that nothing would change his mind now.

"We're going to do this now – this morning. We'll drive to his house in Dalkey and tell him."

"No! It wouldn't be right. I made a mistake – now I'm paying the price – simple as that."

"Aoife – I'm driving you to Kevin Vernon's house – whether you like it or not. Then we'll go on to Larkhaven. Berry's probably getting a bit worried about you. But first I have to finish these papers. So why don't you give her a quick call while you're waiting."

He buried his head once more and Aoife dialled Berry's number but there was no response so she left a message. Then she sat watching as Dermot struggled to the end of the pile of papers. There was that document again – the one she'd half-recognised. And then she did recognise it – fully. But it couldn't be. She leaned forward just to make sure she wasn't seeing things. Perhaps with all the drink the night before, she was just hallucinating. But no – she wasn't.

"How the hell did you get hold of this?" she said, grabbing the page and waving it at him accusingly.

CHAPTER 36

A small crowd of people gathered on the main street of Larkhaven to watch the arrival of the mighty juggernauts. It felt a little bit like the invasion of a hostile army as massive vehicles bearing even more colossal machinery trundled with austere grandeur down the main street, past the little crescent of bay, the jutting stone pier and past the church painted a duck-egg blue. They might as well have carried banners proclaiming that *Resistance Is Futile.*

But resistance is never futile.

Outside the church High Court Judge Patricia de Vere, dressed today in a horribly imposing dark green Chanel suit and a pair of judiciously imprudent high heels, together with the other stalwarts of the Larkhaven Residents' Association gathered. The mood was one of grim determination. Where six months ago Charlotte Pobjoy and her colleagues had all been at each other's throats, they now stood united with a fine sense of purpose.

An enemy was coming amongst them.

They would fight and they would be right!

The colossal machines swept slowly through the village, manoeuvred by stolid blank-faced men in hard hats.

Berry stood on the footpath outside her café and observed their progress with a dull ache. Inside, Harry Robson was completing an online exam in animal husbandry. Old Jim who owned the second-hand bookstore next door leaned on the little sill. Through the glass at his back, you could see piles of dusty books and prints.

Then Berry heard him pronounce:

"My heart is dark and black as a sloe
Or a lump of coal from the smithy's forge
Or the shape of a shoe on gleaming halls,
And a dark cloud hangs over my outward smile.
My heart is sore and broken
Like ice on top of a lake . . ."

He often spoke his feelings in verse.

"That's nice, Jim," Berry said. "It just about sums up how I feel."

"I found it in a book of old Irish poems."

"Don't suppose there'll be much call for poetry or anything else old in the new fabulously fabulous world of HyperShop," Berry said, feeling sorry for Jim. His quaint and dusty world would soon be nothing but a vague memory in old people's heads, something people might reminisce about in *The County Sentinel*.

"I don't mind so much," he said, surprising her. "I was selling up anyhow. I'm getting too old for this malarkey. Guess it's about time I retired and backed out gracefully from life on the main street. But how will you make out?"

Berry shrugged. She was overcome by a suffocating despair. She watched Jim disappear into his dusty world of folklore and myths and legends and romance, where poetry was a common everyday occurrence, where the past was revered and nurtured, not banished and ignored. She was about to turn on her heel and set about hanging up the *'Business for Sale'* sign, when she saw a sight infinitely more terrifying than the procession of juggernauts.

Patricia de Vere was spearheading the members of the Larkhaven Association as they marched in double file down the main street of the village. Berry watched with anxious fascination as they storm-trooped dourly into each little village shop and emerged some minutes later to move on to the next store. Then it was old Jim's turn and Berry couldn't quite suppress a smile as Patricia emerged brushing a fine coating of cobwebs from her Chanel suit and Sheila examined her nails with thinly disguised horror. It would undoubtedly take several deep cleanses and a deluxe manicure to restore them to their former glory.

"Berry," Patricia barked by way of a greeting as she bore down on the little Internet café.

"Hi," said Berry.

"Mind if we step inside?" Patricia asked before sweeping in and positioning herself at the counter. The others stood in a little semi-circle behind her.

From a far corner of the room, Harry Robson finished the last question in his on-line exam and emerged from cyberspace to note the height of Patricia's heels.

"Black patent, class!" he whispered softly to himself before exchanging a fleeting glance with the High Court Judge.

"Coffee anyone?" Berry offered.

"Well, I didn't manage to –" Sheila began.

"No coffee!" Patricia announced as if she was putting an end to a nasty unsocial habit once and for all. "We want you to take a look at this."

She passed a document to Berry and watched carefully as she read through it.

"Well, what do you think?"

"Is it true?"

"Absolutely! Spent weeks checking it out. It was Harry here who put me on to it. What do you think I was doing in here all those afternoons? Finding love on line?"

"I wasn't really sure. I thought you were kind of checking up on me," Berry said. "But now I see it all makes sense."

"They've mucked up the planning permission. They bought the field from Harry but they overlooked an old bye-law preventing the building of any commercial property in the fields behind the church."

"But surely they checked?" Berry said.

"They didn't check carefully enough and once he'd sold the land to them, Harry didn't feel any great need to put them straight. So in a way Harry Robson is the hero of the hour."

They all turned round and peered curiously at Harry. He leaned back in his chair, basking in the attention.

"That's why you wanted me so badly on the Larkhaven Association," he said, giving Patricia a knowing wink. She ignored it.

"I predict that if we look out the window round about now," she said, "you'll see that convoy of trucks and cranes driving back the way they came."

Sure enough they all peeped out the window – and the stony-faced hard-hatted men were driving sheepishly back through the village.

Berry smiled ruefully. It was great. It would buy the shopkeepers some time to ensure that HyperShop didn't trample them into oblivion. But they would be back in any case at some point in the future – not too far away. It wouldn't make any difference to her – since she was virtually bankrupt anyhow.

"Well, that's great news," she said hiding the *Business For Sale* sign under the counter.

When the delegation had left she drew out the sign once more and hung it on the door. It felt like she was putting her own child up for sale.

"Hey, Berry – will you come and have a look at this!" Harry said, chuckling happily to himself. "I've scored! Come and have a look at my bride-to-be!"

"Give it a rest. I'm not in the mood for any more of your wind-ups," she said, wondering if Harry wasn't taking this whole Internet bride thing a bit too seriously.

"It's not a wind-up. I'm engaged! Look – Yelena Tolstoy Dostoevsky of Vladograd – originally from Saint Petersburg – of old aristocratic Russian stock – is coming to Ireland and wants to meet me. And that's not all – would you look at her – I mean, Berry, she's just perfect!"

He brought up the picture of Yelena. Berry had to admit that she was genuinely beautiful. She wrote that her dearest dream was to live on a farm and rear cattle and sheep and hens. She was by her own admission a fantastic cook but she also loved to read and do a little landscape painting on the side.

"I mean I only filled in the form as a joke – but she's

magnificent. And what have I got to lose by meeting up with her? Listen to this, Berry . . . *'My dariling Harold'* – isn't her spelling cute? – *'My dariling Harold, I long to be with you, man of my dreams. There is not a man in hole of Vladograd in Zachistan that is like you, Mel Gibson of my most erotic fantasy. I yearnings to hold you to soothe the savage desires of your beast. But first I must go to university tomorrow and collect degree honours in agricultural scientist from President of our country. It has been difficult time for me – as I only can finance my educations by dancing in the Lapps and on the Poles. Last year, I win first prize in Zachistan Pole dancing championship. I too have suffered the long night of worry over sheep – since my father was chief shepherd to the famous Commissar in bad old days of Communism. Soon, my dariling, I must come to you and bring with me many greatest recipes of my mother who was cook to the famous Commissar also. We will eat blinis and Beluga caviar and drink vodka and then after I have cleaned your palace from top to bottom, and after we have discussed five year plan for your family estate, I will show you some astonishing tricks I have with baby oil . . .'* Like I said – what have I got to lose? *'So my dariling, I come to the Haven of the Larks and we will be together by the weekend – your beloved – with plentiful love and devotion – Yelena XXXX."*

They both stared at the screen for a few moments.

"There you are, Harry – you asked for her – and you got her," Berry said at last, trying to suppress a giggle.

Harry saw her laughing behind her hand and he frowned for a second. Then suddenly he grinned broadly at her. "Hey – you must think I'm a big eejit! You did this, didn't you?"

"How do you mean?" she said innocently.

"Berry, I know this is from you – just to teach me a lesson – teach me to respect women more – isn't it?"

"What? I had nothing to do with it."

He wagged a scolding finger at her as he fished out his wallet to pay. "You made up Yelena – I get it – and point taken. I just enjoy being a rake sometimes. And where's the harm in a little Internet fun until the hottest babe in Larkhaven can no longer resist me?"

Berry stared at him wide-eyed. *Was* he flirting? "I promise you, Harry – cross my heart and all the rest of it – I had absolutely nothing to do with this email from Yelena!"

With a knowing wink, he disappeared out the door.

When she was alone, she ran the regular systems update. Then she carried out a virus check and wiped anything unimportant. She checked her own email box and there was still no reply from Conor. Somehow she sensed that he had reached the same conclusion as her – that it was better to let the past be and not to hanker after it and she was very glad for that. She stepped out into the bright afternoon sun and locked the door behind her.

She was walking towards her car when she bumped straight into Ben.

"What's all this about premises for sale?" he said, examining the sign in the window.

"It's hardly any of your business." She was still smarting from being taken to bed as a gesture of sympathy.

"Just curious."

She fished out her car keys and unhooked the rusting door of her battered old car before sitting into the driving seat. Then she stuck the key in the ignition and jigged it round, trying to coax the engine into life. It coughed and spluttered a few times and just as things were about to get very embarrassing, it started up with a comforting hum.

Then Ben opened the passenger door and slid in beside her.

"Mind if I cadge a lift?" he said, slamming the door firmly.

"Suit yourself," she said, looking over her shoulder to check for traffic before pulling out onto the street and chugging through the village.

"I saw all the cranes and the lorries today," he said. "HyperShop – is that why you're quitting the business?"

She responded with a mild disinterested shrug. The last thing she wanted now was to start to feel anything about this man – nothing – not even annoyance. She needed every shred of emotional energy for the imminent demise of her business, her credit rating, her home, her self-respect and the happiness she'd striven so hard to build for herself. She would stay indifferent to him and save her despair for what really mattered.

He ignored her coolness and continued. "Yes – it's a scary business battling against global corporations. And closing down is probably the most sensible option for you. But . . ."

They had reached his little cottage and she swung the car awkwardly into the driveway. Here they were – all she had to do was to say goodbye and chug off up the rest of the pot-holed avenue. She thought of the kitchen and suddenly longed to be there – where she'd grown up – where she'd sat at the big table splashing paint on big sheets of paper while her mother prepared the dinner, where she'd made elaborate castles out of Lego for her father – sometimes asking him to build a palace for her, swinging her fat little legs at the dinner table and sneaking unwanted chunks of meat to the old dog.

"But what?" she said applying the brake.

"But there might be another way."

"Yeah – like you'd know – you being such a good business man and all!"

Her sarcasm seemed to wash right over him. The car juddered, then slammed into a sudden halt.

"Would you trust me?" he said quietly.

Berry laughed sourly. "You don't exactly inspire trust. You went from riches to rags through your own stupidity. You lost your company and your girl to your business partner. You spent time in prison for burglary and premeditated assault. – you wormed your way into my bedroom for a quick one-night shag on the slimy pretext of feeling sorry for me – and you want to know if I would trust you to advise me about business!"

"It's quite a list of crimes and misdemeanours, I freely admit. Oh and while we're at it – there was one thing I left out of that little yarn I told you."

Berry shrugged. "I don't need to know – hey, your crimes and your life – knowing about them will only clutter up my head."

"Suit yourself. But why don't I call round in the morning anyway."

She didn't even bother to reply, only sat impassively waiting for him to leave.

"Look – I promise I won't try to get into your bedroom again – don't worry – that definitely was a one-off."

Now he was beginning to really annoy her.

"Suit yourself," she said as he clambered out of the car.

CHAPTER 37

Aoife waved the sheet of paper in the air.

"How did you get this?" she repeated, her voice rising and cracking with annoyance.

Dermot observed the paper for a moment and said: "I guess it must have fallen out of the brochure."

"What?"

"Now what did I do with that brochure?" He ambled across the room and began rummaging through a drawer. "Here we are!" He waved a large brown envelope at her triumphantly.

"What's going on, Dermot? I'm fed up with all this – disappearing, turning out to be gay, and now snooping around in my business. I want answers and I want them now!" She almost stamped her foot she was so cross.

He stared at her coldly. "I'm getting a bit fed up with all your smart comments about me being gay."

"Sorry – I won't say it again."

Their eyes locked briefly. Might he at last begin to tell her what the hell was going on?

"I'll explain everything later, after we've been to Kevin's."

"No!" she said, sinking down into the large white leather sofa once more. "I'm not going anywhere until you explain why you have a sales brochure for the house in Talavera Road."

"Aoife, please – we need to get to Kevin's. It's important for you to sort it out before it's too late."

"Not budging!" she said folding her arms, clamping her lips together and tucking in her chin like a wilful turkey.

Dermot let out a long weary sigh.

"You've been spying on me, haven't you?" she clipped.

"Nope!"

"What then?"

"Do you really want to know?"

She unclamped her lips briefly to let out an impatient puff of air.

"Right then. I had a personal interest in the sale of that house on Talavera Road. I didn't want to tell you because – well – lots of reasons – the main one being, you didn't deserve to know."

Aoife's brain juddered quickly into action. It was one of her most appealing qualities, Dermot used to say – that she could go from airhead to mastermind in thirty seconds flat when the situation demanded. And this situation certainly demanded. She closed her eyes, lightly massaged her cheekbones as she considered the possibilities of Dermot's interest in a property like Talavera Road. Even on his good salary he couldn't afford a house like that. She shuffled all the information round in her head once more, glanced round the large white apartment and suddenly it all made perfect sense.

"Now I understand!"

"You do?" he said, a little surprised.

"I've been such a fool! Your lover – he must be incredibly rich!"

"Lover? Rich?"

"I mean he sets you up here in his own private version of The North Pole – no smutty pun intended and he trades up to a splendid house in Dublin 4. Well – lucky you – landing on your feet like that – it's nice." She stood up, unable to say any more, wanting suddenly to be out of the room and far away. "Goodbye, Dermot – have a good life," she said, unable to resist a dramatic exit line.

"What? No! Wait! You've got it all wrong!"

She smiled wanly at him. "I seriously doubt it."

At that point he took the rather unusual step of striding, not mincing, across the room and taking her rather too roughly by the shoulders. "I do not have a gay lover! I am not gay!"

Denial – acceptance issues – *blah blah blah*! It was nice the way he held her shoulders though. And perhaps he was just the tiniest bit bisexual. Could she cope with that? Maybe! Definitely possibly!

"Remember when Kevin told you he wanted the house to fetch a good solid price at auction – it was for me. It was my house."

"Your house? Don't be ridiculous!"

"It's true," he said, then grabbed his car keys. "Come on – I'll tell you on the way to Dalkey."

Outside everything was splashed and dappled in

bright sunshine. They sat into his car and Aoife insisted he stop at the nearest service station before going any further. She bought a large bottle of Lucozade and a packet of jelly babies and sat back into the car once more.

"Go on so," she said swigging thirstily from the dayglo orange bottle and gobbling up jelly babies like some giant vengeful anti-jelly god.

"You remember my Uncle Charlie?"

"Vaguely. I never met him. Jelly baby?"

He shook his head and continued. "Well, he died a few weeks ago."

"I'm sorry to hear that. But what's all this got to do with Talavera Road?"

"Now – Uncle Charlie *was* gay – but it's worth repeating once more – I'm not. Uncle Charlie liked me. I used to come and stay with him when I was in college and no one else in the family would talk to him."

"Why wouldn't they talk to him?"

"On account of him being gay! But I always thought he was the best fun. He used to take me to all the gay bars and introduce me to all his friends and guard me fiercely from the more predatory ones."

"Wait! So that was your Uncle Charlie, the one with the fedora and the spats?"

"I thought you said you'd never seen him?"

"Oh – caught a glimpse of him one day. So that was him?"

"Yes, wouldn't be seen dead without his fedora – literally – we put it in his coffin."

"But Cla – someone told me they'd seen him holding hands with you and kissing you!"

"Well, he was always very demonstrative and those

final months were very emotional, of course. On the other hand, it might all have been more casual than it appeared to Claire. You know? He might have been camping it up just for fun."

"Claire? I didn't say it was Claire!"

He slid her a knowing look and continued with his story as she subsided blushing. "Right, where was I? Yes . . . so I daren't tell my mother about my friendship with Uncle Charlie – because you couldn't even mention Charlie's name in the same room as her. Anyway, as he had no family, he spent all his money on doing up that house. He filled it up with beautiful paintings and furniture and priceless ornaments."

Aoife groaned! "The vase!"

"Yes – well – anyway, he bought this apartment here for his lover. The lover used it to entertain his own fleet of lovers and Charlie was broken-hearted when he found out. Needless to say that relationship didn't work out. Dimitri went back to Thessalonika and Charlie vowed that he would never again take another lover. Soon afterwards he took ill suddenly and then a few months ago before he died, he informed me that he'd put everything he owned into my name."

Aoife couldn't think of anything to say. Her mind was racing. If what Dermot said was true – then he was the vendor of the house. It must have been him sitting in the negotiating room waiting anxiously for the result of the auction. It must have been him who had drunk champagne to celebrate when the house sold for four and a quarter million. She stared across at him and found that she was looking at a stranger.

"Charlie left everything in as much order as he could,"

Dermot continued. "I didn't have to do probate or anything like that – but still the amount of paperwork is amazing – I have a case full of it. And it was all wrecking my head – so I decided to take a few weeks' unpaid leave and sort it all out. Then it was a long time since I'd had a decent holiday – so that's how you ended up getting an email from Spain."

Dermot drove down Booterstown Avenue into Blackrock and then headed out the coast road. They sat in silence as Aoife digested all that she'd been told, assessed all the new things she'd learned about Dermot in the past hour. Some blokes would have bragged about it all over town but he'd kept news of the inheritance all to himself for months on end, hadn't told anyone outside of his family. He'd shown kindness and love to his uncle without any thought of reward when he could easily have ignored him.

She opened her mouth to say something but he interrupted.

"And to be honest, Aoife, most of all *you* were wrecking my head." There was a cold hard edge to his voice.

"I can see that now, and I'm truly sorry," she said, staring out at the sea and the sky and for the first time in her life feeling horribly overcome with remorse. There was nothing else she could say.

They drove in silence for a while, along the narrow winding roads of Dalkey until they came to the turn-off to Kevin's house. Dermot swung his car through the big stone gateway and parked on the driveway.

Remembering all the lies that Flann Slevin had told Kevin about her, remembering the horrible moment in the negotiating room only the night before, and her own stupidity in not telling the truth in the first place, Aoife huddled in the car, unwilling to go in and face the music.

"Off you go!" Dermot said, patting her knee lightly.

"Won't you come in with me? It would make it all so much easier!"

"And that's exactly why I won't go in with you. You are surrounded by people who make things easier for you. It's time you grew up, Aoife, and took responsibility for your own life. Anyway I have things to do. See you later." He nudged her gently from the car.

She stood on the gravelled driveway, alone and palely loitering – watching as he swung the car round and disappeared once more through the gates. It felt to her like their lives were about to sheer off in two very different directions and she would never see him again.

She smoothed her hair down as best she could and rang the brass doorbell. She could hear nothing for a few moments, but then she heard the unmistakable sound of Stella clip-clopping across the marble-floored hall.

Aoife felt that the next hour or two would qualify to feature in any TV compilation of *Top Ten Moments Of Shame*! She tried to straighten up and look proud and determined as the big grand door opened but all she could feel was self-disgust and humiliation.

"Aoife!" Stella said, not beaming out her usual effusive warmth and welcome. "I wasn't expecting to see you here – after all that's gone on."

"Can I come in? Please? Just for a few minutes? I need to speak to Kevin."

Stella raised a well-tended eyebrow. "I'm not sure . . ."

"Please. I'm desperate."

"There's hardly any point. There's no sense in making an ugly scene – it would be pointless. Let me call a cab to take you to the station. You can take the train back into town."

"Stella, I really need to talk to Kevin. It's important. I have to explain."

"There's nothing to explain," Stella said, now a bit tetchily. "Just go home, Aoife – and reflect on what a gift it is to have people who believe in you and trust in you – and how completely you have broken that trust."

Racked with shame and too tired to argue, Aoife turned on her heel to leave.

Then her mobile flashed up a message from Dermot: *"Don't you dare leave without explaining!"*

But it was too late. Stella had shut the door quietly but very firmly in her face.

Nathalie had gone into town that morning to buy something nice to wear for dinner with Mark Tierney's family. She figured that she ought to buy something shimmery and glamorous but everything she tried on made her look overdressed and silly. In the end she bought a flowing peasant skirt in indigo blue with a hip-slinging leather belt and a little blue ballet cardigan to match.

She showered and blow-dried her hair and then sat at the kitchen table painting her nails. Her mother came in, just back from the shops, and bustled around the kitchen emptying bags and filing groceries away in cupboards.

"I'm wrecked. Town was mobbed and it took me ages to get parking. How are you, love?"

"Grand."

"Cup of tea?"

"No, thanks."

"That's a nice colour varnish. Is it new?"

Nathalie shrugged passively. She wished her mother would leave and stop trying to make nice cosy conversation. The atmosphere in the kitchen was stifling and she longed to get up and leave but she had to finish her nails.

"Still no word from your dad," Yvonne said.

"And tell me something I don't know," Nathalie said sourly, wishing her mother wouldn't feel compelled to state the obvious all the time.

Her mobile flashed and she picked it up carefully so as not to smudge the varnish.

"Hi – it's Mark."

"Hi."

"All set?"

"Yes – I think so . . ." she said laughing nervously, aware that her mother was still in the kitchen.

"I'll pick you up at Blackrock Station."

"OK, see you then."

She didn't want her mother knowing about Mark. Only a few weeks ago, she would have dragged Yvonne into town to help her pick a new outfit and they would have sat for hours discussing Mark and whether or not he might be ever really interested in her. But now she couldn't bear the thought of her mother knowing anything about it.

"Who was that?" Yvonne asked, straining to sound casual.

"Just Johanne," she said and switched on her iPod –

putting an end to the prospect of any further conversation.

Outside Kevin Vernon's Dalkey mansion, Aoife shuffled about on the gravelled driveway, wondering if it might not be best all round to just go to the beach at the bottom of the road and fling herself into the sea. She tried Dermot's mobile – but he'd switched it off. She tried Nathalie who had also switched off and she was on the point of calling Berry to come and rescue her, but then she remembered that Berry had enough to be dealing with – putting her business up for sale, and forced to put the family home up for auction as well.

At last she decided that the only sensible thing to do was to call a taxi and get out of Vernon's quickly. The signal was weak to the front of the house and she edged round by the side, trying to get her call through and hoping that no one would see her. Without even realising it, she now found herself in the lovely terraced garden where she'd danced the night away at the Vernon's summer barbeque only a few months earlier. The gardens opened out to the bay and she stood for a few moments, soothed by the bright blue stretch of sea before her.

"Lovely, isn't it?" said a voice behind her.

She swung round to find Kevin sitting on a little deck with a book and glass of beer for company.

"I'm sorry – I was just trying to get a signal. I didn't mean to intrude." She began to back away.

"Stella will organise a cab for you. Sit down here. I'll be back in a moment." He disappeared into the house and reappeared moments later with a second glass of beer.

"It's a hot day. Drink up."

"Thanks."

They stared out at the sea for a while and Aoife felt suddenly lonely for her father. Often when she was a little girl, they'd sat together in companionable silence – just looking out to sea. Sometimes she'd brought little tragedies to him for fixing. Occasionally he would scold her – but he'd always manage to fix things in the end.

"I'm really sorry I let you down, Kevin," she said now. "I feel so ashamed." Kevin didn't say anything and she continued. "The whole truth is that I was trying to put the vase away somewhere for safe keeping – so that it wouldn't get stolen. I knew it must have been overlooked. Flann Slevin sneaked into the house and shouted at me so I dropped it with the fright. Then Flann advised me to say nothing about it, that it wouldn't be noticed. That's the absolute truth. It doesn't much matter now anyway – but I wanted you to know."

"Is that all?" Kevin said after a brief silence. "I thought there was something else you might want to explain to me."

Aoife took a sip of her beer and tried to compose her thoughts. "Something else?"

"Do you really think I'd ask you to leave Vernon's over a silly vase? Sure, I was disappointed that you tried to cover it up but I was prepared to forget about the whole thing. As you probably know now, the owner of the vase was hardly going to kick up a stink. But your father asked us to look out for you and we did. We had such high hopes that you would do well with Vernon's. Then this other thing . . . " His voice trailed away.

Aoife couldn't make out what he was talking about. "Did Flann Slevin say something else about me?"

"Flann said lots of things. And I don't pay much heed to any of them. Flann isn't quite as smart as he thinks. But I knew that when I hired him. He's got the relevant experience – but his six-month contract is up and I won't be renewing it. No doubt he thinks he's going to go off and set up a rival business. But he has neither the money nor the guts or the integrity. And I don't really care what he does. No – it's you – the level of cunning you've shown is breathtaking – way beyond anything he could even dream of. I tell you, Aoife, if you'd only used the same ingenuity to work your way up through the company, you'd be a managing director in five years."

Aoife stared at Kevin. What was he talking about? Maybe Flann Slevin was right and the boss was losing his marbles. She went back over what he'd said, trying to make some sense of it. She thought of all the work she'd done over the past twelve months. Apart from that one silly vase incident and the Monday she'd come in late and smelling of drink after Dermot's thirtieth birthday, she could remember nothing.

"Lucky I caught it in time," he was saying now. "Vernon's could have lost millions. To say nothing of expensive court cases!"

"Caught what?"

"So you're not going to admit it?" he said heavily.

"I can't admit something I know nothing about!" she replied heatedly.

"Very well, then. A pity you won't take the option of being honest with me. I'm referring to the fact you've been trading confidential company information with a commercial buyer over the Internet."

Aoife was astounded. "No, I have not!" Now it was

her turn to be angry. "That's an outrageous accusation!"

"Don't add insult to injury by denying it. We have proof."

"What proof?"

"Your email records."

"Then you've made a mistake."

"No mistake."

Aoife placed her glass very carefully on the wrought-iron table. Then she stood up and looked Kevin straight in the eye. "You're wrong."

He pulled a piece of paper from his pocket – a printout of deleted mails – and handed it to her. She looked down the list and recognised it instantly. There were mails to Nathalie, an occasional one to Dermot, one or two to Berry. But mostly the list comprised of correspondence with potential buyers and vendors or queries with other branches. There was even the correspondence with Mike Mordaunt's detective agency.

She shook her head. "I see nothing wrong with this."

"Take another look," he said.

Aoife took a deep breath to suppress her annoyance. This was getting ridiculous. Still she did as she was told and looked through the list – this time more carefully. Then it felt as if an icy creature from a swamp was slithering down her spine. Her entire body tingled and burned with shock. There in the middle of the list was a mail to Nutopia, Nathalie's old company, and beside it was the little paperclip icon that indicated an attachment. She never had any reason to send Nathalie attachments – not even the silly jokes that sometimes flew round town by email.

As if reading her mind Kevin pointed to the attachment and said calmly: "Our entire client database."

Everybody who had sold a house through Vernon's in the past year was on that list – and the amount of money each vendor had made on the sale of their property. Sending that sort of information to a telesales company like Nutopia was a bit like handing over people's credit cards to a bunch of thieves and robbers.

She sank down into the chair. "Oh God!"

"This Nutopia – they buy up client lists and confidential details from unscrupulous employees. I've heard they pay good money for the lists. But then you'd know all about that."

"How did you find out?"

"Random net security check."

Aoife remembered how Kevin was practically paranoid about Internet security. Vernon's had the most up-to-date firewalls and anti-virus software. Circular jokes and chain letters were not allowed. Kevin was constantly reminding everyone that people were entitled to their privacy – especially when large sums of money were involved.

"Fortunately we got to it before anyone in Nutopia did."

He stood up and walked away from her, taking a path to the rocky shore. It seemed their conversation was at an end. He stood on a large rock and stared out to sea – a light breeze fluttering through his thinning grey hair. Aoife stared after him. She was in a state of utter shock and amazement and for a few moments it felt like her feet had become welded to the ground.

"Wait a minute . . ." she said as an idea dawned.

She hurried swiftly down the gravel path and confronted him on the rock.

"I think I know what happened. I was in a terrible rush

one evening and Head Office was nagging me to email them the updated list of vendors. Well, it was late and I had a lot of things on my mind so Flann offered to stay and make sure it was sent. Well, he must have sent a copy to Nutopia as well – whether by accident or on purpose, I don't suppose we'll ever find out."

Kevin looked at her dubiously.

She went on. "You remember my cousin Nathalie? She worked in Nutopia until a few weeks ago. She would have deleted it without even opening it and mailed me a note to that effect. But look at the date – it was sent a few days before she left Nutopia. On her last week, she was moved to a desk where she could only get internal mails and so she probably never got to see it."

Kevin stared at her for a long moment. "How can I be certain this is not just another elaborate lie?"

"You can't be certain," she said simply. "But it's the truth. Why would I lie? Why would I betray your trust? You've been very good to me. Maybe I haven't always shown my appreciation – but I would never do anything to deliberately betray you or the company."

Kevin stared out across the waves, his wispy hair blustering in across his forehead, his face set in stone. Aoife could see it was no use pleading with him.

"Anyway, I can see you've made up your mind about me – so thanks for everything and I am really sorry for making such a monumental mistake. Goodbye. And don't bother about the taxi – I'll walk."

She set off briskly along the path, feeling as if she'd aged ten years in the past day. She slipped out through the big cast-iron gates onto the narrow windy road. There was no sign of a taxi so she slogged uphill along the narrow footpath. Trudging the half-mile walk to a bus stop was easier than enduring another moment's humiliation at Vernon's. Her green slingbacks were not really made for walking any distance and she hobbled onwards, each step more painful than the last. She could feel blisters forming on her soles and heels and she longed to just flop down on the pavement and cry her eyes out. She took out her mobile to see if she could get hold of a taxi but the signal kept coming and going and she couldn't get through.

A couple of boy racers sped by in open-top convertibles, like they thought they were in Monte Carlo. The road was so narrow that she practically had to cling to the wall to avoid being run over. Still, she envied them as they took the steep hill effortlessly. It seemed to her the hill was getting steeper and if felt as though she'd been walking for hours. The backs of her legs ached from the effort of climbing upwards – and the green slingbacks did not help. Another boy racer came speeding up behind her – *vroom vroom* and the sound of Phil Lynnott belting out "The Old Town".

"This girl is cracking up – this girl has broke down . . ." she sang along with her own version of the lyrics.

The music and the car stopped abruptly.

"Aoife?"

It was Dermot.

"Are you OK?"

She nodded forlornly.

"Come on," he said. "Hop in. We'll grab a couple of bags of chips and eat them on Killiney Strand and talk about what might happen with the rest of our lives."

"OK," she said, climbing in beside him.

CHAPTER 38

Berry was deep in the herbaceous border, digging the last of some rich horse manure through the soil.

Some of the plants needed dividing and cutting back and Berry had assembled a collection of tools for the job. She needed the distraction of physical work now more than ever. The 'For Sale' sign leaned idly against the front wall of the house. It looked like it was loitering with intent. She turned her back to it, hoping to blot it out of her mind – but she was aware of it lurking there behind her all the time like some sinister presence.

Ben had turned up earlier in the day, glanced briefly at the sign, and ambled along the hall into her kitchen. He'd plonked his large frame down at the kitchen table and drew out a big sheet of paper.

She had eyed him coolly and offered coffee.

"Forget the coffee. Sit down – no, I'm not going to beat you senseless with a golf club"

"Well, that's something," she said and sat down opposite him.

"See, Berry – the truly great entrepreneur must be able to take an imaginative leap in the dark – think of the crazy thing and then just do it."

She eyed him doubtfully.

"If you want to be successful, that is – oh, and by the way this can also be applied to other aspects of life."

"What's that supposed to mean?"

"It means that truly great romances are founded on such imaginative risk-taking."

"That's just pure crap," she said. "And I happen to know that for a fact."

"No – no, it's not crap. Love is the most real thing in the world if it happens and is worth the risk."

"And you would be speaking from which experience exactly?" This was a man who'd openly admitted he'd never been in love.

"OK – let's just stick to the business thing so. What you have to do is convince that clever little sister of yours to go into business with you."

"Doing what?"

"That's obvious. A one-stop shop – Estate Agency cum Internet Café. You could even throw in a bookshop. I hear the one next door is closing down. See, it combines both your skills. The important thing then is to make sure you have an option on opening a premises in the new HyperShop centre when it opens."

"Wonderful – and where will the funding come from?" she said dryly.

"Me."

She laughed dryly.

"What I didn't get to tell you is that I had a bad breakdown when I was in prison. People develop all sorts of phobias when they've been traumatised. My lawyers had secured some of my funds and assets – but I couldn't bear to think of them. I figured that success and money had destroyed me and so I tried to pretend that none of it ever existed. And I've been happier in the cottage struggling to make ends meet than I ever was in my old life."

"OK, so you told me a lie or two here and there – it hardly matters now," she said wearily.

"Berry, you're not hearing me. I'm saying I have money. I just tried to pretend to myself that I didn't need it any more. I can put up the money for this thing. It will still be a struggle – but we can do it. Please say yes. It's a chance for both of us."

She looked him straight in the eye and ran her hand lightly along the edge of his chin.

"Thanks, it's a nice thought and you are a good man. But it wouldn't work."

He sighed and stood up. Then he reached into his pocket and fished out the keys to the lodge. He placed them carefully on the table.

Berry tried not to react.

"Anyway, even if you won't take my money I've given you my sound business advice for what it's worth."

"Thanks."

"I've enjoyed my time here. If nothing else, it's helped me to get my head in order."

"That's good."

He bent to kiss her then appeared to think better of it and shook her hand awkwardly instead. Then he strode off down the avenue.

So now she was digging with philosophical determination and forcing her mind to focus on the news in this week's *Larkhaven Notes*. The news would be dominated by the HyperShop planning-permission fiasco, by the announcement that Jim was closing his bookshop after forty years in the business, that the Larkhaven Association was mounting a vigorous campaign to ensure that HyperShop did not set up in business until the wishes and the commercial interests of locals were duly accommodated. She would write about the forthcoming sale of one of the village's loveliest Georgian homes – Bloomfield House. Lastly she would briefly note that local resident, Ben Searson, would be leaving Larkhaven to embark on a new series of travels. She composed the note in her head. *Mr Searson is leaving Larkhaven to pursue a number of business interests. By his own admission his time here has been enjoyable and memorable. He leaves behind new friends and . . .*

Berry looked up and saw the weary figure of her young sister straggling up the pot-holed avenue. Aoife trudged round the side of the house and into the kitchen. Berry followed her.

"You look half dead," Berry said reaching for the kettle.

"It's been an eventful couple of days."

Aoife slung her bag in the corner. She ought to have been feeling sad and depressed and ashamed. But now that she and Dermot were back together again – it felt as if nothing in the world could really hold her down for long.

"How did the auction go? I didn't hear from you except for a couple of garbled messages on my phone and there's been a lot happening here – I hope it all went well."

Aoife was about to embark on the full story – how she'd been practically raped by Flann Slevin who had robbed her commission, all the stuff about Dermot and his gay uncle and her discovering that she actually adored him, and then the entire business of the client database ending up in Nutopia of all places and having no job to go to any more – but she didn't really know where to begin..

"I've been sacked," she said quite cheerfully.

"What?"

"Yes – it's a long story – but never mind that – Dermot and I are back together again."

Berry forced a smile. "That's great. I suppose we'll be having that dinner in Maison de Faux tonight to celebrate?"

Aoife shook her head. "No. We'd end up spending hundreds of euro just so as some snotty head waiter can look down his nose at us."

"I never liked the place anyway."

Berry sank into a chair with a mug of tea and Aoife bustled about the kitchen, tidying things away and wiping down the counter.

Aoife worked quietly for a while and then she turned to Berry and took a deep breath. "We should work together more. I've thought a lot about it."

"How do you mean?"

"I have an idea. Promise you won't laugh. I've been thinking really hard about it all afternoon and all the way home on the train. And it might just work."

"Go on."

"You and I set up in business together in Larkhaven."

It was the eeriest of coincidences.

"What? That makes no sense. We're already broke as it is."

"I contacted Andrew McRory and he told me he'll make good his promise to put up the money for me to set up in business – so long as he can have some share in the profits. Dermot wants to invest in it as well."

Berry was looking quite puzzled now.

"I forgot – I have to tell you all about Dermot and the house in Talavera Road and the gay uncle . . . anyway, back to business. We pay off all your debts and get some essential maintenance done on this house and then we open a one-stop shop in the village. Jim is closing down. We take over his premises and we start up an Estate Agency cum Internet Café. We could even keep on a more up-to-date version of the bookshop. We also make sure that we get an option to move our premises into the HyperShop centre. What do you think?"

"Have you been talking to Ben Searson?"

Aoife looked bewildered. "No! What's he got to do with it?"

"He suggested the same idea – almost word for word."

Aoife shrugged dismissively. "Well, that's probably because it's a brilliant idea. Go on, Berry – say yes – we'll make a great team."

"No, it's too risky," she said.

She was not in the mood for new beginnings. She thought of Ben and felt a horrible wrench in her chest. The smart thing to do would be to go down there right now and beg him to take her with him. There would be nothing to keep her in Larkhaven very soon in any case. Maybe they could set out on a completely new journey together, free from all the baggage of the past. She pictured them for a moment – living in some simple little farmhouse in the Languedoc, growing grapes and growing old. A rosé-tinted dream! It wasn't worth the risk.

"Think about it, Berry," said Aoife. "Seriously."

She went outside and fixed the *For Sale* sign into the lawn, glanced briefly at the cottage and then disappeared into the house to make some sort of dinner. She assembled the ingredients on the table:

> Minced steak
>
> A turnip
>
> Some couscous she had bought on special offer.

There wasn't much in the line of seasoning but rummaging around in the back of the spice cupboard she came across some stale chilli powder. She eyed the odd collection of ingredients and wondered if there might be a suitable recipe on www.epicurious.com.

She whisked out the laptop and, just as she was about to log on to the cookery site, she noticed with some relief that her mail to Conor Lynch had failed to deliver on account of ongoing problems with his server. Thank goodness for technological failure, she told herself, and turned her attention to finding a recipe.

She keyed in all the ingredients and found vegetable couscous or lamb cutlet couscous.

She could do a variation of the two. She didn't actually have the cumin – but chilli powder would do nicely instead. And she could make little meatballs with the mince. Pretty soon a pot of something very strange was simmering on the stove. Every so often Berry lifted the lid to investigate. It looked as if all the ingredients had morphed into a big dirty orange sludge.

She would never be a cook. It was a knack she would never possess. It would have been nice if she'd found a partner who could have brought her to the heights of culinary ecstasy but that was hardly going to happen now.

She poured the orange sludge into a grey serving dish and set it down in the centre of the table. Aoife sniffed at it, poked a spoon into it and deemed it to be possibly the most appalling mess she'd ever seen.

They sent out for a pizza, drank a bottle of cheap wine and Aoife told Berry the whole story about Dermot and about getting the sack from Vernon's.

"Kevin will have you back once he realises it was a mistake."

"It doesn't matter now anyway," Aoife said. "It's time to move on. I've learned a lot in Vernon's – now I'd like the chance to use it. Won't you think about us setting up in business together?"

Berry shook her head. She needed to steer clear of any further money problems. The phone rang and she went to answer it.

"It's for you," she said holding out the receiver to Aoife.

"Who is it?"

"Kevin Vernon."

"Oh God," Aoife said.

Berry held out the phone and Aoife took it. She took a deep breath and listened carefully for several moments.

"I'm very sorry too, Kevin," she said and then listened some more. "Well, I'm glad it's all cleared up anyway," she said after another few minutes. She continued to listen and then she pulled a notebook and pencil from a drawer and sat town at the table. While Kevin talked and talked at the other end of the line, Aoife scribbled notes down on a page – then whole bunches of figures then some diagrams.

After what seemed like an age Aoife said: "Thanks, Kevin – I'll be in touch, bye."

"What was that all about?" Berry asked.

Aoife scratched her head and stared at the pages in front of her. "Now where do I begin?"

A short while later, Berry stared at her little sister, who she had cosseted and protected and half-reared, and she felt fit to burst with pride, overcome with a strange maternal feeling.

"It could just work," she said, examining Aoife's sums carefully. "Now that you've got your commission back – that at least will mean we don't have to sell the house after all. And then if we find a more sympathetic bank manager than tiny Toby Looby – we might just pull it off."

A few phone calls and some hours later Berry let out a whoop of joy.

"Aoife Joyce – my kid sister – you are a genius!"

CHAPTER 39

Dressed in pale lilac velour bottoms and a plain white T-shirt, Nathalie's cast-offs, Yvonne Kelly was bent low, midway through giving the dining-room floor a coat of clear varnish. She crouched on her hands and knees, carefully applying even brush strokes, trying to find comfort and distraction in hard work. It wasn't really working but at least she was keeping busy and doing something useful at the same time. She listened to Andrea Boccelli and when he sang 'Time to Say Goodbye' the tears started coursing down her cheeks. To be honest, for the past few days, every single song that came on the radio brought stinging tears to her eyes – "What a Difference a Day Makes", "Say Hello, Wave Goodbye", "Don't Treat Me This Way", "I Will Always Love You-ou-ou", "More Than Words", "Everybody Hurts". . . even Louis Armstrong crooning "What a Wonderful World" made her sob because it was one of Liam's favourite songs. At this rate of going even "The Teddy Bear's Picnic" would be off limits.

He'd been gone for two weeks now and she would have to face the fact that most probably he would not be coming back. He'd told her that he would only be gone for a few days – but now it looked as if he might only have said that for Nathalie's sake. She hadn't a clue where he had gone and she'd even enquired with the guards, more out of a need to be doing something than out of any real hope of finding him. They had asked her if she thought he might have gone off with someone else. No – she didn't think so. 'You never know, love – the wife is always the last to know!' they had informed her.

She wasn't sleeping well and was finding work a terrible drag. Every time she looked at Alan Halvey in the office, she felt sick.

Most of all she was worried about Nathalie. Almost overnight, their comfortable closeness had evaporated and it felt to Yvonne as though their relationship had ceased to exist – like a death in some ways. Each night she would tap lightly on Nathalie's bedroom door, hoping that her daughter would even call out 'Night, Mum' as she used to and each night she was rewarded with a cold accusing silence. She didn't know how much longer she could stick it. This evening Nathalie had said she was going out with Johanne – but Yvonne suspected that she was meeting someone – a man most likely. It hurt that her daughter wouldn't confide in her any more and she felt excluded and suddenly surplus to requirements.

One half of the dining-room floor was now varnished and Andrea Boccelli had come to the end of his romantic warblings. She'd do the rest tomorrow. Her knees ached, her shoulders and back stiff from bending and crouching. The strong varnish smell had provoked a headache and on top of it all she was plain tired from lack of sleep. She showered, heated a frozen beef curry in the microwave, half-heartedly consumed a few mouthfuls while gazing blankly at an Australian soap opera, then kicked off her slippers and lay out on the couch. In a matter of seconds she was fast asleep.

She woke to shady twilight, the house in quietness. What time was it? Where was Nathalie? She fumbled for the lamp switch and squinted at the face on her watch. Eight o'clock! She'd been asleep for over three hours. She sat up and pushed back the throw that she didn't really remember pulling over her before she fell asleep. It was chilly. She'd forgotten to turn on the heating. That had been one of Liam's jobs.

Then from across the room she distinctly heard a voice say: "You must have been tired."

She rubbed the sleep from her eyes and leaned forward. Slowly her eyes adjusted to the evening light and she came face to face with her recently departed husband, sitting in his favourite armchair, like he'd never left.

"How long have you been there?"

"About two hours."

"Why didn't you wake me?"

"I didn't want to."

"Would you like a cup of tea?"

"Ah no. You're grand."

There was a sudden, choking, suffocating silence. The air seemed to be sucked out of the room. It felt just as if an electrical storm was approaching. Yvonne tensed on the sofa. She chanced a look across at him, fatally meeting his eyes. It was a moment of awesome intensity. But suddenly and without speaking a word, they were both laughing at their own foolishness, and at their silly old married habits.

"Where's Nathalie?" he asked some time later as they lay curled up in bed.

"Out – with a boy – I think. She's not been telling me much lately – a bit like her dad!" Yvonne planted an affectionate kiss on her husband's cheek.

"You know what? I've been a complete fool," he said, squeezing her tightly. "The biggest fool a man could be."

"I could have told you that!" she said, teasing him.

"Yes, but Yvonne, when I tell you the whole story I don't know if you'll ever be able to forgive me."

"I'll forgive you," she said steadily.

He sighed. "It's about Guy Bushell. He lied about me and got me sacked from my job. Did you know that?"

Yvonne stared at her husband, as if she was seeing him for the first time.

"Accused me of stealing – anyway, it's all a long time ago. But, as I told you before I left, I always felt I'd never given you the sort of life you deserved. And I blamed Guy for that."

"Is that who you went to see?"

"Yes! And he's a wreck – I wouldn't be him for all the money in the world. His own kids despise him. He's a worthless sponge."

"Well, there you are then – we're not doing so badly after all."

"I suppose so," he said.

"You big eejit," she said, patting his chest fondly.

"There's a bit more."

Suddenly she could feel him tense. "Yes?"

There was a long silence.

"Yes?" she repeated.

He heaved a great sigh. "When Nathalie was born, Guy called and wanted to meet up. I agreed reluctantly to see him because he said he had something important to tell me." He paused.

"Yes?" Now she was beginning to feel really nervous.

He took a deep breath. "He told me he had slept with you a few times just weeks before we got married . . ."

"What?"

"And that Nathalie was his."

Yvonne stared at her husband in disbelief. This was it – the thing that had been gnawing away at him for so long! No – he was winding her up. Her first instinct was to laugh but something about the grim set of his jaw stifled the laugh in her throat. "You never believed him!"

He didn't answer.

"You did?"

He wouldn't even meet her eyes.

She pulled on a dressing-gown and sat on the edge of the bed, trying to take in the enormity of what her husband had just told her.

"But that means . . ." she began then stopped. She couldn't find the words. It meant that from the start he thought their marriage was a lie. It meant that from the moment Nathalie was born he'd believed her to be someone else's child. No! It couldn't be. "But . . . you loved Nathalie . . . " she whispered.

"Yes, I loved her. I thought she was the most beautiful thing in the world. I wanted her so much to be mine – and I used to forget for weeks on end that she mightn't be."

"I just can't believe that you would think that. How could you not *see* she's yours?"

"She had your colouring – not mine. Then we never had any other children. I thought that proved it, proved that I was infertile and Nathalie was not mine. And, Yvonne, I am so sorry, but I could never allow you to talk about us doing any tests . . . I was afraid of finding out it was my fault . . . then you and I would have to acknowledge openly that Nathalie was not mine." He heaved a huge sigh. "Anyway, I learned to live with it but, after her twenty-first birthday, for some reason it all came rolling back to bother me."

"But why didn't you say or ask? I could have told you straight out. I didn't even *like* Guy Bushell – I did go out with him before I met you but I never ever had sex with him! Or anything close to sex with him! Then I met you – and from that moment on, I was so nuts about you that I never even looked at another man!" She blanched when she thought of the night with Alan Halvey in Sheehy's Shack. But she'd been provoked into doing that and besides nothing had happened. She rounded on Liam once more. "How could you spend all that time not trusting me and thinking I'd lie to you like that?"

"I suppose I was afraid of knowing the answer once and for all – what if you'd said that she was Bushell's? What could I have done about it? As long as I didn't know for sure, I could feel she was mine."

There was such pain in his voice that, despite her own hurt, she was suddenly overcome with pity for him.

"And what if Guy had lied?" he went on. "What if it had never happened and I accused you? What if I wrecked our trust in each other for nothing?" He raised his head and gazed at her. "I suppose that's exactly what I have done now. Do you want me to leave?"

She slid coolly from the bed and stepped into the shower room but emerged moments later.

"Is that what you want?" she said.

He had pulled on a pair of old jeans and a blue cotton shirt. "I've been a complete fool, Yvonne – I just find it hard to talk about things – and I really couldn't bear the thought of you and . . ." He sank down on the bed and buried his face in his hands.

She sat beside him and took his hand in hers.

"I have a lot to put up with," she said. "I'm a pure saint."

He nodded and squeezed her hand.

"But you'd better stay," she said. "It wouldn't be right to let an eejit like you out on the streets. Now I'm going to shower and get dressed and you are going to take me out to dinner and we're going to start all over again and try and put this whole silly business behind us. OK?"

He looked at her with hope and gratitude. "I'd like that very much," he said and kissed her tenderly on the lips.

A while later they waited downstairs for a taxi to take them to Wayne Wong's down the road. Yvonne wore her best black trousers with a green lace and silk top. Liam had let out a low appreciative whistle as she came down the stairs. It felt like old times. She sat on the little hall chair and put the finishing touches to her make-up.

"There is one last thing . . ." he said, slinging a plain brown envelope on the hall table. "You'd better open this."

Yvonne eyed it suspiciously. She'd had so many surprises and shocks in recent weeks that she wasn't really keen on another one. She picked it up and slipped it open. Inside were two return tickets to Portugal.

"What's this all about?"

"You don't think I spent all of the last few weeks with Guy Bushell, do you? I've been in Portugal – checking out villas. But we definitely can't afford a villa. So I've found a lovely apartment right on the seafront – there's a lot of work to be done to it – that's how I've got it cheaply."

Yvonne stared at him in confusion. "What are you saying?"

"You said you wanted a place in Portugal – well, here it is. I can do all the refurbishing work and then we can go there whenever we want. It will be our little place in the sun."

She heard the taxi pulling up outside and the doorbell ringing. She stood up beside him and took his hand.

"My mother always said I should hang on to you," she said, kissing him.

CHAPTER 40

Nathalie sat in the train that would bring her to Blackrock to meet Mark. It was quite a struggle remaining calm – especially when she remembered how he'd flirted with her the last day and sent her home on the giddy possibility that he might after all like her. She tried not to worry about meeting his parents. It was quite stressful enough wondering if he really liked her or not.

Mark was standing on the platform waiting for her. His neat light brown hair curled lightly over a grey polo shirt and loose fitting jeans. His warm green eyes lit up delightedly when he saw her, and it made Nathalie feel like she was the only woman in the world as she stepped down from the train.

"You look pretty," he said admiring her indigo blue skirt with the white blouse and blue ballet shrug.

"Thanks," she said and they stood awkwardly for a

moment. Then before she could even catch her breath, he'd leaned forward and kissed her lightly on the cheek.

"I was afraid you'd change your mind," he said softly.

Nathalie thought she might just float off on a cloud of happiness until she remembered that everyone kissed nowadays and that he probably meant nothing by it.

"I nearly chickened out. I don't know what your family will make of me," she said anxiously.

He grinned at her. "There's nothing to worry about," he said, squeezing her hand reassuringly as they set off down the road to his house.

But as they strolled in the evening sunshine along leafy roads past magnificent houses, each one grander than the last, her heart sank.

"Here we are," he said, stopping at last beside a large pair of black wrought-iron gates. Nathalie tried to peep through but all that was visible was a winding avenue of trees and shrubs – with some barley-sugar chimneys peeping over the tops. It looked enormous – not a house at all but a mansion.

The gate opened electronically and he took her by the hand, noticing her hesitation and tugging her gently forward. "Lest there be any doubt, Miss Nathalie Kelly – I've asked you here because I fancy you something rotten."

He pulled her towards him, took her sweet rounded face in his two hands, then bent his head and planted a long, lingering kiss on her lips. Nathalie felt the world tilt and spin, felt herself responding to him, wishing that the kiss would go on forever. But he pulled away and smiled crookedly at her. "Just remember that and you'll get through the afternoon fine."

"OK," she said.

"We'll continue with the kissing thing later – if that's all right with you," he added. Then he grabbed her hand once more and led her firmly down the winding avenue.

Pretty soon the house came into view and her jaw dropped.

"Not a bad pad, is it?" he said proudly.

"I've never seen a place like it. Your family must be rolling in it."

"Come on," he said, leading her across a wide expanse of well-tended lawn and into a garden to the side of the property. "Mum's probably in the kitchens."

"Kitchens?"

He led her into a maze of corridors and rooms until they came to a large cavernous arched kitchen – and of course there was the little army of servants – bustling about their tasks presided over by a large beaming lady in a white overall.

"Mark – it's chaos here – Sandra's gone AWOL again – and didn't do the soup before she left. I'm trying to do something now with a few packs of Erin – God knows what it will be like. Will you check the meat, Jesus?"

"Yes, Missus Tierney," said a swarthy Spanish-sounding man.

"Here," Mark's mother said as she handed him a large wooden spoon, "you stir this and introduce us."

"Mum, this is Nathalie."

The woman beamed broadly at Nathalie and shook her hand vigorously. Then she took a bag of bread rolls from a cupboard and placed a tub of butter and a knife beside it on the large marble-topped island in the centre of the room.

"Nathalie, would you? Butter the rolls, I mean? Only we'll never get this dinner on the table otherwise."

Mark grinned at Nathalie and rolled his eyes.

"I'd love to," said Nathalie, delighted to be asked to do something with her hands – something to take her mind off the fact it looked like she was facing into sitting down to a banquet with at least twenty other people.

So Mark stirred and Nathalie spread the butter and Jesus carved a huge joint of beef. Maureen – Mark's mother – made the gravy.

At one point, when Maureen left the room, Nathalie abandoned her buttering and went over to Mark. "How many are coming to dinner?" she asked, unable to keep the note of panic from her voice.

"It's about twenty – I think," he said easily.

"You should have told me, Mark! It's not fair on your mother when she has all those other people coming along as well."

"It's not like you think."

"No?"

"Well – I thought you'd have figured it out by now."

"Figured what out?"

He waved his wooden spoon around, almost spattering her with drops of hot soup. "All of this."

"Yes, I have! You and your family live in this mansion and you're all filthy rich and there's a large gang of your friends coming over for dinner – and I haven't the foggiest idea what the hell I'm supposed to be doing in the middle of it all!" She stalked back to the table and resumed her roll-buttering. "You should have more consideration for your mother," she added.

Mark stopped stirring the soup, threw back his head and laughed. "Listen – if we were all so filthy rich – do you honestly think my mother would be brewing up a big saucepan of packet soup for her guests – or spreading butter on a catering batch of bread rolls?"

"Maybe she's just being thrifty. Rich people always are. That's how they get rich."

"Remember I told you she runs the home – well, this is it – the *home*. She's a matron. We don't live in this place – it's a nursing home for people who are recovering from operations." He pointed through the large leaded window at a much smaller building the far side of the garden. "That's our gaff – comes with the job. Not bad, is it?" He grinned impishly at her.

Nathalie glared at him crossly. She felt like she ought to pelt him with the entire batch of bread rolls but that wouldn't be fair on his mother. "But your dad is a big consultant in the Blackrock Clinic!"

"You keep on jumping to conclusions. Just like that first day in Felicity's office – when you assumed I was an office boy. Yes, he does work in the Clinic – he looks after maintaining the building. Anyway – what's that got to do with anything? We'd better help Mum to serve up this lot."

So instead of sitting in a grand dining-room and watching her table manners and struggling to make polite conversation with a bunch of strangers, Nathalie ended up serving dinner to twenty invalids in a bright and cheerful high-ceilinged dining-room. There was a warm happy atmosphere and one or two of the patients teased her about being Mark's girlfriend.

Afterwards, when everything had been cleared away, and Mark's dad had arrived home, the family retired to the little house at the end of the garden and Maureen served up the remains of the roast dinner with a couple of bottles of red wine.

"There now – it wasn't so bad – was it?" Mark said, holding her hand tightly as they walked towards the station later that night.

"They're really nice – your mum and dad." She felt a horrible twinge of sadness as she thought of her own dad. "Mark, there's something you need to know about my family."

"I know all I need to know," he said, squeezing her hand to reassure her.

"No, but – this is something that I want to tell you." She was on the point of telling him about her father and how he had disappeared, on account of her mother having the grubby affair in the expensive thong, when her mobile rang.

"Nathalie – it's Mum."

"Hi,"

"I just wanted you to know – your dad's home."

Nathalie listened carefully as her mother, sounding happier than she'd been in months, described Liam's homecoming. When Nathalie finally hung up they had arrived at the station.

"Sorry," she said to Mark.

"That's OK," he said, then added: "You said there was something you needed to tell me about your family . . ."

"What? My family?" It hardly seemed important now. Her dad was home, safe and well. Her mother was happy once more.

"What you should know about my family – is that they will probably like you a lot," she said and kissed him right on the lips.

CHAPTER 41

Berry and Aoife were sitting with Harry Robson in the lounge of the Bayview Hotel. Harry had received several more emails from Yelena and Berry had finally convinced him that they were none of her doing. Harry had phoned the mobile number Yelena had written in her email and she had assured him that she would be in Ireland this very Saturday to visit her sister in Dublin and to meet Harry Robson, man of her dreams.

Harry wasn't fully convinced, but since he had nothing else planned for the afternoon he waited in the Bayview on the off-chance that someone called Yelena might turn up. And if the Russian lady didn't show, he was more than happy to spend his time with the very attractive Joyce sisters.

But an hour drifted by quite pleasantly and there was no sign of Yelena. A few stragglers came and went in the lounge but generally things were very quiet until, unusually for her, Judge Patricia de Vere swept in, looking as if she'd just come from dispensing a few life sentences. She wore a severe grey overcoat with a half-belt at the back and her black patent stilettos. Her dark golden hair was pulled into a severe knot at the nape of her neck giving her an even haughtier expression than normal. She glanced around the room and waved dismissively at Harry and his two companions. Then she sat at the bar and ordered a large stiff gin.

"Strange woman!" Harry murmured to the Joyce sisters.

"You can say that again!" muttered Aoife.

The bar was quiet except for the low clink of glasses as the barman stacked the shelves in preparation for the busy evening ahead.

Then Harry drained his glass. "Oh well! So much for my Russian bride! Listen, thanks for keeping me company – but I must go now – I've got work to do."

Then just at that moment Judge Patricia swept down from her high bar stool and strode across to Harry and the two girls. "Great news about the HyperShop," she said. "Thanks to you, Harry. We couldn't have done it without you."

"My pleasure," he said absently.

"Mind if I join you?" Patricia said as she tugged at a loose strand of hair.

Berry and Aoife shrugged, none too enthusiastically.

"Fire away," said Harry, "but I was just on the point of leaving."

"That's a shame," Patricia said.

Then, as Harry got to his feet, Patricia placed a long forefinger in the middle of his chest and pushed with such force that he collapsed back into his seat. Then, as he goggled in amazement, she took a step backwards, putting a hand to the back of her neck. In an instant, a long mane of golden tresses tumbled down about her face. She slipped out of the dull grey coat and stood there resplendent in a black velvet dress that showed off a magnificent curvy figure. She tossed the horn-rimmed spectacles aside, and stretching out her long shapely legs, hands on her hips, she purred: "My dariling Harold – I have waited so long for this moment! Since leaving Zuchistan, I long to be with you, Mel Gibson of my fantasies . . ."

Berry and Aoife both stared gobsmacked at the High Court Judge. They'd only ever seen her in the severest of suits, her hair pulled back in a tight bun, a pair of menacing glasses always perched on the end of her aquiline nose. They both looked at her now and realised that there was an awful lot more to Judge Patricia de Vere than either of them would ever have imagined – most especially a wicked sense of humour.

For once, the rakish grin was wiped clear from Harry's face as he took in the soft tumbling waves of Patricia's hair, the smouldering indigo grey of her eyes, the voluptuous curve of her breasts and the magnificent grace of her long elegant legs. And yes, of course, there was only one woman smart enough to have conned him with a fake Russian Bride email.

Three sets of eyes stared at the High Court Judge in utter amazement.

"Yelena?" Harry stammered.

"The Russian bride?" Berry chipped in.

"Judge de Vere!" Aoife gasped.

"Hottest babe in Larkhaven," Harry said, looking directly into her eyes, now he'd got over the shock.

"Why thank you, Mr Harry Robson," Patricia purred.

"Now maybe you'll change your mind and stay for that drink."

"Just the one," Harry said, then added: "And then you've got some big explaining to do. And, by the way, the little matter of astonishing tricks with baby oil? Is that legal?"

CHAPTER 42

Over the next few months, life returned to a manageable rhythm. Together Aoife and Berry worked night and day – preparing to open their new premises. Andrew McRory put up the bulk of the money but Dermot also chipped in – keen to help out with his new fiancée's new business venture.

As the months went by and the building took shape, the Joyce sisters' new business venture became the talk of the village.

But there were other changes also.

At home in Bloomfield House, Aoife stripped the oak floorboards of years of grime and wax and sanded and restored them to their former glory. Then she turned her attention to the kitchen and stripped down the kitchen units before giving them a bright new coat of paint. She used a DIY site on the Internet to show her how to take down the bathroom door and rehang it so that it didn't squeak and jam any more.

Berry brought the garden to a state of delightfulness that could have featured in a magazine. She learned to cook – and at weekends the sisters began to entertain a procession of guests – Patricia and Harry, now head over heels in love; Liam and Yvonne, their happiness restored; Mark and Nathalie, just setting out on their own fantastic voyage of love. Kevin and Stella visited and Gothic Claire from Vernon's with her new boyfriend, Joe the doorman. There were even girlie weekends with Nathalie and Johanne and Claire – when they ate takeaway and drank too much wine and teased Nathalie gently about Mark. And most of all there was Dermot, quietly enjoying his new-found fortune and now happily reunited with Aoife and planning marriage. In short, life for Aoife and Berry was truly bursting with riches – friends, family, neighbours, and their home and new business.

Kevin Vernon came from Dublin on the day of the grand opening and cut the tape and said a few words. Andrew McRory breezed in for twenty minutes on his way to Budapest and praised the sisters and promised his continuing support. Dermot had supplied the champagne and food. Even the general manager of HyperShop showed up to offer his guarded support. The villagers milled about the brand new offices – big open-plan rooms, and already a steady flow of properties for sale and people to buy them.

Jim, whose bookshop they had bought out, was positively poetic about the wonderful changes they'd made He drifted about, glass of wine in hand, and admired the grand curving glass walls and high vaulted ceilings and salvaged oak floors and a little deck to the rear that faced out to the strand with light pouring in from all directions

In the evening, when all the guests and VIPs had left

Aoife and Berry sat in the plush foyer sipping a glass of champagne and savouring their good fortune.

It was dark by the time they got home. Swinging in through the gateway in her brand-new car, Berry felt a little twinge of sadness that the cottage was empty, its rooms in darkness. She thought fleetingly of Ben Searson and wondered where his travels had led him. Would their paths ever cross again? She doubted it. They ought to rent the gatelodge out again if only just to keep it habitable. And it had felt safe when Ben was close by. Somehow he'd been a good neighbour without ever making a big deal about it.

In the kitchen, Aoife yawned and decided that she was too tired to make tea.

"Think I'll have a bath," she said stifling another yawn and disappearing upstairs.

Berry took a cup of tea, the day's crossword and a digestive biscuit into the TV room and curled up on the big old sofa. There was a travel programme she wanted to watch. But the excitement of the day was catching up on her now and she could barely keep her eyes open. She snoozed through most of the travel programme and then the late evening news came on. There was nothing unusual – just the standard politics, crime, surveys and reports, followed by the usual weekly sporting dramas. Programmes for the remainder of the evening were listed – drama with *Desperate Sex in the OC*, followed by highlights of the day's golf, then, *Turning Point – How Prison Changed My Life – Noelle Johnson talks to Ben Pearse*.

She had to wait an hour – and it turned out to be a

terribly long hour, as she grew more and more impatient with both the actors and the golfers. Even Pádraig Harrington who was normally crucial viewing in any golf tournament couldn't hold her attention. The golf ran over by almost half an hour but at last it was time for *Turning Point*.

And there he was – the unruly dark hair, grown slightly gray at the temples, dark-eyed, clean shaven, leaner and more tanned than when she'd seen him last. Her heart leapt to see him and to hear his wounded gravelly voice describe the life he had once led and the crime that had put him in prison.

"So prison forced you to reassess almost every aspect of your life, Ben?"

He nodded and smiled stiffly. Berry knew by him that he was uncomfortable.

"I'm a very different person now. I'm not sure if it's all to do with being sent to prison though."

"How do you mean?"

"When I left prison – I went to live by the sea for a while – in a little cottage – digging the garden, chopping logs, fixing things . . . making new friends . . ."

"And did you find that therapeutic?"

Ben ignored the question and there was an uneasy silence, broken at last by the interviewer.

"What does the future hold for Ben Pearse, do you think? Will you go back to making Reality TV shows? Surely a man of your ambition, your experience and connections won't be happy to stay out of the limelight for much longer?"

Ben shrugged and smiled his wary smile at her. "Who knows? Right now I fancy going back to that little cottage and finishing one or two projects there. But the reality is that a man has to make a living. We've got some interesting programmes in the pipeline. I'm not short of work for the foreseeable future."

"Ben Pearse there – enigmatic as ever – on how a spell in prison became a significant turning point in his life."

So there he was and she had let him go. She glanced out at the little gatelodge and suppressed a gnawing dart of regret.

Weeks passed. Aoife and Berry were so busy that they had scarcely enough time to note the passing of each day. Each night Berry fell into bed exhausted and vowed that some day soon she would allow herself a day off. Sometimes at weekends Aoife stayed in town with Dermot, and Berry had the house to herself. She would use the time to catch up on the accounts or to work in the garden. One evening, Judge Patricia and Harry came over for tea and Berry cooked a simple lasagna and salad. It seemed to her that Patricia and Harry had always been meant for each other. And even now after a few short months, she could scarcely imagine them not being together. She watched them drive off down the short avenue past the little gatelodge and envied their happiness.

Back in the living room, she tried to watch TV but nothing held her interest. She leafed through the little bundle of notes for *The County Sentinel* and vowed faithfully to tackle them in the morning. A badly typed letter informed her that Colin Farrell had been sighted yet again, this time heavily disguised as a biker, scouting for land along the coast. A carefully worded letter from The

Larkhaven Association announced that membership had increased tenfold in the past six months. Father Martin had sent an email saying that he intended to conduct a survey on what colour the church should be painted this year. Nancy Lemon had retired to her sister's house in Ballivor and thanked all her friends and neighbours for the happy times she'd spent in Larkhaven. Harry Robson was applying for planning permission to extend his home. That brought a smile to Berry's face. She replaced the little pile of notes in their folder and then crossed to the window and swiftly drew the curtains.

As she did so, a glimmer of light caught her eye. She pulled the curtain back again. She looked again and, with a leap of her heart, saw that there was a light in the cottage. She suppressed a quick dart of hope and told herself that it was probably one of the local tramps. It wasn't all that hard to force the back door open and borrow a free bed for the night.

She pulled on her old waxed jacket and walking shoes and within minutes she was rapping gently on the door of the little gatelodge.

There was no reply. She pushed against the door and it opened. She stepped inside gingerly. Was she being careless? What if it were somebody dangerous?

And there he was. She stood motionless, afraid to speak.

"I thought it might be someone dangerous," she said at last, her voice trembling. She couldn't tear her eyes away from him.

"It is someone very dangerous," he said and took her hand.

She wanted to say she'd missed him, that she'd longed

for him every single night since he'd left, that there was a very distinct possibility that she might be in love with him.

"You kept a spare key," she said to him instead.

He tugged her forward into his arms. "Yes – I'm sorry about that."

"I saw you on TV."

"Dreadful stuff," he said. "But a bit of public atonement always makes good television."

"So – what next for Ben Pearse?" she said, mimicking the reporter's earnest voice and taking a step towards him.

"Who knows?" he said. "I had no idea I was coming back here until I discovered I was just five miles from Larkhaven. But maybe I should leave again."

"Stay?"

He said nothing, just held her. What words could either of them come up with? What words did either of them need to say?

"OK," he said at last.

THE END

Direct to your home!

If you enjoyed this book why not visit our website:

www.poolbeg.com

and get another book delivered straight to your home or to a friend's home!

www.poolbeg.com

All orders are despatched within 24 hours.

The Little Oxford Dictionary
and Thesaurus

The Little Oxford Dictionary & Thesaurus

REVISED EDITION

Edited by
Sara Hawker

with
Chris Cowley

OXFORD
UNIVERSITY PRESS

OXFORD
UNIVERSITY PRESS

Great Clarendon Street, Oxford OX2 6DP

Oxford University Press is a department of the University of Oxford.
It furthers the University's objective of excellence in research, scholarship,
and education by publishing worldwide in

Oxford New York

Athens Auckland Bangkok Bogotá Buenos Aires Calcutta
Cape Town Chennai Dar es Salaam Delhi Florence Hong Kong Istanbul
Karachi Kuala Lumpur Madrid Melbourne Mexico City Mumbai
Nairobi Paris São Paulo Singapore Taipei Tokyo Toronto Warsaw

with associated companies in Berlin Ibadan

The publishers are grateful to the Reader's Digest Association
Limited for permission to use the respelling pronunciation
system shown in this dictionary

Oxford is a registered trade mark of Oxford University Press
in the UK and in certain other countries

Published in the United States
by Oxford University Press Inc., New York

© Oxford University Press 1996, 1998

First edition 1996
This revised edition 1998
Based on the text of the *Oxford Minireference Dictionary and Thesaurus*, 1995

British Library Cataloguing in Publication Data

Data available

Library of Congress Cataloging in Publication Data

Data available

ISBN 0-19-860246-4

10 9 8 7 6 5 4 3

Printed in Great Britain by
Clay PLC, Bungay, Suffolk

Contents

Preface

The *Little Oxford Dictionary & Thesaurus* combines the information you would expect to find in a conventional dictionary and a thesaurus in a single handy volume. Within an individual entry it offers a guide to the spelling and meaning of a word, together with lists of synonyms from which an alternative word can be selected.

Also included in this revised edition is a special Reverse Dictionary Supplement, providing a guide to related words, a vocabulary builder, and a puzzle solver all in one.

Suitable for use on many occasions, from writing a letter to solving a crossword puzzle, the *Little Oxford Dictionary & Thesaurus* is a convenient and compact quick-reference book.

S. J. H.

How to use the Little Oxford Dictionary & Thesaurus

The 'entry map' below explains the different parts of an entry.

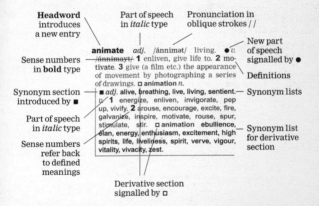

Headword introduces a new entry

Part of speech in *italic* type

Pronunciation in oblique strokes / /

New part of speech signalled by ●

Sense numbers in **bold** type

Definitions

Synonym section introduced by ■

Synonym lists

Part of speech in *italic* type

Sense numbers refer back to defined meanings

Synonym list for derivative section

Derivative section signalled by □

Arrangement of synonym sections

Synonyms are offered for many of the words defined in the *Little Oxford Dictionary & Thesaurus*. The sense numbering in the synonym sections follows the pattern of the defining sections, so that users can easily see which synonyms are appropriate to which meaning of the headword. Synonyms are not always offered for every dictionary sense and in some cases a single list of synonyms is offered for several senses. The sense numbering may then take the form of a list, as, for example, **1, 3, 4**. Wherever a single synonym list covers all the meanings explained in the defining section, sense numbers are dispensed with and the synonym list is simply introduced by the symbol ■.

Within each separate sense synonyms are arranged alphabetically, but a list may be divided by a semicolon to indicate a different 'branch' of meaning.

> **hire** *v.* engage or grant temporary use of, for payment. ● *n.* hiring. □ **hire purchase** system of purchase by paying in instalments. **hirer** *n.*
> ■ *v.* charter, lease, rent; employ, engage, take on. *n.* lease, rental.

semicolon indicates new 'branch' of meaning.

Occasionally, the synonyms offered are for a form other than the exact form of the headword. In these cases, this altered form is given in brackets at the beginning of the synonym list.

> **gut** *n.* **1** intestine. **2** thread made from animal intestines. **3** (*pl.*) abdominal organs. **4** (*pl., colloq.*) courage and determination. ● *v.* (**gutted**) **1** remove guts from (fish). **2** remove or destroy internal fittings or parts of.
> ■ *n.* **3** (**guts**) bowels, entrails, *colloq.* innards, *colloq.* insides, intestines, viscera, vitals. **4** (**guts**) boldness, bravery, courage, daring, fearlessness, *colloq.* grit, mettle, nerve, pluck, spirit, valour. *v.* **1** disembowel, eviscerate. **2** destroy, devastate, ravage; empty, loot, pillage, plunder, ransack, strip.

synonyms offered for a plural form of the headword.

Key to the Pronunciations

This dictionary uses a simple respelling system to show how words are pronounced. The following symbols are used:

a, á	*as in*	**pat** /pat/, **pattern** /páttərn/	
aa, áa	*as in*	**palm** /paam/, **rather** /ra<u>a</u>thər/	
air, áir	*as in*	**fair** /fair/, **fairy** /fáiri/	
aw, áw	*as in*	**law** /law/, **caught** /kawt/, **caution** /káwsh'n/	
awr, áwr	*as in*	**warm** /wawrm/, **warning** /wáwrning/	
ay, áy	*as in*	**gauge** /gayj/, **daily** /dáyli/	
ch	*as in*	**church** /church/, **cello** /chéllō/	
e, é	*as in*	**said** /sed/, **jealous** /jélləss/	
ee, ée	*as in*	**feet** /feet/, **recent** /reéss'nt/	
er, ér	*as in*	**fern** /fern/, **early** /érli/	
érr	*as in*	**ferry** /férri/, **burial** /bérriəl/	
ə	*as in*	**along** /əlóng/, **pollen** /póllən/, **lemon** /lémmən/, **serious** /seériəss/	
g	*as in*	**get** /get/	
i, í	*as in*	**pin** /pin/, **women** /wímmin/	
ī, í	*as in*	**time** /tīm/, **writing** /rīting/	
īr, ír	*as in*	**fire** /fīr/, **choir** /kwīr/, **desire** /dizír/	
írr	*as in*	**lyrics** /lírriks/	
j	*as in*	**judge** /juj/	
<u>kh</u>	*as in*	**loch** /lo<u>kh</u>/	
N	*as in*	**en route** /oN rōōt/	
ng	*as in*	**sing** /sing/, **sink** /singk/	
ngg	*as in*	**single** /síngg'l/, **anger** /ánggər/	
o, ó	*as in*	**rob** /rob/, **robin** /róbbin/	
ō, ố	*as in*	**boat** /bōt/, **motion** /mōsh'n/	

ö, ő	*as in*	**colonel** /kőn'l/
oo	*as in*	**unite** /yoonĭt/
ŏŏ, ŏŏ	*as in*	**wood** /wŏŏd/, **football** /fŏŏtbawl/
ōō, ōō	*as in*	**food** /fōōd/, **music** /myōōzik/
oor, oor	*as in*	**cure** /kyoor/, **jury** /jóori/
or, ór	*as in*	**door** /dor/, **corner** /kórnər/
ow, ów	*as in*	**mouse** /mowss/, **coward** /kówərd/
oy, óy	*as in*	**boy** /boy/, **noisy** /nóyzi/
r̍, rr	*as in*	**run** /run/, **fur** /fur/, **spirit** /spírrit/
sh	*as in*	**shut** /shut/
th	*as in*	**thin** /thin/, **truth** /trōōth/
<u>th</u>	*as in*	**then** /<u>th</u>en/, **mother** /mú<u>th</u>ər/
u, ú	*as in*	**cut** /kut/, **money** /múnni/
ur, úr	*as in*	**curl** /kurl/, **journey** /júrni/
úrr	*as in*	**hurry** /húrri/
y	*as in*	**yet** /yet/, **million** /mílyən/
<u>zh</u>	*as in*	**measure** /mé<u>zh</u>ər/, **vision** /ví<u>zh</u>'n/

Consonants

The consonants *b, d, f, h, k, l, m, n, p, s, t, v, w, z* are pronounced in the usual way. A doubled consonant indicates that the preceding vowel is short, as in **robin** /róbbin/.

Stress

The mark ´ that appears over the vowel symbol in words of more than one syllable indicates the part of the word which carries the stress.

Abbreviations

abbr. abbreviation
adj. adjective
adjs. adjectives
adv. adverb
attrib. attributively
Austr. Australian
colloq. colloquial
conj. conjunction
Dec. December
derog. derogatory
esp. especially
fem. feminine
Fr. French
int. interjection

Ir. Irish
Jan. January
joc. jocularly
n. noun
N. Engl. northern England
Nov. November
ns. nouns
orig. originally
[P.] proprietary term
pl. plural
poss. possessive
pref. prefix

prep. preposition
pron. pronoun
rel.pron. relative pronoun
S. Afr. South African
Sc. Scottish
sing. singular
sl. slang
US United States
usu. usually
v. verb
v. aux. auxiliary verb

Abbreviations that are in general use (such as ft, RC) appear in the dictionary itself.

Proprietary terms

This dictionary includes some words which are, or are asserted to be, proprietary terms or trade marks. Their inclusion does not mean that they have acquired for legal purposes a non-proprietary or general significance, nor is any other judgement implied concerning their legal status. In cases where the editor has some evidence that a word is used as a proprietary name or trade mark this is indicated by a letter [P.], but no judgement concerning the legal status of such words is made or implied thereby.

a *adj.* **1** one, any. **2** in, to, or for each.

aback *adv.* **taken aback** disconcerted.

abacus *n.* (*pl.* **-cuses**) frame with balls sliding on rods, used for counting.

abandon *v.* **1** leave without intending to return. **2** give up. ● *n.* careless freedom of manner. □ **abandonment** *n.*

■ *v.* **1** evacuate, leave, quit, vacate, withdraw from; desert, *sl.* ditch, forsake, jilt, leave behind, leave in the lurch, maroon, strand, wash one's hands of. **2** cede, discontinue, disown, *sl.* ditch, drop, forfeit, forgo, give up, relinquish, renounce, resign, surrender, yield.

abandoned *adj.* **1** deserted. **2** unrestrained.

abase *v.* humiliate, degrade. □ **abasement** *n.*

abashed *adj.* embarrassed, ashamed.

abate *v.* make or become less intense. □ **abatement** *n.*

abattoir /ábbətwaar/ *n.* slaughterhouse.

abbess *n.* head of a community of nuns.

abbey *n.* building occupied by a community of monks or nuns.

abbot *n.* head of a community of monks.

abbreviate *v.* shorten.

■ abridge, condense, cut, edit, précis, reduce, shorten, summarize, truncate.

abbreviation *n.* shortened form of word(s).

ABC *n.* **1** alphabet. **2** alphabetical guide. **3** rudiments (of a subject).

abdicate *v.* renounce the throne. □ **abdication** *n.*

abdomen *n.* part of the body containing the digestive organs. □ **abdominal** *adj.*

abduct *v.* kidnap. □ **abduction** *n.*, **abductor** *n.*

■ carry off, kidnap, seize.

aberrant *adj.* showing aberration. □ **aberrance** *n.*

aberration *n.* **1** deviation from what is normal. **2** distortion.

abet *v.* (**abetted**) encourage or assist in wrongdoing. □ **abettor** *n.*

abeyance *n.* **in abeyance** not being used for a time.

abhor *v.* (**abhorred**) detest. □ **abhorrence** *n.*

■ abominate, despise, detest, execrate, hate, loathe, shudder at.

abhorrent *adj.* detestable.

■ abominable, detestable, execrable, hateful, loathsome, obnoxious, repellent, revolting.

abide *v.* tolerate. □ **abide by 1** keep (a promise). **2** accept (consequences etc.).

■ accept, bear, endure, put up with, stand, stomach, suffer, tolerate. □ **abide by** accept, adhere to, comply with, conform to, heed, honour, keep (to), obey, observe, pay attention to, stick to.

abiding *adj.* lasting, permanent.

ability *n.* **1** power to do something. **2** cleverness.

■ **1** capacity, means, power, resources, scope. **2** aptitude, bent, brains, capability, cleverness, competence, expertise, flair, genius, gift, intelligence, knack, know-how, knowledge, proficiency, prowess, skill, strength, talent, training, wit.

abject *adj.* **1** wretched. **2** lacking pride. □ **abjectly** *adv.*

ablaze *adj.* blazing.

able *adj.* **1** having power or capacity. **2** talented. □ **ably** *adv.*

■ **1** allowed, at liberty, authorized, available, capable, eligible, equipped, fit, free, permitted, prepared, willing. **2** accomplished, adept, capable, clever, competent, effective, efficient, experienced, expert, handy, intelligent, masterly, practised, proficient, skilful, skilled, talented.

ablutions *n.pl.* process of washing oneself.

abnegate *v.* renounce.

abnormal *adj.* not normal. □ **abnormally** *adv.*, **abnormality** *n.*

■ aberrant, anomalous, atypical, bizarre, curious, deviant, eccentric, exceptional, extraordinary, funny, idiosyncratic, irregular, *colloq.* kinky, odd, peculiar, perverted, queer, singular, strange, unnatural, unusual, weird.

aboard *adv.* & *prep.* on board.

abode *n.* home, dwelling place.

abolish v. put an end to. □ **abolition** n.

■ annul, destroy, dispense with, do away with, eliminate, end, eradicate, get rid of, liquidate, nullify, overturn, put an end to, quash, suppress, terminate.

abominable adj. very bad or unpleasant. □ **abominably** adv.

■ abhorrent, appalling, atrocious, awful, colloq. beastly, despicable, detestable, disgusting, dreadful, execrable, foul, hateful, heinous, horrible, loathsome, nasty, obnoxious, odious, repellent, repugnant, repulsive, revolting, terrible, vile.

abominate v. detest. □ **abomination** n.

aboriginal adj. existing in a country from its earliest times.

aborigine /ábbərijini/ n. aboriginal inhabitant.

abort v. 1 (cause to) expel a foetus prematurely. 2 end prematurely and unsuccessfully.

abortion n. 1 premature expulsion of a foetus from the womb. 2 operation to cause this.

abortionist n. person who performs abortions.

abortive adj. 1 causing an abortion. 2 unsuccessful.

■ 2 fruitless, futile, ineffective, unsuccessful, vain.

abound v. be plentiful.

about adv. & prep. 1 near. 2 here and there. 3 in circulation. 4 approximately. 5 in connection with. 6 so as to face in the opposite direction. □ **about-face**, **-turn** ns. reversal of direction or policy. **be about to** be on the point of (doing).

above adv. & prep. 1 at or to a higher point (than). 2 beyond the level or understanding of. □ **above board** without deception.

abracadabra n. magic formula.

abrasion n. 1 rubbing or scraping away. 2 injury caused by this.

abrasive adj. 1 causing abrasion. 2 harsh. ● n. substance used for grinding or polishing surfaces.

abreast adv. side by side.

abridge v. shorten by using fewer words. □ **abridgement** n.

■ abbreviate, condense, cut, précis, reduce, shorten, summarize.

abroad adv. away from one's home country.

abrogate v. repeal, cancel. □ **abrogation** n.

abrupt adj. 1 sudden. 2 curt. 3 steep. □ **abruptly** adv., **abruptness** n.

■ 1 hasty, hurried, precipitate, quick, rapid, sudden, unexpected, unforeseen. 2 blunt, brusque, curt, discourteous, impolite, rude, short, terse, ungracious, sharp, sheer, steep. 3 precipitous.

abscess n. collection of pus formed in the body.

abscond v. go away secretly or illegally.

abseil v. descend by using a rope fixed at a higher point. ● n. such a descent.

absence n. 1 being absent. 2 lack.

absent¹ /ábs'nt/ adj. 1 not present. 2 lacking, non-existent. □ **absent-minded** adj. forgetful, inattentive.

■ 1 away, elsewhere, gone, missing, off, out, playing truant. 2 lacking, missing, non-existent. □ **absent-minded** careless, forgetful, inattentive, preoccupied, scatterbrained, thoughtless.

absent² /əbsént/ v. **absent oneself** stay away.

absentee n. person who is absent from work etc. □ **absenteeism** n.

absinthe n. a green liqueur.

absolute adj. 1 complete. 2 despotic. □ **absolutely** adv.

■ 1 categorical, complete, downright, out and out, perfect, pure, sheer, thorough, total, unadulterated, unconditional, unmitigated, unqualified, unreserved, utter. 2 autocratic, despotic, dictatorial, totalitarian, tyrannical.

absolution n. priest's formal declaration of forgiveness of sins.

absolutism n. principle of government with unrestricted powers. □ **absolutist** n.

absolve v. clear of blame or guilt.

■ acquit, clear, excuse, exonerate, forgive, pardon.

absorb v. 1 take in, combine into itself or oneself. 2 reduce the intensity of. 3 occupy the attention or interest of. □ **absorption** n., **absorptive** adj.

■ 1 assimilate, consume, digest, imbibe, incorporate, soak up, take in. 2 cushion, deaden, lessen, soften. 3 captivate, engage, engross, enthral, fascinate, interest, occupy, preoccupy.

absorbent adj. able to absorb moisture etc.

abstain v. 1 refrain, esp. from drinking alcohol. 2 decide not to use one's vote. □ **abstainer** n., **abstention** n.

abstemious *adj.* not self-indulgent. □ **abstemiously** *adv.*

■ ascetic, frugal, moderate, restrained, self-denying, temperate.

abstinence *n.* abstaining esp. from food or alcohol.

abstract *adj.* /ábstrakt/ **1** having no material existence, theoretical. **2** (of art) not representing things pictorially. ● *n.* /ábstrakt/ **1** summary. **2** abstract quality or idea. **3** piece of abstract art. ● *v.* /əbstrákt/ **1** take out, remove. **2** make a summary of. □ **abstraction** *n.*

■ *adj.* **1** academic, conceptual, intangible, metaphysical, notional, philosophical, theoretical. ● *n.* **1** outline, précis, résumé, summary, synopsis.

abstruse *adj.* hard to understand, profound.

■ complex, cryptic, deep, difficult, enigmatic, esoteric, mysterious, obscure, profound, recondite.

absurd *adj.* not in accordance with common sense, ridiculous. □ **absurdly** *adv.*, **absurdity** *n.*

■ crazy, daft, farcical, foolish, idiotic, illogical, incongruous, irrational, laughable, ludicrous, nonsensical, outlandish, paradoxical, preposterous, ridiculous, senseless, silly, stupid, unreasonable.

abundant *adj.* plentiful. □ **abundant in** having plenty of. **abundantly** *adv.*, **abundance** *n.*

■ ample, bountiful, copious, generous, lavish, liberal, luxuriant, plentiful, profuse. □ **abundant in** full of, overflowing with, rich in, teeming with.

abuse *v.* /əbyōoz/ **1** ill-treat. **2** make bad use of. **3** attack with abusive language. ● *n.* /əbyōoss/ **1** ill-treatment. **2** incorrect use. **3** abusive language.

■ *v.* **1** damage, harm, hurt, ill-treat, injure, maltreat, molest, wrong. **2** exploit, misapply, misuse, pervert, take advantage of. **3** berate, be rude to, curse (at), defame, insult, libel, malign, rail at, revile, slander, swear at, vilify, vituperate. ● *n.* **1** illtreatment, maltreatment, molestation. **2** misapplication, misuse, perversion. **3** curses, insults, invective, vilification, vituperation.

abusive *adj.* using harsh words or insults. □ **abusively** *adv.*

■ censorious, critical, defamatory, derogatory, disparaging, insulting, libellous, offensive, opprobrious, pejorative, rude, scurrilous, slanderous, vituperative.

abut *v.* (**abutted**) **1** border (upon). **2** touch or lean (against).

abysmal *adj.* very bad.

abyss *n.* very deep chasm.

acacia /əkáyshə/ *n.* flowering tree or shrub.

academic *adj.* **1** of a college or university. **2** scholarly, intellectual. **3** of theoretical interest only. ● *n.* academic person. □ **academically** *adv.*

■ *adj.* **2** bookish, brainy, clever, erudite, highbrow, intellectual, learned, scholarly, studious. **3** abstract, hypothetical, speculative, theoretical. ● *n.* don, highbrow, intellectual, lecturer, professor, scholar, thinker.

academician *n.* member of an Academy.

academy *n.* **1** school, esp. for specialized training. **2** (**Academy**) society of scholars or artists.

acanthus *n.* plant with large thistle-like leaves.

accede /akséed/ *v.* agree (to).

accelerate *v.* **1** increase speed (of). **2** (cause to) happen earlier. □ **acceleration** *n.*

■ **1** go faster, hasten, pick up speed, quicken, speed up. **2** expedite, forward, hasten, precipitate, speed up, spur on, stimulate.

accelerator *n.* pedal on a vehicle for increasing speed.

accent *n.* /áks'nt/ **1** particular regional, national, or other way of pronouncing words. **2** emphasis on a word. **3** mark showing how a letter is pronounced. ● *v.* /aksént/ emphasize.

accentuate *v.* **1** emphasize. **2** make prominent. □ **accentuation** *n.*

accept *v.* **1** say yes (to). **2** tolerate. **3** take as true. **4** acknowledge. □ **acceptance** *n.*

■ **1** accede (to), acquiesce (in), agree (to), consent (to). **2** bear, come to terms with, put up with, resign oneself to, stomach, submit to, suffer, tolerate. **3** believe, credit, find credible, have faith in. **4** acknowledge, admit, concede, recognize.

acceptable *adj.* **1** worth accepting, pleasing. **2** adequate. □ **acceptably** *adv.*, **acceptability** *n.*

■ **1** agreeable, gratifying, pleasant, pleasing, suitable, welcome. **2** adequate, admissible, passable, satisfactory, tolerable.

access *n.* **1** way in. **2** right to enter. **3** right to visit.

accessible *adj.* able to be reached or obtained. □ **accessibly** *adv.*, **accessibility** *n.*
■ at hand, attainable, available, close, convenient, handy, to hand, within reach.

accessory *adj.* additional. ● *n.* **1** additional fitment. **2** person who helps in a crime.
■ *adj.* added, additional, extra, supplementary. ● *n.* **2** abettor, accomplice, assistant, associate, collaborator, confederate, conspirator, helper, partner.

accident *n.* **1** unexpected event, chance. **2** unfortunate event.
■ **1** coincidence, fluke; chance, fate, fortune, luck, serendipity. **2** catastrophe, disaster, misadventure, mishap, mischance; collision, crash, pile-up.

accidental *adj.* happening by accident. □ **accidentally** *adv.*
■ casual, chance, coincidental, fortuitous, inadvertent, lucky, random, unexpected, unforeseen, unintended, unintentional, unlooked-for, unlucky, unplanned, unpremeditated.

acclaim *v.* welcome or applaud enthusiastically. ● *n.* shout of welcome, applause. □ **acclamation** *n.*
■ *v.* applaud, extol, hail, honour, praise, salute, welcome.

acclimatize *v.* adapt to a new climate or conditions. □ **acclimatization** *n.*

accolade *n.* **1** bestowal of a knighthood. **2** praise.

accommodate *v.* **1** provide lodging or room for. **2** adapt.
■ **1** billet, harbour, house, lodge, put up, quarter, shelter. **2** adapt, adjust, fit, harmonize, modify, reconcile.

accommodating *adj.* obliging.
■ adaptable, amenable, complaisant, compliant, cooperative, easygoing, flexible, helpful, kind, obliging.

accommodation *n.* place to live.
■ domicile, digs, home, house, housing, lodgings, quarters, residence, rooms, shelter.

accompany *v.* **1** go with. **2** be done or found with. **3** play an instrumental part supporting (singer(s) or an instrument). □ **accompaniment** *n.*, **accompanist** *n.*
■ **1** chaperon, conduct, escort, go with, guide, partner, usher.

accomplice *n.* partner, esp. in a crime.
■ abettor, accessory, associate, collaborator, confederate, conspirator, helper, partner.

accomplish *v.* succeed in doing or achieving.
■ achieve, attain, bring off, carry out, complete, consummate, do successfully, effect, finish, fulfil, realize, succeed in.

accomplished *adj.* **1** skilled. **2** having many accomplishments.
■ able, adept, expert, gifted, practised, proficient, skilful, skilled, talented.

accomplishment *n.* **1** useful ability. **2** thing achieved.
■ **1** ability, gift, skill, talent. **2** achievement, attainment, deed, exploit, feat, *tour de force*.

accord *v.* be consistent. ● *n.* consent, agreement. □ **of one's own accord** without being asked.

accordance *n.* conformity.

according *adv.* **according to 1** as stated by. **2** in proportion to. □ **accordingly** *adv.*

accordion *n.* musical instrument with bellows and a keyboard.

accost *v.* approach and speak to.

account *n.* **1** description, report. **2** statement of money paid or owed. **3** importance. **4** credit arrangement with a bank or firm. ● *v.* **account for 1** explain. **2** kill, overcome. □ **on account of** because of.
■ *n.* **1** commentary, description, explanation, history, log, narration, narrative, record, report, statement, story, tale. **2** bill, *US* check, invoice, statement. **3** consequence, importance, significance, use, value, worth.

accountable *adj.* obliged to account for one's actions. □ **accountability** *n.*

accountant *n.* person who keeps or inspects business accounts. □ **accountancy** *n.*

accoutrements /əkoōtrəmənts/ *n.pl.* equipment, trappings.

accretion *n.* **1** growth. **2** matter added.

accrue *v.* accumulate.

accumulate *v.* **1** acquire more and more of. **2** increase in amount. □ **accumulation** *n.*
■ **1** amass, collect, gather, heap up, hoard, pile up, stockpile, store up. **2** accrue, build up, collect, gather, grow, increase, multiply, pile up. □ **accumulation** collection, heap, hoard, mass, stack, stockpile, store.

accumulator n. **1** rechargeable electric battery. **2** bet on a series of events with winnings restaked.

accurate adj. **1** free from error. **2** careful and precise. □ **accurately** adv., **accuracy** n.

■ **1** correct, exact, faultless, flawless, perfect, right, true, unerring. **2** careful, meticulous, precise, scrupulous.

accuse v. lay the blame for a crime or fault on. □ **accusation** n., **accuser** n.

■ blame, censure, charge, denounce, impeach, indict. □ **accusation** allegation, charge, denunciation, impeachment, indictment.

accustom v. make used (to).

ace n. **1** playing card with one spot. **2** expert. **3** unreturnable service in tennis.

acerbity n. sharpness of manner.

acetate n. synthetic textile fibre.

acetic acid clear liquid acid in vinegar.

acetone n. colourless liquid used as a solvent.

acetylene n. colourless gas burning with a bright flame.

ache n. dull continuous pain. ● v. suffer an ache. □ **achy** adj.

■ n. discomfort, pain, pang, soreness, throbbing, twinge. ● v. hurt, smart, sting, throb.

achieve v. **1** accomplish. **2** reach or gain by effort. □ **achievement** n., **achiever** n.

■ **1** accomplish, bring off, carry out, complete, conclude, do successfully, effect, engineer, execute, finish, fulfil, realize, succeed in. **2** acquire, attain, earn, gain, get, obtain, reach, win.

Achilles heel vulnerable point. □ **Achilles tendon** tendon attaching the calf muscles to the heel.

acid adj. sour. ● n. any of a class of substances that contain hydrogen and neutralize alkalis. □ **acidly** adv., **acidity** n.

■ adj. sharp, sour, tangy, tart, vinegary.

acknowledge v. **1** admit the truth of. **2** confirm receipt of. □ **acknowledgement** n.

■ **1** accept, admit, allow, concede, confess, grant, own, recognize.

acme /ákmi/ n. highest point.

acne /ákni/ n. eruption of pimples.

acolyte n. person assisting a priest in a church service.

acorn n. oval nut of the oak tree.

acoustic adj. of sound. ● n.pl. qualities of a room that affect the way sound carries in it.

acquaint v. **acquaint with** make aware of. □ **be acquainted with** know slightly.

■ □ **acquaint with** apprise of, inform of, familiarize with, make aware of, notify of, tell of.

acquaintance n. **1** slight knowledge. **2** person one knows slightly.

acquiesce v. assent. □ **acquiescent** adj., **acquiescence** n.

acquire v. get possession of.

■ buy, come by, earn, gain, get, obtain, pick up, procure, purchase, secure.

acquisition n. **1** acquiring. **2** thing acquired.

acquisitive adj. eager to acquire things. □ **acquisitiveness** n.

acquit v. (**acquitted**) declare to be not guilty. □ **acquittal** n.

■ absolve, clear, declare innocent, discharge, excuse, exonerate, free, release, reprieve, set free.

acre n. measure of land, 4,840 sq. yds (0.405 hectares).

acreage /áykərij/ n. number of acres.

acrid adj. bitterly pungent.

acrimonious adj. angry and bitter. □ **acrimony** n.

■ biting, bitter, caustic, cutting, harsh, sarcastic, scathing, sharp, spiteful, tart, testy, venomous, virulent, waspish.

acrobat n. performer of acrobatics.

acrobatic adj. involving spectacular gymnastic feats. ● n.pl. acrobatic feats.

acronym n. word formed from the initial letters of others.

acropolis n. upper fortified part of an ancient Greek city.

across prep. & adv. **1** from side to side (of). **2** on the other side (of).

acrostic n. poem in which the first and/or last letters of lines form word(s).

acrylic adj. & n. (synthetic fibre) made from an organic substance.

act n. **1** thing done. **2** law made by parliament. **3** item in a circus or variety show. **4** section of a play. ● v. **1** perform actions, behave. **2** have an effect. **3** play the part of. **4** pretend (to be).

■ n. **1** accomplishment, achievement, action, deed, exploit, feat, operation, step. **2** bill, decree, edict, law, measure, regulation, statute. **3** performance, routine, sketch, turn. ● v. **1** behave, carry on, conduct oneself. **2** be effective, function, operate, take effect, work. **3** appear (as), enact, perform, play, portray, represent. **4** fake, feign, pose (as), pretend (to be), sham, simulate.

action *n.* **1** process of doing something. **2** thing done. **3** battle. **4** lawsuit.
■ **1** activity, movement, performance, practice. **2** act, deed, exploit, feat, step, undertaking. **3** battle, combat, conflict, encounter, engagement, fight, fray, skirmish.

actionable *adj.* giving cause for a lawsuit.

activate *v.* make active. □ **activation** *n.*, **activator** *n.*

active *adj.* **1** doing things, energetic. **2** working. □ **actively** *adv.*
■ **1** animated, brisk, bustling, busy, dynamic, energetic, hyperactive, lively, *colloq.* on the go, tireless, vigorous, vivacious. **2** functioning, in operation, operative, working.

activist *n.* person adopting a policy of vigorous action in politics etc. □ **activism** *n.*

activity *n.* action, occupation.

actor, actress *ns.* performer in play(s) or film(s).

actual *adj.* existing, current.
■ authentic, bona fide, factual, genuine, material, real, tangible, true, verifiable; current, existent, existing.

actuality *n.* reality.

actually *adv.* in fact, really.

actuary *n.* insurance expert who calculates risks and premiums. □ **actuarial** *adj.*

actuate *v.* **1** activate. **2** be a motive for. □ **actuation** *n.*

acumen *n.* shrewdness.

acupuncture *n.* pricking the body with needles to relieve pain. □ **acupuncturist** *n.*

acute *adj.* **1** sharp, intense. **2** (of illness) severe for a time. **3** quick at understanding. □ **acute accent** the accent (´). **acutely** *adv.*, **acuteness** *n.*
■ **1** excruciating, exquisite, intense, keen, penetrating, piercing, severe, sharp, sudden, violent. **2** critical, dangerous, grave, serious, severe. **3** alert, astute, canny, clever, discerning, incisive, intelligent, penetrating, perceptive, sharp, shrewd.

ad *n.* (*colloq.*) advertisement.

adamant *adj.* not yielding to requests.

Adam's apple prominent cartilage at the front of the neck.

adapt *v.* **1** alter or modify. **2** make or become suitable for new use or conditions. □ **adaptable** *adj.*, **adaptation** *n.*, **adaptor** *n.*
■ **1** alter, amend, change, correct, edit, modify, revise, rewrite. **2** adjust, attune, fit; become acclimatized *or* accustomed *or* habituated *or* inured.

add *v.* **1** join as an increase or supplement. **2** put together to get a total. **3** say further. □ **add up** find the total of.
■ **1** affix, annex, append, attach, combine, join (on to), tack on (to), unite with. **2** add up, count up, reckon, total, *colloq.* tot up.

addendum *n.* (*pl.* **-da**) section added to a book.

adder *n.* small poisonous snake.

addict *n.* one who is addicted, esp. to drug(s).

addicted *adj.* doing or using something as a habit or compulsively. □ **addiction** *n.*, **addictive** *adj.*

addition *n.* **1** act or process of adding. **2** thing added.
■ **1** adding-up, calculation, computation, reckoning, *colloq.* totting-up. **2** addendum, appendage, appendix, postscript, supplement; annexe, extension, wing.

additional *adj.* added, extra. □ **additionally** *adv.*
■ added, extra, further, increased, more, new, other, spare, supplementary.

additive *n.* substance added.

addle *v.* **1** (of an egg) become rotten. **2** muddle, confuse.

address *n.* **1** details of where a person lives or where mail should be delivered. **2** speech. ● *v.* **1** write the address on. **2** speak to. **3** apply (oneself) to a task.
■ *n.* **2** discourse, harangue, lecture, oration, sermon, speech, talk. ● *v.* **2** accost, greet, hail, salute; give a speech to; lecture, speak to, talk to. **3** concentrate on, focus on.

addressee *n.* person to whom a letter etc. is addressed.

adduce *v.* cite as proof.

adenoids *n.pl.* enlarged tissue at the back of the throat. □ **adenoidal** *adj.*

adept *adj.* & *n.* skilful (person).
■ *adj.* able, accomplished, adroit, clever, competent, deft, dexterous, expert, gifted, proficient, skilful, talented.

adequate adj. **1** satisfactory but not excellent. **2** enough. □ **adequately** adv., **adequacy** n.
■ **1** acceptable, all right, average, competent, fair, middling, colloq. OK, passable, satisfactory, tolerable. **2** enough, sufficient.

adhere v. **1** stick. **2** continue to give one's support. □ **adherence** n., **adherent** adj. & n.
■ □ **adherent** n. admirer, devotee, disciple, fan, follower, supporter.

adhesion n. process or fact of sticking to something.

adhesive adj. sticking, sticky.

ad hoc for a specific purpose.

adieu /ədyōō/ int. & n. goodbye.

ad infinitum for ever.

adjacent adj. **1** lying near. **2** next to.

adjective n. descriptive word. □ **adjectival** adj.

adjourn v. move (a meeting etc.) to another place or time. □ **adjournment** n.

adjudge v. decide judicially.

adjudicate v. **1** act as judge (of). **2** adjudge. □ **adjudication** n., **adjudicator** n.

adjunct n. thing that is subordinate to another.

adjure v. beg or command.

adjust v. **1** alter slightly so as to be correct or in the proper position. **2** adapt oneself to new conditions. □ **adjustable** adj., **adjustment** n.
■ **1** adapt, alter, amend, change, correct, modify, put right, rearrange, rectify, regulate, reorganize, reset, tailor, tune. **2** acclimatize, accommodate oneself, accustom oneself, adapt, reconcile oneself.

adjutant n. army officer assisting in administrative work.

ad lib 1 as one pleases. **2** improvise(d).

administer v. **1** manage (business affairs). **2** give or hand out.
■ **1** administrate, conduct, control, direct, manage, organize, oversee, preside over, regulate, run, supervise. **2** dispense, distribute, give out, hand out, mete out.

administrate v. act as manager (of). □ **administrator** n.

administration n. **1** administering, esp. of public or business affairs. **2** government in power. □ **administrative** adj.

admirable adj. **1** worthy of admiration. **2** excellent. □ **admirably** adv.
■ **1** commendable, creditable, estimable, laudable, meritorious, praiseworthy, worthy. **2** excellent, great, first-class, first-rate, marvellous, splendid, superb, wonderful.

admiral n. naval officer of the highest rank.

admire v. regard with approval, think highly of. □ **admiration** n.
■ approve of, esteem, honour, idolize, like, look up to, love, respect, revere, value, venerate.

admissible adj. able to be admitted or allowed. □ **admissibility** n.

admission n. **1** process or right of entering. **2** statement admitting something.
■ **1** access, admittance, entrance, entry. **2** acknowledgement, concession, confession, declaration, disclosure, revelation.

admit v. (**admitted**) **1** allow to enter. **2** accept as valid. **3** state reluctantly.
■ **2** accept, acknowledge, allow, concede, grant, recognize. **3** confess, disclose, own up (to), reveal.

admittance n. admitting, esp. to a private place.

admittedly adv. as an acknowledged fact.

admixture n. **1** thing added as an ingredient. **2** adding of this.

admonish v. **1** exhort. **2** reprove. □ **admonition** n.

ad nauseam to a sickening extent.

ado n. fuss, trouble.

adobe /ədóbi/ n. sun-dried brick.

adolescent adj. & n. (person) between childhood and maturity. □ **adolescence** n.

adopt v. **1** take (esp. a child) as one's own. **2** choose. **3** take and use. **4** approve (a report etc.). □ **adoption** n.
■ **2** choose, embrace, select. **3** appropriate, borrow, take over. **4** accept, approve, back, endorse, ratify, sanction, support.

adorable adj. very lovable.

adore v. love deeply. □ **adoration** n.
■ be in love with, dote on, idolize, love, revere, worship.

adorn v. **1** decorate. **2** be an ornament to. □ **adornment** n.
■ **1** beautify, decorate, embellish, garnish, ornament, trim.

adrenal /ədréen'l/ adj. close to the kidneys.

adrenalin /ədrénnəlin/ n. stimulant hormone produced by the adrenal glands.

adrift adj. & adv. **1** drifting. **2** loose.

adroit *adj.* skilful.
■ able, accomplished, adept, clever, deft, dexterous, expert, proficient, resourceful, skilful.

adsorb *v.* attract and hold (a gas or liquid) to a surface.

adulation *n.* excessive admiration or praise.

adult *adj. & n.* fully grown (person etc.). □ **adulthood** *n.*
■ *adj.* fully grown, grown-up, mature, of age.

adulterate *v.* make impure by adding substance(s). □ **adulteration** *n.*
■ contaminate, corrupt, debase, doctor, pollute, taint.

adultery *n.* sexual infidelity to one's wife or husband. □ **adulterer** *n.*, **adulterous** *adj.*

advance *v.* 1 move forward, make progress. 2 put forward. 3 promote. 4 lend (money). ● *n.* 1 forward movement, progress. 2 loan. 3 increase in price. □ **advancement** *n.*
■ *v.* 1 forge ahead, make headway, make progress, proceed, progress. 2 present, propose, put forward, submit, suggest. 3 aid, assist, boost, forward, further, help, improve, promote. 4 lend, loan. ● *n.* 1 breakthrough, development, headway, improvement, progress, progression.

advanced *adj.* 1 well ahead. 2 not elementary.

advantage *n.* 1 beneficial feature, favourable circumstance. 2 benefit. □ **take advantage of** 1 make use of. 2 exploit unfairly.
■ 1 asset, bonus, convenience, feature, good point, plus; superiority, upper hand. 2 benefit, gain, profit, service, use, usefulness. □ **take advantage of** 1 benefit from, build on, make (good) use of, profit from, use. 2 abuse, exploit, impose on, manipulate, trick.

advantageous *adj.* profitable, beneficial.
■ beneficial, favourable, helpful, profitable, useful, valuable, worthwhile.

advent *n.* 1 arrival. 2 (**Advent**) season before Christmas.

adventure *n.* exciting or dangerous experience. □ **adventurer** *n.*, **adventurous** *adj.*
■ deed, escapade, event, experience, exploit, happening, incident; risk, undertaking, venture. □ **adventurous** audacious,

bold, brave, courageous, daredevil, daring, enterprising, intrepid, venturesome.

adverb *n.* word qualifying a verb, adjective, or other adverb. □ **adverbial** *adj.*

adversary *n.* opponent, enemy. □ **adversarial** *adj.*
■ antagonist, attacker, enemy, foe, opponent.

adverse *adj.* 1 unfavourable. 2 harmful. □ **adversely** *adv.*, **adversity** *n.*
■ 1 disadvantageous, hostile, inimical, inauspicious, unfavourable, unpropitious. 2 damaging, deleterious, detrimental, harmful, hurtful, injurious.

advert *n.* (*colloq.*) advertisement.

advertise *v.* make publicly known, esp. to encourage sales.
■ announce, broadcast, make known, make public, proclaim, promulgate; *colloq.* plug, promote, publicize.

advertisement *n.* 1 advertising. 2 public notice about something.

advice *n.* opinion given about what should be done.
■ counsel, guidance, opinion, recommendation, suggestion, tip, view; admonition, warning.

advisable *adj.* worth recommending as a course of action. □ **advisability** *n.*
■ expedient, judicious, prudent, recommendable, sensible, wise.

advise *v.* 1 give advice to, recommend. 2 inform. □ **adviser** *n.*
■ 1 counsel, guide; advocate, recommend, suggest, urge; caution, warn. 2 apprise, inform, make known to, notify, tell.

advisory *adj.* giving advice.

advocacy *n.* speaking in support.

advocate *n.* /ádvəkət/ person who speaks in court on behalf of another. ● *v.* /ádvəkayt/ recommend.
■ *v.* advise, counsel, favour, recommend, support, urge.

aegis /éejiss/ *n.* protection, sponsorship.

aeon /ée-on/ *n.* immense time.

aerate *v.* 1 expose to the action of air. 2 add carbon dioxide to.

aerial *adj.* 1 of or like air. 2 existing or moving in the air. 3 by or from aircraft. ● *n.* wire for transmitting or receiving radio waves. □ **aerially** *adv.*

aerobatics *n.pl.* spectacular feats by aircraft in flight.

aerobics *n.pl.* vigorous exercises designed to increase oxygen intake. □ **aerobic** *adj.*

aerodynamics *n.* science dealing with forces acting on solid objects moving through air. □ **aerodynamic** *adj.*

aerofoil *n.* aircraft wing, fin, or tailplane giving lift in flight.

aeronautics *n.* study of the flight of aircraft. □ **aeronautical** *adj.*

aeroplane *n.* power-driven aircraft with wings.

aerosol *n.* container holding a substance for release as a fine spray.

aerospace *n.* earth's atmosphere and space beyond this.

aesthete /eess-theet/ *n.* person who appreciates beauty.

aesthetic /eess-théttik/ *adj.* **1** of or showing appreciation of beauty. **2** artistic, tasteful. □ **aesthetically** *adv.*

aetiology /éetióllaji/ *n.* study of causes, esp. of disease.

affable *adj.* polite and friendly. □ **affably** *adv.*, **affability** *n.*

affair *n.* **1** thing to be done. **2** (*colloq.*) thing or event. **3** temporary sexual relationship.
■ **1** business, concern, matter. **2** episode, event, happening, incident, occurrence. **3** intrigue, liaison, relationship, romance.

affect *v.* **1** pretend to have or feel. **2** have an effect on. **3** touch the feelings of.
■ **1** counterfeit, fake, feign, imitate, pretend, sham, simulate. **2** alter, change, have an effect on, have an impact on, influence, transform. **3** move, stir, touch, trouble, upset.

affectation *n.* pretence, esp. in behaviour.

affected *adj.* full of affectation.

affection *n.* love, liking.
■ fondness, friendship, goodwill, liking, love, tenderness, warmth.

affectionate *adj.* loving. □ **affectionately** *adv.*
■ caring, devoted, doting, fond, kind, loving, tender.

affidavit *n.* written statement sworn on oath to be true.

affiliate *v.* connect as a subordinate member or branch. □ **affiliation** *n.*

affinity *n.* **1** close resemblance. **2** attraction, natural liking.
■ **1** closeness, correspondence, likeness, resemblance, similarity, similitude. **2** attraction, fondness, like-mindedness, liking, rapport, sympathy.

affirm *v.* **1** state as a fact. **2** declare formally and solemnly. □ **affirmation** *n.*
■ assert, avow, declare, maintain, proclaim, state, swear, testify.

affirmative *adj.* & *n.* saying 'yes'.

affix *v.* /əfíks/ **1** attach. **2** add (a signature etc.). ● *n.* /áffiks/ **1** thing affixed. **2** prefix, suffix.

afflict *v.* distress physically or mentally.
■ beset, burden, distress, oppress, rack, torment, trouble.

affliction *n.* **1** distress, suffering. **2** cause of this.
■ **1** distress, grief, hardship, illness, misery, misfortune, pain, sorrow, suffering, torment, torture, tribulation.

affluent *adj.* rich. □ **affluence** *n.*
■ □ moneyed, prosperous, rich, wealthy, *colloq.* well-heeled, well-off, well-to-do.

afford *v.* **1** have enough money or time for. **2** provide.
■ **2** furnish, give, provide, supply, yield.

afforest *v.* **1** convert into forest. **2** plant with trees. □ **afforestation** *n.*

affray *n.* public fight or riot.

affront *v.* & *n.* insult.

afloat *adv.* & *adj.* **1** floating. **2** on the sea.

afoot *adv.* & *adj.* going on.

aforesaid *adj.* mentioned previously.

afraid *adj.* **1** frightened. **2** regretful.
■ **1** alarmed, anxious, apprehensive, *colloq.* chicken, cowardly, faint-hearted, fearful, frightened, intimidated, *colloq.* jittery, nervous, panicky, panic-stricken, scared, terrified, timid, timorous, trembling, *colloq.* yellow. **2** apologetic, regretful, sorry.

afresh *adv.* anew, with a fresh start.

Afrikaans *n.* language of S. Africa, developed from Dutch.

Afrikaner *n.* Afrikaans-speaking white person in S. Africa.

aft *adv.* at or towards the rear of a ship or aircraft.

after *prep.*, *adv.*, & *adj.* **1** behind. **2** later (than). **3** in pursuit of. **4** concerning. **5** according to. ● *conj.* at a time later than. □ **after-effect** *n.* effect persisting after its cause has gone.

afterbirth *n.* placenta discharged from the womb after childbirth.

aftermath *n.* after-effects.

afternoon *n.* time between midday and evening.

afterthought n. thing thought of or added later.

afterwards adv. at a later time.

again adv. 1 another time, once more. 2 besides.

against prep. 1 in opposition or contrast to. 2 in preparation or return for. 3 into collision or contact with.

age n. 1 length of life or existence. 2 later part of life. 3 historical period. 4 (colloq., usu. pl.) very long time. ● v. (ageing) 1 grow old, show signs of age. 2 cause to do this. □ of age old enough, adult.
  ■ n. 2 maturity, seniority; old age, senescence. 3 epoch, era, period, time(s). ● v. 1 get on, grow older; mature, mellow, ripen.

aged adj. 1 /ayjd/ of the age of. 2 /áyjid/ old.

ageism n. prejudice on grounds of age.

ageless adj. 1 not growing old. 2 not seeming old.

agency n. 1 business or office of an agent. 2 means of action by which something is done.

agenda n. list of things to be dealt with, esp. at a meeting.

agent n. 1 person acting for another. 2 person or thing producing an effect.
  ■ 1 broker, delegate, envoy, executor, go-between, intermediary, mediator, middleman, negotiator, proxy, representative, surrogate.

agent provocateur /aázhoN prə-vókkətör/ person employed to tempt suspected offenders into overt action.

aggrandize v. make seem greater. □ aggrandizement n.

aggravate v. 1 make worse. 2 (colloq.) annoy. □ aggravation n.
  ■ 1 exacerbate, increase, intensify, make worse, worsen. 2 annoy, exasperate, infuriate, irk, irritate, nettle, vex.

aggregate adj. /ágrigət/ combined, total. ● n. /ágrigat/ 1 collected mass. 2 broken stone etc. used in making concrete. ● v. /ágrigayt/ 1 collect into an aggregate, unite. 2 (colloq.) amount to. □ aggregation n.

aggression n. 1 unprovoked attack. 2 hostile action(s) or behaviour.
  ■ 1 attack, assault, onslaught, invasion. 2 belligerence, hostility, pugnacity, truculence.

aggressive adj. 1 openly hostile. 2 forceful. □ aggressively adv.
  ■ 1 antagonistic, bellicose, belligerent, hostile, militant, offensive, pugnacious, quarrelsome, truculent, warlike. 2 assertive, brash, forceful, colloq. pushy.

aggressor n. one who begins hostilities.

aggrieved adj. having a grievance.

aghast adj. filled with horror.

agile adj. nimble, quick-moving. □ agility n.
  ■ acrobatic, active, lissom, lithe, nimble, quick-moving, sprightly, spry, supple, swift.

agitate v. 1 shake or move briskly. 2 cause anxiety to. 3 stir up public concern. □ agitation n., agitator n.
  ■ 1 churn, shake, stir. 2 alarm, discomfit, disconcert, disturb, fluster, perturb, ruffle, trouble, unsettle, upset, worry. 3 campaign, fight.

agnostic adj. & n. (person) holding that nothing can be known about the existence of God. □ agnosticism n.

ago adv. in the past.

agog adj. eager, expectant.

agonize v. 1 cause agony to. 2 suffer agony, worry intensely.

agony n. extreme suffering.
  ■ anguish, distress, pain, suffering, torment, torture.

agoraphobia n. abnormal fear of open spaces or public places.

agrarian adj. of land or agriculture.

agree v. 1 hold or reach a similar opinion. 2 consent. 3 be consistent with. □ agree with suit the health or digestion of.
  ■ 1 be of one mind, be unanimous, concur; accept, admit, allow, concede, grant. 2 accede, acquiesce, assent, consent. 3 accord, correspond, square, tally.

agreeable adj. 1 pleasing. 2 willing to agree. □ agreeably adv.
  ■ 1 congenial, delightful, enjoyable, gratifying, nice, pleasant, pleasing, satisfying. 2 accommodating, acquiescent, amenable, compliant, willing.

agreement n. 1 act or state of agreeing. 2 arrangement agreed between people.
  ■ 1 accord, concord, conformity, consensus, unanimity, unity. 2 arrangement, bargain, compact, contract, covenant, deal, pact, settlement, treaty, truce, understanding.

agriculture n. large-scale cultivation of land. □ **agricultural** adj., **agriculturalist** n.

agronomy n. soil management and crop production.

aground adv. & adj. (of a ship) on the bottom in shallow water.

ahead adv. further forward in position or time.

ahoy int. seaman's shout to call attention.

aid v. & n. help.
■ n. assistance, backing, cooperation, help, relief, succour, support. ● v. abet, assist, back, cooperate with, facilitate, help, promote, relieve, succour, support.

aide n. 1 aide-de-camp. 2 assistant.

aide-de-camp n. officer assisting a senior officer.

Aids abbr. (also **AIDS**) acquired immune deficiency syndrome, a condition developing after infection with the HIV virus, breaking down a person's natural defences against illness.

ail v. make or become ill.

aileron n. hinged flap on an aircraft wing.

ailment n. slight illness.

aim v. 1 direct towards a target. 2 intend, try. ● n. 1 purpose, intention. 2 action of aiming.
■ v. 1 direct, focus, level, point, train. 2 intend, mean, plan, propose, seek, strive, try, want. ● n. 1 ambition, aspiration, design, end, goal, intention, object, objective, plan, purpose, target.

aimless adj. without a purpose. □ **aimlessly** adv., **aimlessness** n.
■ erratic, haphazard, pointless, purposeless, random.

air n. 1 mixture of gases surrounding the earth, atmosphere overhead. 2 light wind. 3 impression given. 4 manner. 5 melody. ● v. 1 expose to air, dry off. 2 express publicly. □ **air-bed** n. inflatable mattress. **airbrick** n. perforated brick for ventilation. **air-conditioned** adj. supplied with **air-conditioning**, system controlling the humidity and temperature of air. **air force** branch of the armed forces using aircraft. **air raid** attack by aircraft dropping bombs. **on the air** broadcasting by radio or television.
■ n. 1 atmosphere, ether. 2 breeze, draught, wind, poetic zephyr. 3 atmosphere, aura, feeling, impression, sense. 4 appearance, aspect, bearing, demeanour,

look, manner. 5 melody, song, strain, tune. ● v. 1 aerate, dry off, freshen, ventilate. 2 broadcast, declare, express, give vent to, make known, make public, vent, voice.

airborne adj. 1 carried by air or aircraft. 2 (of aircraft) in flight.

aircraft n. machine capable of flight in air.

airfield n. area with runways etc. for aircraft.

airgun n. gun with a missile propelled by compressed air.

airlift n. large-scale transport of supplies by aircraft. ● v. transport thus.

airline n. company providing air transport service.

airliner n. passenger aircraft.

airlock n. 1 stoppage of the flow in a pipe, caused by an air-bubble. 2 airtight compartment giving access to a pressurized chamber.

airmail n. mail carried by aircraft. ● v. send by airmail.

airman n. member of an air force.

airport n. airfield with facilities for passengers and goods.

airship n. power-driven aircraft that is lighter than air.

airstrip n. strip of ground for take-off and landing of aircraft.

airtight adj. not allowing air to enter or escape.

airworthy adj. (of aircraft) fit to fly.

airy adj. (-ier, -iest) 1 well-ventilated. 2 light as air. 3 careless and light-hearted.

aisle /īl/ n. 1 side part of a church. 2 gangway between rows of seats or shelves.

ajar adv. & adj. slightly open.

akimbo adv. with hands on hips and elbows pointed outwards.

akin adj. related, similar.

alabaster n. translucent usu. white form of gypsum.

à la carte (of a meal) ordered as separate items from a menu.

alacrity n. eager readiness.

alarm n. 1 warning sound or signal. 2 fear caused by expectation of danger. ● v. cause alarm to.
■ n. 1 red light, siren, tocsin, warning. 2 anxiety, consternation, dismay, dread, fear, fright, nervousness, panic, terror, trepidation, uneasiness. ● v. dismay, frighten, panic, colloq. put the wind up, scare, shock, startle, terrify, worry.

alarmist n. person who raises unnecessary or excessive alarm.

alas *int.* exclamation of sorrow.

albatross *n.* long-winged seabird.

albino *n.* (*pl.* **-os**) person or animal with no natural colouring matter in the hair or skin.

album *n.* **1** blank book for holding photographs, stamps, etc. **2** set of recordings.

albumen *n.* white of egg.

albumin *n.* protein found in egg white, milk, blood, etc.

alchemy *n.* medieval form of chemistry, seeking to turn other metals into gold. □ **alchemist** *n.*

alcohol *n.* **1** colourless inflammable liquid, intoxicant in wine, beer, etc. **2** liquor containing this.

alcoholic *adj.* of alcohol. ● *n.* person addicted to drinking alcohol. □ **alcoholism** *n.*

alcove *n.* recess in a wall or room.

alder *n.* tree related to birch.

ale *n.* beer.

alert *adj.* watchful, observant. ● *v.* rouse to be alert.
■ *adj.* attentive, awake, careful, heedful, observant, on one's guard, on one's toes, on the lookout, vigilant, watchful, *colloq.* wide awake.

alfresco *adv.* & *adj.* in the open air.

alga *n.* (*pl.* **-gae**) water plant with no true stems or leaves.

algebra *n.* branch of mathematics using letters etc. to represent quantities. □ **algebraic** *adj.*

algorithm *n.* step by step procedure for calculation.

alias *n.* (*pl.* **-ases**) false name. ● *adv.* also called.

alibi *n.* **1** proof that one was elsewhere. **2** excuse.

alien *n.* **1** person who is not a citizen of the country where he or she lives. **2** a being from another world. ● *adj.* **1** unfamiliar. **2** foreign.
■ *n.* **1** foreigner, newcomer, outsider, stranger. ● *adj.* **1** peculiar, odd, outlandish, strange, unknown, unfamiliar. **2** exotic, foreign, imported, overseas.

alienate *v.* cause to become unfriendly. □ **alienation** *n.*

alight[1] *v.* **1** get down or off. **2** descend and settle.

alight[2] *adj.* on fire.

align *v.* **1** place or bring into line. **2** join as an ally. □ **alignment** *n.*

alike *adj.* like one another. ● *adv.* in the same way.
■ *adj.* akin, comparable, similar; identical, indistinguishable.

alimentary *adj.* of nourishment.

alimony *n.* money payable to a divorced or separated spouse.

alive *adj.* **1** living. **2** lively. □ **alive to** aware of.
■ **1** animate, breathing, extant, live, living. **2** active, animated, brisk, energetic, lively, spirited, sprightly, vibrant, vigorous, vivacious.

alkali *n.* (*pl.* **-is**) any of a class of substances that neutralize acids. □ **alkaline** *adj.*

alkaloid *n.* a kind of organic compound containing nitrogen.

all *adj.* whole amount, number, or extent of. ● *n.* all those concerned. □ **all but** almost. **all-clear** *n.* signal that danger is over. **all in 1** exhausted. **2** including everything. **all out** using maximum effort. **all right 1** satisfactory, satisfactorily. **2** in good condition.

allay *v.* lessen, alleviate.

allegation *n.* thing alleged.

allege *v.* declare without proof.
■ assert, avow, claim, contend, declare, maintain, profess, state.

allegedly *adv.* according to allegation.

allegiance *n.* support given to a government, sovereign, or cause.
■ constancy, devotion, faithfulness, fidelity, loyalty.

allegory *n.* story symbolizing an underlying meaning. □ **allegorical** *adj.*, **allegorically** *adv.*

allegro *adv.* & *n.* (passage to be played) briskly.

allergen *n.* substance causing an allergic reaction.

allergic *adj.* **1** having or caused by an allergy. **2** (*colloq.*) having a strong dislike.

allergy *n.* unfavourable reaction to certain foods, pollens, etc.

alleviate *v.* lessen (pain or distress). □ **alleviation** *n.*
■ allay, assuage, diminish, ease, lessen, lighten, mitigate, moderate, palliate, reduce, relieve, soften, soothe, subdue.

alley *n.* **1** narrow street. **2** long enclosure for tenpin bowling.

alliance *n.* association formed for mutual benefit.

■ association, bloc, cartel, coalition, confederation, consortium, federation, league, partnership, syndicate, union.

allied *adj.* **1** of an alliance. **2** similar.

alligator *n.* reptile of the crocodile family.

alliteration *n.* occurrence of the same sound at the start of words. □ **alliterative** *adj.*

allocate *v.* allot. □ **allocation** *n.*

allot *v.* (**allotted**) distribute officially, give as a share.

allotment *n.* **1** share allotted. **2** small area of land for cultivation.

allow *v.* **1** permit. **2** give a limited quantity or sum. **3** admit, agree. **4** add or deduct in estimating.

■ **1** agree to, authorize, consent to, give the go-ahead to, *colloq.* give the green light to, grant permission for, let, permit, sanction; put up with, stand (for), tolerate. **2** allocate, allot, assign, give, grant. **3** acknowledge, admit, agree, concede, confess, grant, own.

allowance *n.* **1** amount or sum allowed. **2** deduction, discount. □ **make allowances for** be lenient towards or because of.

■ **1** allocation, portion, quota, ration, share. **2** deduction, discount, rebate, reduction.

alloy *n.* mixture of metals. ● *v.* **1** mix (with another metal). **2** spoil or weaken (pleasure etc.).

allude *v.* **allude to** refer briefly or indirectly to.

■ mention, refer to, speak of, touch on.

allure *v.* entice, attract. ● *n.* attractiveness.

■ *n.* appeal, attractiveness, charisma, charm, magnetism, pull, seductiveness.

allusion *n.* statement alluding to something. □ **allusive** *adj.*

■ hint, innuendo, insinuation, mention, reference.

alluvium *n.* deposit left by a flood. □ **alluvial** *adj.*

ally *n.* /állī/ country or person in alliance with another. ● *v.* /əlī/ join as an ally.

■ *n.* accomplice, associate, collaborator, colleague, comrade, confederate, helper, partner, supporter. ● *v.* combine, join, join forces, team up, unite.

almanac *n.* calendar with astronomical or other data.

almighty *adj.* **1** all-powerful. **2** very great.

almond *n.* **1** kernel of a fruit related to the peach. **2** tree bearing this.

almost *adv.* very little short of, as the nearest thing to.

■ about, all but, approximately, around, as good as, nearly, not quite, practically, virtually.

alms *n.* money given to the poor.

almshouse *n.* charitable institution for the poor.

aloe *n.* plant with bitter juice.

aloft *adv.* **1** high up. **2** upwards.

alone *adj.* **1** without company or help. **2** lonely. ● *adv.* only.

■ *adj.* **1** by oneself, single-handed, solo, unassisted, unaccompanied. **2** desolate, forlorn, forsaken, friendless, isolated, lonely, solitary.

along *adv.* **1** through part or all of a thing's length. **2** onward. **3** in company with others. ● *prep.* beside the length of.

alongside *adv.* close to the side of a ship or wharf etc.

aloof *adv.* apart. ● *adj.* showing no interest, unfriendly.

■ *adj.* chilly, cold, cool, distant, frosty, haughty, indifferent, reserved, reticent, standoffish, supercilious, unapproachable, undemonstrative, unforthcoming, unfriendly, unsociable, unsympathetic, withdrawn.

aloud *adv.* audibly.

alpaca *n.* **1** llama with long wool. **2** its wool. **3** cloth made from this.

alpha *n.* first letter of the Greek alphabet, = a.

alphabet *n.* letters used in writing a language. □ **alphabetical** *adj.*, **alphabetically** *adv.*

alphabetize *v.* put into alphabetical order.

alpine *adj.* of high mountains. ● *n.* plant growing on mountains or in rock gardens.

already *adv.* **1** before this time. **2** as early as this.

Alsatian *n.* German shepherd dog.

also *adv.* in addition, besides.

■ additionally, besides, furthermore, in addition, moreover, too.

altar *n.* table used in religious service.

alter v. make or become different. □ **alteration** n.

■ adapt, adjust, amend, change, convert, modify, reform, remodel, reorganize, reshape, revise, transform, vary. □ **alteration** adjustment, amendment, change, correction, modification, reorganization, revision, transformation.

altercation n. noisy dispute.

alternate adj. /áwltérnət/ first one then the other successively. ● v. /áwltərnayt/ place or occur alternately. □ **alternately** adv., **alternation** n.

alternative adj. **1** usable instead of another. **2** unconventional. ● n. any of two or more possibilities. □ **alternatively** adv.

although conj. though.

altimeter n. instrument in an aircraft showing altitude.

altitude n. height above sea level or above the horizon.

alto n. (pl. **-os**) highest adult male voice.

altogether adv. **1** entirely. **2** on the whole. **3** in total.

■ **1** absolutely, completely, entirely, fully, perfectly, quite, thoroughly, totally, utterly, wholly. **2** by and large, in general, on the whole.

altruism n. unselfishness. □ **altruist** n., **altruistic** adj.

aluminium n. light silvery metal.

always adv. **1** repeatedly, often. **2** for ever. **3** at all times. **4** whatever the circumstances.

■ **1** constantly, continually, perpetually, repeatedly, usually; frequently, often. **2** eternally, evermore, for ever, unceasingly. **3** consistently, every time, invariably, without exception.

alyssum n. plant with small yellow or white flowers.

a.m. abbr. (Latin ante meridiem) before noon.

amalgam n. **1** alloy of mercury. **2** soft pliable mixture.

amalgamate v. mix, combine. □ **amalgamation** n.

■ blend, combine, compound, consolidate, fuse, integrate, join, merge, mix, synthesize, unite.

amaryllis n. lily-like plant.

amass v. heap up, collect.

amateur n. person who does something as a pastime not as a profession.

■ dabbler, dilettante, layperson, nonprofessional.

amateurish adj. lacking professional skill.

amatory adj. of or showing love.

amaze v. fill with surprise or wonder. □ **amazing** adj., **amazement** n.

■ astonish, astound, awe, bowl over, dumbfound, colloq. flabbergast, shock, stagger, startle, stun, stupefy, surprise. □ **amazing** astonishing, astounding, breathtaking, extraordinary, fabulous, marvellous, miraculous, phenomenal, prodigious, remarkable, sensational, staggering, startling, colloq. stunning, stupendous, surprising, wonderful.

amazon n. fierce strong woman.

ambassador n. diplomat representing his or her country abroad.

amber n. **1** hardened brownish-yellow resin. **2** its colour.

ambergris n. waxy substance found in tropical seas, used in perfume manufacture.

ambidextrous adj. able to use either hand equally well.

ambience n. surroundings, atmosphere.

ambiguous adj. having two or more possible meanings. □ **ambiguously** adv., **ambiguity** n.

■ confusing, equivocal, indefinite, obscure, puzzling, uncertain, unclear, vague.

ambit n. bounds, scope.

ambition n. **1** strong desire to achieve something. **2** object of this desire.

■ **1** determination, drive, eagerness, energy, enterprise, enthusiasm, initiative, motivation, zeal. **2** aim, aspiration, desire, dream, goal, hope, intention, object, objective, target, wish.

ambitious adj. full of ambition.

■ determined, eager, enterprising, enthusiastic, go-ahead, go-getting, keen, motivated, colloq. pushy, zealous.

ambivalent adj. with mixed feelings towards something. □ **ambivalence** n.

amble v. & n. walk at a leisurely pace.

ambrosia n. something delicious.

ambulance n. vehicle equipped to carry sick or injured people.

ambuscade n. & v. ambush.

ambush n. surprise attack from a concealed position. ● v. attack thus.

■ n. ambuscade, trap. ● v. ambuscade, ensnare, intercept, pounce on, surprise, trap, waylay.

ameliorate v. make or become better. □ **amelioration** n.

amenable *adj.* accommodating, responsive. □ **amenably** *adv.*
■ accommodating, adaptable, agreeable, biddable, complaisant, compliant, cooperative, docile, persuadable, responsive, tractable, willing.

amend *v.* **1** make minor alterations in. **2** improve. □ **make amends** compensate for something. **amendment** *n.*
■ **1** adjust, alter, correct, emend, modify, polish, refine. **2** change, improve, make better, mend, put right, reform.

amenity *n.* pleasant or useful feature of a place.

American *adj.* **1** of America. **2** of the USA. ● *n.* American person.

Americanism *n.* American word or phrase.

Americanize *v.* make American in character.

amethyst *n.* **1** purple or violet semi-precious stone. **2** its colour.

amiable *adj.* likeable, friendly. □ **amiably** *adv.*, **amiability** *n.*
■ affable, agreeable, amicable, charming, cordial, friendly, genial, good-natured, kind, kind-hearted, kindly, likeable, pleasant.

amicable *adj.* friendly. □ **amicably** *adv.*

amid *prep.* (also **amidst**) in the middle of, during.

amino acid organic acid found in proteins.

amiss *adj.* & *adv.* wrong(ly).

ammonia *n.* **1** strong-smelling gas. **2** solution of this in water.

ammonite *n.* fossil of a spiral shell.

ammunition *n.* bullets, shells, etc.

amnesia *n.* loss of memory. □ **amnesiac** *adj.* & *n.*

amnesty *n.* general pardon.

amniotic fluid fluid surrounding the foetus in the womb.

amoeba /əmeéba/ *n.* (*pl.* **-bae** or **-bas**) simple microscopic organism changing shape constantly.

amok *adv.* **run amok** be out of control and do much damage.

among *prep.* (also **amongst**) **1** surrounded by. **2** in the category of. **3** between.

amoral *adj.* not based on moral standards.

amorous *adj.* showing or feeling sexual love.
■ amatory, ardent, impassioned, loving, lustful, passionate.

amorphous *adj.* shapeless.

amount *n.* total of anything, quantity. ● *v.* **amount to** be equivalent to in number, size, significance, etc.
■ *n.* aggregate, bulk, extent, lot, mass, number, quantity, sum, total, volume. ● *v.* add up to, come to, make, total; be equal or equivalent to.

ampere *n.* unit of electric current.

ampersand *n.* the sign & (= and).

amphetamine *n.* stimulant drug.

amphibian *n.* amphibious animal or vehicle.

amphibious *adj.* able to live or operate on land and in water.

amphitheatre *n.* semicircular unroofed building with tiers of seats round a central arena.

ample *adj.* **1** plentiful. **2** quite enough. **3** large. □ **amply** *adv.*
■ **1** abundant, bountiful, copious, generous, lavish, liberal, plentiful, profuse, unstinting. **2** adequate, enough, sufficient. **3** capacious, commodious, large, spacious, substantial.

amplify *v.* **1** increase the strength or volume of. **2** add details to (a statement). □ **amplification** *n.*, **amplifier** *n.*
■ **1** augment, boost, heighten, increase, intensify, magnify, make louder. **2** add to, broaden, develop, elaborate on, embellish, embroider, enlarge on, expand on, expatiate on, lengthen, make fuller, supplement.

amplitude *n.* **1** breadth. **2** abundance.

amputate *v.* cut off by surgical operation. □ **amputation** *n.*

amulet *n.* thing worn as a charm against evil.

amuse *v.* **1** cause to laugh or smile. **2** make time pass pleasantly for. □ **amusing** *adj.*
■ **1** cheer (up), delight, tickle. **2** absorb, beguile, divert, engross, entertain, interest, please. □ **amusing** comical, droll, enjoyable, entertaining, funny, hilarious, humorous, pleasing, witty.

amusement *n.* **1** being amused. **2** thing that amuses.

an *adj.* form of *a* used before vowel sounds other than long 'u'.

anachronism *n.* thing that does not belong in the period in which it is placed. □ **anachronistic** *adj.*

anaemia /əneémiə/ *n.* lack of haemoglobin in blood.

anaemic /əneémik/ *adj.* **1** suffering from anaemia. **2** lacking strong colour or characteristics.

■ **2** colourless, pale, pallid, pasty, sallow, sickly, unhealthy, wan, washed out.

anaesthesia /ániss-theéziə/ *n.* loss of sensation, esp. induced by anaesthetics.

anaesthetic /ánniss-théttik/ *adj.* & *n.* (substance) causing loss of sensation.

anaesthetist /ənéess-thətist/ *n.* person who administers anaesthetics.

anagram *n.* word formed from the rearranged letters of another.

anal *adj.* of the anus.

analgesic *adj.* & *n.* (drug) relieving pain. □ **analgesia** *n.*

analogous *adj.* similar in certain respects.

analogue *n.* analogous thing.

analogy *n.* partial likeness between things.

■ correlation, correspondence, likeness, parallel, relation, resemblance, similarity.

analyse *v.* **1** make an analysis of. **2** psychoanalyse. □ **analyst** *n.*

analysis *n.* (*pl.* **-lyses**) detailed examination or study.

■ breakdown, critique, dissection, evaluation, examination, inquiry, interpretation, investigation, review, scrutiny, study.

analytical *adj.* (also **analytic**) of or using analysis.

anarchism *n.* belief that government and law should be abolished. □ **anarchist** *n.*

anarchy *n.* **1** total lack of organized control. **2** lawlessness. □ **anarchical** *adj.*

anathema /ənáthəmə/ *n.* **1** formal curse. **2** detested thing.

anatomist *n.* expert in anatomy.

anatomy *n.* **1** bodily structure. **2** study of this. □ **anatomical** *adj.*

ancestor *n.* person from whom another is descended. □ **ancestral** *adj.*

■ antecedent, forebear, forefather, forerunner, precursor, predecessor, progenitor.

ancestry *n.* line of ancestors.

anchor *n.* heavy metal structure for mooring a ship to the sea bottom. ● *v.* **1** moor with an anchor. **2** fix firmly.

anchorage *n.* **1** place for anchoring. **2** lying at anchor.

anchovy *n.* small strong-tasting fish.

ancient *adj.* **1** of long ago. **2** very old.

■ **1** antediluvian, antiquated, archaic, bygone, past, prehistoric, primeval, primitive, primordial. **2** aged, elderly, hoary, old, venerable.

ancillary *adj.* helping in a subsidiary way.

and *conj.* connecting words, phrases, or sentences.

anecdote *n.* short amusing or interesting true story.

anemone *n.* plant with white, red, or purple flowers.

aneurysm *n.* excessive swelling of an artery.

anew *adv.* **1** again. **2** in a new way.

angel *n.* **1** messenger of God. **2** kind person. □ **angelic** *adj.*

angelica *n.* **1** candied stalks of a fragrant plant. **2** this plant.

anger *n.* extreme displeasure. ● *v.* make angry.

■ *n.* annoyance, displeasure, exasperation, fury, indignation, ire, irritation, rage, resentment, vexation, wrath. ● *v.* annoy, *colloq.* aggravate, displease, drive mad, enrage, exasperate, gall, incense, inflame, infuriate, irritate, madden, outrage, provoke, vex.

angina *n.* (in full **angina pectoris**) sharp pain in the chest.

angle[1] *n.* **1** point of view. **2** space between two lines or surfaces that meet. ● *v.* **1** present from a particular point of view. **2** place obliquely.

■ *n.* **1** approach, perspective, point of view, slant, standpoint, viewpoint.

angle[2] *v.* **1** fish with hook and bait. **2** try to obtain by hinting. □ **angler** *n.*

Anglican *adj.* & *n.* (member) of the Church of England. □ **Anglicanism** *n.*

Anglicism *n.* English idiom.

Anglicize *v.* make English in character. □ **Anglicization** *n.*

Anglo- *pref.* English, British.

Anglo-Saxon *n.* & *adj.* **1** (of) English person or language before the Norman Conquest. **2** (of) person of English descent.

angora *n.* **1** long-haired variety of cat, goat, or rabbit. **2** yarn or fabric made from the hair of such goats or rabbits.

angostura *n.* aromatic bitter bark of S. American tree.

angry *adj.* (**-ier**, **-iest**) feeling or showing anger. □ **angrily** *adv.*

■ annoyed, *colloq.* apoplectic, choleric, cross, enraged, exasperated, fuming, furious, heated, in a bad temper, incensed, indignant, infuriated, irate, irritated, *colloq.* livid, *colloq.* mad, outraged, raging, raving, resentful, seething, smouldering, sore, vexed, wrathful.

angstrom *n.* unit of measurement for wavelengths.

anguish *n.* severe physical or mental pain. □ **anguished** *adj.*
■ agony, anxiety, distress, grief, heartache, misery, pain, sorrow, suffering, torment, torture, woe.

angular *adj.* **1** having angles or sharp corners. **2** forming an angle.

aniline *n.* oily liquid used in making dyes and plastics.

animal *n.* & *adj.* (of) a living thing that can move voluntarily.

animate *adj.* /ánnimət/ living. ● *v.* /ánnimayt/ **1** enliven, give life to. **2** motivate. **3** give (a film etc.) the appearance of movement by photographing a series of drawings. □ **animation** *n.*
■ *adj.* alive, breathing, live, living, sentient. ● *v.* **1** energize, enliven, invigorate, pep up, vivify. **2** arouse, encourage, excite, fire, galvanize, inspire, motivate, rouse, spur, stimulate, stir. □ **animation** ebullience, élan, energy, enthusiasm, excitement, high spirits, life, liveliness, spirit, verve, vigour, vitality, vivacity, zest.

animated *adj.* lively, vigorous.
■ active, alive, brisk, bubbly, ebullient, energetic, enthusiastic, excited, exuberant, high-spirited, lively, spirited, sprightly, vibrant, vigorous, vivacious.

animosity *n.* hostility.
■ acrimony, antagonism, animus, antipathy, aversion, bitterness, dislike, enmity, hate, hatred, hostility, ill will, loathing, malevolence, malice, rancour, resentment, spite, unfriendliness, venom, vindictiveness, virulence.

animus *n.* animosity.

aniseed *n.* fragrant seed of a plant (**anise**), used for flavouring.

ankle *n.* joint connecting the foot with the leg.

anklet *n.* chain or band worn round the ankle.

annals *n.pl.* **1** narrative of events year by year. **2** historical records.

anneal *v.* toughen (metal or glass) by heat and slow cooling.

annex *v.* **1** take possession of. **2** add as a subordinate part. □ **annexation** *n.*
■ **1** appropriate, conquer, occupy, seize, take over, usurp.

annexe *n.* additional building.

annihilate *v.* destroy completely. □ **annihilation** *n.*
■ destroy, eliminate, eradicate, exterminate, extinguish, extirpate, obliterate, raze, wipe out.

anniversary *n.* yearly return of the date of an event.

annotate *v.* add explanatory notes to. □ **annotation** *n.*

announce *v.* **1** make known publicly. **2** make known the presence or arrival of. □ **announcement** *n.*
■ **1** advertise, broadcast, declare, disclose, divulge, give notice of, give out, make public, proclaim, promulgate, publicize, publish, reveal, state. **2** introduce, present. □ **announcement** bulletin, communiqué, declaration, proclamation, report, statement.

announcer *n.* person who announces items in a broadcast.

annoy *v.* **1** cause slight anger to. **2** be troublesome to. □ **annoyance** *n.*
■ **1** *colloq.* aggravate, anger, bother, *sl.* bug, displease, drive mad, exasperate, gall, infuriate, irk, irritate, madden, needle, nettle, offend, pique, provoke, *colloq.* rile, ruffle, upset, vex. **2** badger, harass, harry, *colloq.* hassle, molest, pester, *colloq.* plague.

annoyed *adj.* slightly angry.
■ cross, disgruntled, displeased, exasperated, indignant, irritated, nettled, offended, *colloq.* peeved, piqued, *colloq.* shirty, sore, upset, *colloq.* uptight, vexed.

annual *adj.* yearly. ● *n.* **1** plant that lives for one year or one season. **2** book published in yearly issues. □ **annually** *adv.*

annuity *n.* yearly allowance provided by an investment.

annul *v.* (**annulled**) make null and void. □ **annulment** *n.*

annular *adj.* ring-shaped.

Annunciation *n.* announcement by the angel Gabriel to the Virgin Mary that she was to be the mother of Christ.

anode *n.* electrode by which current enters a device.

anodize *v.* coat (metal) with a protective layer by electrolysis.

anodyne *n.* something that relieves pain or distress.

anoint *v.* apply ointment or oil to, esp. ritually.

anomaly *n.* something irregular or inconsistent. □ **anomalous** *adj.*

anon *adv.* (*old use*) soon.

anon. *abbr.* anonymous.

anonymous *adj.* of unknown or undisclosed name or authorship. □ **anonymity** *n.*

anorak *n.* waterproof jacket with hood attached.

anorexia *n.* loss of appetite. □ **anorexia nervosa** obsessive desire to lose weight by refusing to eat. **anorexic** *adj. & n.*

another *adj.* **1** one more. **2** a different. **3** any other. ● *pron.* another one.

answer *n.* **1** thing said, written, needed, or done to deal with a question, accusation, etc. **2** solution to a problem. ● *v.* **1** make an answer or response (to). **2** be suitable for. **3** correspond (to a description). □ **answer for 1** take responsibility for. **2** vouch for.

> ■ *n.* **1** acknowledgement, reaction, rejoinder, reply, response, retort, riposte. **2** explanation, solution. ● *v.* **1** acknowledge, reply (to), rejoin, respond (to), retort. **2** fulfil, meet, satisfy, serve, suffice for, suit. **3** correspond to, fit, match, tally with.

answerable *adj.* having to account for something.

ant *n.* small insect that lives in highly organized groups.

antacid *n. & adj.* (substance) preventing or correcting acidity.

antagonism *n.* active opposition, hostility. □ **antagonistic** *adj.*

> ■ animosity, antipathy, conflict, enmity, friction, hostility, opposition, rivalry, strife.

antagonist *n.* opponent.

antagonize *v.* rouse antagonism in.

Antarctic *adj. & n.* (of) regions round the South Pole.

ante *n.* stake put up by a poker player before receiving cards.

ante- *pref.* before.

anteater *n.* mammal that eats ants.

antecedent *n.* preceding thing or circumstance. ● *adj.* previous.

antedate *v.* **1** put an earlier date on. **2** precede in time.

antediluvian *adj.* **1** before the Flood. **2** antiquated.

antelope *n.* animal resembling a deer.

antenatal *adj.* **1** before birth. **2** of or during pregnancy.

antenna *n.* **1** (*pl.* **-ae**) insect's feeler. **2** (*pl.* **-as**) radio or TV aerial.

anterior *adj.* coming before in position or time.

ante-room *n.* room leading to a more important one.

anthem *n.* piece of music to be sung in a religious service.

anther *n.* part of a flower's stamen containing pollen.

anthology *n.* collection of poems, stories, etc.

anthracite *n.* form of coal burning with little flame or smoke.

anthrax *n.* disease of sheep and cattle, transmissible to people.

anthropoid *adj. & n.* human-like (ape).

anthropology *n.* study of the origin and customs of humankind. □ **anthropological** *adj.*, **anthropologist** *n.*

anthropomorphic *adj.* attributing human form to a god or animal. □ **anthropomorphism** *n.*

anti- *pref.* **1** opposed to. **2** counteracting. □ **anti-aircraft** *adj.* used against enemy aircraft.

antibiotic *n.* substance that destroys bacteria.

antibody *n.* protein formed in the blood in reaction to a substance which it then destroys.

anticipate *v.* **1** deal with in advance. **2** foresee. **3** look forward to. □ **anticipation** *n.*

> ■ **1** forestall, intercept, preclude, pre-empt, prevent. **2** envisage, forecast, foresee, foretell, predict, prophesy. **3** await, expect, look forward to, wait for.

anticlimax *n.* dull ending where a climax was expected.

anticlockwise *adj. & adv.* in the direction opposite to clockwise.

antics *n.pl.* absurd behaviour.

anticyclone *n.* outward flow of air from an area of high pressure, producing fine weather.

antidote *n.* substance that counteracts the effects of poison.

antifreeze *n.* substance added to water to prevent freezing.

antigen *n.* foreign substance stimulating the production of antibodies.

antihistamine *n.* substance counteracting the effect of histamine.

antimony *n.* brittle silvery metallic element.

antipathy *n.* strong dislike.

> ■ abhorrence, aversion, disgust, dislike, hatred, loathing, repugnance, revulsion.

antiperspirant *n.* substance that prevents or reduces sweating.

antipodes /antipp̆ădeez/ *n.pl.* places on opposite sides of the earth, esp. Australia and New Zealand (opposite Europe).

antiquarian *adj.* of the study of antiques. ● *n.* person who studies antiques.

antiquated *adj.* very old-fashioned.
■ antediluvian, archaic, dated, obsolete, old, old-fashioned, outmoded, out of date, unfashionable.

antique *adj.* belonging to the distant past. ● *n.* antique interesting or valuable object.

antiquity *n.* **1** ancient times. **2** object dating from ancient times.

antirrhinum *n.* snapdragon.

anti-Semitic *adj.* hostile to Jews.

antiseptic *adj.* & *n.* (substance) preventing things from becoming septic. □ **antiseptically** *adv.*

antisocial *adj.* destructive or hostile to society.

antistatic *adj.* counteracting the effects of static electricity.

antithesis *n.* (*pl.* **-eses**) **1** opposite. **2** contrast. □ **antithetical** *adj.*

antitoxin *n.* substance neutralizing a toxin. □ **antitoxic** *adj.*

antivivisectionist *n.* person opposed to making experiments on live animals.

antler *n.* branched horn of a deer.

antonym *n.* word opposite to another in meaning.

anus *n.* opening at the excretory end of the alimentary canal.

anvil *n.* iron block on which a smith hammers metal.

anxiety *n.* **1** state of being anxious. **2** anxious desire.
■ **1** agitation, apprehension, concern, consternation, disquiet, distress, dread, fear, foreboding, misgiving, nervousness, panic, solicitude, tension, unease, uneasiness, worry. **2** desire, eagerness, longing, yearning.

anxious *adj.* **1** mentally troubled. **2** eager. □ **anxiously** *adv.*
■ **1** afraid, agitated, apprehensive, concerned, distressed, edgy, fearful, *colloq.* fraught, fretful, *colloq.* jittery, nervous, panicky, perturbed, restless, solicitous, tense, troubled, uneasy, upset, worried. **2** dying, eager, keen, longing, yearning.

any *adj.* **1** one or some from a quantity. **2** every.

anybody *n.* & *pron.* any person.

anyhow *adv.* **1** anyway. **2** not in an orderly manner.

anyone *n.* & *pron.* anybody.

anything *n.* & *pron.* any item.

anyway *adv.* whatever the truth or possible outcome is.

anywhere *adv.* & *pron.* (in or to) any place.

aorta *n.* main artery carrying blood from the heart.

apart *adv.* **1** separately, so as to become separated. **2** to or at a distance. **3** into pieces.

apartheid /əpa´atayt/ *n.* former policy of racial segregation in S. Africa.

apartment *n.* **1** set of rooms. **2** (*US*) flat.

apathy *n.* lack of interest or concern. □ **apathetic** *adj.*
■ indifference, lassitude, lethargy, listlessness, passivity, torpor. □ **apathetic** cool, half-hearted, impassive, indifferent, languid, lethargic, listless, passive, phlegmatic, sluggish, torpid, unconcerned, unenthusiastic, uninterested, unmoved.

ape *n.* tailless monkey. ● *v.* imitate, mimic.

aperitif *n.* alcoholic drink taken as an appetizer.

aperture *n.* opening, esp. one that admits light.

apex *n.* **1** highest point. **2** tip.
■ **1** crest, crown, peak, pinnacle, point, summit, top; acme, climax, culmination, height, zenith.

aphid *n.* small insect destructive to plants.

aphorism *n.* pithy saying.

aphrodisiac *adj.* & *n.* (substance) arousing sexual desire.

apiary *n.* place where bees are kept. □ **apiarist** *n.*

apiece *adv.* to or for or by each.

aplomb /əplóm/ *n.* dignity and confidence.

apocalypse *n.* **1** violent event. **2** revelation, esp. about the end of the world. □ **apocalyptic** *adj.*

Apocrypha *n.pl.* books of the Old Testament not accepted as part of the Hebrew scriptures.

apocryphal *adj.* **1** of doubtful authenticity. **2** invented.

apogee *n.* point in the moon's orbit furthest from the earth.

apologetic *adj.* expressing regret. □ **apologetically** *adv.*
■ conscience-stricken, contrite, penitent, regretful, remorseful, repentant, rueful, sorry.

apologize *v.* make an apology.

apology *n.* **1** statement of regret for having done wrong or hurt. **2** explanation of one's beliefs.

apoplexy *n.* **1** a stroke. **2** (*colloq.*) rush of extreme emotion, esp. anger. □ **apoplectic** *adj.*

apostasy *n.* abandonment of one's former religious belief.

apostate *n.* person who is guilty of apostasy.

Apostle *n.* any of the twelve men sent forth by Christ to preach the gospel. □ **apostolic** *adj.*

apostrophe /apóstrafi/ *n.* the sign ' used to show the possessive case or omission of a letter.

apothecary *n.* (*old use*) pharmacist.

appal *v.* (**appalled**) fill with horror or dismay. □ **appalling** *adj.*

■ disgust, dismay, distress, horrify, outrage, revolt, scandalize, shock, sicken. □ **appalling** abominable, atrocious, awful, deplorable, dreadful, ghastly, grim, grisly, gruesome, hideous, horrible, horrifying, outrageous, revolting, shocking, terrible.

apparatus *n.* equipment for scientific or other work.

■ equipment, gear, implements, instruments, machinery, paraphernalia, tackle, tools, utensils; appliance, contraption, device, gadget, machine.

apparel *n.* clothing.

apparent *adj.* **1** clearly seen or understood. **2** seeming but not real. □ **apparently** *adv.*

■ **1** blatant, clear, conspicuous, discernible, evident, manifest, marked, noticeable, obvious, patent, perceptible, plain, unconcealed, unmistakable, visible. **2** ostensible, outward, seeming.

apparition *n.* **1** ghost. **2** thing appearing, esp. of a startling or remarkable kind.

■ ghost, hallucination, phantom, spectre, spirit, *colloq.* spook, wraith.

appeal *v.* **1** make an earnest or formal request. **2** apply to a higher court. **3** be attractive or of interest. ● *n.* **1** act of appealing. **2** attractiveness.

■ *v.* **1** beg, pray, solicit, supplicate; (**appeal to**) ask, beseech, entreat, implore, petition, plead with. **3** (**appeal to**) allure, attract, fascinate, please, interest. ● *n.* **1** application, cry, entreaty, petition, plea, prayer, request, supplication. **2** allure, attractiveness, charisma, charm, fascination, pull, seductiveness.

appear *v.* **1** be or become visible or evident. **2** seem. **3** take part in a play, film, etc.

■ **1** arrive, *colloq.* show up, turn up; arise, come out, crop up, emerge, materialize, surface. **2** look, seem. **3** act, perform, play a role *or* part in.

appearance *n.* **1** act of appearing. **2** look, semblance.

■ **1** advent, arrival, coming, emergence. **2** air, aspect, bearing, demeanour, look, manner, mien; guise, impression, semblance, show.

appease *v.* soothe or conciliate, esp. by giving what was asked. □ **appeasement** *n.*

■ assuage, calm, conciliate, humour, mollify, pacify, placate, quiet, satisfy, soothe.

appellant *n.* person who appeals to a higher court.

append *v.* add at the end.

appendage *n.* thing appended.

appendicitis *n.* inflammation of the intestinal appendix.

appendix *n.* **1** (*pl.* **-ices**) section at the end of a book, giving extra information. **2** (*pl.* **-ixes**) small blind tube of tissue attached to the intestine.

■ **1** addendum, addition, codicil, postscript, supplement.

appertain *v.* be relevant.

appetite *n.* desire, esp. for food.

■ craving, desire, eagerness, enthusiasm, hankering, hunger, inclination, keenness, liking, longing, passion, predilection, preference, relish, stomach, taste, thirst, yearning, *colloq.* yen.

appetizer *n.* thing eaten or drunk to stimulate the appetite.

appetizing *adj.* stimulating the appetite.

applaud *v.* **1** express approval (of), esp. by clapping. **2** praise. □ **applause** *n.*

■ **1** clap, cheer, give a person an ovation. **2** acclaim, commend, compliment, congratulate, eulogize, extol, hail, pay tribute to, praise, salute.

apple *n.* fruit with firm flesh.

appliance *n.* device, instrument.

■ apparatus, contraption, device, gadget, implement, instrument, machine, tool, utensil.

applicable *adj.* **1** appropriate. **2** relevant. □ **applicability** *n.*

applicant n. person who applies for a job.
■ candidate, job-hunter, job-seeker, interviewee.

application n. **1** act of applying. **2** formal request. **3** sustained effort, diligence. **4** relevance.
■ **2** appeal, request, petition, submission. **3** assiduity, assiduousness, attention, dedication, diligence, effort, industry, perseverance. **4** applicability, bearing, relevance, pertinence.

applied adj. put to practical use.

appliqué /əpleékay/ n. piece of fabric attached ornamentally.

apply v. **1** put or spread on. **2** bring into use or action. **3** be relevant. □ **apply to** or **for** make a formal request for something to be done, given, etc. **apply oneself** give one's attention and energy.
■ **1** put on, rub in, spread on. **2** employ, exercise, implement, practise, use, utilize. **3** be relevant, have a bearing, pertain, relate. □ **apply to** appeal to, make an application to, petition, solicit.

appoint v. **1** choose (a person) for a job, committee, etc. **2** decide on (a time, place, etc.).
■ **1** assign, choose, co-opt, delegate, depute, designate, detail, elect, name, nominate, select. **2** arrange, decide on, determine, establish, fix, ordain, set, settle.

appointee n. person appointed.

appointment n. **1** job. **2** arrangement to meet.
■ **1** job, office, place, position, post, situation. **2** arrangement, assignation, colloq. date, engagement, meeting, rendezvous.

apportion v. divide into shares.

apposite adj. appropriate.

apposition n. juxtaposition, esp. of syntactically parallel words.

appraise v. estimate the value or quality of. □ **appraisal** n.

appreciable adj. **1** perceptible. **2** considerable. □ **appreciably** adv.

appreciate v. **1** value. **2** understand. **3** rise in value. □ **appreciation** n., **appreciative** adj.
■ **1** admire, enjoy, esteem, prize, rate highly, respect, think highly of, treasure, value. **2** comprehend, know, realize, recognize, see, understand.

apprehend v. **1** seize, arrest. **2** understand. **3** expect with fear or anxiety. □ **apprehension** n.
■ **1** arrest, capture, catch, collar, sl. nab, sl. seize, take. **2** colloq. catch on to, comprehend, grasp, perceive, understand.

apprehensive adj. fearful, anxious. □ **apprehensively** adv.
■ afraid, anxious, concerned, edgy, fearful, colloq. jittery, nervous, tense, uneasy, worried.

apprentice n. person learning a craft. □ **apprenticeship** n.
■ beginner, learner, novice, probationer, pupil, starter, trainee.

apprise v. inform.

approach v. **1** come nearer (to). **2** set about doing. **3** go to with a request or offer. ● n. **1** act or means of approaching. **2** way of dealing with a person or thing.
■ v. **1** catch up (with), gain on, move towards, near; advance, loom. **2** address, begin, buckle down to, embark on, set about, tackle. **3** contact, make a proposal to, make overtures to, proposition. ● n. **1** advance, advent, arrival; access, drive, entrance, path, way. **2** manner, method, mode, procedure, style, system, technique, way.

approachable adj. easy to talk to.

approbation n. approval.

appropriate adj. /əprópriət/ suitable, proper. ● v. /əprópriayt/ **1** take and use. **2** set aside (money) for a special purpose. □ **appropriately** adv., **appropriation** n.
■ adj. apposite, apt, befitting, correct, deserved, felicitous, fit, fitting, germane, pertinent, proper, relevant, right, suitable, suited. ● v. **1** commandeer, make off with, pocket, purloin, seize, colloq. snaffle, snatch, steal, take. **2** allot, apportion, earmark, set aside.

approval n. **1** act of approving. **2** consent. □ **on approval** (of goods) returnable if not satisfactory.
■ acceptance, agreement, approbation, assent, authorization, backing, blessing, consent, endorsement, go-ahead, colloq. green light, leave, colloq. OK, permission, sanction.

approve v. agree to, sanction. □ **approve of** say or think (a thing) is good or suitable.
■ accede to, accept, agree to, allow, assent to, authorize, consent to, endorse,

give the go-ahead to, permit, ratify, rubber-stamp, sanction.

approximate *adj.* /əpróksimət/ almost but not quite exact. ● *v.* /əpróksimayt/ be or make almost the same. ▫ **approximately** *adv.*, **approximation** *n.*
■ *adj.* estimated, imprecise, inexact, rough. ● *v.* be similar to, border on, come near to, resemble. ▫ **approximately** about, approaching, around, close to, in the region of, more or less, nearly, roughly, round about.

après-ski /áprayskée/ *adj.* & *n.* (of or for) the social activities following a day's skiing.

apricot *n.* **1** orange-yellow peach-like fruit. **2** its colour.

apron *n.* garment worn over the front of the body to protect clothes.

apropos /ápropṓ/ *adv.* concerning.

apse *n.* recess with an arched or domed roof in a church.

apt *adj.* **1** suitable. **2** having a tendency. **3** quick to learn.
■ **1** apposite, appropriate, befitting, felicitous, fitting, relevant, suitable, well-chosen. **2** disposed, given, inclined, liable, likely, predisposed, prone, ready. **3** able, bright, capable, clever, intelligent, quick.

aptitude *n.* natural ability.
■ ability, bent, capability, flair, gift, knack, skill, talent.

aqualung *n.* portable underwater breathing-apparatus.

aquamarine *n.* **1** bluish-green beryl. **2** its colour.

aquarium *n.* (*pl.* **-ums**) tank for keeping living fish etc.

aquatic *adj.* **1** living in or near water. **2** done in or on water.

aquatint *n.* a kind of etching.

aqueduct *n.* artificial channel on a raised structure, carrying water across country.

aqueous /áykwiəss/ *adj.* of or like water.

aquifer *n.* water-bearing rock or soil.

aquiline *adj.* **1** like an eagle. **2** (of a nose) hooked.

Arab *n.* & *adj.* (member) of a Semitic people of the Middle East.

arabesque *n.* **1** dancer's posture with the body bent forward and leg and arm extended in line. **2** decoration with intertwined lines etc.

Arabian *adj.* of Arabia.

Arabic *adj.* & *n.* (of) the language of the Arabs. ▫ **arabic numerals** the symbols 1, 2, 3, etc.

arable *adj.* & *n.* (land) suitable for growing crops.

arachnid *n.* member of the class to which spiders belong.

arachnophobia *n.* fear of spiders.

arbiter *n.* **1** person with power to decide what shall be done or accepted. **2** arbitrator.

arbitrary *adj.* based on random choice. ▫ **arbitrarily** *adv.*
■ capricious, chance, erratic, inconsistent, irrational, random, subjective, unpredictable, whimsical.

arbitrate *v.* act as arbitrator. ▫ **arbitration** *n.*
■ adjudge, adjudicate, decide, judge, referee, umpire.

arbitrator *n.* impartial person chosen to settle a dispute.
■ adjudicator, arbiter, intermediary, judge, mediator, negotiator, peacemaker, referee, umpire.

arboreal *adj.* of or living in trees.

arboretum *n.* place where trees are grown for study and display.

arbour *n.* shady shelter under trees etc.

arc *n.* **1** part of a curve. **2** luminous electric current crossing a gap between terminals.

arcade *n.* **1** covered walk between shops. **2** place with pin-tables, gambling machines, etc.

arcane *adj.* mysterious.

arch[1] *n.* curved structure, esp. as a support. ● *v.* form into an arch.

arch[2] *adj.* consciously or affectedly playful. ▫ **archly** *adv.*

archaeology *n.* study of civilizations through their material remains. ▫ **archaeological** *adj.*, **archaeologist** *n.*

archaic *adj.* belonging to former or ancient times.

archaism *n.* (use of) an archaic word or phrase.

archangel *n.* angel of the highest rank.

archbishop *n.* chief bishop.

archdeacon *n.* priest ranking next below bishop.

archer *n.* person who shoots with bow and arrows. ▫ **archery** *n.*

archetype /aarkitīp/ n. **1** prototype. **2** typical specimen. □ **archetypal** adj.

■ **1** master, original, pattern, prototype. **2** classic, epitome, exemplar, ideal, model, paradigm, standard.

archipelago n. (pl. **-os**) **1** group of islands. **2** sea round this.

architect n. designer of buildings.

architecture n. **1** designing of buildings. **2** style of building(s). □ **architectural** adj.

architrave n. moulded frame round a doorway or window.

archive /aarkīv/ n. (usu. pl.) historical documents.

archivist /aarkivist/ n. person trained to deal with archives.

archway n. arched entrance or passage.

Arctic adj. **1** of regions round the North Pole. **2** (**arctic**) very cold. ● n. Arctic regions.

ardent adj. full of ardour, enthusiastic. □ **ardently** adv.

■ avid, burning, eager, enthusiastic, fervent, fervid, hot, impassioned, intense, keen, passionate, vehement, warm, zealous.

ardour n. great warmth of feeling, enthusiasm.

■ desire, eagerness, enthusiasm, fervour, intensity, heat, passion, vehemence, warmth, zeal.

arduous adj. needing much effort.

■ demanding, difficult, exhausting, formidable, gruelling, hard, herculean, laborious, onerous, severe, strenuous, taxing, tiring, tough.

area n. **1** extent or measure of a surface. **2** region. **3** range of a subject etc.

■ **1** acreage, expanse, extent, measure, size, space. **2** district, locality, neighbourhood, part, precinct, quarter, region, sector, territory, vicinity, zone. **3** compass, range, scope, sphere.

arena n. **1** level area in the centre of an amphitheatre or sports stadium. **2** scene of conflict.

argon n. an inert gas.

argot /aargō/ n. jargon.

arguable adj. **1** able to be asserted or certain. □ **arguably** adv.

argue v. **1** exchange views or opinions, esp. angrily. **2** maintain by reasoning.

■ **1** bicker, debate, disagree, dispute, fall out, fight, quarrel, row, colloq. scrap, spar,

squabble, wrangle. **2** assert, claim, contend, hold, maintain, reason.

argument n. **1** (angry) exchange of views. **2** reason put forward, reasoning process.

■ **1** altercation, clash, conflict, controversy, debate, disagreement, disputation, dispute, fight, fracas, quarrel, row, colloq. scrap, squabble, tiff, wrangle. **2** case, contention, reasoning, thesis.

argumentative adj. fond of arguing.

aria n. solo in opera.

arid adj. dry, barren. □ **aridly** adv., **aridity** n.

■ barren, desert, dry, lifeless, parched, sterile, unproductive, waste, waterless.

arise v. (**arose, arisen**) **1** come into existence or to people's notice. **2** rise.

■ **1** appear, come up, crop up, develop, emerge, materialize, occur, surface.

aristocracy n. hereditary upper classes. □ **aristocratic** adj.

■ **aristocratic** blue-blooded, elite, noble, titled, upper class, colloq. upper crust.

aristocrat n. member of the aristocracy.

arithmetic n. calculating by means of numbers.

ark n. Noah's boat in which he and his family and animals were saved from the Flood. □ **Ark of the Covenant** wooden chest in which the writings of Jewish Law were kept.

arm¹ n. **1** upper limb of the human body. **2** raised side part of a chair.

arm² v. **1** equip with weapons. **2** make (a bomb) ready to explode. ● n.pl. weapons.

armada n. fleet of warships.

armadillo n. S. American burrowing mammal with a plated body.

Armageddon n. final disastrous conflict.

armament n. **1** military weapons. **2** process of equipping for war.

armature n. wire-wound core of a dynamo.

armchair n. chair with raised sides.

armistice n. agreement to stop fighting temporarily.

■ ceasefire, peace, truce.

armlet n. band worn round an arm or sleeve.

armour n. protective metal covering, formerly worn in fighting. □ **armoured** adj.

armourer n. maker, repairer, or keeper of weapons.

armoury n. arsenal.

armpit n. hollow under the arm at the shoulder.

army n. 1 organized force for fighting on land. 2 vast group.

aroma n. smell, esp. a pleasant one. □ **aromatic** adj.

■ bouquet, fragrance, odour, perfume, redolence, scent, smell.

aromatherapy n. use of fragrant oils etc., esp. in massage.

arose see **arise**.

around adv. & prep. 1 all round, on every side (of). 2 approximately.

arouse v. rouse.

■ awaken, rouse, wake, wake up, waken; encourage, excite, inspire, kindle, provoke, stimulate, stir up, whip up.

arpeggio n. (pl. **-os**) notes of a chord played in succession.

arraign v. 1 indict, accuse. 2 find fault with. □ **arraignment** n.

arrange v. 1 put into order. 2 settle the details of. 3 adapt.

■ 1 align, array, categorize, classify, display, dispose, group, lay out, marshal, order, organize, position, put in order, range, sort (out), systematize. 2 decide on, determine, fix, organize, plan, prepare, see to, settle. 3 adapt, orchestrate, score.

arrangement n. 1 act or process of arranging. 2 settlement between people. 3 (pl.) plans.

■ 1 classification, disposition, grouping, organization, planning. 2 agreement, bargain, contract, settlement, understanding. 3 (**arrangements**) measures, plans, preparations; itinerary, programme, schedule.

array v. 1 arrange in order. 2 adorn. ● n. imposing series, display.

■ v. 1 arrange, assemble, display, dispose, lay out, range. 2 adorn, attire, clothe, deck, decorate, drape, dress, garb, robe. ● n. arrangement, collection, display, exhibition, panoply, parade, range, series, show, variety.

arrears n.pl. 1 money owed and overdue for repayment. 2 work overdue for being finished.

arrest v. 1 stop (a movement or moving thing). 2 seize by authority of law. ● n. legal seizure of an offender.

■ v. 1 block, check, delay, halt, hinder, impede, interrupt, obstruct, restrain, retard, slow, stem, stop. 2 apprehend, capture, catch, collar, detain, sl. nab, sl. nick, seize, take into custody. ● n. apprehension, capture, detention, seizure.

arrival n. 1 act of arriving. 2 person or thing that has arrived.

■ 1 advent, appearance, approach, entrance; disembarkation, landing, touchdown. 2 immigrant, newcomer, visitor.

arrive v. 1 reach a destination. 2 (colloq.) establish one's reputation or success. 3 (of time) come.

■ 1 appear, come, make one's appearance, colloq. show up, turn up; disembark, land, touch down. 2 colloq. make it, make the grade, succeed.

arrogant adj. proud and overbearing. □ **arrogantly** adv., **arrogance** n.

■ boastful, bumptious, cavalier, cocksure, cocky, conceited, contemptuous, disdainful, egotistical, haughty, high-handed, imperious, lofty, overbearing, patronizing, pompous, presumptuous, proud, scornful, self-assertive, self-important, colloq. snooty, supercilious, superior.

arrow n. 1 straight shaft with a sharp point, shot from a bow. 2 line with a V at the end, indicating direction.

arrowroot n. edible starch made from a W. Indian plant.

arsenal n. place where weapons are stored or made.

arsenic n. 1 semi-metallic element. 2 strongly poisonous compound of this.

arson n. intentional and unlawful setting on fire of a building.

art n. 1 creative skill, works such as paintings or sculptures produced by this. 2 (pl.) subjects or activities concerned with creativity (e.g. painting, music, writing). 3 aptitude or knack.

■ 1 artistry, craftsmanship, creativity, imagination, inventiveness. 3 aptitude, knack, skill, talent, technique, trick.

artefact n. man-made object.

arterial adj. of an artery. □ **arterial road** main trunk road.

artery n. blood vessel carrying blood away from the heart.

artesian well a well that is bored vertically into oblique strata so that water rises naturally with little or no pumping.

artful adj. crafty. □ **artfully** adv.

■ crafty, cunning, deceitful, designing, devious, scheming, sly, tricky, wily.

arthritis n. condition in which there is pain and stiffness in the joints. □ **arthritic** adj.

arthropod *n.* animal with a segmented body and jointed limbs (e.g. an insect or crustacean).

artichoke *n.* plant with a flower of leaf-like scales used as a vegetable. □ **Jerusalem artichoke** sunflower with an edible root.

article *n.* **1** particular or separate thing. **2** piece of writing in a newspaper etc. **3** clause in an agreement. □ **definite article** the word 'the'. **indefinite article** 'a' or 'an'.

> ■ **1** commodity, item, object, thing. **2** editorial, essay, feature, item, leader, piece, story.

articulate *adj.* /aartíkyoolət/ **1** spoken distinctly. **2** able to express ideas clearly. ● *v.* /aartíkyoolayt/ **1** say or speak distinctly. **2** form a joint, connect by joints. □ **articulated lorry** one with sections connected by a flexible joint. **articulation** *n.*

> ■ *adj.* **1** clear, coherent, comprehensible, eloquent, intelligible, lucid, understandable. **2** coherent, eloquent, fluent. ● *v.* **1** enunciate, express, pronounce, say, speak, utter, vocalize, voice.

artifice *n.* **1** trickery. **2** device.

artificial *adj.* **1** not originating naturally, not real. **2** insincere. □ **artificially** *adv.*, **artificiality** *n.*

> ■ **1** bogus, fabricated, fake, false, imitation, man-made, manufactured, mock, plastic, simulated, synthetic. **2** affected, feigned, insincere, *colloq.* phoney, pretended, sham, studied, unnatural.

artillery *n.* **1** large guns used in fighting on land. **2** branch of an army using these.

artisan *n.* skilled workman.

artist *n.* **1** person who produces works of art, esp. paintings. **2** one who does something with exceptional skill. **3** artiste. □ **artistry** *n.*, **artistic** *adj.*

artiste /aarteést/ *n.* professional entertainer.

artless *adj.* guileless, ingenuous. □ **artlessly** *adv.*

> ■ childlike, frank, guileless, honest, ingenuous, innocent, naive, natural, simple, sincere, unaffected, unsophisticated.

arty *adj.* (**-ier, -iest**) affectedly or pretentiously artistic.

as *adv. & conj.* **1** in the same degree, similarly. **2** in the form or function of. **3** while, when. **4** because. □ **as for, as to** with regard to. **as well** in addition.

asbestos *n.* **1** soft fibrous mineral substance. **2** fireproof material made from this.

asbestosis *n.* lung disease caused by inhaling asbestos particles.

ascend *v.* go or come up.

> ■ climb, come up, go up, mount, move up, rise, scale, soar.

ascendant *adj.* rising. □ **in the ascendant** rising in power or influence.

ascension *n.* ascent, esp. (**Ascension**) that of Christ to heaven.

ascent *n.* **1** ascending. **2** way up.

ascertain *v.* find out by enquiring. □ **ascertainable** *adj.*

> ■ confirm, determine, discover, establish, find out, learn, make certain, make sure, verify.

ascetic *adj.* not allowing oneself pleasures and luxuries. ● *n.* ascetic person. □ **asceticism** *n.*

> ■ *adj.* abstemious, austere, celibate, frugal, puritanical, rigorous, self-denying, self-disciplined, severe, spartan.

ascorbic acid vitamin C.

ascribe *v.* attribute. □ **ascription** *n.*

asepsis *n.* absence of harmful bacteria. □ **aseptic** *adj.*

asexual *adj.* without sex. □ **asexually** *adv.*

ash¹ *n.* tree with silver-grey bark.

ash² *n.* powder that remains after something has burnt.

ashamed *adj.* feeling shame.

> ■ abashed, conscience-stricken, contrite, embarrassed, humiliated, mortified, penitent, remorseful, repentant, shamefaced, sheepish, sorry.

ashen *adj.* **1** pale as ashes. **2** grey.

ashore *adv.* to or on shore.

ashram *n.* (orig. in India) retreat for religious meditation.

ashy *adj.* (**-ier, -iest**) **1** ashen. **2** covered with ash.

Asian *adj.* of Asia or its people. ● *n.* Asian person.

Asiatic *adj.* of Asia.

aside *adv.* to or on one side, away from the main part or group. ● *n.* words spoken so that only certain people will hear.

asinine /ássinīn/ *adj.* silly.

ask *v.* **1** call for an answer to or about. **2** seek to obtain. **3** invite.

> ■ **1** enquire (of), interrogate, question, quiz. **2** appeal for, apply for, beg, beseech, demand, entreat, implore, petition, plead

for, request, seek, solicit, supplicate. **3** invite, summon.

askance *adv.* **look askance at** regard suspiciously.

askew *adv. & adj.* crooked(ly).

asleep *adv. & adj.* in or into a state of sleep.

asp *n.* small poisonous snake.

asparagus *n.* plant whose shoots are used as a vegetable.

aspect *n.* **1** look or appearance. **2** feature of a problem or situation. **3** direction a thing faces.
■ **1** air, appearance, bearing, countenance, demeanour, expression, face, look, manner, mien. **2** attribute, characteristic, detail, element, facet, feature, ingredient, quality, respect, side. **3** direction, outlook, prospect, view.

aspen *n.* a kind of poplar tree.

asperity *n.* harshness.
■ acerbity, astringency, bitterness, gall, harshness, severity, sharpness.

aspersion *n.* **cast aspersions on** defame, criticize.

asphalt *n.* **1** black substance like coal tar. **2** mixture of this with gravel etc. for paving.

asphyxia *n.* suffocation.

asphyxiate *v.* suffocate. □ **asphyxiation** *n.*

aspic *n.* clear savoury jelly.

aspidistra *n.* house plant with broad tapering leaves.

aspirant *n.* person who aspires to something.

aspirate *n.* /áspirət/ sound of h. ● *v.* /áspiráyt/ pronounce with an h.

aspiration *n.* desire, ambition.
■ aim, ambition, desire, dream, goal, hope, longing, object, objective, wish, yearning.

aspire *v.* **aspire to** have a strong ambition to achieve.
■ aim for, desire, dream of, hanker after, hope for, strive for, want, wish for, yearn for.

aspirin *n.* **1** drug that reduces pain and fever. **2** tablet of this.

ass *n.* **1** donkey. **2** stupid person.

assail *v.* attack violently.

assailant *n.* attacker.

assassin *n.* person who assassinates another.

assassinate *v.* kill (an important person) by violent means. □ **assassination** *n.*

assault *n. & v.* attack.
■ *n.* attack, battering, battery, beating; charge, offensive, onset, onslaught, raid, strike. ● *v.* assail, attack, beat up, go for, hit, *colloq.* lay into, pounce on, set about, strike.

assay *n.* test of metal for quality. ● *v.* make an assay of.

assemble *v.* **1** gather together, collect. **2** put or fit together.
■ **1** collect, congregate, convene, forgather, gather, get together, meet, rally; bring together, marshal, round up. **2** build, construct, erect, fabricate, make, manufacture, put together.

assembly *n.* assembled group.
■ collection, company, congregation, crowd, flock, gathering, group, meeting, rally, throng; committee, congress, convention, convocation, council.

assent *v.* express agreement, consent. ● *n.* approval, consent.
■ *v.* accede, accept, acquiesce, agree, comply, concur, consent. ● *n.* acceptance, acquiescence, agreement, approbation, approval, concurrence, consent, permission, sanction.

assert *v.* **1** state, declare to be true. **2** use (power etc.) effectively. □ **assertion** *n.*
■ **1** affirm, allege, attest, claim, contend, declare, insist, maintain, profess, protest, state, swear, testify.

assertive *adj.* **1** forthright and self-assured. **2** dogmatic. □ **assertiveness** *n.*
■ **1** certain, confident, decided, definite, emphatic, firm, forceful, forthright, insistent, positive, self-assertive, self-assured, self-confident. **2** *colloq.* bossy, dogmatic, opinionated, peremptory, *colloq.* pushy.

assess *v.* estimate the size, value, or quality of. □ **assessment** *n.*, **assessor** *n.*
■ appraise, calculate, consider, estimate, evaluate, gauge, judge, rate, *colloq.* size up, weigh up, work out.

asset *n.* **1** useful or valuable thing or person. **2** (usu. *pl.*) property with money value.
■ **1** advantage, attraction, benefit, plus, resource, strength, talent. **2** (assets) capital, effects, estate, funds, holdings, means, money, possessions, property, resources, savings, valuables, wealth.

assiduous *adj.* diligent and persevering. □ **assiduously** *adv.*, **assiduity** *n.*

assign v. **1** allot. **2** designate to perform a task.
■ **1** allocate, allot, apportion, dispense, distribute, give out, hand (out). **2** appoint, delegate, designate, detail, name, nominate.

assignation n. arrangement to meet.

assignment n. task assigned.
■ chore, duty, errand, job, mission, project, task.

assimilate v. absorb or be absorbed into the body or a group etc., or into the mind as knowledge. □ **assimilation** n.

assist v. help. □ **assistance** n.
■ aid, back (up), cooperate with, help, lend a hand, support; advance, expedite, facilitate, further. □ **assistance** aid, backing, collaboration, cooperation, help, reinforcement, relief, succour, support.

assistant n. **1** helper. **2** person who serves customers in a shop.
■ **1** acolyte, aide, helper, right-hand man or woman; abettor, accessory, accomplice, collaborator, henchman; adjutant, aide-de-camp, auxiliary, deputy, subordinate, underling.

associate v. /əsṓshiayt/ **1** join or combine. **2** connect in one's mind. **3** mix socially. ● n. /əsṓshiət/ **1** companion, partner. **2** subordinate member.
■ v. **1** affiliate, ally, combine, join (together), unite. **2** connect, link, put together, relate. **3** consort, fraternize, hobnob, mingle, socialize. ● n. **1** accomplice, ally, colleague, companion, comrade, crony, fellow worker, friend, mate, partner.

association n. **1** act of associating. **2** group organized for a common purpose. **3** connection between ideas.
■ **1** amalgamation, combination, union. **2** alliance, cartel, club, coalition, confederation, consortium, federation, fellowship, group, guild, league, organization, society, syndicate, union. **3** connection, interconnection, link, relationship.

assonance n. partial resemblance of sound between syllables. □ **assonant** adj.

assorted adj. of different sorts.

assortment n. collection composed of several sorts.
■ array, collection, group, hotchpotch, jumble, medley, miscellany, mixture, potpourri, range, selection, variety.

assuage /əswáyj/ v. soothe, allay.

assume v. **1** take as true. **2** take or put upon oneself. **3** simulate.
■ **1** believe, fancy, imagine, presume, suppose, take it for granted, think. **2** accept, take on, undertake. **3** affect, fake, feign, pretend, simulate.

assumption n. **1** thing assumed to be true. **2** act of assuming.
■ **1** belief, conjecture, guess, hypothesis, postulation, premiss, presumption, presupposition, supposition, surmise, theory.

assurance n. **1** solemn promise or guarantee. **2** self-confidence. **3** life insurance.
■ **1** guarantee, oath, pledge, promise, vow, undertaking, word (of honour). **2** aplomb, confidence, poise, self-assurance, self-confidence.

assure v. **1** convince. **2** tell confidently.

assured adj. **1** sure, confident. **2** insured.

assuredly adv. certainly.

aster n. garden plant with daisy-like flowers.

asterisk n. star-shaped symbol *.

astern adv. **1** at or towards the stern. **2** backwards.

asteroid n. any of the tiny planets revolving round the sun.

asthma /ásmə/ n. chronic condition causing difficulty in breathing. □ **asthmatic** adj. & n.

astigmatism n. defect in an eye, preventing proper focusing. □ **astigmatic** adj.

astonish v. surprise greatly. □ **astonishment** n.
■ amaze, astound, bowl over, confound, dumbfound, colloq. flabbergast, shock, stagger, startle, stun, stupefy, surprise, take aback, take by surprise.

astound v. shock with surprise.

astrakhan n. dark curly fleece of lambs from Russia.

astray adv. & adj. away from the proper path.

astride adv. with one leg on each side.

astringent adj. **1** causing tissue to contract. **2** harsh, severe. ● n. astringent substance. □ **astringency** n., **astringently** adv.

astrology n. study of the supposed influence of stars on human affairs. □ **astrologer** n., **astrological** adj.

astronaut n. space traveller.

astronautics n. study of space travel and its technology.

astronomical adj. **1** of astronomy. **2** enormous in amount. □ **astronomically** adv.

astronomy n. study of stars and planets. □ **astronomer** n.

astute adj. shrewd, quick at seeing how to gain an advantage. □ **astutely** adv., **astuteness** n.
■ acute, clever, discerning, intelligent, observant, perceptive, perspicacious, quick, sagacious, sharp, shrewd, wise; artful, canny, crafty, cunning, sly, wily.

asunder adv. apart, into pieces.

asylum n. **1** refuge. **2** (old use) mental institution.
■ **1** haven, refuge, retreat, sanctuary, shelter.

asymmetry n. lack of symmetry. □ **asymmetrical** adj.

at prep. having as position, time of day, condition, or price.

atavism n. resemblance to remote ancestors. □ **atavistic** adj.

ate see eat.

atheist n. person who does not believe in God. □ **atheism** n.

athlete n. person who is good at athletics.

athletic adj. **1** of athletes. **2** muscular and physically active. □ **athletically** adv., **athleticism** n.
■ **2** energetic, fit, lithe, muscular, powerful, sinewy, strong, supple, vigorous, wiry.

athletics n.pl. sports, esp. running, jumping, and throwing.

atlas n. book of maps.

atmosphere n. **1** feeling conveyed by an environment or group. **2** mixture of gases surrounding a planet. **3** unit of pressure. □ **atmospheric** adj.
■ **1** air, ambience, aura, feeling, mood, spirit, tone. **2** air, ether, heavens, sky, stratosphere.

atoll n. ring-shaped coral reef enclosing a lagoon.

atom n. **1** smallest particle of a chemical element. **2** very small quantity or thing.
■ **2** bit, crumb, grain, iota, jot, mite, morsel, scrap, speck, spot.

atomic adj. of atom(s). □ **atomic bomb** bomb deriving its power from atomic energy. **atomic energy** that obtained from nuclear fission.

atomize v. reduce to atoms or fine particles. □ **atomizer** n.

atonal /áytôn'l/ adj. (of music) not written in any key. □ **atonality** n.

atone v. make amends. □ **atonement** n.
■ compensate, make amends, make reparation, redeem oneself.

atrocious adj. **1** very bad. **2** wicked. □ **atrociously** adv.
■ **1** abominable, abysmal, awful, bad, dreadful, colloq. frightful, colloq. ghastly, horrendous, colloq. horrible, colloq. lousy, colloq. shocking, terrible. **2** appalling, barbaric, brutal, cruel, diabolical, evil, fiendish, heinous, horrific, horrifying, inhuman, savage, sickening, vicious, vile, villainous, wicked.

atrocity n. **1** wickedness. **2** cruel act.
■ **1** cruelty, enormity, evil, inhumanity, iniquity, villainy, wickedness. **2** crime, enormity, outrage.

atrophy n. wasting away, esp. through disuse. ● v. **1** cause atrophy in. **2** suffer atrophy.

attach v. **1** fix or join to something else. **2** attribute, be attributable. □ **attachment** n.
■ **1** add, affix, append, connect, couple, fasten, fix, hitch, join, link, pin, secure, tie, unite. **2** ascribe, assign, attribute, impute.

attaché n. person attached to an ambassador's staff. □ **attaché case** small rectangular case for carrying documents.

attached adj. devoted.

attack v. **1** attempt to hurt or defeat. **2** criticize adversely. ● n. **1** act or process of attacking. **2** sudden onset of illness. □ **attacker** n.
■ v. **1** assail, assault, beat up, go for, jump, lash out at, colloq. lay into, mug, pounce on, set about; charge, rush, storm. **2** abuse, berate, censure, criticize, denounce, sl. knock, colloq. lambaste, colloq. lay into, malign, revile, sl. slag (off), sl. slam, colloq. slate, vilify. ● n. **1** ambush, assault, battery, blitz, bombardment, charge, foray, incursion, invasion, offensive, onset, onslaught, raid, rush, sortie, strike. **2** bout, fit, outbreak, paroxysm, seizure, spasm, colloq. turn. □ **attacker** aggressor, assailant, mugger; critic, detractor.

attain v. achieve. □ **attainable** adj., **attainment** n.
■ accomplish, achieve, arrive at, fulfil, gain, get, grasp, make, obtain, reach, realize, secure, win.

attempt v. make an effort to do. ● n. such an effort.
■ v. endeavour, have a go, make a bid, seek, strive, try. ● n. bid, effort, endeavour, essay, go, shot, *colloq.* stab, try.

attend v. 1 be present at. 2 escort. □ **attend to** give attention to. **attendance** n.
■ 1 be present (at), go (to), *colloq.* show up (at), turn up (at). 2 accompany, chaperon, conduct, escort, usher. □ **attend to** concentrate on, heed, listen to, mark, mind, note, pay attention to, take notice of, watch; deal with, do, handle, look after, see to, take care of.

attendant adj. accompanying. ● n. person present to provide service.
■ n. assistant, chaperon, escort, helper, servant, steward, stewardess, usher, valet.

attention n. 1 consideration, care. 2 applying one's mind. 3 erect attitude in military drill.
■ 1 care, consideration, heed, notice, regard, thought. 2 attentiveness, concentration.

attentive adj. paying attention. □ **attentively** adv.
■ alert, awake, concentrating, heedful, intent, observant, vigilant, watchful.

attenuate v. make slender, thin, or weaker. □ **attenuation** n.

attest v. 1 provide proof of. 2 declare true or genuine. □ **attestation** n.

attic n. room in the top storey of a house.

attire n. clothes. ● v. clothe.
■ n. apparel, clothes, clothing, costume, dress, finery, garb, garments, wear.

attitude n. 1 position of the body. 2 way of thinking or behaving.
■ 1 pose, position, posture, stance. 2 approach, opinion, outlook, perspective, point of view, standpoint, thought, view, viewpoint.

attorney n. (US) lawyer.

attract v. 1 draw to oneself or itself. 2 arouse the interest or pleasure of. □ **attraction** n.
■ 1 catch, capture, draw, invite, pull. 2 allure, appeal to, captivate, charm, enchant, entice, fascinate, interest, lure, tempt.

attractive adj. 1 capable of attracting. 2 pleasing in appearance. □ **attractively** adv.
■ 1 alluring, appealing, captivating, enchanting, engaging, enticing, fascinating, interesting, inviting, pleasing, seductive, tempting, winning. 2 beautiful, *Sc.* bonny, comely, desirable, glamorous, good-looking, *colloq.* gorgeous, handsome, personable, pretty, *colloq.* stunning, taking.

attribute¹ /ətríbyōōt/ v. **attribute to** regard as belonging to or caused by. □ **attributable** adj., **attribution** n.
■ ascribe, assign, impute.

attribute² /átribyōōt/ n. characteristic quality.
■ characteristic, feature, property, quality, trait.

attrition n. wearing away.

attune v. 1 adapt. 2 tune.

atypical adj. not typical. □ **atypically** adv.

aubergine /óbərzheen/ n. 1 deep-purple vegetable. 2 its colour.

aubrietia n. perennial rock-plant.

auburn adj. (of hair) reddish-brown.

auction n. public sale where articles are sold to the highest bidder. ● v. sell by auction.

auctioneer n. person who conducts an auction.

audacious adj. bold, daring. □ **audaciously** adv., **audacity** n.
■ adventurous, bold, brave, courageous, daring, fearless, intrepid, plucky, valiant; daredevil, foolhardy, rash, reckless. □ **audacity** boldness, bravery, courage, daring, *colloq.* guts, nerve, pluck, valour; rashness, recklessness, temerity.

audible adj. loud enough to be heard. □ **audibly** adv.

audience n. 1 group of listeners or spectators. 2 formal interview.
■ 1 assembly, congregation, crowd, gathering, listeners, spectators, turn-out, viewers.

audio n. (reproduction of) sound. □ **audio-visual** adj. using both sight and sound.

audit n. official examination of accounts. ● v. make an audit of.

audition n. test of a prospective performer's ability. ● v. test or be tested in an audition.

auditor n. one who audits accounts.

auditorium n. part of a building where the audience sits.

auditory adj. of hearing.

augment v. increase. □ **augmentation** n., **augmentative** adj.
■ add to, amplify, boost, build up, enlarge, increase, multiply, step up, supplement, swell.

augur v. bode.
■ bode, foreshadow, herald, portend, predict, presage, promise, prophesy.

augury n. divination, omen.

august adj. majestic.

auk n. northern seabird.

aunt n. sister or sister-in-law of one's father or mother.

au pair young person from overseas helping with housework in return for board and lodging.

aura n. atmosphere surrounding a person or thing.

aural adj. of the ear. □ **aurally** adv.

aureole n. halo.

auscultation n. listening to the sound of the heart for diagnosis.

auspice n. 1 omen. 2 (pl.) patronage.

auspicious adj. showing signs that promise success.
■ bright, encouraging, favourable, hopeful, promising, propitious, rosy.

austere adj. 1 severely simple and plain. 2 stern. □ **austerity** n.
■ 1 modest, plain, simple, spartan, stark, unadorned, unostentatious. 2 cold, dour, forbidding, hard, harsh, rigorous, serious, sober, stern, strict.

Australasian adj. & n. (native, inhabitant) of Australia, New Zealand, and neighbouring islands.

Australian adj. & n. (native, inhabitant) of Australia.

authentic adj. genuine, known to be true. □ **authentically** adv., **authenticity** n.
■ actual, bona fide, genuine, legitimate, real, true, valid; authoritative, reliable, truthful.

authenticate v. prove the truth or authenticity of. □ **authentication** n.
■ certify, confirm, corroborate, prove, substantiate, validate, verify.

author n. 1 writer of a book etc. 2 originator. □ **authorship** n.
■ 1 columnist, dramatist, journalist, novelist, playwright, poet, scriptwriter, writer. 2 creator, designer, father, founder, inventor, maker, originator.

authoritarian adj. favouring complete obedience to authority. □ **authoritarianism** n.
■ autocratic, colloq. bossy, despotic, dictatorial, dogmatic, domineering, high-handed, strict, tyrannical.

authoritative adj. 1 recognized as true or reliable. 2 having authority. □ **authoritatively** adv.
■ 1 authentic, definitive, dependable, reliable, true, valid. 2 approved, lawful, legitimate, official, sanctioned.

authority n. 1 power to enforce obedience. 2 delegated power. 3 person(s) with authority. 4 influence. 5 person with specialized knowledge.
■ 1 command, control, dominion, jurisdiction, power, prerogative, right, supremacy. 2 authorization, licence, permission. 3 (**authorities**) the establishment, government, officials. 4 hold, influence, sway, weight. 5 colloq. buff, connoisseur, expert, specialist.

authorize v. give permission for. □ **authorization** n.
■ agree to, allow, approve, consent to, endorse, give the go-ahead to, colloq. give the green light to, legalize, license, colloq. OK, permit, rubber-stamp, sanction.

autism n. mental disorder characterized by self-absorption and withdrawal. □ **autistic** adj.

auto- pref. self-.

autobiography n. story of a person's life written by that person. □ **autobiographical** adj.

autocracy n. despotism.

autocrat n. person with unrestricted power. □ **autocratic** adj., **autocratically** adv.

autocross n. motor racing on dirt tracks.

autograph n. person's signature. ● v. write one's name in or on.

automate v. control by automation.

automatic adj. 1 (of a machine etc.) working by itself. 2 done without thinking. ● n. automatic machine or firearm. □ **automatically** adv.
■ adj. 1 automated, mechanical, robotic. 2 impulsive, instinctive, involuntary, knee-jerk, mechanical, reflex, spontaneous, unconscious, unthinking.

automation n. use of automatic equipment in industry.

automaton n. (pl. **-tons** or **-ta**) robot.

automobile n. (US) car.

automotive adj. concerned with motor vehicles.

autonomous adj. self-governing. □ **autonomy** n.

autopilot n. device for keeping an aircraft on a set course automatically.

autopsy n. post-mortem.

autumn n. season between summer and winter. □ **autumnal** adj.

auxiliary adj. giving help or support. ● n. helper. □ **auxiliary verb** one used in forming tenses of other verbs.

■ adj. additional, ancillary, extra, secondary, subsidiary, supplementary, supporting.

avail v. be of use or help (to). ● n. effectiveness, advantage. □ **avail oneself of** make use of.

available adj. 1 ready to be used. 2 within reach. □ **availability** n.

■ 1 at one's disposal, free, unoccupied. 2 accessible, at hand, handy, obtainable, colloq. on tap, to hand, within reach.

avalanche n. mass of snow pouring down a mountain.

avant-garde /ávvon-gaárd/ n. group of innovators. ● adj. progressive.

avarice n. greed for gain. □ **avaricious** adj., **avariciously** adv.

■ □ avaricious covetous, grasping, greedy, mercenary, rapacious, selfish.

avenge v. take vengeance for.

avenue n. 1 wide street or road. 2 way of approach.

average n. 1 standard regarded as usual. 2 value arrived at by adding several quantities together and dividing by the number of these. ● adj. 1 of ordinary standard. 2 found by making an average.

■ adj. commonplace, everyday, mediocre, medium, middling, moderate, normal, ordinary, run-of-the-mill, standard, typical, unexceptional, usual.

averse adj. unwilling, disinclined.

■ disinclined, indisposed, loath, opposed, reluctant, resistant, unwilling.

aversion n. strong dislike or unwillingness.

■ antipathy, dislike, disinclination, distaste, hatred, loathing, reluctance, unwillingness.

avert v. 1 turn away. 2 ward off.

■ 1 deflect, divert, turn aside or away. 2 fend off, forestall, prevent, stave off, ward off.

aviary n. large cage or building for keeping birds.

aviation n. flying an aircraft.

avid adj. eager, greedy. □ **avidly** adv., **avidity** n.

avocado n. (pl. **-os**) pear-shaped tropical fruit.

avocet n. wading bird with a long upturned bill.

avoid v. refrain or keep away from. □ **avoidable** adj., **avoidance** n.

■ abstain from, refrain from; bypass, circumvent, dodge, elude, escape, evade, give a wide berth to, shun, sidestep, skirt round, steer clear of.

avow v. declare. □ **avowal** n.

avuncular adj. of or like a kindly uncle.

await v. wait for.

awake v. (**awoke, awoken**) wake. ● adj. 1 not asleep. 2 alert.

■ v. awaken, come to, get up, rouse oneself, wake (up). ● adj. 1 conscious, up, wide awake. 2 alert, on one's guard, on one's toes, vigilant, watchful.

awaken v. awake.

award v. give officially as a prize, payment, or penalty. ● n. thing awarded.

■ v. bestow on, confer on, give, grant, present with. ● n. gift, prize, reward, trophy.

aware adj. having knowledge or realization. □ **awareness** n.

awash adj. washed over by water.

away adv. 1 to or at a distance. 2 into non-existence. 3 persistently. ● adj. played on an opponent's ground.

awe n. reverential fear or wonder. ● v. fill with awe.

■ n. admiration, amazement, dread, fear, respect, reverence, veneration, wonder.

aweigh adv. (of anchor) raised just clear of the sea bottom.

awesome adj. causing awe.

awful adj. 1 extremely bad or unpleasant. 2 (colloq.) very great. □ **awfully** adv.

■ 1 abominable, abysmal, appalling, atrocious, bad, colloq. beastly, deplorable, dreadful, colloq. frightful, ghastly, gruesome, horrendous, horrible, colloq. lousy, nasty, obnoxious, repellent, colloq. shocking, terrible, unpleasant.

awhile adv. for a short time.

awkward adj. 1 difficult to use. 2 clumsy. 3 embarrassing. 4 ill at ease. □ **awkwardly** adv., **awkwardness** n.

■ 1 cumbersome, unmanageable, unwieldy; colloq. fiddly. 2 blundering, bungling, clumsy, gauche, gawky, colloq. ham-fisted, inept, maladroit, ungainly, ungraceful, unskilful. **3** delicate, difficult, embarrassing, *colloq.* sticky, ticklish, tricky, troublesome. **4** disconcerted, embarrassed, ill at ease, self-conscious, uncomfortable, uneasy.

awning *n.* roof-like canvas shelter.

awoke, awoken *see* **awake**.

awry /ərí/ *adv. & adj.* **1** twisted to one side. **2** amiss.

axe *n.* chopping tool. ● *v.* (**axing**) abolish, dismiss.

axiom *n.* accepted general truth or principle. □ **axiomatic** *adj.*

axis *n.* (*pl.* **axes**) line through the centre of an object, round which it rotates if spinning. □ **axial** *adj.*

axle *n.* rod on which wheels turn.

ayatollah *n.* religious leader in Iran.

aye *adv.* yes. ● *n.* vote in favour of a proposal.

azalea *n.* shrub-like flowering plant.

Aztec *n.* member of a former Indian people of Mexico.

azure *adj. & n.* sky-blue.

baa n. & v. bleat.

babble v. 1 chatter indistinctly or foolishly. 2 (of a stream) murmur. ● n. babbling talk or sound.

babe n. baby.

babel n. confused noise.

baboon n. large monkey.

baby n. very young child or animal. □ **babyish** adj.

■ babe, child, infant, toddler, tot. □ **babyish** childish, immature, infantile, juvenile, puerile, silly.

babysit v. look after a child while its parents are out. □ **babysitter** n.

baccarat /bákkəraa/ n. gambling card game.

bachelor n. 1 unmarried man. 2 person with university degree.

bacillus n. (pl. **-li**) rod-like bacterium.

back n. 1 surface or part furthest from the front. 2 rear part of the human body from shoulders to hips. 3 corresponding part of an animal's body. 4 defensive player positioned near the goal in football etc. ● adj. 1 situated behind. 2 of or for past time. ● adv. 1 at or towards the rear. 2 in or into a previous time, position, or state. 3 in return. ● v. 1 move backwards. 2 help, support. 3 lay a bet on. □ **back down** withdraw a claim or argument. **back-pedal** v. reverse one's previous action or opinion. **back seat** inferior position or status. **back up** support.

■ adj. 1 end, hind, posterior, rear. ● v. 1 reverse. 2 aid, assist, back up, encourage, endorse, help, promote, second, side with, support, uphold; finance, fund, sponsor, subsidize, underwrite.

backache n. pain in one's back.

backbencher n. MP not entitled to sit on the front benches.

backbiting n. spiteful talk.

backbone n. column of bones down the centre of the back.

backchat n. verbal insolence.

backcloth n. painted cloth at the back of a stage or scene.

backdate v. declare to be valid from an earlier date.

backdrop n. backcloth.

backfire v. 1 make an explosion in an exhaust pipe. 2 produce an undesired effect.

backgammon n. game played on a board with draughts and dice.

background n. 1 conditions surrounding something. 2 person's history. 3 back part of a scene or picture.

■ 1 circumstances, context, setting, surroundings. 2 experience, history, qualifications, training, upbringing.

backhand n. backhanded stroke.

backhanded adj. 1 performed with the back of the hand turned forwards. 2 said with underlying sarcasm.

backhander n. 1 backhanded stroke. 2 (sl.) bribe.

backlash n. violent hostile reaction.

backlog n. arrears of work.

backpack n. rucksack.

backside n. (colloq.) buttocks.

backslide v. slip back from good behaviour into bad.

backstage adj. & adv. behind a theatre stage.

backstroke n. stroke used in swimming on one's back.

backtrack v. 1 retrace one's route. 2 reverse one's opinion.

backward adj. 1 directed backwards. 2 having made less than normal progress. 3 shy. ● adv. backwards.

backwards adv. 1 towards the back. 2 with the back foremost.

backwash n. 1 receding waves created by a ship etc. 2 reaction.

backwater n. 1 stagnant water joining a stream. 2 place unaffected by new ideas or progress.

backwoods n.pl. remote region.

bacon n. salted or smoked meat from a pig.

bacteriology n. study of bacteria. □ **bacteriologist** n.

bacterium n. (pl. **-ia**) microscopic organism. □ **bacterial** adj.

bad adj. (**worse**, **worst**) 1 of poor quality. 2 unpleasant. 3 wicked or offensive. 4 naughty. 5 harmful. 6 serious, severe. 7

decayed, polluted. □ **bad-tempered** irritable. **badly** adv.

■ **1** abominable, abysmal, awful, colloq. chronic, deplorable, disgraceful, dreadful, inadequate, incompetent, inferior, colloq. lousy, poor, second-rate, colloq. shocking, shoddy, substandard, unsatisfactory, useless, worthless. **2** awful, colloq. beastly, disagreeable, dreadful, colloq. lousy, nasty, terrible, unpleasant. **3** corrupt, criminal, cruel, depraved, evil, immoral, malevolent, malicious, offensive, sinful, vicious, vile, villainous, wicked, wrong. **4** disobedient, mischievous, naughty, rebellious, unruly, wayward, wild. **5** dangerous, deleterious, detrimental, harmful, hurtful, injurious, noxious, unhealthy. **6** appalling, awful, dire, disastrous, distressing, dreadful, ghastly, grave, horrible, serious, severe, terrible. **7** decayed, decomposing, foul, mildewed, mouldy, off, polluted, putrid, rancid, rank, rotten, sour, stale, tainted. □ **bad-tempered** cantankerous, crabby, cross, crotchety, disagreeable, fractious, grumpy, irascible, irritable, peevish, petulant, prickly, quarrelsome, snappy, splenetic, surly, testy.

bade see **bid²**.

badge n. thing worn to show membership, rank, etc.
■ crest, emblem, insignia, logo, trade mark, symbol, token.

badger n. burrowing animal. ● v. pester.

badminton n. game like tennis, played with a shuttlecock.

baffle v. **1** be too difficult for. **2** frustrate. □ **bafflement** n.
■ **1** colloq. bamboozle, bewilder, confound, confuse, floor, colloq. flummox, mystify, perplex, puzzle, colloq. stump. **2** baulk, foil, frustrate, stymie, thwart.

bag n. **1** flexible container. **2** handbag. **3** (pl., colloq.) large amount. ● v. (**bagged**) take for oneself.

baggage n. luggage.

baggy adj. (**-ier, -iest**) hanging in loose folds.

bagpipes n.pl. wind instrument with air stored in a bag and pressed out through pipes.

bail¹ n. money pledged as security that an accused person will return for trial. ● v. **bail out 1** obtain or allow the release of (a person) on bail. **2** relieve by financial help.

bail² n. each of two crosspieces resting on the stumps in cricket.

bail³ v. scoop water out of. See also **bale**.

bailey n. outer wall of a castle.

bailiff n. law officer empowered to seize goods for non-payment of fines or debts.

bailiwick n. area of authority.

bait n. an enticement, esp. placed to attract prey. ● v. **1** torment. **2** place bait on or in.
■ n. enticement, decoy, inducement, lure, temptation. ● v. **1** annoy, goad, harass, hound, persecute, pester, provoke, taunt, tease, torment.

baize n. thick green woollen cloth used for covering billiard tables.

bake v. cook or harden by dry heat.

baker n. person who bakes and sells bread.

bakery n. place where bread is baked for sale.

baking powder mixture used to make cakes rise.

balaclava (helmet) woollen cap covering the head and neck.

balalaika n. Russian guitar-like instrument with a triangular body.

balance n. **1** even distribution of weight or amount. **2** remainder. **3** difference between credits and debits. **4** weighing apparatus. **5** regulating apparatus of a clock. ● v. **1** consider by comparing. **2** be, put, or keep in a state of balance.
■ n. **1** equality, equilibrium, evenness, parity, poise, steadiness, symmetry. **2** difference, remainder, residue, rest, surplus. ● v. **1** compare, consider, counterbalance, evaluate, offset, weigh. **2** even up, keep balanced, level, steady, stabilize.

balcony n. **1** projecting platform with a rail or parapet. **2** upper floor of seats in a theatre etc.

bald adj. **1** with scalp wholly or partly hairless. **2** without details. **3** (of tyres) with the tread worn away. □ **baldly** adv., **baldness** n.

balderdash n. nonsense.

balding adj. becoming bald.

bale n. **1** large bound bundle of straw etc. **2** large package of goods. ● v. make into a bale or bales. □ **bale out** (also **bail out**) make an emergency parachute jump from an aircraft etc.

baleful adj. menacing, destructive. □ **balefully** adv.

ball¹ n. **1** spherical object used in games. **2** rounded part or mass. **3** delivery of a ball by a bowler. □ **ball-bearing** n. **1** bearing using small steel balls. **2** one such ball. **ballpoint** *n.* pen with a tiny ball as its writing-point.

ball² *n.* social gathering for dancing.

ballad *n.* song telling a story.

ballast *n.* heavy material placed in a ship's hold to steady it.

ballcock *n.* device with a floating ball controlling the water level in a cistern.

ballerina *n.* female ballet dancer.

ballet *n.* performance of dancing and mime to music.

ballistics *n.pl.* study of projectiles. □ **ballistic** *adj.*

balloon *n.* bag inflated with air or lighter gas. ● *v.* swell like this.

ballot *n.* **1** method of voting by writing on a slip of paper. **2** votes recorded in this way. ● *v.* (**balloted**) (cause to) vote by ballot.

ballroom *n.* large room where dances are held.

ballyhoo *n.* **1** fuss. **2** extravagant publicity.

balm *n.* **1** soothing influence. **2** fragrant herb. **3** ointment.

balmy *adj.* (**-ier, -iest**) **1** fragrant. **2** (of air) soft and warm.

balsa *n.* **1** tropical American tree. **2** its lightweight wood.

balsam *n.* **1** soothing oil. **2** a kind of flowering plant.

baluster *n.* short stone pillar in a balustrade.

balustrade *n.* row of short pillars supporting a rail or coping.

bamboo *n.* giant tropical grass with hollow stems.

bamboozle *v.* (*colloq.*) **1** mystify. **2** trick.

ban *v.* (**banned**) forbid officially. ● *n.* order banning something.

  ■ *v.* bar, debar, disallow, forbid, outlaw, prevent, prohibit, proscribe, stop, suppress, veto. ● *n.* boycott, embargo, interdict, moratorium, prohibition, taboo, veto.

banal *adj.* commonplace, uninteresting. □ **banality** *n.*

  ■ boring, commonplace, *colloq.* corny, dull, hackneyed, humdrum, ordinary, pedestrian, platitudinous, stale, stereotyped, trite, unimaginative, unoriginal.

banana *n.* **1** curved yellow fruit. **2** tropical tree bearing this.

band *n.* **1** strip of material. **2** stripe. **3** organized group of people. **4** group of musicians. **5** range of values or wavelengths. □ **bandmaster** *n.*, **bandsman** *n.*

  ■ **1** belt, ribbon, sash. **2** bar, border, line, ring, streak, striation, strip, stripe. **3** body,

clique, club, company, crew, gang, group, horde, party, team, troop. **4** ensemble, group, orchestra.

bandage *n.* strip of material for binding a wound. ● *v.* bind with this.

bandit *n.* member of a band of robbers.

  ■ brigand, buccaneer, desperado, gangster, highwayman, marauder, outlaw, pirate, robber, thief.

bandstand *n.* covered outdoor platform for musicians.

bandwagon *n.* **climb on the bandwagon** join a movement heading for success.

bandy¹ *v.* pass to and fro.

bandy² *adj.* (**-ier, -iest**) (of legs) curving apart at the knees.

bane *n.* cause of trouble or ruin.

bang *n.* **1** noise of or like an explosion. **2** sharp blow. ● *v.* **1** make this noise. **2** strike. **3** shut noisily. ● *adv.* **1** abruptly. **2** exactly.

  ■ *n.* blast, boom, clap, crash, detonation, explosion, report, shot.

banger *n.* **1** firework that explodes noisily. **2** (*sl.*) noisy old car. **3** (*sl.*) sausage.

bangle *n.* bracelet of rigid material.

banish *v.* **1** condemn to exile. **2** dismiss from one's presence or thoughts. □ **banishment** *n.*

  ■ **1** deport, drive out, eject, exile, expel, oust, outlaw.

banisters *n.pl.* uprights and handrail of a staircase.

banjo *n.* guitar-like musical instrument with a circular body.

bank¹ *n.* **1** slope, esp. at the side of a river. **2** raised mass of earth etc. **3** row of lights, switches, etc. ● *v.* **1** build up into a bank. **2** tilt sideways in rounding a curve.

bank² *n.* **1** establishment for safe keeping of money. **2** storage place. ● *v.* **1** place money in a bank. **2** base one's hopes.

banknote *n.* piece of paper money.

bankrupt *adj.* unable to pay one's debts. ● *n.* bankrupt person. ● *v.* make bankrupt. □ **bankruptcy** *n.*

banner *n.* kind of flag.

  ■ ensign, flag, pennant, pennon, standard, streamer.

banns *n.pl.* announcement in church of an intended marriage.

banquet *n.* elaborate ceremonial public meal.

banquette *n.* long upholstered seat attached to a wall.

banshee *n.* spirit whose wail is said to foretell a death.

bantam *n.* small kind of fowl.

banter *n.* good-humoured joking. ● *v.* joke thus.
∎ *n.* jesting, joking, pleasantries, repartee, teasing.

Bantu *adj.* & *n.* (*pl.* **Bantu** or **-us**) (member) of a group of African Negroid peoples.

bap *n.* large soft bread roll.

baptism *n.* religious rite of sprinkling with water as a sign of purification, usu. with name-giving. □ **baptismal** *adj.*

Baptist *n.* member of a Protestant sect believing that baptism should be by immersion.

baptistery *n.* place where baptism is performed.

baptize *v.* **1** perform baptism on. **2** name, nickname.

bar¹ *n.* **1** long piece of solid material. **2** strip. **3** barrier. **4** place containing a counter where alcohol or refreshments are served, this counter. **5** vertical line dividing music into units, this unit. **6** barristers, their profession. ● *v.* (**barred**) **1** fasten or secure with bar(s). **2** obstruct. **3** prohibit. ● *prep.* except.
∎ *n.* **1** beam, pole, rail, railing, rod, shaft, stake, stick; block, cake, lump, tablet. **2** band, line, streak, strip, stripe. **3** barrier, deterrent, hindrance, impediment, obstacle, obstruction. **4** café, pub, wine bar. ● *v.* **1** barricade, fasten, make fast, secure. **2** block, frustrate, hamper, hinder, impede, obstruct, prevent, stop. **3** ban, debar, exclude, forbid, prohibit.

bar² *n.* unit of atmospheric pressure.

barb *n.* **1** backward-pointing part of an arrow. **2** wounding remark.

barbarian *n.* uncivilized person.
∎ boor, *colloq.* brute, hooligan, ignoramus, lout, oaf, philistine, ruffian, vandal, *sl.* yob; savage.

barbaric *adj.* **1** brutal, cruel. **2** uncivilized.
∎ **1** barbarous, bestial, brutal, brutish, cruel, ferocious, inhuman, ruthless, savage, vicious, violent.

barbarity *n.* savage cruelty.

barbarous *adj.* **1** cruel. **2** uncivilized.

barbecue *n.* **1** frame for grilling food above an open fire. **2** this food. **3** open-air party where such food is served. ● *v.* cook on a barbecue.

barbed *adj.* having barbs. □ **barbed wire** wire with many sharp points.

barber *n.* men's hairdresser.

barbican *n.* **1** outer defence to a city or castle. **2** double tower over a gate or bridge.

barbiturate *n.* sedative drug.

bar code machine-readable striped code identifying a commodity, its price, etc.

bard *n.* **1** Celtic minstrel. **2** poet. □ **bardic** *adj.*

bare *adj.* **1** not clothed or covered. **2** lacking vegetation. **3** not adorned. **4** only just enough. ● *v.* reveal. □ **barely** *adv.*
∎ *adj.* **1** nude, (stark) naked, unclothed, uncovered, undressed; defoliated, denuded, leafless, shorn, stripped. **2** barren, bleak, desolate, open, treeless, windswept. **3** austere, plain, simple, unadorned, undecorated, unfurnished. **4** basic, meagre, mere, minimal, scant, scanty. ● *v.* expose, reveal, show, uncover, unmask, unveil.

bareback *adv.* without a saddle.

barefaced *adj.* shameless, undisguised.

bargain *n.* **1** agreement with obligations on both sides. **2** thing obtained cheaply. ● *v.* discuss the terms of an agreement. □ **bargain for** expect.
∎ *n.* **1** agreement, arrangement, contract, deal, pact, settlement, understanding. **2** good buy, *sl.* snip, *colloq.* steal. ● *v.* barter, haggle, negotiate. □ **bargain for** be prepared for, envisage, expect, foresee.

barge *n.* large flat-bottomed boat used on rivers and canals. ● *v.* move clumsily. □ **barge in** intrude.

baritone *n.* male voice between tenor and bass.

barium *n.* white metallic element.

bark¹ *n.* outer layer of a tree. ● *v.* scrape skin off accidentally.

bark² *n.* sharp harsh cry of a dog. ● *v.* **1** make this sound. **2** utter sharply.

barley *n.* **1** cereal plant. **2** its grain. □ **barley sugar** sweet made of boiled sugar. **barley water** drink made from pearl barley.

barman, barmaid *ns.* person serving in a pub etc.

barmy *adj.* (**-ier, -iest**) (*sl.*) crazy.

barn *n.* building for storing grain or hay etc.

barnacle *n.* shellfish that attaches itself to objects under water.

barometer *n.* instrument measuring atmospheric pressure. □ **barometric** *adj.*

baron *n.* member of the lowest rank of nobility. □ **baroness** *n.*, **baronial** *adj.*

baronet *n*. lowest hereditary title in Britain. □ **baronetcy** *n*.

baroque /bərók/ *adj*. of the ornate architectural style of the 17th–18th centuries. ● *n*. this style.

barque *n*. sailing ship.

barrack *v*. shout or jeer (at).

barracks *n.pl*. building(s) for soldiers to live in.

barracuda *n*. large voracious tropical sea fish.

barrage *n*. **1** heavy bombardment. **2** artificial barrier.

barrel *n*. **1** large round container with flat ends. **2** tube-like part esp. of a gun. □ **barrel organ** musical instrument with a rotating pin-studded cylinder.
　■ **1** butt, cask, churn, drum, keg, tank, tub, water-butt.

barren *adj*. **1** not fertile. **2** without vegetation. □ **barrenness** *n*.
　■ **1** infertile, sterile, unfruitful, unproductive. **2** arid, bare, desert, desolate, dry, lifeless, waste.

barricade *n*. barrier. ● *v*. block or defend with a barricade.

barrier *n*. thing that prevents or controls advance or access.
　■ bar, barricade, boom, bulwark, dam, fence, hurdle, obstruction, railing, stockade, wall; handicap, hindrance, impediment, obstacle, stumbling block.

barrister *n*. lawyer representing clients in court.

barrow[1] *n*. **1** wheelbarrow. **2** cart pushed or pulled by hand.

barrow[2] *n*. prehistoric burial mound.

barter *n*. & *v*. trade by exchange of goods for other goods.

basalt /bássawlt/ *n*. dark rock of volcanic origin.

base *n*. **1** part on which a thing rests or is supported. **2** point from which something is developed. **3** headquarters. **4** substance capable of combining with an acid to form a salt. **5** each of four stations to be reached by a batter in baseball. ● *v*. **1** use as a basis (for). **2** station. ● *adj*. **1** dishonourable. **2** of inferior value.
　■ *n*. **1** bottom, foot, pedestal, plinth, stand, support. **2** basis, foundation, starting point, underlying principle. **3** camp, centre, headquarters. ● *v*. **1** build, establish, found, ground. **2** locate, place, position, station. ● *adj*. **1** contemptible, corrupt, cowardly, despicable, dishonourable, dis-

reputable, ignoble, immoral, low, mean, shabby, shameful, sordid, undignified, unworthy, vile, wicked. **2** cheap, inferior, mean, poor, second-rate, shoddy, worthless.

baseball *n*. American team game played with bat and ball, in which the batter has to hit the ball and run round a circuit.

baseless *adj*. groundless.

basement *n*. storey below ground level.

bash *v*. strike violently. ● *n*. violent blow or knock.

bashful *adj*. shy, self-conscious.
　■ abashed, coy, demure, diffident, embarrassed, meek, reserved, retiring, self-conscious, self-effacing, shamefaced, sheepish, shy, timid.

basic *adj*. **1** very important. **2** simple. **3** lowest in level. **4** deeply rooted. ● *n*. (usu. *pl*.) fundamental fact or principle. □ **basically** *adv*.
　■ *adj*. **1** central, chief, crucial, essential, fundamental, important, intrinsic, key, main, necessary, primary, principal, underlying, vital. **2** bare, crude, primitive, simple, spartan. **3** beginner's, early, elementary, first, initial, introductory, preliminary, primary, rudimentary. **4** elemental, inborn, inherent, innate, instinctive, profound, radical. ● *n*. (**basics**) elements, essentials, first principles, foundations, fundamentals, *sl*. nitty-gritty, rudiments.

basil *n*. sweet-smelling herb.

basilica *n*. oblong hall or church with an apse at one end.

basilisk *n*. **1** American lizard. **2** mythical reptile said to cause death by its glance or breath.

basin *n*. **1** deep open container for liquids. **2** washbasin. **3** sunken place. **4** area drained by a river. □ **basinful** *n*.

basis *n*. (*pl*. **bases**) **1** foundation or support. **2** main principle.
　■ **1** base, footing, foundation, support; grounds, principle, reason. **2** cornerstone, essence, underlying principle.

bask *v*. sit or lie comfortably in warmth and light.

basket *n*. container made of interwoven cane or wire.

basketball *n*. team game in which the aim is to throw the ball through a high net.

basketwork *n*. **1** art of weaving cane etc. **2** work so produced.

Basque n. & adj. **1** (member) of a people living in the western Pyrenees. **2** (of) their language.

bas-relief n. sculpture or carving in low relief.

bass[1] /bass/ n. (pl. **bass**) fish of the perch family.

bass[2] /bayss/ adj. deep-sounding, of the lowest pitch in music. ● n. (pl. **basses**) **1** lowest male voice. **2** bass pitch. **3** double bass.

basset n. short-legged hound.

bassoon n. woodwind instrument with a deep tone.

bast n. **1** inner bark of the lime tree. **2** similar fibre.

bastard n. **1** illegitimate child. **2** (sl.) unpleasant or difficult person or thing. □ **bastardy** n.

baste[1] v. sew together temporarily with loose stitches.

baste[2] v. **1** moisten with fat during cooking. **2** thrash.

bastion n. **1** projecting part of a fortified place. **2** stronghold.

bat[1] n. **1** wooden implement for striking a ball in games. **2** batsman. ● v. (**batted**) perform or strike with the bat in cricket etc. □ **batsman** n. player batting in cricket.

bat[2] n. nocturnal flying animal with a mouse-like body.

batch n. set of people or things dealt with as a group.

bated adj. **with bated breath** anxiously.

bath n. **1** washing (of the whole body) by immersion. **2** container used for this. ● v. wash in a bath. □ **bathroom** n. room with a bath.

bathe v. **1** immerse in liquid. **2** swim for pleasure. ● n. swim.

bathos n. anticlimax, descent from an important thing to a trivial one.

batik n. method of printing designs on textiles by waxing parts not to be dyed.

batman n. soldier acting as an officer's personal servant.

baton n. short stick, esp. used by a conductor or police officer.

batrachian /bətráykian/ n. amphibian that discards gills and tail when fully developed.

battalion n. army unit of several companies.

batten[1] n. bar of wood or metal, esp. holding something in place. ● v. fasten with batten(s).

batten[2] v. **batten on** thrive at another's expense.

batter[1] v. hit hard and often. ● n. beaten mixture of flour, eggs, and milk, used in cooking.

■ v. bash, beat, belabour, bludgeon, sl. clobber, cudgel, hit, pound, pummel, strike, thrash.

batter[2] n. player batting in baseball.

battering ram iron-headed beam formerly used in war for breaking through walls or gates.

battery n. **1** group of big guns. **2** artillery unit. **3** set of similar or connected units of equipment, poultry cages, etc. **4** electric cell(s) supplying current. **5** unlawful blow or touch.

battle n. **1** fight between armed forces. **2** contest, struggle. ● v. struggle.

■ n. **1** action, clash, combat, conflict, encounter, engagement, fight, fray. **2** competition, contest, match; campaign, crusade, fight, struggle, war. ● v. campaign, crusade, fight, struggle, wage war, wrestle.

battleaxe n. **1** medieval weapon. **2** (colloq.) formidable woman.

battlefield n. scene of battle.

battlements n.pl. parapet with gaps for firing from.

battleship n. warship of the most heavily armed kind.

batty adj. (**-ier, -iest**) (sl.) crazy.

bauble n. valueless ornament.

baulk v. **1** shirk. **2** frustrate. ● n. hindrance.

bauxite n. mineral from which aluminium is obtained.

bawdy adj. (**-ier, -iest**) humorously indecent. □ **bawdiness** n.

bawl v. **1** shout. **2** weep noisily. □ **bawl out** (colloq.) reprimand.

■ **1** bellow, roar, shout, thunder, yell. **2** blubber, cry, howl, sob, wail, weep.

bay[1] n. a kind of laurel.

bay[2] n. part of a sea or lake within a wide curve of the shore.

■ cove, creek, estuary, fiord, firth, gulf, harbour, inlet.

bay[3] n. recess, compartment. □ **bay window** one projecting from an outside wall.

■ alcove, booth, compartment, opening, recess.

bay[4] n. deep cry of a large dog or of hounds. ● v. make this sound. □ **at bay** forced to face attackers.

bay[5] adj. & n. reddish-brown (horse).

bayonet n. stabbing blade fixed to the muzzle of a rifle.

bazaar n. **1** oriental market. **2** sale of goods to raise funds.

bazooka n. portable weapon for firing anti-tank rockets.

be v. **1** exist, occur. **2** have a certain position, quality, or condition. ● v.aux. used to form tenses of other verbs.

beach n. sandy or pebbly shore of the sea. ● v. bring on shore from water. □ **beachcomber** n. person who salvages things on a beach. **beachhead** n. fortified position set up on a beach by an invading army.
■ n. coast, littoral, sands, seashore, shore, strand.

beacon n. fire or light used as a signal.

bead n. **1** small shaped piece of hard material pierced for threading with others on a string. **2** drop of liquid.

beading n. strip of trimming for wood.

beadle n. (formerly) minor parish official.

beady adj. (**-ier, -iest**) (of eyes) small and bright.

beagle n. small hound used for hunting hares.

beak n. **1** bird's horny projecting jaws. **2** any similar projection. **3** (sl.) magistrate.

beaker n. tall drinking cup.

beam n. **1** long piece of timber or metal used in house-building etc. **2** ray of light or other radiation. **3** bright smile. **4** ship's breadth. ● v. **1** send out light etc. **2** smile radiantly.
■ n. **1** bar, girder, joist, plank, rafter, support, timber. **2** gleam, ray, shaft. **3** grin, smile. ● v. **1** emit, radiate, send out, shine. **2** grin, smile.

bean n. **1** plant with kidney-shaped seeds in long pods. **2** seed of this or of coffee.

bear[1] n. large heavy animal with thick fur.

bear[2] v. (**bore, borne**) **1** carry. **2** support. **3** keep in thought or memory. **4** endure, tolerate. **5** be fit for. **6** produce, give birth to. **7** take (a specified direction).
■ **1** bring, carry, convey, deliver, take, transport. **2** carry, hold, support, sustain, take. **3** harbour, keep, retain. **4** cope with, endure, experience, go through, suffer, undergo, weather, withstand; abide, brook, put up with, stand, stomach, colloq. stick, tolerate. **5** be worthy of, deserve, merit, rate. **6** develop, generate, produce, yield; give birth to, have, spawn. **7** fork, go, swing, turn, veer.

bearable adj. endurable.
■ acceptable, endurable, supportable, tolerable.

beard n. hair on and round a man's chin. ● v. confront boldly.

bearing n. **1** posture. **2** outward behaviour. **3** relevance. **4** compass direction. **5** device reducing friction where a part turns.
■ **1** carriage, deportment, posture, stance. **2** air, aspect, attitude, behaviour, conduct, demeanour, manner, mien, presence. **3** applicability, application, connection, pertinence, relationship, relevance, significance.

bearskin n. guardsman's tall furry cap.

beast n. **1** large four-footed animal. **2** brutal person.
■ **1** animal, creature. **2** brute, fiend, monster, ogre, savage.

beastly adj. (**-ier, -iest**) (colloq.) very unpleasant.

beat v. (**beat, beaten**) **1** hit repeatedly. **2** mix vigorously. **3** (of the heart) pump rhythmically. **4** do better than, defeat. ● n. **1** recurring emphasis marking rhythm. **2** throbbing action or sound. **3** appointed course of a policeman or sentinel. □ **beat up** assault violently.
■ v. **1** bash, belabour, sl. belt, bludgeon, sl. clobber, clout, flog, hammer, hit, colloq. lambaste, lash, colloq. lay into, pound, pummel, punch, strike, thrash, thump, thwack, sl. wallop, colloq. whack, whip. **2** blend, mix, stir, whip, whisk. **3** palpitate, pound, pulsate, pulse, throb. **4** conquer, crush, defeat, get the better of, colloq. lick, outdo, outstrip, overcome, overpower, overwhelm, rout, subdue, surpass, thrash, trounce, vanquish, worst. ● n. **1** measure, rhythm, stress, tempo. **2** palpitation, pulsation, pulse, throb. **3** circuit, course, path, route, way.

beatific adj. showing great happiness. □ **beatifically** adv.

beatify v. (RC Church) declare blessed, as first step in canonization. □ **beatification** n.

beatitude n. blessedness.

beauteous adj. (poetic) beautiful.

beautician n. person who gives beauty treatment.

beautiful adj. **1** having beauty. **2** excellent. □ **beautifully** adv.
■ **1** alluring, appealing, attractive, poetic beauteous, Sc. bonny, comely, colloq. divine, exquisite, glamorous, good-looking,

colloq. gorgeous, handsome, lovely, pretty, *colloq.* stunning; artistic, charming, decorative, delightful, elegant, fine, graceful, picturesque, scenic, tasteful. **2** admirable, excellent, magnificent, marvellous, splendid, superb, wonderful.

beautify *v.* make beautiful. □ **beautification** *n.*
■ adorn, deck, decorate, embellish, ornament, *colloq.* titivate.

beauty *n.* **1** combination of qualities giving pleasure to the sight, mind, etc. **2** beautiful person or thing.
■ **1** attractiveness, charm, elegance, glamour, grace, loveliness, prettiness, radiance, splendour. **2** belle, *colloq.* knockout, *colloq.* stunner.

beaver *n.* small amphibious rodent. ● *v.* work hard.

becalmed *adj.* unable to move because there is no wind.

because *conj.* for the reason that. □ **because of** by reason of.

beck¹ *n.* **at the beck and call of** ready and waiting to obey.

beck² *n.* mountain stream.

beckon *v.* summon by a gesture.

become *v.* (**became, become**) **1** come to be, begin to be. **2** suit.
■ **1** change into, develop into, grow into, mature into, turn into. **2** flatter, look good on, suit.

bed *n.* **1** thing to sleep or rest on. **2** framework with a mattress and coverings. **3** flat base, foundation. **4** bottom of a sea or river etc. **5** layer. **6** garden plot.

bedbug *n.* bug infesting beds.

bedclothes *n.pl.* sheets, blankets, etc.

bedding *n.* beds and bedclothes.

bedevil *v.* (**bedevilled**) afflict with difficulties.

bedlam *n.* scene of uproar.

Bedouin /bédoo-in/ *n.* (*pl.* **Bedouin**) member of an Arab people living in tents in the desert.

bedpan *n.* pan for use as a lavatory by an invalid in bed.

bedraggled *adj.* limp and untidy.
■ dishevelled, drenched, messy, *colloq.* scruffy, soaked, sodden, unkempt, untidy, wet.

bedridden *adj.* permanently confined to bed through illness.

bedrock *n.* **1** solid rock beneath loose soil. **2** basic facts.

bedroom *n.* room for sleeping in.

bedsit *n.* (also **bedsitter**) room for living and sleeping in.

bedsore *n.* sore developed by lying in bed for a long time.

bedspread *n.* covering spread over a bed during the day.

bedstead *n.* framework of a bed.

bee *n.* insect that produces honey.

beech *n.* tree with smooth bark and glossy leaves.

beef *n.* **1** meat from ox, bull, or cow. **2** muscular strength. **3** (*sl.*) grumble. ● *v.* (*sl.*) grumble.

beefburger *n.* hamburger.

beefeater *n.* warder in the Tower of London.

beefy *adj.* (**-ier, -iest**) having a solid muscular body.

beehive *n.* structure in which bees live.

beeline *n.* **make a beeline for** go straight or rapidly towards.

beep *n.* & *v.* bleep. □ **beeper** *n.*

beer *n.* alcoholic drink made from malt and hops. □ **beery** *adj.*

beeswax *n.* yellow substance secreted by bees, used as polish.

beet *n.* plant with a fleshy root used as a vegetable or for making sugar.

beetle¹ *n.* insect with hard wing-covers.

beetle² *n.* tool for ramming or crushing things.

beetle³ *v.* overhang, project.

beetroot *n.* beet with a dark red root used as a vegetable.

befall *v.* (**befell, befallen**) **1** happen. **2** happen to.

befit *v.* (**befitted**) be suitable for.

before *adv., prep., & conj.* **1** at an earlier time (than). **2** ahead, in front of. **3** in preference to.

beforehand *adv.* in advance.

befriend *v.* show kindness towards.

beg *v.* (**begged**) **1** ask for as a gift or charity. **2** request earnestly.
■ **1** cadge, scrounge, sponge. **2** beseech, crave, entreat, implore, importune, petition, plead with, pray, request, solicit, supplicate.

beggar *n.* person who lives by begging. ● *v.* reduce to poverty.

begin *v.* (**began, begun, beginning**) **1** perform the first part of. **2** come into existence. **3** be the first to do a thing.
■ **1** commence, embark on, get going, inaugurate, initiate, set about, set in motion, set out (on), start. **2** arise, come into being, get under way, originate, start.

beginner *n.* person just beginning to learn a skill.
■ apprentice, initiate, learner, novice, recruit, trainee.

beginning *n.* **1** first part. **2** starting point, source or origin.
■ **1** commencement, inauguration, introduction, opening, start. **2** creation, dawn, dawning, genesis, inception, onset, origin, outset, source, start, starting point.

begonia *n.* garden plant with bright leaves and flowers.

begrudge *v.* be unwilling to give or allow.

beguile *v.* **1** entertain pleasantly. **2** deceive.
■ **1** absorb, amuse, charm, divert, entertain. **2** cheat, deceive, delude, dupe, fool, hoodwink, mislead, trick.

begum *n.* title of a Muslim married woman.

behalf *n.* **on behalf of** as the representative of.

behave *v.* **1** act or react in a specified way. **2** (also **behave oneself**) show good manners.
■ **1** act, conduct oneself, function, operate, perform, react.

behaviour *n.* way of behaving.
■ actions, attitude, bearing, conduct, demeanour, deportment, manners.

behead *v.* cut the head off.

beheld *see* **behold**.

behind *adv. & prep.* **1** in or to the rear (of). **2** in arrears. **3** remaining after others' departure. ● *n.* buttocks.

behold *v.* (**beheld**) (*poetic*) **1** see. **2** observe. □ **beholder** *n.*

beholden *adj.* owing thanks.

behove *v.* be incumbent on.

beige *adj. & n.* light fawn (colour).

being *n.* **1** existence. **2** thing that exists and has life.
■ **1** actuality, existence, life, reality. **2** animal, creature, human being, individual, mortal, person, soul.

belabour *v.* **1** beat. **2** attack.

belated *adj.* coming (too) late.
■ delayed, late, overdue, tardy, unpunctual.

belch *v.* send out wind noisily from the stomach through the mouth. ● *n.* act of belching.

beleaguer *v.* besiege.

belfry *n.* **1** bell tower. **2** space for bells in a tower.

belie *v.* contradict, fail to confirm.

belief *n.* **1** what one believes. **2** trust, confidence.
■ **1** conviction, creed, doctrine, opinion, persuasion, principle(s), tenet, view; faith, religion. **2** certainty, confidence, credence, faith, reliance, sureness, trust.

believe *v.* **1** accept as true or as speaking truth. **2** think, suppose. □ **believe in 1** have faith in the existence of. **2** feel sure of the worth of. **believer** *n.*
■ **1** accept, be certain of, credit, find credible, put one's faith in. **2** assume, feel, gather, hold, imagine, maintain, presume, suppose, think. □ **believe in** have faith in, rely on, swear by, trust in.

belittle *v.* disparage.
■ criticize, decry, denigrate, deprecate, detract from, discredit, disparage, minimize, play down, run down, slight, undervalue.

bell *n.* **1** cup-shaped metal instrument that makes a ringing sound when struck. **2** its sound.

belle *n.* beautiful woman.

belles-lettres /bel-létrə/ *n.pl.* literary studies.

bellicose *adj.* eager to fight.

belligerent *adj.* **1** aggressive. **2** engaged in a war. □ **belligerently** *adv.*, **belligerence** *n.*
■ **1** aggressive, antagonistic, argumentative, bellicose, combative, contentious, fierce, hostile, militant, pugnacious, quarrelsome, truculent. **2** martial, warring.

bellow *v.* utter a deep loud roar. ● *n.* a bellowing sound.
■ *v.* bawl, howl, roar, shout, thunder, trumpet, yell.

bellows *n.pl.* apparatus for driving air into something.

belly *n.* **1** abdomen. **2** stomach.

bellyful *n.* (*colloq.*) as much as one wants or rather more.

belong *v.* have a rightful place. □ **belong to 1** be the property of **2** be a member of.

belongings *n.pl.* possessions.
■ chattels, effects, goods, possessions, property, stuff, things.

beloved *adj. & n.* dearly loved (person).

below *adv. & prep.* at or to a lower position or amount (than).

belt *n.* **1** strip of cloth or leather etc., worn round the waist. **2** distinct region.

● v. 1 put a belt round. 2 (sl.) hit. 3 (sl.) rush.

■ n. 1 girdle, sash. 2 area, district, quarter, region, sector, stretch, strip, tract, zone.

bemoan v. complain about.

bemuse v. bewilder.

bench n. 1 long seat of wood or stone. 2 long working-table. 3 judges or magistrates hearing a case.

benchmark n. 1 surveyor's fixed point. 2 point of reference.

bend v. (**bent**) 1 make or become curved. 2 turn downwards, stoop. 3 turn in a new direction. ● n. curve, turn.

■ v. 1 arch, bow, crook, curl, curve, flex. 2 crouch, duck, lean, stoop. 3 bear, incline, swerve, swing, turn, veer, wind. ● n. angle, arc, corner, crook, curvature, curve, turn, turning, twist.

bender n. (sl.) drinking spree.

beneath adv. & prep. 1 below, underneath. 2 not worthy of.

benediction n. spoken blessing.

benefactor n. one who gives financial or other help. □ **benefaction** n., **benefactress** n.

■ backer, donor, fairy godmother, investor, patron, philanthropist, sponsor, supporter, underwriter.

beneficent adj. 1 doing good. 2 actively kind. □ **beneficence** n.

beneficial adj. helpful, useful. □ **beneficially** adv.

■ advantageous, constructive, favourable, gainful, good, helpful, profitable, useful, valuable, worthwhile; healthy, salutary, salubrious, wholesome.

beneficiary n. one who receives a benefit or legacy.

■ heir, heiress, inheritor, legatee, recipient, successor.

benefit n. 1 something helpful, favourable, or profitable. 2 payment made from government funds etc. ● v. (**benefited**, **benefiting**) 1 do good to. 2 receive benefit.

■ n. 1 advantage, gain, good, help, profit; asset, attraction, plus. ● v. 1 aid, assist, better, boost, enhance, further, help, improve, promote. 2 gain, profit.

benevolent adj. kindly and helpful. □ **benevolence** n.

■ altruistic, beneficent, benign, caring, charitable, compassionate, considerate, friendly, generous, good, helpful, humane, kind, kind-hearted, kindly, sympathetic, thoughtful, unselfish, well-disposed.

benighted adj. 1 in darkness. 2 ignorant.

benign adj. 1 mild and gentle, kindly. 2 (of a tumour) not malignant. □ **benignly** adv.

■ 1 amiable, benevolent, compassionate, gentle, genial, good, friendly, kind, kind-hearted, kindly, mild, well-disposed.

bent see **bend**. adj. 1 curved. 2 (sl.) dishonest. ● n. natural skill or liking. □ **bent on** seeking or determined to do.

benzene n. liquid obtained from coal tar, used as a solvent.

benzine n. liquid mixture of hydrocarbons used in dry-cleaning.

bequeath v. leave as a legacy.

■ hand down, leave, make over, pass on, will.

bequest n. legacy.

■ heritage, gift, inheritance, legacy, patrimony.

berate v. scold.

bereave v. deprive, esp. of a relative, by death. □ **bereavement** n.

bereft adj. deprived.

beret /bérray/ n. round flat cap with no peak.

beriberi n. disease caused by lack of vitamin B.

berry n. small round juicy fruit with no stone.

berserk adj. **go berserk** go into a wild destructive rage.

berth n. 1 sleeping place in a ship. 2 place for a ship to tie up at a wharf. ● v. moor at a berth. □ **give a wide berth** to keep a safe distance from.

beryl n. transparent green gem.

beseech v. (**besought**) implore.

■ appeal to, ask, beg, entreat, implore, importune, plead with, pray, supplicate.

beset v. (**beset**, **besetting**) 1 affect or trouble persistently. 2 hem in, surround.

■ 1 afflict, assail, attack, bedevil, beleaguer, harass, hound, colloq. plague, torment, trouble. 2 besiege, encircle, hem in, surround.

beside prep. 1 at the side of, close to. 2 compared with. □ **beside oneself** frantic with anger or worry etc. **beside the point** irrelevant.

besides prep. in addition to, other than. ● adv. also.

besiege v. **1** lay siege to. **2** crowd round eagerly. **3** harass with requests.

■ **1** beleaguer, blockade, lay siege to. **2** beset, encircle, hem in, surround. **3** beleaguer, beset, bombard, harass, hound, pester, *colloq.* plague.

besotted adj. infatuated.

besought see **beseech**.

bespeak v. (**bespoke, bespoken**) **1** engage beforehand. **2** be evidence of.

bespoke adj. (of clothes) made to a customer's order.

best adj. most excellent. ● adv. **1** in the best way. **2** most usefully. ● n. best thing. □ **best man** bridegroom's chief attendant. **best part of** most of.

■ adj. choicest, excellent, finest, first-class, incomparable, optimum, outstanding, peerless, pre-eminent, superb, superlative, supreme, top, unequalled, unrivalled, unsurpassed.

bestial adj. **1** savage. **2** of or like a beast. □ **bestiality** n.

■ **1** barbarous, barbaric, brutal, cruel, ferocious, fierce, inhuman, savage, vicious, violent.

bestir v. (**bestirred**) **bestir oneself** exert oneself.

bestow v. confer as a gift. □ **bestowal** n.

■ award, confer, give, grant, present.

bestride v. (**bestrode**) stand astride over.

bet n. sum of money etc. risked on the outcome of an unpredictable event. ● v. (**bet** or **betted**) **1** make a bet. **2** risk (money) as a bet. **3** (*colloq.*) predict.

■ n. *colloq.* flutter, stake, wager. ● v. **1** gamble, *colloq.* have a flutter, wager. **2** chance, hazard, risk, stake, venture.

beta n. second letter of the Greek alphabet, = b.

betake v. (**betook, betaken**) **betake oneself** go.

betide v. happen to.

betimes adv. (*poetic*) in good time, early.

betoken v. be a sign of.

betray v. **1** be disloyal to (a person, one's country). **2** reveal involuntarily. □ **betrayal** n.

■ **1** be disloyal to, denounce, double-cross, inform against *or* on, let down, rat on, sell out, *sl.* shop. **2** disclose, divulge, give away, *sl.* let on, reveal, show, tell.

betroth v. cause to be engaged to marry. □ **betrothal** n.

better adj. **1** more excellent. **2** partly or fully recovered from illness. ● adv. **1** in a

better manner. **2** more usefully. ● v. **1** improve. **2** surpass. □ **better part** more than half. **get the better of 1** overcome. **2** outwit.

■ adj. **1** preferable, superior. **2** convalescent, fitter, healthier, on the mend, progressing, recovering; cured, recovered, well. ● v. **1** ameliorate, amend, enhance, improve, mend, polish, rectify, refine, reform. **2** beat, cap, eclipse, exceed, excel, outdo, outshine, outstrip, surpass.

betting shop bookmaker's office.

between prep. **1** in the space, time, or quality bounded by (two limits). **2** separating. **3** to and from. **4** connecting. **5** shared by. ● adv. between points or limits etc.

bevel n. sloping edge. ● v. (**bevelled**) give a sloping edge to.

beverage n. any drink.

bevy n. company, large group.

bewail v. wail over.

beware v. be on one's guard.

■ be careful, be on one's guard, look out, take care, take heed, watch out, watch one's step.

bewilder v. puzzle, confuse. □ **bewilderment** n.

■ baffle, *colloq.* bamboozle, bemuse, confound, confuse, floor, *colloq.* flummox, mystify, perplex, puzzle, *colloq.* stump.

bewitch v. **1** delight very much. **2** cast a spell on.

■ **1** captivate, charm, delight, enchant, enrapture, entrance, fascinate, hypnotize, mesmerize.

beyond adv. & prep. **1** at or to the further side (of). **2** outside the range of.

biannual adj. happening twice a year. □ **biannually** adv.

bias n. predisposition, prejudice. ● v. (**biased**) influence.

■ n. bent, inclination, leaning, partiality, predilection, predisposition, preference, prejudice, proclivity, propensity, tendency. ● v. affect, colour, influence, predispose, prejudice, sway.

bib n. covering put under a child's chin while feeding.

Bible n. Christian or Jewish scripture.

biblical adj. of or in the Bible.

bibliography n. list of books about a subject or by a specified author. □ **bibliographer** n., **bibliographical** adj.

bibliophile n. book-lover.

bibulous adj. fond of drinking.

bicentenary n. 200th anniversary.

bicentennial *adj.* happening every 200 years. ● *n.* bicentenary.

biceps *n.* large muscle at the front of the upper arm.

bicker *v.* quarrel pettily.

bicycle *n.* two-wheeled vehicle driven by pedals. ● *v.* ride a bicycle.

bid¹ *n.* **1** offer of a price, esp. at an auction. **2** (*colloq.*) attempt. **3** statement of the number of tricks a player proposes to win in a card game. ● *v.* (**bid, bidding**) make a bid (of), offer.

> ■ *n.* **1** offer, price, proposal, tender. **2** attempt, effort, endeavour, go, *colloq.* stab, try. ● *v.* offer, proffer, propose, tender.

bid² *v.* (**bid** or **bade, bidden, bidding**) **1** command. **2** say as a greeting.

biddable *adj.* willing to obey.

bide *v.* await (one's time).

bidet /beeday/ *n.* low washbasin that one can sit astride to wash the genital and anal regions.

biennial *adj.* **1** lasting for two years. **2** happening every second year. ● *n.* plant that flowers and dies in its second year.

bier /beer/ *n.* movable stand for a coffin.

biff *v.* & *n.* (*sl.*) hit.

bifocals *n.pl.* spectacles with lenses that have two parts for distant and close focusing.

bifurcate *v.* fork. □ **bifurcation** *n.*

big *adj.* (**bigger, biggest**) **1** large in size, amount, or intensity. **2** important.

> ■ **1** *colloq.* almighty, astronomical, broad, capacious, colossal, commodious, considerable, elephantine, enormous, extensive, gargantuan, giant, gigantic, great, hefty, huge, *colloq.* hulking, immense, king-sized, large, mammoth, massive, mighty, monstrous, monumental, mountainous, oversized, prodigious, roomy, sizeable, spacious, substantial, *colloq.* terrific, titanic, tremendous, vast, voluminous. **2** crucial, important, major, momentous, serious, significant.

bigamy *n.* crime of going through a form of marriage while a previous marriage is still valid. □ **bigamist** *n.*, **bigamous** *adj.*

bigot *n.* intolerant adherent of a creed or view. □ **bigoted** *adj.*, **bigotry** *n.*

bike (*colloq.*) *n.* **1** bicycle. **2** motor cycle. ● *v.* ride a bicycle or motor cycle. □ **biker** *n.*

bikini *n.* (*pl.* -**is**) woman's scanty two-piece beach garment.

bilateral *adj.* **1** having two sides. **2** existing between two groups. □ **bilaterally** *adv.*

bilberry *n.* **1** small dark blue berry. **2** shrub producing this.

bile *n.* bitter yellowish liquid produced by the liver.

bilge *n.* **1** ship's bottom. **2** water collecting there. **3** (*sl.*) nonsense.

bilharzia *n.* disease caused by a tropical parasitic flatworm.

bilingual *adj.* written in or able to speak two languages.

bilious *adj.* sick, esp. from trouble with bile or liver.

bilk *v.* defraud of payment.

bill¹ *n.* **1** written statement of charges to be paid. **2** poster. **3** programme. **4** draft of a proposed law. **5** (*US*) banknote. ● *v.* **1** send a statement of charges to. **2** announce, advertise.

> ■ *n.* **1** account, *US* check, invoice, statement. **2** advertisement, notice, placard, poster, sign.

bill² *n.* bird's beak. ● *v.* **bill and coo** exchange caresses.

billabong *n.* (*Austr.*) backwater.

billet *n.* lodging for troops. ● *v.* (**billeted**) place in a billet.

billhook *n.* pruning-instrument with a concave edge.

billiards *n.* game played with cues and three balls on a table.

billion *n.* one thousand million.

billow *n.* great wave. ● *v.* **1** rise or move like waves. **2** swell out.

> ■ *v.* ripple, roll, surge, swell, undulate.

bin *n.* large rigid container or receptacle.

binary *adj.* of two. □ **binary digit** either of two digits (0 and 1) used in the **binary scale**, system of numbers using only these.

bind *v.* (**bound**) **1** tie or fasten tightly. **2** place under an obligation or legal agreement. **3** edge with braid etc. **4** fasten into a cover. ● *n.* (*colloq.*) nuisance.

> ■ *v.* **1** attach, fasten, hitch, join, make fast, rope, secure, tether, tie (up), truss; bandage, dress. **2** compel, constrain, force, obligate, oblige, require.

binding *n.* **1** book cover. **2** braid etc. used to bind an edge.

bindweed *n.* wild convolvulus.

binge *n.* (*sl.*) bout of excessive eating, drinking, etc.

bingo *n.* gambling game using cards marked with numbered squares.

binocular *adj.* using two eyes.

binoculars *n.pl.* instrument with lenses for both eyes, making distant objects seem larger.

binomial *adj.& n.* (expression or name) consisting of two terms.

biochemistry *n.* chemistry of living organisms. □ **biochemical** *adj.*, **biochemist** *n.*

biodegradable *adj.* able to be decomposed by bacteria.

biography *n.* story of a person's life. □ **biographer** *n.*, **biographical** *adj.*

biology *n.* study of the life and structure of living things. □ **biological** *adj.*, **biologist** *n.*

bionic *adj.* (of a person or faculties) operated electronically.

biopsy *n.* examination of tissue cut from a living body.

biorhythm *n.* any of the recurring cycles of activity in a person's life.

bipartite *adj.* 1 consisting of two parts. 2 involving two groups.

biped *n.* two-footed animal.

biplane *n.* aeroplane with two pairs of wings.

birch *n.* tree with smooth bark.

bird *n.* feathered animal.

birth *n.* 1 emergence of young from the mother's body. 2 parentage. □ **birth control** prevention of unwanted pregnancy.
■ 1 childbirth, confinement, delivery, nativity, parturition. 2 ancestry, blood, descent, extraction, family, line, lineage, origins, parentage, pedigree, stock.

birthday *n.* anniversary of the day of one's birth.

birthmark *n.* unusual coloured mark on the skin at birth.

birthright *n.* thing that is one's right through being born into a certain family or country.

biscuit *n.* small flat thin piece of pastry baked crisp.

bisect *v.* divide into two equal parts. □ **bisection** *n.*, **bisector** *n.*

bisexual *adj.* sexually attracted to members of both sexes. □ **bisexuality** *n.*

bishop *n.* 1 clergyman of high rank. 2 mitre-shaped chess piece.

bishopric *n.* diocese of a bishop.

bismuth *n.* 1 metallic element. 2 compound of this used in medicines.

bison *n.* (*pl.* **bison**) wild ox.

bistro *n.* (*pl.* **-os**) small bar or restaurant.

bit[1] *n.* 1 small piece or quantity. 2 short time or distance. 3 mouthpiece of a bridle. 4 cutting part of a tool etc.
■ 1 atom, chip, crumb, dollop, drop, fraction, fragment, grain, iota, jot, morsel, mouthful, part, particle, piece, pinch, portion, sample, scrap, section, segment, share, shred, slice, sliver, snippet, speck, spot, taste, titbit, trace. 2 instant, minute, moment, second, *colloq.* tick, while; inch, little.

bit[2] *n.* (in computers) binary digit.

bit[3] *see* **bite**.

bitch *n.* 1 female dog. 2 (*sl.*) spiteful woman. ● *v.* (*colloq.*) speak spitefully or sourly. □ **bitchy** *adj.*, **bitchiness** *n.*

bite *v.* (**bit**, **bitten**) 1 cut with the teeth. 2 penetrate. 3 grip or act effectively. ● *n.* 1 act of biting. 2 wound so made. 3 small meal.
■ *v.* 1 champ, chew, gnaw, munch, nibble, nip.

biting *adj.* 1 causing a smarting pain. 2 sharply critical.

bitter *adj.* 1 tasting sharp, not sweet. 2 causing or feeling mental pain or resentment. 3 piercingly cold. ● *n.* bitter beer. □ **bitterly** *adv.*, **bitterness** *n.*
■ *adj.* 1 acid, acrid, harsh, sharp, sour, vinegary. 2 cruel, distressing, grievous, harrowing, heartbreaking, hurtful, painful, upsetting; aggrieved, embittered, rancorous, resentful. 3 biting, cold, freezing, icy, keen, perishing, piercing, raw, wintry.

bittern *n.* a kind of marsh bird.

bitty *adj.* (**-ier**, **-iest**) made up of unrelated bits. □ **bittiness** *n.*

bitumen *n.* black substance made from petroleum. □ **bituminous** *adj.*

bivalve *n.* shellfish with a hinged double shell.

bivouac *n.* temporary camp without tents or other cover. ● *v.* (**bivouacked**) camp thus.

bizarre *adj.* very odd in appearance or effect.
■ curious, eccentric, extraordinary, fantastic, freakish, grotesque, odd, offbeat, outlandish, peculiar, strange, surreal, unconventional, unusual, weird.

blab *v.* (**blabbed**) talk indiscreetly.

black *adj.* 1 of the very darkest colour, like coal or soot. 2 dismal, gloomy. 3 hostile. 4 wicked. 5 having a black skin. ● *n.* 1 black colour or thing. 2 member of a dark-skinned race. □ **black eye** bruised eye. **black hole** region in outer space from which matter and radiation cannot escape. **blacklist** *n.* list of people who are disapproved of. *v.* put on a blacklist. **black market** illegal buying and selling. **black out** cover windows so that no light can penetrate. **black pudding** sausage of blood and suet. **black sheep** scoundrel. **in the black** with a credit balance.

■ *adj.* **1** dusky, ebony, jet-black, pitch-black, pitch-dark, raven, sable, sooty. **2** dark, dismal, gloomy, funereal, murky, overcast, sombre. **3** angry, furious, hostile, resentful, sulky, unfriendly, wrathful. **4** bad, diabolical, evil, iniquitous, nefarious, unspeakable, vile, villainous, wicked.

blackberry *n.* **1** bramble. **2** its edible dark berry.

blackbird *n.* European songbird.

blackboard *n.* board for writing on with chalk in front of a class.

blacken *v.* **1** make or become black. **2** say evil things about.

blackguard /blággaard/ *n.* scoundrel. □ **blackguardly** *adj.*

blackhead *n.* small dark lump blocking a pore in the skin.

blackleg *n.* person refusing to join a strike.

blackmail *v.* demand payment or action from (a person) by threats. ● *n.* money demanded thus. □ **blackmailer** *n.*

blackout *n.* temporary loss of consciousness or memory.

blacksmith *n.* smith who works in iron.

blackthorn *n.* thorny shrub bearing white flowers and sloes.

bladder *n.* **1** sac in which urine collects in the body. **2** inflatable bag.

blade *n.* **1** flattened cutting part of a knife or sword. **2** flat part of an oar or propeller. **3** flat narrow leaf of grass. **4** broad bone.

blame *v.* assign responsibility to. ● *n.* **1** responsibility for a fault. **2** act of blaming.

■ *v.* accuse, censure, condemn, criticize, find fault with, hold responsible, reprehend, reprimand, reproach, reprove, scold. ● *n.* **1** culpability, guilt, *sl.* rap, responsibility. **2** castigation, censure, condemnation, criticism, recrimination, reproach, reproof.

blameless *adj.* not subject to blame.

■ above suspicion, faultless, guiltless, innocent, irreproachable, unimpeachable, upright.

blameworthy *adj.* deserving blame.

blanch *v.* make or become white or pale.

blancmange /bləmónj/ *n.* flavoured jelly-like pudding.

bland *adj.* **1** mild. **2** insipid. □ **blandly** *adv.*

■ **1** gentle, mild, smooth, soothing. **2** boring, characterless, dull, flat, insipid, nondescript, tame, tasteless, unexciting, uninspiring, uninteresting, vapid, wishy-washy.

blandishments *n.pl.* flattering or coaxing words.

blank *adj.* **1** not written or printed on, unmarked. **2** without interest or expression. ● *n.* **1** blank space. **2** cartridge containing no bullet. □ **blank cheque** one with the amount left blank for the payee to fill in. **blank verse** unrhymed verse.

■ *adj.* **1** clean, clear, empty, new, unadorned, undecorated, unmarked, unused, virgin. **2** deadpan, emotionless, expressionless, impassive, poker-faced, vacant, vacuous.

blanket *n.* **1** warm covering made of woollen or similar material. **2** thick covering mass.

blare *v.* sound loudly and harshly. ● *n.* this sound.

blarney *n.* smooth talk that flatters and deceives.

blasé /bláazay/ *adj.* bored or unimpressed by things.

blaspheme *v.* utter blasphemies (about). □ **blasphemer** *n.*

blasphemy *n.* irreverent talk about sacred things. □ **blasphemous** *adj.*

■ □ **blasphemous** disrespectful, impious, irreverent, profane, sacrilegious, sinful, ungodly, wicked.

blast *n.* **1** strong gust. **2** explosion. **3** loud sound of a wind instrument, car horn, whistle, etc. **4** (*colloq.*) severe reprimand. ● *v.* **1** blow up with explosives. **2** cause to wither, destroy. **3** (*colloq.*) reprimand severely. □ **blast off** be launched by firing of rockets.

■ *n.* **1** gale, gust, wind. **2** bang, burst, crack, detonation, eruption, explosion. **3** blare, din, noise, racket. ● *v.* **1** blow up, dynamite, explode. **2** blight, dash, destroy, kill, put an end to, ruin.

blatant *adj.* flagrant, shameless. □ **blatantly** *adv.*

■ barefaced, brazen, flagrant, glaring, obvious, overt, palpable, shameless, sheer, undisguised, unmistakable.

blaze[1] n. **1** bright flame or fire. **2** bright light or display. **3** outburst. ● v. burn or shine brightly.

■ n. **1** conflagration, fire, flame, inferno. **3** eruption, explosion, outbreak, outburst. ● v. burn, flame, flare; flash, gleam, glitter, glow, shine, sparkle.

blaze[2] n. **1** white mark on an animal's face. **2** mark chipped in the bark of a tree to mark a route. □ **blaze a trail 1** make such marks. **2** pioneer.

blazer n. loose-fitting jacket, esp. in the colours or bearing the badge of a school, team, etc.

blazon n. coat of arms. ● v. **1** proclaim. **2** ornament with (a coat of arms).

bleach v. whiten by sunlight or chemicals. ● n. bleaching substance or process.

bleak adj. **1** bare and cold. **2** cheerless. □ **bleakness** n.

■ **1** bare, barren, chilly, cold, desolate, exposed, grim, inhospitable, windswept, wintry. **2** cheerless, dark, depressing, disheartening, dismal, dreary, gloomy, melancholy, miserable, sombre, uninviting, unpromising.

bleary adj. (**-ier**, **-iest**) (of eyes) watery and seeing indistinctly.

bleat n. cry of a sheep or goat. ● v. **1** utter this cry. **2** speak or say plaintively.

bleed v. (**bled**) **1** leak blood or other fluid. **2** draw blood or fluid from. **3** extort money from.

bleep n. short high-pitched sound. ● v. make this sound. □ **bleeper** n.

blemish n. flaw or defect that spoils the perfection of a thing. ● v. spoil with a blemish.

■ n. blot, blotch, defect, disfigurement, fault, flaw, imperfection, mark, scar, smudge, spot, stain. ● v. deface, disfigure, flaw, mar, mark, scar, spoil, stain, tarnish.

blench v. flinch.

blend v. mix into a harmonious compound. ● n. mixture.

■ v. amalgamate, combine, fuse, integrate, merge, mingle, mix, synthesize, unite. ● n. amalgam, amalgamation, combination, composite, compound, fusion, mix, mixture, synthesis, union.

blender n. machine for liquidizing food.

blenny n. sea fish with spiny fins.

bless v. **1** make sacred or holy. **2** praise (God). **3** call God's favour upon.

■ **1** consecrate, dedicate, sanctify. **2** exalt, extol, glorify, praise.

blessed adj. **1** holy, sacred. **2** in paradise. **3** fortunate. **4** (colloq.) damned.

blessing n. **1** act of seeking or giving (esp. divine) favour. **2** something one is glad of.

■ **1** benediction, prayer; approbation, approval, consent, permission, sanction. **2** advantage, asset, boon, godsend, help.

blight n. **1** disease of plants. **2** malignant influence. ● v. **1** affect with blight. **2** spoil.

blind adj. **1** without sight. **2** without adequate foresight, understanding, or information. **3** not governed by purpose. ● v. deprive of sight or of the power of judgement. ● n. **1** screen for a window. **2** pretext. □ **blind to** unwilling or unable to appreciate (a factor). **blindly** adv., **blindness** n.

■ adj. **1** eyeless, sightless, visually handicapped. **2** blinkered, ignorant, imperceptive, insensitive. **3** indiscriminate, mindless, stupid, thoughtless, unreasoning, unthinking. ● n. **1** curtain, screen, shade, shutter(s). **2** front, pretext, smokescreen. □ **blind to** heedless of, impervious to, oblivious of or to, unaffected by, unaware of, unmoved by.

blindfold n. cloth used to cover the eyes and block the sight. ● v. cover the eyes of (a person) thus.

blink v. **1** open and shut one's eyes rapidly. **2** shine unsteadily. ● n. **1** act of blinking. **2** gleam.

■ v. **1** flutter, wink. **2** flash, flicker, gleam, glimmer, shimmer, sparkle, twinkle.

blinker n. leather piece fixed to a bridle to prevent a horse from seeing sideways. ● v. obstruct the sight or understanding of.

blip n. **1** quick sound or movement. **2** small image on a radar screen.

bliss n. perfect happiness. □ **blissful** adj., **blissfully** adv.

■ delight, ecstasy, euphoria, felicity, glee, happiness, joy, pleasure, rapture.

blister n. **1** bubble-like swelling on skin. **2** raised swelling on a surface. ● v. **1** cause blister(s) on. **2** be affected with blister(s).

blithe adj. casual and carefree. □ **blithely** adv.

blitz n. violent attack, esp. from aircraft. ● v. attack in a blitz.

blizzard n. severe snowstorm.

bloat v. inflate, swell.

bloater n. salted smoked herring.

blob n. **1** drop of liquid. **2** round mass.

bloc n. group of parties or countries who combine for a purpose.

block n. **1** solid piece of hard substance. **2** obstruction. **3** (sl.) head. **4** pulley(s) mounted in a case. **5** compact mass of buildings. **6** large building divided into flats or offices. **7** large quantity treated as a unit. **8** pad of paper for drawing or writing on. ● v. obstruct, prevent the movement or use of. □ **block letters** plain capital letters.
■ n. **1** bar, brick, cake, chunk, hunk, ingot, lump, mass, piece, slab. **2** bar, barrier, blockage, impediment, obstacle, obstruction, stumbling block. ● v. bar, barricade, choke, clog, congest, obstruct, stop (up); hamper, hinder, impede, prevent, thwart.

blockade n. blocking of access to a place, to prevent entry of goods. ● v. set up a blockade of.

blockage n. obstruction.

blockhead n. stupid person.

bloke n. (sl.) man.

blond adj. & n. fair-haired (man).

blonde adj. & n. fair-haired (woman).

blood n. **1** red liquid circulating in the bodies of animals. **2** temper, courage. **3** race, descent, parentage. **4** kindred. ● v. **1** give a first taste of blood to (a hound). **2** initiate (a person). □ **blood-curdling** adj. horrifying. **blood sports** sports involving killing. **blood vessel** tubular structure conveying blood within the body.

bloodhound n. large keen-scented dog, used in tracking.

bloodless adj. without bloodshed. □ **bloodlessly** adv.

bloodshed n. killing.

bloodshot adj. (of eyes) red from dilated veins.

bloodstream n. circulating blood.

bloodsucker n. **1** leech. **2** person who extorts money.

bloodthirsty adj. eager for bloodshed.
■ brutal, cruel, ferocious, fierce, homicidal, murderous, pitiless, ruthless, sadistic, savage, vicious, violent, warlike.

bloody adj. (-ier, -iest) **1** bloodstained. **2** with much bloodshed. **3** cursed. ● adv. (sl.) extremely. ● v. stain with blood. □ **bloody-minded** adj. (colloq.) deliberately uncooperative.

bloom n. **1** flower. **2** beauty, perfection. ● v. **1** bear flowers. **2** flourish.
■ n. **1** blossom, bud, efflorescence, floret, flower. **2** beauty, perfection, prime. ● v.

blossom, bud, burgeon, come out, effloresce, flower, open. **2** blossom, flourish, prosper, thrive.

blossom n. flower(s), esp. of a fruit tree. ● v. **1** open into flowers. **2** develop and flourish.

blot n. **1** spot of ink etc. **2** something ugly or disgraceful. ● v. (**blotted**) make blot(s) on. □ **blot out** cross out thickly, obscure.
■ n. **1** blob, blotch, mark, smear, smudge, splodge, splotch, spot, stain. **2** blemish, defect, eyesore, fault, flaw, imperfection. ● v. blemish, mar, mark, smudge, spot, stain; discredit, dishonour, disgrace, spoil, sully, tarnish. □ **blot out** cross out, delete, erase, obliterate, score out; conceal, cover up, hide, obscure.

blotch n. large irregular mark. □ **blotchy** adj.

blouse n. shirt-like garment worn by women.

blow[1] v. (**blew**, **blown**) **1** send out a current of air or breath. **2** drive or be driven by a current of air. **3** sound (a wind instrument). **4** puff and pant. **5** break with explosives. **6** make or shape by blowing. **7** (of a fuse) melt. ● n. blowing. □ **blow-out** n. burst tyre. **blow up 1** explode. **2** inflate. **3** enlarge (a photograph). **5** (colloq.) lose one's temper. **6** (colloq.) reprimand severely.
■ v. **1** breathe, exhale, puff. **2** drive, move, toss, waft, whirl; blast, flutter, stream, wave. **3** play, sound, toot. □ **blow up 1** burst, explode, go off, shatter; blast, bomb, detonate, dynamite, set off. **2** dilate, expand, inflate, pump up. **3** amplify, exaggerate, overstate. **4** enlarge, magnify. **5** explode, flare up, get angry, lose one's temper.

blow[2] n. **1** hard stroke with a hand, tool, or weapon. **2** shock, disaster.
■ **1** bang, bash, colloq. clip, clout, cuff, hit, knock, punch, rap, slap, smack, stroke, colloq. swipe, thump, colloq. whack. **2** bombshell, calamity, disappointment, disaster, misfortune, shock, surprise, upset.

blowfly n. bluebottle.

blowlamp n. portable burner for directing a very hot flame.

blowpipe n. tube through which air etc. is blown, e.g. to heat a flame or send out a missile.

blowy adj. (-ier, -iest) windy.

blowzy adj. (-ier, -iest) red-faced and coarse-looking.

blub v. (**blubbed**) (sl.) weep.

blubber¹ n. whale fat.

blubber² v. weep noisily.

bludgeon n. heavy club. ● v. 1 strike with this. 2 coerce.

blue adj. 1 of a colour like the cloudless sky. 2 unhappy. 3 indecent. ● n. 1 blue colour or thing. 2 (pl.) melancholy jazz melodies. 3 (**the blues**) state of depression. □ **blue-blooded** adj. of aristocratic descent. **out of the blue** unexpectedly. **bluish** adj.

■ adj. 1 aquamarine, azure, cerulean, cobalt, indigo, navy, sapphire, saxe-blue, sky-blue, turquoise, ultramarine. 2 dejected, depressed, despondent, dispirited, downcast, gloomy, glum, melancholy, sad, unhappy.

bluebell n. plant with blue bell-shaped flowers.

blueberry n. 1 edible blue berry. 2 shrub bearing this.

bluebottle n. large bluish fly.

blueprint n. 1 blue photographic print of building plans. 2 detailed scheme.

bluff¹ adj. 1 with a broad steep front. 2 abrupt, frank, hearty. ● n. bluff cliff etc.

bluff² v. pretend to have strength, knowledge, etc. ● n. bluffing.

blunder v. 1 move clumsily and uncertainly. 2 make a bad mistake. ● n. bad mistake.

■ v. 1 flounder, lurch, stagger, stumble. 2 sl. screw up, colloq. slip up. ● n. colloq. boob, error, faux pas, gaffe, howler, miscalculation, misjudgement, mistake, slip, colloq. slip-up.

blunderbuss n. old type of gun firing many balls at one shot.

blunt adj. 1 without a sharp edge or point. 2 speaking or expressed plainly. ● v. make blunt. □ **bluntly** adv., **bluntness** n.

■ adj. 1 blunted, dull, unsharpened, worn. 2 abrupt, bluff, brusque, candid, curt, direct, downright, forthright, frank, impolite, outspoken, rude, straightforward, tactless, undiplomatic, ungracious.

blur n. something that appears indistinct. ● v. (**blurred**) 1 smear. 2 make or become indistinct.

■ v. 1 smear, smudge. 2 cloud, conceal, dim, hide, mask, obscure, veil.

blurb n. written description praising something.

blurt v. **blurt out** utter abruptly or tactlessly.

blush v. become red-faced from shame or embarrassment. ● n. 1 blushing. 2 pink tinge.

■ v. colour, flush, go red, redden.

blusher n. rouge.

bluster v. 1 talk aggressively. 2 blow in gusts. ● n. blustering talk. □ **blustery** adj.

BMX n. 1 bicycle racing on a dirt track. 2 bicycle for this.

boa /bô'ə/ n. large snake that crushes its prey.

boar n. male pig.

board n. 1 flat piece of wood or other stiff material. 2 committee. 3 daily meals supplied in return for payment or services. ● v. 1 enter (a ship etc.). 2 provide with or receive meals and accommodation for payment. 3 cover with boards. □ **on board** on or in a ship etc.

■ n. 1 beam, plank, slat, timber. 2 cabinet, committee, council, directorate, panel. 3 food, meals. ● v. 1 embark, enter, get on, go aboard. 2 accommodate, billet, lodge, put up, quarter.

boarder n. 1 person who boards with someone. 2 resident pupil.

boarding house, boarding school one taking boarders.

boardroom n. room where a board of directors meets.

boast v. 1 speak with great pride, trying to impress people. 2 possess something to be proud of. ● n. 1 boastful statement. 2 thing one is proud of. □ **boastful** adj.

■ v. 1 brag, crow, show off, swagger, vaunt. □ **boastful** bragging, bumptious, colloq. cocky, conceited, egotistical, pompous, proud, vain.

boat n. vessel for travelling on water. ● v. travel in a boat, esp. for pleasure.

■ craft, cruiser, launch, motor boat, rowing boat, ship, skiff, speedboat, vessel, yacht.

boater n. flat-topped straw hat.

boathouse n. shed at the water's edge for boats.

boatman n. man who rows, sails, or rents out boats.

boatswain /bô'sn/ n. ship's officer in charge of rigging, boats, etc.

bob v. (**bobbed**) 1 move quickly up and down. 2 cut (hair) short to hang loosely. ● n. 1 bobbing movement. 2 bobbed hair.

bobbin n. small spool holding thread or wire in a machine.

bobble n. small woolly ball on a hat etc.

bobsleigh n. sledge with two sets of runners in tandem.

bode v. be a sign of, promise.

bodice n. 1 part of a dress from shoulder to waist. 2 undergarment for this part of the body.

bodily adj. of the human body or physical nature. ● adv. 1 in person, physically. 2 as a whole.

body n. 1 physical structure of a person or animal. 2 corpse. 3 main part. 4 group regarded as a unit. 5 strong texture or quality. 6 separate piece of matter. 7 woman's one-piece garment covering the torso. □ **body-blow** n. severe blow. **bodywork** n. outer shell of a vehicle.

> ■ 2 cadaver, carcass, corpse, remains, *sl.* stiff. 3 core, essence, heart, main part, substance. 4 association, band, committee, company, corporation, council, federation, group, league, party, society. 5 firmness, fullness, richness, solidity, substance.

bodyguard n. escort or personal guard of an important person.

> ■ escort, guard, *sl.* minder, protector.

Boer /bṓər/ n. Afrikaner.

boffin n. (*colloq.*) person engaged in scientific research.

bog n. permanently wet spongy ground. ● v. **bog down** make or become stuck and unable to progress. □ **boggy** adj.

> ■ n. fen, marsh, mire, morass, quagmire, quicksand, slough, swamp.

bogey n. thing causing fear.

boggle v. be bewildered.

bogie n. undercarriage on wheels, pivoted at each end.

bogus adj. false.

> ■ counterfeit, fake, false, fraudulent, imitation, *colloq.* phoney, sham, spurious.

bohemian adj. socially unconventional.

boil[1] n. inflamed swelling producing pus.

boil[2] v. 1 bubble up with heat. 2 heat so that liquid does this. 3 be very angry.

boiler n. container in which water is heated. □ **boiler suit** protective one-piece garment.

boisterous adj. 1 noisily exuberant. 2 violent, rough. □ **boisterously** adv.

> ■ 1 exuberant, frisky, high-spirited, irrepressible, lively, noisy, rollicking, rowdy, *colloq.* rumbustious, unruly, wild. 2 blustery, rough, squally, stormy, tempestuous, turbulent, violent.

bold adj. 1 confident, courageous. 2 impudent. 3 distinct, vivid. □ **boldly** adv., **boldness** n.

> ■ 1 adventurous, audacious, brave, confident, courageous, daring, dauntless, fearless, gallant, heroic, intrepid, plucky, spirited, unafraid, valiant, valorous; daredevil, foolhardy, rash, reckless. 2 brash, brazen, cheeky, forward, impertinent, impudent, insolent, pert, presumptuous, rude. 3 clear, conspicuous, distinct, prominent, pronounced, striking, strong, vivid.

bole n. trunk of a tree.

bolero n. 1 Spanish dance. 2 woman's short jacket with no fastening.

boll n. round seed vessel of cotton, flax, etc.

bollard n. short thick post.

boloney n. (*sl.*) nonsense.

bolster n. long pad placed under a pillow. ● v. support, prop up.

> ■ v. buttress, hold up, prop up, reinforce, shore up, strengthen, support, sustain.

bolt n. 1 sliding bar for fastening a door. 2 strong metal pin. 3 sliding part of a rifle-breech. 4 shaft of lightning. 5 roll of cloth. 6 arrow from a crossbow. ● v. 1 fasten with bolt(s). 2 run away. 3 gulp (food) hastily. □ **bolt-hole** n. place into which one can escape.

> ■ v. 1 fasten, latch, lock, secure. 2 dash away, *sl.* do a bunk, escape, flee, run away, rush away, *colloq.* skedaddle, take to one's heels. 3 gobble, gulp, *colloq.* scoff, wolf.

bomb n. case of explosive or incendiary material to be set off by impact or a timing device. ● v. attack with bombs.

bombard v. 1 attack with artillery. 2 attack with questions etc. □ **bombardment** n.

bombardier n. artillery non-commissioned officer.

bombastic adj. using pompous words.

> ■ flowery, grandiloquent, pompous, pretentious, rhetorical, turgid.

bomber n. 1 aircraft that carries and drops bombs. 2 person who throws or places bombs.

bombshell n. great shock.

bona fide /bṓnə fīdi/ genuine.

bonanza n. sudden great wealth.

bond n. 1 uniting force. 2 (usu. *pl.*) thing that restrains. 3 binding agreement. 4 document issued by a government or company acknowledging that money has been lent to it and will be repaid with interest. ● v. unite with a bond. □ **in bond** stored in a customs warehouse until duties are paid.

■ n. **1** attachment, connection, link, relationship, tie, union. **2** (**bonds**) chains, cords, fetters, manacles, restraints, ropes, shackles, ties. **3** agreement, contract, covenant, pact; guarantee, oath, pledge, promise, word.

bondage n. slavery, captivity.

■ captivity, confinement, enslavement, servitude, slavery.

bone n. each of the hard parts making up the vertebrate skeleton. ● v. remove bones from. □ **bone china** made of clay and bone ash.

bonfire n. open-air fire.

bongo n. each of a pair of small drums played with the fingers.

bonhomie /bónnomeé/ n. geniality.

bonnet n. **1** hat with strings that tie under the chin. **2** hinged cover over the engine of a motor vehicle.

bonny adj. (**-ier, -iest**) **1** healthy-looking. **2** (Sc.) attractive.

bonsai n. **1** miniature tree or shrub. **2** art of growing these.

bonus n. extra payment or benefit.

■ commission, dividend, gratuity, handout, colloq. perk, reward, tip; advantage, benefit, extra, plus.

bony adj. (**-ier, -iest**) **1** like bones. **2** having bones with little flesh.

boo int. exclamation of disapproval. ● v. shout 'boo' (at).

boob n. & v. (colloq.) blunder.

booby n. foolish person. □ **booby prize** one given as a joke to the competitor with the lowest score. **booby trap 1** practical joke in the form of a trap. **2** hidden bomb.

book n. **1** written or printed work bound into a cover. **2** main division of a literary work. ● v. **1** reserve (a seat etc.) in advance. **2** enter in a book or list. □ **booking** n. reservation.

■ n. **1** hardback, paperback, publication, tome, volume, work. ● v. **1** earmark, order, reserve, save.

bookcase n. piece of furniture with shelves for books.

bookie n. (colloq.) bookmaker.

bookish adj. fond of reading.

bookkeeping n. systematic recording of business transactions.

booklet n. small thin book.

bookmaker n. person whose business is the taking of bets.

bookmark n. strip of paper etc. to mark a place in a book.

bookworm n. **1** grub that eats holes in books. **2** person fond of reading.

boom¹ v. **1** make a deep resonant sound. **2** be suddenly prosperous or successful. ● n. **1** booming sound. **2** period of prosperity.

■ v. **1** bellow, resonate, resound, reverberate, roar, rumble, thunder. **2** burgeon, flourish, grow, increase, prosper, succeed, thrive. ● n. **1** reverberation, roar, rumble. **2** growth, improvement, increase, upsurge, upturn.

boom² n. **1** long pole. **2** floating barrier.

boomerang n. Australian missile of curved wood that returns to the thrower.

boon¹ n. benefit.

boon² adj. **boon companion** close companion.

boor n. ill-mannered person. □ **boorish** adj., **boorishness** n.

■ □ **boorish** churlish, coarse, crude, ill-mannered, loutish, uncivilized, uncouth, vulgar.

boost v. **1** increase the strength or reputation of. **2** push upwards. ● n. **1** an increase. **2** upward thrust. □ **booster** n.

■ v. **1** aid, assist, build up, enhance, help, improve, increase, promote, strengthen, support.

boot n. **1** sturdy shoe covering both foot and ankle. **2** luggage compartment in a car. **3** (colloq.) dismissal. ● v. kick.

bootee n. baby's woollen boot.

booth n. **1** small shelter. **2** cubicle.

bootleg adj. smuggled, illicit. □ **bootlegger** n., **bootlegging** n.

booty n. loot.

■ contraband, haul, loot, plunder, spoils, sl. swag.

booze (colloq.) v. drink alcohol. ● n. alcoholic drink. □ **boozer** n., **boozy** adj.

borage n. blue-flowered plant.

borax n. compound of boron used in detergents.

border n. **1** edge, boundary, or part near it. **2** flower bed round part of a garden. ● v. put or be a border to. □ **border on 1** be next to. **2** come close to being.

■ n. **1** edge, fringe, margin, perimeter, periphery, rim, verge; borderline, boundary, frontier; edging, frame, frieze, surround.

borderline n. line of demarcation.

bore¹ *see* **bear²**.

bore² *v.* make (a hole), esp. with a revolving tool or by excavation. ● *n.* **1** hole bored. **2** hollow inside of a cylinder. **3** its diameter.
■ *v.* dig (out) drill, excavate, gouge (out), sink, tunnel.

bore³ *v.* weary by dullness. ● *n.* boring person or thing. □ **boredom** *n.*, **boring** *adj.*
■ □ **boring** dreary, dry, dull, flat, humdrum, interminable, monotonous, mundane, repetitive, soporific, stodgy, tedious, tiresome, unexciting, uninspiring, uninteresting, wearisome.

bore⁴ *n.* tidal wave in an estuary.

born *adj.* **1** brought forth by birth. **2** having a specified natural quality. □ **born-again** *adj.* reconverted to religion.

borne *see* **bear²**.

boron *n.* chemical element very resistant to high temperatures.

borough *n.* town or district with rights of local government.

borrow *v.* get temporary use of (a thing or money). ■ **borrower** *n.*

Borstal *n.* former name of an institution for young offenders.

borzoi *n.* Russian wolfhound.

bosom *n.* breast. □ **bosom friend** very dear friend.

boss¹ (*colloq.*) *n.* employer, manager, person in charge. ● *v.* give orders to.
■ *n.* chief, director, employer, foreman, forewoman, *colloq.* gaffer, head, leader, manager, overseer, superintendent, supervisor.

boss² *n.* projecting knob.

bossy *adj.* (**-ier**, **-iest**) (*colloq.*) fond of giving orders to people. □ **bossily** *adv.*, **bossiness** *n.*
■ authoritarian, dictatorial, domineering, high-handed, imperious, officious, overbearing.

botany *n.* study of plants. □ **botanical** *adj.*, **botanist** *n.*

botch *v.* spoil by poor work.

both *adj.*, *pron.*, & *adv.* the two.

bother *v.* **1** trouble, worry, annoy. **2** take trouble. **3** feel concern. ● *n.* worry, minor trouble. □ **bothersome** *adj.*
■ *v.* **1** concern, disconcert, distress, disturb, perturb, trouble, unsettle, upset, worry; *colloq.* bug, *sl.* harass, inconvenience, irritate; badger, *sl.* harass, *colloq.* hassle, nag, pester, *colloq.* plague.

● *n.* annoyance, bind, *colloq.* hassle, headache, inconvenience, irritation, nuisance, trouble, worry; ado, commotion, disturbance, fuss, to-do.

bottle *n.* glass or plastic container for liquid. ● *v.* **1** store in bottles. **2** preserve in jars.

bottleneck *n.* **1** narrow place where traffic cannot flow freely. **2** obstruction to an even flow of work etc.

bottom *n.* **1** lowest part or place. **2** buttocks. **3** ground under a stretch of water. ● *adj.* lowest in position, rank, or degree.
■ *n.* **1** base, bed, floor, foot, foundation, underside.

bottomless *adj.* extremely deep.

botulism *n.* poisoning by bacteria in food.

bougainvillaea *n.* tropical shrub with red or purple bracts.

bough *n.* large branch coming from the trunk of a tree.

bought *see* **buy**.

boulder *n.* large rounded stone.

boulevard *n.* wide street.

bounce *v.* **1** rebound. **2** move energetically. **3** (*sl.*, of a cheque) be sent back by a bank as worthless. ● *n.* **1** bouncing movement or power. **2** (*colloq.*) liveliness. □ **bouncy** *adj.*
■ *v.* **1** rebound, ricochet. **2** bound, caper, gambol, hop, jump, leap, prance, skip, spring. ● *n.* **1** bound, hop, jump, leap, spring; elasticity, springiness. **2** animation, energy, go, life, liveliness, pep, spirit, verve, vigour, *colloq.* vim, vitality, vivacity, zest, zip.

bouncer *n.* (*sl.*) person employed to eject troublemakers.

bound¹ *v.* limit, be a boundary of. ● *n.* (usu. *pl.*) limit. □ **out of bounds** beyond the permitted area.

bound² *v.* leap, spring. ● *n.* bounding movement.
■ *v.* bounce, caper, gambol, hop, jump, leap, prance, romp, skip, spring, vault.

bound³ *see* **bind**. *adj.* obstructed by a specified thing (*snow-bound*). □ **bound to** certain to.

bound⁴ *adj.* going in a specified direction.

boundary *n.* **1** line that marks a limit. **2** hit to the boundary in cricket.
■ **1** border, borderline, frontier; bounds, confines, edge, fringe, limit, margin, perimeter.

bounden adj. **bounden duty** duty dictated by conscience.

boundless adj. without limits.
■ endless, immeasurable, incalculable, inexhaustible, infinite, limitless, unbounded, unending, unlimited, untold.

bountiful adj. **1** giving generously. **2** abundant.

bounty n. **1** generosity. **2** official reward. □ **bounteous** adj.
■ **1** beneficence, charity, generosity, largesse, liberality, munificence, philanthropy.

bouquet /bookáy/ n. **1** bunch of flowers. **2** perfume of wine.
■ **1** arrangement, bunch, corsage, nosegay, posy, spray. **2** aroma, fragrance, perfume, scent, smell.

bouquet garni /bookáy gaárni/ bunch of herbs for flavouring.

bourbon /búrb'n/ n. whisky made mainly from maize.

bourgeois /boorzhwaá/ adj. urban middle-class.

bourgeoisie /boorzhwaazee/ n. bourgeois society.

bout n. **1** period of exercise, work, or illness. **2** boxing contest.
■ **1** period, run, session, spell, stint, stretch, time; attack, fit. **2** competition, contest, encounter, fight, match, round.

boutique n. small shop selling fashionable clothes etc.

bovine adj. **1** of cattle. **2** dull and stupid.

bow¹ /bō/ n. **1** weapon for shooting arrows. **2** rod with horsehair stretched between its ends, for playing a violin etc. **3** knot with loops in a ribbon etc.

bow² /bow/ v. **1** incline the head or body in greeting, acknowledgement, etc. **2** submit. ● n. act of bowing.
■ v. **1** curtsy, genuflect; nod. **2** capitulate, defer, give in, give way, submit, succumb, surrender, yield.

bow³ /bow/ n. **1** front end of a boat or ship. **2** oarsman nearest the bow.

bowdlerize v. expurgate. □ **bowdlerization** n.

bowel n. **1** (often pl.) intestine. **2** (pl.) innermost parts.
■ **1** (bowels) entrails, guts, colloq. innards, colloq. insides, intestines, viscera, vitals. **2** (bowels) centre, core, depths, heart, inside, interior.

bower n. leafy shelter.

bowie knife long hunting knife.

bowl¹ n. **1** basin. **2** hollow rounded part of a spoon etc.

bowl² n. **1** heavy ball weighted to roll in a curve. **2** (pl.) game played with such balls. **3** ball used in skittles. ● v. **1** roll (a ball etc.). **2** go rapidly. **3** send a ball to a batsman, dismiss by knocking bails off with this. **4** play bowls. □ **bowl over 1** knock down. **2** overwhelm.

bowler¹ n. player who bowls.

bowler² n. (in full **bowler hat**) hard felt hat with a rounded top.

bowling n. playing bowls, skittles, or a similar game.

box¹ n. **1** container or receptacle with a flat base. **2** facility at a newspaper office for holding replies to an advertisement. **3** compartment in a theatre, stable, etc. **4** small shelter. ● v. put into a box. □ **box office** office for booking seats at a theatre etc.
■ n. **1** caddy, carton, case, casket, chest, coffer, container, crate, receptacle, trunk.

box² v. fight with fists as a sport, usu. in padded gloves. ● n. slap. □ **boxing** n.

box³ n. **1** small evergreen shrub. **2** its wood. □ **boxwood** n.

boxer n. **1** person who engages in the sport of boxing. **2** dog of a breed resembling a bulldog.

boy n. male child. □ **boyfriend** n. person's regular male companion or lover. **boyhood** n., **boyish** adj.

boycott v. refuse to deal with or trade with. ● n. such a refusal.
■ v. avoid, ostracize, reject, shun; blacklist. ● n. ban, blacklist, embargo, prohibition.

bra n. woman's undergarment worn to support the breasts.

brace n. **1** device that holds things together or in position. **2** pair. **3** (pl.) straps supporting trousers from the shoulders. ● v. give support or firmness to.

bracelet n. ornamental band worn on the arm.

bracing adj. invigorating.
■ crisp, exhilarating, fresh, invigorating, refreshing, restorative, stimulating, tonic.

bracken n. **1** large fern growing on open land. **2** mass of such ferns.

bracket n. **1** projecting support. **2** any of the marks used in pairs for enclosing words or figures, (), [], {}. ● v. **1** enclose by brackets. **2** put together as similar.

brackish adj. slightly salty.

bract n. leaf-like part of a plant.

brag v. (**bragged**) boast. ● n. boastful statement.

braggart n. person who brags.

Brahman n. (also **Brahmin**) member of the Hindu priestly caste.

braid n. 1 woven ornamental trimming. 2 plait of hair. ● v. 1 trim with braid. 2 plait.

Braille n. system of representing letters etc. by raised dots which blind people read by touch.

brain n. 1 mass of soft grey matter in the skull, centre of the nervous system in animals. 2 (also pl.) mind, intelligence.

brainchild n. person's invention or plan.

brainstorm n. 1 violent mental disturbance. 2 (US) bright idea.

brainwash v. force (a person) to change their views by subjecting them to great mental pressure.

brainwave n. bright idea.

brainy adj. (**-ier, -iest**) clever.

braise v. cook slowly with little liquid in a closed container.

brake n. device for reducing speed or stopping motion. ● v. slow by use of this.

bramble n. wild thorny shrub, esp. the blackberry.

bran n. ground inner husks of grain, sifted from flour.

branch n. 1 arm-like part of a tree. 2 subdivision of a river, subject, family, etc. 3 local shop or office belonging to a large organization. ● v. send out or divide into branches.
■ n. 1 bough, limb. 2 department, division, offshoot, part, ramification, section, subdivision.

brand n. 1 goods of a particular make. 2 trade mark. 3 identifying mark made with hot metal. ● v. mark with a brand.
□ **brand new** new, unused.

brandish v. wave, flourish.

brandy n. strong alcoholic spirit distilled from wine or fermented fruit juice.

brash adj. vulgarly self-assertive.
□ **brashly** adv., **brashness** n.

brass n. 1 yellow alloy of copper and zinc. 2 musical wind instruments made of this. ● adj. made of brass.

brasserie n. restaurant (orig. one serving beer with food).

brassière /brázziər/ n. bra.

brassy adj. (**-ier, -iest**) 1 like brass. 2 bold and vulgar.

brat n. (derog.) child.

bravado n. show of boldness.

brave adj. 1 able to face and endure danger or pain. 2 spectacular. ● v. face and endure bravely. □ **bravely** adv.
■ adj. 1 adventurous, audacious, bold, courageous, daring, dauntless, fearless, gallant, game, colloq. gutsy, heroic, indomitable, intrepid, mettlesome, plucky, resolute, spirited, stout, unafraid, undaunted, valiant, valorous, venturesome. ● v. confront, endure, face, stand up to, weather, withstand.

bravery n. brave conduct.
■ audacity, boldness, courage, daring, determination, fearlessness, firmness, fortitude, gallantry, colloq. grit, colloq. guts, heroism, intrepidity, mettle, nerve, pluck, resoluteness, spirit, valour.

bravo int. well done!

brawl n. noisy quarrel or fight. ● v. take part in a brawl.
■ n. affray, altercation, colloq. bust-up, commotion, fight, fracas, fray, mêlée, quarrel, row, rumpus, colloq. scrap, scuffle, squabble, tussle. ● v. fight, quarrel, row, colloq. scrap, scuffle, squabble, tussle, wrangle.

brawn n. 1 muscular strength. 2 pressed meat from a pig's or calf's head.
□ **brawny** adj.

bray n. 1 donkey's cry. 2 similar sound.
● v. make a bray.

braze v. solder with an alloy of brass.

brazen adj. 1 shameless, impudent. 2 like or made of brass. ● v. **brazen it out** be defiantly unrepentant. □ **brazenly** adv.
■ adj. 1 barefaced, blatant, flagrant, shameless, unashamed; cheeky, forward, impertinent, impudent, insolent, presumptuous, rude.

brazier n. basket-like stand for holding burning coals.

breach n. 1 breaking or neglect of a rule or contract. 2 estrangement. 3 broken place, gap. ● v. 1 break through. 2 make a breach in.
■ n. 1 break, contravention, infringement, transgression, violation. 2 break, estrangement, rift, rupture, separation, split. 3 aperture, break, crack, fissure, gap, hole, opening, space.

bread n. baked dough of flour and liquid, usu. leavened by yeast. □ **breadfruit** n. tropical fruit with bread-like pulp.
breadwinner n. person whose work supports a family.

breadline n. **on the breadline** living in extreme poverty.

breadth n. width, broadness.

break v. (**broke, broken**) **1** separate into pieces under a blow or strain. **2** become unusable. **3** fail to keep (a promise or law). **4** make or become discontinuous. **5** make or become weak. **6** reveal (news). **7** surpass (a record). **8** appear suddenly. **9** (of a ball) change direction after touching the ground. ● n. **1** act or instance of breaking. **2** sudden dash. **3** gap. **4** interval. **5** opportunity, piece of luck. **6** points scored continuously in snooker. □ **break down 1** fail, collapse. **2** give way to emotion. **3** analyse. **break even** make gains and losses that balance exactly.

■ v. **1** burst, colloq. bust, crack, crumble, fracture, fragment, shatter, smash, snap, splinter, split. **2** break down, sl. conk out. **3** contravene, defy, disobey, disregard, fail to observe, flout, infringe, transgress, violate. **4** cut off, discontinue, interrupt, suspend. **5** debilitate, drain, exhaust, sap, weaken, wear out, weary. **6** announce, disclose, divulge, make public, reveal, tell. **7** beat, better, cap, exceed, outdo, outstrip, surpass. ● n. **1** breach, breakage, burst, fracture, rift, rupture, split. **2** bolt, dart, dash, run, rush. **3** aperture, chink, crack, gap, hole, opening, slit, space. **4** breather, interlude, intermission, interval, lull, pause, respite, rest. **5** chance, opening, opportunity, piece of luck.

breakable adj. easily broken.

breakage n. breaking.

breakdown n. **1** mechanical failure. **2** analysis. **3** collapse of health or mental stability.

breaker n. heavy ocean wave.

breakfast n. first meal of the day. ● v. eat breakfast.

breakneck adj. dangerously fast.

breakthrough n. major advance in knowledge or negotiation.

breakwater n. barrier to break the force of waves.

bream n. fish of the carp family.

breast n. **1** upper front part of the body. **2** either of the two milk-producing organs on a woman's chest. □ **breastfeed** v. feed (a baby) from the breast.

breaststroke n. swimming stroke performed face downwards.

breastbone n. bone down the upper front of the body.

breath n. **1** air drawn into and sent out of the lungs in breathing. **2** breathing in. **3** gentle blowing. □ **out of breath** panting after exercise. **under one's breath** in a whisper.

breathalyse v. test by a breathalyser.

breathalyser n. [P.] device measuring the alcohol in a person's breath.

breathe v. **1** draw (air) into the lungs and send it out again. **2** utter.

■ **1** exhale, inhale, pant, respire. **2** murmur, say, tell, utter, whisper.

breather n. **1** pause for rest. **2** short period in fresh air.

breathless adj. out of breath.

breathtaking adj. amazing.

bred see breed.

breech n. **1** buttocks. **2** back part of a gun barrel, where it opens.

breeches n.pl. trousers reaching to just below the knees.

breed v. (**bred**) **1** produce offspring. **2** raise (livestock). **3** give rise to. **4** train, bring up. ● n. **1** variety of animals etc. within a species. **2** sort. □ **breeder** n.

■ v. **1** procreate, reproduce, spawn. **2** farm, raise, rear. **3** cause, create, engender, foster, generate, give rise to. **4** bring up, raise, rear, train. ● n. **1** stock, strain. **2** kind, sort, species, type, variety.

breeding n. good manners resulting from training or background.

breeze n. light wind. □ **breezy** adj.

■ draught, flurry, gust, wind, poetic zephyr. □ **breezy** airy, blowy, draughty, fresh, gusty, windy.

breeze-blocks n.pl. lightweight building blocks.

brethren n.pl. brothers.

Breton adj. & n. (native) of Brittany.

breve n. **1** mark (˘) over a short vowel. **2** (in music) long note.

breviary n. book of prayers to be said by RC priests.

brevity n. briefness.

brew v. **1** make (beer) by boiling and fermentation. **2** make (tea) by infusion. **3** concoct, plan. **4** be forming. ● n. liquid or amount brewed.

■ v. **3** concoct, contrive, colloq. cook up, devise, hatch, plan, plot. **4** be imminent, be in the wind, develop, form, gather force, impend, loom. ● n. concoction, drink, infusion, potion.

brewer n. person whose trade is brewing beer.

brewery n. building where beer is brewed commercially.

briar n. = **brier**.

bribe n. thing offered to influence a person to act in favour of the giver. ● v. persuade by this. □ **bribery** n.

■ n. *sl.* backhander, inducement, payola, *colloq.* sweetener. ● v. corrupt, *sl.* nobble, *colloq.* square, suborn.

bric-à-brac n. odd items of ornaments, furniture, etc.

brick n. **1** block of baked or dried clay used to build walls. **2** rectangular block. ● v. block with a brick structure.

brickbat n. **1** missile hurled at someone. **2** criticism.

bricklayer n. person who builds with bricks.

bridal adj. of a bride or wedding.

bride n. woman on her wedding day or when newly married.

bridegroom n. man on his wedding day or when newly married.

bridesmaid n. girl or unmarried woman attending a bride.

bridge[1] n. **1** structure providing a way across something. **2** something that joins or connects different things. **3** captain's platform on a ship. **4** bony upper part of the nose. ● v. make or be a bridge over.

■ n. **1** aqueduct, causeway, flyover, footbridge, overpass, viaduct. **2** connection, link, tie. ● v. cross, pass over, span, traverse; connect, join, link, unite.

bridge[2] n. card game developed from whist.

bridgehead n. position held on the enemy's side of a river.

bridle n. harness on a horse's head. ● v. **1** put a bridle on. **2** restrain. **3** show offence or resentment. □ **bridle path** path suitable for horse-riding.

brief adj. **1** lasting only for a short time. **2** concise. **3** scanty. ● n. set of instructions and information, esp. to a barrister about a case. ● v. **1** inform or instruct in advance. **2** employ a barrister. □ **briefly** adv., **briefness** n.

■ adj. **1** ephemeral, fleeting, fugitive, momentary, short, transient, transitory; cursory, hasty, quick, rapid, speedy, swift. **2** compact, concise, pithy, succinct, to the point. ● n. directions, instructions. ● v. **1** advise, apprise, *colloq.* fill in, inform, instruct, prepare, prime.

briefcase n. flat document case.

briefs n.pl. short pants or knickers.

brier n. thorny bush, wild rose.

brigade n. army unit forming part of a division.

brigadier n. officer commanding a brigade or of similar status.

brigand n. member of a band of robbers.

bright adj. **1** giving out or reflecting much light, shining. **2** cheerful. **3** promising. **4** clever. □ **brightly** adv., **brightness** n.

■ **1** beaming, dazzling, gleaming, glistening, glittering, glowing, incandescent, light, luminous, radiant, resplendent, shimmering, shining, sparkling, twinkling; glossy, lustrous, polished, shiny. **2** cheerful, cheery, gay, happy, light-hearted, perky, merry, sunny. **3** auspicious, favourable, hopeful, optimistic, promising, rosy. **4** brainy, clever, gifted, intelligent, quick, sharp, smart, talented.

brighten v. make or become brighter.

brilliant adj. **1** very bright, sparkling. **2** very clever. ● n. cut diamond with many facets. □ **brilliantly** adv., **brilliance** n.

■ adj. **1** bright, dazzling, glittering, radiant, resplendent, shining, sparkling. **2** bright, clever, gifted, intelligent, talented.

brim n. **1** edge of a cup or hollow. **2** projecting edge of a hat. ● v. (**brimmed**) be full to the brim.

brimstone n. (*old use*) sulphur.

brindled adj. brown with streaks of another colour.

brine n. **1** salt water. **2** sea water.

bring v. (**brought**) **1** convey. **2** cause to come or be present. □ **bring about** cause to happen. **bring off** do successfully. **bring out 1** show clearly. **2** publish. **bring up 1** look after and train. **2** draw attention to.

■ **1** bear, carry, convey, deliver, fetch, take, transport. **2** attract, draw, lead. □ **bring about** cause, engender, generate, give rise to, occasion, produce, work. **bring off** accomplish, achieve, carry out, do, pull off, succeed in. **bring up 1** care for, look after, nurture, raise, rear, train. **2** broach, draw attention to, introduce, mention, raise.

brink n. **1** edge of a steep place or of a stretch of water. **2** point just before a change.

■ **1** border, brim, edge, lip, margin, rim. **2** threshold, verge.

brinkmanship n. policy of pursuing a dangerous course to the brink of catastrophe.

briny adj. of brine or sea water.

briquette n. block of compressed coal dust.

brisk adj. lively, quick. □ **briskly** adv.
■ energetic, fast, lively, quick, rapid, snappy, speedy, spirited, sprightly, spry, vigorous; active, bustling, busy.

brisket n. joint of beef from the breast.

bristle n. **1** short stiff hair. **2** one of the stiff pieces of hair or wire in a brush.
● v. **1** raise bristles in anger or fear. **2** show indignation. **3** be thickly set with bristles. □ **bristly** adj.

British adj. of Britain or its people.

Briton n. British person.

brittle adj. easily broken.
■ breakable, crisp, delicate, fragile, friable.

broach v. **1** raise for discussion. **2** open and start using.

broad adj. **1** large across, wide. **2** in general terms. **3** full and clear. **4** (of humour) rather coarse. □ **broad bean** edible bean with flat seeds. **broad-minded** adj. having tolerant views. **broadly** adv.
■ **1** expansive, extensive, large, spacious, vast, wide. **2** approximate, general, generalized, rough. **4** coarse, improper, indecent, indelicate, rude, vulgar. □ **broad-minded** liberal, permissive, tolerant, unbiased, unprejudiced.

broadcast v. (**broadcast**) **1** send out by radio or television. **2** make generally known. **3** scatter (seed) etc. ● n. broadcast programme. □ **broadcaster** n., **broadcasting** n.
■ v. **1** radio, relay, televise, transmit. **2** advertise, announce, circulate, disseminate, make known, make public, proclaim, promulgate, publish, report. □ **broadcaster** announcer, commentator, newsreader, presenter.

broaden v. make or become broader.

broadsheet n. large-sized newspaper.

broadside n. firing of all guns on one side of a ship.

brocade n. fabric woven with raised patterns.

broccoli n. vegetable with green or purple flower heads.

brochure /brōshər/ n. booklet or leaflet giving information.

brogue n. **1** strong shoe with ornamental perforated bands. **2** dialectal esp. Irish accent.

broil v. **1** grill. **2** make or become very hot.

broiler n. chicken suitable for broiling.

broke see **break**. adj. (colloq.) **1** having no money. **2** bankrupt.

broken see **break**. adj. (of a language) badly spoken by a foreigner.

broken-hearted adj. overwhelmed with grief.

broker n. agent who buys and sells on behalf of others.

bromide n. chemical compound used to calm nerves.

bromine n. poisonous liquid element.

bronchial adj. of the branched tubes into which the windpipe divides.

bronchitis n. inflammation of the bronchial tubes.

bronco n. (pl. -os) wild or half-tamed horse of western N. America.

brontosaurus n. large plant-eating dinosaur.

bronze n. **1** brown alloy of copper and tin. **2** thing made of this. **3** its colour.
● v. make or become suntanned.

brooch /brōch/ n. ornamental hinged pin fastened with a clasp.

brood n. young produced at one hatching or birth. ● v. **1** sit on (eggs) and hatch them. **2** worry or ponder, esp. resentfully.
■ n. litter, offspring, progeny, young. ● v. **1** agonize, fret, worry; meditate, muse, ponder, reflect, ruminate.

broody adj. **1** (of a hen) wanting to brood. **2** thoughtful and depressed.

brook¹ n. small stream.
■ beck, Sc. burn, rivulet, stream, watercourse.

brook² v. tolerate, allow.

broom n. **1** long-handled brush for sweeping floors. **2** shrub with white, yellow, or red flowers.

broomstick n. broom-handle.

broth n. thin meat or fish soup.

brothel n. house where women work as prostitutes.

brother n. **1** son of the same parents as another person. **2** man who is a fellow member of a group, trade union, or Church. **3** monk who is not a priest.
□ **brother-in-law** n. (pl. **brothers-in-law**) **1** brother of one's husband or wife. **2** husband of one's sister. **brotherly** adj.

brotherhood n. **1** relationship of brothers. **2** comradeship.

brought see **bring**.

brow n. **1** eyebrow. **2** forehead. **3** projecting or overhanging part.

browbeat v. (-**beat**, -**beaten**) intimidate.
■ bully, cow, frighten, hector, intimidate, persecute, terrorize, threaten, tyrannize.

brown adj. of the colour of dark wood. ● v. make or become brown. □ **browned off** (colloq.) bored, fed up. **brownish** adj.

browse v. **1** feed on leaves or grass. **2** read or look around casually.

bruise n. injury that discolours skin without breaking it. ● v. cause bruise(s) on.

bruiser n. (colloq.) tough brutal person.

brunch n. meal combining breakfast and lunch.

brunette n. woman with brown hair.

brunt n. chief stress or strain.

brush n. **1** implement with bristles. **2** the action of brushing. **3** skirmish. **4** undergrowth. **5** fox's tail. ● v. **1** use a brush on. **2** touch lightly in passing. □ **brush off 1** reject curtly. **2** snub. **brush up 1** smarten. **2** revise one's knowledge of.
■ n. **1** besom, broom. **3** altercation, clash, conflict, confrontation, dispute, encounter, fracas, scrimmage, skirmish, tussle. **4** bracken, brushwood, scrub, undergrowth. ● v. **1** clean, scrub, sweep; groom. **2** graze, touch. □ **brush off** dismiss, put down, rebuff, reject, snub, spurn.

brushwood n. **1** undergrowth. **2** cut or broken twigs.

brusque /brŏosk/ adj. curt and offhand. □ **brusquely** adv.

Brussels sprout edible bud of a kind of cabbage.

brutal adj. cruel, without mercy. □ **brutally** adv., **brutality** n.
■ barbaric, bestial, bloodthirsty, callous, cold-blooded, cruel, ferocious, hard-hearted, heartless, inhuman, inhumane, merciless, murderous, pitiless, ruthless, sadistic, savage, severe, vicious, violent, wild.

brutalize v. **1** make brutal. **2** treat brutally. □ **brutalization** n.

brute n. **1** animal other than a human being. **2** brutal person. **3** (colloq.) unpleasant person. ● adj. **1** unable to reason. **2** unreasoning. □ **brutish** adj.

bryony n. climbing hedge plant.

BSE abbr. bovine spongiform encephalopathy (cattle disease).

Bt. abbr. Baronet.

bubble n. **1** thin ball of liquid enclosing air or gas. **2** air-filled cavity. ● v. rise in bubbles.
■ n. **1** (bubbles) effervescence, foam, froth, lather, spume, suds. ● v. boil, effervesce, fizz, foam, froth, seethe.

bubbly adj. **1** full of bubbles. **2** lively, vivacious.
■ **1** effervescent, fizzy, foaming, frothy, sparkling. **2** animated, colloq. bouncy, buoyant, cheerful, ebullient, exuberant, high-spirited, lively, vivacious.

bubonic adj. (of plague) characterized by swellings.

buccaneer n. **1** pirate. **2** adventurer. □ **buccaneering** n. & adj.

buck[1] n. male of deer, hare, or rabbit. ● v. (of a horse) jump with the back arched. □ **buck up** (colloq.) **1** make haste. **2** make or become more cheerful.

buck[2] n. article placed before the dealer in a game of poker. □ **pass the buck** shift the responsibility.

buck[3] n. (US & Austr. sl.) dollar.

bucket n. open container with a handle, for carrying or holding liquid. ● v. pour heavily.

buckle n. device through which a belt or strap is threaded to secure it. ● v. **1** fasten with a buckle. **2** crumple under pressure. □ **buckle down** to set about doing.

buckwheat n. **1** cereal plant. **2** its seed.

bucolic adj. rustic.

bud n. leaf or flower not fully open. ● v. (budded) **1** put forth buds. **2** begin to develop.

Buddhism n. Asian religion based on the teachings of Buddha. □ **Buddhist** adj. & n.

buddleia n. tree or shrub with purple or yellow flowers.

buddy n. (colloq.) friend.

budge v. move slightly.

budgerigar n. a kind of Australian parakeet.

budget n. **1** plan of income and expenditure. **2** amount allowed. ● v. (budgeted) allow or arrange in a budget.

buff n. **1** fawn colour. **2** (colloq.) enthusiast. ● v. polish with soft material.

buffalo n. (pl. buffalo or -oes) wild ox.

buffer n. **1** thing that lessens the effect of impact. **2** (sl.) man.

buffet[1] /bŏoffay/ n. **1** counter where food and drink are served. **2** self-service meal.

buffet[2] /bŭffit/ n. blow, esp. with a hand. ● v. (buffeted) deal blows to.

buffoon n. foolish person. □ **buffoonery** n.

bug n. **1** small unpleasant insect. **2** (sl.) virus, infection. **3** (colloq.) defect. **4** secret microphone. ● v. (**bugged**) **1** install a secret microphone in. **2** (sl.) annoy.

■ n. **1** creepy-crawly, insect. **2** bacterium, germ, microbe, micro-organism, virus; disease, infection. **4** tap.

bugbear n. thing feared or disliked.

buggy n. **1** light carriage. **2** small sturdy vehicle. **3** pushchair.

bugle n. brass instrument like a small trumpet. □ **bugler** n.

build v. (**built**) construct by putting parts or material together. ● n. bodily shape. □ **build up 1** establish gradually. **2** increase. **build-up** n. this process. **builder** n.

■ v. assemble, construct, erect, fabricate, make, put together, put up, set up. ● n. body, figure, physique. □ **build up 1** develop, establish, expand, extend. **2** increase, intensify, strengthen.

building n. house or similar structure. □ **building society** organization that accepts deposits of money and lends to people buying houses.

■ construction, edifice, pile, structure.

built see **build**. □ **built-in** adj. forming part of a structure. **built-up** adj. covered with buildings.

bulb n. **1** rounded base of the stem of certain plants. **2** (esp. an electric lamp) shaped like this. □ **bulbous** adj.

bulge n. rounded swelling. ● v. swell outwards.

■ n. bump, distension, excrescence, knob, lump, projection, protrusion, protuberance, swelling. ● v. project, protrude, stick out, swell out.

bulk n. **1** size, magnitude (esp. large). **2** greater part. ● v. increase the size or thickness of.

■ n. **1** amount, extent, magnitude, mass, quantity, size, volume, weight. **2** best part, body, greater part, majority, preponderance.

bulkhead n. partition in a ship etc.

bulky adj. (**-ier**, **-iest**) **1** large. **2** unwieldy.

■ **1** beefy, big, brawny, burly, chunky, corpulent, heavy, hefty, large. **2** awkward, cumbersome, unwieldy, voluminous.

bull[1] n. **1** male of ox, whale, elephant, etc. **2** bull's-eye. □ **bull's-eye** n. centre of a target. **bull terrier** terrier resembling a bulldog.

bull[2] n. pope's official edict.

bull[3] n. (sl.) absurd statement.

bulldog n. powerful dog with a short thick neck.

bulldozer n. powerful tractor with a device for clearing ground.

bullet n. small missile fired from a rifle or revolver.

bulletin n. short official statement of news.

■ announcement, communication, communiqué, dispatch, message, newsflash, report, statement.

bullfighting n. baiting and killing bulls as entertainment.

bullfinch n. songbird with a strong beak and pinkish breast.

bullion n. gold or silver in bulk or bars, before manufacture.

bullock n. castrated bull.

bully[1] n. person who hurts or intimidates others. ● v. behave as a bully towards.

■ v. browbeat, hector, intimidate, persecute, terrorize, threaten, torment, tyrannize, victimize.

bully[2] v. **bully off** put the ball into play in hockey.

bulrush n. a kind of tall rush.

bulwark n. **1** wall of earth built as a defence. **2** ship's side above the deck.

bum[1] n. (sl.) buttocks.

bum[2] n. (US sl.) beggar, loafer.

bumble v. move or act in a blundering way.

bumble-bee n. large bee.

bump n. **1** dull-sounding blow or collision. **2** swelling caused by this. ● v. **1** hit or come against with a bump. **2** travel with a jolting movement. □ **bumpy** adj.

■ n. **1** blow, collision, knock, thud, thump. **2** bulge, lump, protuberance, swelling, welt. ● v. **1** bang, collide with, hit, knock against, ram, run into, strike. **2** bounce, jerk, jolt, lurch.

bumper n. **1** horizontal bar at the front and back of a motor vehicle to lessen the effect of collision. **2** something unusually large.

bumpkin n. country person with awkward manners.

bumptious adj. conceited.

bun n. **1** small sweet cake. **2** coil of hair at the back of the head.

bunch n. cluster of things growing or fastened together. ● v. **1** make into bunch(es). **2** form a group.

■ n. batch, bundle, clump, cluster, sheaf, tuft; bouquet, nosegay, posy, spray.

bundle n. collection of things loosely fastened or wrapped together. ● v. 1 make into a bundle. 2 push hurriedly.

■ n. bale, bunch, collection, package, packet, parcel, sheaf. ● v. 1 gather together, package, pack up, tie up. 2 cram, push, ram, shove, squeeze, thrust.

bung n. stopper for the hole in a barrel or jar. ● v. (sl.) throw.

bungalow n. one-storeyed house.

bungle v. mismanage. ● n. bungled attempt. □ **bungler** n.

■ v. botch, sl. fluff, colloq. make a hash of, make a mess of, mess up, mismanage, colloq. muff, sl. screw up, spoil.

bunion n. swelling at the base of the big toe, with thickened skin.

bunk[1] n. shelf-like bed.

bunk[2] n. **do a bunk** (sl.) run away.

bunker n. 1 container for fuel. 2 sandy hollow on a golf course. 3 reinforced underground shelter.

bunkum n. nonsense, humbug.

Bunsen burner device burning mixed air and gas in a single very hot flame.

bunting[1] n. bird related to the finches.

bunting[2] n. decorative flags.

buoy /boy/ n. anchored floating object serving as a navigation mark. ● v. **buoy up** 1 keep afloat. 2 sustain, hearten.

buoyant /bóyənt/ adj. 1 able to float. 2 cheerful, lively. □ **buoyancy** n.

■ 2 carefree, cheerful, cheery, ebullient, exuberant, happy, high-spirited, jaunty, light-hearted, lively, vivacious.

bur n. plant's seed case that clings to clothing etc.

burble v. 1 make a gentle murmuring sound. 2 speak lengthily.

burden n. 1 load, esp. a heavy one. 2 oppressive duty, obligation, etc. ● v. put a burden on. □ **burdensome** adj.

■ n. 1 cargo, load, weight. 2 cross, duty, imposition, millstone, obligation, onus, responsibility, trial, trouble, worry. ● v. encumber, load, lumber, oppress, overload, saddle, tax, trouble, weigh down. □ **burdensome** arduous, difficult, exacting, onerous, oppressive, taxing, tiring, troublesome, wearisome, worrying.

bureau /byoóró/ n. (pl. **-eaux**) 1 writing desk with drawers. 2 office, department.

bureaucracy /byoorókrəsi/ n. 1 government by unelected officials. 2 excessive administration.

bureaucrat n. government official. □ **bureaucratic** adj.

burgeon v. begin to grow rapidly.

burglar n. person who breaks into a building, esp. in order to steal. □ **burglary** n.

■ housebreaker, intruder, robber, thief.

burgle v. rob as a burglar.

burial n. burying.

burlesque n. mocking imitation. ● v. imitate mockingly.

■ n. caricature, imitation, mockery, parody, satire, colloq. spoof, take-off.

burly adj. (**-ier, -iest**) large and sturdy. □ **burliness** n.

■ beefy, brawny, heavy, hefty, muscular, powerful, stocky, strapping, strong, sturdy, thickset.

burn[1] v. (**burned** or **burnt**) 1 (cause to) be destroyed by fire. 2 blaze or glow with fire. 3 (cause to) be injured or damaged by fire, sun, etc. 4 feel a sensation (as) of heat. 5 use or be used as fuel. ● n. mark or sore made by burning.

■ v. 1 cremate, fire, ignite, incinerate, set fire to, set on fire. 2 blaze, flame, glow, smoulder. 3 · char, scald, scorch, sear, singe.

burn[2] n. (Sc.) brook.

burner n. part that shapes the flame in a lamp or cooker etc.

burning adj. 1 on fire, very hot. 2 intense. 3 hotly discussed.

■ 1 ablaze, alight, blazing, fiery, flaming, on fire, smouldering. 2 ardent, fervent, fervid, fierce, impassioned, intense, passionate, vehement.

burnish v. polish by rubbing.

burnt see **burn**[1].

burp n. & v. (colloq.) belch.

burr n. 1 whirring sound. 2 rough pronunciation of 'r'. 3 country accent using this.

burrow n. hole dug by a fox or rabbit as a dwelling. ● v. 1 dig a burrow. 2 search deeply, delve.

bursar n. treasurer of a college etc.

bursary n. 1 grant, esp. a scholarship. 2 bursar's office.

burst v. (**burst**) 1 break violently apart, explode. 2 appear, move, speak, etc. suddenly or violently. ● n. 1 bursting. 2 outbreak. 3 brief violent effort, spurt.

■ v. 1 break apart, blow up, colloq. bust, explode, give way, rupture, shatter, split.

bury v. **1** place (a dead body) in the earth or a tomb. **2** put or hide underground, cover up. **3** involve (oneself) deeply.
■ **1** inter, lay to rest. **2** hide, secrete, *colloq.* stash away; conceal, cover up, obscure, shroud. **3** engross, immerse, occupy, plunge.

bus n. (*pl.* **buses**) large passenger vehicle.
● v. (**bussed**) travel or transport by bus.

bush¹ n. **1** shrub. **2** thick growth. **3** wild uncultivated land.

bush² n. **1** metal lining for a hole in which something fits. **2** electrically insulating sleeve.

bushy adj. (**-ier, -iest**) **1** covered with bushes. **2** growing thickly.

business n. **1** occupation, trade. **2** task, duty. **3** thing to be dealt with. **4** buying and selling, trade. **5** commercial establishment. □ **businessman, businesswoman** ns. person engaged in trade or commerce.
■ **1** calling, career, employment, field, job, line of work, occupation, profession, trade, vocation. **2** duty, function, responsibility, role, task. **3** affair, issue, matter(s) in hand, question, problem, subject; agenda. **4** commerce, industry, trade; dealings, transactions. **5** company, concern, corporation, enterprise, firm, organization, partnership, practice, venture.

businesslike adj. practical, systematic.
■ down-to-earth, efficient, hard-headed, level-headed, logical, methodical, orderly, practical, pragmatic, professional, sensible, systematic, well-organized.

busk v. perform esp. music in the street for tips. □ **busker** n.

bust¹ n. **1** sculptured head, shoulders, and chest. **2** bosom.

bust² v. (**busted** or **bust**) (*colloq.*) burst, break. □ **bust-up** n. (*colloq.*) quarrel. **go bust** (*colloq.*) become bankrupt.

bustle¹ v. move busily and energetically.
● n. excited activity.
■ v. dash, hasten, hurry, hustle, rush, scamper, scramble, scurry, scuttle. ● n. activity, commotion, excitement, flurry, fuss, haste, hurly-burly, hustle, stir, to-do.

bustle² n. (*old use*) padding to puff out the top of a skirt at the back.

busy adj. (**-ier, -iest**) **1** working, having much to do. **2** full of activity. □ **busily** adv.
■ **1** hard-working, industrious, *colloq.* on the go, tireless, working; engaged, occu-

pied, tied up. **2** active, brisk, bustling, eventful, full, hectic.

busybody n. meddlesome person.

but adv. only. ● prep. & conj. **1** however. **2** except.

butane n. inflammable liquid used as fuel.

butch adj. (*sl.*) strongly masculine.

butcher n. **1** person who cuts up and sells meat. **2** brutal murderer. ● v. kill needlessly or brutally. □ **butchery** n.

butler n. chief manservant, in charge of the wine cellar.

butt¹ n. large cask or barrel.

butt² n. **1** thicker end of a tool or weapon. **2** short remnant, stub.

butt³ n. **1** target for ridicule or teasing. **2** mound behind a target. **3** (*pl.*) shooting range.

butt⁴ v. **1** push with the head. **2** meet or place edge to edge. □ **butt in 1** interrupt. **2** meddle.

butter n. fatty food substance made from cream. ● v. spread with butter. □ **butter up** flatter.

buttercup n. wild plant with yellow cup-shaped flowers.

butterfly n. **1** insect with four large often brightly coloured wings. **2** swimming stroke with both arms lifted at the same time.

buttermilk n. liquid left after butter is churned from milk.

butterscotch n. hard toffee-like sweet.

buttock n. either of the two fleshy rounded parts at the lower end of the back of the body.

button n. **1** disc or knob sewn to a garment as a fastener or ornament. **2** small rounded object. **3** knob etc. pressed to operate a device. ● v. fasten with button(s).

buttonhole n. **1** slit through which a button is passed to fasten clothing. **2** flower worn in the buttonhole of a lapel. ● v. accost and talk to.

buttress n. **1** support built against a wall. **2** thing that supports. ● v. reinforce, prop up.
■ n. prop, support. ● v. bolster, brace, prop up, reinforce, shore up, strengthen, support, sustain.

buxom adj. plump and healthy.

buy v. (**bought**) obtain in exchange for money. ● n. purchase. □ **buyer** n.
■ v. acquire, come by, get, obtain, pay for, procure, purchase. □ **buyer** client, con-

sumer, customer, *colloq.* punter, purchaser, shopper.

buzz *n.* **1** vibrating humming sound. **2** rumour. **3** thrill. ● *v.* **1** make or be filled with a buzz. **2** go about busily. □ **buzzword** *n.* (*colloq.*) fashionable word.

buzzard *n.* a kind of hawk.

buzzer *n.* device that produces a buzzing sound as a signal.

by *prep.* & *adv.* **1** near, beside, in reserve. **2** along, via, past. **3** during. **4** through the agency or means of. **5** not later than. □ **by and by** before long. **by and large** on the whole. **by-election** *n.* election of an MP to replace one who has died or resigned. **by-law** *n.* regulation made by a local authority or corporation. **by oneself** alone, without help. **by-product** *n.* thing produced while making something else.

bye *n.* **1** run scored from a ball not hit by the batsman. **2** having no opponent for one round of a tournament.

bygone *adj.* belonging to the past. ● *n.pl.* bygone things.

bypass *n.* road taking traffic round a town. ● *v.* avoid.

byre *n.* cowshed.

byroad *n.* minor road.

bystander *n.* person standing near when something happens.

■ eyewitness, observer, onlooker, passer-by, spectator, witness.

byte *n.* (in computers) group of bits.

byway *n.* minor road.

byword *n.* **1** notable example. **2** familiar saying.

Byzantine *adj.* **1** of Byzantium. **2** complicated, underhand.

Cc

C *abbr.* **1** Celsius. **2** centigrade.

cab *n.* **1** taxi. **2** compartment for the driver of a train, lorry, etc.

cabaret /kábbaray/ *n.* entertainment in a nightclub etc.

cabbage *n.* vegetable with a round head of green or purple leaves.

cabby *n.* (*colloq.*) taxi driver.

caber *n.* trimmed tree trunk.

cabin *n.* **1** small hut. **2** compartment in a ship or aircraft.
■ **1** chalet, hut, lodge, shack, shanty, shelter. **2** berth, compartment, room, stateroom.

cabinet *n.* **1** cupboard with drawers or shelves. **2** (**Cabinet**) group of senior ministers in government.

cable *n.* **1** thick rope of fibre or wire. **2** set of insulated wires for carrying electricity or signals. □ **cable car** car of a **cable railway** drawn on an endless cable by a stationary engine. **cable television** transmission by cable to subscribers.
■ **1** chain, guy, hawser, mainstay, rope, wire. **2** cord, flex, lead.

cacao *n.* **1** seed from which cocoa and chocolate are made. **2** tree producing this.

cache /kash/ *n.* **1** hiding place for treasure or stores. **2** things in this. ● *v.* put into a cache.

cachet /káshay/ *n.* **1** prestige. **2** distinctive mark or feature.

cackle *n.* **1** clucking of hens. **2** chattering talk. **3** loud silly laugh. ● *v.* utter a cackle.

cacophony *n.* harsh discordant sound. □ **cacophonous** *adj.*
■ □ **cacophonous** discordant, dissonant, grating, harsh, jangling, noisy, raucous, strident.

cactus *n.* (*pl.* **-ti** or **-tuses**) fleshy plant, usu. with spines.

cadaver *n.* corpse.

cadaverous *adj.* gaunt and pale.

caddie *n.* golfer's attendant carrying clubs. ● *v.* act as caddie.

caddis-fly *n.* four-winged insect living near water.

caddy *n.* small box for tea.

cadence *n.* **1** rhythm. **2** rise and fall of the voice in speech. **3** end of a musical phrase.
■ **1** accent, beat, lilt, measure, metre, rhythm, tempo.

cadenza *n.* elaborate passage for a solo instrument or singer.

cadet *n.* young trainee in the armed forces or police.

cadge *v.* ask for as a gift, beg.

cadmium *n.* metallic element.

cadre *n.* small group, esp. of soldiers.

caecum /seékam/ *n.* (*pl.* **-ca**) pouch between the small and large intestines.

Caesarean section delivery of a child by cutting into the mother's abdomen.

café *n.* informal restaurant.

cafeteria *n.* self-service restaurant.

caffeine *n.* stimulant found in tea and coffee.

caftan *n.* long loose robe or dress.

cage *n.* enclosure of wire or with bars, esp. for birds or animals.

cagey *adj.* (**-ier**, **-iest**) (*colloq.*) cautious and noncommittal. □ **cagily** *adv.*, **caginess** *n.*

cagoule *n.* light hooded waterproof jacket.

cahoots *n.* (*sl.*) partnership.

cairn *n.* mound of stones as a memorial or landmark. □ **cairn terrier** small shaggy short-legged terrier.

caisson *n.* watertight chamber used in underwater construction work.

cajole *v.* persuade by flattery. □ **cajolery** *n.*
■ coax, entice, inveigle, persuade, seduce, wheedle.

cake *n.* **1** baked sweet bread-like food. **2** small flattened mass. ● *v.* form into a compact mass.

calamine *n.* lotion containing zinc carbonate.

calamity *n.* disaster. □ **calamitous** *adj.*, **calamitously** *adv.*
■ cataclysm, catastrophe, disaster, misfortune, tragedy.

calcify *v.* harden by a deposit of calcium salts. □ **calcification** *n.*

calcium *n.* whitish metallic element.

calculate v. 1 reckon mathematically. 2 estimate. 3 plan deliberately. □ **calculation** n.
■ 1 add up, compute, determine, reckon, work out. 2 assess, estimate, evaluate, gauge, weigh up.

calculator n. electronic device for making calculations.

calculus n. (pl. -li) 1 method of calculating in mathematics. 2 stone formed in the body.

Caledonian adj. of Scotland. ● n. Scottish person.

calendar n. chart showing dates of days of the year.

calf¹ n. (pl. **calves**) young of cattle, also of elephant, whale, and seal.

calf² n. (pl. **calves**) fleshy part of the human leg below the knee.

calibrate v. 1 mark or correct the units of measurement on (a gauge). 2 find the calibre of. □ **calibration** n.

calibre n. 1 diameter of a gun, tube, or bullet. 2 level of ability.
■ 1 bore, diameter, gauge, size. 2 ability, capability, capacity, competence, merit, proficiency, quality, stature, talent.

calico n. a kind of cotton cloth.

caliph n. (formerly) Muslim ruler.

call v. 1 shout to attract attention. 2 summon. 3 rouse from sleep. 4 communicate (with) by telephone or radio. 5 name, describe, or address as. 6 make a brief visit. 7 utter a characteristic cry. ● n. 1 shout. 2 invitation. 3 need. 4 demand. 5 telephone conversation. 6 short visit. 7 bird's cry. □ **call box** telephone kiosk. **call off** cancel. **caller** n.
■ v. 1 bawl, bellow, cry (out), hail, shout, yell. 2 assemble, convene, convoke, rally, summon. 3 awake, awaken, get up, knock up, rouse, wake. 4 dial, colloq. phone, ring up, telephone. 5 baptize, christen, designate, dub, name, nickname. 6 drop in, pay a visit, visit. ● n. 1 bellow, cry, shout, yell. 2 command, invitation, request, summons. 3 cause, justification, need, occasion, reason. 4 demand, desire, market.

calligraphy n. (beautiful) handwriting. □ **calligraphic** adj.

calling n. vocation, profession.

calliper n. splint for a weak leg.

callisthenics n.pl. exercises to develop strength and grace.

callous adj. feeling no pity or sympathy. □ **callously** adv., **callousness** n.
■ cold, cruel, hard, hard-boiled, hardhearted, heartless, inhumane, insensitive, stony, uncaring, unfeeling, unsympathetic.

callow adj. immature and inexperienced.
■ green, immature, inexperienced, juvenile, naive, unsophisticated.

callus n. patch of hardened skin.

calm adj. 1 still, not windy. 2 not excited or agitated. ● n. calm condition. ● v. make calm. □ **calmly** adv., **calmness** n.
■ adj. 1 peaceful, quiet, still, tranquil, windless. 2 collected, composed, controlled, cool, dispassionate, equable, impassive, imperturbable, nonchalant, relaxed, sedate, self-controlled, self-possessed, serene, stoical, colloq. unflappable, unperturbed, unruffled, untroubled. ● n. calmness, composure, equanimity, peace, peacefulness, placidity, quiet, quietness, serenity, stillness, tranquillity. ● v. appease, assuage, lull, mollify, pacify, placate, quiet, quieten, settle, soothe.

calorie n. 1 unit of heat. 2 unit of the energy-producing value of food.

calorific adj. heat-producing.

calumniate v. slander.

calumny n. slander.

calve v. give birth to a calf.

Calvinism n. teachings of the Protestant reformer John Calvin or his followers. □ **Calvinist** n.

calypso n. topical W. Indian song.

calyx n. ring of sepals covering a flower bud.

cam n. device changing rotary to to-and-fro motion. □ **camshaft** n.

camaraderie n. comradeship.

camber n. slight convex curve given to a surface esp. of a road.

cambric n. thin linen or cotton cloth.

camcorder n. combined video and sound recorder.

came see **come**.

camel n. 1 four-legged animal with one hump or two. 2 fawn colour.

camellia n. evergreen flowering shrub.

cameo n. 1 stone in a ring or brooch with coloured layers carved in a raised design. 2 small part in a play or film taken by a famous actor or actress.

camera n. apparatus for taking photographs or film pictures. □ **in camera** in private.

camiknickers *n.pl.* woman's undergarment combining camisole and knickers.

camisole *n.* woman's cotton bodice-like garment.

camomile *n.* aromatic herb.

camouflage *n.* disguise, concealment, by colouring or covering. ● *v.* disguise or conceal in this way.

■ *n.* concealment, cover, disguise, façade, front, mask, screen. ● *v.* cloak, conceal, cover (up), disguise, hide, mask, screen, veil.

camp[1] *n.* **1** temporary accommodation in tents. **2** place where troops are lodged or trained. **3** fortified site. ● *v.* encamp, be in a camp. □ **camp bed** portable folding bed. **camper** *n.*

camp[2] *adj.* **1** affected, exaggerated. **2** homosexual. ● *n.* camp behaviour. ● *v.* act or behave in a camp way.

campaign *n.* **1** organized course of action. **2** series of military operations. ● *v.* take part in a campaign. □ **campaigner** *n.*

■ *n.* **1** crusade, drive, effort, move, movement, plan, push, scheme. **2** manoeuvre(s), offensive, operation(s).

campanology *n.* **1** study of bells. **2** bell-ringing. □ **campanologist** *n.*

campanula *n.* plant with bell-shaped flowers.

camphor *n.* strong-smelling white substance used in medicine and moth-balls. □ **camphorated** *adj.*

campion *n.* wild plant with pink or white flowers.

campus *n.* (*pl.* **-puses**) grounds of a university or college.

can[1] *n.* container in which food etc. is sealed and preserved. ● *v.* (**canned**) preserve in a can.

can[2] *v.aux.* is or are able or allowed to.

Canadian *adj.* & *n.* (native, inhabitant) of Canada.

canal *n.* **1** artificial watercourse. **2** duct.

canalize *v.* **1** convert into a canal. **2** channel. □ **canalization** *n.*

canapé /kánnəpi/ *n.* small piece of bread etc. with savoury topping.

canary *n.* small yellow songbird.

cancan *n.* high-kicking dance.

cancel *v.* (**cancelled**) **1** declare that (something arranged) will not take place. **2** order to be discontinued, make invalid.

3 cross out. □ **cancel out** neutralize. **cancellation** *n.*

■ **1** call off, postpone, *colloq.* scrub. **2** abolish, annul, countermand, do away with, invalidate, nullify, quash, repeal, rescind, retract, revoke, withdraw. **3** cross out, delete, erase, rub out. □ **cancel out** compensate for, counterbalance, make up for, neutralize, offset.

cancer *n.* **1** malignant tumour. **2** spreading evil. □ **cancerous** *adj.*

candela *n.* unit measuring the brightness of light.

candelabrum *n.* (also **-bra**) large branched candlestick.

candid *adj.* frank. □ **candidly** *adv.*

■ blunt, direct, forthright, frank, honest, ingenuous, open, outspoken, plain, sincere, straightforward, truthful, unequivocal.

candidate *n.* person applying for a job or taking an exam. □ **candidacy** *n.,* **candidature** *n.*

■ applicant, aspirant, competitor, contender, examinee, interviewee.

candied *adj.* encrusted or preserved in sugar.

candle *n.* stick of wax enclosing a wick which is burnt to give light.

candlestick *n.* holder for a candle.

candlewick *n.* fabric with a tufted pattern.

candour *n.* frankness.

candy *n.* (*US*) sweets, a sweet.

candyfloss *n.* fluffy mass of spun sugar.

candy stripe alternate stripes of white and esp. pink.

candytuft *n.* garden plant with flowers in flat clusters.

cane *n.* **1** stem of a tall reed or grass or slender palm. **2** light walking stick.

canine /káynīn/ *adj.* of dog('s). ● *n.* (in full **canine tooth**) a pointed tooth between incisors and molars.

canister *n.* small metal container.

canker *n.* **1** disease of animals or plants. **2** influence that corrupts.

cannabis *n.* **1** hemp plant. **2** drug made from this.

cannibal *n.* person who eats human flesh. □ **cannibalism** *n.*

cannibalize *v.* use parts from (a machine) to repair another.

cannon *n.* **1** large gun. **2** hitting of two balls in one shot in billiards. ● *v.* bump heavily (into).

cannonade *n.* continuous gunfire. ● *v.* bombard with this.

cannot negative form of **can²**.

canny adj. (**-ier, -iest**) shrewd. □ **cannily** adv.

canoe n. light boat propelled by paddle(s). ● v. go in a canoe. □ **canoeist** n.

canon n. **1** member of cathedral clergy. **2** general rule or principle. **3** set of writings accepted as genuine. □ **canonical** adj.

canonize v. declare officially to be a saint. □ **canonization** n.

canopy n. covering hung up over a throne, bed, person, etc.

cant n. **1** insincere talk. **2** jargon.

cantaloup n. small ribbed melon.

cantankerous adj. bad-tempered. □ **cantankerously** adv.

> ■ bad-tempered, choleric, crabby, cross, crotchety, gruff, grumpy, fractious, irascible, irritable, peevish, petulant, prickly, quarrelsome, surly, testy, waspish.

cantata n. choral composition.

canteen n. **1** restaurant for employees. **2** case of cutlery.

canter n. gentle gallop. ● v. go at a canter.

cantilever n. projecting beam or girder supporting a structure.

canto n. division of a long poem.

canton n. division of Switzerland.

canvas n. **1** strong coarse cloth. **2** a painting on this.

canvass v. **1** ask for political support. **2** ascertain opinions of.

canyon n. deep gorge.

> ■ defile, gorge, pass, ravine.

cap n. **1** soft brimless hat, often with a peak. **2** headdress worn as part of a uniform. **3** cover or top. **4** explosive device for a toy pistol. ● v. (**capped**) **1** put a cap on. **2** form the top of. **3** surpass.

capable adj. competent, able. □ **capably** adv., **capability** n.

> ■ able, accomplished, adept, clever, competent, efficient, experienced, practised, proficient, qualified, skilful, skilled, talented.

capacious adj. roomy.

> ■ ample, commodious, roomy, sizeable, spacious.

capacitance n. ability to store an electric charge.

capacitor n. device storing a charge of electricity.

capacity n. **1** amount that can be contained or produced. **2** mental power. **3** function or position. **4** ability to contain, receive, experience, or produce.

> ■ **1** content, dimensions, magnitude, proportions, size, volume. **2** ability, brains, capability, cleverness, competence, intelligence, perspicacity, wit. **3** duty, function, job, office, place, position, post, responsibility, role. **4** potential.

cape¹ n. a short cloak.

cape² n. coastal promontory.

caper¹ v. move friskily. ● n. **1** frisky movement. **2** (sl.) activity.

> ■ v. bound, cavort, frisk, frolic, gambol, hop, jump, leap, prance, skip, spring.

caper² n. **1** bramble-like shrub. **2** one of its pickled buds.

capercaillie n. (also **capercailzie**) large grouse.

capillary n. very fine hair-like tube or blood vessel.

capital adj. **1** chief, very important. **2** involving the death penalty. **3** (of a letter of the alphabet) of the kind used to begin a name or sentence. ● n. **1** chief city of a country etc. **2** money with which a business is started. **3** capital letter. **4** top part of a pillar.

> ■ adj. **1** cardinal, central, chief, foremost, leading, main, major, paramount, pre-eminent, primary, prime, principal. ● n. **2** assets, cash, finances, funds, means, money, principal, resources, savings, stocks, wealth, colloq. wherewithal.

capitalism n. system in which trade and industry are controlled by private owners.

capitalist n. person who has money invested in businesses.

capitalize v. **1** convert into or provide with capital. **2** write as or with a capital letter. □ **capitalize on** make advantageous use of. **capitalization** n.

capitulate v. surrender, yield. □ **capitulation** n.

> ■ acquiesce, concede, give in, relent, submit, succumb, surrender, throw in the towel, yield.

caprice /kəpreess/ n. **1** whim. **2** lively piece of music.

capricious adj. impulsive and unpredictable. □ **capriciously** adv., **capriciousness** n.

> ■ changeable, erratic, fickle, impulsive, inconsistent, inconstant, mercurial, moody, temperamental, unpredictable, unreliable, unstable, variable, volatile, wayward.

capsicum n. tropical plant with pungent seeds.

capsize v. overturn.
■ flip over, keel over, overturn, tip over, turn turtle, turn upside down.

capstan n. revolving post or spindle on which a cable etc. winds.

capsule n. **1** small soluble case containing medicine. **2** detachable compartment of a spacecraft. **3** plant's seed case.

captain n. **1** leader of a group or sports team. **2** person commanding a ship or civil aircraft. **3** naval officer next below rear admiral. **4** army officer next below major. ● v. be captain of. □ **captaincy** n.

caption n. **1** short title or heading. **2** explanation on an illustration.

captious adj. fond of finding fault, esp. about trivial matters.

captivate v. fascinate, charm. □ **captivation** n.
■ attract, bewitch, charm, dazzle, delight, enchant, enrapture, enthral, entrance, fascinate, hypnotize, mesmerize.

captive adj. taken prisoner, confined, unable to escape. ● n. captive person or animal. □ **captivity** n.
■ adj. caged, captured, confined, imprisoned, incarcerated, jailed, locked up. ● n. detainee, hostage, internee, prisoner. □ **captivity** bondage, confinement, custody, detention, imprisonment, incarceration, internment, slavery.

captor n. one who takes a captive.

capture v. **1** take prisoner. **2** take or obtain by force or skill. **3** cause (data) to be stored in a computer. ● n. act of capturing.
■ v. **1** apprehend, arrest, catch, collar, ensnare, kidnap, sl. nab, sl. nick, seize, take prisoner. **2** carry, carry off, gain, get, obtain, secure, take, win.

car n. **1** motor vehicle for a small number of passengers. **2** (US) railway carriage. **3** compartment in a cable railway, lift, etc.
■ **1** US automobile, sl. banger, motor, motor car, vehicle.

carafe /kəráf/ n. glass bottle for serving wine or water.

caramel n. **1** brown syrup made from heated sugar. **2** toffee tasting like this. □ **caramelize** v.

carapace n. upper shell of a tortoise.

carat n. unit of purity of gold.

caravan n. **1** dwelling on wheels, able to be towed by a horse or car. **2** company travelling together across desert. □ **caravanner** n., **caravanning** n.

caraway n. (plant with) spicy seeds used for flavouring cakes.

carbine n. automatic rifle.

carbohydrate n. energy-producing compound in food.

carbolic n. a kind of disinfectant.

carbon n. non-metallic element occurring as diamond, graphite, and charcoal, and in all living matter. □ **carbon 1** copy made with carbon paper. **2** exact copy. **carbon paper** paper coated with pigment for making a copy as something is typed or written.

carbonate n. compound releasing carbon dioxide when mixed with acid. ● v. impregnate with carbon dioxide.

carboniferous adj. producing coal.

carborundum n. compound of carbon and silicon used for grinding and polishing things.

carbuncle n. **1** severe abscess. **2** bright red gem.

carburettor n. apparatus mixing air and petrol in a motor engine.

carcass n. dead body of an animal.

carcinogen n. cancer-producing substance. □ **carcinogenic** adj.

carcinoma n. cancerous tumour.

card¹ n. **1** piece of cardboard or thick paper. **2** this printed with a greeting or invitation. **3** postcard. **4** playing card. **5** credit card. **6** (pl., colloq.) employee's official documents, held by his employer. □ **card-sharp** n. swindler at card games.

card² v. clean or comb (wool) with a wire brush.

cardboard n. stiff substance made by pasting together sheets of paper.

cardiac adj. of the heart.

cardigan n. knitted jacket.

cardinal adj. chief, most important. ● n. prince of the RC Church. □ **cardinal number** whole number (1, 2, 3, etc.).

cardiogram n. record of heart movements. □ **cardiograph** n. instrument producing this.

cardiology n. study of diseases of the heart. □ **cardiologist** n.

cardphone n. public telephone operated by a plastic machine-readable card.

care n. **1** serious attention and thought. **2** caution to avoid damage or loss. **3** (cause of) worry, anxiety. **4** protection. ● v. feel concern or interest. □ **care for 1** like, love. **2** look after.
■ n. **1** attention, consideration, deliberation, diligence, heed, meticulousness,

pains, prudence, punctiliousness, thought. **2** caution, circumspection, mindfulness, vigilance, watchfulness. **3** anxiety, concern, disquiet, distress, worry; problem, sorrow, trouble, woe. **4** charge, custody, guardianship, keeping, protection, responsibility, trust. □ **care for 1** adore, be fond of, be in love with, cherish, dote on, like, love, treasure. **2** look after, mind, minister to, nurse, provide for, see to, support, take care of, tend.

careen v. tilt or keel over.

career n. **1** way of making one's living, profession. **2** course through life. **3** swift course. ● v. go swiftly or wildly.
■ n. **1** calling, job, line of work, livelihood, occupation, profession, trade, vocation. ● v. dash, fly, hurtle, race, rush, shoot, speed, sprint, tear, zoom.

careerist n. person intent on advancement in a career.

carefree adj. light-hearted, free from anxieties.
■ airy, blithe, cheerful, debonair, easy-going, happy, happy-go-lucky, insouciant, light-hearted, nonchalant, relaxed.

careful adj. acting or done with care. □ **carefully** adv., **carefulness** n.
■ alert, cautious, chary, circumspect, guarded, on one's guard, prudent, vigilant, wary, watchful; accurate, conscientious, diligent, methodical, meticulous, orderly, organized, painstaking, precise, punctilious, scrupulous, systematic, thorough, well-organized.

careless adj. not careful. □ **carelessly** adv., **carelessness** n.
■ absent-minded, heedless, inattentive, incautious, irresponsible, neglectful, negligent, remiss, scatterbrained, thoughtless, unguarded, unthinking; casual, cursory, perfunctory; disorganized, inaccurate, shoddy, slapdash, slipshod, sloppy, slovenly.

carer n. person who looks after a sick or disabled person at home.

caress n. loving touch, kiss. ● v. give a caress to.
■ v. cuddle, embrace, fondle, hug, kiss, nuzzle, pat, pet, stroke.

caret n. omission mark.

caretaker n. person employed to look after a building.

careworn adj. showing signs of prolonged worry.

cargo n. (pl. **-oes**) goods carried by ship or aircraft.
■ consignment, freight, goods, load, payload, shipment.

Caribbean adj. of the W. Indies or their inhabitants.

caribou n. N. American reindeer.

caricature n. exaggerated portrayal of a person for comic effect. ● v. make a caricature of.
■ n. burlesque, cartoon, parody, satire, colloq. spoof, take-off. ● v. burlesque, lampoon, parody, satirize, send up, take off.

caries n. decay of tooth or bone.

carillon /kəˈrilyən/ n. **1** set of bells sounded mechanically. **2** tune played on these.

Carmelite n. member of an order of white-cloaked friars or nuns.

carmine adj. & n. vivid crimson.

carnage n. great slaughter.
■ bloodshed, butchery, killing, massacre, slaughter.

carnal adj. **1** of the body or flesh, worldly. **2** sensual.
■ **1** animal, bodily, corporeal, physical; earthly, material, worldly. **2** erotic, lascivious, lustful, sensual, sexual.

carnation n. clove-scented pink.

carnival n. public festivities, usu. with a procession.

carnivore n. carnivorous animal.

carnivorous adj. feeding on flesh.

carol n. Christmas hymn. ● v. (**carolled**) **1** sing carols. **2** sing joyfully.

carotid adj. & n. (artery) carrying blood to the head.

carouse v. drink and be merry. □ **carousal** n., **carouser** n.

carousel n. **1** (US) merry-go-round. **2** rotating conveyor.

carp[1] n. freshwater fish.

carp[2] v. keep finding fault.
■ cavil, complain, colloq. gripe, grumble, colloq. nit-pick, pick holes, colloq. whinge.

carpenter n. person who makes or repairs wooden objects and structures. □ **carpentry** n.

carpet n. fabric for covering a floor. ● v. (**carpeted**) **1** cover with a carpet. **2** reprimand.

carport n. roofed open-sided shelter for a car.

carpus n. set of small bones forming the wrist joint.

carriage n. **1** railway passenger vehicle. **2** horse-drawn vehicle. **3** conveying of goods etc., cost of this. **4** bearing, deportment. □ **carriage clock** small portable clock with a handle on top.

■ **1** US car, coach, wagon. **2** coach, gig, landau, trap. **3** conveyance, haulage, shipping, transport, transportation. **4** bearing, demeanour, deportment, posture, stance.

carriageway n. that part of the road on which vehicles travel.

carrier n. **1** person or thing carrying something. **2** paper or plastic bag with handles.

carrion n. dead decaying flesh.

carrot n. **1** plant with edible tapering orange root. **2** this root. **3** incentive.

carry v. **1** transport, convey. **2** support. **3** involve, entail. **4** stock (goods for sale). **5** take (a process etc.) to a specified point. **6** win acceptance for (a motion etc.). **7** get the support of. **8** be audible at a distance. □ **carry off** remove by force. **2** win. **carry on 1** continue. **2** (colloq.) behave excitedly. **carry out** put into practice.

■ **1** bear, bring, sl. cart, convey, deliver, ferry, haul, lug, move, ship, take, transfer, transport; conduct, transmit. **2** bear, hold, support, take. **3** entail, include, involve. **4** have in stock, keep, sell, stock. □ **carry off** abduct, capture, kidnap, make off with, snatch. **2** gain, secure, win. **carry out** effect, execute, implement, perform, put into practice.

cart n. wheeled structure for carrying loads. ● v. (sl.) carry.

carte blanche /kaart blónsh/ complete freedom to do as one thinks best.

cartel n. manufacturer's or producer's union to control prices.

carthorse n. horse of heavy build.

cartilage n. firm elastic tissue in skeletons of vertebrates, gristle.

cartography n. map-drawing. □ **cartographer** n.

carton n. cardboard or plastic container.

cartoon n. **1** humorous drawing. **2** film consisting of an animated sequence of drawings. **3** sketch for a painting. □ **cartoonist** n.

cartridge n. **1** case containing explosive for firearms. **2** sealed cassette. □ **cartridge paper** thick strong paper.

cartwheel n. sideways somersault with arms and legs extended.

carve v. **1** make, inscribe, or decorate by cutting. **2** cut (meat) into slices for eating.

■ **1** chisel, engrave, fashion, hew, inscribe, sculpt, sculpture, whittle.

cascade n. **1** waterfall. **2** thing falling or hanging like this. ● v. fall in this way.

case[1] n. **1** instance of a thing's occurring. **2** situation. **3** lawsuit. **4** set of facts or arguments supporting something. □ **in case** lest.

■ **1** example, illustration, instance, occurrence. **2** occasion, position, situation, state of affairs; eventuality. **3** action, lawsuit, suit.

case[2] n. **1** container or covering enclosing something. **2** item of luggage. ● v. **1** enclose in a case. **2** (sl.) examine (a building etc.) in preparation for a crime.

■ n. **1** box, carton, casket, container, crate, holder, receptacle. **2** bag, grip, holdall, suitcase, trunk.

casement n. window opening on vertical hinges.

cash n. money in the form of coins or banknotes. ● v. give or obtain cash for (a cheque etc.). □ **cash in (on)** get profit or advantage (from).

■ n. banknotes, US bills, change, coins, currency, sl. dough, money, notes.

cash card plastic card with magnetic code for drawing money from a machine.

cashew n. a kind of edible nut.

cashier[1] n. person employed to receive money.

cashier[2] v. dismiss from military service in disgrace.

cashmere n. **1** very fine soft wool. **2** fabric made from this.

cashpoint n. machine dispensing cash.

casino n. (pl. **-os**) public building or room for gambling.

cask n. barrel for liquids.

casket n. **1** small box for valuables. **2** (US) coffin.

cassava n. **1** tropical plant. **2** flour made from its roots.

casserole n. **1** covered dish in which meat etc. is cooked and served. **2** food cooked in this. ● v. cook in a casserole.

cassette n. small case containing a reel of film or magnetic tape.

cassock n. long robe worn by clergy and choristers.

cassowary n. large flightless bird related to the emu.

cast v. (**cast**) 1 throw. 2 shed. 3 direct (a glance). 4 register (one's vote). 5 select actors for a play or film, assign a role to. 6 shape (molten metal) in a mould. ● n. 1 throw of dice, fishing line, etc. 2 set of actors in a play etc. 3 type, quality. 4 moulded mass of solidified material. 5 slight squint. □ **cast-iron** adj. very strong. **cast-off** adj. & n. discarded (thing).

■ v. 1 colloq. chuck, fling, hurl, lob, pitch, colloq. sling, throw, toss. ● n. 1 pitch, shy, toss, throw. 2 company, performers, players, troupe. 3 kind, quality, sort, style, type, variety.

castanets n.pl. pair of shell-shaped pieces of wood clicked in the hand to accompany dancing.

castaway n. shipwrecked person.

caste n. exclusive social class, esp. in the Hindu system.

castigate v. punish or rebuke severely. □ **castigation** n.

■ berate, colloq. blast, chastise, chide, criticize, rebuke, reprimand, reproach, scold, upbraid; discipline, punish.

casting vote deciding vote when those on each side are equal.

castle n. large fortified residence.

castor n. 1 small swivelling wheel on a leg of furniture. 2 small container with a perforated top for sprinkling sugar etc.

castor oil laxative and lubricant vegetable oil.

castrate v. remove the testicles of. □ **castration** n.

casual adj. 1 chance. 2 not regular or permanent. 3 not interested or concerned. 4 careless. 5 (of clothes etc.) informal. □ **casually** adv.

■ 1 accidental, chance, coincidental, fortuitous, random, unexpected, unforeseen, unlooked-for, unplanned. 2 irregular, occasional, part-time, temporary. 3 blasé, blithe, dispassionate, indifferent, insouciant, lackadaisical, nonchalant, offhand, relaxed, unconcerned, unenthusiastic, uninterested. 4 careless, disorganized, haphazard, hit-or-miss, colloq. slap-happy, unmethodical, unsystematic.

casualty n. 1 person killed or injured. 2 thing lost or destroyed.

■ 1 fatality, victim; (**casualties**) dead, injured, wounded.

casuist n. 1 theologian who studies moral problems. 2 sophist, quibbler. □ **casuistic** adj., **casuistry** n.

cat n. 1 small furry domesticated animal. 2 wild animal related to this. 3 whip with knotted lashes. □ **cat's cradle** child's game with string. **cat's-paw** n. person used as a tool by another.

cataclysm n. violent upheaval or disaster. □ **cataclysmic** adj.

catacomb /káttəkoom/ n. underground cemetery.

catafalque n. decorated bier, esp. for a state funeral.

catalepsy n. seizure or trance with rigidity of the body. □ **cataleptic** adj.

catalogue n. systematic list of items. ● v. list in a catalogue.

■ n. directory, index, inventory, list, record, register, roll. ● v. index, itemize, list, make an inventory of, record, register.

catalyse v. subject to the action of a catalyst. □ **catalysis** n.

catalyst n. substance that aids a chemical reaction while remaining unchanged.

catamaran n. boat with twin hulls.

catapult n. device with elastic for shooting small stones. ● v. hurl from or as if from a catapult.

cataract n. 1 large waterfall. 2 opaque area clouding the eye.

catarrh n. inflammation of mucous membrane, esp. of the nose, with a watery discharge.

catastrophe /kətástrəfi/ n. sudden great disaster. □ **catastrophic** adj., **catastrophically** adv.

■ accident, calamity, cataclysm, disaster, fiasco, misfortune, mishap, tragedy.

catcall n. whistle of disapproval.

catch v. (**caught**) 1 capture. 2 detect or surprise. 3 reach or overtake. 4 grasp and hold. 5 become infected with. 6 perceive. 7 be in time for. ● n. 1 act of catching. 2 amount of thing caught. 3 thing or person caught or worth catching. 4 concealed difficulty. 5 fastener. □ **catch on** (colloq.) 1 become popular. 2 understand what is meant. **catch out** detect in a mistake etc. **catchphrase** n. phrase in frequent current use, slogan. **catch-22** n. dilemma where the victim is bound to suffer. **catch up** 1 come abreast with. 2 do arrears of work.

■ v. 1 apprehend, arrest, capture, collar, sl. cop, sl. nab, sl. nick, take prisoner; ensnare, hook, land, net, snare, trap. 2 detect, discover, find, surprise. 3 draw level with, overtake, pass, reach. 4 clasp, clutch, grab, grasp, grip, intercept, seize, snatch, take hold of. **5** contract, develop, get, pick up. **6** comprehend, follow, grasp, hear, make out, perceive, understand, take in. ● *n.* **2** harvest, haul, take, yield. **3** acquisition, conquest, find, trophy. **4** difficulty, disadvantage, drawback, hitch, problem, snag, stumbling block. **5** bolt, clasp, clip, fastener, fastening, hook, latch, lock.

catching *adj.* infectious.

catchment area **1** area from which rainfall drains into a river. **2** area from which a hospital draws patients or a school draws pupils.

catchword *n.* catchphrase.

catchy *adj.* (**-ier, -iest**) (of a tune) pleasant and easy to remember.

catechism *n.* series of questions and answers.

catechize *v.* put a series of questions to.

categorical *adj.* absolute, explicit. □ **categorically** *adv.*

■ absolute, complete, decided, definite, direct, downright, emphatic, explicit, express, firm, flat, point-blank, positive, unambiguous, unconditional, unequivocal, unmitigated, unqualified.

categorize *v.* place in a category. □ **categorization** *n.*

category *n.* class of things.

■ class, grade, group, kind, league, order, rank, set, sort, type, variety.

cater *v.* **1** supply food. **2** provide what is needed or wanted. □ **caterer** *n.*

caterpillar *n.* larva of butterfly or moth. □ **Caterpillar track** [P.] steel band with treads, passing round a vehicle's wheels.

caterwaul *v.* howl like a cat.

catgut *n.* gut as thread.

catharsis *n.* **1** purgation. **2** emotional release. □ **cathartic** *adj.*

cathedral *n.* principal church of a diocese.

Catherine wheel rotating firework.

catheter *n.* tube inserted into the bladder to extract urine.

cathode *n.* electrode by which current leaves a device. □ **cathode ray** beam of electrons from the cathode of a vacuum tube.

catholic *adj.* **1** universal. **2** of wide sympathies or interests. **3** of all Churches or all Christians. **4** (**Catholic**) Roman Catholic. ● *n.* (**Catholic**) Roman Catholic. □ **Catholicism** *n.*

■ *adj.* **1** general, universal, widespread. **2** broad-minded, eclectic, inclusive, liberal, tolerant, varied, wide, wide-ranging.

cation *n.* positively charged ion.

catkin *n.* hanging flower of willow, hazel, etc.

catmint *n.* strong-smelling plant attractive to cats.

catnap *n.* short nap.

catnip *n.* catmint.

Catseye *n.* [P.] reflector stud on a road.

cattery *n.* (*pl.* **-ies**) boarding place for cats.

cattle *n.pl.* large animals with horns and cloven hoofs.

catty *adj.* (**-ier, -iest**) spiteful. □ **cattily** *adv.*, **cattiness** *n.*

catwalk *n.* narrow strip for walking on.

caucus *n.* **1** (often *derog.*) local committee of a political party. **2** (*US*) meeting of party leaders.

caught *see* **catch**.

cauldron *n.* large deep pot for boiling things in.

cauliflower *n.* cabbage with a white flower head.

caulk *v.* stop up (a ship's seams) with waterproof material.

causal *adj.* relating to cause (and effect). □ **causality** *n.*

causation *n.* causality.

cause *n.* **1** that which produces an effect. **2** reason or motive for action. **3** lawsuit. **4** principle supported. ● *v.* be the cause of.

■ *n.* **1** basis, genesis, origin, root, source; initiator, instigator, originator. **2** grounds, justification, motive, occasion, reason. ● *v.* bring about, create, effect, engender, generate, give rise to, induce, lead to, occasion, precipitate, produce, provoke, result in, trigger off.

causeway *n.* raised road across low or wet ground.

caustic *adj.* **1** burning, corrosive. **2** sarcastic, biting. ● *n.* caustic substance. □ **caustically** *adv.*

■ **2** biting, bitter, critical, cutting, mordant, sarcastic, sardonic, scathing, sharp.

cauterize *v.* burn (tissue) to destroy infection or stop bleeding. □ **cauterization** *n.*

caution *n.* **1** avoidance of rashness. **2** warning. ● *v.* **1** warn. **2** admonish. □ **cautionary** *adj.*

■ *n.* **1** care, carefulness, circumspection, forethought, heed, prudence, vigilance, wariness, watchfulness. **2** advice, caveat, counsel, warning. ● *v.* **1** advise, counsel, forewarn, warn. **2** admonish, reprimand, *colloq.* tell off, *colloq.* tick off.

cautious *adj.* having or showing caution. □ **cautiously** *adv.*
■ alert, *colloq.* cagey, careful, chary, circumspect, discreet, guarded, heedful, prudent, vigilant, wary, watchful.

cavalcade *n.* procession.

Cavalier *n.* supporter of Charles I in the English Civil War.

cavalier *adj.* arrogant, offhand.

cavalry *n.* troops who fight on horseback.

cave *n.* natural hollow. ●*v.* explore caves. □ **cave in 1** collapse. **2** yield.
■ *n.* cavern, grotto, hole, pothole. □ **cave in 1** buckle, collapse, crumble, crumple, give (way), subside. **2** capitulate, give in *or* up *or* way, submit, surrender, yield.

caveat /kávviat/ *n.* warning.

caveman *n.* person of prehistoric times living in a cave.

cavern *n.* large cave.

cavernous *adj.* like a cavern.

caviar *n.* pickled roe of sturgeon or other large fish.

cavil *v.* (**cavilled**) raise petty objections. ●*n.* petty objection.

cavity *n.* hollow within a solid body.
■ crater, gap, hole, hollow, pit.

cavort *v.* caper excitedly.

caw *n.* harsh cry of a rook etc. ●*v.* utter a caw.

cayenne *n.* hot red pepper.

cayman *n.* S. American alligator.

CB *abbr.* citizens' band.

cc *abbr.* cubic centimetre(s).

CD *abbr.* compact disc.

cease *v.* bring or come to an end, stop. □ **ceasefire** *n.* signal to stop firing guns.
■ desist (from), discontinue, *US* quit, refrain (from), stop, suspend, terminate; come to an end, die away, end, finish.

ceaseless *adj.* not ceasing.
■ constant, continual, continuous, endless, incessant, interminable, never-ending, non-stop, perpetual, unceasing, unending, unremitting.

cedar *n.* **1** evergreen tree. **2** its hard fragrant wood.

cede *v.* surrender (territory etc.).

cedilla *n.* mark written under c (ç) pronounced as s.

ceilidh /káyli/ *n.* informal gathering for music and dancing.

ceiling *n.* **1** surface of the top of a room. **2** upper limit or level.

celandine *n.* small wild plant with yellow flowers.

celebrate *v.* mark with or engage in festivities. □ **celebration** *n.*
■ commemorate, keep, observe, solemnize. □ **celebration** commemoration, observance, solemnization; festival, gala, jamboree, party; festivities, merrymaking, revelry.

celebrated *adj.* famous.

celebrity *n.* **1** famous person. **2** fame.
■ **1** luminary, notable, personage, personality, public figure, star. **2** eminence, fame, glory, prominence, stardom, renown.

celeriac *n.* variety of celery.

celerity *n.* swiftness.

celery *n.* plant with edible crisp juicy stems.

celestial *adj.* **1** of the sky or heavenly bodies. **2** heavenly.
■ **1** planetary, stellar. **2** divine, ethereal, heavenly, immortal, spiritual, sublime.

celibate *adj.* abstaining from sexual intercourse. □ **celibacy** *n.*

cell *n.* **1** small room for a monk or prisoner. **2** compartment in a honeycomb. **3** device for producing electric current chemically. **4** microscopic unit of living matter. **5** small group as a nucleus of political activities.

cellar *n.* **1** underground room. **2** stock of wine.

cello /chéllō/ *n.* bass instrument of the violin family. □ **cellist** *n.*

Cellophane *n.* [P.] thin transparent wrapping material.

celluloid *n.* plastic made from cellulose nitrate and camphor.

cellulose *n.* substance in plant tissues used in making plastics.

Celsius *adj.* of a scale of temperature on which water freezes at 0° and boils at 100°.

Celt *n.* member of an ancient European people or their descendants. □ **Celtic** *adj.*

cement *n.* **1** substance of lime and clay setting like stone. **2** adhesive. ●*v.* **1** join with cement. **2** unite firmly.

cemetery *n.* burial ground other than a churchyard.

cenotaph *n.* tomb-like monument to people buried elsewhere.

censer *n.* container for burning incense.

censor *n.* person authorized to examine letters, books, films, etc., and remove or ban anything regarded as harmful. ● *v.* remove or ban thus. □ **censorship** *n.*

censorious *adj.* severely critical.

censure *n.* severe criticism and rebuke. ● *v.* criticize and rebuke severely.
■ *n.* castigation, condemnation, criticism, stricture. ● *v.* admonish, berate, castigate, condemn, criticize, denounce, rebuke, reproach, scold, take to task, upbraid.

census *n.* official counting of population.

cent *n.* **1** 100th part of a dollar or other currency. **2** coin worth this.

centaur *n.* mythical creature half man, half horse.

centenarian *n.* person 100 years old or more.

centenary *n.* 100th anniversary.

centennial *adj.* of a centenary. ● *n.* (US) centenary.

centigrade *adj.* Celsius.

centilitre *n.* 100th of a litre.

centimetre *n.* 100th of a metre.

centipede *n.* small crawling creature with many legs.

central *adj.* **1** of, at, or forming a centre. **2** most important. □ **central heating** heating of a building from one source. **centrally** *adv.*, **centrality** *n.*
■ **1** inner, medial, mid, middle. **2** basic, cardinal, chief, crucial, essential, fundamental, key, main, major, primary, principal, vital.

centralize *v.* bring under the control of a central authority. □ **centralization** *n.*

centre *n.* middle point or part. ● *v.* (**centred**, **centring**) place in or at a centre.
■ *n.* core, focus, heart, hub, kernel, middle, nub, nucleus.

centrifugal *adj.* moving away from the centre.

centrifuge *n.* machine using centrifugal force for separating substances.

centripetal *adj.* moving towards the centre.

centurion *n.* commander in the ancient Roman army.

century *n.* **1** period of 100 years. **2** 100 runs at cricket.

cephalic *adj.* of the head.

cephalopod *n.* mollusc with tentacles (e.g. an octopus).

ceramic *adj.* of pottery or a similar substance. ● *n.* (**ceramics**) art of making pottery.

cereal *n.* **1** grass plant with edible grain. **2** this grain. **3** breakfast food made from it.

cerebral *adj.* **1** of the brain. **2** intellectual. □ **cerebrally** *adv.*

cerebrum *n.* main part of the brain.

ceremonial *adj.* of or used in ceremonies, formal. ● *n.* **1** ceremony. **2** rules for this.
■ *adj.* commemorative, ritual, state; ceremonious, dignified, formal, majestic, solemn, stately.

ceremonious *adj.* full of ceremony. □ **ceremoniously** *adv.*

ceremony *n.* **1** formal occasion. **2** formalities.
■ **1** ceremonial, rite(s), ritual, service; celebration, function, pageant. **2** conventions, formalities, protocol.

cerise /səreéz/ *adj.* & *n.* light red.

certain *adj.* **1** feeling sure. **2** indisputable. **3** that may be relied on to happen or be effective. **4** specific but not named. **5** some.
■ **1** assured, confident, convinced, positive, satisfied, sure. **2** definite, incontestable, incontrovertible, indubitable, irrefutable, undeniable, undisputed, undoubted, unquestionable. **3** bound, destined, fated, sure; dependable, infallible, reliable, unfailing. **4** unnamed, unspecified.

certainly *adv.* **1** without doubt. **2** yes.

certainty *n.* **1** being certain. **2** thing that is certain.
■ **1** assurance, certitude, confidence, conviction, sureness. **2** actuality, fact, reality, truth; *colloq.* cinch, foregone conclusion.

certificate *n.* official document attesting certain facts.

certify *v.* **1** declare formally. **2** officially declare insane. □ **certifiable** *adj.*, **certifiably** *adv.*
■ **1** affirm, attest (to), confirm, guarantee, swear (to), testify (to), verify, vouch for.

certitude *n.* feeling of certainty.

cerulean *adj.* sky-blue.

cervix *n.* **1** neck. **2** neck-like structure, esp. of the womb. □ **cervical** *adj.*

cessation *n.* ceasing.

cesspit *n.* (also **cesspool**) pit for liquid waste or sewage.

cetacean /sitáysh'n/ *adj.* & *n.* (member) of the whale family.

cf. *abbr.* compare.

CFC *abbr.* chlorofluorocarbon, gaseous compound that harms the earth's atmosphere.

chafe *v.* **1** warm by rubbing. **2** make or become sore by rubbing. **3** show irritation.

chafer *n.* large beetle.

chaff *n.* **1** corn husks separated from seed. **2** chopped hay and straw. **3** banter. ● *v.* banter, tease.

chaffinch *n.* European finch.

chafing dish heated pan for keeping food warm at the table.

chagrin *n.* annoyance and embarrassment.

chain *n.* **1** series of connected metal links. **2** (*pl.*) restraining force. **3** connected series or sequence. ● *v.* fasten with chain(s). □ **chain reaction** change causing further changes.
  ■ *n.* **2** (chains) bonds, fetters, shackles; constraints, restraints, restrictions. **3** combination, concatenation, sequence, series, set, string, succession, train; line, range, row. ● *v.* bind, confine, fasten, fetter, manacle, restrain, shackle, tie up.

chair *n.* **1** movable seat for one person. **2** (position of) chairman. **3** position of a professor. ● *v.* act as chairman of. □ **chairlift** *n.* series of chairs on a cable for carrying people up a mountain. **chairman, chairperson, chairwoman** *ns.* person who presides over a meeting or committee.

chaise longue /sháyz lóngg/ sofa with one armrest.

chalcedony *n.* type of quartz.

chalet /shállay/ *n.* **1** Swiss hut or cottage. **2** small villa. **3** small hut in a holiday camp etc.

chalice *n.* large goblet.

chalk *n.* **1** white soft limestone. **2** piece of this or similar coloured substance used for drawing. □ **chalky** *adj.*

challenge *n.* **1** call to try one's skill or strength. **2** demand to respond or identify oneself. **3** formal objection. **4** demanding task. ● *v.* **1** make a challenge to. **2** question the truth or rightness of. □ **challenger** *n.*
  ■ *v.* **1** dare, defy, invite. **2** contest, dispute, object to, oppose, protest against, query, question, take exception to.

chamber *n.* **1** hall used for meetings of an assembly. **2** (*old use*) room, bedroom. **3** (*pl.*) set of rooms. **4** cavity or compartment. □ **chamber music** music for performance in a room rather than a

hall. **chamber pot** bedroom receptacle for urine.

chamberlain *n.* official managing a royal or noble household.

chambermaid *n.* cleaner of hotel bedrooms.

chameleon /kəmméelian/ *n.* small lizard that changes colour according to its surroundings.

chamfer *v.* (chamfered) bevel the edge of.

chamois *n.* **1** /shámwaa/ small mountain antelope. **2** /shámmi/ a kind of soft leather.

champ *v.* **1** munch noisily. **2** show impatience.

champagne *n.* **1** sparkling white wine. **2** its pale straw colour.

champion *n.* **1** person or thing that defeats all others in a competition. **2** person who fights or speaks in support of another or of a cause. ● *v.* support as champion. □ **championship** *n.*
  ■ *n.* **1** prizewinner, title-holder, victor, winner. **2** advocate, backer, defender, patron, protector, supporter, upholder. ● *v.* back, defend, fight for, protect, stand up for, support, uphold.

chance *n.* **1** way things happen, luck. **2** unplanned occurrence. **3** likelihood. **4** opportunity. ● *adj.* happening by chance. ● *v.* **1** happen. **2** risk.
  ■ *n.* **1** destiny, fate, fortune, kismet, luck. **2** accident, coincidence, fluke. **3** likelihood, odds, possibility, probability, prospect. **4** occasion, opportunity, turn. ● *adj.* accidental, arbitrary, casual, coincidental, fortuitous, inadvertent, random, unexpected, unforeseen, unlooked-for, unplanned, unpremeditated. ● *v.* **1** befall, come about, happen, occur, take place. **2** hazard, risk, venture.

chancel *n.* part of a church near the altar.

chancellor *n.* **1** government minister in charge of the nation's budget. **2** state or law official of various other kinds. **3** nonresident head of a university. □ **chancellorship** *n.*

Chancery *n.* division of the High Court of Justice.

chancy *adj.* (**-ier, -iest**) risky.

chandelier *n.* hanging support for several lights.

chandler *n.* dealer in ropes, canvas, etc., for ships.

change *v.* **1** make or become different. **2** take or use another instead of, go from one to another. **3** put fresh clothes or coverings on. **4** get or give money or different currency for. ●*n.* **1** act or instance of changing. **2** money in small units or returned as balance. □ **changeable** *adj.*

■ *v.* **1** adapt, adjust, alter, amend, convert, modify, modulate, transfigure, transform, transmute; mutate, metamorphose; fluctuate, shift, oscillate, vary; affect, have an impact on, influence. **2** exchange, interchange, replace, swap, switch, substitute, transpose. ●*n.* **1** adaptation, adjustment, alteration, amendment, conversion, fluctuation, metamorphosis, modification, modulation, mutation, shift, swing, transfiguration, transformation, transition, transposition; U-turn, volte-face; exchange, interchange, replacement, substitution. **2** cash, coins, coppers, silver.

changeling *n.* child believed to be a substitute for another.

channel *n.* **1** stretch of water connecting two seas. **2** passage for liquid. **3** medium of communication. **4** band of broadcasting frequencies. ●*v.* (**channelled**) direct through a channel.

■ *n.* **1** sound, strait. **2** canal, conduit, ditch, duct, groove, gully, gutter, moat, pipe, sluice, trench, watercourse, waterway. **3** avenue, means, medium, method, path, route, way.

chant *n.* **1** melody for psalms. **2** monotonous singing. **3** rhythmic shout. ●*v.* **1** sing, esp. to a chant. **2** shout rhythmically.

chantry *n.* chapel founded for priests to sing masses for the founder's soul.

chaos *n.* great disorder. □ **chaotic** *adj.*, **chaotically** *adv.*

■ bedlam, confusion, disarray, disorder, disorganization, havoc, mayhem, pandemonium, shambles, tumult, turmoil, uproar. □ **chaotic** confused, disorderly, disorganized, haphazard, haywire, higgledy-piggledy, jumbled, topsy-turvy, untidy, upside down.

chap¹ *n.* (*colloq.*) man.

chap² *n.* crack in skin. ●*v.* (**chapped**) **1** cause chaps in. **2** suffer chaps.

chaparral *n.* (*US*) dense tangled brushwood.

chapatti *n.* (*pl.* **-is**) small flat cake of unleavened bread.

chapel *n.* **1** place used for Christian worship, other than a cathedral or par-

ish church. **2** place with a separate altar within a church.

chaperon *n.* person looking after another or others in public. ●*v.* act as chaperon to.

chaplain *n.* clergyman of an institution, private chapel, ship, regiment, etc. □ **chaplaincy** *n.*

chapter *n.* **1** division of a book. **2** canons of a cathedral.

char¹ *n.* charwoman.

char² *v.* (**charred**) make or become black by burning.

character *n.* **1** qualities making a person or thing what he, she, or it is. **2** moral strength. **3** person in a novel or play etc. **4** letter or sign used in writing, printing, etc. **5** noticeable or eccentric person. **6** reputation.

■ **1** disposition, make-up, nature, personality, spirit, temperament; attributes, features, properties, qualities, traits; distinctiveness, flavour, stamp. **2** decency, fibre, honesty, honour, integrity, morality, rectitude, respectability. **3** part, role. **4** figure, hieroglyph, letter, mark, rune, sign, symbol.

characteristic *adj. & n.* (feature) forming part of the character of a person or thing. □ **characteristically** *adv.*

■ *adj.* distinctive, distinguishing, idiosyncratic, representative, symptomatic, typical. ●*n.* aspect, attribute, feature, hallmark, idiosyncrasy, peculiarity, property, quality, symptom, trait.

characterize *v.* **1** describe the character of. **2** be characteristic of. □ **characterization** *n.*

■ **1** delineate, depict, describe, identify, mark, paint, portray, present, represent.

charade /ʃəraad/ *n.* **1** (*pl.*) game which involves guessing words from acted clues. **2** absurd pretence.

charcoal *n.* black substance made by burning wood slowly.

charge *n.* **1** price asked for goods or services. **2** accusation. **3** rushing attack. **4** task, duty. **5** custody. **6** person or thing entrusted. **7** quantity of explosive. **8** electricity contained in a substance. ●*v.* **1** ask (an amount) as a price. **2** ask (a person) for an amount as a price. **3** accuse formally. **4** give as a task or duty. **5** rush forward in attack. **6** load or fill with explosive. **7** give an electric charge to. □ **charge card** a kind of credit card. **in**

charge in command. **take charge** take control.
■ *n.* **1** cost, fare, fee, payment, price, rate, tariff, toll. **2** accusation, allegation, imputation, indictment. **3** assault, attack, foray, incursion, onslaught, raid, sally, sortie. **4** burden, duty, obligation, responsibility, task. **5** care, control, custody, guardianship, keeping, protection, safe-keeping, trust. **6** protégé, ward. ● *v.* **1** ask, claim, demand, expect. **2** bill, invoice. **3** accuse, arraign, impeach, indict. **4** entrust, trust; burden, saddle. **5** assail, assault, attack, rush, storm.

chargé d'affaires (*pl.* **-gés**) ambassador's deputy.

chariot *n.* two-wheeled horse-drawn vehicle used in ancient times in battle and in racing.

charioteer *n.* driver of a chariot.

charisma /karízma/ *n.* power to inspire or attract others. □ **charismatic** *adj.*

charitable *adj.* **1** generous to those in need. **2** lenient in judging others. **3** of or belonging to charities. □ **charitably** *adv.*
■ **1** beneficent, bountiful, generous, liberal, munificent, open-handed, philanthropic, public-spirited, unselfish. **2** kind, indulgent, lenient, magnanimous, sympathetic, tolerant.

charity *n.* **1** loving kindness. **2** lenience in judging others. **3** help given voluntarily to those in need. **4** organization etc. for helping those in need.
■ **1** altruism, beneficence, benevolence, generosity, humanity, kindness, love, philanthropy, unselfishness. **2** indulgence, lenience, magnanimity, sympathy, tolerance, understanding. **3** aid, alms, assistance, help, largesse, relief, support.

charlady *n.* charwoman.

charlatan *n.* person falsely claiming to be an expert.

charlotte *n.* pudding of cooked fruit with breadcrumbs.

charm *n.* **1** attractiveness, power of arousing love or admiration. **2** act, object, or words believed to have magic power. **3** small ornament worn on a bracelet etc. ● *v.* **1** give pleasure to. **2** influence by personal charm or as if by magic. □ **charmer** *n.*
■ *n.* allure, appeal, attraction, attractiveness, charisma, fascination, magnetism, pull, seductiveness. **2** amulet, mascot, talisman; incantation, spell. ● *v.* **1** captivate, delight, enrapture, enchant, entrance,

please. **2** bewitch, enthral, fascinate, hold spellbound, hypnotize, mesmerize, seduce.

charming *adj.* delightful.

charnel house place containing corpses or bones.

chart *n.* **1** map for navigators. **2** table, diagram, or outline map. **3** list of recordings that are currently most popular. ● *v.* make a chart of.

charter *n.* **1** official document granting rights. **2** chartering of aircraft etc. ● *v.* **1** grant a charter to. **2** let or hire (an aircraft, ship, or vehicle). □ **chartered accountant** one qualified according to the rules of an association holding a royal charter.

chartreuse /shaartrő́z/ *n.* fragrant green or yellow liqueur.

charwoman *n.* woman employed to clean a house etc.

chary *adj.* (**-ier, -iest**) cautious.

chase *v.* go quickly after in order to capture, overtake, or drive away. ● *n.* **1** chasing, pursuit. **2** hunting. **3** steeplechase.
■ *v.* follow, hound, hunt, pursue, run after, track, trail. ● *n.* **1** hunt, pursuit, search.

chasm *n.* deep cleft.
■ abyss, canyon, cleft, crater, crevasse, fissure, hole, opening, pit, ravine, rift, split.

chassis /shássi/ *n.* (*pl.* **chassis**) base frame of a vehicle.

chaste *adj.* **1** celibate. **2** virtuous. **3** simple in style, not ornate. □ **chastely** *adv.*
■ **1** celibate, pure, virginal, unsullied. **2** decent, good, irreproachable, moral, sinless, virtuous. **3** austere, plain, severe, simple, unadorned.

chasten *v.* **1** discipline by punishment. **2** subdue the pride of.
■ **1** castigate, chastise, discipline, punish. **2** humble, subdue.

chastise *v.* **1** rebuke. **2** punish, beat. □ **chastisement** *n.*
■ **1** berate, castigate, chide, rebuke, reprimand, reproach, reprove, scold, take to task, upbraid. **2** castigate, chasten, discipline, punish; beat, cane, flog, spank, thrash, whip.

chastity *n.* being chaste.

chat *n.* informal conversation. ● *v.* (**chatted**) have a chat.
■ *n.* chatter, conversation, gossip, *colloq.* natter, talk, tête-à-tête. ● *v.* chatter, gossip, *colloq.* natter, prattle, talk.

chateau n. (pl. **-eaux**) French castle or large country house.

chatelaine n. mistress of a large house.

chattel n. movable possession.

chatter v. 1 talk quickly and continuously about unimportant matters. 2 (of teeth) rattle together. ● n. chattering talk.

chatterbox n. talkative person.

chatty adj. (**-ier, -iest**) 1 fond of chatting. 2 resembling chat.

chauffeur n. person employed to drive a car.

chauvinism n. exaggerated patriotism. □ **male chauvinism** prejudiced belief in male superiority over women. **chauvinist** n., **chauvinistic** adj.

cheap adj. 1 low in cost or value. 2 poor in quality. □ **cheaply** adv., **cheapness** n.
■ 1 inexpensive, knock-down, low-priced, reasonable. 2 base, inferior, poor, second-rate, shoddy, tawdry, trashy, worthless.

cheapen v. 1 make or become cheap. 2 degrade.

cheat v. 1 deceive or trick. 2 gain unfair advantage. ● n. 1 person who cheats. 2 deception.
■ v. 1 colloq. bamboozle, beguile, sl. con, deceive, defraud, double-cross, dupe, colloq. fiddle, fleece, hoodwink, colloq. rip off, short-change, swindle, take in, trick. ● n. 1 charlatan, deceiver, fraud, impostor, quack, swindler. 2 sl. con, confidence trick, deception, colloq. fiddle, colloq. rip-off, ruse, swindle, trick.

check[1] v. 1 test or examine, inspect. 2 stop, slow the motion (of). ● n. 1 inspection. 2 pause. 3 restraint. 4 exposure of a chess king to capture. 5 (US) bill in a restaurant. 6 (US) cheque. □ **check in** register on arrival. **check out** register on departure or dispatch. **check-out** n. desk where goods are paid for in a supermarket. **checker** n.
■ v. 1 examine, go over, inspect, investigate, look into, monitor, scrutinize, test; authenticate, confirm, corroborate, validate, verify. 2 arrest, brake, control, curb, halt, slow (down), stanch, stem, stop; block, hamper, hinder, impede, obstruct; contain, hold back, repress, restrain. ● n. 1 examination, inspection, investigation, colloq. once-over, scrutiny, test. 2 break, delay, halt, hesitation, interruption, pause, stop, stoppage. 3 constraint, curb, hindrance, impediment, restraint, restriction.

check[2] n. pattern of squares or crossing lines. □ **checked** adj.

checkmate n. 1 situation in chess where capture of a king is inevitable. 2 complete defeat, deadlock. ● v. 1 put into checkmate. 2 defeat, foil.

cheek n. 1 side of the face below the eye. 2 impudent speech, arrogance. ● v. speak cheekily to. □ **cheek by jowl** close together.

cheeky adj. (**-ier, -iest**) showing cheerful lack of respect. □ **cheekily** adv.
■ disrespectful, forward, impertinent, impudent, irreverent, pert, presumptuous, rude, saucy.

cheep n. weak shrill cry like that of a young bird. ● v. make this cry.

cheer n. 1 shout of applause. 2 cheerfulness. ● v. 1 utter a cheer, applaud with a cheer. 2 gladden. □ **cheer up** make or become more cheerful.
■ n. 1 cry, hooray, hurrah, shout, whoop. 2 cheerfulness, gaiety, gladness, happiness, joy. ● v. 1 applaud, clap, shout, whoop, yell. 2 colloq. buck up, buoy up, cheer up, comfort, encourage, gladden, hearten, uplift.

cheerful adj. 1 in good spirits. 2 pleasantly bright. □ **cheerfully** adv., **cheerfulness** n.
■ 1 buoyant, cheery, chirpy, exuberant, gay, glad, happy, jaunty, jolly, jovial, joyful, light-hearted, merry, optimistic, perky, sunny, colloq. upbeat. 2 appealing, attractive, bright, gay, pleasant.

cheerless adj. gloomy, dreary.
■ bleak, dark, depressing, dingy, dismal, dispiriting, drab, dreary, gloomy, grim, melancholy, miserable, sombre.

cheery adj. (**-ier, -iest**) cheerful.

cheese n. food made from pressed milk curds. □ **cheese-paring** adj. stingy.

cheeseburger n. hamburger with cheese on it.

cheesecake n. 1 open tart filled with flavoured cream cheese. 2 (sl.) sexually stimulating display of women.

cheesecloth n. thin loosely-woven cotton fabric.

cheetah n. a kind of leopard.

chef n. professional cook.

chemical adj. of or made by chemistry. ● n. substance obtained by or used in a chemical process. □ **chemically** adv.

chemise n. woman's loose-fitting undergarment or dress.

chemist *n.* **1** expert in chemistry. **2** dealer in medicinal drugs.

chemistry *n.* **1** study of substances and their reactions. **2** structure and properties of a substance.

chemotherapy *n.* treatment of disease by drugs etc.

chenille *n.* velvety fabric.

cheque *n.* **1** written order to a bank to pay out money from an account. **2** printed form for this. □ **cheque card** card guaranteeing payment of cheques.

chequer *n.* pattern of squares, esp. of alternating colours.

chequered *adj.* **1** marked with a chequer pattern. **2** having frequent changes of fortune.

cherish *v.* **1** tend lovingly. **2** be fond of. **3** cling to (hopes etc.).

■ **1** care for, look after, nurse, protect, take care of, tend. **2** hold dear, love, prize, treasure, value.

cheroot *n.* cigar with both ends open.

cherry *n.* **1** small soft round fruit with a stone. **2** tree bearing this. **3** deep red.

cherub *n.* **1** (*pl.* **cherubim**) angelic being. **2** (in art) chubby infant with wings. **3** angelic child. □ **cherubic** *adj.*

chervil *n.* herb with aniseed flavour.

chess *n.* game for two players using 32 **chessmen** on a chequered **chessboard** with 64 squares.

chest *n.* **1** large strong box. **2** upper front surface of the body. □ **chest of drawers** piece of furniture with drawers for clothes etc.

chesterfield *n.* sofa with a padded back, seat, and ends.

chestnut *n.* **1** tree with a hard brown nut. **2** this nut. **3** reddish-brown. **4** horse of this colour. **5** (*colloq.*) old joke or anecdote.

chevron *n.* V-shaped symbol.

chew *v.* work or grind between the teeth.

■ bite, champ, crunch, gnaw, masticate, munch, nibble.

chewing gum flavoured gum used for prolonged chewing.

chewy *adj.* (**-ier, -iest**) needing much chewing. □ **chewiness** *n.*

chiaroscuro /kiaáraskoórō/ *n.* **1** light and shade effects. **2** use of contrast.

chic *adj.* stylish and elegant. ● *n.* stylishness, elegance.

■ *adj.* elegant, fashionable, modish, sophisticated, stylish, tasteful.

chicane /shikáyn/ *n.* barriers on a motor racing course.

chicanery *n.* trickery.

chick *n.* newly hatched bird.

chicken *n.* **1** young domestic fowl. **2** its flesh as food. ● *adj.* (*colloq.*) cowardly. ● *v.* **chicken out** (*colloq.*) withdraw through cowardice. □ **chicken feed** (*colloq.*) trifling amount of money. **chickenpox** *n.* disease with a rash of small red blisters.

chickpea *n.* pea with yellow seeds used as a vegetable.

chicory *n.* blue-flowered plant grown for its salad leaves.

chide *v.* (**chided** or **chid, chidden**) rebuke.

chief *n.* **1** leader, ruler. **2** person with the highest rank. ● *adj.* **1** highest in rank. **2** most important.

■ *n. colloq.* boss, captain, commander, director, *colloq.* gaffer, governor, head, leader, manager, master, overseer, president, principal, ringleader, ruler, superintendent, supervisor, supremo, *colloq.* top dog. ● *adj.* **1** first, foremost, greatest, head, highest, leading, premier, senior, supreme, top. **2** cardinal, central, essential, fundamental, key, main, major, overriding, paramount, predominant, primary, prime, principal.

chiefly *adv.* mainly.

■ by and large, especially, essentially, largely, mainly, mostly, on the whole, particularly, predominantly, primarily, principally.

chieftain *n.* chief of a clan or tribe.

chiffon *n.* diaphanous fabric.

chignon /sheényoN/ *n.* coil of hair at the back of the head.

chihuahua /chiwaáwə/ *n.* very small smooth-haired dog.

chilblain *n.* painful swelling caused by exposure to cold.

child *n.* (*pl.* **children**) **1** young human being. **2** son or daughter. □ **childhood** *n.*, **childless** *adj.*

■ **1** adolescent, babe, baby, boy, *derog.* brat, chit, girl, infant, juvenile, *colloq.* kid, lad, lass, minor, stripling, teenager, toddler, tot, urchin, youngster, youth. **2** daughter, descendant, heir, son; (**children**) family, issue, offspring, progeny. □ **childhood** adolescence, boyhood, girlhood, infancy, minority, puberty, teens, youth.

childbirth *n.* process of giving birth to a child.

childish adj. **1** of or like a child. **2** immature, silly.
 ■ **1** childlike, boyish, girlish, youthful. **2** babyish, immature, infantile, juvenile, puerile, silly.

childlike adj. simple and innocent.
 ■ artless, guileless, ingenuous, innocent, naive, simple, trustful, unsophisticated, youthful.

chill n. **1** unpleasant coldness. **2** illness with feverish shivering. ● adj. chilly. ● v. **1** make or become chilly. **2** preserve (food or drink) by cooling.

chilli n. (pl. **-ies**) dried pod of red pepper.

chilly adj. (**-ier, -iest**) **1** rather cold. **2** unfriendly in manner.
 ■ **1** cold, cool, crisp, frosty, icy, colloq. nippy, raw, wintry. **2** aloof, cold, cool, distant, frigid, frosty, reserved, standoffish, unforthcoming, unfriendly.

chime n. **1** tuned set of bells. **2** series of notes from these. ● v. ring as a chime. □ **chime in** put in a remark.

chimera /kīmeerə/ n. **1** legendary monster with a lion's head, goat's body, and serpent's tail. **2** fantastic product of the imagination.

chimney n. (pl. **-eys**) structure for carrying off smoke or gases. □ **chimney pot** pipe on top of a chimney.

chimpanzee n. African ape.

chin n. front of the lower jaw.

china n. **1** fine earthenware, porcelain. **2** things made of this.

chinchilla n. **1** S. American rodent. **2** its soft grey fur.

chine n. **1** animal's backbone. **2** ravine in southern England.

Chinese adj. & n. (native, language) of China.

chink[1] n. narrow opening, slit.
 ■ aperture, cleft, crack, cranny, crevice, fissure, gap, opening, rift, slit, split.

chink[2] n. sound of glasses or coins striking together. ● v. make this sound.

chintz n. glazed cotton cloth used for furnishings.

chip n. **1** small piece cut or broken off something hard. **2** fried oblong strip of potato. **3** counter used in gambling. ● v. (**chipped**) **1** break or cut the edge or surface of. **2** shape in this way. □ **chip in** (colloq.) **1** interrupt. **2** contribute money.

chipboard n. board made of compressed wood chips.

chipmunk n. striped squirrel-like animal of N. America.

chipolata n. small sausage.

chiropody /kiróppədi/ n. treatment of minor ailments of the feet. □ **chiropodist** n.

chiropractic /kīrōpráktik/ n. treatment of physical disorders by manipulation of the spinal column. □ **chiropractor** n.

chirp n. short sharp sound made by a small bird or grasshopper. ● v. make this sound.

chirpy adj. (**-ier, -iest**) cheerful.

chisel n. tool with a sharp bevelled end for shaping wood or stone etc. ● v. (**chiselled**) cut with this.

chit[1] n. young child.

chit[2] n. short written note.

chivalry n. courtesy and consideration, inclination to help weaker people. □ **chivalrous** adj.
 ■ □ **chivalrous** considerate, courteous, courtly, gallant, gentlemanly, gracious, kind, well-mannered.

chive n. small herb with onion-flavoured leaves.

chivvy v. urge to hurry.

chloride n. compound of chlorine and another element.

chlorinate v. treat or sterilize with chlorine. □ **chlorination** n.

chlorine n. poisonous gas used for bleaching and disinfecting.

chloroform n. liquid giving off vapour that causes unconsciousness when inhaled.

chlorophyll n. green colouring matter in plants.

choc n. (colloq.) chocolate. □ **choc ice** bar of ice cream coated with chocolate.

chock n. block or wedge for preventing something from moving. ● v. wedge with chock(s). □ **chock-a-block** adj. & adv. crammed, crowded together.

chocolate n. **1** edible substance made from cacao seeds. **2** sweet made or coated with this, drink made with this. **3** dark brown.

choice n. **1** act of choosing. **2** power to choose. **3** variety from which to choose. **4** person or thing chosen. ● adj. of especially good quality. □ **choicely** adv.
 ■ n. **1** election, pick, selection. **2** alternative, option. **3** assortment, diversity, range, selection, variety. ● adj. excellent, exceptional, fine, first-class, first-rate, prime, outstanding, splendid, superior.

choir n. **1** group of singers, esp. in church. **2** part of a church where these sit, chancel.

choirboy *n.* boy singer in a church choir.

choke *v.* **1** stop (a person) breathing by squeezing or blocking the windpipe. **2** be unable to breathe. **3** clog, block. ● *n.* valve controlling the flow of air into a petrol engine.
■ *v.* **1** asphyxiate, garrotte, smother, strangle, suffocate, throttle. **2** gag, retch. **3** block, clog, congest, constrict, dam, fill, obstruct, silt up.

choker *n.* close-fitting necklace.

cholera *n.* serious often fatal bacterial disease.

choleric *adj.* easily angered.

cholesterol *n.* fatty animal substance thought to cause hardening of arteries.

choose *v.* (**chose, chosen**) **1** select out of a greater number. **2** decide.
■ **1** adopt, decide on, go for, opt for, pick, plump for, select, single out. **2** decide, determine, elect, make up one's mind, resolve.

choosy *adj.* (**-ier, -iest**) (*colloq.*) careful in choosing, hard to please. □ **choosiness** *n.*

chop *v.* (**chopped**) **1** cut by a blow with an axe or knife. **2** hit with a short downward movement. ● *n.* **1** chopping stroke. **2** thick slice of meat, usu. including a rib.

chopper *n.* **1** chopping tool. **2** (*colloq.*) helicopter.

choppy *adj.* (**-ier, -iest**) **1** full of short broken waves. **2** jerky.

chopstick *n.* each of a pair of sticks used in China, Japan, etc., to lift food to the mouth.

chop suey Chinese dish of meat or fish fried with vegetables.

choral *adj.* for or sung by a chorus.

chorale *n.* choral composition using the words of a hymn.

chord[1] *n.* **1** string of a harp etc. **2** straight line joining two points on a curve.

chord[2] *n.* combination of notes sounded together.

chore *n.* routine task.

choreography *n.* composition of stage dances. □ **choreographer** *n.*, **choreographic** *adj.*

chorister *n.* member of a choir.

chortle *n.* gleeful chuckle. ● *v.* utter a chortle.

chorus *n.* **1** group of singers. **2** simultaneous utterance. **3** refrain of a song. **4** group of singing dancers in a musical comedy etc. ● *v.* say as a group.

chose, chosen see **choose**.

choux pastry /shōō/ light pastry for making small cakes.

chow *n.* **1** long-haired dog of a Chinese breed. **2** (*sl.*) food.

chowder *n.* stew of shellfish with bacon and onions etc.

chow mein Chinese dish of fried noodles and shredded meat etc.

christen *v.* **1** admit to the Christian Church by baptism. **2** name.

Christendom *n.* all Christians or Christian countries.

Christian *adj.* **1** of or believing in Christianity. **2** kindly, humane. ● *n.* believer in Christianity. □ **Christian name** personal name given at a christening. **Christian Science** religious system by which health and healing are sought by prayer alone.

Christianity *n.* religion based on the teachings of Christ.

Christmas *n.* festival (25 Dec.) commemorating Christ's birth. □ **Christmas tree** tree decorated at Christmas.

chromatic *adj.* of colour, in colours. □ **chromatic scale** music scale proceeding by semitones. **chromatically** *adv.*

chrome *n.* **1** chromium. **2** yellow pigment from a compound of chrome.

chromium *n.* metallic element that does not rust.

chromosome *n.* thread-like structure carrying genes in animal and plant cells.

chronic *adj.* **1** (of a disease) long-lasting. **2** (of a patient) having a chronic illness. **3** (*colloq.*) bad. □ **chronically** *adv.*

chronicle *n.* record of events. ● *v.* record in a chronicle. □ **chronicler** *n.*
■ *n.* account, annals, archive, diary, history, journal, narrative, record, story.

chronological *adj.* arranged in the order in which things occurred. □ **chronologically** *adv.*

chronology *n.* arrangement of events in order of occurrence.

chronometer *n.* time-measuring instrument.

chrysalis *n.* **1** form of an insect in the stage between larva and adult insect. **2** case enclosing it.

chrysanthemum *n.* garden plant flowering in autumn.

chub *n.* river fish.

chubby *adj.* (**-ier**, **-iest**) round and plump. □ **chubbiness** *n.*
■ dumpy, fat, plump, podgy, pudgy, roly-poly, stout, tubby.

chuck¹ *v.* (*colloq.*) throw carelessly or casually.

chuck² *n.* **1** part of a lathe holding the drill. **2** part of a drill holding the bit. **3** cut of beef from neck to ribs.

chuckle *n.* quiet laugh. ● *v.* utter a chuckle.

chug *v.* (**chugged**) make or move with a dull short repeated sound. ● *n.* this sound.

chukka *n.* period of play in a polo game.

chum *n.* (*colloq.*) close friend. □ **chummy** *adj.*

chump *n.* (*colloq.*) foolish person. □ **chump chop** chop from the thick end of a loin of mutton.

chunk *n.* **1** thick piece. **2** substantial amount.

chunky *adj.* (**-ier**, **-iest**) **1** short and thick. **2** in chunks, containing chunks. □ **chunkiness** *n.*

church *n.* **1** building for public Christian worship. **2** religious service in this. **3** (**the Church**) Christians collectively, particular denomination of these.

churchwarden *n.* parish representative, assisting with church business.

churchyard *n.* enclosed land round a church, used for burials.

churlish *adj.* ill-mannered, surly.

churn *n.* **1** machine in which milk is beaten to make butter. **2** very large milk can. ● *v.* **1** beat (milk) or make (butter) in a churn. **2** stir or swirl violently. □ **churn out** produce rapidly.

chute *n.* slide for sending things to a lower level.

chutney *n.* (*pl.* **-eys**) seasoned mixture of fruit, vinegar, spices, etc., eaten with meat or cheese.

cicada *n.* chirping insect resembling a grasshopper.

cicatrice *n.* scar.

cider *n.* fermented drink made from apples.

cigar *n.* roll of tobacco leaf for smoking.

cigarette *n.* roll of shredded tobacco in thin paper for smoking.

cinch *n.* (*colloq.*) **1** certainty. **2** easy task.

cinder *n.* piece of partly burnt coal or wood.

cine *adj.* cinematographic.

cinema *n.* **1** theatre where films are shown. **2** films as an art form or industry.

cinematography *n.* art of making films. □ **cinematographic** *adj.*

cinnamon *n.* spice made from the bark of a south-east Asian tree.

cipher *n.* **1** symbol 0 representing nought or zero. **2** numeral. **3** person of no importance. **4** secret or disguised writing.

circa *prep.* about.

circle *n.* **1** perfectly round plane figure. **2** group with similar interests. **3** curved tier of seats at a theatre etc. ● *v.* **1** move in a circle. **2** form a circle round.
■ *n.* **1** disc, ring, round. **2** clique, coterie, faction, group, set, society. ● *v.* **1** gyrate, loop, orbit, revolve, rotate, spin, spiral. **2** encircle, enclose, encompass, girdle, hem in, ring, surround.

circlet *n.* **1** small circle. **2** circular band worn as an ornament.

circuit *n.* **1** line, route, or distance round a place. **2** path of an electric current.
■ **1** lap, orbit, revolution.

circuitous *adj.* roundabout, indirect. □ **circuitously** *adv.*
■ indirect, meandering, roundabout, serpentine, tortuous, twisting, winding.

circuitry *n.* circuits.

circular *adj.* shaped like or moving round a circle. ● *n.* letter or leaflet sent to a circle of people. □ **circularity** *n.*

circulate *v.* **1** go or send round. **2** mingle among guests etc.
■ **1** course, flow, go round, move round; advertise, broadcast, disseminate, distribute, issue, make known, promulgate, publicize, send round, spread. **2** fraternize, mingle, mix, socialize.

circulation *n.* **1** movement from and back to a starting point, esp. that of blood to and from the heart. **2** transmission, distribution. **3** number of copies sold.

circumcise *v.* cut off the foreskin of. □ **circumcision** *n.*

circumference *n.* **1** boundary of a circle. **2** distance round this.

circumflex accent *n.* the accent (ˆ).

circumlocution *n.* roundabout, verbose, or evasive expression. □ **circumlocutory** *adj.*

circumnavigate *v.* sail round. □ **circumnavigation** *n.*

circumscribe *v.* **1** draw a line round. **2** restrict.

circumspect *adj.* cautious and watchful, wary. □ **circumspection** *n.*, **circumspectly** *adv.*

circumstance *n.* occurrence or fact.
■ affair, episode, event, fact, happening, incident, occasion, occurrence, situation.

circumstantial *adj.* **1** detailed. **2** consisting of facts that suggest something but do not prove it.

circumvent *v.* evade (a difficulty etc.). □ **circumvention** *n.*

circus *n.* travelling show with performing animals, acrobats, etc.

cirrhosis /sirṓsiss/ *n.* disease of the liver.

cirrus *n.* (*pl.* **cirri**) high wispy white cloud.

cistern *n.* tank for storing water.

citadel *n.* fortress overlooking a city.

cite *v.* quote or mention as an example etc. □ **citation** *n.*
■ adduce, bring up, mention, name, quote, refer to.

citizen *n.* **1** inhabitant of a city. **2** person with full rights in a country. □ **citizen's band** system of local intercommunication by radio. **citizenship** *n.*
■ **2** denizen, inhabitant, national, native, resident, subject.

citric acid acid in the juice of lemons, limes, etc.

citrus *n.* tree of a group including lemon, orange, etc.

city *n.* **1** important town. **2** town with special rights given by charter.
■ **1** borough, conurbation, metropolis, municipality, town.

civet *n.* **1** cat-like animal of central Africa. **2** musky substance obtained from its glands.

civic *adj.* of a city or citizenship.

civil *adj.* **1** of ordinary citizens, not of the armed forces or the Church. **2** polite and obliging. □ **civil engineering** designing and construction of roads, bridges, etc. **Civil List** annual allowance for the sovereign's household expenses. **civil servant** employee of the **civil service**, government departments other than the armed forces. **civil war** war between citizens of the same country. **civilly** *adv.*
■ **1** civilian, lay, non-military, secular. **2** affable, civilized, cordial, courteous, gracious, obliging, pleasant, polite, respectful, urbane, well-mannered.

civilian *n.* & *adj.* (of) person(s) not in the armed forces.

civility *n.* politeness.

civilization *n.* **1** advanced stage or system of social development. **2** peoples regarded as having achieved this. **3** making or becoming civilized.

civilize *v.* **1** improve the behaviour of. **2** bring out of a primitive stage of society.

clack *n.* short sharp sound. ● *v.* make this sound.

clad *adj.* clothed.

cladding *n.* boards or metal plates as a protective covering.

claim *v.* **1** demand as one's right. **2** assert. ● *n.* **1** demand. **2** assertion. **3** right or title.
■ *v.* **1** ask for, demand, exact, insist on, request, require. **2** affirm, allege, assert, contend, declare, insist, maintain, profess, state. ● *n.* **1** demand, petition, request, requisition. **2** affirmation, assertion, contention, declaration.

claimant *n.* person making a claim.

clairvoyance *n.* power of seeing the future. □ **clairvoyant** *n.*

clam *n.* shellfish with a hinged shell. ● *v.* (**clammed**) **clam up** (*colloq.*) refuse to talk.

clamber *v.* climb with difficulty.

clammy *adj.* (**-ier**, **-iest**) unpleasantly moist and sticky.
■ damp, dank, humid, moist, muggy, sticky, sweaty.

clamour *n.* **1** loud confused noise. **2** loud protest etc. □ **clamorous** *adj.*
■ **1** babel, commotion, din, hubbub, hullabaloo, noise, outcry, racket, uproar.

clamp *n.* **1** device for holding things tightly. **2** device for immobilizing an illegally parked car. ● *v.* **1** grip with a clamp, fix firmly. **2** immobilize an illegally parked car with a clamp. □ **clamp down on** become firmer about, put a stop to.

clan *n.* group of families with a common ancestor. □ **clannish** *adj.*
■ dynasty, family, house, line, tribe.

clandestine *adj.* secret.

clang *n.* loud ringing sound. ● *v.* make this sound.

clanger *n.* (*sl.*) blunder.

clangour *n.* clanging noise.

clank *n.* sound like metal striking metal. ● *v.* make or cause to make this sound.

clap *v.* (**clapped**) **1** strike the palms together, esp. in applause. **2** put or place quickly or vigorously. ● *n.* **1** act or

sound of clapping. **2** explosive noise, esp. of thunder. □ **clapped out** (sl.) worn-out.
■ v. **1** applaud, cheer. **2** fling, place, put, slap, colloq. stick.

clapper n. tongue or striker of a bell.

clapperboard n. device in film-making for making a sharp clap to synchronize picture and sound at the start of a scene.

claptrap n. insincere talk.

claret n. a dry red wine.

clarify v. make or become clear. □ **clarification** n.
■ clear up, elucidate, explain, make plain, simplify, spell out.

clarinet n. woodwind instrument with finger-holes and keys. □ **clarinettist** n.

clarion adj. loud, rousing.

clarity n. clearness.

clash n. **1** conflict. **2** discordant sounds or colours. ● v. **1** make a clashing sound. **2** come into conflict, be at variance.
■ n. **1** altercation, argument, conflict, disagreement, dispute, fight, quarrel, squabble. ● v. **1** bang, clang, clank, crash, smash. **2** argue, conflict, differ, disagree, dispute, quarrel, squabble.

clasp n. **1** device for fastening things, with interlocking parts. **2** grasp, handshake. ● v. **1** fasten, join with a clasp. **2** grasp, embrace closely.
■ n. **1** brooch, buckle, catch, clip, fastener, fastening, hook, pin. **2** embrace, grasp, grip, handshake, hold, hug. ● v. **1** clip, fasten, pin, secure. **2** clutch, embrace, grasp, grip, hold, hug, seize, take hold of.

class n. **1** set of people or things with characteristics in common. **2** rank of society. **3** high quality. **4** set of students taught together. ● v. place in a class.
■ n. **1** category, denomination, genre, genus, group, kind, league, set, sort, species, type. **2** caste, grade, level, order, rank, stratum. ● v. categorize, classify, grade, group, order, rank, rate.

classic adj. **1** of recognized high quality. **2** typical. **3** having enduring worth. **4** simple in style. ● n. **1** classic author or work etc. **2** (pl.) study of ancient Greek and Roman literature, history, etc. □ **classicism** n., **classicist** n.
■ adj. excellent, exemplary, first-rate, noteworthy, outstanding, superior. **2** archetypal, standard, typical. **3** ageless, enduring, immortal, time-honoured, timeless, undying, vintage.

classical adj. **1** classic. **2** of the ancient Greeks and Romans. **3** traditional and standard. □ **classically** adv.

classify v. **1** arrange systematically, class. **2** designate as officially secret. □ **classifiable** adj., **classification** n.
■ **1** arrange, catalogue, categorize, class, grade, group, order, organize, pigeon-hole, sort, systematize, tabulate.

classroom n. room where a class of students is taught.

classy adj. (colloq.) superior.

clatter n. rattling sound. ● v. make this sound.

clause n. **1** single part in a treaty, law, or contract. **2** distinct part of a sentence, with its own verb.

claustrophobia n. abnormal fear of being in an enclosed space. □ **claustrophobic** adj.

clavichord n. early small keyboard instrument.

claw n. **1** pointed nail on an animal's or bird's foot. **2** claw-like device for gripping and lifting things. ● v. scratch or pull with a claw or hand.

clay n. stiff sticky earth, used for making bricks and pottery. □ **clay pigeon** breakable disc thrown up as a target for shooting. **clayey** adj.

claymore n. Scottish two-edged broadbladed sword.

clean adj. free from dirt or impurities, not soiled or used. ● v. make clean. □ **cleaner** n., **cleanly** adv.
■ adj. decontaminated, disinfected, pure, purified, sanitary, sterile, sterilized, uncontaminated, undefiled, unpolluted, unsoiled, unstained, unsullied, untainted; laundered, scrubbed, washed; immaculate, spotless, unmarked, untouched, unused. ● v. cleanse, launder, mop, scour, scrub, sponge, sweep, wash, wipe.

cleanly /klénli/ adj. attentive to cleanness. □ **cleanliness** n.

cleanse /klenz/ v. make clean. □ **cleanser** n.

clear adj. **1** not clouded. **2** transparent. **3** convinced. **4** not confused or doubtful. **5** easily seen, heard, or understood. **6** not obstructed. ● v. **1** make or become clear. **2** prove innocent. **3** get past or over. **4** make as net profit. □ **clear off** (colloq.) go away. **clear out 1** empty. **2** remove. **3** (colloq.) go away. **clearly** adv.
■ adj. **1** cloudless, fair, fine, sunny. **2** crystalline, limpid, pellucid, translucent, transparent. **3** assured, certain, confident,

convinced, positive, sure. **4** definite, evident, incontrovertible, indisputable, manifest, obvious, palpable, patent, plain, undeniable, unmistakable. **5** distinct, sharp, vivid, well-defined; legible, readable, coherent, comprehensible, explicit, intelligible, lucid, precise, unambiguous, understandable. **6** free, open, passable, unblocked, unobstructed. ● v. **1** brighten, lighten; clarify, purify; open up, unblock, unclog. **2** absolve, acquit, exonerate, vindicate. **3** jump over, leap over, vault over.

clearance n. **1** clearing. **2** permission. **3** space allowed for one object to pass another.

clearing n. space cleared of trees in a forest.

clearway n. road where vehicles must not stop.

cleat n. projecting piece for fastening ropes to.

cleavage n. **1** split, separation. **2** hollow between full breasts.

cleave v. (**cleaved**, **clove**, or **cleft**; **cloven** or **cleft**) split.

cleaver n. butcher's chopper.

clef n. symbol on a stave in music, showing the pitch of notes.

cleft adj. & n. split.

clematis n. climbing plant with showy flowers.

clemency n. **1** mildness. **2** mercy. □ **clement** adj.

clementine n. a kind of small orange.

clench v. close tightly.

clergy n. people ordained for religious duties. □ **clergyman** n., **clergywoman** n.

cleric n. member of the clergy.

clerical adj. **1** of clerks. **2** of clergy.

■ **1** secretarial, white-collar. **2** canonical, ecclesiastical, episcopal, ministerial, priestly.

clerk n. person employed to do written work in an office.

clever adj. **1** quick to learn and understand. **2** skilful. **3** ingenious. □ **cleverly** adv., **cleverness** n.

■ **1** able, acute, astute, brainy, bright, brilliant, canny, discerning, gifted, intellectual, intelligent, perceptive, quick, sharp, shrewd, smart. **2** adept, adroit, deft, dexterous, handy, skilful, skilled, talented. **3** cunning, imaginative, ingenious, inventive, resourceful.

cliché /kléeshay/ n. hackneyed phrase or idea. □ **clichéd** adj.

■ banality, colloq. chestnut, platitude, stereotype, truism.

click n. short sharp sound. ● v. **1** make or cause to make a click. **2** (colloq.) be a success. **3** (colloq.) be understood.

client n. **1** customer. **2** person using the services of a professional person.

clientele /klée-ontél/ n. clients.

cliff n. steep rock face, esp. on a coast. □ **cliffhanger** n. story or contest full of suspense.

■ bluff, crag, escarpment, precipice, scarp.

climacteric n. period of life when physical powers begin to decline.

climate n. regular weather conditions of an area.

climax n. point of greatest interest or intensity.

■ acme, culmination, height, high point, peak, summit, zenith.

climb v. go up or over. ● n. ascent made by climbing. □ **climber** n.

■ v. ascend, clamber up, go up, mount, scale, shin up.

clime n. **1** climate. **2** region.

clinch v. **1** fasten securely. **2** settle conclusively. **3** (of boxers) hold on to each other. ● n. clinching. □ **clincher** n.

cling v. (**clung**) **1** stick. **2** hold on tightly. □ **cling film** thin polythene wrapping.

clinic n. **1** place or occasion for giving medical treatment. **2** private or specialized hospital.

clinical adj. of or used in treatment of patients. □ **clinically** adv.

clink n. thin sharp sound. ● v. make this sound.

clinker n. fused coal ash.

clip[1] n. device for holding things tightly or together. ● v. (**clipped**) fix or fasten with clip(s).

clip[2] v. (**clipped**) **1** cut with shears or scissors. **2** (colloq.) hit sharply. ● n. **1** act of clipping. **2** piece clipped from something. **3** (colloq.) sharp blow.

■ v. **1** crop, cut, lop, prune, shear, snip, trim.

clipper n. **1** fast sailing ship. **2** (pl.) instrument for clipping.

clipping n. **1** piece clipped off. **2** newspaper cutting.

clique /kleek/ n. small exclusive group.

clitoris n. small erectile part of female genitals.

cloak n. loose sleeveless outer garment. ● v. cover, conceal.

■ n. cape, mantle, wrap. ● v. conceal, cover, disguise, hide, mask, screen, shroud, veil, wrap.

cloakroom n. room where outer garments can be left, often containing a lavatory.

clobber (sl.) n. 1 equipment. 2 belongings. ● v. 1 hit hard. 2 defeat heavily.

cloche n. translucent cover for protecting plants.

clock n. instrument indicating time. □ **clock in** or **on**, **out** or **off** register one's time of arrival or departure. **clock up** achieve.

clockwise adv. & adj. moving in the direction of the hands of a clock.

clockwork n. mechanism with wheels and springs.

clod n. lump of earth.

clog n. wooden-soled shoe. ● v. (**clogged**) 1 cause an obstruction in. 2 become blocked.

cloister n. 1 covered walk along the side of a church etc. 2 life in a monastery or convent.

cloistered adj. secluded.

clone n. group of plants or organisms produced asexually from one ancestor. ● v. grow in this way.

close¹ /klōss/ adj. 1 situated at a short distance or interval. 2 dear to each other. 3 dense, compact. 4 concentrated. 5 secretive. 6 stingy. 7 stuffy or humid. 8 (of a danger etc.) narrowly avoided. ● adv. 1 closely. 2 in a near position. ● n. street closed at one end. 2 grounds round a cathedral or abbey. □ **close-up** n. photograph etc. taken at close range.

closely adv., **closeness** n.

■ adj. 1 adjacent, near. 2 affectionate, devoted, friendly, inseparable, intimate, loving, colloq. pally, colloq. thick. 3 compact, cramped, dense, tight. 4 assiduous, careful, concentrated, minute, painstaking, precise, rigorous, searching, thorough. 5 reserved, reticent, secretive, uncommunicative. 6 mean, miserly, niggardly, parsimonious, stingy, colloq. tight, tight-fisted. 7 airless, fuggy, fusty, humid, muggy, oppressive, stale, stifling, stuffy, suffocating, unventilated.

close² /klōz/ v. 1 shut. 2 bring or come to an end. 3 come nearer together. ● n. conclusion, end.

■ v. 1 bolt, fasten, lock, padlock, seal, secure, shut. 2 complete, conclude, end,

finish, terminate, wind up. ● n. completion, conclusion, culmination, end, finish, halt, termination.

closet n. 1 cupboard. 2 store room. ● v. (**closeted**) shut away in private conference or study.

closure n. closing, closed state.

clot n. 1 thickened mass of liquid. 2 (colloq.) stupid person. ● v. (**clotted**) form clot(s).

cloth n. 1 woven or felted material. 2 piece of this.

clothe v. put clothes on, provide with clothes.

■ attire, dress, garb, kit out, robe, colloq. tog out.

clothes n.pl. things worn to cover the body.

■ apparel, attire, clothing, finery, garb, garments, get-up, kit, colloq. togs, vestments, wardrobe.

clothier n. person who deals in cloth and men's clothes.

clothing n. clothes for the body.

cloud n. 1 visible mass of watery vapour floating in the sky. 2 mass of smoke or dust. ● v. 1 become covered with clouds or gloom. 2 make unclear.

cloudburst n. violent storm of rain.

cloudy adj. (**-ier, -iest**) 1 covered with clouds. 2 (of liquid) not transparent. □ **cloudiness** n.

■ 1 clouded, dark, dull, gloomy, grey, leaden, murky, overcast, starless, sunless. 2 muddy, opaque, turbid.

clout n. 1 blow. 2 (colloq.) power of effective action. ● v. hit.

clove¹ n. dried bud of a tropical tree, used as spice.

clove² n. one division of a compound bulb such as garlic.

clove³, **cloven** see **cleave¹**.

clove hitch knot used to fasten a rope round a pole etc.

cloven hoof divided hoof like that of sheep, cows, etc.

clover n. plant with three-lobed leaves. □ **in clover** in luxury.

clown n. 1 comic entertainer. 2 foolish or playful person. ● v. perform or behave as a clown.

■ n. 1 comedian, comedienne, comic, jester, joker. 2 buffoon, fool, idiot.

cloy v. sicken by glutting with sweetness or pleasure.

club n. 1 heavy stick used as a weapon. 2 group who meet for social or sporting purposes, their premises. **3** organization offering benefit to subscribers. **4** stick with a wooden or metal head, used in golf. **5** playing card of the suit marked with black clover leaves. ● *v.* (**clubbed**) strike with a club. □ **club together** join in subscribing.

■ *n.* **1** bat, baton, cosh, cudgel, truncheon. **2** association, circle, federation, fellowship, group, guild, organization, society, union. ● *v.* beat, belabour, bludgeon, cudgel, thrash.

cluck *n.* throaty cry of hen. ● *v.* utter a cluck.

clue *n.* fact or idea giving a guide to the solution of a problem.

■ hint, indication, lead, pointer, suggestion, tip-off; idea, inkling.

clump *n.* cluster, esp. of trees. ● *v.* **1** form a clump. **2** tread heavily.

clumsy *adj.* (**-ier, -iest**) **1** awkward in movement or shape. **2** tactless. □ **clumsily** *adv.*, **clumsiness** *n.*

■ **1** awkward, blundering, bungling, fumbling, gangling, gawky, graceless, *colloq.* ham-fisted, *colloq.* hulking, inept, lumbering, maladroit, uncoordinated, ungainly, ungraceful; bulky, cumbersome, ponderous, unmanageable, unwieldy. **2** gauche, ill-judged, insensitive, tactless, thoughtless, undiplomatic.

clung *see* **cling.**

cluster *n.* close group of similar people or things. ● *v.* form a cluster.

■ *n.* batch, bunch, clump, collection; flock, gathering, group, huddle, knot, swarm, throng. ● *v.* assemble, bunch, collect, congregate, flock, gather, group.

clutch[1] *v.* grasp tightly. ● *n.* **1** tight grasp. **2** device for connecting and disconnecting moving parts.

■ *v.* clasp, grab, grasp, grip, seize, snatch, take hold of.

clutch[2] *n.* **1** set of eggs for hatching. **2** chickens hatched from these.

clutter *n.* things lying about untidily. ● *v.* fill with clutter.

■ *n.* confusion, disorder, jumble, litter, mess, muddle. ● *v.* litter, mess up, strew.

Co. *abbr.* **1** Company. **2** County.

c/o *abbr.* care of.

co- *pref.* joint, jointly.

coach *n.* **1** single-decker bus. **2** large horse-drawn carriage. **3** railway carriage. **4** private tutor. **5** instructor in sports. ● *v.* train, teach.

■ *n.* **3** *US* car, carriage, wagon. **4** instructor, teacher, trainer, tutor. ● *v.* drill, guide, instruct, prepare, school, teach, train, tutor.

coagulate *v.* change from liquid to semi-solid, clot. □ **coagulant** *n.*, **coagulation** *n.*

■ clot, congeal, curdle, *colloq.* jell, set, solidify, thicken.

coal *n.* hard black mineral used for burning as fuel. □ **coalfield** *n.* area yielding coal.

coalesce *v.* combine. □ **coalescence** *n.*

coalition *n.* union, esp. temporary union of political parties.

coarse *adj.* **1** rough or loose in texture or grain. **2** crude in manner, vulgar. □ **coarse fish** freshwater fish other than salmon and trout. **coarsely** *adv.*, **coarseness** *n.*

■ **1** bristly, prickly, rough, scratchy. **2** boorish, crude, loutish, rude, uncouth, vulgar.

coarsen *v.* make or become coarse.

coast *n.* seashore and land near it. ● *v.* **1** sail along a coast. **2** ride a bicycle or drive a motor vehicle without using power. □ **coastal** *adj.*

■ *n.* beach, littoral, seashore, seaside, shore, strand.

coaster *n.* **1** ship trading along a coast. **2** mat for a glass.

coastguard *n.* officer of an organization that keeps watch on the coast.

coat *n.* **1** outdoor garment with sleeves. **2** fur or hair covering an animal's body. **3** covering layer. ● *v.* cover with a layer. □ **coat of arms** design on a shield as the emblem of a family etc.

■ *n.* **1** *colloq.* mac, mackintosh, overcoat, raincoat, topcoat. **2** fleece, fur, hide, pelt, skin. **3** coating, covering, film, layer. ● *v.* cover, paint, spread.

coating *n.* covering layer.

coax *v.* **1** persuade gently. **2** manipulate carefully or slowly.

■ **1** cajole, inveigle, manipulate, persuade, talk into, wheedle.

coaxial *adj.* (of cable) containing two conductors, one surrounding but insulated from the other.

cob *n.* **1** sturdy short-legged horse. **2** large hazelnut. **3** stalk of an ear of maize. **4** small round loaf.

cobalt n. **1** metallic element. **2** deep-blue pigment made from it.

cobber n. (*Austr. & NZ colloq.*) friend, mate.

cobble¹ n. rounded stone formerly used for paving roads.

cobble² v. mend roughly.

cobbler n. shoe-mender.

cobra n. poisonous snake.

cobweb n. network spun by a spider.

cocaine n. drug used illegally as a stimulant.

coccyx /kóksiks/ n. bone at the base of the spinal column.

cochineal n. red colouring matter used in food.

cock n. **1** male bird. **2** tap or valve controlling a flow. ● v. **1** tilt or turn upwards. **2** set (a gun) for firing. □ **cock-a-hoop** adj. very pleased. **cock-eyed** adj. (*colloq.*) **1** askew. **2** absurd.

cockade n. rosette worn on a hat.

cockatoo n. crested parrot.

cocker n. breed of spaniel.

cockerel n. young male fowl.

cockle n. edible shellfish.

cockney n. native or dialect of the East End of London.

cockpit n. compartment for the pilot in a plane, or for the driver in a racing car.

cockroach n. beetle-like insect.

cockscomb n. cock's crest.

cocksure adj. very self-confident.

cocktail n. mixed alcoholic drink.

cocky adj. (**-ier, -iest**) conceited and arrogant. □ **cockily** adv.

cocoa n. **1** powder of crushed cacao seeds. **2** drink made from this.

coconut n. **1** nut of a tropical palm. **2** its edible lining.

cocoon n. **1** silky sheath round a chrysalis. **2** protective wrapping.

cod n. large edible sea fish.

coda n. final part of a musical composition.

coddle v. cherish and protect.

code n. **1** system of signals or symbols etc. used for secrecy, brevity, etc. **2** systematic set of laws, rules, etc.

codeine n. substance made from opium, used to relieve pain.

codicil n. appendix to a will.

codify v. arrange (laws etc.) into a code. □ **codification** n.

coeducation n. education of boys and girls in the same classes. □ **coeducational** adj.

coefficient n. **1** multiplier. **2** mathematical factor.

coeliac disease /séeliak/ disease causing inability to digest gluten.

coerce v. compel by threats or force. □ **coercion** n., **coercive** adj.

■ blackmail, bludgeon, browbeat, bully, compel, constrain, dragoon, drive, force, pressurize, railroad.

coeval adj. of the same age or epoch.

coexist v. exist together, esp. harmoniously. □ **coexistence** n., **coexistent** adj.

coffee n. **1** bean-like seeds of a tropical shrub, roasted and ground for making a drink. **2** this drink. **3** light brown. □ **coffee table** small low table.

coffer n. **1** large strong box for holding money and valuables. **2** (*pl.*) financial resources.

coffin n. box in which a corpse is placed for burial or cremation.

cog n. one of a series of projections on the edge of a wheel, engaging with those of another.

cogent adj. convincing. □ **cogently** adv., **cogency** n.

■ compelling, convincing, effective, forceful, persuasive, potent, powerful, strong, weighty.

cogitate v. think deeply. □ **cogitation** n.

cognac n. French brandy.

cognate adj. akin, related. ● n. **1** relative. **2** cognate word.

cognition n. knowing, perceiving. □ **cognitive** adj.

cognizant adj. aware, having knowledge. □ **cognizance** n.

cohabit v. live together as man and wife. □ **cohabitation** n.

cohere v. stick together.

coherent adj. **1** connected logically. **2** intelligible. □ **coherently** adv., **coherence** n.

■ **1** consistent, orderly, organized, logical, rational, reasonable. **2** articulate, clear, comprehensible, intelligible, lucid, understandable.

cohesion n. tendency to cohere.

cohesive adj. cohering.

cohort n. **1** tenth part of a Roman legion. **2** people banded together.

coiffure /kwaafyóor/ n. hairstyle.

coil v. wind into rings or a spiral. ● n. **1** something coiled. **2** one ring or turn in this.

■ v. curl, loop, snake, spiral, twine, twirl, twist, wind. ● n. convolution, curl, helix, loop, spiral, twist, whirl, whorl.

coin n. piece of metal money. ● v. **1** make (coins) by stamping metal. **2** invent (a word). □ **coiner** n.

coinage n. **1** coining. **2** coins, system of these. **3** invented word.

coincide v. **1** occur at the same time. **2** agree or be identical.
■ **2** accord, agree, correspond, match, tally.

coincidence n. **1** occurring together. **2** remarkable concurrence of events etc., apparently by chance. □ **coincidental** adj., **coincidentally** adv.

coition n. coitus.

coitus n. sexual intercourse.

coke¹ n. solid substance left after gas and tar have been extracted from coal, used as fuel.

coke² n. (sl.) cocaine.

col n. depression in a range of mountains.

colander n. bowl-shaped perforated vessel for draining food.

cold adj. **1** at or having a low temperature. **2** not affectionate, enthusiastic, or kind. ● n. **1** cold conditions, weather etc. **2** illness causing catarrh and sneezing. □ **cold-blooded** adj. **1** having a blood temperature varying with that of the surroundings. **2** unfeeling, ruthless. **cold feet** fear. **cold-shoulder** v. treat with deliberate unfriendliness. **coldly** adv., **coldness** n.
■ adj. arctic, bitter, bleak, chill, chilly, cool, draughty, freezing, frigid, frosty, glacial, icy, keen, colloq. nippy, raw, wintry; chilled, frozen, shivering, shivery. **2** aloof, apathetic, chilly, cool, distant, frigid, frosty, indifferent, lukewarm, standoffish, undemonstrative, unemotional, unfriendly, unresponsive; callous, hard-hearted, heartless, stony, uncaring, unfeeling, unsympathetic.

coleslaw n. salad of shredded raw cabbage coated in dressing.

colic n. severe abdominal pain.

colitis n. inflammation of the colon.

collaborate v. work in partnership. □ **collaboration** n., **collaborator** n., **collaborative** adj.

collage /kóllaazh/ n. picture made by gluing pieces of paper etc. to a backing.

collapse v. **1** fall down suddenly. **2** lose strength suddenly. ● n. **1** collapsing. **2** breakdown.
■ v. **1** cave in, crumble, crumple, fall apart, fall down, give way, subside, tumble down.

2 faint, keel over, pass out; colloq. crack up.

collapsible adj. made so as to fold up.

collar n. **1** band round the neck of a garment. **2** leather band round an animal's neck. **3** band holding part of a machine. ● v. seize, take for oneself.

collate v. collect and arrange systematically. □ **collator** n.

collateral adj. **1** parallel. **2** additional but subordinate. ● n. additional security pledged. □ **collaterally** adv.

collation n. **1** collating. **2** light meal.

colleague fellow worker esp. in a business or profession.

collect v. **1** bring or come together. **2** fetch. **3** obtain specimens of, esp. as a hobby. □ **collector** n.
■ **1** assemble, congregate, convene, converge, gather, meet, rally; accumulate, amass, compile, garner, heap up, hoard, pile up, save, stockpile, store up. **2** bring, fetch, get, pick up.

collected adj. calm and controlled.
■ calm, composed, controlled, cool, imperturbable, level-headed, nonchalant, sedate, self-possessed, serene, tranquil, unperturbed, unruffled.

collection n. **1** act or process of collecting. **2** things collected.
■ **2** accumulation, assortment, heap, hoard, pile, stack, store; anthology, compendium, compilation, miscellany.

collective adj. of or denoting a group taken or working as a unit. ● **collective noun** noun (singular in form) denoting a group (e.g. army, herd). **collectively** adv.

colleen n. (Ir.) girl.

college n. **1** establishment for higher or professional education. **2** organized group of professional people. □ **collegiate** adj.

collide v. come into collision.

collie n. dog with a pointed muzzle and shaggy hair.

colliery n. coal mine.

collision n. violent striking of one thing against another.
■ accident, bump, crash, pile-up, smash.

collocate v. place (words) together. □ **collocation** n.

colloquial adj. suitable for informal speech or writing. □ **colloquially** adv., **colloquialism** n.

collude v. conspire. □ **collusion** n., **collusive** adj.

colon[1] n. lower part of the large intestine. □ **colonic** adj.

colon[2] n. punctuation mark (:).

colonel /kŏn'l/ n. army officer next below brigadier.

colonial adj. of a colony or colonies. ● n. inhabitant of a colony.

colonialism n. policy of acquiring or maintaining colonies.

colonize v. establish a colony in. □ **colonization** n., **colonist** n.

colonnade n. row of columns.

colony n. **1** settlement or settlers in new territory, remaining subject to the parent state. **2** people of one nationality or occupation living in a particular area. **3** group of animals living close together.

coloration n. colouring.

colossal adj. immense. □ **colossally** adv.

■ enormous, gargantuan, giant, gigantic, huge, immense, mammoth, massive, monumental, prodigious, titanic, vast.

colossus n. (pl. **colossi**) immense statue.

colour n. **1** one, or any mixture, of the constituents into which light is separated in a rainbow etc. **2** pigment, paint. **3** (usu. pl.) flag of a ship or regiment. ● v. **1** apply colour to. **2** blush. **3** influence. □ **colour-blind** adj. unable to distinguish between certain colours.

■ n. **1** hue, shade, tincture, tint, tone. **2** dye, paint, pigment. **3** (**colours**) banner, flag, ensign, pennant, standard. ● v. **1** dye, paint, stain, tinge, tint. **2** blush, flush, go red, redden. **3** affect, bias, distort, influence, prejudice, slant, sway.

colourant n. colouring matter.

colourful adj. **1** full of colour. **2** full of interest, vivid. □ **colourfully** adv.

■ **1** bright, gay, iridescent, multicoloured, vivid. **2** graphic, interesting, picturesque, vivid.

colourless adj. **1** without colour. **2** lacking interest.

■ **1** ashen, pale, pallid, wan, washed out, white. **2** bland, boring, drab, dreary, dull, insipid, lacklustre, lifeless, tame, uninspiring, uninteresting, vapid.

colt n. young male horse.

coltsfoot n. wild plant with yellow flowers.

columbine n. garden flower with pointed projections on its petals.

column n. **1** round pillar. **2** thing shaped like this. **3** vertical division of a page, printed matter in this. **4** long narrow formation of troops, vehicles, etc.

columnist n. journalist contributing regularly to a newspaper.

coma n. deep unconsciousness.

comatose adj. **1** in a coma. **2** drowsy.

comb n. **1** toothed strip of stiff material for tidying hair. **2** fowl's fleshy crest. **3** honeycomb. ● v. **1** tidy with a comb. **2** search thoroughly.

combat n. battle, contest. ● v. (**combated**) counter. □ **combative** adj.

■ n. action, battle, conflict, contest, duel, encounter, engagement, fight, skirmish, struggle. ● v. counter, fight, oppose, resist, strive against, struggle against.

combatant adj. & n. (person or nation) engaged in fighting.

combination n. **1** act or process of combining. **2** set of things or people combined. □ **combination lock** lock controlled by a series of positions of dial(s).

■ amalgamation, blend, mix, mixture, synthesis, union.

combine v. /kəmbín/ join into a group, set, or mixture. ● n. /kómbīn/ combination of people or firms acting together.

■ v. associate, club together, gang up, join forces, link, team up, unite; add together, amalgamate, blend, integrate, join, merge, mix, pool, put together, synthesize.

combustible adj. capable of catching fire.

combustion n. **1** burning. **2** process in which substances combine with oxygen and produce heat.

come v. (**came**, **come**) **1** move towards or reach a place, time, situation, etc. **2** occur. □ **come about** happen. **come across** meet or find unexpectedly. **comeback** n. **1** return to a former successful position. **2** retort. **come by** obtain. **come-down** n. fall in status. **come down with** contract (an illness). **come into** inherit. **come off** be successful. **come out 1** become visible. **2** emerge. **come round 1** recover from fainting. **2** be converted to the speaker's opinion. **come to 1** regain consciousness. **2** amount to. **come up** arise for discussion.

■ **1** appear, approach, arrive, draw near, colloq. show up, turn up. □ **come about** befall, happen, occur, take place. **come across** chance on, discover, encounter, find, happen on, hit on, light on, run into. **come by** acquire, get, obtain, procure, secure. **come to 1** awake, revive, wake up.

comedian *n.* humorous entertainer or actor.

comedienne *n.* female comedian.

comedy *n.* **1** light amusing drama. **2** humour.

comely *adj.* (**-ier, -iest**) good-looking. □ **comeliness** *n.*

comestibles *n.pl.* things to eat.

comet *n.* heavenly body with a luminous 'tail'.

comfort *n.* **1** state of ease and contentment. **2** relief of suffering or grief. **3** person or thing giving this. ● *v.* give comfort to. □ **comforter** *n.*

■ *n.* **1** content, contentment, ease. **2** consolation, reassurance, relief, solace, support. ● *v.* cheer (up), console, gladden, hearten, reassure, relieve, solace, soothe.

comfortable *adj.* giving or having ease and contentment. □ **comfortably** *adv.*

■ congenial, cosy, pleasant, relaxing, snug; contented, easy, relaxed, untroubled.

comic *adj.* **1** causing amusement. **2** of comedy. ● *n.* **1** comedian. **2** periodical with a series of strip cartoons. □ **comical** *adj.*, **comically** *adv.*

■ *adj.* amusing, comical, diverting, droll, funny, hilarious, humorous, *sl.* priceless, witty.

comma *n.* punctuation mark (,).

command *n.* **1** statement, given with authority, that an action must be performed. **2** holding of authority. **3** mastery. **4** forces or district under a commander. ● *v.* **1** give a command to. **2** have authority over.

■ *n.* **1** decree, dictate, direction, directive, edict, injunction, instruction, order. **2** authority, control, dominion, government, jurisdiction, leadership, management, mastery, power, sovereignty, supervision, sway. **3** grasp, knowledge, mastery. ● *v.* **1** adjure, bid, direct, instruct, order, require. **2** be in charge of, control, dominate, govern, head, hold sway over, lead, preside over, rule.

commandant *n.* officer in command of a fortress etc.

commandeer *v.* seize for use.

■ appropriate, confiscate, hijack, requisition, seize.

commander *n.* **1** person in command. **2** naval officer next below captain.

commandment *n.* divine command.

commando *n.* member of a military unit specially trained for making raids and assaults.

commemorate *v.* keep in the memory by a celebration or memorial. □ **commemoration** *n.*, **commemorative** *adj.*

■ celebrate, observe, solemnize; honour, pay homage to, pay tribute to, salute.

commence *v.* begin. □ **commencement** *n.*

■ begin, embark on, inaugurate, initiate, launch, open, start.

commend *v.* **1** praise. **2** entrust. □ **commendation** *n.*

commendable *adj.* worthy of praise. □ **commendably** *adv.*

■ admirable, creditable, deserving, laudable, meritorious, praiseworthy, worthy.

commensurable *adj.* measurable by the same standard. □ **commensurability** *n.*

commensurate *adj.* **1** of the same size. **2** proportionate.

comment *n.* **1** opinion, remark. **2** explanatory note. ● *v.* make comment(s).

■ *n.* **1** observation, opinion, remark, view. **2** annotation, explanation, footnote, note. ● *v.* observe, opine, remark, say.

commentary *n.* spoken or written description of something.

commentate *v.* act as commentator.

commentator *n.* person who writes or speaks a commentary.

commerce *n.* buying and selling, trading.

commercial *adj.* of, engaged in, or financed by commerce. □ **commercially** *adv.*

commercialize *v.* **1** make commercial. **2** make profitable. □ **commercialization** *n.*

commingle *v.* mix.

commiserate *v.* express or feel sympathy. □ **commiseration** *n.*

commission *n.* **1** committing. **2** giving of authority to perform a task. **3** task given. **4** group of people given such authority. **5** warrant conferring authority on an officer in the armed forces. **6** payment to an agent selling goods or services. ● *v.* **1** give commission to. **2** place an order for. □ **in commission** ready for service. **out of commission** not in working order.

commissionaire *n.* uniformed door attendant.

commissioner *n.* **1** member of a commission. **2** government official in charge of a district abroad.

commit v. (**committed**) **1** do, perform. **2** entrust, consign. **3** pledge to a course of action. □ **committal** n.

■ **1** carry out, do, execute, perform, perpetrate. **2** assign, consign, deliver, entrust, give, hand over, transfer. **3** pledge, promise, swear, undertake, vow.

commitment n. **1** committing. **2** obligation or pledge, state of being involved in this.

committee n. group of people appointed for a special function.

■ board, body, cabinet, commission, council, panel.

commode n. **1** chest of drawers. **2** chamber pot in a chair or box.

commodious adj. roomy.

commodity n. article of trade.

commodore n. **1** naval officer next below rear admiral. **2** president of a yacht club.

common adj. **1** of or affecting all. **2** occurring often. **3** ordinary. **4** of inferior quality. ● n. area of unfenced grassland for all to use. □ **common law** unwritten law based on custom and precedent. **common room** room shared by students or teachers for social purposes. **common sense** normal good sense in practical matters. **common time** 4 crotchets in the bar in music.

■ adj. **1** communal, general, joint, colloq. mutual, public, shared, universal. **2** customary, familiar, frequent, habitual, prevalent, usual; hackneyed, overused, stale, trite. **3** average, commonplace, conventional, everyday, mediocre, middling, normal, ordinary, run-of-the-mill, standard, stock, typical, unexceptional, workaday.

commoner n. person below the rank of peer.

commonly adv. usually, frequently.

commonplace adj. **1** lacking originality. **2** ordinary.

■ average, banal, hackneyed, humdrum, ordinary, pedestrian, predictable, prosaic, run-of-the-mill, standard, stock, trite, undistinguished, unremarkable.

commonwealth n. **1** independent state. **2** federation of states.

commotion n. fuss and disturbance.

■ ado, bother, din, fracas, furore, fuss, hubbub, hullabaloo, hurly-burly, colloq. kerfuffle, colloq. palaver, rumpus, stir, to-do, upheaval, uproar.

communal adj. shared among a group. □ **communally** adv.

commune[1] /kəmyoōn/ v. communicate mentally or spiritually.

commune[2] /kómyoōn/ n. **1** group sharing accommodation and goods. **2** district of local government in France etc.

communicant n. person who receives Holy Communion.

communicate v. **1** make known. **2** pass news etc. to and fro. **3** transmit (disease etc.). □ **communicator** n., **communicable** adj.

■ **1** announce, broadcast, convey, disclose, divulge, impart, intimate, make known, pass on, proclaim, promulgate, reveal, spread, transfer, transmit. **2** be in communication, be in touch, commune, converse, correspond, talk.

communication n. **1** act of communicating. **2** letter or message. **3** means of access.

■ **1** disclosure, intimation, promulgation, spread, transmission. **2** communiqué, dispatch, epistle, letter, line, message, note.

communicative adj. talkative, willing to give information.

■ chatty, expansive, forthcoming, frank, informative, open, outgoing, sociable, talkative.

communion n. **1** fellowship. **2** social dealings. **3** branch of the Christian Church. **4** (**Holy Communion**) Eucharist.

communiqué /kəmyoōnikay/ n. **1** official report. **2** agreed statement.

communism n. **1** social system based on common ownership of property etc. **2** political doctrine or movement advocating this. □ **communist** n.

community n. group of people living in one district or having common interests or origins.

commute v. **1** exchange for something else. **2** travel regularly by train or bus to and from one's work. □ **commuter** n.

compact[1] /kómpakt/ n. pact, contract.

compact[2] adj. /kəmpákt/ **1** closely or neatly packed together. **2** concise. ● v. /kəmpákt/ make compact. ● n. /kómpakt/ small flat case for face powder. □ **compact disc** small disc from which sound etc. is reproduced by laser action.

■ adj. **1** compressed, dense, firm, solid. **2** brief, compendious, concise, condensed, laconic, pithy, succinct, terse.

companion n. **1** person who accompanies or associates with another. **2** handbook, reference book. □ **companionway** *n.* staircase from a ship's deck to cabins etc. **companionship** *n.*

■ **1** associate, *colloq.* buddy, *colloq.* chum, comrade, confidant(e), crony, fellow, friend, mate, *colloq.* pal, partner; chaperon, escort. **2** guide, handbook, manual, reference book.

companionable *adj.* sociable.

company *n.* **1** being with another or others. **2** people assembled. **3** guest(s). **4** actors etc. working together. **5** commercial business. **6** subdivision of an infantry battalion. □ **keep company with** associate with habitually.

■ **1** companionship, fellowship, society. **2** assembly, audience, band, crowd, gathering, party, throng, troop; entourage, retinue, suite, train. **3** caller(s), guest(s), visitor(s). **4** cast, ensemble, performers, troupe. **5** business, concern, corporation, establishment, firm, house, partnership.

comparable *adj.* suitable to be compared, similar. □ **comparability** *n.*, **comparably** *adv.*

comparative *adj.* **1** involving comparison. **2** of the grammatical form expressing 'more'. ● *n.* comparative form of a word. □ **comparatively** *adv.*

compare *v.* **1** estimate the similarity of. **2** declare to be similar. **3** bear comparison.

■ **1** contrast, correlate, juxtapose, relate, weigh up. **2** equate, liken.

comparison *n.* **1** act or instance of comparing. **2** similarity.

■ **2** analogy, comparability, correspondence, likeness, parallel, relation, relationship, resemblance, similarity.

compartment *n.* partitioned space. □ **compartmental** *adj.*

■ alcove, bay, booth, cubby hole, cubicle, niche, pigeon-hole, section, slot, space.

compass *n.* **1** device showing the direction of the magnetic or true north. **2** range, scope. **3** (*pl.*) hinged instrument for drawing circles. ● *v.* encompass.

compassion *n.* feeling of pity. □ **compassionate** *adj.*

compatible *adj.* **1** able to coexist. **2** consistent. □ **compatibly** *adv.*, **compatibility** *n.*

■ **1** like-minded, similar, well-matched, well-suited. **2** congruent, consistent, consonant.

compatriot *n.* person from one's own country.

compel *v.* (**compelled**) **1** force. **2** arouse (a feeling) irresistibly.

■ **1** coerce, constrain, dragoon, drive, force, make, oblige, order, press-gang, pressure, pressurize, railroad, require.

compendious *adj.* giving much information concisely.

compendium *n.* (*pl.* **-dia** or **-s**) **1** summary. **2** collection of information etc.

compensate *v.* **1** make a suitable payment in return for loss or damage. **2** counterbalance. □ **compensation** *n.*, **compensatory** *adj.*

■ **1** recompense, reimburse, repay, requite; atone, make amends.

compère *n.* person who introduces performers in a variety show. ● *v.* act as compère to.

compete *v.* **1** strive. **2** take part in a contest etc.

■ **1** battle, contend, fight, strive, struggle, vie. **2** participate, take part.

competence *n.* ability, authority.

competent *adj.* **1** having ability or authority to do what is required. **2** satisfactory. **3** proficient. □ **competently** *adv.*

■ **1** capable, fit, qualified. **2** acceptable, adequate, all right, *colloq.* OK, satisfactory. **3** able, accomplished, adept, capable, experienced, expert, practised, proficient, skilled.

competition *n.* **1** friendly contest. **2** competing. **3** those who compete.

■ **1** championship, contest, event, game, match, race, tournament. **2** contention, rivalry, struggle.

competitive *adj.* involving competition. □ **competitively** *adv.*, **competitiveness** *n.*

competitor *n.* one who competes.

■ contender, contestant; adversary, opponent, rival.

compile *v.* collect and arrange into a list or book. □ **compilation** *n.*, **compiler** *n.*

complacent *adj.* self-satisfied. □ **complacency** *n.*

complain *v.* **1** express dissatisfaction. **2** say one is suffering from pain. □ **complainant** *n.*

■ **1** *sl.* beef, carp, *colloq.* gripe, *colloq.* grouch, *colloq.* grouse, grumble, moan, object, protest, whine, *colloq.* whinge.

complaint n. **1** cause of dissatisfaction. **2** illness.

■ **1** sl. beef, grievance, colloq. gripe, colloq. grouse, grumble. **2** ailment, disease, disorder, illness, malady, sickness.

complaisant adj. willing to please others. □ **complaisance** n.

complement n. thing that completes. ● v. form a complement to. □ **complementary** adj.

complete adj. **1** having all its parts. **2** finished. **3** thorough, in every way. ● v. **1** finish, make complete. **2** fill in (a form etc.). □ **completely** adv., **completeness** n., **completion** n.

■ adj. **1** entire, full, intact, total, unabridged, unbroken, uncut, undivided, unexpurgated, whole. **2** concluded, done, finished, over. **3** absolute, out and out, perfect, pure, thorough, total, unmitigated, unqualified, utter. ● v. **1** accomplish, achieve, clinch, conclude, finalize, finish, end, settle; crown, perfect, round off.

complex adj. **1** made up of many parts. **2** complicated. ● n. **1** complex whole. **2** set of feelings that influence behaviour. **3** set of buildings. □ **complexity** n.

■ adj. **1** composite, compound. **2** complicated, difficult, intricate, involved, knotty, labyrinthine.

complexion n. **1** colour and texture of the skin of the face. **2** general character of things.

compliant adj. complying, obedient. □ **compliance** n.

complicate v. make complicated. □ **complication** n.

complicated adj. complex and difficult.

■ Byzantine, complex, difficult, elaborate, intricate, involved, knotty, labyrinthine, tangled.

complicity n. involvement in wrongdoing.

compliment n. **1** polite expression of praise. **2** (pl.) formal greetings. ● v. congratulate.

■ n. **1** commendation, tribute. **2** (compliments) best wishes, felicitations, greetings, regards, salutations. ● v. commend, congratulate, eulogize, felicitate, laud, pay tribute to, praise, salute.

complimentary adj. **1** expressing a compliment. **2** free of charge.

■ **1** appreciative, congratulatory, eulogistic, favourable, flattering, laudatory. **2** free, gratis.

comply v. act in accordance (with a request etc.).

■ accede, acquiesce, agree, assent, concur, conform, consent, obey, submit, yield.

component n. one of the parts of which a thing is composed.

comport v. **comport oneself** behave.

compose v. **1** create in music or literature. **2** constitute, make up. **3** arrange in good order. □ **compose oneself** become calm. **composer** n.

■ **1** create, write. **2** constitute, form, make up. **3** arrange, dispose, lay out, order, organize. □ **compose oneself** calm down, control oneself, quieten down, settle down.

composite adj. & n. (thing) made up of parts.

composition n. **1** act of composing. **2** structure. **3** thing composed.

■ **1** creation, writing. **2** arrangement, construction, formation, layout, make-up, organization, structure. **3** essay, piece, work.

compositor n. typesetter.

compost n. mixture of decayed organic matter used as fertilizer.

composure n. calmness.

compote n. fruit in syrup.

compound adj. /kómpownd/ made up of two or more ingredients. ● n. /kómpownd/ compound substance. ● v. /kampównd/ **1** combine. **2** increase. **3** settle by agreement.

■ adj. complex, composite. ● n. alloy, amalgam, blend, combination, mixture, synthesis. ● v. **1** amalgamate, blend, combine, fuse, mix, put together, synthesize, unite. **2** add to, aggravate, augment, exacerbate, heighten, increase, intensify, worsen.

comprehend v. **1** understand. **2** include.

■ **1** appreciate, apprehend, fathom, grasp, realize, see, take in, understand. **2** comprise, embrace, include, take in.

comprehensible adj. intelligible.

comprehension n. understanding.

comprehensive adj. including much or all. ● n. (in full **comprehensive school**) secondary school for children of all abilities. □ **comprehensively** adv.

■ adj. broad, complete, encyclopedic, exhaustive, extensive, full, inclusive, sweeping, thorough, wide-ranging.

compress v. /kampréss/ squeeze, force into less space. ● n. /kómpress/ pad to stop bleeding or to relieve inflammation. □ **compression** n., **compressor** n.

comprise v. 1 include. 2 consist of.

compromise n. settlement reached by mutual concessions. ● v. 1 make a settlement in this way. 2 expose to suspicion.

compulsion n. 1 compelling, being compelled. 2 irresistible urge.

compulsive adj. 1 compelling. 2 resulting or acting (as if) from compulsion. 3 irresistible. □ **compulsively** adv.

■ 1 compelling, overwhelming, uncontrollable, urgent. 2 habitual, incorrigible, incurable, inveterate, obsessive. 3 compelling, fascinating, gripping, irresistible.

compulsory adj. required by law or rule. □ **compulsorily** adv.

compunction n. regret, scruple.

■ misgiving, qualm, regret, second thought, scruple.

compute v. 1 calculate. 2 use a computer. □ **computation** n.

computer n. electronic apparatus for analysing or storing data, making calculations, etc.

computerize v. equip with or perform or operate by computer. □ **computerization** n.

comrade n. companion, associate. □ **comradeship** n.

■ associate, colleague, companion, compatriot, crony, partner.

con[1] (sl.) v. (**conned**) swindle, deceive. ● n. confidence trick.

con[2] v. (**conned**) direct the steering of (a ship).

con[3] see pro and con.

concatenation n. combination.

concave adj. curved like the inner surface of a ball.

conceal v. hide, keep secret. □ **concealment** n.

■ camouflage, cloak, cover (up), disguise, hide, keep secret, mask; bury, secrete, tuck away; gloss over, whitewash.

concede v. 1 admit to be true. 2 admit defeat. 3 grant.

■ 1 accept, acknowledge, admit, allow, confess, grant, own, recognize. 2 capitulate, give in, submit, surrender, throw in the towel, yield.

conceit n. too much pride in oneself. □ **conceited** adj.

■ arrogance, egotism, narcissism, pride, self-admiration, self-love, vanity. □ **conceited** arrogant, bumptious, cocky, egot-

istical, narcissistic, proud, self-important, self-satisfied, smug, colloq. stuck-up, vain.

conceive v. 1 become pregnant. 2 form (a plan etc.). □ **conceive of** imagine.

conceivable adj.

■ 2 contrive, design, devise, dream up, form, hatch, plan, colloq. think up. □ **conceive of** envisage, imagine, think of.

concentrate v. 1 employ all one's attention or effort. 2 bring together. 3 make less dilute. ● n. concentrated substance.

■ v. 1 apply oneself, focus, think. 2 cluster, collect, congregate, gather, group. 3 condense, distil.

concentration n. 1 concentrating. 2 concentrated thing. □ **concentration camp** camp for political prisoners in Nazi Germany.

concentric adj. having the same centre. □ **concentrically** adv.

concept n. idea, general notion.

conception n. 1 conceiving. 2 idea.

conceptual adj. of concepts.

conceptualize v. form a concept of. □ **conceptualization** n.

concern v. 1 be relevant or important to. 2 worry. ● n. 1 matter of interest or importance. 2 care, consideration. 3 anxiety. 4 business. □ **concern oneself** interest or involve oneself.

■ v. 1 affect, have a bearing on, interest, involve, matter to, pertain to, refer to, relate to. 2 bother, disturb, perturb, trouble, upset, worry. ● n. 1 affair, business, duty, problem, responsibility, task. 2 attention, care, consideration, heed, regard, thought. 3 anxiety, disquiet, distress, solicitude, uneasiness, worry. 4 business, company, establishment, firm, house, organization.

concerned adj. anxious.

■ anxious, bothered, distressed, perturbed, troubled, uneasy, upset, worried.

concerning prep. with reference to.

■ about, apropos, as regards, re, regarding, relating to, with reference to, with regard to, with respect to.

concert n. musical entertainment.

concerted adj. done in combination.

concertina n. portable musical instrument with bellows and keys.

concerto /kǒnchaírtō/ n. musical composition for solo instrument and orchestra.

concession n. 1 conceding. 2 thing conceded. 3 special privilege. 4 right granted.

conch n. spiral shell.

conciliate v. **1** soothe the hostility of. **2** reconcile. □ **conciliation** n., **conciliatory** adj.

concise adj. brief and comprehensive. □ **concisely** adv., **conciseness** n.

■ brief, compact, compendious, laconic, pithy, short, succinct, terse; abbreviated, abridged, shortened.

conclude v. **1** end. **2** infer. **3** settle finally.

■ **1** close, complete, end, finish, halt, stop, terminate, wind up. **2** assume, deduce, draw the conclusion, gather, infer, judge, presume, suppose, surmise, understand. **3** clinch, negotiate, pull off, settle.

conclusion n. **1** ending. **2** opinion reached.

■ **1** cessation, close, completion, end, finish, termination, denouement, ending, finale. **2** decision, deduction, inference, judgement, verdict.

conclusive adj. ending doubt, convincing. □ **conclusively** adv.

■ certain, convincing, decisive, definite, incontrovertible, indisputable, irrefutable, undeniable, unequivocal, unquestionable.

concoct v. **1** prepare from ingredients. **2** invent. □ **concoction** n.

concomitant adj. accompanying.

concord n. agreement, harmony.

concordance n. **1** agreement. **2** index of words.

concordant adj. being in concord.

concourse n. **1** crowd. **2** open area at a railway station etc.

concrete n. mixture of gravel and cement etc. used for building. ● adj. **1** existing in material form. **2** definite. ● v. cover with or embed in concrete.

■ adj. actual, definite, genuine, material, physical, real, substantial, tangible.

concretion n. solidified mass.

concubine n. woman who lives with a man as his wife.

concur v. (**concurred**) **1** agree in opinion. **2** happen together, coincide. □ **concurrence** n., **concurrent** adj., **concurrently** adv.

concuss v. affect with concussion.

concussion n. injury to the brain caused by a hard blow.

condemn v. **1** express strong disapproval of. **2** doom. **3** convict. **4** sentence.

5 declare unfit for use. □ **condemnation** n.

■ **1** blame, censure, criticize, decry, denounce, disparage, rebuke, reprove, revile, colloq. slam, colloq. slate, upbraid. **2** destine, doom, fate, ordain.

condense v. **1** make denser or briefer. **2** change from gas or vapour to liquid. □ **condensation** n.

condescend v. **1** consent to do something less dignified or fitting than is usual. **2** pretend to be on equal terms with (an inferior). □ **condescension** n.

■ **1** deign, demean oneself, lower oneself, stoop.

condiment n. seasoning for food.

condition n. **1** thing that must exist if something else is to exist or occur. **2** state of being. **3** ailment. **4** (pl.) circumstances. ● v. **1** bring to the desired condition. **2** have a strong effect on. **3** accustom. □ **conditioner** n.

■ n. **1** prerequisite, proviso, requirement, requisite, stipulation. **2** fitness, form, health, shape, state. **3** ailment, complaint, disease, disorder, illness. **4** (conditions) circumstances, environment, surroundings. ● v. **1** adapt, get ready, make ready, modify, prepare. **2** affect, determine, govern, influence, shape. **3** acclimatize, accustom, habituate, inure.

conditional adj. subject to specified conditions. □ **conditionally** adv.

condole v. express sympathy. □ **condolence** n.

condom n. contraceptive sheath.

condone v. forgive, overlook.

conducive adj. helping to cause or produce.

conduct v. /kəndúkt/ **1** lead, guide. **2** manage. **3** transmit (heat or electricity). **4** be the conductor of. ● n. /kóndukt/ **1** behaviour. **2** way of conducting business, war, etc.

■ v. **1** escort, guide, lead, show, usher. **2** administer, control, direct, handle, manage, operate, run, supervise. **3** carry, channel, convey, transmit. ● n. **1** actions, attitude, behaviour, demeanour, deportment, manners. **2** administration, control, direction, government, handling, management, regulation, supervision.

conduction n. conducting of heat or electricity. □ **conductive** adj., **conductivity** n.

conductor n. **1** director of orchestra etc. **2** thing that conducts heat or electricity.

conduit n. **1** pipe or channel for liquid. **2** tube protecting wires.

cone n. **1** tapering object with a circular base. **2** cone-shaped thing. **3** dry fruit of pine or fir.

confection n. prepared dish or delicacy.

confectioner n. maker or seller of confectionery.

confectionery n. sweets, cakes, and pastries.

confederacy n. league of states.

confederate adj. joined by treaty or agreement. ● n. **1** member of a confederacy. **2** accomplice.

confederation n. union of states, people, or organizations.

confer v. (**conferred**) **1** grant. **2** hold a discussion. □ **conferment** n.
■ **1** award, bestow, give, grant, present. **2** consult, converse, negotiate, parley, talk.

conference n. meeting for discussion.

confess v. **1** acknowledge, admit. **2** declare one's sins to a priest.
■ **1** acknowledge, admit, concede, own (up to); disclose, divulge, reveal.

confession n. **1** act of confessing. **2** statement of principles.

confessional n. enclosed stall in a church for hearing confessions.

confessor n. priest who hears confessions and gives counsel.

confetti n. bits of coloured paper thrown at a bride and groom.

confidant n. (fem. **confidante**) person one confides in.

confide v. **1** tell or talk confidentially. **2** entrust.

confidence n. **1** firm trust. **2** feeling of certainty, trust in one's own ability. **3** thing told confidentially. □ **confidence trick** swindle worked by gaining a person's trust.
■ **1** belief, faith, trust. **2** certainty, certitude, conviction; aplomb, assurance, courage, nerve, panache, self-assurance, self-possession, self-reliance.

confident adj. feeling confidence. □ **confidently** adv.
■ assured, certain, convinced, positive, sure; bold, cocksure, cool, courageous, fearless, self-assured, self-possessed, unafraid.

confidential adj. **1** to be kept secret. **2** entrusted with secrets. □ **confidentially** adv., **confidentiality** n.

configuration n. shape, outline.

confine v. **1** keep within limits. **2** keep shut up.
■ **1** limit, restrict. **2** cage, coop up, immure, imprison, shut in.

confinement n. **1** confining, being confined. **2** childbirth.

confines n.pl. boundaries.

confirm v. make firmer or definite. □ **confirmatory** adj.
■ authenticate, back up, corroborate, prove, reinforce, ratify, strengthen, substantiate, support, validate, verify.

confirmation n. **1** confirming. **2** thing that confirms.

confiscate v. take or seize by authority. □ **confiscation** n.
■ appropriate, commandeer, expropriate, impound, remove, seize, sequestrate, take away.

conflagration n. great fire.

conflate v. blend or fuse together. □ **conflation** n.

conflict n. /kónflikt/ **1** state of opposition. **2** fight, struggle. ● v. /kanflíkt/ be in disagreement.
■ n. **1** battle, combat, war; antagonism, disagreement, discord, friction, opposition. **2** affray, fracas, fray, skirmish, struggle; altercation, dispute, feud, quarrel, row, squabble, wrangle. ● v. be at odds, be at variance, be incompatible, clash, differ, disagree.

confluence n. place where two rivers unite. □ **confluent** adj.

conform v. comply with rules or general custom. □ **conformity** n.
■ comply, keep in step, obey, toe the line.

conformist n. person who conforms to rules or custom. □ **conformism** n.

confound v. **1** astonish and perplex. **2** confuse.

confront v. **1** be, come, or bring face to face with. **2** face boldly. □ **confrontation** n.

confuse v. **1** bewilder. **2** mix up. **3** make unclear. □ **confusion** n.
■ **1** baffle, bemuse, bewilder, confound, daze, discomfit, disconcert, floor, colloq. flummox, fluster, mystify, nonplus, perplex, puzzle, colloq. stump, colloq. throw. **2** disarrange, disorder, jumble, mess up, mix up, muddle. **3** blur, cloud, obscure. □ **confusion** bemusement, bewilderment, discomfiture, mystification, perplexity, puzzlement; chaos, disarray, disorder, jumble, mess, muddle, shambles, turmoil.

confute v. prove wrong. □ **confutation** n.

conga n. dance in which people form a long winding line.

congeal v. coagulate, solidify.
■ clot, coagulate, curdle, harden, set, solidify, stiffen, thicken.

congenial adj. pleasant, agreeable.
□ **congenially** adv.
■ agreeable, amiable, friendly, genial, likeable, nice, pleasant, pleasing, sympathetic.

congenital adj. being so from birth.
□ **congenitally** adv.

conger n. large sea eel.

congest v. make abnormally full.
□ **congestion** n.

conglomerate adj. /kənglómmərət/ gathered into a mass. ● n. /kənglómmərət/ coherent mass. ● v. /kənglómmərayt/ collect into a coherent mass. □ **conglomeration** n.

congratulate v. tell (a person) that one admires his or her success. □ **congratulation** n., **congratulatory** adj.
■ applaud, compliment, felicitate, praise.

congregate v. flock together.
■ assemble, cluster, collect, convene, converge, gather, mass, meet, rally, swarm, throng.

congregation n. people assembled at a church service.

congress n. 1 formal meeting of delegates for discussion. 2 (**Congress**) law-making assembly, esp. of the USA.
□ **congressional** adj.

congruent adj. 1 suitable, consistent. 2 having exactly the same shape and size.
□ **congruence** n.

conic adj. of a cone.

conical adj. cone-shaped.

conifer n. tree bearing cones. □ **coniferous** adj.

conjecture n. & v. guess.

conjugal adj. of marriage.

conjunction n. word such as 'and' or 'or' that connects others.

conjunctivitis n. inflammation of the membrane (**conjunctiva**) connecting eyeball and eyelid.

conjure v. do sleight-of-hand tricks.
□ **conjuror** n.

conk n. (sl.) nose, head. ● v. (sl.) hit.
□ **conk out** (colloq.) break down.

connect v. 1 join, be joined. 2 associate mentally. 3 (of a train etc.) arrive so that passengers are in time to catch another.
□ **connection** n., **connective** adj., **connector** n.
■ 1 attach, combine, couple, fasten, fit together, fix, join, link, put together, tie, unite. 2 associate, link, relate, tie in. □ **connection** association, bond, link, linkage, relationship, tie, tie-up, union.

connive v. **connive at** tacitly consent to.
□ **connivance** n.

connoisseur /kónnəsőr/ n. person with expert understanding.

connote v. imply in addition to its basic meaning. □ **connotation** n.

conquer v. overcome in war or by effort.
□ **conqueror** n.
■ beat, crush, defeat, get the better of, colloq. lick, master, overpower, overthrow, rout, subjugate, thrash, triumph over, trounce, vanquish; overcome, surmount.

conquest n. 1 conquering. 2 thing won by conquering.

conscience n. person's sense of right and wrong.

conscientious adj. diligent, careful.
□ **conscientiously** adv., **conscientiousness** n.
■ attentive, careful, diligent, meticulous, painstaking, punctilious, rigorous, scrupulous, sedulous, thorough.

conscious adj. 1 with mental faculties awake. 2 intentional. 3 aware. □ **consciously** adv., **consciousness** n.
■ 1 alert, awake. 2 calculated, deliberate, intentional, purposeful, studied, wilful.

conscript v. /kənskrípt/ summon for compulsory military service. ● n. /kónskript/ conscripted person. □ **conscription** n.

consecrate v. 1 make sacred. 2 dedicate to the service of God. □ **consecration** n.

consecutive adj. following continuously. □ **consecutively** adv.

consensus n. general agreement.

consent v. say one is willing to do or allow what is asked. ● n. agreement, permission.
■ v. accede, acquiesce, agree, comply, concede, concur. ● n. acquiescence, agreement, approval, assent, authorization, compliance, concurrence, go-ahead, colloq. OK, permission.

consequence n. 1 result. 2 importance.
■ 1 effect, outcome, repercussion, result, upshot. 2 account, import, importance, moment, note, significance.

consequent adj. resulting.

consequential adj. **1** consequent. **2** important. **3** self-important.

consequently adv. as a result.

conservancy n. commission controlling a river etc.

conservation n. conserving, esp. of the natural environment. □ **conservationist** n.

■ care, maintenance, preservation, protection, safeguarding, upkeep.

conservative adj. **1** opposed to change. **2** (of an estimate) purposely low. ● n. conservative person. □ **conservatism** n.

■ **1** conventional, hidebound, old-fashioned, orthodox, reactionary, traditional, unadventurous. **2** cautious, tentative.

conservatory n. greenhouse built on to a house.

conserve¹ /kənsérv/ v. keep from harm, decay, or loss.

■ husband, keep, preserve, save, store up; maintain, protect, safeguard, take care of.

conserve² /kónserv/ n. jam made from fresh fruit and sugar.

consider v. **1** think about, esp. in order to decide. **2** be of the opinion. **3** allow for.

■ **1** contemplate, deliberate, mull over, ponder, reflect (on), ruminate (on), study, think about. **2** believe, deem, judge, reckon, regard, think. **3** allow for, take into account or consideration, respect.

considerable adj. fairly great in amount or importance. □ **considerably** adv.

■ appreciable, large, respectable, sizeable, substantial; distinguished, important, notable, noteworthy.

considerate adj. careful not to hurt or inconvenience others. □ **considerately** adv.

■ caring, courteous, gracious, helpful, kind, kindly, neighbourly, obliging, polite, solicitous, sympathetic, tactful, thoughtful, unselfish.

consideration n. **1** careful thought. **2** being considerate. **3** fact that must be kept in mind. **4** payment given as a reward.

considering prep. taking into account.

consign v. **1** deposit, entrust. **2** send (goods etc.).

consignee n. person to whom goods are sent.

consignment n. **1** consigning. **2** batch of goods.

consist v. **consist of** be composed of.

consistency n. **1** being consistent. **2** degree of thickness or solidity.

consistent adj. **1** unchanging. **2** not contradictory. □ **consistently** adv.

■ **1** constant, dependable, predictable, reliable, steady, unchanging, undeviating. **2** compatible, consonant, harmonious, in accordance, in agreement, in harmony, of a piece.

consolation n. **1** consoling. **2** thing that consoles.

console¹ /kənsól/ v. comfort in time of sorrow.

■ cheer (up), comfort, hearten, reassure, solace, soothe.

console² /kónsol/ n. **1** bracket supporting a shelf. **2** panel for switches, controls, etc.

consolidate v. **1** combine. **2** make or become secure and strong. □ **consolidation** n.

consommé /kənsómmay/ n. clear soup.

consonant n. **1** letter other than a vowel. **2** sound it represents. ● adj. consistent, harmonious.

consort n. /kónsort/ husband or wife, esp. of a monarch. ● v. /kənsórt/ keep company.

consortium n. (pl. **-tia**) combination of firms acting together.

conspicuous adj. easily seen, attracting attention. □ **conspicuously** adv.

■ apparent, blatant, clear, evident, flagrant, glaring, manifest, marked, noticeable, obtrusive, obvious, perceptible, prominent, pronounced, salient, striking, unmistakable, visible.

conspiracy n. **1** secret plan to commit a crime or do harm. **2** act of conspiring.

■ **1** intrigue, machination, plot, scheme.

conspirator n. one who conspires. □ **conspiratorial** adj.

conspire v. **1** plan secretly against others. **2** (of events) seem to combine.

constable n. policeman or policewoman of the lowest rank.

constabulary n. police force.

constancy n. **1** quality of being unchanging. **2** faithfulness.

constant adj. **1** happening repeatedly or all the time. **2** unchanging. **3** faithful. ● n. unvarying quantity. □ **constantly** adv.

■ adj. **1** ceaseless, continual, continuous, endless, incessant, non-stop, perpetual, persistent, steady, unending, uninterrupted, unremitting. **2** fixed, invariable, unchanging, uniform, unvarying. **3** dependable, devoted, faithful, loyal, reliable, staunch, steadfast, true, trustworthy, trusty, unswerving.

constellation *n.* group of stars.

consternation *n.* great surprise and anxiety.

constipation *n.* difficulty in emptying the bowels.

constituency *n.* **1** group of voters who elect a representative. **2** area represented in this way.

constituent *adj.* forming part of a whole. ● *n.* **1** constituent part. **2** member of a constituency.

constitute *v.* be the parts of.

constitution *n.* **1** principles by which a state is organized. **2** bodily condition.

constitutional *adj.* in accordance with a constitution. ● *n.* walk taken for exercise.

constrain *v.* compel, oblige.

constraint *n.* **1** constraining. **2** restriction. **3** strained manner.

constrict *v.* make narrow or tight, squeeze. □ **constriction** *n.*

construct *v.* fit together, build. ● *n.* thing constructed, esp. in the mind. □ **constructor** *n.*

■ *v.* assemble, build, create, erect, fabricate, fashion, frame, make, put up, set up.

construction *n.* **1** constructing. **2** thing constructed. **3** words put together to form a phrase. **4** interpretation.

constructive *adj.* helpful, useful. □ **constructively** *adv.*

■ beneficial, helpful, positive, practical, useful, valuable, worthwhile.

construe *v.* interpret.

consul *n.* official representative of a state in a foreign city. □ **consular** *adj.*

consulate *n.* consul's position or premises.

consult *v.* seek information or advice from. □ **consultation** *n.*

■ ask, confer with, deliberate with, refer to, speak to, talk to.

consultant *n.* specialist consulted for professional advice. □ **consultancy** *n.*

consultative *adj.* **1** of or for consultation. **2** advisory.

consume *v.* **1** eat or drink. **2** use up. **3** destroy.

■ **1** devour, drink, eat, gobble, guzzle, *colloq.* scoff. **2** deplete, drain, exhaust,

expend, go through, use up. **3** destroy, devastate, gut, lay waste, ravage, ruin.

consumer *n.* person who buys or uses goods or services.

consummate *v.* accomplish, complete (esp. marriage by sexual intercourse). □ **consummation** *n.*

consumption *n.* **1** consuming. **2** (*old use*) tuberculosis.

consumptive *adj. & n.* (person) suffering from tuberculosis.

contact *n.* **1** touching, communication. **2** electrical connection. **3** one who may be contacted for information or help. ● *v.* get in touch with. □ **contact lens** very small lens worn in the eye.

■ *v.* get in touch with, reach, ring (up), speak to, telephone, write to.

contagion *n.* spreading of disease by contact. □ **contagious** *adj.*

contain *v.* **1** have within itself. **2** include. **3** control, restrain.

■ **1** carry, hold. **2** comprise, consist of, include. **3** check, control, curb, hold back, repress, restrain, stifle, suppress.

container *n.* receptacle, esp. to transport goods.

containment *n.* prevention of hostile expansion.

contaminate *v.* pollute. □ **contamination** *n.*

■ adulterate, corrupt, debase, defile, infect, poison, pollute, soil, spoil, taint.

contemplate *v.* **1** survey with the eyes or the mind. **2** consider as a possibility, intend. □ **contemplation** *n.*

■ **1** eye, gaze at, look at, observe, scrutinize, survey, view; brood on, cogitate on, consider, meditate on, mull over, muse on, ponder on, reflect on, ruminate on, think about. **2** consider, intend, plan, propose, think about or of.

contemplative *adj.* **1** meditative. **2** of religious meditation.

contemporaneous *adj.* existing or occurring at the same time.

contemporary *adj.* **1** of the same period or age. **2** modern in style. ● *n.* person of the same age.

■ *adj.* **1** coeval, coexistent, concurrent. **2** fashionable, in, modern, new, stylish, *colloq.* trendy, up to date.

contempt *n.* **1** feeling of despising a person or thing. **2** the condition of being

despised. **3** disrespect. □ **contemptible**
adj.

■ **1** abhorrence, disdain, disgust, hatred,
loathing, odium, scorn. □ **contemptible**
dastardly, despicable, disgraceful, dishonourable, low, shabby, shameful,
wretched.

contemptuous *adj.* showing contempt.
□ **contemptuously** *adv.*

■ derisive, disdainful, insolent, insulting,
scornful, sneering, *colloq.* snooty, supercilious.

contend *v.* **1** strive, compete. **2** assert.
□ **contender** *n.*

■ **1** compete, contest, strive, struggle, vie.
2 affirm, allege, argue, assert, claim,
maintain.

content[1] /kəntént/ *adj.* satisfied. ● *n.*
being content. ● *v.* make content.
□ **contented** *adj.*, **contentment** *n.*

■ *adj.* contented, happy, glad, gratified,
pleased, satisfied. ● *v.* gladden, gratify,
please, satisfy. □ **contentment** gratification, happiness, pleasure, satisfaction.

content[2] /kóntent/ *n.* what is contained
in something.

contention *n.* **1** contending. **2** assertion
made in argument.

contentious *adj.* **1** quarrelsome. **2** likely
to cause contention.

contest *v.* /kəntést/ **1** compete for or in.
2 dispute. ● *n.* /kóntest/ **1** struggle for
victory. **2** competition. □ **contestant** *n.*

■ *v.* **1** compete for, contend for, fight for,
vie for. **2** argue against, challenge, dispute,
oppose, query, question. ● *n.* **1** battle,
conflict, fight, struggle. **2** championship,
competition, game, match, tournament.

context *n.* **1** what precedes or follows a
word or statement. **2** circumstances.
□ **contextual** *adj.*

contiguous *adj.* adjacent.

continent *n.* one of the main land
masses of the earth. □ **continental** *adj.*

contingency *n.* **1** something unforeseen.
2 thing that may occur.

contingent *adj.* **1** fortuitous. **2** possible
but not certain. **3** conditional. ● *n.* group
of troops etc. contributed to a larger
group.

continual *adj.* constantly or frequently
recurring. □ **continually** *adv.*

■ ceaseless, constant, continuous, endless, *colloq.* eternal, everlasting, incessant,
non-stop, perennial, perpetual, persistent,
recurrent, repeated, steady, unbroken,

uninterrupted, unceasing, unending, unremitting.

continuance *n.* continuing.

continue *v.* **1** not cease. **2** remain in existence. **3** resume. □ **continuation** *n.*

■ **1** carry on (with), keep up, maintain,
persevere (in), persist (in), proceed (with),
pursue, sustain. **2** endure, go on, last,
remain. **3** carry on (with), resume, return
to, take up.

continuous *adj.* without interval, uninterrupted. □ **continuously** *adv.*, **continuity** *n.*

■ ceaseless, constant, continual, endless,
incessant, interminable, non-stop, unbroken, unceasing, uninterrupted, unremitting.

continuum *n.* (*pl.* **-tinua**) continuous
thing.

contort *v.* force or twist out of normal
shape. □ **contortion** *n.*

contortionist *n.* performer who adopts
contorted postures.

contour *n.* **1** outline. **2** line on a map
showing height above sea level.

contra- *pref.* against.

contraband *n.* smuggled goods.

contraception *n.* prevention of conception, birth control.

contraceptive *adj.* & *n.* (drug or device)
preventing conception.

contract *n.* /kóntrakt/ formal agreement. ● *v.* /kəntrákt/ **1** enter into an
agreement. **2** catch (an illness). **3** make
or become smaller or shorter. □ **contraction** *n.*, **contractor** *n.*, **contractual**
adj.

■ *n.* agreement, arrangement, bargain,
compact, deal, pact. ● *v.* **1** agree, covenant, promise, undertake. **2** catch, come or
go down with, develop, get. **3** draw together, narrow, reduce, shrink.

contradict *v.* **1** deny, oppose verbally. **2**
be contrary to. □ **contradiction** *n.*, **contradictory** *adj.*

contraflow *n.* flow (esp. of traffic) in a
direction opposite to and alongside the
usual flow.

contralto *n.* lowest female voice.

contraption *n.* strange device or machine.

contrapuntal *adj.* of or in counterpoint.

contrariwise *adv.* **1** on the other hand. **2**
in the opposite way.

contrary /kóntrəri/ *adj.* **1** opposite in
nature, tendency, or direction. **2**
/kəntráiri/ perverse. ● *n.* the opposite.

● *adv.* in opposition. □ **on the contrary** the opposite is true.

■ *adj.* **1** conflicting, contradictory, different, opposed, opposing, opposite. **2** awkward, *colloq.* cussed, difficult, obstinate, perverse, refractory, self-willed, stubborn, uncooperative, unhelpful.

contrast *n.* /kóntraast/ difference shown by comparison. ● *v.* /kɒntraást/ **1** compare to reveal contrast. **2** show contrast.

■ *n.* comparison, juxtaposition; difference, disparity, dissimilarity, distinction. ● *v.* **1** compare, juxtapose; differentiate, distinguish. **2** conflict, differ, diverge.

contravene *v.* break (a rule etc.). □ **contravention** *n.*

contretemps /káwntrətɒn/ *n.* unfortunate happening.

contribute *v.* **1** give to a common fund or effort. **2** help to bring about. □ **contribution** *n.*, **contributor** *n.*, **contributory** *adj.*

■ **1** bestow, *colloq.* chip in, donate, give, grant, present, provide, supply.

contrite *adj.* **1** penitent. **2** sorry. □ **contritely** *adv.*, **contrition** *n.*

contrivance *n.* **1** contriving. **2** contrived thing, device.

contrive *v.* plan, make, or do something resourcefully.

control *n.* **1** power to give orders or restrain. **2** means of restraining or regulating. **3** standard of comparison for checking results of an experiment. ● *v.* **(controlled) 1** have control of, regulate. **2** restrain.

■ *n.* **1** authority, charge, command, direction, guidance, jurisdiction, leadership, management, mastery, power, rule, supervision, sway; restraint, self-restraint. **2** brake, check, curb. ● *v.* **1** be in charge (of), command, conduct, direct, dominate, govern, guide, hold sway over, lead, manage, oversee, regulate, rule, run, superintend, steer, supervise. **2** check, contain, curb, hold back, keep in check, master, repress, restrain, subdue.

controversial *adj.* causing controversy. □ **controversially** *adv.*

controversy *n.* prolonged dispute.

■ argument, debate, disagreement, dispute, quarrel, wrangle.

controvert *v.* deny the truth of.

contusion *n.* bruise.

conundrum *n.* riddle, puzzle.

conurbation *n.* large urban area formed where towns have spread and merged.

convalesce *v.* regain health after illness. □ **convalescence** *n.*, **convalescent** *adj.* & *n.*

■ get better, improve, recover, recuperate, regain strength.

convection *n.* transmission of heat within a liquid or gas by movement of heated particles.

convene *v.* assemble.

convenience *n.* **1** being convenient. **2** convenient thing. **3** lavatory.

convenient *adj.* **1** serving one's comfort or interests. **2** well situated. □ **conveniently** *adv.*

■ **1** expedient, helpful, suitable, useful. **2** accessible, available, at hand, handy, nearby, well situated, within reach.

convent *n.* residence of a community of nuns.

convention *n.* **1** accepted custom. **2** assembly. **3** formal agreement.

■ **1** custom, practice, rule, tradition, usage. **2** assembly, conference, congress, convocation, gathering, meeting, symposium.

conventional *adj.* **1** depending on or according with convention. **2** bound by social conventions. **3** usual. □ **conventionally** *adv.*

■ **1** agreed, established, orthodox, traditional. **2** conservative, old-fashioned, strait-laced, *colloq.* stuffy. **3** customary, everyday, habitual, normal, ordinary, standard, usual.

converge *v.* come to or towards the same point. □ **convergence** *n.*, **convergent** *adj.*

conversant *adj.* **conversant with** having knowledge of.

conversation *n.* informal talk between people. □ **conversational** *adj.*

■ chat, dialogue, discourse, discussion, gossip, *colloq.* natter, talk, tête-à-tête.

converse¹ *v.* /kənvérss/ talk.

converse² /kónverss/ *adj.* opposite, contrary. ● *n.* converse idea or statement. □ **conversely** *adv.*

convert *v.* /kənvért/ **1** change from one form or use to another. **2** cause to change an attitude or belief. ● *n.* /kónvert/ person converted, esp. to a religious faith. □ **conversion** *n.*

■ *v.* **1** alter, change, modify, remodel, transform, transmute.

convertible *adj.* able to be converted. ● *n.* car with a folding or detachable roof.

convex *adj.* curved like the outer surface of a ball. □ **convexity** *n.*

convey *v.* **1** carry, transport, transmit. **2** communicate (meaning etc.).

■ **1** bear, bring, carry, deliver, ferry, send, ship, take, transfer, transport; conduct, transmit. **2** communicate, get *or* put across, impart, make known.

conveyance *n.* **1** conveying. **2** means of transport, vehicle.

conveyancing *n.* branch of law dealing with the transfer of property.

conveyor *n.* **1** person or thing that conveys. **2** continuous moving belt conveying objects.

convict *v.* /kənvíkt/ prove or declare guilty. ● *n.* /kónvikt/ sentenced criminal.

conviction *n.* **1** convicting. **2** firm opinion.

convince *v.* make (a person) feel certain that something is true.

convivial *adj.* sociable and lively.

convocation *n.* **1** convoking. **2** assembly convoked.

convoke *v.* summon to assemble.

convoluted *adj.* coiled, twisted.

convolution *n.* coil, twist.

convolvulus *n.* twining plant with trumpet-shaped flowers.

convoy *n.* ships or vehicles travelling together.

convulse *v.* cause violent movement or a fit of laughter in.

convulsion *n.* **1** violent involuntary movement of the body. **2** upheaval. □ **convulsive** *adj.*

coo *v.* make a soft murmuring sound like a dove. ● *n.* this sound.

cook *v.* **1** prepare (food) by heating. **2** undergo this process. **3** (*colloq.*) falsify (accounts etc.). ● *n.* person who cooks, esp. as a job. □ **cook up** (*colloq.*) concoct.

cooker *n.* stove for cooking food.

cookery *n.* art of cooking.

cookie *n.* (*US*) sweet biscuit.

cool *adj.* **1** fairly cold. **2** calm. **3** not enthusiastic. **4** unfriendly. ● *n.* **1** coolness. **2** (*sl.*) calmness. ● *v.* make or become cool. □ **coolly** *adv.*, **coolness** *n.*

■ *adj.* **1** chilly, cold, *colloq.* nippy. **2** calm, collected, composed, imperturbable, level-headed, phlegmatic, quiet, relaxed, self-possessed, serene, unemotional, unexcited, *colloq.* unflappable, unflustered, unruffled. **3** apathetic, half-hearted, lukewarm, unenthusiastic, uninterested. **4** aloof, cold, detached, distant, frosty,

standoffish, unfriendly, unsociable, unwelcoming.

coolant *n.* fluid for cooling machinery.

coomb /kōom/ *n.* valley.

coop *n.* cage for poultry. ● *v.* confine, shut in.

co-op *n.* (*colloq.*) **1** cooperative society. **2** shop run by this.

cooper *n.* person who makes or repairs casks and barrels.

cooperate *v.* work or act together. □ **cooperation** *n.*

■ collaborate, join forces, team up, unite, work together.

cooperative *adj.* **1** willing to help. **2** based on economic cooperation. ● *n.* farm or firm etc. run on this basis.

■ *adj.* **1** accommodating, amenable, considerate, helpful, obliging, willing.

co-opt *v.* appoint to a committee by invitation of existing members, not election.

coordinate¹ /kō-órdinət/ *adj.* equal in importance. ● *n.* either of two numbers or letters used to give the position of a point on a graph or map.

coordinate² /kō-órdinayt/ *v.* cause to function together efficiently. □ **coordination** *n.*, **coordinator** *n.*

coot *n.* a kind of waterbird.

cop (*sl.*) *n.* **1** police officer. **2** capture. ● *v.* (**copped**) catch.

cope *v.* deal effectively, manage.

■ get by, make do, manage, muddle through, survive.

copier *n.* copying machine.

coping *n.* sloping top row of masonry in a wall.

copious *adj.* plentiful. □ **copiously** *adv.*

■ abundant, ample, bountiful, generous, lavish, liberal, luxuriant, overflowing, plentiful, profuse, unstinting, voluminous.

copper¹ *n.* **1** reddish-brown metal. **2** coin containing this. **3** its colour. ● *adj.* made of copper.

copper² *n.* (*sl.*) policeman.

coppice *n.* (also **copse**) group of small trees and undergrowth.

copulate *v.* have sexual intercourse. □ **copulation** *n.*

copy *n.* **1** thing made to look like another. **2** specimen of a book etc. ● *v.* **1** make a copy of. **2** imitate.

■ *n.* **1** duplicate, facsimile, imitation, likeness, replica, reproduction, transcript; carbon copy, photocopy; counterfeit, fake, forgery. ● *v.* **1** duplicate, replicate, reproduce, transcribe. **2** ape, echo, imitate, impersonate, mimic.

copyright *n.* sole right to publish a work. ● *v.* secure copyright for.

coquette *n.* woman who flirts. □ **coquettish** *adj.*, **coquetry** *n.*

coracle *n.* small wicker boat.

coral *n.* **1** hard red, pink, or white substance built by tiny sea creatures. **2** reddish-pink.

cor anglais /kór óngglay/ woodwind instrument like the oboe but lower in pitch.

corbel *n.* stone or wooden support projecting from a wall.

cord *n.* **1** long thin flexible material made from twisted strands. **2** piece of this. **3** corduroy.

■ **1** cable, flex, rope, string, twine.

cordial *adj.* warm and friendly. ● *n.* fruit-flavoured drink. □ **cordially** *adv.*

■ *adj.* affable, amiable, courteous, friendly, genial, hospitable, pleasant, polite, warm.

cordon *n.* **1** line or circle of police etc. **2** fruit tree pruned to grow as a single stem. ● *v.* enclose by a cordon.

cordon bleu /kórdon blö/ of the greatest excellence in cookery.

corduroy *n.* cloth with velvety ridges.

core *n.* **1** central or most important part. **2** horny central part of an apple etc., containing seeds. ● *v.* remove the core from.

■ *n.* **1** centre, crux, essence, heart, kernel, *sl.* nitty-gritty, nub, quintessence.

co-respondent *n.* person with whom the respondent in a divorce suit is said to have committed adultery.

corgi *n.* dog of a small Welsh breed with short legs.

coriander *n.* plant whose leaves and seeds are used for flavouring.

cork *n.* **1** light tough bark of a Mediterranean oak. **2** piece of this used as a float. **3** bottle stopper. ● *v.* stop up with a cork.

corkage *n.* restaurant's charge for serving wine.

corkscrew *n.* **1** tool for extracting corks from bottles. **2** spiral thing.

corm *n.* bulb-like underground stem from which buds grow.

cormorant *n.* large black seabird.

corn[1] *n.* **1** wheat, oats, or maize. **2** its grain.

corn[2] *n.* small area of horny hardened skin, esp. on the foot.

corncrake *n.* bird with a harsh cry.

cornea *n.* transparent outer covering of the eyeball.

cornelian *n.* reddish or white semi-precious stone.

corner *n.* **1** angle or area where two lines, sides, or streets meet. **2** free kick or hit from the corner of the field in football or hockey. ● *v.* **1** force into a position from which there is no escape. **2** obtain a monopoly of. **3** drive fast round a corner.

cornerstone *n.* **1** basis. **2** vital foundation.

cornet *n.* **1** brass instrument like a small trumpet. **2** cone-shaped wafer holding ice cream.

cornflour *n.* flour made from maize.

cornflower *n.* blue-flowered plant growing among corn.

cornice *n.* ornamental moulding round the top of an indoor wall.

Cornish *adj.* of Cornwall. ● *n.* Celtic language of Cornwall.

cornucopia *n.* horn-shaped container overflowing with fruit and flowers, symbol of abundance.

corny *adj.* (**-ier**, **-iest**) (*colloq.*) hackneyed.

corollary *n.* proposition that follows logically from another.

corona *n.* (*pl.* **-nae**) ring of light round something.

coronary *n.* **1** one of the arteries supplying blood to the heart. **2** thrombosis in this.

coronation *n.* ceremony of crowning a monarch or consort.

coroner *n.* officer holding inquests.

coronet *n.* small crown.

corporal[1] /kórpral/ *n.* non-commissioned officer next below sergeant.

corporal[2] /kórpərəl/ *adj.* of the body. □ **corporal punishment** whipping or beating.

corporate *adj.* of or belonging to a corporation or group.

corporation *n.* group in business or elected to govern a town.

corporeal *adj.* having a body, tangible. □ **corporeally** *adv.*

corps /kor/ *n.* **1** military unit. **2** organized group of people.

corpse *n.* dead body.

■ body, cadaver, carcass, remains, *sl.* stiff.

corpulent *adj.* having a bulky body, fat. □ **corpulence** *n.*

corpus *n.* (*pl.* **corpora**) set of writings.

corpuscle *n.* blood cell.

corral *n.* (*US*) enclosure for cattle. ● *v.* (**coralled**) put or keep in a corral.

correct *adj.* **1** true, accurate. **2** in accordance with an approved way of behaving or working. ● *v.* **1** make correct. **2** mark errors in. **3** reprove. □ **correctly** *adv.*, **correctness** *n.*
■ *adj.* **1** accurate, exact, factual, faithful, precise, right, true. **2** acceptable, appropriate, decent, decorous, fitting, proper, seemly, suitable. ● *v.* **1** amend, cure, fix, put right, rectify, redress, remedy, repair. **2** grade, mark. **3** admonish, berate, rebuke, reprimand, reprove, scold.

correction *n.* **1** correcting. **2** alteration correcting something.

corrective *adj.* & *n.* (thing) correcting what is bad or harmful.

correlate *v.* compare, connect, or be connected systematically. □ **correlation** *n.*

correspond *v.* **1** be similar or equivalent. **2** exchange letters.
■ **1** accord, agree, concur, coincide, match, square, tally. **2** communicate, write.

correspondence *n.* **1** similarity. **2** (exchange of) letters.

correspondent *n.* **1** person who writes letters. **2** person employed to write or report for a newspaper or TV news station.

corridor *n.* **1** passage in a building or train. **2** strip of territory giving access to somewhere.

corroborate *v.* give support to, confirm. □ **corroboration** *n.*, **corroborative** *adj.*
■ authenticate, back up, confirm, prove, substantiate, support, validate, verify.

corrode *v.* destroy (metal etc.) gradually by chemical action. □ **corrosion** *n.*, **corrosive** *adj.*

corrugated *adj.* shaped into ridges. □ **corrugation** *n.*

corrupt *adj.* **1** dishonest, accepting bribes. **2** immoral, wicked. **3** decaying. ● *v.* **1** make corrupt. **2** spoil, taint. □ **corruption** *n.*
■ *adj.* **1** *sl.* bent, *colloq.* crooked, dishonest, dishonourable, unscrupulous, untrustworthy, venal. **2** decadent, degenerate, depraved, dissolute, evil, immoral, perverted, wicked. ● *v.* **1** bribe, suborn; deprave, pervert. **2** contaminate, defile, poison, pollute, spoil, taint.

corsage /korsaÃazh/ *n.* (*US*) flowers worn by a woman.

corset *n.* close-fitting undergarment to shape or support the body.

cortège /kortáyzh/ *n.* funeral procession.

cortex *n.* (*pl.* **-ices**) outer part of the brain.

cortisone *n.* hormone produced by adrenal glands or synthetically.

corvette *n.* small fast gunboat.

cos¹ *n.* long-leaved lettuce.

cos² *abbr.* cosine.

cosh *n.* weighted weapon for hitting people. ● *v.* hit with a cosh.

cosine *n.* ratio of the side adjacent to an acute angle in a right-angled triangle to the hypotenuse.

cosmetic *n.* substance for beautifying the complexion etc. ● *adj.* improving the appearance.

cosmic *adj.* of the universe. □ **cosmic rays** radiation from outer space.

cosmogony *n.* (theory of) the origin of the universe.

cosmology *n.* science or theory of the universe. □ **cosmological** *adj.*, **cosmologist** *n.*

cosmopolitan *adj.* **1** of or from all parts of the world. **2** free from national prejudices. ● *n.* cosmopolitan person.

cosmos *n.* universe.

Cossack *n.* member of a S. Russian people, famous as horsemen.

cost *v.* (**cost**) **1** have as its price. **2** involve the sacrifice or loss of. **3** (**costed**) estimate the cost of. ● *n.* what a thing costs.
■ *n.* charge, expenditure, expense, outlay, payment, price, rate, tariff.

costermonger *n.* person selling fruit etc. from a barrow.

costly *adj.* (**-ier, -iest**) expensive.

costume *n.* **1** style of clothes, esp. that of a historical period. **2** clothing for a specified activity.

cosy *adj.* (**-ier, -iest**) warm and comfortable. ● *n.* cover to keep a teapot hot. □ **cosily** *adv.*, **cosiness** *n.*
■ *adj.* comfortable, homely, relaxing, restful, snug, warm.

cot *n.* child's bed with high sides. □ **cot death** unexplained death of a sleeping baby.

coterie *n.* select group.

cotoneaster /kətóniástər/ *n.* shrub or tree with red berries.

cottage *n.* small simple house in the country. □ **cottage cheese** mild white lumpy cheese. **cottage pie** shepherd's pie.

cotton *n.* **1** soft white substance round the seeds of a tropical plant. **2** this plant. **3** thread or fabric made from cotton. ● *v.* **cotton on** (*colloq.*) understand. □ **cotton wool** fluffy material orig. made from raw cotton.

couch *n.* long piece of furniture for lying or sitting on. ● *v.* express in a specified way.

couch grass weed with long creeping roots.

cougar /kōōgər/ *n.* (*US*) puma.

cough *v.* expel air etc. from lungs with a sudden sharp sound. ● *n.* **1** act or sound of coughing. **2** illness causing coughing.

could *see* can².

coulomb /kōōlom/ *n.* unit of electric charge.

council *n.* **1** (meeting of) an advisory or administrative body. **2** local administrative body of a town etc.
■ **1** assembly, conference, congress, convention, meeting; board, body, committee, panel.

councillor *n.* member of a council.

counsel *n.* **1** advice. **2** barrister(s). ● *v.* (**counselled**) advise, recommend. □ **counsellor** *n.*
■ *n.* **1** advice, guidance, judgement, opinion, recommendation. ● *v.* advise, advocate, exhort, recommend, suggest, urge.

count¹ *v.* **1** say numbers in order. **2** find the total of. **3** include or be included in a reckoning. **4** regard as. **5** be important. ● *n.* **1** counting, number reached by this. **2** point being considered. □ **count on 1** rely on. **2** expect confidently.
■ *v.* **2** add up, calculate, compute, reckon, total, *colloq.* tot up. **3** allow for, include, take into account. **4** consider, deem, judge, rate, reckon, regard as. **5** be important, matter, signify. □ **count on** bank on, be sure of, depend on, lean on, rely on, swear by, trust.

count² *n.* foreign nobleman corresponding to earl.

countdown *n.* counting seconds backwards to zero.

countenance *n.* **1** face. **2** expression. **3** approval. ● *v.* give approval to.

counter¹ *n.* **1** flat-topped fitment in a shop etc. over which business is conducted. **2** small disc used in board games.

counter² *adv.* in the opposite direction. ● *adj.* opposed. ● *v.* take opposing action against.

counter- *pref.* **1** rival. **2** retaliatory. **3** reversed. **4** opposite.

counteract *v.* neutralize. □ **counteraction** *n.*
■ cancel out, counterbalance, nullify, offset.

counter-attack *n.* & *v.* attack in reply to an opponent's attack.

counterbalance *n.* weight or influence balancing another. ● *v.* act as a counterbalance to.

counterfeit *adj.*, *n.*, & *v.* fake.
■ *adj.* artificial, bogus, fake, false, forged, fraudulent, imitation, *colloq.* phoney, sham, spurious; feigned, insincere, pretended, simulated. ● *n.* fake, forgery, imitation, *colloq.* phoney. ● *v.* copy, fake, falsify, forge, imitate; feign, pretend, simulate.

counterfoil *n.* section of a cheque or receipt kept as a record.

countermand *v.* cancel.

counterpane *n.* bedspread.

counterpart *n.* person or thing corresponding to another.

counterpoint *n.* method of combining melodies.

counter-productive *adj.* having the opposite of the desired effect.

countersign *n.* password. ● *v.* add a confirming signature to.

countersink *v.* (**-sunk**) sink (a screwhead) into a shaped cavity so that the surface is level.

counter-tenor *n.* male alto.

countervail *v.* avail against.

countess *n.* **1** count's or earl's wife or widow. **2** woman with the rank of count or earl.

countless *adj.* too many to be counted.

countrified *adj.* rustic.

country *n.* **1** nation's territory, a state. **2** land of a person's birth or citizenship. **3** land consisting of fields etc. with few buildings. **4** region with regard to its associations etc. **5** national population.
■ **1** kingdom, nation, power, realm, state. **2** fatherland, homeland, motherland, native land. **3** countryside, green belt. **4** land, terrain, territory.

countryman, countrywoman *ns.* **1** person living in the country. **2** person of one's own country.

countryside *n.* rural district.

county n. **1** major administrative division of a country. **2** families of high social class long established in a county.

coup /koo/ n. sudden action taken to obtain power etc.

coup de grâce /koo də graass/ finishing stroke.

coup d'état /koo daytaa/ sudden overthrow of a government by force or illegal means.

couple n. **1** two people or things. **2** married or engaged pair. ● v. **1** link together. **2** copulate.
■ n. **1** brace, pair. **2** duo, pair, twosome. ● v. **1** connect, fasten, hitch, join, link, unite, yoke.

couplet n. two successive rhyming lines of verse.

coupling n. connecting device.

coupon n. **1** form or ticket entitling the holder to something. **2** entry form for a football pool.

courage n. ability to control fear, bravery. □ **courageous** adj., **courageously** adv.
■ boldness, bravery, daring, fearlessness, fortitude, gallantry, colloq. grit, colloq. guts, heroism, intrepidity, mettle, nerve, pluck, spirit, valour. □ **courageous** bold, brave, daring, dauntless, fearless, gallant, game, colloq. gutsy, heroic, intrepid, mettlesome, plucky, spirited, valiant, valorous.

courgette n. small vegetable marrow.

courier n. **1** messenger carrying documents. **2** person employed to guide and assist tourists.

course n. **1** direction taken or intended. **2** onward progress. **3** golf course, racecourse, etc. **4** series of lessons or treatments. **5** layer of stone etc. in a building. **6** one part of a meal. ● v. move or flow freely. □ **of course** without doubt.
■ n. **1** direction, passage, path, route, tack, track, way.

court n. **1** courtyard. **2** area where tennis, squash, etc., are played. **3** sovereign's establishment with attendants. **4** room or building where legal cases are heard or judged. ● v. **1** try to win the favour, support, or love of. **2** invite (danger etc.). □ **court martial** judicial court of military officers. **court-martial** v. (**-martialled**) try by court martial.

courteous adj. polite. □ **courteously** adv., **courteousness** n.
■ chivalrous, civil, considerate, gentlemanly, ladylike, polite, respectful, urbane, well-mannered.

courtesan n. prostitute with wealthy or upper-class clients.

courtesy n. courteous behaviour or act.

courtier n. person who attends a sovereign at court.

courtly adj. dignified and polite.

courtship n. courting.

courtyard n. space enclosed by walls or buildings.

cousin n. (also **first cousin**) child of one's uncle or aunt. □ **second cousin** child of one's parent's cousin.

couture n. design and making of fashionable clothes.

couturier /kootyooriay/ n. designer of fashionable clothes.

cove n. small bay.

coven n. assembly of witches.

covenant n. formal agreement, contract. ● v. make a covenant.

cover v. **1** place or be or spread over. **2** conceal or protect thus. **3** travel over (a distance). **4** be enough to pay for. **5** deal with (a subject etc.). **6** protect by insurance etc. **7** report for a newspaper etc. ● n. **1** thing that covers, esp. a lid, wrapper, etc. **2** screen, shelter, protection. **3** place laid at a meal. □ **cover up** conceal. **cover-up** n.
■ v. **1** coat, extend over, spread over. **2** bury, camouflage, cloak, conceal, hide, mask, shroud, veil; enclose, envelop, swaddle, wrap; protect, screen, shelter, shield. **3** travel, traverse. **4** be enough for, defray, pay for. **5** comprise, deal with, encompass, include, incorporate, take in. ● n. **1** cap, covering, lid, top; binding, dust cover or jacket, wrapper. **2** camouflage, cloak, cover-up, disguise, front, mask, pretence, screen, smokescreen; hiding place, refuge, retreat, shelter; concealment, protection.

coverage n. **1** process of covering. **2** area or risk etc. covered.

coverlet n. bedspread.

covert n. thick undergrowth where animals hide. ● adj. done secretly. □ **covertly** adv.

covet v. (**coveted**) desire (a thing belonging to another person). □ **covetous** adj.

covey n. group of partridges.

cow[1] n. fully grown female of cattle or other large animals.

cow[2] v. intimidate.

coward n. person who lacks courage. □ **cowardly** adj.

■ □ **cowardly** afraid, colloq. chicken, craven, faint-hearted, fearful, frightened, pusillanimous, spineless, scared, timid, timorous, unheroic, colloq. yellow.

cowardice n. lack of courage.

cowboy n. 1 man in charge of cattle on a ranch. 2 (colloq.) person with reckless methods in business.

cower v. crouch or shrink in fear.

cowl n. 1 monk's hood or hooded robe. 2 hood-shaped covering.

cowling n. removable metal cover on an engine.

cowrie n. a kind of seashell.

cowslip n. wild plant with small fragrant yellow flowers.

cox n. coxswain. ● v. act as cox of.

coxswain /kóks'n/ n. steersman.

coy adj. pretending to be shy or embarrassed. □ **coyly** adv.

coyote /koyóti/ n. N. American wild dog.

coypu n. beaver-like water animal.

crab n. ten-legged shellfish. □ **crab apple** small sour apple.

crabbed adj. 1 bad-tempered. 2 (of handwriting) hard to read.

crabby adj. bad-tempered.

crack n. 1 sudden sharp noise. 2 sharp blow. 3 narrow opening. 4 line where a thing is broken but not separated. 5 (colloq.) joke. ● adj. (colloq.) first-rate. ● v. 1 make or cause to make the sound of a crack. 2 break without parting completely. 3 knock sharply. 4 find a solution to (a problem). 5 collapse under strain. 6 tell (a joke). 7 (of the voice) become harsh. □ **crack-brained** adj. (colloq.) crazy. **crack down on** (colloq.) take severe measures against. **crack up** (colloq.) have a physical or mental breakdown.

■ n. 1 bang, clap, report, snap, shot. 2 bang, blow, colloq. clip, clout, knock, rap, smack. 3 breach, break, chink, cleft, cranny, crevice, fissure, gap, opening, rift, rupture, slit, split. ● v. 2 break, fracture, rupture, split. 3 bang, bash, hit, knock, strike, colloq. whack. 4 decipher, figure out, solve, work out. 5 break down, cave in, collapse, give way, yield.

crackdown n. (colloq.) severe measures against something.

cracker n. 1 small explosive firework. 2 toy paper tube made to give an explosive crack when pulled apart. 3 thin dry biscuit.

crackers adj. (sl.) crazy.

crackle v. make light cracking sounds. ● n. these sounds.

crackling n. crisp skin on roast pork.

crackpot (sl.) n. eccentric person. ● adj. 1 crazy. 2 unworkable.

cradle n. 1 baby's bed usu. on rockers. 2 place where something originates. 3 supporting structure. ● v. hold or support gently.

craft n. 1 skill, technique. 2 occupation requiring this. 3 cunning, deceit. 4 (pl. **craft**) vessel, aircraft, or spacecraft.

■ 1 ability, craftsmanship, dexterity, expertise, flair, know-how, skill, talent, technique. 2 calling, occupation, profession, trade, vocation. 3 artfulness, craftiness, cunning, deceit, guile, trickery, wiliness. 4 boat, ship, vessel; aeroplane, aircraft, plane; rocket, spacecraft, spaceship.

craftsman n. person skilled in a craft. □ **craftsmanship** n.

crafty adj. (**-ier, -iest**) cunning, using underhand methods. □ **craftily** adv., **craftiness** n.

■ artful, canny, clever, cunning, deceitful, designing, devious, guileful, machiavellian, scheming, shrewd, sly, underhand, wily.

crag n. steep or rugged rock.

craggy adj. (**-ier, -iest**) rugged.

cram v. (**crammed**) 1 fill to bursting. 2 force into a space. 3 study intensively for an exam. □ **crammer** n.

■ 1 jam, overcrowd, pack, stuff. 2 push, ram, shove, squeeze, thrust. 3 study, colloq. swot.

cramp n. painful involuntary tightening of a muscle. ● v. keep within too narrow limits.

crampon n. spiked plate worn on boots for climbing on ice.

cranberry n. 1 small red sharp-tasting berry. 2 shrub bearing this.

crane n. 1 large wading bird. 2 apparatus for lifting and moving heavy objects. ● v. stretch (one's neck) to see something. □ **crane-fly** n. long-legged flying insect.

crank[1] n. L-shaped part for converting to-and-fro into circular motion. ● v. turn with a crank. □ **crankshaft** n. shaft turned in this way.

crank² *n.* person with very strange ideas. □ **cranky** *adj.*

cranny *n.* crevice.

craps *n.pl.* (*US*) gambling game played with a pair of dice.

crash *n.* **1** sudden loud noise. **2** violent collision. **3** financial collapse. ● *v.* **1** make a crashing noise. **2** be or cause to be involved in a collision. **3** undergo financial ruin. **4** (*colloq.*) gatecrash. ● *adj.* involving intense effort to achieve something rapidly. □ **crash helmet** padded helmet worn to protect the head in a crash. **crash-land** *v.* land (an aircraft) in emergency, causing damage.

■ *n.* **1** bang, boom, clash, explosion, smash. **2** accident, collision, pile-up, smash. ● *v.* **1** bang, boom, clash, explode, smash. **2** bang together, collide; smash, wreck. **3** collapse, fail, fold, go bankrupt, *colloq.* go bust, *colloq.* go broke, go out of business, go under.

crass *adj.* **1** very stupid. **2** insensitive.

crate *n.* **1** packing-case made of wooden slats. **2** (*sl.*) old aircraft or car. ● *v.* pack in crate(s).

crater *n.* bowl-shaped cavity.

cravat *n.* **1** short scarf. **2** necktie.

crave *v.* long or beg for.

craven *adj.* cowardly.

craving *n.* intense longing.

craw *n.* bird's crop.

crawfish *n.* large spiny sea lobster.

crawl *v.* **1** move on hands and knees or with the body on the ground. **2** move very slowly. **3** (*colloq.*) seek favour by servile behaviour. ● *n.* **1** crawling movement or pace. **2** overarm swimming stroke. □ **crawler** *n.*

crayfish *n.* **1** freshwater shellfish like a small lobster. **2** crawfish.

crayon *n.* stick of coloured wax etc. ● *v.* draw or colour with crayon(s).

craze *n.* **1** temporary enthusiasm. **2** object of this.

■ enthusiasm, fad, fashion, mania, obsession, trend.

crazy *adj.* (**-ier, -iest**) **1** insane. **2** very foolish. **3** (*colloq.*) madly eager. □ **crazy paving** paving made of irregular pieces. **crazily** *adv.*, **craziness** *n.*

■ **1** *sl.* barmy, *sl.* batty, *colloq.* crackbrained, *sl.* crackers, demented, deranged, insane, lunatic, mad, *sl.* nuts, *sl.* nutty, out of one's mind, *sl.* potty, unbalanced. **2** absurd, asinine, *sl.* crackpot, daft, foolish, hare-brained, idiotic, illogical, imbecilic, impractical, inane, laughable, ludicrous,

nonsensical, preposterous, ridiculous, senseless, silly, stupid, unrealistic, unreasonable, unwise.

creak *n.* harsh squeak. ● *v.* make this sound. □ **creaky** *adj.*

cream *n.* **1** fatty part of milk. **2** its colour, yellowish-white. **3** cream-like substance. **4** best part. ● *adj.* creamcoloured. ● *v.* **1** remove the cream from. **2** make creamy. □ **cream cheese** soft rich cheese. **cream cracker** crisp unsweetened biscuit. **creamy** *adj.*

crease *n.* **1** line made by crushing or pressing. **2** line marking the limit of the bowler's or batsman's position in cricket. ● *v.* **1** make a crease in. **2** develop creases.

create *v.* **1** bring into existence. **2** invest with a new rank. **3** (*sl.*) make a fuss. □ **creation** *n.*, **creator** *n.*

■ **1** bring into being, cause, design, devise, dream up, engender, fashion, forge, generate, give rise to, imagine, invent, make, manufacture, originate, produce, spawn, *colloq.* think up.

creative *adj.* inventive, imaginative. □ **creatively** *adv.*, **creativity** *n.*

■ artistic, imaginative, ingenious, inventive, original, resourceful.

creature *n.* animal, person.

crèche /kresh/ *n.* day nursery.

credence *n.* belief.

credentials *n.pl.* documents showing that a person is who or what he or she claims to be.

credible *adj.* believable. □ **credibly** *adv.*, **credibility** *n.*

■ believable, conceivable, feasible, likely, plausible, possible, probable.

credit *n.* **1** belief that a thing is true. **2** acknowledgement of merit. **3** good reputation. **4** system of allowing payment to be deferred. **5** sum at a person's disposal in a bank. **6** entry in an account for a sum received. **7** acknowledgement in a book or film. ● *v.* (**credited**) **1** believe. **2** enter as credit. □ **credit card** plastic card containing machine-readable magnetic code enabling the holder to make purchases on credit. **credit a person with** ascribe to a person.

■ *n.* **1** belief, credence, faith, trust. **2** acclaim, commendation, praise, recognition, tribute. **3** name, reputation, repute, standing, stature, status. ● *v.* **1** accept, believe, have faith in, rely on, trust.

creditable *adj.* deserving praise. □ **creditably** *adv.*
■ admirable, commendable, estimable, laudable, meritorious, praiseworthy.

creditor *n.* person to whom money is owed.

credulous *adj.* too ready to believe things. □ **credulity** *n.*

creed *n.* set of beliefs.
■ belief(s), doctrine, dogma, philosophy, principles.

creek *n.* **1** narrow inlet of water, esp. on a coast. **2** (*US*) tributary.

creep *v.* (**crept**) **1** move with the body close to the ground. **2** move timidly, slowly, or stealthily. **3** develop gradually. **4** (of a plant) grow along the ground or a wall etc. **5** (of flesh) shudder with horror etc. ● *n.* **1** creeping. **2** (*sl.*) unpleasant person. **3** (*pl.*) nervous sensation.
■ *v.* **1** crawl, slither, squirm, worm, wriggle. **2** edge, inch, sidle, slink, sneak, steal, tip-toe.

creepy *adj.* (**-ier, -iest**) causing horror or fear. □ **creepy-crawly** *n.* (*pl.* **-crawlies**) small insect.

cremate *v.* burn (a corpse) to ashes. □ **cremation** *n.*

crematorium *n.* (*pl.* **-ia**) place where corpses are cremated.

crenellated *adj.* having battlements.

Creole *n.* **1** descendant of European settlers in the W. Indies or S. America. **2** their dialect. **3** hybrid language.

creosote *n.* oily wood-preservative distilled from coal tar.

crêpe /krayp/ *n.* fabric with a wrinkled surface.

crept *see* **creep**.

crepuscular *adj.* active at twilight.

crescendo /krishéndō/ *adv. & n.* (*pl.* **-os**) increasing in loudness.

crescent *n.* **1** narrow curved shape tapering to a point at each end. **2** curved street of houses.

cress *n.* plant with hot-tasting leaves used in salads.

crest *n.* **1** tuft or outgrowth on a bird's or animal's head. **2** plume on a helmet. **3** top of a mountain, wave, etc. **4** design above a shield on a coat of arms.

crestfallen *adj.* dejected.

cretaceous *adj.* chalky.

cretin *n.* person who is deformed and mentally retarded as the result of a thyroid deficiency. □ **cretinous** *adj.*

crevasse *n.* deep open crack esp. in a glacier.

crevice *n.* narrow gap in a surface.
■ chink, cleft, crack, cranny, fissure, gap, opening, rift, split.

crew¹ *see* **crow**.

crew² *n.* group of people working together, esp. manning a ship, aircraft, etc. □ **crew-cut** *n.* closely cropped haircut.
■ band, body, company, corps, gang, group, party, team.

crib *n.* **1** model of the manger scene at Bethlehem. **2** cot. **3** (*colloq.*) translation for students' use. ● *v.* (**cribbed**) copy unfairly.

cribbage *n.* a card game.

crick *n.* painful stiffness in the neck or back.

cricket¹ *n.* outdoor game for two teams of 11 players with ball, bats, and wickets. □ **cricketer** *n.*

cricket² *n.* brown insect resembling a grasshopper.

crime *n.* **1** act that breaks a law. **2** illegal acts.
■ **1** misdeed, misdemeanour, offence, transgression, wrong. **2** lawlessness, wrongdoing.

criminal *n.* person guilty of a crime. ● *adj.* of or involving crime. □ **criminally** *adv.*, **criminality** *n.*
■ *n.* convict, *colloq.* crook, culprit, desperado, lawbreaker, malefactor, miscreant, offender, thug, transgressor, villain, wrongdoer. ● *adj. sl.* bent, *colloq.* crooked, dishonest, illegal, illicit, lawless, unlawful.

criminology *n.* study of crime. □ **criminologist** *n.*

crimp *v.* press into ridges.

crimson *adj. & n.* deep red.

cringe *v.* **1** cower. **2** behave obsequiously.
■ **1** blench, cower, flinch, quail, recoil, shrink back, wince. **2** crawl, fawn, grovel, kowtow.

crinkle *n. & v.* wrinkle.

crinoline *n.* hooped petticoat.

cripple *n.* lame person. ● *v.* **1** make lame. **2** weaken seriously.
■ *v.* **1** disable, handicap, incapacitate, lame, maim. **2** damage, debilitate, hamstring, impair, paralyse, weaken.

crisis n. (pl. **crises**) **1** time of acute difficulty. **2** decisive moment.
■ **1** calamity, catastrophe, disaster, emergency. **2** critical moment, turning point, watershed.

crisp adj. **1** brittle. **2** cold and bracing. **3** brisk and decisive. ● n. thin slice of potato fried crisp. □ **crisply** adv., **crispness** n., **crispy** adj.
■ adj. **1** brittle, crispy, crunchy, friable. **2** bracing, exhilarating, fresh, invigorating, refreshing, stimulating. **3** brisk, decisive, incisive, vigorous.

criss-cross n. pattern of crossing lines. ● adj. & adv. in this pattern. ● v. mark, form, or move in this way, intersect.

criterion n. (pl. **-ia**) standard of judgement.

critic n. **1** person who points out faults. **2** one skilled in criticism.

critical adj. **1** looking for faults. **2** of or at a crisis. **3** expressing criticism. □ **critically** adv.
■ **1** captious, censorious, deprecatory, derogatory, disparaging, colloq. nit-picking, uncomplimentary. **2** dangerous, grave, perilous, serious, severe, touch-and-go; crucial, important, momentous, vital.

criticism n. **1** pointing out of faults. **2** judging of merit of literary or artistic works.
■ **1** censure, condemnation, disapproval, disparagement, fault-finding. **2** analysis, appraisal, assessment, evaluation, judgement.

criticize v. **1** find fault with. **2** discuss the merit of literary or artistic works.
■ **1** carp at, cast aspersions on, censure, condemn, disparage, colloq. get at, find fault with, impugn, sl. knock, colloq. pan, pick holes in, sl. slam, colloq. slate. **2** analyse, appraise, assess, evaluate, judge, review.

critique n. critical essay.

croak n. deep hoarse cry or sound like that of a frog. ● v. **1** utter or speak with a croak. **2** (sl.) die.

crochet /krṓshay/ n. handiwork done with a thread and a hooked needle. ● v. make by crochet.

crock[1] n. **1** earthenware pot. **2** broken piece of this.

crock[2] n. (colloq.) old or worn-out person or vehicle.

crockery n. household china.

crocodile n. large amphibious reptile. □ **crocodile tears** pretence of sorrow.

crocus n. spring-flowering plant growing from a corm.

croft n. small rented farm in Scotland.

crofter n. tenant of a croft.

croissant /krwússon/ n. rich crescent-shaped roll.

crone n. withered old woman.

crony n. close friend or companion.

crook n. **1** hooked stick. **2** bent thing. **3** (colloq.) criminal. ● v. bend.

crooked adj. **1** not straight. **2** (colloq.) dishonest. □ **crookedly** adv.
■ **1** askew, bent, contorted, gnarled, lop-sided, misshapen, twisted, warped. **2** bent, criminal, dishonest, illegal, illicit, unlawful, wrong.

croon v. sing softly. □ **crooner** n.

crop n. **1** batch of plants grown for their produce. **2** harvest from this. **3** group or amount produced at one time. **4** pouch in a bird's gullet where food is broken up for digestion. **5** whip-handle. **6** very short haircut. ● v. (**cropped**) **1** cut or bite off. **2** produce or gather as harvest. □ **crop up** occur unexpectedly.

cropper n. (sl.) heavy fall.

croquet /krṓkay/ n. game played on a lawn with balls and mallets.

croquette /krɒkét/ n. fried ball or roll of potato, meat, or fish.

cross n. **1** stake with a transverse bar used in crucifixion, this as an emblem of Christianity. **2** affliction. **3** hybrid animal or plant. **4** mixture of or compromise between two things. **5** mark made by drawing one line across another. **6** thing shaped like this. ● v. **1** go or extend across. **2** pass in different directions. **3** draw line(s) across (a cheque) so that it must be paid into a bank. **4** oppose the wishes of. **5** cause to interbreed. ● adj. **1** peevish, angry. **2** reaching from side to side. **3** reciprocal. □ **at cross purposes** misunderstanding each other. **cross out** obliterate by drawing lines across. □ **crossly** adv., **crossness** n.
■ n. **1** crucifix. **2** affliction, burden, misfortune, problem, trial, tribulation, trouble, woe, worry. **3** cross-breed, hybrid, mixture, mongrel. ● v. **1** cross over, go across, pass over, span, traverse. **2** intersect, join, meet. ● adj. **1** angry, annoyed, bad-tempered, cantankerous, crabby, crotchety, fractious, grumpy, huffy, irascible, irate, irritable, irritated, peevish, pettish, colloq. shirty, testy, vexed. □ **cross out**

blot out, cancel, delete, erase, obliterate, score out, strike out.

crossbar n. horizontal bar.

crossbow n. mechanical bow fixed across a wooden stock.

cross-breed n. animal produced by interbreeding. ● v. cause to interbreed. □ **cross-bred** adj.

cross-check v. check again by a different method.

cross-examine v. question, esp. in a law court. □ **cross-examination** n.

cross-eyed adj. squinting.

crossfire n. gunfire crossing another line of fire.

crossing n. 1 journey across water. 2 place where things cross. 3 place for pedestrians to cross a road.

crosspatch n. (colloq.) bad-tempered person.

cross-ply adj. (of a tyre) having fabric layers with cords lying crosswise.

cross-question v. cross-examine.

cross-reference n. reference to another place in the same book.

crossroads n. place where roads intersect.

cross-section n. 1 diagram showing internal structure. 2 representative sample.

crosswise adv. in the form of a cross.

crossword n. puzzle in which intersecting words have to be inserted into a diagram.

crotch n. place where things fork, esp. where legs join the trunk.

crotchet n. note in music, half a minim.

crotchety adj. peevish.

crouch v. stoop low with legs tightly bent. ● n. this position.

croupier /krōōpiar/ n. person in charge of a gaming table.

croûton /krōōton/ n. small piece of fried or toasted bread.

crow n. 1 large black bird. 2 cock's cry. ● v. (crowed or crew) 1 (of a cock) utter a loud cry. 2 express gleeful triumph.

crowbar n. bar of iron, usually with a bent end, used as a lever.

crowd n. large group. ● v. 1 come together in a crowd. 2 fill or occupy fully.
  ■ n. cluster, drove, flock, herd, horde, host, mob, multitude, pack, swarm, throng. ● v. 1 assemble, cluster, collect, congregate, flock, gather, herd, mass, press, swarm, throng.

crown n. 1 monarch's ceremonial headdress, usu. a circlet of gold. 2 (the

Crown) supreme governing power in a monarchy. 3 top part of a head, hat, etc. ● v. 1 place a crown on. 2 make king or queen. 3 be a climax to. 4 (sl.) hit on the head.
  ■ n. 1 circlet, coronet, diadem. 2 (the Crown) king, monarch, queen, ruler, sovereign. ● v. 2 enthrone. 3 cap, complete, perfect, round off, top.

crucial adj. very important, decisive. □ **crucially** adv.
  ■ critical, decisive, essential, key, momentous, vital.

crucible n. pot in which metals are melted.

crucifix n. model of a cross with a figure of Christ on it.

crucifixion n. 1 crucifying. 2 (the Crucifixion) that of Christ.

cruciform adj. cross-shaped.

crucify v. 1 put to death by nailing or binding to a transverse bar. 2 cause extreme pain to.

crude adj. 1 in a natural or raw state. 2 rough, unpolished. 3 lacking good manners, vulgar. □ **crudely** adv., **crudity** n.
  ■ 1 natural, raw, unprocessed, unrefined. 2 primitive, rough, rudimentary, simple, unfinished, unpolished. 3 boorish, coarse, uncouth, vulgar.

cruel adj. (crueller, cruellest) 1 feeling pleasure in another's suffering. 2 causing pain or suffering, esp. deliberately. □ **cruelly** adv., **cruelty** n.
  ■ 1 callous, cold-blooded, hard, hard-hearted, harsh, heartless, merciless, pitiless, ruthless, sadistic, unkind, unmerciful. 2 barbaric, bloodthirsty, brutal, diabolical, ferocious, fiendish, inhuman, savage, vicious.

cruet n. set of containers for oil, vinegar, and salt at the table.

cruise v. 1 sail for pleasure or on patrol. 2 travel at a moderate speed. ● n. cruising voyage.

cruiser n. 1 fast warship. 2 motor boat with a cabin.

crumb n. small fragment of bread etc.

crumble v. break into small fragments. ● n. dish of cooked fruit with crumbly topping.

crumbly adj. easily crumbled.

crummy adj. (-ier, -iest) (sl.) 1 dirty, squalid. 2 inferior.

crumpet n. flat soft yeasty cake eaten toasted.

crumple v. **1** crush or become crushed into creases. **2** collapse.
■ **1** crease, crinkle, crush, rumple. **2** cave in, collapse, give way.

crunch v. **1** crush noisily with the teeth. **2** make this sound. ● n. **1** crunching sound. **2** decisive event. □ **crunchy** adj.

crupper n. strap looped under a horse's tail from the saddle.

crusade n. **1** campaign against an evil. **2** medieval Christian military expedition to recover the Holy Land from Muslims. ● v. take part in a crusade. □ **crusader** n.
■ n. **1** battle, campaign, drive, offensive, war. ● v. battle, campaign, fight, lobby.

crush v. **1** press so as to break, injure, or wrinkle. **2** pound into fragments. **3** defeat or subdue completely. ● n. **1** crowded mass of people. **2** (colloq.) infatuation.
■ v. **1** break, shatter, smash; mangle, mash, press, pulp, squeeze; crease, crinkle, crumple, rumple, wrinkle. **2** crumble, pound, pulverize. **3** beat, conquer, defeat, overcome, overwhelm, quash, quell, subdue, suppress, thrash, vanquish; devastate, humiliate, mortify.

crust n. hard outer layer, esp. of bread.

crustacean n. animal with a hard shell (e.g. lobster).

crusty adj. (**-ier, -iest**) **1** with a crisp crust. **2** irritable, curt.

crutch n. **1** support for a lame person. **2** crotch.

crux n. (pl. **cruces**) **1** vital part of a problem. **2** difficult point.

cry n. **1** loud wordless sound. **2** urgent appeal. **3** spell of weeping. ● v. **1** shed tears. **2** call loudly. **3** appeal for help.
■ n. **1** bellow, howl, roar, scream, screech, shout, shriek, whoop, wail, yell, yelp, yowl. **2** appeal, entreaty, plea, request, supplication. ● v. **1** bawl, blubber, grizzle, shed tears, snivel, sob, wail, weep, whimper. **2** bellow, call, roar, scream, shout, shriek, yell.

cryogenics n. branch of physics dealing with very low temperatures. □ **cryogenic** adj.

crypt n. underground room, esp. beneath a church, used usu. as a burial place.
■ catacomb, sepulchre, mausoleum, tomb, vault.

cryptic adj. **1** obscure in meaning. **2** secret, mysterious.
■ **1** mystifying, obscure, puzzling. **2** arcane, enigmatic, esoteric, mysterious, occult, secret.

cryptogram n. thing written in cipher.

crystal adj. **1** glass-like mineral. **2** high-quality glass. **3** symmetrical piece of a solidified substance.

crystalline adj. **1** like or made of crystal. **2** clear.

crystallize v. **1** form into crystals. **2** make or become definite in form. □ **crystallization** n.

cub n. young of certain animals.

cubby hole small compartment.

cube n. **1** solid object with six equal square sides. **2** product of a number multiplied by itself twice. □ **cube root** number of which a given number is the cube.

cubic adj. of three dimensions.

cubicle n. small division of a large room, screened for privacy.

cubism n. style of painting in which objects are shown as geometrical shapes. □ **cubist** n.

cuckold n. man whose wife commits adultery. ● v. make a cuckold of.

cuckoo n. bird with a call sounding similar to its name.

cucumber n. long green fleshy fruit used in salads.

cud n. food that cattle bring back from the stomach into the mouth and chew again.

cuddle v. **1** hug lovingly. **2** nestle together. ● n. gentle hug. □ **cuddly** adj. pleasant to cuddle.
■ v. **1** caress, embrace, hug. **2** nestle, snuggle.

cudgel n. short thick stick used as a weapon. ● v. (**cudgelled**) beat with a cudgel.

cue[1] n. & v. (**cueing**) signal to do something.
■ n. hint, reminder, sign, signal.

cue[2] n. long rod for striking balls in billiards etc. ● v. strike with a cue.

cuff n. **1** end part of a sleeve. **2** blow with the open hand. ● v. strike with the open hand. □ **cuff link** fastener to hold shirt cuffs together.

cuisine /kwizeen/ n. style of cooking.

cul-de-sac n. (pl. **culs-de-sac**) street closed at one end.

culinary adj. of or for cooking.

cull v. **1** gather, select. **2** select and kill (surplus animals). ● n. **1** culling. **2** animal(s) culled.

culminate v. reach its highest point or degree. □ **culmination** n.

culottes n.pl. women's trousers styled to resemble a skirt.

culpable adj. deserving blame. □ **culpably** adv., **culpability** n.

culprit n. guilty person.

■ criminal, malefactor, miscreant, offender, wrongdoer.

cult n. **1** system of religious worship. **2** excessive admiration of a person or thing.

cultivate v. **1** prepare and use (land) for crops. **2** raise (crops). **3** further one's acquaintance with (a person). **4** improve (manners etc.). □ **cultivation** n., **cultivator** n.

■ **1** farm, plough, till, work. **2** grow, produce, raise, tend. **3** develop, encourage, foster, further, nurture, promote. **4** civilize, educate, polish, refine.

culture n. **1** developed appreciation of the arts etc. **2** customs and civilization of a particular time or people. **3** rearing of organisms. **4** bacteria grown for study. ● v. grow in artificial conditions. □ **cultural** adj., **culturally** adv.

■ n. **1** education, erudition, learning, refinement, taste. **2** civilization, customs, way of life.

cultured adj. educated to appreciate the arts etc.

culvert n. drain under a road.

cumbersome adj. clumsy to carry or use.

cumin n. plant with aromatic seed.

cummerbund n. sash for the waist.

cumulative adj. increasing by additions. □ **cumulatively** adv.

cumulus n. (pl. **-li**) cloud in heaped-up rounded masses.

cuneiform n. ancient writing done in wedge-shaped strokes.

cunning adj. **1** deceitful, crafty. **2** ingenious. ● n. craftiness, ingenuity. □ **cunningly** adv.

■ adj. **1** artful, crafty, deceitful, devious, guileful, machiavellian, sly, tricky, wily. **2** adroit, clever, ingenious, shrewd, skilful, subtle. ■ n. artfulness, chicanery, craftiness, deceit, deviousness, duplicity, guile, trickery; cleverness, ingenuity, skill.

cup n. **1** drinking vessel usu. with a handle at the side. **2** prize. **3** wine or fruit juice with added flavourings. ● v. (**cupped**) make cup-shaped. □ **cupful** n.

cupboard n. recess or piece of furniture with a door, in which things may be stored.

cupidity n. greed for gain.

cupola n. small dome.

cur n. bad-tempered or scruffy dog.

curacy n. position of curate.

curare /kyooraá ri/ n. vegetable poison that induces paralysis.

curate n. member of the clergy who assists a parish priest.

curator n. person in charge of a museum or other collection.

curb n. means of restraint. ● v. restrain.

■ v. bridle, check, contain, control, hold back, repress, restrain, subdue, suppress.

curds n.pl. thick soft substance formed when milk turns sour.

curdle v. (cause to) form curds.

cure v. **1** restore to health. **2** rid (of a disease, trouble, etc.). **3** preserve by salting, drying, etc. ● n. **1** curing. **2** substance or treatment that cures disease etc.

■ v. **1** heal, make better, restore to health. **3** dry, pickle, preserve, salt, smoke. ● n. **2** antidote, medicine, remedy; therapy, treatment.

curette n. surgical scraping instrument. □ **curettage** n.

curfew n. signal or time after which people must stay indoors.

curio n. (pl. **-os**) unusual and therefore interesting object.

curiosity n. **1** desire to find out and know things. **2** curio.

■ **1** inquisitiveness, interest, colloq. nosiness. **2** curio, objet d'art, oddity, rarity.

curious adj. **1** eager to learn or know something. **2** strange, unusual. □ **curiously** adv.

■ **1** inquiring, inquisitive, interested, colloq. nosy. **2** bizarre, extraordinary, funny, odd, offbeat, outlandish, peculiar, quaint, queer, singular, strange, surprising, unusual, weird.

curl v. curve, esp. in a spiral shape or course. ● n. **1** curled thing or shape. **2** coiled lock of hair.

curler n. device for curling hair.

curlew n. wading bird with a long curved bill.

curling n. game like bowls played on ice.

curly adj. (**-ier, -iest**) full of curls.

curmudgeon *n.* bad-tempered person.
□ **curmudgeonly** *adj.*

currant *n.* **1** dried grape used in cookery.
2 small round edible berry. **3** shrub producing this.

currency *n.* **1** money in use. **2** state of being widely known.

current *adj.* **1** belonging to the present time. **2** in general use. ● *n.* **1** body of water or air moving in one direction. **2** flow of electricity. □ **currently** *adv.*

■ *adj.* **1** contemporary, latest, ongoing, present, up to date. **2** accepted, common, popular, prevailing, prevalent, widespread. ● *n.* **1** flow, stream, tide.

curriculum *n.* (*pl.* **-la**) course of study.
□ **curriculum vitae** brief account of one's career.

curry¹ *n.* **1** seasoning made with hot-tasting spices. **2** dish flavoured with this.

curry² *v.* groom (a horse) with a **curry-comb**, a pad with rubber or plastic projections. □ **curry favour** win favour by flattery.

curse *n.* **1** call for evil to come on a person or thing. **2** violent exclamation of anger. **3** thing causing evil or harm. ● *v.* **1** utter a curse (against). **2** afflict.

■ *n.* **1** execration, imprecation. **2** blasphemy, expletive, oath, obscenity, profanity, swear word. **3** bane, blight, evil, misfortune. ● *v.* **1** damn, execrate, blaspheme (at), swear (at). **2** afflict, burden, saddle, weigh down.

cursive *adj.* & *n.* (writing) done with joined letters.

cursor *n.* movable indicator on a VDU screen.

cursory *adj.* hasty, hurried. □ **cursorily** *adv.*

■ desultory, hasty, hurried, perfunctory, quick, rapid, summary, superficial.

curt *adj.* noticeably or rudely brief.
□ **curtly** *adv.*, **curtness** *n.*

■ abrupt, blunt, brusque, laconic, rude, short, terse, ungracious.

curtail *v.* cut short, reduce. □ **curtailment** *n.*

■ abbreviate, abridge, cut, cut short, shorten; cut down, reduce.

curtain *n.* piece of cloth hung as a screen, esp. at a window.

curtsy *n.* movement of respect made by bending the knees. ● *v.* make a curtsy.

curvaceous *adj.* (*colloq.*) shapely.

curvature *n.* **1** curving. **2** curved form.

curve *n.* line or surface with no part straight or flat. ● *v.* form (into) a curve.

cushion *n.* **1** stuffed bag used as a seat, esp. for leaning against. **2** padded part. **3** body of air supporting a hovercraft. ● *v.* **1** protect with a pad. **2** lessen the impact of.

cushy *adj.* (**-ier**, **-iest**) (*colloq.*) pleasant and easy.

cusp *n.* pointed part where curves meet.

cuss (*colloq.*) *n.* **1** curse. **2** awkward person. ● *v.* curse.

cussed /kússid/ *adj.* (*colloq.*) awkward and stubborn.

custard *n.* sauce made with milk and eggs or flavoured cornflour.

custodian *n.* guardian, keeper.

custody *n.* **1** guardianship. **2** imprisonment.

■ **1** care, charge, guardianship, keeping, protection, safe-keeping. **2** confinement, detention, imprisonment, incarceration.

custom *n.* **1** usual way of behaving or acting. **2** regular dealing by customer(s). **3** (*pl.*) duty on imported goods.

■ **1** convention, fashion, form, habit, practice, routine, tradition, usage, way, wont. **2** business, patronage, support, trade.

customary *adj.* usual. □ **customarily** *adv.*

■ accepted, accustomed, common, conventional, everyday, habitual, normal, ordinary, regular, routine, traditional, usual.

customer *n.* person buying goods or services from a shop etc.

■ buyer, client, consumer, patron, purchaser.

cut *v.* (**cut**, **cutting**) **1** divide, wound, or penetrate with a sharp-edged instrument. **2** reduce the length of, edit. **3** reduce (prices, wages, etc.). **4** intersect. **5** ignore (a person). **6** divide (a pack of cards). **7** stop filming. ● *n.* **1** wound or mark made by a sharp edge. **2** reduction. **3** (*colloq.*) share. **4** piece cut off. **5** style of cutting hair, clothes, etc. **6** hurtful remark. □ **cut in 1** interrupt. **2** pull in too closely in front of another vehicle.

■ *v.* **1** carve, slice; gash, lacerate, slash, slit, wound. **2** chop off, clip, crop, lop, shear, snip, trim; mow; abbreviate, abridge, curtail, edit, précis, shorten, truncate. **3** lower, reduce, slash. **4** cross, intersect, join, meet. **5** cold-shoulder, ignore, rebuff, snub. ● *n.* **1** gash, graze, incision, laceration, nick, slash, wound. **2** curtailment, decrease, reduction. **3** percentage, portion, share.

cute *adj.* (*colloq.*) **1** clever. **2** ingenious. **3** attractive, pretty. □ **cutely** *adv.*, **cuteness** *n.*

cuticle *n.* skin at the base of a nail.

cutlass *n.* short curved sword.

cutler *n.* maker of cutlery.

cutlery *n.* table knives, forks, and spoons.

cutlet *n.* **1** neck-chop. **2** mince cooked in this shape. **3** thin piece of veal.

cutthroat *adj.* merciless. ● *n.* murderer.

cutting *adj.* (of remarks) hurtful. ● *n.* **1** passage cut through high ground for a railway etc. **2** piece of a plant for re-planting.

■ *adj.* biting, caustic, harsh, hurtful, malicious, sarcastic, sardonic, scathing, scornful, venomous, wounding.

cuttlefish *n.* sea creature that ejects black fluid when attacked.

cyanide *n.* a strong poison.

cybernetics *n.* science of systems of control and communication in animals and machines.

cyclamen *n.* plant with petals that turn back.

cycle *n.* **1** recurring series of events etc. **2** bicycle, tricycle. ● *v.* ride a bicycle. □ **cyclist** *n.*

■ *n.* **1** course, pattern, rotation, round, series, sequence.

cyclic *adj.* (also **cyclical**) happening in cycles. □ **cyclically** *adv.*

cyclone *n.* violent wind rotating round a central area. □ **cyclonic** *adj.*

cyclotron *n.* apparatus for accelerating charged particles in a spiral path.

cygnet *n.* young swan.

cylinder *n.* object with straight sides and circular ends. □ **cylindrical** *adj.*, **cylindrically** *adv.*

cymbal *n.* brass plate struck with another to make a ringing sound.

cynic *n.* person who believes people's motives are usually bad or selfish. □ **cynical** *adj.*, **cynically** *adv.*, **cynicism** *n.*

cypress *n.* evergreen tree with dark feathery leaves.

cyst *n.* sac of fluid or soft matter on or in the body.

cystic *adj.* of the bladder. □ **cystic fibrosis** hereditary disease usu. resulting in respiratory infections.

cystitis *n.* inflammation of the bladder.

cytology *n.* study of biological cells. □ **cytological** *adj.*

czar *n.* = **tsar**.

Dd

dab[1] *n.* quick light blow or pressure. ● *v.* (**dabbed**) strike or press lightly or feebly.

dab[2] *n.* a kind of small flatfish.

dabble *v.* **1** splash about gently or playfully. **2** work at something in an amateur way. □ **dabbler** *n.*

dace *n.* (*pl.* **dace**) small freshwater fish.

dachshund *n.* small dog with a long body and short legs.

dad *n.* (*colloq.*) father.

daddy *n.* (*colloq.*) father.

daddy-long-legs *n.* crane-fly.

daffodil *n.* yellow flower with a trumpet-shaped central part.

daft *adj.* silly, crazy.

■ absurd, asinine, *sl.* barmy, crazy, fatuous, foolish, hare-brained, idiotic, imbecilic, ludicrous, mad, nonsensical, *sl.* potty, ridiculous, risible, senseless, silly, stupid, unwise.

dagger *n.* short pointed two-edged weapon used for stabbing.

dahlia *n.* garden plant with bright flowers.

daily *adj.* happening or appearing on every day or every weekday. ● *adv.* once a day. ● *n.* **1** daily newspaper. **2** (*colloq.*) charwoman.

dainty *adj.* (**-ier, -iest**) **1** delicately pretty. **2** choice. **3** fastidious. □ **daintily** *adv.*, **daintiness** *n.*

■ **1** charming, delicate, elegant, exquisite, fine, graceful, pretty. **2** appetizing, choice, delectable, delicious, tasty. **3** *colloq.* choosy, fastidious, fussy, sensitive, squeamish.

daiquiri /dákkəri/ *n.* cocktail of rum and lime juice.

dairy *n.* place where milk and its products are processed or sold.

dais /dáyiss/ *n.* low platform, esp. at the end of a hall.

daisy *n.* small white flower with a yellow centre. □ **daisy wheel** printing device with radiating spokes.

dale *n.* valley.

dally *v.* **1** idle, dawdle. **2** flirt. □ **dalliance** *n.*

■ **1** dawdle, delay, *colloq.* dilly-dally, idle, linger, loiter.

Dalmatian *n.* large white dog with dark spots.

dam[1] *n.* barrier built across a river to hold back water. ● *v.* (**dammed**) **1** hold back with a dam. **2** obstruct (a flow).

dam[2] *n.* mother of an animal.

damage *n.* **1** something done that reduces the value or usefulness of the thing affected or spoils its appearance. **2** (*pl.*) money as compensation for injury. ● *v.* cause damage to.

■ *n.* **1** destruction, harm, hurt, injury, impairment, mutilation. ● *v.* deface, harm, hurt, impair, injure, mar, mutilate, sabotage, spoil, vandalize.

damask *n.* fabric woven with a pattern visible on either side.

dame *n.* **1** (*US sl.*) woman. **2** (**Dame**) title of a woman with an order of knighthood.

damn /dam/ *v.* **1** condemn to hell. **2** condemn as a failure. **3** swear at. ● *int.* & *n.* uttered curse. ● *adj.* & *adv.* damned.

damnable *adj.* hateful, annoying.

damnation *n.* eternal punishment in hell. ● *int.* exclamation of annoyance.

damp *n.* moisture. ● *adj.* slightly wet. ● *v.* **1** make damp. **2** take the force or vigour out of. **3** stop the vibration of. □ **dampness** *n.*

■ *adj.* clammy, dank, humid, moist, muggy, steamy, wet. ● *v.* **1** dampen, moisten, wet. **2** dampen, diminish, discourage, dull, lessen, moderate, subdue, reduce, temper.

dampen *v.* **1** make or become damp. **2** make less forceful or vigorous.

damper *n.* **1** plate controlling the draught in a flue. **2** depressing influence. **3** pad that damps the vibration of a piano string.

damsel *n.* (*old use*) young woman.

damson *n.* small purple plum.

dance *v.* **1** move with rhythmical steps and gestures, usu. to music. **2** move in a quick or lively way. ● *n.* **1** social gathering for dancing. **2** piece of dancing music for this. □ **dance attendance on** follow about and help dutifully. **dancer** *n.*

dandelion *n.* wild plant with bright yellow flowers.

dandified *adj.* like a dandy.

dandle *v.* dance or nurse (a child) in one's arms.

dandruff *n.* scurf from the scalp.

dandy *n.* man who pays excessive attention to his appearance.

Dane *n.* native or inhabitant of Denmark.

danger *n.* **1** likelihood of harm or death. **2** thing causing this.
■ hazard, jeopardy, peril, risk, threat.

dangerous *adj.* causing danger, not safe.
□ **dangerously** *adv.*
■ chancy, *sl.* dicey, hazardous, perilous, precarious, risky, treacherous, unsafe.

dangle *v.* **1** hang or swing loosely. **2** hold out temptingly.

Danish *adj.* & *n.* (language) of Denmark.

dank *adj.* damp and cold.

dapper *adj.* neat and smart.
■ fashionable, neat, smart, spruce, stylish, trim, well-dressed.

dapple *v.* mark with patches of colour or shade. □ **dapple-grey** *adj.* grey with darker markings.

dare *v.* **1** be bold enough (to do something). **2** challenge to do something. ● *n.* this challenge.
■ **1** hazard, risk, venture. **2** challenge, defy.

daredevil *adj.* & *n.* recklessly daring (person).

daring *adj.* bold. ● *n.* boldness.

dark *adj.* **1** with little or no light. **2** of a deep or sombre colour. **3** having dark hair or skin. **4** gloomy. **5** secret, mysterious. ● *n.* **1** absence of light. **2** time of darkness, night. □ **dark horse** competitor of whom little is known. **darkroom** *n.* darkened room for processing photographs. **darkly** *adv.,* **darkness** *n.*
■ *adj.* **1** black, pitch-black, pitch-dark, sunless, starless, unlit, unlighted, unilluminated; dim, dusky, gloomy, murky, overcast, shadowy. **2** inky, sooty; drab, dreary, dull, funereal, sombre. **3** brunette; brown, swarthy, tanned. **4** bleak, cheerless, depressing, dismal, gloomy, melancholy, mournful, pessimistic. **5** arcane, deep, incomprehensible, mysterious, obscure, secret, unfathomable.

darken *v.* make or become dark.

darling *n.* & *adj.* **1** loved or lovable (person or thing). **2** favourite.

darn *v.* mend by weaving thread across a hole. ● *n.* place darned.

dart *n.* **1** small pointed missile, esp. for throwing at the target in the game of darts. **2** darting movement. **3** tapering tuck. ● *v.* **1** run suddenly. **2** send out (a glance etc.) rapidly.

dartboard *n.* target in the game of darts.

dash *v.* **1** run rapidly, rush. **2** knock or throw forcefully against something. **3** destroy (hopes). ● *n.* **1** rapid run, rush. **2** small amount of liquid or flavouring added. **3** vigour. **4** dashboard. **5** punctuation mark (—) showing a break in the sense.
■ *v.* **1** bolt, bound, dart, flash, fly, hasten, hurry, hurtle, race, run, rush, scoot, scurry, speed, sprint, tear, whiz, zoom. **2** knock, smash, strike; cast, fling, hurl, pitch, throw, toss. **3** destroy, put paid to, ruin, spoil. ● *n.* **1** bolt, bound, dart, run, rush, sprint. **2** bit, drop, hint, pinch, sprinkling, suggestion, touch, trace. **3** élan, energy, impetuosity, liveliness, spirit, verve, vigour, vivacity.

dashboard *n.* instrument panel of a motor vehicle.

dashing *adj.* spirited, showy.

dastardly *adj.* contemptible.

data *n.pl.* **1** facts on which a decision is to be based. **2** facts to be processed by computer.

data bank large store of computerized data.

database *n.* organized store of computerized data.

date¹ *n.* **1** day, month, or year of a thing's occurrence. **2** period to which a thing belongs. **3** (*colloq.*) appointment to meet socially. **4** (*colloq.*) person to be met thus. ● *v.* **1** mark with a date. **2** assign a date to. **3** originate from a particular date. **4** become out of date. **5** (*colloq.*) make a social appointment (with). □ **out of date** old-fashioned, obsolete. **to date** until now. **up to date** fashionable, modern.
■ *n.* **2** age, day, epoch, era, season, time, year. □ **out of date** anachronistic, antiquated, behind the times, obsolete, old, old-fashioned, outdated, outmoded. **up to date** contemporary, current, fashionable, modern, *colloq.* trendy.

date² *n.* small brown edible fruit. □ **date palm** tree bearing this.

datum *n.* (*pl.* **data**) item of data.

daub *v.* smear roughly. ● *n.* **1** clumsily painted picture. **2** smear.

daughter *n.* female in relation to her parents. □ **daughter-in-law** *n.* (*pl.* **daughters-in-law**) son's wife.

daunt v. discourage, intimidate.

■ demoralize, deter, discourage, dishearten, dismay, frighten, intimidate, overawe, put off, scare, unnerve.

dauntless adj. brave.

dauphin n. title of the eldest son of former kings of France.

davit n. small crane on a ship.

dawdle v. walk slowly and idly, take one's time. □ **dawdler** n.

■ dally, delay, colloq. dilly-dally, hang about, idle, lag behind, linger, loiter, straggle, take one's time, waste time.

dawn n. **1** first light of day. **2** beginning. ● v. begin to grow light. □ **dawn on** become evident to. **dawning** n.

■ n. **1** break of day, daybreak, first light, sunrise. **2** beginning, commencement, dawning, emergence, genesis, inception, origin, start.

day n. **1** time while the sun is above the horizon. **2** period of 24 hours. **3** hours given to work during a day. **4** specified day. **5** time, period.

daybreak n. first light of day.

daydream n. pleasant idle thoughts. ● v. have daydreams.

■ n. dream, fancy, fantasy, pipedream, reverie. ● v. dream, fantasize.

daylight n. **1** light of day. **2** dawn.

daytime n. part of the day when there is natural daylight.

daze v. cause to feel stunned or bewildered. ● n. dazed state.

■ v. amaze, astonish, astound, bowl over, dumbfound, colloq. flabbergast, stagger, startle, stun, stupefy, surprise, take aback; baffle, bemuse, bewilder, confuse, nonplus, perplex, puzzle.

dazzle v. **1** blind temporarily with bright light. **2** impress with skill, beauty, etc.

de- pref. implying removal or reversal.

deacon n. **1** member of the clergy ranking below priest. **2** lay officer in Nonconformist churches.

dead adj. **1** no longer alive. **2** obsolete, extinct. **3** numb. **4** without brightness or resonance. **5** dull. **6** abrupt, complete. ● adv. completely. □ **dead beat** tired out. **dead end** road closed at one end. **dead heat** race in which two or more competitors finish exactly even. **dead letter** law or rule no longer observed.

■ adj. **1** deceased, defunct, departed, gone, late, lifeless. **2** disused, extinct, obsolete, outmoded. **3** deadened, numb, paralysed. **5** boring, dull, flat, lifeless, te-

dious, uninteresting. **6** abrupt, sudden; absolute, complete, downright, entire, out and out, outright, total, unqualified. ● adv. absolutely, completely, entirely, totally, utterly.

deaden v. deprive of or lose vitality, loudness, feeling, etc.

■ blunt, cushion, dampen, dull, moderate, muffle, soften; numb, paralyse.

deadline n. time limit.

deadlock n. state of unresolved conflict. ● v. reach this.

■ n. impasse, stalemate, standstill.

deadly adj. (-ier, -iest) **1** causing death or serious damage. **2** death-like. **3** very dreary. ● adv. **1** as if dead. **2** extremely. □ **deadly nightshade** plant with poisonous black berries.

■ **1** dangerous, fatal, lethal, mortal, poisonous, toxic. **2** deathly, ghastly, ghostly, livid. **3** boring, dreary, dull, tedious, tiresome.

deadpan adj. expressionless.

deaf adj. **1** wholly or partly unable to hear. **2** refusing to listen. □ **deafness** n.

deafen v. make unable to hear by a very loud noise.

deal¹ n. fir or pine timber.

deal² v. (**dealt**) **1** distribute. **2** cause to be received. **3** hand out (cards) to players in a card game. ● n. **1** business transaction. **2** large amount. **3** player's turn to deal in a card game. □ **deal in** sell. **deal with 1** take action about. **2** be about or concerned with. **3** do business with.

■ v. **1** allot, dispense, distribute, dole out, give out, hand out, mete out, share out. **2** administer, deliver, inflict. ● n. **1** agreement, arrangement, bargain, contract, transaction, understanding. □ **deal with 1** attend to, do, look after, organize, see to, sort out, take care of, take charge of. **2** analyse, consider, discuss, examine, explore, investigate, study, treat.

dealer n. **1** person who deals. **2** trader.

dealings n.pl. conduct or transactions.

dean n. **1** head of a cathedral chapter. **2** university official.

deanery n. dean's position or residence.

dear adj. **1** much loved. **2** expensive. ● n. dear person. ● int. exclamation of surprise or distress. □ **dearly** adv.

■ adj. **1** adored, beloved, cherished, darling, loved, precious, prized, treasured, valued. **2** costly, exorbitant, expensive, high-priced, colloq. steep.

dearth *n.* scarcity, lack.

death *n.* **1** process of dying, end of life. **2** ending. **3** destruction. **4** state of being dead. □ **death duty** tax levied on property after the owner's death. **death trap** very dangerous place. **death-watch beetle** beetle whose larvae bore into wood and make a ticking sound.

■ **1** decease, demise, dying, end, expiration, passing away. **2** cessation, ending, finish, termination. **3** annihilation, destruction, extinction, obliteration.

deathly *adj.* (**-ier, -iest**) like death.

debacle /daybaák'l/ *n.* general collapse.

debar *v.* (**debarred**) exclude.

debase *v.* lower in quality or value. □ **debasement** *n.*

■ cheapen, degrade, demean, devalue, diminish, lower, reduce.

debatable *adj.* questionable.

■ arguable, controversial, disputable, doubtful, dubious, open to question, problematic(al), questionable, uncertain.

debate *n.* formal discussion. ● *v.* **1** discuss or dispute. **2** consider.

■ *n.* argument, discussion, disputation, dispute. ● *v.* **1** argue about, discuss, dispute, wrangle over. **2** consider, deliberate, meditate on, mull over, ponder, reflect on, think over.

debauchery over-indulgence in harmful or immoral pleasures.

debilitate *v.* weaken. □ **debilitation** *n.*

debility *n.* weakness of health.

debit *n.* entry in an account for a sum owing. ● *v.* (**debited**) enter as a debit, charge. □ **direct debit** instruction allowing an organization to take regular payments from one's bank account.

debonair *adj.* having a carefree self-confident manner.

debouch *v.* come out from a narrow into an open area.

debrief *v.* question to obtain facts about a completed mission.

debris /débree/ *n.* scattered broken pieces or rubbish.

■ flotsam, fragments, litter, pieces, refuse, remains, rubbish, rubble, ruins, waste, wreckage.

debt /det/ *n.* something owed. □ **in debt** owing something.

debtor *n.* person who owes money.

debug *v.* (**debugged**) remove bugs from.

debunk *v.* (*colloq.*) show up as exaggerated or false.

debut /dáy-byōō/ *n.* first public appearance.

deca- *pref.* ten.

decade *n.* ten-year period.

decadent *adj.* in a state of moral deterioration. □ **decadence** *n.*

■ corrupt, debased, degenerate, dissipated, dissolute, immoral.

decaffeinated *adj.* with caffeine removed or reduced.

decagon *n.* geometric figure with ten sides. □ **decagonal** *adj.*

decamp *v.* go away suddenly or secretly.

decant *v.* pour off (wine etc.) leaving sediment behind.

decanter *n.* bottle for decanted wine etc.

decapitate *v.* behead. □ **decapitation** *n.*

decarbonize *v.* remove carbon deposit from (an engine). □ **decarbonization** *n.*

decathlon *n.* athletic contest involving ten events.

decay *v.* **1** rot. **2** lose quality or strength. ● *n.* **1** rotten state. **2** decline.

● *v.* **1** decompose, go bad, go off, moulder, perish, putrefy, rot, spoil. **2** atrophy, crumble, decline, degenerate, deteriorate, disintegrate, waste away, wither. ● *n.* **1** decomposition, putrefaction, rot. **2** atrophy, decline, degeneration, deterioration, disintegration.

decease *n.* death.

deceased *adj.* dead.

deceit *n.* **1** process of deceiving. **2** trick.

■ **1** cheating, chicanery, craftiness, cunning, deceitfulness, deception, dishonesty, dissimulation, double-dealing, duplicity, fraud, guile, hypocrisy, slyness, treachery, trickery. **2** artifice, deception, manoeuvre, ploy, ruse, stratagem, subterfuge, trick, wile.

deceitful *adj.* intending to deceive. □ **deceitfully** *adv.*

■ crafty, cunning, dishonest, disingenuous, double-dealing, false, fraudulent, guileful, hypocritical, insincere, lying, scheming, sly, treacherous, two-faced, underhand, untrustworthy, wily.

deceive *v.* **1** cause to believe what is false. **2** be sexually unfaithful to. □ **deceiver** *n.*

■ **1** *colloq.* bamboozle, beguile, betray, cheat, *sl.* con, delude, double-cross, dupe, fool, fox, hoax, hoodwink, mislead, pull the wool over somone's eyes, swindle, take in, trick.

decelerate *v.* reduce the speed (of). □ **deceleration** *n.*

decennial adj. **1** happening every tenth year. **2** lasting ten years. □ **decennially** adv.

decent adj. **1** conforming to accepted standards of what is proper. **2** respectable. **3** kind. □ **decently** adv., **decency** n.
■ **1** acceptable, appropriate, correct, fitting, proper, right, suitable. **2** decorous, presentable, respectable, seemly. **3** accommodating, considerate, courteous, generous, kind, nice, obliging, pleasant, thoughtful.

decentralize v. transfer from central to local control. □ **decentralization** n.

deception n. **1** deceit. **2** trick.

deceptive adj. misleading.
■ deceiving, delusive, false, illusory, misleading, unreliable; deceitful, dishonest, untruthful.

deci- pref. one-tenth.

decibel n. unit for measuring the relative loudness of sound.

decide v. **1** make up one's mind. **2** settle a contest or argument. □ **decide or** choose.
■ **1** determine, make up one's mind, resolve. **2** adjudicate, arbitrate, judge, resolve, settle. □ **decide on** choose, go for, opt for, pick out, plump for, select.

decided adj. **1** having firm opinions. **2** clear, definite. □ **decidedly** adv.
■ **1** decisive, determined, firm, resolute, uncompromising, unswerving, unwavering. **2** clear, definite, evident, indisputable, marked, obvious, pronounced, undeniable, unequivocal, unmistakable, unquestionable.

deciduous adj. shedding its leaves annually.

decimal adj. reckoned in tens or tenths. ● n. decimal fraction. □ **decimal fraction** fraction based on powers of ten, shown as figures after a dot. **decimal point** this dot.

decimalize v. convert into a decimal. □ **decimalization** n.

decimate v. destroy a large proportion of. □ **decimation** n.

decipher v. make out the meaning of (code, bad handwriting).
■ decode, disentangle, figure out, interpret, make out, unravel, work out.

decision n. **1** deciding. **2** judgement so reached. **3** resoluteness.
■ **1** arbitration, determination, resolution, settlement. **2** conclusion, judgement, resolution; decree, finding, ruling, verdict. **3** decisiveness, determination, resoluteness, resolution, resolve.

decisive adj. **1** conclusive. **2** quick to decide. □ **decisively** adv., **decisiveness** n.
■ **1** conclusive, convincing, definitive, incontrovertible, irrefutable, unquestionable. **2** definite, determined, firm, forthright, resolute.

deck[1] n. floor or storey of a ship or bus. □ **deckchair** n. folding canvas chair.

deck[2] v. decorate, dress up.

declaim v. speak or say impressively. □ **declamation** n., **declamatory** adj.

declare v. **1** announce openly or formally. **2** state firmly. □ **declaration** n., **declaratory** adj.
■ **1** announce, broadcast, make known, proclaim, promulgate, pronounce. **2** affirm, assert, attest, avow, claim, profess, protest, state, swear. □ **declaration** announcement, proclamation, promulgation, pronouncement; affirmation, assertion, avowal, deposition, profession, protestation, statement, testimony.

declassify v. cease to classify as secret. □ **declassification** n.

decline v. **1** refuse. **2** slope downwards. **3** decrease, lose strength or vigour. ● n. gradual decrease or loss of strength.
■ v. **1** colloq. pass up, refuse, turn down. **2** descend, dip, slope downwards. **3** decrease, diminish, drop, dwindle, ebb, flag, lessen, subside, tail off, taper off, wane; decay, degenerate, deteriorate, fail, weaken. ● n. decrease, diminution, drop, fall, lessening, reduction.

declivity n. downward slope.

declutch v. disengage the clutch of a motor.

decode v. **1** put (a coded message) into plain language. **2** make (an electronic signal) intelligible. □ **decoder** n.

decompose v. (cause to) rot or decay. □ **decomposition** n.

decompress v. **1** release from compression. **2** reduce air pressure in. □ **decompression** n.

decongestant n. medicinal substance that relieves congestion.

decontaminate v. rid of contamination. □ **decontamination** n.

decor n. style of decoration used in a room.

decorate v. **1** make look attractive by adding objects or details. **2** paint or paper the walls of. **3** confer a medal or award on. ◻ **decoration** n.

■ **1** adorn, beautify, deck, dress, embellish, embroider, festoon, garnish, ornament, smarten up, spruce up, *colloq.* tart up, trim. **2** do up, paper, paint, redecorate, refurbish, renovate.

decorative *adj.* ornamental. ◻ **decoratively** *adv.*

decorator n. person who decorates professionally.

decorous *adj.* having or showing decorum. ◻ **decorously** *adv.*

■ correct, decent, demure, dignified, gentlemanly, ladylike, polite, proper, refined, respectable, seemly, well-behaved.

decorum n. correctness and dignity of behaviour.

■ correctness, decency, dignity, good manners, politeness, propriety, respectability, seemliness.

decoy n. person or animal used to lure others into danger. ● v. lure by a decoy.

■ n. bait, enticement, lure, trap. ● v. attract, draw, entice, inveigle, lure, seduce, tempt, trick.

decrease v. reduce, diminish. ● n. **1** decreasing. **2** amount of this.

■ v. curtail, cut, lessen, lower, reduce; abate, decline, diminish, drop, dwindle, ebb, fall, go down, shrink, subside, tail off, taper off, wane. ● n. abatement, curtailment, cut, decline, diminution, drop, dwindling, ebb, fall, lessening, reduction, shrinkage.

decree n. order given by a government or other authority. ● v. (**decreed**) order by decree.

■ n. command, dictate, dictum, directive, edict, injunction, law, order, ordinance, proclamation, regulation, ruling, statute. ● v. command, dictate, direct, ordain, order, proclaim, pronounce, rule.

decrepit *adj.* **1** made weak by age or infirmity. **2** dilapidated. ◻ **decrepitude** n.

■ **1** debilitated, doddery, feeble, frail, infirm, weak, worn-out. **2** crumbling, decaying, derelict, dilapidated, ramshackle, rickety, tumbledown.

decry v. disparage.

dedicate v. devote to a person, use, or cause. ◻ **dedication** n.

■ commit, consecrate, devote, give, pledge. ◻ **dedication** allegiance, commitment, devotion, faithfulness, fidelity, loyalty.

deduce v. infer. ◻ **deducible** *adj.*

■ assume, conclude, gather, infer, presume, suppose, surmise, understand.

deduct v. subtract.

deduction n. **1** deducting. **2** thing deducted. **3** deducing. **4** conclusion deduced.

deductive *adj.* based on reasoning.

deed n. **1** thing done, act. **2** legal document.

■ **1** accomplishment, achievement, act, action, exploit, feat.

deem v. consider to be.

deep *adj.* **1** going or situated far down or in. **2** (of colours) intense. **3** low-pitched. **4** heartfelt. **5** absorbed. **6** profound. ◻ **deeply** *adv.*

■ **1** bottomless, unfathomable, unfathomed. **2** dark, intense, rich, strong. **3** bass, booming, low, low-pitched, resonant, resounding, sonorous. **4** ardent, earnest, genuine, heartfelt, intense, profound, sincere. **5** absorbed, engrossed, immersed, intent, involved, lost, preoccupied, rapt. **6** abstruse, difficult, esoteric, heavy, profound, weighty.

deepen v. make or become deeper.

deer n. (*pl.* **deer**) hoofed animal, male of which usu. has antlers.

deerstalker n. cloth cap with a peak in front and at the back.

deface v. disfigure. ◻ **defacement** n.

■ blemish, damage, disfigure, harm, impair, injure, mar, mutilate, ruin, spoil.

de facto existing in fact.

defamatory *adj.* defaming.

defame v. attack the good reputation of. ◻ **defamation** n.

default v. fail to fulfil one's obligations or to appear. ● n. this failure. ◻ **defaulter** n.

defeat v. **1** win victory over. **2** cause to fail. ● n. act or process of defeating or being defeated.

■ v. **1** beat, be victorious over, conquer, crush, destroy, get the better of, *colloq.* lick, overcome, overpower, overthrow, overwhelm, prevail over, rout, subdue, suppress, thrash, triumph over, trounce, vanquish. **2** end, foil, frustrate, stop, thwart. ● n. beating, conquest, overthrow, rout, trouncing; end, frustration.

defeatism n. readiness to accept defeat. ◻ **defeatist** n. & *adj*

defecate v. discharge faeces from the body. □ **defecation** n.

defect n. /deéfekt/ shortcoming, imperfection. ● v. /difékt/ desert one's country etc. for another. □ **defection** n., **defector** n.

■ n. deficiency, failing, fault, imperfection, shortcoming, weakness, weak point; blemish, flaw, mark, spot, stain.

defective adj. having defect(s). □ **defectiveness** n.

■ broken, deficient, faulty, flawed, impaired, imperfect, incomplete, out of order.

defence n. 1 (means of) defending. 2 arguments against an accusation. □ **defenceless** adj.

■ 1 barrier, cover, guard, protection, safeguard, shelter, shield. 2 argument, excuse, explanation, justification, plea, reason, vindication.

defend v. 1 protect from attack. 2 speak or write in favour of. 3 represent (the defendant). □ **defender** n.

■ 1 guard, keep safe, preserve, protect, safeguard, screen, shelter, shield, watch over. 2 argue for, back, champion, plead for, stand by, stand up for, colloq. stick up for, support, uphold.

defendant n. person accused or sued in a lawsuit.

defensible adj. able to be defended.

defensive adj. 1 intended for defence. 2 in an attitude of defence. □ **defensively** adv., **defensiveness** n.

defer¹ v. (**deferred**) postpone. □ **deferment** n., **deferral** n.

■ adjourn, delay, postpone, put off, shelve, suspend.

defer² v. (**deferred**) yield to a person's wishes etc.

■ bow, capitulate, give way, submit, yield.

deference n. polite respect. □ **deferential** adj.

■ civility, consideration, courtesy, politeness, regard, respect.

defiance n. 1 bold resistance. 2 open disobedience. □ **defiant** adj., **defiantly** adv.

■ □ **defiant** aggressive, antagonistic, belligerent, bold, pugnacious, truculent; disobedient, insubordinate, mutinous, obstinate, rebellious, recalcitrant, refractory.

deficiency n. 1 lack, shortage. 2 thing or amount lacking.

deficient adj. incomplete or insufficient.

■ defective, faulty, incomplete, lacking, imperfect, inadequate, insufficient, short, unsatisfactory, wanting.

deficit n. amount by which a total falls short.

defile¹ v. make dirty, pollute.

■ contaminate, corrupt, dirty, foul, poison, pollute, soil, stain, sully, taint.

defile² n. narrow pass or gorge.

define v. 1 state or explain precisely. 2 mark the boundary of.

■ 1 describe, detail, explain, specify, spell out. 2 bound, circumscribe, delineate, demarcate, outline.

definite adj. 1 exact. 2 clear and distinct. 3 certain, sure. □ **definitely** adv.

■ 1 exact, precise, specific. 2 clear, explicit, distinct, obvious, plain, unambiguous, unequivocal, well-defined. 3 certain, fixed, positive, settled, sure.

definition n. 1 statement of meaning. 2 clearness of outline.

definitive adj. 1 finally fixing or settling something. 2 most authoritative. □ **definitively** adv.

■ 1 conclusive, decisive, final, ultimate. 2 authoritative, reliable.

deflate v. (cause to) collapse through release of air. □ **deflation** n.

deflect v. turn aside. □ **deflection** n., **deflector** n.

■ avert, divert, fend off, head off, sidetrack, turn aside; deviate, swerve, swing away, veer.

defoliate v. remove the leaves of. □ **defoliant** n., **defoliation** n.

deforest v. clear of trees. □ **deforestation** n.

deform v. spoil the shape of. □ **deformation** n.

deformity n. abnormality of shape, esp. of a part of the body.

defraud v. cheat by fraud.

■ cheat, sl. con, dupe, fleece, colloq. rip off, swindle, trick.

defray v. provide money to pay (costs). □ **defrayal** n.

defrost v. thaw.

deft adj. skilful, esp. with one's hands. □ **deftly** adv.

■ adept, adroit, clever, dexterous, expert, handy, skilful.

defunct adj. 1 dead. 2 no longer existing or functioning.

defuse v. **1** remove the fuse from (a bomb). **2** reduce the tension in (a situation).

defy v. **1** refuse to obey. **2** present insuperable obstacles to. **3** challenge to do something.

■ **1** disobey, flout, go against. **2** defeat, foil, frustrate, resist, thwart, withstand. **3** challenge, dare.

degenerate v. /dijénnərayt/ become worse. ● adj. /dijénnərət/ having lost normal or good qualities. □ **degeneration** n., **degeneracy** n.

■ v. become worse, decay, decline, deteriorate, colloq. go to pot, go to rack and ruin, retrogress, run to seed, worsen. ● adj. corrupt, corrupted, debased, decadent, depraved, rotten.

degrade v. **1** reduce to a lower rank. **2** humiliate, disgrace. □ **degradation** n.

■ **1** demote, downgrade. **2** abase, cheapen, debase, demean, disgrace, dishonour, humiliate, shame.

degree n. **1** stage in a scale or series. **2** stage in intensity or amount. **3** academic award for proficiency. **4** unit of measurement for angles or temperature.

■ **1** level, place, point, stage, step. **2** amount, extent, intensity, magnitude, measure.

dehumanize v. **1** remove human qualities from. **2** make impersonal. □ **dehumanization** n.

dehydrate v. **1** make dry. **2** lose moisture. □ **dehydration** n.

de-ice v. free from ice. □ **de-icer** n.

deify v. treat as a god. □ **deification** n.

deign v. condescend.

■ condescend, demean oneself, lower oneself, stoop.

deity n. god, goddess.

déjà vu /dáyzhaa vōo/ feeling of having experienced the present situation before.

dejected adj. in low spirits.

■ blue, crestfallen, depressed, despondent, disconsolate, dispirited, downcast, downhearted, glum, heavy-hearted, in the doldrums, melancholy, miserable, sad, unhappy, woebegone.

dejection n. lowness of spirits.

delay v. **1** make or be late. **2** postpone. ● n. delaying.

■ v. **1** hinder, hold up, impede, retard, set back, slow up or down; dally, dawdle, colloq. dilly-dally, hang about or back, hesitate, lag behind, linger, loiter, mark

time, procrastinate, stall, temporize. **2** defer, postpone, put off, shelve, suspend. ● n. hiatus, hold-up, interlude, interruption, lull, stoppage, wait; deferment, deferral, postponement.

delectable adj. delightful.

delectation n. enjoyment.

delegate n. /délligət/ representative. ● v. /délligayt/ entrust (a task or power) to an agent.

■ n. agent, ambassador, emissary, envoy, go-between, plenipotentiary, representative, spokesperson. ● v. assign, entrust, give, hand over, transfer.

delegation n. **1** delegating. **2** group of representatives.

delete v. strike out (a word etc.). □ **deletion** n.

■ blot out, cancel, cross out, efface, erase, expunge, obliterate, remove, rub out, strike out.

deleterious adj. harmful.

deliberate adj. /dilíbbərət/ **1** intentional. **2** slow and careful. ● v. /dilíbbərayt/ **1** think carefully. **2** discuss. □ **deliberately** adv.

■ adj. **1** calculated, conscious, considered, intended, intentional, planned, preconceived, premeditated, purposeful, studied, wilful. **2** careful, cautious, methodical, orderly, painstaking, punctilious, systematic, thoughtful, thorough, unhurried. ● v. cogitate, meditate, ponder, reflect, ruminate, think. **2** consider, debate, discuss.

deliberation n. **1** deliberating. **2** being deliberate.

delicacy n. **1** being delicate. **2** choice food.

■ **1** beauty, daintiness, grace; fragility, frailty, weakness; awkwardness, difficulty, sensitivity, trickiness; consideration, discretion, tact, thoughtfulness. **2** luxury, titbit, treat.

delicate adj. **1** exquisite. **2** not robust or strong. **3** requiring or using tact. □ **delicately** adv.

■ **1** beautiful, dainty, elegant, exquisite, fine, graceful. **2** feeble, fragile, frail, sickly, unhealthy, weak. **3** awkward, difficult, embarrassing, sensitive, colloq. sticky, ticklish, tricky; considerate, discreet, tactful, thoughtful.

delicatessen n. shop selling prepared delicacies.

delicious adj. delightful, esp. to taste or smell. □ **deliciously** adv.
■ appetizing, choice, delectable, delightful, luscious, savoury, colloq. scrumptious, tasty, colloq. yummy.

delight n. **1** great pleasure. **2** thing giving this. ● v. please greatly. □ **delight in** take great pleasure in. **delightful** adj., **delightfully** adv.
■ n. **1** bliss, ecstasy, enjoyment, gratification, joy, pleasure, rapture, satisfaction. **2** joy, pleasure, treat. ● v. amuse, captivate, charm, enchant, entertain, entrance, gladden, gratify, please, satisfy, thrill. □ **delight in** enjoy, glory in, like, love, relish, revel in. **delightful** agreeable, amusing, captivating, charming, enchanting, enjoyable, entertaining, colloq. heavenly, colloq. lovely, pleasant, pleasing.

delimit v. determine the limits or boundaries of. □ **delimitation** n.

delineate v. outline. □ **delineation** n., **delineator** n.

delinquent adj. & n. (person) guilty of persistent law-breaking. □ **delinquency** n.

delirium n. **1** disordered state of mind. **2** wild excitement. □ **delirious** adj., **deliriously** adv.
■ □ **delirious** crazy, demented, frantic, frenzied, hysterical, incoherent, irrational, rambling, raving, unhinged; beside oneself, ecstatic, thrilled, wild.

deliver v. **1** distribute (letters, goods, etc.) to their destination. **2** hand over. **3** utter. **4** launch or aim (a blow etc.). **5** rescue, set free. **6** assist in the birth (of). □ **deliverer** n., **delivery** n.
■ **1** bring, carry, convey, distribute, give or hand out, take round, transport. **2** commit, give up, hand over, relinquish, surrender, yield. **3** give, make, present, read, recite, utter. **4** administer, aim, deal, direct, inflict, launch, send, throw. **5** emancipate, liberate, release, rescue, save, set free.

deliverance n. rescue, freeing.

dell n. small wooded hollow.

delphinium n. tall garden plant with usu. blue flowers.

delta n. **1** fourth letter of the Greek alphabet. = d. **2** triangular patch of alluvial land at the mouth of a river.

delude v. deceive.

deluge n. & v. flood.

delusion n. false belief or impression. □ **delusive** adj.
■ error, illusion, misapprehension, misconception, mistake.

de luxe **1** of superior quality. **2** luxurious.

delve v. search deeply.

demagogue n. person who wins support by appealing to popular feelings and prejudices. □ **demagogic** adj., **demagogy** n.

demand n. **1** firm or official request. **2** desire for goods or services. **3** urgent claim. ● v. **1** make a demand for. **2** need.
■ n. **1** call, command, order, request. **2** call, desire, market, need, requirement. **3** call, claim. ● v. **1** ask for, claim, insist on, require, requisition. **2** necessitate, need, require, want.

demanding adj. **1** making demands, hard to satisfy. **2** requiring great skill or effort.
■ **1** difficult, importunate, insistent, persistent, troublesome, trying. **2** arduous, challenging, difficult, exacting, hard, laborious, onerous, strenuous, taxing, tough.

demarcation n. marking of a boundary or limits.

demean v. lower the dignity of.

demeanour n. behaviour.

demented adj. mad.

dementia n. a type of insanity.

demerara n. brown raw cane sugar.

demi- pref. half.

demilitarize v. remove military forces from. □ **demilitarization** n.

demise n. death.

demist v. clear mist from (a windscreen etc.). □ **demister** n.

demobilize v. disband (troops) etc. □ **demobilization** n.

democracy n. **1** government by all the people, usu. through elected representatives. **2** country governed in this way.

democrat n. person favouring democracy.

democratic adj. of or according to democracy. □ **democratically** adv.

demography n. statistical study of human populations. □ **demographic** adj.

demolish v. **1** pull or knock down. **2** destroy. □ **demolition** n.
■ **1** destroy, dismantle, knock down, level, pull to pieces, raze, tear down, topple, wreck. **2** destroy, put an end to, put paid to, ruin, shatter, spoil, wreck.

demon n. **1** devil, evil spirit. **2** cruel or forceful person. □ **demonic** adj., **demoniac(al)** adj.

demonstrable adj. able to be demonstrated. □ **demonstrability** n., **demonstrably** adv.

demonstrate v. **1** show evidence of, prove. **2** show the working of. **3** take part in a public protest. □ **demonstration** n., **demonstrator** n.
■ **1** display, establish, evidence, evince, exhibit, indicate, make evident, manifest, prove, show. **2** describe, explain, illustrate. **3** march, parade, protest.

demonstrative adj. showing one's feelings readily, affectionate. □ **demonstratively** adv.
■ affectionate, effusive, emotional, expansive, open, uninhibited, unreserved.

demoralize v. dishearten. □ **demoralization** n.

demote v. reduce to a lower rank or category. □ **demotion** n.

demur v. (**demurred**) raise objections. ● n. objection raised.

demure adj. **1** quiet, modest. **2** coy. □ **demurely** adv.

den n. **1** wild animal's lair. **2** person's small private room.

denationalize v. privatize. □ **denationalization** n.

denature v. **1** change the properties of. **2** make (alcohol) unfit for drinking.

denial n. act or instance of denying or refusing.
■ contradiction, disavowal, disclaimer, negation, refutation, repudiation; refusal, rejection.

denier /dényər/ n. unit of weight measuring the fineness of yarn.

denigrate v. disparage the reputation of. □ **denigration** n.

denim n. **1** strong twilled fabric. **2** (pl.) trousers made of this.

denizen n. inhabitant or occupant.

denominate v. **1** name. **2** describe as.

denomination n. **1** specified Church or sect. **2** class of units of measurement or money. **3** name. □ **denominational** adj.
■ **1** Church, faith, order, persuasion, sect. **2** class, kind, size, sort, type, value. **3** designation, name, term, title.

denominator n. number below the line in a vulgar fraction.

denote v. **1** be the sign or symbol of. **2** indicate. □ **denotation** n.
■ **1** betoken, represent, signify, stand for, symbolize. **2** connote, imply, indicate, mean, suggest.

denouement /daynoomon/ n. final outcome of a play or story.

denounce v. **1** speak against, condemn. **2** inform against.
■ **1** attack, castigate, censure, condemn, criticize, impugn, pillory, rail against, vilify, vituperate. **2** betray, incriminate, inform against, report.

dense adj. **1** closely compacted in substance, thick. **2** crowded together. **3** stupid. □ **densely** adv., **denseness** n.
■ **1** close, compact, compressed, heavy, impenetrable, solid, thick. **2** congested, crammed, crowded, packed. **3** colloq. dim, obtuse, slow, stupid, colloq. thick.

density n. **1** denseness. **2** relation of weight to volume.

dent n. hollow left by a blow or pressure. ● v. make or become dented.

dental adj. **1** of or for teeth. **2** of dentistry.

dentifrice n. substance for cleaning teeth.

dentist n. person qualified to treat, extract, etc., teeth.

dentistry n. dentist's work.

denture n. set of artificial teeth.

denude v. strip of covering or property. □ **denudation** n.

denunciation n. denouncing.

deny v. **1** say that (a thing) is untrue or does not exist. **2** disown. **3** prevent from having.
■ **1** challenge, contradict, controvert, disclaim, dispute, gainsay. **2** disown, renounce, repudiate. **3** deprive of, forbid, refuse.

deodorant n. substance that removes or conceals smells.

deodorize v. destroy the odour of. □ **deodorization** n.

depart v. go away, leave.
■ go, go away, leave, retire, retreat, set off or out, withdraw.

department n. section of an organization. □ **department store** large shop selling many kinds of goods. **departmental** adj.

departure n. **1** departing. **2** new course of action.

depend v. **depend on 1** be determined by. **2** rely on. **3** be unable to do without.

■ **1** be conditional or dependent on, be subject to, hang on, hinge on. **2** bank on, count on, lean on, put one's faith in, reckon on, rely on, trust (in).

dependable adj. reliable.

dependant n. one who depends on another for support.

dependence n. depending.

dependency n. dependent state.

dependent adj. **1** depending. **2** controlled by another.

depict v. represent in a picture or in words. □ **depiction** n.

■ characterize, delineate, describe, draw, paint, picture, portray, represent, show.

depilatory adj. & n. (substance) removing hair.

deplete v. reduce by using quantities of. □ **depletion** n.

deplorable adj. **1** regrettable. **2** very bad. □ **deplorably** adv.

■ **1** despicable, disgraceful, lamentable, regrettable, reprehensible, scandalous, shameful, shocking. **2** abominable, appalling, atrocious, awful, bad, dreadful, execrable, terrible.

deplore v. find or call deplorable.

deploy v. spread out, organize for effective use. □ **deployment** n.

depopulate v. reduce the population of. □ **depopulation** n.

deport v. remove (a person) from a country. □ **deportation** n.

deportment n. behaviour, bearing.

depose v. remove from power.

deposit v. (**deposited**) **1** put or lay down. **2** entrust for safe keeping. **3** pay as a deposit. **4** leave as a layer of matter. ● n. **1** sum entrusted or left as guarantee. **2** something deposited. □ **depositor** n.

■ v. **1** dump, lay (down), leave, park, place, put (down), set (down). **2** bank, consign, entrust, lodge, save, set aside, colloq. stash, store. ● n. **2** accumulation, alluvium, dregs, precipitate, sediment, silt.

deposition n. **1** deposing. **2** depositing. **3** sworn statement.

depository n. storehouse.

depot /déppō/ n. **1** storage area, esp. for vehicles. **2** (US) bus or railway station.

deprave v. corrupt morally.

depravity n. moral corruption.

deprecate v. express disapproval of. □ **deprecation** n., **deprecatory** adj.

depreciate v. make or become lower in value. □ **depreciation** n.

depredation n. plundering.

depress v. **1** press down. **2** reduce (trade etc.). **3** make sad. □ **depressant** adj. & n.

■ **3** demoralize, discourage, dishearten, dismay, dispirit, sadden.

depression n. **1** extreme dejection. **2** long period of inactivity in trading. **3** sunken place. **4** area of low atmospheric pressure. □ **depressive** adj.

■ **1** dejection, despair, despondency, gloom, glumness, melancholy, sadness, the blues, unhappiness. **2** economic decline, recession, slump. **3** cavity, dent, dimple, dip, hollow, indentation.

deprive v. prevent from having or enjoying. □ **deprivation** n.

■ dispossess, divest, rob, strip.

depth n. **1** deepness, measure of this. **2** deepest or most central part. □ **depth charge** bomb that explodes under water. **in depth** thoroughly. **out of one's depth** in water too deep to stand in.

deputation n. group of people sent to represent others.

depute v. appoint to act as one's representative.

deputize v. act as deputy.

deputy n. person appointed to act as a substitute or representative.

■ proxy, replacement, reserve, stand-in, substitute, surrogate; agent, delegate, emissary, envoy, spokesperson.

derail v. cause (a train) to leave the rails. □ **derailment** n.

derange v. **1** disrupt. **2** make insane. □ **derangement** n.

derelict adj. left to fall into ruin.

■ abandoned, decaying, decrepit, deserted, dilapidated, neglected, ruined, tumbledown.

dereliction n. **1** abandonment. **2** neglect (of duty).

deride v. scoff at.

■ jeer at, laugh at, make fun of, mock (at), poke fun at, ridicule, scoff at, taunt.

derision n. scorn, ridicule.

derisive adj. scornful, showing derision. □ **derisively** adv.

derisory adj. **1** showing derision. **2** deserving derision.

derivative adj. & n. derived (thing).

derive v. **1** obtain from a source. **2** have its origin. □ **derivation** n.

■ **1** draw, extract, gain, get, obtain, procure, secure. **2** arise, develop, emanate, originate, proceed, spring, stem.

dermatitis n. inflammation of the skin.

dermatology n. study of skin diseases. □ **dermatologist** n.

derogatory adj. disparaging.

derrick n. **1** crane. **2** framework over an oil well etc.

derv n. fuel for diesel engines.

dervish n. member of a Muslim religious order known for their whirling dance.

desalinate v. remove salt from. □ **desalination** n.

descant n. treble accompaniment to a main melody.

descend v. **1** come, go, or slope down. **2** stoop to unworthy behaviour. ■ be **descended from** have as one's ancestor(s).

■ **1** climb down, come down, go down, move down; decline, drop, fall, plunge, sink, slope down. **2** condescend, lower oneself, stoop.

descendant n. person descended from another.

descent n. **1** descending. **2** downward slope. **3** lineage.

■ **1** drop, fall. **2** declivity, dip, incline, slant, slope. **3** ancestry, blood, extraction, family, heredity, lineage, origins, parentage, pedigree, stock.

describe v. **1** give a description of. **2** mark the outline of.

■ **1** chronicle, give an account of, narrate, outline, recount, relate, report, speak of, tell of; characterize, depict, paint, portray.

description n. **1** representation of a person or thing. **2** sort, kind.

■ **1** account, narrative, report, story; characterization, depiction, portrait, portrayal, representation, sketch. **2** category, character, kind, nature, sort, type, variety.

descriptive adj. describing.

descry v. catch sight of, discern.

desecrate v. violate the sanctity of. □ **desecration** n., **desecrator** n.

desegregate v. abolish segregation in or of. □ **desegregation** n.

deselect v. decline to select or retain as a constituency candidate. □ **deselection** n.

desert[1] /dézzert/ n. barren uninhabited often sandy area. ● adj. desolate, barren.

■ n. waste, wilderness. ● adj. arid, bare, barren, desolate, empty, lonely, uncultivated, uninhabited, unpeopled, wild.

desert[2] /dizért/ v. **1** abandon. **2** leave one's service in the armed forces without permission. □ **deserter** n., **desertion** n.

■ **1** abandon, sl. ditch, jilt, forsake, leave, leave in the lurch, walk out on; maroon, strand. **2** abscond, defect, run away.

deserts n.pl. what one deserves.

deserve v. be worthy of or entitled to. □ **deservedly** adv.

■ be entitled to, be worthy of, earn, justify, merit, rate, warrant.

desiccate v. dry out moisture from. □ **desiccation** n.

design n. **1** plan or sketch for a product. **2** general form or arrangement. **3** lines or shapes as decoration. **4** mental plan. ● v. **1** prepare a design for. **2** intend. □ **designedly** adv., **designer** n.

■ n. **1** blueprint, draft, drawing, model, pattern, plan, sketch. **2** arrangement, composition, configuration, form, format, layout, organization, shape, style. **3** motif, pattern. **4** aim, goal, intention, object, objective, plan, purpose, target. ● v. **1** conceive (of), create, devise, invent, originate, plan; develop, draft, draw, fashion, form, make, shape, sketch. **2** aim, intend, mean, plan, purpose.

designate adj. /dézzignat/ appointed but not yet installed. ● v. /dézzignayt/ **1** name as. **2** specify. **3** appoint to a position. □ **designation** n.

■ v. **1** call, christen, describe as, dub, label, name, nickname. **2** appoint, establish, fix, pinpoint, set, specify, state, stipulate. **3** appoint, assign, choose, elect, name, nominate, select.

designing adj. scheming.

■ artful, calculating, crafty, cunning, devious, guileful, machiavellian, scheming, sly, wily.

desirable adj. arousing desire, worth desiring. □ **desirability** n.

■ alluring, attractive, captivating, seductive, sexy; covetable, enviable; advantageous, beneficial, preferable, profitable, worthwhile.

desire n. **1** feeling of wanting something strongly. **2** thing desired. ● v. feel a desire for.

■ n. **1** appetite, craving, hankering, hunger, itch, longing, thirst, yearning, *colloq.* yen; lasciviousness, lust, passion. ● v. covet, crave, hanker after, *colloq.* have a yen for, hope for, hunger for, itch for, long for, lust after, pine for, want, wish for, yearn for.

desirous adj. desiring.

desist v. cease.

desk n. **1** piece of furniture for reading or writing at. **2** counter. **3** section of a newspaper office.

desolate adj. **1** left alone. **2** ruined, uninhabited. **3** miserable. □ **desolation** n., **desolated** adj.

■ **1** abandoned, alone, bereft, lonely, neglected, solitary. **2** bare, barren, bleak, deserted, dreary, empty, ruined, uninhabited. **3** dejected, despondent, disconsolate, forlorn, melancholy, miserable, mournful, sad, sorrowful, unhappy, woebegone, wretched.

despair n. complete lack of hope. ● v. feel despair.

■ n. dejection, depression, desperation, despondency, hopelessness, misery, wretchedness.

desperado n. (pl. **-oes**) reckless criminal.

desperate adj. **1** reckless through despair. **2** extremely serious or dangerous. □ **desperately** adv., **desperation** n.

■ **1** foolhardy, impetuous, rash, reckless, wild; at one's wits' end, despairing, frantic. **2** acute, critical, grave, pressing, serious, urgent; dangerous, hazardous, hopeless, perilous, precarious.

despicable adj. contemptible. □ **despicably** adv.

despise v. regard as worthless.

■ abhor, be contemptuous of, detest, disdain, hate, loathe, look down on, scorn.

despite prep. in spite of.

despoil v. plunder. □ **despoliation** n.

despondent adj. dejected. □ **despondently** adv., **despondency** n.

despot n. dictator. □ **despotic** adj., **despotism** n.

dessert n. sweet course of a meal. □ **dessertspoon** n. medium-sized spoon for dessert.

destination n. place to which a person or thing is going.

destine v. settle the future of, set apart for a purpose.

destiny n. **1** fate. **2** one's future destined by fate.

■ doom, fate, fortune, kismet, lot.

destitute adj. without means to live. □ **destitution** n.

■ down-and-out, impecunious, impoverished, indigent, needy, penniless, poor, poverty-stricken.

destroy v. **1** pull or break down. **2** ruin. **3** kill (an animal). **4** defeat. □ **destruction** n., **destructive** adj.

■ **1** annihilate, demolish, devastate, knock down, lay waste, obliterate, pull down, ravage, raze, ruin, tear down, vandalize, wipe out, wreak havoc on, wreck. **2** bring to an end, dash, end, finish, kill, put an end to, ruin, shatter, spoil, terminate. □ **destruction** annihilation, demolition, devastation, ruin, ruination.

destroyer n. **1** one who destroys. **2** fast warship.

destruct v. destroy deliberately. □ **destructible** adj.

desultory adj. going from one subject to another.

detach v. release or separate. □ **detachable** adj.

■ cut off, disconnect, disengage, disentangle, free, pull off, release, remove, separate, uncouple, undo, unfasten.

detached adj. **1** separate. **2** impartial, unemotional.

■ **1** disconnected, separate, separated, unattached. **2** disinterested, dispassionate, impartial, neutral, objective, unbiased, unemotional, unprejudiced.

detachment n. **1** detaching. **2** being detached. **3** military group.

detail n. **1** small fact or item. **2** such items collectively. **3** small military detachment. ● v. **1** relate in detail. **2** assign to special duty.

■ n. **1** aspect, component, element, fact, factor, feature, item, nicety, particular, point, respect, technicality; (**details**) minutiae, specifics. **3** detachment, group, party, squad, unit. ● v. **1** enumerate, itemize, list, recount, relate, specify, spell out.

detailed adj. containing many details.

detain v. **1** keep in custody. **2** cause delay to. □ **detainment** n.

■ **1** confine, imprison, intern, keep in custody, remand. **2** delay, hold back or up, impede, keep, retard, slow down.

detainee n. person detained in custody.

detect v. discover or perceive the existence or presence of. □ **detection** n., **detector** n.

■ ascertain, discover, ferret out, find, locate, uncover, unearth; become aware of, discern, feel, identify, note, notice, observe, perceive, scent, sense, smell.

detective n. person, esp. a police officer, who investigates crimes.

détente /daytónt/ n. easing of tension between states.

detention n. **1** detaining. **2** imprisonment.

deter v. (**deterred**) **1** discourage from action. **2** prevent.

■ **1** discourage, dissuade, frighten off, put off, scare off. **2** hinder, impede, obstruct, prevent, stop.

detergent n. & adj. cleansing (substance, esp. other than soap).

deteriorate v. become worse. □ **deterioration** n.

■ decline, degenerate, get worse, colloq. go to pot, worsen; decay, disintegrate, fall apart.

determination n. **1** firmness of purpose. **2** process of deciding.

■ **1** firmness, fortitude, colloq. grit, colloq. guts, perseverance, persistence, resoluteness, resolution, resolve, tenacity, willpower.

determine v. **1** establish precisely. **2** decide, settle. **3** be a decisive factor in.

■ **1** ascertain, discover, establish, find out, learn. **2** choose, decide, resolve, select, settle. **3** affect, govern, influence, shape.

determined adj. resolute.

deterrent n. thing that deters. □ **deterrence** n.

detest v. dislike intensely. □ **detestable** adj., **detestation** n.

■ abhor, abominate, despise, execrate, hate, loathe.

dethrone v. remove from a throne. □ **dethronement** n.

detonate v. explode. □ **detonation** n., **detonator** n.

detour n. deviation from a direct or intended course.

detract v. **detract from** reduce, diminish. □ **detraction** n.

■ devalue, diminish, lessen, reduce, take away from.

detractor n. person who criticizes a thing unfavourably.

detriment n. harm. □ **detrimental** adj., **detrimentally** adv.

■ damage, disadvantage, harm, hurt, impairment, injury. □ **detrimental** adverse, damaging, deleterious, disadvantageous, harmful, hurtful, injurious, prejudicial, unfavourable.

deuterium n. heavy form of hydrogen.

Deutschmark /dóychmaark/ n. unit of money in Germany.

devalue v. reduce the value of. □ **devaluation** n.

devastate v. **1** cause great destruction to. **2** upset deeply. □ **devastation** n.

■ **1** annihilate, demolish, destroy, lay waste, obliterate, ravage, raze, ruin, wreck. **2** overwhelm, shatter, shock, stagger.

devastating adj. overwhelming.

develop v. (**developed**) **1** make or become larger or more mature or organized. **2** begin to exhibit or suffer from. **3** come into existence. **4** make usable or profitable, build on (land). **5** treat (a film) so as to make a picture visible. □ **developer** n., **development** n.

■ **1** broaden, build up, extend, increase, promote, strengthen; amplify, elaborate on, enlarge on, expand on; advance, evolve, improve, mature, progress. **2** acquire, contract, get, pick up. **3** arise, begin, come about, happen, occur. □ **development** enlargement, evolution, expansion, extension, growth, increase; advance, improvement, progress.

deviant adj. & n. (person or thing) deviating from normal behaviour.

deviate v. turn aside. □ **deviation** n.

■ diverge, stray, swerve, turn aside, veer; digress, drift, get off the subject, wander.

device n. **1** thing made or used for a purpose. **2** scheme.

■ **1** apparatus, appliance, contraption, contrivance, gadget, implement, instrument, invention, machine, tool, utensil. **2** gambit, manoeuvre, plan, ploy, ruse, scheme, stratagem, tactic, trick.

devil n. **1** evil spirit. **2** (**the Devil**) supreme spirit of evil. **3** cruel or annoying person. **4** person of mischievous energy or cleverness. □ **devil's advocate** person who tests a proposition by arguing against it. **devilish** adj.

devilled adj. cooked with hot spices.

devilment n. mischief.

devilry n. **1** wickedness. **2** devilment.

devious *adj.* **1** indirect. **2** underhand. □ **deviously** *adv.*, **deviousness** *n.*
■ **1** circuitous, indirect, roundabout, serpentine, tortuous, winding, zigag. **2** artful, crafty, cunning, deceitful, deceptive, designing, dishonest, insincere, misleading, scheming, slippery, sly, treacherous, underhand, untrustworthy, wily.

devise *v.* plan, invent.
■ conceive, concoct, contrive, *colloq.* cook up, create, design, dream up, form, invent, make up, plan, scheme, *colloq.* think up, work out.

devoid *adj.* **devoid of** lacking, free from.

devolution *n.* **1** devolving. **2** delegation of power from central to local administration.

devolve *v.* pass or be passed to a deputy or successor.

devote *v.* give or use for a particular purpose.

devoted *adj.* showing devotion.
■ ardent, constant, dedicated, faithful, loving, loyal, staunch, steadfast, true, zealous.

devotee *n.* enthusiast.

devotion *n.* **1** great love or loyalty. **2** worship. **3** (*pl.*) prayers.
■ **1** ardour, fervour, love, passion, zeal; adherence, allegiance, commitment, constancy, dedication, fidelity, loyalty.

devotional *adj.* used in worship.

devour *v.* **1** eat hungrily or greedily. **2** (of fire etc.) destroy. **3** take in avidly. □ **devourer** *n.*
■ **1** bolt, consume, gobble, gulp, guzzle, *colloq.* scoff, wolf. **2** annihilate, consume, destroy, engulf, ravage. **3** absorb, drink in, take in.

devout *adj.* earnestly religious or sincere. □ **devoutly** *adv.*
■ faithful, God-fearing, pious, religious, reverent, staunch; earnest, genuine, heartfelt, sincere.

dew *n.* drops of condensed moisture on a surface.

dewclaw *n.* small claw on the inner side of a dog's leg.

dewlap *n.* fold of loose skin at the throat of cattle etc.

dexterity *n.* skill.

dexterous *adj.* (also **dextrous**) skilful. □ **dexterously** *adv.*
■ adept, adroit, clever, deft, expert, handy, skilful.

diabetes *n.* disease in which sugar and starch are not properly absorbed by the body. □ **diabetic** *adj.* & *n.*

diabolic *adj.* of the Devil.

diabolical *adj.* very cruel or wicked. □ **diabolically** *adv.*

diabolism *n.* worship of the Devil.

diaconate *n.* **1** office of deacon. **2** body of deacons. □ **diaconal** *adj.*

diadem *n.* crown.

diagnose *v.* make a diagnosis of.

diagnosis *n.* (*pl.* **-oses**) identification of a disease or condition from its symptoms. □ **diagnostic** *adj.*

diagonal *adj.* & *n.* (line) crossing from corner to corner. □ **diagonally** *adv.*

diagram *n.* drawing that shows the parts or operation of something. □ **diagrammatic** *adj.*

dial *n.* **1** face of a clock or watch. **2** similar plate or disc with a movable pointer. **3** movable disc on the front of a telephone. ● *v.* (**dialled**) select by using a dial or numbered buttons.

dialect *n.* local form of a language. □ **dialectal** *adj.*
■ idiom, language, patois, speech, tongue, vernacular.

dialectic *n.* investigation of truths in philosophy etc. by systematic reasoning. □ **dialectical** *adj.*

dialogue *n.* talk between people.

dialysis *n.* purification of blood by causing it to flow through a suitable membrane.

diamanté /diəmóntay/ *adj.* decorated with artificial jewels.

diameter *n.* **1** straight line from side to side through the centre of a circle or sphere. **2** its length.

diametrical *adj.* **1** of or along a diameter. **2** (of opposition) direct. □ **diametrically** *adv.*

diamond *n.* **1** very hard brilliant precious stone. **2** four-sided figure with equal sides and with angles that are not right angles. **3** playing card marked with such shapes. □ **diamond wedding** 60th anniversary.

diaper *n.* (*US*) baby's nappy.

diaphanous *adj.* almost transparent. □ **diaphanously** *adv.*

diaphragm /díəfram/ *n.* **1** a muscular partition between chest and abdomen. **2** contraceptive cap fitting over the cervix.

diarrhoea /díərée′ə/ *n.* condition with frequent fluid faeces.

diary n. **1** daily record of events. **2** book for this. □ **diarist** n.
■ **1** annals, chronicle, journal, log, memoirs, record.

diatribe n. violent verbal attack.

dibber n. tool to make holes in ground for young plants.

dice n. (pl. **dice**) small cube marked on each side with 1–6 spots, used in games of chance. ● v. cut into small cubes.
□ **dice with death** take great risks.

dicey adj. (**-ier**, **-iest**) (sl.) **1** risky. **2** unreliable.

dichotomy /dīkóttəmi/ n. division into two parts or kinds.

dicky adj. (**-ier**, **-iest**) (sl.) shaky, unsound.

dictate v. **1** state or order authoritatively. **2** give orders officiously. **3** say (words) aloud to be written or recorded. ● n. command. □ **dictation** n.
■ v. **1** command, decree, ordain, order, prescribe, state. ● n. command, decree, edict, instruction, order, requirement.

dictator n. **1** ruler with unrestricted authority. **2** domineering person. □ **dictatorship** n.
■ **1** autocrat, despot, tyrant.

dictatorial adj. of or like a dictator. □ **dictatorially** adv.
■ authoritarian, autocratic, despotic, totalitarian, tyrannical; colloq. bossy, dogmatic, domineering, high-handed, imperious, overbearing.

diction n. manner of uttering or pronouncing words.

dictionary n. book that lists and explains the words of a language or the topics of a subject.

dictum n. (pl. **-ta**) formal saying.

did see **do**.

didactic adj. meant or meaning to instruct. □ **didactically** adv.

die¹ v. (**dying**) **1** cease to be alive. **2** cease to exist or function. □ **be dying to** or **for** feel an intense longing to or for.
■ **1** sl. croak, expire, go, lose one's life, pass away, perish, sl. snuff it. **2** cease, come to an end, decline, diminish, disappear, dwindle, ebb, end, fade (away), fizzle out, stop, subside, vanish, wane, wilt, wither (away).

die² n. device that stamps a design or that cuts or moulds material into shape.

diehard n. very conservative or stubborn person.

diesel n. **1** diesel engine. **2** vehicle driven by this. □ **diesel-electric** adj. using an electric generator driven by a diesel engine. **diesel engine** oil-burning engine in which ignition is produced by the heat of compressed air.

diet¹ n. **1** usual food. **2** restricted selection of food. ● v. limit one's diet. □ **dietary** adj., **dieter** n.

diet² n. congress, parliamentary assembly in certain countries.

dietetic adj. of diet and nutrition. ● n.pl. study of diet and nutrition.

dietitian n. expert in dietetics.

differ v. **1** be unlike. **2** disagree.
■ **1** be different, be dissimilar, contrast. **2** argue, be at odds, be at variance, clash, conflict, disagree, fall out, quarrel.

difference n. **1** being different. **2** way in which things differ. **3** remainder after subtraction. **4** disagreement. **5** notable change.
■ **1** discrepancy, dissimilarity, dissimilitude, diversity, inconsistency, variation. **2** contrast, disparity, distinction. **3** balance, remainder, residue, rest, surplus. **4** argument, conflict, disagreement, dispute, quarrel, tiff. **5** alteration, change, transformation.

different adj. **1** not the same. **2** distinct, separate. **3** unusual. □ **differently** adv.
■ **1** conflicting, contrasting, dissimilar, divergent, diverse, inconsistent, opposite, unalike, unlike. **2** disparate, distinct, separate. **3** bizarre, extraordinary, new, offbeat, original, peculiar, singular, strange, unconventional, unique, unorthodox, unusual.

differential adj. of, showing, or depending on a difference. ● n. **1** agreed difference in wage-rates. **2** arrangement of gears allowing a vehicle's wheels to revolve at different speeds when cornering.

differentiate v. **1** be a difference between. **2** distinguish between. **3** develop differences. □ **differentiation** n.

difficult adj. **1** needing much effort or skill to do, deal with, or understand. **2** troublesome. □ **difficulty** n.
■ **1** arduous, burdensome, challenging, demanding, exacting, laborious, onerous, taxing, tough; awkward, delicate, sensitive, ticklish, tricky; baffling, complex, complicated, hard, intricate, knotty, perplexing, problematic(al), puzzling. **2** colloq. bloody-minded, demanding, intractable, naughty, obstinate, obstreperous, obstructive, re-

calcitrant, refractory, stubborn, tiresome, troublesome, trying, uncooperative, unmanageable. □ **difficulty** catch, hindrance, impediment, obstacle, pitfall, problem, snag.

diffident *adj.* lacking confidence. □ **diffidently** *adv.*, **diffidence** *n.*

■ bashful, hesitant, inhibited, meek, modest, reserved, reticent, retiring, selfconscious, self-effacing, shy, tentative, timid, unassertive, unassuming.

diffract *v.* break up a beam of light into a series of coloured or dark and light bands. □ **diffraction** *n.*, **diffractive** *adj.*

diffuse *adj.* /difyŏŏss/ not concentrated. ● *v.* /difyŏŏz/ spread widely or thinly. □ **diffusion** *n.*, **diffusive** *adj.*, **diffusible** *adj.*

■ *v.* circulate, disperse, disseminate, distribute, scatter, spread.

dig *v.* (**dug**, **digging**) **1** break up and move soil. **2** make (a way or hole) thus. **3** poke. ● *n.* **1** excavation. **2** poke. **3** cutting remark. **4** (*pl.*) lodgings. □ **dig out** or **up** find by investigation.

■ *v.* **1** fork over, hoe, plough, till, turn over. **2** burrow, excavate, gouge (out), hollow (out), scoop (out), tunnel. **3** elbow, jab, nudge, poke, prod, stab. □ **dig out** bring to light, discover, ferret out, find, turn up, unearth.

digest *v.* /dījést/ **1** break down (food) in the body. **2** absorb into the mind. ● *n.* /dījest/ methodical summary. □ **digestible** *adj.*

digestion *n.* process or power of digesting food.

digestive *adj.* of or aiding digestion. □ **digestive biscuit** wholemeal biscuit.

digger *n.* **1** one who digs. **2** mechanical excavator.

digit *n.* **1** any numeral from 0 to 9. **2** finger or toe.

digital *adj.* of or using digits. □ **digital clock** one that shows the time as a row of figures. **digitally** *adv.*

digitalis *n.* heart stimulant prepared from foxglove leaves.

dignified *adj.* showing dignity.

■ august, courtly, distinguished, elegant, formal, grave, lofty, majestic, noble, regal, sedate, serious, sober, solemn, stately.

dignify *v.* give dignity to.

dignitary *n.* person holding high rank or position.

dignity *n.* **1** calm and serious manner. **2** high rank or position.

■ **1** decorum, grandeur, gravity, majesty, nobility, seriousness, solemnity, stateliness.

digress *v.* depart from the main subject. □ **digression** *n.*

■ deviate, drift, go off at a tangent, ramble, wander.

dike *n.* = **dyke**.

dilapidated *adj.* in disrepair.

■ crumbling, decaying, decrepit, derelict, falling down, gone to rack and ruin, gone to seed, in disrepair, in ruins, ramshackle, rickety, ruined, tumbledown.

dilapidation *n.* dilapidated state.

dilate *v.* make or become wider. □ **dilation** *n.*, **dilatation** *n.*

dilatory /díllətəri/ *adj.* delaying, not prompt.

dilemma *n.* **1** situation in which a difficult choice must be made. **2** difficult situation.

■ **1** catch-22. **2** deadlock, fix, impasse, *colloq.* pickle, plight, predicament, quandary.

dilettante /dillitánti/ *n.* person who dabbles in a subject.

diligent *adj.* working or done with care and effort. □ **diligently** *adv.*, **diligence** *n.*

■ assiduous, careful, conscientious, earnest, hard-working, industrious, meticulous, painstaking, punctilious, scrupulous, sedulous, thorough.

dill *n.* herb with spicy seeds.

dilly-dally *v.* (*colloq.*) **1** dawdle. **2** waste time by indecision.

dilute *v.* **1** reduce the strength of (fluid) by adding water etc. **2** weaken in effect. □ **dilution** *n.*

dim *adj.* (**dimmer**, **dimmest**) **1** lit faintly, not bright. **2** indistinct. **3** (*colloq.*) stupid. ● *v.* (**dimmed**) make or become dim. □ **dimly** *adv.*, **dimness** *n.*

■ *adj.* **1** faint, pale, weak; dark, dusky, gloomy, murky, shadowy, sombre. **2** blurred, clouded, foggy, fuzzy, hazy, illdefined, indistinct, misty, nebulous, obscure, unclear, vague. ● *v.* cloud, darken, obscure, shade.

dime *n.* 10-cent coin of the USA.

dimension *n.* **1** measurable extent. **2** scope. □ **dimensional** *adj.*

diminish v. make or become smaller or less.
- ■ abate, decline, decrease, dwindle, ease off, ebb, fade, lessen, shrink, subside, taper off, wane; curtail, lower, reduce.

diminuendo adv. & n. (pl. **-os**) decreasing in loudness.

diminution n. decrease.

diminutive adj. tiny. ● n. affectionate form of a name.

dimple n. small dent, esp. in the skin. ● v. 1 show dimple(s). 2 produce dimples in.

din n. loud annoying noise. ● v. (**dinned**) force (information) into a person by constant repetition.
- ■ n. babel, clamour, clatter, commotion, hubbub, hullabaloo, noise, racket, row, rumpus, shouting, tumult, uproar, yelling.

dinar /deénaar/ n. unit of money in some Balkan and Middle Eastern countries.

dine v. eat dinner. □ **diner** n.

dinghy n. small open boat or inflatable rubber boat.

dingle n. deep dell.

dingo n. (pl. **-oes**) Australian wild dog.

dingy adj. (**-ier, -iest**) drab, dirty-looking. □ **dinginess** n.
- ■ cheerless, dark, depressing, dim, dirty, dismal, drab, dreary, dull, frowzy, gloomy.

dining room room in which meals are eaten.

dinky adj. (**-ier, -iest**) (colloq.) attractively small and neat.

dinner n. 1 chief meal of the day. 2 formal evening meal. □ **dinner jacket** man's usu. black jacket for evening wear.

dinosaur n. prehistoric reptile.

dint n. dent. □ **by dint of** by means of.

diocese n. district under the care of a bishop. □ **diocesan** adj.

diode n. semiconductor allowing the flow of current in one direction only.

dioxide n. oxide with two atoms of oxygen to one of a metal or other element.

dip v. (**dipped**) 1 plunge briefly into liquid. 2 lower, go downwards. ● n. 1 dipping. 2 short bathe. 3 downward slope. 4 liquid or mixture into which something is dipped. □ **dip into** read briefly from (a book).
- ■ v. 1 bathe, douse, duck, dunk, immerse, plunge, submerge. 2 decline, descend, drop, fall, go down, sag, sink, slump, subside. ● n. 1 immersion; decline, drop, fall, slump. 2 bathe, swim. 3 declivity, incline, slope.

diphtheria n. infectious disease with inflammation of the throat.

diphthong n. compound vowel sound (as ou in loud).

diploma n. certificate awarded on completion of a course of study.

diplomacy n. 1 handling of international relations. 2 tact.
- ■ 1 statesmanship. 2 delicacy, discretion, finesse, politeness, sensitivity, tact, tactfulness.

diplomat n. 1 member of the diplomatic service. 2 tactful person.

diplomatic adj. 1 of or engaged in diplomacy. 2 tactful. □ **diplomatically** adv.
- ■ 2 considerate, discreet, judicious, polite, prudent, sensitive, tactful, thoughtful.

dipper n. 1 diving bird. 2 ladle.

dipsomania n. uncontrollable craving for alcohol. □ **dipsomaniac** n.

diptych /díptik/ n. pair of pictures on two hinged panels.

dire adj. 1 dreadful. 2 extreme and urgent. 3 ominous.
- ■ 1 appalling, awful, calamitous, disastrous, dreadful, frightful, grim, horrible, terrible, unfortunate, wretched. 2 acute, desperate, drastic, extreme, grievous, serious, urgent. 3 dark, fateful, ominous, sinister, threatening.

direct adj. 1 straight, not roundabout. 2 with nothing or no one between. 3 straightforward, frank. ● adv. by a direct route. ● v. 1 tell how to do something or reach a place. 2 address (a letter etc.). 3 control. 4 order. 5 cause to move in a certain direction. □ **directness** n.
- ■ adj. 1 shortest, straight, through, undeviating, unswerving. 3 blunt, candid, forthright, frank, honest, open, outspoken, plain, sincere, straightforward. ● v. 1 advise, counsel, instruct; escort, guide, give directions, lead, show the way, usher. 3 administer, be in charge of, conduct, control, govern, handle, manage, oversee, regulate, run, steer, superintend, supervise. 4 bid, command, instruct, order, require. 5 aim, level, point, target, train, turn.

direction n. 1 directing. 2 line along which a person or thing moves or faces. 3 (usu. pl.) instruction. □ **directional** adj.
- ■ 1 administration, control, guidance, management, regulation, supervision. 2

bearing, course, path, route, way. **3 (dir-ections)** guidelines, instructions, orders.

directive *n.* general instruction issued by authority.

directly *adv.* **1** in a direct way. **2** very soon. ● *conj.* as soon as.

director *n.* **1** supervisor. **2** member of a board directing a business. **3** one who supervises acting and filming. □ **directorship** *n.*

directorate *n.* **1** office of director. **2** board of directors.

directory *n.* list of telephone subscribers, members, etc.

dirge *n.* song of mourning.

dirigible *n.* airship.

dirk *n.* a kind of dagger.

dirndl *n.* full gathered skirt.

dirt *n.* **1** unclean matter. **2** soil. **3** foul words. **4** scandal.

dirty *adj.* **(-ier, -iest) 1** soiled, not clean. **2** dishonest. **3** lewd, obscene. ● *v.* make or become dirty. □ **dirtily** *adv.*, **dirtiness** *n.*
   ■ *adj.* **1** dingy, dusty, filthy, foul, grimy, grubby, insanitary, marked, messy, *colloq.* mucky, muddy, polluted, smeary, soiled, sooty, sordid, squalid, stained, sullied, tainted, tarnished, unclean, unwashed. **2** dishonest, dishonourable, ignoble, low-down, mean, sordid, treacherous, unfair, unscrupulous, unsporting. ● *v.* defile, foul, mark, muddy, pollute, smear, smudge, soil, stain, sully, tarnish.

disability *n.* thing that disables.

disable *v.* **1** deprive of some ability. **2** make unfit. □ **disablement** *n.*

disabled *adj.* having a disability.

disabuse *v.* disillusion.

disadvantage *n.* something that hinders or is unhelpful. □ **disadvantaged** *adj.*, **disadvantageous** *adj.*
   ■ drawback, handicap, liability, set-back, weakness; detriment, disservice, harm, hurt, injury, loss.

disaffected *adj.* discontented, no longer loyal. □ **disaffection** *n.*

disagree *v.* **1** have a different opinion. **2** quarrel. **3** fail to correspond. □ **disagreement** *n.*
   ■ **1** be at odds, be at variance, differ, dissent. **2** argue, bicker, dispute, fall out, fight, quarrel, squabble, wrangle. **3** be different, be incompatible, conflict. □ **disagreement** conflict, controversy, dissension, dissent; altercation, argument, clash, dispute, quarrel, squabble, strife, tiff, wrangle; dif-

ference, divergence, incompatibility, disparity, dissimilarity.

disagreeable *adj.* **1** unpleasant. **2** bad-tempered. □ **disagreeably** *adv.*
   ■ **1** displeasing, distasteful, nasty, objectionable, offensive, repellent, unpleasant, unsavoury. **2** bad-tempered, cantankerous, crabby, cross, grumpy, impolite, irritable, quarrelsome, rude, sour, surly, uncooperative, unfriendly.

disallow *v.* refuse to sanction.

disappear *v.* pass from sight or existence. □ **disappearance** *n.*
   ■ become invisible, dissolve, evaporate, fade (away), melt (away), vanish.

disappoint *v.* fail to do what was desired or expected. □ **disappointment** *n.*
   ■ disenchant, disillusion, dissatisfy, fail, let down.

disapprobation *n.* disapproval.

disapprove *v.* **disapprove of** have or express an unfavourable opinion of. □ **disapproval** *n.*
   ■ censure, condemn, criticize, deplore, frown on, object to, take exception to. □ **disapproval** censure, condemnation, criticism, disapprobation, disfavour, displeasure, dissatisfaction.

disarm *v.* **1** deprive of weapon(s). **2** reduce armed forces. **3** make less hostile.

disarmament *n.* reduction of a country's forces or weapons.

disarrange *v.* put into disorder.

disarray *n.* & *v.* disorder.

disaster *n.* **1** sudden great misfortune. **2** complete failure. □ **disastrous** *adj.*, **disastrously** *adv.*
   ■ **1** accident, calamity, cataclysm, catastrophe, misfortune, mishap, tragedy. **2** debacle, fiasco, *sl.* flop, *colloq.* wash-out. □ **disastrous** appalling, calamitous, cataclysmic, catastrophic, devastating, dire, dreadful, horrendous, ruinous, terrible, tragic.

disavow *v.* disclaim. □ **disavowal** *n.*

disband *v.* separate, disperse.

disbelieve *v.* refuse or be unable to believe. □ **disbelief** *n.*

disburse *v.* pay out (money). □ **disbursement** *n.*

disc *n.* **1** thin circular plate or layer. **2** record bearing recorded sound. **3** = **disk**. □ **disc jockey** person who introduces and plays pop records at a disco or on the radio.

discard v. /diskaárd/ reject as useless or unwanted. ● n. /diskaard/ discarded thing.
■ v. abandon, cast off, dispose of, sl. ditch, get rid of, jettison, reject, scrap, throw away.

discern v. perceive with the mind or senses. □ **discernible** adj., **discernment** n.
■ become aware of, catch sight of, descry, detect, distinguish, glimpse, make out, notice, observe, perceive, pick out, see, colloq. spot, spy.

discerning adj. perceptive, showing sensitive insight.
■ astute, clever, discriminating, intelligent, judicious, perceptive, perspicacious, sagacious, sage, sharp, shrewd, wise.

discharge v. **1** emit, pour out. **2** release. **3** dismiss. **4** pay (a debt). **5** perform (a duty etc.). ● n. **1** discharging. **2** substance discharged.
■ v. **1** emit, exude, leak, ooze, pour out, produce, send out. **2** free, let go, liberate, release, set free. **3** cashier, dismiss, eject, expel, fire, lay off, colloq. sack, throw out. **4** pay, settle, square. **5** accomplish, carry out, do, execute, fulfil, perform. ● n. **1** dismissal, ejection, expulsion; payment, settlement; execution, fulfilment, performance.

disciple n. **1** person following the teachings of another. **2** one of the original followers of Christ.
■ **1** adherent, admirer, devotee, follower; apprentice, learner, pupil, student.

disciplinarian n. person who enforces strict discipline.

disciplinary adj. of or for discipline.

discipline n. **1** control exercised over people or animals. **2** mental or moral training. **3** branch of learning. ● v. **1** train to be orderly. **2** punish.
■ n. **1** authority, control, order, regulation, restraint, rule. **2** drill, drilling, instruction, schooling, training. ● v. **1** coach, drill, indoctrinate, instruct, school, teach, train; control, curb, govern, keep in check, restrain. **2** castigate, chastise, penalize, punish, rebuke, reprimand, reprove.

disclaim v. disown.
■ deny, disown, reject, renounce, repudiate.

disclaimer n. statement disclaiming something.

disclose v. reveal. □ **disclosure** n.
■ blurt out, betray, divulge, leak, make known, reveal, tell.

disco n. (pl. **-os**) nightclub, party, etc. where people dance to recorded pop music.

discolour v. **1** change in colour. **2** stain. □ **discoloration** n.

discomfit v. (**discomfited**) disconcert. □ **discomfiture** n.

discomfort n. **1** being uncomfortable. **2** thing causing this.

discommode v. inconvenience.

disconcert v. disturb the composure of, fluster.
■ agitate, bewilder, confuse, discomfit, disturb, fluster, nonplus, perplex, perturb, puzzle, colloq. rattle, unsettle, upset, worry.

disconnect v. **1** break the connection of. **2** cut off power supply of. □ **disconnection** n.

disconsolate adj. unhappy, disappointed. □ **disconsolately** adv.

discontent n. dissatisfaction. □ **discontented** adj.
■ displeasure, dissatisfaction, unhappiness. □ **discontented** annoyed, colloq. browned off, disaffected, disgruntled, displeased, dissatisfied, fed up, unhappy.

discontinue v. **1** put an end to. **2** cease. □ **discontinuance** n.

discontinuous adj. not continuous. □ **discontinuity** n.

discord n. **1** disagreement, strife. **2** harsh sound. □ **discordance** n., **discordant** adj.
■ **1** conflict, disagreement, disharmony, dissension, strife. **2** cacophony, din, dissonance, jangle. □ **discordant** conflicting, contrary, differing, disagreeing, divergent, incompatible, opposed, opposite; cacophonous, dissonant, grating, harsh, jangling, jarring, shrill, strident, tuneless, unharmonious, unmusical.

discount n. /diskownt/ amount deducted from the full price. ● v. /diskównt/ disregard.
■ n. allowance, deduction, rebate, reduction. ● v. dismiss, disregard, ignore, omit, overlook, pay no attention to.

discourage v. **1** dishearten. **2** dissuade. □ **discouragement** n.
■ **1** daunt, demoralize, depress, dishearten, dismay, unnerve. **2** deter, dissuade.

discourse n. /diskorss/ **1** conversation. **2** lecture. **3** treatise. ● v. /diskórss/ utter or write a discourse.

discourteous adj. lacking courtesy. □ **discourteously** adv., **discourtesy** n.

discover v. find or find out, by effort or chance. □ **discovery** n.

■ come across, detect, dig up, ferret out, find, happen on, hit on, locate, track down, turn up, uncover, unearth; ascertain, determine, discern, find out, learn, notice, perceive, realize.

discredit v. (**discredited**) **1** damage the reputation of. **2** cause to be disbelieved. ● n. (thing causing) damage to a reputation.

■ v. **1** bring into disrepute, defame, disgrace, dishonour. **2** colloq. debunk, disprove, explode, rebut, refute. ● n. disgrace, disrepute, dishonour, humiliation, ignominy, shame.

discreditable adj. bringing discredit.

discreet adj. **1** circumspect, tactful. **2** unobtrusive. □ **discreetly** adv.

■ **1** careful, cautious, chary, circumspect, guarded, prudent, wary; considerate, delicate, diplomatic, judicious, tactful, thoughtful. **2** inconspicuous, low-key, unobtrusive.

discrepancy n. failure to tally.

discrete adj. separate, not continuous. □ **discretely** adv.

discretion n. **1** being discreet. **2** freedom to decide something.

discretionary adj. done or used at a person's discretion.

discriminate v. make a distinction (between). □ **discriminate against** treat unfairly. **discriminatory** adj.

■ differentiate, distinguish, tell apart, tell the difference.

discriminating adj. having good judgement.

■ astute, discerning, keen, perceptive, perspicacious, selective, shrewd.

discrimination n. **1** unfavourable treatment based on prejudice. **2** good taste or judgement.

■ **1** bias, bigotry, favouritism, prejudice, unfairness. **2** acumen, astuteness, discernment, insight, judgement, perception, perceptiveness, perspicacity, shrewdness, taste.

discursive adj. rambling, not keeping to the main subject.

discus n. heavy disc thrown in contests of strength.

discuss v. talk or write about. □ **discussion** n.

■ chat about, confer about, converse about, consider, debate, deliberate, examine, talk about, thrash out. □ **discussion** chat, conference, consultation, conversation, debate, deliberation, dialogue, discourse, parley.

disdain v. & n. scorn. □ **disdainful** adj., **disdainfully** adv.

■ □ **disdainful** contemptuous, derisive, haughty, hoity-toity, scornful, snobbish, colloq. stuck-up, supercilious, superior.

disease n. **1** unhealthy condition. **2** specific illness. □ **diseased** adj.

■ **1** affliction, ailment, complaint, disorder, illness, infection, malady, sickness. **2** sl. bug, infection, colloq. virus.

disembark v. put or go ashore. □ **disembarkation** n.

disembodied adj. (of a voice) apparently not produced by anyone.

disembowel v. (**disembowelled**) take out the bowels of. □ **disembowelment** n.

disenchant v. disillusion. □ **disenchantment** n.

disenfranchise v. deprive of the right to vote. □ **disenfranchisement** n.

disengage v. detach or separate. □ **disengagement** n.

disentangle v. free or become free from tangles or confusion. □ **disentanglement** n.

disfavour n. dislike, disapproval.

disfigure v. spoil the appearance of. □ **disfigurement** n.

■ blemish, damage, deface, deform, distort, impair, injure, mar, mutilate, ruin, scar, spoil.

disgorge v. eject, pour forth.

disgrace n. **1** loss of reputation or respect. **2** shameful or very bad person or thing. ● v. bring disgrace upon. □ **disgraceful** adj., **disgracefully** adv.

■ n. degradation, discredit, dishonour, disrepute, embarrassment, humiliation, ignominy, mortification, opprobrium, scandal, shame. ● v. discredit, dishonour, embarrass, humiliate, mortify, shame. □ **disgraceful** bad, base, contemptible, degrading, deplorable, despicable, discreditable, dishonourable, humiliating, ignominious, outrageous, scandalous, shameful, shocking.

disgruntled adj. discontented.

disguise v. conceal the identity of. ● n. **1** thing that disguises. **2** disguising, disguised condition.

■ v. camouflage, conceal, cover up, hide, mask, screen, veil. ● n. **1** camouflage, cover, front, guise, mask, smokescreen.

disgust n. strong dislike. ● v. cause disgust in. □ **disgusting** adj.

■ n. abhorrence, aversion, contempt, dislike, distaste, hatred, loathing, repugnance, revulsion. ● v. appal, repel, revolt, shock, sicken. ● **disgusting** abhorrent, distasteful, foul, loathsome, nasty, obnoxious, offensive, colloq. off-putting, repellent, repugnant, repulsive, sickening, vile.

dish n. **1** shallow bowl, esp. for food. **2** food prepared for the table. □ **dish out** (colloq.) distribute. **dish up** serve out food.

disharmony n. lack of harmony.

dishearten v. cause to lose hope or confidence.

■ daunt, demoralize, depress, deter, discourage, dismay.

dishevelled adj. ruffled and untidy. □ **dishevelment** n.

■ bedraggled, messy, ruffled, rumpled, colloq. scruffy, tangled, tousled, untidy, windswept.

dishonest adj. not honest. □ **dishonestly** adv., **dishonesty** n.

■ sl. bent, cheating, corrupt, criminal, colloq. crooked, deceitful, deceptive, dishonourable, double-dealing, false, fraudulent, hypocritical, insincere, lying, mendacious, perfidious, shady, slippery, treacherous, two-faced, underhand, unprincipled, unscrupulous, untrustworthy, untruthful.

dishonour v. & n. disgrace.

dishonourable adj. **1** causing disgrace, ignominious. **2** unprincipled. □ **dishonourably** adv.

■ **1** degrading, discreditable, disgraceful, humiliating, ignominious, shameful. **2** base, contemptible, despicable, dishonest, disloyal, faithless, ignoble, low, mean, perfidious, shabby, shameless, treacherous, two-faced, unprincipled, unscrupulous, untrustworthy, unworthy.

disillusion v. free from pleasant but mistaken beliefs. □ **disillusionment** n.

disincentive n. thing that discourages an action or effort.

disinclination n. unwillingness.

disincline v. make unwilling.

disinfect v. cleanse of infection. □ **disinfection** n.

■ clean, cleanse, decontaminate, fumigate, purify, sanitize, sterilize.

disinfectant n. substance used for disinfecting things.

disinformation n. deliberately misleading information.

disingenuous adj. insincere.

disinherit v. reject from being one's heir. □ **disinheritance** n.

disintegrate v. **1** separate into small pieces. **2** decay. □ **disintegration** n.

■ **1** break up, come or fall apart, crumble, fall to pieces, fragment, shatter. **2** decay, decompose, rot.

disinter v. (**disinterred**) dig up, unearth. □ **disinterment** n.

disinterested adj. unbiased.

■ detached, dispassionate, fair, impartial, neutral, objective, unbiased, uninvolved, unprejudiced.

disjointed adj. lacking orderly connection.

disk n. flat circular device on which computer data can be stored.

dislike n. feeling of not liking something. ● v. feel dislike for.

■ n. antipathy, aversion, detestation, disgust, distaste, hatred, loathing, repugnance. ● v. despise, detest, hate, loathe.

dislocate v. **1** displace from its position. **2** disrupt. □ **dislocation** n.

dislodge v. move or force from an established position.

disloyal adj. not loyal. □ **disloyally** adv., **disloyalty** n.

■ faithless, false, perfidious, traitorous, treacherous, two-faced, unfaithful, untrustworthy.

dismal adj. **1** gloomy. **2** (colloq.) feeble. □ **dismally** adv.

■ **1** bleak, cheerless, dark, depressing, dreary, dull, funereal, gloomy, grim, solemn, sombre; lugubrious, miserable, morose, mournful, sad, unhappy.

dismantle v. take to pieces.

dismay n. feeling of anxiety and discouragement. ● v. cause dismay to.

■ n. alarm, anxiety, apprehension, consternation, disappointment, discouragement, trepidation. ● v. alarm, disconcert, discourage, frighten, horrify, startle, take aback, unnerve.

dismember v. **1** remove the limbs of. **2** split into pieces. □ **dismemberment** n.

dismiss v. **1** send away from one's presence or employment. **2** reject. □ **dismissal** n., **dismissive** adj.

■ **1** pack off, send away, send packing; discharge, fire, colloq. give a person the boot, colloq. kick out, lay off, make redundant, colloq. sack, send packing, throw out. **2** discount, disregard, reject.

dismount v. get off a thing on which one is riding.

disobedient adj. not obedient. □ **disobediently** adv., **disobedience** n.

■ badly behaved, contrary, defiant, headstrong, insubordinate, intractable, mischievous, mutinous, naughty, obstinate, obstreperous, perverse, rebellious, recalcitrant, refractory, self-willed, uncontrollable, unmanageable, unruly, wayward, wilful.

disobey v. disregard orders.

■ break, contravene, defy, disregard, flout, ignore, infringe, transgress, violate.

disoblige v. fail to help or oblige. □ **disobliging** adj.

disorder n. **1** lack of order or of discipline. **2** ailment. ● v. throw into disorder. □ **disorderly** adj.

■ n. **1** chaos, clutter, confusion, disarray, disorganization, jumble, mess, muddle, shambles, tangle, untidiness; bedlam, commotion, disturbance, fracas, hullabaloo, pandemonium, riot, rumpus, tumult, turmoil, unrest, upheaval, uproar. **2** ailment, disease, illness, malady, sickness.

disorganize v. upset the arrangement of. □ **disorganization** n.

disorientate v. cause (a person) to lose his or her sense of direction. □ **disorientation** n.

disown v. **1** refuse to acknowledge. **2** reject all connection with.

disparage v. suggest that something is of little value or importance. □ **disparagement** n.

■ belittle, criticize, decry, denigrate, deprecate, minimize, run down, undervalue.

disparate adj. different in kind. □ **disparately** adv., **disparity** n.

dispassionate adj. **1** not emotional. **2** impartial. □ **dispassionately** adv.

■ **1** calm, composed, cool, equable, eventempered, level-headed, placid, self-controlled, sober, unemotional, colloq. unflappable. **2** detached, disinterested, impartial, neutral, objective, unbiased, unprejudiced.

dispatch v. **1** send off to a destination or for a purpose. **2** kill. **3** complete (a task) quickly. ● n. **1** dispatching. **2** promptness. **3** news report. **4** official message. □ **dispatch box** container for official documents. **dispatch rider** motorcyclist carrying messages.

dispel v. (**dispelled**) **1** drive away. **2** scatter. □ **dispeller** n.

dispensable adj. not essential.

dispensary n. place where medicines are dispensed.

dispensation n. **1** dispensing. **2** distributing. **3** exemption.

dispense v. **1** deal out. **2** prepare and give out (medicine etc.). □ **dispense with 1** do without. **2** make unnecessary. **dispenser** n.

disperse v. go or send in different directions, scatter. □ **dispersal** n., **dispersion** n.

■ diffuse, disseminate, distribute, spread; disband, dismiss, scatter, send away.

dispirited adj. dejected. □ **dispiriting** adj.

displace v. **1** shift. **2** take the place of. **3** oust. □ **displacement** n.

display v. show, arrange conspicuously. ● n. **1** act or instance of displaying. **2** thing(s) displayed. □ **displayer** n.

■ v. demonstrate, evince, manifest, reveal, show; arrange, dispose, exhibit, present, unveil; flash, flaunt, parade, show off. ● n. **1** demonstration, manifestation, revelation. **2** array, exhibit, exhibition, panoply, parade, presentation, show, spectacle.

displease v. irritate, annoy.

■ colloq. aggravate, anger, annoy, sl. bug, exasperate, infuriate, irk, irritate, nettle, offend, put out, colloq. rile, upset, vex.

displeasure n. disapproval.

disport v. disport oneself frolic.

disposable adj. **1** that can be disposed of. **2** designed to be thrown away after use. □ **disposability** n.

disposal n. disposing. □ **at one's disposal** available for one's use.

dispose v. **1** place, arrange. **2** make willing or ready to do something. □ **dispose of 1** get rid of. **2** finish. **be well disposed** be friendly or favourable.

■ **1** arrange, array, distribute, organize, place, position, put, range. **2** incline, induce, influence, lead, move, persuade, tempt. □ **dispose of 1** discard, dump, get rid of, jettison, scrap, throw away or out. **2** complete, conclude, finish, settle.

disposition n. **1** arrangement. **2** person's character. **3** tendency.
■ **1** arrangement, disposal, grouping, organization. **2** attitude, character, make-up, nature, personality, temperament. **3** inclination, leaning, predisposition, preference, proclivity, propensity, tendency.

dispossess v. deprive of the possession of. □ **dispossession** n.

disproportionate adj. relatively too large or too small. □ **disproportionately** adv.

disprove v. show to be wrong.
■ confute, colloq. debunk, destroy, demolish, discredit, explode, invalidate, negate, rebut, refute.

disputable adj. questionable.

disputant n. person engaged in a dispute.

disputation n. argument, debate.

disputatious adj. argumentative.

dispute v. **1** question the validity of. **2** argue, quarrel. ● n. **1** debate. **2** quarrel.
■ v. **1** challenge, contest, deny, disagree with, object to, oppose, query, question. **2** argue, debate, fight, quarrel, squabble, wrangle. ● n. **1** argument, controversy, debate, discussion, disputation. **2** altercation, clash, disagreement, fight, quarrel, squabble, wrangle.

disqualify v. make ineligible or unsuitable. □ **disqualification** n.

disquiet n. uneasiness, anxiety. ● v. cause disquiet to.

disregard v. ignore, treat as unimportant. ● n. lack of attention.
■ v. discount, dismiss, ignore, overlook, pass over, pay no attention to, take no notice of.

disrepair n. bad condition caused by neglect.

disreputable adj. not respectable. □ **disreputably** adv.
■ discreditable, disgraceful, dishonourable, shady, shameful, sleazy, unprincipled, unscrupulous, untrustworthy.

disrepute n. discredit.

disrespect n. lack of respect. □ **disrespectful** adj.
■ □ **disrespectful** cheeky, discourteous, impolite, impudent, insolent, irreverent, pert, rude, saucy, uncivil.

disrobe v. undress.

disrupt v. **1** cause to break up. **2** interrupt the continuity of. □ **disruption** n., **disruptive** adj.

dissatisfaction n. lack of satisfaction or of contentment.
■ annoyance, chagrin, disappointment, discontent, displeasure, exasperation, frustration, irritation, unhappiness.

dissatisfied adj. not satisfied.
■ colloq. browned off, disaffected, disappointed, discontented, disgruntled, displeased, fed up, frustrated, unhappy.

dissect v. cut apart so as to examine the internal structure. □ **dissection** n., **dissector** n.

dissemble v. conceal (feelings).

disseminate v. spread widely. □ **dissemination** n.

dissension n. disagreement that gives rise to strife.

dissent v. have a different opinion. ● n. difference in opinion. □ **dissenter** n., **dissentient** adj. & n.

dissertation n. detailed discourse.

disservice n. unhelpful or harmful action.

dissident adj. disagreeing. ● n. person who disagrees, esp. with the authorities. □ **dissidence** n.

dissimilar adj. unlike. □ **dissimilarity** n., **dissimilitude** n.
■ contrasting, different, distinct, distinguishable, diverse, unalike, unlike, unrelated.

dissimulate v. dissemble. □ **dissimulation** n.

dissipate v. fritter away. □ **dissipation** n.

dissipated adj. dissolute.

dissociate v. **1** regard as separate. **2** declare to be unconnected. □ **dissociation** n.

dissolute adj. lacking moral restraint or self-discipline.
■ corrupt, debauched, decadent, degenerate, depraved, dissipated, immoral, licentious, profligate, rakish, wanton.

dissolution n. dissolving of an assembly or partnership.

dissolve v. **1** make or become liquid or dispersed in liquid. **2** disappear gradually. **3** disperse (an assembly). **4** end (a partnership, esp. marriage).
■ **1** disintegrate, liquefy, melt. **2** disappear, fade (away), melt (away), vanish. **3** disband, dismiss, disperse, wind up.

dissonant adj. discordant. □ **dissonance** n.

dissuade v. persuade against a course of action. □ **dissuasion** n.

distaff *n.* cleft stick holding wool etc. in spinning. □ **distaff side** female branch of a family.

distance *n.* **1** length of space between two points. **2** distant part. **3** aloofness. **4** remoteness. ● *v.* separate.
■ **1** gap, interval, space, span, stretch. **3** aloofness, coolness, detachment, reserve, stiffness.

distant *adj.* **1** at a specified or considerable distance away. **2** aloof. □ **distantly** *adv.*
■ **1** far, far-away, far-off, outlying, remote. **2** aloof, chilly, cold, cool, detached, haughty, reserved, reticent, standoffish, stiff, unapproachable, unfriendly, withdrawn.

distaste *n.* dislike, disapproval.

distasteful *adj.* arousing distaste.
■ disagreeable, disgusting, displeasing, nasty, objectionable, offensive, *colloq.* off-putting, unpalatable, unpleasant, unsavoury.

distemper *n.* **1** disease of dogs. **2** paint for use on walls. ● *v.* paint with distemper.

distend *v.* swell from pressure within. □ **distension** *n.*

distil *v.* (**distilled**) **1** treat or make by distillation. **2** undergo distillation.

distillation *n.* **1** process of vaporizing and condensing a liquid so as to purify it or to extract elements. **2** something distilled.

distiller *n.* one who makes alcoholic liquor by distillation.

distillery *n.* place where alcohol is distilled.

distinct *adj.* **1** clearly perceptible. **2** different in kind. □ **distinctly** *adv.*
■ **1** apparent, clear, definite, evident, manifest, noticeable, obvious, palpable, patent, perceptible, plain, recognizable, sharp, unambiguous, unequivocal, unmistakable, visible, well-defined. **2** contrasting, different, dissimilar, unalike, unlike.

distinction *n.* **1** act or instance of distinguishing. **2** difference. **3** thing that differentiates. **4** excellence. **5** mark of honour.
■ **1** discrimination, differentiation. **2** contrast, difference, dissimilarity, disparity. **3** characteristic, feature, mark, peculiarity. **4** eminence, excellence, fame, glory, greatness, honour, importance, merit, note, prestige, renown, reputation, significance, superiority, value, worth.

distinctive *adj.* distinguishing, characteristic. □ **distinctively** *adv.*, **distinctiveness** *n.*

distinguish *v.* **1** be or see a difference between. **2** discern. **3** make notable. □ **distinguishable** *adj.*
■ **1** differentiate, separate, tell apart; set apart, single out. **2** descry, detect, discern, identify, make out, notice, perceive, pick out, recognize.

distinguished *adj.* famous for great achievements.
■ celebrated, eminent, famous, great, honoured, illustrious, notable, noted, prominent, renowned.

distort *v.* **1** pull out of shape. **2** misrepresent. □ **distortion** *n.*
■ **1** bend, contort, deform, disfigure, twist, warp. **2** falsify, misrepresent, twist.

distract *v.* draw away the attention of.

distracted *adj.* distraught.

distraction *n.* **1** distracting. **2** thing that distracts. **3** entertainment. **4** distraught state.

distraught *adj.* nearly crazy with grief or worry.
■ agitated, at one's wits' end, beside oneself, distracted, distressed, disturbed, frantic, frenetic, hysterical, overwrought, troubled, wild.

distress *n.* suffering, unhappiness. ● *v.* cause distress to. □ **in distress** in danger and needing help.
■ *n.* affliction, agony, anguish, anxiety, desolation, grief, heartache, misery, pain, sadness, sorrow, suffering, torment, trouble, unhappiness, woe, wretchedness. ● *v.* afflict, disturb, grieve, hurt, pain, perturb, sadden, torment, torture, trouble, upset, worry.

distribute *v.* **1** divide and share out. **2** scatter, place at different points. □ **distribution** *n.*
■ **1** allocate, allot, apportion, assign, *colloq.* dish out, dispense, divide up, dole out, give out, hand out, issue, partition, share (out). **2** disperse, disseminate, scatter, spread, strew.

distributor *n.* **1** one who distributes. **2** device for passing electric current to spark plugs.

district *n.* part (of a country, county, or city) with a particular feature or regarded as a unit.
■ area, locality, neighbourhood, parish, part, province, quarter, region, sector, ward, zone.

distrust *n.* lack of trust, suspicion. ● *v.* feel distrust in. ☐ **distrustful** *adj.*, **distrustfully** *adv.*
■ *n.* doubt, misgiving, mistrust, scepticism, suspicion, uncertainty. ● *v.* be sceptical of, doubt, have misgivings about, have qualms about, mistrust, question, suspect.

disturb *v.* **1** break the quiet, rest, or calm of. **2** disorganize. ☐ **disturbance** *n.*
■ **1** agitate, alarm, bother, concern, disconcert, distress, fluster, perturb, ruffle, shake, trouble, unsettle, upset, worry; disrupt, interrupt, intrude on; distract, inconvenience, put out. **2** disarrange, disorder, disorganize, jumble (up), move, muddle (up).

disturbed *adj.* mentally or emotionally unstable or abnormal.

disuse *n.* state of not being used.

disused *adj.* no longer used.

ditch *n.* long narrow trench for drainage. ● *v.* **1** make or repair ditches. **2** (*sl.*) abandon.

dither *v.* hesitate indecisively.

ditto *n.* (in lists) the same again.

ditty *n.* short simple song.

diuretic *adj.* & *n.* (substance) causing more urine to be excreted.

diurnal *adj.* of or in the day.

divan *n.* **1** couch without back or arms. **2** bed resembling this.

dive *v.* **1** plunge head first into water. **2** plunge or move quickly downwards. **3** go under water. **4** rush headlong. ● *n.* **1** diving. **2** sharp downward movement or fall. **3** (*colloq.*) disreputable place.

diver *n.* **1** one who dives. **2** person who works underwater.

diverge *v.* **1** separate and go in different directions. **2** depart from a path etc. ☐ **divergence** *n.*, **divergent** *adj.*
■ **1** branch, divide, fork, ramify, separate, split. **2** deviate, drift, stray, turn aside, wander.

diverse *adj.* of differing kinds.
■ assorted, heterogeneous, miscellaneous, mixed, multifarious, varied, various, varying.

diversify *v.* **1** introduce variety into. **2** vary. ☐ **diversification** *n.*

diversion *n.* **1** act of diverting. **2** thing that diverts attention. **3** entertainment. **4** route round a closed road.
■ **1** deviation, digression. **2** distraction, interruption. **3** amusement, entertainment, game, pastime, recreation, relaxation.

diversity *n.* variety.

divert *v.* **1** turn from a course or route. **2** entertain, amuse.
■ **1** avert, deflect, redirect, sidetrack, switch, turn aside. **2** absorb, amuse, beguile, engage, entertain, interest, occupy.

divest *v.* **divest of** strip of.

divide *v.* **1** separate into parts or from something else. **2** distribute. **3** cause to disagree. **4** find how many times one number contains another. **5** be able to be divided. ● *n.* dividing line.
■ *v.* **1** break up, cut up, partition, separate, split (up), subdivide. **2** apportion, distribute, dole out, share (out). **3** alienate, estrange, part, separate, split.

dividend *n.* **1** share of profits payable. **2** number to be divided.

divider *n.* **1** thing that divides. **2** (*pl.*) measuring compasses.

divination *n.* divining.

divine *adj.* **1** of, from, or like God or a god. **2** (*colloq.*) excellent, beautiful. ● *v.* discover by intuition or magic. ☐ **divinely** *adv.*, **diviner** *n.*
■ *adj.* **1** celestial, godlike, heavenly, holy. ● *v.* forecast, foresee, foretell, predict, prognosticate.

divining rod dowser's stick.

divinity *n.* **1** being divine. **2** god.

divisible *adj.* able to be divided. ☐ **divisibility** *n.*

division *n.* **1** act or instance of dividing. **2** dividing line. **3** one of the parts into which a thing is divided. ☐ **divisional** *adj.*
■ **1** dividing, partition, separation, splitting. **2** border, borderline, boundary, frontier. **3** compartment, part, section, segment.

divisive *adj.* tending to cause disagreement.

divisor *n.* number by which another is to be divided.

divorce *n.* **1** legal termination of a marriage. **2** separation. ● *v.* **1** end the marriage of (a person) by divorce. **2** separate.

divorcee *n.* divorced person.

divulge *v.* reveal (information).

Diwali *n.* Hindu festival at which lamps are lit, held between September and November.

dizzy *adj.* (**-ier, -iest**) **1** giddy, dazed. **2** causing giddiness. □ **dizzily** *adv.*, **dizziness** *n.*

djellaba /jéllǝbǝ/ *n.* Arab cloak.

do *v.* (**did, done**) **1** perform, complete. **2** deal with. **3** act, behave. **4** fare. **5** be suitable. **6** suffice. ● *v.aux.* used to form present or past tense, for emphasis, or to avoid repeating a verb just used. ● *n.* (*pl.* **dos** or **do's**) entertainment, party. □ **do away with 1** abolish, get rid of. **2** kill. **do down** (*colloq.*) swindle. **do for** (*colloq.*) ruin, destroy. **do-gooder** *n.* well-meaning but unrealistic promoter of social work or reform. **do in** (*sl.*) **1** ruin, kill. **2** tire out. **do out** clean, redecorate. **do up 1** fasten. **2** repair, redecorate. **do without** manage without.

■ *v.* **1** accomplish, achieve, bring off, carry out, complete, discharge, execute, finish, fulfil, perform, pull off. **2** attend to, deal with, look after, organize, see to, sort out, take charge of. **3** act, behave, conduct oneself. **4** get on, fare, manage. **5** be acceptable, be suitable, satisfy, serve. **6** be enough, suffice. □ **do away with 1** abolish, cancel, dispense with, dispose of, eliminate, get rid of.

Dobermann pinscher dog of a large smooth-coated breed.

docile *adj.* willing to obey. □ **docilely** *adv.*, **docility** *n.*

■ biddable, complaisant, compliant, cooperative, manageable, meek, obedient, passive, submissive, tame, tractable, yielding.

dock[1] *n.* enclosed harbour for loading, unloading, and repair of ships. ● *v.* **1** bring or come into dock. **2** connect (spacecraft) in space, be joined thus.

dock[2] *n.* enclosure for the prisoner in a criminal court.

dock[3] *v.* **1** cut short. **2** reduce, take away part of.

dock[4] *n.* weed with broad leaves.

docker *n.* labourer who loads and unloads ships in a dockyard.

docket *n.* **1** document listing goods delivered. **2** voucher. ● *v.* (**docketed**) label with a docket.

dockyard *n.* area and buildings round a shipping dock.

doctor *n.* **1** qualified medical practitioner. **2** holder of a doctorate. ● *v.* **1** tamper with. **2** castrate, spay.

doctorate *n.* highest degree at a university.

doctrinaire *adj.* applying theories or principles rigidly.

doctrine *n.* principle(s) of a religious, political, or other group. □ **doctrinal** *adj.*

■ belief, conviction, creed, dogma, precept, principle, tenet.

document *n.* piece of paper giving information or evidence. ● *v.* provide or prove with documents. □ **documentation** *n.*

documentary *adj.* **1** consisting of documents. **2** giving a factual report. ● *n.* documentary film.

dodder *v.* totter, esp. from age. □ **dodderer** *n.*, **doddery** *adj.*

dodge *v.* **1** move quickly to one side so as to avoid (a thing). **2** evade. ● *n.* **1** clever trick, ingenious action. **2** quick evasive action. □ **dodger** *n.*

■ *v.* **1** bob, duck, sidestep, swerve, veer. **2** avoid, elude, escape from, evade, get away from, get out of. ● *n.* **1** device, manoeuvre, ploy, ruse, scheme, stratagem, subterfuge, trick.

dodgem *n.* small car at a funfair, driven so as to bump others in an enclosure.

dodo *n.* (*pl.* **-os**) large extinct bird.

doe *n.* female of deer, hare, or rabbit.

doff *v.* take off (one's hat).

dog *n.* **1** four-legged carnivorous wild or domesticated animal. **2** male of this or of fox or wolf. **3** (**the dogs**) greyhound racing. ● *v.* (**dogged**) follow persistently. □ **dog collar** (*colloq.*) clerical collar fastening at the back of the neck. **dog-eared** *adj.* with page-corners crumpled.

dog cart two-wheeled cart with back-to-back seats.

dogfish *n.* a kind of small shark.

dogged *adj.* determined. □ **doggedly** *adv.*

doggerel *n.* bad verse.

doggo *adv.* **lie doggo** (*sl.*) remain motionless or making no sign.

doggy *adj.* & *n.* (of) a dog. □ **doggy bag** bag for carrying away leftovers.

dogma *n.* doctrine(s) put forward by authority.

dogmatic *adj.* imposing personal opinions. □ **dogmatically** *adv.*

■ arrogant, assertive, dictatorial, domineering, high-handed, imperious, intolerant, opinionated, overbearing, peremptory.

dog rose wild hedge-rose.

dogsbody n. (colloq.) drudge.

doh n. name for the keynote of a scale in music, or the note C.

doily n. small ornamental mat.

doldrums n.pl. equatorial regions with little or no wind. □ **in the doldrums** in low spirits.

dole v. **dole out** distribute. ● n. (colloq.) unemployment benefit.

doleful adj. mournful. □ **dolefully** adv., **dolefulness** n.

doll n. small model of a human figure, esp. as a child's toy.

dollar n. unit of money in the USA, Australia, etc.

dollop n. mass of a soft substance.

dolly n. **1** (children's use) doll. **2** movable platform for a cine camera.

dolman sleeve tapering sleeve cut in one piece with the body of a garment.

dolmen n. megalithic structure of a large flat stone laid on two upright ones.

dolomite n. a type of limestone rock. □ **dolomitic** adj.

dolphin n. sea animal like a large porpoise, with a beak-like snout.

dolt n. stupid person. □ **doltish** adj.

domain n. **1** area under a person's control. **2** field of activity.

dome n. **1** rounded roof with a circular base. **2** thing shaped like this. □ **domed** adj.

domestic adj. **1** of home or household. **2** of one's own country. **3** domesticated. ● n. household servant. □ **domestically** adv.

domesticate v. **1** train (an animal) to live with humans. **2** accustom to household work and home life. □ **domestication** n.

domesticity n. domestic life.

domicile n. place of residence. □ **domiciliary** adj.

dominant adj. dominating, prevailing. □ **dominance** n.

> ■ authoritative, commanding, dominating, influential, leading, ruling; chief, main, outstanding, predominant, pre-eminent, prevailing, primary, principal.

dominate v. **1** have a commanding influence over. **2** be the most influential or conspicuous person or thing. **3** tower over. □ **domination** n.

> ■ **1** command, control, direct, govern, have under one's thumb, keep, reign over, rule; be at the wheel, be in control, have the upper hand. **2** predominate, preponderate, prevail. **3** dwarf, overshadow, tower over.

domineer v. behave forcefully, making others obey.

dominion n. **1** authority to rule, control. **2** ruler's territory.

domino n. (pl. **-oes**) small oblong piece marked with pips, used in the game of **dominoes**.

don[1] v. (**donned**) put on.

don[2] n. head, fellow, or tutor of a college. □ **donnish** adj.

donate v. give as a donation.

> ■ contribute, give, grant, pledge, present, provide, supply.

donation n. gift (esp. of money) to a fund or institution.

done see **do**. adj. (colloq.) socially acceptable.

donkey n. animal of the horse family, with long ears. □ **donkey jacket** thick weatherproof jacket. **donkey's years** (colloq.) a very long time. **donkey work** drudgery.

donor n. one who gives or donates something.

doodle v. scribble idly. ● n. drawing or marks made thus.

doom n. terrible and inevitable fate. ● v. destine to a grim fate.

> ■ n. destiny, fate, fortune, kismet, lot; death, destruction, downfall, end, ruin.

doomsday n. Judgement Day.

door n. **1** hinged, sliding, or revolving barrier closing an opening. **2** doorway.

doorway n. opening filled by a door.

dope n. (sl.) **1** drug. **2** information. **3** stupid person. ● v. drug.

dopey adj. (**-ier**, **-iest**) **1** half asleep. **2** stupid.

dormant adj. **1** sleeping, temporarily inactive. **2** in abeyance. □ **dormancy** n.

> ■ **1** asleep, at rest, hibernating, inactive, inert, quiescent, quiet, resting, sleeping. **2** hidden, in abeyance, latent, potential, untapped.

dormer n. upright window under a small gable on a sloping roof.

dormitory n. room with several beds, esp. in a school. □ **dormitory town** commuter town or suburb.

dormouse n. (pl. **-mice**) mouse-like animal that hibernates.

dorsal adj. of or on the back.

dory n. edible sea fish.

dosage n. size of a dose.

dose n. **1** amount of medicine to be taken at one time. **2** amount of radiation received. ● v. give dose(s) of medicine to.

doss v. (sl.) sleep in a doss-house or on a makeshift bed etc. □ **dosser** n.

doss-house n. cheap hostel.

dossier n. set of documents about a person or event.

dot n. small round mark. ● v. (**dotted**) **1** mark with dot(s). **2** scatter here and there. **3** (sl.) hit. □ **on the dot** exactly on time.

dotage n. senility.

dote v. **dote on** feel great fondness for. □ **doting** adj.
■ adore, be fond of, be infatuated with, idolize, love, worship.

dotty adj. (**-ier**, **-iest**) (colloq.) **1** feeble-minded. **2** eccentric. **3** silly. □ **dottily** adv., **dottiness** n.

double adj. **1** consisting of two things or parts. **2** twice as much or as many. **3** designed for two people or things. ● adv. **1** twice as much. **2** in twos. ● n. **1** person or thing very like another. **2** double quantity or thing. **3** (pl.) game with two players on each side. ● v. **1** make or become twice as much or as many. **2** fold in two. **3** turn back sharply. **4** act two parts. **5** have two uses. □ **at the double** running, hurrying. **double bass** lowest-pitched instrument of the violin family. **double-breasted** adj. (of a coat) with fronts overlapping. **double chin** chin with a roll of fat below. **double cream** thick cream. **double-cross** v. cheat, deceive. **double-dealing** n. deceit, esp. in business. adj. deceitful. **double-decker** n. bus with two decks. **double Dutch** gibberish. **double figures** numbers from 10 to 99. **double glazing** two sheets of glass in a window. **double take** delayed reaction just after one's first reaction. **double-talk** n. talk with deliberately ambiguous meaning. **doubly** adv.

double entendre /doob'l aantaándra/ phrase with two meanings, one usu. indecent.

doublet n. **1** each of a pair of similar things. **2** (old use) man's close-fitting jacket.

doubt n. **1** feeling of uncertainty or disbelief. **2** being undecided. ● v. feel doubt about, hesitate to believe. □ **doubter** n.
■ n. **1** anxiety, apprehension, disquiet, distrust, hesitation, incredulity, misgiving, mistrust, qualm(s), reservation(s), scepticism, suspicion, uncertainty. **2** indecision, irresolution. ● v. be sceptical of, distrust, feel uncertain about, have misgivings about, mistrust, query, question, suspect.

doubtful adj. **1** feeling or causing doubt. **2** unreliable. □ **doubtfully** adv.
■ **1** distrustful, hesitant, incredulous, mistrustful, sceptical, suspicious, uncertain, unconvinced, undecided, unsure; ambiguous, debatable, disputable, dubious, equivocal, problematic(al), questionable, suspect. **2** unpredictable, unreliable, untrustworthy.

doubtless adj. certainly.

douche /doosh/ n. **1** jet of water applied to the body. **2** device for applying this. ● v. use a douche (on).

dough /do/ n. **1** thick mixture of flour etc. and liquid, for baking. **2** (sl.) money. □ **doughy** adj.

doughnut /dónut/ n. small cake of fried sweetened dough.

dour /door/ adj. stern, gloomy-looking.

douse /dowss/ v. **1** extinguish (a light). **2** throw water on. **3** put into water.

dove n. **1** bird with a thick body and short legs. **2** advocate of peaceful policies.

dovecote n. shelter for domesticated pigeons.

dovetail n. wedge-shaped joint interlocking two pieces of wood. ● v. combine neatly.

dowager n. woman holding a title or property from her dead husband.

dowdy adj. (**-ier**, **-iest**) **1** dull, not stylish. **2** dressed dowdily. □ **dowdily** adv., **dowdiness** n.
■ drab, dull, frowzy, frumpish, frumpy, unfashionable.

dowel n. headless wooden or metal pin holding pieces of wood or stone together.

dowelling n. rods for cutting into dowels.

down[1] n. area of open undulating land, esp. (pl.) chalk uplands.

down[2] n. very fine soft furry feathers or short hairs.

down[3] adv. **1** to, in, or at a lower place or state etc. **2** to a smaller size. **3** from an earlier to a later time. **4** recorded in writing. **5** to the source or place where a thing is. **6** as (partial) payment at the time of purchase. ● prep. **1** downwards along or through or into. **2** at a lower part of. ● adj. **1** directed downwards. **2** travelling away from a central place. ● v. (colloq.) **1** knock, bring, or put down. **2** swallow. □ **down-and-out** adj. & n. destitute (person). **have a down on** (colloq.) be hostile to. **down-to-earth** adj. sensible, practical. **down under** in the antipodes, esp. Australia.

downcast *adj.* **1** dejected. **2** (of eyes) looking downwards.

downfall *n.* **1** fall from prosperity or power. **2** thing causing this.

downgrade *v.* reduce to a lower grade.

downhearted *adj.* in low spirits.

■ blue, dejected, depressed, despondent, dispirited, downcast, gloomy, glum, melancholy, miserable, sad, unhappy.

downhill *adj. & adv.* going or sloping downwards.

downpour *n.* great fall of rain.

downright *adj.* **1** frank, straightforward. **2** utter. ● *adv.* thoroughly.

■ **1** blunt, candid, direct, forthright, frank, honest, open, outspoken, plain, straightforward. **2** absolute, categorical, complete, out and out, outright, sheer, total, thorough, unmitigated, utter.

Down's syndrome abnormal congenital condition causing physical abnormalities and learning difficulties.

downstairs *adv. & adj.* to or on a lower floor.

downstream *adj. & adv.* in the direction in which a stream flows.

downtrodden *adj.* oppressed.

downward *adj.* moving or leading down. ● *adv.* downwards.

downwards *adv.* towards a lower place etc.

downy *adj.* (**-ier**, **-iest**) of, like, or covered with soft down.

dowry *n.* property brought by a bride to her husband.

dowse /dowz/ *v.* search for underground water or minerals by using a stick which dips when these are present. □ **dowser** *n.*

doxology *n.* hymn of praise to God.

doyen *n.* (*fem.* **doyenne**) senior member of a group.

doze *v.* sleep lightly. ● *n.* short light sleep.

dozen *n.* **1** set of twelve. **2** (*pl.*, *colloq.*) very many.

Dr *abbr.* Doctor.

drab *adj.* dull, uninteresting.

■ cheerless, colourless, depressing, dingy, dismal, dreary, dull, grey, sombre; boring, lacklustre, lifeless, tedious, uninspiring, uninteresting.

drachm /dram/ *n.* one-eighth of an ounce or of a fluid ounce.

drachma *n.* (*pl.* **-as** or **-ae**) unit of money in Greece.

draconian *adj.* (of laws) harsh.

draft[1] *n.* **1** preliminary written version. **2** written order to a bank to pay money. **3** (*US*) conscription. ● *v.* **1** prepare a draft of. **2** (*US*) conscript.

draft[2] *n.* (*US*) draught.

drag *v.* (**dragged**) **1** pull along with effort or difficulty. **2** trail on the ground. **3** (of time etc.) pass slowly or tediously. **4** search (water) with nets or hooks. ● *n.* **1** thing that slows progress. **2** (*colloq.*) draw at a cigarette. **3** (*sl.*) women's clothes worn by men. □ **dragnet** *n.* net for dragging water.

■ *v.* **1** draw, haul, lug, pull, tow, trail, tug.

dragon *n.* **1** mythical reptile able to breathe fire. **2** fierce person.

dragonfly *n.* long-bodied insect with gauzy wings.

dragoon *n.* cavalryman. ● *v.* force into action.

drain *v.* **1** draw off (liquid) by channels or pipes etc. **2** flow away. **3** deprive gradually (of strength or resources). **4** drink all of. ● *n.* **1** channel or pipe carrying away water or sewage. **2** thing that drains one's strength etc.

■ *v.* **1** draw off, extract, pump out, remove, tap. **2** drip, ebb, flow away, seep, trickle. **3** debilitate, deplete, exhaust, sap, weaken. ● *n.* **1** channel, conduit, ditch, drainpipe, gutter, outlet, pipe, sewer, trench, watercourse.

drainage *n.* **1** draining. **2** system of drains. **3** what is drained off.

drake *n.* male duck.

dram *n.* **1** drachm. **2** small drink of spirits.

drama *n.* **1** play(s) for acting on the stage or broadcasting. **2** dramatic quality or series of events.

dramatic *adj.* **1** of drama. **2** exciting and unexpected, impressive. □ **dramatically** *adv.*

■ **1** histrionic, theatrical. **2** breathtaking, exciting, impressive, sensational, spectacular, striking, sudden, thrilling.

dramatist *n.* writer of plays.

dramatize *v.* make into a drama. □ **dramatization** *n.*

drank *see* **drink**.

drape *v.* cover or arrange loosely.

drastic *adj.* having a strong or violent effect. □ **drastically** *adv.*

draught *n.* **1** current of air. **2** single act of drinking. **3** amount so drunk. **4** pulling. **5** depth of water needed to float a ship. **6** (*pl.*) game played with 24 round pieces on a chessboard. □ **draught beer** beer drawn from a cask.

■ **1** breeze, current, puff, wind. **2** drink, gulp, pull, sip, swallow.

draughtsman *n.* one who draws plans or sketches.

draughty *adj.* (**-ier, -iest**) letting in sharp currents of air.

draw *v.* (**drew, drawn**) **1** pull. **2** attract. **3** take in (breath etc.). **4** take from or out. **5** produce (a picture etc.) by making marks. **6** finish a contest with scores equal. **7** make one's way, come. **8** obtain by lottery. **9** infuse. **10** promote or allow a draught of air (in). ● *n.* **1** act of drawing. **2** thing that draws custom or attention. **3** drawing of lots. **4** drawn game. □ **draw in** (of days) become shorter. **draw out** prolong. **2** (of days) become longer. **drawstring** *n.* string that can be pulled to tighten an opening. **draw the line at** refuse to do or tolerate. **draw up 1** halt. **2** compose (a contract etc.). **3** make (oneself) stiffly erect.

■ *v.* **1** drag, haul, lug, pull, tow, tug. **2** attract, entice, lure, pull. **3** breathe, inhale, take in. **4** extract, pull out, remove, take out, withdraw. **5** paint, sketch; delineate, depict, outline, portray, represent. **6** finish equal, tie. ● *n.* **1** pull, tug. **2** attraction, lure. **3** lottery, raffle. **4** stalemate, tie. □ **draw out** extend, prolong, protract, spin out, stretch out. **draw up 1** halt, pull up, stop. **2** compose, draft, prepare, put together.

drawback *n.* disadvantage.
■ catch, difficulty, disadvantage, hindrance, hitch, obstacle, problem, snag, stumbling block.

drawbridge *n.* bridge over a moat, hinged for raising.

drawer *n.* **1** person who draws. **2** one who writes a cheque. **3** horizontal sliding compartment. **4** (*pl.*) knickers, underpants.

drawing *n.* picture made with a pencil etc. □ **drawing-pin** *n.* pin for fastening paper to a surface. **drawing room** formal sitting room.

drawl *v.* speak lazily or with drawn-out vowel sounds. ● *n.* drawling manner of speaking.

drawn *see* **draw**. *adj.* looking tired and strained.

dread *n.* great fear. ● *v.* be in great fear of. ● *adj.* dreaded.

■ *n.* alarm, apprehension, awe, dismay, fear, fright, horror, terror, trepidation. ● *v.* be afraid of, fear, recoil from, shrink from.

dreadful *adj.* **1** appalling. **2** very bad. □ **dreadfully** *adv.*

■ **1** alarming, appalling, dire, frightening, frightful, ghastly, grim, gruesome, harrowing, hideous, horrible, horrifying, shocking, terrible. **2** atrocious, awful, bad, *colloq.* chronic, deplorable, disgraceful, *colloq.* frightful, *colloq.* lousy, terrible.

dream *n.* **1** series of scenes in a sleeping person's mind. **2** fantasy. **3** aspiration. ● *v.* (**dreamed** or **dreamt**) **1** have dream(s). **2** think of as a possibility. □ **dream up** imagine, invent. **dreamer** *n.*, **dreamless** *adj.*

■ *n.* daydream, delusion, fantasy, hallucination, illusion, mirage, pipedream, reverie. **3** ambition, aspiration, hope, ideal, wish. ● *v.* **1** daydream, fantasize, hallucinate. □ **dream up** conceive, *colloq.* cook up, create, devise, hatch, imagine, invent, make up, *colloq.* think up.

dreamy *adj.* (**-ier, -iest**) daydreaming. □ **dreamily** *adv.*

dreary *adj.* (**-ier, -iest**) dull, gloomy. □ **drearily** *adv.*, **dreariness** *n.*

■ boring, colourless, dull, monotonous, tedious, tiresome, uninteresting, wearisome; bleak, cheerless, depressing, dismal, gloomy, miserable, sombre.

dredge *v.* **1** remove (silt) from (a river or channel). **2** sprinkle with flour etc.

dredger *n.* **1** boat that dredges. **2** container with perforated lid for sprinkling flour etc.

dregs *n.pl.* **1** sediment. **2** worst part.
■ **1** deposit, grounds, lees, remains, residue, sediment

drench *v.* wet thoroughly.

dress *n.* **1** outer clothing. **2** woman's or girl's garment with a bodice and skirt. ● *v.* **1** put clothes on. **2** clothe oneself. **3** arrange, decorate, trim. **4** put a dressing on. □ **dress circle** first gallery in a theatre. **dress rehearsal** final one, in costume. **dress shirt** shirt for wearing with evening dress.

■ *n.* **1** apparel, attire, clothes, clothing, costume, garb, garments, get-up, outfit. **2** frock, gown. ● *v.* **1** attire, clothe, garb, robe. **2** dress oneself, get dressed. **3** adorn, arrange, deck, decorate, embellish, garnish, trim. **4** bandage, bind up, swathe.

dressage /dréssazh/ n. management of a horse to show its obedience and deportment.

dresser[1] n. one who dresses a person or thing.

dresser[2] n. kitchen sideboard with shelves for dishes etc.

dressing n. **1** sauce for food. **2** fertilizer etc. spread over land. **3** bandage or ointment etc. for a wound. □ **dressing down** scolding. **dressing gown** loose robe worn when one is not fully dressed. **dressing table** table with a mirror, for use while dressing.

dressmaker n. person who makes women's clothes.

dressy adj. (**-ier, -iest**) smart, elegant.

drew see draw.

drey n. squirrel's nest.

dribble v. **1** have saliva flowing from the mouth. **2** flow or let flow in drops. **3** (in football etc.) move the ball forward with slight touches. ● n. act or flow of dribbling.

dried adj. (of food etc.) preserved by removal of moisture.

drift v. **1** be carried by a current of water or air. **2** go casually or aimlessly. ● n. **1** mass of snow, sand, etc. piled up by the wind. **2** general meaning of a speech etc. **3** slow movement or variation.

■ v. **1** coast, float, waft. **2** maunder, meander, ramble, roam, stray, wander. ● n. **1** bank, dune, heap, mound, pile. **2** essence, gist, import, meaning, purport, significance, substance.

drifter n. aimless person.

driftwood n. wood floating on the sea or washed ashore.

drill[1] n. **1** tool or machine for boring holes or sinking wells. **2** training. **3** (colloq.) routine procedure. ● v. **1** use a drill, make (a hole) with a drill. **2** train, be trained.

■ n. **2** discipline, exercise, instruction, practice, training. **3** custom, procedure, routine. ● v. **1** bore, perforate, pierce. **2** coach, discipline, exercise, instruct, school, teach, train.

drill[2] n. strong twilled fabric.

drily adv. in a dry way.

drink v. (**drank, drunk**) **1** swallow (liquid). **2** take alcoholic drink, esp. in excess. **3** pledge good wishes (to) by drinking. ● n. **1** (specified amount of) liquid for drinking. **2** (glass of) alcoholic liquor. □ **drink in** watch or listen to eagerly. **drinker** n.

■ v. **1** colloq. down, gulp, imbibe, lap (up), quaff, sip, swallow, swill. **2** colloq. booze, carouse, tipple. ● n. **1** draught, gulp, sip, swallow; beverage, potation. **2** dram, nightcap, nip, sl. snifter, colloq. tipple, tot; alcohol, colloq. booze, liquor, spirits.

drip v. (**dripped**) fall or let fall in drops. ● n. **1** liquid falling in drops. **2** sound of this. **3** device administering a liquid at a very slow rate, esp. intravenously. □ **drip-dry** v. & adj. (able to) dry easily without ironing. **drip-feed** n. & v. feed(-ing) by a drip.

dripping n. fat melted from roast meat.

drive v. (**drove, driven**) **1** send or urge onwards. **2** operate (a vehicle) and direct its course. **3** travel or convey in a private vehicle. **4** cause, compel. **5** (of wind etc.) carry along. **6** make (a bargain). ● n. **1** journey in a private vehicle. **2** energy, motivation. **3** organized effort. **4** track for a car, leading to a private house. **5** transmission of power to machinery. □ **drive at** intend to convey as a meaning. **drive-in** adj. (of a cinema etc.) able to be used without getting out of one's car.

■ v. **1** propel, push, send, urge; herd, shepherd. **2** control, handle, manoeuvre, operate, steer. **3** go, journey, move, ride, travel; bring, convey, give a person a lift, take. **4** compel, constrain, coerce, force, impel, make, press, pressurize. ● n. **1** excursion, jaunt, journey, outing, ride, run, spin, trip. **2** ambition, determination, energy, enterprise, enthusiasm, go, initiative, keenness, motivation, vigour, colloq. vim, zeal. **3** campaign, crusade, effort.

drivel n. silly talk, nonsense.

driver n. **1** person who drives. **2** golf club for driving from a tee.

drizzle n. & v. rain in very fine drops.

droll adj. amusing in an odd way. □ **drolly** adv., **drollery** n.

dromedary n. camel with one hump, bred for riding.

drone n. **1** male bee. **2** deep humming sound. ● v. **1** make this sound. **2** speak monotonously.

drool v. **1** slaver, dribble. **2** show gushing appreciation.

droop v. bend or hang down limply. ● n. drooping attitude. □ **droopy** adj.

drop n. **1** small rounded mass of liquid. **2** very small quantity. **3** steep descent, distance of this. **4** fall. **5** (*pl.*) medicine measured by drops. ● *v.* (**dropped**) **1** shed, let fall. **2** allow to fall. **3** make or become lower. **4** omit. **5** abandon. **6** set down (a passenger etc.). **7** utter casually. □ **drop in** pay a casual visit. **drop off** fall asleep. **drop out** cease to participate. **drop-out** *n.* one who drops out from a course of study or from conventional society.

■ *n.* **1** bead, blob, drip, droplet, globule, tear. **2** bit, dash, pinch, spot, touch. **3** declivity, descent, fall, slope. **4** decline, decrease, fall, reduction. ● *v.* **1** dribble, drip, fall, trickle. **3** descend, dive, fall, plummet, plunge, sink. **4** eliminate, exclude, leave out, omit.

droplet *n.* small drop of liquid.

dropper *n.* device for releasing liquid in drops.

droppings *n.pl.* animal dung.

dropsy *n.* oedema. □ **dropsical** *adj.*

dross *n.* **1** scum on molten metal. **2** impurities, rubbish.

drought *n.* long spell of dry weather.

drove *see* **drive**. *n.* moving herd, flock, or crowd.

drover *n.* herder of cattle.

drown *v.* **1** kill or be killed by submersion in liquid. **2** flood, drench. **3** deaden (grief etc.) with drink. **4** overpower (sound) with greater loudness.

■ **2** deluge, drench, engulf, flood, immerse, inundate, overwhelm, submerge, swamp.

drowse *v.* be lightly asleep. □ **drowsy** *adj.*, **drowsily** *adv.*, **drowsiness** *n.*

drudge *n.* person who does laborious or menial work. ● *v.* do such work. □ **drudgery** *n.*

drug *n.* substance used in medicine or as a stimulant or narcotic. ● *v.* (**drugged**) add or give a drug to.

■ *n.* medicament, medicine; narcotic, opiate, stimulant, tranquillizer. ● *v.* anaesthetize, dope, dose, knock out, sedate.

drugstore *n.* (*US*) combined chemist's shop and café.

Druid *n.* priest of an ancient Celtic religion. □ **Druidical** *adj.*

drum *n.* **1** hollow percussion instrument covered at one or both ends with skin etc. **2** cylindrical object. **3** eardrum. ● *v.* (**drummed**) **1** tap continually. **2** din. □ **drum up** obtain by vigorous effort.

drummer *n.* player of drum(s).

drumstick *n.* **1** stick for beating a drum. **2** lower part of a cooked fowl's leg.

drunk *see* **drink**. *adj.* excited or stupefied by alcoholic drink. ● *n.* drunken person.

■ *adj.* fuddled, inebriated, intoxicated, *sl.* sloshed, *colloq.* sozzled, *colloq.* tiddly, *colloq.* tight, tipsy.

drunkard *n.* person who is often drunk.

drunken *adj.* **1** drunk. **2** often in this condition. □ **drunkenly** *adv.*, **drunkenness** *n.*

dry *adj.* (**drier, driest**) **1** without water, moisture, or rainfall. **2** uninteresting. **3** (of a sense of humour) ironic, understated. **4** not allowing the sale of alcohol. **5** (of wine) not sweet. **6** (*colloq.*) thirsty. ● *v.* **1** make or become dry. **2** preserve (food) by removing its moisture. □ **dry-clean** *v.* clean by solvent that evaporates quickly. **dry rot** decay of wood that is not ventilated. **dry run** (*colloq.*) dummy run. **dry up 1** dry washed dishes. **2** (*colloq.*) cease talking. **dryness** *n.*

■ *adj.* **1** arid, dehydrated, desiccated, parched, waterless. **2** boring, dreary, dull, prosaic, tedious, uninspired, uninteresting. **3** droll, ironic, subtle, understated, wry.

dryad *n.* wood nymph.

dual *adj.* composed of two parts, double. □ **dual carriageway** road with a dividing strip between traffic travelling in opposite directions. **duality** *n.*

dub[1] *v.* (**dubbed**) give a nickname to.

dub[2] *v.* (**dubbed**) replace the soundtrack of a film.

dubbin *n.* grease for softening and waterproofing leather.

dubiety *n.* feeling of doubt.

dubious *adj.* doubtful. □ **dubiously** *adv.*

ducal *adj.* of a duke.

ducat /dúkkət/ *n.* former gold coin of various European countries.

duchess *n.* **1** duke's wife or widow. **2** woman with the rank of duke.

duchy *n.* territory of a duke.

duck *n.* **1** swimming bird of various kinds. **2** female of this. **3** batsman's score of 0. **4** ducking movement. ● *v.* **1** push (a person) or dip one's head under water. **2** bob down, esp. to avoid being seen or hit. **3** dodge (a task etc.).

■ *v.* **1** dip, dunk, immerse, push under, submerge. **2** bend, bob down, crouch, dodge, stoop.

duckboards *n.pl.* boards forming a narrow path.

duckling *n.* young duck.

duct *n.* channel or tube conveying liquid or air. □ **ductless** *adj.*

ductile *adj.* (of metal) able to be drawn into fine strands.

dud *n. & adj.* (*sl.*) (thing) that is counterfeit or fails to work.

dude *n.* (*sl.*) **1** fellow. **2** dandy. □ **dude ranch** ranch used as a holiday centre.

dudgeon *n.* indignation.

due *adj.* **1** owing or payable as a debt. **2** merited, appropriate. **3** scheduled to do something or to arrive. ● *adv.* exactly. ● *n.* **1** a person's right, what is owed to him or her. **2** (*pl.*) fees. □ **be due to** be attributable to.

■ *adj.* **1** outstanding, owed, owing, payable, unpaid. **2** correct, deserved, fitting, just, merited, proper, right, rightful, suitable, well-earned; adequate, appropriate, enough, necessary, sufficient. ● *n.* **1** prerogative, privilege, right.

duel *n.* contest between two people or sides. □ **duellist** *n.*

duenna *n.* older woman acting as chaperon to girls, esp. in Spain.

duet *n.* musical composition for two performers.

duff *adj.* (*sl.*) dud.

duffer *n.* (*colloq.*) inefficient or stupid person.

duffle-coat *n.* heavy woollen coat with a hood.

dug[1] *see* **dig**.

dug[2] *n.* udder, teat.

dugong *n.* Asian sea mammal.

dugout *n.* **1** underground shelter. **2** canoe made from a hollowed tree trunk.

duke *n.* **1** nobleman of the highest hereditary rank. **2** ruler of certain small states. □ **dukedom** *n.*

dulcet *adj.* sounding sweet.

dulcimer *n.* musical instrument with strings struck by two hammers.

dull *adj.* **1** not bright. **2** stupid. **3** boring. **4** not sharp. **5** not resonant. ● *v.* make or become dull. □ **dully** *adv.*, **dullness** *n.*

■ *adj.* **1** dark, drab, dreary; cloudy, dismal, gloomy, grey, murky, overcast, sombre, sunless. **2** dense, *colloq.* dim, obtuse, slow, stupid, unintelligent. **3** boring, humdrum, monotonous, pedestrian, tedious, unimaginative, uninspiring, uninteresting. **4** blunt, blunted. **5** deadened, muffled, muted.

dullard *n.* stupid person.

duly *adv.* in a suitable way.

dumb *adj.* **1** unable to speak. **2** silent. **3** (*colloq.*) stupid. □ **dumb-bell** *n.* short bar with weighted ends, lifted to exercise muscles. **dumbly** *adv.*, **dumbness** *n.*

■ **1** mute, voiceless. **2** *colloq.* mum, quiet, silent, speechless, tongue-tied.

dumbfound *v.* astonish.

dumdum bullet soft-nosed bullet that expands on impact.

dummy *n.* **1** sham article. **2** model of the human figure, esp. as used to display clothes. **3** rubber teat for a baby to suck. ● *adj.* sham. □ **dummy run 1** trial attempt. **2** rehearsal.

dump *v.* **1** dispose of as rubbish. **2** put down carelessly. **3** sell abroad at a lower price. ● *n.* **1** rubbish heap. **2** temporary store. **3** (*colloq.*) dull place.

dumpling *n.* ball of dough cooked in stew or with fruit inside.

dumpy *adj.* (**-ier, -iest**) short and fat. □ **dumpiness** *n.*

dun *adj. & n.* greyish-brown.

dunce *n.* person slow at learning.

dune *n.* mound of drifted sand.

dung *n.* animal excrement.

dungarees *n.pl.* overalls of coarse cotton cloth.

dungeon *n.* strong underground cell for prisoners.

dunk *v.* dip into liquid.

duo *n.* (*pl.* **-os**) pair of performers.

duodecimal *adj.* reckoned in twelves or twelfths.

duodenum *n.* part of the intestine next to the stomach. □ **duodenal** *adj.*

dupe *v.* deceive, trick. ● *n.* duped person.

duple *adj.* **1** having two parts. **2** (in music) having two beats to the bar.

duplex *adj.* having two elements.

duplicate *n.* /dyōōplikət/ exact copy. ● *adj.* /dyōōplikət/ exactly alike. ● *v.* /dyōōplikayt/ **1** make or be a duplicate. **2** do twice. □ **duplication** *n.*

■ *n.* clone, copy, double, facsimile, match, replica, reproduction, twin; carbon copy, photocopy. ● *adj.* identical, matching, twin. ● *v.* **1** imitate, reproduce; copy, photocopy.

duplicity *n.* deceitfulness.

durable *adj.* likely to last. ● *n.pl.* durable goods. □ **durably** *adv.*, **durability** *n.*

■ *adj.* dependable, enduring, hardwearing, long-lasting, reliable, stout, strong, sturdy, substantial, tough.

duration *n.* time during which a thing continues.

duress *n.* use of force or threats.

during *prep.* **1** throughout. **2** at a point in the continuance of.

dusk *n.* darker stage of twilight.

dusky *adj.* (**-ier, -iest**) **1** shadowy. **2** dark-coloured. □ **duskiness** *n.*

dust *n.* fine particles of earth or other matter. ● *v.* **1** sprinkle with dust or powder. **2** clear of dust by wiping, clean a room etc. thus. □ **dust bowl** area denuded of vegetation and reduced to desert. **dust cover, jacket** paper jacket on a book. **dusty** *adj.*

dustbin *n.* bin for household rubbish.

duster *n.* cloth for dusting things.

dustman *n.* person employed to empty dustbins.

dustpan *n.* container into which dust is brushed from a floor.

Dutch *adj.* & *n.* (language) of the Netherlands. □ **Dutch courage** that obtained by drinking alcohol. **go Dutch** share expenses on an outing. **Dutchman** *n.*, **Dutchwoman** *n.*

dutiable *adj.* on which customs or other duties must be paid.

dutiful *adj.* doing one's duty, obedient. □ **dutifully** *adv.*

■ compliant, conscientious, considerate, deferential, diligent, faithful, loyal, obedient, reliable, respectful, responsible.

duty *n.* **1** moral or legal obligation. **2** task, action to be performed. **3** tax on goods or imports. □ **on duty** at work.

■ **1** obligation, responsibility; burden, charge, onus. **2** assignment, chore, function, job, task. **3** customs, excise, levy, tariff, tax.

duvet /dōōvay/ *n.* thick soft quilt used as bedclothes.

dwarf *n.* (*pl.* **-fs**) **1** person or thing much below the usual size. **2** (in fairy tales) small being with magic powers. ● *adj.* very small. ● *v.* **1** stunt. **2** make seem small.

dwell *v.* (**dwelt**) live as an inhabitant. □ **dwell on** speak or think lengthily about. **dweller** *n.*

■ live, lodge, reside, stay. □ **dwell on** elaborate on, emphasize, harp on, labour; agonize over, brood on, fret about, worry about.

dwelling *n.* house etc. to live in.

■ abode, domicile, habitation, home, house, lodging, quarters, residence.

dwindle *v.* become less or smaller.

dye *v.* (**dyeing**) colour, esp. by dipping in liquid. ● *n.* **1** substance used for dyeing things. **2** colour given by dyeing. □ **dyer** *n.*

dying *see* **die**[1].

dyke *n.* **1** embankment to prevent flooding. **2** drainage ditch.

dynamic *adj.* **1** energetic, forceful. **2** of force producing motion. □ **dynamically** *adv.*

■ **1** active, animated, energetic, enterprising, enthusiastic, forceful, go-ahead, go-getting, lively, powerful, spirited, vigorous, vital, zealous.

dynamics *n.* branch of physics dealing with matter in motion.

dynamism *n.* energizing power.

dynamite *n.* powerful explosive made of nitroglycerine. ● *v.* fit or blow up with dynamite.

dynamo *n.* (*pl.* **-os**) small generator producing electric current.

dynasty *n.* line of hereditary rulers. □ **dynastic** *adj.*

dysentery *n.* disease causing severe diarrhoea.

dysfunction *n.* malfunction.

dyslexia *n.* condition causing difficulty in reading and spelling. □ **dyslexic** *adj.* & *n.*

dyspepsia *n.* indigestion. □ **dyspeptic** *adj.* & *n.*

dystrophy *n.* wasting of a part of the body.

E. *abbr.* **1** east. **2** eastern.

each *adj.* & *pron.* every one of two or more.

eager *adj.* full of desire, enthusiastic. □ **eagerly** *adv.*, **eagerness** *n.*
■ animated, ardent, avid, earnest, enthusiastic, excited, fervent, fervid, hungry, keen, passionate, zealous. □ **eagerness** animation, appetite, ardour, avidity, desire, enthusiasm, excitement, fervour, hunger, keenness, longing, passion, thirst, zeal, zest.

eagle *n.* large bird of prey.

ear¹ *n.* **1** organ of hearing. **2** external part of this. **3** ability to distinguish sounds accurately. □ **eardrum** *n.* membrane inside the ear.

ear² *n.* seed-bearing part of corn.

earl *n.* British nobleman ranking between marquess and viscount. □ **earldom** *n.*

early *adj.* & *adv.* (**-ier, -iest**) **1** before the usual or expected time. **2** not far on in development or in a series.
■ *adj.* **1** premature, untimely. **2** basic, first, initial, introductory, original. ● *adv.* **1** ahead of time, beforehand, in advance, prematurely; *poetic* betimes, in good time.

earmark *n.* distinguishing mark. ● *v.* **1** put such mark on. **2** set aside for a particular purpose.

earn *v.* **1** get or deserve for work or merit. **2** (of money) gain as interest.
■ **1** be paid, clear, get, gross, make, net, receive; be entitled to, be worthy of, deserve, merit, warrant, win. **2** pay, yield.

earnest *adj.* showing serious feeling or intention. □ **in earnest** seriously. **earnestly** *adv.*
■ assiduous, committed, conscientious, dedicated, determined, devoted, diligent, hard-working, industrious, serious, sober, solemn, thoughtful; fervent, heartfelt, profound, sincere, wholehearted.

earshot *n.* range of hearing.

earth *n.* **1** the planet we live on. **2** soil. **3** land and sea as opposed to sky. **4** fox's den. **5** connection of an electrical circuit to ground. ● *v.* connect an electrical circuit to earth. □ **run to earth** find after a long search.
■ *n.* **1** globe, planet, world. **2** clay, dirt, loam, sod, soil, turf.

earthen *adj.* made of earth or of baked clay. □ **earthenware** *n.* pottery made of baked clay.

earthly *adj.* **1** of the earth. **2** of human life on earth, worldly.
■ **1** terrestrial. **2** human, material, mortal, physical, secular, temporal, worldly.

earthquake *n.* violent movement of part of the earth's crust.

earthwork *n.* bank built of earth.

earthworm *n.* worm living in the soil.

earthy *adj.* (**-ier, -iest**) **1** like earth or soil. **2** coarse, crude.

earwig *n.* small insect with pincers at the end of its body.

ease *n.* freedom from pain, worry, or effort. ● *v.* **1** relieve from pain, anxiety, etc. **2** make easier. **3** become less burdensome or severe. **4** move gently or gradually.
■ *n.* calmness, comfort, composure, contentment, peace, peace and quiet, relaxation, relief, repose, rest, serenity, tranquillity; easiness, effortlessness, facility; aplomb, insouciance, naturalness, nonchalance. ● *v.* **1** calm, comfort, pacify, quieten, relieve, soothe; allay, alleviate, appease, assuage, mollify. **2** aid, assist, expedite, facilitate, help. **3** abate, decrease, drop, diminish, lessen, *colloq.* let up, moderate, subside. **4** edge, guide, inch, manoeuvre.

easel *n.* frame to support a painting or blackboard etc.

east *n.* **1** point on the horizon where the sun rises. **2** direction in which this lies. **3** eastern part. ● *adj.* **1** in the east. **2** (of wind) from the east. ● *adv.* towards the east.

Easter *n.* festival commemorating Christ's resurrection. □ **Easter egg** chocolate egg given at Easter.

easterly *adj.* towards or blowing from the east.

eastern *adj.* of or in the east.

easternmost *adj.* furthest east.

eastward adj. towards the east. □ **eastwards** adv.

easy adj. (**-ier, -iest**) **1** not difficult. **2** free from pain, trouble, or anxiety. **3** easygoing. ● adv. in an easy way. □ **easy chair** large comfortable chair. **easily** adv., **easiness** n.

■ adj. **1** basic, effortless, elementary, rudimentary, simple, straightforward, uncomplicated, undemanding. **2** carefree, comfortable, colloq. cushy, peaceful, relaxing, restful, serene, tranquil, untroubled. **3** agreeable, affable, amiable, easygoing, friendly, genial, natural, pleasant.

easygoing adj. relaxed in manner, tolerant.

■ accommodating, agreeable, affable, amenable, amiable, carefree, casual, cheerful, even-tempered, flexible, friendly, genial, happy-go-lucky, natural, placid, pleasant, relaxed; indulgent, lenient, permissive, tolerant.

eat v. (**ate, eaten**) **1** chew and swallow (food). **2** have a meal. □ **eat away (at)** destroy gradually.

■ **1** bolt, consume, devour, gobble, gulp, guzzle, munch, nibble, colloq. scoff, colloq. tuck into, wolf. **2** breakfast, dine, have a bite, have a meal, lunch. □ **eat away (at)** consume, corrode, destroy, erode, wear away.

eatables n.pl. food.

eau-de-Cologne /ódəkəlón/ n. a delicate perfume.

eaves n.pl. overhanging edge of a roof.

eavesdrop v. (**-dropped**) listen secretly to a private conversation. □ **eavesdropper** n.

ebb n. **1** outflow of the tide, away from the land. **2** decline. ● v. **1** flow away. **2** decline.

■ v. **1** drain away, flow back, go down, recede, subside. **2** decline, decrease, diminish, dwindle, flag, lessen, wane.

ebony n. hard black wood of a tropical tree. ● adj. black as ebony.

ebullient adj. full of high spirits. □ **ebulliently** adv., **ebullience** n.

EC abbr. **1** European Community. **2** European Commission.

eccentric adj. **1** unconventional. **2** not concentric. **3** (of an orbit or wheel) not circular. ● n. eccentric person. □ **eccentrically** adv., **eccentricity** n.

■ adj. aberrant, abnormal, bizarre, curious, odd, offbeat, outlandish, out of the ordinary, peculiar, quaint, queer, quirky, singular, strange, unconventional, unusual, weird.

ecclesiastical adj. of the Church or clergy.

echelon /éshəlon/ n. **1** staggered formation of troops etc. **2** level of rank or authority.

echo n. (pl. **-oes**) **1** repetition of sound by reflection of sound waves. **2** close imitation. ● v. (**echoed, echoing**) **1** repeat by an echo. **2** imitate.

■ v. **1** resound, reverberate, ring. **2** ape, copy, emulate, imitate, mimic, repeat.

éclair n. finger-shaped cake with cream filling.

eclectic adj. choosing or accepting from various sources.

eclipse n. **1** blocking of light from one heavenly body by another. **2** loss of brilliance or power etc. ● v. **1** cause an eclipse of. **2** outshine.

■ v. **1** block, blot out, conceal, cover, hide, obscure, shroud, veil. **2** outshine, outstrip, overshadow, surpass, top.

eclogue n. short pastoral poem.

ecology n. **1** (study of) relationships of living things to their environment. **2** protection of the natural environment. □ **ecological** adj., **ecologically** adv., **ecologist** n.

economic adj. **1** of economics. **2** enough to give a good return for money or effort outlaid.

economical adj. thrifty, avoiding waste. □ **economically** adv.

■ careful, frugal, provident, prudent, sparing, thrifty; cheap, inexpensive, reasonable.

economics n. **1** the science of the production and use of goods or services. **2** (as pl.) the financial aspects of something.

economist n. expert in economics.

economize v. use or spend less.

■ cut back, retrench, save, scrimp, skimp, spend less.

economy n. **1** being economical. **2** community's system of using its resources to produce wealth. **3** state of a country's prosperity.

■ **1** frugality, husbandry, prudence, thrift, thriftiness.

ecstasy n. intense delight. □ **ecstatic** adj., **ecstatically** adv.

■ bliss, delight, elation, euphoria, exultation, happiness, joy, rapture. □ **ecstatic** delighted, elated, enraptured, euphoric, exhilarated, exultant, happy, joyful, overjoyed, rapturous, thrilled.

ecu /ékyoo/ *abbr.* European currency unit.

ecumenical *adj.* **1** of the whole Christian Church. **2** seeking worldwide Christian unity.

eczema *n.* skin disease causing scaly itching patches.

eddy *n.* swirling patch of water or air etc. ● *v.* swirl in eddies.

edelweiss /áydˈlvīss/ *n.* alpine plant with woolly white bracts.

edge *n.* **1** outer limit of a surface or area, narrow surface of a thin object. **2** sharpness. **3** sharpened side of a blade. ● *v.* **1** border. **2** move gradually.
■ *n.* **1** boundary, fringe, margin, perimeter, periphery; border, brim, brink, lip, rim, side, verge. **2** acuteness, keenness, sharpness. ● *v.* **1** border, fringe, trim. **2** crawl, creep, inch, sidle, steal, worm.

edgeways *adv.* (also **edgewise**) with the edge forwards or outwards.

edging *n.* thing placed round an edge to define or decorate it.

edgy *adj.* (**-ier**, **-iest**) tense and irritable.

edible *adj.* suitable for eating.
■ eatable, palatable, wholesome.

edict /eédikt/ *n.* order proclaimed by authority.

edifice *n.* large building.

edify *v.* be an uplifting influence on the mind of. □ **edification** *n.*

edit *v.* (**edited**) **1** prepare for publication. **2** prepare (a film) by arranging sections in sequence.

edition *n.* **1** form in which something is published. **2** number of objects issued at one time.

editor *n.* **1** person responsible for the contents of a newspaper etc. or a section of this. **2** one who edits.

editorial *adj.* of an editor. ● *n.* newspaper article giving the editor's comments.

educate *v.* **1** train the mind and abilities of. **2** provide such training for. □ **education** *n.,* **educational** *adj.*
■ bring up, civilize, edify, enlighten, inform, instruct, school, teach, train, tutor. □ **education** instruction, schooling, teaching, training, tuition, upbringing.

Edwardian *adj.* of the reign of Edward VII (1901–10).

EEC *abbr.* European Economic Community.

eel *n.* snake-like fish.

eerie *adj.* (**-ier**, **-iest**) mysterious and frightening. □ **eerily** *adv.*
■ creepy, frightening, ghostly, mysterious, *colloq.* scary, *colloq.* spooky, strange, uncanny, unearthly, weird.

efface *v.* **1** rub out, obliterate. **2** make inconspicuous. □ **effacement** *n.*

effect *n.* **1** result of an action etc. **2** efficacy. **3** impression. **4** (*pl.*) property. **5** state of being operative. ● *v.* cause to occur.
■ *n.* **1** conclusion, consequence, outcome, repercussion, result, upshot. **2** effectiveness, efficacy, impact, influence, force, power. **3** feeling, impression, sense. **4** (**effects**) belongings, chattels, possessions, property, things. ● *v.* accomplish, achieve, bring about, carry out, cause, create, execute, make, produce, secure.

effective *adj.* **1** producing the intended result. **2** striking. **3** operative. □ **effectively** *adv.,* **effectiveness** *n.*
■ **1** effectual, efficacious, efficient, functional, serviceable, useful. **2** impressive, outstanding, powerful, striking. **3** functioning, in operation, operational, operative.

effectual *adj.* answering its purpose. □ **effectually** *adv.*

effeminate *adj.* (of a man) feminine in appearance or manner. □ **effeminacy** *n.*

effervesce *v.* give off bubbles. □ **effervescence** *n.,* **effervescent** *adj.*
■ bubble, fizz, foam, froth. □ **effervescent** bubbling, bubbly, carbonated, fizzy, foaming, frothing, frothy, sparkling.

effete *adj.* having lost its vitality.

efficacious *adj.* producing the desired result. □ **efficacy** *n.*

efficient *adj.* **1** producing results with little waste of effort. **2** capable, competent. □ **efficiently** *adv.,* **efficiency** *n.*
■ **1** effective, effectual, efficacious. **2** businesslike, capable, competent, organized, professional, proficient, skilled, systematic, well-organized.

effigy *n.* model of person.

effloresce *v.* flower. □ **efflorescence** *n.*

effluent *n.* outflow, sewage.

effluvium *n.* (*pl.* **-ia**) outflow, esp. unpleasant or harmful.

effort n. **1** strenuous use of energy. **2** attempt. □ **effortless** adj.

■ **1** exertion, pains, strain, striving, struggle, toil, trouble, work. **2** attempt, endeavour, essay, shot, try, venture.

effrontery n. bold insolence.

effusion n. outpouring.

effusive adj. expressing emotion in an unrestrained way. □ **effusively** adv., **effusiveness** n.

e.g. abbr. (Latin exempli gratia) for example.

egalitarian adj. & n. (person) holding the principle of equal rights for all. □ **egalitarianism** n.

egg¹ n. **1** hard-shelled oval body produced by the female of birds, esp. that of the domestic hen. **2** ovum. □ **eggshell** n.

egg² v. **egg on** urge on.

eggplant n. aubergine.

ego n. **1** self. **2** self-esteem.

egocentric adj. self-centred.

egoism n. self-centredness. □ **egoist** n., **egoistic** adj.

egotism n. conceit, selfishness. □ **egotist** n., **egotistic(al)** adj.

■ conceit, narcissism, pride, self-admiration, self-importance, selfishness, self-love, vanity.

egregious /igreéjass/ adj. **1** shocking. **2** (old use) remarkable.

egress n. **1** departure. **2** way out.

egret n. a kind of heron.

Egyptian adj. & n. (native) of Egypt.

Egyptology n. study of Egyptian antiquities. □ **Egyptologist** n.

eider n. northern species of duck.

eiderdown n. quilt stuffed with soft material.

eight adj. & n. one more than seven. □ **eighth** adj. & n.

eighteen adj. & n. one more than seventeen. □ **eighteenth** adj. & n.

eighty adj. & n. ten times eight. □ **eightieth** adj. & n.

either adj. & pron. **1** one or other of two. **2** each of two. ● adv. & conj. as one alternative.

ejaculate v. **1** utter suddenly. **2** eject (semen). □ **ejaculation** n.

eject v. **1** drive out forcefully. **2** emit. □ **ejection** n., **ejector** n.

■ **1** drive out, evict, expel, colloq. kick out, oust, remove, send packing, throw out; banish, deport, exile, send away; discharge, dismiss, fire, colloq. sack. **2** disgorge, emit, exude, send out, spew out, spout.

eke v. **eke out 1** supplement. **2** make (a living) laboriously.

elaborate adj. /ilábbərət/ **1** carefully worked out. **2** with many parts or details. ● v. /ilábbərayt/ add detail to. □ **elaborately** adv., **elaboration** n.

■ adj. **1** careful, detailed, exhaustive, meticulous, painstaking, thorough. **2** baroque, decorative, fancy, fussy, ornamental, ornate, rococo, showy; complex, complicated, intricate, involved. ● v. add to, amplify, develop, embellish, embroider, enlarge on, expand, fill out.

élan /aylón/ n. vivacity, vigour.

eland /eéland/ n. large African antelope.

elapse v. (of time) pass away.

elastic adj. **1** able to go back to its original length or shape after being stretched or squeezed. **2** adaptable. ● n. cord or material made elastic by interweaving strands of rubber etc. □ **elasticity** n.

■ adj. **1** bendable, flexible, pliable, pliant, resilient, springy, stretchable, stretchy. **2** adaptable, adjustable, flexible.

elate v. cause to feel very pleased or proud. □ **elation** n.

elbow n. **1** joint between the forearm and upper arm. **2** part of a sleeve covering this. **3** sharp bend. ● v. thrust with one's elbow. □ **elbow grease** (joc.) vigorous polishing. **elbow room** enough space to move or work in.

elder¹ adj. older. ● n. **1** older person. **2** official in certain Churches.

elder² n. tree with dark berries.

elderberry n. fruit of the elder tree.

elderly adj. rather old.

eldest adj. first-born or oldest surviving (son, daughter, etc.).

elect v. **1** choose by vote. **2** choose. ● adj. chosen.

■ v. **1** appoint, choose, designate, name, nominate, pick, select, vote for. **2** adopt, choose, decide on, go for, opt for, pick, select.

election n. **1** process of electing. **2** occasion for this.

■ **1** choice, nomination, selection. **2** ballot, plebiscite, poll, referendum, vote.

electioneer v. busy oneself in an election campaign.

elective adj. **1** chosen by election. **2** entitled to elect. **3** optional.

elector n. person entitled to vote in an election. □ **electoral** adj.

electorate n. body of electors.

electric *adj.* of, producing, or worked by electricity.

electrical *adj.* of or worked by electricity. □ **electrically** *adv.*

electrician *n.* person who installs or maintains electrical equipment.

electricity *n.* **1** form of energy occurring in certain particles. **2** supply of electric current.

electrify *v.* **1** charge with electricity. **2** convert to electric power. □ **electrification** *n.*

electrocardiogram *n.* record of the electric current generated by heartbeats.

electrocute *v.* kill by electricity. □ **electrocution** *n.*

electrode *n.* solid conductor through which electricity enters or leaves a vacuum tube etc.

electroencephalogram *n.* record of the electrical activity of the brain.

electrolyte *n.* solution that conducts electric current.

electromagnet *n.* magnet consisting of a metal core magnetized by a current-carrying coil round it.

electromagnetism *n.* magnetic forces produced by electricity. □ **electromagnetic** *adj.*

electron *n.* particle with a negative electric charge. □ **electron microscope** very powerful one using a focused beam of electrons instead of light.

electronic *adj.* **1** produced or worked by a flow of electrons. **2** of electronics. □ **electronically** *adv.*

electronics *n.* science concerned with the movement of electrons in a vacuum, gas, semiconductor, etc.

elegant *adj.* tasteful and dignified. □ **elegantly** *adv.*, **elegance** *n.*

■ dignified, exquisite, fine, graceful, refined, tasteful; debonair, polished, sophisticated, suave, urbane; artistic, beautiful, chic, fashionable, smart, stylish, *colloq.* swish.

elegy *n.* sorrowful or serious poem. □ **elegiac** *adj.*

element *n.* **1** component part. **2** suitable or satisfying environment. **3** (*pl.*) basic principles. **4** substance that cannot be broken down into other substances. **5** trace. **6** wire that gives out heat in an electrical appliance. **7** (*pl.*) atmospheric forces. □ **elemental** *adj.*

■ **1** component, constituent, detail, factor, feature, ingredient, part, piece, unit. **2** domain, environment, habitat, medium,

sphere, surroundings, territory. **3** (**elements**) basics, essentials, first principles, foundations, fundamentals, rudiments.

elementary *adj.* dealing with the simplest facts of a subject.

■ basic, fundamental, initial, introductory, primary, rudimentary; easy, simple, straightforward, uncomplicated.

elephant *n.* very large animal with a trunk and ivory tusks.

elephantine *adj.* **1** of or like elephants. **2** very large, clumsy.

elevate *v.* raise to a higher position or level.

■ lift, raise; advance, exalt, promote, upgrade.

elevation *n.* **1** elevating. **2** altitude. **3** hill. **4** drawing showing one side of a structure.

elevator *n.* **1** thing that hoists something. **2** (*US*) lift.

eleven *n.* one more than ten. □ **eleventh** *adj.* & *n.*

elevenses *n.* mid-morning snack.

elf *n.* (*pl.* **elves**) imaginary small being with magic powers. □ **elfin** *adj.*

elicit *v.* draw out.

■ bring out, draw out, evoke, extract, get, wrest, wring.

eligible *adj.* qualified to be chosen or allowed something. □ **eligibility** *n.*

■ appropriate, entitled, fit, qualified, suitable, worthy.

eliminate *v.* **1** get rid of. **2** exclude. □ **elimination** *n.*, **eliminator** *n.*

■ **1** dispense with, dispose of, do away with, eradicate, get rid of, remove, root out, stamp out. **2** drop, exclude, leave out, omit, rule out.

elite /ayleét/ *n.* group regarded as superior and favoured.

elitism /ayleétiz'm/ *n.* favouring of or dominance by a selected group. □ **elitist** *n.*

elixir *n.* fragrant liquid used as medicine or flavouring.

Elizabethan *adj.* of Elizabeth I's reign (1558–1603).

elk *n.* large deer.

ellipse *n.* regular oval.

ellipsis *n.* (*pl.* **-pses**) omission of words.

elliptical *adj.* **1** shaped like an ellipse. **2** having omissions. □ **elliptically** *adv.*

elm *n.* **1** tree with rough serrated leaves. **2** its wood.

elocution *n.* art of speaking.

elongate v. lengthen.

elope v. run away secretly with a lover. □ **elopement** n.

eloquence n. fluent speaking. □ **eloquent** adj., **eloquently** adv.
■ □ **eloquent** articulate, expressive, fluent, lucid.

else adv. 1 besides. 2 otherwise.

elsewhere adv. somewhere else.

elucidate v. throw light on, explain. □ **elucidation** n.

elude v. 1 escape skilfully from. 2 avoid. 3 escape the memory or understanding of. □ **elusion** n.
■ 1 avoid, dodge, escape, evade, get away from, give a person the slip. 2 avoid, duck, sidestep.

elusive adj. difficult to find, catch, or remember.

elver n. young eel.

emaciated adj. thin from illness or starvation. □ **emaciation** n.
■ bony, cadaverous, gaunt, haggard, scraggy, scrawny, skeletal, skinny, starved, thin, underfed, undernourished, wizened.

emanate v. issue, originate from a source. □ **emanation** n.

emancipate v. liberate, free from restraint. □ **emancipation** n.
■ deliver, free, liberate, release, set free.

emasculate v. deprive of force, weaken. □ **emasculation** n.

embalm v. preserve (a corpse) by using spices or chemicals.

embankment n. bank constructed to confine water or carry a road or railway.

embargo n. (pl. **-oes**) order forbidding commerce or other activity.

embark v. board a ship. □ **embark on** begin an undertaking. **embarkation** n.

embarrass v. cause to feel awkward or ashamed. □ **embarrassment** n.
■ abash, discomfit, disconcert; disgrace, humiliate, mortify, shame. □ **embarrassment** awkwardness, discomfort, self-consciousness; chagrin, mortification.

embassy n. 1 ambassador and staff. 2 their headquarters.

embed v. (**embedded**) fix firmly in a surrounding mass.

embellish v. 1 ornament. 2 improve (a story) with invented details. □ **embellishment** n.
■ 1 adorn, beautify, deck, decorate, dress (up), embroider, ornament, trim. 2 elaborate, embroider, exaggerate.

embers n.pl. small pieces of live coal or wood in a dying fire.

embezzle v. take (money etc.) fraudulently for one's own use. □ **embezzler** n.

embitter v. rouse bitter feelings in. □ **embitterment** n.

emblem n. symbol, design used as a badge etc.
■ badge, crest, insignia, mark, seal, sign, symbol, token; logo, trade mark.

emblematic adj. serving as an emblem. □ **emblematically** adv.

embody v. 1 express (principles or ideas) in visible form. 2 incorporate. □ **embodiment** n.
■ 1 epitomize, exemplify, express, manifest, personify, represent, typify. 2 comprise, embrace, encompass, include, incorporate.

embolden v. encourage.

embolism n. obstruction of an artery by a blood clot etc.

emboss v. 1 decorate by a raised design. 2 mould in relief.

embrace v. 1 hold closely and lovingly, hold each other thus. 2 accept, adopt. 3 include. ● n. act of embracing, hug.
■ v. 1 clasp, cuddle, enfold, grasp, hold, hug. 2 accept, adopt, espouse, welcome. 3 comprise, embody, encompass, include, incorporate. ● n. clasp, cuddle, hug, squeeze.

embrocation n. liquid for rubbing on the body to relieve muscular pain.

embroider v. 1 ornament with needlework. 2 embellish (a story). □ **embroidery** n.

embroil v. involve in an argument or quarrel etc.

embryo n. (pl. **-os**) animal developing in a womb or egg. □ **embryonic** adj.

embryology n. study of embryos.

emend v. alter to remove errors. □ **emendation** n.

emerald n. 1 bright green precious stone. 2 its colour.

emerge v. **1** come up or out into view. **2** become known. □ **emergence** n., **emergent** adj.

■ **1** appear, arise, come into view, come out, surface. **2** become known, be revealed, come to light, transpire, turn out.

emergency n. serious situation needing prompt attention.

■ crisis, danger, difficulty, exigency, predicament.

emery n. coarse abrasive. □ **emery board** emery-coated cardboard strip for filing the nails.

emetic n. medicine used to cause vomiting.

emigrate v. leave one country and go to settle in another. □ **emigration** n., **emigrant** n.

eminence n. **1** state of being eminent. **2** rising ground.

eminent adj. famous, distinguished. □ **eminently** adv.

■ celebrated, distinguished, esteemed, exalted, famous, great, honoured, illustrious, important, notable, noteworthy, outstanding, pre-eminent, prominent, renowned, respected, well-known.

emir /emeer/ n. Muslim ruler. □ **emirate** n. his territory.

emissary n. person sent to conduct negotiations.

emit v. (**emitted**) **1** send out (light, heat, fumes, etc.). **2** utter. □ **emission** n., **emitter** n.

■ **1** discharge, eject, expel, exude, give off or out, radiate, send out.

emollient adj. softening, soothing. ● n. emollient substance.

emolument n. **1** fee. **2** salary.

emotion n. strong instinctive feeling.

■ feeling, passion, sensation, sentiment.

emotional adj. **1** of, expressing, or arousing great emotion. **2** liable to excessive emotion. □ **emotionally** adv., **emotionalism** n.

■ **1** ardent, fervent, fervid, heartfelt, heated, impassioned, passionate; emotive, moving, pathetic, poignant, touching. **2** excitable, highly-strung, temperamental, volatile.

emotive adj. rousing emotion.

empathize v. show empathy.

empathy n. ability to identify oneself mentally with, and so understand, a person or thing.

emperor n. ruler of an empire.

emphasis n. (pl. **-ases**) **1** special importance. **2** vigour of expression etc. **3** stress on word(s).

■ **1** importance, priority, prominence, significance, stress, weight.

emphasize v. lay emphasis on.

■ accent, accentuate, draw attention to, feature, highlight, point up, spotlight, stress, underline.

emphatic adj. using or showing emphasis. □ **emphatically** adv.

■ assertive, categorical, decided, definite, explicit, firm, forceful, insistent, strong, uncompromising, unequivocal, vigorous.

emphysema n. disease of the lungs, causing breathlessness.

empire n. **1** group of countries ruled by a supreme authority. **2** large organization controlled by one person or group.

empirical adj. based on observation or experiment, not on theory. □ **empirically** adv., **empiricism** n., **empiricist** n.

emplacement n. place or platform for a gun or guns.

employ v. **1** use the services of. **2** make use of. □ **employer** n.

■ **1** engage, hire, recruit, take on. **2** make use of, use, utilize. □ **employer** colloq. boss, chief, colloq. gaffer, head, manager, owner, proprietor.

employee n. person employed by another in return for wages.

■ hand, member of staff, worker; (**employees**) staff, workforce.

employment n. **1** act of employing or state of being employed. **2** person's trade or profession.

■ **1** engagement, hire, hiring, recruitment; application, use, utilization. **2** business, craft, job, occupation, profession, trade, vocation, work.

empower v. authorize, enable.

empress n. **1** woman emperor. **2** wife of an emperor.

empty adj. (**-ier, -iest**) **1** containing nothing. **2** without occupant(s). **3** meaningless, insincere. ● v. make or become empty. □ **emptiness** n.

■ adj. **1** unfilled, void; blank, clean, new, unused; drained, emptied; unfurnished. **2** deserted, uninhabited, unoccupied, vacant; bare, barren, desolate, waste. **3** hollow, hypocritical, insincere, meaningless, pointless, shallow, valueless, worthless. ● v. clear (out), evacuate, vacate; drain; discharge, unload, void.

emu *n.* large Australian bird resembling an ostrich.

emulate *v.* try to do as well as. □ **emulation** *n.*, **emulator** *n.*

emulsify *v.* convert or be converted into emulsion. □ **emulsification** *n.*, **emulsifier** *n.*

emulsion *n.* 1 creamy liquid. 2 light-sensitive coating on photographic film.

enable *v.* give the authority or means to do something.
■ allow, authorize, empower, entitle, license, permit, qualify.

enact *v.* 1 make into a law. 2 perform (a play etc.). □ **enactment** *n.*

enamel *n.* 1 glass-like coating for metal or pottery. 2 glossy paint. 3 hard outer covering of teeth. ● *v.* (**enamelled**) coat with enamel.

enamoured *adj.* fond.

en bloc /on blôk/ all together.

encamp *v.* settle in a camp.

encampment *n.* camp.

encapsulate *v.* 1 enclose (as) in a capsule. 2 summarize.

encase *v.* enclose in a case.

encephalitis *n.* inflammation of the brain.

enchant *v.* bewitch. □ **enchantment** *n.*, **enchanter** *n.*, **enchantress** *n.*
■ bewitch, captivate, cast a spell on, charm, delight, enthral, entrance, fascinate, hold spellbound.

encircle *v.* surround. □ **encirclement** *n.*

enclave *n.* small territory wholly within the boundaries of another.

enclose *v.* 1 shut in on all sides. 2 include with other contents.
■ 1 bound, circle, confine, encircle, encompass, envelop, fence in, hedge in, hem in, immure, pen, ring, shut in, surround, wall in.

enclosure *n.* 1 enclosing. 2 enclosed area. 3 thing enclosed.

encompass *v.* 1 encircle. 2 include.

encore *n.* a (call for) repetition of a performance. ● *int.* this call.

encounter *v.* 1 meet by chance. 2 be faced with. ● *n.* 1 chance meeting. 2 meeting in conflict.
■ *v.* 1 come across, meet, run into. 2 be faced with, experience, face, meet (with). ● *n.* 2 altercation, battle, brush, clash, conflict, confrontation, dispute, fight, *colloq.* scrap, skirmish, struggle, tussle.

encourage *v.* 1 give hope, confidence, or stimulus to. 2 urge. □ **encouragement** *n.*
■ 1 buoy up, cheer (up), embolden, fortify, hearten, inspire, pep up, reassure, support; advance, aid, assist, boost, foster, help, promote, stimulate. 2 egg on, exhort, incite, spur on, urge. □ **encouragement** help, inspiration, moral support, reassurance, stimulation, support; exhortation, incitement.

encroach *v.* **encroach on** intrude on someone's territory or rights. □ **encroachment** *n.*
■ impinge on, infringe on, intrude on, invade, trespass on.

encrust *v.* cover with a crust of hard material. □ **encrustation** *n.*

encumber *v.* be a burden to, hamper. □ **encumbrance** *n.*

encyclical *n.* pope's letter for circulation to churches.

encyclopedia *n.* book of information on many subjects. □ **encyclopedic** *adj.*

end *n.* 1 extreme limit, furthest point or part. 2 final part. 3 destruction, death. 4 objective. ● *v.* bring or come to an end. □ **end up** reach a certain place or condition eventually. **make ends meet** live within one's income.
■ *n.* 1 boundary, edge, extremity, limit, tip. 2 cessation, completion, conclusion, culmination, finish, termination; close, coda, denouement, finale. 3 annihilation, death, destruction, extinction, ruin. 4 aim, aspiration, design, goal, intention, object, objective, plan, purpose; destination. ● *v.* bring to an end, conclude, discontinue, halt, put paid to, stop, terminate, wind up; cease, come to an end, die (away), fizzle out.

endanger *v.* cause danger to.
■ expose to risk, imperil, jeopardize, put in jeopardy, threaten.

endear *v.* cause to be loved.

endearment *n.* word(s) expressing love.

endeavour *v.* & *n.* attempt.

endemic *adj.* commonly found in a specified area or people.

ending *n.* final part.

endive *n.* 1 curly-leaved plant used in salads. 2 (*US*) chicory.

endless *adj.* 1 infinite. 2 continual. □ **endlessly** *adv.*
■ 1 boundless, immeasurable, infinite, unbounded, unlimited; eternal, everlasting, perpetual. 2 ceaseless, constant, continual, continuous, everlasting, incessant,

interminable, never-ending, non-stop, perpetual, unceasing, unending, unremitting.

endocrine gland gland secreting hormones into the blood.

endorse v. **1** declare approval of. **2** sign the back of (a cheque). **3** note an offence on (a driving licence etc.). □ **endorsement** n.
■ **1** agree to, approve, assent to, authorize, back, give the go-ahead to, colloq. OK, rubber-stamp, sanction.

endow v. provide with a permanent income. □ **endowment** n.

endurance n. power of enduring.
■ durability, colloq. grit, fortitude, patience, perseverance, persistence, resilience, stamina, staying power, strength, tenacity.

endure v. **1** experience and survive (pain or hardship). **2** tolerate. **3** last. □ **endurable** adj.
■ **1** brave, face, survive, take, undergo, weather, withstand. **2** abide, bear, cope with, put up with, stand, stomach, suffer, tolerate. **3** carry on, continue, last, persist, remain, stay, survive.

enema n. liquid injected into the rectum.

enemy n. one who is hostile to and seeks to harm another.
■ adversary, antagonist, foe, opponent, rival.

energetic adj. full of energy. □ **energetically** adv.
■ active, animated, brisk, bubbly, dynamic, enthusiastic, go-ahead, go-getting, indefatigable, lively, spirited, sprightly, spry, tireless, unflagging, untiring, vibrant, vigorous, vivacious, zestful.

energize v. **1** give energy to. **2** cause electricity to flow into.

energy n. **1** vigour. **2** capacity for activity. **3** ability of matter or radiation to do work. **4** oil etc. as fuel.
■ **1** animation, colloq. bounce, drive, dynamism, élan, enthusiasm, go, gusto, life, liveliness, pep, spirit, verve, colloq. vim, vigour, vitality, vivacity, zeal, zest, zip. **2** force, forcefulness, might, power, strength.

enervate v. cause to lose vitality. □ **enervation** n.

enfant terrible /ónfon teréebla/ person whose behaviour is embarrassing or irresponsible.

enfeeble v. make feeble. ■ **enfeeblement** n.

enfold v. **1** wrap up. **2** clasp.

enforce v. compel obedience to. □ **enforcement** n.

enfranchise v. give the right to vote. □ **enfranchisement** n.

engage v. **1** employ (a person). **2** occupy the attention of. **3** reserve. **4** begin a battle with. **5** interlock.
■ **1** employ, hire, recruit, sign, take on. **2** absorb, attract, capture, catch, draw, hold, occupy. **3** book, reserve, take. **4** clash (with), encounter, fight (against), join in battle (with), wage war (against).

engaged adj. **1** having promised to marry a specified person. **2** occupied. **3** in use.

engagement n. **1** act of engaging something. **2** appointment. **3** promise to marry a specified person. **4** battle.
■ **2** appointment, assignation, colloq. date, meeting, rendezvous. **3** betrothal. **4** battle, combat, conflict, encounter, fight, fray, skirmish, war.

engaging adj. attractive.

engender v. give rise to.

engine n. **1** machine using fuel and supplying power. **2** railway locomotive.

engineer n. **1** person skilled in engineering. **2** one in charge of machines and engines. ● v. contrive, bring about.

engineering n. application of science for the design and building of machines etc.

English adj. & n. (language) of England. □ **Englishman** n., **Englishwoman** n.

engrave v. **1** cut (a design) into a hard surface. **2** ornament thus. □ **engraver** n.
■ **1** carve, chisel, cut, etch, inscribe.

engraving n. print made from an engraved metal plate.

engross v. occupy fully by absorbing the attention.

engulf v. swamp, overwhelm.

enhance v. intensify, improve. □ **enhancement** n.
■ add to, augment, boost, heighten, improve, increase, intensify, raise, strengthen.

enigma n. puzzling person or thing. □ **enigmatic** adj.
■ conundrum, mystery, problem, puzzle, riddle.

enjoy v. **1** get pleasure from. **2** have the use or benefit of. □ **enjoyable** adj., **enjoyment** n.
■ **1** appreciate, colloq. be into, be keen on, be partial to, delight in, like, love, relish, revel in, savour, take pleasure in. **2** benefit from, have, make use of, possess, use,

utilize. □ **enjoyable** agreeable, amusing, delightful, entertaining, pleasant, pleasing, pleasurable, satisfying.

enlarge v. make or become larger. □ **enlarge upon** say more about. **enlargement** n.

■ add to, augment, broaden, develop, elongate, expand, extend, increase, lengthen, magnify, stretch, supplement, widen; dilate, distend, inflate, swell. □ **enlarge upon** amplify, go into detail about, elaborate on, embellish, embroider, expand on, expatiate on.

enlighten v. 1 inform. 2 free from ignorance. □ **enlightenment** n.

■ 1 advise, apprise, inform, make aware. 2 civilize, edify, educate, instruct, teach.

enlist v. 1 enrol for military service. 2 get the support of. □ **enlistment** n.

enliven v. make more lively. □ **enlivenment** n.

■ animate, arouse, energize, galvanize, inspire, invigorate, kindle, pep up, refresh, rouse, stimulate, stir (up), vivify.

en masse /on máss/ all together.

enmesh v. entangle.

enmity n. hostility, hatred.

ennoble v. make noble. □ **ennoblement** n.

ennui /onwee/ n. boredom.

enormity n. (act of) great wickedness.

enormous adj. very large.

■ colossal, elephantine, gargantuan, giant, gigantic, huge, immense, mammoth, massive, monstrous, mountainous, prodigious, stupendous, titanic, vast.

enough adj., adv., & n. as much or as many as necessary.

■ adj. adequate, ample, sufficient.

enquire v. ask. □ **enquiry** n.

enrage v. make furious.

■ anger, drive berserk, exasperate, incense, inflame, infuriate, madden.

enrapture v. delight intensely.

enrich v. make richer. □ **enrichment** n.

enrol v. (**enrolled**) admit as or become a member. □ **enrolment** n.

en route /on root/ on the way.

ensconce v. establish securely or comfortably.

ensemble /onsómb'l/ n. 1 thing viewed as a whole. 2 set of performers. 3 outfit.

enshrine v. set in a shrine.

ensign n. military or naval flag.

enslave v. make slave(s) of. □ **enslavement** n.

ensnare v. trap.

ensue v. happen afterwards or as a result.

en suite /on sweet/ forming a unit.

ensure v. make certain or safe.

entail v. necessitate or involve.

■ demand, involve, mean, necessitate, require.

entangle v. 1 tangle. 2 entwine and trap. □ **entanglement** n.

entente /ontónt/ n. friendly understanding between countries.

enter v. 1 go or come in or into. 2 penetrate. 3 put on a list or into a record etc. 4 register as a competitor.

■ 2 go through, penetrate, perforate, pierce, puncture; infiltrate, invade. 3 jot down, list, log, note, put down, record, register, write down.

enteritis n. inflammation of the intestines.

enterprise n. 1 bold undertaking. 2 initiative. 3 business activity.

■ 1 adventure, endeavour, project, scheme, undertaking, venture. 2 ambition, courage, daring, determination, drive, dynamism, energy, initiative, resourcefulness. 3 business, company, concern, corporation, firm, organization.

enterprising adj. full of initiative.

■ adventurous, ambitious, bold, courageous, daring, determined, dynamic, eager, energetic, enthusiastic, go-ahead, go-getting, imaginative, ingenious, innovative, inventive, keen, colloq. pushy, resourceful, spirited, vigorous, zealous.

entertain v. 1 amuse, occupy pleasantly. 2 receive with hospitality. 3 consider (an idea etc.). □ **entertainer** n.

■ 1 amuse, delight, make laugh, please, tickle; absorb, beguile, divert, engage, interest, occupy. 2 accommodate, feed, fête, receive, regale, treat. 3 consider, contemplate.

entertainment n. 1 entertaining, being entertained. 2 thing that entertains, performance.

■ 1 amusement, distraction, diversion; enjoyment, fun, pleasure, recreation. 2 extravaganza, performance, presentation, show, spectacle.

enthral v. (**enthralled**) hold spellbound. □ **enthralment** n.

enthrone v. place on a throne. □ **enthronement** n.

enthuse v. fill with or show enthusiasm.

enthusiasm n. **1** eager liking or interest. **2** object of this. □ **enthusiastic** adj., **enthusiastically** adv.
■ **1** appetite, ardour, devotion, eagerness, fervour, gusto, interest, keenness, liking, love, passion, predilection, relish, zeal, zest. **2** craze, fad, mania, passion; hobby, pastime. □ **enthusiastic** animated, ardent, avid, committed, dedicated, devoted, eager, ebullient, exuberant, fervent, hearty, impassioned, keen, passionate, vehement, vigorous, warm, wholehearted, zealous; *colloq.* crazy, excited, mad, wild.

enthusiast n. person who is full of enthusiasm for something.

entice v. attract by offering something pleasant. □ **enticement** n.
■ allure, attract, coax, inveigle, lure, seduce, tempt, wheedle.

entire adj. complete. □ **entirely** adv.
■ complete, full, total, whole, unabridged, uncut; intact, perfect, unbroken, undamaged.

entirety n. **in its entirety** as a whole.

entitle v. **1** give a title to (a book etc.). **2** give (a person) a right or claim. □ **entitlement** n.
■ **1** call, name. **2** allow, authorize, empower, enable, license, permit, qualify.

entity n. a separate thing.

entomology n. study of insects. □ **entomological** adj., **entomologist** n.

entourage /óntooraazh/ n. people accompanying an important person.

entrails n.pl. intestines.

entrance[1] /éntranss/ n. **1** act or instance of entering. **2** door or passage by which one enters. **3** right of admission, fee for this.
■ **1** appearance, arrival, entry. **2** access, door, doorway, entry, gate, way in. **3** admission, admittance, ingress, right of entry.

entrance[2] /intraanss/ v. fill with intense delight.

entreat v. request earnestly or emotionally. □ **entreaty** n.
■ □ **entreaty** appeal, call, cry, petition, plea, request, supplication.

entrench v. establish firmly. □ **entrenchment** n.

entrepreneur n. person who organizes a commercial undertaking. □ **entrepreneurial** adj.

entrust v. give as a responsibility, place in a person's care.

entry n. **1** act or instance of entering. **2** entrance. **3** item entered in a list etc.

entwine v. twine round.

enumerate v. mention (items) one by one. □ **enumeration** n.

enunciate v. **1** pronounce. **2** state clearly. □ **enunciation** n.

envelop v. (**enveloped**) wrap, cover on all sides. □ **envelopment** n.
■ clothe, cover, encase, enclose, enfold, sheathe, swaddle, swathe, wrap; bury, cloak, conceal, hide, mask, shroud, veil.

envelope n. folded gummed cover for a letter.

enviable adj. desirable enough to arouse envy. □ **enviably** adv.

envious adj. full of envy. □ **enviously** adv.
■ begrudging, bitter, covetous, grudging, jaundiced, jealous, resentful.

environment n. **1** surroundings. **2** natural world. □ **environmental** adj., **environmentally** adv.
■ **1** ambience, conditions, environs, surroundings; element, habitat, medium, milieu; background, context, setting, situation.

environmentalist adj. & n. (person) seeking to protect the natural environment.

environs n.pl. surrounding districts, esp. of a town.

envisage v. imagine, foresee.

envoy n. messenger, esp. to a foreign government.

envy n. **1** discontent aroused by another's possessions or success. **2** object of this. ● v. feel envy of.
■ n. **1** bitterness, ill will, jealousy, resentment; craving, hankering, longing. ● v. begrudge, be jealous of, grudge, resent; covet, crave, hanker after, long for.

enzyme n. protein formed in living cells (or produced synthetically) and assisting chemical processes.

epaulette n. ornamental shoulder-piece.

ephemeral adj. lasting only a short time. □ **ephemerally** adv.
■ brief, fleeting, fugitive, momentary, passing, short, transient, transitory.

epic n. long poem, story, or film about heroic deeds or history. ● adj. of or like an epic.

epicentre n. point where an earthquake reaches the earth's surface.

epicure n. person with refined tastes in food and drink. □ **epicurean** adj. & n.

epidemic *n.* outbreak of a disease etc. spreading through a community.

epidermis *n.* outer layer of the skin.

epidural *n.* anaesthetic injected close to the spinal cord.

epiglottis *n.* cartilage that covers the larynx in swallowing.

epigram *n.* short witty saying. □ **epigrammatic** *adj.*

epilepsy *n.* disorder of the nervous system, causing fits. □ **epileptic** *adj.* & *n.*

epilogue *n.* short concluding section.

episcopal *adj.* of or governed by bishop(s).

episcopalian *adj.* & *n.* (member) of an episcopal church.

episode *n.* **1** event forming one part of a sequence. **2** one part of a serial. □ **episodic** *adj.*

■ **1** event, happening, incident, occasion, occurrence. **2** chapter, instalment, part.

epistle *n.* letter. □ **epistolary** *adj.*

epitaph *n.* words in memory of a dead person, esp. on a tomb.

epithet *n.* descriptive word(s).

epitome /ɪpɪttəmi/ *n.* person or thing embodying a quality etc.

■ archetype, embodiment, incarnation, personification, quintessence.

epitomize *v.* be an epitome of.

epoch /éepok/ *n.* particular period.

eponymous *adj.* after whom something is named.

equable *adj.* moderate, even-tempered. □ **equably** *adv.*

equal *adj.* **1** same in size, amount, value, etc. **2** evenly matched. **3** having the same rights or status. ● *n.* person or thing equal to another. ● *v.* (**equalled**) **1** be equal to. **2** do something equal to. □ **equally** *adv.*, **equalness** *n.*

■ *adj.* **1** commensurate, equivalent, identical, indistinguishable, interchangeable, level, on a par, similar, the same. **2** balanced, matched, proportionate, symmetrical; level pegging, neck and neck. ● *n.* counterpart, equivalent, fellow, match, peer. ● *v.* **2** be on a par with, compare with, match, parallel, resemble, rival. □ **equality** equivalence, identity, parity, sameness, similarity.

equalize *v.* **1** make or become equal. **2** equal an opponent's score. □ **equalization** *n.*

equalizer *n.* equalizing goal etc.

equanimity *n.* composure.

equate *v.* consider to be equal or equivalent.

equation *n.* mathematical statement that two expressions are equal.

equator *n.* imaginary line round the earth at an equal distance from the North and South Poles. □ **equatorial** *adj.*

equestrian *adj.* **1** of horse-riding. **2** on horseback.

equidistant *adj.* at an equal distance.

equilateral *adj.* having all sides equal.

equilibrium *n.* state of balance.

equine /ékwīn/ *adj.* of or like a horse.

equinox *n.* time of year when night and day are of equal length. □ **equinoctial** *adj.*

equip *v.* (**equipped**) supply with what is needed.

■ arm, fix up, furnish, kit (out), provide, rig (out), stock, supply.

equipment *n.* **1** necessary tools, clothing, etc. for a purpose. **2** process of equipping or being equipped.

■ **1** accoutrements, apparatus, *sl.* clobber, gear, kit, materials, outfit, paraphernalia, stuff, tackle, things, tools, trappings.

equipoise *n.* equilibrium.

equitable *adj.* fair and just. □ **equitably** *adv.*

equitation *n.* horse-riding.

equity *n.* **1** fairness, impartiality. **2** (*pl.*) stocks and shares not bearing fixed interest.

equivalent *adj.* equal in importance, value, or meaning etc. ● *n.* equivalent thing. □ **equivalence** *n.*

■ *adj.* akin, analogous, commensurate, comparable, corresponding, equal, identical, interchangeable, parallel, similar, the same, tantamount.

equivocal *adj.* **1** ambiguous. **2** questionable. □ **equivocally** *adv.*

■ **1** ambiguous, evasive, indefinite, misleading, vague. **2** doubtful, dubious, questionable, suspect, suspicious.

equivocate *v.* use words ambiguously. □ **equivocation** *n.*

■ be evasive, evade the issue, hedge, prevaricate, quibble.

era *n.* period of history.

■ age, day(s), epoch, period, time.

eradicate *v.* wipe out, destroy. □ **eradication** *n.*

■ destroy, eliminate, expunge, extirpate, get rid of, obliterate, remove, root out, stamp out, uproot, wipe out.

erase v. rub out, obliterate. □ **eraser** n., **erasure** n.

■ cancel, cross out, delete, efface, expunge, obliterate, rub out, strike out.

erect adj. **1** upright. **2** (of a part of the body) rigid, esp. from sexual excitement. ● v. set up, build. □ **erection** n.

■ adj. **1** perpendicular, standing, straight, upright, upstanding, vertical. ● v. assemble, build, construct, put together, put up, set up; pitch.

ergonomics n. study of work and its environment in order to improve efficiency. □ **ergonomic** adj., **ergonomically** adv.

ermine n. **1** stoat. **2** its white winter fur.

erode v. wear away gradually. □ **erosion** n., **erosive** adj.

■ corrode, eat away (at), gnaw away, grind down, wash away, wear away, whittle away.

erogenous adj. (of a part of the body) sexually sensitive.

erotic adj. of or arousing sexual desire. □ **erotically** adv., **eroticism** n.

err v. (**erred**) **1** be mistaken or incorrect. **2** sin.

■ **1** be in the wrong, be mistaken, be wrong, blunder, make a mistake, miscalculate, colloq. slip up. **2** do wrong, sin, transgress.

errand n. **1** short journey to take or fetch something. **2** its purpose.

errant adj. misbehaving.

erratic adj. inconsistent or uncertain in conduct, movement, etc. □ **erratically** adv.

■ capricious, changeable, fickle, inconsistent, unpredictable, unreliable, wayward; aimless, haphazard, meandering, wandering; fitful, irregular, spasmodic, sporadic, uneven, variable.

erroneous adj. incorrect. □ **erroneously** adv.

error n. **1** mistake. **2** condition of being wrong. **3** amount of inaccuracy.

■ **1** blunder, colloq. boob, sl. clanger, fault, flaw, gaffe, colloq. howler, inaccuracy, mistake, oversight, slip, colloq. slip-up; misprint, misapprehension, miscalculation, misconception, misunderstanding. **2** misconduct, sin, transgression, wrongdoing.

erstwhile adj. former.

erudite adj. learned. □ **erudition** n.

erupt v. **1** break out or through. **2** eject lava. □ **eruption** n.

■ **1** break out, burst forth, explode, flare up. **2** gush, shoot out, spew, spout.

escalate v. increase in intensity or extent. □ **escalation** n.

escalator n. moving staircase.

escalope n. slice of boneless meat, esp. veal.

escapade n. piece of reckless or mischievous conduct.

escape v. **1** get free. **2** leak out of its container. **3** avoid. **4** be forgotten or unnoticed by. ● n. **1** act or means of escaping. **2** leakage.

■ v. **1** abscond, bolt, decamp, sl. do a bunk, flee, fly, get away, get free, run away, colloq. skedaddle, slip away, take to one's heels. **2** drain, leak, ooze, pour, seep. **3** avoid, dodge, elude, evade. ● n. **1** flight, flit, getaway.

escapee n. one who escapes.

escapism n. escape from the realities of life. □ **escapist** n. & adj.

escapologist n. person who entertains by escaping from confinement.

escarpment n. steep slope at the edge of a plateau etc.

eschew v. abstain from.

escort n. /éskort/ **1** person(s) or vehicle(s) accompanying another as a protection or honour. **2** person accompanying a person of the opposite sex socially. **3** person acting as a guide on a journey etc. ● v. /iskórt/ act as escort to.

■ n. **1** bodyguard, chaperon, guard, guardian, protector; entourage, retinue, suite, train. **2** companion, colloq. date, partner. **3** guide, leader. ● v. chaperon, guard, protect, watch over; accompany, attend, conduct, shepherd, take, usher.

escudo n. (pl. **-os**) unit of money in Portugal.

Eskimo n. (pl. **Eskimo** or **-os**) member or language of a people living in Arctic regions. ● adj. of Eskimos or their language. (The Eskimos of N. America prefer the name **Inuit**.)

esoteric adj. intended only for people with special knowledge.

espadrille n. canvas shoe with a sole of plaited fibre.

espalier n. **1** trellis. **2** shrub or tree trained on this.

esparto n. a kind of grass used in making paper.

especial adj. special, notable.

especially *adv.* **1** in particular. **2** more than in other cases.

espionage *n.* spying.

esplanade *n.* promenade.

espouse *v.* **1** support (a cause). **2** marry. □ **espousal** *n.*

espresso *n.* (*pl.* **-os**) coffee made by forcing steam through powdered coffee beans.

esprit de corps /esprée də kór/ loyalty uniting a group.

espy *v.* catch sight of.

Esq. *abbr.* Esquire, courtesy title placed after a man's surname.

essay *n.* /éssay/ short piece of writing. ● *v.* /esáy/ attempt.

essence *n.* **1** indispensable quality or element. **2** concentrated extract.

■ **1** core, crux, heart, pith, quintessence, soul, substance. **2** concentrate, distillation, extract.

essential *adj.* **1** absolutely necessary. **2** fundamental. ● *n.* essential thing. □ **essentially** *adv.*

■ **1** crucial, indispensable, key, necessary, requisite, vital. **2** basic, fundamental, inherent, innate, intrinsic, quintessential.

establish *v.* **1** set up. **2** settle. **3** prove. **4** cause to be accepted.

■ **1** begin, create, form, found, inaugurate, institute, organize, set up, start. **2** ensconce, entrench, install, settle. **3** authenticate, certify, confirm, corroborate, demonstrate, determine, prove, show, substantiate, validate, verify.

establishment *n.* **1** establishing. **2** firm or institution. **3** premises or personnel of this. **4** (**the Establishment**) people established in authority.

■ **1** creation, formation, foundation, inauguration, institution, introduction, setting up. **2** business, company, concern, enterprise, firm, institution, organization.

estate *n.* **1** landed property. **2** property left at one's death. **3** residential or industrial district planned as a unit. □ **estate car** car that can carry passengers and goods in one compartment.

■ **2** assets, belongings, capital, effects, fortune, possessions, property, wealth.

esteem *v.* think highly of. ● *n.* favourable opinion, respect.

■ *v.* admire, appreciate, honour, prize, regard highly, respect, revere, treasure, value. ● *n.* admiration, favour, (high) opinion, (high) regard, respect, reverence, veneration.

estimable *adj.* worthy of esteem.

estimate *n.* /éstimat/ judgement of a thing's approximate value, amount, cost, etc. ● *v.* /éstimayt/ form an estimate of. □ **estimation** *n.*

■ *n.* approximation, calculation, estimation, guess; appraisal, assessment, evaluation. ● *v.* appraise, assess, calculate, consider, evaluate, gauge, guess, judge, reckon, *colloq.* size up, surmise, work out.

estrange *v.* make hostile or indifferent. □ **estrangement** *n.*

estuary *n.* mouth of a large river, affected by tides.

etc. *abbr.* = **et cetera** and other things of the same kind.

etch *v.* engrave with acids. □ **etcher** *n.*, **etching** *n.*

eternal *adj.* **1** existing always. **2** unchanging. **3** (*colloq.*) constant. □ **eternally** *adv.*

■ **1** endless, everlasting, immortal, perpetual, undying, unending. **2** enduring, lasting, immutable, unchangeable, unchanging.

eternity *n.* **1** infinite time. **2** endless period of life after death. □ **eternity ring** jewelled finger ring symbolizing eternal love.

ether *n.* **1** upper air. **2** liquid used as an anaesthetic and solvent.

ethereal *adj.* **1** light and delicate. **2** heavenly. □ **ethereally** *adv.*

ethic *n.* **1** moral principle. **2** (*pl.*) moral philosophy.

ethical *adj.* **1** morally correct, honourable. **2** relating to morals or ethics. □ **ethically** *adv.*

■ **1** correct, decent, fair, good, honest, honourable, just, moral, noble, principled, righteous, upright, virtuous.

ethnic *adj.* of a group sharing a common origin, culture, or language. □ **ethnic cleansing** mass expulsion or killing of people from opposing ethnic groups. **ethnically** *adv.*, **ethnicity** *n.*

ethnology *n.* comparative study of human races. □ **ethnological** *adj.*, **ethnologist** *n.*

ethos /éethoss/ *n.* characteristic spirit and beliefs.

etiolate /éetiōlayt/ *v.* make pale through lack of light. □ **etiolation** *n.*

etiquette *n.* rules of correct behaviour.

etymology n. account of a word's origin and development. □ **etymological** adj.

eucalyptus n. (pl. **-tuses** or **-ti**) evergreen tree with leaves that yield a strong-smelling oil.

Eucharist n. **1** Christian sacrament in which bread and wine are consumed. **2** this bread and wine. □ **Eucharistic** adj.

eugenics n. science of improving the human race by control of inherited characteristics.

eulogy n. piece of spoken or written praise. □ **eulogistic** adj., **eulogize** v.

eunuch n. castrated man.

euphemism n. mild word(s) substituted for improper or blunt one(s). □ **euphemistic** adj., **euphemistically** adv.

euphonium n. tenor tuba.

euphony n. pleasantness of sounds, esp. in words. □ **euphonious** adj.

euphoria n. feeling of happiness. □ **euphoric** adj.

Eurasian adj. **1** of Europe and Asia. **2** of mixed European and Asian parentage. ● n. Eurasian person.

eureka int. I have found it! (announcing a discovery etc.).

Euro- pref. European.

European adj. of Europe or its people. ● n. European person.

Eustachian tube /yōōstáysh'n/ passage between the ear and the throat.

euthanasia n. bringing about an easy death, esp. to end suffering.

evacuate v. **1** remove from a dangerous place. **2** empty or leave (a place). □ **evacuation** n.
■ **2** abandon, desert, leave, move out of, pull out of, quit, vacate, withdraw from.

evacuee n. evacuated person.

evade v. avoid, escape from.
■ avoid, circumvent, dodge, duck, elude, escape from, get away from, get out of, shirk, sidestep.

evaluate v. **1** find out or state the value of. **2** assess. □ **evaluation** n.
■ **1** calculate, estimate, gauge, judge, reckon. **2** appraise, assess, value.

evangelical adj. of or preaching the gospel. □ **evangelicalism** n.

evangelist n. **1** author of one of the Gospels. **2** person who preaches the gospel. □ **evangelism** n., **evangelistic** adj.

evaporate v. **1** turn into vapour. **2** (cause to) disappear. □ **evaporation** n.
■ **1** vaporize. **2** disappear, dissolve, fade (away), melt away, vanish.

evasion n. **1** evading. **2** evasive answer or excuse.

evasive adj. seeking to evade something. □ **evasively** adv., **evasiveness** n.
■ ambiguous, colloq. cagey, equivocal, indirect, misleading, oblique, prevaricating.

eve n. evening, day, or time just before a special event.

even adj. **1** level, smooth. **2** uniform. **3** calm. **4** equal. **5** exactly divisible by two. ● v. make or become even. ● adv. (used for emphasis or in comparing things). □ **evenly** adv.
■ adj. **1** flat, flush, level, plane, smooth, straight. **2** consistent, constant, measured, regular, rhythmical, steady, unbroken, uniform, unvarying. **3** calm, cool, equable, even-tempered, imperturbable, placid, sedate, self-possessed, serene, tranquil. **4** equal, identical, the same.

evening n. latter part of the day, before nightfall.

event n. **1** something that happens, esp. something important. **2** item in a sports programme, or the programme as a whole.
■ **1** affair, circumstance, episode, experience, happening, incident, occurrence. **2** championship, competition, contest, game, match, tournament.

eventful adj. full of incidents.

eventual adj. coming at last, ultimate. □ **eventually** adv.

eventuality n. possible event.

ever adv. **1** always. **2** at any time.

evergreen adj. having green leaves throughout the year. ● n. evergreen tree or shrub.

everlasting adj. lasting for ever or for a very long time.
■ endless, eternal, immortal, perpetual, timeless, undying; ceaseless, constant, continual, continuous, incessant, interminable, never-ending, unceasing.

evermore adv. for ever, always.

every adj. **1** each one without exception. **2** each in a series. **3** all possible.

everybody pron. every person.

everyday adj. **1** worn or used on ordinary days. **2** ordinary.

everyone pron. everybody.

everything pron. **1** all things. **2** all that is important.

everywhere *adv.* in every place.

evict *v.* expel (a tenant) by legal process. □ **eviction** *n.*, **evictor** *n.*

evidence *n.* **1** anything that gives reason for believing something. **2** statements made in a law court to support a case.
● *v.* be evidence of. □ **be in evidence** be conspicuous. **evidential** *adj.*
■ *n.* **1** data, documentation, facts, grounds, indication, proof, sign. **2** affidavit, attestation, deposition, statement, testimony. ● *v.* attest, demonstrate, display, evince, exhibit, manifest, prove, show.

evident *adj.* obvious to the eye or mind. □ **evidently** *adv.*
■ apparent, clear, discernible, manifest, noticeable, obvious, palpable, patent, perceptible, plain, unmistakable, visible.

evil *adj.* **1** morally bad. **2** harmful. **3** very unpleasant. ● *n.* evil thing, sin, harm. □ **evilly** *adv.*, **evildoer** *n.*
■ *adj.* **1** bad, base, corrupt, depraved, diabolical, heinous, immoral, iniquitous, malevolent, nefarious, perverted, sinful, vicious, vile, villainous, wicked, wrong. **2** harmful, hurtful, injurious, malignant, pernicious. **3** disagreeable, disgusting, foul, nasty, offensive, repulsive, unpleasant, vile. ● *n.* depravity, immorality, iniquity, sin, turpitude, vice, viciousness, villainy, wickedness, wrongdoing.

evince *v.* show, indicate.

eviscerate *v.* disembowel. □ **evisceration** *n.*

evoke *v.* inspire (feelings etc.). □ **evocation** *n.*, **evocative** *adj.*
■ arouse, awaken, draw forth, elicit, excite, inspire, provoke, stir up.

evolution *n.* **1** process of evolving. **2** development of species from earlier forms. □ **evolutionary** *adj.*
■ develop, grow, mature, progress, unfold.

ewe *n.* female sheep.

ewer *n.* pitcher, water jug.

ex- *pref.* former.

exacerbate /igzássərbayt/ *v.* **1** make worse. **2** irritate. □ **exacerbation** *n.*

exact *adj.* accurate, correct in all details. ● *v.* insist on and obtain. □ **exaction** *n.*, **exactness** *n.*
■ *adj.* accurate, correct, faithful, faultless, identical, perfect, precise, true. ● *v.* claim, compel, demand, extort, extract, get, insist on, require.

exacting *adj.* making great demands, requiring great effort.

exactly *adv.* **1** in an exact manner. **2** quite so, as you say.

exaggerate *v.* make seem greater or larger than it really is. □ **exaggeration** *n.*, **exaggerator** *n.*
■ blow up, magnify, overemphasize, overstate, overstress; amplify, embellish, embroider.

exalt *v.* **1** raise in rank. **2** praise highly. **3** make more excellent or sublime. □ **exaltation** *n.*

exam *n.* examination.

examination *n.* **1** examining. **2** test of knowledge or ability.
■ **1** analysis, appraisal, assessment, inspection, investigation, *colloq.* once-over, probe, scrutiny, study, survey; cross-examination, grilling, interrogation, questioning.

examine *v.* **1** inquire into. **2** look at closely. **3** question formally. □ **examiner** *n.*
■ **1** analyse, check, explore, inquire into, look into, investigate, probe, research, sift (through), *colloq.* vet. **2** go over, inspect, peruse, pore over, scan, scrutinize, study. **3** catechize, cross-examine, cross-question, grill, interrogate, pump, question, quiz.

examinee *n.* person being tested in an examination.

example *n.* **1** thing characteristic of its kind or illustrating a general rule. **2** person or thing worthy of imitation. □ **make an example of** punish as a warning to others.
■ **1** case, illustration, instance, occurrence, sample, specimen. **2** exemplar, model, pattern.

exasperate *v.* annoy greatly. □ **exasperation** *n.*
■ *colloq.* aggravate, anger, annoy, *sl.* bug, drive mad, enrage, gall, infuriate, irk, irritate, madden, nettle, *colloq.* rile, vex.

excavate *v.* **1** make (a hole) by digging, dig out. **2** reveal by digging. □ **excavation** *n.*, **excavator** *n.*
■ **1** dig (out), gouge (out), hollow (out), scoop (out). **2** disinter, exhume, reveal, uncover, unearth.

exceed *v.* **1** be greater than. **2** go beyond the limit of.
■ **1** beat, better, excel, outdo, outstrip, overtake, pass, surpass, top, transcend.

exceedingly *adv.* very.

excel *v.* (**excelled**) **1** be or do better than. **2** be very good at something.
■ **1** beat, be superior to, eclipse, outclass, outdo, outshine, surpass, top.

excellent *adj.* extremely good. □ **excellently** *adv.*, **excellence** *n.*
■ admirable, *colloq.* divine, exceptional, *colloq.* fabulous, *colloq.* fantastic, fine, first-class, first-rate, *colloq.* great, magnificent, marvellous, outstanding, *colloq.* smashing, splendid, sterling, *colloq.* super, superb, superlative, *colloq.* terrific, *colloq.* tremendous, wonderful.

except *prep.* not including. ● *v.* exclude from a statement etc.

excepting *prep.* except.

exception *n.* **1** excepting. **2** thing that does not follow the general rule. □ **take exception** object.

exceptionable *adj.* offensive.

exceptional *adj.* **1** unusual. **2** very good. □ **exceptionally** *adv.*
■ **1** anomalous, atypical, extraordinary, odd, out of the ordinary, peculiar, rare, singular, special, strange, surprising, uncommon, unexpected, unheard-of, unprecedented, unusual. **2** excellent, first-rate, outstanding, magnificent, marvellous, splendid, superb, wonderful.

excerpt *n.* extract from a book, film, etc.
■ citation, extract, passage, quotation, selection.

excess *n.* **1** exceeding of due limits. **2** amount by which one quantity etc. exceeds another. **3** intemperance in eating and drinking. ● *adj.* exceeding a limit.
■ *n.* **1** glut, over-abundance, overflow, plethora, superfluity, surfeit, surplus. **2** balance, difference. **3** extravagance, immoderation, intemperance, overindulgence.

excessive *adj.* too much. □ **excessively** *adv.*
■ disproportionate, exorbitant, extravagant, extreme, immoderate, inordinate, outrageous, superfluous, undue, unjustifiable, unreasonable.

exchange *v.* give or receive in place of another thing. ● *n.* **1** exchanging. **2** price at which one currency is exchanged for another. **3** place where merchants, brokers, or dealers assemble to do business. **4** centre where telephone lines are connected. □ **exchangeable** *adj.*
■ *v.* barter, change, interchange, substitute, swap, switch, trade. ● *n.* **1** swap, trade, transfer.

excise[1] /ˈɛksɪz/ *n.* duty or tax on certain goods and licences.

excise[2] /ɪkˈsɪz/ *v.* cut out or away. □ **excision** *n.*

excitable *adj.* easily excited. □ **excitably** *adv.*, **excitability** *n.*
■ emotional, fiery, highly-strung, mercurial, nervous, quick-tempered, temperamental, volatile.

excitation *n.* **1** exciting, arousing. **2** stimulation.

excite *v.* **1** rouse the emotions or feelings of. **2** provoke an (action etc.). □ **excitement** *n.*
■ **1** animate, arouse, fire, inflame, inspire, intoxicate, kindle, rouse, stimulate; thrill, titillate, *colloq.* turn on. **2** cause, give rise to, instigate, occasion, provoke, stir up.

exclaim *v.* cry out suddenly.
■ bellow, call, cry out, shout, shriek, yell.

exclamation *n.* **1** exclaiming. **2** word(s) exclaimed. □ **exclamation mark** punctuation mark (!) placed after an exclamation. **exclamatory** *adj.*

exclude *v.* **1** keep out from a place or group or privilege etc. **2** omit, ignore as irrelevant. **3** make impossible. □ **exclusion** *n.*
■ **1** ban, bar, debar, forbid, keep out, prohibit, proscribe, shut out, veto. **2** eliminate, except, leave out, omit, rule out.

exclusive *adj.* **1** excluding others. **2** catering only for the wealthy. **3** not obtainable elsewhere. □ **exclusive of** not including. **exclusively** *adv.*, **exclusiveness** *n.*

excommunicate *v.* cut off from a Church or its sacraments. □ **excommunication** *n.*

excoriate *v.* **1** strip skin from. **2** censure severely. □ **excoriation** *n.*

excrement *n.* faeces.

excrescence *n.* outgrowth on an animal or plant.

excreta *n.pl.* matter (esp. faeces) excreted from the body.

excrete *v.* expel (waste matter) from the body or tissues. □ **excretion** *n.*, **excretory** *adj.*

excruciating *adj.* intensely painful.

excursion *n.* short journey to and from a place, made for pleasure.
■ expedition, jaunt, journey, outing, tour, trip.

excuse *v.* /ikskyōōz/ **1** try to lessen the blame attaching to (a person, act, etc.). **2** overlook (a fault). **3** exempt. ● *n.* /ikskyōōs/ reason put forward to justify a fault etc. □ **excusable** *adj.*
■ *v.* **1** condone, extenuate, explain, justify, mitigate, palliate, vindicate, warrant. **2** disregard, forgive, ignore, overlook, pardon, pass over. ● *n.* apology, defence, explanation, justification, plea, pretext, reason, vindication.

ex-directory *adj.* deliberately not listed in a telephone directory.

execrable *adj.* abominable.

execrate *v.* **1** express loathing for. **2** curse. □ **execration** *n.*

execute *v.* **1** carry out. **2** put (a condemned person) to death. □ **execution** *n.*
■ **1** accomplish, bring off, carry out, discharge, do, effect, implement, perform, pull off.

executioner *n.* one who executes condemned person(s).

executive *n.* person or group with managerial powers, or with authority to put government decisions into effect. ● *adj.* having such power or authority.

executor *n.* person appointed to carry out the terms of one's will.

exemplar *n.* **1** model. **2** typical instance.

exemplary *adj.* **1** fit to be imitated, outstandingly good. **2** serving as a warning to others.
■ **1** model, perfect; admirable, commendable, excellent, outstanding, meritorious, praiseworthy. **2** cautionary, warning.

exemplify *v.* serve as an example of. □ **exemplification** *n.*
■ demonstrate, depict, embody, epitomize, illustrate, personify, represent, show, typify.

exempt *adj.* free from a customary obligation or payment etc. ● *v.* make exempt. □ **exemption** *n.*

exercise *n.* **1** use of one's powers or rights. **2** activity, esp. designed to train the body or mind. ● *v.* **1** use (powers etc.). **2** (cause to) take exercise. □ **exercise book** book for writing in.
■ *n.* **1** application, employment, use, utilization. **2** activity, exertion, movement, practice, training; (**exercises**) aerobics, callisthenics, gymnastics. ● *v.* **1** apply,

employ, put to use, use, utilize, wield. **2** drill, keep fit, train, warm up, work out.

exert *v.* use. □ **exert oneself** make an effort. **exertion** *n.*
■ deploy, employ, exercise, put to use, use, utilize, wield. □ **exert oneself** apply oneself, do one's best, make an effort, push oneself, strive, try. **exertion** action, diligence, effort, endeavour, industry, labour, strain, struggle, toil, trouble, work.

exfoliate *v.* come off in scales or layers. □ **exfoliation** *n.*

ex gratia /eks gráyshə/ done or given as a concession, without legal obligation.

exhale *v.* **1** breathe out. **2** give off in vapour. □ **exhalation** *n.*

exhaust *v.* **1** use up completely. **2** tire out. ● *n.* **1** waste gases from an engine etc. **2** device through which they are expelled. □ **exhaustible** *adj.*, **exhaustion** *n.*
■ *v.* **1** consume, deplete, expend, go through, finish, fritter away, squander, spend, use up. **2** debilitate, drain, enervate, fatigue, *sl.* knacker, prostrate, sap, tire (out), wear out, weary. □ **exhaustion** debilitation, enervation, fatigue, lassitude, tiredness, weariness.

exhaustive *adj.* thorough, comprehensive. □ **exhaustively** *adv.*
■ complete, comprehensive, extensive, far-reaching, sweeping, thorough, wide-ranging.

exhibit *v.* **1** display, present for the public to see. **2** manifest. ● *n.* thing exhibited. □ **exhibitor** *n.*
■ *v.* **1** display, offer, present, show. **2** demonstrate, display, evidence, evince, manifest, reveal, show.

exhibition *n.* **1** public display. **2** act or instance of exhibiting.
■ demonstration, display, exposition, presentation, show.

exhibitionism *n.* tendency to behave in a way designed to attract attention. □ **exhibitionist** *n.*

exhilarate *v.* make joyful or lively. □ **exhilaration** *n.*
■ □ **exhilaration** animation, elation, exuberance, gaiety, glee, happiness, joy, joyfulness.

exhort *v.* urge or advise earnestly. □ **exhortation** *n.*, **exhortative** *adj.*
■ advise, counsel, encourage, press, recommend, urge.

exhume v. dig up (a buried corpse).
□ **exhumation** n.

exigency n. (also **exigence**) **1** urgent need. **2** emergency.

exigent adj. **1** urgent. **2** requiring much, exacting.

exiguous adj. very small.

exile n. **1** banishment or long absence from one's country or home. **2** exiled person. ● v. send into exile.
■ n. **1** banishment, deportation, expatriation, expulsion. **2** expatriate, refugee. ● v. banish, deport, drive out, eject, expatriate, expel.

exist v. **1** have being. **2** be found. **3** maintain life. □ **existence** n., **existent** adj.
■ **1** be extant, live. **2** be found, be present, occur. **3** get by, keep going, stay alive, subsist, survive.

existentialism n. philosophical theory emphasizing that individuals are free to choose their actions. □ **existentialist** n.

exit n. **1** departure from a stage or place. **2** way out. ● v. make one's exit.
■ n. **1** departure, leave-taking, retreat, withdrawal. **2** door, egress, gate, way out.

exodus n. departure of many people.

ex officio /éks əfishiō/ because of one's official position.

exonerate v. declare or show to be blameless. □ **exoneration** n.

exorbitant adj. (of a price or demand) much too great.
■ disproportionate, excessive, extortionate, extravagant, immoderate, inordinate, outrageous, unjustifiable, unreasonable.

exorcize v. **1** drive out (an evil spirit) by prayer. **2** free a person or place) of an evil spirit. □ **exorcism** n., **exorcist** n.

exotic adj. **1** brought from abroad. **2** strange, unusual. □ **exotically** adv.
■ **1** alien, foreign, imported. **2** different, extraordinary, odd, outlandish, out of the ordinary, peculiar, remarkable, singular, strange, unfamiliar, unusual.

expand v. **1** increase in size or importance. **2** become more genial. **3** spread out flat. □ **expand on** give a fuller account of. □ **expandable** adj., **expansion** n.
■ **1** dilate, distend, enlarge, extend, increase, inflate, spread (out), stretch, swell; augment, broaden, develop, widen. □ **expand on** amplify, develop, elaborate on, embellish, embroider, enlarge on.

expanse n. wide area or extent.
■ area, extent, range, space, spread, stretch, tract.

expansive adj. **1** able to expand. **2** genial, communicative.

expatiate /ikspáyshiayt/ v. speak or write at length.

expatriate adj. living abroad. ● n. expatriate person.

expect v. **1** believe that (a person or thing) will come or (a thing) will happen. **2** be confident of receiving. **3** think, suppose.
■ **1** anticipate, await, look forward to, wait for; bargain for, contemplate, envisage, foresee. **2** count on, demand, hope for, rely on, require, want. **3** assume, believe, conjecture, guess, imagine, presume, suppose, surmise, think.

expectant adj. filled with expectation.
□ **expectant mother** pregnant woman.
expectantly adv., **expectancy** n.

expectation n. **1** expecting. **2** thing expected. **3** probability.

expectorant n. medicine for causing a person to expectorate.

expectorate v. cough and spit phlegm.
□ **expectoration** n.

expedient adj. advantageous rather than right or just. ● n. means of achieving an end. □ **expediency** n.
■ adj. advantageous, advisable, beneficial, desirable, helpful, opportune, practical, prudent, useful. ● n. contrivance, device, manoeuvre, means, measure, method, resort, stratagem.

expedite v. help or hurry the progress of.

expedition n. **1** journey for a purpose. **2** people and equipment for this. □ **expeditionary** adj.
■ **1** excursion, exploration, journey, pilgrimage, tour, trek, trip, voyage.

expeditious adj. speedy and efficient.
□ **expeditiously** adv.

expel v. (**expelled**) **1** deprive of membership. **2** compel to leave.
■ **1** ban, bar, debar, exclude. **2** dismiss, drive out, eject, evict, force out, colloq. kick out, oust, push out, throw out, colloq. turf out, turn out; banish, deport, exile.

expend v. **1** spend. **2** use up.

expendable adj. **1** able to be expended. **2** not worth saving.

expenditure n. **1** expending of money etc. **2** amount expended.

expense n. **1** cost. **2** (pl.) amount spent doing a job, reimbursement of this.

expensive adj. costing or charging more than average. □ **expensively** adv.
■ costly, dear, over-priced, colloq. steep.

experience n. **1** personal observation or contact. **2** knowledge or skill gained by this. **3** event that affects one. ● v. **1** have experience of. **2** feel.
■ n. **1** involvement, observation, participation, practice. **2** expertise, know-how, knowledge, judgement, skill, wisdom. **3** adventure, episode, event, happening, incident, occurrence; ordeal, trial. ● v. **1** encounter, endure, face, go through, live through, meet, suffer, undergo. **2** be aware of, feel, sense, taste.

experienced adj. having had much experience.

experiment n. & v. test to find out or prove something. □ **experimentation** n.
■ n. investigation, test, trial, try-out.

experimental adj. **1** of or used in experiments. **2** still being tested. □ **experimentally** adv.

expert adj. well-informed or skilful in a subject. ● n. expert person. □ **expertly** adv.
■ adj. accomplished, adept, adroit, dexterous, experienced, knowledgeable, masterly, practised, proficient, qualified, skilful, skilled, trained. ● n. ace, authority, connoisseur, master, professional, pundit, specialist, virtuoso, wizard.

expertise n. expert knowledge or skill.
■ adroitness, dexterity, judgement, know-how, knowledge, mastery, proficiency, skill.

expiate v. make amends for. □ **expiation** n., **expiatory** adj.

expire v. **1** cease to be valid. **2** die. **3** exhale. □ **expiration** n.
■ **1** cease, come to an end, finish, run out, terminate. **2** decease, die, pass away, perish.

expiry n. termination of validity.

explain v. **1** make clear, show the meaning of. **2** account for. □ **explanation** n., **explanatory** adj.
■ **1** clarify, clear up, define, disentangle, elucidate, expound, interpret, make clear, make plain, simplify, spell out, unravel. **2** account for, excuse, give reasons for, justify, rationalize. □ **explanation** account, definition, description, exposition, interpretation; excuse, justification, rationalization.

expletive n. violent exclamation, oath.

explicable adj. explainable.

explicit adj. stated plainly. □ **explicitly** adv., **explicitness** n.
■ categorical, clear, definite, distinct, express, overt, plain, positive, precise, specific, unambiguous, unequivocal, unmistakable.

explode v. **1** (cause to) expand and break with a loud noise. **2** show sudden violent emotion. **3** discredit. **4** increase suddenly. □ **explosion** n.
■ **1** blow up, burst, erupt, go off, fly apart, shatter; blast, detonate, set off. **2** colloq. blow up, flare up, lose one's temper. **3** colloq. debunk, discredit, disprove, refute. □ **explosion** bang, blast, boom, clap, crack, eruption, report; detonation; outbreak, outburst, paroxysm, spasm.

exploit n. /éksployt/ notable deed. ● v. /iksplóyt/ **1** make good use of. **2** use selfishly. □ **exploitation** n., **exploiter** n.
■ n. accomplishment, achievement, attainment, deed, feat. ● v. **1** capitalize on, cash in on, make use of, profit from, take advantage of, use, utilize. **2** abuse, manipulate, misuse, take advantage of.

explore v. **1** travel into (a country etc.) in order to learn about it. **2** inquire into. **3** examine (a part of the body). □ **exploration** n., **exploratory** adj., **explorer** n.
■ **1** reconnoitre, survey, tour, travel through, traverse. **2** analyse, examine, inquire into, inspect, investigate, look into, probe, research, study.

explosive adj. & n. (substance) able or liable to explode.

exponent n. one who favours a specified theory etc.

export v. /ekspórt/ send (goods etc.) to another country for sale. ● n. /éksport/ **1** exporting. **2** thing exported. □ **exportation** n., **exporter** n.

expose v. **1** leave uncovered or unprotected. **2** disclose, make public. **3** allow light to reach (film etc.). □ **expose to** subject to a risk etc. **exposure** n.
■ **2** bring to light, disclose, make known, make public, reveal, uncover, unmask, unveil. □ **expose to** lay open to, make vulnerable to, put at risk of, subject to.

exposé /ekspózay/ n. **1** statement of facts. **2** disclosure.

exposition n. 1 expounding. 2 explanation. 3 large exhibition.

expostulate v. protest, remonstrate. □ **expostulation** n.

expound v. explain in detail.

express adj. 1 definitely stated. 2 travelling rapidly, designed for high speed. ● adv. at high speed. ● n. fast train or bus making few or no stops. ● v. 1 make (feelings, thoughts, etc.) known by words, gestures, etc. 2 represent by symbols. 3 squeeze out. □ **express oneself** say what one thinks, feels, or means. **expressible** adj.

■ adj. 1 clear, definite, explicit, plain, specific, unambiguous, unmistakable. ● v. 1 air, articulate, communicate, enunciate, give vent to, put into words, state, utter, verbalize, voice; phrase, put, word; betoken, convey, demonstrate, denote, evince, indicate, intimate, make known, manifest, reveal, show. 2 denote, represent, signify, symbolize. 3 extract, squeeze out, wring out.

expression n. 1 act or instance of expressing. 2 word or phrase. 3 look or manner that expresses feeling.

■ 1 articulation, utterance, voicing; indication, manifestation, sign, token. 2 idiom, phrase, saying, term. 3 air, appearance, aspect, countenance, face, look, mien.

expressionism n. style of art seeking to express feelings rather than represent objects realistically. □ **expressionist** n.

expressive adj. 1 expressing something. 2 full of expression. □ **expressively** adv.

expressly adv. 1 explicitly. 2 for a particular purpose.

expropriate v. 1 seize (property). 2 dispossess. □ **expropriation** n.

expulsion n. 1 expelling. 2 being expelled. □ **expulsive** adj.

expunge v. wipe out.

expurgate v. remove (objectionable matter) from (a book etc.). □ **expurgation** n., **expurgator** n., **expurgatory** adj.

exquisite adj. 1 having exceptional beauty. 2 acute, keenly felt. □ **exquisitely** adv.

■ 1 beautiful, delicate, fine, colloq. heavenly, colloq. gorgeous, lovely, perfect, colloq. stunning. 2 acute, agonizing, excruciating, intense, keen, sharp.

extant adj. still existing.

extemporize v. speak, perform, or produce without preparation. □ **extemporary** adj., **extemporization** n.

extend v. 1 make longer. 2 stretch out. 3 reach. 4 offer. □ **extendible** adj., **extensible** adj.

■ 1 add to, broaden, elongate, enlarge, expand, increase, lengthen, widen; prolong, protract. 2 give, hold out, offer, present, proffer, reach out, stretch out. 3 range, reach, stretch.

extension n. 1 extending. 2 extent. 3 additional part or period. 4 subsidiary telephone, its number.

extensive adj. large in area or scope. □ **extensively** adv.

■ big, considerable, enormous, great, huge, immense, large, sizeable, spacious, substantial, vast; broad, catholic, comprehensive, far-reaching, sweeping, wide, widespread.

extent n. 1 space over which a thing extends. 2 width of application.

■ 1 amplitude, area, dimensions, expanse, length, magnitude, size, space, span. 2 breadth, compass, degree, range, scope.

extenuate v. make (an offence) seem less great by providing a partial excuse. □ **extenuation** n.

exterior adj. on or coming from the outside. ● n. exterior aspect or surface.

■ adj. external, outer, outside, outward, superficial, surface. ● n. façade, face, front, outside, shell, surface.

exterminate v. destroy utterly. □ **extermination** n., **exterminator** n.

■ annihilate, destroy, eliminate, eradicate, extirpate, get rid of, liquidate, obliterate, wipe out.

external adj. of or on the outside. □ **externally** adv.

■ exterior, outer, outside, outward, superfical; apparent, perceptible, visible.

extinct adj. 1 no longer existing or burning. 2 (of a volcano) no longer active.

extinction n. 1 extinguishing. 2 making or becoming extinct.

extinguish v. 1 put out (a flame or light). 2 end the existence of.

■ 1 blow out, douse, put out, quench, snuff out; switch off, turn off. 2 annihilate, destroy, eliminate, end, eradicate, exterminate, kill, obliterate, wipe out.

extinguisher n. device for discharging liquid chemicals or foam to extinguish a fire.

extirpate v. root out, destroy. □ **extirpation** n.

extol v. (**extolled**) praise enthusiastically.

extort v. obtain by force or threats. □ **extortion** n.

extortionate adj. exorbitant.

extra adj. additional, more than is usual or expected. ● adv. 1 more than usually. 2 in addition. ● n. 1 extra thing. 2 person employed as one of a crowd in a film. ■ adj. added, additional, auxiliary, further, spare, supplementary.

extra- pref. outside, beyond.

extract v. /ɪkˈstrakt/ 1 take out or obtain by force or effort. 2 obtain by suction, pressure, distillation, etc. 3 derive (pleasure etc.). ● n. /ˈekstrakt/ 1 substance extracted from another. 2 passage from a book, play, film, or music. □ **extractor** n.
■ v. 1 draw out, pull out, remove, take out, withdraw; extort, obtain, wrest, wring. ● n. 1 concentrate, distillation, essence. 2 citation, excerpt, passage, quotation, selection.

extraction n. 1 extracting. 2 lineage.

extradite v. hand over (an accused person) for trial in the country where a crime was committed. □ **extradition** n.

extramarital adj. (of sexual relationships) outside marriage.

extramural adj. additional to ordinary teaching or studies.

extraneous adj. 1 of external origin. 2 not relevant.

extraordinary adj. unusual, remarkable. □ **extraordinarily** adv.
■ abnormal, exceptional, rare, remarkable, singular, special, uncommon, unheard-of, unprecedented, unusual; bizarre, curious, odd, peculiar, strange, uncanny; amazing, astonishing, astounding, incredible, marvellous, miraculous, notable, noteworthy, outstanding, phenomenal, sensational, unbelievable.

extrapolate v. estimate on the basis of available data. □ **extrapolation** n.

extrasensory adj. achieved by some means other than the known senses.

extraterrestrial adj. of or from outside the earth or its atmosphere.

extravagant adj. 1 spending excessively. 2 going beyond what is reasonable. □ **extravagantly** adv., **extravagance** n.
■ 1 improvident, lavish, prodigal, profligate, spendthrift, wasteful. 2 excessive, immoderate, inordinate, unjustifiable, unreasonable.

extravaganza n. lavish spectacular display or entertainment.

extreme adj. 1 very great or intense. 2 severe, not moderate. 3 at the end(s), outermost. ● n. 1 either of two things as different or as remote as possible. 2 highest degree. 3 thing at either end of anything. □ **extremely** adv.
■ adj. 1 considerable, enormous, great, immense, tremendous. 2 draconian, drastic, excessive, harsh, immoderate, severe, stiff, stringent, unreasonable. 3 endmost, farthest, furthermost, outermost, utmost. ● n. 2 apex, extremity, height, peak, pinnacle, summit, zenith; depth, nadir.

extremist n. person holding extreme views. □ **extremism** n.

extremity n. 1 extreme point. 2 extreme degree of need or danger. 3 (pl.) hands and feet.

extricate v. free from an entanglement or difficulty. □ **extrication** n., **extricable** adj.

extrinsic adj. 1 not intrinsic. 2 extraneous. □ **extrinsically** adv.

extrovert n. lively sociable person. □ **extroversion** n.

extrude v. thrust or squeeze out. □ **extrusion** n., **extrusive** adj.

exuberant adj. 1 high-spirited. 2 growing profusely. □ **exuberantly** adv., **exuberance** n.
■ 1 animated, boisterous, bubbly, buoyant, cheerful, ebullient, effusive, energetic, enthusiastic, exhilarated, happy, high-spirited, joyful, lively, spirited, sprightly, spry, vigorous, vivacious. 2 abundant, copious, lush, luxuriant, plentiful, profuse, prolific.

exude v. 1 ooze. 2 give off like sweat or a smell. □ **exudation** n.

exult v. rejoice greatly. □ **exultant** adj., **exultation** n.
■ □ **exultant** delighted, ecstatic, elated, gleeful, joyful, jubilant, overjoyed, rejoicing, triumphant.

eye n. 1 organ of sight. 2 iris of this. 3 region round it. 4 power of seeing. 5 thing like an eye, spot, hole. ● v. (**eyed**, **eyeing**) look at, watch. □ **eye-opener** n. thing that brings enlightenment or great surprise. **eye-shade** n. device to protect the eyes from strong light. **eye-shadow** n. cosmetic applied to the skin round the eyes. **eye-tooth** n. canine tooth in the upper jaw.

eyeball *n.* whole of the eye within the eyelids.

eyebrow *n.* fringe of hair on the ridge above the eye socket.

eyelash *n.* one of the hairs fringing the eyelids.

eyelet *n.* **1** small hole. **2** ring strengthening this.

eyelid *n.* upper or lower fold of skin closing to cover the eye.

eyepiece *n.* lens(es) to which the eye is applied in a telescope or microscope etc.

eyesight *n.* **1** ability to see. **2** range of vision.

eyesore *n.* ugly object.

eyewitness *n.* person who actually saw something happen.

eyrie /īri/ *n.* **1** eagle's nest. **2** house etc. perched high up.

Ff

F *abbr.* Fahrenheit.

fable *n.* fictional tale, often legendary or moral. □ **fabled** *adj.*

fabric *n.* **1** cloth or knitted material. **2** walls etc. of a building.
■ **1** cloth, material, textile.

fabricate *v.* **1** construct, manufacture. **2** invent (a story etc.). □ **fabrication** *n.*, **fabricator** *n.*

fabulous *adj.* **1** incredibly great. **2** legendary. **3** (*colloq.*) excellent. □ **fabulously** *adv.*
■ **1** amazing, astonishing, astounding, extraordinary, inconceivable, incredible, phenomenal, unbelievable. **2** fabled, fictional, fictitious, imaginary, legendary, mythical.

façade /fəsaád/ *n.* **1** front of a building. **2** outward appearance.

face *n.* **1** front of the head. **2** expression shown by its features. **3** front or main side. **4** outward aspect. **5** dial of a clock. **6** coalface. ● *v.* **1** have or turn the face towards. **2** meet firmly. **3** put a facing on. □ **face flannel** cloth for washing one's face. **facelift** *n.* **1** operation for tightening the skin of the face. **2** improvement in appearance. **face up to** accept bravely.
■ *n.* **1** countenance, features, *sl.* mug, physiognomy, visage. **2** appearance, aspect, expression, look. **3** exterior, façade, front, outside, surface. **4** façade, front, mask, veneer. ● *v.* **1** be opposite, front onto, look towards, overlook. **2** brave, confront, cope with, deal with, encounter, meet.

faceless *adj.* **1** without identity. **2** purposely not identifiable.

facet *n.* **1** one of many sides of a cut stone or jewel. **2** one aspect.

facetious *adj.* intended or intending to be amusing. □ **facetiously** *adv.*, **facetiousness** *n.*

facia /fáyshə/ *n.* **1** dashboard. **2** nameplate over a shop front.

facial *adj.* of the face. ● *n.* beauty treatment for the face.

facile /fássɪl/ *adj.* **1** easily achieved. **2** superficial.

facilitate *v.* make easy or easier. □ **facilitation** *n.*

facility *n.* **1** absence of difficulty. **2** means for doing something.
■ **1** ease, effortlessness, smoothness. **2** amenity, convenience, resource.

facing *n.* **1** outer covering. **2** material at the edge of a garment for strength or contrast.

facsimile *n.* a reproduction of a document etc.

fact *n.* **1** reality. **2** (*pl.*) evidence. **3** thing known to have happened or to be true.
■ **1** actuality, certainty, reality, truth. **2** (facts) data, details, evidence, information, *colloq.* low-down, particulars.

faction *n.* small united group within a larger one.

factitious *adj.* **1** made for a special purpose. **2** artificial.

factor *n.* **1** circumstance that contributes towards a result. **2** number by which a given number can be divided exactly.
■ **1** aspect, circumstance, consideration, element, fact, influence, ingredient.

factory *n.* building(s) in which goods are manufactured.

factotum *n.* servant or assistant doing all kinds of work.

factual *adj.* based on or containing facts. □ **factually** *adv.*
■ accurate, actual, authentic, bona fide, faithful, genuine, objective, real, realistic, true, unbiased, unvarnished, verifiable.

faculty *n.* **1** any of the powers of the body or mind. **2** university department.

fad *n.* craze, whim.

faddy *adj.* having petty likes and dislikes, esp. about food.

fade *v.* **1** (cause to) lose colour, freshness, or vigour. **2** disappear gradually.
■ **1** blanch, discolour, (grow) dim *or* pale; droop, wilt, wither; decline, deteriorate, die away, diminish, dwindle, ebb, flag, languish, wane. **2** disappear, dissolve, melt away, vanish.

faeces /feesseez/ *n.pl.* waste matter discharged from the bowels. □ **faecal** *adj.*

fag (*colloq.*) *v.* (**fagged**) exhaust. ● *n.* **1** tedious task. **2** cigarette.

faggot n. **1** tied bundle of sticks or twigs. **2** ball of chopped seasoned liver, baked or fried.

Fahrenheit adj. of a temperature scale on which water freezes at 32° and boils at 212°.

faience /fíonss/ n. painted glazed earthenware.

fail v. **1** be unsuccessful. **2** become weak, cease functioning. **3** disappoint. **4** become bankrupt. **5** neglect or be unable. **6** declare to be unsuccessful. ● n. failure.
　▪ v. **1** be unsuccessful, come to grief, fall through, sl. flop, founder, go wrong, miscarry, misfire. **2** deteriorate, diminish, disappear, dwindle, ebb, fade, give out, wane, weaken. **3** disappoint, let down. **4** crash, fold, go bankrupt, colloq. go bust, colloq. go broke, go under. **5** neglect, omit.

failing n. weakness or fault. ● prep. in default of.
　▪ n. blemish, defect, fault, flaw, imperfection, shortcoming, weakness, weak spot.

failure n. **1** lack of success. **2** person or thing that fails.
　▪ **1** collapse, defeat, disappointment. **2** disaster, fiasco, sl. flop, colloq. wash-out.

faint adj. **1** indistinct, not intense. **2** about to faint. **3** slight. ● v. collapse unconscious. ● n. act or state of fainting. □ **faint-hearted** adj. timid. **faintly** adv., **faintness** n.
　▪ adj. **1** blurred, dim, feeble, hazy, ill-defined, indistinct, pale, subdued, weak; hushed, low, muffled, muted, quiet, soft, stifled. **2** dizzy, giddy, light-headed, unsteady, weak. **3** remote, slight. ● v. black out, collapse, colloq. flake out, keel over, pass out.

fair[1] n. **1** funfair. **2** gathering for a sale of goods, often with entertainments. **3** trade exhibition. □ **fairground** n. open space where a funfair is held.

fair[2] adj. **1** just, unbiased. **2** light in colour, having light-coloured hair. **3** of moderate quality or amount. **4** (of weather) fine and dry, (of wind) favourable. ● adv. fairly.
　▪ adj. **1** disinterested, equitable, honest, honourable, impartial, just, lawful, legitimate, proper, right, unbiased, unprejudiced. **2** light, pale; blond(e), fair-haired, flaxen-haired. **3** acceptable, adequate, average, mediocre, middling, colloq. OK, passable, satisfactory, tolerable. **4** bright, clear, cloudless, dry, fine, pleasant, sunny.

fairing n. streamlining structure.

fairy n. imaginary small being with magical powers. □ **fairy godmother** benefactress. **fairy lights** strings of small coloured lights used as decorations. **fairy story, tale** n. **1** tale about fairies or magic. **2** falsehood.

fairyland n. **1** world of fairies. **2** very beautiful place.

fait accompli /fáyt əkómplee/ thing already done and not reversible.

faith n. **1** complete trust. **2** (system of) religious belief. **3** loyalty. □ **faith healing** cure etc. dependent on faith.
　▪ **1** belief, certainty, certitude, confidence, conviction, credence, trust. **2** denomination, sect; belief, creed, religion. **3** allegiance, dedication, devotion, faithfulness, fidelity, loyalty.

faithful adj. **1** loyal, trustworthy. **2** true, accurate. □ **faithfully** adv., **faithfulness** n.
　▪ **1** constant, dedicated, dependable, devoted, loyal, reliable, staunch, steadfast, trusted, trustworthy. **2** accurate, exact, perfect, precise, true.

faithless adj. disloyal.

fake n. a person or thing that is not genuine. ● adj. faked. ● v. **1** make an imitation of. **2** pretend.
　▪ n. charlatan, cheat, fraud, impostor, colloq. phoney, quack; copy, counterfeit, forgery, imitation, sham. ● adj. artificial, bogus, counterfeit, false, forged, fraudulent, imitation, mock, colloq. phoney, sham, simulated, spurious. ● v. **1** counterfeit, fabricate, forge. **2** affect, feign, pretend, simulate.

fakir /fáykeer/ n. Muslim or Hindu religious mendicant or ascetic.

falcon n. a kind of small hawk.

falconry n. breeding and training of hawks. □ **falconer** n.

fall v. (**fell, fallen**) **1** come or go down freely. **2** lose balance and come suddenly to the ground. **3** decrease. **4** be captured or conquered. **5** die in battle. **6** pass into a specified state. **7** occur. **8** lose power or status. **9** (of the face) show dismay. ● n. **1** act or an instance of falling. **2** amount of this. **3** (US) autumn. **4** (pl.) waterfall. □ **fall back on** have recourse to. **fall for 1** fall in love with. **2** be deceived by. **fall out** quarrel. **2** happen. **fallout** n. airborne radioactive debris. **fall short** be inadequate. **fall through** (of a plan) fail to be achieved.

■ v. **1** come down, descend, dive, drop down, nosedive, plummet, plunge; cascade. **2** collapse, keel over, overbalance, stumble, topple (over), trip (over), tumble. **3** decline, decrease, diminish, drop, dwindle, sink, slump, subside. **4** be defeated, be captured, be overthrown; capitulate, succumb, surrender, yield. **5** die, perish. **6** become, grow, get. **7** happen, occur, take place. ● n. **1** descent, dive, drop, nosedive, plunge, tumble; collapse, decline, decrease, diminution, slump; capture, conquest, defeat, overthrow; capitulation, submission, surrender. □ **fall out 1** clash, disagree, dispute, fight, quarrel, squabble, wrangle.

fallacy n. false belief or reasoning. □ **fallacious** adj.

■ delusion, error, miscalculation, misconception, misjudgement, mistake.

fallible adj. liable to make mistakes. □ **fallibility** n.

Fallopian tube either of the two tubes from the ovary to the womb.

fallow adj. (of land) left unplanted. ● n. such land.

fallow deer reddish-brown deer with white spots.

false adj. **1** incorrect. **2** deceitful, unfaithful. **3** not genuine, sham. □ **falsely** adv., **falseness** n.

■ **1** erroneous, fallacious, fictitious, flawed, imprecise, inaccurate, incorrect, invalid, misleading, mistaken, untrue, wrong. **2** deceitful, dishonest, disloyal, double-dealing, faithless, lying, treacherous, two-faced, unfaithful, untrustworthy. **3** affected, artificial, bogus, counterfeit, fake, forged, imitation, insincere, mock, colloq. phoney, sham, simulated, spurious, synthetic.

falsehood n. lie(s).

falsetto n. (pl. **-os**) unusually high male voice.

falsify v. **1** alter fraudulently. **2** misrepresent. □ **falsification** n.

■ **1** alter, colloq. cook, doctor. **2** distort, misrepresent, twist.

falsity n. **1** falseness. **2** falsehood.

falter v. **1** stumble, go unsteadily. **2** lose courage. **3** speak hesitantly.

fame n. **1** condition of being famous. **2** reputation.

■ celebrity, eminence, illustriousness, prominence, renown, repute, stardom; notoriety.

familial adj. of a family.

familiar adj. **1** well-known. **2** too informal. □ **familiar with** knowing a thing well. **familiarly** adv., **familiarity** n.

■ **1** common, commonplace, customary, everyday, habitual, traditional, usual, well-known. **2** disrespectful, forward, impertinent, impudent, insolent, over-friendly, presumptuous. □ **familiar with** acquainted with, at home with, aware of, conversant with, knowledgeable about, versed in, well-informed about.

familiarize v. make familiar. □ **familiarization** n.

family n. **1** set of relations, esp. parents and children. **2** a person's children. **3** lineage. **4** group of related plants, animals, or things.

■ **1** flesh and blood, folk, kindred, kinsfolk, kith and kin, relations, relatives. **2** brood, children, colloq. kids, offspring, progeny. **3** ancestors, forebears, forefathers; ancestry, descent, dynasty, genealogy, house, line, lineage, parentage, pedigree, stock.

famine n. extreme scarcity (esp. of food) in a region.

famished adj. extremely hungry.

famous adj. known to very many people. □ **famously** adv.

■ celebrated, distinguished, eminent, illustrious, colloq. legendary, notable, noted, prominent, renowned, well-known; notorious.

fan¹ n. hand-held or mechanical device to create a current of air. ● v. (**fanned**) **1** cool with a fan. **2** spread from a central point. □ **fan belt** belt driving a fan that cools a car engine.

fan² n. enthusiastic admirer or supporter. □ **fan mail** letters from fans.

■ admirer, colloq. buff, devotee, enthusiast, fanatic, fiend, follower, lover, supporter.

fanatic n. person filled with excessive enthusiasm for something. □ **fanatical** adj., **fanatically** adv., **fanaticism** n.

■ □ **fanatical** excessive, extreme, fervent, fervid, maniacal, obsessive, passionate, rabid, zealous.

fanciful adj. **1** imaginative. **2** imaginary. □ **fancifully** adv.

fancy n. **1** inclination. **2** unfounded idea. **3** imagination. ● adj. ornamental, elaborate. ● v. **1** imagine. **2** suppose. **3** (colloq.) desire, find attractive. □ **fancy dress** costume representing an animal,

historical character, etc., worn for a party.
■ *n.* **1** fondness, inclination, liking, partiality, penchant, predilection, taste. **2** caprice, notion, vagary, whim. **3** creativity, imagination, inventiveness. ● *adj.* decorated, decorative, elaborate, embellished, embroidered, intricate, ornamental, ornate, rococo. ● *v.* **1** envisage, imagine, picture, visualize. **2** conjecture, guess, imagine, presume, suppose, surmise, think.

fandango *n.* (*pl.* **-oes**) lively Spanish dance.

fanfare *n.* short showy or ceremonious sounding of trumpets.

fang *n.* **1** long sharp tooth. **2** snake's tooth that injects venom.

fanlight *n.* small window above a door or larger window.

fantasia *n.* imaginative musical or other composition.

fantasize *v.* daydream.

fantastic *adj.* **1** absurdly fanciful. **2** (*colloq.*) excellent. □ **fantastically** *adv.*
■ **1** absurd, extravagant, fanciful, illusory, imaginary, irrational, strange, whimsical, wild.

fantasy *n.* **1** imagination. **2** thing(s) imagined. **3** fanciful design.
■ **1** fancy, imagination, inventiveness. **2** chimera, delusion, hallucination, illusion, mirage; daydream, dream, pipedream.

far *adv.* at or to or by a great distance. ● *adj.* distant, remote. □ **far-away**, **far-off** *adjs.* remote. **Far East** countries of east and south-east Asia. **far-fetched** *adj.* very unlikely.

farad *n.* unit of capacitance.

farce *n.* **1** light comedy. **2** absurd and useless proceedings, pretence. □ **farcical** *adj.*

fare *n.* **1** price charged for a passenger to travel. **2** passenger paying this. **3** food provided. ● *v.* get on or be treated.

farewell *int.* & *n.* goodbye.

farinaceous *adj.* starchy.

farm *n.* unit of land used for raising crops or livestock. ● *v.* **1** grow crops, raise livestock. **2** use (land) for this. □ **farmer** *n.*

farmhouse *n.* farmer's house.

farmyard *n.* enclosed area round farm buildings.

farrago /fəráagō/ *n.* (*pl.* **-os**) hotchpotch.

farrier *n.* smith who shoes horses.

farrow *v.* give birth to piglets. ● *n.* litter of piglets.

farther *adv.* & *adj.* at or to a greater distance, more remote.

farthest *adv.* & *adj.* at or to the greatest distance, most remote.

fascinate *v.* **1** capture the interest of. **2** attract irresistibly. □ **fascination** *n.*
■ bewitch, captivate, charm, enchant, enthral, entrance, hold spellbound, intrigue, mesmerize, rivet, transfix.

fascism /fáshiz'm/ *n.* system of extreme right-wing dictatorship. □ **fascist** *n.*

fashion *n.* **1** manner of doing something. **2** style popular at a given time. ● *v.* shape, make.
■ *n.* **1** manner, method, mode, style, way. **2** craze, custom, fad, style, trend, vogue. ● *v.* build, carve, construct, create, form, frame, make, shape.

fashionable *adj.* **1** of or conforming to current fashion. **2** used by stylish people. □ **fashionably** *adv.*
■ chic, in, in fashion, in vogue, *sl.* snazzy, stylish, *colloq.* swish, *colloq.* trendy, up to date.

fast[1] *adj.* **1** moving or done quickly. **2** firmly fixed or attached. **3** capable of or intended for high speed. **4** showing a time ahead of the correct one. ● *adv.* **1** quickly. **2** firmly, tightly.
■ *adj.* **1** brisk, expeditious, *colloq.* nippy, quick, rapid, speedy, swift; hasty, hurried, precipitate. **2** attached, bound, fastened, fixed, secured, tied; firm, lasting, secure, settled, unshakeable, unwavering.

fast[2] *v.* go without food. ● *n.* act or period of fasting.

fasten *v.* make or become fixed or secure.
■ affix, anchor, attach, bind, bolt, clasp, close, connect, do up, join, link, lock, pin, secure, stick, tether, tie.

fastener *n.* (also **fastening**) device that fastens something.

fastidious *adj.* **1** choosing only what is good. **2** easily disgusted.
■ **1** *colloq.* choosy, dainty, finicky, fussy, nice, particular, *colloq.* pernickety, selective. **2** queasy, squeamish.

fastness *n.* stronghold, fortress.

fat *n.* white or yellow substance found in animal bodies and certain seeds. ● *adj.* (**fatter**, **fattest**) **1** excessively plump. **2** containing much fat. **3** thick, substantial. □ **fatness** *n.*, **fatty** *adj.*
■ *adj.* **1** bulky, chubby, corpulent, dumpy, flabby, fleshy, heavy, obese, overweight,

plump, podgy, portly, pot-bellied, pudgy, roly-poly, rotund, stout, tubby.

fatal adj. causing or ending in death or disaster. □ **fatally** adv.
■ deadly, final, lethal, mortal, terminal.

fatalism n. belief that all events are determined by fate and therefore inevitable. □ **fatalist** n.

fatality n. death caused by accident or in war etc.

fate n. **1** power thought to control all events. **2** person's destiny.
■ **1** chance, destiny, fortune, kismet, luck. **2** destiny, lot.

fated adj. **1** destined by fate. **2** doomed.
■ **1** destined, ineluctable, predestined, preordained, unavoidable.

fateful adj. bringing great usu. unpleasant events.

father n. **1** male parent or ancestor. **2** founder, originator. **3** title of certain priests. ● v. **1** be the father of. **2** originate. □ **father-in-law** n. (pl. **fathers-in-law**) father of one's wife or husband. **fatherhood** n., **fatherless** adj., **fatherly** adj.
■ n. **2** author, creator, designer, founder, inventor, originator.

fatherland n. native country.

fathom n. measure (1.82 m) of the depth of water. ● v. understand. □ **fathomable** adj.

fatigue n. **1** tiredness. **2** weakness in metal etc., caused by stress. **3** soldier's non-military task. ● v. cause fatigue to.
■ n. **1** enervation, exhaustion, lassitude, lethargy, listlessness, tiredness, weakness, weariness.

fatstock n. livestock fattened for slaughter as food.

fatten v. make or become fat.

fatuous adj. foolish, silly. □ **fatuously** adv., **fatuousness** n.

faucet n. tap.

fault n. **1** defect, imperfection. **2** error, offence. **3** responsibility for something wrong. **4** break in layers of rock. ● v. find fault(s) in. □ **at fault** responsible for a mistake etc. **faultless** adj., **faulty** adj.
■ n. **1** blemish, defect, deficiency, failing, flaw, imperfection, shortcoming, weakness. **2** error, mistake, oversight, slip, colloq. slip-up; misdeed, misdemeanour, offence, sin, transgression. **3** blame, culpability, liability, responsibility. □ **faultless** exemplary, flawless, immaculate, impeccable, irreproachable, perfect. **faulty** broken,

damaged, defective, flawed, impaired, imperfect, out of order, unsound.

faun n. Latin rural deity with a goat's legs and horns.

fauna n.pl. animals of an area or period.

faux pas /fō paá/ (pl. **faux pas** /paás/) embarrassing blunder.

favour n. **1** liking, approval. **2** kindly or helpful act. **3** favouritism. ● v. **1** regard or treat with favour. **2** facilitate.
■ n. **1** approbation, approval, goodwill, liking. **2** courtesy, good turn, kindness. **3** bias, favouritism, partiality, partisanship. ● v. **1** have a liking for, incline to, like, opt for, side with, support; advocate, back, endorse, prefer, recommend. **2** advance, aid, assist, benefit, encourage, facilitate, help, promote.

favourable adj. **1** approving. **2** promising. **3** pleasing, satisfactory. □ **favourably** adv.
■ **1** approving, complimentary, encouraging, enthusiastic, good, laudatory, positive, sympathetic. **2** auspicious, hopeful, promising, propitious. **3** good, pleasing, satisfactory.

favourite adj. liked above others. ● n. **1** favoured person or thing. **2** competitor expected to win.
■ adj. beloved, best-liked, chosen, favoured, pet, preferred. ● n. **1** beloved, darling, idol, pet.

favouritism n. unfair favouring of one at the expense of others.

fawn[1] n. **1** a deer in its first year. **2** light yellowish-brown. ● adj. fawn-coloured.

fawn[2] v. **1** (of a dog) show affection. **2** try to win favour by obsequiousness.

fax n. **1** facsimile transmission by electronic scanning. **2** document produced thus. ● v. transmit by this process.

fear n. unpleasant sensation caused by nearness of danger or pain. ● v. **1** feel fear of. **2** be afraid.
■ n. alarm, apprehension, consternation, dismay, dread, fright, horror, panic, terror, trepidation.

fearful adj. **1** feeling fear. **2** terrible, extremely unpleasant. □ **fearfully** adv.
■ **1** afraid, alarmed, anxious, apprehensive, edgy, frightened, jumpy, nervous, panicky, panic-stricken, scared, terrified. **2** appalling, atrocious, awful, disgusting, dreadful, frightful, ghastly, gruesome, horrendous, horrible, horrific, horrifying,

loathsome, monstrous, repugnant, repulsive, revolting, terrible.

fearless *adj.* feeling no fear. □ **fearlessly** *adv.*

■ bold, brave, courageous, daring, dauntless, gallant, game, *colloq.* gutsy, heroic, intrepid, plucky, resolute, spirited, unafraid, undaunted, valiant, valorous.

fearsome *adj.* frightening.

feasible *adj.* **1** able to be done. **2** plausible. □ **feasibly** *adv.*, **feasibility** *n.*

■ **1** attainable, possible, practicable, practical, viable, workable. **2** believable, credible, likely, plausible, reasonable.

feast *n.* **1** large elaborate meal. **2** sensual or mental pleasure. **3** joyful festival. ● *v.* **1** eat heartily. **2** give a feast to.

■ *n.* **1** banquet, *colloq.* spread. **2** delight, gratification, pleasure, treat. ● *v.* **1** dine, gorge (oneself). **2** entertain, feed, regale.

feat *n.* remarkable achievement.

■ accomplishment, achievement, act, action, attainment, deed, exploit, performance, *tour de force*.

feather *n.* each of the structures with a central shaft and fringe of fine strands, growing from a bird's skin. ● *v.* **1** cover or fit with feathers. **2** turn (an oar-blade etc.) to pass through the air edgeways. □ **feather-bed** *v.* make things financially easy for. **feather one's nest** enrich oneself. **feathery** *adj.*

featherweight *n.* very lightweight thing or person.

feature *n.* **1** characteristic or distinctive part. **2** (usu. *pl.*) part of the face. **3** prominent article in a newspaper etc. **4** full-length cinema film. ● *v.* **1** give prominence to. **2** be a feature of or in.

■ *n.* **1** aspect, attribute, characteristic, facet, hallmark, idiosyncrasy, mark, peculiarity, property, quality, trait. **2** (**features**) countenance, face, *sl.* mug, physiognomy, visage. **3** article, column, piece. ● *v.* call attention to, emphasize, highlight, spotlight, stress. **2** act, perform, star.

febrile /féebrīl/ *adj.* of fever.

feckless *adj.* incompetent and irresponsible. □ **fecklessness** *n.*

fecund *adj.* fertile. □ **fecundity** *n.*

fed *see* **feed**. *adj.* **fed up** discontented, bored.

federal *adj.* of a system in which states unite under a central authority but are independent in internal affairs. □ **federalism** *n.*, **federalist** *n.*, **federally** *adv.*

federate *v.* /féddrayt/ unite on a federal basis. ● *adj.* /féddərət/ united thus. □ **federative** *adj.*

federation *n.* **1** federating. **2** federal group.

fee *n.* payment for professional advice or services.

feeble *adj.* **1** weak. **2** ineffective. □ **feebly** *adv.*, **feebleness** *n.*

■ **1** ailing, debilitated, decrepit, delicate, enfeebled, fragile, frail, infirm, puny, sickly, weak. **2** flimsy, insubstantial, lame, poor, thin, unconvincing, weak; impotent, ineffective, ineffectual, namby-pamby, spineless, *colloq.* wet, wishy-washy.

feed *v.* (**fed**) **1** give food to. **2** (of animals) take food. **3** supply (material) to a machine etc. ● *n.* **1** meal. **2** food for animals.

■ *v.* **1** nourish, nurture; breast-feed, suckle; cater for, provide for, support, sustain. **2** browse, eat, graze, pasture.

feedback *n.* **1** return of part of a system's output to its source. **2** return of information about a product etc. to its supplier.

feeder *n.* **1** one that feeds. **2** baby's feeding bottle. **3** feeding apparatus in a machine. **4** road or railway line linking outlying areas to a central system.

feel *v.* (**felt**) **1** explore or perceive by touch. **2** be conscious of (being). **3** experience. **4** have an impression, think. **5** give a sensation. ● *n.* **1** sense of touch. **2** act of feeling. **3** sensation produced by a thing touched. □ **feel like** be in the mood for.

■ *v.* **1** finger, handle, manipulate, touch; caress, fondle, *colloq.* paw, stroke. **2** be aware of, be conscious of, detect, discern, notice, perceive, sense. **3** bear, endure, experience, go through, undergo. **4** believe, consider, have a feeling, have a hunch, get the impression, judge, think. **5** appear, seem, strike one as.

feeler *n.* **1** long slender organ of touch in certain animals. **2** tentative suggestion.

feeling *n.* **1** power to feel things. **2** mental or physical awareness. **3** (*pl.*) emotional susceptibilities. **4** opinion or notion, esp. a vague one. **5** readiness to feel sympathy or compassion. **6** impression.

■ **1** sensation, sense of touch, sensitivity. **2** awareness, consciousness, perception, sensation, sense. **3** (**feelings**) emotions, susceptibilities, sympathies. **4** hunch, idea, impression, inkling, instinct, intuition, notion, suspicion; premonition, presentiment. **5** empathy, sensibility, sensitivity, sympathy, understanding. **6** air, ambience, atmosphere, aura, impression.

feet see **foot.**

feign /fayn/ v. pretend.

feint /faynt/ n. sham attack made to divert attention. ● v. make a feint. ● adj. (of ruled lines) faint.

feldspar n. white or red mineral containing silicates.

felicitate v. congratulate. □ **felicitation** n.

felicitous adj. well-chosen, apt.

felicity n. **1** happiness. **2** pleasing manner or style.

feline adj. of cats, cat-like. ● n. animal of the cat family.

fell[1] n. stretch of moor or hilly land, esp. in northern England.

fell[2] v. strike or cut down.

■ cut down, floor, knock down, prostrate, strike down.

fell[3] see **fall.**

fellow n. **1** associate, comrade. **2** (colloq.) man, boy. **3** thing like another. **4** member of a learned society or governing body of a college. □ **fellow feeling** sympathy.

fellowship n. **1** friendly association with others. **2** society, membership of this. **3** position of a college fellow.

felt[1] n. cloth made by matting and pressing fibres. ● v. **1** make or become matted. **2** cover with felt.

felt[2] see **feel.**

female adj. **1** of the sex that can bear offspring or produce eggs. **2** (of plants) fruit-bearing. **3** (of a socket etc.) hollow. ● n. female animal or plant.

feminine adj. **1** of, like, or traditionally considered suitable for women. **2** of the grammatical form suitable for names of females. ● n. feminine word. □ **femininity** n.

feminism n. belief in the principle that women should have the same rights and opportunities as men. □ **feminist** n. & adj.

femur n. thigh-bone. □ **femoral** adj.

fen n. low-lying marshy land.

fence n. barrier round the boundary of a field or garden etc. ● v. **1** surround with a fence. **2** engage in the sport of fencing. □ **fencer** n.

■ n. barricade, barrier, hedge, palisade, railing, rampart, stockade, wall. ● v. **1** bound, circumscribe, encircle, enclose, hedge, surround.

fencing n. **1** fences, their material. **2** sport of fighting with foils.

fend v. **1** fend for look after (esp. oneself). **2** fend off ward off.

■ **2** deflect, fight off, hold at bay, keep away, parry, repel, stave off, ward off.

fender n. **1** low frame bordering a fireplace. **2** pad hung over a moored vessel's side to protect against bumping. **3** (US) mudguard or bumper of a vehicle.

feral adj. wild.

ferment v. **1** undergo or subject to fermentation. **2** stir up, excite.

■ **1** boil, bubble, effervesce, foam, froth, seethe. **2** excite, foment, incite, inflame, instigate, provoke, rouse, stir up.

fermentation n. breakdown of a substance by yeasts, bacteria, etc.

fern n. flowerless plant with feathery green leaves.

ferocious adj. fierce, savage. □ **ferociously** adv., **ferocity** n.

■ barbaric, bestial, bloodthirsty, brutal, cruel, fierce, inhuman, merciless, murderous, pitiless, savage, vicious, violent, wild.

ferret n. small animal of the weasel family. ● v. (**ferreted**) search, rummage. □ **ferret out** discover by searching.

ferroconcrete n. reinforced concrete.

ferrous adj. containing iron.

ferrule n. metal ring or cap on the end of a stick or tube.

ferry v. **1** convey in a boat across water. **2** transport. ● n. **1** boat used for ferrying. **2** place where it operates. **3** service it provides.

fertile adj. **1** able to produce vegetation, fruit, or young. **2** capable of growth. **3** inventive. □ **fertility** n.

■ **1** fecund, fruitful, productive, prolific, rich.

fertilize v. **1** make fertile. **2** introduce pollen or sperm into. □ **fertilization** n.

fertilizer n. material added to soil to make it more fertile.

fervent adj. showing fervour. □ **fervently** adv., **fervency** n.

■ ardent, burning, eager, emotional, enthusiastic, fanatical, fervid, fiery, impassioned, intense, keen, passionate, spirited, vehement, zealous.

fervid adj. fervent. □ **fervidly** adv.

fervour *n.* intensity of feeling.

■ ardour, eagerness, enthusiasm, fervency, gusto, intensity, passion, spirit, vehemence, warmth, zeal, zest.

fester *v.* **1** make or become septic. **2** cause continuing resentment. **3** rot.

■ **1** suppurate. **2** rankle, smoulder. **3** decay, decompose, putrefy, rot.

festival *n.* **1** day or period of celebration. **2** series of cultural events in a town etc.

■ **1** anniversary, carnival, feast, fête, fiesta, gala, jubilee.

festive *adj.* **1** of or suitable for a festival. **2** joyful.

■ **2** cheerful, cheery, convivial, gay, happy, jolly, jovial, joyful, joyous, light-hearted, merry, mirthful.

festivity *n.* **1** gaiety. **2** festive proceedings.

■ **1** gaiety, glee, jollity, joyfulness, jubilation, merriment, merrymaking, mirth, rejoicing, revelry.

festoon *n.* hanging chain of flowers or ribbons etc. ● *v.* decorate with hanging ornaments.

fetch *v.* **1** go for and bring back. **2** be sold for (a price).

■ **1** bring (back), get, go for, retrieve. **2** earn, make, sell for.

fête /fayt/ *n.* **1** festival. **2** outdoor entertainment or sale, esp. in aid of charity. ● *v.* entertain in celebration of an achievement.

fetid *adj.* stinking.

fetish *n.* **1** object worshipped as having magical powers. **2** thing given excessive respect.

fetter *n.* & *v.* shackle.

feud *n.* prolonged hostility. ● *v.* conduct a feud.

■ *n.* argument, conflict, dispute, falling out, quarrel, vendetta.

feudal *adj.* of or like the feudal system. □ **feudal system** medieval system of holding land by giving one's services to the owner. **feudalism** *n.*, **feudalistic** *adj.*

fever *n.* **1** abnormally high body temperature. **2** disease causing it. **3** nervous excitement. □ **fevered** *adj.*

feverish *adj.* **1** having symptoms of fever. **2** excited, restless.

■ **1** febrile, fevered, flushed, hot. **2** excited, frantic, frenetic, frenzied, hectic, restless.

few *adj.* & *n.* not many. □ **a few** some. **quite a few** (*colloq.*) a fairly large number.

fey *adj.* having a strange dreamy charm, whimsical.

fez *n.* (*pl.* **fezzes**) Muslim man's high flat-topped red cap.

fiancé (*fem.* **fiancée**) *n.* person one is engaged to marry.

fiasco *n.* (*pl.* **-os**) ludicrous failure.

fib *n.* unimportant lie. ● *v.* (**fibbed**) tell a fib. □ **fibber** *n.*

fibre *n.* **1** thread-like strand. **2** substance formed of fibres. **3** fibrous matter in food. **4** strength of character. □ **fibre optics** transmission of information by infra-red signals along thin glass fibres. **fibrous** *adj.*

fibreglass *n.* material made of or containing glass fibres.

fibroid *adj.* consisting of fibrous tissue. ● *n.* benign fibroid tumour.

fibrositis *n.* rheumatic pain in fibrous tissue.

fibula *n.* (*pl.* **-lae**) bone on the outer side of the shin.

fiche /feesh/ *n.* microfiche.

fickle *adj.* often changing, not loyal. □ **fickleness** *n.*

■ capricious, changeable, disloyal, erratic, faithless, inconstant, mutable, unfaithful, unpredictable, unreliable, unstable, unsteady.

fiction *n.* **1** invented story. **2** non-factual literature, esp. novels. □ **fictional** *adj.*

fictitious *adj.* **1** imaginary. **2** not genuine.

■ **1** apocryphal, fictional, imaginary, imagined, invented, made-up, unreal, untrue. **2** bogus, false, *colloq.* phoney, spurious.

fiddle *n.* **1** violin. **2** (*colloq.*) swindle. ● *v.* **1** fidget with something. **2** (*colloq.*) cheat, falsify. **3** play the violin. □ **fiddler** *n.*

fiddlesticks *n.* nonsense.

fiddly *adj.* (**-ier, -iest**) (*colloq.*) awkward to do or use.

fidelity *n.* **1** faithfulness, loyalty. **2** accuracy.

fidget *v.* (**fidgeted**) **1** move restlessly. **2** make or be uneasy. ● *n.* **1** one who fidgets. **2** (*pl.*) restless mood. □ **fidgety** *adj.*

■ *v.* **1** jig about, squirm, wiggle, wriggle. □ **fidgety** *colloq.* jittery, jumpy, nervous, nervy, restive, restless, uneasy.

fiduciary *adj.* held or given etc. in trust. ● *n.* trustee.

fief n. land held under the feudal system.

field n. **1** piece of open ground, esp. for pasture or cultivation. **2** sports ground. **3** all competitors in a race or contest. **4** sphere of action or interest. **5** area rich in a natural product. ● v. **1** be a fielder, stop and return (a ball). **2** put (a team) into a contest. **field day** day of much activity. **field events** athletic contests other than races. **field glasses** binoculars. **Field Marshal** army officer of the highest rank.

■ n. **1** poetic lea, meadow, paddock, pasture. **2** ground, pitch, playing field. **3** competition, competitors, contestants, participants, players. **4** area, domain, province, realm, speciality, sphere, subject, territory.

fielder n. **1** person who fields a ball. **2** member of the side not batting.

fieldwork n. practical work done by surveyors, social workers, etc. □ **fieldworker** n.

fiend /feend/ n. **1** evil spirit. **2** devotee. **3** wicked, mischievous, or annoying person. □ **fiendish** adj.

fierce adj. **1** violent in manner or action. **2** eager, intense. □ **fiercely** adv., **fierceness** n.

■ **1** aggressive, barbaric, barbarous, bestial, bloodthirsty, brutal, brutish, cruel, dangerous, ferocious, homicidal, inhuman, murderous, savage, vicious, violent, wild. **2** ardent, eager, fiery, furious, intense, vehement.

fiery adj. (**-ier, -iest**) **1** consisting of or like fire. **2** spirited.

■ **1** blazing, burning, flaming; gleaming, glowing, incandescent; hot, red-hot, white-hot. **2** eager, excitable, excited, fierce, lively, passionate, spirited.

fiesta n. festival in Spanish-speaking countries.

fife n. small shrill flute.

fifteen adj. & n. one more than fourteen. □ **fifteenth** adj. & n.

fifth adj. & n. next after fourth. □ **fifthly** adv.

fifty adj. & n. five times ten. □ **fifty-fifty** adj. & adv. half-and-half, equally. **fiftieth** adj. & n.

fig n. **1** soft fruit with many seeds. **2** tree bearing this.

fight v. (**fought**) **1** struggle against, esp. in physical combat or war. **2** argue, quarrel. **3** strive to overcome. **4** strive to achieve something. ● n. **1** combat,

struggle. **2** battle. **3** argument. **4** boxing match.

■ v. **1** battle, brawl, clash, conflict, contend, engage, grapple, colloq. scrap, scuffle, skirmish, spar, tussle, wage war, wrestle. **2** argue, bicker, disagree, dispute, fall out, quarrel, row, squabble, wrangle. **3** confront, defy, make a stand against, oppose, resist, struggle against. **4** campaign, strive, struggle. ● n. **1** brawl, brush, clash, combat, contest, fracas, fray, mêlée, colloq. scrap, scrimmage, scuffle, skirmish, struggle, tussle. **2** battle, conflict, encounter, engagement. **3** altercation, argument, colloq. bust-up, disagreement, dispute, quarrel, row, squabble, tiff, wrangle.

fighter n. **1** one who fights. **2** aircraft designed for attacking others.

figment n. thing that does not exist except in the imagination.

figurative adj. metaphorical. □ **figuratively** adv.

figure n. **1** external form, bodily shape. **2** representation of a person or animal. **3** numerical symbol or number. **4** diagram. **5** value, amount of money. **6** (pl.) arithmetic. **7** geometric shape. ● v. **1** appear or be mentioned. **2** represent in a diagram etc. **3** calculate. □ **figurehead** n. **1** carved image at the prow of a ship. **2** leader with only nominal power. **figure of speech** word(s) used for effect and not literally. **figure out** work out by arithmetic or logic.

■ n. **1** body, build, form, physique, shape. **2** bust, effigy, image, representation, sculpture, statue. **3** cipher, digit, number, numeral, symbol. **4** diagram, drawing, illustration, picture, plate, sketch.

figured adj. with a woven pattern.

figurine n. statuette.

filament n. **1** strand. **2** wire giving off light in an electric lamp.

filbert n. nut of a cultivated hazel.

filch v. pilfer, steal.

file¹ n. tool with a rough surface for smoothing things. ● v. shape or smooth with a file.

file² n. **1** cover or box etc. for holding documents. **2** its contents. **3** line of people or things one behind another. **4** set of data in a computer. ● v. **1** place in a file or among records. **2** march in a file.

■ n. **1** case, folder, portfolio. **2** documents, dossier, papers. **3** column, line, queue, rank, row.

filial *adj.* of or due from a son or daughter. □ **filially** *adv.*

filigree *n.* lace-like work in metal.

filings *n.pl.* particles filed off.

fill *v.* **1** make or become full. **2** block. **3** occupy completely. **4** spread over or through. **5** appoint to (a vacant post). ● *n.* **1** enough to fill a thing. **2** enough to satisfy a person's appetite or desire. □ **fill in 1** complete. **2** act as substitute. **3** (*colloq.*) inform more fully. **fill out 1** enlarge. **2** become enlarged or plumper. **fill up** fill completely.

> ■ *v.* **1** fill up, top up. **2** block, close, plug, stop (up). **3** cram, crowd (into), occupy, pack, squeeze into, stuff. **4** permeate, pervade, suffuse.

filler *n.* thing or material used to fill a gap or increase bulk.

fillet *n.* piece of boneless meat or fish. ● *v.* (**filleted**) remove bones from.

filling *n.* substance used to fill a cavity etc. □ **filling station** place selling petrol to motorists.

filly *n.* young female horse.

film *n.* **1** thin layer. **2** motion picture. **3** sheet or rolled strip of light-sensitive material for taking photographs. ● *v.* **1** make a film of. **2** cover or become covered with a thin layer.

> ■ *n.* **1** coat, coating, covering, layer, membrane, skin. **2** motion picture, *US colloq.* movie, picture; video.

filmy *adj.* (**-ier, -iest**) thin and almost transparent.

filter *n.* **1** device or substance for holding back impurities in liquid or gas passing through it. **2** screen for absorbing or modifying light or electrical or sound waves. ● *v.* **1** pass through a filter. **2** pass gradually in or out. **3** (of traffic) be allowed to pass while other traffic is held up.

> ■ *v.* **1** filtrate, leach, percolate, sieve, sift, strain; clarify, purify, refine.

filth *n.* **1** disgusting dirt. **2** obscenity. □ **filthy** *adj.*

> ■ **1** dirt, filthiness, grime, *colloq.* muck, slime; dung, excrement, ordure; garbage, refuse, rubbish. □ **filthy** dirty, grimy, grubby, *colloq.* mucky, muddy, polluted, slimy, soiled, sooty, sordid, squalid, stained, unclean, unwashed.

filtrate *n.* filtered liquid. ● *v.* filter. □ **filtration** *n.*

fin *n.* **1** thin projection from a fish's body, used for propelling and steering itself. **2** similar projection to improve the stability of aircraft etc.

final *adj.* **1** at the end, coming last. **2** conclusive. ● *n.* **1** last heat or game. **2** last edition of a day's newspaper. **3** (*pl.*) final exams. □ **finally** *adv.*, **finality** *n.*

> ■ *adj.* **1** closing, concluding, eventual, finishing, last, terminal, terminating, ultimate. **2** conclusive, decisive, definitive, irrevocable, unalterable.

finale /finaáli/ *n.* final section of a drama or musical composition.

finalist *n.* competitor in a final.

finalize *v.* **1** bring to an end. **2** put in final form.

> ■ clinch, complete, conclude, put the finishing touches to, settle.

finance *n.* **1** management of money. **2** (*pl.*) money resources. ● *v.* provide money for. □ **financial** *adj.*, **financially** *adv.*

> ■ *n.* **2** (**finances**) assets, capital, cash, funds, money, resources, wealth, *colloq.* wherewithal. ● *v.* back, fund, invest in, pay for, subsidize, underwrite.

financier *n.* person engaged in financing businesses.

finch *n.* a kind of small bird.

find *v.* (**found**) **1** discover by effort or chance. **2** succeed in obtaining. **3** discover by experience. **4** consider to be. **5** (of a jury etc.) decide and declare. ● *n.* **1** discovery. **2** thing found. □ **find out** detect, discover. **finder** *n.*

> ■ *v.* **1** chance on, come across, dig out, dig up, discover, encounter, ferret out, happen on, hit on, light on, locate, trace, track down, turn up, uncover, unearth. **2** achieve, acquire, gain, get, obtain, procure, secure, win. **3** discover, note, notice, observe, perceive, realize, see. **4** consider, deem, judge, think.

fine[1] *n.* money paid as a penalty. ● *v.* punish by a fine.

fine[2] *adj.* **1** of high quality or merit. **2** bright, free from rain. **3** thin, delicate. **4** subtle. **5** in small particles. ● *adv.* finely. □ **finely** *adv.*, **fineness** *n.*

> ■ *adj.* **1** choice, first-class, first-rate, prime, select, superior, supreme; admirable, commendable, excellent, exceptional, exquisite, good, great, magnificent, marvellous, meritorious, outstanding, splendid. **2** bright, clear, cloudless, dry, fair, nice, pleasant, sunny. **3** delicate, diaphanous,

filmy, flimsy, fragile, gauzy, thin, translucent. **4** nice, precise, subtle. **5** powdery.

finery n. showy clothes etc.

finesse n. **1** delicate manipulation. **2** tact.

finger n. **1** each of the five parts extending from each hand. **2** any of these other than the thumb. **3** finger-like object. **4** measure (about 20 mm) of alcohol in a glass. ● v. touch or feel with the fingers. □ **finger-stall** n. sheath to cover an injured finger.

fingerprint n. impression of ridges on the pad of a finger.

finish v. **1** bring to an end, complete. **2** consume or use all of. **3** come to an end, cease. **4** reach the end, esp. of a race. ● n. **1** last stage. **2** point where a race etc. ends. **3** completed state. □ **finish off 1** (*colloq.*) kill, overcome completely. **2** consume the whole of.

■ v. **1** accomplish, achieve, bring to an end, carry out, clinch, complete, fulfil, round off. **2** consume, devour, drain, drink (up), eat (up), finish off, get *or* go through, polish off, use (up). **3** cease, close, come to an end, conclude, end, halt, stop, terminate, wind up; culminate. ● n. **1** close, completion, conclusion, culmination, end, ending, finale, termination, winding-up.

finite adj. limited.

■ bounded, countable, delimited, limited, measurable, restricted.

fiord /fyord/ n. narrow inlet of the sea esp. in Norway.

fir n. evergreen cone-bearing tree.

fire n. **1** state of combustion. **2** flame. **3** destructive burning. **4** burning fuel. **5** electric or gas heater. **6** firing of guns. **7** angry or excited feeling. ● v. **1** send a bullet or shell from a (gun). **2** detonate. **3** discharge (a missile). **4** dismiss from a job. **5** set fire to. **6** catch fire. **7** excite. **8** bake (pottery etc.). □ **fire brigade** organized group of people employed to extinguish fires. **fire engine** vehicle with equipment for putting out fires. **fire escape** special staircase or apparatus for escape from a burning building.

■ n. **3** blaze, conflagration, flames, holocaust, inferno. **6** barrage, bombardment, cannonade, firing, fusillade, gunfire, salvo, shelling, volley. **7** animation, ardour, energy, enthusiasm, excitement, fervour, intensity, passion, spirit, vigour. ● v. **1** open fire, shoot. **2** detonate, explode, let off, set off. **3** catapult, discharge, launch, propel. **4**

discharge, dismiss, *colloq.* give a person the boot *or* the sack, give a person notice, lay off, make redundant, *colloq.* sack, throw out. **5** burn, ignite, kindle, set alight, set fire to, set on fire. **7** animate, awaken, excite, inflame, inspire, motivate, rouse, stimulate, stir (up).

firearm n. gun, pistol, etc.

firebreak n. open space as an obstacle to the spread of fire.

firedamp n. explosive mixture of methane and air in mines.

firefly n. phosphorescent beetle.

fireman n. member of a fire brigade.

fireplace n. recess with a chimney for a domestic fire.

fireside n. space round a fireplace.

firework n. device containing chemicals that burn or explode spectacularly.

firing squad group detailed to shoot a condemned person.

firm¹ n. business company.

■ business, company, concern, corporation, establishment, organization, partnership.

firm² adj. **1** not yielding when pressed or pushed. **2** fixed, steady. **3** resolute. **4** securely established. ● v. make or become firm. □ **firmness** n.

■ adj. **1** compact, compressed, dense, hard, inflexible, rigid, set, solid, solidified, stiff, unyielding. **2** anchored, fast, fixed, immovable, moored, secure, stable, steady, tight. **3** adamant, decided, determined, dogged, resolute, resolved, stubborn, unshakeable, unwavering. **4** abiding, constant, devoted, enduring, faithful, longstanding, staunch, steadfast.

firmament n. sky with its clouds and stars.

first adj. coming before all others in time or order or importance. ● n. **1** first thing or occurrence. **2** first day of a month. ● adv. before all others or another. □ **at first** at the beginning. **first aid** treatment given for an injury etc. before a doctor arrives. **first-class** adj. & adv. **1** of the best quality. **2** in the best category of accommodation. **first cousin** (see **cousin**). **first name** personal name. **first-rate** adj. excellent.

■ adj. earliest, oldest, original; basic, elementary, fundamental, initial, introductory, opening, preliminary, rudimentary; chief, foremost, head, key, leading, main, paramount, pre-eminent, premier, primary, prime, principal.

firstly *adv.* first.

firth *n.* estuary, inlet.

fiscal *adj.* of public revenue.

fish *n.* (*pl.* usu. **fish**) **1** cold-blooded vertebrate living in water. **2** its flesh as food. • *v.* **1** try to catch fish (from). **2** search by reaching into something.

fishery *n.* **1** place where fish are caught or reared. **2** business of fishing.

fishmeal *n.* dried ground fish used as a fertilizer.

fishmonger *n.* shopkeeper who sells fish.

fishy *adj.* (**-ier, -iest**) **1** like fish. **2** causing disbelief or suspicion.

fissile *adj.* **1** tending to split. **2** capable of undergoing nuclear fission.

fission *n.* splitting (esp. of an atomic nucleus, with release of energy).

fissure *n.* cleft.

fist *n.* hand when tightly closed.

fisticuffs *n.* fighting with fists.

fistula *n.* abnormal or artificial passage in the body.

fit[1] *n.* **1** sudden attack of illness or its symptoms, or of convulsions or loss of consciousness. **2** sudden short bout of activity, feeling, etc.
■ **1** attack, bout, convulsion, paroxysm, seizure, spasm. **2** bout, burst, outbreak, outburst, spell.

fit[2] *adj.* (**fitter, fittest**) **1** suitable. **2** right and proper. **3** in good health. • *v.* (**fitted**) **1** be the right shape and size for. **2** put into place. **3** make or be suitable or competent. • *n.* way a thing fits. □ **fitly** *adv.*, **fitness** *n.*
■ *adj.* **1** adapted, appropriate, apt, fitting, suitable, suited. **2** becoming, correct, proper, right. **3** hale, healthy, in good health, *colloq.* in the pink, robust, strong, well. • *v.* **1** connect, insert, join, position, put in place, put together. **3** adapt, adjust, alter, change, modify; prepare, prime, qualify, train.

fitful *adj.* spasmodic, intermittent. □ **fitfully** *adv.*

fitment *n.* piece of fixed furniture.

fitter *n.* **1** person who supervises the fitting of clothes. **2** mechanic.

fitting *adj.* right and proper.

fittings *n.pl.* fixtures, fitments.

five *adj.* & *n.* one more than four.

fiver *n.* (*colloq.*) five-pound note.

fix *v.* **1** put something firmly in place. **2** establish, specify. **3** repair. **4** direct (eyes etc.) steadily. **5** (*colloq.*) arrange fraudulently. • *n.* **1** awkward situation. **2** position determined by taking bearings. □ **fix up 1** organize. **2** provide. **fixer** *n.*
■ *v.* **1** affix, anchor, attach, fasten, make fast, secure, stick, pin. **2** agree on, arrange, arrive at, conclude, decide, establish, name, organize, set, settle, specify. **3** adjust, cure, emend, mend, patch up, put right, rectify, remedy, repair. **5** *colloq.* fiddle, rig. • *n.* **1** catch-22, difficulty, dilemma, *colloq.* hole, *colloq.* jam, mess, *colloq.* pickle, plight, predicament, quandary.

fixated *adj.* having an obsession.

fixation *n.* **1** fixing. **2** obsession.

fixative *n.* & *adj.* (substance) for keeping things in position, or preventing fading or evaporation.

fixedly *adv.* intently.

fixity *n.* fixed state, stability, permanence.

fixture *n.* **1** thing fixed in position. **2** firmly established person or thing.

fizz *v.* hiss or splutter, esp. when gas escapes in bubbles from a liquid. • *n.* **1** effervescence. **2** fizzing drink. □ **fizziness** *n.*, **fizzy** *adj.*
■ *v.* bubble, effervesce, fizzle, froth, hiss, sizzle, splutter, sputter.

fizzle *v.* fizz feebly. □ **fizzle out** end feebly or unsuccessfully.

flab *n.* (*colloq.*) flabbiness, fat.

flabbergast *v.* (*colloq.*) astound.

flabby *adj.* (**-ier, -iest**) fat and limp, not firm. □ **flabbiness** *n.*

flaccid *adj.* loose or wrinkled, not firm. □ **flaccidity** *n.*

flag *n.* **1** piece of cloth attached by one edge to a staff or rope, used as a signal or symbol. **2** similarly shaped device. **3** flagstone. • *v.* (**flagged**) **1** droop. **2** lose vigour. **3** mark or signal (as) with a flag. □ **flag day** day on which small emblems are sold for a charity.
■ *n.* **1** banner, colours, ensign, pennant, pennon, standard, streamer. • *v.* **1** droop, sag, wilt. **2** grow tired, tire, weaken; decline, die away, diminish, dwindle, ebb, fade, fail, languish, subside, wane.

flagellate *v.* whip, flog. □ **flagellant** *n.*, **flagellation** *n.*

flageolet /flájǝlét/ *n.* small flute.

flagged *adj.* paved with flagstones.

flagon *n.* large bottle or other vessel for wine, cider, etc.

flagrant /fláygrǝnt/ *adj.* (of an offence or offender) very bad and obvious. □ **flagrantly** *adv.*

flagship n. 1 admiral's ship. 2 principal shop, product, etc.

flagstone n. large paving-stone.

flail n. implement formerly used for threshing grain. ● v. thrash or swing about wildly.

flair n. natural ability.

> ■ ability, aptitude, bent, genius, gift, instinct, knack, skill, talent.

flak n. 1 anti-aircraft shells. 2 barrage of criticism.

flake n. small thin piece. ● v. come off in flakes. □ **flake out** (colloq.) faint, fall asleep from exhaustion. **flaky** adj.

> ■ bit, chip, fragment, particle, piece, scale, shaving, sliver, wafer.

flamboyant adj. showy in appearance or manner. □ **flamboyantly** adv., **flamboyance** n.

> ■ colourful, elaborate, extravagant, flashy, gaudy, ornate, ostentatious, showy, theatrical.

flame n. bright tongue-shaped portion of gas burning visibly. ● v. 1 burn with flames. 2 become bright red. □ **old flame** (colloq.) former sweetheart.

flamenco n. (pl. **-os**) Spanish style of singing and dancing.

flamingo n. (pl. **-os**) wading bird with long legs and pink feathers.

flammable adj. able to be set on fire. □ **flammability** n.

flan n. open pastry or sponge case with filling.

flange n. projecting rim.

flank n. side, esp. of the body between ribs and hip. ● v. place or be at the side of.

flannel n. 1 woollen fabric. 2 face flannel. 3 (pl.) trousers of flannel. 4 (sl.) nonsense, flattery. ● v. (flannelled) (sl.) flatter.

flannelette n. napped cotton fabric like flannel.

flap v. (flapped) 1 move up and down with a sharp sound. 2 (colloq.) show agitation. ● n. 1 act or sound of flapping. 2 hanging or hinged piece. 3 (colloq.) agitation.

flare v. 1 blaze with bright unsteady flame. 2 burst into activity or anger. 3 widen outwards. ● n. 1 sudden blaze. 2 device producing flame as a signal or illumination. 3 flared shape.

> ■ v. 1 blaze, burn, flame, flash, flicker, gleam, glitter, shine, sparkle. 2 blow up, erupt, explode. 3 broaden, spread out, swell, widen.

flash v. 1 (cause to) emit a sudden bright light. 2 move rapidly. 3 show suddenly or ostentatiously. 4 come suddenly into sight or mind. ● n. 1 sudden burst of flame or light. 2 very brief time. 3 sudden show of wit or feeling. 4 device producing a brief bright light in photography. ● adj. (colloq.) flashy. □ **flash flood** sudden destructive flood.

> ■ v. 1 beam, blaze, flare, flicker, glare, gleam, glimmer, glint, glitter, shimmer, shine, sparkle, twinkle. 2 dart, dash, fly, hasten, hurry, race, run, rush, shoot, speed, sprint, streak, tear, whiz, zoom. 3 display, flaunt, flourish, show off. ● n. 1 blaze, flare, flickering, gleam, glimmer, glint, glitter, shimmer, sparkle, twinkle. 2 instant, minute, moment, split second.

flashback n. change of scene in a story or film to an earlier period.

flashing n. strip of metal covering a joint in a roof etc.

flashlight n. electric torch.

flashpoint n. temperature at which a vapour ignites.

flashy adj. (**-ier, -iest**) showy, gaudy. □ **flashily** adv.

flask n. 1 narrow-necked bottle. 2 vacuum flask.

flat adj. (flatter, flattest) 1 horizontal, level. 2 absolute. 3 monotonous. 4 dejected. 5 having lost effervescence or power to generate electric current. 6 below the correct pitch in music. ● adv. 1 lying at full length. 2 completely, exactly. ● n. 1 flat surface, level ground. 2 set of rooms on one floor, used as a residence. 3 (sign indicating) music note lowered by a semitone. □ **flatfish** n. fish with a flattened body, swimming on its side. **flat out** 1 at top speed. 2 with maximum effort.

> ■ adj. 1 even, horizontal, level, plane, smooth, unbroken. 2 absolute, categorical, definite, direct, downright, firm, outright, plain, unambiguous, unequivocal, unqualified. 3 boring, dead, dull, featureless, insipid, lacklustre, lifeless, monotonous, prosaic, tedious, unexciting, uninteresting. 4 dejected, depressed, dispirited, listless, low. ● adv. 1 outstretched, prone, prostrate, recumbent, spread-eagled, supine.

flatlet n. small flat.

flatten v. make or become flat.

flatter v. **1** compliment insincerely. **2** enhance the appearance of. □ **flatterer** n., **flattery** n.
■ **1** butter up, compliment, curry favour with, fawn on, sl. flannel, overpraise, colloq. suck up to, toady to. **2** become, set off, suit.

flatulent adj. causing or suffering from formation of gas in the digestive tract. □ **flatulence** n.

flaunt v. display proudly or ostentatiously.

flautist n. flute player.

flavour n. **1** distinctive taste. **2** characteristic quality. ● v. give flavour to.
■ n. **1** piquancy, savour, tang, taste. **2** air, atmosphere, character, feeling, quality, spirit, stamp, style. ● v. season, spice.

flavouring n. substance used to give flavour to food.

flaw n. imperfection. ● v. spoil with a flaw. □ **flawless** adj.
■ n. blemish, blot, defect, error, failing, fault, imperfection, mistake, shortcoming, weakness. □ **flawless** clean, faultless, immaculate, impeccable, perfect, pristine, pure, spotless, undamaged, unsoiled, unsullied, untarnished.

flax n. **1** blue-flowered plant. **2** textile fibre from its stem.

flaxen adj. **1** made of flax. **2** (of hair) pale yellow.

flay v. **1** strip off the skin or hide of. **2** criticize severely.

flea n. small jumping blood-sucking insect. □ **flea market** market for second-hand goods.

fleck n. **1** small patch of colour or light. **2** speck. ● v. mark with flecks.

fled see **flee**.

fledged adj. (of a young bird) able to fly.

fledgeling n. young bird.

flee v. (**fled**) run away (from).
■ abscond, bolt, dash away, decamp, sl. do a bunk, escape, fly, make a getaway, make off, run away, rush away, colloq. scram, colloq. skedaddle, take flight, take to one's heels, vanish.

fleece n. sheep's woolly coat. ● v. rob by trickery. □ **fleecy** adj.

fleet¹ n. **1** navy. **2** ships sailing together. **3** vehicles or aircraft under one command or ownership.
■ **2** armada, convoy, flotilla, squadron.

fleet² adj. moving swiftly, nimble.

fleeting adj. transitory, brief.
■ brief, ephemeral, fugitive, impermanent, momentary, passing, short, transient, transitory.

flesh n. **1** soft substance of animal bodies. **2** body as opposed to mind or soul. **3** pulpy part of fruits and vegetables. □ **flesh and blood 1** human nature. **2** one's relatives. **flesh wound** superficial wound.

fleshy adj. (-**ier**, -**iest**) **1** of or like flesh. **2** having much flesh.

flew see **fly**².

flex¹ v. **1** bend. **2** move (a muscle) to bend a joint. □ **flexion** n.

flex² n. flexible insulated wire for carrying electric current.

flexible adj. **1** able to bend easily. **2** adaptable. □ **flexibly** adv., **flexibility** n.
■ **1** bendable, elastic, lithe, plastic, pliable, pliant, resilient, springy, stretchable, supple, whippy, willowy, yielding. **2** accommodating, adaptable, amenable, compliant, cooperative, easygoing.

flexitime n. system of flexible working hours.

flick n. quick light blow. ● v. move or strike with a flick. □ **flick knife** knife with a blade that springs out. **flick through** glance through by turning over (pages etc.) rapidly.

flicker v. **1** burn or shine unsteadily. **2** occur briefly. **3** quiver. ● n. **1** flickering light or movement. **2** brief occurrence.

flier n. = **flyer**.

flight¹ n. **1** flying. **2** movement or path of a thing through the air. **3** journey by air. **4** birds or aircraft flying together. **5** series of stairs. **6** feathers etc. on a dart or arrow. □ **flight deck 1** cockpit of a large aircraft. **2** deck of an aircraft carrier. **flight recorder** electronic device in an aircraft recording details of its flight.

flight² n. hasty retreat.
■ departure, escape, exit, exodus, getaway, retreat.

flightless adj. unable to fly.

flighty adj. (-**ier**, -**iest**) frivolous.

flimsy adj. (-**ier**, -**iest**) **1** light and thin. **2** fragile. **3** unconvincing. □ **flimsily** adv., **flimsiness** n.
■ **1** delicate, diaphanous, filmy, fine, light, sheer, thin. **2** breakable, fragile, frail, gimcrack, makeshift, ramshackle, rickety, shaky. **3** feeble, implausible, inadequate, lame, poor, unbelievable, unconvincing, unsatisfactory, weak.

flinch v. draw back in fear, wince.
■ blench, cower, cringe, draw back, quail, recoil, shrink back, shy away, start, wince.

fling v. (**flung**) 1 throw violently or hurriedly. 2 rush angrily or violently. ● n. spell of indulgence in pleasure.
■ v. 1 cast, colloq. chuck, colloq. heave, hurl, launch, lob, pitch, colloq. sling, throw, toss.

flint n. 1 very hard stone. 2 piece of hard alloy producing sparks when struck.

flip v. (**flipped**) 1 flick. 2 toss with a sharp movement. ● n. action of flipping. ● adj. (colloq.) glib, flippant.

flippant adj. not showing proper seriousness. □ **flippantly** adv., **flippancy** n.
■ cheeky, disrespectful, facetious, colloq. flip, frivolous, impertinent, impudent, irreverent, pert, saucy.

flipper n. 1 sea animal's limb used in swimming. 2 large flat rubber attachment to the foot for underwater swimming.

flirt v. 1 behave in a frivolously amorous way. 2 toy (with an idea etc.). ● n. person who flirts. □ **flirtation** n., **flirtatious** adj.
■ v. 1 dally, philander. 2 play, toy, trifle. ● n. coquette, philanderer, tease.

flit v. (**flitted**) 1 fly or move lightly and quickly. 2 decamp stealthily. ● n. act of flitting.

flitter v. flit about.

float v. 1 rest or drift on the surface of liquid. 2 start (a company or scheme). 3 have or allow (currency) to have a variable rate of exchange. ● n. 1 thing designed to float on liquid. 2 money for minor expenditure or giving change.

flocculent adj. like tufts of wool.

flock[1] n. 1 number of animals or birds together. 2 large number of people, congregation. ● v. gather or go in a flock.
■ n. 1 drove, gaggle, herd, pack, pride, school, shoal, skein, swarm. 2 assembly, band, body, bunch, cluster, company, congregation, crowd, gang, gathering, group, horde, host, multitude, throng, troop. ● v. assemble, collect, congregate, crowd, gather, herd, mass, meet, swarm, throng.

flock[2] n. shredded wool, cotton, etc. used as stuffing.

floe n. sheet of floating ice.

flog v. (**flogged**) 1 beat severely. 2 (sl.) sell. □ **flogging** n.
■ 1 beat, cane, flagellate, flay, lash, scourge, thrash, whip.

flood n. 1 overflow of water on a place usually dry. 2 great outpouring. 3 inflow of the tide. 4 (**the Flood**) the flood described in the Old Testament. ● v. 1 cover or fill with a flood, overflow. 2 come in great quantities.
■ n. 1 deluge, inundation, overflow, overflowing. 2 flow, outpouring, rush, spate, stream, surge, tide, torrent. ● v. 1 deluge, drown, engulf, fill, inundate, overflow, submerge, swamp. 2 flow, gush, pour, surge, swarm.

floodlight n. lamp producing a broad bright beam. ● v. (**floodlit**) illuminate with this.

floor n. 1 lower surface of a room. 2 right to speak in an assembly. 3 storey. ● v. 1 provide with a floor. 2 knock down. 3 baffle. □ **floor show** cabaret.

flooring n. material for a floor.

flop v. (**flopped**) 1 hang or fall heavily and loosely. 2 (sl.) be a failure. ● n. 1 flopping movement or sound. 2 (sl.) failure.

floppy adj. (**-ier**, **-iest**) tending to flop. □ **floppy disk** flexible disk for storing computer data.

flora n. plants of an area or period.

floral adj. of flowers.

floret n. each of the small flowers of a composite flower.

florid adj. 1 ornate. 2 ruddy.

florist n. person who sells or grows flowers as a business.

flotation n. floating, esp. of a commercial venture.

flotilla n. 1 small fleet. 2 fleet of small ships.

flotsam n. floating wreckage. □ **flotsam and jetsam** odds and ends.

flounce[1] v. go in an impatient annoyed manner. ● n. flouncing movement.

flounce[2] n. deep frill attached by its upper edge. □ **flounced** adj.

flounder[1] n. small flatfish.

flounder[2] v. 1 move clumsily, as in mud. 2 become confused when trying to do something.
■ 1 blunder, fumble, grope, lurch, stagger, struggle, stumble.

flour n. fine powder made from grain, used in cooking. ● v. cover with flour. □ **floury** adj.

flourish v. **1** grow vigorously. **2** prosper. **3** wave dramatically. ● n. **1** dramatic gesture. **2** ornamental curve. **3** fanfare.
  ■ v. **1** bloom, blossom, burgeon, flower, thrive. **2** be successful, boom, do well, prosper, succeed, thrive. **3** brandish, flaunt, shake, swing, twirl, wave, wield.

flout v. disobey openly.

flow v. **1** glide along as a stream. **2** gush out. **3** proceed evenly. **4** hang loosely. ● n. **1** flowing movement or liquid. **2** amount flowing. **3** inflow of the tide. □ **flow chart** diagram showing a sequence of processes.
  ■ v. **1** course, glide, go, run, stream, swirl, trickle. **2** cascade, flood, gush, spew, spout, spurt, squirt, stream, well. ● n. **1** current, drift, movement, stream. **2** gush, outflow, outpouring, rush, surge.

flower n. **1** part of a plant where fruit or seed develops. **2** plant grown for this. **3** best part. ● v. produce flowers.
  ■ n. **1** bloom, blossom, floret. ● v. bloom, blossom, burgeon, come out, effloresce, open, unfold.

flowered adj. ornamented with a design of flowers.

flowery adj. **1** full of flowers. **2** full of ornamental phrases.

flown see **fly²**.

flu n. (colloq.) influenza.

fluctuate v. vary, esp. irregularly. □ **fluctuation** n.
  ■ alternate, change, oscillate, see-saw, shift, swing, vacillate, vary, waver.

flue n. **1** smoke-duct in a chimney. **2** channel for conveying heat.

fluent adj. speaking or spoken smoothly and readily. □ **fluently** adv., **fluency** n.
  ■ articulate, eloquent, glib, voluble; effortless, flowing, smooth.

fluff n. soft mass of fibres or down. ● v. **1** shake into a soft mass. **2** (sl.) bungle. □ **fluffy** adj.

fluid adj. **1** consisting of particles that move freely among themselves. **2** not stable. ● n. fluid substance. □ **fluidity** n.
  ■ adj. **1** aqueous, flowing, liquefied, liquid, molten, runny. **2** changeable, fluctuating, shifting, uncertain, unstable, variable.

fluke¹ n. success due to luck.

fluke² n. **1** barbed arm of an anchor etc. **2** lobe of a whale's tail.

flummox v. (colloq.) baffle.

flung see **fling**.

fluoresce v. be or become fluorescent.

fluorescent adj. taking in radiations and sending them out as light. □ **fluorescence** n.

fluoridate v. add fluoride to (a water supply). □ **fluoridation** n.

fluoride n. compound of fluorine with metal.

fluorine n. pungent corrosive gas.

flurry n. **1** short rush of wind, rain, or snow. **2** commotion. **3** nervous agitation. ● v. fluster.

flush¹ v. **1** become red in the face. **2** cleanse or dispose of with a flow of water. ● n. **1** blush. **2** rush of emotion. **3** rush of water. ● adj. **1** level, in the same plane. **2** (colloq.) having plenty of money.
  ■ v. **1** blush, colour, glow, go red, redden.

flush² v. drive out from cover.

fluster v. make nervous or confused. ● n. flustered state.
  ■ v. agitate, bewilder, bother, confuse, discomfit, disconcert, disturb, perplex, perturb, put off, puzzle, colloq. rattle, ruffle, colloq. throw, unsettle, upset.

flute n. **1** wind instrument, pipe with a mouth-hole at the side. **2** ornamental groove.

flutter v. **1** move wings hurriedly. **2** wave or flap quickly. **3** (of the heart) beat irregularly. ● n. **1** fluttering movement or beat. **2** nervous excitement. **3** (sl.) small bet.

fluvial adj. of or found in rivers.

flux n. **1** flow. **2** continuous succession of changes. **3** substance mixed with metal etc. to assist fusion.

fly¹ n. two-winged insect. □ **fly-blown** adj. tainted by flies' eggs.

fly² v. (flew, flown) **1** move through the air on wings or in an aircraft. **2** control the flight of. **3** go quickly. **4** flee. **5** display (a flag). ● n. **1** flying. **2** (pl.) fastening down the front of trousers. □ **fly-post** v. display (posters etc.) in unauthorized places. **fly-tip** v. dump (waste) illegally.
  ■ v. **1** soar, take to the air, take wing, wing. **2** control, operate, pilot. **3** dart, dash, hasten, hurry, race, run, scoot, shoot, speed, sprint, tear, whiz, zoom. **4** abscond, bolt, decamp, sl. do a bunk, escape, flee, make a getaway, make off, run away, rush away, colloq. skedaddle, take flight, take to one's heels.

flyer n. **1** one that flies. **2** airman. **3** fast animal or vehicle.

flying adj. able to fly. □ **flying buttress** one based on separate structure, usu.

forming an arch. **flying colours** great credit. **flying fox** fruit-eating bat. **flying saucer** unidentified object reported as seen in the sky.

flyleaf *n.* blank leaf at the beginning or end of a book.

flyover *n.* bridge carrying one road or railway over another.

flywheel *n.* heavy wheel revolving on a shaft to regulate machinery.

foal *n.* young of the horse. ● *v.* give birth to a foal.

foam *n.* **1** collection of small bubbles. **2** spongy rubber or plastic. ● *v.* form foam. □ **foamy** *adj.*

■ *n.* **1** bubbles, effervescence, fizz, froth, lather, spume, suds.

fob *v.* (**fobbed**) **fob off 1** palm off. **2** get (a person) to accept something inferior.

focal *adj.* of or at a focus.

fo'c's'le /fóks'l/ *n.* forecastle.

focus *n.* (*pl.* **-cuses** or **-ci**) **1** point where rays meet. **2** distance at which an object is most clearly seen. **3** adjustment on a lens to produce a clear image. **4** centre of activity or interest. ● *v.* (**focused**) **1** adjust the focus of. **2** bring into focus. **3** concentrate.

fodder *n.* food for animals.

foe *n.* enemy.

foetus /féetəss/ *n.* (*pl.* **-tuses**) developed embryo in a womb or egg. □ **foetal** *adj.*

fog *n.* thick mist. ● *v.* (**fogged**) cover or become covered with fog or condensed vapour. □ **foghorn** *n.* horn warning ships in fog. **foggy** *adj.*

fogey *n.* (also **fogy**) (*pl.* **-eys** or **-ies**) old-fashioned person.

foible *n.* harmless peculiarity in a person's character.

foil[1] *n.* **1** paper-thin sheet of metal. **2** person or thing emphasizing another's qualities by contrast.

foil[2] *v.* thwart, frustrate.

■ baffle, baulk, check, defeat, frustrate, hamper, hinder, impede, outwit, *sl.* scupper, stymie, thwart.

foil[3] *n.* long thin sword with a button on the point.

foist *v.* impose (an unwelcome person or thing).

fold[1] *v.* **1** bend so that one part lies on another. **2** clasp, embrace. **3** cease to function. ● *n.* **1** folded part. **2** line or hollow made by folding. ■ *v.* **1** bend, crease, crimp, gather, pleat. **2** clasp, embrace, enclose, enfold, envelop, hold, hug, wrap. **3** close down, go bank-

rupt, *colloq.* go broke, go out of business, go under, fail. ● *n.* **1** crease, pleat; crinkle, pucker, wrinkle.

fold[2] *n.* enclosure for sheep. ● *v.* enclose (sheep) in a fold.

folder *n.* **1** folding cover for loose papers. **2** leaflet.

foliage *n.* leaves.

foliate *v.* split into thin layers. □ **foliation** *n.*

folk *n.* **1** people. **2** (*pl.*) one's relatives. □ **folk dance, song** dance or song in the traditional style of a country. **folk-tale** *n.* popular or traditional story.

■ **1** citizenry, people, population; clan, ethnic group, race, tribe. **2** (**folks**) family, parents, kin, kinsfolk, kith and kin, relations, relatives.

folklore *n.* traditional beliefs and tales of a community.

folksy *adj.* informal and friendly.

follicle *n.* small cavity, esp. for a hair-root. □ **follicular** *adj.*

follow *v.* **1** go or come after. **2** go along (a road etc.). **3** accept the ideas of. **4** take an interest in the progress of. **5** grasp the meaning of. **6** be a natural consequence of. □ **follow suit** follow a person's example. **follow up** investigate further. **follow-up** *n.* **follower** *n.*

■ **1** come or go after, walk behind; chase, dog, pursue, shadow, stalk, *colloq.* tail, track, trail; replace, succeed, supersede, supplant, take the place of. **3** abide by, accept, adhere to, be guided by, comply with, conform to, heed, obey, observe. **5** appreciate, comprehend, fathom, *colloq.* get, grasp, see, take in, understand. **6** develop, ensue, result.

following *n.* group of supporters. ● *adj.* now to be mentioned. ● *prep.* as a sequel to.

folly *n.* **1** foolishness. **2** foolish act. **3** ornamental building.

■ **1** absurdity, foolishness, idiocy, insanity, lunacy, madness, silliness, stupidity.

foment *v.* stir up (trouble). □ **fomentation** *n.*

■ excite, ferment, incite, instigate, kindle, provoke, stimulate, stir up, whip up.

fond *adj.* **1** affectionate, doting. **2** foolishly optimistic. □ **fondly** *adv.*, **fondness** *n.*

■ **1** adoring, affectionate, caring, devoted, doting, loving, tender, warm. **2** credulous, foolish, naive.

fondant n. soft sugary sweet.

fondle v. handle lovingly.

  ■ caress, cuddle, pat, pet, stroke.

fondue n. dish of flavoured melted cheese.

font n. basin in a church, holding water for baptism.

fontanelle n. soft spot where the bones of an infant's skull have not yet grown together.

food n. substance (esp. solid) taken into the body of an animal or plant to maintain its life.

  ■ nourishment, nutriment, sustenance; comestibles, eatables, foodstuffs, sl. grub, provisions, refreshments.

foodstuff n. substance used as food.

fool n. 1 foolish person. 2 creamy fruit-flavoured pudding. ● v. 1 joke, tease. 2 trick. □ **fool about** play about idly. **make a fool of** make (a person) look foolish, trick.

  ■ n. 1 ass, blockhead, booby, buffoon, colloq. chump, colloq. clot, dolt, sl. dope, colloq. duffer, halfwit, idiot, imbecile, jackass, ninny, colloq. nitwit, sl. sap, simpleton, sl. twerp, sl. twit, sl. wally. ● v. 1 banter, jest, joke, colloq. kid, tease. 2 colloq. bamboozle, sl. con, deceive, delude, dupe, hoax, hoodwink, make a fool of, pull the wool over someone's eyes, take in, trick.

foolery n. foolish acts.

foolhardy adj. taking foolish risks.

foolish adj. lacking good sense or judgement. □ **foolishly** adv., **foolishness** n.

  ■ absurd, asinine, sl. barmy, sl. batty, crazy, daft, fatuous, foolhardy, harebrained, idiotic, ill-considered, imbecilic, imprudent, inane, incautious, laughable, ludicrous, mad, misguided, nonsensical, rash, reckless, ridiculous, senseless, short-sighted, silly, stupid, thoughtless, unintelligent, unwise, witless.

foolproof adj. simple and easy to use, unable to go wrong.

foot n. (pl. **feet**) 1 part of the leg below the ankle. 2 lower part or end. 3 measure of length, = 12 inches (30.48 cm). 4 unit of rhythm in verse. ● v. 1 walk. 2 be the one to pay (a bill). □ **foot-and-mouth disease** contagious virus disease of cattle.

football n. 1 large round or elliptical inflated ball. 2 game played with this.

□ **football pool** form of gambling on the results of football matches. **footballer** n.

footfall n. sound of footsteps.

foothills n.pl. low hills near the bottom of a mountain or range.

foothold n. 1 place just wide enough for one's foot. 2 small but secure position gained.

footing n. 1 foothold. 2 balance. 3 status, conditions.

footlights n.pl. row of lights along the front of a stage floor.

footling adj. (sl.) trivial.

footloose adj. independent, without responsibilities.

footman n. manservant, usu. in livery.

footnote n. note printed at the bottom of a page.

footpath n. path for pedestrians.

footprint n. impression left by a foot or shoe.

footsore adj. with feet sore from walking.

footstep n. 1 step. 2 sound of this.

footwork n. manner of moving or using the feet in sports etc.

fop n. dandy.

for prep. 1 in place of. 2 as the price or penalty of. 3 in defence or favour of. 4 with a view to. 5 in the direction of. 6 intended to be received or used by. 7 because of. 8 during. ● conj. because.

forage v. 1 go searching. 2 rummage. ● n. 1 foraging. 2 food for horses and cattle.

foray n. sudden attack, raid. ● v. make a foray.

forbade see **forbid**.

forbear v. (**forbore**, **forborne**) refrain (from).

forbearance n. patience, tolerance.

forbearing adj. patient, tolerant.

forbid v. (**forbade**, **forbidden**) 1 refuse to allow. 2 order not to.

  ■ 1 ban, bar, disallow, outlaw, prohibit, proscribe, rule out, veto.

forbidding adj. having an uninviting appearance, stern.

  ■ grim, hostile, menacing, ominous, sinister, stern, threatening, unfriendly, uninviting.

force n. 1 strength, power. 2 intense effort. 3 compulsion. 4 effectiveness. 5 group of troops or police. 6 organized or available group. 7 influence tending to cause movement. ● v. 1 use force upon, esp. in order to get or do something. 2 break open by force. 3 propel. 4 strain to the utmost, overstrain. **5** produce by effort. **6** impose.

■ *n.* **1** dynamism, energy, impact, intensity, might, muscle, potency, power, strength, vigour, violence. **2** effort, exertion, strain. **3** coercion, compulsion, constraint, pressure. **4** cogency, effectiveness, persuasiveness, power, validity, weight. **5** army, corps, detachment, division, squad, squadron, regiment, unit. ● *v.* **1** coerce, compel, constrain, dragoon, drive, impel, make, oblige, press-gang, pressurize, railroad. **2** break open, jemmy, prise open, wrench open. **3** drive, propel, push, thrust. **6** foist, impose, inflict.

forceful *adj.* **1** powerful and vigorous. **2** cogent. □ **forcefully** *adv.*, **forcefulness** *n.*
■ **1** dynamic, energetic, mighty, potent, powerful, strong, vigorous. **2** cogent, compelling, convincing, effective, persuasive.

forceps *n.* (*pl.* **forceps**) pincers used in surgery etc.

forcible *adj.* done by force. □ **forcibly** *adv.*

ford *n.* shallow place where a stream may be crossed. ● *v.* cross thus.

fore *adj.* & *adv.* in, at, or towards the front. ● *n.* fore part. □ **to the fore** in front, conspicuous.

forearm¹ *n.* arm from the elbow downwards.

forearm² *v.* arm or prepare in advance against possible danger.

forebears *n.pl.* ancestors.

foreboding *n.* feeling that trouble is coming.
■ intimation, premonition, presentiment; anxiety, apprehension, dread, fear, misgiving.

forecast *v.* (**forecast**) tell in advance (what is likely to happen). ● *n.* statement that does this. □ **forecaster** *n.*
■ *v.* foresee, foretell, predict, presage, prognosticate, prophesy. ● *n.* prediction, prognosis, prognostication, prophecy.

forecastle /fōks'l/ *n.* forward part of certain ships.

foreclose *v.* repossess property when a loan is not duly repaid. □ **foreclosure** *n.*

forecourt *n.* enclosed space in front of a building.

forefathers *n.pl.* ancestors.

forefinger *n.* finger next to the thumb.

forefoot *n.* animal's front foot.

forefront *n.* the very front.

foregoing *adj.* preceding.

foregone *adj.* **foregone conclusion** predictable result.

foreground *n.* part of a scene etc. that is nearest to the observer.

forehand *n.* stroke played with the palm of the hand turned forwards. ● *adj.* of or made with this stroke. □ **forehanded** *adj.*

forehead *n.* part of the face above the eyes.

foreign *adj.* **1** of, from, or dealing with a country that is not one's own. **2** not belonging naturally.
■ **1** alien, exotic, imported, overseas; international.

foreigner *n.* person born in or coming from another country.

foreknowledge *n.* knowledge of a thing before it occurs.

foreleg *n.* animal's front leg.

forelock *n.* lock of hair just above the forehead.

foreman *n.* **1** worker superintending others. **2** president and spokesperson of a jury.

foremost *adj.* **1** most important. **2** most advanced in position or rank. ● *adv.* in the foremost position.
■ *adj.* chief, first, leading, main, paramount, pre-eminent, primary, prime, principal, supreme, top.

forename *n.* first name.

forensic *adj.* of or used in law courts. □ **forensic medicine** medical knowledge used in police investigations etc.

foreplay *n.* stimulation preceding sexual intercourse.

forerunner *n.* person or thing that comes in advance of another which it foreshadows.
■ ancestor, antecedent, herald, precursor, predecessor.

foresee *v.* (**foresaw**, **foreseen**) be aware of or realize beforehand. □ **foreseeable** *adj.*
■ anticipate, envisage, forecast, foretell, predict, prophesy.

foreshadow *v.* be an advance sign of (a future event etc.).

foreshore *n.* shore that the tide flows over.

foreshorten *v.* show or portray with apparent shortening giving an effect of distance.

foresight *n.* ability to foresee and prepare for future needs.

foreskin *n.* loose skin at the end of the penis.

forest n. trees and undergrowth covering a large area.

forestall v. prevent or foil by taking action first.

forestry n. science of planting and caring for forests.

foretaste n. experience in advance of what is to come.

foretell v. (**foretold**) forecast.

forethought n. careful thought and planning for the future.

forewarn v. warn beforehand.

foreword n. introductory remarks in a book.

forfeit n. thing that has to be paid or given up as a penalty. ● v. give or lose as a penalty. ● adj. forfeited. □ **forfeiture** n.
■ n. fee, fine, penalty. ● v. concede, give up, lose, relinquish, surrender.

forgather v. assemble.

forgave see **forgive**.

forge¹ v. advance by effort.

forge² n. 1 blacksmith's workshop. 2 furnace where metal is heated. ● v. 1 shape (metal) by heating and hammering. 2 make a fraudulent copy of. □ **forger** n.
■ v. 1 construct, fashion, hammer out, make, manufacture, shape. 2 copy, counterfeit, fake, falsify.

forgery n. 1 forging. 2 thing forged.
■ 2 copy, counterfeit, fake, imitation, colloq. phoney, sham.

forget v. (**forgot**, **forgotten**) cease to remember or think about. □ **forget-me-not** n. plant with small blue flowers.

forgetful adj. apt to forget. □ **forgetfully** adv., **forgetfulness** n.

forgive v. (**forgave**, **forgiven**) cease to feel angry or resentful towards, pardon. □ **forgivable** adj., **forgiveness** n.
■ absolve, acquit, clear, exonerate, let off, reprieve; condone, disregard, ignore, overlook, pass over; excuse, pardon, make allowances for.

forgo v. (**forwent**, **forgone**) give up, go without.
■ abandon, abstain from, deny oneself, do without, eschew, give up, go without, colloq. pass up, refrain from, sacrifice.

fork n. 1 pronged instrument or tool. 2 thing or part divided like this. 3 each of its divisions. ● v. 1 lift or dig with a fork. 2 separate into two branches. 3 follow one of these branches. □ **fork-lift truck** truck with a forked device for lifting and carrying loads.

forlorn adj. left alone and unhappy. □ **forlorn hope** the only faint hope left. **forlornly** adv.
■ abandoned, alone, bereft, dejected, deserted, desolate, forsaken, friendless, lonely, melancholy, miserable, sad, solitary, sorrowful, unhappy, woebegone, woeful, wretched.

form n. 1 shape, arrangement of parts. 2 visible aspect. 3 kind or variety. 4 customary or correct behaviour. 5 condition of health and training. 6 way in which a thing exists. 7 school class. 8 document with blank spaces for details. 9 bench. ● v. 1 shape, produce. 2 bring into existence. 3 constitute. 4 take shape, be formed. 5 develop.
■ n. 1 appearance, configuration, construction, shape, structure. 2 body, build, figure, physique, shape. 3 brand, category, class, genre, kind, make, sort, type, variety. 4 code, convention, custom, etiquette, manners, practice, procedure, protocol, routine, ritual, rule, tradition, way. 5 condition, health, shape, state. ● v. 1 construct, fabricate, fashion, forge, make, manufacture, model, mould, produce, shape, turn. 2 conceive, concoct, contrive, create, design, devise, dream up, colloq. think up. 3 constitute, make up. 4 appear, arise, develop, emerge, grow, materialize, take shape. 5 acquire, contract, develop.

formal adj. 1 in accordance with rules, convention, or ceremony. 2 regular in design. □ **formally** adv.
■ 1 conventional, customary, correct, established, official, prescribed, proper, set, standard; ceremonial, ceremonious, dignified, solemn, stately.

formaldehyde n. colourless gas used in solution as a preservative and disinfectant.

formality n. 1 being formal. 2 formal act, esp. one required by rules.

formalize v. make formal or official. □ **formalization** n.

format n. 1 shape and size of a book etc. 2 style of arrangement. ● v. (**formatted**) arrange in a format.

formation n. 1 forming. 2 thing formed. 3 particular arrangement.

formative adj. 1 forming. 2 of formation.

former adj. 1 of an earlier period. 2 mentioned first of two.
■ 1 bygone, old, past; earlier, erstwhile, ex-, previous, prior, recent, sometime.

formerly *adv.* in former times.

formidable *adj.* **1** inspiring fear, awe, or respect. **2** difficult to do. □ **formidably** *adv.*

■ **1** alarming, dreadful, fearsome, frightening, frightful, intimidating, terrible, terrifying; awesome, imposing, impressive, redoubtable. **2** arduous, challenging, daunting, difficult, onerous, tough.

formula *n.* (*pl.* **-ae** or **-as**) **1** symbols showing chemical constituents or a mathematical statement. **2** fixed series of words for use on social or ceremonial occasions. **3** list of ingredients. **4** classification of a racing car. □ **formulaic** *adj.*

formulate *v.* express systematically. □ **formulation** *n.*

fornicate *v.* have extramarital sexual intercourse. □ **fornication** *n.,* **fornicator** *n.*

forsake *v.* (**forsook, forsaken**) withdraw one's help or companionship etc. from.

■ abandon, desert, *sl.* ditch, drop, jilt, leave, leave in the lurch, reject.

fort *n.* fortified place or building.

forth *adv.* **1** out. **2** onwards. □ **back and forth** to and fro.

forthcoming *adj.* **1** about to occur or appear. **2** communicative.

forthright *adj.* frank, outspoken.

■ blunt, candid, direct, frank, honest, open, outspoken, plain, straightforward, unequivocal.

forthwith *adv.* immediately.

fortification *n.* **1** fortifying. **2** defensive wall or building etc.

fortify *v.* **1** provide with fortifications. **2** strengthen.

■ **1** defend, guard, protect, safeguard, strengthen. **2** buoy up, cheer, embolden, encourage, hearten, inspire, invigorate, strengthen, sustain.

fortitude *n.* courage in bearing pain or trouble.

■ bravery, courage, determination, endurance, *colloq.* grit, *colloq.* guts, nerve, pluck, resilience, resoluteness, stoicism, strength, valour, will-power.

fortnight *n.* period of two weeks.

fortnightly *adj.* & *adv.* (happening or appearing) once a fortnight.

fortress *n.* fortified building or town.

fortuitous *adj.* happening by chance. □ **fortuitously** *adv.*

fortunate *adj.* lucky, auspicious. □ **fortunately** *adv.*

■ blessed, lucky; advantageous, auspicious, favourable, fortuitous, happy, opportune, promising, propitious, providential, timely.

fortune *n.* **1** chance as a power in humankind's affairs. **2** destiny. **3** prosperity, wealth. **4** (*colloq.*) large sum of money. □ **fortune-teller** *n.* person claiming to foretell one's destiny.

■ **1** accident, chance, destiny, fate, luck. **2** destiny, fate, kismet, lot. **3** affluence, prosperity, riches, wealth.

forty *adj.* & *n.* four times ten. □ **fortieth** *adj.* & *n.*

forum *n.* place or meeting where a public discussion is held.

forward *adj.* **1** directed towards the front or its line of motion. **2** having made more than normal progress. **3** presumptuous. ● *n.* attacking player in football or hockey. ● *adv.* **1** forwards. **2** towards the future. **3** in advance, ahead. ● *v.* **1** send on (a letter, goods) to a final destination. **2** help to advance, promote.

■ *adj.* **1** advancing, onward, progressing. **2** advanced, precocious, well-developed. **3** bold, brash, brazen, cheeky, familiar, impertinent, impudent, insolent, pert, presumptuous, saucy. ● *adv.* **1** ahead, forwards, on, onward, onwards, towards the front. ● *v.* **1** dispatch, mail, post, send on. **2** accelerate, advance, aid, assist, benefit, expedite, further, help the progress of, promote, speed up.

forwards *adv.* **1** towards the front. **2** with forward motion. **3** so as to make progress. **4** with the front foremost.

fossil *n.* hardened remains or traces of a prehistoric animal or plant. ● *adj.* **1** of or like a fossil. **2** (of fuel) extracted from the ground.

fossilize *v.* turn or be turned into a fossil. □ **fossilization** *n.*

foster *v.* **1** promote the growth of. **2** rear (a child that is not one's own). □ **foster-child** *n.* child reared thus. **foster home** home in which a foster-child is reared. **foster-parent** *n.* person who fosters a child.

■ **1** advance, aid, assist, encourage, forward, further, help, promote, stimulate. **2** bring up, look after, raise, rear, take care of.

fought *see* **fight**.

foul *adj.* **1** causing disgust. **2** unfair, against the rules of a game. ● *adv.* unfairly. ● *n.* action that breaks rules. ● *v.* **1** make or become foul. **2** (cause to) become entangled or blocked. **3** commit a foul against. □ **foul-mouthed** *adj.* using foul language. **foully** *adv.*, **foulness** *n.*

■ *adj.* **1** disgusting, *colloq.* horrible, horrid, loathsome, nasty, obnoxious, odious, offensive, repellent, repulsive, revolting, unpleasant, vile; fetid, putrid, rancid, rank, rotten, stinking; contaminated, defiled, dirty, filthy, grimy, polluted, soiled, sordid, squalid, unclean. **2** dirty, dishonest, underhand, unfair, unscrupulous, unsporting, unsportsmanlike.

found¹ *see* **find**.

found² *v.* **1** establish (an institution etc.). **2** base.

■ **1** create, establish, inaugurate, initiate, institute, launch, organize, originate, set up, start. **2** base, build, construct, ground.

found³ *v.* **1** melt or mould (metal or glass). **2** make (an object) in this way.

foundation *n.* **1** base, first layer. **2** (*pl.*) basic principles. **3** act or instance of founding. **4** institution or fund founded.

■ **1** base, bottom, substructure. **2** (**foundations**) basics, elements, essentials, fundamentals, groundwork, principles, rudiments. **3** creation, establishment, formation, founding, inauguration, initiation, institution, origination, setting up. **4** establishment, institute, institution.

founder *v.* **1** stumble or fall. **2** (of a ship) sink. **3** fail completely. ● *n.* person who has founded an institution etc.

■ **1** collapse, fall, lurch, stumble, topple, trip. **2** go down or under, sink. **3** come to grief, go wrong, fail, fall through, *sl.* flop, miscarry, misfire.

foundling *n.* deserted child of unknown parents.

foundry *n.* workshop where metal or glass founding is done.

fount *n.* **1** fountain, source. **2** one size and style of printing type.

fountain *n.* **1** spring or jet of water. **2** structure provided for this. **3** source. □ **fountainhead** *n.* source. **fountain pen** pen that can be filled with ink.

four *adj.* & *n.* one more than three. □ **four-poster** *n.* bed with four posts that support a canopy. **four-wheel drive** motive power acting on all four wheels of a vehicle.

fourfold *adj.* & *adv.* four times as much or as many.

foursome *n.* group of four people.

fourteen *adj.* & *n.* one more than thirteen. □ **fourteenth** *adj.* & *n.*

fourth *adj.* next after the third. ● *n.* **1** fourth thing, class, etc. **2** quarter. □ **fourthly** *adv.*

fowl *n.* kind of bird kept to supply eggs and flesh for food.

fox *n.* **1** wild animal of the dog family with a bushy tail. **2** its fur. **3** crafty person. ● *v.* deceive or puzzle by acting craftily.

foxglove *n.* tall plant with purple or white flowers.

foxhole *n.* small trench as a military shelter.

foxtrot *n.* **1** dance with slow and quick steps. **2** music for this.

foyer /fóyər/ *n.* entrance hall of a theatre, cinema, or hotel.

fracas /frákkaa/ *n.* (*pl.* **fracas**) noisy quarrel or disturbance.

fraction *n.* **1** number that is not a whole number. **2** small part or amount. □ **fractional** *adj.*, **fractionally** *adv.*

fractious *adj.* irritable, peevish.

fracture *n.* break, esp. of bone. ● *v.* break.

fragile *adj.* **1** easily broken. **2** not strong. □ **fragility** *n.*

■ **1** breakable, brittle, delicate, flimsy, frail, insubstantial, rickety. **2** delicate, feeble, frail, weak.

fragment *n.* /frágmənt/ **1** piece broken off something. **2** isolated part. ● *v.* /fragmént/ break into fragments. □ **fragmentation** *n.*

■ *n.* bit, chip, crumb, part, particle, piece, scrap, shard, shred, sliver, snippet, splinter.

fragmentary *adj.* consisting of fragments.

fragrant *adj.* having a pleasant smell. □ **fragrance** *n.*

■ aromatic, balmy, perfumed, redolent, scented, sweet-smelling.

frail *adj.* **1** fragile. **2** physically weak. □ **frailty** *n.*

■ **1** breakable, brittle, delicate, flimsy, fragile, insubstantial. **2** ailing, delicate, feeble, ill, infirm, sickly, unwell, weak.

frame *n.* **1** rigid structure supporting other parts. **2** case or border enclosing a picture or pane of glass etc. **3** single exposure on cine film. ● *v.* **1** put or form a frame round. **2** construct. **3** (*sl.*) arrange false evidence against. □ **frame of mind** temporary state of mind.

■ *n.* **1** framework, shell, skeleton, structure; bodywork, chassis. **2** border, edge, edging, frieze, mount, surround. ● *v.* **1** box in, encase, enclose, surround. **2** assemble, build, construct, fabricate, fashion, make, put up.

framework *n.* supporting frame.

franc *n.* unit of money in France, Belgium, and Switzerland.

franchise *n.* **1** right to vote in public elections. **2** authorization to sell a company's goods or services in a certain area. ● *v.* grant a franchise to.

Franco- *pref.* French.

frank[1] *adj.* showing one's thoughts and feelings openly. □ **frankly** *adv.*, **frankness** *n.*

■ artless, blunt, candid, direct, downright, forthright, honest, open, outspoken, plain, sincere, straightforward, truthful.

frank[2] *v.* mark (a letter etc.) to show that postage has been paid.

frankfurter *n.* smoked sausage.

frankincense *n.* sweet-smelling gum burnt as incense.

frantic *adj.* wildly excited or agitated. □ **frantically** *adv.*

■ delirious, excited, feverish, frenetic, frenzied, hysterical, wild, worked up; agitated, anxious, at one's wits' end, beside oneself, desperate, distraught, *colloq.* fraught, overwrought, panicky, panic-stricken.

fraternal *adj.* of a brother or brothers. □ **fraternally** *adv.*

fraternity *n.* brotherhood.

fraternize *v.* associate with others in a friendly way. □ **fraternization** *n.*

fratricide *n.* killing or killer of own brother or sister. □ **fratricidal** *adj.*

fraud *n.* **1** criminal deception. **2** dishonest trick. **3** person carrying this out.

■ **1** cheating, chicanery, deceit, deception, dishonesty, double-dealing, duplicity, sharp practice, swindling, trickery. **2** hoax, *colloq.* rip-off, ruse, swindle, trick. **3** charlatan, cheat, deceiver, fake, impostor, swindler.

fraudulent *adj.* of, involving, or guilty of fraud. □ **fraudulence** *n.*, **fraudulently** *adv.*

■ bogus, counterfeit, fake, false, falsified, forged, *colloq.* phoney, spurious; cheating,

deceitful, deceptive, dishonest, double-dealing, duplicitous.

fraught *adj.* (*colloq.*) causing or suffering anxiety. □ **fraught with** filled with, involving.

fray[1] *n.* fight, conflict.

fray[2] *v.* **1** make or become worn so that there are loose threads. **2** strain (nerves or temper).

frazzle *n.* exhausted state.

freak *n.* abnormal person or thing. ● *v.* **freak out** (*colloq.*) (cause to) hallucinate or become wildly excited. □ **freakish** *adj.*, **freaky** *adj.*

freckle *n.* light brown spot on the skin. ● *v.* spot or become spotted with freckles. □ **freckled** *adj.*

free *adj.* (**freer**, **freest**) **1** not in the power of another, not a slave. **2** unrestricted, not confined. **3** without charge. **4** not occupied, not in use. **5** lavish. ● *v.* (**freed**) **1** make free. **2** disentangle. □ **free fall** unrestricted fall under the force of gravity. **free from** without, not subject to. **free hand** right of taking what action one chooses. **freehand** *adj.* (of drawing) done without ruler or compasses etc. **free house** pub not controlled by one brewery. **freelance** *v.* & *n.* (person) selling services to various employers. **free-range** *adj.* **1** (of hens) allowed to range freely in search of food. **2** (of eggs) from such hens. **freewheel** *v.* ride a bicycle without pedalling.

■ *adj.* **1** autonomous, democratic, independent, self-governing, self-ruling, sovereign. **2** at large, at liberty, loose, out, unconfined, unconstrained, unencumbered, unfettered, unimpeded, unrestricted, untrammelled; emancipated, liberated, released. **3** complimentary, free of charge, gratis. **4** available, empty, not in use, unoccupied, vacant. **5** bountiful, generous, lavish, liberal, munificent, open-handed, unstinting. ● *v.* **1** emancipate, let go, let loose, liberate, loose, release, set free; unchain, unfetter, unleash, unloose, untie. **2** disengage, disentangle, extricate, release.

freedom *n.* **1** being free. **2** right or power to do as one pleases. **3** unrestricted use. **4** honorary citizenship.

■ **1** autonomy, independence, liberty, self-determination, self-government, sovereignty; emancipation, liberation. **2** ability, authority, discretion, free hand, latitude, leeway, licence, permission, power, privilege, right, scope.

freehold *n.* holding of land or a house etc. in absolute ownership. □ **freeholder** *n.*

Freemason *n.* member of a fraternity for mutual help, with elaborate secret rituals. □ **Freemasonry** *n.*

freesia *n.* fragrant flower.

freeze *v.* (**froze, frozen**) 1 change from liquid to solid by extreme cold. 2 be so cold that water turns to ice. 3 chill or be chilled by extreme cold or fear. 4 preserve by refrigeration. 5 make (assets) unable to be realized. 6 hold (prices or wages) at a fixed level. 7 stop, stand very still. ● *n.* 1 period of freezing weather. 2 freezing of prices etc. □ **freeze-dry** *v.* freeze and dry by evaporation of ice in a vacuum.

freezer *n.* refrigerated container for preserving and storing food.

freight *n.* 1 cargo. 2 transport of goods. ● *v.* 1 load with freight. 2 transport as freight.

freighter *n.* ship or aircraft carrying mainly freight.

French *adj.* & *n.* (language) of France. □ **French horn** brass wind instrument with a coiled tube. **French-polish** *v.* polish (wood) with shellac polish. **French window** one reaching to the ground, used also as a door. **Frenchman** *n.*, **Frenchwoman** *n.*

frenetic *adj.* in a state of frenzy. □ **frenetically** *adv.*

frenzy *n.* violent excitement or agitation. □ **frenzied** *adj.*

frequency *n.* 1 frequent occurrence. 2 rate of recurrence (of a vibration etc.).

frequent¹ /fréekwənt/ *adj.* happening or appearing often. □ **frequently** *adv.*

■ common, constant, continual, customary, familiar, habitual, persistent, recurrent, regular, repeated, usual.

frequent² /frikwént/ *v.* go frequently to, be often in (a place).

fresco *n.* (*pl.* **-os**) picture painted on a wall or ceiling before the plaster is dry.

fresh *adj.* 1 new, not stale or faded. 2 different. 3 additional. 4 refreshing, invigorating. 5 pure. 6 not preserved by tinning or freezing etc. 7 not salty. □ **freshly** *adv.*, **freshness** *n.*

■ 1 brand new, new, newly-made. 2 alternative, different, innovative, new, novel, original, unconventional, unfamiliar, unusual, up to date. 3 additional, extra, fur-

ther, new, supplementary. 4 bracing, breezy, cool, crisp, exhilarating, invigorating, refreshing. 5 clean, pure, uncontaminated, unpolluted.

freshen *v.* make or become fresh.

fresher *n.* first-year university student.

fret¹ *v.* (**fretted**) be worried or distressed. □ **fretful** *adj.*

fret² *n.* each of the ridges on the finger-board of a guitar etc.

fretsaw *n.* very narrow saw used for fretwork.

fretwork *n.* woodwork cut in decorative patterns.

friable *adj.* easily crumbled. □ **friability** *n.*

friar *n.* member of certain religious orders of men.

friary *n.* monastery of friars.

fricassee *n.* dish of pieces of meat served in a thick sauce. ● *v.* make a fricassee of.

friction *n.* 1 rubbing of one thing against another. 2 resistance so encountered. 3 conflict of people who disagree. □ **frictional** *adj.*

■ 1 abrasion, chafing, grating, rubbing, scraping. 3 animosity, antagonism, bad feeling, bickering, conflict, discord, dispute, dissension, dissent, hostility, ill will, quarrelling, strife, wrangling.

fridge *n.* (*colloq.*) refrigerator.

fried *see* **fry¹**.

friend *n.* 1 person (other than a relative or lover) with whom one is on terms of mutual affection. 2 helper, sympathizer. □ **friendship** *n.*

■ 1 *colloq.* buddy, *colloq.* chum, companion, confidant(e), crony, intimate, mate, *colloq.* pal. 2 backer, benefactor, helper, patron, supporter, sympathizer. □ **friendship** closeness, fellowship, harmony, intimacy, rapport.

friendly *adj.* (**-ier, -iest**) 1 kind and pleasant. 2 on good terms. □ **friendliness** *n.*

■ 1 affable, affectionate, agreeable, amiable, amicable, approachable, benevolent, benign, civil, companionable, congenial, convivial, cordial, easygoing, genial, good-natured, gracious, helpful, hospitable, kind, kind-hearted, kindly, likeable, neighbourly, outgoing, pleasant, sociable, sympathetic, warm, welcoming, well-disposed. 2 *colloq.* chummy, close, intimate, on good terms, *colloq.* pally, *colloq.* thick.

frieze *n.* band of decoration round the top of a wall.

frigate *n.* small fast naval ship.

fright *n.* **1** sudden great fear. **2** instance of this. **3** ridiculous-looking person or thing.

■ **1** alarm, dread, fear, horror, panic, terror, trepidation. **2** scare, shock, start.

frighten *v.* **1** cause fright to. **2** drive or compel by fright.

■ **1** alarm, daunt, horrify, intimidate, petrify, *colloq.* put the wind up, scare, shock, startle, terrify.

frightful *adj.* **1** causing horror. **2** ugly. **3** (*colloq.*) extremely great or bad. □ **frightfully** *adv.*

■ **1** appalling, awful, dreadful, fearsome, ghastly, grisly, gruesome, hideous, horrendous, horrible, horrid, horrific, horrifying, loathsome, shocking, terrible, vile.

frigid *adj.* **1** intensely cold. **2** very cold in manner. **3** unresponsive sexually. □ **frigidity** *n.*

frill *n.* **1** gathered or pleated strip of trimming attached at one edge. **2** unnecessary extra. □ **frilled** *adj.*, **frilly** *adj.*

fringe *n.* **1** ornamental edging of hanging threads or cords. **2** front hair cut short to hang over the forehead. **3** edge of an area or group etc. ● *v.* edge. □ **fringe benefit** one provided by an employer in addition to wages.

frippery *n.* showy finery.

frisk *v.* **1** leap or skip playfully. **2** (*sl.*) search (a person) for concealed weapons etc. ● *n.* playful leap or skip.

frisky *adj.* (**-ier, -iest**) lively, playful. □ **friskily** *adv.*

fritter[1] *n.* fried batter-coated slice of fruit or meat etc.

fritter[2] *v.* waste little by little on trivial things.

frivolous *adj.* **1** trivial. **2** not serious, silly. □ **frivolously** *adv.*, **frivolity** *n.*

■ **1** *sl.* footling, inconsequential, insignificant, minor, petty, trifling, trivial, unimportant. **2** flighty, *colloq.* flip, flippant, foolish, giddy, shallow, silly, superficial.

frizz *v.* curl into a wiry mass. □ **frizzy** *adj.*, **frizziness** *n.*

frizzle *v.* fry crisp.

fro *see* **to and fro**.

frock *n.* woman's or girl's dress. □ **frockcoat** *n.* man's long-skirted coat.

frog *n.* small amphibian with long webfooted hind legs. □ **frog in one's throat** hoarseness.

frogman *n.* swimmer with a rubber suit and oxygen supply for use under water.

frogmarch *v.* hustle (a person) forcibly, holding the arms.

frolic *v.* (**frolicked**) play about in a lively way. ● *n.* such play.

■ *v.* caper, cavort, frisk, gambol, leap, play, prance, romp, skip.

from *prep.* **1** having as the starting point, source, or cause. **2** as separated, distinguished, or unlike. □ **from time to time** at intervals of time.

frond *n.* leaf-like part of a fern or palm tree etc.

front *n.* **1** side or part normally nearer or towards the spectator or line of motion. **2** battle line. **3** outward appearance. **4** cover for secret activities. **5** promenade of a seaside resort. **6** boundary between warm and cold air-masses. ● *adj.* of or at the front. ● *v.* **1** face, have the front towards. **2** (*sl.*) serve as a cover for secret activities. □ **front runner** leading contestant. **in front** at the front.

■ *n.* **1** façade, face, fore, forefront, frontage. **2** van, vanguard. **3** appearance, aspect, façade, face, look, show. ● *adj.* first, foremost, leading. ● *v.* **1** face, look out on, lie opposite, overlook.

frontage *n.* **1** front of a building. **2** land bordering this.

frontal *adj.* of or on the front.

frontier *n.* boundary between countries.

frontispiece *n.* illustration opposite the title-page of a book.

frost *n.* **1** freezing weather condition. **2** white frozen dew or vapour. ● *v.* **1** injure with frost. **2** cover (as) with frost. **3** make (glass) opaque by roughening its surface. □ **frostbite** *n.* injury to body tissue from freezing. **frostbitten** *adj.*

frosting *n.* sugar icing.

frosty *adj.* (**-ier, -iest**) **1** covered with frost. **2** unfriendly.

froth *n.* & *v.* foam. □ **frothy** *adj.*

frown *v.* wrinkle one's brow in thought or disapproval. ● *n.* frowning movement or look. □ **frown on** disapprove of.

■ *v.* & *n.* glare, glower, grimace, scowl.

frowzy *adj.* (**-ier, -iest**) **1** fusty. **2** dingy. □ **frowziness** *n.*

froze, frozen *see* **freeze**.

frugal *adj.* **1** careful and economical. **2** scanty, costing little. □ **frugally** *adv.*, **frugality** *n.*

■ **1** abstemious, careful, economical, provident, prudent, sparing, thrifty. **2** meagre, paltry, poor, scanty, skimpy, small.

fruit n. **1** seed-containing part of a plant. **2** this used as food. **3** (usu. pl.) product of labour. ● v. produce or allow to produce fruit. □ **fruit machine** coin-operated gambling machine.

fruiterer n. shopkeeper selling fruit.

fruitful adj. **1** producing much fruit. **2** successful. □ **fruitfully** adv.

■ **1** fecund, fertile, productive, rich. **2** beneficial, productive, profitable, rewarding, successful, useful, worthwhile.

fruition /froo-ish'n/ n. realization of aims or hopes.

fruitless adj. producing little or no result. □ **fruitlessly** adv.

■ abortive, futile, ineffective, pointless, profitless, unprofitable, unrewarding, unsuccessful, useless, vain.

fruity adj. (-ier, -iest) like fruit in smell or taste. □ **fruitiness** n.

frump n. dowdy woman. □ **frumpish** adj., **frumpy** adj.

frustrate v. prevent from achieving something or from being achieved. □ **frustration** n.

■ baulk, block, check, defeat, foil, hamper, hinder, impede, prevent, sl. scupper, stop, stymie, thwart.

frustrated adj. discontented, not satisfied.

fry[1] v. (**fried**) cook or be cooked in very hot fat.

fry[2] n. (pl. **fry**) young fish. □ **small fry** people of little importance.

ft abbr. foot or feet (as a measure).

fuchsia /fyoosha/ n. ornamental shrub with drooping flowers.

fuddle v. stupefy, esp. with drink.

fuddy-duddy adj. & n. (sl.) (person who is) old-fashioned.

fudge n. soft sweet made of milk, sugar, and butter. ● v. make or do clumsily or dishonestly.

fuel n. **1** material burnt as a source of energy. **2** thing that increases anger etc. ● v. (**fuelled**) supply with fuel.

fug n. stuffy atmosphere in a room etc. □ **fuggy** adj.

fugitive n. person who is fleeing or escaping. ● adj. **1** fleeing. **2** transient.

■ n. deserter, escapee, refugee, runaway. ● adj. **1** escaped, fleeing, runaway. **2** brief, ephemeral, fleeting, momentary, passing, short, transient, transitory.

fulcrum n. (pl. **-cra**) point of support on which a lever pivots.

fulfil v. (**fulfilled**) **1** accomplish, carry out (a task). **2** satisfy, do what is required by (a contract etc.). □ **fulfil oneself** realize one's potential. □ **fulfilment** n.

■ **1** accomplish, achieve, carry out, complete, discharge, do, effect, execute, perform, realize. **2** answer, comply with, meet, satisfy.

full adj. **1** holding or having as much as is possible. **2** copious. **3** complete. **4** plump. **5** (of tone) deep and mellow. **6** (of clothes) made with plenty of material. ● adv. **1** completely. **2** exactly. □ **full-blooded** adj. vigorous, hearty. **full-blown** adj. fully developed. **full moon** moon with the whole disc illuminated. **full-scale** adj. of actual size, not reduced. **full stop 1** dot used as a punctuation mark at the end of a sentence or abbreviation. **2** complete stop. **fullness** n.

■ adj. **1** brimming, chock-a-block, crammed, crowded, filled, jam-packed, packed, stuffed; replete, sated, satiated. **2** abundant, ample, copious, extensive, plentiful. **3** complete, comprehensive, exhaustive, detailed, thorough, unabridged. **4** buxom, plump, rounded, shapely, voluptuous. **5** deep, mellow, resonant, rich, sonorous.

fully adv. completely. □ **fully-fledged** adj. mature.

fulminate v. protest loudly and bitterly. □ **fulmination** n.

fulsome adj. **1** excessive. **2** insincere.

fumble v. **1** touch or handle (a thing) awkwardly. **2** grope about.

fume n. pungent smoke or vapour. ● v. **1** emit fumes. **2** seethe with anger. **3** subject to fumes.

fumigate v. disinfect by fumes. □ **fumigation** n., **fumigator** n.

fun n. **1** light-hearted amusement. **2** source of this. □ **funfair** n. group of stalls, amusements, sideshows, etc. **make fun of** tease, ridicule.

■ amusement, enjoyment, gaiety, glee, jollity, joy, merriment, mirth, pleasure. □ **make fun of** deride, jeer at, laugh at, mock, poke fun at, sl. rag, colloq. rib, ridicule, send up, taunt, tease.

function n. **1** special activity or purpose of a person or thing. **2** important ceremony. **3** (in mathematics) quantity whose value depends on varying values of others. ● v. **1** fulfil a function. **2** be in action.

■ n. **1** activity, business, capacity, duty, job, occupation, office, place, position, responsibility, role, task; purpose, use. **2** ceremony, *colloq.* do, occasion, party, reception. ● v. **1** act, serve. **2** be in working order, go, operate, run, work.

functional *adj.* **1** of or serving a function. **2** practical, not decorative. **3** able to function. □ **functionally** *adv.*

■ **2** practical, serviceable, useful, utilitarian. **3** functioning, going, operating, operational, running.

functionary *n.* official.

fund *n.* **1** sum of money for a special purpose. **2** stock, supply. **3** (*pl.*) money resources. ● v. provide with money.

■ n. **1** collection, kitty; endowment, nest egg. **2** cache, hoard, mine, pool, reserve, stock, store, supply. **3** (**funds**) assets, capital, cash, investments, means, money, resources, savings, wealth, *colloq.* wherewithal. ● v. back, finance, pay for, subsidize, support.

fundamental *adj.* **1** basic. **2** essential. ● n. fundamental fact or principle. □ **fundamentally** *adv.*

■ *adj.* basic, central, chief, crucial, essential, important, inherent, intrinsic, main, necessary, primary, prime, principal, quintessential, underlying, vital.

fundamentalism *n.* strict adherence to traditional religious beliefs. □ **fundamentalist** *n.*

funeral *n.* ceremonial burial or cremation of the dead.

funerary *adj.* of or used for a burial or funeral.

funereal *adj.* **1** suitable for a funeral. **2** dismal, dark.

fungicide *n.* substance that kills fungus. □ **fungicidal** *adj.*

fungus *n.* (*pl.* **-gi**) plant without green colouring matter (e.g. mushroom, mould). □ **fungal** *adj.*, **fungous** *adj.*

funnel *n.* **1** tube with a wide top for pouring liquid into small openings. **2** chimney on a steam engine or ship. ● v. (**funnelled**) move through a narrowing space.

funny *adj.* (**-ier, -iest**) **1** causing amusement. **2** puzzling, odd. □ **funny bone** part of the elbow where a very sensitive nerve passes. **funnily** *adv.*

■ **1** amusing, comic, comical, diverting, droll, entertaining, hilarious, humorous,

witty. **2** bizarre, curious, mysterious, mystifying, odd, peculiar, perplexing, puzzling, queer, surprising, weird.

fur *n.* **1** short fine hair of certain animals. **2** skin with this used for clothing. **3** coating, incrustation. ● v. (**furred**) cover or become covered with fur.

furbish *v.* **1** clean up. **2** renovate.

furious *adj.* **1** full of anger. **2** violent, intense. □ **furiously** *adv.*

■ **1** angry, beside oneself, cross, enraged, fuming, incensed, infuriated, irate, *colloq.* livid, *colloq.* mad, seething, wild. **2** fierce, intense, savage, violent, wild.

furl *v.* roll up and fasten.

furlong *n.* one-eighth of a mile.

furnace *n.* enclosed fireplace for intense heating or smelting.

furnish *v.* **1** equip with furniture. **2** provide, supply.

furnishings *n.pl.* furniture and fitments etc.

furniture *n.* movable articles (e.g. chairs, beds) for use in a room.

furore /fyooróri/ *n.* uproar of enthusiastic admiration or fury.

furrier *n.* person who deals in furs or fur clothes.

furrow *n.* **1** trench made by a plough. **2** groove. ● v. make furrows in.

furry *adj.* (**-ier, -iest**) **1** like fur. **2** covered with fur. □ **furriness** *n.*

further *adv.* & *adj.* **1** more distant. **2** to a greater extent. **3** additional(ly). ● v. help the progress of. □ **further education** that provided for people above school age. **furtherance** *n.*

■ *adv.* **3** additionally, also, besides, furthermore, in addition, moreover, too. ● *adj.* **3** additional, auxiliary, extra, fresh, more, new, supplementary. ● v. advance, aid, assist, expedite, facilitate, forward, foster, help, promote.

furthermore *adv.* moreover.

furthest *adj.* most distant. ● *adv.* at or to the greatest distance.

furtive *adj.* sly, stealthy. □ **furtively** *adv.*, **furtiveness** *n.*

■ clandestine, covert, crafty, secret, secretive, sly, stealthy, surreptitious, underhand.

fury *n.* **1** wild anger. **2** violence.

■ **1** anger, ire, rage, wrath. **2** ferocity, fierceness, savagery, violence.

furze *n.* gorse.

fuse¹ *v.* **1** melt with intense heat. **2** blend by melting. **3** fit with a fuse. **4** stop functioning through melting of a fuse. ● *n.* strip of wire placed in an electric circuit to melt and interrupt the current when the circuit is overloaded.

fuse² *n.* length of easily burnt material for igniting a bomb or explosive. ● *v.* fit a fuse to.

fuselage *n.* body of an aeroplane.

fusible *adj.* able to be fused. □ **fusibility** *n.*

fusion *n.* **1** fusing. **2** union of atomic nuclei, with release of energy.

fuss *n.* **1** excited commotion, nervous activity. **2** excessive concern about a trivial thing. **3** vigorous protest. ● *v.* **1** make a fuss. **2** agitate.

■ *n.* **1** ado, ballyhoo, bother, bustle, commotion, excitement, flap, flurry, fluster, hubbub, *colloq.* kerfuffle, *colloq.* palaver, stir, to-do. **3** complaint, objection, protest, *colloq.* stink.

fussy *adj.* (**-ier**, **-iest**) **1** often fussing. **2** fastidious. **3** with much unnecessary detail or decoration. □ **fussily** *adv.*

■ **2** *colloq.* choosy, faddy, fastidious, finicky, particular, *colloq.* pernickety. **3** elaborate, fancy, ornate, over-decorated.

fusty *adj.* (**-ier**, **-iest**) smelling stale and stuffy. □ **fustiness** *n.*

futile *adj.* producing no result. □ **futilely** *adv.*, **futility** *n.*

■ abortive, fruitless, profitless, unprofitable, unsuccessful, useless, vain.

futon /ˈfuːton/ *n.* light orig. Japanese kind of mattress.

future *adj.* belonging to the time after the present. ● *n.* **1** future time, events, or condition. **2** prospect of success etc. □ **in future** from now on.

futuristic *adj.* suitable for the future, not traditional.

fuzz *n.* fluff, fluffy or frizzy thing.

fuzzy *adj.* (**-ier**, **-iest**) **1** like or covered with fuzz. **2** blurred, indistinct. □ **fuzzily** *adv.*

Gg

g *abbr.* gram(s).

gabardine *n.* strong twilled fabric.

gabble *v.* talk quickly and indistinctly. ● *n.* gabbled talk.

gable *n.* triangular part of a wall, between sloping roofs. □ **gabled** *adj.*

gad *v.* (**gadded**) **gad about** go about idly in search of pleasure. □ **gadabout** *n.* idle pleasure-seeker.

gadfly *n.* fly that bites cattle.

gadget *n.* small mechanical device or tool. □ **gadgetry** *n.*

■ apparatus, appliance, contraption, device, implement, invention, machine, tool, utensil.

Gaelic /gáylik/ *n.* Celtic language of Scots or Irish.

gaff *n.* stick with a hook for landing large fish. ● *v.* seize with a gaff.

gaffe *n.* blunder.

gaffer *n.* **1** elderly man. **2** (*colloq.*) boss, foreman.

gag *n.* **1** thing put in or over a person's mouth to silence them. **2** device to hold the mouth open. **3** joke. ● *v.* (**gagged**) **1** put a gag on. **2** deprive of freedom of speech. **3** retch.

gaggle *n.* **1** flock (of geese). **2** disorderly group.

gaiety *n.* **1** cheerfulness. **2** merrymaking. **3** bright appearance.

■ **1** cheerfulness, glee, happiness, high spirits, jollity, joy, joyfulness, light-heartedness, merriment, mirth. **2** celebration, festivity, fun, jollification, merrymaking, revelry.

gaily *adv.* with gaiety.

gain *v.* **1** obtain, secure. **2** acquire more of something. **3** earn. **4** reach. **5** (of a clock) become fast. ● *n.* increase, profit. □ **gain on** get nearer to in pursuit.

■ *v.* **1** achieve, acquire, attain, come by, get, obtain, secure, pick up, procure, reap, win. **2** gather, pick up; put on. **3** clear, earn, get, make. **4** arrive at, come to, get to, reach.

gainful *adj.* profitable. □ **gainfully** *adv.*

■ advantageous, lucrative, profitable, productive, remunerative.

gainsay *v.* (**gainsaid**) deny, contradict.

gait *n.* manner of walking or running.

gaiter *n.* cloth or leather covering for the lower part of the leg.

gala /gaála/ *n.* **1** festive occasion. **2** fête.

galaxy *n.* system of stars, esp. (**the Galaxy**) the one of which the solar system is a part. □ **galactic** *adj.*

gale *n.* **1** very strong wind. **2** noisy outburst.

gall[1] *n.* **1** impudence. **2** bitterness of feeling. **3** bile. □ **gall bladder** organ storing bile.

■ **1** cheek, effrontery, impertinence, impudence, insolence, temerity. **2** acrimony, asperity, bitterness, rancour, resentment.

gall[2] *n.* sore made by rubbing. ● *v.* **1** rub and make sore. **2** vex.

■ *v.* **1** chafe, rub, scrape, scratch. **2** *colloq.* aggravate, annoy, *sl.* bug, exasperate, irk, irritate, nettle, *colloq.* rile, vex.

gall[3] *n.* abnormal growth on a plant, esp. on an oak tree.

gallant *adj.* **1** brave. **2** chivalrous, attentive to women. □ **gallantly** *adv.*, **gallantry** *n.*

■ **1** bold, brave, courageous, daring, dauntless, fearless, heroic, intrepid, plucky, unafraid, valorous. **2** attentive, chivalrous, considerate, courteous, courtly, gentlemanly, gracious, polite.

galleon *n.* large Spanish sailing ship in the 15th–17th centuries.

gallery *n.* **1** balcony in a hall or theatre etc. **2** long room or passage, esp. used for special purpose. **3** room or building for showing works of art.

galley *n.* (*pl.* -**eys**) **1** ancient ship, esp. propelled by oars. **2** kitchen in a ship or aircraft. **3** (also **galley proof**) printer's proof in a long narrow form.

Gallic *adj.* **1** of ancient Gaul. **2** French.

gallon *n.* measure for liquids, = 4 quarts (4.546 litres).

gallop *n.* **1** horse's fastest pace. **2** ride at this. ● *v.* (**galloped**) **1** go or ride at a gallop. **2** progress rapidly.

gallows *n.* framework with a noose for hanging criminals.

gallstone *n.* small hard mass formed in the gall bladder.

galore *adv.* in plenty.

galosh n. rubber overshoe.

galvanize v. **1** stimulate into activity. **2** coat with zinc.

gambit n. opening move.

gamble v. **1** play games of chance for money. **2** bet (a sum of money). **3** risk in hope of gain. ● n. **1** gambling. **2** risky undertaking. □ **gambler** n.
■ v. **1** bet, game, colloq. have a flutter. **2** bet, hazard, risk, stake, venture, wager.

gambol v. (**gambolled**) jump about in play. ● n. gambolling movement.

game[1] n. **1** play or sport, esp. with rules. **2** section of this as a scoring unit. **3** scheme. **4** wild animals hunted for sport or food. **5** their flesh as food. ● v. gamble for money stakes. ● adj. **1** brave. **2** willing. □ **gamely** adv.
■ n. **1** recreation, sport; competition, contest. **2** bout, heat, match, round. **3** design, plan, plot, ploy, scheme, stratagem, strategy. ● adj. **1** adventurous, bold, brave, courageous, daring, colloq. gutsy, plucky, spirited. **2** eager, enthusiastic, prepared, ready, willing.

game[2] adj. lame.

gamekeeper n. person employed to protect and breed game.

gamesmanship n. art of winning games by dubious means.

gamete n. cell able to unite with another in sexual reproduction.

gamine n. girl with mischievous charm.

gamma n. third letter of the Greek alphabet, = g.

gammon n. cured or smoked ham.

gammy adj. (sl.) = **game**[2].

gamut n. whole range or scope.

gamy adj. smelling or tasting like high game. □ **gaminess** n.

gander n. male goose.

gang n. group of people working or going about together. ● v. **gang up** combine in a gang.
■ n. band, company, crew, crowd, group, party, team, troop; circle, clique, coterie, set.

gangling adj. tall and awkward.

ganglion n. (pl. **-ia**) **1** group of nerve cells. **2** cyst on a tendon.

gangplank n. plank placed for walking into or out of a boat.

gangrene n. decay of body tissue. □ **gangrenous** adj.

gangster n. member of a gang of violent criminals.

gangway n. **1** passage, esp. between rows of seats. **2** passageway on a ship. **3** bridge from a ship to land.

gannet n. large seabird.

gantry n. overhead bridge-like framework supporting railway signals or a travelling crane etc.

gaol n. = **jail**.

gap n. **1** opening, space, interval. **2** wide difference. **3** deficiency.
■ **1** aperture, breach, cavity, chink, crack, cranny, crevice, hole, opening, rift, space; break, hiatus, interlude, intermission, interruption, interval, lull, pause, recess, respite. **2** difference, discrepancy, disparity, divergence, inconsistency.

gape v. **1** open the mouth wide. **2** stare in surprise. **3** be wide open. ● n. **1** yawn. **2** stare.

garage n. **1** building for storing motor vehicle(s). **2** commercial establishment for refuelling or repairing motor vehicles. ● v. put or keep in a garage.

garb n. clothing. ● v. clothe.

garbage n. domestic rubbish.

garble v. distort or confuse (a message or story etc.).
■ confuse, distort, jumble, mix up, scramble, twist.

garden n. **1** piece of cultivated ground, esp. attached to a house. **2** (pl.) ornamental public grounds. ● v. tend a garden. □ **gardener** n.

gardenia n. tree or shrub with fragrant flowers.

gargantuan adj. gigantic.

gargle v. wash the inside of the throat with liquid held there by the breath. ● n. liquid for this.

gargoyle n. grotesque carved face or figure on a building.

garish adj. gaudy. □ **garishly** adv., **garishness** n.

garland n. wreath of flowers etc. as a decoration. ● v. adorn with garland(s).

garlic n. onion-like plant. □ **garlicky** adj.

garment n. article of clothing.

garner v. store up, collect.

garnet n. red semiprecious stone.

garnish v. decorate (esp. food). ● n. thing used for garnishing.

garret n. attic, poor room.

garrison n. **1** troops stationed in a town or fort. **2** building they occupy. ● v. occupy this.

garrotte n. wire or metal collar used to strangle a victim. ● v. strangle with this.

garrulous adj. talkative. □ **garrulously** adv., **garrulousness** n.

garter n. band worn round the leg to keep a stocking up.

gas n. (pl. **gases**) **1** substance with particles that can move freely. **2** such a substance used as a fuel or anaesthetic. **3** (colloq.) empty talk. **4** (US) petrol. ● v. (**gassed**) **1** kill or overcome by poisonous gas. **2** (colloq.) talk lengthily. □ **gas chamber** room filled with poisonous gas to kill people. **gas mask** device worn over face as a protection against poisonous gas. **gassy** adj.

gaseous adj. of or like a gas.

gash n. long deep cut. ● v. make a gash in.

gasify v. convert or be converted into gas. □ **gasification** n.

gasket n. piece of rubber etc. sealing a joint between metal surfaces.

gasoline n. (US) petrol.

gasp v. **1** breathe quickly and noisily. **2** breathe in sharply as in surprise or pain. ● n. breath drawn in thus.

■ v. **1** blow, heave, pant, puff, wheeze.

gastric adj. of the stomach.

gastropod n. mollusc, such as a snail, that moves by means of a ventral organ.

gate n. **1** hinged movable barrier in a wall or fence etc. **2** gateway. **3** number of spectators paying to attend a sporting event, amount of money taken.

gateau /gáttō/ n. (pl. **-eaux**) large rich cream cake.

gatecrash v. go to (a party) uninvited. □ **gatecrasher** n.

gateway n. **1** opening or structure framing a gate. **2** entrance.

gather v. **1** bring or come together. **2** collect. **3** understand, conclude. **4** develop a higher degree of. **5** draw together in folds.

■ **1** assemble, cluster, collect, come together, congregate, convene, flock, forgather, group, mass, meet, throng; bring together, marshal, rally, round up. **2** accumulate, amass, collect, garner, heap (up), pile (up), stockpile. **3** assume, conclude, deduce, infer, surmise, understand. **4** gain, increase, pick up.

gathering n. people assembled.

■ assembly, conference, congregation, convention, colloq. get-together, meeting, rally.

gauche /gōsh/ adj. socially awkward. □ **gaucherie** n.

gaucho /gówchō/ n. (pl. **-os**) S. American cowboy.

gaudy adj. (**-ier, -iest**) showy or bright in a tasteless way. □ **gaudily** adv., **gaudiness** n.

■ garish, colloq. flash, flashy, loud, ostentatious, showy, tasteless, tawdry, vulgar.

gauge /gayj/ n. **1** standard measure to which thing must conform. **2** device for measuring things. **3** distance between pairs of rails or wheels. ● v. **1** measure. **2** estimate.

■ n. **1** benchmark, measure, rule, pattern, yardstick. ● v. **1** calculate, compute, determine, measure. **2** assess, estimate, evaluate, judge, rate.

gaunt adj. lean and haggard. □ **gauntness** n.

■ bony, cadaverous, emaciated, haggard, lean, scraggy, scrawny, skeletal, thin.

gauntlet[1] n. **1** glove with a long wide cuff. **2** this cuff.

gauntlet[2] n. **run the gauntlet** be exposed to criticism or risk.

gauze n. **1** thin transparent fabric. **2** fine wire mesh. □ **gauzy** adj.

gave see **give**.

gavel n. mallet used by an auctioneer or chairman etc. to call for attention or order.

gawky adj. (**-ier, -iest**) awkward and ungainly. □ **gawkiness** n.

gawp v. (colloq.) stare stupidly.

gay adj. **1** happy and full of fun. **2** brightly coloured. **3** homosexual. ● n. homosexual person. □ **gayness** n.

■ adj. **1** bubbly, buoyant, carefree, cheerful, cheery, chirpy, ebullient, exuberant, gleeful, happy, high-spirited, jolly, jovial, joyful, light-hearted, lively, merry, vivacious. **2** bright, colourful, vivid.

gaze v. look long and steadily. ● n. long steady look.

■ v. gape, colloq. gawp, goggle, look fixedly, stare.

gazebo /gazéebō/ n. (pl. **-os**) summer house with a wide view.

gazelle n. small antelope.

gazette n. **1** newspaper. **2** official journal containing public notices.

gazetteer n. index of places, rivers, mountains, etc.

gazump v. disappoint (an intended house buyer) by raising the price agreed.

GB abbr. Great Britain.

gear n. **1** equipment. **2** set of toothed wheels working together in machinery.

● *v.* **1** provide with gear(s). **2** adapt (to a purpose). ▢ **in gear** with gear mechanism engaged.

■ *n.* **1** accoutrements, apparatus, *sl.* clobber, equipment, kit, materials, paraphernalia, stuff, tackle, things, tools, trappings.

gearbox *n.* case enclosing gear mechanism.

gecko *n.* (*pl.* **-os**) tropical lizard.

geese *see* **goose**.

Geiger counter /gígər/ device for measuring radioactivity.

geisha /gáysha/ *n.* Japanese woman trained to entertain men.

gel *n.* jelly-like substance.

gelatine *n.* clear substance made by boiling bones. ▢ **gelatinous** *adj.*

geld *v.* castrate, spay.

gelding *n.* gelded horse.

gelignite *n.* explosive containing nitroglycerine.

gem *n.* **1** precious stone. **2** thing of great beauty or excellence.

gender *n.* **1** one's sex. **2** grammatical classification corresponding roughly to sex.

gene *n.* one of the factors controlling heredity.

genealogy *n.* **1** list of ancestors. **2** study of pedigrees. ▢ **genealogical** *adj.*, **genealogist** *n.*

genera *see* **genus**.

general *adj.* **1** including or affecting all or most parts, things, or people. **2** prevalent, usual. **3** not detailed or specific. **4** (in titles) chief. ● *n.* army officer next below field marshal. ▢ **general election** election of parliamentary representatives from the whole country. **general practitioner** community doctor treating cases of all kinds. **in general 1** usually. **2** for the most part. **generally** *adv.*

■ *adj.* **1** comprehensive, extensive, global, universal, worldwide; communal, popular, public, shared. **2** common, familiar, habitual, normal, ordinary, prevailing, prevalent, regular, usual, widespread. **3** approximate, generalized, imprecise, indefinite, inexact, loose, rough, vague.

generality *n.* **1** being general. **2** general statement.

generalize *v.* **1** draw a general conclusion. **2** speak in general terms. ▢ **generalization** *n.*

generate *v.* bring into existence, produce.

■ breed, bring about, cause, create, engender, give rise to, produce.

generation *n.* **1** generating. **2** single stage in descent or pedigree. **3** all people born at about the same time. **4** period of about 30 years.

generator *n.* machine converting mechanical energy into electricity.

generic *adj.* of a whole genus or group. ▢ **generically** *adv.*

generous *adj.* **1** giving or given freely. **2** magnanimous. **3** plentiful. ▢ **generously** *adv.*, **generosity** *n.*

■ **1** bountiful, charitable, free, lavish, liberal, munificent, open-handed, unstinting. **2** benevolent, forgiving, humane, magnanimous, noble, philanthropic, public-spirited, selfless, unselfish. **3** abundant, ample, bountiful, copious, lavish, overflowing, plentiful; big, considerable, large, sizeable, substantial. ▢ **generosity** bounty, largesse, liberality, munificence.

genesis *n.* origin.

genetic *adj.* of genes or genetics. ▢ **genetically** *adv.*

genetics *n.* science of heredity.

genial *adj.* kindly and cheerful. ▢ **genially** *adv.*, **geniality** *n.*

■ agreeable, affable, amiable, cheerful, congenial, convivial, cordial, easygoing, friendly, good-humoured, good-natured, hospitable, kindly, likeable, nice, pleasant, sociable, sympathetic.

genie *n.* (*pl.* **genii**) magical spirit or goblin.

genital *adj.* of animal reproduction or sex organs. ● *n.pl.* external sex organs.

genius *n.* (*pl.* **-uses**) **1** exceptionally great natural ability. **2** person having this.

■ **1** ability, aptitude, capability, flair, gift, knack, talent; brains, brilliance, intellect, intelligence. **2** adept, expert, maestro, mastermind, prodigy, virtuoso, wizard, *colloq.* whiz-kid.

genocide *n.* deliberate extermination of a race of people.

genre /zhónrə/ *n.* kind, esp. of art or literature.

genteel *adj.* affectedly polite and refined. ▢ **genteelly** *adv.*

gentian /jénsh'n/ *n.* alpine plant with usu. deep-blue flowers.

gentile *n.* non-Jewish person.

gentility *n.* good manners and elegance.

gentle adj. **1** mild or kind. **2** moderate, not severe. ●v. coax. □ **gently** adv., **gentleness** n.

■ adj. **1** benign, humane, kind, kindly, lenient, mellow, merciful, mild, peaceful, placid, serene, sweet-tempered, tender, tranquil. **2** light, mild, moderate, soft.

gentleman n. **1** man, esp. of good social position. **2** well-mannered man. □ **gentlemanly** adj.

gentrify v. alter (an area) to conform to middle-class tastes. □ **gentrification** n.

gentry n.pl. **1** people next below nobility. **2** (derog.) people.

genuflect v. bend the knee and lower the body, esp. in worship. □ **genuflection** n.

genuine adj. really what it is said to be. □ **genuinely** adv., **genuineness** n.

■ authentic, bona fide, legitimate, real, true, veritable.

genus n. (pl. **genera**) **1** group of animals or plants, usu. containing several species. **2** kind.

geocentric adj. **1** having the earth as a centre. **2** as viewed from the earth's centre.

geode n. **1** cavity lined with crystals. **2** rock containing this.

geography n. **1** study of earth's physical features, climate, etc. **2** features of a place. □ **geographical** adj., **geographically** adv., **geographer** n.

geology n. **1** study of earth's crust. **2** features of earth's crust. □ **geological** adj., **geologist** n.

geometry n. branch of mathematics dealing with lines, angles, surfaces, and solids. □ **geometric(al)** adj., **geometrician** n.

Georgian adj. of the time of the Georges, kings of England, esp. 1714–1830.

geranium n. garden plant with red, pink, or white flowers.

gerbil n. rodent with long hind legs.

geriatrics n. branch of medicine dealing with the diseases and care of old people. □ **geriatric** adj. & n.

germ n. **1** micro-organism, esp. one capable of causing disease. **2** portion of an organism capable of developing into a new organism. **3** basis from which a thing may develop.

■ **1** bacterium, sl. bug, microbe, micro-organism, virus. **3** basis, beginning, origin, root, seed, source, start.

German adj. & n. (native, language) of Germany. □ **German measles** disease with symptoms like mild measles. **German shepherd dog** dog of a large strong smooth-haired breed.

germane adj. relevant.

germinate v. begin or cause to grow. □ **germination** n.

gerontology n. study of ageing.

gerrymander v. arrange boundaries of (a constituency etc.) so as to gain unfair electoral advantage.

gerund n. English verbal noun ending in -ing.

Gestapo n. Nazi secret police.

gestation n. **1** carrying in the womb between conception and birth. **2** period of this.

gesticulate v. make expressive movements with the hands and arms. □ **gesticulation** n.

gesture n. expressive movement or action. ●v. make a gesture.

■ n. gesticulation, motion, movement, sign, signal. ●v. gesticulate, indicate, motion, signal, wave.

get v. (**got**, **getting**) **1** come into possession of. **2** earn. **3** win. **4** fetch. **5** capture. **6** contract (an illness). **7** bring or come into a certain state. **8** persuade. **9** (colloq.) understand. **10** (colloq.) annoy. **11** prepare (a meal). □ **get across** manage to communicate. **get along** live harmoniously, be on good terms. **get away** escape. **get at 1** reach. **2** (colloq.) imply. **3** (colloq.) nag. **get by** manage to survive. **get off** be acquitted. **get on 1** manage. **2** make progress. **3** be on harmonious terms. **4** advance in age. **get out of** evade. **get-out** n. means of evading something. **get over 1** recover from. **2** surmount. **3** communicate. **get round 1** successfully coax or cajole. **2** evade (a law or rule). **get through 1** pass (an exam etc.). **2** use up (resources). **3** make contact by telephone. **get-together** n. (colloq.) social gathering. **get up 1** rise, esp. from bed. **2** prepare, organize. **get-up** n. outfit.

■ **1** acquire, be given, come by, obtain, pick up, procure, receive, secure; buy, purchase. **2** be paid, clear, earn, gross, make, net. **3** achieve, attain, find, gain, win. **4** collect, fetch, go for, retrieve. **5** apprehend, arrest, capture, grab, seize, take. **6** be afflicted with, catch, come down with, contract, develop, fall ill with, have, suffer from. **7** become, come to, grow, turn. **8** cajole, coax, convince, induce, persuade, prevail on, talk into, wheedle into. **9** appreciate, comprehend, follow, grasp, see, understand. □ **get across** communicate, convey, get over, impart, make clear, put over. **get by** cope, exist, make do, make ends meet, manage, pull through, scrape by, struggle along, survive. **get on 1** cope, fare, manage. **2** advance, be successful, do well, make progress, progress, succeed. **3** be friendly, be on good terms, get along, hit it off. **get out of** avoid, dodge, escape, evade, shirk, sidestep.

getaway *n.* escape after a crime.

gewgaw *n.* gaudy ornament etc.

geyser /geezər/ *n.* **1** spring that spouts hot water or steam. **2** a kind of water heater.

ghastly *adj.* (**-ier, -iest**) **1** causing horror. **2** pale and ill-looking. **3** (*colloq.*) very bad.

■ **1** appalling, awful, dreadful, grim, grisly, gruesome, frightful, hideous, horrendous, horrible, horrid, horrifying, shocking, terrible, terrifying. **2** ashen, livid, pale, pallid, wan.

gherkin *n.* small cucumber used for pickling.

ghetto *n.* (*pl.* **-os**) slum area occupied by a particular group. □ **ghetto-blaster** *n.* large portable cassette player.

ghost *n.* dead person's spirit. ● *v.* write as a ghost writer. □ **ghost writer** person who writes a book etc. for another to pass off as his or her own. **ghostly** *adj.*, **ghostliness** *n.*

■ *n.* apparition, phantom, spectre, spirit, *colloq.* spook, wraith.

ghoul /gool/ *n.* **1** person who enjoys gruesome things. **2** (in Muslim stories) spirit preying on corpses. □ **ghoulish** *adj.*

giant *n.* **1** (in fairy tales) a being of superhuman size. **2** abnormally large person, animal, or thing. **3** person of outstanding ability. ● *adj.* very large.

gibber *v.* make meaningless sounds, esp. in shock or terror.

gibberish *n.* unintelligible talk, nonsense.

gibbet *n.* gallows.

gibbon *n.* long-armed ape.

gibe /jīb/ *n.* & *v.* jeer.

giblets *n.pl.* edible organs from a bird.

giddy *adj.* (**-ier, -iest**) **1** having or causing the feeling that everything is spin-

ning round. **2** excitable, flighty. □ **giddily** *adv.*, **giddiness** *n.*

■ **1** dizzy, faint, light-headed, unsteady. **2** capricious, excitable, impulsive, volatile; flighty, foolish, frivolous, irresponsible, scatterbrained, silly.

gift *n.* **1** thing given or received without payment. **2** natural ability. **3** easy task. ● *v.* bestow.

■ *n.* **1** benefaction, bequest, donation, handout, offering, present. **2** ability, aptitude, capability, capacity, flair, genius, instinct, knack, skill, talent.

gifted *adj.* talented.

■ able, accomplished, bright, brilliant, capable, clever, expert, skilful, skilled, talented.

gig[1] *n.* light two-wheeled horse-drawn carriage.

gig[2] (*colloq.*) *n.* engagement to play music. ● *v.* (**gigged**) perform a gig.

giga- *pref.* multiplied by 10^9 (as in *gigametre*).

gigantic *adj.* very large.

■ colossal, enormous, gargantuan, giant, huge, immense, mammoth, massive, monumental, titanic, vast.

giggle *v.* give small bursts of half-suppressed laughter. ● *n.* this laughter.

■ *v.* & *n.* cackle, chortle, chuckle, laugh, snicker, snigger, titter.

gigolo /zhíggəlō/ *n.* (*pl.* **-os**) man paid by a woman to be her escort or lover.

gild *v.* (**gilded**) cover with a thin layer of gold or gold paint.

gill[1] /gil/ *n.* **1** (usu. *pl.*) respiratory organ of a fish etc. **2** each of the vertical plates on the underside of a mushroom cap.

gill[2] /jil/ *n.* one-quarter of a pint.

gilt *adj.* gilded, gold-coloured. ● *n.* **1** substance used in gilding. **2** gilt-edged investment. □ **gilt-edged** *adj.* (of an investment etc.) very safe.

gimbals *n.pl.* contrivance of rings to keep instruments horizontal in a moving ship etc.

gimcrack /jímcrak/ *adj.* cheap and flimsy.

gimlet *n.* small tool with a screw-like tip for boring holes.

gimmick *n.* trick or device to attract attention. □ **gimmicky** *adj.*

gin *n.* alcoholic spirit flavoured with juniper berries.

ginger *n.* **1** hot-tasting root of a tropical plant. **2** this plant. **3** reddish-yellow. ● *adj.* ginger-coloured. □ **ginger ale, beer**

ginger-flavoured fizzy drinks. **ginger group** group urging a more active policy.

gingery *adj.*

gingerbread *n.* ginger-flavoured cake or biscuit.

gingerly *adj.* & *adv.* cautious(ly).

gingham *n.* cotton fabric with a checked or striped pattern.

ginseng *n.* plant with a fragrant root used in medicine.

gipsy *n.* = **gypsy**.

giraffe *n.* long-necked African animal.

girder *n.* metal beam supporting part of a building or bridge.

girdle *n.* **1** cord worn round the waist. **2** elastic corset. **3** connected ring of bones in the body. ● *v.* surround.

girl *n.* **1** female child. **2** young woman. **3** female assistant or employee. **4** man's girlfriend. □ **girlfriend** *n.* female friend, esp. man's usual companion. **girlhood** *n.*, **girlish** *adj.*

giro /jī́rō/ *n.* (*pl.* **-os**) **1** banking system by which payment can be made by transferring credit from one account to another. **2** cheque or payment made by this.

girth *n.* **1** distance round something. **2** band under a horse's belly, holding a saddle in place.

gist /jist/ *n.* essential points or general sense of a speech etc.

■ core, heart, essence, nub, substance; drift, import, meaning, purport, sense.

give *v.* (**gave**, **given**) **1** cause to receive or have. **2** provide with. **3** make or perform (an action etc.). **4** yield as a product or result. **5** yield to pressure, collapse. ● *n.* springiness, elasticity. □ **give and take** willingness to make reciprocal concessions. **give away 1** give as a gift. **2** reveal (a secret etc.) unintentionally. **give-away** *n.* (*colloq.*) unintentional disclosure. **give in** acknowledge defeat. **give off** emit. **give out 1** announce. **2** distribute. **3** become exhausted or used up. **give over 1** devote. **2** (*colloq.*) cease. **give up 1** cease. **2** abandon hope or an attempt. **3** part with. **give way 1** yield. **2** collapse. **3** allow other traffic to go first. **giver** *n.*

■ *v.* **1** award, bestow, confer, contribute, donate, grant, hand over, make over, present; bequeath, leave, will; commit, consign, entrust; communicate, convey, deliver, impart, pass on, send. **2** furnish with, provide with, supply with. **3** emit, utter. **4** afford, make, produce, yield. **5** break,

buckle, collapse, come or fall apart, give way. □ **give away 2** disclose, divulge, leak, reveal; betray, grass on, inform on. **give in** admit defeat, capitulate, concede, give up, submit, surrender, throw in the towel, yield. **give out 1** announce, broadcast, declare, make known, make public. **2** allocate, allot, deal out, *colloq.* dish out, distribute, dole out, hand out. **give up 1** abandon, cease, desist from, *colloq.* stop. **2** admit defeat, capitulate, give in, submit, surrender. **give way 1** back down, capitulate, give in, submit, surrender, yield. **2** buckle, cave in, collapse, crumple, subside.

given *see* **give**. *adj.* **1** specified. **2** having a tendency.

gizzard *n.* bird's second stomach, in which food is ground.

glacé /glássay/ *adj.* (of fruit) preserved in sugar.

glacial *adj.* **1** icy. **2** of or from glaciers. □ **glacially** *adv.*

glaciated *adj.* covered with or affected by a glacier. □ **glaciation** *n.*

glacier *n.* mass or river of ice moving very slowly.

glad *adj.* **1** pleased. **2** cheerful. **3** giving joy. □ **gladly** *adv.*, **gladness** *n.*

■ **1** delighted, elated, gratified, happy, overjoyed, pleased, thrilled; eager, keen, ready, willing. **2** cheerful, cheery, gay, joyful, joyous, merry. **3** cheering, gratifying, pleasing, welcome.

gladden *v.* make glad.

glade *n.* open space in a forest.

gladiator *n.* man trained to fight at public shows in ancient Rome. □ **gladiatorial** *adj.*

gladiolus *n.* (*pl.* **-li**) garden plant with spikes of flowers.

glamour *n.* alluring or exciting beauty or charm. □ **glamorize** *v.*, **glamorous** *adj.*

■ allure, attraction, beauty, charisma, charm, fascination, excitement, romance. □ **glamorous** alluring, attractive, beautiful, fascinating, romantic.

glance *v.* **1** look briefly. **2** strike and bounce off. ● *n.* brief look.

■ *v.* **1** peek, peep. **2** bounce, rebound, ricochet.

gland *n.* organ that secretes substances to be used or expelled by the body. □ **glandular** *adj.*

glare *v.* **1** shine with a harsh dazzling light. **2** stare angrily. ● *n.* glaring light or stare.

glaring adj. conspicuous.
■ blatant, conspicuous, flagrant, obvious, manifest, obtrusive, patent, prominent.

glass n. **1** hard brittle usu. transparent substance. **2** things made of this. **3** mirror. **4** glass drinking vessel. **5** barometer. **6** (pl.) spectacles, binoculars. ● v. fit or cover with glass.

glasshouse n. **1** greenhouse. **2** (sl.) military prison.

glassy adj. **1** like glass. **2** (of eyes etc.) dull, expressionless.

glaze v. **1** fit or cover with glass. **2** coat with a glossy surface. **3** become glassy. ● n. shiny surface or coating.
■ n. coat, coating; gloss, lustre, patina, polish, sheen, shine.

glazier n. person whose trade is to fit glass in windows etc.

gleam n. **1** faint or brief light. **2** brief show of a quality. ● v. shine faintly, send out gleams.
■ v. flicker, glimmer, glint, glisten, glitter, glow, shimmer, shine, sparkle, twinkle.

glean v. **1** pick up (grain left by harvesters). **2** gather scraps of. □ **gleaner** n., **gleanings** n.pl.

glee n. lively or triumphant joy. □ **gleeful** adj., **gleefully** adv.
■ delight, elation, exultation, gaiety, joy, joyfulness, jubilation, merriment, mirth. □ **gleeful** delighted, elated, exultant, joyful, jubilant, merry, mirthful, triumphant.

glen n. narrow valley.

glib adj. speaking or spoken fluently but insincerely.
■ colloq. flip, fluent, insincere, slick, smooth.

glide v. **1** move smoothly. **2** fly in a glider or aircraft without engine power. ● n. gliding movement.
■ v. **1** coast, float, flow, sail, skim, slide, slip, stream.

glider n. aeroplane with no engine.

glimmer n. faint gleam. ● v. gleam faintly.

glimpse n. brief view. ● v. have a brief view of.

glint n. very brief flash of light. ● v. send out a glint.

glisten v. shine like something wet.
■ gleam, glint, glitter, shimmer, shine, sparkle, twinkle.

glitter v. & n. sparkle.

gloaming n. evening twilight.

gloat v. be full of greedy or malicious delight.

global adj. covering or affecting the whole world. □ **global warming** increase in temperature of the earth's atmosphere. **globally** adv.
■ international, universal, world, worldwide.

globe n. **1** ball-shaped object, esp. with a map of the earth on it. **2** the world. **3** hollow round glass object. □ **globetrotting** n. travelling widely as a tourist.

globular adj. shaped like a globe.

globule n. small rounded drop.

glockenspiel n. musical instrument of tuned steel bars or tubes struck by hammers.

gloom n. **1** semi-darkness. **2** melancholy, depression.
■ **1** dark, darkness, dimness, dusk, murk, obscurity, shade, shadow. **2** dejection, depression, despair, despondency, melancholy, misery, sadness, sorrow, unhappiness.

gloomy adj. (-ier, -iest) **1** dark. **2** depressed. **3** depressing.
■ **1** dark, dim, dusky, murky, shadowy, shady. **2** dejected, depressed, disconsolate, dispirited, downcast, downhearted, forlorn, glum, lugubrious, melancholy, miserable, morose, sad, sorrowful, unhappy. **3** bleak, cheerless, depressing, dismal, dreary.

glorify v. **1** praise highly. **2** make seem grander than it is. □ **glorification** n.
■ **1** acclaim, applaud, commend, eulogize, extol, honour, laud, pay tribute to, praise.

glorious adj. **1** having or bringing glory. **2** (colloq.) excellent. □ **gloriously** adv.
■ **1** celebrated, distinguished, eminent, famed, famous, honoured, illustrious, renowned; admirable, excellent, impressive, magnificent, marvellous, outstanding, spectacular, splendid, superb.

glory n. **1** fame, honour, and praise. **2** thing bringing this. **3** magnificence. ● v. rejoice. □ **glory in** take pride in.
■ n. **1** celebrity, distinction, eminence, fame, honour, kudos, prestige, renown. **3** grandeur, magnificence, majesty, pomp, splendour. □ **glory in** delight in, exult in, rejoice in, relish, revel in, take pride in.

gloss n. shine on a smooth surface. ● v. make glossy. □ **gloss over** cover up (a mistake etc.).

■ n. gleam, lustre, patina, sheen, shine. ● v. buff, burnish, polish, shine. □ **gloss over** camouflage, conceal, cover up, disguise, hide, whitewash.

glossary n. list of technical or special words, with definitions.

glossy adj. (**-ier, -iest**) shiny.

■ gleaming, lustrous, shining, shiny, sleek.

glottis n. opening at the upper end of the windpipe between the vocal cords. □ **glottal** adj.

glove n. covering for the hand, usu. with separate divisions for fingers and thumb.

glow v. **1** send out light and heat without flame. **2** have a warm or flushed look, colour, or feeling. ● n. glowing state, look, or feeling. □ **glow-worm** n. beetle that can give out a greenish light.

■ v. **1** gleam, glimmer, shine. **2** blush, colour, flush, go red, redden. ● n. **2** brightness, incandescence, radiance; blush, flush, rosiness, ruddiness; ardour, enthusiasm, fervour, passion, warmth.

glower /glowr/ v. scowl.

glucose n. form of sugar found in fruit juice.

glue n. sticky substance used for joining things together. ● v. (**gluing**) **1** fasten with glue. **2** attach closely. □ **gluey** adj.

glum adj. (**glummer, glummest**) sad and gloomy.

■ crestfallen, dejected, depressed, despondent, disconsolate, dispirited, downcast, downhearted, gloomy, low, melancholy, miserable, morose, sad, sorrowful, unhappy, woebegone.

glut v. (**glutted**) **1** supply with more than is needed. **2** overload with food. ● n. excessive supply.

■ v. **1** deluge, flood, inundate, overload, oversupply, saturate, swamp. **2** overfeed, sate, satiate, surfeit. ● n. excess, overabundance, oversupply, superfluity, surfeit, surplus.

gluten n. sticky protein substance found in cereals.

glutinous adj. glue-like, sticky.

glutton n. **1** greedy person. **2** one who is eager for something. □ **gluttonous** adj., **gluttony** n.

■ **1** gourmand, colloq. hog, colloq. pig. □ **gluttonous** greedy, colloq. gutsy, insa-

tiable, colloq. piggy, voracious. **gluttony** greed, greediness, insatiability, voracity.

glycerine n. thick sweet liquid used in medicines etc.

gnarled /naarld/ adj. knobbly, twisted.

■ contorted, crooked, knobbed, knobbly, knotty, misshapen, twisted.

gnash /nash/ v. grind (one's teeth).

gnat /nat/ n. small biting fly.

gnaw /naw/ v. bite persistently.

■ bite, champ, chew, crunch, masticate, munch.

gnome /nōm/ n. dwarf, goblin.

gnomic /nōmik/ adj. sententious.

gnu /nōō/ n. ox-like antelope.

go v. (**went, gone**) **1** walk, travel, proceed. **2** depart. **3** extend. **4** function. **5** (of time) pass. **6** belong in a specified place. **7** become. **8** match. **9** be spent or used up. **10** collapse, fail, die. **11** make (a specified movement or sound). **12** be sold. ● n. (pl. **goes**) **1** energy. **2** turn, try. □ **go-ahead** n. signal to proceed. ● adj. enterprising. **go back on** fail to keep (a promise). **go-between** n. one who acts as messenger or negotiator. **go down with** become ill with. **go for 1** go to fetch. **2** choose. **3** (sl.) attack. **go-getter** n. pushily enterprising person. **go-getting** adj. aggressively ambitious. **go-kart** n. miniature racing car. **go off 1** explode. **2** decay. **go out** be extinguished. **go over** inspect the details of. **go round 1** spin, revolve. **2** be enough for everyone. **go slow** work at a deliberately slow pace as a protest. **go-slow** n. this procedure. **go through 1** undergo. **2** use up. **go under 1** succumb. **2** fail. **go up 1** rise in price. **2** explode, burn rapidly. **go with 1** accompany. **2** match, harmonize with. **on the go** (colloq.) in constant motion, active.

■ v. **1** advance, betake oneself, journey, move, proceed, progress, travel, walk, wend one's way. **2** depart, leave, make off, move away, retire, retreat, withdraw; set off or out. **3** extend, lead, stretch. **4** be operational, function, operate, run, work. **5** elapse, pass, slip by or away. **6** become, get, grow, turn. **8** be compatible, be suited, complement each other, harmonize, match, suit each other. ● n. **1** animation, drive, dynamism, energy, enthusiasm, initiative, pep, verve, vigour, colloq. vim, vitality, vivacity, zest. **2** attempt, bid, shot, colloq. stab, try; chance, opportunity, turn. □ **go-ahead** n. approval, authorization, colloq.

green light, *colloq.* OK, permission. *adj.* ambitious, dynamic, enterprising, go-getting, keen, *colloq.* pushy, resourceful. **go back on** break, fail to keep, renege on, repudiate, retract. **go-between** intermediary, mediator, messenger, middleman, negotiator, representative. **go off 1** blow up, burst, erupt, explode. **2** decay, decompose, go bad, go stale, moulder, rot, spoil. **go over** examine, inspect, investigate, look at, read, review, scrutinize, study. **go through 1** bear, endure, experience, live through, put up with, stand, suffer, undergo, withstand. **2** consume, exhaust, spend, use up. **go under 2** collapse, fail, fold, go bankrupt, *colloq.* go bust, go out of business.

goad *n.* **1** pointed stick for driving cattle. **2** stimulus to activity. ● *v.* stimulate by annoying.
■ *n.* **2** impetus, incitement, instigation, motivation, provocation, spur, stimulus.

goal *n.* **1** structure or area into which players try to send the ball in certain games. **2** point scored thus. **3** objective. □ **goalpost** *n.* either of the posts marking the limit of a goal.
■ **3** aim, ambition, aspiration, design, end, intention, object, objective, purpose, target.

goalie *n.* (*colloq.*) goalkeeper.
goalkeeper *n.* player whose task is to keep the ball out of the goal.
goat *n.* small horned animal.
gobble *v.* **1** eat quickly and greedily. **2** make a throaty sound like a turkeycock.
■ **1** bolt, gulp, guzzle, *colloq.* scoff, wolf.

gobbledegook *n.* (*colloq.*) pompous language used by officials.
goblet *n.* drinking glass with a stem and foot.
goblin *n.* mischievous ugly elf.
god *n.* **1** superhuman being worshipped as having power over nature and human affairs. **2** (**God**) creator and ruler of the universe in Christian, Jewish, and Muslim teaching. **3** person or thing that is greatly admired or adored. □ **God-fearing** *adj.* sincerely religious. **godforsaken** *adj.* wretched, dismal.
godchild *n.* child in relation to its godparent(s).
god-daughter *n.* female godchild.
goddess *n.* female god.
godfather *n.* male godparent.
godhead *n.* **1** divine nature. **2** deity.
godmother *n.* female godparent.

godparent *n.* person who promises at a child's baptism to see that it is brought up as a Christian.
godsend *n.* piece of unexpected good fortune.
godson *n.* male godchild.
goggle *v.* stare with wide-open eyes.
goggles *n.pl.* spectacles for protecting the eyes.
goitre /góytər/ *n.* enlarged thyroid gland.
gold *n.* **1** yellow metal of high value. **2** coins or articles made of this. **3** its colour. ● *adj.* made of, coloured, or shining like gold. □ **goldfield** *n.* area where gold is found. **gold rush** rush to a newly discovered goldfield.
golden *adj.* **1** made of gold. **2** like gold in colour. **3** precious, excellent. □ **golden handshake** generous cash payment to a person dismissed or forced to retire. **golden jubilee, wedding** 50th anniversary.
goldfinch *n.* songbird with a band of yellow across each wing.
goldfish *n.* (*pl.* **goldfish**) reddish carp kept in a bowl or pond.
goldsmith *n.* person whose trade is making articles in gold.
golf *n.* game in which a ball is struck with clubs into a series of holes. ● *v.* play golf. □ **golf course** land on which golf is played. **golfer** *n.*
golliwog *n.* black-faced soft doll with fuzzy hair.
gonad *n.* animal organ producing gametes.
gondola *n.* Venetian canal-boat.
gondolier *n.* man who propels a gondola by means of a pole.
gone *see* go.
gong *n.* **1** metal plate that resounds when struck. **2** (*sl.*) medal.
gonorrhoea *n.* a venereal disease.
goo *n.* (*colloq.*) sticky wet substance. □ **gooey** *adj.*
good *adj.* (**better, best**) **1** having the right or desirable qualities, satisfactory. **2** proper, expedient. **3** morally correct, kindly. **4** well-behaved. **5** enjoyable. **6** beneficial. **7** efficient. **8** thorough. **9** considerable, full. **10** valid. ● *n.* **1** that which is beneficial or morally good. **2** (*pl.*) movable property, articles of trade, things to be carried by road or rail. □ **as good as** practically, almost. **good-for-nothing** *adj.* & *n.* worthless (person). **Good Friday** Friday before Easter, commemorating the Crucifixion. **good-looking** *adj.* attractive. **good name** good

reputation. **good-natured** adj. kind, friendly.

■ adj. **1** acceptable, adequate, commendable, fine, colloq. OK, satisfactory. **2** appropriate, correct, expedient, fitting, proper, right, suitable. **3** ethical, honourable, moral, noble, respectable, righteous, upright, virtuous, worthy; benevolent, charitable, considerate, humane, kind, kind-hearted, kindly, nice. **4** manageable, obedient, well-behaved, well-mannered. **5** agreeable, amusing, enjoyable, entertaining, pleasant, pleasing, pleasurable. **6** beneficial, healthy, salutary, wholesome. **7** accomplished, adept, capable, competent, proficient, skilful, skilled; efficient, reliable, safe, sound, trustworthy. **8** careful, methodical, meticulous, painstaking, scrupulous, systematic, thorough. **9** considerable, large, respectable, sizeable, substantial. **10** authentic, believable, credible, genuine, legitimate, sound, valid. ● n. **1** advantage, benefit, gain, profit, use. **2** (**goods**) belongings, effects, possessions, property, things; commodities, stocks, wares; cargo, freight. □ **good-looking** attractive, beautiful, Sc. bonny, comely, handsome, personable, pretty, colloq. stunning. **good-natured** amiable, charitable, friendly, generous, genial, helpful, kind, kind-hearted, kindly, likeable, nice, pleasant.

goodbye int. & n. expression used when parting.

goodness n. **1** quality of being good. **2** good part of something.

goodwill n. **1** friendly feeling. **2** established popularity of a business, treated as a saleable asset.

goody n. (colloq.) something good or attractive, esp. to eat. □ **goody-goody** adj. & n. smugly virtuous (person).

goose n. (pl. **geese**) **1** web-footed bird larger than a duck. **2** female of this. □ **goose-flesh, -pimples** ns. bristling skin caused by cold or fear. **goose-step** n. way of marching without bending the knees.

gooseberry n. **1** thorny shrub. **2** its edible (usu. green) berry.

gore¹ n. clotted blood from a wound.

gore² v. pierce with a horn or tusk.

gore³ n. triangular or tapering section of a skirt or sail.

gorge n. narrow steep-sided valley. ● v. **1** devour greedily. **2** satiate.

■ n. canyon, defile, pass, ravine. ● v. **1** bolt, devour, gobble, guzzle, wolf. **2** fill, glut, satiate, surfeit.

gorgeous adj. **1** richly coloured, magnificent. **2** (colloq.) beautiful. □ **gorgeously** adv.

■ **1** brilliant, exquisite, magnificent, resplendent, rich, splendid, sumptuous. **2** attractive, beautiful, good-looking, lovely, colloq. stunning.

gorgon n. terrifying woman.

gorilla n. large powerful ape.

gorse n. wild evergreen thorny shrub with yellow flowers.

gory adj. (-**ier**, -**iest**) **1** covered with blood. **2** involving bloodshed.

gosling n. young goose.

gospel n. **1** teachings of Christ. **2** (**Gospel**) any of the first four books of the New Testament. **3** thing regarded as definitely true.

gossamer n. **1** fine filmy piece of cobweb. **2** flimsy delicate material.

gossip n. **1** casual talk, esp. about other people's affairs. **2** person fond of gossiping. ● v. (**gossiped**) engage in gossip.

■ n. **1** chat, conversation, small talk, talk; hearsay, rumour, scandal, tittle-tattle. ● v. chat, chatter, colloq. natter, prattle, talk; spread rumours, tell tales, tittle-tattle.

got see **get**.

Gothic adj. **1** of an architectural style of the 12th–16th centuries, with pointed arches. **2** (of a novel etc.) in a horrific style popular in the 18th–19th centuries.

gouge n. chisel with a concave blade. ● v. **1** cut out with a gouge. **2** scoop or force out.

goulash n. stew of meat and vegetables, seasoned with paprika.

gourd n. **1** fleshy fruit of a climbing plant. **2** container made from its dried rind.

gourmand n. glutton.

gourmet /goormay/ n. connoisseur of good food and drink.

gout n. disease causing inflammation of the joints. □ **gouty** adj.

govern v. **1** rule with authority. **2** keep under control. **3** influence, determine. □ **governable** adj., **governor** n.

■ **1** be in charge of, command, control, direct, hold sway over, manage, rule, run, preside over, steer. **2** bridle, check, control, curb, repress, restrain, subdue, suppress. **3** affect, determine, influence.

governance *n.* governing, control.

government *n.* **1** governing. **2** group or organization governing a country. □ **governmental** *adj.*
■ **1** administration, command, control, direction, governance, management, rule. **2** administration, leadership, regime.

gown *n.* **1** loose flowing garment. **2** woman's long dress. **3** official robe.

GP *abbr.* general practitioner.

grab *v.* (**grabbed**) **1** grasp suddenly. **2** take greedily. ● *n.* **1** sudden clutch or attempt to seize. **2** mechanical device for gripping things.
■ *v.* **1** clutch, grasp, grip, seize, take hold of. **2** appropriate, *sl.* nab, seize, snap up, snatch.

grace *n.* **1** attractiveness and elegance, esp. of manner or movement. **2** courteous good will. **3** mercy. **4** short prayer of thanks for a meal. ● *v.* **1** add grace to, enhance. **2** confer honour or dignity on.
■ *n.* **1** attractiveness, ease, elegance, finesse, gracefulness, poise, polish, refinement, suavity, tastefulness; agility, suppleness. **2** courtesy, decency, manners, politeness, tact. **3** clemency, compassion, forgiveness, leniency, mercifulness, mercy. ● *v.* **1** adorn, beautify, decorate, embellish, enhance. **2** dignify, distinguish, honour.

graceful *adj.* having or showing grace. □ **gracefully** *adv.*
■ agile, lissom, lithe, nimble, supple; elegant, polished, refined.

graceless *adj.* lacking grace or charm.

gracious *adj.* kind and pleasant towards inferiors. □ **graciously** *adv.*, **graciousness** *n.*
■ affable, agreeable, beneficent, benevolent, charitable, civil, considerate, cordial, courteous, friendly, good-natured, kind, kindly, obliging, pleasant, polite.

gradation *n.* **1** stage in a process of gradual change. **2** this process.

grade *n.* **1** level of rank, quality, or value. **2** mark given to a student for his or her standard of work. ● *v.* **1** arrange in grades. **2** assign a grade to. □ **make the grade** be successful.
■ *n.* **1** class, degree, echelon, level, position, rank, stage, standing, station, status. **2** mark, score. ● *v.* **1** categorize, class,

classify, group, order, organize, sort. **2** assess, evaluate, mark, rate.

gradient *n.* slope, amount of this.

gradual *adj.* taking place by degrees. □ **gradually** *adv.*
■ progressive, slow, steady, step by step.

graduate *n.* /grádyooat/ person who holds a university degree. ● *v.* /grádyoo-ayt/ **1** take a university degree. **2** divide into graded sections. **3** mark into regular divisions. □ **graduation** *n.*

graffiti *n.pl.* words or drawings scribbled on a wall etc.

graft *n.* **1** shoot fixed into a cut in a tree to form a new growth. **2** living tissue transplanted surgically. **3** (*sl.*) hard work. ● *v.* **1** put a graft in or on. **2** join inseparably. **3** (*sl.*) work hard.

grain *n.* **1** small hard seed(s) of a food plant such as wheat or rice. **2** these plants. **3** small hard particle. **4** unit of weight (0.065 g). **5** texture or pattern made by fibres or particles. □ **grainy** *adj.*

gram *n.* one-thousandth of a kilogram.

grammar *n.* use of words in their correct forms and relationships.

grammatical *adj.* according to the rules of grammar. □ **grammatically** *adv.*

grampus *n.* dolphin-like sea animal.

gran *n.* (*colloq.*) grandmother.

granary *n.* storehouse for grain.

grand *adj.* **1** splendid, imposing. **2** of chief importance. **3** (*colloq.*) very good. ● *n.* grand piano. □ **grand piano** large full-toned piano with horizontal strings.

grandly *adv.*, **grandness** *n.*
■ *adj.* **1** dignified, fine, imposing, impressive, lofty, luxurious, magnificent, majestic, monumental, noble, palatial, splendid, stately, sumptuous. **2** chief, head, leading, main, principal.

grandad *n.* (*colloq.*) grandfather.

grandchild *n.* child of one's son or daughter.

granddaughter *n.* female grandchild.

grandeur *n.* **1** splendour. **2** nobility of character.
■ **1** magnificence, majesty, pomp, splendour. **2** dignity, eminence, greatness, nobility.

grandfather *n.* male grandparent. □ **grandfather clock** one in a tall wooden case.

grandiloquent *adj.* using pompous language. □ **grandiloquence** *n.*

grandiose adj. 1 imposing. 2 planned on a large scale. □ **grandiosely** adv., **grandiosity** n.
■ 1 imposing, impressive, magnificent, majestic, splendid. 2 ambitious, extravagant, flamboyant, ostentatious, pretentious.

grandma n. (colloq.) grandmother.

grandmother n. female grandparent.

grandpa n. (colloq.) grandfather.

grandparent n. parent of one's father or mother.

grandson n. male grandchild.

grandstand n. main stand for spectators at sports ground.

grange n. country house with farm buildings that belong to it.

granite n. hard grey stone.

granny n. (colloq.) grandmother. □ **granny flat** self-contained accommodation in one's house for a relative.

grant v. 1 consent to fulfil. 2 give or allow as a privilege. 3 admit to be true. ● n. money given for a particular purpose, esp. from public funds. □ **take for granted** assume to be true or sure to happen or continue.
■ v. accede to, agree to, assent to, concede to, consent to. 2 allow, award, give, permit. 3 acknowledge, admit, allow, concede, confess. ● n. allocation, allowance, award; subsidy, subvention; bursary, scholarship.

granular adj. like grains.

granulate v. 1 form into grains. 2 roughen the surface of. □ **granulation** n.

granule n. small grain.

grape n. green or purple berry used for making wine. □ **grapevine** n. 1 vine bearing grapes. 2 way news spreads unofficially.

grapefruit n. large round yellow citrus fruit.

graph n. diagram showing the relationship between quantities.

graphic adj. 1 of drawing, painting, or engraving. 2 giving a vivid description. ● n.pl. diagrams etc. used in calculation and design. □ **graphically** adv.
■ adj. 2 clear, colourful, detailed, lifelike, picturesque, realistic, striking, vivid.

graphite n. a form of carbon.

graphology n. study of handwriting. □ **graphologist** n.

grapnel n. 1 small anchor with several hooks. 2 hooked device for dragging a river bed.

grapple v. fight at close quarters, struggle. □ **grapple with** try to manage or overcome. **grappling-iron** n. grapnel.

grasp v. 1 seize and hold. 2 understand. ● n. 1 firm hold or grip. 2 understanding.
■ v. 1 clasp, clutch, grab, grip, hold, seize, snatch, take hold of. 2 comprehend, fathom, follow, colloq. get, colloq. get the hang of, see, take in, understand.

grasping adj. greedy, avaricious.
■ acquisitive, avaricious, greedy, rapacious.

grass n. 1 wild plant with green blades eaten by animals. 2 species of this (e.g. a cereal plant). 3 ground covered with grass. ● v. cover with grass. □ **grass roots** 1 fundamental level or source. 2 rank-and-file members. **grass widow** wife whose husband is absent temporarily. **grassy** adj.

grasshopper n. jumping insect that makes a chirping noise.

grassland n. wide grass-covered area with few trees.

grate¹ n. 1 metal frame keeping fuel in a fireplace. 2 hearth.

grate² v. 1 shred finely by rubbing against a jagged surface. 2 make a harsh noise by rubbing. □ **grate on** have an irritating effect on.
■ 1 grind, shred, rasp, scrape, scratch. □ **grate on** annoy, get on one's nerves, irk, irritate, jar on.

grateful adj. feeling that one values a kindness or benefit received. □ **gratefully** adv.
■ appreciative, thankful; beholden, indebted, obliged.

grater n. device for grating food.

gratify v. 1 please. 2 satisfy (wishes). □ **gratification** n.
■ 1 delight, gladden, please. 2 fulfil, indulge, pander to, satisfy.

grating n. screen of spaced bars placed across an opening.

gratis adj. & adv. free of charge.

gratitude n. being grateful.

gratuitous adj. 1 given or done free. 2 uncalled-for. □ **gratuitously** adv.
■ 2 needless, uncalled-for, unjustified, unprovoked, unsolicited, unwarranted.

gratuity n. money given in recognition of services rendered.

grave¹ n. hole dug to bury a corpse.

grave² *adj.* **1** serious, causing great anxiety. **2** solemn. □ **grave accent** /graav/ the accent (`). **gravely** *adv.*

■ **1** important, pressing, serious, urgent, weighty; acute, critical, dangerous, perilous, severe, threatening. **2** earnest, serious, sober, solemn, sombre, unsmiling.

gravel *n.* coarse sand with small stones. □ **gravelly** *adj.*

gravestone *n.* stone placed over a grave.

graveyard *n.* burial ground.

gravitate *v.* move or be attracted towards something.

gravitation *n.* **1** gravitating. **2** force of gravity. □ **gravitational** *adj.*

gravity *n.* **1** seriousness, importance. **2** solemnity. **3** force that attracts bodies towards the centre of the earth.

■ **1** importance, magnitude, seriousness, significance; acuteness, severity, urgency. **2** dignity, soberness, solemnity, sombreness.

gravy *n.* **1** juice from cooked meat. **2** sauce made from this.

gray *adj.* & *n.* = **grey**.

graze¹ *v.* **1** feed on growing grass. **2** pasture animals in (a field).

graze² *v.* **1** injure by scraping the skin. **2** touch or scrape lightly in passing. ● *n.* abrasion.

■ *v.* **1** bark, scrape, scratch, skin. **2** brush, shave, touch. ● *n.* abrasion, scrape, scratch.

grease *n.* fatty or oily matter, esp. as a lubricant. ● *v.* put grease on. □ **greasepaint** *n.* make-up used by actors. **greasy** *adj.*

great *adj.* **1** much above average in size, amount, or intensity. **2** of remarkable ability etc. **3** important, distinguished. **4** (*colloq.*) very good. □ **greatness** *n.*

■ **1** big, colossal, enormous, extensive, gigantic, huge, immense, large, massive, prodigious, tremendous, vast; considerable, extreme, intense, marked, pronounced. **2** accomplished, brilliant, excellent, exceptional, gifted, outstanding, skilled, talented. **3** celebrated, distinguished, eminent, famous, illustrious, important, notable, prominent, renowned, well-known.

great- *pref.* (of a family relationship) one generation removed in ancestry or descent.

greatly *adv.* very much.

grebe *n.* a diving bird.

Grecian *adj.* Greek.

greed *n.* excessive desire, esp. for food or wealth. □ **greedy** *adj.*, **greedily** *adv.*, **greediness** *n.*

■ acquisitiveness, avarice, cupidity, greediness; gluttony, voracity. □ **greedy** acquisitive, avaricious, covetous, grasping, materialistic; gluttonous, *colloq.* gutsy, insatiable, ravenous, voracious.

Greek *adj.* & *n.* (native, language) of Greece.

green *adj.* **1** of the colour of growing grass. **2** unripe. **3** inexperienced, easily deceived. **4** concerned with protecting the environment. ● *n.* **1** green colour or thing. **2** piece of grassy public land. **3** (*pl.*) green vegetables. □ **green belt** area of open land round a town. **green fingers** skill in growing plants. **green light** signal or (*colloq.*) permission to proceed. **Green Paper** government report of proposals being considered. **green-room** *n.* room in a theatre for the use of actors when off stage. **greenish** *adj.*

■ *adj.* **2** unready, unripe, unripened. **3** callow, credulous, gullible, immature, inexperienced, innocent, naive, unsophisticated.

greenery *n.* green foliage or plants.

greenfinch *n.* finch with green and yellow feathers.

greenfly *n.* (*pl.* **-fly**) small green insect that sucks juices from plants.

greengage *n.* round plum with a greenish skin.

greengrocer *n.* shopkeeper selling vegetables and fruit.

greenhorn *n.* novice.

greenhouse *n.* glass building for rearing plants. □ **greenhouse effect** trapping of the sun's radiation by pollution in the atmosphere. **greenhouse gas** gas contributing to this.

greet *v.* **1** address politely on meeting or arrival. **2** receive or acknowledge in a particular way. **3** become apparent to (the eye or ear).

■ **1,2** hail, meet, receive, salute, welcome; acknowledge.

gregarious *adj.* **1** fond of company. **2** living in flocks etc. □ **gregariousness** *n.*

■ **1** companionable, convivial, friendly, outgoing, sociable.

gremlin *n.* (*colloq.*) mischievous spirit blamed for faults or problems.

grenade *n.* small bomb thrown by hand or fired from a rifle.

grenadine n. flavouring syrup made from pomegranates etc.

grew see **grow**.

grey adj. of the colour between black and white. ●n. grey colour or thing. ●v. make or become grey. □ **greyish** adj.

greyhound n. slender dog noted for its swiftness.

grid n. 1 grating. 2 system of numbered squares for map references. 3 network of lines, power cables, etc. 4 gridiron.

gridiron n. 1 framework of metal bars for cooking on. 2 field for American football, marked with parallel lines.

grief n. deep sorrow. □ **come to grief** meet with disaster.
- ■ anguish, desolation, distress, heartache, misery, pain, sadness, sorrow, unhappiness.

grievance n. cause for complaint.
- ■ sl. beef, complaint, colloq. gripe, colloq. grouse, objection.

grieve v. (cause to) feel grief.
- ■ distress, hurt, sadden, upset, wound; be in mourning, cry, mourn, sorrow, weep.

grievous adj. 1 causing grief. 2 serious. □ **grievously** adv.

griffin n. mythological creature with an eagle's head and wings and a lion's body.

griffon n. 1 small terrier-like dog. 2 a kind of vulture. 3 griffin.

grill n. 1 metal grid, grating. 2 device on a cooker for radiating heat downwards. 3 grilled food. ●v. 1 cook under a grill or on a gridiron. 2 question closely and severely.

grille n. grating, esp. in a door or window.

grim adj. (**grimmer, grimmest**) 1 stern, severe. 2 ghastly. 3 cheerless, uninviting. □ **grimly** adv., **grimness** n.
- ■ 1 dour, fierce, forbidding, implacable, relentless, severe, sombre, stern, stony, unrelenting, unsmiling, unyielding. 2 appalling, awful, dire, dreadful, ghastly, grisly, gruesome, hideous, horrendous, horrible, horrid, shocking, terrible. 3 bleak, cheerless, depressing, dismal, dreary, gloomy, uninviting.

grimace n. contortion of the face in pain or disgust, or to amuse. ●v. make a grimace.

grime n. ingrained dirt. ●v. blacken with grime. □ **grimy** adj.

grin v. (**grinned**) smile broadly, showing the teeth. ●n. broad smile.

grind v. (**ground**) 1 crush into grains or powder. 2 sharpen or smooth by friction. 3 rub harshly together. ●n. 1 grinding process. 2 hard monotonous work. □ **grind down** oppress by cruelty. **grinder** n.
- ■ v. 1 crush, granulate, mince, pound, powder, pulverize. 2 sharpen, whet; file, polish, smooth. 3 gnash, grate. □ **grind down** crush, oppress, persecute, subdue, suppress.

grindstone n. thick revolving disc for sharpening or grinding.

grip v. (**gripped**) 1 take or keep firm hold of. 2 hold the attention of. ●n. 1 firm grasp or hold. 2 way of or thing for gripping. 3 understanding. 4 travelling bag.
- ■ v. 1 clasp, clutch, grab, grasp, hold, take hold of. 2 absorb, captivate, enthral, entrance, fascinate, hold spellbound, hypnotize, mesmerize, rivet. ●n. 1 clasp, grasp, hold. 2 foothold, purchase, toe-hold; handle. 3 apprehension, awareness, comprehension, grasp, perception, understanding.

gripe v. (colloq.) grumble. ●n. 1 colic pain. 2 (colloq.) grievance.

grisly adj. (-**ier, -iest**) causing fear, horror, or disgust.

gristle n. tough tissue of animal bodies, esp. in meat. □ **gristly** adj.

grit n. 1 particles of stone or sand. 2 (colloq.) courage and endurance. ●v. (**gritted**) 1 make a grating sound. 2 clench. 3 spread grit on. □ **gritty** adj.

grizzle v. & n. whimper, whine.

grizzled adj. grey-haired.

grizzly bear large brown bear of N. America.

groan v. make a long deep sound in pain, grief, or disapproval. ●n. sound made by groaning.
- ■ v. cry out, moan, sigh, wail, whimper.

grocer n. shopkeeper selling foods and household stores.

grocery n. grocer's shop or goods.

grog n. drink of spirits mixed with water.

groggy adj. (-**ier, -iest**) weak and unsteady, esp. after illness. □ **groggily** adv., **grogginess** n.

groin n. 1 groove where each thigh joins the trunk. 2 curved edge where two vaults meet.

grommet n. 1 insulating washer. 2 tube placed through the eardrum.

groom n. 1 person employed to look after horses. 2 bridegroom. ● v. 1 clean and brush (an animal). 2 make neat and trim. 3 prepare (a person) for a career or position.

■ v. 1 brush, clean, curry. 2 neaten up, smarten up, spruce up, tidy up, colloq. titivate. 3 coach, drill, make ready, prepare, prime, school, train.

groove n. long narrow channel. ● v. make groove(s) in.

grope v. feel about as one does in the dark.

gross adj. 1 thick, large-bodied. 2 vulgar. 3 outrageous. 4 total, without deductions. ● n. (pl. **gross**) twelve dozen. ● v. produce or earn as total profit. □ **grossly** adv.

■ adj. 1 bloated, bulky, corpulent, fat, fleshy, heavy, large, massive, obese, overfed, overweight. 2 coarse, crude, indecent, indelicate, obscene, offensive, rude, vulgar. 3 blatant, flagrant, glaring, monstrous, outrageous, shocking. 4 entire, inclusive, overall, total, whole.

grotesque adj. very odd or ugly. ● n. 1 comically distorted figure. 2 design using fantastic forms. □ **grotesquely** adv.

■ adj. bizarre, freakish, hideous, misshapen, monstrous, odd, outlandish, peculiar, strange, ugly, unnatural.

grotto n. (pl. **-oes**) picturesque cave.

grouch v. & n. (colloq.) grumble.

ground[1] n. 1 solid surface of earth. 2 soil. 3 (pl.) reason for a belief or action. 4 (pl.) enclosed land attached to a house etc. 5 area designated for special use. 6 (pl.) dregs. ● v. 1 prevent (an aircraft or pilot) from flying. 2 base. 3 give basic training to. □ **ground-rent** n. rent paid for land leased for building. **ground swell** slow heavy waves.

■ n. 1 earth, land, terra firma. 2 clay, dirt, earth, loam, sod, soil. 3 (grounds) basis, cause, excuse, foundation, justification, motive, reason. 4 (grounds) estate, lands; campus. 5 field, pitch, playing field. 5 (grounds) dregs, lees, sediment. ● v. 2 base, establish, found. 3 coach, inform, instruct, prepare, teach, train.

ground[2] see **grind**.

grounding n. basic training.

groundless adj. without foundation.

groundnut n. peanut.

groundsheet n. waterproof sheet for spreading on the ground.

groundsman n. person employed to look after a sports ground.

groundwork n. preliminary or basic work.

group n. number of people or things near, belonging, classed, or working together. ● v. form or gather into group(s).

■ n. assortment, batch, category, class, collection, series, set; alliance, assembly, association, band, body, circle, clique, club, cluster, company, congregation, corps, coterie, crew, crowd, faction, flock, gang, gathering, league, party, society, team, throng, troop, union. ● v. categorize, class, classify, grade, rank, sort; assemble, bring together, collect, gather.

grouse[1] n. a kind of game bird.

grouse[2] v. & n. (colloq.) grumble.

grout n. thin fluid mortar. ● v. fill with grout.

grove n. group of trees.

grovel v. (**grovelled**) 1 behave obsequiously. 2 crawl face downwards.

■ 1 abase oneself, crawl, cringe, fawn, kowtow, toady.

grow v. (**grew**, **grown**) 1 increase in size or amount. 2 develop or exist as a living plant. 3 become. 4 produce by cultivation. □ **grow up** become adult or mature. **grown-up** adj. & n. adult. **grower** n.

■ 1 broaden, develop, enlarge, evolve, expand, extend, lengthen, multiply, spread, stretch, swell, widen; flourish, prosper, thrive. 2 bud, burgeon, germinate, shoot up, spring up, sprout. 3 become, get. 4 cultivate, farm, produce, propagate, raise.

growl v. make a low threatening sound. ● n. this sound.

grown see **grow**.

growth n. 1 process of growing. 2 thing that grows or has grown. 3 tumour. □ **growth industry** one developing faster than others.

■ 1 broadening, development, enlargement, evolution, expansion, extension, increase, proliferation, spread.

groyne n. wall built out into the sea to prevent erosion.

grub n. 1 larva of certain insects. 2 (sl.) food. ● v. (**grubbed**) 1 dig the surface of soil. 2 dig up by the roots. 3 rummage.

grubby adj. (**-ier**, **-iest**) dirty.

grudge n. feeling of resentment or ill will. ● v. begrudge, resent.

■ v. begrudge, be jealous of, envy, mind, resent.

gruel n. thin oatmeal porridge.

gruelling adj. very tiring.

■ arduous, demanding, draining, exhausting, hard, laborious, strenuous, taxing, tiring, tough.

gruesome adj. filling one with horror or disgust.

■ abhorrent, appalling, awful, disgusting, dreadful, fearful, frightful, ghastly, grim, grisly, hideous, horrendous, horrible, horrid, horrific, loathsome, repellent, repugnant, repulsive, revolting, shocking, terrible.

gruff adj. **1** (of the voice) low and hoarse. **2** surly. □ **gruffly** adv.

■ **1** deep, guttural, hoarse, husky, low, throaty. **2** bad-tempered, blunt, brusque, cantankerous, churlish, crabby, crotchety, crusty, curt, grumpy, irascible, short-tempered, surly, terse.

grumble v. **1** complain peevishly. **2** rumble. ● n. **1** complaint. **2** rumble. □ **grumbler** n.

■ v. **1** carp, complain, colloq. gripe, colloq. grouch, colloq. grouse, make a fuss, moan, colloq. whinge.

grumpy adj. (**-ier**, **-iest**) bad-tempered. □ **grumpily** adv.

■ bad-tempered, cantankerous, crabby, cross, crotchety, crusty, disagreeable, gruff, fractious, irritable, peevish, snappy, splenetic, surly, testy.

grunt n. gruff snorting sound made by a pig. ● v. make this or a similar sound.

gryphon n. = **griffin**.

G-string n. narrow strip of cloth covering the genitals, attached to a string round the waist.

guano /gwaáno/ n. dung of seabirds, used as manure.

guarantee n. **1** formal promise to do something or that a thing is of specified quality and durability. **2** thing offered as security. **3** guarantor. ● v. **1** give or serve as a guarantee for. **2** promise.

■ n. **1** assurance, oath, pledge, promise, word; warrant, warranty. **2** bond, pledge, security, surety. ● v. **1** answer for, attest to, certify, vouch for. **2** give one's word, pledge, promise, swear.

guarantor n. giver of a guarantee.

guard v. **1** watch over and protect or supervise. **2** restrain. ● n. **1** state of watchfulness. **2** person(s) guarding something. **3** protecting part or device. **4** railway official in charge of a train. **5** defensive attitude in boxing, cricket, etc.

□ **guard against** take precautions against. **on** or **off one's guard** prepared (or unprepared) for some surprise or difficulty.

■ v. **1** defend, keep safe, look after, mind, patrol, protect, shield, supervise, watch over. **2** contain, control, curb, keep in check, restrain. ● n. **1** lookout, vigil, watch. **2** bodyguard, custodian, guardian, sl. minder, protector; sentinel, sentry, watchman; jailer, warder. **3** defence, protection, safeguard, shield.

guarded adj. cautious, discreet.

■ colloq. cagey, careful, cautious, chary, circumspect, discreet, noncommittal, reticent, wary.

guardian n. **1** one who guards or protects. **2** person undertaking legal responsibility for an orphan. □ **guardianship** n.

■ **1** custodian, defender, keeper, preserver, protector.

guardsman n. soldier acting as guard.

guava /gwaáva/ n. orange-coloured fruit of a tropical tree.

gudgeon[1] n. small freshwater fish.

gudgeon[2] n. **1** a kind of pivot. **2** socket for a rudder. **3** metal pin.

guerrilla n. member of a small fighting force, taking independent irregular action.

guess v. **1** estimate without calculation or measurement. **2** think likely. ● n. opinion formed by guessing. □ **guesser** n.

■ v. **1** estimate, make a guess (at). **2** assume, believe, conjecture, deduce, fancy, feel, infer, reckon, suppose, surmise, suspect, think. ● n. conjecture, estimate, speculation, supposition, surmise.

guesswork n. guessing.

guest n. **1** person entertained at another's house or table etc., or lodging at a hotel. **2** visiting performer. □ **guest house** superior boarding house.

guffaw n. coarse noisy laugh. ● v. utter a guffaw.

guidance n. **1** guiding. **2** advising or advice on problems.

■ **1** conduct, control, direction, leadership. **2** advice, briefing, counsel, counselling, information, instruction, teaching.

guide n. **1** person who shows others the way, esp. one employed to point out interesting sights to travellers. **2** adviser. **3** book of information. **4** thing directing actions or movements. ● v. 1 act as guide to. 2 lead, direct.

■ n. 1 conductor, director, escort, leader; courier. 2 adviser, counsellor, guru, mentor, teacher. 3 companion, guidebook, handbook, manual. 4 example, model, pattern, standard; beacon, indicator, landmark, light, marker, sign, signal, signpost. ● v. conduct, direct, lead, manoeuvre, pilot, shepherd, show, steer, usher; advise, counsel, instruct, teach, train.

guidebook n. book of information about a place.

guild n. 1 society for mutual aid or with a common purpose. 2 medieval association of craftsmen.

guilder n. unit of money of the Netherlands.

guile n. treacherous cunning, craftiness. □ **guileful** adj., **guileless** adj.

guillotine n. 1 machine for beheading criminals. 2 machine for cutting paper or metal. 3 fixing of times for voting in Parliament, to prevent a lengthy debate. ● v. use a guillotine on.

guilt n. 1 fact of having committed an offence. 2 responsibility for an offence. 3 feeling that one is to blame. □ **guiltless** adj.

■ 1 criminality, misconduct, sinfulness, wrongdoing. 2 blame, culpability, responsibility. 3 contrition, penitence, regret, remorse, repentance, self-reproach, shame.

guilty adj. (-ier, -iest) 1 having done wrong. 2 feeling or showing guilt. □ **guiltily** adv.

■ 1 at fault, blameworthy, culpable, responsible. 2 ashamed, conscience-stricken, contrite, penitent, remorseful, repentant, rueful, shamefaced, sheepish, sorry.

guinea n. 1 former British coin worth 21 shillings (£1.05). 2 this amount. □ **guinea pig** 1 rodent kept as a pet or for biological experiments. 2 person used in an experiment.

guise n. 1 false outward manner or appearance. 2 pretence.

guitar n. a kind of stringed musical instrument. □ **guitarist** n.

gulf n. 1 large area of sea partly surrounded by land. 2 deep hollow. 3 wide difference in opinion.

gull n. seabird with long wings.

gullet n. passage by which food goes from mouth to stomach.

gullible adj. easily deceived. □ **gullibility** n.

■ credulous, green, innocent, naive, unsuspecting.

gully n. narrow channel cut by water or carrying rainwater from a building.

gulp v. 1 swallow (food etc.) hastily or greedily. 2 make a gulping movement. ● n. 1 act of gulping. 2 large mouthful.

■ v. 1 bolt, devour, gobble, guzzle, colloq. scoff, swallow, wolf; quaff, swill.

gum¹ n. firm flesh in which teeth are rooted.

gum² n. 1 sticky substance exuded by certain trees. 2 adhesive. 3 chewing gum. 4 gumdrop. ● v. (**gummed**) smear or stick together with gum. □ **gum tree** tree that exudes gum, esp. eucalyptus. **gummy** adj.

gumboil n. abscess on the gum.

gumboot n. rubber boot.

gumdrop n. hard gelatine sweet.

gumption n. (colloq.) resourcefulness, common sense.

gun n. 1 weapon that sends shells or bullets from a metal tube. 2 device operating similarly. ● v. (**gunned**) shoot with a gun.

gunfire n. firing of guns.

gunman n. man armed with a gun.

gunner n. 1 artillery soldier. 2 naval officer in charge of a battery of guns.

gunnery n. construction and operating of large guns.

gunny n. 1 coarse sackcloth. 2 sack made of this.

gunpowder n. explosive of saltpetre, sulphur, and charcoal.

gunrunning n. smuggling of firearms. □ **gunrunner** n.

gunshot n. shot fired from a gun.

gunsmith n. maker and repairer of small firearms.

gunwale /gúnn'l/ n. upper edge of a small ship's or boat's side.

guppy n. very small brightly coloured tropical fish.

gurgle n. low bubbling sound. ● v. make or utter with this sound.

guru n. (pl. **-us**) 1 Hindu spiritual teacher. 2 revered teacher.

gush v. 1 flow or pour suddenly or in great quantities. 2 talk effusively. ● n. 1 sudden or great outflow. 2 effusiveness.

■ v. 1 cascade, flood, flow, pour, rush, spout, spurt, stream, surge. 2 be effusive, enthuse. ● *n.* **1** cascade, flood, flow, jet, rush, spout, spurt, stream, torrent.

gusset *n.* piece of cloth inserted to strengthen or enlarge a garment etc. □ **gusseted** *adj.*

gust *n.* sudden rush of wind, rain, smoke, or sound. ● *v.* blow in gusts. □ **gusty** *adj.*

gustatory *adj.* of the sense of taste.

gusto *n.* zest.

■ delight, eagerness, enjoyment, enthusiasm, pleasure, relish, verve, vigour, zest.

gut *n.* **1** intestine. **2** thread made from animal intestines. **3** (*pl.*) abdominal organs. **4** (*pl., colloq.*) courage and determination. ● *v.* (**gutted**) **1** remove guts from (fish). **2** remove or destroy internal fittings or parts of.

■ *n.* **3** (**guts**) bowels, entrails, *colloq.* innards, *colloq.* insides, intestines, viscera, vitals. **4** (**guts**) boldness, bravery, courage, daring, fearlessness, *colloq.* grit, mettle, nerve, pluck, spirit, valour. ● *v.* **1** disembowel, eviscerate. **2** destroy, devastate, ravage; empty, loot, pillage, plunder, ransack, strip.

gutsy *adj.* (*colloq.*) **1** courageous. **2** greedy.

gutta-percha *n.* rubbery substance made from latex.

gutter *n.* **1** trough round a roof, or channel at a roadside, for carrying away rainwater. **2** (**the gutter**) slum environment. ● *v.* (of a candle) burn unsteadily.

guttural *adj.* throaty, harsh-sounding. □ **gutturally** *adv.*

guy[1] *n.* **1** effigy of Guy Fawkes burnt on 5 Nov. **2** (*colloq.*) man. ● *v.* ridicule.

guy[2] *n.* rope or chain used to keep a thing steady or secured.

guzzle *v.* eat or drink greedily.

■ bolt, devour, gobble, gulp, *colloq.* scoff, wolf.

gybe *v.* **1** (of a sail or boom) swing across. **2** (of a boat) change course thus.

gym *n.* (*colloq.*) **1** gymnasium. **2** gymnastics.

gymkhana *n.* horse-riding competition.

gymnasium *n.* room equipped for physical training and gymnastics.

gymnast *n.* expert in gymnastics.

gymnastics *n.pl.* exercises to develop the muscles or demonstrate agility. □ **gymnastic** *adj.*

gynaecology /gínikóllaji/ *n.* study of the physiological functions and diseases of women. □ **gynaecological** *adj.*, **gynaecologist** *n.*

gypsophila *n.* garden plant with many small white flowers.

gypsum *n.* chalk-like substance.

gypsy *n.* member of a nomadic people of Europe.

gyrate *v.* move in circles or spirals, revolve. □ **gyration** *n.*

■ circle, revolve, rotate, spin, swirl, swivel, twirl, wheel, whirl.

gyratory *adj.* gyrating, following a circular or spiral path.

gyro *n.* (*pl.* **-os**) (*colloq.*) gyroscope.

gyroscope *n.* rotating device used to keep navigation instruments steady.

ha *int.* exclamation of triumph.

habeas corpus order requiring a person to be brought into court.

habit *n.* **1** usual behaviour or practice. **2** tendency to act in a particular way. **3** monk's or nun's long dress. **4** a woman's riding-dress.

■ **1** convention, custom, practice, routine, rule, usage, wont. **2** idiosyncrasy, mannerism, quirk, peculiarity, tendency, trick.

habitable *adj.* suitable for living in.

habitat *n.* animal's or plant's natural environment.

■ domain, element, environment, surroundings, territory.

habitation *n.* place to live in.

habitual *adj.* **1** done or doing something constantly, esp. as a habit. **2** usual. □ **habitually** *adv.*

■ **1** constant, continual, perpetual, persistent; chronic, compulsive, inveterate. **2** accustomed, common, conventional, customary, established, everyday, familiar, normal, regular, routine, set, settled, standard, traditional, usual.

habituate *v.* accustom. □ **habituation** *n.*

hacienda *n.* ranch or large estate in S. America.

hack¹ *n.* **1** horse for ordinary riding. **2** person doing routine work, esp. as a writer. ● *v.* ride on horseback at an ordinary pace.

hack² *v.* cut, chop, or hit roughly. ● *n.* blow given thus.

hacker *n.* (*colloq.*) computer enthusiast, esp. one gaining unauthorized access to files.

hacking *adj.* (of a cough) dry and frequent.

hackles *n.pl.* feathers or hairs on some birds or animals, raised in anger.

hackneyed *adj.* (of sayings) over-used and therefore lacking impact.

hacksaw *n.* saw for metal.

haddock *n.* (*pl.* **haddock**) edible sea fish like a small cod.

haematology /hee-/ *n.* study of blood. □ **haematologist** *n.*

haemoglobin /hee-/ *n.* red oxygen-carrying substance in blood.

haemophilia /hee-/ *n.* failure of the blood to clot causing excessive bleeding. □ **haemophiliac** *n.*

haemorrhage /hém-/ *n.* profuse bleeding. ● *v.* bleed profusely.

haemorrhoids /hém-/ *n.pl.* varicose veins at or near the anus.

haft *n.* handle of a knife etc.

hag *n.* ugly old woman.

haggard *adj.* looking ugly from exhaustion. □ **haggardness** *n.*

■ careworn, drawn, exhausted, gaunt, run down, worn.

haggis *n.* Scottish dish made from sheep's offal.

haggle *v.* argue about price or terms when settling a bargain.

ha-ha *n.* sunk fence.

hail¹ *v.* **1** greet. **2** acclaim. **3** signal to and summon.

■ **1** accost, address, call, greet, salute. **2** acclaim, applaud, extol, honour, laud, praise.

hail² *n.* **1** pellets of frozen rain falling in a shower. **2** shower of blows, questions, etc. ● *v.* pour down as or like hail. □ **hailstone** *n.*, **hailstorm** *n.*

■ *n.* **2** barrage, onslaught, shower, storm, torrent, volley. ● *v.* pelt, pour, rain, shower, volley.

hair *n.* **1** fine thread-like strand growing from the skin. **2** mass of these, esp. on the head. □ **hair-raising** *adj.* terrifying. **hair-trigger** *n.* trigger operated by the slightest pressure.

haircut *n.* **1** shortening of hair by cutting it. **2** style of this.

hairdo *n.* (*pl.* **-dos**) arrangement of the hair.

hairdresser *n.* person who cuts and arranges hair. □ **hairdressing** *n.*

hairgrip *n.* springy hairpin.

hairline *n.* **1** edge of the hair on the forehead etc. **2** very narrow crack or line.

hairpin *n.* U-shaped pin for keeping hair in place. □ **hairpin bend** sharp U-shaped bend in a road.

hairy adj. (-ier, -iest) 1 covered with hair. 2 (sl.) unpleasant, difficult. □ **hairiness** n.
■ 1 bearded, bristly, hirsute, shaggy, unshaven, whiskered, whiskery.

Haitian adj. & n. (native) of Haiti.

hajji n. Muslim who has been to Mecca on pilgrimage.

hake n. (pl. **hake**) edible sea fish of the cod family.

halal n. meat from an animal killed according to Muslim law.

halcyon adj. (of a period) happy and peaceful.

hale adj. strong and healthy.

half n. (pl. **halves**) 1 each of two equal parts. 2 this amount. 3 (colloq.) half-back, half-pint, etc. ● adj. amounting to a half. ● adv. to the extent of a half, partly. □ **half a dozen** six. **half and half** half one thing and half another. **half-back** n. player between forwards and full back(s). **half-brother, -sister** ns. one having only one parent in common. **half-hearted** adj. not very enthusiastic. **half-life** n. time after which radioactivity etc. is half its original level. **at half-mast** (of a flag) lowered in mourning. **half nelson** wrestling hold. **half-term** n. short holiday halfway through a school term. **half-timbered** adj. built with a timber frame with brick or plaster filling. **half-time** n. interval between two halves of a game. **halfway** adj. & adv. at a point equidistant between two others. **halfwit** n. halfwitted person. **halfwitted** adj. stupid.

halfpenny /háypni/ n. (pl. **-pennies** for single coins, **-pence** for a sum of money) coin worth half a penny.

halibut n. (pl. **halibut**) large edible flatfish.

halitosis n. breath that smells unpleasant.

hall n. 1 large room or building for meetings, concerts, etc. 2 space inside the front entrance of a house etc. 3 large country house.
■ 1 auditorium, lecture hall, theatre. 2 corridor, entrance hall, lobby, passage, passageway, vestibule.

hallmark n. 1 official mark on precious metals to indicate their standard. 2 distinguishing characteristic.

hallo int. & n. = **hello**.

Hallowe'en n. 31 Oct., eve of All Saints' Day.

hallucinate v. experience hallucinations.

hallucination n. illusion of seeing or hearing something not actually present. □ **hallucinatory** adj.
■ apparition, chimera, illusion, mirage, vision.

hallucinogenic adj. causing hallucinations.

halo n. (pl. **-oes**) circle of light esp. round the head of a sacred figure.

halogen n. any of a group of certain nonmetallic elements.

halt n. & v. stop.
■ n. cessation, close, end, interruption, standstill, stop, stoppage, termination. ● v. bring to an end, discontinue, end, finish, put an end to, terminate; come to a standstill, draw up, pull up, stop; cease, come to an end, finish.

halter n. strap round the head of a horse for leading or fastening it.

halting adj. slow and hesitant.

halve v. 1 divide or share equally between two. 2 reduce by half.

halyard n. rope for raising or lowering a sail or flag.

ham n. 1 upper part of a pig's leg cured for food. 2 (colloq.) poor actor or performer. 3 (colloq.) amateur radio operator. ● v. (**hammed**) (colloq.) overact. □ **ham-fisted** adj. (colloq.) clumsy.

hamburger n. flat round cake of minced beef.

hamlet n. small village.

hammer n. 1 tool with a head for hitting things or driving nails in. 2 metal ball attached to a wire for throwing as an athletic contest. ● v. 1 hit or beat with a hammer. 2 strike loudly.

hammock n. hanging bed of canvas or netting.

hamper[1] n. large basket, usu. with a hinged lid and containing food.

hamper[2] v. 1 obstruct the movement of. 2 hinder.
■ 1 block, encumber, impede, inhibit, obstruct, prevent. 2 baulk, check, delay, frustrate, handicap, hinder, hold up, restrict, retard, slow down, thwart.

hamster n. small rodent with cheekpouches.

hamstring n. tendon at the back of a knee or hock. ● v. (**hamstrung**) 1 cripple by cutting hamstring(s). 2 cripple the activity of.

hand n. 1 end part of the arm, below the wrist. 2 (often pl.) control. 3 influence, or help in doing something. 4 manual worker. **5** style of handwriting. **6** pointer on a dial etc. **7** (*colloq.*) round of applause. **8** (right or left) side. **9** round of a card game, player's cards. ● *v.* give or pass. □ **at hand** close by. **handout** *n.* thing distributed free of charge. **hands down** easily. **in hand** receiving attention. **lend a hand** help. **on hand** available. **out of hand** out of control. **to hand** within reach.

■ *n.* **2** (**hands**) care, charge, control, custody, guardianship, hold, jurisdiction, keeping, possession, power. **3** agency, influence, involvement. **4** employee, labourer, operative, worker. **5** handwriting, writing. **6** indicator, needle, pointer. **7** clap, ovation, round of applause. ● *v.* deliver, give, pass, present. □ **at hand** accessible, at one's disposal, available, close (by), convenient, handy, near, nearby, on hand, *colloq.* on tap, to hand, within reach. **hands down** comfortably, easily, effortlessly, without difficulty.

handbag *n.* bag to hold a purse and small personal articles.

handbill *n.* printed notice circulated by hand.

handbook *n.* small book giving useful facts.

handcuff *n.* metal ring linked to another, for securing a prisoner's wrists. ● *v.* put handcuffs on.

handful *n.* **1** quantity that fills the hand. **2** a few. **3** (*colloq.*) difficult person or task.

handicap *n.* **1** disadvantage imposed on a superior competitor to equalize chances. **2** race etc. in which handicaps are imposed. **3** physical or mental disability. **4** thing that makes progress difficult. ● *v.* (**handicapped**) impose or be a handicap on.

■ *n.* **4** bar, barrier, disadvantage, encumbrance, hindrance, impediment, limitation, obstacle, stumbling block. ● *v.* encumber, hamper, hinder, hold back, impede, limit, put at a disadvantage, restrict.

handkerchief *n.* (*pl.* **-fs**) small square of cloth for wiping the nose etc.

handle *n.* part by which a thing is to be held, carried, or controlled. ● *v.* **1** touch or move with the hands. **2** deal with, manage. **3** deal in.

■ *v.* **1** feel, finger, *colloq.* paw, touch. **2** attend to, deal with, do, look after, manage, organize, see to, sort out, take charge of;

control, cope with. **3** deal in, sell, stock, trade in.

handlebar *n.* steering bar of a bicycle etc.

handler *n.* person in charge of a trained dog etc.

handrail *n.* rail beside stairs etc.

handshake *n.* act of shaking hands as a greeting etc.

handsome *adj.* **1** good-looking. **2** generous. **3** considerable.

■ **1** attractive, good-looking, personable. **2** generous, lavish, liberal, munificent, princely. **3** big, considerable, large, sizeable, substantial.

handstand *n.* balancing on one's hands with feet in the air.

handwriting *n.* **1** writing by hand. **2** style of this.

handy *adj.* (**-ier, -iest**) **1** convenient. **2** clever with one's hands. □ **handily** *adv.*

■ **1** accessible, at hand, available, close by, convenient, nearby, to hand, within reach; helpful, serviceable, useful. **2** adept, adroit, clever, deft, dexterous, skilful, skilled, proficient.

handyman *n.* person who does odd jobs.

hang *v.* (**hung**) **1** support or be supported from above with the lower end free. **2** let droop. **3** remain or be hung. **4** (**hanged**) kill or be killed by suspension from a rope round the neck. ● *n.* way a thing hangs. □ **get the hang of** (*colloq.*) get the knack of, understand. **hang about** loiter. **hang back** hesitate. **hang-glider** *n.* frame used in hang-gliding. **hang-gliding** *n.* sport of gliding in an airborne frame in which the pilot is suspended. **hang on 1** hold tightly. **2** depend on. **3** (*sl.*) wait. **hang-up** *n.* (*sl.*) emotional problem or inhibition.

■ *v.* **1** attach, fasten, put up, suspend; be suspended, dangle, sway, swing. **2** droop, drop, let fall. **4** execute, string up. □ **hang about** dally, dawdle, *colloq.* dilly-dally, hover, idle, linger, loaf about, loiter, wait.

hangar *n.* shed for aircraft.

hangdog *adj.* shamefaced.

hanger *n.* **1** loop or hook by which a thing is hung. **2** shaped piece of wood etc. to hang a garment on.

hangings *n.pl.* draperies hung on walls.

hangman *n.* person who hangs people condemned to death.

hangnail *n.* torn skin at the root of a fingernail.

hangover *n.* after-effects of an excess of alcohol.

hank *n.* coil or length of thread.

hanker *v.* **hanker after** long for. □ **hankering** *n.*

> ■ crave, desire, hunger for, long for, thirst for, want, yearn for.

hanky *n.* (*colloq.*) handkerchief.

Hanukkah *n.* Jewish festival of lights, beginning in December.

haphazard *adj.* done or chosen at random. □ **haphazardly** *adv.*

> ■ aimless, arbitrary, chaotic, hit-or-miss, indiscriminate, random, unmethodical, unplanned, unsystematic.

hapless *adj.* unlucky.

happen *v.* occur. □ **happen on** discover by chance. **happen to** be the fate or experience of.

> ■ come about, occur, take place. □ **happen on** come across, discover, encounter, find, hit on, light on, meet by chance. **happen to** become of, befall, betide.

happy *adj.* (-**ier**, -**iest**) **1** contented, pleased. **2** fortunate. □ **happy-go-lucky** *adj.* taking events cheerfully. **happily** *adv.*, **happiness** *n.*

> ■ **1** buoyant, carefree, cheerful, cheery, chirpy, content, contented, delighted, ecstatic, elated, euphoric, exhilarated, gay, glad, gleeful, high-spirited, in high spirits, jovial, joyful, jubilant, merry, overjoyed, pleased, sunny, thrilled. **2** auspicious, favourable, fortunate, lucky, propitious. □ **happy-go-lucky** blithe, carefree, easygoing, insouciant, light-hearted, relaxed. **happiness** bliss, cheerfulness, delight, elation, euphoria, exhilaration, felicity, gaiety, glee, high spirits, joy, joyfulness, jubilation, pleasure.

harangue *n.* lengthy earnest speech. ● *v.* make a harangue to.

> ■ *n.* address, declamation, diatribe, exhortation, lecture, oration, sermon, speech, tirade.

harass *v.* **1** worry or annoy continually. **2** make repeated attacks on. □ **harassment** *n.*

> ■ **1** annoy, badger, bait, bother, harry, *colloq.* hassle, hound, nag, pester, *colloq.* plague, torment, trouble, worry.

harbour *n.* place of shelter for ships. ● *v.* **1** shelter. **2** keep in one's mind.

hard *adj.* **1** firm, not easily cut. **2** difficult. **3** not easy to bear. **4** harsh. **5** strenuous. **6** (of drugs) strong and ad-dictive. **7** (of currency) not likely to drop suddenly in value. **8** (of drinks) strongly alcoholic. **9** (of water) containing mineral salts that prevent soap from lathering freely. ● *adv.* **1** strenuously, intensively, copiously. **2** with difficulty. □ **hard-boiled** *adj.* **1** (of eggs) boiled until yolk and white are set. **2** callous. **hard copy** material produced in printed form by a computer. **hard-headed** *adj.* shrewd and practical. **hard-hearted** *adj.* unfeeling. **hard of hearing** slightly deaf. **hard sell** aggressive salesmanship. **hard shoulder** extra strip of road beside a motorway, for use in an emergency. **hard up** short of money. **hardness** *n.*

> ■ *adj.* **1** dense, firm, impenetrable, rigid, set, solid, solidified, stiff, tough, unmalleable, unyielding; flinty, rocky, steely, stony. **2** baffling, complex, complicated, difficult, intricate, knotty, perplexing, problematic(al), puzzling. **3** calamitous, distressing, grievous, insupportable, intolerable, painful, unbearable, unendurable, unpleasant. **4** callous, cold, cruel, hard-boiled, hard-hearted, harsh, heartless, insensitive, ruthless, severe, stern, stony, strict, unfeeling, unkind, unsympathetic. **5** arduous, demanding, exacting, exhausting, gruelling, herculean, laborious, onerous, strenuous, taxing, tiring, tough. □ **hard-headed** astute, businesslike, level-headed, practical, pragmatic, realistic, sensible, sharp, shrewd. **hard up** *colloq.* broke, impecunious, impoverished, penniless, poor, short of money, *sl.* skint.

hardbitten *adj.* tough and tenacious.

hardboard *n.* stiff board made of compressed wood pulp.

harden *v.* become or make hard or hardy.

> ■ cake, coagulate, congeal, set, solidify, stiffen; strengthen, toughen.

hardly *adv.* **1** only with difficulty. **2** scarcely.

hardship *n.* harsh circumstance.

> ■ adversity, affliction, deprivation, difficulty, misfortune, privation, trouble.

hardware *n.* **1** tools and household implements sold by a shop. **2** weapons. **3** machinery used in a computer system.

hardwood *n.* hard heavy wood of deciduous trees.

hardy adj. (**-ier**, **-iest**) capable of enduring cold or harsh conditions. □ **hardiness** n.
∎ fit, hale, healthy, robust, stalwart, strong, sturdy, tough.

hare n. field animal like a large rabbit. ● v. run rapidly. □ **hare-brained** adj. wild, rash.

harem /háareem/ n. **1** women of a Muslim household. **2** their apartments.

haricot bean /hárrikō/ white dried seed of a kind of bean.

hark v. listen. □ **hark back** return to an earlier subject.

harlequin adj. in varied colours.

harm n. damage, injury. ● v. cause harm to. □ **harmful** adj. **harmless** adj.
∎ n. damage, hurt, injury, mischief, misfortune. ● v. abuse, damage, deface, hurt, ill-treat, impair, injure, maltreat, mar, wound. □ **harmful** bad, damaging, dangerous, deleterious, destructive, detrimental, hurtful, injurious, noxious, pernicious, poisonous, toxic. **harmless** benign, innocuous, mild, safe.

harmonic adj. full of harmony.

harmonica n. mouth-organ.

harmonious adj. **1** sweet-sounding. **2** forming a pleasing or consistent whole. **3** free from ill feeling. □ **harmoniously** adv.
∎ **1** dulcet, euphonious, mellifluous, melodious, musical, sweet-sounding, tuneful. **2** compatible, complementary, concordant, consonant. **3** amicable, cordial, friendly, peaceable, peaceful.

harmonium n. musical instrument like a small organ.

harmonize v. **1** make or be harmonious. **2** add notes to form chords. □ **harmonization** n.

harmony n. **1** combination of musical notes to form chords, esp. with a pleasing effect. **2** agreement between people or things.
∎ **1** euphony, melodiousness, tunefulness. **2** accord, agreement, compatibility, concord, consistency; friendship, rapport.

harness n. **1** straps and fittings by which a horse is controlled. **2** similar fastenings. ● v. **1** put harness on, attach by this. **2** control and use.

harp n. musical instrument with strings in a triangular frame. ● v. **harp on** dwell on tediously. □ **harpist** n.

harpoon n. spear-like missile with a rope attached. ● v. spear with a harpoon.

harpsichord n. piano-like instrument.

harpy n. grasping unscrupulous woman.

harridan n. bad-tempered old woman.

harrow n. heavy frame with metal spikes or discs for breaking up clods. ● v. **1** draw a harrow over. **2** distress greatly.

harry v. harass.

harsh adj. **1** unpleasantly rough to the senses. **2** severe, cruel. □ **harshly** adv., **harshness** n.
∎ **1** bristly, coarse, rough, scratchy; cacophonous, discordant, dissonant, grating, guttural, hoarse, jangling, jarring, rasping, raucous, shrill, strident; acrid, bitter, sour. **2** cruel, draconian, hard, heartless, inhuman, merciless, pitiless, ruthless, severe, stern, stringent; austere, bleak, comfortless, grim, spartan, stark.

hart n. adult male deer.

hartebeest n. large African antelope.

harum-scarum adj. & n. wild and reckless (person).

harvest n. **1** gathering of crop(s). **2** season for this. **3** season's yield of a natural product. ● v. **1** gather a crop. **2** receive as the consequence of actions. □ **harvester** n.
∎ v. **1** collect, garner, gather, glean, pick, reap. **2** earn, gain, get, make, obtain.

hash n. **1** dish of chopped re-cooked meat. **2** jumble. ● v. make into hash. □ **make a hash of** (colloq.) bungle.

hashish n. narcotic drug obtained from hemp.

hasp n. clasp fitting over a staple, secured by a pin or padlock.

hassle n. & v. (colloq.) **1** quarrel. **2** trouble, inconvenience.

hassock n. thick firm cushion for kneeling on in church.

haste n. hurry. □ **make haste** hurry.

hasten v. hurry.
∎ dash, hurry, fly, make haste, race, run, rush, scamper, scurry, scuttle, speed, sprint.

hasty adj. (**-ier**, **-iest**) **1** hurried. **2** acting or done too quickly. □ **hastily** adv., **hastiness** n.
∎ **1** brisk, fast, hurried, quick, rapid, speedy, swift. **2** heedless, impetuous, impulsive, incautious, precipitate, rash, reckless, unthinking; careless, cursory, perfunctory, slapdash.

hat n. covering for the head, worn out of doors. □ **hat trick** three successes in a row, esp. in sports.

hatch¹ *n.* **1** opening in a door, floor, ship's deck, etc. **2** its cover.

hatch² *v.* **1** emerge or produce (young) from an egg. **2** devise (a plot). ● *n.* brood hatched.

> ■ *v.* **2** conceive, concoct, contrive, *colloq.* cook up, devise, dream up, form, invent, plan, *colloq.* think up.

hatch³ *v.* mark with close parallel lines. □ **hatching** *n.* these marks.

hatchback *n.* a car with a back door that opens upwards.

hatchery *n.* place for hatching eggs.

hatchet *n.* small axe. □ **bury the hatchet** cease quarrelling and become friendly.

hatchway *n.* = **hatch¹**.

hate *n.* hatred. ● *v.* dislike greatly.

> ■ *v.* abhor, abominate, despise, detest, dislike, execrate, loathe.

hateful *adj.* arousing hatred.

> ■ abhorrent, abominable, contemptible, despicable, detestable, disgusting, execrable, foul, loathsome, odious, repugnant, repulsive, revolting.

hatred *n.* violent dislike.

> ■ abhorrence, antagonism, antipathy, aversion, contempt, detestation, disgust, dislike, hate, hostility, ill will, loathing, odium, repugnance, revulsion.

haughty *adj.* (**-ier, -iest**) proud, superior. □ **haughtily** *adv.*, **haughtiness** *n.*

> ■ aloof, arrogant, conceited, contemptuous, disdainful, hoity-toity, lofty, pretentious, proud, scornful, self-important, snobbish, *colloq.* snooty, *colloq.* stuck-up, supercilious, superior, *colloq.* uppity.

haul *v.* **1** pull or drag forcibly. **2** transport by truck etc. ● *n.* **1** process of hauling. **2** amount gained by effort, booty.

> ■ *v.* **1** drag, draw, heave, lug, pull, tow, tug. **2** carry, cart, convey, move, transport.

haulage *n.* transport of goods.

haulier *n.* person or firm that transports goods by road.

haunch *n.* **1** fleshy part of the buttock and thigh. **2** leg and loin of meat.

haunt *v.* **1** linger in the mind of. **2** (esp. of a ghost) repeatedly visit (a person or place). ● *n.* place frequented by a particular person.

> ■ *v.* **1** beset, obsess, preoccupy, prey on, torment, trouble.

haute couture /ốt kootyóor/ high fashion.

have *v.* **1** possess. **2** contain. **3** experience, undergo. **4** give birth to. **5** cause to be or do or be done. **6** allow. **7** receive, accept. **8** (*colloq.*) cheat, deceive. ● *v.aux.* used with past participle to form past tenses. □ **have it out** settle a problem by frank discussion. **have up** bring (a person) to trial. **haves and have-nots** people with and without wealth or privilege.

> ■ *v.* **1** hold, keep, own, possess. **2** consist of, contain, include. **3** endure, experience, feel, suffer, undergo. **4** bear, deliver, give birth to. **6** allow, brook, permit, put up with, *colloq.* stand for, tolerate. **7** accept, acquire, get, obtain, receive, take.

haven *n.* **1** refuge. **2** harbour.

> ■ **1** asylum, refuge, retreat, sanctuary, shelter. **2** anchorage, harbour, port.

haversack *n.* strong bag carried on the back or shoulder.

havoc *n.* great destruction or disorder.

> ■ damage, destruction, devastation, ruin; chaos, confusion, disorder, disruption, turmoil.

haw *n.* hawthorn berry.

hawk¹ *n.* **1** bird of prey. **2** person who favours an aggressive policy. □ **hawk-eyed** *adj.* having very keen sight.

hawk² *v.* clear one's throat of phlegm noisily.

hawser *n.* heavy rope or cable for mooring or towing a ship.

hawthorn *n.* thorny tree or shrub with small red berries.

hay *n.* grass mown and dried for fodder. □ **hay fever** irritation of nose, throat, etc. caused by pollen or dust.

haymaking *n.* mowing grass and spreading it to dry.

haystack *n.* regular pile of hay firmly packed for storing.

haywire *adj.* badly disorganized.

hazard *n.* **1** risk, danger. **2** source of this. ● *v.* risk. □ **hazardous** *adj.*

> ■ *n.* danger, jeopardy, peril, pitfall, risk, threat. ● *v.* endanger, imperil, jeopardize, put in jeopardy, risk. □ **hazardous** dangerous, *sl.* dicey, perilous, precarious, risky, uncertain, unpredictable, unreliable, unsafe.

haze *n.* thin mist.

hazel *n.* **1** bush with small edible nuts. **2** light brown. □ **hazelnut** *n.*

hazy adj. (-ier, -iest) 1 misty. 2 vague, confused. □ **hazily** adv., **haziness** n.
■ 1 foggy, misty. 2 dim, faint, fuzzy, indistinct, nebulous, vague; confused, muddled, uncertain, unclear.

H-bomb n. hydrogen bomb.

he pron. male previously mentioned. ● n. male animal.

head n. 1 part of the body containing the eyes, nose, mouth, and brain. 2 intellect. 3 thing like the head in form or position. 4 top or leading part or position. 5 person in charge, esp. of a school. 6 (colloq.) headache. 7 individual person or animal. 8 foam on beer etc. 9 body of water or steam confined for exerting pressure. 10 (pl.) side of a coin showing a head, turned upwards after being tossed. ● adj. chief, principal. ● v. 1 be at the head or top of. 2 direct one's course. 3 strike (a ball) with one's head. □ **head-hunt** v. seek to recruit (senior staff) from another firm. **head off** force to turn by getting in front. **head-on** adj. & adv. with head or front foremost. **head wind** wind blowing from directly in front.
■ n. 1 sl. block, sl. conk, sl. nut, skull. 2 brain(s), intellect, intelligence, sl. loaf, mind, wit. 4 apex, brow, crest, crown, peak, summit, tip, top; fore, forefront, front, van, vanguard. 5 colloq. boss, chairman, chairwoman, chief, director, governor, leader, manager, president, supervisor; headmaster, headmistress, principal. ● adj. chief, first, foremost, leading, main, pre-eminent, prime, principal, senior. ● v. 1 be in charge of, be in control of, command, direct, lead, supervise. 2 aim, face, go, move, point, proceed, steer, turn.

headache n. 1 continuous pain in the head. 2 worrying problem.

headdress n. ornamental covering worn on the head.

header n. 1 dive with the head first. 2 heading of the ball in football.

headgear n. hat or headdress.

heading n. word(s) at the top of written matter as a title.

headlamp n. headlight.

headland n. promontory.

headlight n. powerful light on the front of a vehicle etc.

headline n. 1 heading in a newspaper. 2 (pl.) summary of broadcast news.

headlong adj. & adv. 1 falling or plunging with the head first. 2 in a hasty and rash way.

headmaster, **headmistress** ns. teacher in charge of a school.

headphone n. receiver held over the ear(s) by a band over the head.

headquarters n.pl. organization's administrative centre.

headstone n. stone set up at the head of a grave.

headstrong adj. self-willed and obstinate.
■ defiant, disobedient, intractable, intransigent, obstinate, pigheaded, recalcitrant, refractory, self-willed, stubborn, wilful.

headway n. progress.

heady adj. (-ier, -iest) likely to cause intoxication.

heal v. 1 make or become healthy after injury or illness. 2 put right (differences). □ **healer** n.
■ 1 cure; be on the mend, get better, improve, mend. 2 mend, patch up, put right, reconcile, rectify, remedy, repair, settle.

health n. 1 state of being well and free from illness. 2 condition of the body.
■ 1 fitness, healthiness, robustness, strength, vigour, well-being. 2 condition, constitution, form, shape.

healthful adj. health-giving.

healthy adj. (-ier, -iest) having, showing, or producing good health. □ **healthily** adv., **healthiness** n.
■ blooming, fit, flourishing, hale, in good health, colloq. in the pink, robust, strong, thriving, vigorous, well; healthful, nourishing, nutritious, salubrious, wholesome.

heap n. 1 a number of things or particles lying one on top of another. 2 (usu. pl., colloq.) plenty. ● v. 1 pile or become piled in a heap. 2 load copiously.
■ n. 1 accumulation, collection, mass, mound, mountain, pile, stack. ● v. 1 accumulate, amass, collect, gather, pile up, stack. 2 burden, load, lumber, overwhelm, weigh down.

hear v. (**heard**) 1 perceive (sounds) with the ear. 2 pay attention to. 3 receive information. □ **hear! hear!** I agree. **hearer** n.
■ 1 catch, perceive. 2 attend to, heed, listen to, mark, note, pay attention to, take notice of. 3 be informed, be told, discover, find out, get wind of, learn.

hearing n. 1 ability to hear. 2 opportunity to be heard. 3 trial of a lawsuit. □ **hearing aid** small sound-amplifier worn by a partially deaf person.

hearsay n. rumour, gossip.

hearse n. vehicle for carrying the coffin at a funeral.

heart n. 1 muscular organ that keeps blood circulating. 2 centre of a person's emotions or inmost thoughts. 3 courage or enthusiasm. 4 central part. 5 figure representing a heart. 6 playing card of the suit marked with these. □ **break the heart of** cause overwhelming grief to. **by heart** memorized thoroughly. **heart attack** sudden failure of the heart to function normally. **heart-searching** n. examination of one's own feelings and motives. **heart-to-heart** adj. frank and personal. **heart-warming** adj. emotionally moving and encouraging.

■ 3 bravery, boldness, courage, colloq. guts, mettle, nerve, pluck; enthusiasm, spirit, verve. 4 centre, core, hub, middle, nucleus; crux, essence, kernel, nub, pith, quintessence, substance. □ **heart-to-heart** candid, frank, intimate, personal. **heart-warming** cheering, encouraging, moving, poignant, touching, uplifting.

heartache n. mental anguish.

heartbeat n. pulsation of the heart.

heartbreak n. overwhelming grief.

heartbroken adj. broken-hearted.

■ broken-hearted, desolate, devastated, grief-stricken, inconsolable, miserable, sad, sorrowful.

heartburn n. burning sensation in the chest from indigestion.

hearten v. encourage.

heartfelt adj. felt deeply, sincere.

■ ardent, deep, devout, earnest, genuine, honest, profound, sincere, unfeigned, wholehearted.

hearth n. 1 floor of a fireplace. 2 fireside.

heartless adj. not feeling pity or sympathy. □ **heartlessly** adv.

■ brutal, callous, cold, cold-blooded, cruel, hard, hard-hearted, inhuman, inhumane, insensitive, merciless, pitiless, ruthless, unfeeling, unkind, unsympathetic.

heart-throb n. (colloq.) object of romantic affection.

hearty adj. (-ier, -iest) 1 vigorous. 2 enthusiastic. 3 (of meals) large. 4 warm, friendly. □ **heartily** adv., **heartiness** n.

■ 1 energetic, full-blooded, hale, healthy, robust, strong, vigorous. 2 eager, enthusiastic, spirited, vigorous. 3 ample, large, satisfying, sizeable, substantial. 4 affectionate, friendly, genial, warm.

heat n. 1 condition or sensation of being hot. 2 form of energy produced by movement of molecules. 3 passion, anger. 4 preliminary contest. ● v. make or become hot. □ **heatstroke** n. illness caused by overexposure to sun.

■ n. 1 warmness, warmth. 3 ardour, eagerness, fervour, intensity, passion, vehemence, warmth, zeal; anger, fury. 4 game, round.

heated adj. (of a person or discussion) angry. □ **heatedly** adv.

heater n. device supplying heat.

heath n. flat uncultivated land with low shrubs.

heathen n. person who does not believe in an established religion. ● adj. of or relating to heathens.

heather n. evergreen plant with purple, pink, or white flowers.

heave v. 1 lift or haul with great effort. 2 utter (a sigh). 3 (colloq.) throw. 4 rise and fall like waves. 5 pant, retch. ● n. act of heaving.

■ v. 1 hoist, lift, raise; drag, draw, haul, pull, tug. 2 breathe, utter.

heaven n. 1 abode of God. 2 place or state of bliss. 3 (**the heavens**) the sky as seen from the earth.

heavenly adj. 1 of heaven, divine. 2 of or in the heavens. 3 (colloq.) very pleasing. □ **heavenly bodies** sun, moon, stars, etc.

■ 1 angelic, celestial, divine, ethereal, holy, immortal, seraphic, spiritual. 2 celestial, planetary, stellar.

heavy adj. (-ier, -iest) 1 having great weight, force, or intensity. 2 dense. 3 hard to digest or understand. 4 dull, tedious. 5 serious. □ **heavy-hearted** adj. sad. **heavy industry** that producing metal or heavy machines etc. **heavily** adv., **heaviness** n.

■ 1 hefty, massive, ponderous, weighty; bulky, burly, corpulent, fat, large, overweight, portly, stout, tubby; forceful, intense, severe, torrential, violent. 2 dense, solid, thick. 3 indigestible, stodgy; abstruse, complex, deep, difficult, esoteric, profound. 4 boring, dull, tedious, uninteresting, wearisome. 5 grave, important, serious, weighty.

heavyweight adj. having great weight or influence. ● n. heavyweight person.

Hebrew n. & adj. 1 (member) of a Semitic people in ancient Palestine. 2 (of) their language or a modern form of this. □ **Hebraic** adj.

heckle v. interrupt (a public speaker) with aggressive questions and abuse. □ **heckler** n.

hectare n. unit of area, 10,000 sq. metres (about 2½ acres).

hectic adj. with feverish activity. □ **hectically** adv.
■ busy, chaotic, confused, excited, feverish, frantic, frenetic, turbulent, wild.

hectogram n. 100 grams.

hector v. intimidate by bullying.

hedge n. **1** fence of bushes or shrubs. **2** barrier. ● v. **1** surround with a hedge. **2** make or trim hedges. **3** avoid giving a direct answer or commitment.

hedgehog n. small animal covered in stiff spines.

hedgerow n. bushes etc. forming a hedge.

hedonist n. person who believes pleasure is the chief good. □ **hedonism** n., **hedonistic** adj.

heed v. pay attention to. ● n. careful attention. □ **heedful** adj., **heedless** adj.
■ v. attend to, be mindful of, listen to, mark, mind, note, pay attention to, take notice of. ● n. attention, consideration, notice, thought. □ **heedful** alert, attentive, careful, cautious, mindful, observant, on the lookout, vigilant, watchful. **heedless** careless, inattentive, incautious, thoughtless, unmindful, unobservant, unthinking.

heel[1] n. **1** back part of the human foot. **2** part of a stocking or shoe covering or supporting this. **3** (sl.) dishonourable man. ● v. make or repair the heel(s) of. □ **down at heel** shabby. **take to one's heels** run away.

heel[2] v. tilt (a ship) or become tilted to one side. ● n. this tilt.

hefty adj. (**-ier, -iest**) large and heavy.
■ beefy, big, brawny, burly, muscular, powerful, robust, strapping; bulky, heavy, large, massive, substantial, weighty.

hegemony /hijémməni/ n. leadership, esp. by one country.

Hegira /héjirə/ n. Muhammad's flight from Mecca (AD 622), from which the Muslim era is reckoned.

heifer /héffər/ n. young cow.

height n. **1** measurement from base to top. **2** distance above ground or sea level. **3** highest degree of something.
■ **2** altitude, elevation. **3** acme, climax, culmination, high point, peak, pinnacle, summit, zenith.

heighten v. make or become higher or more intense.
■ elevate, lift, raise; add to, amplify, augment, deepen, enhance, increase, intensify, strengthen.

heinous /háynəss/ adj. very wicked.

heir /air/ n. person entitled to inherit property or a rank etc.

heiress /áiriss/ n. female heir, esp. to great wealth.

heirloom /áirloom/ n. possession handed down in a family for several generations.

held see **hold**[1].

helical adj. like a helix.

helicopter n. aircraft with blades that revolve horizontally.

heliport n. helicopter station.

helium n. light colourless gas that does not burn.

helix n. (pl. **-ices**) spiral.

hell n. **1** place of punishment for the wicked after death. **2** place or state of supreme misery. □ **hell-bent** adj. recklessly determined.

Hellenistic adj. of Greece in the 4th–1st centuries BC.

hello int. & n. exclamation used in greeting or to call attention.

helm n. tiller or wheel by which a ship's rudder is controlled.

helmet n. protective head-covering.

helmsman n. person controlling a ship's helm.

help v. **1** provide with the means to what is sought or needed. **2** be useful (to). **3** improve (a situation). **4** serve with food. ● n. **1** act of helping. **2** person or thing that helps. □ **helper** n.
■ v. **1** aid, assist, lend a hand; encourage, fortify, succour, support; back, finance, fund, sponsor, subsidize. **2** be of use (to), be useful (to), serve. **3** alleviate, ease, improve, mitigate, relieve, remedy; expedite, facilitate, further. ● n. aid, assistance, backing, succour, support. □ **helper** accessory, accomplice, aide, assistant, helper, partner, right-hand man or woman, supporter.

helpful adj. giving help, useful. □ **helpfully** adv., **helpfulness** n.
■ accommodating, cooperative, kind, neighbourly, obliging, supportive; beneficial, constructive, practical, useful, valuable.

helping n. portion of food served.

helpless adj. **1** unable to manage without help. **2** powerless. □ **helplessly** adv., **helplessness** n.

■ **1** feeble, incapable, infirm, weak. **2** defenceless, exposed, powerless, unprotected, vulnerable.

helpline n. telephone service providing help with problems.

helter-skelter adv. in disorderly haste. ● n. spiral slide at a funfair.

hem n. edge (of cloth) turned under and sewn or fixed down. ● v. (**hemmed**) sew thus. □ **hem in** surround and restrict.

hemisphere n. **1** half a sphere. **2** half the earth. □ **hemispherical** adj.

hemlock n. poisonous plant.

hemp n. **1** plant with coarse fibres used in making rope etc. **2** narcotic drug made from it.

hempen adj. made of hemp.

hen n. female bird, esp. of the domestic fowl. □ **hen-party** n. (colloq.) party for women only.

hence adv. **1** from this time. **2** for this reason.

henceforth adv. (also **henceforward**) from this time on.

henchman n. trusty supporter.

henna n. **1** reddish dye used esp. on the hair. **2** tropical plant from which it is made. □ **hennaed** adj.

henpecked adj. (of a man) nagged by his wife.

henry n. unit of inductance.

hepatic adj. of the liver.

hepatitis n. inflammation of the liver.

heptagon n. geometric figure with seven sides. □ **heptagonal** adj.

heptathlon n. athletic contest involving seven events.

her pron. objective case of she. ● adj. belonging to her.

herald n. person or thing heralding something. ● v. proclaim the approach of.

heraldic adj. of heraldry.

heraldry n. study of armorial bearings.

herb n. plant used in making medicines or flavourings.

herbaceous adj. soft-stemmed. □ **herbaceous border** border containing esp. perennial plants.

herbal adj. of herbs. ● n. book about herbs.

herbalist n. dealer in medicinal herbs.

herbicide n. substance used to destroy plants. □ **herbicidal** adj.

herbivore n. plant-eating animal. □ **herbivorous** adj.

herculean adj. needing or showing great strength or effort.

herd n. **1** group of animals feeding or staying together. **2** mob. ● v. **1** gather, stay, or drive as a group. **2** tend (a herd). □ **herdsman** n.

■ n. **1** drove, flock, pack. **2** crowd, group, horde, mob, multitude, swarm, throng. ● v. **1** assemble, collect, congregate, flock, gather, huddle; drive, round up. **2** look after, take care of, tend.

here adv. **1** in, at, or to this place. **2** at this point. ● n. this place.

hereabouts adv. near here.

hereafter adv. from now on. ● n. **1** the future. **2** the next world.

hereby adv. by this act.

hereditary adj. **1** inherited. **2** holding a position by inheritance.

heredity n. inheritance of characteristics from parents.

herein adv. in this place or book etc.

heresy n. **1** opinion contrary to accepted beliefs. **2** holding of this.

heretic n. person who holds a heresy. □ **heretical** adj.

hereto adv. to this.

herewith adv. with this.

heritage n. **1** thing(s) inherited. **2** nation's historic buildings etc.

■ **1** bequest, birthright, inheritance, legacy, patrimony.

hermaphrodite n. creature with male and female sexual organs.

hermetic adj. with an airtight seal. □ **hermetically** adv.

hermit n. person living in solitude.

hermitage n. hermit's dwelling.

hernia n. protrusion of part of an organ through the wall of the cavity containing it.

hero n. (pl. -oes) **1** man admired for his brave deeds. **2** chief male character in a story etc.

heroic adj. very brave. ● n.pl. overdramatic behaviour. □ **heroically** adv.

■ adj. bold, brave, courageous, daring, dauntless, fearless, gallant, intrepid, manly, spirited, valiant, valorous.

heroin n. powerful drug prepared from morphine.

heroine n. female hero.

heroism n. heroic conduct.

heron n. long-legged wading bird.

herpes /hérpeez/ *n.* virus disease causing blisters.

herring *n.* edible N. Atlantic fish. □ **herringbone** *n.* zigzag pattern or arrangement.

hers *poss.pron.* belonging to her.

herself *pron.* emphatic and reflexive form of *she* and *her.*

hertz *n.* (*pl.* **hertz**) unit of frequency of electromagnetic waves.

hesitant *adj.* hesitating. □ **hesitantly** *adv.,* **hesitancy** *n.*

■ ambivalent, cautious, doubtful, hesitating, in two minds, irresolute, tentative, undecided, unsure.

hesitate *v.* **1** pause doubtfully. **2** be reluctant. □ **hesitation** *n.*

■ **1** be in two minds, be uncertain *or* undecided, dither, hang back, pause, shilly-shally, vacillate, waver. **2** be disinclined, be reluctant, have misgivings *or* qualms, scruple.

hessian *n.* strong coarse cloth of hemp or jute.

heterodox *adj.* not orthodox.

heterogeneous *adj.* made up of people or things of various sorts. □ **heterogeneity** *n.*

heterosexual *adj.* & *n.* (person) sexually attracted to people of the opposite sex. □ **heterosexuality** *n.*

hew *v.* (**hewn**) **1** chop or cut with an axe etc. **2** cut into shape.

hexagon *n.* geometric figure with six sides. □ **hexagonal** *adj.*

hey *int.* exclamation of surprise or interest, or to attract attention.

heyday *n.* time of greatest success.

hi *int.* exclamation calling attention or greeting.

hiatus *n.* (*pl.* **-tuses**) break or gap in a sequence or series.

hibernate *v.* spend the winter in sleep-like state. □ **hibernation** *n.*

Hibernian *adj.* & *n.* (native) of Ireland.

hibiscus *n.* shrub or tree with trumpet-shaped flowers.

hiccup *n.* cough-like stopping of breath. ● *v.* (**hiccuped**) make this sound.

hide[1] *v.* (**hid**, **hidden**) **1** put or keep out of sight. **2** keep secret. **3** conceal oneself. □ **hideout** *n.* (*colloq.*) hiding place.

■ **1** bury, conceal, cover up, put out of sight, secrete, *colloq.* stash away. **2** camouflage, conceal, cover up, disguise, keep secret, mask, suppress. **3** go into hiding, *sl.* lie doggo, lie low, lurk.

hide[2] *n.* animal's skin.

hidebound *adj.* rigidly conventional.

■ conservative, conventional, narrow-minded, reactionary, set in one's ways, strait-laced.

hideous *adj.* very ugly. □ **hideously** *adv.,* **hideousness** *n.*

■ disgusting, ghastly, grisly, grotesque, gruesome, monstrous, repellent, repulsive, revolting, ugly, unsightly.

hiding *n.* (*colloq.*) thrashing.

hierarchy *n.* system with grades of status. □ **hierarchical** *adj.*

hieroglyph *n.* pictorial symbol used in ancient Egyptian and other writing. □ **hieroglyphic** *adj.,* **hieroglyphics** *n.pl.*

hi-fi *adj.* & *n.* (*colloq.*) high fidelity, (equipment) reproducing sound with little or no distortion.

higgledy-piggledy *adj.* & *adv.* in complete confusion.

high *adj.* **1** extending far or a specified distance upwards. **2** far above ground or sea level. **3** ranking above others. **4** greater than normal. **5** (of sound or a voice) not deep or low. **6** (of meat) slightly decomposed. **7** (*sl.*) intoxicated, under the influence of a drug. ● *n.* **1** high level. **2** area of high pressure. ● *adv.* in, at, or to a high level. □ **higher education** education at university etc. **high-handed** *adj.* using authority arrogantly. **high-rise** *adj.* with many storeys. **high road** main road. **high sea(s)** sea outside a country's territorial waters. **high season** busiest season. **high-spirited** *adj.* lively, cheerful. **high spirits** liveliness, cheerfulness. **high street** principal shopping street. **high tea** early evening meal with tea and cooked food. **high-tech** *adj.* involving advanced technology and electronics. **high-water mark** level reached by the tide at its highest level.

■ *adj.* **1** elevated, lofty, tall, towering. **2** chief, distinguished, eminent, foremost, important, leading, principal, superior. **4** excessive, exorbitant, extreme, *colloq.* steep, stiff. **5** high-pitched, penetrating, piercing, piping, shrill, squeaky, treble. **6** gamy. ● *n.* **1** height, peak, record, summit. □ **high-handed** arrogant, autocratic, *colloq.* bossy, dictatorial, domineering, imperious, overbearing, peremptory. **high-spirited** animated, bubbly, buoyant, cheerful, ebullient, exuberant, lively, spirited, vivacious.

highbrow adj. very intellectual, cultured. ● n. highbrow person.
■ adj. cultured, erudite, intellectual, learned, scholarly.

highlands n.pl. mountainous region. □ **highland** adj., **highlander** n.

highlight n. 1 bright area in a picture. 2 best feature. ● v. emphasize.
■ v. accent, accentuate, draw attention to, emphasize, feature, focus attention on, point up, spotlight, stress, underline.

highly adv. 1 in a high degree, extremely. 2 very favourably. □ **highly-strung** adj. sensitive, nervous.
■ 1 exceptionally, extraordinarily, extremely, immensely, tremendously. 2 admiringly, appreciatively, favourably, warmly, well. □ **highly-strung** emotional, excitable, jumpy, nervous, nervy, sensitive, temperamental, touchy, volatile.

highway n. 1 public road. 2 main route.

highwayman n. person (usu. on horseback) who robbed travellers in former times.

hijack v. seize control illegally of (a vehicle or aircraft in transit). ● n. hijacking. □ **hijacker** n.

hike n. long walk. ● v. go for a hike. □ **hiker** n.

hilarious adj. 1 extremely funny. 2 boisterous and merry. □ **hilariously** adv., **hilarity** n.
■ 1 comical, funny, sl. priceless. 2 boisterous, jolly, merry, rollicking, uproarious.

hill n. 1 raised part of earth's surface, lower than a mountain. 2 slope in a road etc. 3 mound. □ **hill-billy** n. (US) rustic person.
■ 1 elevation, hillock, hummock, knoll, mound. 2 gradient, incline, rise, slope. 3 heap, mound, pile, stack.

hillock n. small hill, mound.

hilt n. handle of a sword or dagger. □ **to the hilt** completely.

him pron. objective case of he.

Himalayan adj. of the Himalaya Mountains.

himself pron. emphatic and reflexive form of he and him.

hind¹ n. female deer.

hind² adj. situated at the back.

hinder v. delay progress of.
■ baulk, delay, foil, forestall, frustrate, hamper, handicap, hold up, impede, obstruct, prevent, set back, slow down, thwart.

Hindi n. group of languages of northern India.

hindmost adj. furthest behind.

hindrance n. 1 thing that hinders. 2 hindering, being hindered.
■ 1 catch, drawback, hitch, impediment, obstacle, obstruction, snag, stumbling block.

hindsight n. wisdom about an event after it has occurred.

Hindu n. person whose religion is Hinduism. ● adj. of Hindus or Hinduism.

Hinduism n. principal religion and philosophy of India.

Hindustani n. language of much of northern India and Pakistan.

hinge n. movable joint on which a door or lid turns. ● v. attach or be attached by hinge(s). □ **hinge on** depend on.

hint n. 1 slight or indirect indication or suggestion. 2 piece of practical information. 3 faint trace. ● v. make a hint.
■ n. 1 allusion, clue, implication, indication, inkling, innuendo, insinuation, intimation, suggestion. 2 piece of advice, suggestion, tip. 3 shade, suggestion, touch, trace. ● v. imply, indicate, insinuate, intimate, suggest.

hinterland n. district behind that lying along a coast etc.

hip¹ n. projection of the pelvis on each side of body.

hip² n. fruit of wild rose.

hippopotamus n. (pl. **-muses**) large African river animal with a thick skin.

hire v. engage or grant temporary use of, for payment. ● n. hiring. □ **hire purchase** system of purchase by paying in instalments. **hirer** n.
■ v. charter, lease, rent; employ, engage, take on. ● n. lease, rental.

hireling n. (derog.) hired helper.

hirsute /húrsyoot/ adj. hairy.

his adj. & poss.pron. belonging to him.

Hispanic adj. & n. (native) of Spain or a Spanish-speaking country.

hiss n. sound like 's'. ● v. 1 make this sound. 2 utter with a hiss. 3 express disapproval in this way.

histamine n. substance present in the body associated with allergic reactions.

histology n. study of organic tissues. □ **histological** adj.

historian n. expert in or writer of history.

historic *adj.* famous in history.
■ celebrated, famous, great, important, memorable, momentous, notable, noteworthy, significant, unforgettable.

historical *adj.* of or concerned with history. □ **historically** *adv.*
■ authentic, documented, factual, recorded, true, verifiable.

history *n.* **1** continuous record of (esp. public) events. **2** study of past events. **3** series of events, facts, etc. connected with a person, thing, or place.
■ **1** account, annals, chronicle, description, narrative, record, story. **3** antecedents, background, life, past.

histrionic *adj.* **1** of acting. **2** theatrical in manner. ● *n.pl.* **1** theatricals. **2** theatrical behaviour.

hit *v.* (**hit, hitting**) **1** strike with a blow or missile. **2** come forcefully against. **3** affect badly. **4** reach. **5** encounter. ● *n.* **1** blow, stroke. **2** shot that hits its target. **3** success. □ **hit it off** get on well together. **hit on** find, esp. by chance. **hit-or-miss** *adj.* aimed or done carelessly. **hitter** *n.*
■ *v.* bash, batter, beat, *sl.* belt, *sl.* biff, box, buffet, *colloq.* clip, *sl.* clobber, clout, cuff, pound, pummel, slap, smack, *colloq.* sock, spank, strike, swat, *colloq.* swipe, thrash, thump, thwack, *sl.* wallop, *colloq.* whack. **2** bang into, collide with, crash into, knock against, run into, smash into, strike. **3** affect, have an impact on, leave a mark on. **4** arrive at, come *or* get to, reach. **5** be faced with, encounter, experience, meet (with). □ **hit on** come across, discover, find, happen on, light on.

hitch *v.* **1** fasten with a loop or hook. **2** move (a thing) with a slight jerk. **3** hitchhike, obtain (a lift) in this way. ● *n.* **1** snag. **2** slight jerk. **3** noose or knot of various kinds.
■ *v.* **1** attach, connect, couple, fasten, hook, join, link, tether, tie. ● *n.* **1** catch, difficulty, hindrance, impediment, obstacle, problem, snag, stumbling block.

hitchhike *v.* travel by seeking free lifts in passing vehicles. □ **hitchhiker** *n.*

hi-tech *adj.* high-tech.

hither *adv.* to or towards this place.

hitherto *adv.* until this time.

HIV *abbr.* human immunodeficiency virus (causing Aids).

hive *n.* structure in which bees live. ● *v.* **hive off** separate from a larger group.

hives *n.pl.* skin eruption, esp. nettle-rash.

hoard *v.* save and put away. ● *n.* things hoarded. □ **hoarder** *n.*
■ *v.* accumulate, amass, collect, lay up, put by, reserve, save, *colloq.* stash away, stockpile, store (up). ● *n.* accumulation, cache, collection, reserve, stock, stockpile, store, supply.

hoarding *n.* fence of boards, often bearing advertisements.

hoar-frost *n.* white frost.

hoarse *adj.* **1** (of a voice) sounding rough as if from a dry throat. **2** having such a voice. □ **hoarsely** *adv.*, **hoarseness** *n.*
■ croaking, gruff, guttural, husky, rough, throaty.

hoary *adj.* (**-ier, -iest**) **1** grey with age. **2** (of a voice etc.) old.

hoax *v.* deceive jokingly. ● *n.* joking deception. □ **hoaxer** *n.*
■ *v.* *colloq.* bamboozle, deceive, dupe, fool, hoodwink, pull the wool over someone's eyes, swindle, trick. ● *n.* cheat, *sl.* con, joke, practical joke, trick.

hob *n.* top of a cooker, with hotplates.

hobble *v.* **1** walk lamely. **2** fasten the legs of (a horse) to limit its movement. ● *n.* **1** hobbling walk. **2** rope etc. used to hobble a horse.

hobby *n.* thing done often and for pleasure in one's spare time.
■ interest, leisure activity, pastime, pursuit, recreation, sideline.

hobby horse **1** stick with a horse's head, as a toy. **2** favourite topic.

hobgoblin *n.* mischievous imp.

hobnail *n.* heavy-headed nail for bootsoles. □ **hobnailed** *adj.*

hobnob *v.* (**-nobbed**) spend time together in a friendly way.
■ consort, fraternize, keep company, mingle, mix, socialize.

hock[1] *n.* middle joint of an animal's hind leg.

hock[2] *n.* German white wine.

hockey *n.* **1** field game played with curved sticks and a small hard ball. **2** ice hockey.

hocus-pocus *n.* trickery.

hod *n.* **1** trough on a pole for carrying mortar or bricks. **2** portable container for coal.

hoe *n.* tool for loosening soil or scraping up weeds. ● *v.* (**hoeing**) dig or scrape with a hoe.

hog *n.* **1** castrated male pig reared for meat. **2** (*colloq.*) greedy person. ● *v.*

(**hogged**) (*colloq.*) **1** take greedily. **2** hoard selfishly.

hoick *v.* (*colloq.*) lift or jerk.

hoi polloi ordinary people.

hoist *v.* raise or haul up. ● *n.* apparatus for hoisting things.

■ *v.* elevate, haul up, heave up, lift, raise, winch. ● *n.* crane, davit, lift, winch.

hoity-toity *adj.* haughty.

hokum *n.* (*sl.*) nonsense.

hold[1] *v.* (**held**) **1** keep in one's arms or hands etc. **2** keep in a particular position. **3** contain. **4** possess (property etc.). **5** bear the weight of. **6** detain. **7** continue. **8** occupy, engross. **9** cause to take place. **10** believe. ● *n.* **1** act, manner, or means of holding. **2** means of exerting influence. □ **hold back** impede the progress of. **hold dear** regard with affection. **hold out 1** offer. **2** last. **3** continue to make a demand. **hold up 1** support. **2** hinder. **3** stop and rob by use of threats or force. **hold-up** *n.* **1** delay. **2** robbery. **hold with** (*colloq.*) approve of. **holder** *n.*

■ *v.* **1** clasp, clench, clutch, grasp, grip, hang on to; cradle, embrace, enfold, hug. **2** keep, maintain, sustain. **3** accommodate, carry, contain, take. **4** have, keep, own, possess, retain. **5** bear, carry, support, sustain, take. **6** confine, detain, keep in custody, shut up, restrain. **7** carry on, continue, go on, keep up, last, persist. **8** absorb, engage, engross, involve, occupy. **9** assemble, call, convene, convoke. **10** believe, consider, deem, judge, maintain, think. ● *n.* **1** clasp, clutch, grasp, grip; foothold, purchase. **2** ascendancy, authority, *colloq.* clout, control, dominance, influence, leverage, mastery, power, sway. □ **hold back** check, control, curb, hinder, impede, inhibit, restrain. **hold out 1** extend, offer, present, proffer, reach out, stretch out. **2** carry on, continue, last, persevere, persist. **hold up 1** bolster, buttress, prop up, shore up, support. **2** delay, hinder, impede, obstruct, set back, slow down.

hold[2] *n.* storage cavity below a ship's deck.

holdall *n.* large soft travel bag.

holding *n.* **1** something held or owned. **2** land held by an owner or tenant.

hole *n.* **1** hollow place. **2** burrow. **3** aperture. **4** (*colloq.*) wretched place. **5** (*colloq.*) awkward situation. ● *v.* make hole(s) in.

■ *n.* **1** cave, cavity, crater, dent, depression, dip, hollow, indentation, niche, nook, pit, pocket, pothole, recess. **2** burrow, den, lair, sett, tunnel. **3** aperture, breach, fissure, gap, opening, orifice, perforation, puncture, rip, slit, slot, tear, vent.

holey *adj.* full of holes.

holiday *n.* day(s) of recreation. ● *v.* spend a holiday. □ **holiday-maker** *n.* person on holiday.

■ *n.* leave, recess, *colloq.* vac, *US* vacation. □ **holiday-maker** sightseer, tourist, traveller, tripper, visitor.

holiness *n.* being holy.

holistic *adj.* (of treatment) involving the mind, body, social factors, etc.

hollow *adj.* **1** empty within, not solid. **2** sunken. **3** echoing as if in something hollow. **4** worthless. **5** insincere. ● *n.* **1** cavity. **2** sunken place. **3** valley. ● *v.* make hollow.

■ *adj.* **1** empty, void, unfilled. **2** cavernous, concave, indented, recessed, sunken. **3** echoing, low, rumbling. **4** empty, fruitless, futile, meaningless, pointless, profitless, useless, vain, valueless, worthless. **5** empty, false, hypocritical, insincere. ● *n.* **1,2** cavity, concavity, crater, dent, depression, dip, hole, indentation, pit, trough. **3** coomb, dale, dell, dingle, glen, valley. ● *v.* dig, excavate, furrow, gouge.

holly *n.* evergreen shrub with prickly leaves and red berries.

hollyhock *n.* plant with large flowers on a tall stem.

holocaust *n.* large-scale destruction, esp. by fire.

hologram *n.* three-dimensional photographic image.

holograph[1] *v.* record as a hologram. □ **holography** *n.*

holograph[2] *adj.* & *n.* (document) written wholly in the handwriting of the author.

holster *n.* leather case holding a pistol or revolver.

holy *adj.* (**-ier, -iest**) **1** belonging to or devoted to God. **2** consecrated. **3** morally and spiritually excellent. □ **holy of holies** most sacred place.

■ **1** divine, sacred. **2** blessed, consecrated, sacred, sanctified. **3** devout, God-fearing, pious, religious, reverent, saintly, virtuous.

homage *n.* things said or done as a mark of respect or loyalty.

home *n.* **1** place where one lives. **2** dwelling house. **3** native land. **4** institution where those needing care may live. ● *adj.* **1** of one's home or country. **2** played on one's own ground. ● *adv.* **1** at or to one's home. **2** to the point aimed at. ● v. make its way home. □ **home in on** be guided to a destination. **at home 1** in one's own home. **2** at ease. **3** well-informed. **home truth** unpleasant truth about oneself.

■ n. **1** abode, domicile, habitation, house, lodging, quarters, residence. **2** US apartment, digs, dwelling, flat, house, lodgings. **3** country, fatherland, homeland, motherland, native land. **4** almshouse, hospice, institution, nursing home. □ **home in on** aim at or for, head for, make a beeline for, target, zero in on.

homeland n. native land.

homeless adj. lacking a home. □ **homelessness** n.

homely adj. (**-ier, -iest**) **1** simple and informal. **2** (US) plain, not beautiful. □ **homeliness** n.

■ **1** modest, ordinary, plain, simple, unassuming, unpretentious, unsophisticated; comfortable, cosy, folksy, friendly, informal, relaxed, snug, welcoming. **2** plain, ugly, unattractive.

homesick adj. longing for home.

homeward adj. & adv. going towards home. □ **homewards** adv.

homework n. work set for a pupil to do away from school.

homicide n. killing of one person by another. □ **homicidal** adj.

homily n. moralizing lecture. □ **homiletic** adj.

hominid adj. & n. (member) of the family including humans and their fossil ancestors.

homoeopathy /hōmióppəthi/ n. treatment of a disease by very small doses of a substance that would produce the same symptoms in a healthy person. □ **homoeopathic** adj.

homogeneous adj. of the same kind, uniform. □ **homogeneously** adv., **homogeneity** n.

homogenize v. treat (milk) so that cream does not separate and rise to the top.

homonym n. word with the same spelling as another.

homophobia n. hatred or fear of homosexuals.

homophone n. word with the same sound as another.

homosexual adj. & n. (person) sexually attracted to people of the same sex. □ **homosexuality** n.

hone v. sharpen on a whetstone.

honest adj. **1** truthful. **2** trustworthy. **3** fairly earned. □ **honestly** adv., **honesty** n.

■ **1** candid, direct, forthright, frank, colloq. on the level, open, sincere, straight, straightforward, truthful, veracious. **2** decent, dependable, ethical, fair, good, honourable, just, law-abiding, loyal, moral, principled, reliable, trustworthy, upright, virtuous. **3** above board, bona fide, legitimate. □ **honesty** candour, directness, forthrightness, frankness, sincerity, truthfulness, veracity; equity, fairness, goodness, honour, integrity, probity, rectitude, trustworthiness, virtue, virtuousness.

honey n. (pl. **-eys**) **1** sweet substance made by bees from nectar. **2** darling. □ **honey bee** common bee living in a hive.

honeycomb n. **1** bees' wax structure for holding their honey and eggs. **2** pattern of six-sided sections.

honeydew melon melon with pale skin and sweet green flesh.

honeyed adj. sweet, sweet-sounding.

honeymoon n. **1** holiday spent together by a newly married couple. **2** initial period of goodwill. ● v. spend a honeymoon.

honeysuckle n. climbing shrub with fragrant flowers.

honk n. **1** sound of a car horn. **2** cry of a wild goose. ● v. make this noise.

honorary adj. **1** given as an honour. **2** unpaid.

honour n. **1** great respect or public regard. **2** mark of this, privilege. **3** adherence to what is right. **4** reputation, good name. ● v. **1** respect highly. **2** confer honour on. **3** pay (a cheque) or fulfil (a promise etc.).

■ n. **1** distinction, esteem, glory, kudos, prestige, regard, renown, respect, reverence, veneration. **2** award, reward, tribute; distinction, pleasure, privilege. **3** decency, fairness, goodness, honesty, justice, integrity, morality, probity, rectitude, righteousness, virtue, virtuousness. ● v. **1** admire, esteem, respect, revere, venerate. **2** acclaim, applaud, eulogize, glorify, laud, pay tribute to, praise. **3** pay, redeem; carry out, discharge, fulfil.

honourable adj. deserving, possessing, or showing honour. □ **honourably** adv.

■ decent, ethical, fair, good, honest, incorruptible, just, moral, noble, principled, respectable, trustworthy, upright, virtuous, worthy.

hood¹ n. **1** covering for the head and neck, esp. forming part of a garment. **2** hood-like thing or cover. **3** folding roof over a car. □ **hooded** adj.

hood² n. (US) gangster, gunman.

hoodlum n. hooligan.

hoodoo n. (US) **1** bad luck. **2** thing causing this.

hoodwink v. deceive.

■ cheat, sl. con, deceive, double-cross, dupe, hoax, mislead, pull the wool over someone's eyes, take in, trick.

hoof n. (pl. **hoofs** or **hooves**) horny part of a horse's foot.

hook n. **1** bent or curved device for catching hold or hanging things on. **2** short blow made with the elbow bent. ● v. **1** grasp, catch, or fasten with hook(s). **2** (in sports) send (a ball) in a curving or deviating path. □ **hook-up** n. interconnection. **off the hook** freed from a difficulty.

hookah n. tobacco pipe with a long tube passing through water.

hooked adj. hook-shaped. □ **hooked on** (sl.) addicted to.

hookworm n. parasitic worm with hooklike mouthparts.

hooligan n. young ruffian. □ **hooliganism** n.

■ delinquent, hoodlum, lout, ruffian, tearaway, thug, tough, vandal, sl. yob.

hoop n. **1** circular band of metal or wood. **2** metal arch used in croquet.

hoopla n. game in which rings are thrown to encircle a prize.

hoopoe n. bird with a crest and striped plumage.

hooray int. & n. = hurrah.

hoot n. **1** owl's cry. **2** sound of a hooter. **3** cry of laughter or disapproval. **4** cause of laughter. ● v. (cause to) make a hoot.

hooter n. thing that hoots, esp. a siren or car's horn.

Hoover n. [P.] a kind of vacuum cleaner. ● v. (**hoover**) clean with a vacuum cleaner.

hop¹ v. (**hopped**) **1** (of a person) jump on one foot. **2** (of an animal) jump from both or all feet. **3** (colloq.) make a quick short trip. ● n. **1** hopping movement. **2** informal dance. **3** short journey.

hop² n. **1** climbing plant cultivated for its cones. **2** (pl.) these cones, used to give a bitter flavour to beer.

hope n. **1** feeling of expectation and desire. **2** person or thing giving cause for this. **3** what one hopes for. ● v. feel hope.

■ n. **1** anticipation, expectancy, expectation. **3** ambition, aspiration, dream, wish.

hopeful adj. **1** feeling or inspiring hope. **2** promising. □ **hopefully** adv.

■ **1** confident, full of hope, optimistic, sanguine. **2** auspicious, bright, encouraging, favourable, promising, propitious, rosy.

hopeless adj. **1** feeling no hope. **2** inadequate, incompetent. **3** not likely to improve or succeed. □ **hopelessly** adv., **hopelessness** n.

■ **1** dejected, desolate, despairing, despondent, downcast, inconsolable, in despair, melancholy, miserable, wretched. **2** bad, inadequate, incompetent, inept, poor. **3** beyond hope, desperate, irremediable, irreparable, irretrievable; futile, impossible, impracticable, pointless, useless, vain, worthless.

hopper n. **1** one who hops. **2** container with an opening at its base through which its contents can be discharged.

hopscotch n. game involving hopping over marked squares.

horde n. large group or crowd.

■ crowd, flock, gang, herd, host, mob, multitude, swarm, throng.

horizon n. **1** line at which earth and sky appear to meet. **2** limit of knowledge or interests.

horizontal adj. parallel to the horizon, going straight across. □ **horizontally** adv.

hormone n. secretion (or synthetic substance) that stimulates an organ or growth. □ **hormonal** adj.

horn n. **1** hard pointed growth on the heads of certain animals. **2** substance of which this is made. **3** similar projection. **4** wind instrument with a trumpet-shaped end. **5** device for sounding a warning signal. □ **horn-rimmed** adj. with frames of material like horn or tortoiseshell.

hornblende n. dark mineral constituent of granite etc.

hornet n. a kind of large wasp.

hornpipe n. lively solo dance associated esp. with sailors.

horny adj. (**-ier, -iest**) **1** of or like horn. **2** hardened and calloused. □ **horniness** n.

horology n. art of making clocks etc. □ **horologist** n.

horoscope *n.* forecast of events based on the positions of stars.

horrendous *adj.* horrifying. □ **horrendously** *adv.*

horrible *adj.* **1** causing horror. **2** (*colloq.*) unpleasant. □ **horribly** *adv.*
■ **1** appalling, awful, dreadful, fearful, frightful, ghastly, grim, grisly, gruesome, hideous, horrendous, horrid, horrific, horrifying, repulsive, revolting, shocking, terrible. **2** awful, *colloq.* beastly, disagreeable, disgusting, *colloq.* frightful, horrid, nasty, objectionable, obnoxious, offensive, *colloq.* off-putting, repellent, unpleasant.

horrid *adj.* horrible.

horrific *adj.* horrifying. □ **horrifically** *adv.*

horrify *v.* arouse horror in, shock.
■ appal, disgust, dismay, frighten, outrage, repel, revolt, scandalize, scare, shock, startle, terrify.

horror *n.* **1** extreme fear, dread. **2** intense dislike or dismay. **3** person or thing causing horror.
■ **1** alarm, dread, fear, fright, panic, perturbation, terror, trepidation. **2** abhorrence, antipathy, aversion, detestation, dislike, distaste, hatred, hostility, loathing, odium, repugnance, revulsion.

hors d'oeuvre /or dɔ́rvrə/ food served as an appetizer.

horse *n.* **1** four-legged animal with a mane and tail. **2** padded structure for vaulting over in a gymnasium. ● *v.* (*colloq.*) fool, play. □ **horse chestnut 1** brown shiny nut. **2** tree bearing this. **horse sense** (*colloq.*) common sense.

horseback *n.* **on horseback** riding on a horse.

horsebox *n.* closed vehicle for transporting a horse.

horseman, horsewoman *ns.* rider on horseback. □ **horsemanship** *n.*

horseplay *n.* boisterous play.

horsepower *n.* unit for measuring the power of an engine.

horseradish *n.* plant with a hot-tasting root used to make sauce.

horseshoe *n.* **1** U-shaped strip of metal nailed to a horse's hoof. **2** thing shaped like this.

horsy *adj.* **1** of or like a horse. **2** interested in horses.

horticulture *n.* art of garden cultivation. □ **horticultural** *adj.*, **horticulturist** *n.*

hose *n.* **1** (also **hosepipe**) flexible tube for conveying water. **2** stockings and socks. ● *v.* water or spray with a hosepipe.

hosiery *n.* stockings, socks, etc.

hospice *n.* hospital or home for the terminally ill.

hospitable *adj.* giving hospitality. □ **hospitably** *adv.*
■ convivial, genial, friendly, kind, neighbourly, sociable, warm, welcoming.

hospital *n.* institution for treatment of sick or injured people.
■ clinic, infirmary, sanatorium.

hospitality *n.* friendly and generous entertainment of guests.

hospitalize *v.* send or admit to a hospital. □ **hospitalization** *n.*

host¹ *n.* large number of people or things.
■ army, crowd, herd, horde, legion, mass, mob, multitude, pack, swarm, throng.

host² *n.* **1** person who entertains guest(s). **2** organism on which another lives as a parasite. ● *v.* act as host to.

hostage *n.* person held as security that the holder's demands will be satisfied.

hostel *n.* lodging house for students, nurses, etc.

hostess *n.* woman who entertains guests.

hostile *adj.* **1** of an enemy. **2** unfriendly, opposed.
■ **1** aggressive, belligerent, combative, militant, opposing, warring. **2** inhospitable, inimical, malevolent, unfriendly, unsympathetic, unwelcoming; antagonistic, averse, opposed.

hostility *n.* **1** being hostile, enmity. **2** (*pl.*) acts of warfare.
■ **1** animosity, animus, antagonism, antipathy, aversion, enmity, hatred, ill will, malevolence, opposition, unfriendliness. **2** (**hostilities**) action, combat, fighting, war, warfare.

hot *adj.* (**hotter, hottest**) **1** at or having a high temperature. **2** producing a burning sensation to the taste. **3** excited. **4** eager. ● *v.* (**hotted**) **hot up** (*colloq.*) make or become hot or exciting. □ **hot air** (*colloq.*) excited or boastful talk. **hot dog** hot sausage in a bread roll. **hot line** direct line for speedy communication. **hot-tempered** *adj.* impulsively angry. **in hot water** in trouble.
■ *adj.* **1** burning, fiery, red-hot, scorching, sultry, sweltering, torrid, white-hot. **2** peppery, piquant, sharp, spicy. **3** ardent, enthusiastic, excited, fervent, fervid, impassioned, intense, passionate, vehement.

4 anxious, avid, eager, keen. □ **hot-tempered** excitable, irascible, irritable, quick-tempered, stormy, temperamental, volatile.

hotbed n. place encouraging vice, intrigue, etc.

hotchpotch n. jumble.

hotel n. building providing meals and rooms for travellers.

hotelier n. hotel-keeper.

hotfoot adv. in eager haste.
■ hastily, helter-skelter, hurriedly, pell-mell, rapidly, swiftly.

hothead n. impetuous person.

hotheaded adj. impetuous.
■ foolhardy, hasty, impetuous, impulsive, madcap, precipitate, rash, reckless, thoughtless, wild.

hothouse n. heated greenhouse.

hotplate n. heated surface on a cooker.

hotpot n. stew of meat and vegetables.

houmous n. = **hummus**.

hound n. dog used in hunting. ● v. pursue, harass.
■ v. chase, hunt, pursue; annoy, badger, harass, harry, colloq. hassle, nag, persecute, pester, colloq. plague.

hour n. **1** one twenty-fourth part of a day and night. **2** point of time. **3** occasion. **4** (pl.) period for daily work. □ **hourly** adj. & adv.

hourglass n. glass containing sand that takes one hour to trickle from upper to lower section through a narrow opening.

houri /hoōri/ n. (pl. **-is**) beautiful young woman of the Muslim paradise.

house n. /howss/ **1** building for people (usu. one family) to live in, or for a specific purpose. **2** household. **3** legislative assembly. **4** business firm. **5** family, dynasty. **6** theatre audience or performance. ● v. /howz/ **1** provide accommodation or storage space for. **2** encase. □ **house arrest** detention in one's own home. **house-proud** adj. attentive to the appearance of one's home. **house-trained** adj. trained to be clean in the house. **house-warming** n. party celebrating a move to a new home.
■ n. **1** abode, domicile, dwelling, habitation, home, lodging(s), residence; building, edifice, structure. **2** household, ménage. **3** legislature, parliament. **4** business, company, concern, corporation, enterprise, establishment, firm, organization. **5** clan, dynasty, family, line, lineage. ● v. **1** accommodate, harbour, lodge, put up, quar-

ter, shelter. **2** contain, cover, encase, enclose.

houseboat n. barge-like boat equipped for living in.

housebound adj. confined to one's house through illness etc.

housebreaker n. burglar. □ **housebreaking** n.

housecoat n. woman's garment for informal wear in the house.

household n. occupants of a house. □ **household word** familiar saying or name.

householder n. person owning or renting a house or flat.

housekeeper n. person employed to look after a household.

housekeeping n. **1** management of household affairs. **2** money to be used for this.

housemaster, **housemistress** ns. teacher in charge of a school boarding house.

housewife n. woman managing a household. □ **housewifely** adj.

housework n. cleaning and cooking etc. done in the home.

housing n. **1** accommodation. **2** rigid case enclosing machinery.

hovel n. small miserable dwelling.

hover v. **1** (of a bird etc.) remain in one place in the air. **2** linger, wait close at hand. □ **hover fly** wasp-like insect that hovers.

hovercraft n. (pl. **-craft**) vehicle supported by air thrust downwards from its engines.

how adv. **1** by what means, in what way. **2** to what extent or amount etc. **3** in what condition.

howdah n. seat, usu. with a canopy, on an elephant's back.

however adv. **1** in whatever way, to whatever extent. **2** nevertheless.

howitzer n. short gun firing shells at high elevation.

howl n. long loud wailing cry or sound. ● v. **1** make or utter with a howl. **2** weep loudly.
■ n. cry, scream, ululation, wail, yelp, yowl. ● v. **1** bay, bellow, cry, scream, ululate, wail, yelp, yowl. **2** bawl, cry, wail, weep.

howler n. **1** animal etc. that howls. **2** (colloq.) stupid mistake.

hoyden n. boisterous girl.

h.p. abbr. **1** hire purchase. **2** horsepower.

hub n. **1** central part of a wheel. **2** centre of activity, interest, etc. □ **hubcap** n. cover for the hub of a car wheel.

■ **2** centre, core, focal point, focus, heart, nucleus.

hubbub n. confused noise of voices.

hubris /hyōobriss/ n. arrogant pride.

huckleberry n. **1** N. American shrub. **2** its fruit.

huddle v. crowd into a small place. ● n. close mass.

■ v. cluster, crowd, flock, gather, squeeze. ● n. bunch, clump, cluster, crowd, group, throng.

hue[1] n. colour.

■ colour, shade, tincture, tinge, tint, tone.

hue[2] n. **hue and cry** outcry.

huff n. fit of annoyance. ● v. blow. □ **huffy** adj., **huffily** adv.

hug v. (**hugged**) **1** squeeze tightly in one's arms. **2** keep close to. ● n. hugging movement.

■ v. **1** clasp, cuddle, embrace, squeeze.

huge adj. extremely large. □ **hugely** adv., **hugeness** n.

■ colossal, enormous, gargantuan, giant, gigantic, huge, immense, mammoth, massive, monumental, prodigious, titanic, tremendous, vast.

hula n. Polynesian women's dance. □ **hula hoop** large hoop for spinning round the body.

hulk n. **1** body of an old ship. **2** large clumsy-looking person or thing.

hulking adj. (colloq.) large and clumsy.

hull[1] n. framework of a ship.

hull[2] n. **1** pod of a pea or bean. **2** cluster of leaves on a strawberry. ● v. remove the hull of.

hullabaloo n. uproar.

■ clamour, commotion, din, disorder, disturbance, fracas, furore, hubbub, pandemonium, racket, rumpus, tumult, uproar.

hullo int. = hello.

hum v. (**hummed**) **1** make a low continuous sound like a bee. **2** sing with closed lips. **3** (colloq.) be in state of activity. ● n. humming sound.

■ v. **1** buzz, drone, murmur, purr, whirr.

human adj. **1** of humankind. **2** having the weaknesses or strengths of humankind. ● n. human being. ■ **human being** man, woman, or child.

humane adj. kind-hearted, merciful. □ **humanely** adv.

■ benevolent, caring, charitable, compassionate, considerate, forbearing, forgiving, generous, good, good-natured, kind, kind-hearted, kindly, lenient, merciful, sympathetic, tender, warm.

humanism n. non-religious philosophy based on liberal human values. □ **humanist** n., **humanistic** adj.

humanitarian adj. promoting human welfare and reduction of suffering. □ **humanitarianism** n.

humanity n. **1** human nature or qualities. **2** kindness. **3** human race. **4** (pl.) arts subjects.

humanize v. make human or humane. □ **humanization** n.

humankind n. human beings in general.

■ human beings, humanity, man, mankind, the human race.

humble adj. **1** having or showing a modest estimate of one's own importance. **2** of low rank. **3** not large or expensive. ● v. lower the rank or self-importance of. □ **humbly** adv.

■ adj. **1** modest, self-effacing, unassuming; deferential, meek, obsequious, servile, submissive, subservient. **2** inferior, insignificant, low, lowly, mean, undistinguished, unimportant. ● v. demote, downgrade; chasten, humiliate, subdue.

humbug n. **1** misleading behaviour or talk to win support or sympathy. **2** person behaving thus. **3** peppermint-flavoured boiled sweet. ● v. (**humbugged**) delude.

humdrum adj. dull, commonplace.

■ boring, commonplace, dull, mundane, ordinary, routine, run-of-the-mill, tedious, tiresome, uneventful, unexciting, uninteresting, wearisome.

humerus n. (pl. **-ri**) bone of the upper arm. □ **humeral** adj.

humid adj. (of air) damp. □ **humidity** n.

■ clammy, close, damp, moist, muggy, oppressive, steamy, sticky, sultry.

humidify v. keep (air) moist in a room etc. □ **humidifier** n.

humiliate v. cause to feel disgraced. □ **humiliation** n.

■ abase, chasten, crush, degrade, demean, disgrace, embarrass, humble, mortify, shame. □ **humiliation** degradation, disgrace, dishonour, embarrassment, ignominy, indignity, mortification, shame.

humility *n.* humble condition or attitude of mind.

■ lowliness, meekness, modesty, self-effacement, servility, submissiveness, subservience.

hummock *n.* hillock.

hummus /hŏŏmməss/ *n.* (also **houmous**) dip of chickpeas, sesame oil, lemon juice, and garlic.

humour *n.* **1** quality of being amusing. **2** state of mind. ● *v.* keep (a person) contented by doing as he or she wishes. □ **sense of humour** ability to perceive and enjoy humour. **humorous** *adj.*, **humorously** *adv.*

■ *n.* **1** comedy, drollery, hilarity, jocularity, wit, wittiness. **2** disposition, mood, state of mind, spirits, temper. ● *v.* appease, gratify, indulge, mollify, pander to, placate, please. □ **humorous** amusing, comic(al), droll, entertaining, funny, hilarious, witty.

hump *n.* **1** rounded projecting part. **2** curved deformity of the spine. ● *v.* **1** form into a hump. **2** hoist and carry. □ **humpback bridge** small steeply arched bridge.

■ *n.* **1** bulge, bump, knob, lump, node, projection, protrusion, protuberance, swelling; hillock, hummock, mound. ● *v.* **2** arch, bend, crook, curve, hunch.

humus *n.* soil-fertilizing substance formed by decay of dead leaves and plants etc.

hunch *v.* bend into a hump. ● *n.* **1** intuitive feeling. **2** hump.

■ *n.* **1** feeling, impression, intuition, premonition, presentiment, suspicion.

hundred *n.* ten times ten. □ **hundredth** *adj.* & *n.*

hundredfold *adj.* & *adv.* 100 times as much or as many.

hundredweight *n.* measure of weight, 112 lb (50.80 kg).

hung *see* **hang**. *adj.* (of a council, parliament, etc.) with no party having a clear majority. □ **hung-over** *adj.* (*colloq.*) having a hangover.

Hungarian *adj.* & *n.* (native, language) of Hungary.

hunger *n.* **1** pain or discomfort felt when one has not eaten for some time. **2** strong desire. ● *v.* feel hunger. □ **hunger for** have a strong desire for. **hunger strike** refusal of food as a protest.

■ *n.* **2** appetite, craving, desire, hankering, itch, longing, thirst, yearning, *colloq.* yen.

□ **hunger for** crave, desire, hanker after, long for, thirst for, want, wish for, yearn for.

hungry *adj.* (**-ier**, **-iest**) feeling hunger. □ **hungrily** *adv.*

■ famished, *colloq.* peckish, ravenous, *colloq.* starving; avid, desirous, eager, greedy, longing, thirsty, yearning.

hunk *n.* large piece cut off.

hunt *v.* **1** pursue (wild animals) for food or sport. **2** (of animals) pursue prey. ● *n.* **1** process of hunting. **2** hunting group. □ **hunt for** seek, search for.

■ *v.* chase, pursue, stalk, track, trail. ● *n.* **1** chase, pursuit, search, quest. □ **hunt for** go in search of, look for, search for, seek.

hunter *n.* **1** one who hunts. **2** horse used for hunting.

hurdle *n.* **1** portable frame with bars, used as a temporary fence. **2** frame to be jumped over in a race. **3** obstacle, difficulty. □ **hurdler** *n.*

■ **3** barrier, complication, difficulty, hindrance, impediment, obstacle, obstruction, problem, snag, stumbling block.

hurl *v.* throw violently. ● *n.* violent throw.

■ *v.* cast, *colloq.* chuck, fling, *colloq.* heave, lob, pitch, *colloq.* sling, throw, toss.

hurly-burly *n.* boisterous activity.

hurrah *int.* & *n.* (also **hurray**) exclamation of joy or approval.

hurricane *n.* storm with violent wind. □ **hurricane lamp** lamp with the flame protected from the wind.

■ cyclone, storm, tornado, typhoon, whirlwind.

hurried *adj.* done with great haste. □ **hurriedly** *adv.*

hurry *v.* **1** act or move with eagerness or too quickly. **2** cause to do this. ● *n.* hurrying.

■ *v.* **1** dash, hasten, fly, make haste, race, run, rush, scurry, scuttle, shoot, speed, tear, zoom. **2** accelerate, expedite, quicken, speed up.

hurt *v.* (**hurt**) **1** cause pain, harm, or distress (to). **2** feel pain. ● *n.* injury, harm. □ **hurtful** *adj.*

■ *v.* **1** injure, wound; damage, harm, impair, mar, spoil; afflict, distress, grieve, pain, upset. **2** ache, be painful *or* sore, smart, sting, throb. ● *n.* damage, harm, injury; agony, anguish, distress, pain, suffering. □ **hurtful** cruel, cutting, malicious, mean, nasty, spiteful, unkind, wounding;

damaging, deleterious, detrimental, harmful, injurious.

hurtle v. move or hurl rapidly.

husband n. married man in relation to his wife. ● v. use economically, try to save.

husbandry n. 1 farming. 2 management of resources.

hush v. make or become silent. ● n. silence. □ **hush-hush** adj. secret.
■ v. quieten, colloq. shush, silence; fall silent, colloq. shut up. ● n. peace, quiet, silence, stillness, tranquillity.

husk n. dry outer covering of certain seeds and fruits. ● v. remove the husk from.

husky[1] adj. (-ier, -iest) 1 hoarse. 2 burly. □ **huskily** adv.

husky[2] n. Arctic sledge-dog.

hustle v. 1 push roughly. 2 hurry. ● n. hustling.
■ v. 1 elbow, jostle, push, shove, thrust. 2 hasten, hurry, rush, scurry, scuttle, sprint.

hut n. small simple or roughly made house or shelter.

hutch n. box-like pen for rabbits.

hyacinth n. plant with fragrant bell-shaped flowers.

hybrid n. 1 offspring of two different species or varieties. 2 thing made by combining different elements. ● adj. produced in this way. □ **hybridism** n.
■ n. 1 cross, cross-breed, mongrel. 2 blend, composite, compound, mix, mixture.

hybridize v. 1 cross-breed. 2 produce hybrids. 3 interbreed. □ **hybridization** n.

hydrangea n. shrub with pink, blue, or white flowers in clusters.

hydrant n. outlet for drawing water from a main.

hydrate n. chemical compound of water with another substance.

hydraulic adj. operated by pressure of fluid conveyed in pipes. ● n. (**hydraulics**) science of hydraulic operations.

hydrocarbon n. compound of hydrogen and carbon.

hydrochloric acid solution of hydrogen chloride in water.

hydrodynamics n. science of forces acting or exerted by liquids. □ **hydrodynamic** adj.

hydroelectric adj. using water-power to produce electricity.

hydrofoil n. 1 boat with a structure that raises its hull out of the water when the boat is in motion. 2 this structure.

hydrogen n. odourless gas, the lightest element. □ **hydrogen bomb** powerful bomb releasing energy by fusion of hydrogen nuclei.

hydrolysis n. decomposition by chemical reaction with water. □ **hydrolytic** adj.

hydrometer n. device measuring the density of liquids.

hydrophobia n. 1 abnormal fear of water. 2 rabies.

hydroponics n. art of growing plants in water impregnated with chemicals.

hydrostatic adj. of the pressure and other characteristics of liquid at rest.

hydrotherapy n. use of water to treat diseases etc.

hydrous adj. containing water.

hyena n. wolf-like animal with a howl that sounds like laughter.

hygiene n. cleanliness as a means of preventing disease. □ **hygienic** adj., **hygienically** adv., **hygienist** n.
■ □ **hygienic** aseptic, clean, disinfected, sanitary, sterile.

hymen n. membrane partly closing the opening of the vagina of a virgin girl or woman.

hymn n. song of praise to God or a sacred being.

hyper- pref. excessively.

hyperactive adj. abnormally active. □ **hyperactivity** n.

hypermarket n. very large supermarket.

hypersonic adj. of speeds more than five times that of sound.

hypertension n. 1 abnormally high blood pressure. 2 extreme tension.

hyphen n. the sign - used to join words together or divide a word into parts. ● v. hyphenate.

hyphenate v. join or divide with a hyphen. □ **hyphenation** n.

hypnosis n. sleep-like condition produced in a person who then obeys suggestions.

hypnotic adj. of or producing hypnosis. □ **hypnotically** adv.

hypnotism n. hypnosis.

hypnotize v. 1 produce hypnosis in. 2 fascinate. □ **hypnotist** n.
■ 1 mesmerize. 2 bewitch, captivate, entrance, fascinate, hold spellbound, mesmerize.

hypochondria n. state of constantly imagining that one is ill. □ **hypochondriac** n. & adj.

hypocrisy *n.* **1** falsely pretending to be virtuous. **2** insincerity.
■ deceit, deceitfulness, deception, duplicity, falseness, falsity, insincerity, sanctimoniousness.

hypocrite *n.* person guilty of hypocrisy.
□ **hypocritical** *adj.*, **hypocritically** *adv.*
■ □ **hypocritical** deceitful, dishonest, disingenuous, dissembling, duplicitous, insincere, sanctimonious, two-faced.

hypodermic *adj.* (of a drug, syringe, etc.) introduced under the skin. ● *n.* hypodermic syringe.

hypotenuse *n.* longest side of a right-angled triangle.

hypothermia *n.* abnormally low body temperature.

hypothesis *n.* (*pl.* **-theses**) supposition put forward as a basis for reasoning or investigation.
■ assumption, premiss, proposition, supposition, theory.

hypothetical *adj.* supposed but not necessarily true. □ **hypothetically** *adv.*
■ notional, putative, speculative, supposed, theoretical, unproven.

hysterectomy *n.* surgical removal of the womb.

hysteria *n.* wild uncontrollable emotion.
□ **hysterical** *adj.*, **hysterically** *adv.*

hysterics *n.pl.* hysterical outburst.

Hz *abbr.* hertz.

I *pron.* person speaking or writing and referring to himself or herself.

iambic *adj.* & *n.* (verse) using iambuses, metrical feet of one long and one short syllable.

iatrogenic *adj.* (of disease) caused unintentionally by medical treatment.

Iberian *adj.* of the peninsula comprising Spain and Portugal.

ibex *n.* (*pl.* **ibex** or **ibexes**) mountain goat with curving horns.

ibis *n.* wading bird found in warm climates.

ice *n.* **1** frozen water. **2** portion of ice cream. ● *v.* **1** become frozen. **2** make very cold. **3** decorate with icing. □ **ice cream** sweet creamy frozen food. **ice hockey** game like hockey played on ice by skaters. **ice lolly** water ice or ice cream on a stick.

iceberg *n.* mass of ice floating in the sea.

Icelandic *adj.* & *n.* (language) of Iceland.

ichthyology /ikthiólləji/ *n.* study of fish. □ **ichthyologist** *n.*

icicle *n.* hanging ice formed when dripping water freezes.

icing *n.* mixture of powdered sugar etc. used to decorate food.

icon *n.* sacred painting, mosaic, etc.

iconoclast *n.* person who attacks cherished beliefs. □ **iconoclasm** *n.*, **iconoclastic** *adj.*

icy *adj.* (**-ier, -iest**) **1** very cold. **2** covered with ice. **3** very unfriendly. □ **icily** *adv.*, **iciness** *n.*
■ **1** arctic, bitter, chilling, chilly, cold, freezing, frigid, frosty, glacial, raw. **2** frosty, frozen, slippery. **3** aloof, chilly, cold, cool, frigid, unfriendly, unwelcoming.

idea *n.* **1** plan etc. formed by mental effort. **2** opinion. **3** mental impression, vague belief.
■ **1** brainwave, inspiration; concept, conception, design, notion, plan, scheme, stratagem, thought. **2** belief, conviction, opinion, theory, view. **3** feeling, hunch, impression, inkling, intimation, notion, suspicion.

ideal *adj.* satisfying one's idea of what is perfect. ● *n.* person or thing regarded as perfect or as a standard to aim at. □ **ideally** *adv.*
■ *adj.* excellent, exemplary, faultless, flawless, model, perfect.

idealist *n.* person with high ideals. □ **idealism** *n.*, **idealistic** *adj.*

idealize *v.* regard or represent as perfect. □ **idealization** *n.*

identical *adj.* **1** the same. **2** exactly alike. □ **identically** *adv.*
■ **1** selfsame, (very) same. **2** alike, corresponding, duplicate, equal, equivalent, indistinguishable, interchangeable, like, matching, twin.

identify *v.* establish the identity of. □ **identify with 1** closely associate with. **2** associate (oneself) with in feeling or interest. **identifiable** *adj.*, **identification** *n.*
■ discern, distinguish, pick out, recognize; diagnose, establish, find out. □ **identify with 2** empathize with, relate to, sympathize with.

identity *n.* **1** who or what a person or thing is. **2** sameness.
■ **1** distinctiveness, individuality, personality, uniqueness. **2** congruence, correspondence, likeness, sameness.

ideology *n.* ideas that form the basis of a political or economic theory. □ **ideological** *adj.*
■ beliefs, convictions, doctrine, ideas, philosophy, principles, teachings, tenets.

idiocy *n.* **1** state of being an idiot. **2** extreme foolishness.

idiom *n.* **1** phrase etc. established by usage and not immediately comprehensible from the words used. **2** form of expression peculiar to a language. □ **idiomatic** *adj.*
■ **1** expression, phrase, saying. **2** dialect, jargon, parlance, patois, phraseology.

idiosyncrasy *n.* person's own characteristic way of behaving. □ **idiosyncratic** *adj.*
■ characteristic, foible, habit, mannerism, peculiarity, quirk.

idiot *n.* very stupid person. ▫ **idiotic** *adj.*, **idiotically** *adv.*

■ ass, blockhead, *colloq.* clot, dolt, *sl.* dope, *colloq.* duffer, dullard, ignoramus, imbecile, ninny, *colloq.* nitwit, *sl.* twit, *sl.* wally.

idle *adj.* **1** not employed or in use. **2** lazy. **3** aimless. ● *v.* **1** be idle. **2** (of an engine) run slowly in neutral gear. ● *v.* pass (time) aimlessly. **idly** *adv.*, **idleness** *n.*, **idler** *n.*

■ *adj.* **1** inactive, not in use, not working, stationary; jobless, out of work, redundant, unemployed. **2** indolent, lazy, shiftless, slothful. **3** aimless, casual, offhand, purposeless. ● *v.* **1** hang about, laze around, loaf about, lounge about. **2** tick over. ▫ **idle away** fritter away, squander, waste, while away.

idol *n.* **1** image worshipped as a god. **2** idolized person or thing.

■ **1** fetish, icon, totem. **2** hero, heroine, star.

idolatry *n.* worship of idols. ▫ **idolater** *n.*, **idolatrous** *adj.*

idolize *v.* love or admire excessively. ▫ **idolization** *n.*

■ admire, adore, deify, lionize, love, revere, venerate, worship.

idyll /iddil/ *n.* **1** peaceful or romantic scene or incident. **2** description of this, usu. in verse. ▫ **idyllic** *adj.*, **idyllically** *adv.*

i.e. *abbr.* (Latin *id est*) that is.

if *conj.* **1** on condition that. **2** supposing that. **3** whether. ● *n.* condition, supposition.

igloo *n.* Eskimo snow house.

igneous *adj.* (of rock) formed by volcanic action.

ignite *v.* **1** set fire to. **2** catch fire.

■ **1** light, set alight, set fire to, set on fire. **2** burst into flames, catch fire, kindle.

ignition *n.* **1** igniting. **2** mechanism producing a spark to ignite the fuel in an engine.

ignoble *adj.* not noble in character, aims, or purpose.

ignominy *n.* disgrace, humiliation. ▫ **ignominious** *adj.*, **ignominiously** *adv.*

■ discredit, disgrace, dishonour, humiliation, infamy, mortification, obloquy, opprobrium, shame.

ignoramus *n.* (*pl.* **-muses**) ignorant person.

ignorant *adj.* **1** lacking knowledge. **2** rude through lack of respect for good manners. ▫ **ignorantly** *adv.*, **ignorance** *n.*

■ **1** benighted, illiterate, uneducated, unenlightened, uninformed, unlettered, unschooled. **2** bad-mannered, boorish, ill-mannered, rude, uncouth.

ignore *v.* take no notice of.

■ cold-shoulder, cut, snub; discount, disregard, leave out, omit, overlook, pass over, pay no attention to, take no notice of.

iguana *n.* tropical tree lizard.

il- *pref. see* **in-**.

ileum *n.* part of the small intestine.

ill *adj.* **1** unwell. **2** bad. **3** harmful. **4** hostile, unkind. ● *adv.* badly. ● *n.* evil, harm, injury. ▫ **ill-advised** *adj.* unwise. **ill at ease** uncomfortable, embarrassed. **ill-gotten** *adj.* gained by evil or unlawful means. **ill-mannered** *adj.* having bad manners. **ill-treat** *v.* treat badly or cruelly. **ill will** hostility, unkind feeling.

■ *adj.* **1** ailing, in bad health, indisposed, infirm, not well, off colour, poorly, sick, sickly, under the weather, unhealthy, unwell. **2** bad, inauspicious, unfavourable, unfortunate, unlucky, unpromising. **3** adverse, damaging, dangerous, deleterious, detrimental, harmful, hurtful, injurious, noxious, pernicious. **4** antagonistic, cruel, hostile, malevolent, malicious, unfriendly, unkind. ● *adv.* adversely, badly, critically, unfavourably. ● *n.* evil, injustice, wrong; damage, harm, hurt, injury, mischief, misfortune. ▫ **ill-advised** foolhardy, foolish, impolitic, imprudent, incautious, misguided, rash, reckless, short-sighted, unwise. **ill-mannered** discourteous, ignorant, impertinent, impolite, impudent, insolent, rude, uncivil, uncouth, ungentlemanly, ungracious, unladylike. **ill-treat** abuse, harm, hurt, injure, knock about, maltreat, misuse. **ill will** acrimony, animosity, animus, antipathy, bad feeling, dislike, enmity, hate, hatred, hostility, loathing, malevolence, malice, rancour, resentment, unfriendliness, venom.

illegal *adj.* against the law. ▫ **illegally** *adv.*, **illegality** *n.*

■ actionable, banned, criminal, forbidden, illegitimate, illicit, outlawed, prohibited, unauthorized, unlawful, unlicensed.

illegible *adj.* not legible. ▫ **illegibly** *adv.*, **illegibility** *n.*

■ crabbed, indecipherable, scrawled, scribbled, unintelligible, unreadable.

illegitimate *adj.* **1** born of parents not married to each other. **2** against the law, illegal. □ **illegitimately** *adv.*, **illegitimacy** *n.*

illicit *adj.* unlawful, illegal. □ **illicitly** *adv.*

illiterate *adj.* **1** unable to read and write. **2** uneducated. □ **illiteracy** *n.*

illness *n.* **1** state of being ill. **2** particular form of ill health.
  ■ **1** bad health, ill health, infirmity, sickness. **2** ailment, *sl.* bug, complaint, condition, disorder, indisposition, infection, infirmity, sickness, *colloq.* virus.

illogical *adj.* not logical. □ **illogically** *adv.*, **illogicality** *n.*

illuminate *v.* **1** light up. **2** throw light on (a subject). **3** decorate with lights. □ **illumination** *n.*
  ■ **1** brighten, light (up), lighten, illumine, irradiate, shed or throw light on. **2** clarify, elucidate, explain, shed or throw light on.

illumine *v.* **1** light up. **2** enlighten.

illusion *n.* **1** false belief. **2** thing wrongly supposed to exist. □ **illusive** *adj.*, **illusory** *adj.*
  ■ **1** delusion, fallacy, misapprehension, misconception, mistake, mistaken impression. **2** chimera, fantasy, figment of the imagination, hallucination, mirage, vision. □ **illusory** deceptive, delusive, fallacious, false, fanciful, illusive, imaginary, imagined, misleading, unreal, untrue.

illusionist *n.* conjuror.

illustrate *v.* **1** supply (a book etc.) with drawings or pictures. **2** make clear by example(s) or picture(s) etc. **3** serve as an example of. □ **illustrative** *adj.*, **illustrator** *n.*
  ■ **2** clarify, elucidate, explain, illuminate, shed or throw light on. **3** demonstrate, epitomize, exemplify, represent, typify.

illustration *n.* **1** drawing etc. in a book. **2** explanatory example. **3** act or instance of illustrating.
  ■ **1** diagram, drawing, figure, picture, plate, sketch. **2** case, example, exemplification, instance. **3** depiction, representation; clarification, elucidation, explication.

illustrious *adj.* distinguished.
  ■ acclaimed, celebrated, distinguished, eminent, esteemed, famed, famous, great, *colloq.* legendary, notable, noted, renowned, well-known.

im- *pref. see* **in-**.

image *n.* **1** representation of an object. **2** reputation. **3** appearance of a thing as

seen in a mirror or through a lens. **4** mental picture. ● *v.* picture.
  ■ *n.* **1** effigy, figure, icon, likeness, portrait, representation, sculpture, statue. **2** character, persona, reputation. **3** reflection. **4** concept, conception, idea, impression, mental picture, vision.

imaginary *adj.* existing only in the imagination, not real.
  ■ fabulous, fanciful, fictional, fictitious, illusory, imagined, invented, made-up, unreal.

imagination *n.* **1** process of imagining. **2** ability to imagine or to plan creatively. □ **imaginative** *adj.*, **imaginatively** *adv.*
  ■ **1** conception, visualization. **2** creativity, ingenuity, invention, inventiveness. □ **imaginative** creative, ingenious, innovative, inspired, inventive.

imagine *v.* **1** form a mental image of. **2** think, suppose.
  ■ **1** conceive of, envisage, picture, think of, visualize. **2** assume, be of the opinion, believe, expect, guess, presume, reckon, suppose, surmise, suspect.

imago /imáygō/ *n.* (*pl.* **-gines** or **-os**) insect in its fully developed adult stage.

imam *n.* Muslim spiritual leader.

imbalance *n.* lack of balance.

imbecile *n.* extremely stupid person. ● *adj.* idiotic. □ **imbecilic** *adj.*, **imbecility** *n.*

imbibe *v.* **1** drink. **2** absorb (ideas).

imbroglio /imbrṓliō/ *n.* (*pl.* **-os**) confused situation.

imbue *v.* fill with feelings, qualities, or emotions.

imitate *v.* **1** try to act or be like. **2** copy. □ **imitable** *adj.*, **imitator** *n.*
  ■ **1** copy, echo, emulate. **2** ape, copy, impersonate, mimic, parody, take off.

imitation *n.* **1** act or instance of imitating. **2** copy. ● *adj.* counterfeit, fake.
  ■ *n.* **1** emulation, impersonation, mimicry, parody. **2** copy, replica, reproduction; counterfeit, fake, forgery. ● *adj.* artificial, counterfeit, fake, mock, *colloq.* phoney, sham, simulated, synthetic.

imitative *adj.* imitating.

immaculate *adj.* **1** spotlessly clean. **2** free from blemish or fault. □ **immaculately** *adv.*

immanent *adj.* inherent. □ **immanence** *n.*

immaterial *adj.* **1** having no physical substance. **2** of no importance.

immature *adj.* not mature. □ **immaturity** *n.*

■ young, youthful; babyish, callow, childish, green, inexperienced, infantile, juvenile, naive, puerile.

immeasurable *adj.* not measurable, immense. □ **immeasurably** *adv.*, **immeasurability** *n.*

immediate *adj.* **1** with no delay. **2** nearest. □ **immediately** *adv.*, **immediacy** *n.*

■ **1** instant, instantaneous, on the spot, prompt, rapid, speedy, swift. **2** adjacent, closest, nearest, next, proximate.

immemorial *adj.* existing from before what can be remembered.

immense *adj.* extremely great. □ **immensely** *adv.*, **immensity** *n.*

■ colossal, enormous, extensive, gargantuan, giant, gigantic, great, huge, mammoth, massive, monumental, prodigious, titanic, tremendous, vast.

immerse *v.* **1** put completely into liquid. **2** involve deeply.

■ **1** bathe, dip, douse, duck, dunk, plunge, sink, submerge. **2** absorb, bury, engage, engross, involve, occupy.

immersion *n.* immersing. □ **immersion heater** electric heater placed in the liquid to be heated.

immigrate *v.* come into a foreign country as a permanent resident. □ **immigrant** *n.* & *n.*, **immigration** *n.*

imminent *adj.* about to occur. □ **imminence** *n.*, **imminently** *adv.*

■ approaching, drawing near, forthcoming, impending, looming.

immobile *adj.* **1** immovable. **2** not moving. □ **immobility** *n.*

immobilize *v.* make or keep immobile. □ **immobilization** *n.*

immoderate *adj.* excessive. □ **immoderately** *adv.*

immolate *v.* kill as a sacrifice. □ **immolation** *n.*

immoral *adj.* morally wrong. □ **immorally** *adv.*, **immorality** *n.*

■ bad, corrupt, decadent, degenerate, depraved, dishonest, dissipated, dissolute, evil, iniquitous, nefarious, sinful, unprincipled, unscrupulous, wicked.

immortal *adj.* **1** living or lasting for ever. **2** divine. **3** famous for all time. ● *n.* immortal being. □ **immortality** *n.*

■ *adj.* **1** endless, enduring, eternal, everlasting, incorruptible, indestructible, lasting, perpetual, undying. **2** celestial, divine, heavenly. **3** celebrated, classic, famous, *colloq.* legendary, timeless.

immortalize *v.* make immortal.

immovable *adj.* **1** unable to be moved. **2** unyielding. □ **immovably** *adv.*, **immovability** *n.*

■ **1** anchored, fast, fixed, immobile, riveted, rooted, set, unmovable; immutable, unalterable, unchangeable. **2** adamant, determined, dogged, firm, inflexible, obdurate, resolute, steadfast, stubborn, unbending, uncompromising, unshakeable, unswerving, unwavering, unyielding.

immune *adj.* having immunity. □ **immune from** or **to** free or exempt from.

immunity *n.* **1** ability to resist infection. **2** special exemption.

immunize *v.* make immune to infection. □ **immunization** *n.*

immunodeficiency *n.* reduction in normal resistance to infection.

immure *v.* imprison, shut in.

immutable *adj.* unchangeable. □ **immutability** *n.*

imp *n.* **1** small devil. **2** mischievous child.

impact *n.* /ímpakt/ **1** collision, force of this. **2** strong effect. ● *v.* /impákt/ press or wedge firmly. □ **impaction** *n.*

■ *n.* **1** bang, bump, collision, crash, smash; brunt, force, weight, thrust. **2** effect, impression, influence.

impair *v.* damage, weaken. □ **impairment** *n.*

■ damage, debilitate, harm, hurt, injure, mar, ruin, spoil, weaken.

impala *n.* (*pl.* **impala**) small antelope.

impale *v.* fix or pierce with a pointed object. □ **impalement** *n.*

impalpable *adj.* intangible.

impart *v.* **1** give. **2** make (information etc.) known.

impartial *adj.* not favouring one more than another. □ **impartially** *adv.*, **impartiality** *n.*

■ detached, disinterested, dispassionate, equitable, fair, just, neutral, objective, unbiased, unprejudiced.

impassable *adj.* impossible to travel or over.

impasse /ámpass/ *n.* deadlock.

impassioned *adj.* passionate.

impassive *adj.* not feeling or showing emotion. □ **impassively** *adv.*

impatient *adj.* **1** feeling or showing lack of patience. **2** restlessly eager. □ **impatiently** *adv.*, **impatience** *n.*

■ **1** abrupt, brusque, curt, irritable, quick-tempered, short-tempered, snappy. **2** edgy, fidgety, nervous, restive, restless; agog, anxious, eager, keen.

impeach *v.* accuse of a serious crime against the state and bring for trial. □ **impeachment** *n.*

impeccable *adj.* faultless. □ **impeccably** *adv.*, **impeccability** *n.*

impecunious *adj.* having little or no money.

impedance *n.* resistance of an electric circuit to the flow of current.

impede *v.* hinder.

■ bar, baulk, block, check, delay, frustrate, hamper, handicap, hinder, hold up, obstruct, retard, slow down, stymie, thwart.

impediment *n.* **1** hindrance, obstruction. **2** defect in speech, esp. a lisp or stammer.

impel *v.* (**impelled**) **1** drive, force. **2** propel.

impending *adj.* imminent.

impenetrable *adj.* unable to be penetrated. □ **impenetrably** *adv.*, **impenetrability** *n.*

imperative *adj.* **1** essential. **2** (of a verb) expressing a command. ● *n.* **1** command. **2** essential thing.

■ *adj.* **1** compulsory, essential, indispensable, mandatory, necessary, obligatory, required, vital.

imperceptible *adj.* too slight to be noticed. □ **imperceptibly** *adv.*

■ inaudible, indiscernible, indistinguishable, invisible, undetectable, unnoticeable.

imperfect *adj.* **1** not perfect. **2** (of a tense) implying action going on but not completed. □ **imperfectly** *adv.*, **imperfection** *n.*

■ **1** damaged, defective, faulty, flawed; deficient, inadequate, incomplete, patchy, rudimentary, sketchy, unfinished, unpolished. □ **imperfection** blemish, defect, failing, fault, flaw, shortcoming.

imperial *adj.* **1** of an empire. **2** majestic. **3** (of measures) belonging to the British official non-metric system. □ **imperially** *adv.*

imperialism *n.* policy of having or extending an empire. □ **imperialist** *n.*, **imperialistic** *adj.*

imperil *v.* (**imperilled**) endanger.

imperious *adj.* domineering. □ **imperiously** *adv.*

■ *colloq.* bossy, dictatorial, domineering, high-handed, magisterial, overbearing, peremptory.

impersonal *adj.* not showing or influenced by personal feeling. □ **impersonally** *adv.*, **impersonality** *n.*

■ cold, cool, formal, starchy, stiff, stilted, unfriendly; detached, disinterested, dispassionate, impartial, neutral, objective, unbiased, unprejudiced.

impersonate *v.* pretend to be (another person). □ **impersonation** *n.*, **impersonator** *n.*

impertinent *adj.* not showing proper respect. □ **impertinently** *adv.*, **impertinence** *n.*

■ brazen, cheeky, disrespectful, forward, impolite, impudent, insolent, pert, rude, saucy, uncivil.

imperturbable *adj.* not excitable, calm. □ **imperturbably** *adv.*, **imperturbability** *n.*

impervious *adj.* **impervious to** not able to be penetrated or influenced by.

impetigo /impitīgō/ *n.* contagious skin disease.

impetuous *adj.* acting or done on impulse. □ **impetuously** *adv.*, **impetuosity** *n.*

■ abrupt, hasty, hotheaded, impromptu, impulsive, precipitate, quick, rash, reckless, spontaneous, sudden, unplanned, unpremeditated, unthinking.

impetus *n.* moving or driving force.

■ energy, force, momentum; goad, impulse, incentive, inducement, motivation, spur, stimulation, stimulus.

impinge *v.* **1** make an impact. **2** encroach. □ **impingement** *n.*

impious *adj.* not reverent, wicked. □ **impiously** *adv.*

■ blasphemous, irreligious, irreverent, profane, sacrilegious, sinful, ungodly, unholy, wicked.

implacable *adj.* relentless. □ **implacably** *adv.*

■ hard, inexorable, inflexible, merciless, pitiless, relentless, ruthless, unforgiving, unrelenting, unyielding.

implant *v.* /implaʹnt/ **1** plant, insert. **2** insert (tissue) in a living thing. ● *n.* /implaant/ implanted tissue. □ **implantation** *n.*

implement n. tool. ● v. put into effect.
□ **implementation** n.
■ n. appliance, device, gadget, instrument, tool utensil. ● v. accomplish, achieve, bring about, carry out, effect, execute, fulfil, perform, put into practice, realize.

implicate v. show or cause to be involved in a crime etc.
■ associate, connect, embroil, entangle, include, incriminate, involve.

implication n. 1 thing implied. 2 implicating.
■ 1 hint, inference, innuendo, insinuation, intimation, suggestion.

implicit adj. 1 implied. 2 absolute. □ **implicitly** adv.
■ 1 implied, indirect, tacit, undeclared, unspoken. 2 absolute, complete, entire, perfect, total, unquestioning, unreserved, utter.

implode v. (cause to) burst inwards.
□ **implosion** n.

implore v. request earnestly.

imply v. 1 suggest without stating directly. 2 mean.
■ 1 hint (at), insinuate, intimate, make out, suggest. 2 connote, denote, indicate, mean, signify; entail, involve, necessitate.

impolitic adj. not advisable.

imponderable adj. not able to be estimated. ● n. imponderable thing. □ **imponderably** adv., **imponderability** n.

import v. /impórt/ 1 bring in from abroad or from an outside source. 2 imply. ● n. /import/ 1 importing. 2 thing imported. 3 meaning. 4 importance. □ **importation** n., **importer** n.

important adj. 1 having a great effect. 2 having great authority or influence. □ **importance** n.
■ 1 consequential, grave, momentous, pressing, serious, significant, urgent, weighty. 2 distinguished, eminent, foremost, high-ranking, influential, leading, notable, noted, noteworthy, outstanding, powerful, prominent, respected, worthy. □ **importance** consequence, gravity, import, momentousness, seriousness, significance, weight; distinction, eminence, influence, note, prominence, standing, status, worth.

importunate adj. making persistent requests. □ **importunity** n.

importune v. solicit.

impose v. 1 inflict (a tax etc.). 2 enforce compliance with. □ **impose on** take advantage of.

imposing adj. impressive.

imposition n. 1 act of imposing. 2 unfair demand or burden.

impossible adj. 1 not possible. 2 unendurable. □ **impossibly** adv., **impossibility** n.
■ 1 impracticable, out of the question, unfeasible, unworkable. 2 insupportable, intolerable, unbearable, unendurable.

impostor n. person who assumes a false identity.

imposture n. fraudulent deception.

impotent adj. 1 powerless. 2 (of a male) incapable of sexual intercourse. □ **impotently** adv., **impotence** n.

impound v. 1 take (property) into legal custody. 2 confiscate.

impoverish v. 1 cause to become poor. 2 exhaust the strength or fertility of. □ **impoverishment** n.

imprecation n. spoken curse.

impregnable adj. safe against attack. □ **impregnability** n.
■ impenetrable, invincible, inviolable, invulnerable, safe, secure, unassailable, unconquerable.

impregnate v. 1 make pregnant. 2 saturate. □ **impregnation** n.

impresario n. (pl. -os) organizer of public entertainments.

impress v. 1 affect or influence deeply. 2 arouse admiration or respect in. 3 press a mark into.
■ 1 affect, influence, inspire, move, strike, sway, touch.

impression n. 1 effect produced on the mind. 2 uncertain idea. 3 imitation done for entertainment. 4 impressed mark. 5 reprint.
■ 1 awareness, consciousness, feeling, sensation, sense; effect, impact, influence. 2 feeling, hunch, idea, notion, suspicion. 3 imitation, impersonation, parody, take-off. 4 brand, mark, stamp. 5 edition, reprint.

impressionable adj. easily influenced.
■ persuadable, receptive, suggestible, susceptible.

impressionism n. style of painting etc. giving a general impression without detail. □ **impressionist** n., **impressionistic** adj.

impressive *adj.* arousing respect or admiration. □ **impressively** *adv.*
■ awe-inspiring, awesome, breathtaking, formidable, imposing, magnificent, majestic, redoubtable, splendid, striking.

imprint *n.* /imprint/ **1** mark made by pressing on a surface. **2** publisher's name etc. on a title-page. ● *v.* /imprint/ impress or stamp a mark etc. on.

imprison *v.* **1** put into prison. **2** confine. □ **imprisonment** *n.*
■ **1** detain, incarcerate, jail, lock up, remand. **2** confine, coop up, immure, shut in or up. □ **imprisonment** confinement, custody, detention, incarceration.

improbable *adj.* not likely to be true or to happen. □ **improbably** *adv.*, **improbability** *n.*
■ doubtful, dubious, far-fetched, implausible, incredible, unbelievable, unconvincing, unlikely.

impromptu *adj.* & *adv.* without preparation or rehearsal.
■ *adj.* ad lib, extemporary, improvised, spontaneous, unprepared, unrehearsed.

improper *adj.* **1** indecent, unseemly. **2** not conforming to social conventions. □ **improperly** *adv.*, **impropriety** *n.*
■ **1** immodest, indecent, indecorous, indelicate, unbecoming, ungentlemanly, unladylike, unseemly. **2** inappropriate, unacceptable, unfitting, unsuitable.

improve *v.* make or become better. □ **improvement** *n.*
■ ameliorate, better, enhance, perfect, polish, put right, rectify, refine; modernize, overhaul, refurbish, renovate, repair, revamp, touch up; amend, correct, edit, emend; be on the mend, get better, look up, make progress, pick up, rally, recover, recuperate. □ **improvement** amelioration, amendment, correction, enhancement, rectification, reform; modernization, overhaul, refurbishment; rally, recovery, upswing, upturn.

improvident *adj.* not providing for future needs. □ **improvidently** *adv.*, **improvidence** *n.*
■ careless, heedless, imprudent, incautious, injudicious, short-sighted; extravagant, prodigal, spendthrift, thriftless, uneconomical, wasteful.

improvise *v.* **1** compose impromptu. **2** provide from whatever materials are at hand. □ **improvisation** *n.*

imprudent *adj.* unwise. □ **imprudently** *adv.*, **imprudence** *n.*
■ foolhardy, foolish, hasty, heedless, ill-advised, impolitic, incautious, injudicious, irresponsible, misguided, precipitate, rash, reckless, short-sighted, thoughtless, unwise, wild.

impudent *adj.* impertinent. □ **impudently** *adv.*, **impudence** *n.*
■ cheeky, disrespectful, forward, impertinent, impolite, insolent, pert, rude, saucy.

impugn /impyōōn/ *v.* express doubts about the truth or honesty of.

impulse *n.* **1** impetus. **2** stimulating force in a nerve. **3** sudden urge to do something.
■ **1** impetus, incentive, motivation, spur, stimulation, stimulus. **3** caprice, desire, fancy, instinct, urge, whim.

impulsive *adj.* acting or done on impulse. □ **impulsively** *adv.*, **impulsiveness** *n.*
■ impetuous, involuntary, snap, spontaneous, spur-of-the-moment, unplanned, unpremeditated; hasty, hotheaded, madcap, precipitate, quick, rash, reckless.

impunity *n.* freedom from punishment or injury.

impure *adj.* not pure.
■ adulterated, contaminated, dirty, polluted, tainted, unclean; immoral, sinful, unchaste, wanton.

impurity *n.* **1** being impure. **2** impure thing or part.

impute *v.* attribute (a fault etc.). □ **imputation** *n.*

in *prep.* **1** having as a position or state within (limits of space, time, surroundings, etc.). **2** having as a state or manner. **3** into, towards. ● *adv.* **1** in or to a position bounded by limits. **2** inside. **3** in fashion, season, or office. ● *adj.* **1** internal. **2** living etc. inside. **3** fashionable. □ **in for 1** about to experience. **2** competing in. **ins and outs** details. **in so far as** to the extent that.

in- *pref.* (**il-** before *l*; **im-** before *b, m, p*; **ir-** before *r*) **1** not. **2** without, lacking.

in. *abbr.* inch(es).

inability *n.* being unable.

inaction *n.* lack of action.

inactive *adj.* not active. □ **inactivity** *n.*
■ dormant, immobile, inert, motionless, passive, quiescent, stagnant, static, stationary, still, unmoving; idle, inoperative, unoccupied.

inadequate *adj.* **1** not adequate. **2** not sufficiently able. □ **inadequately** *adv.*, **inadequacy** *n.*
■ **1** deficient, insufficient, meagre, scanty, skimpy, sparse. **2** incapable, incompetent, ineffective, ineffectual, inept, not up to scratch, *colloq.* pathetic, useless.

inadmissible *adj.* not allowable.

inadvertent *adj.* unintentional.
■ accidental, chance, unconscious, unintended, unintentional, unplanned, unpremeditated, unthinking.

inalienable *adj.* not able to be given or taken away.

inane *adj.* silly, lacking sense. □ **inanely** *adv.*, **inanity** *n.*

inanimate *adj.* **1** lacking animal life. **2** showing no signs of life.

inappropriate *adj.* unsuitable.
■ inapt, inapposite, infelicitous, inopportune, out of keeping, unsuitable, unsuited, untimely.

inarticulate *adj.* **1** unable to express oneself clearly. **2** (of speech) not clear or well-expressed.
■ **1** incoherent, speechless, tongue-tied. **2** disjointed, garbled, faltering, incoherent, indistinct, muddled, muffled, mumbled, muttered, rambling, unclear, unintelligible.

inasmuch *adv.* **inasmuch as** seeing that, because.

inattentive *adj.* not paying attention. □ **inattentiveness** *n.*

inaugural *adj.* of an inauguration.

inaugurate *v.* **1** admit to office ceremonially. **2** open (a building etc.) formally. **3** begin, introduce. □ **inauguration** *n.*
■ **1** enthrone, induct, install, invest, ordain. **3** begin, initiate, introduce, launch, start.

inborn *adj.* existing in a person or animal from birth, natural.
■ congenital, hereditary, inbred, inherent, inherited, innate, native, natural.

inbred *adj.* **1** produced by inbreeding. **2** inborn.

inbreeding *n.* breeding from closely related individuals.

Inc. *abbr.* (*US*) Incorporated.

incalculable *adj.* unable to be calculated. □ **incalculably** *adv.*

incandescent *adj.* glowing with heat. □ **incandescence** *n.*

incantation *n.* words or sounds uttered as a magic spell.

incapable *adj.* **1** not capable. **2** helpless. □ **incapability** *n.*

incapacitate *v.* **1** disable. **2** make ineligible. □ **incapacitation** *n.*

incapacity *n.* inability, lack of sufficient strength or power.

incarcerate *v.* imprison. □ **incarceration** *n.*

incarnate *adj.* embodied, esp. in human form.

incarnation *n.* **1** embodiment, esp. in human form. **2** (**the Incarnation**) that of God as Christ.

incautious *adj.* rash. □ **incautiously** *adv.*

incendiary *adj.* designed to cause fire. ● *n.* **1** incendiary bomb. **2** arsonist. □ **incendiarism** *n.*

incense¹ /ínsenss/ *n.* **1** substance burnt to produce fragrant smoke, esp. in religious ceremonies. **2** this smoke.

incense² /insénss/ *v.* make angry.
■ anger, drive berserk, enrage, exasperate, inflame, infuriate, madden, outrage.

incentive *n.* thing that encourages an action or effort.
■ carrot, encouragement, impetus, inducement, lure, motivation, spur, stimulus.

inception *n.* beginning.

incessant *adj.* not ceasing. □ **incessantly** *adv.*
■ ceaseless, constant, continual, continuous, endless, *colloq.* eternal, everlasting, interminable, never-ending, non-stop, perpetual, persistent, relentless, unbroken, unceasing, unending, uninterrupted, unremitting.

incest *n.* sexual intercourse between very closely related people. □ **incestuous** *adj.*

inch *n.* measure of length (= 2.54 cm). ● *v.* move gradually.

incidence *n.* **1** rate at which a thing occurs. **2** falling of a ray, line, etc. on a surface.

incident *n.* event, esp. one causing trouble.
■ *colloq.* affair, circumstance, episode, experience, event, happening, occasion, occurrence; clash, confrontation, contretemps, disturbance, fight, fracas, quarrel, row, skirmish, to-do.

incidental *adj.* **1** occurring in connection with something more important. **2** casual.
■ **1** peripheral, secondary, subordinate, subsidiary, supplementary. **2** accidental, casual, chance, fortuitous, unexpected, unforeseen, unlooked-for.

incidentally adv. **1** in an incidental way. **2** by the way.

incinerate v. burn to ashes. □ **incineration** n., **incinerator** n.

incipient adj. beginning to exist.

incise v. **1** make a cut in. **2** engrave. □ **incision** n.

incisive adj. **1** mentally sharp. **2** clear and effective. □ **incisively** adv., **incisiveness** n.
> ■ **1** acute, astute, canny, clever, intelligent, keen, penetrating, perceptive, percipient, perspicacious, sharp, shrewd. **2** clear, concise, effective, pithy, succinct, terse, to the point.

incisor n. any of the front teeth.

incite v. **1** urge on. **2** stir up. □ **incitement** n.
> ■ **1** drive on, egg on, encourage, goad, prod, rouse, spur, urge. **2** foment, instigate, provoke, stir up, whip up.

incivility n. rudeness.

inclination n. **1** slope. **2** bending. **3** tendency. **4** liking, preference.
> ■ **1** angle, gradient, incline, list, slant, slope, tilt. **2** bending, bow, bowing, nod, nodding. **3** bent, bias, disposition, leaning, predisposition, proclivity, propensity, tendency. **4** affection, fondness, liking, love, partiality, penchant, predilection, soft spot, weakness.

incline v. /inklīn/ **1** slope. **2** bend. **3** (cause to) have a certain tendency, influence. ● n. /inklīn/ slope.
> ■ v. **1** angle, bank, lean, list, slant, slope, tilt. **2** bend, bow, nod, stoop. **3** cause, convince, dispose, induce, influence, persuade, predispose; gravitate, swing, tend. ● n. ascent, descent, dip, gradient, hill, ramp, slant, slope.

include v. **1** have or treat as part of a whole. **2** put into a specified category. □ **inclusion** n.
> ■ **1** comprehend, comprise, contain, embody, embrace, encompass, incorporate, take in; allow for, count, number, take into account. **2** catalogue, categorize, classify, group.

inclusive adj. **1** including what is mentioned. **2** including everything. □ **inclusively** adv., **inclusiveness** n.

incognito adj. & adv. with one's identity kept secret. ● n. (pl. **-os**) pretended identity.

incoherent adj. rambling in speech or reasoning. □ **incoherently** adv., **incoherence** n.
> ■ confused, delirious, inarticulate, incomprehensible, rambling, raving, unintelligible; disconnected, disjointed, disordered, disorganized, garbled, illogical, jumbled, mixed-up, muddled.

incombustible adj. not able to be burnt. □ **incombustibility** n.

income n. money received during a period as wages, interest, etc.
> ■ pay, remuneration, salary; earnings, proceeds, profits, returns, revenue, takings, turnover.

incoming adj. coming in.

incommunicado adj. not allowed or not wishing to communicate with others.

incomparable adj. beyond comparison, without an equal.
> ■ inimitable, matchless, peerless, perfect, unequalled, unique, unmatched, unparalleled, unrivalled, unsurpassable, unsurpassed.

incomprehensible adj. not able to be understood. □ **incomprehension** n.
> ■ illegible, inarticulate, incoherent, indecipherable, unintelligible; abstruse, arcane, baffling, cryptic, dark, deep, enigmatic, mysterious, mystifying, obscure, perplexing, puzzling, recondite, unaccountable, unfathomable.

inconceivable adj. unable to be imagined.

inconclusive adj. not fully convincing. □ **inconclusively** adv.

incongruous adj. unsuitable, not harmonious. □ **incongruously** adv., **incongruity** n.
> ■ discordant, inappropriate, incompatible, inconsistent, inharmonious, out of keeping, out of place, unsuitable.

inconsequential adj. **1** unimportant. **2** not following logically. □ **inconsequentially** adv.

inconsiderable adj. negligible.

inconsolable adj. not able to be consoled. □ **inconsolably** adv.

inconstant adj. **1** fickle. **2** variable. □ **inconstancy** n.
> ■ **1** capricious, changeable, fickle, flighty, mercurial, moody, temperamental, volatile. **2** erratic, fluctuating, inconsistent, irregular, unsettled, unstable, unsteady, variable, wavering.

incontestable adj. indisputable. □ **incontestably** adv.

incontinent adj. **1** unable to control one's bowels or bladder. **2** lacking self-restraint. □ **incontinence** n.

incontrovertible adj. indisputable. □ **incontrovertibly** adv.

inconvenience n. **1** lack of convenience. **2** thing causing this. ● v. cause inconvenience to.
■ n. **1** awkwardness, discomfort, disruption, disturbance, trouble. **2** annoyance, colloq. bind, bore, bother, burden, colloq. hassle, hindrance, irritation, nuisance. ● v. bother, discommode, disturb, colloq. hassle, put out, trouble.

inconvenient adj. not convenient, slightly troublesome. □ **inconveniently** adv.
■ annoying, awkward, bothersome, ill-timed, inappropriate, inexpedient, inopportune, irritating, troublesome, untimely.

incorporate v. **1** include as a part. **2** form into a corporation. □ **incorporation** n.

incorrigible adj. not able to be reformed. □ **incorrigibly** adv.
■ habitual, hardened, incurable, inveterate, irredeemable.

incorruptible adj. **1** not liable to decay. **2** not corruptible morally. □ **incorruptibility** n.

increase v. /inkréess/ make or become greater. ● n. /inkreess/ **1** increasing. **2** amount by which a thing increases.
■ v. add to, amplify, augment, boost, broaden, build up, develop, enlarge, expand, extend, heighten, intensify, lengthen, lift, maximize, raise, step up, strengthen, widen; dilate, distend, inflate, swell; accumulate, burgeon, escalate, flourish, grow, mount, multiply, mushroom, pile up, proliferate, snowball, spread. ● n. **1** addition, amplification, augmentation, development, enlargement, escalation, expansion, extension, multiplication, proliferation, spread. **2** gain, growth, increment, jump, rise.

increasingly adv. more and more.

incredible adj. unbelievable. □ **incredibly** adv., **incredibility** n.
■ far-fetched, implausible, improbable, inconceivable, unbelievable, unimaginable, unlikely; amazing, astonishing, astounding, extraordinary, marvellous, miraculous, wonderful.

incredulous adj. unbelieving, showing disbelief. □ **incredulously** adv., **incredulity** n.
■ disbelieving, distrustful, doubtful, dubious, mistrustful, sceptical, suspicious, unconvinced.

increment n. increase, added amount. □ **incremental** adj.

incriminate v. indicate as guilty. □ **incrimination** n., **incriminatory** adj.

incrustation n. **1** encrusting. **2** crust or deposit formed on a surface.

incubate v. **1** hatch (eggs) by warmth. **2** cause (bacteria etc.) to develop. □ **incubation** n.

incubator n. apparatus providing warmth for hatching eggs, rearing premature babies, or developing bacteria.

inculcate v. implant (a habit etc.) by constant urging. □ **inculcation** n.

incumbent adj. forming an obligation or duty. ● n. holder of an office, esp. a rector or a vicar.

incur v. (**incurred**) become subject to (something unpleasant) as a result of one's own behaviour.

incursion n. brief invasion, raid.
■ attack, foray, invasion, raid, sally, sortie.

indebted /indéttid/ adj. owing a debt.
■ beholden, grateful, obligated, obliged, thankful.

indecent adj. **1** offending against standards of decency. **2** unseemly. □ **indecently** adv., **indecency** n.
■ **1** blue, coarse, crude, dirty, indelicate, lewd, naughty, obscene, offensive, ribald, risqué, rude, salacious, smutty, suggestive, vulgar. **2** improper, inappropriate, indecorous, unbecoming, unseemly, unsuitable.

indecipherable adj. unable to be read or deciphered.

indecision n. inability to decide something, hesitation.

indecorous adj. improper.

indeed adv. in truth, really.

indefatigable adj. untiring. □ **indefatigably** adv.
■ assiduous, indomitable, industrious, tenacious, tireless, unflagging, untiring.

indefensible adj. unable to be defended or justified.
■ inexusable, reprehensible, unforgivable, unjustifiable, unjustified, unpardonable.

indefinable adj. unable to be defined or described clearly. □ **indefinably** adv.

indefinite *adj.* not clearly stated or fixed, vague. □ **indefinite article** the word 'a' or 'an'.

■ ambiguous, equivocal, uncertain, unclear, unsure, vague; indeterminate, undecided, undefined, unfixed, unsettled, unspecified; blurred, dim, fuzzy, hazy, indistinct, indistinguishable, obscure, unrecognizable.

indefinitely *adv.* **1** in an indefinite way. **2** for an unlimited period.

indelible *adj.***1** (of a mark) unable to be removed. **2** permanent. □ **indelibly** *adv.*

indelicate *adj.* **1** slightly indecent. **2** tactless. □ **indelicately** *adv.*, **indelicacy** *n.*

indemnify *v.* provide indemnity to. □ **indemnification** *n.*

indemnity *n.* **1** compensation for loss or damage. **2** legal exemption from penalties incurred by one's own actions.

indent *v.* **1** start inwards from a margin. **2** place an official order (for goods etc.). □ **indentation** *n.*

indenture *n.* written contract, esp. of apprenticeship. ● *v.* bind by this.

independent *adj.* not dependent on or not controlled by another person or thing. □ **independently** *adv.*, **independence** *n.*

■ autonomous, free, self-governing, sovereign; footloose, individualistic, self-reliant, self-sufficient; disinterested, impartial, neutral, unbiased, unprejudiced. □ **independence** autonomy, freedom, liberty, self-determination, self-government; individualism, self-sufficiency.

indescribable *adj.* unable to be described. □ **indescribably** *adv.*

indestructible *adj.* unable to be destroyed. □ **indestructibly** *adv.*

■ enduring, eternal, everlasting, immortal, undying; durable, shatter-proof, tough, unbreakable.

indeterminable *adj.* impossible to discover or decide.

indeterminate *adj.* not fixed in extent or character.

index *n.* (*pl.* **indexes** or **indices**) **1** list (usu. alphabetical) of names, subjects, etc., with references. **2** figure showing the current level of prices etc. compared with a previous level. ● *v.* **1** make an index to. **2** enter in an index. **3** adjust (wages etc.) according to a price index. □ **index finger** forefinger. **indexation** *n.*

■ *n.* **1** catalogue, concordance, directory, inventory, list, register, table of contents.

Indian *adj.* of India or Indians. ● *n.* **1** native of India. **2** any of the original inhabitants of the American continent or their descendants. □ **Indian ink** a black pigment. **Indian summer** dry sunny weather in autumn.

indiarubber *n.* rubber for rubbing out pencil or ink marks.

indicate *v.* **1** point out. **2** be a sign of. **3** state briefly. □ **indication** *n.*, **indicative** *adj.*

■ **1** direct attention to, display, identify, point out, point to, show. **2** bespeak, betoken, denote, evidence, evince, imply, manifest, reveal, signify, suggest. **3** express, make known, state. □ **indication** clue, hint, inkling, intimation, manifestation, mark, omen, sign, signal, symptom, token, warning.

indicator *n.* **1** thing that indicates. **2** pointer. **3** device on a vehicle showing the direction in which it is about to turn.

indict /indít/ *v.* accuse formally. □ **indictment** *n.*

■ accuse, arraign, charge, impeach, summons.

indifferent *adj.* **1** showing no interest. **2** neither good nor bad. **3** not very good. □ **indifferently** *adv.*, **indifference** *n.*

■ **1** aloof, apathetic, blasé, casual, cool, detached, impassive, lackadaisical, lukewarm, uncaring, unconcerned, uninterested, unmoved, unsympathetic. **2** average, commonplace, fair, mediocre, middling, ordinary, undistinguished, uninspired. **3** all right, *colloq.* OK, passable, tolerable.

indigenous *adj.* native.

indigent *adj.* needy, poor. □ **indigence** *n.*

indigestible *adj.* difficult or impossible to digest.

indigestion *n.* pain caused by difficulty in digesting food.

indignant *adj.* feeling or showing indignation. □ **indignantly** *adv.*

■ annoyed, disgruntled, exasperated, huffy, in a huff, irked, irritated, piqued, *colloq.* peeved, sore, *colloq.* uptight.

indignation *n.* anger aroused by a supposed injustice.

■ anger, annoyance, displeasure, exasperation, irritation, pique, resentment, vexation.

indignity *n.* unworthy treatment, humiliation.

indigo *n.* deep blue dye or colour.

indiscernible *adj.* unable to be discerned. □ **indiscernibly** *adv.*

indiscreet *adj.* 1 revealing secrets. 2 not judicious. □ **indiscreetly** *adv.*, **indiscretion** *n.*

■ 1 garrulous, talkative; irresponsible, untrustworthy. 2 ill-advised, ill-judged, impolitic, imprudent, incautious, injudicious, insensitive, tactless, thoughtless, undiplomatic, unguarded, unwise.

indiscriminate *adj.* 1 not discriminating. 2 haphazard. □ **indiscriminately** *adv.*

■ 1 undiscriminating, unselective. 2 aimless, arbitrary, haphazard, hit-or-miss, random, unmethodical, unsystematic, wholesale.

indispensable *adj.* essential.

■ crucial, essential, imperative, key, necessary, requisite, vital.

indisposed *adj.* 1 slightly ill. 2 unwilling. □ **indisposition** *n.*

indisputable *adj.* undeniable. □ **indisputably** *adv.*

■ certain, incontestable, incontrovertible, indubitable, irrefutable, undeniable, unquestionable.

indissoluble *adj.* firm and lasting, not able to be destroyed.

individual *adj.* 1 single, separate. 2 characteristic of one particular person or thing. ● *n.* 1 one person, animal, or plant considered separately. 2 (*colloq.*) person. □ **individually** *adv.*, **individuality** *n.*

■ *adj.* 1 distinct, particular, separate, single, specific. 2 characteristic, distinctive, idiosyncratic, peculiar, personal, special, unique. ● *n.* 2 child, human being, man, mortal, person, soul, woman.

individualist *n.* person who is independent in thought etc. □ **individualistic** *adj.*, **individualism** *n.*

indoctrinate *v.* fill (a person's mind) with particular ideas or doctrines. □ **indoctrination** *n.*

indolent *adj.* lazy. □ **indolently** *adv.*, **indolence** *n.*

indomitable *adj.* 1 unconquerable. 2 unyielding. □ **indomitably** *adv.*

■ 1 invincible, unassailable, unconquerable. 2 brave, courageous, dauntless, determined, indefatigable, persistent, resolute, staunch, steadfast, tireless, undaunted, unflagging, untiring, unyielding.

indoor *adj.* situated, used, or done inside a building. □ **indoors** *adv.*

indubitable *adj.* that cannot be doubted. □ **indubitably** *adv.*

induce *v.* 1 persuade. 2 cause. 3 bring on (labour) artificially.

■ 1 cajole, coax, convince, get, influence, inveigle, lead, persuade, press, prevail on, push, talk into, wheedle. 2 bring about, cause, create, engender, give rise to, lead to.

inducement *n.* 1 inducing. 2 incentive.

induct *v.* install (a clergyman) ceremonially into a benefice.

inductance *n.* amount of induction of electric current.

induction *n.* 1 inducting. 2 inducing. 3 reasoning (from observed examples) that a general law exists. 4 production of an electric or magnetic state by proximity of an electrified or magnetic object. 5 drawing of a fuel mixture into the cylinder(s) of an engine. □ **inductive** *adj.*

indulge *v.* 1 allow (a person) to have or do what he or she wishes. 2 gratify. □ **indulge in** allow oneself to enjoy the pleasure of. **indulgence** *n.*

■ 1 mollycoddle, pamper, spoil, treat. 2 cater to, gratify, humour, minister to, pander to, satisfy. □ **indulge in** luxuriate in, succumb to, treat oneself to, wallow in, yield to.

indulgent *adj.* lenient, willing to overlook faults. □ **indulgently** *adv.*

■ easygoing, forbearing, forgiving, kind, lax, lenient, liberal, patient, permissive, soft, tolerant, understanding.

industrial *adj.* of, for, or full of industries. □ **industrially** *adv.*

industrialist *n.* owner or manager of an industrial business. □ **industrialism** *n.*

industrialized *adj.* full of highly developed industries.

industrious *adj.* hard-working. □ **industriously** *adv.*

■ assiduous, conscientious, diligent, dogged, hard-working, indefatigable, painstaking, sedulous, tireless, zealous.

industry n. **1** manufacture or production of goods. **2** business activity. **3** being industrious.

inebriated adj. drunken. □ **inebriation** n.

inedible adj. not edible.

ineducable adj. incapable of being educated.

ineffable adj. too great to be described. □ **ineffably** adv.

ineluctable adj. inescapable, unavoidable.

inept adj. **1** unskilful. **2** unsuitable. **3** absurd. □ **ineptly** adv., **ineptitude** n.

■ **1** amateurish, awkward, bumbling, bungling, clumsy, colloq. ham-fisted, incompetent, inefficient, inexpert, maladroit, unskilled, unskilful. **2** inapt, inappropriate, out of keeping, out of place, unsuitable.

inequality n. lack of equality.

■ difference, discrepancy, disparity, disproportion, dissimilarity, imbalance, incongruity, inconsistency; bias, partiality, prejudice, unfairness, injustice.

inequitable adj. unfair, unjust. □ **inequitably** adv.

ineradicable adj. not able to be eradicated. □ **ineradicably** adv.

inert adj. **1** without the power of moving. **2** sluggish, slow. **3** chemically inactive. □ **inertly** adv., **inertness** n.

■ **1** immobile, inanimate, lifeless, motionless, quiescent, static, stationary, still. **2** idle, inactive, indolent, languid, languorous, lazy, leaden, listless, passive, slothful, slow, sluggish, torpid.

inertia n. **1** being inert. **2** property by which matter continues in its state of rest or line of motion.

■ **1** immobility, inactivity, quiescence, stasis, stillness; idleness, indolence, lassitude, laziness, listlessness, sloth, sluggishness, torpor.

inescapable adj. unavoidable. □ **inescapably** adv.

inessential adj. not necessary. ● n. inessential thing.

■ adj. dispensable, expendable, needless, superfluous, unnecessary, unneeded.

inestimable adj. too great to be estimated. □ **inestimably** adv.

inevitable adj. unavoidable, sure to happen or appear. □ **inevitably** adv., **inevitability** n.

■ destined, fated, ineluctable, inescapable, unavoidable; assured, certain, guaranteed, sure.

inexact adj. not exact. □ **inexactly** adv., **inexactitude** n.

■ approximate, estimated, general, imprecise, rough, vague; erroneous, false, inaccurate, incorrect, mistaken, wrong.

inexhaustible adj. available in unlimited quantity.

■ boundless, endless, infinite, limitless, unbounded, unlimited, unrestricted.

inexorable adj. relentless. □ **inexorably** adv., **inexorability** n.

inexperience n. lack of experience. □ **inexperienced** adj.

■ □ inexperienced callow, green, immature, innocent, naive, unsophisticated, unworldly; amateurish, inexpert, unseasoned, unskilled, untrained, unversed.

inexpert adj. not expert, unskilful. □ **inexpertly** adv.

inexplicable adj. unable to be explained. □ **inexplicably** adv.

■ baffling, incomprehensible, mysterious, mystifying, perplexing, puzzling, unaccountable, unexplainable.

inextricable adj. unable to be extricated or disentangled. □ **inextricably** adv.

infallible adj. **1** incapable of being wrong. **2** never failing. □ **infallibly** adv., **infallibility** n.

■ certain, dependable, faultless, flawless, foolproof, guaranteed, perfect, reliable, sure, unerring, unfailing.

infamous /ínfəməss/ adj. having a bad reputation. □ **infamously** adv., **infamy** n.

■ disreputable, ill-famed, notorious.

infancy n. **1** early childhood. **2** early stage of development.

infant n. child during the earliest part of its life.

infanticide n. killing or killer of an infant soon after its birth. □ **infanticidal** adj.

infantile adj. **1** of infants or infancy. **2** very childish.

■ **2** babyish, childish, immature, juvenile, puerile.

infantry n. troops who fight on foot.

infatuated adj. filled with intense love. □ **infatuation** n.

infect v. **1** affect or contaminate with a disease or its germs. **2** affect with one's feeling.

■ **1** blight, contaminate, poison, pollute, taint.

infection n. **1** infecting, being infected. **2** disease or condition so caused.

■ **1** contamination, pollution, tainting. **2** sl. bug, disease, disorder, sickness, colloq. virus.

infectious adj. **1** (of disease) able to spread by air or water. **2** infecting others.

■ **1** catching, communicable, contagious, transmissible.

infer v. (**inferred**) reach (an opinion) from facts or reasoning. □ **inference** n.

■ conclude, deduce, draw the conclusion, gather, surmise, understand.

inferior adj. low or lower in rank, importance, quality, or ability. ● n. person inferior to another, esp. in rank. □ **inferiority** n.

■ adj. lesser, lower, junior, minor, lowly, subordinate; bad, cheap, disappointing, faulty, gimcrack, low-quality, mediocre, poor, second-class, second-rate, shoddy, slipshod, substandard, tawdry, trashy. ● n. junior, subordinate, underling; colloq. dogsbody, drudge, menial.

infernal adj. **1** of hell. **2** (colloq.) tiresome. □ **infernally** adv.

inferno n. (pl. **-os**) **1** hell. **2** intensely hot place. **3** raging fire.

infest v. overrun in large numbers. □ **infestation** n.

■ invade, overrun, pervade, swarm over, take over.

infidel n. **1** person with no religious faith. **2** opponent of a religion, esp. Christianity.

infidelity n. unfaithfulness.

■ adultery, deceit, deception, disloyalty, faithlessness, falseness, treachery, unfaithfulness.

infighting n. hidden conflict within an organization.

infiltrate v. enter gradually and unperceived. □ **infiltration** n., **infiltrator** n.

infinite /infinit/ adj. **1** having no limit. **2** too great or too many to be measured. □ **infinitely** adv.

■ bottomless, boundless, countless, immeasurable, incalculable, inestimable, inexhaustible, innumerable, limitless, numberless, unbounded, unlimited, untold.

infinitesimal adj. extremely small. □ **infinitesimally** adv.

infinitive n. form of a verb not indicating tense, subject, etc. (e.g. to go).

infinity n. infinite number, extent, or time.

infirm adj. physically weak.

■ ailing, debilitated, decrepit, doddery, enfeebled, feeble, frail, ill, sick, unwell, weak.

infirmary n. hospital.

infirmity n. **1** being infirm. **2** particular physical weakness.

■ **1** debilitation, debility, decrepitude, feebleness, frailty, weakness. **2** affliction, ailment, complaint, condition, disease, disorder, illness, indisposition, malady, sickness.

inflame v. **1** arouse strong feeling in. **2** cause inflammation in.

■ **1** arouse, excite, fire, incite, kindle, provoke, stimulate, stir up, whip up; anger, enrage, exasperate, incense, infuriate, madden.

inflammable adj. able to be set on fire. □ **inflammability** n.

inflammation n. redness and heat in a part of the body.

inflammatory adj. arousing strong feeling or anger.

inflatable adj. able to be inflated.

inflate v. **1** fill with air or gas so as to swell. **2** increase artificially.

■ **1** blow up, pump up; dilate, distend, swell.

inflation n. **1** inflating. **2** general rise in prices and fall in the purchasing power of money. □ **inflationary** adj.

inflect v. **1** change the pitch of (a voice) in speaking. **2** change the ending or form of (a word) grammatically. □ **inflection** n.

inflexible adj. **1** not flexible. **2** unyielding. □ **inflexibly** adv., **inflexibility** n.

■ **1** firm, hard, inelastic, rigid, stiff, unbendable, unmalleable. **2** adamant, determined, firm, immovable, obdurate, resolute, rigid, stiff-necked, stubborn, unbending, uncompromising, unyielding.

inflict v. cause (a blow, penalty, etc.) to be suffered. □ **infliction** n.

■ administer, deal, deliver, impose, levy, wreak.

influence n. **1** effect a person or thing has on another. **2** moral power, ascendancy. **3** person or thing with this. ● v. exert influence on.

■ n. **1** bearing, effect, impact, impression. **2** ascendancy, authority, colloq. clout, control, leverage, mastery, power, pull, sway, weight. ● v. affect, alter, change, have an effect on, modify, sway; drive, force, impel, induce, motivate, move, persuade; manipulate, pressurize, pull strings with.

influential adj. having great influence. □ **influentially** adv.
■ authoritative, controlling, dominant, important, leading, powerful, strong; persuasive, significant, telling.

influenza n. virus disease causing fever, muscular pain, and catarrh.

influx n. inward flow.

inform v. tell. □ **inform against** or **on** give incriminating evidence about a person to police etc. **informer** n.
■ advise, apprise, brief, communicate to, enlighten, fill in, let know, notify, tell, tip off. □ **inform on** betray, denounce, incriminate, rat on, sl. shop, sl. squeal on.

informal adj. not formal, without formality or ceremony. □ **informally** adv., **formality** n.

informant n. giver of information.

information n. facts told, heard, or discovered.
■ data, details, facts, intelligence, knowledge, colloq. low-down, news, tidings, word.

informative adj. giving information. □ **informatively** adv.
■ edifying, educational, enlightening, helpful, illuminating, instructive; chatty, communicative, forthcoming.

infra-red adj. of or using radiation with a wavelength longer than that of visible light rays.

infrastructure n. subordinate parts forming the basis of an enterprise.

infringe v. 1 break (a rule or agreement). 2 encroach, trespass. □ **infringement** n.
■ 1 break, contravene, disobey, flout, violate.

infuriate v. make very angry.

infuse v. 1 fill (with a quality). 2 soak to bring out flavour.

infusion n. 1 infusing. 2 liquid made by this.

ingenious adj. 1 clever at inventing things. 2 cleverly contrived. □ **ingeniously** adv., **ingenuity** n.
■ adept, adroit, astute, brilliant, clever, creative, cunning, deft, dexterous, imaginative, inventive, original, resourceful, shrewd, skilful, skilled.

ingenuous adj. without artfulness. □ **ingenuously** adv.
■ artless, childlike, guileless, innocent, naive, trustful, unsophisticated, unsuspecting.

ingest v. take in as food.

ingot n. oblong lump of cast metal.

ingrained adj. deeply fixed in a surface or character.

ingratiate v. bring (oneself) into a person's favour, esp. to gain advantage. □ **ingratiation** n.

ingratitude n. lack of gratitude.

ingredient n. one element in a mixture or combination.
■ component, constituent, element, factor, part.

ingress n. 1 going in. 2 right of entry.

ingrowing adj. growing abnormally into the flesh.

inhabit v. live in, occupy. □ **inhabitable** adj., **inhabitant** n.
■ dwell in, live in, lodge in, occupy, reside in; people, populate. □ **inhabitant** householder, inmate, occupant, occupier, resident, tenant; citzen, denizen, local, native.

inhalant n. medicinal substance to be inhaled.

inhale v. 1 breathe in. 2 draw tobacco smoke into the lungs.

inhaler n. device producing a medicinal vapour to be inhaled.

inherent adj. existing in a thing as a permanent quality. □ **inherently** adv.
■ congenital, inborn, ingrained, inherited, innate, native, natural; essential, fundamental, intrinsic.

inherit v. 1 receive from a predecessor, esp. someone who has died. 2 derive from parents etc. □ **inheritance** n.
■ □ **inheritance** bequest, birthright, heritage, legacy, patrimony.

inhibit v. 1 restrain, prevent. 2 cause inhibitions in.
■ 1 check, deter, discourage, frustrate, hamper, hinder, hold back, impede, interfere with, obstruct, prevent, restrain, stop.

inhibition n. 1 inhibiting. 2 inability to act naturally or spontaneously.
■ 1 prevention, repression, suppression. 2 embarrassment, reticence, self-consciousness, shyness; sl. hang-up.

inhospitable adj. 1 not hospitable. 2 giving no shelter.

inhuman *adj.* brutal, cruel. □ **inhumanly** *adv.*, **inhumanity** *n.*

■ barbaric, barbarous, bestial, bloodthirsty, brutal, cruel, ferocious, harsh, heartless, inhumane, merciless, pitiless, ruthless, savage, vicious.

inhumane *adj.* callous. □ **inhumanely** *adv.*, **inhumanity** *n.*

■ brutal, callous, cold, cold-blooded, cruel, hard, hard-hearted, harsh, heartless, inconsiderate, inhuman, merciless, pitiless, remorseless, ruthless, uncaring, unforgiving, unkind, unsympathetic.

inimical *adj.* hostile. □ **inimically** *adv.*

inimitable *adj.* impossible to imitate. □ **inimitably** *adv.*

iniquity *n.* 1 great injustice. 2 wickedness. □ **iniquitous** *adj.*

initial *n.* first letter of a word or name. ● *v.* (**initialled**) mark or sign with initials. ● *adj.* of the beginning. □ **initially** *adv.*

■ *adj.* early, first, inaugural, introductory, opening, original.

initiate *v.* /iníshiayt/ 1 begin, originate. 2 admit into membership. 3 give instruction to. ● *n.* /iníshiət/ initiated person. □ **initiation** *n.*, **initiator** *n.*, **initiatory** *adj.*

■ *v.* 1 begin, instigate, institute, introduce, launch, originate, pioneer, set up, start. 2 accept, admit, enrol, install, introduce. 3 coach, drill, instruct, school, teach, train, tutor.

initiative *n.* 1 ability to initiate. 2 first step in a process.

■ 1 drive, dynamism, energy, enterprise, go, *colloq.* gumption, resourcefulness.

inject *v.* force (liquid) into the body with a syringe. □ **injection** *n.*

■ **injection** inoculation, *colloq.* jab, shot, vaccination.

injudicious *adj.* unwise. □ **injudiciously** *adv.*

■ foolhardy, foolish, ill-advised, impolitic, improvident, imprudent, incautious, misguided, rash, reckless, short-sighted, unwise.

injunction *n.* court order.

injure *v.* 1 damage physically. 2 impair. 3 do wrong to.

■ 1 break, bruise, burn, cut, damage, disfigure, fracture, gash, harm, hurt, lacerate, maim, wound. 2 damage, impair, harm,

mar, ruin, spoil, undermine, weaken. 3 abuse, ill-treat, maltreat, wrong.

injurious *adj.* hurtful, wrongful.

■ adverse, bad, damaging, dangerous, deleterious, destructive, detrimental, harmful, hurtful; unfair, unjust, wrongful.

injury *n.* 1 damage, harm. 2 form of this. 3 wrong or unjust act.

■ 1 damage, disfigurement, harm, hurt, impairment. 2 abrasion, break, bruise, contusion, cut, fracture, gash, laceration, wound. 3 disservice, injustice, ill, mischief, wrong.

injustice *n.* 1 lack of justice. 2 unjust action or treatment.

■ 1 inequality, iniquity, unfairness, unjustness, wrong; bias, discrimination, favouritism, partiality, partisanship, prejudice. 2 bad turn, disservice, injury, wrong.

ink *n.* coloured liquid used in writing, printing, etc. ● *v.* apply ink to. □ **inky** *adj.*

inkling *n.* slight suspicion, hint.

■ clue, hint, indication, intimation, suggestion, suspicion.

inlaid *see* **inlay**.

inland *adj.* & *adv.* in or towards the interior of a country.

in-laws *n.pl.* one's relatives by marriage.

inlay *v.* /inláy/ (**inlaid**) set (one thing in another) so that the surfaces are flush. ● *n.* /ínlay/ inlaid material or design.

inlet *n.* 1 strip of water extending inland. 2 way of admission.

inmate *n.* inhabitant, esp. of an institution.

inmost *adj.* furthest inward.

inn *n.* pub, esp. one in the country offering accommodation.

innards *n.pl.* (*colloq.*) 1 entrails. 2 inner parts.

innate *adj.* inborn. □ **innately** *adv.*

inner *adj.* interior, internal. □ **inner city** central densely populated urban area.

innermost *adj.* furthest inward.

innocent *adj.* 1 not guilty, free of evil. 2 naive, foolishly trustful. □ **innocently** *adv.*, **innocence** *n.*

■ 1 blameless, guiltless, irreproachable, not guilty, unimpeachable; chaste, good, moral, pure, righteous, sinless, virtuous. 2 artless, childlike, guileless, gullible, inexperienced, ingenuous, naive, simple, trustful, unsophisticated, unsuspecting, unworldly.

innocuous *adj.* harmless. □ **innocuously** *adv.*

innovate *v.* introduce something new. □ **innovation** *n.*, **innovative** *adj.*, **innovator** *n.*

innuendo *n.* (*pl.* **-oes**) insinuation.

innumerable *adj.* too many to be counted.
■ countless, incalculable, infinite, many, numberless, *sl.* umpteen, unnumbered, untold.

innumerate *adj.* not knowing basic mathematics. □ **innumeracy** *n.*

inoculate *v.* protect (against disease) with vaccines or serums. □ **inoculation** *n.*

inoperable *adj.* unable to be cured by surgical operation.

inoperative *adj.* not functioning.

inopportune *adj.* happening at an unsuitable time.
■ badly-timed, inappropriate, inconvenient, unfavourable, unfortunate, unseasonable, unsuitable, untimely, untoward.

inordinate *adj.* excessive. □ **inordinately** *adv.*

inorganic *adj.* of mineral origin, not organic. □ **inorganically** *adv.*

in-patient *n.* patient staying in a hospital during treatment.

input *n.* what is put in. ● *v.* (**input** or **inputted**) **1** put in. **2** supply (data etc.) to a computer.

inquest *n.* judicial investigation, esp. of a sudden death.

inquire *v.* seek information formally. □ **inquire into** make an investigation into. **inquirer** *n.*
■ □ **inquire into** examine, explore, investigate, look into, probe, research, scrutinize, study.

inquiry *n.* investigation.
■ examination, exploration, inquest, investigation, probe, scrutiny, study, survey.

inquisition *n.* detailed or relentless questioning. □ **inquisitor** *n.*, **inquisitorial** *adj.*

inquisitive *adj.* **1** eagerly seeking knowledge. **2** prying. □ **inquisitively** *adv.*, **inquisitiveness** *n.*
■ **1** curious, inquiring, interested. **2** intrusive, meddlesome, *colloq.* nosy, prying.

inroad *n.* incursion.

insalubrious *adj.* unhealthy.

insane *adj.* **1** mad. **2** very foolish. □ **insanely** *adv.*, **insanity** *n.*
■ **1** *sl.* barmy, *sl.* batty, certifiable, *sl.* crackers, crazy, demented, deranged, lunatic, mad, *sl.* nuts, *sl.* nutty, out of one's mind, *sl.* potty, psychotic, unbalanced. **2** absurd, asinine, crazy, daft, foolish, idiotic, imbecile, inane, ludicrous, nonsensical, ridiculous, senseless, silly, stupid. □ **insanity** dementia, lunacy, madness, psychosis; folly, foolishness, idiocy, senselessness, stupidity.

insanitary *adj.* not clean, not hygienic.
■ dirty, filthy, insalubrious, sordid, squalid, unclean, unhealthy, unhygienic.

insatiable *adj.* unable to be satisfied. □ **insatiably** *adv.*, **insatiability** *n.*

inscribe *v.* write or engrave.

inscription *n.* words inscribed.

inscrutable *adj.* baffling, impossible to interpret. □ **inscrutably** *adv.*, **inscrutability** *n.*
■ baffling, enigmatic, mysterious, mystifying, perplexing, puzzling, unfathomable.

insect *n.* small creature with six legs, no backbone, and a segmented body.

insecticide *n.* substance for killing insects.

insectivorous *adj.* insect-eating.

inseminate *v.* insert semen into. □ **insemination** *n.*

insensible *adj.* **1** unconscious. **2** unaware. **3** callous. **4** imperceptible. □ **insensibly** *adv.*
■ **1** comatose, out, senseless, unconscious. **2** heedless, oblivious, unaware, unconscious, unmindful.

insensitive *adj.* not sensitive.
■ callous, inconsiderate, tactless, thick-skinned, thoughtless, uncaring, unfeeling, unsympathetic.

inseparable *adj.* unable to be separated or kept apart. □ **inseparably** *adv.*, **inseparability** *n.*

insert *v.* /insért/ put into or between or among. ● *n.* /ínsert/ thing inserted. □ **insertion** *n.*
■ *v.* implant, inset, introduce, place in, pop in, put in, *colloq.* stick in; interject, interpose.

inset *v.* /insét/ (**inset**, **insetting**) **1** place in. **2** decorate with an inset. ● *n.* /ínset/ thing set into a larger thing.

inshore *adj.* & *adv.* near or nearer to the shore.

inside n. **1** inner side, surface, or part. **2** (pl., colloq.) stomach and bowels. ● adj. of or from the inside. ● adv. on, in, or to the inside. ● prep. **1** on or to the inside of. **2** within. □ **inside out 1** with the inner side outwards. **2** thoroughly.
■ n. **1** centre, core, heart, interior, middle. **2** (insides) bowels, entrails, guts, colloq. innards, intestines, viscera, vitals. ● adj. inner, interior, internal; indoor.

insidious adj. proceeding inconspicuously but harmfully. □ **insidiously** adv., **insidiousness** n.

insight n. perception and understanding of a thing's nature.
■ acumen, discernment, perception, perceptiveness, percipience, perspicacity, sensitivity, sharpness, shrewdness, understanding.

insignia n.pl. badges or marks of office etc.

insignificant adj. unimportant. □ **insignificantly** adv., **insignificance** n.
■ sl. footling, inconsequential, little, minor, petty, trifling, trivial, unimportant.

insinuate v. **1** insert gradually or craftily. **2** hint artfully. □ **insinuation** n., **insinuator** n.
■ **1** insert, introduce, slip. **2** hint, imply, indicate, intimate, suggest. □ **insinuation** allusion, hint, implication, innuendo, intimation, suggestion.

insipid adj. dull, lifeless, flavourless. □ **insipidity** n.
■ boring, characterless, colourless, dull, flat, lacklustre, lifeless, tedious, unexciting, uninspiring, uninteresting, vapid; bland, flavourless, tasteless.

insist v. declare or demand emphatically.
■ assert, avow, declare, emphasize, hold, maintain, stress, swear; demand, require.

insistent adj. **1** tending to insist. **2** demanding attention. □ **insistently** adv., **insistence** n.
■ **1** determined, dogged, emphatic, firm, positive, resolute, tenacious, unrelenting, unyielding. **2** intrusive, obtrusive; demanding, importunate, nagging, persistent.

in situ /in sityoō/ in its original place.

insolent adj. impertinently insulting. □ **insolently** adv., **insolence** n.
■ brazen, cheeky, contemptuous, disrespectful, impertinent, impudent, insulting, offensive, pert, presumptuous, rude.

insoluble adj. **1** unable to be dissolved. **2** unable to be solved.

insolvent adj. unable to pay one's debts. □ **insolvency** n.
■ bankrupt, colloq. broke, colloq. gone bust, failed.

insomnia n. inability to sleep.

insomniac n. sufferer from insomnia.

insouciant adj. carefree, unconcerned. □ **insouciantly** adv., **insouciance** n.

inspect v. examine critically or officially. □ **inspection** n.
■ check, examine, go over, investigate, look into, peruse, pore over, scan, scrutinize, study, survey, colloq. vet. □ **inspection** check, examination, investigation, colloq. once-over, scrutiny, study, survey, colloq. vetting.

inspector n. **1** person who inspects. **2** police officer above sergeant.

inspiration n. **1** creative force or influence. **2** sudden brilliant idea. □ **inspirational** adj.
■ **1** creativity, imagination, originality, spark; encouragement, impetus, spur, stimulation, stimulus. **2** US brainstorm, brainwave, bright idea.

inspire v. **1** stimulate to activity. **2** animate. **3** instil (a feeling or idea) into.
■ **1,2** animate, arouse, encourage, energize, enliven, excite, fortify, galvanize, invigorate, motivate, move, rouse, stimulate, stir.

install v. **1** place (a person) into office ceremonially. **2** set in position and ready for use. **3** establish. □ **installation** n.
■ **1** enthrone, inaugurate, induct, initiate, ordain. **2** fit, put in. **3** ensconce, establish, place, position, seat, settle, station.

instalment n. one of the parts in which a thing is presented or a debt paid over a period of time.

instance n. **1** example. **2** particular case. ● v. mention as an instance.
■ n. **1** example, exemplar, exemplification, illustration. **2** case, circumstance, event, occasion, occurrence, situation. ● v. adduce, allude to, cite, quote.

instant adj. **1** immediate. **2** (of food) quickly and easily prepared. ● n. exact moment. □ **instantly** adv.
■ adj. **1** immediate, instantaneous, on the spot, prompt, quick, speedy, sudden, swift, unhesitating. ● n. minute, moment, point, split second.

instantaneous adj. occurring or done instantly. □ **instantaneously** adv.

instead adv. as an alternative.

instep n. **1** middle part of the foot. **2** part of a shoe etc. covering this.

instigate v. **1** incite. **2** initiate. □ **instigation** n., **instigator** n.
■ **1** encourage, foment, incite, provoke, stir up, whip up. **2** begin, get under way, initiate, set in motion, start.

instil v. (**instilled**) implant (ideas etc.) gradually. □ **instillation** n.

instinct n. **1** inborn pattern of behaviour. **2** innate impulse. **3** unconscious skill, intuition.
■ **3** aptitude, bent, flair, gift, knack, skill, talent; feeling, intuition, sixth sense.

instinctive adj. **1** of or prompted by instinct. **2** apparently unconscious or automatic. □ **instinctively** adv.
■ **1** inborn, inbred, inherent, innate, intuitive, native, natural. **2** automatic, involuntary, knee-jerk, mechanical, spontaneous, subconscious, unconscious.

institute n. **1** organization for promotion of a specified activity. **2** its premises. ● v. **1** establish. **2** initiate. □ **institutor** n.
■ n. **1** association, company, establishment, foundation, institution, organization, society. ● v. **1** create, establish, form, found, inaugurate, launch, set up. **2** begin, get under way, initiate, instigate, set in motion, start.

institution n. **1** process of instituting. **2** organization founded esp. for educational or social purposes. **3** established rule or custom. □ **institutional** adj.
■ **1** creation, establishment, formation, foundation, inauguration, initiation, instigation, launch, start. **2** establishment, foundation, institute, organization; academy, college, school; clinic, hospital, (nursing) home, sanatorium. **3** convention, custom, habit, practice, routine, rule, tradition.

institutionalize v. accustom to living in an institution.

instruct v. **1** teach (a person) a subject or skill. **2** give instructions to. □ **instructor** n.
■ **1** coach, drill, educate, ground, school, teach, train, tutor. **2** bid, command, direct, order, require, tell.

instruction n. **1** process of teaching. **2** (pl.) statements telling a person what to do.
■ **1** coaching, education, grounding, schooling, teaching, training. **2** (**instructions**) advice, commands, dictates, directions, directives, guidelines, orders, recommendations.

instructive adj. giving instruction, enlightening.
■ edifying, educational, enlightening, helpful, illuminating, informative, revealing.

instrument n. **1** implement, esp. for delicate work. **2** measuring device of an engine or vehicle. **3** device for producing musical sounds.
■ **1** appliance, device, gadget, implement, tool, utensil.

instrumental adj. **1** serving as a means. **2** performed on musical instruments.

instrumentalist n. player of a musical instrument.

insubordinate adj. disobedient, rebellious. □ **insubordination** n.
■ defiant, disobedient, insurgent, intractable, mutinous, obstreperous, rebellious, recalcitrant, refractory, uncooperative, ungovernable, unruly.

insubstantial adj. **1** not real. **2** weak, flimsy. □ **insubstantiality** n.
■ **1** fanciful, illusive, illusory, imaginary, unreal. **2** fragile, frail, rickety, shaky; feeble, flimsy, tenuous, unconvincing, weak; diaphanous, filmy, thin.

insufferable adj. intolerable. □ **insufferably** adv.

insular adj. **1** of an island. **2** narrow-minded. □ **insularity** n.

insulate v. **1** cover with a substance that prevents the passage of electricity, sound, or heat. **2** isolate from influences. □ **insulation** n., **insulator** n.
■ **1** cover, lag, wrap. **2** keep apart, isolate, segregate, separate; cushion, shelter.

insulin n. hormone controlling the body's absorption of sugar.

insult v. /insúlt/ speak or act so as to offend someone. ● n. /ínsult/ insulting remark or action. □ **insulting** adj.
■ v. abuse, be rude to, calumniate, defame, malign, put down, revile, sl. slag (off), slander, vilify; affront, hurt, injure, offend, slight. ● n. affront, rebuff, slander, slight, slur, snub.

insuperable *adj.* unable to be overcome. □ **insuperably** *adv.*, **insuperability** *n.*
■ insurmountable, invincible, overwhelming, unconquerable.

insupportable *adj.* intolerable.

insurance *n.* **1** contract to provide compensation for loss, damage, or death. **2** sum payable as a premium or in compensation. **3** safeguard against loss or failure.

insure *v.* protect by insurance.

insurgent *adj.* in revolt, rebellious. ● *n.* rebel. □ **insurgency** *n.*

insurmountable *adj.* insuperable.

insurrection *n.* rebellion. □ **insurrectionist** *n.*

intact *adj.* undamaged, complete.
■ complete, entire, flawless, perfect, unbroken, undamaged, unharmed, unscathed, whole.

intake *n.* **1** taking things in. **2** place or amount of this.

integral *adj.* forming or necessary to form a whole.
■ complete, entire, intact, integrated, unified, whole; basic, essential, fundamental, indispensable, intrinsic, necessary.

integrate *v.* **1** combine (parts) into a whole. **2** bring or come into full membership of a community. □ **integration** *n.*

integrity *n.* honesty.
■ decency, goodness, honesty, honour, morality, principle, probity, rectitude, righteousness, trustworthiness, virtue.

intellect *n.* faculty of reasoning and acquiring knowledge.
■ brains, intelligence, *sl.* loaf, mind, reason, understanding.

intellectual *adj.* **1** of or using the intellect. **2** having a strong intellect. ● *n.* intellectual person. □ **intellectually** *adv.*
■ *adj.* **1** cerebral, mental. **2** academic, bookish, brainy, clever, erudite, highbrow, learned, scholarly. ● *n.* academic, highbrow, professor, scholar, thinker.

intelligence *n.* **1** the intellect. **2** quickness of understanding. **3** information, esp. that of military value. **4** people collecting this.
■ **1** brains, intellect, *sl.* loaf, mind, reason, understanding. **2** acumen, acuteness, astuteness, brightness, cleverness, common sense, insight, *colloq.* nous, perception, percipience, perspicacity, sharpness, shrewdness, smartness, wit.

intelligent *adj.* mentally able, clever. □ **intelligently** *adv.*
■ able, astute, brainy, bright, brilliant, canny, clever, discerning, penetrating, perceptive, quick, sharp, shrewd, smart.

intelligible *adj.* able to be understood. □ **intelligibly** *adv.*, **intelligibility** *n.*
■ articulate, audible, clear, coherent, comprehensible, legible, lucid, plain, rational, readable, understandable.

intend *v.* have in mind as what one wishes to do or achieve.
■ aim, contemplate, design, have in mind, mean, plan, propose, purpose.

intense *adj.* **1** strong in quality or degree. **2** feeling, or apt to feel, strong emotion. □ **intensely** *adv.*, **intensity** *n.*
■ **1** acute, ardent, burning, exquisite, extreme, fervent, fierce, great, heartfelt, keen, overpowering, powerful, profound, severe, sharp, strong, vehement, violent. **2** emotional, impassioned, passionate; highly-strung, moody, sensitive, temperamental, touchy.

intensify *v.* make or become more intense. □ **intensification** *n.*
■ add to, amplify, augment, deepen, double, enhance, escalate, heighten, increase, redouble, reinforce, step up, strengthen; aggravate, exacerbate, worsen.

intensive *adj.* employing much effort. □ **intensively** *adv.*, **intensiveness** *n.*
■ assiduous, concentrated, exhaustive, meticulous, painstaking, rigorous, thorough.

intent *n.* intention. ● *adj.* with concentrated attention. □ **intent on** determined to. **intently** *adv.*, **intentness** *n.*
■ *adj.* absorbed, concentrating, engrossed, involved, rapt.

intention *n.* purpose, aim.
■ aim, ambition, design, goal, end, intent, object, objective, purpose, target.

intentional *adj.* done on purpose. □ **intentionally** *adv.*
■ calculated, conscious, deliberate, intended, meant, planned, preconceived, premeditated, purposeful, wilful.

inter *v.* (**interred**) bury.

inter- *prep.* between, among.

interact *v.* have an effect upon each other. □ **interaction** *n.*, **interactive** *adj.*

interbreed *v.* (**interbred**) breed with each other, cross-breed.

intercede v. intervene on someone's behalf.

intercept v. stop or catch in transit. □ **interception** n., **interceptor** n.

intercession n. interceding.

interchange v. /intercháynj/ **1** cause to change places. **2** alternate. ● n. /íntərchaynj/ **1** process of interchanging. **2** road junction where streams of traffic do not cross on the same level. □ **interchangeable** adj.

intercom n. (colloq.) communication system operating by telephone or radio.

interconnect v. connect with each other. □ **interconnection** n.

intercontinental adj. between continents.

intercourse n. **1** dealings between people or countries. **2** sexual intercourse, copulation.

interdict n. formal prohibition.

interest n. **1** feeling of curiosity or concern. **2** hobby etc. in which one is concerned. **3** advantage. **4** legal share. **5** money paid for use of money borrowed. ● v. arouse the interest of.

▪ n. **1** attention, attentiveness, concern, curiosity, eagerness, enthusiasm, fascination, inquisitiveness. **2** amusement, hobby, pastime, pursuit. **3** advantage, avail, benefit, gain, good, profit, use. **4** claim, entitlement, share, stake, title. ● v. absorb, appeal to, attract, captivate, engage, engross, fascinate, grip, intrigue, occupy, rivet; amuse, divert, entertain.

interested adj. **1** feeling interest. **2** having an interest, not impartial.

▪ **1** absorbed, curious, gripped, engrossed, fascinated, intrigued, riveted. **2** biased, concerned, involved, partial, partisan, prejudiced.

interesting adj. arousing interest.

▪ absorbing, compelling, engrossing, entertaining, exciting, fascinating, gripping, intriguing, stimulating.

interface n. place where interaction occurs.

interfere v. take part in others' affairs, esp. without right or invitation. □ **interfere with 1** obstruct, hinder. **2** assult sexually.

▪ barge in, butt in, intercede, interpose, intervene, intrude, meddle. □ **interfere with 1** block, get in the way of, hamper, handicap, hinder, hold back, impede, inhibit, obstruct, slow down.

interference n. **1** interfering. **2** disturbance of radio signals.

interferon n. protein preventing the development of a virus.

interim n. intervening period. ● adj. temporary.

▪ n. interval, meantime, meanwhile. ● adj. makeshift, provisional, temporary.

interior adj. inner. ● n. interior part.

interject v. put in (a remark) when someone is speaking.

interjection n. exclamation.

interlace v. weave or lace together.

interlink v. link together.

interlock v. fit into each other. ● n. fine machine-knitted fabric.

interloper n. intruder.

interlude n. **1** interval. **2** thing happening or performed in this.

▪ **1** break, hiatus, intermission, interval, lull, pause, respite, stop.

intermarry v. (of families, races, etc.) become connected by marriage. □ **intermarriage** n.

intermediary n. mediator. ● adj. **1** acting as intermediary. **2** intermediate.

▪ n. agent, arbitrator, go-between, mediator, middleman, negotiator, peacemaker, representative.

intermediate adj. coming between in time, place, or order.

▪ halfway, intermediary, median, mid, middle, midway, transitional.

interment n. burial.

intermezzo /intərmétsō/ n. (pl. **-os**) short piece of music.

interminable adj. very long and boring. □ **interminably** adv.

intermission n. interval, pause.

intermittent adj. occurring at intervals. □ **intermittently** adv.

▪ discontinuous, fitful, irregular, occasional, on and off, periodic, spasmodic, sporadic.

intern v. compel (esp. an enemy alien) to live in a special area.

internal adj. **1** of or in the inside. **2** of a country's domestic affairs. □ **internal-combustion engine** engine producing motive power from fuel exploded within a cylinder. **internally** adv.

international adj. between countries. ● n. **1** sports contest between players representing different countries. **2** one of these players. □ **internationally** adv.

■ adj. cosmopolitan, global, intercontinental, universal, world, worldwide.

internecine /intərneéssīn/ adj. mutually destructive.

internee n. interned person.

internment n. interning.

interplay n. interaction.

interpolate v. **1** interject. **2** insert. □ **interpolation** n.

interpose v. **1** insert. **2** intervene. □ **interposition** n.

interpret v. **1** explain the meaning of. **2** act as interpreter. □ **interpretation** n.

■ **1** clarify, elucidate, explain, illuminate, make clear, shed or throw light on, simplify; decipher, decode. **2** translate. □ **interpretation** clarification, elucidation, explanation, illumination, simplification, translation.

interpreter n. person who orally translates speech between people speaking different languages.

interregnum n. period between the rule of two successive rulers.

interrogate v. question closely or formally. □ **interrogation** n., **interrogator** n.

■ catechize, cross-examine, cross-question, examine, grill, pump, question, quiz. □ **interrogation** cross-examination, debriefing, examination, grilling, questioning, quizzing.

interrogative adj. forming or having the form of a question.

interrupt v. **1** break the continuity of. **2** break the flow of (speech etc.) by a remark. □ **interruption** n.

■ **1** adjourn, bring to a halt, discontinue, halt, stop, suspend. **2** barge in on, butt in on, cut in on, disrupt, disturb, intrude on; chime in, colloq. chip in. □ **interruption** disruption, disturbance, intrusion; adjournment, break, discontinuance, suspension.

intersect v. divide or cross by passing or lying across. □ **intersection** n.

intersperse v. insert here and there.

interval n. **1** intervening time or space. **2** pause or break. **3** difference in musical pitch.

■ **1** interim, meantime, meanwhile, period, time; gap, space. **2** break, interlude, intermission, pause.

intervene v. **1** enter a situation to change its course or resolve it. **2** occur between events. □ **intervention** n.

■ **1** intercede, mediate, step in; interfere, intrude, meddle.

interview n. formal meeting with a person to assess his or her merits or to obtain information. ● v. hold an interview with. □ **interviewer** n., **interviewee** n.

■ n. appraisal, assessment, evaluation, examination, grilling; audience, conversation, discussion, pre-conference, talk.

interweave v. (-**wove**, -**woven**) weave together.

intestate adj. not having made a valid will. □ **intestacy** n.

intestine n. section of the alimentary canal between stomach and anus. □ **intestinal** adj.

intimate¹ /íntimət/ adj. **1** closely acquainted or familiar. **2** private and personal. **3** having a sexual relationship (esp. outside marriage). ● n. intimate friend. □ **intimately** adv., **intimacy** n.

■ adj. **1** attached, close, devoted, friendly, inseparable, colloq. pally, colloq. thick; cherished, dear. **2** confidential, personal, private, secret. ● n. bosom friend, colloq. chum, confidant(e), crony, friend, mate, colloq. pal.

intimate² /íntimayt/ v. make known, esp. by hinting. □ **intimation** n.

■ hint, imply, indicate, insinuate, suggest. □ **intimation** hint, implication, indication, insinuation, suggestion.

intimidate v. influence by frightening. □ **intimidation** n.

■ browbeat, bully, cow, daunt, frighten, colloq. lean on, menace, overawe, pressure, pressurize, railroad, scare, terrify, terrorize, threaten.

into prep. **1** to the inside of, to a point within. **2** to a particular state or occupation. **3** dividing (a number) mathematically. **4** (colloq.) interested in.

intolerable adj. too bad to be endured. □ **intolerably** adv.

■ insufferable, insupportable, unbearable, unendurable.

intonation n. **1** pitch of the voice in speaking. **2** act of intoning.

■ **1** accent, cadence, inflection, modulation, pitch, tonality, tone.

intone v. chant, esp. on one note.

intoxicate v. **1** make drunk. **2** make greatly excited. □ **intoxication** n.
■ **1** fuddle, inebriate, stupefy. **2** arouse, elate, enrapture, excite, exhilarate, inflame, thrill.

intra- pref. within.

intractable adj. hard to deal with or control. □ **intractability** n.
■ disobedient, headstrong, insubordinate, obdurate, obstinate, recalcitrant, refractory, uncontrollable, ungovernable, unmanageable, unruly, wild.

intransigent adj. stubborn. □ **intransigence** n.

intra-uterine adj. within the uterus.

intravenous adj. into a vein. □ **intravenously** adv.

intrepid adj. fearless, brave. □ **intrepidly** adv., **intrepidity** n.

intricate adj. very complicated. □ **intricately** adv., **intricacy** n.
■ Byzantine, complex, complicated, difficult, involved, knotty, labyrinthine; detailed, elaborate, fancy, ornate, rococo.

intrigue v. **1** plot secretly. ● n. **1** underhand plot or plotting. **2** secret love affair.
■ v. **1** conspire, plot, scheme. **2** attract, captivate, charm, enthral, fascinate, interest. ● n. **1** conspiracy, machination, plot, scheme.

intrinsic adj. belonging to the basic nature of. □ **intrinsically** adv.
■ basic, fundamental, essential, inborn, inherent, innate, native, natural.

introduce v. **1** make (a person) known to another. **2** present to an audience. **3** bring into use. **4** insert.
■ **1** make acquainted, present. **2** announce, present. **3** establish, inaugurate, initiate, instigate, institute, launch, set in motion. **4** add, insert, interpolate, interpose.

introduction n. **1** introducing. **2** introductory section or treatise.
■ **1** presentation; inauguration, initiation, institution. **2** foreword, preamble, preface, prelude, prologue.

introductory adj. preliminary.

introspection n. examination of one's own thoughts and feelings. □ **introspective** adj.

introvert n. introspective and shy person. □ **introverted** adj.

intrude v. come or join in without being invited or wanted. □ **intruder** n., **intrusion** n., **intrusive** adj.
■ encroach, impinge, infringe, invade, trespass; barge in, butt in, interfere, meddle, colloq. muscle in. □ **intruder** burglar, housebreaker, robber, thief; gatecrasher, interloper, invader, prowler, trespasser.

intuition n. (power of) knowing without learning or reasoning. □ **intuitive** adj., **intuitively** adv.
■ instinct, sixth sense; feeling, foreboding, hunch, inkling, premonition, presentiment.

Inuit /ínyoo-it/ n. (pl. **Inuit** or **-s**) N. American Eskimo.

inundate v. flood. □ **inundation** n.

inure v. accustom, esp. to something unpleasant.

invade v. **1** enter (territory) with hostile intent. **2** swarm into. **3** encroach on. **4** (of disease etc.) attack. □ **invader** n.
■ **1** occupy, overrun, storm, take over. **2** infest, permeate, pervade, swarm into. **3** encroach on, infringe on, intrude on, trespass on.

invalid[1] /ínvaleed/ n. person suffering from ill health.

invalid[2] /inválid/ adj. not valid.
■ null and void, void, worthless; baseless, false, groundless, illogical, incorrect, irrational, spurious, unreasonable.

invalidate v. make no longer valid. □ **invalidation** n.
■ annul, cancel, nullify, quash, repeal, rescind, revoke; discredit, disprove, negate, rebut.

invaluable adj. having value too great to be measured.

invariable adj. not variable, always the same. □ **invariably** adv.
■ changeless, constant, enduring, eternal, fixed, immutable, permanent, unalterable, unchangeable, unchanging, unvarying; even, level, regular, stable, steady, uniform.

invasion n. hostile or harmful intrusion.
■ encroachment, infiltration, intrusion, occupation; attack, foray, incursion, inroad, offensive, onslaught, raid.

invective n. abusive language.

inveigle v. entice.

invent v. **1** make or design (something new). **2** make up (a lie, a story). □ **inventor** n.
■ **1** coin, conceive, contrive, create, design, devise, dream up, imagine, improvise, colloq. think up. **2** concoct, colloq. cook up, fabricate, make up.

invention n. **1** process of inventing. **2** thing invented. **3** inventiveness.
■ **1** conception, creation, design, origination. **2** brainchild, contraption, contrivance, device, gadget; fib, lie, story, tale, untruth. **3** creativity, imagination, imaginativeness, ingenuity, inspiration, inventiveness, originality, resourcefulness.

inventive adj. able to invent things. □ **inventiveness** n.
■ clever, creative, imaginative, ingenious, innovative, original, resourceful.

inventory n. detailed list of goods or furniture.

inverse adj. inverted. □ **inversely** adv.

invert v. **1** turn upside down. **2** reverse the position, order, or relationship of. □ **inverted commas** quotation marks. **inversion** n.

invertebrate adj. & n. (animal) having no backbone.

invest v. **1** use (money, time, etc.) to earn interest or bring profit. **2** confer rank or power upon. **3** endow with a quality. □ **investment** n., **investor** n.
■ **1** contribute, devote, donate, expend, give, lay out, sink, spend.

investigate v. **1** study carefully. **2** inquire into. □ **investigation** n., **investigator** n., **investigative** adj.
■ analyse, examine, explore, go over, inquire into, inspect, look into, probe, research, scrutinize, study, survey. □ **investigation** analysis, examination, exploration, inquiry, inspection, review, scrutiny, study, survey.

inveterate adj. **1** habitual. **2** firmly established.

invidious adj. liable to cause resentment. □ **invidiously** adv.

invigilate v. supervise examinees. □ **invigilator** n.

invigorate v. fill with vigour, give strength or courage to.
■ animate, brace, energize, enliven, fortify, hearten, pep up, perk up, refresh, rejuvenate, restore, revive, strengthen, vivify.

invincible adj. unconquerable. □ **invincibly** adv., **invincibility** n.
■ impenetrable, impregnable, indestructible, indomitable, invulnerable, unassailable, unbeatable, unconquerable.

invisible adj. not able to be seen. □ **invisibly** adv., **invisibility** n.
■ imperceptible, indiscernible, indistinguishable, undetectable, unnoticeable; concealed, hidden, out of sight.

invite v. **1** ask (a person) politely to come or to do something. **2** ask for. **3** attract. □ **invitation** n.
■ **1** ask, bid, summon. **2** appeal for, ask for, call for, request, solicit. **3** allure, attract, tempt.

inviting adj. attractive and tempting. □ **invitingly** adv.
■ alluring, appealing, attractive, captivating, engaging, fascinating, intriguing, seductive, tempting.

in vitro in a test-tube or other laboratory environment.

invoice n. bill for goods or services. ● v. send an invoice to.

invoke v. **1** call for the help or protection of. **2** summon (a spirit).

involuntary adj. done without intention. □ **involuntarily** adv.
■ automatic, impulsive, instinctive, knee-jerk, mechanical, spontaneous, unconscious, unintentional, unpremeditated, unthinking, unwitting.

involve v. **1** engross, occupy fully. **2** have as a consequence. **3** include or affect. **4** implicate. □ **involvement** n.
■ **1** absorb, engage, engross, immerse, interest, occupy. **2** entail, imply, mean, necessitate, presuppose. **3** comprehend, comprise, cover, embody, embrace, encompass, include, incorporate; affect, apply to, be relevant to, concern, have a bearing on. **4** connect, embroil, entangle, implicate.

involved adj. **1** complicated. **2** concerned.
■ **1** complex, complicated, difficult, elaborate, intricate, knotty, labyrinthine, tangled. **2** affected, concerned, interested.

invulnerable adj. not vulnerable. □ **invulnerability** n.
■ impenetrable, impregnable, invincible, safe, secure, unassailable, unconquerable.

inward adj. **1** situated on or going towards the inside. **2** in the mind or spirit.

● *adv.* inwards. □ **inwardly** *adv.*, **inwards** *adv.*

iodine *n.* chemical used in solution as an antiseptic.

ion *n.* electrically charged particle. □ **ionic** *adj.*

ionize *v.* convert or be converted into ions. □ **ionization** *n.*

ionosphere *n.* ionized region of the atmosphere. □ **ionospheric** *adj.*

iota *n.* 1 ninth letter of the Greek alphabet, = i. 2 very small amount.

IOU *n.* signed paper given as a receipt for money borrowed.

ir- *see* **in-**.

irascible *adj.* hot-tempered, irritable. □ **irascibly** *adv.*, **irascibility** *n.*

irate *adj.* angry. □ **irately** *adv.*

ire *n.* anger.

iridescent *adj.* 1 coloured like a rainbow. 2 shimmering. □ **iridescence** *n.*

iris *n.* 1 coloured part of the eyeball, round the pupil. 2 plant with showy flowers and sword-shaped leaves.

Irish *adj.* & *n.* (language) of Ireland. □ **Irishman** *n.*, **Irishwoman** *n.*

irk *v.* annoy, be tiresome to.
■ *colloq.* aggravate, annoy, *sl.* bug, exasperate, gall, get on a person's nerves, grate on, infuriate, irritate, madden, nettle, pique, *colloq.* rile, vex.

irksome *adj.* tiresome.
■ annoying, bothersome, exasperating, infuriating, irritating, maddening, tiresome, troublesome, trying, vexatious.

iron *n.* 1 hard grey metal. 2 tool etc. made of this. 3 implement with a flat base heated for smoothing cloth or clothes. 4 (*pl.*) fetters. ● *adj.* 1 made of iron. 2 strong as iron. ● *v.* smooth (clothes etc.) with an iron. □ **ironing board** narrow folding table for ironing clothes on.

ironic *adj.* (also **ironical**) using irony. □ **ironically** *adv.*

ironmonger *n.* shopkeeper selling tools and household implements.

ironstone *n.* 1 hard iron ore. 2 a kind of hard white pottery.

irony *n.* 1 expression of meaning by use of words normally conveying the opposite. 2 apparent perversity of fate or circumstances.

irradiate *v.* 1 throw light or other radiation on. 2 treat (food) by radiation. □ **irradiation** *n.*

irrecoverable *adj.* unable to be recovered. □ **irrecoverably** *adv.*

irrefutable *adj.* unable to be refuted. □ **irrefutably** *adv.*

irregular *adj.* 1 not regular. 2 contrary to rules or custom. □ **irregularly** *adv.*, **irregularity** *n.*
■ 1 asymmetrical, lopsided; bumpy, craggy, pitted, rocky, rough, rugged, uneven; erratic, fitful, fluctuating, inconsistent, intermittent, on and off, spasmodic, sporadic, unsteady, variable. 2 improper, incorrect, unauthorized; abnormal, anomalous, exceptional, odd, peculiar, strange, uncommon, unconventional, unorthodox, unusual.

irrelevant *adj.* not relevant. □ **irrelevance** *n.*
■ beside the point, immaterial, inapplicable, inapposite, inappropriate, unconnected, unrelated.

irreparable *adj.* unable to be repaired. □ **irreparably** *adv.*

irreplaceable *adj.* unable to be replaced.

irrepressible *adj.* unable to be repressed. □ **irrepressibly** *adv.*
■ boisterous, bubbly, buoyant, ebullient, exuberant, headstrong, lively, spirited, vivacious.

irreproachable *adj.* blameless, faultless. □ **irreproachably** *adv.*

irresistible *adj.* too strong or delightful to be resisted. □ **irresistibly** *adv.*, **irresistibility** *n.*

irresolute *adj.* unable to make up one's mind. □ **irresolutely** *adv.*, **irresolution** *n.*
■ doubtful, dubious, hesitant, indecisive, in two minds, uncertain, unsure, wavering.

irrespective *adj.* **irrespective of** not taking (a thing) into account.

irresponsible *adj.* not showing a proper sense of responsibility. □ **irresponsibly** *adv.*, **irresponsibility** *n.*
■ careless, feckless, flighty, giddy, heedless, reckless, thoughtless, unreliable, unthinking, untrustworthy.

irreverent *adj.* 1 not reverent. 2 not respectful. □ **irreverently** *adv.*, **irreverence** *n.*

irreversible *adj.* not reversible, unable to be altered or revoked. □ **irreversibly** *adv.*

irrevocable *adj.* unalterable. □ **irrevocably** *adv.*
■ decided, fixed, immutable, irreversible, settled, unalterable, unchangeable.

irrigate v. supply (land) with water by streams, pipes, etc. □ **irrigation** n.

irritable adj. easily annoyed. □ **irritably** adv., **irritability** n.

■ bad-tempered, cantankerous, crabby, cross, crotchety, crusty, disagreeable, fractious, grumpy, huffy, irascible, peevish, pettish, petulant, prickly, quarrelsome, querulous, short-tempered, snappy, splenetic, testy, touchy, waspish.

irritant adj. & n. (thing) causing irritation.

irritate v. **1** annoy. **2** cause discomfort in. □ **irritation** n.

■ **1** colloq. aggravate, annoy, sl. bug, exasperate, gall, colloq. get, get on a person's nerves, grate on, infuriate, irk, nettle, pique, provoke, colloq. rile, vex. **2** chafe, hurt, sting.

Islam n. **1** Muslim religion. **2** Muslim world. □ **Islamic** adj.

island n. piece of land surrounded by water.

islander n. inhabitant of an island.

isle n. island.

islet n. small island.

isobar n. line on a map, connecting places with the same atmospheric pressure. □ **isobaric** adj.

isolate v. **1** place apart or alone. **2** separate (esp. an infectious patient from others). □ **isolation** n.

■ insulate, keep apart, maroon, seclude, segregate, separate, sequester; quarantine.

isolationism n. policy of holding aloof from other countries or groups. □ **isolationist** n.

isosceles /Isóssileez/ adj. (of a triangle) having two sides equal.

isotherm n. line on a map, connecting places with the same temperature.

isotope n. one of two or more forms of a chemical element differing in their atomic weight. □ **isotopic** adj.

issue n. **1** outflow. **2** issuing, quantity issued. **3** one edition (e.g. of a magazine). **4** important topic. **5** offspring. ● v. **1** flow out. **2** supply for use. **3** send out. **4** publish.

■ n. **2** circulation, dissemination, distribution, issuing, promulgation, publication. **3** copy, edition, impression, number. **4** affair, business, matter, point, question, subject, topic. **5** children, descendants, heirs, offspring, progeny. ● v. **1** emanate, escape, flow, pour, stream. **2** furnish, provide, supply. **3** broadcast, circulate, deliver, disseminate, distribute, hand out, make public, release, send out.

isthmus /ismass/ n. (pl. **-muses**) narrow strip of land connecting two larger masses of land.

it pron. **1** thing mentioned or being discussed. **2** impersonal subject of a verb.

Italian adj. & n. (native, language) of Italy.

italic adj. (of type) sloping like this. ● n.pl. italic type.

italicize v. print in italics.

itch n. **1** tickling sensation in the skin, causing a desire to scratch. **2** restless desire. ● v. feel an itch. □ **itchy** adj.

item n. **1** single thing in a list or collection. **2** single piece of news.

■ **1** article, object, thing; component, detail, element, entry, particular. **2** article, feature, piece, report, story.

itemize v. list, state the individual items of. □ **itemization** n.

itinerant adj. travelling from place to place.

■ migrant, migratory, nomadic, peripatetic, roaming, roving, travelling, wandering.

itinerary n. route, list of places to be visited on a journey.

its poss.pron. of it.

it's it is, it has.

itself pron. emphatic and reflexive form of it.

ivory n. **1** hard creamy-white substance forming tusks of elephant etc. **2** object made of this. **3** its colour. ● adj. creamy-white. □ **ivory tower** seclusion from the harsh realities of life.

ivy n. climbing evergreen shrub.

Jj

jab v. (**jabbed**) poke roughly. ● n. **1** rough poke. **2** (*colloq.*) injection.

jabber v. talk rapidly, often unintelligibly. ● n. jabbering talk.

jack n. **1** portable device for raising heavy weights off the ground. **2** playing card next below queen. **3** ship's small flag showing nationality. **4** electrical connection with a single plug. **5** small ball aimed at in bowls. **6** male donkey. ● v. **jack up** raise with a jack.

jackal n. dog-like wild animal.

jackass n. **1** male ass. **2** stupid person.

jackboot n. large high boot.

jackdaw n. bird of the crow family.

jacket n. **1** short coat. **2** outer covering.

jackknife n. large folding knife. ● v. (of an articulated vehicle) fold against itself in an accident.

jackpot n. large prize of money that has accumulated until won. □ **hit the jackpot** (*colloq.*) have a sudden success.

Jacobean adj. of the reign of James I of England (1603–25).

Jacuzzi n. [P.] large bath with underwater jets of water.

jade n. **1** hard green, blue, or white stone. **2** its green colour.

jaded adj. tired and bored.

jagged adj. having sharp projections.
■ craggy, crenellated, irregular, ragged, rough, serrated, spiky, uneven.

jaguar n. large flesh-eating animal of the cat family.

jail n. prison. ● v. put into jail.
■ n. gaol, lock-up, prison, reformatory. ● v. detain, imprison, incarcerate, remand, send to prison.

jailer n. person in charge of a jail or its prisoners.

jam¹ n. thick sweet substance made by boiling fruit with sugar.

jam² v. (**jammed**) **1** squeeze or wedge into a space. **2** become wedged. **3** crowd or block (an area). **4** make (a broadcast) unintelligible by causing interference. ● n. **1** crowded mass of people, vehicles, etc. **2** stoppage caused by jamming. **3** (*colloq.*) difficult situation. □ **jam-packed** adj. (*colloq.*) very full.
■ v. **1** cram, crowd, force, pack, push, ram, shove, squash, squeeze, stuff, thrust, wedge. **3** block, clog, congest, obstruct, stop (up). ● n. **1** crowd, crush, horde, mass, mob, multitude, pack, swarm, throng. **2** blockage, congestion, obstruction.

jamb n. side post of a door or window.

jamboree n. **1** large party. **2** rally.

jangle n. harsh metallic sound. ● v. (cause to) make this sound.

janitor n. caretaker of a building.

japan n. hard usu. black varnish. ● v. (**japanned**) coat with this.

Japanese adj. & n. (native, language) of Japan.

jar¹ n. cylindrical glass or earthenware container.
■ crock, ewer, flagon, jug, pitcher, urn.

jar² v. (**jarred**) jolt. ● n. jolt. □ **jar on** have a harsh or disagreeable effect on.
■ v. bounce, bump, jerk, jog, joggle, jolt, judder, knock, rock, shake. □ **jar on** annoy, grate on, irritate.

jargon n. words or expressions developed for use within a particular group of people.
■ cant, dialect, idiom, language, parlance, patois, slang, speech.

jasmine n. shrub with white or yellow flowers.

jasper n. a kind of quartz.

jaundice n. yellowing of the skin caused by liver disease etc.

jaundiced adj. **1** affected by jaundice. **2** envious, resentful.

jaunt n. short pleasure trip. ● v. make a jaunt.

jaunty adj. (**-ier**, **-iest**) cheerful, self-confident. □ **jauntily** adv., **jauntiness** n.
■ buoyant, cheerful, cheery, chirpy, high-spirited, jolly, jovial, lively, merry, perky, pert, self-confident, spirited, sprightly, vivacious.

javelin n. light spear.

jaw n. **1** bone(s) forming the framework of the mouth. **2** (*pl.*) gripping-parts. **3**

(*colloq.*) lengthy talk. ● *v.* (*colloq.*) talk lengthily.

jay *n.* bird of the crow family.

jaywalking *n.* crossing a road carelessly. □ **jaywalker** *n.*

jazz *n.* type of music with strong rhythm and much syncopation.

jealous *adj.* 1 suspicious or resentful of rivalry in love. 2 envious. 3 taking watchful care. □ **jealously** *adv.*, **jealousy** *n.*

■ 1 distrustful, mistrustful, suspicious. 2 covetous, envious, grudging, resentful. 3 careful, mindful, protective, vigilant, watchful.

jeans *n.pl.* denim trousers.

Jeep *n.* [P.] small sturdy motor vehicle with four-wheel drive.

jeer *v.* laugh or shout rudely or scornfully (at). ● *n.* jeering.

■ *v.* barrack, boo, deride, gibe (at), heckle, laugh (at), mock (at), ridicule, scoff (at), taunt.

Jehovah *n.* name of God in the Old Testament.

jell *v.* (*colloq.*) 1 set as a jelly. 2 take definite form.

jelly *n.* 1 soft solid food made of liquid set with gelatine. 2 substance of similar consistency. 3 jam made of strained fruit juice.

jellyfish *n.* sea animal with a jelly-like body.

jemmy *n.* burglar's short crowbar. ● *v.* open with this.

jenny *n.* female donkey.

jeopardize /jéppərdīz/ *v.* endanger.

■ endanger, imperil, put at risk, put in jeopardy, risk, threaten.

jeopardy /jéppərdi/ *n.* danger.

jerboa *n.* rat-like desert animal with long hind legs.

jerk *n.* sudden sharp movement or pull. ● *v.* move, pull, or stop with jerk(s). □ **jerky** *adj.*, **jerkily** *adv.*, **jerkiness** *n.*

■ *n.* bump, jolt, lurch; pull, tug, tweak, wrench, *colloq.* yank. ● *v.* jiggle, jolt, lurch, start, twitch; pull, tug, tweak, wrench, *colloq.* yank.

jerkin *n.* sleeveless jacket.

jerrycan *n.* five-gallon can for petrol or water.

jersey *n.* (*pl.* **-eys**) 1 knitted woollen pullover. 2 machine-knitted fabric.

jest *n.* & *v.* joke.

jester *n.* 1 person who makes jokes. 2 entertainer at a medieval court.

jet¹ *n.* 1 hard black mineral. 2 glossy black. □ **jet-black** *adj.*

jet² *n.* 1 stream of water, gas, or flame from a small opening. 2 burner on a gas cooker. 3 engine or aircraft using jet propulsion. ● *v.* (**jetted**) travel by jet. □ **jet lag** delayed tiredness etc. after a long flight. **jet-propelled** *adj.* using jet propulsion. **jet propulsion**, propulsion by engines that send out a high-speed jet of gases at the back.

jetsam *n.* goods jettisoned by a ship and washed ashore.

jettison *v.* 1 throw overboard, eject. 2 discard.

jetty *n.* 1 breakwater. 2 landing-stage.

Jew *n.* person of Hebrew descent or whose religion is Judaism. □ **Jewish** *adj.*

jewel *n.* 1 precious stone cut or set as an ornament. 2 person or thing that is highly valued. □ **jewelled** *adj.*

■ 1 brilliant, gem, precious stone, stone. 2 gem, marvel, treasure.

jeweller *n.* person who makes or deals in jewels or jewellery.

jewellery *n.* jewels or similar ornaments to be worn.

Jewry *n.* the Jewish people.

jib *n.* 1 triangular sail set forward from a mast. 2 projecting arm of a crane. ● *v.* (**jibbed**) refuse to proceed. □ **jib at** object to.

jig *n.* 1 lively dance. 2 device that holds work and guides tools working on it. 3 template. ● *v.* (**jigged**) move quickly up and down.

jiggery-pokery *n.* (*colloq.*) trickery.

jiggle *v.* rock or jerk lightly.

jigsaw *n.* machine fretsaw. □ **jigsaw puzzle** picture cut into pieces which are then shuffled and reassembled for amusement.

jilt *v.* abandon (a lover).

■ abandon, desert, *sl.* ditch, drop, leave (in the lurch), walk out on.

jingle *v.* (cause to) make a ringing or clinking sound. ● *n.* 1 this sound. 2 simple rhyme.

■ *n.* 1 chink, clink, jangle, ring, tinkle. 2 ditty, rhyme, song, tune.

jingoism *n.* excessive patriotism and contempt for other countries. □ **jingoist** *n.*, **jingoistic** *adj.*

jinx *n.* (*colloq.*) influence causing bad luck.

jitters *n.pl.* (*colloq.*) nervousness. □ **jittery** *adj.*

jive n. **1** fast lively jazz. **2** dance to this. ● v. dance to this music.

job n. **1** piece of work. **2** paid position of employment. **3** function or responsibility. **4** (colloq.) difficult task. □ **good** or **bad job** fortunate or unfortunate state of affairs. **job lot** miscellaneous articles sold together.

■ **1** assignment, chore, piece of work, project, task, undertaking. **2** appointment, employment, occupation, position, post, situation; career, profession, trade. **3** duty, function, responsibility, role.

jobbing adj. doing single pieces of work for payment.

jobless adj. out of work.

jockey n. (pl. **-eys**) person who rides in horse races. ● v. manoeuvre to gain advantage.

jocose adj. jocular.

jocular adj. **1** fond of joking. **2** humorous. □ **jocularly** adv., **jocularity** n.

jocund adj. merry, cheerful.

jodhpurs n.pl. riding-breeches fitting closely below the knee.

jog v. (**jogged**) **1** nudge. **2** stimulate. **3** run at a slow regular pace. ● n. **1** slow run. **2** nudge. □ **jogger** n.

■ v. **1** elbow, knock, nudge, poke, prod, push. **2** prompt, refresh, stimulate, stir. **3** lope, run, trot.

joggle v. shake slightly. ● n. slight shake.

jogtrot n. slow regular trot.

joie de vivre /zhwáa də véevrə/ exuberant enjoyment of life.

join v. **1** unite. **2** come into the company of. **3** become a member of. **4** take one's place in. ● n. place where things join. □ **join forces** combine efforts. **join in** take part. **join up** enlist for military service.

■ v. **1** attach, combine, connect, couple, fasten, fuse, link, marry, merge, splice, tie, unify, unite, wed, yoke. **2** accompany, go with. **3** become a member of, enlist in, enrol in, enter. **4** ally oneself with, associate oneself with, team up with. ● n. connection, intersection, joint, junction, juncture. □ **join forces** club together, collaborate, cooperate, team up.

joiner n. maker of wooden doors, windows, etc. □ **joinery** n.

joint adj. shared by two or more people. ● n. **1** join. **2** structure where parts or bones fit together. **3** large piece of meat. ● v. **1** connect by joint(s). **2** divide into

joints. □ **out of joint 1** dislocated. **2** in disorder. **jointly** adv.

■ adj. collaborative, collective, combined, common, communal, colloq. mutual, shared.

jointure n. estate settled on a widow for her lifetime.

joist n. one of the beams supporting a floor or ceiling.

jojoba /hōhṓbə/ n. plant producing seeds containing oil used in cosmetics.

joke n. **1** thing said or done to cause laughter. **2** ridiculous person or thing. ● v. make jokes.

■ n. **1** colloq. crack, gag, jest, pun, quip, colloq. wisecrack, witticism; hoax, jape, lark, practical joke, prank, trick. ● v. banter, jest; fool about, colloq. kid, tease.

joker n. **1** person who jokes. **2** extra playing card in a pack.

jollification n. merrymaking.

jollity n. **1** being jolly. **2** merrymaking.

jolly adj. (**-ier, -iest**) **1** cheerful, merry. **2** very pleasant. ● adv. (colloq.) very. ● v. **jolly along** keep in good humour.

■ adj. **1** buoyant, cheerful, cheery, chirpy, happy, gay, glad, gleeful, high-spirited, jocular, jovial, joyful, merry, sunny.

jolt v. **1** shake or dislodge with a jerk. **2** move jerkily. **3** shock. ● n. **1** jolting movement. **2** shock.

■ v. **1** bump, jerk, jog, joggle, knock, rock, shake. **2** bounce, bump, jerk, judder, lurch. **3** disturb, perturb, shake, shock, startle, unnerve, unsettle, upset. ● n. **1** bang, bump, jerk, judder, knock, lurch. **2** blow, bombshell, shock, start, surprise.

jonquil n. a kind of narcissus.

joss-stick n. thin stick that burns with a smell of incense.

jostle v. push roughly.

■ elbow, hustle, push, shoulder, shove, thrust.

jot n. very small amount. ● v. (**jotted**) write down briefly.

jotter n. notepad, notebook.

joule n. unit of energy.

journal n. **1** daily record of events. **2** newspaper, periodical.

■ **1** chronicle, diary, log, record. **2** daily, gazette, magazine, monthly, newspaper, paper, periodical, quarterly, derog. rag, weekly.

journalese n. style of language used in inferior journalism.

journalist *n.* person employed in writing for a newspaper or magazine. □ **journalism** *n.*

■ columnist, correspondent, hack, reporter.

journey *n.* (*pl.* **-eys**) act of going from one place to another. ● *v.* make a journey.

■ *n.* crossing, excursion, expedition, jaunt, odyssey, outing, passage, pilgrimage, tour, trek, trip, voyage. ● *v.* go, make a trip, tour, travel, voyage.

joust *v.* & *n.* fight on horseback with lances.

jovial *adj.* merry, cheerful. □ **jovially** *adv.*, **joviality** *n.*

jowl *n.* **1** jaw, cheek. **2** dewlap, loose skin on the throat.

joy *n.* **1** deep feeling of pleasure. **2** thing causing delight.

■ **1** delight, ecstasy, elation, euphoria, exhilaration, exultation, gratification, happiness, jubilation, pleasure, rapture. **2** delight, pleasure, treat.

joyful *adj.* full of joy. □ **joyfully** *adv.*, **joyfulness** *n.*

■ cheerful, ecstatic, elated, euphoric, exhilarated, exultant, gay, glad, gleeful, happy, joyous, jubilant, merry, overjoyed, pleased, rapturous, thrilled.

joyous *adj.* joyful. □ **joyously** *adv.*

joyride *n.* (*colloq.*) ride for pleasure, esp. in a stolen car. □ **joyriding** *n.*

joystick *n.* **1** aircraft's control lever. **2** device for moving a cursor on a VDU screen.

jubilant *adj.* rejoicing, joyful. □ **jubilantly** *adv.*, **jubilation** *n.*

jubilee *n.* special anniversary.

Judaic *adj.* Jewish.

Judaism *n.* religion of the Jewish people.

judder *v.* shake noisily or violently. ● *n.* this movement.

judge *n.* **1** public officer appointed to hear and try legal cases. **2** person appointed to decide a dispute etc. **3** person able to give an authoritative opinion. ● *v.* **1** try a legal case. **2** act as judge of. **3** form an opinion about. **4** consider.

■ *n.* **1** *sl.* beak, justice, magistrate. **2** ajudicator, arbiter, arbitrator, assessor, examiner, mediator, referee, umpire. **3** authority, connoisseur, expert, pundit, specialist. ● *v.* **1** adjudge, adjudicate, try. **2** adjudicate, arbitrate, referee, umpire. **3** appraise, assess, estimate, evaluate, gauge, rate, weigh (up). **4** believe, consider, deem, hold, regard, think.

judgement *n.* (in law contexts **judgment**) **1** discernment, good sense. **2** opinion or estimate. **3** judge's decision. □ **Judgement Day** day on which God will judge humankind. **judgemental** *adj.*

■ **1** acumen, discernment, discrimination, good sense, insight, intelligence, judiciousness, perception, perceptiveness, sagacity, understanding, wisdom, wit. **2** belief, conviction, feeling, opinion, view; appraisal, assessment, estimate, estimation, evaluation. **3** decision, finding, ruling, verdict.

judicial *adj.* **1** of the administration of justice. **2** of a judge or judgement. □ **judicially** *adv.*

judiciary *n.* the whole body of judges in a country.

judicious *adj.* judging wisely, showing good sense. □ **judiciously** *adv.*, **judiciousness** *n.*

■ astute, canny, careful, diplomatic, discerning, discreet, intelligent, logical, perceptive, percipient, perspicacious, prudent, sagacious, sensible, shrewd, sound, tactful, wise.

judo *n.* Japanese system of unarmed combat. □ **judoist** *n.*

jug *n.* vessel with a handle and a shaped lip, for holding and pouring liquids. □ **jugful** *n.*

juggernaut *n.* **1** large heavy lorry. **2** overwhelming force or object.

juggle *v.* **1** toss and catch objects skilfully for entertainment. **2** manipulate skilfully. □ **juggler** *n.*

jugular vein either of the two large veins in the neck.

juice *n.* **1** fluid content of fruits, vegetables, or meat. **2** fluid secreted by an organ of the body. □ **juicy** *adj.*

ju-jitsu *n.* Japanese system of unarmed combat.

jukebox *n.* coin-operated record player.

julep *n.* drink of spirits and water flavoured esp. with mint.

jumble *v.* mix in a confused way. ● *n.* **1** jumbled articles. **2** items for a jumble sale. □ **jumble sale** sale of second-hand articles, esp. to raise money for charity.

■ *v.* confuse, disarrange, disorder, disorganize, mess up, mix (up), muddle, scramble, shuffle. ● *n.* clutter, confusion, disarray, disorder, hotchpotch, mêlée, mess, muddle, tangle.

jumbo *n.* (*pl.* **-os**) very large thing. □ **jumbo jet** large jet aircraft.

jump v. **1** move up off the ground etc. by muscular movement of the legs. **2** move suddenly. **3** rise suddenly. **4** pass over by jumping. **5** pounce on. **6** leave (rails or track) accidentally. ● n. **1** jumping movement. **2** sudden rise or change. **3** gap in a series. **4** obstacle to be jumped. □ **jump-lead** n. cable for conveying current from one battery to another. **jump suit** one-piece garment for the whole body. **jump the gun** start prematurely. **jump the queue** take unfair precedence.

■ v. **1,2** bound, hop, leap, skip, spring, vault. **3** escalate, go up, increase, rise, rocket, shoot up. **4** clear, leap-frog, leap (over), vault (over). **5** attack, mug, pounce on, take unawares. ● n. **1** bound, hop, leap, skip, spring, vault. **2** escalation, increase, rise, surge, upsurge. **3** break, hiatus, interval, space. **4** fence, hurdle, obstacle.

jumper n. knitted pullover.

jumpy adj. (**-ier**, **-iest**) nervous.
■ agitated, anxious, edgy, fidgety, fretful, ill at ease, colloq. jittery, keyed up, nervous, nervy, overwrought, restless, tense, uneasy, colloq. uptight.

junction n. **1** join. **2** place where roads or railway lines unite.
■ **1** connection, join, union. **2** crossroads, interchange, intersection.

juncture n. point of time, convergence of events.

jungle n. **1** tropical forest with tangled vegetation. **2** scene of ruthless struggle.

junior adj. **1** younger in age. **2** lower in rank or authority. **3** for younger children. ● n. junior person.

juniper n. evergreen shrub with dark berries.

junk¹ n. useless or discarded articles, rubbish. □ **junk food** food with low nutritional value.

junk² n. flat-bottomed ship with sails, used in China seas.

junket n. sweet custard-like food made of milk and rennet.

junkie n. (sl.) drug addict.

junta n. group taking power after a coup d'état.

jurisdiction n. authority to administer justice or exercise power.
■ authority, control, dominion, influence, power, rule, sovereignty.

jurist n. person skilled in law.

juror n. member of a jury.

jury n. group of people sworn to give a verdict on a case in a court of law.

just adj. **1** fair to all concerned. **2** right in amount etc., deserved. ● adv. **1** exactly. **2** by only a short amount etc. **3** only a moment ago. **4** merely. **5** positively. □ **just now** a very short time ago. **justly** adv.

■ adj. **1** disinterested, dispassionate, equitable, ethical, fair, impartial, honest, honourable, moral, objective, principled, unbiased, unprejudiced, upright. **2** appropriate, apt, correct, deserved, due, fitting, justified, legitimate, merited, proper, reasonable, rightful, suitable. ● adv. **1** exactly, precisely. **2** barely, scarcely. **3** just now, not long ago, recently. **4** but, merely, only. **5** absolutely, altogether, positively, thoroughly, utterly.

justice n. **1** just treatment, fairness. **2** legal proceedings. **3** judge.
■ **1** equity, fairness, impartiality, objectivity, right, rightfulness.

justifiable adj. able to be justified. □ **justifiably** adv.
■ defensible, excusable, just, legitimate, reasonable, sound, tenable, valid, well-founded.

justify v. **1** show to be right or reasonable. **2** be sufficient reason for. **3** adjust (a line of type) to fill a space neatly. □ **justification** n.
■ **1** defend, legitimize, substantiate, validate, vindicate, warrant. **2** account for, excuse, explain.

jut v. (**jutted**) project.

jute n. fibre from the bark of certain tropical plants.

juvenile adj. **1** youthful. **2** childish. **3** for young people. ● n. young person. □ **juvenility** n.
■ adj. **1** adolescent, boyish, girlish, teenage(d), under age, young, youthful. **2** callow, childish, immature, infantile, naive, puerile, unsophisticated. ● n. adolescent, boy, child, girl, minor, teenager, youngster, youth.

juxtapose v. put (things) side by side. □ **juxtaposition** n.

Kk

kale *n.* cabbage with curly leaves.

kaleidoscope *n.* toy tube containing mirrors and coloured fragments reflected to produce changing patterns. □ **kaleidoscopic** *adj.*

kamikaze /kámmikaázi/ *n.* (in the Second World War) Japanese explosive-laden aircraft deliberately crashed on its target.

kangaroo *n.* Australian marsupial with strong hind legs for jumping. □ **kangaroo court** illegal court held by strikers etc.

kaolin *n.* fine white clay used in porcelain and medicine.

kapok *n.* fluffy fibre used for padding things.

karate /kəraáti/ *n.* Japanese system of unarmed combat.

karma *n.* (in Buddhism & Hinduism) person's actions as affecting his or her next reincarnation.

kayak /kíak/ *n.* small covered canoe.

kc/s *abbr.* kilocycle(s) per second.

kebabs *n.pl.* small pieces of meat cooked on a skewer.

kedge *n.* small anchor. ● *v.* move by hauling on a kedge.

kedgeree *n.* cooked dish of rice and fish or eggs.

keel *n.* timber or steel structure along the base of a ship. ● *v.* **1** overturn. **2** become tilted.

keen *adj.* **1** eager, ardent. **2** penetrating. **3** sharp. **4** very cold. **5** intense. □ **keen on** liking greatly. **keenly** *adv.*, **keenness** *n.*

■ **1** ardent, avid, dedicated, devoted, eager, enthusiastic, fervent, fervid, passionate, zealous. **2** acute, astute, clever, discerning, discriminating, intelligent, penetrating, perceptive, percipient, perspicacious, sharp. **3** sharp, sharpened. **4** biting, bitter, chilling, chilly, icy, piercing. **5** acute, extreme, excruciating, fierce, intense; deep, heartfelt, profound, strong. □ **keen on** devoted to, enamoured of, enthusiastic about, fond of, interested in.

keep *v.* (**kept**) **1** retain possession of, have charge of. **2** remain or cause to remain in a specified state or position. **3** detain. **4** observe or respect (a law, secret, etc.). **5** provide with food and other necessities. **6** own and look after (animals). **7** manage (a shop etc.). **8** continue doing something. **9** stock (goods for sale). **10** remain in good condition. **11** put aside for a future time. ● *n.* **1** person's food and other necessities. **2** strongly fortified structure in a castle. □ **keep house** look after a house or household. **keep up 1** progress at the same pace as others. **2** continue. **3** maintain.

■ *v.* **1** conserve, have, hold, maintain, preserve, retain, save; accumulate, amass, hoard, put by; look after, mind, protect, safeguard, take care of, take charge of, tend. **2** remain, stay. **3** delay, detain, hold up, slow up. **4** abide by, comply with, follow, obey, observe, stick to; fulfil, honour, respect; celebrate, commemorate. **5** feed, maintain, nourish, nurture, provide for, support, sustain. **6** look after, own, raise, rear. **7** be responsible for, manage, run. **8** carry on, continue, go on, persevere in, persist in. **9** carry, sell, stock. **10** last, stay fresh.

keeper *n.* person who keeps or looks after something, custodian.

■ caretaker, curator, custodian, guardian, warden; guard, jailer, warder.

keeping *n.* custody, charge. □ **in** or **out of keeping with** suited or unsuited to.

■ care, charge, custody, guardianship, protection, safe-keeping.

keepsake *n.* memento, esp. of a person.

keg *n.* small barrel. □ **keg beer** beer in a pressurized metal keg.

kelp *n.* large brown seaweed.

kelvin *n.* degree of the **Kelvin scale** of temperature which has zero at absolute zero (−273.15°C).

kendo *n.* Japanese sport of fencing with bamboo swords.

kennel *n.* **1** shelter for a dog. **2** (*pl.*) boarding place for dogs.

kept *see* **keep**.

kerb *n.* stone edging to a pavement.

kerfuffle *n.* (*colloq.*) fuss, commotion.

kermes *n.* insect used in making a red dye.

kernel n. **1** seed within a husk, nut, or fruit stone. **2** central or important part.
■ **1** nut, pip, seed, stone. **2** centre, core, essence, heart, nub, nucleus, pith.

kerosene n. paraffin oil.

kestrel n. a kind of small falcon.

ketch n. two-masted sailing boat.

ketchup n. thick sauce made from tomatoes and vinegar.

kettle n. container with a spout and handle, for boiling water in.

kettledrum n. large bowl-shaped drum.

Kevlar n. [P.] synthetic fibre used to reinforce rubber etc.

key n. **1** piece of metal shaped for moving the bolt of a lock, tightening a spring, etc. **2** thing giving access or control or insight. **3** system of related notes in music. **4** lever for a finger to press on a piano, typewriter, etc. ● adj. important, essential. □ **keyed up** tense, excited.
■ adj. central, chief, crucial, essential, important, leading, main, necessary, principal, vital.

keyboard n. set of keys on a piano, typewriter, or computer. ● v. enter (data) by using a keyboard. □ **keyboarder** n.

keyhole n. hole by which a key is put into a lock.

keynote n. **1** note on which a key in music is based. **2** prevailing tone.

keypad n. small keyboard or set of buttons for operating an electronic device, telephone, etc.

keyring n. ring on which keys are threaded.

keystone n. central stone of an arch.

keyword n. key to a cipher etc.

kg abbr. kilogram(s).

khaki adj. & n. dull brownish-yellow, colour of military uniforms.

kHz abbr. kilohertz.

kibbutz n. (pl. **-im**) communal settlement in Israel.

kick v. **1** strike or propel with the foot. **2** (of a gun) recoil when fired. ● n. **1** kicking action or blow. **2** (colloq.) thrill, interest. □ **kick-off** n. start of a football game. **kick out** (colloq.) expel or dismiss forcibly. **kick-start** n. lever pressed with the foot to start a motor cycle. **kick up** (colloq.) create (a fuss or noise).

kid n. **1** young goat. **2** (colloq.) child. ● v. (kidded) (colloq.) hoax, tease.

kidnap v. (kidnapped) carry off (a person) illegally in order to obtain a ransom. □ **kidnapper** n.
■ abduct, capture, carry off, make off with, seize, snatch.

kidney n. (pl. **-eys**) either of a pair of organs that remove waste products from the blood and secrete urine. □ **kidney bean** kidney-shaped bean.

kill v. **1** cause the death of. **2** put an end to. **3** spend (time) unprofitably when waiting. ● n. **1** killing. **2** animal(s) killed by a hunter. □ **killer** n.
■ v. **1** assassinate, butcher, dispatch, do away with, sl. do in, execute, colloq. finish off, liquidate, massacre, murder, put to death, slaughter, slay; destroy, put down. **2** bring to an end, dash, destroy, end, eradicate, extinguish, put an end to, ruin, scotch, shatter. **3** fritter away, idle away, pass, spend, squander, waste, while away.

killjoy n. person who spoils the enjoyment of others.

kiln n. oven for hardening or drying things (e.g. pottery, hops).

kilo n. (pl. **-os**) kilogram.

kilo- pref. one thousand.

kilocycle n. kilohertz.

kilogram n. unit of weight or mass in the metric system (2.205 lb).

kilohertz n. 1000 hertz.

kilometre n. 1000 metres (0.62 mile).

kilovolt n. 1000 volts.

kilowatt n. 1000 watts.

kilt n. knee-length pleated skirt of tartan wool, esp. as part of Highland man's dress.

kimono n. (pl. **-os**) **1** loose Japanese robe worn with a sash. **2** dressing gown resembling this.

kin n. person's relatives.
■ family, folks, kindred, kinsfolk, kinsmen, kinswomen, kith and kin, relations, relatives.

kind¹ n. class of similar things. □ **in kind** (of payment) in goods etc. instead of money.
■ brand, category, class, genre, genus, make, sort, species, type, variety.

kind² adj. gentle and considerate towards others. □ **kind-hearted** adj., **kindness** n.
■ accommodating, altruistic, benevolent, benign, caring, charitable, compassionate, considerate, decent, forbearing, forgiving, generous, gentle, good-natured, gracious, helpful, humane, indulgent, kind-hearted, kindly, lenient, magnanimous, merciful,

neighbourly, obliging, sympathetic, thoughtful, tolerant, understanding, unselfish, warm-hearted.

kindergarten *n.* school for very young children.

kindle *v.* **1** set on fire. **2** arouse, stimulate. **3** become kindled.

■ **1** fire, ignite, light, set alight, set fire to, set on fire. **2** arouse, excite, foment, incite, inflame, instigate, rouse, stimulate, stir (up), whip up. **3** burst into flames, catch fire, ignite.

kindling *n.* small pieces of wood for lighting fires.

kindly *adj.* (-**ier**, -**iest**) kind. ● *adv.* **1** in a kind way. **2** please.

kindred *n.* kin. ● *adj.* **1** related. **2** of similar kind.

kinetic *adj.* of movement.

king *n.* **1** male ruler of a country by right of birth. **2** man or thing regarded as supreme. **3** chess piece to be protected. **4** playing card next above queen. □ **king-size(d)** *adj.* extra large. **kingly** *adj.*, **kingship** *n.*

kingdom *n.* **1** country ruled by a king or queen. **2** division of the natural world.

kingfisher *n.* small bird that dives to catch fish.

kingpin *n.* indispensable person or thing.

kink *n.* **1** short twist in thread or wire etc. **2** mental peculiarity. ● *v.* form or cause to form kink(s).

■ *n.* **1** bend, coil, corkscrew, curl, knot, tangle, twist. **2** eccentricity, foible, idiosyncrasy, quirk.

kinky *adj.* **1** having kinks. **2** eccentric. **3** (*colloq.*) deviant.

kinsfolk *n.pl.* kin. □ **kinsman** *n.*, **kinswoman** *n.*

kiosk *n.* booth where newspapers or refreshments are sold, or containing a public telephone.

kipper *n.* smoked herring.

kirk *n.* (*Sc.*) church.

kirsch /keersh/ *n.* colourless liqueur made from wild cherries.

kismet *n.* destiny, fate.

kiss *n.* & *v.* touch or caress with the lips.

kissogram *n.* novelty greetings message delivered with a kiss.

kit *n.* **1** set of clothing, tools, etc. **2** set of parts to be assembled. ● *v.* (**kitted**) equip with kit.

■ *n.* **1** clothes, outfit, *colloq.* rig-out, uniform; accoutrements, apparatus, equipment, gear, implements, instruments, paraphernalia, stuff, supplies, tackle, things, tools, trappings, utensils.

kitbag *n.* bag for holding kit.

kitchen *n.* room where meals are prepared. □ **kitchen garden** vegetable garden.

kitchenette *n.* small kitchen.

kite *n.* **1** large bird of prey. **2** light framework flown on a long string in the wind.

kith *n.* **kith and kin** relatives.

kitsch /kich/ *n.* art perceived as being of poor quality, esp. when garish or sentimental.

kitten *n.* young of cat, rabbit, or ferret. □ **kittenish** *adj.*

kitty *n.* communal fund.

kiwi *n.* (*pl.* -**is**) flightless New Zealand bird.

kleptomania *n.* compulsive desire to steal. □ **kleptomaniac** *n.*

km *abbr.* kilometre(s).

knack *n.* ability to do something skilfully.

■ ability, aptitude, bent, flair, genius, gift, instinct, skill, talent.

knacker *n.* person who buys and slaughters usu. old horses etc. ● *v.* (*sl.*) exhaust.

knapsack *n.* bag worn strapped on the back.

knave *n.* **1** rogue. **2** jack in playing cards.

knead *v.* **1** press and stretch (dough) with the hands. **2** massage with similar movements.

knee *n.* **1** joint between the thigh and the lower part of the leg. **2** part of a garment covering this. ● *v.* (**kneed**) touch or strike with the knee. □ **knee-jerk** *adj.* (of a reaction) automatic and predictable. **knees-up** *n.* (*colloq.*) lively party.

kneecap *n.* small bone over the front of the knee. ● *v.* (**kneecapped**) shoot in the knee as a punishment.

kneel *v.* (**knelt**) lower one's body to rest on the knees.

knell *n.* sound of a bell tolled after a death or at a funeral.

knelt *see* **kneel**.

knew *see* **know**.

knickerbockers *n.pl.* loose breeches gathered in at the knee.

knickers *n.pl.* woman's or girl's undergarment for the lower body.

knick-knack *n.* small ornament.

■ bauble, gewgaw, ornament, trinket.

knife n. (pl. **knives**) cutting instrument with a sharp blade and a handle. ● v. cut or stab with a knife.

knight n. **1** man given a rank below baronet, with the title 'Sir'. **2** chess piece shaped like horse's head. ● v. confer a knighthood on.

knighthood n. rank of knight.

knit v. (**knitted** or **knit**) **1** form (yarn) into fabric of interlocking loops. **2** make in this way. **3** grow together so as to unite. □ **knitter** n., **knitting** n.

knob n. **1** rounded projecting part, esp. as a handle. **2** small lump. □ **knobbly** adj.
  ■ **1** dial, handle, switch. **2** boss, bump, knot, lump, node, protrusion, protuberance, stud.

knock v. **1** strike with an audible sharp blow. **2** strike a door to gain admittance. **3** drive or make by knocking. **4** (sl.) criticize insultingly. ● n. **1** act or sound of knocking. **2** sharp blow. □ **knock about 1** treat roughly. **2** wander casually. **knock-down** adj. (of price) very low. **knock-kneed** adj. having an abnormal inward curvature of the legs at the knees (**knock knees**). **knock off 1** (colloq.) cease work. **2** (colloq.) complete quickly. **3** (sl.) steal. **knock-on effect** secondary or cumulative effect. **knockout** n. **1** knocking a person out. **2** (colloq.) outstanding or irresistible person or thing. **knock out 1** make unconscious. **2** eliminate. **knock up 1** rouse by knocking at a door. **2** make or arrange hastily. **knock-up** n. practice or casual game at tennis etc.
  ■ v. **1** bang, bash, hammer, hit, pound, rap, old use smite, strike, tap, thump. ● n. **1** rap, tap, thump. **2** blow, colloq. clip, clout, cuff, rap, smack.

knocker n. hinged flap for rapping on a door.

knoll n. hillock, mound.

knot n. **1** intertwining of one or more pieces of thread or rope etc. as a fastening. **2** tangle. **3** hard mass esp. where a branch joins a tree trunk. **4** round spot in timber. **5** cluster. **6** unit of speed used by ships and aircraft, = one nautical mile per hour. ● v. (**knotted**) **1** tie or fasten with a knot. **2** entangle.
  ■ n. **2** snarl, tangle. **3** knob, lump, node, nodule, protuberance. **5** bunch, clump, cluster, collection, crowd, gathering, group, throng. ● v. **1** attach, bind, fasten, lash,

secure, tie. **2** entangle, entwine, snarl, twist.

knotty adj. (**-ier, -iest**) **1** full of knots. **2** puzzling, difficult.
  ■ **1** gnarled, knotted, lumpy, nodular; ravelled, tangled, twisted. **2** baffling, complex, complicated, difficult, perplexing, puzzling.

know v. (**knew, known**) **1** have in one's mind or memory. **2** feel certain. **3** recognize, be familiar with. **4** understand. □ **in the know** (colloq.) having inside information. **know-how** n. practical knowledge or skill.
  ■ **1** be familiar with, comprehend, grasp, understand. **3** recall, recognize, recollect, remember; be acquainted with, be a friend of, be friendly with. **4** be aware of, realize, understand. □ **know-how** ability, capability, experience, expertise, knowledge, proficiency, skill.

knowing adj. **1** aware. **2** cunning. □ **knowingly** adv.
  ■ **1** astute, aware, clever, intelligent, knowledgeable, perceptive, sagacious, shrewd, wise. **2** artful, canny, crafty, cunning, sly, wily.

knowledge n. **1** knowing about things. **2** information. **3** all a person knows. **4** all that is known.
  ■ **1** awareness, cognition, comprehension, consciousness, familiarity, grasp, insight, know-how, understanding; experience, expertise, proficiency. **2** data, facts, information, intelligence.

knowledgeable adj. **1** intelligent. **2** well-informed.
  ■ **1** erudite, intelligent, learned, sagacious, well-educated, well-read, wise. **2** aware, enlightened, colloq. in the know, up to date, well-informed.

knuckle n. **1** finger-joint. **2** animal's leg-joint as meat. ● v. **knuckle under** yield, submit.

knuckleduster n. metal device worn over the knuckles to increase the effect of a blow.

koala n. (in full **koala bear**) Australian tree-climbing animal with thick grey fur.

kohl n. black powder used as eye make-up.

kohlrabi n. cabbage with a turnip-like edible stem.

kookaburra n. Australian giant kingfisher with a harsh cry.

kopeck *n.* Russian coin, one-hundredth of a rouble.

Koran *n.* Islamic sacred book.

kosher *adj.* conforming to Jewish dietary laws.

kowtow *v.* behave with exaggerated respect.

k.p.h. *abbr.* kilometres per hour.

krill *n.* tiny plankton crustaceans that are food for whales etc.

kudos *n.* honour and glory.

kudu *n.* African antelope.

kummel /koõmm'l/ *n.* liqueur flavoured with caraway seeds.

kumquat *n.* tiny variety of orange.

kung fu Chinese form of unarmed combat similar to karate.

Kurd *n.* member of a people of SW Asia. □ **Kurdish** *adj.*

kV *abbr.* kilovolt(s).

kW *abbr.* kilowatt(s).

l *abbr.* litre(s).

lab *n.* (*colloq.*) laboratory.

label *n.* note fixed on or beside an object to show its nature, destination, etc. ● *v.* (**labelled**) **1** fix a label to. **2** describe as.
■ *n.* docket, mark, marker, sticker, tab, tag, ticket. ● *v.* **1** docket, mark, tag, ticket. **2** brand, call, classify as, characterize as, describe as, designate, dub, name.

labial *adj.* of the lips.

laboratory *n.* room or building equipped for scientific work.

laborious *adj.* needing or showing much effort. □ **laboriously** *adv.*
■ arduous, demanding, difficult, exhausting, gruelling, hard, herculean, onerous, strenuous, taxing, tiring; forced, laboured, ponderous, strained.

labour *n.* **1** work, exertion. **2** workers. **3** contractions of the womb at childbirth. ● *v.* **1** work hard. **2** emphasize lengthily.
■ *n.* **1** donkey work, drudgery, effort, exertion, *sl.* graft, grind, industry, slog, toil, work. **2** employees, labourers, workers, workforce. ● *v.* **1** beaver (away), drudge, *sl.* graft, *colloq.* plug (away), slave (away), slog (away), strive, struggle, sweat, toil, work. **2** dwell on, harp on, overdo, overemphasize.

laboured *adj.* showing signs of great effort, not spontaneous.

labourer *n.* person employed to do unskilled work.

Labrador *n.* dog of the retriever breed with a black or golden coat.

laburnum *n.* tree with hanging clusters of yellow flowers.

labyrinth *n.* maze. □ **labyrinthine** *adj.*

lace *n.* **1** ornamental openwork fabric or trimming. **2** cord etc. threaded through holes or hooks to pull opposite edges together. ● *v.* **1** fasten with lace(s). **2** intertwine. **3** add a dash of spirits to (drink).
■ *n.* **1** filigree, net, netting, openwork. **2** cord, shoelace, shoestring, string, thong. ● *v.* **1** do up, fasten, knot, tie (up). **2** intertwine, string, thread, weave. **3** flavour, fortify, *colloq.* spike, strengthen.

lacerate *v.* **1** tear (flesh). **2** wound (feelings). □ **laceration** *n.*
■ **1** cut, gash, mangle, rip, slash, tear, wound.

lachrymose *adj.* tearful.

lack *n.* state or fact of not having something. ● *v.* be without.
■ *n.* absence, dearth, deficiency, insufficiency, need, paucity, scarcity, shortage, want. ● *v.* be deficient in, be short of, be without, need, want.

lackadaisical *adj.* lacking vigour, unenthusiastic.
■ apathetic, casual, cool, half-hearted, indifferent, indolent, languid, languorous, lazy, lethargic, listless, lukewarm, sluggish, unenthusiastic, uninterested.

lackey *n.* (*pl.* **-eys**) **1** footman, servant. **2** servile follower.

lacking *adj.* **1** undesirably absent. **2** without.

lacklustre *adj.* lacking brightness or enthusiasm.
■ bland, boring, colourless, dreary, dull, flat, insipid, prosaic, tedious, unimaginative, uninspired, uninteresting, vapid, wishy-washy.

laconic *adj.* terse. □ **laconically** *adv.*
■ brief, concise, pithy, short, succinct, terse, to the point.

lacquer *n.* hard glossy varnish. ● *v.* coat with lacquer.

lactation *n.* **1** suckling. **2** secretion of milk.

lacy *adj.* (**-ier, -iest**) of or like lace.

lad *n.* boy, young fellow.

ladder *n.* **1** set of crossbars between uprights, used as a means of climbing. **2** vertical ladder-like flaw where stitches become undone in a stocking etc. ● *v.* cause or develop a ladder (in).

laden *adj.* loaded.

ladle *n.* deep long-handled spoon for transferring liquids. ● *v.* transfer with a ladle.

lady *n.* **1** woman, esp. of good social position. **2** well-mannered woman. **3** (**Lady**) title of wives, widows, or daughters of certain noblemen.

ladybird *n.* small flying beetle, usu. red with black spots.

ladylike *adj.* polite and appropriate to a lady.

ladyship *n.* title used of or to a woman with rank of *Lady*.

lag¹ *v.* (**lagged**) go too slow, not keep up. ● *n.* lagging, delay.
■ *v.* dally, dawdle, *colloq.* dilly-dally, hang back, linger, straggle, trail.

lag² *v.* (**lagged**) encase in material that prevents loss of heat.

lager *n.* light beer. □ **lager lout** (*colloq.*) youth who behaves badly after drinking too much.

laggard *n.* person who lags behind.

lagging *n.* material used to lag a boiler etc.

lagoon *n.* **1** salt-water lake beside a sea. **2** freshwater lake beside a river or larger lake.

laid *see* **lay²**.

lain *see* **lie²**.

lair *n.* wild animal's resting-place.
■ burrow, covert, den, nest, sett, tunnel.

laird *n.* (*Sc.*) landowner.

laissez-faire /léssayfáir/ *n.* policy of non-interference.

laity *n.* laymen.

lake¹ *n.* large body of water surrounded by land.

lake² *n.* reddish pigment.

lam *v.* (**lammed**) (*sl.*) hit hard.

lama *n.* Buddhist priest in Tibet and Mongolia.

lamb *n.* **1** young sheep. **2** its flesh as food. **3** gentle or endearing person. ● *v.* give birth to a lamb.

lambaste *v.* (*colloq.*) **1** thrash. **2** reprimand severely.

lame *adj.* **1** unable to walk normally. **2** weak, unconvincing. ● *v.* make lame. □ **lame duck** helpless person etc. **lamely** *adv.*, **lameness** *n.*
■ *adj.* **1** crippled, disabled, game, *sl.* gammy, handicapped, incapacitated. **2** feeble, flimsy, inadequate, poor, thin, unconvincing, unsatisfactory, weak.

lamé /laamay/ *n.* fabric with gold or silver thread interwoven.

lament *n.* **1** passionate expression of grief. **2** song or poem expressing grief. ● *v.* feel or express grief or regret. □ **lamentation** *n.*
■ *n.* **1** lamentation, moan, moaning, wail, wailing. **2** dirge, elegy, requiem. ● *v.*

grieve, moan, mourn, sorrow, wail, weep; bemoan, regret, rue.

lamentable *adj.* regrettable, deplorable. □ **lamentably** *adv.*
■ awful, deplorable, dreadful, pitiful, regrettable, sad, terrible, unfortunate, wretched.

laminate *n.* laminated material.

laminated *adj.* made of layers joined one upon another.

lamp *n.* device for giving light.

lamplight *n.* light from a lamp.

lampoon *n.* piece of writing that attacks a person by ridiculing him. ● *v.* ridicule in a lampoon.
■ *n.* burlesque, caricature, parody, satire, take-off. ● *v.* burlesque, caricature, make fun of, parody, ridicule, satirize, send up, take off.

lamppost *n.* tall post of a street lamp.

lamprey *n.* (*pl.* **-eys**) small eel-like water animal.

lampshade *n.* shade placed over a lamp to screen its light.

lance *n.* long spear. ● *v.* prick or cut open with a lancet. □ **lance-corporal** *n.* army rank below corporal.

lanceolate *adj.* tapering to each end like a spearhead.

lancet *n.* **1** surgeon's pointed two-edged knife. **2** tall narrow pointed arch or window.

land *n.* **1** part of earth's surface not covered by water. **2** expanse of this. **3** ground, soil. **4** country, state. **5** (*pl.*) estates. ● *v.* **1** set or go ashore. **2** come or bring to the ground. **3** bring to or reach a place or situation. **4** deal (a person) a blow. **5** bring (a fish) to land. **6** obtain (a prize, appointment, etc.). □ **landlocked** *adj.* surrounded by land.
■ *n.* **1** earth, ground, terra firma. **2** country, terrain. **3** dirt, earth, loam, sod, soil, turf. **4** country, fatherland, homeland, motherland, nation, native land, state, territory. **5** (**lands**) estates, grounds, property. ● *v.* **1** berth, dock, disembark, go ashore. **2** alight, arrive, come to rest, settle, touch down. **4** administer, deal, give. **5** catch, hook, net. **6** gain, get, obtain, procure, secure, win.

landau /lándaw/ *n.* a kind of horse-drawn carriage.

landed *adj.* **1** owning land. **2** consisting of land.

landfall *n.* approach to land after a journey by sea or air.

landfill n. **1** waste material etc. used in landscaping or reclaiming ground. **2** use of this.

landing n. **1** coming or bringing ashore or to ground. **2** place for this. **3** level area at the top of a flight of stairs. □ **landing-stage** n. platform for landing from a boat.

■ **1** arrival, disembarkation, touchdown. **2** dock, jetty, landing-stage, pier, quay, wharf.

landlord, landlady ns. **1** person who lets land or a house or room to a tenant. **2** person who keeps an inn or boarding house.

■ **1** lessor, owner, proprietor. **2** host, hotelier, innkeeper, manager, proprietor, publican.

landlubber n. person unfamiliar with the sea and ships.

landmark n. **1** conspicuous feature of a landscape. **2** event marking a stage in a thing's history.

landscape n. **1** scenery of a land area. **2** picture of this. ● v. lay out (an area) attractively with natural-looking features.

landslide n. **1** landslip. **2** overwhelming majority of votes.

landslip n. sliding down of a mass of land on a slope.

landward adj. & adv. towards the land. □ **landwards** adv.

lane n. **1** narrow road, track, or passage. **2** strip of road for a single line of traffic. **3** track to which ships or aircraft etc. must keep.

■ **1** alley, footpath, passage, passageway, path, road, track.

language n. **1** words and their use. **2** system of this used by a nation or group.

■ **1** diction, speech, talk, words. **2** dialect, idiom, jargon, parlance, patois, slang, tongue, vernacular.

languid adj. lacking vigour or vitality. □ **languidly** adv.

■ apathetic, half-hearted, indolent, inert, lackadaisical, languorous, lazy, lethargic, listless, sluggish, torpid, unenthusiastic.

languish v. lose or lack vitality. □ **languish under** live under (miserable conditions).

■ decline, droop, fade, flag, waste away, wilt.

languor n. **1** state of being languid. **2** tender mood or effect. □ **languorous** adj.

lank adj. **1** tall and lean. **2** straight and limp. □ **lanky** adj.

■ **1** lanky, lean, scrawny, skinny, spindly, tall, thin. **2** limp, straggling, straight.

lanolin n. fat extracted from sheep's wool, used in ointments.

lantern n. transparent case for holding and shielding a light.

lanyard n. **1** short rope for securing things on a ship. **2** cord for hanging a whistle etc. round the neck or shoulder.

lap¹ n. **1** flat area over the thighs of a seated person. **2** single circuit. **3** section of a journey. ● v. (**lapped**) wrap round. **2** be lap(s) ahead of (a competitor). □ **lapdog** n. small pampered dog.

lap² v. (**lapped**) **1** take up (liquid) by movements of tongue. **2** flow (against) with ripples.

lapel n. flap folded back at the front of a coat etc.

lapidary adj. of stones.

lapis lazuli blue semiprecious stone.

Lapp n. native or language of Lapland.

lapse n. **1** pass gradually into a worse state or condition. **2** become void or no longer valid. ● n. **1** slight error. **2** lapsing. **3** passage of time.

■ v. **1** decline, degenerate, deteriorate, sink. **2** expire, run out, terminate. ● n. **1** blunder, error, mistake, omission, oversight, slip, colloq. slip-up. **2** decline, degeneration, deterioration. **3** break, gap, interval, period, space.

laptop n. portable microcomputer.

lapwing n. kind of plover.

larch n. deciduous tree of the pine family.

lard n. white greasy substance prepared from pig-fat. ● v. put strips of fat bacon in or on (meat) before cooking.

larder n. storeroom for food.

large adj. of great size or extent. □ **at large 1** free to roam about. **2** in general. **largeness** n.

■ ample, big, broad, capacious, considerable, enormous, extensive, great, huge, immense, massive, roomy, sizeable, spacious, substantial, vast, voluminous; brawny, burly, heavy, hefty, stocky, strapping, thickset.

largely adv. to a great extent.

largesse n. (also **largess**) **1** money or gifts generously given. **2** generosity.

lariat n. lasso.

lark¹ n. small brown bird, skylark.

lark² n. **1** light-hearted adventurous action. **2** amusing incident. **3** type of activity. ● v. **lark about** play light-heartedly.

larkspur n. plant with spur-shaped blue or pink flowers.

larva n. (pl. **-vae**) insect in the first stage after coming out of the egg. □ **larval** adj.

laryngitis n. inflammation of the larynx.

larynx n. part of the throat containing the vocal cords. □ **laryngeal** adj.

lasagne /ləsányə/ n.pl. pasta in wide ribbon-like strips.

lascivious adj. lustful. □ **lasciviously** adv., **lasciviousness** n.

laser n. device emitting an intense narrow beam of light.

lash v. **1** move in a whip-like movement. **2** beat with a whip. **3** strike violently. **4** fasten with a cord etc. ● n. **1** flexible part of a whip. **2** stroke with this. **3** eyelash. □ **lash out** attack with blows or words. **2** spend lavishly.

■ v. **2** beat, sl. belt, birch, cane, flog, scourge, thrash, whip. **3** batter, buffet, beat, dash, pound, strike. **4** attach, bind, fasten, hitch, rope, secure, strap, tether, tie.

lashings n.pl. (colloq.) a lot.

lass n. (also **lassie**) (Sc. & N. Engl.) girl, young woman.

lassitude n. tiredness, languor.

lasso n. (pl. **-oes**) rope with a noose for catching cattle. ● v. (**lassoed**, **lassoing**) catch with a lasso.

last¹ n. foot-shaped block used in making and repairing shoes.

last² adj. & adv. **1** coming after all others. **2** most recent(ly). ● n. last person or thing. □ **at (long) last** after much delay. **last post** military bugle-call sounded at sunset or military funerals. **last straw** slight addition to difficulties, making them unbearable. **last word 1** final statement in a dispute. **2** latest fashion.

■ adj. **1** closing, concluding, final, terminal, ultimate; hindmost, rearmost.

last³ v. **1** continue, endure. **2** suffice for a period of time. □ **lasting** adj.

■ **1** carry on, continue, go on, endure, hold out, persist, remain, survive; keep, stay fresh. **2** do, serve, suffice.

lastly adv. finally.

latch n. **1** bar lifted from its catch by a lever, used to fasten a gate etc. **2** spring-lock that catches when a door is closed. ● v. fasten with a latch.

latchkey n. key of an outer door.

late adj. & adv. **1** after the proper or usual time. **2** far on in a day or night or period. **3** recent. **4** no longer living or holding a position. □ **of late** lately. **lateness** n.

■ adj. **1** belated, delayed, overdue, tardy, unpunctual. **4** dead, deceased, departed; erstwhile, ex-, former, past, sometime.

lately adv. recently.

latent adj. existing but not developed or visible. □ **latency** n.

■ concealed, dormant, hidden, potential, quiescent, undeveloped, unrevealed.

lateral adj. of, at, to, or from the side(s). □ **laterally** adv.

latex n. milky fluid from certain plants, esp. the rubber tree. **2** similar synthetic substance.

lath n. (pl. **laths**) narrow thin strip of wood, e.g. in trellis.

lathe n. machine for holding and turning pieces of wood or metal etc. while they are worked.

lather n. **1** froth from soap and water. **2** frothy sweat. ● v. cover with or form lather.

Latin n. language of the ancient Romans. ● adj. **1** of or in Latin. **2** speaking a language based on Latin. □ **Latin America** parts of Central and S. America where Spanish or Portuguese is the main language.

latitude n. **1** distance of a place from the equator, measured in degrees. **2** region. **3** freedom from restrictions.

■ **3** freedom, leeway, liberty, license, scope.

latrine n. lavatory in a camp or barracks.

latter adj. **1** mentioned after another. **2** nearer to the end. **3** recent. □ **latter-day** adj. modern, recent.

latterly adv. **1** recently. **2** nowadays.

lattice n. framework of crossed strips.

laud v. praise.

laudable adj. praiseworthy.

■ admirable, commendable, creditable, estimable, meritorious, praiseworthy.

laudanum n. opium prepared for use as a sedative.

laudatory adj. praising.

laugh v. make sounds and movements of the face that express amusement or scorn. ● n. **1** act or manner of laughing. **2** (colloq.) amusing incident. **laugh off** make light of (something embarrassing or humiliating). **laughing-stock** *n.* person or thing that is ridiculed.

■ *v. colloq.* be in stitches, cackle, chortle, chuckle, giggle, guffaw, hoot, snicker, snigger, titter. ● *n.* **1** cackle, chortle, chuckle, giggle, guffaw, hoot, snicker, snigger, titter. **2** joke, hoot, lark, *sl.* scream. □ **laugh at** deride, jeer (at), make fun of, mock, *colloq.* rib, ridicule, scoff at, taunt, tease.

laughable *adj.* ridiculous.

■ *absurd*, farcical, ludicrous, nonsensical, preposterous, ridiculous, risible.

laughter *n.* act or sound of laughing.

launch¹ *v.* **1** put or go into action. **2** cause (a ship) to slide into the water. **3** send forth (a weapon, rocket, etc.). ● *n.* process of launching something.

■ *v.* **1** begin, embark on, establish, inaugurate, initiate, institute, introduce, set up, start. **2** float, set afloat. **3** fire, hurl, project, propel, shoot, throw.

launch² *n.* large motor boat.

launder *v.* **1** wash and iron (clothes etc.). **2** (*colloq.*) transfer (funds) to conceal their origin.

launderette *n.* establishment fitted with washing machines to be used for a fee.

laundry *n.* **1** place where clothes etc. are laundered. **2** batch of clothes etc. sent to or from this.

laurel *n.* **1** evergreen shrub with smooth glossy leaves. **2** (*pl.*) victories or honours gained.

lava *n.* flowing or hardened molten rock from a volcano.

lavatory *n.* **1** fixture into which urine and faeces are discharged for disposal. **2** room equipped with this.

lavender *n.* **1** shrub with fragrant purple flowers. **2** light purple. □ **lavender-water** *n.* perfume made from lavender.

laver *n.* edible seaweed.

lavish *adj.* **1** generous. **2** abundant, plentiful. ● *v.* bestow lavishly. □ **lavishly** *adv.*

■ *adj.* **1** bountiful, free, generous, liberal, munificent, unstinting. **2** abundant, copious, plentiful, prolific, profuse. ● *v.* bestow, pour, rain, shower.

law *n.* **1** rule(s) established by authority or custom. **2** their observance or operation. **3** statement of what always happens in certain circumstances. □ **law-abiding** *adj.* obeying the law.

■ **1** act, decree, directive, edict, injunction, order, ordinance, precept, regulation, rule, statute. **2** equity, justice. **3** axiom, principle, theorem, theory. □ **law-abiding** decent, good, honest, honourable, obedient, orderly, peaceable, principled, upright, virtuous.

lawful *adj.* permitted or recognized by law. □ **lawfully** *adv.*, **lawfulness** *n.*

■ *allowable*, authorized, constitutional, legal, legitimate, permissible, proper, rightful, valid.

lawless *adj.* disregarding the law. □ **lawlessness** *n.*

lawn¹ *n.* fine woven cotton fabric.

lawn² *n.* area of closely cut grass. □ **lawnmower** *n.* machine for cutting the grass of lawns. **lawn tennis** (*see* **tennis**).

lawsuit *n.* process of bringing a problem or claim etc. before a court of law for settlement.

lawyer *n.* person trained and qualified in legal matters.

lax *adj.* slack, not strict or severe. □ **laxity** *n.*

■ *careless*, casual, hit-or-miss, lackadaisical, neglectful, negligent, remiss, slipshod, sloppy; easygoing, indulgent, lenient, liberal, permissive.

laxative *adj. & n.* (medicine) stimulating the bowels to empty.

lay¹ *adj.* **1** not ordained into the clergy. **2** non-professional.

lay² *v.* (**laid**) **1** place on a surface. **2** arrange ready for use. **3** cause to be in a certain position or state. **4** (of a hen) produce (an egg or eggs). ● *n.* way a thing lies. □ **lay about one** hit out on all sides. **lay bare** expose, reveal. **lay into** (*colloq.*) **1** thrash. **2** scold harshly. **lay off 1** discharge (workers) temporarily. **2** (*colloq.*) cease. **lay-off** *n.* temporary discharge. **lay on** provide. **lay out 1** arrange. **2** prepare (a body) for burial. **3** spend (money) for a purpose. **4** knock unconscious. **lay up 1** store. **2** cause (a person) to be ill. **lay to rest** bury in a grave. **lay waste** devastate (an area).

■ *v.* **1** deposit, park, place, put (down), set (down). **2** arrange, prepare, set. **3** fit, put in place. □ **lay bare** disclose, divulge, expose, make known, reveal, show, uncover, unmask, unveil. **lay off 1** discharge, dismiss, fire, make redundant, *colloq.* sack. **lay on** furnish, give, provide, supply. **lay out 1** arrange, array, display, spread out. **2** expend, invest, spend. **3** floor, knock out, prostrate. **lay up 1** hoard, put by, save, set aside, stockpile, store. **lay waste** destroy, devastate, ravage, wreak havoc on, wreck.

lay³ see **lie².**

layabout n. loafer, one who lazily avoids working for a living.

lay-by n. place beside a road where vehicles may stop.

layer n. **1** one thickness of material laid over a surface. **2** attached shoot fastened down to take root. **3** hen that lays eggs. ● v. **1** arrange in layers. **2** propagate (a plant) by layers.
  ■ n. **1** coat, coating, covering, film, sheet, skin, thickness.

layette n. clothes etc. for a newborn baby.

lay figure artist's jointed model of the human body.

layout n. arrangement of parts etc. according to a plan.

layperson n. non-professional person.

laze v. spend time idly. ● n. act or period of lazing.
  ■ v. do nothing, idle, loaf, lounge, loll.

lazy adj. (**-ier, -iest**) **1** unwilling to work, doing little work. **2** showing little energy. □ **lazybones** n. (colloq.) lazy person. **lazily** adv., **laziness** n.
  ■ **1** idle, shiftless, slothful. **2** inactive, indolent, lackadaisical, languid, languorous, lethargic, listless, sluggish, torpid.

lb abbr. pound(s) weight.

lea n. (poetic) piece of meadow etc.

leach v. **1** percolate (liquid) through soil etc. **2** remove (soluble matter) or be removed in this way.

lead¹ /leed/ v. (**led**) **1** guide. **2** influence into an action, opinion, or state. **3** be a route or means of access. **4** pass (one's life). **5** be in first place or ahead. **6** be in charge of. ● n. **1** guidance. **2** clue. **3** leading place, amount by which one competitor is in front. **4** wire conveying electric current. **5** strap or cord for leading an animal. **6** chief role in a play etc. □ **lead to** have as a consequence, result in. **lead up to 1** serve as introduction to or preparation for. **2** direct conversation towards. **leading question** one worded to prompt the desired answer.
  ■ v. **1** accompany, conduct, convey, escort, guide, pilot, shepherd, show, steer, take, usher. **2** bring, cause, dispose, induce, influence, move, persuade, prompt. **3** extend, go, run. **4** have, live, pass, spend. **5** be ahead, be at the front, head. **6** be in charge of, command, control, direct, govern, head, manage, oversee, preside

over, superintend, supervise. ● n. **1** direction, guidance, leadership; example, model, pattern. **2** clue, hint, pointer, suggestion, tip-off. **3** first or leading place, front, pole position, van, vanguard; gap, margin. **4** cable, cord, flex, wire. **5** chain, cord, leash, rope, tether. □ **lead to** bring about, cause, create, engender, give rise to, produce, result in.

lead² /led/ n. **1** heavy grey metal. **2** graphite in a pencil. **3** lump of lead used for sounding depths. **4** (pl.) strips of lead.

leaden adj. **1** made of lead. **2** heavy, slow. **3** lead-coloured.

leader n. **1** one that leads. **2** newspaper article giving editorial opinions. □ **leadership** n.
  ■ **1** chief, commander, director, governor, head, manager, ruler, supremo; captain, skipper; guide, escort; pioneer, trail-blazer, trend-setter.

leaf n. **1** flat (usu. green) organ growing from the stem, branch, or root of a plant. **2** single thickness of paper as a page of a book. **3** very thin sheet of metal. **4** hinged flap or extra section of a table. ● v. **leaf through** turn over the leaves of (a book). □ **leaf-mould** n. soil consisting of decayed leaves. **leafy** adj.

leaflet n. **1** small leaf of a plant. **2** printed sheet of paper giving information. ● v. (**leafleted**) distribute leaflets to.
  ■ n. **2** booklet, brochure, circular, handbill, pamphlet.

league n. **1** union of people or countries. **2** class of contestants. **3** association of sports clubs which compete against each other. □ **in league** allied, conspiring.
  ■ **1** alliance, association, body, coalition, confederacy, confederation, federation, fellowship, group, guild, organization, society, union. **2** category, class, grade, level, rank. □ **in league** allied, collaborating, conspiring, in alliance, sl. in cahoots, in collusion.

leak n. **1** hole through which liquid or gas makes its way wrongly. **2** liquid etc. passing through this. **3** process of leaking. **4** similar escape of an electric charge. **5** disclosure of secret information. ● v. **1** escape or let out from a container. **2** disclose. □ **leak out** become known. **leakage** n., **leaky** adj.
  ■ n. aperture, chink, crack, crevice, fissure, hole, opening, perforation, puncture. **2,3** discharge, escape, leakage, outflow, seepage, spillage. **5** disclosure, revelation.

● *v.* **1** dribble, escape, flow, issue, pour, ooze, seep, stream, trickle. **2** disclose, divulge, impart, give away, make known, reveal, tell.

lean[1] *adj.* **1** without much flesh. **2** (of meat) with little or no fat. **3** scanty. ● *n.* lean part of meat. □ **leanness** *n.*

■ *adj.* **1** bony, lanky, rangy, scraggy, scrawny, skinny, slender, slim, thin. **3** inadequate, insufficient, meagre, poor, scant, scanty, sparse.

lean[2] *v.* (**leaned**, **leant**) **1** put or be in a sloping position. **2** rest for support against. □ **lean on 1** depend on for help. **2** (*colloq.*) influence by intimidating. **lean-to** *n.* shed etc. against the side of a building. **lean towards** have a tendency towards.

■ **1** bend, incline, slant, slope, tilt, tip. **2** lay, place, prop, put, rest; be propped *or* supported, lie. □ **lean on 1** be dependent on, count on, depend on, rely on.

leaning *n.* inclination, preference.

■ bent, bias, disposition, inclination, liking, partiality, penchant, predilection, predisposition, preference, prejudice, proclivity, propensity, tendency.

leap *v.* (**leaped**, **leapt**) jump vigorously. ● *n.* vigorous jump. □ **leap year** year with an extra day (29 Feb.).

■ *n. & v.* bound, hop, jump, skip, spring.

leap-frog *n.* game in which each player vaults over another who is bending down. ● *v.* (**-frogged**) **1** perform this vault (over). **2** overtake alternately.

learn *v.* (**learned** *or* **learnt**) **1** gain knowledge of or skill in. **2** become aware of. □ **learner** *n.*

■ **1** become proficient in, *colloq.* get the hang of, master, pick up; study, take lessons in. **2** ascertain, discover, find out, gather, hear, realize, see.

learned /lérnid/ *adj.* having or showing great learning.

■ academic, cultured, erudite, highbrow, intellectual, knowledgeable, scholarly, well-educated, well-read.

learning *n.* knowledge obtained by study.

■ education, erudition, knowledge, lore, scholarship, wisdom.

lease *n.* contract allowing the use of land or a building for a specified time. ● *v.* allow, obtain, or hold by lease. □ **leasehold** *n.*, **leaseholder** *n.*

leash *n.* dog's lead.

least *adj.* **1** smallest in amount or degree. **2** lowest in importance. ● *n.* least amount etc. ● *adv.* in the least degree.

leather *n.* **1** material made by treating animal skins. **2** piece of soft leather for polishing with. ● *v.* thrash. □ **leatherjacket** *n.* crane-fly grub with tough skin.

leathery *adj.* **1** like leather. **2** tough.

leave *v.* (**left**) **1** go away (from). **2** cease to live at, belong to, work for, etc. **3** deposit or entrust with. **4** abandon. **5** bequeath. **6** let remain. ● *n.* **1** permission. **2** official permission to be absent from duty, period for which this lasts. □ **on leave** absent in this way. **leave out** not insert or include.

■ *v.* **1** be on one's way, depart, *sl.* do a bunk, go, go away, move away, *sl.* push off, set off; decamp, pull out, retire, retreat, withdraw; abandon, evacuate, quit, vacate. **2** give up, *US* quit. **3** consign, deposit, entrust, place, put. **4** abandon, desert, *sl.* ditch, forsake, jilt, leave in the lurch, walk out on. **5** bequeath, hand down, will. ● *n.* **1** authorization, consent, dispensation, permission, sanction.

leaven *n.* **1** raising agent. **2** enlivening influence. ● *v.* **1** add leaven to. **2** enliven.

lecher *n.* lecherous man.

lecherous *adj.* lustful. □ **lechery** *n.*

lectern *n.* stand with a sloping top from which a bible etc. is read.

lecture *n.* **1** speech giving information about a subject. **2** lengthy reproof or warning. ● *v.* **1** give lecture(s). **2** reprove at length. □ **lecturer** *n.*

■ *n.* **1** address, discourse, harangue, speech, talk. **2** dressing down, scolding, talking-to, *colloq.* telling-off, *colloq.* ticking-off. ● *v.* **1** discourse, deliver a speech, speak, talk. **2** *colloq.* bawl out, berate, carpet, castigate, rebuke, remonstrate with, reprimand, reprove, scold, *colloq.* tell off, *colloq.* tick off, upbraid.

led *see* **lead**[1].

ledge *n.* narrow horizontal shelf or projection.

■ overhang, projection, ridge, shelf, sill.

ledger *n.* book in which accounts are kept.

lee *n.* **1** sheltered side. **2** shelter in this.

leech *n.* small blood-sucking worm.

leek *n.* plant related to the onion, with a long cylindrical white bulb.

leer *v.* look slyly, maliciously, or lustfully. ● *n.* leering look.

lees *n.pl.* sediment in wine.

leeward adj. & n. (on) the side away from the wind.

leeway n. degree of freedom of action.
■ freedom, latitude, room, scope, space.

left[1] see leave.

left[2] adj. & adv. of, on, or to the side or region opposite right. ● n. 1 left side or region. 2 left hand or foot. 3 people supporting a more extreme form of socialism than others in their group. □ **left-handed** adj. using the left hand.

leftovers n.pl. things remaining when the rest is finished.
■ leavings, remainders, remains, remnants, scraps.

leg n. 1 each of the limbs on which a person, animal, etc., stands or moves. 2 part of a garment covering a person's leg. 3 projecting support of piece of furniture. 4 one section of a journey or contest.

legacy n. thing left to someone in a will, or handed down by a predecessor.
■ bequest, heritage, inheritance, patrimony.

legal adj. 1 of or based on law. 2 authorized or required by law. □ **legally** adv., **legality** n.
■ 1 forensic, judicial. 2 above board, acceptable, admissible, authorized, lawful, legitimate, permissible, rightful, valid; constitutional, statutory.

legalize v. make legal. □ **legalization** n.
■ allow, authorize, legitimize, license, permit, sanction.

legate n. envoy.

legatee n. recipient of a legacy.

legation n. 1 diplomatic minister and staff. 2 their headquarters.

legend n. 1 story handed down from the past. 2 such stories collectively. 3 inscription, esp. on a coin or medal.
■ 1 epic, fable, folk-tale, myth, romance, saga. 2 folklore, myth, tradition.

legendary adj. 1 of or described in legend. 2 (colloq.) famous.
■ 1 epic, fabled, mythical, traditional; fabulous, fictional, fictitious, imaginary, fairytale.

legerdemain /léjərdəmáyn/ n. sleight of hand.

legible adj. clear enough to be deciphered, readable. □ **legibly** adv., **legibility** n.
■ clear, decipherable, easy to read, intelligible, readable.

legion n. 1 division of the ancient Roman army. 2 organized group. 3 multitude.

legionnaire n. member of a legion. □ **legionnaires' disease** form of bacterial pneumonia.

legislate v. make laws. □ **legislator** n.

legislation n. 1 legislating. 2 law(s) made.

legislative adj. making laws.

legislature n. country's legislative assembly.

legitimate adj. 1 in accordance with a law or rule. 2 justifiable. 3 born of parents married to each other. □ **legitimately** adv., **legitimacy** n.
■ 1 allowable, authorized, lawful, legal, permissible, rightful; authentic, bona fide, genuine, proper, real, true. 2 justifiable, logical, rational, reasonable, valid.

legitimize v. make legitimate. □ **legitimization** n.

legume n. 1 leguminous plant. 2 pod of this.

leguminous adj. of the family of plants bearing seeds in pods.

leisure n. time free from work. □ **at one's leisure** when one has time.

leisured adj. having plenty of leisure.

leisurely adj. & adv. without hurry.
■ adj. easy, easygoing, gentle, relaxed, slow, unhurried.

lemming n. mouse-like Arctic rodent (said to rush headlong into the sea and drown during migration).

lemon n. 1 oval fruit with acid juice. 2 tree bearing it. 3 pale yellow colour. 4 (colloq.) useless person or thing. □ **lemony** adj.

lemonade n. lemon-flavoured soft drink.

lemon sole a kind of plaice.

lemur n. nocturnal monkey-like animal of Madagascar.

lend v. (**lent**) 1 give or allow to use temporarily. 2 provide (money) temporarily in return for payment of interest. 3 contribute as a help or effect. □ **lend itself to** be suitable for. **lender** n.
■ 1 loan. 2 advance, loan. 3 add, bestow, confer, contribute, furnish, give, impart.

length n. 1 measurement or extent from end to end. 2 extent of time. 3 piece (of cloth etc.). □ **at length** after or taking a long time.

■ **1** distance, extent, size, span. **2** duration, period, stretch, time. □ **at length** at last, eventually, finally, in the end, ultimately; endlessly, interminably.

lengthen v. make or become longer.

■ elongate, extend; draw out, pad out, prolong, protract, spin out, stretch out.

lengthways adv. in the direction of a thing's length. **lengthwise** adv. & adj.

lengthy adj. (**-ier**, **-iest**) **1** very long. **2** long and boring. □ **lengthily** adv.

■ **1** extended, long, prolonged. **2** boring, dull, endless, interminable, long-winded, protracted, tedious.

lenient adj. merciful, not severe. □ **leniently** adv., **lenience** n.

■ charitable, compassionate, easygoing, forbearing, forgiving, generous, humane, indulgent, kind, kind-hearted, magnanimous, merciful, permissive, tolerant.

lens n. piece of glass or similar substance shaped for use in an optical instrument.

Lent n. Christian period of fasting and repentance before Easter.

lent see **lend**.

lentil n. a kind of bean.

leonine adj. of or like a lion.

leopard /léppərd/ n. large flesh-eating animal of the cat family, with a dark-spotted yellowish or a black coat.

leotard n. close-fitting garment worn by gymnasts, dancers, etc.

leper n. person with leprosy.

leprechaun n. (in Irish folklore) elf resembling a little old man.

leprosy n. contagious disease of the skin and nerves. □ **leprous** adj.

lesbian adj. & n. homosexual (woman). □ **lesbianism** n.

lesion n. harmful change in the tissue of an organ of the body.

less adj. **1** not so much of. **2** smaller in amount or degree. ● adv. to a smaller extent. ● n. smaller amount. ● prep. minus.

lessee n. person holding property by lease.

lessen v. make or become less.

■ allay, alleviate, assuage, deaden, dull, ease, relieve, soothe; abate, decrease, diminish, ebb, colloq. let up, moderate, subside, wane.

lesser adj. not so great as the other.

lesson n. **1** amount of teaching given at one time. **2** thing to be learnt. **3** experience by which one can learn. **4** passage from the Bible read aloud in church.

lessor n. person who lets property on lease.

lest conj. for fear that.

let v. (**let**, **letting**) **1** allow, enable, or cause to. **2** allow the use of (rooms or land) in return for payment. ● v.aux. used in requests, commands, assumptions, or challenges. ● n. letting of property etc. □ **let alone 1** refrain from interfering with or doing. **2** not to mention. **let down 1** let out air from (a tyre etc.). **2** fail to support, disappoint. **let-down** n. disappointment. **let in** allow to enter. **let off 1** fire or explode (a weapon etc.). **2** not punish or compel. **let on** (sl.) reveal a secret. **let out 1** allow to go out. **2** make looser. **let up** (colloq.) relax, become less intense.

■ v. **1** allow, authorize, give permission, permit, sanction. **2** hire (out), lease, rent (out), sublet. □ **let down 1** disappoint, disenchant, disillusion, dissatisfy, fail. **let off 1** discharge, fire; detonate, explode, set off. **2** exempt from, excuse (from), forgive, pardon, reprieve, spare. **let up** relax, slow down, take a break; abate, decrease, diminish, ease, lessen, moderate, subside.

lethal adj. causing death.

■ deadly, fatal, mortal.

lethargy n. extreme lack of energy or vitality. □ **lethargic** adj., **lethargically** adv.

■ apathy, fatigue, indolence, inertia, languidness, languor, lassitude, laziness, sloth, sluggishness, torpor, weariness.

letter n. **1** symbol representing a speech sound. **2** written message, usu. sent by post. **3** (pl.) literature. ● v. inscribe letters (on). □ **letter box 1** slit in a door, with a movable flap, through which letters are delivered. **2** postbox.

■ n. **1** character, rune, sign, symbol. **2** dispatch, epistle, line, message, note.

letterhead n. printed heading on stationery.

lettuce n. plant with broad crisp leaves used in salads.

leucocyte n. white blood cell.

leukaemia /lōōkeemia/ n. disease in which leucocytes multiply uncontrollably.

levee n. (US) **1** embankment against floods. **2** quay.

level adj. **1** horizontal. **2** without projections or hollows. **3** having equality with something else. **4** steady, uniform. ● *n.* **1** horizontal line or plane. **2** device for testing this. **3** measured height or value etc. **4** relative position. **5** level surface or area. ● *v.* **(levelled) 1** make or become level. **2** knock down (a building). **3** aim (a gun etc.). □ **level crossing** place where a road and railway cross at the same level. **level-headed** *adj.* sensible, calm. **level pegging** equality in score. **on the level** (*colloq.*) honest(ly).

■ *adj.* **1** flat, horizontal. **2** even, flat, flush, plane, smooth, straight, unbroken, uninterrupted. **3** even, flush, parallel; equal, equivalent, level-pegging, neck and neck, on a par, the same. **4** consistent, even, regular, stable, steady, unchanging, uniform, unvarying. ● *v.* **1** even (out or up), flatten (out), iron (out), smooth (out); equalize, make equal. **2** demolish, destroy, knock down, raze. **3** aim, direct, focus, point, train, turn. □ **level-headed** calm, collected, composed, cool, equable, imperturbable, rational, reasonable, sensible, *colloq.* unflappable.

lever *n.* **1** bar pivoted on a fixed point to lift something. **2** pivoted handle used to operate machinery. **3** means of power or influence. ● *v.* **1** use a lever. **2** lift by this.

leverage *n.* **1** action or power of a lever. **2** power, influence.

leveret /lévvərit/ *n.* young hare.

leviathan *n.* thing of enormous size and power.

levitate *v.* (cause to) rise and float in the air. □ **levitation** *n.*

levity *n.* humorous attitude.

levy *v.* impose (payment) or collect (an army etc.) by authority or force. ● *n.* **1** levying. **2** payment or (*pl.*) troops levied.

■ *v.* charge, demand, exact, impose, inflict; conscript, mobilize, raise.

lewd *adj.* **1** treating sexual matters vulgarly. **2** lascivious. □ **lewdly** *adv.*, **lewdness** *n.*

lexical *adj.* of words. □ **lexically** *adv.*

lexicography *n.* process of compiling a dictionary. □ **lexicographer** *n.*

lexicon *n.* dictionary.

liability *n.* **1** being liable. **2** troublesome person or thing. **3** (*pl.*) debts.

■ **1** accountability, responsibility; susceptibility, vulnerability. **2** burden, disadvantage, drawback, encumbrance, hindrance, impediment, millstone.

liable *adj.* **1** held responsible by law, legally obliged to pay a tax or penalty etc. **2** likely to do or suffer something.

■ **1** accountable, answerable, responsible. **2** apt, disposed, inclined, likely, prone; open, subject, susceptible, vulnerable.

liaise *v.* act as liaison.

liaison *n.* **1** communication and cooperation. **2** illicit sexual relationship.

■ **1** communication, connection, contact, cooperation, link, relationship. **2** affair, intrigue, relationship.

liana *n.* climbing plant of tropical forests.

liar *n.* person who tells lies.

libation *n.* drink-offering to a god.

libel *n.* **1** published false statement that damages a person's reputation. **2** act of publishing it. **3** false defamatory statement. ● *v.* **(libelled) 1** publish a libel against. **2** accuse falsely and maliciously. □ **libellous** *adj.*

■ *n.* **3** calumny, defamation, denigration, obloquy, slander, vilification. ● *v.* **2** abuse, calumniate, cast aspersions on, defame, denigrate, malign, slander, traduce, vilify.

liberal *adj.* **1** given or giving freely. **2** tolerant. □ **liberally** *adv.*, **liberality** *n.*

■ **1** abundant, ample, copious, plentiful, profuse; bountiful, generous, free, lavish, magnanimous, munificent, open-handed, unsparing, unstinting. **2** broad-minded, indulgent, lax, lenient, permissive, tolerant, unprejudiced.

liberalize *v.* make less strict. □ **liberalization** *n.*, **liberalizer** *n.*

liberate *v.* set free. □ **liberation** *n.*, **liberator** *n.*

■ deliver, emancipate, free, let go, (let) loose, release, rescue, set free.

libertine *n.* man who lives an irresponsible immoral life.

liberty *n.* freedom. □ **take liberties** behave with undue freedom or familiarity.

■ autonomy, freedom, independence, self-determination, sovereignty; emancipation, liberation; authority, latitude, licence, permission, power, privilege, right, scope.

librarian *n.* person in charge of or assisting in a library.

library *n.* **1** collection of books (or records, films, etc.) for consulting or borrowing. **2** room or building containing these.

lice *see* **louse**.

licence *n.* **1** official permit to own or do something. **2** permission. **3** disregard of rules etc.

> ■ **1** certificate, pass, permit, warrant. **2** authorization, authority, dispensation, entitlement, leave, liberty, permission, right.

license *v.* grant a licence to or for.

> ■ allow, authorize, empower, enable, entitle, permit, sanction.

licensee *n.* holder of a licence.

licentiate *n.* holder of a certificate of competence in a profession.

licentious *adj.* sexually immoral. □ **licentiousness** *n.*

> ■ debauched, decadent, depraved, dissipated, dissolute, immoral, lascivious, lecherous, lustful, wanton.

lichen /líkən/ *n.* dry-looking plant that grows on rocks etc.

lick *v.* **1** pass the tongue over. **2** (of waves or flame) touch lightly. **3** (*colloq.*) defeat. ● *n.* **1** act of licking. **2** slight application (of paint etc.). **3** (*colloq.*) fast pace.

lid *n.* **1** hinged or removable cover for a box, pot, etc. **2** eyelid.

lie[1] *n.* statement the speaker knows to be untrue. ● *v.* (**lied**, **lying**) tell lie(s).

> ■ *n.* falsehood, fib, untruth, *sl.* whopper. ● *v.* commit perjury, fib, perjure oneself, tell lies.

lie[2] *v.* (**lay**, **lain**, **lying**) **1** have or put one's body in a flat or resting position. **2** be at rest on something. **3** be in a specified state. **4** be situated. ● *n.* way a thing lies. □ **lie in** lie in bed late in the morning. **lie-in** *n.* **lie low** conceal oneself or one's intentions.

> ■ *v.* **1** be recumbent *or* prone *or* prostrate *or* supine, prostrate oneself, recline, sprawl, stretch out. **2** be supported, lean, rest. □ **lie low** go into hiding, hide, keep out of sight, *sl.* lie doggo.

lieu /lyoo/ *n.* **in lieu** instead.

lieutenant /lefténnənt/ *n.* **1** army officer next below captain. **2** naval officer next below lieutenant commander. **3** rank just below a specified officer. **4** chief assistant.

life *n.* (*pl.* **lives**) **1** animals' and plants' ability to function and grow, state of being alive. **2** period during which life lasts. **3** living things. **4** way of living. **5** liveliness. **6** biography. □ **life cycle** series of forms into which a living thing changes. **life-jacket** *n.* jacket of buoyant material to keep a person afloat. **life-size(d)** *adj.* of the same size as a real

person. **life-support** *adj.* (of equipment etc.) enabling the body to function in a hostile environment or in cases of physical failure.

> ■ **1** being, existence, sentience. **2** lifetime. **3** fauna, flora, living things, people. **4** existence, lifestyle, way of life. **5** animation, *colloq.* bounce, energy, enthusiasm, exuberance, go, liveliness, pep, spirit, verve, vigour, *colloq.* vim, vitality, vivacity, zest. **6** autobiography, biography, memoir.

lifebelt *n.* belt of buoyant material to keep a person afloat.

lifeboat *n.* **1** boat for rescuing people in danger on the sea. **2** ship's boat for emergency use.

lifebuoy *n.* buoyant device to keep a person afloat.

lifeguard *n.* expert swimmer employed to rescue bathers who are in danger.

lifeless *adj.* **1** without life. **2** unconscious. **3** lacking liveliness.

> ■ **1** dead, deceased; arid, barren, desert, desolate, empty, sterile, uninhabited, waste; inanimate. **2** comatose, insensible, out, unconscious. **3** boring, colourless, dull, flat, lacklustre, tedious, uninspiring, vapid, wooden.

lifelike *n.* closely resembling a real person or thing.

lifeline *n.* **1** rope used in rescue. **2** vital means of communication.

lifelong *adj.* for all one's life.

lifestyle *n.* way of life of a person or group.

lifetime *n.* duration of a person's life.

lift *v.* **1** raise. **2** rise. **3** remove (restrictions). **4** steal, plagiarize. ● *n.* **1** lifting. **2** apparatus for transporting people or goods from one level to another. **3** free ride in a motor vehicle. **4** feeling of elation. □ **lift-off** *n.* vertical take-off of a spacecraft etc.

> ■ *v.* **1** heave (up), hoist (up), pick up; boost, buoy up, elevate, raise, uplift. **2** disappear, disperse, dissipate, rise, vanish. **3** cancel, discontinue, end, put an end to, remove, rescind. **4** filch, *sl.* knock off, *sl.* nick, pilfer, *sl.* pinch, pocket, purloin, steal, *colloq.* swipe, thieve, *sl.* whip; copy, pirate, plagiarize.

ligament *n.* tough flexible tissue holding bones together.

ligature *n.* thing that ties something, esp. in surgical operations. ● *v.* tie with a ligature.

light¹ *n.* **1** a kind of radiation that stimulates sight. **2** brightness. **3** source of light, electric lamp. **4** flame or spark. **5** enlightenment. **6** aspect, way a thing appears to the mind. ● *adj.* **1** full of light, not in darkness. **2** pale. ● *v.* (**lit** or **lighted**) **1** set burning, begin to burn. **2** provide with light. ▫ **bring** or **come to light** reveal or be revealed. **light-pen** *n.* **1** light-emitting device for reading bar codes. **2** (also **light-gun**) device for passing information to a computer screen. **light up 1** put lights on at dusk. **2** brighten. **3** make or become animated. **4** begin to smoke a cigarette etc. **light year** distance light travels in one year.

■ *n.* **2** brightness, brilliance, gleam, glow, illumination, incandescence, luminosity, phosphorescence, radiance; daylight, lamplight, moonlight, sunlight. **3** beacon, candle, flashlight, lamp, lantern, taper, torch; headlamp, headlight. **4** flame, spark. **5** elucidation, enlightenment, illumination. **6** aspect, perspective. ● *adj.* **1** bright, illuminated, sunny, well-lit. **2** pale, pastel-coloured. ● *v.* **1** fire, ignite, set alight, set fire to. **2** brighten, cast light on, illuminate, illumine, irradiate, lighten.

light² *adj.* **1** not heavy, easy to lift, carry, or do. **2** of less than average weight, force, or intensity. **3** not profound or serious. **4** cheerful. **5** (of food, meals, etc.) easy to digest. ● *adv.* lightly, with little load. ● *v.* (**lit** or **lighted**) **light on** find accidentally. ▫ **light-fingered** *adj.* apt to steal. **light-headed** *adj.* **1** feeling faint. **2** delirious. **light-hearted** *adj.* cheerful. **light industry** that producing small or light articles. **make light of** treat as unimportant. **lightly** *adv.*, **lightness** *n.*

■ *adj.* **1** lightweight, portable; bearable, *colloq.* cushy, easy, manageable, undemanding. **2** delicate, faint, gentle, mild, slight, soft. **3** frivolous, lightweight, inconsequential, trivial. **4** cheerful, cheery, gay, glad, happy, merry, sunny. **5** digestible; modest, simple, small. ● *v.* chance on, come across, discover, encounter, find, happen on, hit on. ▫ **light-hearted** airy, carefree, cheerful, cheery, gay, glad, happy, in good spirits, jolly, joyful, merry, sunny, *colloq.* upbeat.

lighten¹ *v.* **1** shed light on. **2** make or become brighter.

■ brighten, cast or shed light on, illuminate, illumine, light up.

lighten² *v.* make or become less heavy.

■ alleviate, ease, lessen, reduce.

lighter¹ *n.* device for lighting cigarettes and cigars.

lighter² *n.* flat-bottomed boat for unloading ships.

lighthouse *n.* tower with a beacon light to warn or guide ships.

lighting *n.* **1** means of providing light. **2** the light itself.

lightning *n.* flash of bright light produced from cloud by natural electricity. ● *adj.* very quick.

lights *n.pl.* lungs of certain animals, used as animal food.

lightship *n.* moored ship with a light, serving as a lighthouse.

lightweight *adj.* not having great weight or influence. ● *n.* lightweight person.

lignite *n.* brown coal of woody texture.

like¹ *adj.* **1** having the qualities or appearance of. **2** characteristic of. ● *prep.* in the manner of, to the same degree as. ● *conj.* **1** (*colloq.*) as. **2** (*US*) as if. ● *adv.* (*colloq.*) likely. ● *n.* person or thing like another. ▫ **like-minded** *adj.* with similar tastes or opinions.

■ *adj.* **1** akin (to), analogous (to), comparable (to or with), equivalent (to), of a piece (with), similar (to). **2** characteristic of, typical of. ● *n.* counterpart, equal, equivalent, match, peer, twin.

like² *v.* **1** find pleasant or satisfactory. **2** be fond of. **3** choose to have, prefer. ● *n.pl.* things one likes or prefers.

■ *v.* **1** be keen on, be partial to, delight in, have a liking for, have a weakness for, enjoy, love. **2** be attracted to, be fond of, be keen on, have a soft spot for.

likeable *adj.* pleasant, easy to like.

■ agreeable, amiable, charming, endearing, friendly, genial, good-natured, nice, pleasant, pleasing, sympathetic, winning, winsome.

likelihood *n.* probability.

■ chance, likeliness, possibility, probability, prospect.

likely *adj.* (**-ier, -iest**) **1** such as may reasonably be expected to occur or be true. **2** seeming to be suitable or have a chance of success. ● *adv.* probably. ▫ **likeliness** *n.*

■ *adj.* **1** possible, probable; apt, disposed, liable, prone; believable, credible, feasible, plausible, reasonable. **2** appropriate, fit, fitting, promising, suitable.

liken v. point out the likeness of (one thing to another).
■ compare, correlate, equate, parallel.

likeness n. **1** being like. **2** portrait, representation.
■ **1** correspondence, resemblance, similarity, similitude. **2** copy, drawing, image, model, painting, picture, portrait, portrayal, representation, reproduction, sketch.

likewise adv. **1** also. **2** in the same way.

liking n. condition of being fond of a person or thing.
■ affection, fancy, fondness, inclination, love, partiality, penchant, predilection, preference, proclivity, propensity, soft spot, taste, weakness.

lilac n. **1** shrub with fragrant purple or white flowers. **2** pale purple. ● adj. pale purple.

lilt n. **1** light rhythm. **2** song with this. □ **lilting** adj.

lily n. plant growing from a bulb, with large flowers.

limb n. **1** projecting part of a person's or animal's body, used in movement or in grasping things. **2** large branch of a tree.

limber v. **limber up** exercise in preparation for athletic activity.

limbo[1] n. intermediate inactive or neglected state.

limbo[2] n. (pl. **-os**) W. Indian dance in which the dancer bends back to pass under a bar.

lime[1] n. white substance used in making cement etc.

lime[2] n. **1** round yellowish-green fruit like a lemon. **2** its colour.

lime[3] n. tree with heart-shaped leaves.

limelight n. great publicity.

limerick n. a type of humorous poem with five lines.

limestone n. a kind of rock from which lime is obtained.

limit n. **1** point beyond which something does not continue. **2** greatest amount allowed. ● v. set or serve as a limit, keep within limits. □ **limitation** n.
■ n. **1** border, boundary, edge, frontier, perimeter, periphery; end, extent, limitation. ● v. check, curb, restrain, restrict; confine, delimit.

limousine n. large luxurious car.

limp[1] v. walk or proceed lamely. ● n. limping walk.

limp[2] adj. **1** not stiff or firm. **2** wilting. □ **limply** adv., **limpness** n.
■ **1** drooping, droopy, flaccid, floppy, loose, slack. **2** enervated, fatigued, spent, tired, weary, wilting, worn-out.

limpet n. small shellfish that sticks tightly to rocks.

limpid adj. (of liquids) clear. □ **limpidly** adv., **limpidity** n.

linchpin n. **1** pin passed through the end of an axle to secure a wheel. **2** person or thing vital to something.

linctus n. soothing cough mixture.

linden n. lime tree.

line[1] n. **1** long narrow mark. **2** furrow, wrinkle. **3** boundary. **4** row of people or things. **5** brief letter. **6** series, several generations of a family. **7** course or manner of procedure, conduct, etc. **8** type of activity, business, or goods. **9** piece of cord for a particular purpose. **10** row of words. **11** (pl.) words of an actor's part. **12** service of ships, buses, or aircraft. **13** railway track. **14** electrical or telephone cable, connection by this. **15** each of a set of military fieldworks. **16** (**the Line**) the equator. ● v. **1** mark with lines. **2** form a line along.
■ n. **1** diagonal, slash, stroke. **2** crease, crinkle, furrow, groove, wrinkle. **3** contour, outline, profile, silhouette. **4** border, borderline, boundary, edge, frontier, limit, perimeter. **5** column, file, procession, queue, rank, row, train; band, bar, belt, strip, stripe. **6** card, letter, note, postcard. **7** series, succession; ancestry, descent, family, house, lineage, parentage, stock. **8** approach, course (of action), path, policy, procedure, strategy, tack, tactic, way. **9** area, department, field, province, speciality; business, job, profession, work; brand, kind, make, type, variety. **10** cable, cord, rope, string, wire. ● v. **1** crease, furrow, wrinkle. **2** border, edge, fringe.

line[2] v. cover the inside surface of. □ **line one's pockets** make money, esp. in underhand ways.

lineage n. line of ancestors or descendants.
■ ancestry, descent, extraction, family, genealogy, line, parentage, pedigree, stock.

lineal adj. of or in a line.

linear adj. **1** of a line, of length. **2** arranged in a line.

linen n. **1** cloth made of flax. **2** articles (e.g. sheets, tablecloths) formerly made of this.

liner¹ n. passenger ship or aircraft of a regular line.

liner² n. removable lining.

linesman n. **1** umpire's assistant at the boundary line. **2** workman who maintains railway, electrical, or telephone lines.

ling¹ n. a kind of heather.

ling² n. sea fish of north Europe.

linger v. **1** be slow or reluctant to depart. **2** dawdle.

■ **1** hang about, sl. hang on, hover, loiter, remain, stay behind, wait. **2** dally, dawdle, colloq. dilly-dally, pause.

lingerie /lánzhəri/ n. women's underwear.

lingua franca language used among people whose native languages are different.

lingual adj. **1** of the tongue. **2** of speech or languages.

linguist n. person who is skilled in languages or linguistics.

linguistic adj. of language. □ **linguistically** adv.

linguistics n. study of language.

liniment n. embrocation.

lining n. material used to cover a surface.

link n. **1** each ring of a chain. **2** person or thing connecting others. **3** means of connection. ● v. **1** connect. **2** intertwine (hands etc.). □ **linkage** n.

■ n. **3** association, connection, linkage, relation, relationship. ● v. **1** attach, connect, fasten, join, tie, unite. **2** clasp, intertwine.

linnet n. a kind of finch.

lino n. linoleum.

linocut n. **1** design cut in relief on a block of linoleum. **2** print made from this.

linoleum n. a kind of smooth covering for floors.

linseed n. seed of flax.

lint n. **1** soft fabric for dressing wounds. **2** fluff.

lintel n. horizontal timber or stone over a doorway etc.

lion n. large flesh-eating animal of the cat family. □ **lion's share** largest part.

lionize v. treat as a celebrity.

lip n. **1** either of the fleshy edges of the opening of the mouth. **2** edge of a container or opening. **3** slight projection shaped for pouring from. □ **lip-read** v.

understand what is said from movements of a speaker's lips.

lipsalve n. ointment for the lips.

lipstick n. cosmetic for colouring the lips.

liquefy v. make or become liquid. □ **liquefaction** n.

liqueur /likyóor/ n. strong sweet alcoholic spirit.

liquid n. flowing substance like water or oil. ● adj. **1** in the form of liquid. **2** (of assets) easy to convert into cash. □ **liquidity** n.

■ n. fluid, juice, liquor, sap, solution. ● adj. **1** aqueous, fluid, liquefied, molten, runny, watery.

liquidate v. **1** pay (a debt). **2** close down (a business) and divide its assets between creditors. **3** get rid of, esp. by killing. □ **liquidation** n., **liquidator** n.

liquidize v. reduce to liquid.

liquidizer n. machine for making purées etc.

liquor n. **1** alcoholic drink. **2** juice from cooked food.

liquorice n. **1** black substance used in medicine and as a sweet. **2** plant from whose root it is made.

lira n. (pl. **lire**) unit of money in Italy and Turkey.

lisp n. speech defect in which s and z are pronounced like th. ● v. speak or utter with a lisp.

lissom adj. lithe.

list¹ n. written or printed series of names, items, figures, etc. ● v. **1** make a list of. **2** enter in a list.

■ n. catalogue, directory, index, inventory, register, roll, roster, rota, schedule. ● v. **1** catalogue, index, itemize. **2** enter, log, note, record, register.

list² v. (of a ship) lean over to one side. ● n. listing position.

■ v. careen, heel, incline, keel, lean (over), lurch, slant, tilt, tip.

listen v. **1** make an effort to hear. **2** pay attention. □ **listen in 1** eavesdrop. **2** listen to a broadcast. **listen to** take notice of, be persuaded by advice etc. **listener** n.

■ **1** hark. **2** attend, pay attention. □ **listen to** be mindful of, heed, mark, mind, note, take notice of.

listless adj. without energy or enthusiasm. □ **listlessly** adv., **listlessness** n.

■ apathetic, drained, enervated, exhausted, lackadaisical, languid, lethargic, lifeless, sluggish, tired, torpid, unenthusiastic, weary.

lit see **light**[1], **light**[2].

litany n. a set form of prayer.

literacy n. being literate.

literal adj. taking the primary meaning of a word or words, not a metaphorical or exaggerated one. □ **literally** adv.

literary adj. of literature.

literate adj. able to read and write.

literature n. writings, esp. great novels, poetry, and plays.

lithe adj. supple, agile.
■ agile, athletic, flexible, graceful, lissom, supple, willowy.

litho adj. & n. lithographic (process).

lithograph n. picture printed by lithography.

lithography n. printing from a design on a smooth surface. □ **lithographic** adj.

litigant adj. & n. (person) involved in or initiating a lawsuit.

litigate v. 1 carry on a lawsuit. 2 contest in law.

litigious adj. fond of litigation.

litmus n. substance turned red by acids and blue by alkalis. □ **litmus paper** paper stained with this.

litre n. metric unit of capacity (about 1¾ pints).

litter n. 1 rubbish left lying about. 2 young animals born at one birth. 3 material used as bedding for animals or to absorb their excrement. ● v. 1 scatter as litter. 2 make untidy by litter. 3 give birth to (a litter).
■ n. 1 garbage, junk, refuse, rubbish, trash. 2 brood. ● v. 1 scatter, spread, strew, throw. 2 clutter (up), mess up.

little adj. 1 small in size or amount etc. ● n. small amount, time, or distance. ● adv. 1 to a small extent. 2 not at all.
■ adj. 1 diminutive, mini-, miniature, minuscule, petite, short, slight, small, colloq. teeny, tiny, Sc. wee. 2 inconsequential, insignificant, minor, petty, negligible, trifling, trivial, unimportant. ● n. bit, dash, drop, hint, modicum, piece, pinch, scrap, spot, taste, trace, touch; minute, moment, second, while. ● adv. 1 barely, hardly, scarcely.

littoral adj. & n. (region) of or by the shore.

liturgy n. set form of public worship. □ **liturgical** adj.

live[1] /lɪv/ adj. 1 alive. 2 burning. 3 unexploded. 4 charged with electricity. 5 (of broadcasts) transmitted while actually happening. □ **live wire** energetic forceful person.
■ 1 alive, animate, living. 2 burning, flaming, glowing, hot, smouldering.

live[2] /lɪv/ v. 1 have life, remain alive. 2 have one's home. 3 pass, spend. 4 conduct (one's life) in a certain way. 5 enjoy life fully. □ **live down** live until (scandal etc.) is forgotten. **live on** keep oneself alive on. **live through** survive. **live with** 1 share a home with. 2 tolerate.
■ 1 be alive, exist; endure, keep going, last, stay alive, subsist, survive, sustain oneself. 2 dwell, lodge, reside, stay. 3 have, lead, pass, spend. □ **live through** endure, experience, go through, survive, weather, withstand.

livelihood n. 1 means of living. 2 job, income.

lively adj. (-ier, -iest) full of energy or action. □ **liveliness** n.
■ active, animated, colloq. bouncy, bubbly, buoyant, chirpy, ebullient, energetic, exuberant, frisky, full of life, high-spirited, irrepressible, perky, playful, skittish, spirited, sprightly, spry, vibrant, vivacious; brisk, fast, quick, rapid, snappy, swift; busy, bustling, crowded, hectic.

liven v. make or become lively.

liver n. 1 large organ in the abdomen, secreting bile. 2 animal's liver as food.

liveried adj. wearing livery.

livery n. distinctive uniform worn by male servants.

livestock n. farm animals.

livid adj. 1 bluish-grey. 2 (colloq.) furiously angry.

living adj. 1 having life, not dead. 2 currently in use. ● n. 1 manner of life. 2 livelihood. □ **living room** room for general daytime use.

lizard n. reptile with four legs and a long tail.

llama n. S. American animal related to the camel.

load n. 1 thing or quantity carried. 2 burden of responsibility or worry. 3 (pl., colloq.) plenty. 4 amount of electric current supplied. ● v. 1 put a load in or on. 2 receive a load. 3 weight. 4 put ammunition into (a gun) or film into (a camera). 5 put (data etc.) into (a computer).
■ n. 1 cargo, consignment, freight, shipment. 2 burden, cross, millstone, onus,

responsibility, weight, worry. ● v. **1** cram, fill, pack, stuff; heap, pile, stack. **3** burden, encumber, overload, lumber, saddle, weigh down, weight.

loaf[1] n. (pl. **loaves**) **1** mass of baked bread. **2** (sl.) head.

loaf[2] v. spend time idly.

loam n. rich soil. □ **loamy** adj.

loan n. **1** lending. **2** thing lent, esp. money. ● v. grant a loan of.

loath adj. unwilling.
■ disinclined, reluctant, unwilling.

loathe v. hate, detest. □ **loathing** n., **loathsome** adj.
■ abhor, abominate, despise, detest, execrate, hate, shudder at. □ **loathing** abhorrence, antipathy, detestation, disgust, hatred, odium, repugnance, revulsion. **loathsome** abhorrent, abominable, contemptible, despicable, detestable, disgusting, execrable, hateful, nasty, odious, repellent, repugnant, repulsive, revolting, sickening, vile.

lob v. (**lobbed**) send or strike (a ball) slowly in a high arc. ● n. lobbed ball.

lobar adj. of a lobe, esp. of the lung.

lobby n. **1** porch, entrance hall, anteroom. **2** group of people seeking to influence legislation. ● v. seek to persuade (an MP etc.) to support one's cause.

lobbyist n. person who lobbies an MP etc.

lobe n. **1** rounded part or projection. **2** lower soft part of the ear.

lobelia n. garden plant.

lobster n. **1** shellfish with large claws. **2** its flesh as food.

local adj. of or affecting a particular place or small area. ● n. **1** inhabitant of a particular district. **2** (colloq.) nearby pub. □ **local government** administration of a district by representatives elected locally. **locally** adv.
■ adj. endemic, indigenous, native; municipal, regional, provincial; nearby, neighbouring. ● n. denizen, native, national, resident, townsman, townswoman.

locality n. **1** thing's position. **2** district or neighbourhood.
■ **1** location, place, position, whereabouts. **2** area, district, environs, neighbourhood, region, vicinity.

localize v. **1** confine within an area. **2** decentralize.

locate v. **1** discover the position of. **2** situate in a particular location.
■ **1** ascertain, determine, detect, discover, find out, identify, pinpoint, track down. **2** place, position, put, site, situate, station.

location n. **1** place where a thing is situated. **2** act or process of locating. □ **on location** (of filming) in a suitable environment, not in a film studio.
■ **1** locality, place, position, setting, site, situation, spot, venue.

loch n. (Sc.) lake, arm of the sea.

lock[1] n. **1** device (opened by a key) for fastening a door or lid etc. **2** gated section of a canal where the water level can be changed. **3** secure hold in wrestling. **4** interlocked or jammed state. ● v. **1** fasten with a lock. **2** make or become rigidly fixed. □ **in lock** in a locked place. **lock out** shut out by locking a door. **lock-up** n. **1** premises that can be locked. **2** place where prisoners can be kept temporarily. **lockable** adj.
■ n. **1** combination lock, latch, padlock, mortise lock. ● v. **1** fasten, latch, padlock, secure. **2** jam, seize up, stick. □ **lock up** confine, detain, imprison, incarcerate, jail, shut in or up.

lock[2] n. **1** portion of hair that hangs together. **2** (pl.) hair.
■ **1** curl, ringlet, strand, tress.

locker n. cupboard where things can be stowed securely.

locket n. small ornamental case worn on a chain round the neck.

lockjaw n. tetanus.

lockout n. employer's procedure of locking out employees during a dispute.

locksmith n. maker and mender of locks.

locomotion n. ability to move from place to place.

locomotive n. self-propelled engine for moving railway trains. ● adj. of or effecting locomotion.

locum n. temporary stand-in for a doctor, clergyman, etc.

locus n. (pl. **-ci**) **1** thing's exact place. **2** line or curve etc. formed by certain points or by the movement of a point or line.

locust n. a kind of grasshopper that devours vegetation.

lode n. vein of metal ore.

lodestar n. star (esp. pole star) used as a guide in navigation.

lodestone n. oxide of iron used as a magnet.

lodge n. **1** cabin for use by hunters, skiers, etc. **2** gatekeeper's house. **3** porter's room at the entrance to a building. **4** members or meeting place of a branch of certain societies. **5** beaver's or otter's lair. ● v. **1** provide with sleeping quarters or temporary accommodation. **2** live as a lodger. **3** deposit. **4** be or become embedded.

■ n. **1** cabin, chalet, cottage. ● v. **1** accommodate, billet, house, put up. **2** board, dwell, live, reside, stay. **3** deposit, store, *colloq.* stash.

lodger n. person paying for accommodation in another's house.

lodging n. **1** temporary accommodation. **2** (pl.) room(s) rented for living in.

■ **1** accommodation, shelter. **2** (**lodgings**) accommodation, digs, quarters, rooms.

loft n. **1** space under a roof. **2** gallery in a church. ● v. send (a ball) in a high arc.

lofty adj. (**-ier, -iest**) **1** very tall. **2** noble. **3** haughty. □ **loftily** adv., **loftiness** n.

■ **1** high, tall, towering. **2** exalted, grand, noble, sublime. **3** aloof, arrogant, contemptuous, condescending, disdainful, haughty, hoity-toity, patronizing, scornful, snobbish, *colloq.* snooty, supercilious, superior, *colloq.* uppity.

log[1] n. **1** piece cut from a trunk or branch of a tree. **2** device for gauging a ship's speed. **3** logbook, entry in this. ● v. (**logged**) enter (facts) in a logbook. □ **logbook** n. book in which details of a voyage or journey are recorded. **log on** or **off** begin or finish operations on a computer terminal.

log[2] n. logarithm.

loganberry n. large dark red fruit resembling a blackberry.

logarithm n. one of a series of numbers set out in tables, used to simplify calculations.

logic n. **1** science or method of reasoning. **2** correct reasoning.

logical adj. **1** of or according to logic. **2** reasonable. **3** reasoning correctly. □ **logically** adv., **logicality** n.

■ **1** rational, reasoned. **2** defensible, justifiable, legitimate, reasonable, right, sensible, sound, valid. **3** intelligent, judicious, rational, sensible, wise.

logician n. person skilled in logic.

logistics n. organization of supplies and services. □ **logistical** adj.

logo n. (pl. **-os**) design used as an emblem.

loin n. side and back of the body between ribs and hip bone.

loincloth n. cloth worn round the loins.

loiter v. linger, stand about idly. □ **loiterer** n.

loll v. **1** stand, sit, or rest lazily. **2** hang loosely.

lollipop n. large usu. flat boiled sweet on a small stick. □ **lollipop lady, man** official using a circular sign on a stick to halt traffic for children to cross a road.

lollop v. (**lolloped**) (*colloq.*) **1** move in clumsy bounds. **2** flop.

lolly n. **1** (*colloq.*) lollipop, ice lolly. **2** (*sl.*) money.

lone adj. solitary.

lonely adj. **1** solitary. **2** sad because lacking companions. **3** not much frequented. □ **loneliness** n.

■ **1** lone, single, sole, solitary. **2** alone, companionless, forlorn, friendless, lonesome. **3** desolate, isolated, out of the way, remote, solitary, unfrequented.

loner n. person who prefers not to associate with others.

lonesome adj. lonely.

long[1] adj. of great or specified length. ● adv. **1** for a long time. **2** throughout a specified time. □ **as** or **so long as** provided that. **long-distance** adj. travelling or operated between distant places. **long face** dismal expression. **long johns** (*colloq.*) underpants with long legs. **long-life** adj. (of milk etc.) treated to prolong its shelf-life. **long-lived** adj. living or lasting for a long time. **long-range** adj. **1** having a relatively long range. **2** relating to a long period of future time. **long shot** wild guess or venture. **long-sighted** adj. able to see clearly only what is at a distance. **long-standing** adj. having existed for a long time. **long-suffering** adj. bearing provocation patiently. **long-term** adj. of or for a long period. **long ton** (*see* ton). **long wave** radio wave of frequency less than 300 kHz. **long-winded** adj. talking or writing at tedious length.

■ adj. drawn-out, extended, interminable, lengthy, prolonged, protracted; in length, lengthwise. □ **long-suffering** forbearing, patient, resigned, stoical, uncomplaining. **long-winded** lengthy, rambling, verbose, wordy.

long[2] v. **long for** feel a longing for.

■ crave, desire, hanker after, hunger for, itch for, thirst for, want, wish for, yearn for.

longevity /lonjévviti/ n. long life.

longhand *n.* ordinary writing, not shorthand or typing etc.

longhorn *n.* one of a breed of cattle with long horns.

longing *n.* intense wish.

■ craving, desire, hankering, hunger, itch, thirst, wish, yearning, *colloq.* yen.

longitude *n.* distance east or west (measured in degrees on a map) from the Greenwich meridian.

longitudinal *adj.* 1 of longitude. 2 of length, lengthwise. □ **longitudinally** *adv.*

loo *n.* (*colloq.*) lavatory.

loofah *n.* dried pod of a gourd, used as a rough sponge.

look *v.* 1 direct one's sight. 2 make a search. 3 face. 4 seem. ● *n.* 1 act of looking. 2 inspection, search. 3 appearance. □ **look after** 1 take care of. 2 attend to. **look at** 1 turn one's eyes in a particular direction. 2 consider. **look down** on despise. **look for** seek. **look forward to** await eagerly. **look into** investigate. **lookout** *n.* 1 watch. 2 watcher(s). 3 observation post. 4 prospect. 5 person's own concern. **look out** be vigilant. **look up** 1 search for information about. 2 improve in prospects. 3 go to visit. **look up to** admire and respect.

■ *v.* 1 gaze, glance, peek, peep, peer, stare. 2 hunt, search. 3 face, point. 4 appear, seem. ● *n.* 1 gaze, glance, glimpse, peek, peep, squint, stare. 2 check, examination, inspection, once-over; hunt, search. 3 air, appearance, aspect, bearing, countenance, demeanour, expression, mien. □ **look after** 1 care for, guard, mind, nurse, tend, take care of. 2 attend to, deal with, do, handle, see to, sort out, take charge of. **look at** 1 contemplate, eye, examine, inspect, observe, regard, scan, scrutinize, study, survey, view, watch. **look for** hunt for, search for, seek, try to find. **look into** examine, explore, go over, investigate, inquire into, research, scrutinize, study. **look up to** admire, esteem, idolize, respect, revere, venerate, worship.

looker-on *n.* (*pl.* **lookers-on**) mere spectator.

loom[1] *n.* apparatus for weaving.

loom[2] *v.* 1 appear, esp. close at hand or threateningly. 2 be ominously close.

■ 1 appear, become visible, emerge, materialize, take shape.

loop *n.* 1 curve that is U-shaped or crosses itself. 2 thing shaped like this, esp. length of cord or wire etc. fastened at the crossing. ● *v.* 1 form into loop(s). 2 fasten or join with loop(s). 3 enclose in a loop. □ **loop the loop** fly in a vertical circle.

loophole *n.* means of evading a rule or contract.

loose *adj.* 1 not tight. 2 not fastened, held, or fixed. 3 inexact. ● *adv.* loosely. ● *v.* 1 release. 2 untie, loosen. □ **at a loose end** without a definite occupation. **loose-leaf** *adj.* with each page removable. **loosely** *adv.*

■ *adj.* 1 baggy. 2 flowing, unbound, untied; at large, free, unconfined; unattached, unconnected, unfastened. 3 broad, general, imprecise, inexact, rough. ● *v.* 1 let go, release, set free. 2 ease, loosen, slacken, undo, unfasten, untie.

loosen *v.* make or become loose or looser.

■ ease, loose, release, slacken, undo, unfasten, unlace, untie.

loot *n.* goods taken from an enemy or by theft. ● *v.* 1 take loot (from). 2 take as loot. □ **looter** *n.*

■ *n.* booty, haul, plunder, spoils, *sl.* swag. ● *v.* pillage, plunder, raid, ransack, rob, sack.

lop *v.* (**lopped**) 1 cut branches or twigs of. 2 cut off.

lope *v.* run with a long bounding stride. ● *n.* this stride.

lop-eared *adj.* with drooping ears.

lopsided *adj.* with one side lower, smaller, or heavier.

■ askew, asymmetrical, awry, *colloq.* cockeyed, crooked, unbalanced, uneven, unsymmetrical.

loquacious *adj.* talkative. □ **loquaciously** *adv.*, **loquacity** *n.*

■ chatty, garrulous, talkative, voluble.

lord *n.* 1 master, ruler. 2 nobleman. 3 (**Lord**) title of certain peers or high officials. 4 (**the Lord**) God. 5 (**Our Lord**) Christ.

lordship *n.* title used of or to a man with the rank of *Lord.*

lore *n.* body of traditions and knowledge.

■ beliefs, folklore, mythology, myths, tradition(s); knowledge, learning.

lorgnette /lornyét/ *n.* eyeglasses or opera-glasses held to the eyes on a long handle.

lorry *n.* large motor vehicle for transporting heavy loads.

lose v. (**lost**) **1** cease to have or maintain. **2** become unable to find. **3** forfeit (right to something). **4** waste (time or an opportunity). **5** get rid of. **6** be defeated in a contest etc. **7** suffer loss (of). **8** cause the loss of. □ **loser** n.

■ **1,2** mislay, misplace. **3** forfeit, give up. **4** miss, squander, waste. **5** elude, escape from, evade, get rid of, give a person the slip.

loss n. **1** act or instance of losing. **2** person or thing or amount lost. **3** disadvantage caused by losing something. □ **be at a loss** not know what to do or say. **loss-leader** n. article sold at a loss to attract customers.

■ **1** forfeiture, mislaying, misplacing, privation. **2** casualty, fatality; depletion, diminution, reduction; debit, deficit. **3** damage, detriment, disadvantage, harm, injury.

lost see **lose**. adj. strayed or separated from its owner.

lot n. **1** each of a set of objects drawn at random to decide something. **2** item being sold at auction. **3** person's share or destiny. **4** piece of land. **5** number of people or things of the same kind. **6** (pl.) large number or amount, much. **7** (**the lot**) the total quantity. □ **bad lot** person of bad character.

■ **3** colloq. cut, part, portion, quota, ration, share; destiny, fate, fortune. **4** piece of land, plot. **5** batch, collection, consignment, group, set. **6** (**lots**) heaps, colloq. loads, colloq. oodles, colloq. piles, plenty, quantities, colloq. stacks.

lotion n. medicinal or cosmetic liquid applied to the skin.

■ balm, cream, embrocation, emollient, liniment, moisturizer, salve, unguent.

lottery n. **1** system of raising money by selling numbered tickets and giving prizes to holders of numbers drawn at random. **2** thing where the outcome is governed by luck.

lotus n. (pl. **-uses**) **1** tropical water lily. **2** mythical fruit.

loud adj. **1** producing much noise. **2** gaudy. ● adv. loudly. □ **loudly** adv., **loudness** n.

■ adj. **1** blaring, booming, deafening, noisy, raucous, stentorian, thunderous. **2** flashy, garish, gaudy, showy, tasteless, tawdry.

loudspeaker n. apparatus that converts electrical impulses into audible sound.

lough /lok/ n. (Ir.) = **loch**.

lounge v. **1** loll. **2** sit or stand about idly. ● n. **1** sitting room. **2** waiting-room at an airport etc. □ **lounge suit** man's ordinary suit for day wear. **lounger** n.

■ v. **1** laze, lie, loll, recline, sprawl. **2** idle, hang about, loaf, loiter. ● n. drawing room, living room, salon, sitting room.

louse n. **1** (pl. **lice**) small parasitic insect. **2** (pl. **louses**) contemptible person.

lousy adj. (**-ier, -iest**) **1** infested with lice. **2** (colloq.) very bad.

lout n. clumsy ill-mannered young man. □ **loutish** adj.

louvre n. each of a set of overlapping slats arranged to admit air but exclude light or rain. □ **louvred** adj.

lovable adj. easy to love.

■ adorable, appealing, charming, colloq. cute, darling, dear, enchanting, endearing, engaging, likeable, colloq. sweet, taking, winning, winsome.

lovage n. herb used for flavouring.

love n. **1** warm liking or affection. **2** sexual passion. **3** loved person. **4** (in games) no score, nil. ● v. **1** feel love for. **2** like greatly. □ **in love** feeling (esp. sexual) love for another person. **love affair** romantic or sexual relationship between two people. **lovebird** n. kind of parakeet. **make love** have sexual intercourse.

■ n. **1** adoration, affection, devotion, fondness, tenderness, warmth; liking, partiality, relish, taste. **2** ardour, lust, passion. **3** beloved, darling, dear, lover, sweet, sweetheart. ● v. **1** adore, be devoted to, be in love with, be infatuated with, care for, cherish, dote on, colloq. have a crush on, hold dear, idolize, treasure, worship. **2** be fond of, be partial to, delight in, have a soft spot for, have a weakness for, like, relish. □ **love affair** affair, intrigue, liaison, relationship, romance.

lovelorn adj. pining with love.

lovely adj. (**-ier, -iest**) **1** beautiful, attractive. **2** (colloq.) delightful. □ **loveliness** n.

■ **1** attractive, beautiful, comely, exquisite, good-looking, colloq. gorgeous, pretty, colloq. stunning. **2** agreeable, delightful, enjoyable, nice, pleasant, pleasurable, colloq. super.

lover n. **1** person in love with another or having an illicit love affair. **2** one who likes or enjoys something.

loving adj. feeling or showing love. □ **lovingly** adv.

■ adoring, affectionate, caring, devoted, doting, fond, tender; amorous, ardent, passionate.

low¹ n. deep sound made by cattle. ● v. make this sound.

low² adj. **1** not high, not extending or lying far up. **2** ranking below others. **3** ignoble, vulgar. **4** less than normal in amount or intensity. **5** not loud or shrill. **6** lacking vigour, depressed. ● n. **1** low level. **2** area of low pressure. ● adv. in, at, or to a low level. □ **low-down** adj. dishonourable. n. (colloq.) relevant information. **low-key** adj. restrained, not intense or emotional. **low season** season that is least busy.

■ adj. **1** little, short, small, stubby, stumpy. **2** humble, inferior, lowly, menial. **3** base, contemptible, despicable, dishonourable, ignoble, mean; coarse, crude, rude, vulgar. **4** inadequate, insufficient, limited, short, scant, scanty, sparse. **5** hushed, indistinct, muffled, muted, quiet, soft, subdued. **6** dejected, depressed, despondent, dispirited, downcast, downhearted, heavy-hearted, gloomy, glum, miserable, sad, unhappy.

lowbrow adj. not intellectual or cultured. ● n. lowbrow person.

lower v. **1** let or haul down. **2** make or become lower. □ **lower case** letters that are not capitals.

■ **1** drop, haul down, let down, put down. **2** cut, decrease, diminish, lessen, mark down, reduce, slash.

lowlands n.pl. low-lying land. □ **lowland** adj., **lowlander** n.

lowly adj. (**-ier, -iest**) of humble rank or condition. □ **lowliness** n.

loyal adj. firm in one's allegiance. □ **loyally** adv., **loyalty** n.

■ constant, dependable, devoted, faithful, reliable, staunch, steadfast, steady, true, trusted, trustworthy, trusty, unswerving, unwavering.

loyalist n. person who is loyal, esp. while others revolt.

lozenge n. **1** four-sided diamond-shaped figure. **2** small tablet to be dissolved in the mouth.

Ltd. abbr. Limited.

lubricant n. lubricating substance.

lubricate v. oil or grease (machinery etc.). □ **lubrication** n.

lubricious adj. **1** slippery. **2** lewd.

lucid adj. **1** clearly expressed. **2** sane. □ **lucidly** adv., **lucidity** n.

■ **1** clear, coherent, comprehensible, eloquent, intelligible, understandable. **2** rational, sane.

luck n. **1** chance regarded as the bringer of good or bad fortune. **2** success due to chance.

■ **1** chance, destiny, fate, fortune. **2** good fortune, serendipity.

luckless adj. unlucky.

■ hapless, unfortunate, unlucky.

lucky adj. (**-ier, -iest**) having, bringing, or resulting from good luck. □ **lucky dip** tub containing articles which people may choose at random. **luckily** adv.

■ blessed, favoured, fortunate; fortuitous, happy, opportune, timely.

lucrative adj. producing much money, profitable.

lucre /lookər/ n. (derog.) money.

ludicrous adj. ridiculous. □ **ludicrously** adv., **ludicrousness** n.

■ absurd, asinine, crazy, farcical, foolish, laughable, nonsensical, preposterous, ridiculous, risible, silly, stupid.

ludo n. simple game played with counters on a special board.

lug¹ v. (**lugged**) drag or carry with great effort.

lug² n. **1** ear-like projection. **2** (colloq.) ear.

luggage n. suitcases, bags, etc. for a traveller's belongings.

■ baggage, bags, belongings, cases, paraphernalia, suitcases, things.

lugubrious adj. dismal, mournful. □ **lugubriously** adv.

■ dismal, forlorn, gloomy, melancholy, miserable, mournful, sad, woebegone, woeful.

lukewarm adj. **1** only slightly warm. **2** not enthusiastic.

■ **1** tepid. **2** apathetic, cool, half-hearted, indifferent, lackadaisical, unenthusiastic, uninterested.

lull v. **1** soothe or send to sleep. **2** calm. **3** become quiet. ● n. period of quiet or inactivity.

■ v. **2** allay, assuage, calm, ease, quiet, quieten, pacify, soothe. **3** abate, decrease, diminish, lessen, quieten, colloq. let up, moderate, subside. ● n. break, hiatus, intermission, interval, pause, respite; calm, calmness, hush, quiet, quietness, silence, stillness.

lullaby *n.* soothing song sung to send a child to sleep.

lumbago *n.* rheumatic pain in muscles of the lower back.

lumbar *adj.* of or in the lower back.

lumber *n.* **1** useless or cumbersome articles. **2** timber sawn into planks. ● *v.* **1** encumber. **2** move heavily and clumsily.
■ *n.* **1** clutter, junk, odds and ends, white elephants. **2** planks, timber, wood. ● *v.* **1** burden, encumber, load, overload, saddle. **2** clump, plod, stump, trudge.

lumberjack *n.* (*US*) workman cutting or conveying lumber.

luminary *n.* **1** natural light-giving body, esp. the sun or moon. **2** eminent person.

luminescent *adj.* emitting light without heat. □ **luminescence** *n.*

luminous *adj.* emitting light, glowing in the dark. □ **luminously** *adv.*, **luminosity** *n.*
■ bright, brilliant, gleaming, glistening, radiant, shimmering, shining; fluorescent, glowing, incandescent, luminescent, phosphorescent.

lump *n.* **1** hard or compact mass. **2** swelling. ● *v.* put or consider together. □ **lump sum** money paid as a single amount.
■ *n.* **1** cake, chunk, clod, clot, nugget, pat, piece, wedge, *colloq.* wodge. **2** bulge, bump, excrescence, growth, knob, nodule, protrusion, protuberance, swelling, tumescence, tumour.

lumpectomy *n.* surgical removal of a lump from the breast.

lumpy *adj.* (**-ier, -iest**) **1** full of lumps. **2** covered in lumps. □ **lumpiness** *n.*

lunacy *n.* **1** insanity. **2** great folly.
■ **1** dementia, derangement, insanity, madness. **2** craziness, folly, foolishness, idiocy, insanity, madness, senselessness, stupidity.

lunar *adj.* of the moon. □ **lunar month** period between new moons (29⅓ days), four weeks.

lunatic *n.* **1** insane person. **2** wildly foolish person. ● *adj.* **1** insane. **2** very foolish.

lunation *n.* lunar month

lunch *n.* midday meal. ● *v.* eat lunch.

luncheon *n.* lunch. □ **luncheon meat** tinned cured meat ready for serving. **luncheon voucher** voucher given to an employee, exchangeable for food.

lung *n.* either of the pair of breathing organs in the chest.

lunge *n.* **1** sudden forward movement of the body. **2** thrust. ● *v.* make this movement.

lupin *n.* garden plant with tall spikes of flowers.

lurch[1] *n.* **leave in the lurch** leave (a person) in difficulties.

lurch[2] *v. & n.* (make) an unsteady swaying movement, stagger.
■ *v.* reel, stagger, stumble, sway; heel, list, pitch, roll.

lure *v.* entice. ● *n.* **1** enticement. **2** bait or decoy to attract wild animals.
■ *v.* attract, coax, draw, entice, inveigle, seduce, tempt. ● *n.* **1** enticement, inducement, temptation. **2** bait, decoy.

lurid *adj.* **1** in glaring colours. **2** sensational or shocking. □ **luridly** *adv.*
■ **1** garish, gaudy, loud. **2** graphic, melodramatic, sensational, shocking, startling, vivid; ghastly, gory, grisly, gruesome.

lurk *v.* **1** wait furtively or keeping out of sight. **2** be latent.

luscious *adj.* **1** delicious. **2** voluptuously attractive.
■ **1** appetizing, delectable, delicious, *colloq.* scrumptious, succulent, tasty, *colloq.* yummy.

lush *adj.* **1** (of grass etc.) luxuriant. **2** luxurious.

lust *n.* **1** intense sexual desire. **2** any intense desire. ● *v.* **lust after** or **for** feel lust for. □ **lustful** *adj.*, **lustfully** *adv.*
■ *n.* **1** desire, passion; lasciviousness, lechery, licentiousness. **2** craving, desire, greed, hunger, longing, thirst, yearning. ● *v.* covet, crave, desire, hanker after, hunger for, thirst for, yearn for. □ **lustful** amorous, passionate; lascivious, lecherous, lewd, licentious, salacious.

lustre *n.* **1** soft brightness of a surface. **2** glory. **3** metallic glaze on pottery. □ **lustrous** *adj.*

lusty *adj.* (**-ier, -iest**) strong and vigorous. □ **lustily** *adv.*
■ full-blooded, hale, healthy, hearty, robust, strong, vigorous.

lute *n.* guitar-like instrument. □ **lutenist** *n.*

luxuriant *adj.* growing profusely. □ **luxuriantly** *adv.*, **luxuriance** *n.*
■ abundant, copious, lush, profuse, rich, thick.

luxuriate *v.* **luxuriate in** feel great enjoyment in something.
■ bask in, delight in, indulge in, relish, revel in, wallow in.

luxurious *adj.* supplied with luxuries, very comfortable. □ **luxuriously** *adv.*
■ de luxe, grand, magnificent, opulent, palatial, plush, *colloq.* posh, splendid, sumptuous.

luxury *n.* **1** choice and costly surroundings, food, etc. **2** self-indulgence. **3** thing that is enjoyable but not essential.
■ **1** grandeur, magnificence, opulence, splendour, sumptuousness. **2** hedonism, indulgence, self-indulgence, voluptuousness. **3** extra, frill, treat.

lying *see* **lie¹, lie².**

lymph *n.* colourless fluid from body tissue. □ **lymphatic** *adj.*

lynch *v.* execute or punish violently by a mob, without trial.

lynx *n.* wild animal of the cat family with keen sight.

lyre *n.* ancient musical instrument with strings in a U-shaped frame. □ **lyre-bird** *n.* Australian bird with a lyre-shaped tail.

lyric *adj.* of poetry that expresses the poet's emotions. ● *n.* **1** lyric poem. **2** (*pl.*) words of a song.

lyrical *adj.* **1** resembling or using language suitable for lyric poetry. **2** (*colloq.*) highly enthusiastic. □ **lyrically** *adv.*

lyricist *n.* writer of lyrics.

Mm

m *abbr.* **1** metre(s). **2** mile(s). **3** million(s).

ma *n.* (*colloq.*) mother.

ma'am *n.* madam.

mac *n.* (*colloq.*) mackintosh.

macabre *adj.* gruesome.
■ appalling, awful, dreadful, fearsome, frightening, frightful, ghastly, gory, gruesome, grotesque, grisly, horrific, terrible.

macadam *n.* layers of broken stone used in road-making.

macadamize *v.* pave with macadam.

macaroni *n.* tube-shaped pasta.

macaroon *n.* biscuit or small cake made with ground almonds.

macaw *n.* American parrot.

mace[1] *n.* ceremonial staff carried or placed before an official.

mace[2] *n.* spice made from the dried outer covering of nutmeg.

machete /məchétti/ *n.* broad heavy knife.

machiavellian *adj.* elaborately cunning or deceitful.

machination *n.* (*usu. pl.*) intrigue, plot.

machine *n.* **1** apparatus for applying mechanical power. **2** thing operated by this. **3** controlling system of an organization etc. ● *v.* produce or work on with a machine. □ **machine-gun** *n.* gun that can fire continuously. **machine-readable** *adj.* in a form that a computer can process.
■ *n.* **1** apparatus, appliance, contraption, device, gadget, mechanism. **2** engine, motor; car, vehicle; automaton, robot.

machinery *n.* **1** machines. **2** mechanism.

machinist *n.* person who works machinery.

machismo *n.* **1** manly courage. **2** show of this.

macho *adj.* ostentatiously manly.

mackerel *n.* (*pl.* **mackerel**) edible sea fish.

mackintosh *n.* **1** cloth waterproofed with rubber. **2** raincoat.

macramé /məkrámi/ *n.* **1** art of knotting cord in patterns. **2** items made in this way.

macrocosm *n.* **1** the universe. **2** any great whole.

mad *adj.* (**madder, maddest**) **1** not sane. **2** extremely foolish. **3** wildly enthusiastic. **4** frenzied. **5** (*colloq.*) very annoyed. □ **madly** *adv.*, **madness** *n.*
■ **1** *sl.* barmy, *sl.* batty, certifiable, *sl.* crackers, crazy, demented, deranged, insane, lunatic, *colloq.* mental, *sl.* nuts, *sl.* nutty, out of one's mind, *sl.* potty, psychotic, unbalanced, unhinged. **2** absurd, asinine, *sl.* barmy, *colloq.* crack-brained, crazy, daft, foolhardy, foolish, hare-brained, idiotic, ludicrous, madcap, nonsensical, reckless, ridiculous, senseless, silly, stupid, unwise. **3** ardent, *colloq.* crazy, enthusiastic, fanatical, fervent, fervid, keen, passionate, wild. **4** frantic, frenzied, frenetic, uncontrolled, unrestrained, wild. **5** angry, annoyed, cross, enraged, exasperated, furious, fuming, irate, incensed, irritated, *colloq.* livid. □ **madness** dementia, derangement, lunacy, mania, mental illness, psychosis; absurdity, craziness, folly, foolishness, idiocy, insanity, senselessness, stupidity.

madam *n.* polite form of address to a woman.

madcap *adj.* & *n.* wildly impulsive (person).

madden *v.* make mad or angry.
■ *colloq.* aggravate, anger, annoy, *sl.* bug, enrage, exasperate, gall, incense, inflame, infuriate, irk, irritate, nettle, *colloq.* rile, vex.

made *see* **make**.

Madeira *n.* fortified wine from Madeira. □ **Madeira cake** rich plain cake.

madonna *n.* picture or statue of the Virgin Mary.

madrigal *n.* song for several voices.

maelstrom /máylstram/ *n.* great whirlpool.

maestro /místrō/ *n.* (*pl.* **-ri**) **1** great conductor or composer of music. **2** master of any art.

magazine *n.* **1** illustrated periodical. **2** store for arms or explosives. **3** chamber holding cartridges in a gun, slides in a projector, etc.
■ **1** journal, monthly, periodical, publication, quarterly, weekly. **2** armoury, arsenal.

magenta *adj.* & *n.* purplish-red.

maggot *n.* larva, esp. of the bluebottle.

magic n. **1** supposed art of controlling things by supernatural power. **2** conjuring tricks. ● adj. using or used in magic. □ **magical** adj., **magically** adv.

■ n. **1** necromancy, sorcery, voodoo, witchcraft, wizardry. **2** conjuring, legerdemain, sleight of hand.

magician n. **1** person skilled in magic. **2** conjuror.

■ **1** enchanter, enchantress, necromancer, sorcerer, sorceress, witch, wizard. **2** conjuror, illusionist.

magisterial adj. **1** of a magistrate. **2** imperious.

magistrate n. official or citizen with authority to hold preliminary hearings and judge minor cases. □ **magistracy** n.

magnanimous adj. noble and generous in conduct, not petty. □ **magnanimity** n.

■ beneficent, benevolent, charitable, generous, forgiving, good, humane, kind, merciful, noble, philanthropic, unselfish.

magnate n. wealthy influential person, esp. in business.

■ colloq. mogul, tycoon.

magnesia n. compound of magnesium used in medicine.

magnesium n. silvery metallic element.

magnet n. **1** piece of iron or steel that can attract iron and point north when suspended. **2** thing exerting powerful attraction.

magnetic adj. **1** having the properties of a magnet. **2** produced or acting by magnetism. □ **magnetic tape** strip of plastic with magnetic particles, used in recording, computers, etc. **magnetically** adv.

magnetism n. **1** properties and effects of magnetic substances. **2** great charm and attraction.

■ **2** allure, appeal, attraction, attractiveness, charisma, charm, pull, seductiveness.

magnetize v. **1** make magnetic. **2** attract. □ **magnetization** n.

magneto /magnéetō/ n. (pl. **-os**) small electric generator using magnets.

magnification n. magnifying.

magnificent adj. **1** splendid in appearance etc. **2** excellent in quality. □ **magnificently** adv., **magnificence** n.

■ **1** glorious, gorgeous, grand, imposing, impressive, majestic, regal, resplendent, splendid, stately, striking; luxurious, opulent, palatial, sumptuous. **2** excellent, fine,

marvellous, outstanding, splendid, superb, colloq. terrific, wonderful.

magnify v. **1** make (an object) appear larger by use of a lens. **2** exaggerate. □ **magnifier** n.

magnitude n. **1** largeness, size. **2** importance.

■ **1** extent, greatness, immensity, largeness, size. **2** consequence, importance, significance.

magnolia n. tree with large wax-like white or pink flowers.

magnum n. wine bottle twice the standard size.

magpie n. kind of crow with black and white plumage.

Magyar adj. & n. (member, language) of a people now predominant in Hungary.

maharajah n. former title of certain Indian princes. □ **maharanee** n. maharajah's wife or widow.

maharishi n. great Hindu sage.

mahatma n. (in India etc.) title of a man regarded with reverence.

mah-jong n. Chinese game played with 136 or 144 pieces.

mahogany n. **1** hard reddish-brown wood. **2** its colour.

maid n. woman servant.

maiden n. (old use) young unmarried woman, virgin. ● adj. **1** unmarried. **2** first. □ **maiden name** woman's surname before marriage. **maidenly** adj.

maidenhair n. fern with very thin stalks and delicate foliage.

maidservant n. female servant.

mail¹ n. = post³. ● v. send by post. □ **mail order** purchase of goods by post. **mailshot** n. material sent to potential customers in an advertising campaign.

mail² n. body-armour made of metal rings or chains.

maim v. wound or injure so that a part of the body is useless.

■ cripple, disable, hamstring, injure, incapacitate, lame, mutilate, wound.

main adj. principal, most important, greatest in size or extent. ● n. main pipe or channel conveying water, gas, or (pl.) electricity. □ **mainly** adv.

■ adj. basic, cardinal, chief, dominant, first, foremost, fundamental, key, leading, major, paramount, predominant, preeminent, primary, prime, principal.

mainframe n. large computer.

mainland n. country or continent without its adjacent islands.

mainmast n. principal mast.

mainsail n. lowest sail or sail set on the after part of the mainmast.

mainspring n. **1** chief spring of a watch or clock. **2** chief motivating force.

mainstay n. **1** cable securing the mainmast. **2** chief support.

mainstream n. dominant trend of opinion or style etc.

maintain v. **1** cause to continue, keep in existence. **2** keep in repair. **3** bear the expenses of. **4** assert.

■ **1** carry on, continue, keep up, perpetuate, persevere in, persist in, preserve, sustain. **2** keep in good condition, keep up, look after, service, take care of. **3** keep, provide for, support. **4** assert, avow, claim, declare, hold, insist, profess, state.

maintenance n. **1** process of maintaining something. **2** provision of means to support life, allowance of money for this.

maisonette n. **1** small house. **2** flat on more than one floor.

maize n. **1** tall cereal plant. **2** its grain.

majestic adj. stately and dignified, imposing. □ **majestically** adv.

■ dignified, glorious, grand, imperial, imposing, kingly, magnificent, noble, princely, queenly, regal, royal, splendid, stately.

majesty n. **1** impressive stateliness. **2** sovereign power. **3** title of a king or queen.

■ **1** dignity, glory, grandeur, magnificence, nobility, pomp, splendour, stateliness.

major adj. **1** greater or relatively great. **2** very important. ● n. army officer next below lieutenant colonel. ● v. (US) specialize (in a subject) at college. □ **major-general** n. army officer next below lieutenant general.

■ adj. **1** bigger, greater, larger, main. **2** crucial, foremost, important, leading, paramount, primary, prime, principal, significant, vital.

majority n. **1** greatest part of a group or class. **2** number by which votes for one party etc. exceed those for the next or for all combined. **3** age when a person legally becomes adult.

■ **1** best or better part, bulk, lion's share, preponderance.

make v. (**made**) **1** form, prepare, produce. **2** cause to exist, be, or become. **3** succeed in arriving at or achieving. **4** gain, acquire. **5** amount to. **6** calculate or estimate. **7** compel. **8** execute or perform (an action, speech, etc.). ● n. brand of goods. □ **make believe** pretend. **make-believe** n. pretence. **make do** manage with something not fully satisfactory. **make for 1** try to reach. **2** tend to bring about. **make good 1** become successful. **2** repair or pay compensation for. **make it** (colloq.) **1** arrive in time. **2** be successful. **make much of 1** treat as important. **2** give flattering attention to. **make off** go away hastily. **make off with** carry away, steal. **make out 1** write out (a list etc.). **2** manage to see or understand. **3** imply, suggest. **make over 1** transfer the ownership of. **2** refashion (a garment etc.). **make up 1** form, constitute. **2** invent (a story). **3** become reconciled after (a quarrel). **4** complete (an amount). **5** apply cosmetics (to). **make up for** compensate for. **make-up** n. **1** cosmetics applied to the skin. **2** way a thing is made. **3** person's character. **make up one's mind** decide.

■ v. **1** assemble, build, construct, create, erect, fabricate, fashion, forge, form, frame, manufacture, produce, shape; cook, get, prepare; compose, draft, draw up. **2** bring about, cause, engender, generate, give rise to, occasion, produce; appoint, designate, elect, name, nominate. **3** arrive at, reach, get to; achieve, accomplish, attain. **4** acquire, clear, gain, get, gross, net, obtain, reap, win; fetch, sell for. **5** add up to, amount to, come to, total. **6** calculate, estimate, gauge, reckon, think. **7** cause, compel, force, impel, induce, oblige, persuade, press, pressure, pressurize, prevail on. **8** execute, perform; give, deliver, present. ● n. brand, kind, sort, type, variety. □ **make believe** daydream, dream, fantasize, pretend. **make do** cope, get by, manage, muddle through, scrape by, survive. **make off** abscond, colloq. clear off, dash away, decamp, flee, fly, make a getaway, run away, colloq. scram, colloq. skedaddle, take to one's heels. **make out 2** descry, detect, discern, distinguish, espy, perceive, pick out, see; comprehend, fathom, figure out, follow, grasp, understand. **3** imply, insinuate, intimate, suggest. **make up 1** compose, comprise, consitute, form. **2** concoct, dream up, fabricate, invent, manufacture. **3** be reconciled, bury the hatchet. **make up for** atone for, compensate for, make amends or reparation for, make good. **make-up 1** cosmetics, greasepaint. **2** arrangement, composition, configuration, construction, format. **3** character, disposition, personality, temper, temperament.

maker *n.* **1** one who makes something. **2** manufacturer.

■ **1** author, creator, designer, father, inventor, originator.

makeshift *adj. & n.* (thing) used as an improvised substitute.

■ *adj.* improvised, provisional, stopgap, temporary.

makeweight *n.* something added to make up for a deficiency.

maladjusted *adj.* not happily adapted to one's circumstances. □ **maladjustment** *n.*

maladminister *v.* manage badly or improperly.

maladroit *adj.* bungling, clumsy.

malady *n.* illness, disease.

malaise *n.* feeling of illness or uneasiness.

malapropism *n.* comical confusion of words.

malaria *n.* disease causing a recurring fever. □ **malarial** *adj.*

Malay *adj. & n.* (member, language) of a people of Malaysia and Indonesia.

malcontent *n.* discontented person.

male *adj.* **1** of the sex that can fertilize egg cells produced by a female. **2** (of a plant) producing pollen, not seeds. **3** (of a screw etc.) for insertion into a corresponding hollow part. ● *n.* male person, animal, or plant.

malefactor /málifaktər/ *n.* wrongdoer.

malevolent *adj.* wishing evil to others. □ **malevolently** *adv.*, **malevolence** *n.*

■ baleful, evil, hostile, malign, malicious, spiteful, venomous, vicious, vindictive.

malformation *n.* faulty formation. □ **malformed** *adj.*

malfunction *n.* faulty functioning. ● *v.* function faultily.

malice *n.* desire to harm others. □ **malicious** *adj.*, **maliciously** *adv.*

■ animosity, hatred, hostility, ill will, malevolence, rancour, spite, spitefulness, venom, vindictiveness. □ **malicious** *colloq.* bitchy, bitter, hurtful, malign, malignant, mean, nasty, spiteful, unkind, venomous, vicious, vindictive, vitriolic.

malign /məlín/ *adj.* **1** harmful. **2** showing malice. ● *v.* slander.

■ *v.* blacken the reputation of, calumniate, defame, denigrate, slander, smear, traduce, vilify.

malignant *adj.* **1** showing great ill will. **2** (of a tumour) growing harmfully and uncontrollably. □ **malignancy** *n.*

malinger *v.* pretend illness to avoid work. □ **malingerer** *n.*

mall *n.* **1** sheltered walk or promenade. **2** shopping precinct.

mallard *n.* wild duck, male of which has a glossy green head.

malleable *adj.* **1** able to be hammered into shape. **2** easy to influence. □ **malleability** *n.*

■ **1** ductile, plastic. **2** adaptable, biddable, compliant, impressionable, tractable.

mallet *n.* **1** hammer, usu. of wood. **2** instrument for striking the ball in croquet or polo.

malmsey /maamzi/ *n.* strong sweet wine.

malnutrition *n.* insufficient nutrition.

malodorous *adj.* stinking.

malpractice *n.* **1** wrongdoing. **2** improper professional conduct.

malt *n.* **1** barley or other grain prepared for brewing or distilling. **2** (*colloq.*) whisky made with this. □ **malted milk** drink made from dried milk and malt.

maltreat *v.* ill-treat. □ **maltreatment** *n.*

mamba *n.* poisonous S. African snake.

mammal *n.* member of the class of animals that suckle their young. □ **mammalian** *adj.*

mammary *adj.* of the breasts.

mammoth *n.* large extinct elephant. ● *adj.* huge.

man *n.* (*pl.* **men**) **1** adult male person. **2** human being, person. **3** humankind. **4** male servant or employee. **5** (usu. *pl.*) soldier, sailor, etc. **6** piece in chess, draughts, etc. ● *v.* (**manned**) supply with people to guard or operate something. □ **man-hour** *n.* one hour's work by one person. **manhunt** *n.* organized search for a person, esp. a criminal. **man-made** *adj.* synthetic.

■ *n.* **1** *sl.* bloke, *colloq.* chap, *colloq.* fellow, gentleman, *colloq.* guy, male. **2** human being, individual, mortal, person, soul. **3** human beings, humanity, humankind, mankind, the human race. **4** batman, footman, manservant, valet; employee, hand, worker.

manacle *n. & v.* handcuff.

manage *v.* **1** have control of. **2** contrive. **3** deal with (a person) tactfully. **4** succeed with limited resources. **5** operate (a tool etc.) effectively. □ **manageable** adj.

■ **1** administer, be in charge of, conduct, direct, govern, handle, head, organize, oversee, preside over, run, supervise. **2** contrive, succeed. **3** control, cope with, deal with, handle. **4** cope, get by, make do, make ends meet, muddle through, scrape by, survive. **5** handle, use, wield.

management n. **1** managing. **2** people managing a business.

■ **1** administration, conduct, control, direction, handling, operation, running. **2** colloq. bosses, directorate, directors, executives.

manager n. person in charge of a business etc. □ **managerial** adj.

■ administrator, colloq. boss, director, employer, head, overseer, superintendent, supervisor.

manageress n. woman manager, esp. of a shop, hotel, etc.

manatee n. large tropical aquatic mammal.

Mandarin n. northern variety of the Chinese language.

mandarin n. **1** senior influential official. **2** small orange.

mandate n. & v. (give) authority to perform certain tasks.

mandatory adj. compulsory.

■ compulsory, essential, necessary, obligatory, required, requisite.

mandible n. jaw or jaw-like part.

mandolin n. guitar-like musical instrument.

mandrake n. poisonous plant with a large yellow fruit.

mandrill n. large baboon.

mane n. long hair on a horse's or lion's neck.

manganese n. hard brittle grey metal or its black oxide.

mange n. skin disease affecting hairy animals.

mangel-wurzel n. large beet used as cattle food.

manger n. open trough for horses or cattle to feed from.

mangle v. damage by cutting or crushing roughly, mutilate.

■ crush, damage, disfigure, lacerate, maim, mutilate.

mango n. (pl. **-oes**) **1** tropical fruit with juicy flesh. **2** tree bearing it.

mangrove n. tropical tree growing in shore-mud and swamps.

mangy adj. **1** having mange. **2** squalid.

manhandle v. **1** move by human effort alone. **2** treat roughly.

manhole n. opening through which a person can enter a drain etc. to inspect it.

manhood n. **1** state of being a man. **2** manly qualities.

mania n. **1** violent madness. **2** extreme enthusiasm, obsession.

■ **1** dementia, derangement, insanity, lunacy, madness. **2** craze, fad, fixation, obsession, passion.

maniac n. person with a mania.

■ lunatic, psychopath; enthusiast, fan, fanatic, fiend.

maniacal adj. of or like a mania or maniac.

manic adj. of or affected by mania.

manicure n. cosmetic treatment of fingernails. ● v. apply such treatment to. □ **manicurist** n.

manifest adj. clear and unmistakable. ● v. show clearly, give signs of. ● n. list of cargo or passengers carried by a ship or aircraft. □ **manifestation** n.

■ adj. apparent, blatant, clear, conspicuous, discernible, evident, obvious, palpable, patent, perceptible, plain, unambiguous, unmistakable, visible. ● v. demonstrate, display, evince, exhibit, indicate, reveal, show. □ **manifestation** demonstration, display, exhibition, indication, show, sign.

manifesto n. (pl. **-os**) public declaration of policy.

manifold adj. of many kinds. ● n. (in a machine) pipe or chamber with several openings.

manikin n. little man, dwarf.

manila n. brown paper used for wrapping and for envelopes.

manipulate v. handle or manage skilfully or cunningly. □ **manipulation** n., **manipulator** n.

■ control, handle, operate, use; exploit, influence, manoeuvre; colloq. cook, doctor, falsify, colloq. fiddle, juggle, rig, tamper with.

mankind n. humankind.

manly adj. **1** brave, strong. **2** considered suitable for a man. □ **manliness** n.

mannequin /mánnikin/ n. **1** fashion model. **2** dummy for display of clothes.

manner n. **1** way a thing is done or happens. **2** person's way of behaving towards others. **3** kind, sort. **4** (*pl.*) polite behaviour.

■ **1** fashion, method, mode, procedure, style, technique, way. **2** air, attitude, bearing, behaviour, conduct, demeanour. **3** class, kind, sort, type, variety. **4** (**manners**) decorum, etiquette, (good) form, politeness.

mannered *adj.* **1** having manners of a certain kind. **2** stilted.

mannerism *n.* distinctive personal habit or way of doing something.

■ characteristic, foible, habit, idiosyncrasy, peculiarity, quirk, trick.

manoeuvre *n.* **1** planned movement of a vehicle, troops, etc. **2** skilful or crafty proceeding. ● *v.* **1** perform manoeuvre(s). **2** move skilfully. **3** manipulate by scheming. □ **manoeuvrable** *adj.*

■ *n.* **1** deployment, movement. **2** dodge, gambit, move, plan, plot, ploy, scheme, stratagem, tactic, trick. ● *v.* **1** guide, navigate, steer. **2** contrive, engineer, manipulate, *colloq.* wangle.

manor *n.* large country house, usu. with lands. □ **manorial** *adj.*

manpower *n.* number of people available for work or service.

manservant *n.* (*pl.* **menservants**) male servant.

mansion *n.* large stately house.

manslaughter *n.* act of killing a person unlawfully but not intentionally.

mantelpiece *n.* shelf above a fireplace.

mantilla *n.* Spanish lace veil worn over a woman's hair and shoulders.

mantis *n.* grasshopper-like insect.

mantle *n.* **1** loose cloak. **2** covering.

manual *adj.* **1** of the hands. **2** done or operated by the hand(s). ● *n.* handbook. □ **manually** *adv.*

manufacture *v.* **1** make or produce (goods) on a large scale by machinery. **2** invent. ● *n.* process of manufacturing. □ **manufacturer** *n.*

■ *v.* **1** assemble, construct, fabricate, make, produce. **2** concoct, fabricate, invent, make up. ● *n.* assembly, building, construction, fabrication, production.

manure *n.* substance, esp. dung, used as a fertilizer. ● *v.* apply manure to.

manuscript *n.* book or document written by hand or typed, not printed.

Manx *adj.* & *n.* (language) of the Isle of Man.

many *adj.* numerous, great in number. ● *n.* many people or things.

■ *adj.* a lot of, countless, innumerable, lots of, multitudinous, numerous, *sl.* umpteen. ● *n.* a lot, crowds, droves, *colloq.* heaps, hordes, *colloq.* loads, lots, masses, multitudes, *colloq.* oodles, plenty, quantities, *colloq.* stacks.

Maori /mówrī/ *n.* & *adj.* (*pl.* **Maori** or **-is**) (member, language) of the indigenous race of New Zealand.

map *n.* representation of earth's surface or a part of it. ● *v.* (**mapped**) make a map of. □ **map out** plan in detail.

maple *n.* tree with broad leaves.

mar *v.* (**marred**) damage, spoil.

■ blemish, damage, disfigure, impair, spoil, stain, tarnish.

maraca *n.* club-like gourd containing beads etc., shaken as a musical instrument.

marathon *n.* **1** long-distance foot race. **2** long test of endurance.

marauding *adj.* & *n.* pillaging. □ **marauder** *n.*

marble *n.* **1** a kind of limestone that can be polished. **2** piece of sculpture in this. **3** small ball of glass or clay used in children's games. ● *v.* give a veined or mottled appearance to.

marcasite *n.* crystals of iron pyrites, used in jewellery.

march *v.* **1** walk in a regular rhythm or an organized column. **2** walk purposefully. **3** cause to march or walk. **4** take part in a protest march. ● *n.* **1** act or instance of marching. **2** procession as a protest or demonstration. **3** progress. **4** music suitable for marching to. □ **marcher** *n.*

■ *v.* **1** file, parade. **2** stalk, stride, walk. ● *n.* **1** parade, procession, walk. **2** demonstration, parade, rally. **3** advance, passage, progress.

marchioness *n.* **1** wife or widow of a marquess. **2** woman with the rank of marquess.

mare *n.* female of the horse or a related animal.

margarine *n.* substance made from animal or vegetable fat and used like butter.

marge *n.* (*colloq.*) margarine.

margin *n.* **1** edge or border of a surface. **2** blank space round the edges of a page.

3 amount by which a thing exceeds, falls short, etc.

■ **1** border, brink, edge, lip, perimeter, rim, side, verge.

marginal *adj.* **1** of or in a margin. **2** insignificant. □ **marginally** *adv.*

■ **2** insignificant, minimal, negligible, slight, small.

marginalize *v.* make or treat as insignificant. □ **marginalization** *n.*

marguerite *n.* large daisy.

marigold *n.* plant with golden or bright yellow flowers.

marijuana /márrihwaánə/ *n.* dried hemp, smoked as a drug.

marimba *n.* a kind of xylophone.

marina *n.* harbour for yachts and pleasure boats.

marinade *n.* flavoured liquid in which meat or fish is steeped before cooking.
● *v.* steep in a marinade.

marine *adj.* **1** of the sea. **2** of shipping.
● *n.* **1** soldier trained to serve on land or sea. **2** a country's shipping.

mariner *n.* sailor, seaman.

marionette *n.* puppet worked by strings.

marital *adj.* of marriage.

maritime *adj.* **1** living or found near the sea. **2** of seafaring.

marjoram *n.* fragrant herb.

mark¹ *n.* **1** thing that visibly breaks the uniformity of a surface. **2** distinguishing feature of a person or animal. **3** thing indicating the presence of a quality or feeling etc. **4** symbol. **5** point given for merit. **6** lasting effect. **7** object, target, goal. **8** line or object serving to indicate a position. **9** numbered design of a piece of equipment etc. ● *v.* **1** make a mark on. **2** characterize. **3** assign marks of merit to. **4** pay attention to. **5** keep close to (an opponent in football etc.). □ **mark time** move the feet as if marching but without advancing.

■ *n.* **1** blemish, blot, blotch, bruise, scar, smear, smudge, splodge, splotch, spot, stain, streak; dent, nick, scratch. **2** blaze, marking, stripe; birthmark. **3** indication, sign, symbol, token. **4** brand, emblem, hallmark, logo, seal, symbol, trademark, watermark. **5** grade, rating, score. **6** effect, impact, impression. **7** aim, end, goal, object, objective, purpose, target. **8** indicator, landmark, marker, milestone, signpost.
● *v.* **1** blemish, smear, smudge, splodge, splotch, spot, stain, streak; nick, scratch. **2** characterize, distinguish. **3** appraise, assess, correct, evaluate, grade. **4** attend to,

heed, mind, note, pay attention to, take notice of.

mark² *n.* Deutschmark.

marked *adj.* clearly noticeable. □ **markedly** *adv.*

■ conspicuous, decided, distinct, noticeable, perceptible, pronounced, unmistakable.

marker *n.* person or object that marks something.

market *n.* **1** gathering or place for the sale of provisions, livestock, etc. **2** demand (for a commodity). ● *v.* **1** sell in a market. **2** offer for sale. □ **market garden** one in which vegetables are grown for market. **on the market** offered for sale.

marking *n.* **1** mark(s). **2** colouring of feathers, fur, etc.

marksman *n.* person who is a skilled shot. □ **marksmanship** *n.*

marl *n.* soil composed of clay and lime, used as a fertilizer.

marmalade *n.* preserve made from citrus fruit, esp. oranges.

marmoset *n.* small bushy-tailed monkey of tropical America.

marmot *n.* small burrowing animal of the squirrel family.

maroon¹ *n.* **1** brownish-red colour. **2** explosive device used as a warning signal.
● *adj.* brownish-red.

maroon² *v.* **1** put and leave (a person) ashore in a desolate place. **2** leave stranded.

marquee *n.* large tent used for a party or exhibition etc.

marquess *n.* nobleman ranking between duke and earl.

marquetry *n.* inlaid work in wood etc.

marquis *n.* foreign nobleman ranking between duke and count.

marram *n.* type of grass that grows esp. in sand.

marriage *n.* **1** legal union of a man and woman. **2** act or ceremony of marrying.

■ **1** matrimony, wedlock. **2** nuptials, wedding.

marriageable *adj.* suitable or old enough for marriage.

marrow *n.* **1** soft fatty substance in the cavities of bones. **2** large gourd used as a vegetable.

marry *v.* **1** take, join, or give in marriage. **2** unite (things).

■ **1** espouse, get married to, wed. **2** amalgamate, combine, couple, join, link, unify, unite.

marsh n. low-lying watery ground. □ **marshy** adj.
■ bog, fen, morass, quagmire, slough, swamp.

marshal n. 1 high-ranking officer. 2 official controlling an event or ceremony. ● v. (**marshalled**) 1 arrange in proper order. 2 assemble. 3 usher.

marshmallow n. soft sweet made from sugar, egg white, and gelatine.

marsupial n. mammal that usu. carries its young in a pouch.

mart n. market.

marten n. weasel-like animal with thick soft fur.

martial adj. 1 of war. 2 warlike. □ **martial law** military government suspending ordinary law.
■ 1 military, soldierly. 2 aggressive, bellicose, belligerent, militant, pugnacious, warlike.

martin n. bird of the swallow family.

martinet n. person who demands strict obedience.

martyr n. person who undergoes death or suffering for his or her beliefs. ● v. kill or torment as a martyr. □ **martyrdom** n.

marvel n. wonderful thing. ● v. (**marvelled**) feel wonder.
■ n. miracle, phenomenon, sensation, wonder. ● v. be amazed or awed, wonder.

marvellous adj. wonderful. □ **marvellously** adv.
■ amazing, astounding, breathtaking, extraordinary, incredible, magnificent, miraculous, outstanding, phenomenal, remarkable, sensational, stupendous, superb, wonderful; excellent, colloq. fabulous, colloq. fantastic, glorious, colloq. great, colloq. heavenly, colloq. smashing, splendid, colloq. super, colloq. terrific, colloq. tremendous.

Marxism n. socialist theories of Karl Marx. □ **Marxist** adj. & n.

marzipan n. edible paste made from ground almonds.

mascara n. cosmetic for darkening the eyelashes.

mascot n. thing believed to bring good luck to its owner.

masculine adj. 1 of, like, or traditionally considered suitable for men. 2 of the grammatical form suitable for the names of males. ● n. masculine word. □ **masculinity** n.

mash n. 1 soft mixture of grain or bran. 2 mashed potatoes. ● v. beat into a soft mass.

mask n. 1 covering worn over the face as a disguise or protection. 2 disguise. ● v. 1 cover with a mask. 2 conceal.
■ n. 2 camouflage, cover-up, disguise, guise, pretence, semblance, show. ● v. 2 camouflage, cloak, conceal, cover (up), disguise, hide, screen, shroud, veil.

masochism n. pleasure in suffering pain. □ **masochist** n., **masochistic** adj.

mason n. person who builds or works with stone.

masonry n. stonework.

masquerade n. false show or pretence. ● v. pretend to be what one is not.

mass[1] n. 1 celebration (esp. in the RC Church) of the Eucharist. 2 form of liturgy used in this.

mass[2] n. 1 quantity of matter without a regular shape. 2 large quantity, heap, or expanse. 3 quantity of matter a body contains. 4 (**the masses**) ordinary people. ● v. gather or assemble into a mass. □ **mass-produce** v. manufacture in large quantities by a standardized process.
■ n. 1 block, chunk, concretion, lump, piece. 2 crowd, herd, horde, host, multitude, swarm, throng; abundance, accumulation, assortment, bunch, collection, conglomeration, heap, mound, mountain, pile, profusion, quantity, colloq. stack. ● v. accumulate, amass, collect, gather, pile up; assemble, congregate, convene, flock together, group; marshal, mobilize, rally.

massacre n. great slaughter. ● v. slaughter in large numbers.
■ n. annihilation, butchery, killing, slaughter. ● v. annihilate, butcher, exterminate, kill, murder, slaughter, slay.

massage n. rubbing and kneading the body to reduce pain or stiffness. ● v. treat in this way.

masseur n. (fem. **masseuse**) person who practises massage professionally.

massive adj. 1 large and heavy or solid. 2 huge. □ **massively** adv.
■ big, bulky, colossal, enormous, gargantuan, gigantic, huge, immense, large, mammoth, mighty, monstrous, monumental, mountainous, titanic, vast.

mast[1] n. tall pole, esp. supporting a ship's sails.

mast[2] n. fruit of beech, oak, etc., used as food for pigs.

mastectomy *n.* surgical removal of a breast.

master *n.* **1** man who has control of people or things. **2** male teacher. **3** person with very great skill, great artist. **4** thing from which a series of copies is made. **6** (**Master**) title of a boy not old enough to be called *Mr.* ● *adj.* **1** superior. **2** principal. **3** controlling others. ● *v.* **1** bring under control. **2** acquire knowledge or skill in. □ **master-key** *n.* key that opens a number of different locks. **master-stroke** *n.* very skilful act of policy.

■ *n.* **1** *colloq.* boss, captain, chief, commander, governor, head, leader, owner, ruler, skipper. **2** instructor, schoolmaster, teacher, tutor. **3** adept, authority, expert, genius, maestro, mastermind, virtuoso, wizard. ● *adj.* **1** excellent, exceptional, expert, outstanding, superior, supreme. **2** chief, main, principal. ● *v.* **1** check, conquer, control, curb, defeat, overcome, quell, repress, subdue, subjugate, suppress. **2** become proficient in, *colloq.* get the hang of, grasp, learn.

masterful *adj.* domineering. □ **masterfully** *adv.*

masterly *adj.* very skilful.

mastermind *n.* **1** person of outstanding mental ability. **2** one directing an enterprise. ● *v.* plan and direct.

masterpiece *n.* outstanding piece of work.

mastery *n.* **1** control, supremacy. **2** thorough knowledge or skill.

■ **1** ascendancy, command, control, dominance, supremacy, superiority, the upper hand. **2** command, comprehension, grasp, knowledge, understanding.

mastic *n.* **1** gum or resin from certain trees. **2** a kind of cement.

masticate *v.* chew. □ **mastication** *n.*

mastiff *n.* large strong dog.

mastodon *n.* extinct animal resembling an elephant.

mastoid *n.* part of a bone behind the ear.

masturbate *v.* stimulate the genitals (of) manually. □ **masturbation** *n.*

mat *n.* **1** piece of material placed on a floor or other surface as an ornament or to protect it. ● *v.* (**matted**) make or become tangled into a thick mass.

matador *n.* bullfighter.

match¹ *n.* short stick tipped with material that catches fire when rubbed on a rough surface.

match² *n.* **1** contest in a game or sport. **2** person or thing exactly like or corresponding or equal to another. **3** matrimonial alliance. ● *v.* **1** equal in ability or achievement. **2** be alike. **3** find a match for. □ **match against** or **with** place in competition with.

■ *n.* **1** bout, competition, contest, game, tournament. **2** equal, equivalent, like, peer; copy, counterpart, double, duplicate, twin. **3** marriage, partnership, union. ● *v.* **1** be in the same league as, be on a par with, compare with, equal, measure up to, rival, touch. **2** agree, correspond, tally.

matchmaking *n.* scheming to arrange marriages. □ **matchmaker** *n.*

matchstick *n.* stick of a match.

matchwood *n.* **1** wood that splinters easily. **2** wood broken into splinters.

mate¹ *n.* **1** companion or fellow worker. **2** male or female of mated animals. **3** merchant ship's officer. ● *v.* come or bring (animals) together to breed.

■ *n.* **1** *colloq.* buddy, *colloq.* chum, companion, crony, friend, *colloq.* pal; associate, colleague, comrade, fellow worker.

mate² *n.* checkmate.

material *n.* **1** that from which something is or can be made. **2** cloth, fabric. ● *adj.* **1** of matter. **2** not spiritual. **3** significant. □ **materially** *adv.*

■ *n.* **1** matter, stuff, substance. **2** cloth, fabric, textile. ● *adj.* **1** concrete, palpable, physical, real, solid, tangible. **2** earthly, mundane, secular, temporal, worldly. **3** consequential, important, relevant, significant.

materialism *n.* **1** belief that only the material world exists. **2** excessive concern with material possessions. □ **materialist** *n.*, **materialistic** *adj.*

materialize *v.* **1** appear, become visible. **2** become a fact, happen. □ **materialization** *n.*

■ **1** appear, become visible, emerge, take shape. **2** come about, happen, occur, take place.

maternal *adj.* **1** of a mother. **2** motherly. **3** related through one's mother. □ **maternally** *adv.*

■ **2** affectionate, caring, gentle, kind, loving, motherly, nurturing, protective, tender, warm.

maternity *n.* motherhood. ● *adj.* of or for women in pregnancy and childbirth.

mathematician *n.* person skilled in mathematics.

mathematics *n.* science of numbers, quantities, and measurements. □ **mathematical** *adj.*

maths *n.* mathematics.

matinée *n.* afternoon performance. □ **matinée coat** baby's jacket.

matriarch *n.* female head of a family or tribe. □ **matriarchal** *adj.*

matriarchy *n.* social organization in which a female is head of the family.

matricide *n.* killing or killer of own mother. □ **matricidal** *adj.*

matriculate *v.* admit or be admitted to a university. □ **matriculation** *n.*

matrimony *n.* marriage. □ **matrimonial** *adj.*

matrix *n.* (*pl.* **matrices**) **1** mould in which a thing is cast or shaped. **2** rectangular array of mathematical quantities.

matron *n.* **1** married woman. **2** woman in charge of domestic affairs or nursing in a school etc.

matronly *adj.* like or characteristic of a staid or dignified married woman.

matt *adj.* dull, not shiny.

matter *n.* **1** that which occupies space in the visible world. **2** specified substance, material, or things. **3** business etc. being discussed. **4** pus. ● *v.* be of importance. □ **what is the matter?** what is amiss?
■ *n.* **2** material, stuff, substance. **3** affair, business, concern, issue, question, subject, topic. ● *v.* be important, be of consequence, count, signify.

mattress *n.* fabric case filled with padding or springy material, used on or as a bed.

maturation *n.* maturing.

mature *adj.* **1** fully grown or developed. **2** (of a bill etc.) due for payment. ● *v.* make or become mature. □ **maturity** *n.*
■ *adj.* **1** adult, developed, experienced, fully-fledged, fully-grown, grown-up, of age; mellow, ready, ripe, ripened. ● *v.* age, grow up, mellow, ripen.

maudlin *adj.* sentimental in a silly or tearful way.
■ mawkish, mushy, sentimental, *colloq.* soppy.

maul *v.* treat roughly, injure by tearing flesh.
■ maltreat, manhandle, mistreat, molest; claw, lacerate, mutilate, savage.

maunder *v.* **1** talk in a dreamy or rambling way. **2** move idly.

mausoleum *n.* magnificent tomb.

mauve /mōv/ *adj.* & *n.* pale purple.

maverick *n.* unorthodox or undisciplined person.

mawkish *adj.* sentimental in a sickly way.

maxim *n.* sentence giving a general truth or rule of conduct.
■ aphorism, axiom, motto, proverb, saw, saying.

maximize *v.* increase to a maximum. □ **maximization** *n.*

maximum *adj.* & *n.* (*pl.* **-ima**) greatest (amount) possible. □ **maximal** *adj.*, **maximally** *adv.*
■ *adj.* greatest, highest, most, top, topmost, utmost, uttermost. ● *n.* limit, peak, top, utmost, uttermost.

may[1] *v.aux.* (**might**) used to express a wish, possibility, or permission.

may[2] *n.* hawthorn blossom.

maybe *adv.* perhaps.
■ conceivably, perhaps, possibly.

mayday *n.* international radio signal of distress.

May Day 1 May, esp. as a festival.

mayfly *n.* insect with long hair-like tails, living in spring.

mayhem *n.* violent action.

mayonnaise *n.* creamy sauce made with eggs and oil.

mayor *n.* head of the municipal corporation of a city or borough. □ **mayoral** *adj.*, **mayoralty** *n.*

mayoress *n.* **1** female mayor. **2** mayor's wife, or other woman with her ceremonial duties.

maypole *n.* tall pole for dancing round on May Day.

maze *n.* complex and baffling network of paths, lines, etc.

me *pron.* objective case of *I.*

mead *n.* alcoholic drink of fermented honey and water.

meadow *n.* field of grass.
■ field, *poetic* lea, paddock.

meagre *adj.* scant in amount.
■ inadequate, insufficient, *sl.* measly, *colloq.* pathetic, poor, scant, scanty, skimpy, sparse.

meal[1] *n.* **1** occasion when food is eaten. **2** the food itself.
■ banquet, feast, *formal* repast, *colloq.* spread; bite, snack.

meal[2] *n.* coarsely ground grain.

mealy *adj.* of or like meal. □ **mealy-mouthed** *adj.* afraid to speak plainly.

mean¹ *adj.* **1** miserly, not generous. **2** ignoble. **3** of low degree or poor quality. **4** malicious, unkind. **5** (*US*) vicious. □ **meanly** *adv.*, **meanness** *n.*

■ **1** close, miserly, near, niggardly, parsimonious, penny-pinching, stingy, *colloq.* tight, tight-fisted, ungenerous. **2** base, dishonourable, ignoble, low, small-minded. **3** humble, inferior, lowly; miserable, poor, *colloq.* scruffy, seedy, shabby, squalid, wretched. **4** cruel, malicious, nasty, spiteful, unkind.

mean² *adj.* & *n.* **1** (thing) midway between two extremes. **2** average.

mean³ *v.* (**meant**) **1** have as one's purpose. **2** have as an equivalent in another language, signify. **3** entail, involve. **4** portend, be likely to result in. **5** be of specified importance.

■ **1** aim, contemplate, design, intend, plan, propose, purpose. **2** connote, denote, indicate, represent, signify. **3** entail, imply, involve. **4** augur, foreshadow, portend, presage, promise.

meander *v.* **1** follow a winding course. **2** wander in a leisurely way. ● *n.* winding course.

■ *v.* **1** snake, turn, twist, wind. **2** amble, drift, ramble, stroll, wander.

meaning *n.* **1** what is meant. **2** significance. ● *adj.* expressive.

■ *n.* **1** connotation, denotation, drift, gist, import, purport, sense, signification, substance. **2** consequence, importance, significance, value, worth.

meaningful *adj.* **1** full of meaning. **2** significant.

■ **1** expressive, pointed, pregnant, suggestive. **2** consequential, important, serious, significant.

meaningless *adj.* having no meaning or significance.

■ empty, hollow, inconsequential, insignificant, pointless, purposeless, senseless, trivial, unimportant, valueless, worthless.

means *n.pl* (often treated as *sing.*) **1** that by which a result is brought about. **2** resources. □ **by all means** certainly. **by no means** not at all. **means test** official inquiry to establish need before giving financial help from public funds.

■ **1** agency, manner, medium, method, mode, process, technique, vehicle, way. **2** capital, cash, funds, money, resources, *colloq.* wherewithal.

meant *see* **mean³**.

meantime *adv.* meanwhile.

meanwhile *adv.* **1** in the intervening period. **2** at the same time.

measles *n.* infectious disease producing red spots on the body.

measly *adj.* (*sl.*) meagre.

measure *n.* **1** size or quantity found by measuring. **2** unit, device, or system used in measuring. **3** rhythm. **4** (usu. *pl.*) action taken for a purpose. **5** (proposed) law. ● *v.* **1** find the size etc. of by comparison with a known standard. **2** be of a certain size. □ **measure out** distribute in measured quantities. **measure up to** reach the standard required by. **measurable** *adj.*, **measurably** *adv.*

■ *n.* **1** amount, amplitude, bulk, dimension(s), extent, magnitude, measurement(s), quantity, proportions, scope, size, weight; breadth, depth, height, length, width; capacity, volume. **2** gauge, rule, ruler, tape-measure; scale, system. **3** beat, cadence, metre, rhythm. **4** (**measures**) action, expedients, procedures, steps, tactics. **5** act, bill, statute. ● *v.* **1** ascertain, assess, calculate, calibrate, compute, determine, evaluate, gauge, size up, weigh. □ **measure out** allocate, allot, apportion, dispense, distribute, deal out, dole out, give out, hand out, mete out, share out. **measure up to** be equal to, equal, fulfil, match, meet.

measured *adj.* **1** rhythmical. **2** carefully considered.

measurement *n.* **1** measuring. **2** size etc. found by measuring.

■ **1** assessment, calculation, computation, evaluation, gauging, mensuration. **2** amount, amplitude, dimension, extent, magnitude, measure, size; breadth, depth, height, length, width; capacity, volume; acreage, yardage.

meat *n.* animal flesh as food.

meaty *adj.* (**-ier, -iest**) **1** like meat. **2** full of meat. **3** full of subject-matter. □ **meatiness** *n.*

mechanic *n.* person skilled in using or repairing machinery.

mechanical *adj.* **1** of or worked by machinery. **2** done without conscious thought. □ **mechanically** *adv.*

■ **1** automated, robotic. **2** automatic, instinctive, involuntary, knee-jerk, unconscious, unthinking.

mechanics *n.* **1** study of motion and force. **2** science of machinery. **3** (as *pl.*) way a thing works.

mechanism *n.* **1** structure or parts of a machine. **2** system of parts working together.

mechanize *v.* equip with machinery. □ **mechanization** *n.*

medal *n.* coin-like piece of metal commemorating an event or awarded for an achievement.

medallion *n.* **1** large medal. **2** circular ornamental design.

medallist *n.* winner of a medal.

meddle *v.* interfere in people's affairs.
■ butt in, interfere, intervene, intrude, pry.

meddlesome *adj.* often meddling.

media *see* **medium**. *n.pl.* (**the media**) newspapers and broadcasting as conveying information to the public.

mediaeval *adj.* = **medieval**.

medial *adj.* situated in the middle. □ **medially** *adv.*

median *adj.* in or passing through the middle. ● *n.* median point or line.

mediate *v.* **1** act as peacemaker between disputants. **2** bring about (a settlement) in this way. □ **mediation** *n.*, **mediator** *n.*
■ **1** arbitrate, intercede, intervene, liaise, negotiate. □ **mediator** arbitrator, arbiter, go-between, intermediary, middleman, negotiator, peacemaker.

medical *adj.* of the science of medicine. ● *n.* (*colloq.*) medical examination. □ **medically** *adv.*

medicament *n.* any medicine, ointment, etc.

medicate *v.* treat with a medicinal substance.

medication *n.* **1** medicinal drug. **2** treatment using drugs.

medicinal *adj.* having healing properties. □ **medicinally** *adv.*
■ healing, health-giving, restorative, therapeutic.

medicine *n.* **1** science of the prevention and cure of disease. **2** substance used to treat disease. ■ **medicine man** witch-doctor.
■ **2** drug, medicament, medication, remedy.

medieval *adj.* of the Middle Ages.

mediocre *adj.* **1** of medium quality. **2** second-rate. □ **mediocrity** *n.*
■ **1** average, commonplace, fair, indifferent, middling, ordinary, pedestrian, run-of-the-mill, undistinguished, unremarkable. **2** inferior, poor, second-rate.

meditate *v.* think deeply. □ **meditation** *n.*, **meditative** *adj.*
■ cogitate, muse, ponder, reflect, ruminate, think.

medium *n.* (*pl.* **-dia** or **-s**) **1** middle size, quality, etc. **2** substance or surroundings in which a thing exists. **3** agency, means. ● *adj.* **1** intermediate. **2** average.
■ *n.* **2** ambience, atmosphere, environment, milieu. **3** agency, avenue, channel, means, method, mode, vehicle. ● *adj.* **1** intermediate, median, mid, middle. **2** average, middling, standard.

medley *n.* (*pl.* **-eys**) assortment.
■ assortment, collection, hotchpotch, miscellany, mixture, pot-pourri.

medulla *n.* **1** spinal or bone marrow. **2** hindmost segment of the brain. ■ **medullary** *adj.*

meek *adj.* quiet and obedient, not protesting. □ **meekly** *adv.*, **meekness** *n.*
■ acquiescent, compliant, deferential, docile, humble, manageable, obedient, quiet, submissive, timid, tractable, unassuming.

meerschaum /meérshəm/ *n.* **1** tobacco pipe with a white clay bowl. **2** this clay.

meet *v.* (**met**) **1** come into contact (with). **2** come together. **3** make the acquaintance of. **4** experience. **5** satisfy (needs etc.). **6** be present at the arrival of. ● *n.* assembly for a hunt etc.
■ *v.* **1** come across, encounter, happen on, run into. **2** converge, intersect, join, link up with; assemble, collect, congregate, convene, gather. **3** be introduced to, make the acquaintance of. **4** encounter, endure, experience, go through, undergo. **5** comply with, fulfil, measure up to, satisfy. **6** greet, receive, welcome.

meeting *n.* **1** coming together. **2** an assembly for discussion.
■ **1** appointment, assignation, *colloq.* date, encounter, engagement, rendezvous; confluence, conjunction, convergence, intersection, junction. **2** assembly, conference, convention, convocation, gathering, *colloq.* get-together, session.

mega- *pref.* **1** large. **2** one million (as in *megavolts, megawatts*).

megabyte *n.* one million bytes.

megalith *n.* large stone, esp. as a prehistoric monument. □ **megalithic** *adj.*

megalomania *n.* excessive self-esteem, esp. as a form of insanity. □ **megalomaniac** *adj.* & *n.*

megaphone *n.* funnel-shaped device for amplifying the voice.

megaton *n.* unit of explosive power equal to one million tons of TNT.

melancholy *n.* mental depression, sadness. ● *adj.* sad, gloomy.

■ *n.* dejection, depression, despondency, gloom, misery, sadness, sorrow, unhappiness. ● *adj.* blue, cheerless, crestfallen, dejected, depressed, despondent, downcast, downhearted, gloomy, glum, forlorn, heavy-hearted, in low spirits, in the doldrums, lugubrious, miserable, morose, mournful, sad, sorrowful, unhappy, woebegone, woeful.

melanin *n.* dark pigment in the skin, hair, etc.

mêlée /méllay/ *n.* 1 confused fight, scuffle. 2 muddle.

mellifluous *adj.* sweet-sounding.

mellow *adj.* 1 (of fruit) ripe and sweet. 2 (of sound or colour) soft and rich. 3 (of people) having become kindly, e.g. with age. ● *v.* make or become mellow.

■ *adj.* 1 mature, ripe, sweet. 2 deep, full, resonant, rich, sonorous; muted, soft, subtle. 3 easygoing, genial, good-natured, friendly, kind, pleasant, warm. ● *v.* age, mature, ripen.

melodic *adj.* 1 of melody 2 melodious. □ **melodically** *adv.*

melodious *adj.* full of melody. □ **melodiously** *adv.*

■ dulcet, euphonious, harmonious, melodic, musical, silvery, sweet-sounding, tuneful.

melodrama *n.* sensational drama. □ **melodramatic** *adj.*, **melodramatically** *adv.*

■ **melodramatic** exaggerated, overdone, over-dramatic, sensational, theatrical.

melody *n.* 1 (piece of) sweet music. 2 main part in a piece of harmonized music.

■ 1 air, song, strain, tune; euphony, harmony, melodiousness, tunefulness.

melon *n.* large sweet fruit.

melt *v.* 1 make into or become liquid, esp. by heat. 2 soften through pity or love. 3 disappear unobtrusively.

■ 1 dissolve, liquefy, thaw. 2 disarm, mellow, soften, thaw. 3 disappear, disperse, evaporate, fade (away), vanish.

meltdown *n.* melting of an overheated reactor core.

member *n.* person or thing belonging to a particular group or society. □ **membership** *n.*

membrane *n.* thin flexible skin-like tissue. □ **membranous** *adj.*

memento *n.* (*pl.* **-oes**) souvenir.

■ keepsake, reminder, souvenir, token.

memo *n.* (*pl.* **-os**) (*colloq.*) memorandum.

memoir /mémwaar/ *n.* historical account written from personal knowledge.

■ account, biography, chronicle, journal, life, record.

memorable *adj.* 1 worth remembering. 2 easy to remember. □ **memorably** *adv.*

■ 1 great, historic, important, momentous, notable, noteworthy, remarkable, significant. 2 catchy, unforgettable.

memorandum *n.* 1 (*pl.* **-da**) note written as a reminder. 2 (*pl.* **-dums**) written message from one colleague to another.

memorial *n.* object or custom etc. established in memory of an event or person(s). ● *adj.* serving as a memorial.

■ *n.* cairn, cenotaph, monument, plaque, statue.

memorize *v.* learn (a thing) so as to know it from memory.

memory *n.* 1 ability to remember things. 2 thing(s) remembered. 3 computer store for data etc.

■ 2 recollection, remembrance, reminiscence.

men *see* **man**.

menace *n.* 1 threat. 2 annoying or troublesome person or thing. ● *v.* threaten. □ **menacingly** *adv.*

■ *n.* 1 danger, hazard, peril, risk, threat. 2 annoyance, nuisance, pest, troublemaker. ● *v.* browbeat, bully, cow, intimidate, threaten, terrorize.

ménage /maynáazh/ *n.* household.

menagerie *n.* small zoo.

mend *v.* 1 repair. 2 make or become better. ● *n.* repaired place. □ **on the mend** recovering after illness.

■ *v.* 1 darn, fix, patch (up), repair. 2 correct, improve, put *or* set right, rectify, remedy; convalesce, get better, heal, recover, recuperate. □ **on the mend** convalescent, improving, recovering, recuperating.

mendacious *adj.* untruthful. □ **mendacity** *n.*

mendicant *adj.* & *n.* (person) living by begging.

menfolk *n.* **1** men in general. **2** men of one's family.

menhir /ménheer/ *n.* tall stone set up in prehistoric times.

menial *adj.* lowly, degrading. ● *n.* person who does menial tasks. □ **menially** *adv.*

■ *adj.* degrading, demeaning, humble, lowly, servile. ● *n.* drudge, *colloq.* dogsbody, lackey, minion, slave, underling.

meningitis *n.* inflammation of the membranes covering the brain and spinal cord.

meniscus *n.* **1** curved surface of a liquid. **2** lens convex on one side and concave on the other.

menopause *n.* **1** ceasing of menstruation. **2** time in a woman's life when this occurs. □ **menopausal** *adj.*

menorah *n.* seven-armed candelabrum used in Jewish worship.

menstrual *adj.* of or in menstruation.

menstruate *v.* experience a monthly discharge of blood from the womb. □ **menstruation** *n.*

mensuration *n.* **1** measuring. **2** mathematical rules for this.

mental *adj.* **1** of, in, or performed by the mind. **2** (*colloq.*) mad. □ **mentally** *adv.*

mentality *n.* characteristic attitude of mind.

■ attitude, character, disposition, frame of mind, make-up, outlook.

menthol *n.* camphor-like substance.

mentholated *adj.* impregnated with menthol.

mention *v.* **1** speak or write about briefly. **2** refer to by name. ● *n.* act of mentioning.

■ *v.* **1** allude to, bring up, broach, refer to, speak about, touch on, write about. **2** cite, name, quote. ● *n.* allusion, citation, reference.

mentor *n.* trusted adviser.

menu *n.* (*pl.* **-us**) **1** list of dishes to be served. **2** list of options displayed on a computer screen.

mercantile *adj.* trading, of trade or merchants.

mercenary *adj.* primarily concerned with money or reward. ● *n.* professional soldier hired by a foreign country.

■ *adj.* acquisitive, avaricious, covetous, grasping, greedy.

merchandise *n.* goods bought and sold or for sale. ● *v.* **1** trade. **2** promote sales of (goods).

■ *n.* commodities, goods, products, stock, wares. ● *v.* **1** market, retail, sell, trade. **2** advertise, promote, publicize.

merchant *n.* **1** wholesale trader. **2** (*US & Sc.*) retail trader. □ **merchant bank** one dealing in commercial loans and the financing of businesses. **merchant navy** shipping employed in commerce. **merchant ship** ship carrying merchandise.

merchantable *adj.* saleable.

merchantman *n.* merchant ship.

merciful *adj.* showing mercy. □ **mercifulness** *n.*

■ charitable, clement, compassionate, forbearing, forgiving, humane, kind, kind-hearted, kindly, magnanimous, lenient.

mercifully *adv.* **1** in a merciful way. **2** (*colloq.*) fortunately.

merciless *adj.* showing no mercy. □ **mercilessly** *adv.*

■ barbaric, barbarous, brutal, callous, cold, cruel, hard, hard-hearted, harsh, heartless, inhuman, inhumane, implacable, pitiless, ruthless, savage, unforgiving, unmerciful.

mercurial *adj.* **1** volatile. **2** of or containing mercury.

■ **1** capricious, changeable, inconstant, temperamental, unpredictable, volatile.

mercury *n.* heavy silvery usu. liquid metal. □ **mercuric** *adj.*

mercy *n.* **1** kindness shown to an offender or enemy etc. who is in one's power. **2** merciful act. □ **at the mercy of** wholly in the power of or subject to.

■ **1** charity, clemency, compassion, forbearance, forgiveness, generosity, humanity, kindness, leniency, magnanimity, pity, quarter.

mere¹ *adj.* no more or no better than what is specified. □ **merely** *adv.*

mere² *n.* (*poetic*) lake.

merge *v.* **1** combine into a whole. **2** blend gradually.

■ **1** amalgamate, coalesce, combine, consolidate, join, unite. **2** blend, mingle, mix.

merger *n.* combining of commercial companies etc. into one.

■ alliance, amalgamation, coalition, combination, merging, union.

meridian *n.* any of the circles round the earth that pass through both the North and South Poles.

meringue /məráng/ n. **1** baked mixture of sugar and egg white. **2** small cake of this.

merino n. (pl. -os) **1** a kind of sheep with fine soft wool. **2** soft woollen fabric.

merit n. **1** feature or quality that deserves praise. **2** worthiness. ● v. (**merited**) deserve.
  ■ n. **1** advantage, asset, good point. **2** excellence, value, worth, worthiness. ● v. be entitled to, be worthy of, deserve, earn, rate, warrant.

meritocracy n. government by people selected for merit.

meritorious adj. deserving praise.
  ■ admirable, commendable, creditable, estimable, excellent, exemplary, laudable, outstanding, praiseworthy.

merlin n. a kind of falcon.

mermaid n. imaginary half-human sea creature with a fish's tail instead of legs.

merry adj. (-ier, -iest) cheerful and lively, joyous. □ **merry-go-round** n. roundabout at a funfair. **merrymaking** n. revelry. **merrily** adv., **merriment** n.
  ■ bubbly, buoyant, carefree, cheerful, cheery, chirpy, gay, gleeful, happy, in good spirits, jolly, joyful, light-hearted, lively, vivacious. ● **merriment** cheer, cheerfulness, gaiety, glee, high spirits, joyfulness, mirth.

mesh n. **1** network fabric. **2** space between threads in net, sieve, etc. ● v. (of a toothed wheel) engage with another.

mesmerize v. **1** hypnotize. **2** fascinate.
  ■ **2** bewitch, captivate, enthral, fascinate, grip, hold spellbound.

mesolithic adj. of the period between palaeolithic and neolithic.

mess n. **1** dirty or untidy condition. **2** difficult or confused situation, trouble. **3** something split etc. **4** (in the armed forces) group who eat together, their dining room. ● v. **mess up 1** make untidy or dirty. **2** muddle, bungle. □ **make a mess of** bungle. **mess about 1** potter. **2** fool about.
  ■ n. **1** chaos, clutter, confusion, disarray, disorder, disorganization, hotchpotch, jumble, muddle, shambles, tangle, untidiness. **2** difficulty, fix, colloq. hole, colloq. jam, colloq. pickle, plight, predicament, quandary, trouble. ● v. **1** clutter up, disarrange, disarray, disorder; dishevel, ruffle, rumple, tousle. **2** botch, bungle, colloq. make a hash of, make a mess of, colloq. muff, ruin, sl. screw up, spoil.

message n. **1** spoken or written communication. **2** moral or social teaching.
  ■ **1** communication, communiqué, dispatch; letter, colloq. memo, memorandum, note.

messenger n. bearer of a message.
  ■ courier, emissary, envoy, go-between, intermediary.

Messiah n. **1** deliverer expected by Jews. **2** Christ as this. □ **Messianic** adj.

Messrs see **Mr**.

messy adj. (-ier, -iest) untidy or dirty. □ **messily** adv.
  ■ chaotic, cluttered, disordered, disorderly, in a muddle, in disarray, topsy-turvy, untidy; dishevelled, rumpled, colloq. scruffy, unkempt; dirty, grubby, colloq. mucky.

met see **meet**.

metabolism n. process by which nutrition takes place. □ **metabolic** adj., **metabolically** adv.

metabolize v. process (food) in metabolism.

metal n. **1** any of a class of mineral substances such as gold, silver, iron, etc., or an alloy of these. **2** road-metal. ● v. make or mend (a road) with road-metal.

metallic adj. of or like metal.

metallurgy n. science of extracting and working metals.

metamorphose v. change by metamorphosis.

metamorphosis n. (pl. -phoses) change of form or character. □ **metamorphic** adj.

metaphor n. application of a word or phrase to something that it does not apply to literally (e.g. the evening of one's life, food for thought). □ **metaphorical** adj., **metaphorically** adv.

metaphysics n. branch of philosophy dealing with the nature of existence and of knowledge. □ **metaphysical** adj.

mete v. **mete out** deal out.

meteor n. small mass of matter from outer space.

meteoric adj. **1** of meteors. **2** swift and brilliant.

meteorite n. meteor fallen to earth.

meteorology n. study of atmospheric conditions in order to forecast weather. □ **meteorological** adj., **meteorologist** n.

meter¹ n. device measuring and indicating the quantity supplied, distance travelled, time elapsed, etc. ● v. measure by a meter.

meter² n. (US) = **metre**.

methane n. colourless inflammable gas.

method n. **1** procedure or way of doing something. **2** orderliness.

■ **1** approach, manner, means, mode, procedure, process, system, technique, way. **2** neatness, order, orderliness, organization, regularity, system.

methodical adj. orderly, systematic. □ **methodically** adv.

■ businesslike, careful, deliberate, ordered, orderly, organized, painstaking, systematic.

meths n. (colloq.) methylated spirit.

methylated spirit form of alcohol used as a solvent and for heating.

meticulous adj. very careful and exact. □ **meticulously** adv.

■ careful, exact, painstaking, particular, precise, punctilious, scrupulous, thorough.

metre n. **1** metric unit of length (about 39.4 inches). **2** rhythm in poetry.

metric adj. **1** of or using the metric system. **2** of poetic metre. □ **metric system** decimal system of weights and measures, using the metre, litre, and gram as units.

metrical adj. of or composed in rhythmic metre, not prose.

metronome n. device used to indicate tempo while practising music.

metropolis n. chief city of country or region.

metropolitan adj. of a metropolis.

mettle n. courage, strength of character.

mettlesome adj. spirited, brave.

mew n. cat's characteristic cry. ● v. make this sound.

mews n. set of stables converted into dwellings etc.

mezzanine n. extra storey set between two others.

mezzotint n. method of engraving.

mg abbr. milligram(s).

MHz abbr. megahertz.

miaow n. & v. = mew.

miasma n. unpleasant or unwholesome air.

mica /míkə/ n. transparent mineral with a layered structure.

mice see mouse.

micro- pref. **1** extremely small. **2** one-millionth part of (as in microgram).

microbe n. micro-organism.

microbiology n. study of micro-organisms.

microchip n. tiny piece of a semiconductor holding a complex electronic circuit.

microcomputer n. computer in which the central processor is contained on microchip(s).

microcosm n. community or complex resembling something else but on a very small scale.

microfiche /míkrōfeesh/ n. (pl. -fiche) small sheet of microfilm.

microfilm n. length of film bearing miniature photographs of document(s). ● v. photograph on this.

microlight n. a kind of motorized hang-glider.

micrometer n. gauge for small-scale measurement.

micron n. one-millionth of a metre.

micro-organism n. organism invisible to the naked eye.

microphone n. instrument for amplifying or broadcasting sound.

microprocessor n. data processor contained on microchip(s).

microscope n. instrument with lenses that magnify very small things and make them visible.

microscopic adj. **1** of a microscope. **2** very small. **3** visible only with a microscope. □ **microscopically** adv., **microscopy** n.

microsurgery n. surgery using a microscope.

microwave n. **1** electromagnetic wave of length between about 50 cm and 1 mm. **2** oven using such waves to cook or heat food quickly.

mid adj. middle.

midday n. noon.

middle adj. occurring at an equal distance from extremes or outer limits. ● n. middle point, position, area, etc. □ **middle age** part of life between youth and old age. **Middle Ages** period of European history from c. 1000–1453. **middle class** class of society between upper and working classes. **Middle East** area from Egypt to Iran inclusive.

■ adj. central, halfway, medial, median, mid. ● n. centre, halfway point, heart, midst.

middleman n. **1** trader handling a commodity between producer and consumer. **2** intermediary.

middling adj. moderately good.

■ adequate, average, fair, indifferent, mediocre, moderate, colloq. OK, ordinary, passable, run-of-the-mill, tolerable, unremarkable.

midge n. small biting insect.

midget *n.* extremely small person or thing. ● *adj.* extremely small.

Midlands *n.pl.* inland counties of central England. □ **midland** *adj.*

midnight *n.* 12 o'clock at night.

midriff *n.* front part of the body just above the waist.

midshipman *n.* naval rank just below sub-lieutenant.

midst *n.* middle. □ **in the midst of** among.

midway *adv.* halfway.

midwife *n.* person trained to assist at childbirth.

mien /meen/ *n.* person's manner or bearing.

might[1] *n.* great strength or power.

■ energy, force, muscle, potency, power, strength.

might[2] *see* **may**[1]. *v.aux.* used to request permission or (like *may*) to express possibility.

mighty *adj.* (**-ier, -iest**) **1** very strong or powerful. **2** very great. □ **mightily** *adv.*

■ **1** potent, powerful, strong; brawny, burly, hefty, muscular, robust, strapping, sturdy. **2** big, colossal, enormous, gigantic, great, huge, large, massive, monumental, tremendous.

migraine /meegrayn/ *n.* severe form of headache.

migrant *adj.* & *n.* migrating (person or animal).

migrate *v.* **1** leave one place and settle in another. **2** (of birds etc.) go from one place to another at each season. □ **migration** *n.*, **migratory** *adj.*

mihrab *n.* niche or slab in a mosque, showing the direction of Mecca.

mild *adj.* **1** gentle. **2** moderate in intensity, not harsh or drastic. **3** not strongly flavoured. □ **mildly** *adv.*, **mildness** *n.*

■ **1** affable, amiable, benign, easygoing, gentle, good-natured, inoffensive, kind, kindly, peaceable, peaceful, placid, serene, tranquil. **2** gentle, light, moderate, soft. **3** bland, insipid.

mildew *n.* tiny fungi forming a coating on things exposed to damp. □ **mildewed** *adj.*

mile *n.* **1** measure of length, 1760 yds (about 1.609 km). **2** (*colloq.*) great distance. □ **nautical mile** unit used in navigation, 2025 yds (1.852 km).

mileage *n.* distance in miles.

milestone *n.* **1** stone showing the distance to a certain place. **2** significant event or stage reached.

milieu /milyó/ *n.* (*pl.* **-eus**) environment, surroundings.

■ background, environment, setting, surroundings.

militant *adj.* & *n.* (person) prepared to take aggressive action. □ **militancy** *n.*

■ *adj.* aggressive, belligerent, combative, pugnacious. ● *n.* activist, extremist, fighter.

militarism *n.* reliance on military attitudes. □ **militaristic** *adj.*

military *adj.* of soldiers or the army or all armed forces.

militate *v.* serve as a strong influence.

militia /milísha/ *n.* a military force, esp. of trained civilians available in an emergency.

milk *n.* **1** white fluid secreted by female mammals as food for their young. **2** cow's milk as food for human beings. **3** milk-like liquid. ● *v.* **1** draw milk from. **2** exploit. □ **milk teeth** first (temporary) teeth in young mammals.

milkman *n.* person who delivers milk to customers.

milky *adj.* **1** of or like milk. **2** containing much milk. □ **Milky Way** broad luminous band of stars.

mill *n.* **1** machinery for grinding or processing specified material. **2** building containing this. ● *v.* **1** process in a mill. **2** produce grooves in (metal). **3** move in a confused mass. □ **miller** *n.*

millennium *n.* (*pl.* **-ums**) **1** period of 1000 years. **2** future period of great happiness for everyone.

millepede *n.* small crawling creature with many legs.

millet *n.* **1** cereal plant. **2** its seeds.

milli- *pref.* one-thousandth part of (as in *milligram, millilitre, millimetre*).

milliner *n.* maker or seller of women's hats. □ **millinery** *n.*

million *n.* one thousand thousand. □ **millionth** *adj.* & *n.*

millionaire *n.* person who possesses a million pounds.

millstone *n.* **1** circular stone for grinding corn. **2** great burden.

milometer *n.* instrument measuring the distance in miles travelled by a vehicle.

milt *n.* sperm of male fish.

mime *n.* acting with gestures without words. ● *v.* act with mime.

mimic v. (**mimicked**) imitate, esp. playfully or for entertainment. ● n. person who is clever at mimicking others. ▫ **mimicry** n.

▪ v. ape, caricature, copy, imitate, impersonate, parody, send up, take off. ● n. imitator, impersonator, impressionist.

mimosa n. tropical shrub with small ball-shaped flowers.

minaret n. tall slender tower on or beside a mosque.

mince v. 1 cut into small pieces in a mincer. 2 walk or speak with affected refinement. ● n. minced meat. ▫ **mince pie** pie containing mincemeat.

mincemeat n. mixture of dried fruit, sugar, etc., used in pies.

mincer n. machine with revolving blades for cutting food into very small pieces.

mind n. 1 ability to be aware of things and to think and reason. 2 person's attention or ability to remember. 3 normal condition of one's mental faculties. ● v. 1 have charge of. 2 object to. 3 remember and be careful (about). 4 heed. ▫ **be in two minds** be undecided. **be of one mind** agree. **have (it) in mind** intend. **out of one's mind** mad. **to my mind** in my opinion.

▪ n. 1 brain(s), intellect, intelligence, reason, sense, understanding, wit. 2 attention, attentiveness, concentration; memory. ● v. 1 care for, have charge of, look after, take care of, tend, watch. 2 be annoyed by, be offended by, be upset by, object to, resent, take offence at. 4 heed, listen to, mark, note, pay attention to, take note of. ▫ **be in two minds** be undecided, dither, hesitate, shilly-shally, vacillate, waver. **have (it) in mind** aim, intend, mean, plan, propose, purpose.

minded adj. having inclinations or interests of a certain kind.

minder n. 1 person employed to look after a person or thing. 2 (sl.) bodyguard.

mindful adj. taking thought or care (of something).

mindless adj. without intelligence. ▫ **mindlessness** n.

▪ asinine, fatuous, foolish, idiotic, senseless, silly, stupid, thoughtless, witless.

mine¹ adj. & poss.pron. belonging to me.

mine² n. 1 excavation for extracting metal or coal etc. 2 abundant source (of information etc.). 3 explosive device laid in or on the ground or in water. ● v. 1

dig for minerals, extract in this way. 2 lay explosive mines under or in.

▪ n. 1 colliery, excavation, quarry, pit. 2 fund, repository, reserve, source, store. ● v. 1 dig, excavate, quarry.

minefield n. area where explosive mines have been laid.

miner n. worker in a mine.

mineral n. 1 inorganic natural substance. 2 fizzy soft drink. ● adj. of or containing minerals. ▫ **mineral water** water naturally containing dissolved mineral salts or gases.

mineralogy n. study of minerals. ▫ **mineralogist** n.

minesweeper n. ship for clearing away mines laid in the sea.

mingle v. 1 blend together. 2 mix socially.

▪ 1 amalgamate, blend, combine, intermingle, merge, mix, unite. 2 circulate, fraternize, hobnob, mix, socialize.

mini- pref. miniature.

miniature adj. very small, on a small scale. ● n. small-scale portrait, copy, or model.

▪ adj. diminutive, little, microscopic, mini-, minuscule, minute, small, tiny, colloq. wee.

miniaturize v. make miniature, produce in a very small version. ▫ **miniaturization** n.

minibus n. small bus-like vehicle with seats for only a few people.

minim n. 1 note in music, lasting half as long as a semibreve. 2 one-sixtieth of a fluid drachm.

minimal adj. very small, least possible. ▫ **minimally** adv.

minimize v. 1 reduce to a minimum. 2 represent as small or unimportant. ▫ **minimization** n.

▪ 1 curtail, cut, decrease, diminish, lessen, reduce. 2 belittle, deprecate, make light of, play down, underestimate, undervalue.

minimum adj. & n. (pl. **-ima**) smallest (amount) possible.

minion n. (derog.) assistant.

minister n. 1 head of a government department. 2 clergyman. 3 senior diplomatic representative. ● v. **minister to** attend to the needs of. ▫ **ministerial** adj.

▪ n. 2 chaplain, clergyman, clergywoman, cleric, padre, colloq. parson, pastor, priest, rector, vicar. 3 ambassador, chargé d'affaires, consul, diplomat, emissary, plenipotentiary. ● v. attend to, care for, look after, see to, take care of.

ministry n. **1** government department headed by a minister. **2** period of government under one leader. **3** work of a clergyman.

mink n. **1** small stoat-like animal. **2** its fur. **3** coat made of this.

minnow n. small freshwater carp.

minor adj. lesser or comparatively small in size or importance. ● n. person not yet legally of adult age.
■ adj. lesser, secondary, smaller, subordinate, subsidiary; inconsequential, inconsiderable, insignificant, negligible, slight, trifling, trivial, unimportant. ● n. adolescent, boy, child, girl, juvenile, teenager, youngster, youth.

minority n. **1** smallest part of a group or class. **2** small group differing from others. **3** age when a person is not yet legally adult.

minstrel n. medieval singer and musician.

mint¹ n. place authorized to make a country's coins. ● v. make (coins). □ **in mint condition** new-looking.

mint² n. **1** fragrant herb. **2** peppermint. **3** sweet flavoured with mint. □ **minty** adj.

minuet /mínyoo-ét/ n. slow stately dance.

minus prep. **1** reduced by subtraction of. **2** below zero. **3** (colloq.) without. ● adj. **1** less than zero. **2** less than the amount indicated.

minuscule adj. extremely small.

minute¹ /mínnit/ n. **1** one-sixtieth of an hour or degree. **2** moment of time. **3** (pl.) official summary of an assembly's proceedings. ● v. record in the minutes.
■ n. **2** flash, instant, moment, split second, colloq. tick.

minute² /mÿnyóot/ adj. **1** extremely small. **2** very precise. □ **minutely** adv., **minuteness** n.
■ **1** diminutive, infinitesimal, little, microscopic, mini-, miniature, minuscule, small, colloq. teeny, tiny, colloq. wee. **2** accurate, detailed, exact, meticulous, painstaking, precise.

minutiae /mÿnyóoshi-ee/ n.pl. very small details.

miracle n. **1** wonderful event attributed to a supernatural agency. **2** remarkable event or thing. □ **miraculous** adj., **miraculously** adv.
■ marvel, phenomenon, prodigy, wonder. □ **miraculous** amazing, astonishing, astounding, breathtaking, extraordinary, incredible, magical, marvellous, phenomenal, remarkable, stupendous, wonderful.

mirage n. optical illusion caused by atmospheric conditions.
■ hallucination, illusion, vision.

mire n. **1** swampy ground, bog. **2** mud or sticky dirt. □ **miry** adj.

mirror n. glass coated so that reflections can be seen in it. ● v. reflect in a mirror.

mirth n. merriment, laughter.
■ cheerfulness, gaiety, glee, fun, high spirits, jollity, joviality, joyousness, laughter, merriment.

mis- pref. badly, wrongly.

misadventure n. piece of bad luck.

misanthrope n. (also **misanthropist**) person who hates humankind. □ **misanthropy** n., **misanthropic** adj.

misapply v. apply (esp. funds) wrongly. □ **misapplication** n.

misapprehend v. misunderstand. □ **misapprehension** n.

misappropriate v. take dishonestly. □ **misappropriation** n.
■ embezzle, filch, sl. nick, pilfer, sl. pinch, pocket, purloin, steal.

misbehave v. behave badly. □ **misbehaviour** n.

miscalculate v. calculate incorrectly. □ **miscalculation** n.

miscarriage n. abortion occurring naturally.

miscarry v. **1** have a miscarriage. **2** go wrong, be unsuccessful.
■ **2** be unsuccessful, come to grief, colloq. come unstuck, fall through, founder, go amiss, go wrong, misfire.

miscellaneous adj. assorted.
■ assorted, diverse, heterogeneous, mixed, motley, multifarious, sundry, varied, various.

miscellany n. collection of assorted items.
■ assortment, diversity, hotchpotch, jumble, medley, mixture, pot-pourri, variety.

mischance n. misfortune.

mischief n. **1** children's annoying but not malicious conduct. **2** playful malice. **3** harm, damage.
■ **1,2** devilment, devilry, misbehaviour, mischievousness, naughtiness, playfulness. **3** damage, detriment, harm, hurt, injury, trouble.

mischievous *adj.* full of mischief.
□ **mischievously** *adv.*, **mischievousness**
n.
■ devilish, disobedient, naughty, playful,
rascally, roguish, wicked.

misconception *n.* wrong interpretation.
■ error, misapprehension, misconstruction,
misinterpretation, misjudgement,
mistake, misunderstanding, wrong idea.

misconduct *n.* **1** bad behaviour. **2**
mismanagement.
■ **1** bad behaviour, disobedience, mischief,
misdeeds, misdemeanours, naughtiness.

misconstrue *v.* misinterpret. □ **misconstruction** *n.*

miscreant *n.* wrongdoer.
■ blackguard, criminal, *colloq.* crook,
knave, lawbreaker, malefactor, offender,
reprobate, rogue, ruffian, scoundrel, villain,
wretch, wrongdoer.

misdeed *n.* wrongful act.
■ crime, misdemeanour, offence, sin,
transgression, wrong.

misdemeanour *n.* misdeed.

miser *n.* person who hoards money and
spends as little as possible. □ **miserly**
adj., **miserliness** *n.*
■ hoarder, niggard, skinflint. □ **miserly**
cheese-paring, close, mean, niggardly,
parsimonious, penny-pinching, stingy,
colloq. tight, tight-fisted.

miserable *adj.* **1** full of misery. **2**
wretchedly poor in quality or surroundings.
□ **miserably** *adv.*
■ **1** blue, broken-hearted, dejected, depressed,
desolate, despondent, disconsolate,
downcast, downhearted, forlorn,
gloomy, glum, heartbroken, melancholy,
mournful, sad, sorrowful, tearful, unhappy,
upset, woebegone, woeful, wretched. **2**
mean, poor, shabby, sordid, sorry, squalid,
wretched.

misery *n.* **1** great unhappiness or discomfort.
2 thing causing this. **3** (*colloq.*)
disagreeable person.
■ **1** anguish, depression, desolation,
despair, despondency, distress, gloom,
heartache, melancholy, sadness, sorrow,
unhappiness, woe, wretchedness. **2** adversity,
affliction, hardship, misfortune,
suffering, trial, tribulation. **3** killjoy, moaner,
pessimist, *colloq.* sourpuss, spoilsport.

misfire *v.* **1** (of a gun or engine) fail to
fire correctly. **2** go wrong.

misfit *n.* person not well suited to his or
her environment.

misfortune *n.* **1** bad luck. **2** unfortunate
event.
■ **1** bad luck, ill luck. **2** accident, calamity,
catastrophe, disaster, misadventure, mischance,
mishap, reverse, tragedy.

misgiving *n.* slight feeling of doubt, fear,
or mistrust.
■ anxiety, apprehension, concern, disquiet,
doubt, mistrust, suspicion, uncertainty,
unease; qualm, reservation, scruple.

misguided *adj.* mistaken in one's opinions
or actions.
■ foolish, ill-advised, impolitic, imprudent,
injudicious, misled, mistaken, unwise,
wrong.

mishap *n.* unlucky accident.
■ accident, calamity, disaster, misadventure,
mischance, misfortune, reverse.

misinform *v.* give wrong information to,
mislead. □ **misinformation** *n.*

misinterpret *v.* interpret incorrectly.
□ **misinterpretation** *n.*
■ misapprehend, misconstrue, misjudge,
misread, mistake, misunderstand.

misjudge *v.* form a wrong opinion or estimate
of. □ **misjudgement** *n.*

mislay *v.* (**mislaid**) lose temporarily.

mislead *v.* (**misled**) **1** cause to form a
wrong impression. **2** deceive.
■ deceive, delude, fool, hoodwink, lead
astray, misinform, pull the wool over
someone's eyes, take in, trick.

mismanage *v.* manage badly or wrongly.
□ **mismanagement** *n.*
■ botch, bungle, *sl.* fluff, *colloq.* make a
hash of, make a mess of, mess up, *colloq.*
muff.

misnomer *n.* wrongly applied name or
description.

misogynist *n.* person who hates women.
□ **misogyny** *n.*

misplace *v.* **1** put in a wrong place,
mislay. **2** place (confidence etc.) unwisely.

misprint *n.* error in printing.

misquote *v.* quote incorrectly. □ **misquotation**
n.

misread *v.* (**-read**) read or interpret incorrectly.

misrepresent *v.* represent wrongly.
□ **misrepresentation** *n.*

misrule *n.* bad government.

Miss *n.* (*pl.* **Misses**) title of a girl or unmarried
woman.

miss v. **1** fail to hit, catch, see, hear, understand, etc. **2** notice or regret the absence or loss of. ● n. failure to hit or attain what is aimed at.

■ v. **2** feel nostalgic for, long for, pine for, yearn for.

misshapen adj. badly shaped.

■ contorted, crooked, distorted, gnarled, grotesque, malformed, twisted, warped.

missile n. object thrown or fired at a target.

missing adj. **1** not present. **2** not in its place, lost.

mission n. **1** task assigned to a person or group. **2** this group. **3** missionaries' headquarters.

■ **1** assignment, commission, duty, errand, job, task. **2** commission, delegation, deputation, group.

missionary n. person sent to spread religious faith.

misspell v. (**misspelt**) spell incorrectly. □ **misspelling** n.

mist n. **1** water vapour near the ground or clouding a window etc. **2** thing resembling this. ● v. cover or become covered with mist.

■ n. **1** cloud, fog, haze, vapour.

mistake n. **1** incorrect idea or opinion. **2** thing done incorrectly. ● v. (**mistook**, **mistaken**) **1** misunderstand. **2** choose or identify wrongly.

■ n. **1** misapprehension, miscalculation, misconception, misjudgement. **2** colloq. boob, blunder, sl. clanger, error, faux pas, gaffe, howler, oversight, slip, colloq. slip-up. ● v. **1** misconstrue, misinterpret, misjudge, misunderstand.

mistle thrush large thrush.

mistletoe n. plant with white berries, growing on trees.

mistral n. cold north or north-west wind in southern France.

mistress n. **1** woman who has control of people or things. **2** female teacher. **3** man's illicit female lover.

mistrust v. feel no trust in. ● n. lack of trust. □ **mistrustful** adj.

■ v. be suspicious or doubtful of, distrust, doubt, have reservations about, question, suspect. ● n. distrust, doubt, scepticism, suspicion, wariness.

misty adj. (**-ier**, **-iest**) **1** full of mist. **2** indistinct. □ **mistily** adv.

■ **1** cloudy, foggy, hazy. **2** blurred, dim, fuzzy, indistinct, unclear, vague.

misunderstand v. (**-stood**) fail to understand correctly. □ **misunderstanding** n.

■ misapprehend, misconstrue, misinterpret, misjudge, misread.

misuse v. /missyōoz/ **1** use wrongly. **2** treat badly. ● n. /missyōoss/ wrong use.

■ v. **1** abuse, misapply. **2** abuse, harm, hurt, ill-treat, knock about, maltreat, mistreat. ● n. abuse, misapplication.

mite n. **1** very small spider-like animal. **2** small creature, esp. a child. **3** small amount.

mitigate v. make seem less serious or severe. □ **mitigation** n.

■ allay, alleviate, assuage, decrease, ease, lessen, lighten, moderate, palliate, reduce, relieve, soften, temper, tone down.

mitre n. **1** pointed headdress of bishops and abbots. **2** join with tapered ends that form a right angle. ● v. join in this way.

mitt n. mitten.

mitten n. glove with no partitions between the fingers, or leaving the fingertips bare.

mix v. **1** combine (different things). **2** prepare by doing this. **3** be compatible. **4** come or be together socially. ● n. mixture. □ **mix up 1** mix thoroughly. **2** confuse. **mixer** n.

■ v. **1** alloy, amalgamate, blend, combine, intermingle, merge, mingle, mix, unite. **4** associate, consort, fraternize, hobnob, keep company, socialize.

mixed adj. **1** composed of various elements. **2** of or for both sexes. □ **mixed-up** adj. **1** muddled. **2** (colloq.) not well-adjusted emotionally.

■ **1** assorted, diverse, diversified, heterogeneous, miscellaneous, motley, sundry, varied, various.

mixture n. **1** thing made by mixing. **2** process of mixing things.

■ **1** alloy, amalgam, amalgamation, blend, compound, mix; assortment, collection, hotchpotch, jumble, medley, miscellany, pot-pourri, variety.

ml abbr. millilitre(s).

mm abbr. millimetre(s).

mnemonic /nimónnik/ adj. & n. (verse etc.) aiding the memory.

moan n. **1** low mournful sound. **2** grumble. ● v. **1** make or utter with a moan. **2** grumble. □ **moaner** n.

■ n. **1** groan, lament, lamentation, sigh, sough, wail. **2** sl. beef, complaint, grievance, *colloq.* gripe, *colloq.* grouse, grumble. ● *v.* **1** groan, lament, sigh, sough, wail. **2** *sl.* beef, complain, *colloq.* gripe, *colloq.* grouse, grumble, whine, *colloq.* whinge.

moat *n.* deep wide usu. water-filled ditch round a castle.

mob *n.* **1** large disorderly crowd. **2** (*sl.*) gang. ● *v.* (**mobbed**) crowd round in great numbers.
■ *n.* **1** crowd, herd, horde, gaggle, multitude, rabble, swarm, throng. ● *v.* besiege, crowd around, surround, swarm around.

mobile *adj.* able to move or be moved easily. ● *n.* artistic hanging structure whose parts move in currents of air. □ **mobility** *n.*

mobilize *v.* assemble (troops etc.) for active service. □ **mobilization** *n.*, **mobilizer** *n.*
■ assemble, marshal, organize, prepare, rally, ready.

moccasin *n.* soft flat-soled leather shoe.

mock *v.* **1** ridicule, scoff at. **2** mimic contemptuously. ● *adj.* imitation. □ **mock-up** *n.* model for testing or study.
■ *v.* **1** deride, gibe (at), jeer (at), laugh at, make fun of, poke fun at, *colloq.* rib, ridicule, scoff at, taunt, tease. **2** ape, burlesque, caricature, imitate, mimic, parody, satirize, send up, take off. ● *adj.* artificial, fake, false, imitation, *colloq.* phoney, simulated, synthetic.

mockery *n.* **1** derision. **2** absurd or unsatisfactory imitation.
■ **1** derision, ridicule, scorn, taunting. **2** charade, farce, parody, travesty.

mode *n.* **1** way a thing is done. **2** current fashion.
■ **1** approach, manner, method, procedure, system, technique, way. **2** fashion, style, trend, vogue.

model *n.* **1** three-dimensional reproduction, usu. on a smaller scale. **2** exemplary person or thing. **3** particular design or style. **4** person employed to pose for an artist or display clothes in a shop etc. by wearing them. ● *adj.* exemplary. ● *v.* (**modelled**) **1** make a model of. **2** work as artist's or fashion model, display (clothes) in this way.
■ *n.* **1** miniature, mock-up, replica, reproduction; dummy, effigy. **2** archetype, epitome, exemplar, ideal, paragon, pattern, prototype, standard, type. **3** design, kind, style, type, version. **4** sitter, subject;

mannequin. ● *adj.* archetypal, exemplary, ideal, inimitable, perfect. ● *v.* **1** fashion, form, make, mould, sculpt, sculpture, shape. **2** pose, sit; display, show.

modem *n.* device for sending and receiving computer data through a telephone line.

moderate *adj.* /móddərət/ **1** avoiding extremes, temperate in conduct etc. **2** fairly large or good. ● *n.* /móddərət/ holder of moderate views. ● *v.* /móddərayt/ make or become moderate. □ **moderately** *adv.*
■ *adj.* **1** calm, controlled, cool, mild, reasonable, restrained, sensible, temperate. **2** acceptable, average, fair, medium, mediocre, middling, modest, unexceptional. ● *v.* cushion, decrease, diminish, lessen, mitigate, reduce, relieve, soften, temper, tone down; abate, ease, *colloq.* let up, subside.

moderation *n.* moderating. □ **in moderation** in moderate amounts.

modern *adj.* **1** of present or recent times. **2** in current style. □ **modernity** *n.*
■ **1** contemporary, current, today's. **2** fashionable, in, in fashion, in vogue, new, newfangled, *colloq.* trendy, up to date.

modernist *n.* person who favours modern ideas or methods. □ **modernism** *n.*

modernize *v.* make modern, adapt to modern ways. □ **modernization** *n.*, **modernizer** *n.*
■ do up, redecorate, redesign, refurbish, renovate, update.

modest *adj.* **1** not vain or boastful. **2** moderate in size etc. **3** not showy. **4** showing regard for conventional decencies. □ **modestly** *adv.*, **modesty** *n.*
■ **1** humble, self-effacing, unassuming. **2** adequate, moderate, unexceptional. **3** homely, humble, ordinary, plain, simple, unpretentious. **4** decent, decorous, demure, proper, seemly.

modicum *n.* small amount.

modify *v.* **1** make less severe. **2** make partial changes in. □ **modification** *n.*
■ **1** decrease, diminish, lessen, moderate, reduce, soften, temper, tone down. **2** adapt, adjust, alter, amend, change, revise.

modish /módish/ *adj.* fashionable.

modulate *v.* **1** regulate, moderate. **2** vary in tone or pitch. □ **modulation** *n.*
■ **1** adjust, moderate, modify, regulate, temper. **2** lower, soften, tone down, turn down.

module n. **1** standardized part or independent unit. **2** unit of training or education. □ **modular** adj.

mogul n. (colloq.) important or influential person.

mohair n. **1** fine silky hair of the angora goat. **2** yarn or fabric made from this.

moiety /móyeti/ n. half.

moist adj. slightly wet.
■ clammy, damp, humid, muggy, wet.

moisten v. make or become moist.
■ damp, dampen, water, wet.

moisture n. water or other liquid diffused through a substance or as vapour or condensation on a surface.
■ condensation, damp, dampness, liquid, water, wetness.

moisturize v. make (skin) less dry. □ **moisturizer** n.

molar n. back tooth with a broad top, used in chewing.

molasses n. **1** syrup from raw sugar. **2** (US) treacle.

mole¹ n. small dark spot on human skin.

mole² n. **1** small burrowing animal with dark fur. **2** spy established within an organization.

molecule n. very small unit (usu. a group of atoms) of a substance. □ **molecular** adj.

molehill n. mound of earth thrown up by a mole.

molest v. attack or interfere with, esp. sexually. □ **molestation** n.

mollify v. soothe the anger of. □ **mollification** n.
■ appease, calm, pacify, placate, soothe.

mollusc n. animal with a soft body and often a hard shell.

mollycoddle v. pamper.

molten adj. liquefied by heat.

molybdenum n. hard metal used in steel.

moment n. **1** point or brief portion of time. **2** importance.
■ **1** juncture, point; flash, instant, minute, split second, colloq. tick. **2** consequence, import, importance, seriousness, significance, weight.

momentary adj. lasting only a moment. □ **momentarily** adv.
■ brief, ephemeral, fleeting, fugitive, impermanent, passing, short, transient, transitory.

momentous adj. of great importance. □ **momentously** adv.
■ consequential, critical, crucial, historic, important, serious, significant, weighty.

momentum n. impetus gained by a moving body.
■ drive, energy, force, impetus, power, push, thrust.

monarch n. ruler with the title of king, queen, emperor, or empress. □ **monarchic** adj., **monarchical** adj.
■ emperor, empress, king, potentate, queen, ruler, sovereign.

monarchist n. supporter of monarchy. □ **monarchism** n.

monarchy n. **1** government headed by a monarch. **2** country governed thus.

monastery n. residence of a community of monks.

monastic adj. of monks or monasteries. □ **monasticism** n.

monetarism n. control of the money supply as a method of curbing inflation. □ **monetarist** n.

monetary adj. of money or currency.

money n. **1** coins and banknotes. **2** (pl. -eys) sums of money. **3** wealth. □ **money-spinner** n. profitable thing.
■ **1** banknotes, US bills, cash, change, coins, currency, sl. dough, legal tender, sl. lolly, lucre, notes, colloq. wherewithal. **3** assets, funds, means, resources, riches, wealth.

moneyed adj. wealthy.
■ affluent, prosperous, rich, wealthy, colloq. well-heeled, well-off, well-to-do.

Mongol n. & adj. (native) of Mongolia.

mongoose n. (pl. -gooses) small flesh-eating tropical mammal.

mongrel n. animal (esp. a dog) of mixed breed. ● adj. of mixed origin or character.

monitor n. **1** device used to observe or test the operation of something. **2** pupil with special duties in a school. ● v. **1** act as monitor of. **2** maintain regular surveillance over.
■ v. examine, colloq. keep tabs on, observe, oversee, study, supervise, survey, watch.

monk n. member of a male religious community. □ **monkish** adj.

monkey n. (pl. -eys) **1** any of various primates, esp. a long-tailed one. **2** mischievous person. ● v. (monkeyed) tamper mischievously. □ **monkey-nut** n.

peanut. **monkey-puzzle** n. evergreen tree with sharp stiff leaves. **monkey wrench** wrench with an adjustable jaw.

mono adj. & n. (pl. **-os**) monophonic (sound or recording).

mono- pref. one, alone, single.

monochrome adj. done in only one colour or in black and white.

monocle n. single eyeglass.

monocular adj. with or for one eye.

monogamy n. system of being married to only one person at a time. □ **monogamous** adj.

monogram n. letters (esp. a person's initials) combined in a design. □ **monogrammed** adj.

monolith n. **1** single upright block of stone. **2** massive organization etc. □ **monolithic** adj.

monologue n. long speech.

monomania n. obsession with one idea or interest. □ **monomaniac** n.

monophonic adj. using only one transmission channel for reproduction of sound.

monoplane n. aeroplane with only one set of wings.

monopolize v. **1** have a monopoly of. **2** not allow others to share in. □ **monopolization** n.

■ control, corner, dominate, take control of, take over.

monopoly n. sole possession or control of something, esp. of trade in a specified commodity. □ **monopolist** n.

monorail n. railway in which the track is a single rail.

monosodium glutamate substance added to food to enhance its flavour.

monosyllable n. word of one syllable. □ **monosyllabic** adj.

monotheism n. doctrine that there is only one God. □ **monotheist** n., **monotheistic** adj.

monotone n. level unchanging tone of voice.

monotonous adj. lacking in variety. □ **monotonously** adv., **monotony** n.

■ boring, colourless, dreary, dull, repetitious, repetitive, soporific, tedious, unchanging, uneventful, unexciting, uninteresting, unvaried, unvarying, wearisome.

monsoon n. **1** seasonal wind in S. Asia. **2** rainy season accompanying this.

monster n. **1** imaginary creature, usually large and frightening. **2** very cruel

or wicked person. **3** misshapen animal or plant. **4** large ugly animal or thing.

■ **1** dragon, giant, ogre, troll. **2** beast, brute, demon, fiend, ogre. **3** freak, mutant, mutation. **4** eyesore, horror, monstrosity.

monstrosity n. monstrous thing.

monstrous adj. **1** like a monster. **2** huge. **3** outrageous, atrocious.

■ **1** disgusting, dreadful, frightful, ghastly, grotesque, gruesome, hideous, horrible, nightmarish, repellent, repulsive, revolting, ugly. **2** colossal, enormous, gargantuan, giant, gigantic, huge, immense, mammoth, massive, titanic, tremendous, vast. **3** appalling, atrocious, barbaric, barbarous, disgraceful, dreadful, evil, foul, heinous, outrageous, scandalous, shameful, shocking, terrible, vile, wicked.

montage n. **1** making of a composite picture from pieces of others. **2** this picture. **3** joining of disconnected pictures in a cinema film.

month n. **1** each of the twelve portions into which the year is divided. **2** period of 28 days.

monthly adj. & adv. (produced or occurring) once a month. ● n. monthly periodical.

monument n. thing that commemorates, esp. a structure, building, or memorial stone.

■ cairn, memorial, obelisk, shrine, statue; cenotaph, mausoleum, sepulchre, tomb; gravestone, headstone, tombstone.

monumental adj. **1** extremely great, stupendous. **2** massive. **3** of or serving as a monument.

■ **1** amazing, awesome, awe-inspiring, impressive, magnificent, marvellous, outstanding, prodigious, remarkable, spectacular, splendid, stupendous, wonderful. **2** colossal, enormous, gigantic, huge, immense, massive, tremendous, vast. **3** commemorative, memorial.

moo n. cow's low deep cry. ● v. make this sound.

mooch v. (colloq.) walk slowly and aimlessly.

mood n. **1** temporary state of mind or spirits. **2** fit of bad temper or depression.

■ **1** disposition, frame of mind, humour, state of mind, temper.

moody adj. (-ier, -iest) **1** given to changes of mood. **2** bad-tempered, sullen.

■ **1** capricious, changeable, erratic, mercurial, temperamental, unpredictable, volatile. **2** bad-tempered, cantankerous, crabby, crotchety, irritable, peevish, petulant, snappy, testy, touchy; dour, gloomy, glum, lugubrious, morose, saturnine, sulky, sullen.

moon n. **1** earth's satellite, made visible by light it reflects from the sun. **2** natural satellite of any planet. ● v. behave dreamily.

moonlight n. light from the moon. ● v. (colloq.) have two paid jobs, one by day and the other in the evening.

moonlit adj. lit by the moon.

moonstone n. pearly semiprecious stone.

Moor n. member of a Muslim people of north-west Africa. □ **Moorish** adj.

moor¹ n. stretch of open uncultivated land with low shrubs.

moor² v. secure (a boat etc.) to a fixed object.

moorhen n. small waterbird.

moorings n.pl. cables or place for mooring a boat.

moose n. (pl. **moose**) elk of N. America.

mop n. **1** pad or bundle of yarn on a stick, used for cleaning things. **2** thick mass of hair. ● v. (**mopped**) clean with a mop. □ **mop up** wipe up with a mop or cloth etc.

mope v. be unhappy and listless.

moped n. motorized bicycle.

moraine n. mass of stones etc. deposited by a glacier.

moral adj. **1** concerned with right and wrong conduct. **2** virtuous. ● n. **1** moral lesson or principle. **2** (pl.) person's standards of behaviour. □ **moral support** encouragement. **moral victory** a triumph though without concrete gain. **morally** adv.

■ adj. **1** ethical. **2** decent, ethical, fair, good, honest, honourable, incorruptible, principled, proper, righteous, upright, virtuous. ● n. **1** lesson, message, point, teaching. **2** (**morals**) ethics, morality, principles, standards, values.

morale /mərraal/ n. state of a person's or group's spirits and confidence.

moralist n. person who expresses or teaches moral principles.

morality n. **1** moral principles or rules. **2** goodness or rightness.

■ **1** ethics, morals, principles, standards. **2** decency, goodness, honesty, honour, integrity, probity, rectitude, right, virtue.

moralize v. talk or write about the morality of something, esp. in a self-righteous way.

■ pontificate, preach, sermonize.

morass n. **1** complex entanglement. **2** marsh, bog.

■ **1** confusion, entanglement, muddle, tangle. **2** bog, fen, marsh, mire, quagmire, slough, swamp.

moratorium n. (pl. **-ums**) temporary agreed ban on an activity.

morbid adj. (of mind, ideas, etc.) having or showing an interest in gloomy or unpleasant things. □ **morbidly** adv., **morbidity** n.

■ ghoulish, gruesome, macabre, sick, unhealthy, unwholesome.

mordant adj. (of wit etc.) caustic.

■ biting, caustic, cutting, sarcastic, scathing, stinging, trenchant, vitriolic.

more adj. greater in quantity or intensity etc. ● n. greater amount or number. ● adv. **1** to a greater extent. **2** again. □ **more or less** approximately.

■ adj. added, additional, extra, fresh, further, supplementary.

moreover adv. besides.

■ also, besides, further, furthermore, in addition, what is more.

morgue /morg/ n. mortuary.

moribund adj. in a dying state.

Mormon n. member of a Christian sect founded in the USA.

morning n. part of the day before noon or the midday meal.

morocco n. goatskin leather.

moron n. **1** adult with a mental age of 8–12. **2** (colloq.) stupid person. □ **moronic** adj.

morose adj. gloomy, sullen. □ **morosely** adv., **moroseness** n.

■ dejected, depressed, gloomy, glum, lugubrious, melancholy, miserable, moody, sad, saturnine, sombre, sulky, sullen, unhappy.

morphia n. morphine.

morphine n. drug made from opium, used to relieve pain.

morphology n. study of forms of animals and plants or of words. □ **morphological** adj.

morris dance English folk dance by people in costume.

Morse code code of signals using short and long sounds or flashes of light.

morsel n. **1** mouthful. **2** small piece (esp. of food).

■ **1** bite, mouthful, nibble, spoonful, taste. **2** bit, crumb, grain, fragment, particle, piece, scrap, shred, sliver.

mortal adj. **1** subject to death. **2** fatal. **3** implacable. ● n. mortal being. □ **mortally** adv.

■ adj. **1** earthly, human, temporal, worldly; ephemeral, transient, transitory. **2** deadly, fatal, lethal, terminal. **3** bitter, implacable, relentless, unrelenting. ● n. creature, human (being), individual, man, person, soul, woman.

mortality n. **1** being mortal. **2** loss of life on a large scale. **3** death rate.

mortar n. **1** mixture of lime or cement with sand and water for joining bricks or stones. **2** bowl in which substances are pounded with a pestle. **3** short cannon.

mortarboard n. stiff square cap worn as part of academic dress.

mortgage /mórgij/ n. **1** loan for purchase of property, in which the property itself is pledged as security. **2** agreement effecting this. ● v. pledge (property) as security in this way.

mortgagee /mórgijee/ n. borrower in a mortgage.

mortgager /mórgijər/ n. (also **mortgagor**) lender in a mortgage.

mortify v. **1** humiliate greatly. **2** (of flesh) become gangrenous. □ **mortification** n.

■ **1** abash, chasten, crush, embarrass, humble, humiliate, shame.

mortise n. hole in one part of a framework shaped to receive the end of another part. □ **mortise lock** lock set in (not on) a door.

mortuary n. place where dead bodies may be kept temporarily.

mosaic n. pattern or picture made with small pieces of glass or stone of different colours.

Moslem adj. & n. = **Muslim**.

mosque n. Muslim place of worship.

mosquito n. (pl. **-oes**) small biting insect.

moss n. small flowerless plant forming a dense growth in moist places. □ **mossy** adj.

most adj. greatest in quantity or intensity etc. ● n. greatest amount or number. ● adv. **1** to the greatest extent. **2** very. □ **at most** not more than. **for the most part 1** mainly. **2** usually.

mostly adv. for the most part.

motel n. roadside hotel for motorists.

moth n. **1** nocturnal insect like a butterfly. **2** similar insect whose larvae feed on cloth or fur. □ **moth-eaten** adj. damaged by moths.

mothball n. small ball of pungent substance for keeping moths away from clothes.

mother n. **1** female parent. **2** title of the female head of a religious community. ● v. look after in a motherly way. □ **mother-in-law** n. (pl. **mothers-in-law**) mother of one's wife or husband. **mother-of-pearl** n. pearly substance lining shells of oysters and mussels etc. **mother tongue** one's native language. **motherhood** n., **motherless** adj.

motherland n. native country.

motherly adj. showing a mother's kindness.

■ affectionate, caring, devoted, fond, gentle, kind, loving, maternal, nurturing, protective, tender, warm.

motif n. recurring design, feature, or melody.

motion n. **1** moving. **2** movement. **3** formal proposal put to a meeting for discussion. **4** emptying of the bowels, faeces. ● v. make a gesture directing (a person) to do something. □ **motion picture** cinema film.

■ n. **1** action, movement, moving, progress, transit, travelling. **2** gesticulation, gesture, movement, sign, signal. **3** proposal, proposition, suggestion. ● v. gesticulate, gesture, sign, signal, wave.

motionless adj. not moving.

■ immobile, static, stationary, still, stock-still, unmoving.

motivate v. **1** supply a motive to. **2** cause to feel active interest. □ **motivation** n.

■ **1** cause, drive, encourage, incite, induce, influence, inspire, lead, move, persuade, prompt, spur, stimulate. **2** excite, galvanize, inspire, rouse, stir.

motive n. that which induces a person to act in a certain way. ● adj. producing movement or action.

■ n. incentive, inducement, motivation, stimulus; ground(s), justification, rationale, reason.

motley adj. **1** multicoloured **2** assorted. ● n. (old use) jester's particoloured costume.

motor n. **1** machine supplying motive power. **2** car. ● adj. **1** producing motion. **2** driven by a motor. □ **motor bike**

(*colloq.*) motor cycle. **motor cycle** motor-driven two-wheeled vehicle. **motor cyclist** rider of a motor cycle. **motor vehicle** vehicle with a motor engine, for use on ordinary roads.

motorcade *n.* procession or parade of motor vehicles.

motorist *n.* driver of a car.

motorize *v.* equip with motor(s) or motor vehicles.

motorway *n.* road designed for fast long-distance traffic.

mottled *adj.* patterned with irregular patches of colour.

■ blotched, blotchy, brindled, dappled, flecked, freckled, marbled, piebald, pied, speckled, spotted, stippled, streaked.

motto *n.* (*pl.* **-oes**) **1** short sentence or phrase expressing an ideal or rule of conduct. **2** maxim, riddle, etc., inside a paper cracker.

■ **1** aphorism, axiom, maxim, proverb, saw, saying.

mould[1] *n.* **1** hollow container into which a liquid is poured to set in a desired shape. ● *v.* **1** shape. **2** pudding etc. made in this. ● *v.* **1** shape. **2** influence the development of.

■ *n.* **1** cast, die, matrix. ● *v.* **1** fashion, form, make, model, sculpt, sculpture, shape, work. **2** control, direct, form, guide, influence, shape.

mould[2] *n.* furry growth of tiny fungi on a damp substance. □ **mouldy** *adj.*

mould[3] *n.* soft fine earth rich in organic matter.

moulder *v.* decay and rot away.

moult *v.* shed feathers, hair, or skin before new growth. ● *n.* process of moulting.

mound *n.* **1** mass of piled-up earth, stones, etc. **2** heap, pile. **3** small hill.

■ **1** barrow. **2** heap, mountain, pile, stack. **3** hill, hillock, hummock, knoll, rise.

mount[1] *n.* mountain, hill.

mount[2] *v.* **1** go up. **2** get on a horse etc. **3** increase. **4** fix on or in support(s) or setting. **5** organize, arrange. ● *n.* **1** thing on which something is fixed. **2** horse for riding.

■ *v.* **1** ascend, clamber up, climb (up), go up, make one's way up, scale. **3** escalate, grow, increase, intensify, rise; accumulate, build up, multiply, pile up. **4** frame. **5** arrange, coordinate, organize, prepare, stage.

mountain *n.* **1** mass of land rising to a great height. **2** large heap or pile.

□ **mountain ash** rowan tree. **mountain bike** strong bicycle suitable for riding on rough hilly ground.

■ **1** elevation, eminence, mount, peak, tor. **2** heap, mass, mound, pile, stack.

mountaineer *n.* person who climbs mountains. ● *v.* climb mountains as a recreation.

mountainous *adj.* **1** full of mountains. **2** huge.

■ **1** alpine, craggy, hilly. **2** colossal, enormous, gigantic, high, huge, immense, massive, mighty, towering.

mourn *v.* feel or express sorrow or regret about (a dead person or lost thing). □ **mourner** *n.*

■ grieve, lament, sorrow, weep; regret, rue.

mournful *adj.* sorrowful. □ **mournfully** *adv.*

■ desolate, despondent, disconsolate, dispirited, doleful, downcast, downhearted, forlorn, heavy-hearted, lugubrious, melancholy, miserable, sad, sorrowful, woebegone, woeful.

mourning *n.* **1** expression of sorrow for a dead person, esp. by wearing dark clothes. **2** such clothes.

mouse *n.* (*pl.* **mice**) **1** small rodent with a long tail. **2** quiet timid person. **3** small rolling device for moving the cursor on a VDU screen.

moussaka *n.* Greek dish of minced meat and aubergine.

mousse *n.* **1** frothy creamy dish. **2** substance of similar texture.

moustache /məstaásh/ *n.* hair on the upper lip.

mousy *adj.* **1** dull greyish-brown. **2** quiet and timid.

mouth *n.* /mowth/ **1** opening in the head through which food is taken in and sounds uttered. **2** opening of a bag, cave, cannon, etc. **3** place where a river enters the sea. ● *v.* /mowth/ form (words) soundlessly with the lips. □ **mouth-organ** *n.* small instrument played by blowing and sucking.

mouthful *n.* **1** quantity of food etc. that fills the mouth. **2** small quantity.

mouthpiece *n.* **1** part of an instrument placed between or near the lips. **2** spokesperson.

mouthwash *n.* liquid for cleansing the mouth.

move *v.* **1** (cause to) be in motion, or change place or position. **2** progress. **3** change one's residence. **4** provoke an emotion or reaction in. **5** take action. **6** propose for discussion. ● *n.* **1** act of moving. **2** calculated action. **3** moving of a piece in chess etc. □ **movable** *adj.*, **mover** *n.*

▪ *v.* **1** budge, make a move, stir; carry, shift, transfer, transport. **2** advance, go, pass, proceed, progress, travel, walk. **3** emigrate, leave, relocate. **4** affect, have an effect on, have an impact on, hit, impress, make an impression on, touch; dispose, incline, influence, inspire, lead, motivate, persuade, prompt, provoke, rouse. **5** act, take action, take the initiative. **6** advance, propose, put forward, submit, suggest. ● *n.* **1** action, motion, movement; relocation, shift, transfer. **2** act, gambit, manoeuvre, ploy, ruse, stratagem, tactic; initiative, step.

movement *n.* **1** act or instance of moving or being moved. **2** moving parts. **3** group with a common cause. **4** campaign undertaken by such a group. **5** section of a long piece of music.

▪ **1** flow, migration, move, relocation, shift, transfer; action, activity, stir, stirring; gesticulation, gesture, motion, sign, signal. **2** machinery, mechanism, works. **3** faction, group, lobby, party. **4** campaign, crusade, drive.

movie *n.* (*US colloq.*) cinema film.

moving *adj.* arousing pity or sympathy. □ **movingly** *adv.*

▪ affecting, emotional, emotive, pathetic, poignant, touching.

mow *v.* (**mown**) cut (grass etc.) with a scythe or a machine. □ **mow down** kill or destroy by a moving force. **mower** *n.*

m.p.h. *abbr.* miles per hour.

Mr *n.* (*pl.* **Messrs**) title prefixed to a man's name.

Mrs *n.* (*pl.* **Mrs**) title prefixed to a married woman's name.

Ms *n.* title prefixed to a married or unmarried woman's name.

much *adj. & n.* (existing in) great quantity. ● *adv.* **1** in a great degree. **2** to a great extent.

mucilage *n.* **1** sticky substance obtained from plants. **2** adhesive gum.

muck *n.* **1** farmyard manure. **2** (*colloq.*) dirt. □ **mucky** *adj.*

muckraking *n.* seeking and exposing scandal.

mucous *adj.* like or covered with mucus.

mucus *n.* slimy substance coating the inner surface of hollow organs of the body.

mud *n.* wet soft earth.

▪ dirt, mire, *colloq.* muck, silt, sludge.

muddle *v.* **1** bring into disorder. **2** bewilder. ● *n.* muddled condition or things. □ **muddle along** progress in a haphazard way. **muddle through** succeed by perseverance rather than skill.

▪ *v.* **1** confuse, disarrange, disorganize, jumble, mess up, mix up, scramble. **2** bemuse, bewilder, confuse, confound, mystify, perplex, puzzle. ● *n.* clutter, confusion, disarray, disorder, hotchpotch, jumble, mess, tangle.

muddy *adj.* (**-ier, -iest**) **1** like mud. **2** covered in or full of mud. **3** (of liquid etc.) not clear. ● *v.* make muddy.

▪ *adj.* **2** dirty, filthy, grubby, miry, *colloq.* mucky, muddied, soiled; boggy, marshy, swampy. **3** clouded, cloudy, opaque, turbid.

mudguard *n.* curved cover above a wheel as a protection against mud.

muesli *n.* food of mixed crushed cereals, dried fruit, nuts, etc.

muezzin /moo-ézzin/ *n.* man who proclaims the hours of prayer for Muslims.

muff[1] *n.* tube-shaped usu. furry covering for the hands.

muff[2] *v.* (*colloq.*) bungle.

muffin *n.* light round cake eaten toasted and buttered.

muffle *v.* wrap for warmth or protection, or to deaden sound.

▪ cloak, cover, envelop, swaddle, swathe, wrap; deaden, dull, silence, quieten, smother, stifle, suppress.

muffler *n.* scarf worn for warmth.

mufti *n.* civilian clothes.

mug *n.* **1** large drinking vessel with a handle, for use without a saucer. **2** (*sl.*) face. **3** (*sl.*) person who is easily outwitted. ● *v.* (**mugged**) attack and rob, esp. in a public place. □ **mugger** *n.*

muggy *adj.* (**-ier, -iest**) (of weather) oppressively damp and warm. □ **mugginess** *n.*

▪ close, damp, humid, oppressive, steamy, sticky, sultry.

mulberry *n.* **1** edible purple or white fruit. **2** tree bearing this. **3** dull purplish-red.

mulch *n.* mixture of wet straw, leaves, etc., spread on ground to protect plants or retain moisture. ● v. cover with mulch.

mulct v. take money from (a person) by a fine, taxation, etc.

mule[1] n. animal that is the offspring of a horse and a donkey.

mule[2] n. backless slipper.

mull[1] v. heat (wine etc.) with sugar and spices, as a drink.

mull[2] v. **mull over** think over.

■ cogitate on, consider, contemplate, meditate on, muse on, ponder, reflect on, ruminate on, think about or over, weigh.

mullah n. Muslim learned in Islamic law.

mullet n. small edible sea fish.

mulligatawny n. highly seasoned soup.

mullion n. upright bar between the sections of a tall window.

multi- pref. many.

multicultural adj. of or involving several cultural or ethnic groups. □ **multiculturalism** n.

multifarious adj. very varied.

multinational adj. & n. (business company) operating in several countries.

multiple adj. having or affecting many parts. ● n. quantity exactly divisible by another.

multiplex adj. having many elements.

multiplication n. multiplying.

multiplicity n. great variety.

■ abundance, diversity, profusion, range, variety.

multiply v. **1** add a quantity to itself a specified number of times. **2** increase in number.

■ **2** grow, increase, mushroom, pile up, proliferate, snowball, spread.

multiracial adj. of or involving people of several races.

multitude n. great number of things or people.

■ crowd, flock, horde, host, legion, mass, myriad, swarm, throng.

multitudinous adj. very numerous.

mum[1] adj. (colloq.) silent.

mum[2] n. (colloq.) mother.

mumble v. speak or utter indistinctly. ● n. indistinct speech.

mumbo-jumbo n. **1** meaningless ritual. **2** deliberately obscure language.

mummify v. preserve (a corpse) by embalming as in ancient Egypt. □ **mummification** n.

mummy[1] n. corpse embalmed and wrapped for burial, esp. in ancient Egypt.

mummy[2] n. (colloq.) mother.

mumps n. virus disease with painful swellings in the neck.

munch v. chew vigorously.

■ champ, chew, crunch, masticate, scrunch.

mundane adj. **1** dull, routine. **2** worldly.

■ **1** boring, commonplace, dull, everyday, humdrum, ordinary, pedestrian, prosaic, routine, run-of-the-mill, tedious, unexciting, uninteresting. **2** earthly, secular, temporal, worldly.

municipal adj. of a town or city.

municipality n. self-governing town or district.

■ borough, city, district, metropolis, town.

munificent adj. splendidly generous. □ **munificence** n.

munitions n.pl. weapons, ammunition, etc., used in war.

mural adj. of or on a wall. ● n. a painting made on a wall.

murder n. intentional unlawful killing. ● v. kill intentionally and unlawfully. □ **murderer** n.

■ n. assassination, butchery, genocide, homicide, infanticide, killing, massacre, matricide, parricide, patricide, regicide, slaughter. ● v. assassinate, butcher, sl. do in, exterminate, kill, liquidate, massacre, put to death, slaughter, slay.

murderous adj. involving or capable of murder.

■ deadly, fatal, lethal, mortal; barbarous, bloodthirsty, brutal, cruel, ferocious, fierce, inhuman, homicidal, savage, vicious.

murk n. darkness, gloom. □ **murky** adj.

■ □ murky clouded, cloudy, dark, dim, dismal, dreary, funereal, gloomy, overcast, shadowy.

murmur n. **1** low continuous sound. **2** softly spoken words. ● v. **1** make a murmur. **2** speak or utter softly.

■ n. **1** hum, humming, murmuring, rumble, whirr. **2** mumble, whisper. ● v. **1** hum, rumble, whirr. **2** mumble, mutter, whisper.

murrain n. infectious disease of cattle.

muscle /múss'l/ n. **1** strip of fibrous tissue able to contract and so move a part of the body. **2** muscular power. **3** strength. ● v. **muscle in** (colloq.) force one's way.

muscular *adj.* **1** of muscles. **2** having well-developed muscles. □ **muscularity** *n.*
■ **2** athletic, beefy, brawny, burly, husky, powerful, robust, sinewy, strapping, strong, sturdy.

muse *v.* ponder.
■ brood, cogitate, consider, deliberate, meditate, ponder, reflect, ruminate, think.

museum *n.* place where objects of historical interest are collected and displayed.

mush *n.* soft pulp.

mushroom *n.* edible fungus with a stem and a domed cap. ● *v.* appear or develop rapidly.

mushy *adj.* **1** as or like mush. **2** feebly sentimental.

music *n.* **1** arrangement of sounds of one or more voices or instruments. **2** written form of this.

musical *adj.* **1** of or involving music. **2** fond of or skilled in music. **3** sweet-sounding. ● *n.* play with songs and dancing. □ **musically** *adv.*
■ **3** dulcet, euphonious, mellifluous, melodic, melodious, sweet-sounding, tuneful.

musician *n.* person skilled in music.

musicology *n.* study of the history and forms of music. □ **musicologist** *n.*

musk *n.* substance secreted by certain animals or produced synthetically, used in perfumes. □ **musky** *adj.*

musket *n.* long-barrelled gun formerly used by infantry.

Muslim *n.* of or believing in Muhammad's teaching. ● *n.* believer in this faith.

muslin *n.* thin cotton cloth.

musquash *n.* **1** N. American water animal. **2** its fur.

mussel *n.* edible bivalve mollusc.

must *v.aux.* used to express necessity or obligation, certainty, or insistence. ● *n.* (*colloq.*) thing that must be done or visited etc.

mustang *n.* wild horse of Mexico and California.

mustard *n.* **1** sharp-tasting yellow condiment made from the seeds of a plant. **2** this plant.

musty *adj.* (**-ier, -iest**) mouldy, stale. □ **mustiness** *n.*
■ damp, mildewed, mouldy; airless, fusty, stale.

mutable *adj.* liable to change. □ **mutability** *n.*

mutant *adj.* & *n.* (living thing) differing from its parents as a result of genetic change.

mutate *v.* change in form.

mutation *n.* **1** change in form. **2** mutant.
■ **1** alteration, change, metamorphosis, modification, transformation, transmutation. **2** freak, monstrosity, mutant.

mute *adj.* **1** silent. **2** dumb. ● *n.* **1** dumb person. **2** device muffling the sound of a musical instrument. ● *v.* deaden or muffle the sound of. □ **mutely** *adv.*
■ *adj.* **1** *colloq.* mum, quiet, silent, speechless, tongue-tied; tacit, undeclared, unspoken. **2** dumb, voiceless.

mutilate *v.* injure or disfigure by cutting off a part. □ **mutilation** *n.*
■ cripple, damage, disable, disfigure, maim, mangle.

mutineer *n.* person who mutinies.

mutinous *adj.* rebellious, ready to mutiny. □ **mutinously** *adv.*
■ insurgent, rebellious, revolutionary, seditious, subversive; defiant, disobedient, insubordinate, recalcitrant, refractory, uncontrollable, ungovernable, unruly.

mutiny *n.* rebellion against authority, esp. by members of the armed forces. ● *v.* engage in mutiny.
■ *n.* insurgency, insurrection, rebellion, revolt, uprising. ● *v.* rebel, revolt.

mutter *v.* **1** speak or utter in a low unclear tone. **2** utter subdued grumbles. ● *n.* muttering.
■ *v.* **1** mumble, murmur, whisper. **2** complain, grumble, *colloq.* grouch, *colloq.* gripe, moan.

mutton *n.* flesh of sheep as food.

mutual *adj.* **1** felt or done by each to the other. **2** (*colloq.*) common to two or more. □ **mutually** *adv.*, **mutuality** *n.*
■ **1** reciprocal, reciprocated. **2** common, communal, joint, shared.

muzzle *n.* **1** projecting nose and jaws of certain animals. **2** open end of a firearm. **3** strap etc. over an animal's head to prevent it from biting or feeding. ● *v.* **1** put a muzzle on. **2** prevent from expressing opinions freely.

muzzy *adj.* dazed, confused.

my *adj.* belonging to me.

mycology *n.* study of fungi.

myna *n.* bird of the starling family that can mimic sounds.

myopia /mī́ópiə/ *n.* short sight. □ **myopic** /-óppik/ *adj.*

myriad *n.* vast number.

myrrh /mur/ *n.* gum resin used in perfumes, incense, etc.

myrtle *n.* evergreen shrub.

myself *pron.* emphatic and reflexive form of *I* and *me.*

mysterious *adj.* full of mystery, puzzling. □ **mysteriously** *adv.*

■ baffling, bewildering, confusing, curious, enigmatic, inexplicable, incomprehensible, inscrutable, mystifying, perplexing, puzzling, strange, uncanny, unfathomable, weird; abstruse, arcane, dark, occult, recondite, secret.

mystery *n.* **1** a matter that remains unexplained. **2** quality of being unexplained or obscure. **3** story dealing with a puzzling crime.

■ **1** conundrum, enigma, puzzle, riddle. **2** ambiguity, inscrutability, obscurity, secrecy. **3** detective story, thriller, *colloq.* whodunit.

mystic *adj.* **1** having a hidden or symbolic meaning, esp. in religion. **2** inspiring a sense of mystery and awe. ● *n.*

person who seeks to obtain union with God by spiritual contemplation. □ **mystical** *adj.*, **mystically** *adv.*, **mysticism** *n.*

mystify *v.* cause to feel puzzled. □ **mystification** *n.*

■ baffle, *colloq.* bamboozle, bewilder, confound, confuse, *colloq.* flummox, perplex, puzzle, *colloq.* stump.

mystique *n.* aura of mystery or mystical power.

myth *n.* **1** traditional tale(s) containing beliefs about ancient times or natural events. **2** imaginary person or thing. □ **mythical** *adj.*

■ **1** fable, legend, story, folk-tale. □ **mythical** fabled, fabulous, fairy-tale, legendary, mythological.

mythology *n.* **1** myths. **2** study of myths. □ **mythological** *adj.*

■ **1** folklore, legend, lore, myth(s), tradition.

myxomatosis *n.* fatal virus disease of rabbits.

Nn

N. abbr. **1** north. **2** northern.

nab v. (**nabbed**) (sl.) **1** catch in wrong-doing, arrest. **2** seize.

nadir n. lowest point.

naevus /néevəss/ n. (pl. **-vi**) red birth-mark.

nag¹ n. (colloq.) horse.

nag² v. (**nagged**) **1** criticize or scold per-sistently. **2** (of pain) be felt persistently.
> ■ **1** berate, carp at, criticize, *colloq.* get at, find fault with, *colloq.* keep on at, pick on, scold.

naiad /níad/ n. water nymph.

nail n. **1** layer of horny substance over the outer tip of a finger or toe. **2** claw. **3** small metal spike. ● v. **1** fasten with nail(s). **2** catch, arrest.

naive /naa-éev/ adj. showing lack of ex-perience or judgement. □ **naively** adv., **naivety** n.
> ■ artless, childlike, guileless, ingenuous, innocent, trustful, unsophisticated, un-worldly; callow, credulous, green, gullible, immature, inexperienced.

naked adj. **1** without clothes on. **2** without coverings. □ **naked eye** the eye unassisted by a telescope or microscope etc. **nakedness** n.
> ■ **1** bare, nude, unclothed, undressed. **2** uncovered, unprotected, unsheathed.

namby-pamby adj. & n. feeble or un-manly (person).

name n. **1** word(s) by which a person, place, or thing is known or indicated. **2** reputation. ● v. **1** give as a name. **2** nominate. **3** mention, specify. □ **in name only** as a mere formality.
> ■ n. **1** denomination, designation, term, title; alias, nickname, *nom de plume*, pen-name, pseudonym. ● v. **1** call, dub, label; baptize, christen. **2** appoint, choose, desig-nate, elect, nominate, select. **3** cite, identify, mention, specify.

namely adv. that is to say.

namesake n. person or thing with the same name as another.

nanny n. child's nurse. □ **nanny goat** female goat.

nano- pref. one thousand millionth.

nap¹ n. short sleep, esp. during the day. ● v. (**napped**) have a nap. □ **catch a person napping** catch him or her un-awares.
> ■ n. catnap, doze, rest, siesta, sleep, snooze.

nap² n. short raised fibres on the surface of cloth or leather.

napalm /náypaam/ n. jelly-like petrol substance used in incendiary bombs.

nape n. back part of neck.

naphtha /náftha/ n. inflammable oil.

naphthalene n. pungent white substance obtained from coal tar.

napkin n. **1** piece of cloth or paper used to protect clothes or for wiping one's lips at meals. **2** nappy.

nappy n. piece of absorbent material worn by a baby to absorb or retain its excreta.

narcissism n. abnormal self-admiration. □ **narcissistic** adj.
> ■ conceit, egotism, self-admiration, self-love, vanity.

narcissus n. (pl. **-cissi**) flower of the group including the daffodil.

narcotic adj. & n. (drug) causing sleep or drowsiness.

narrate v. tell (a story), give an account of. □ **narration** n., **narrator** n.
> ■ chronicle, describe, detail, recount, re-late, report, tell.

narrative n. spoken or written account of something. ● adj. in this form.
> ■ n. account, chronicle, description, his-tory, report, story, tale.

narrow adj. **1** small across, not wide. **2** of limited scope. **3** with little margin. ● v. make or become narrower. □ **narrow-minded** adj. restricted in one's views, intolerant. **narrowly** adv., **narrowness** n.
> ■ adj. **1** attenuated, slender, slim, tapering, thin; confined, constricted, cramped. **2** circumscribed, limited, restricted. **3** close, lucky, near. ● v. constrict, limit, reduce, restrict; contract, decrease, diminish, lessen. □ **narrow-minded** bigoted, con-servative, hidebound, insular, intolerant, parochial, prejudiced, provincial, small-minded, strait-laced, *colloq.* stuffy.

narwhal n. Arctic whale with a spirally grooved tusk.

nasal adj. **1** of the nose. **2** sounding as if breath came out through the nose. □ **nasally** adv.

nascent adj. just coming into existence. □ **nascence** n.

nasty adj. (**-ier, -iest**) **1** unpleasant. **2** unkind. **3** difficult. □ **nastily** adv., **nastiness** n.
■ **1** disagreeable, disgusting, distasteful, foul, colloq. horrible, horrid, loathsome, objectionable, obnoxious, odious, offensive, repellent, repugnant, repulsive, revolting, unpleasant, unsavoury, vile. **2** cruel, malicious, mean, spiteful, unkind. **3** difficult, problematic(al), tricky.

natal adj. of or from one's birth.

nation n. people of mainly common descent and history usu. inhabiting a particular country under one government.
■ country, land, realm, state.

national adj. of or common to a nation. ● n. citizen of a particular country. □ **nationally** adv.

nationalism n. **1** patriotic feeling. **2** policy of national independence. □ **nationalist** n., **nationalistic** adj.

nationality n. condition of belonging to a particular nation.

nationalize v. convert from private to state ownership. □ **nationalization** n.

native adj. **1** natural, inborn. **2** belonging to a place by birth. ● n. **1** person born in a specified place. **2** local inhabitant.
■ adj. **1** inborn, inherent, innate, instinctive, natural. **2** aboriginal, indigenous. ● n. **2** citizen, inhabitant, local, national, resident.

nativity n. **1** birth. **2** (**the Nativity**) that of Christ.

natter v. & n. (colloq.) chat.

natural adj. **1** of or produced by nature. **2** normal. **3** innate. **4** not seeming artificial or affected. ● n. person or thing that seems naturally suited for something. ■ **natural history** study of animals and plants. **naturalness** n.
■ adj. **2** common, customary, everyday, habitual, normal, regular, routine, standard, typical, usual. **3** inborn, inherent, innate, instinctive, native. **4** artless, easy, genuine, guileless, ingenuous, spontaneous, straightforward, unaffected, unsophisticated, unstudied.

naturalism n. realism in art and literature. □ **naturalistic** adj.

naturalist n. expert in natural history.

naturalize v. **1** admit (a foreigner) to full citizenship of a country. **2** introduce (a plant etc.) into a region. **3** make look natural. □ **naturalization** n.

naturally adv. **1** in a natural manner. **2** as might be expected, of course.

nature n. **1** the world with all its features and living things. **2** physical power producing these. **3** kind, sort. **4** thing's or person's essential qualities or character.
■ **3** category, class, description, kind, sort, type, variety. **4** character, disposition, make-up, personality, temperament; attributes, essence, features, properties, qualities.

naturist n. nudist. □ **naturism** n.

naughty adj. (**-ier, -iest**) **1** behaving badly, disobedient. **2** slightly indecent. □ **naughtily** adv., **naughtiness** n.
■ **1** devilish, disobedient, mischievous, obstreperous, rascally, refractory, roguish, uncooperative, unmanageable, ungovernable, unruly, wayward, wicked.

nausea n. feeling of sickness.

nauseate v. affect with nausea.

nauseous adj. affected with or causing nausea.

nautical adj. of sailors or seamanship.

nautilus n. (pl. **-luses**) mollusc with a spiral shell.

naval adj. of a navy.

nave n. main part of a church.

navel n. small hollow in the centre of the abdomen.

navigable adj. **1** suitable for ships. **2** able to be steered and sailed. □ **navigability** n.

navigate v. **1** sail in or through (a sea or river etc.). **2** direct the course of (a ship or vehicle etc.). □ **navigation** n., **navigator** n.
■ **1** cross, cruise, sail (across). **2** direct, guide, manoeuvre, pilot, steer.

navvy n. labourer making roads etc. where digging is necessary.

navy n. **1** a country's warships. **2** crew of these. **3** navy blue. □ **navy blue** very dark blue.

NB abbr. (Latin nota bene) note well.

NE abbr. **1** north-east. **2** north-eastern.

neap tide tide when there is least rise and fall of water.

near adv. **1** at, to, or within a short distance or interval. **2** nearly. ● prep. near to. ● adj. **1** close to, in place or time. **2**

closely related. **3** with little margin. **4** of the left side of a horse, vehicle, or road. **5** stingy. ● *v.* draw near. □ **nearness** *n.*
■ *adv.* **1** close (by), nearby, in the vicinity, not far away, within reach. ● *adj.* **1** adjacent, nearby, neighbouring; approaching, close, forthcoming, imminent, impending, looming. **2** close, intimate. **3** close, lucky, narrow. **5** close, mean, miserly, niggardly, parsimonious, penny-pinching, stingy, *colloq.* tight, tight-fisted.

nearby *adj.* & *adv.* near in position.

nearly *adv.* **1** closely. **2** almost.
■ **2** about, all but, almost, approximately, around, as good as, more or less, practically, virtually, well-nigh.

neat *adj.* **1** orderly in appearance or workmanship. **2** undiluted. □ **neatly** *adv.*, **neatness** *n.*
■ **1** orderly, organized, shipshape, smart, spruce, straight, tidy, trim, uncluttered. **2** pure, straight, unadulterated, undiluted.

neaten *v.* make neat.
■ put in order, smarten up, spruce up, straighten, tidy.

nebula *n.* (*pl.* **-ae**) a cloud of gas or dust in space. □ **nebular** *adj.*

nebulous *adj.* indistinct. □ **nebulously** *adv.*, **nebulosity** *n.*
■ dim, faint, foggy, fuzzy, hazy, indistinct, obscure, shadowy, unclear, vague.

necessarily *adv.* as a necessary result, inevitably.

necessary *adj.* **1** essential in order to achieve something. **2** happening or existing by necessity.
■ **1** compulsory, essential, imperative, indispensable, needed, needful, obligatory, required, requisite, vital. **2** inescapable, inevitable, unavoidable.

necessitate *v.* **1** make necessary. **2** involve as a condition or result.

necessitous *adj.* needy.

necessity *n.* **1** indispensable thing. **2** state of being indispensable. **3** pressure of circumstances. **4** poverty.
■ **1** essential, fundamental, need, prerequisite, requirement, requisite. **3** exigency, need, urgency. **4** destitution, hardship, indigence, need, penury, poverty, want.

neck *n.* **1** narrow part connecting the head to the body. **2** part of a garment round this. **3** narrow part of a bottle, cavity, etc. □ **neck and neck** running level in a race.

necklace *n.* piece of jewellery etc. worn round the neck.

neckline *n.* outline formed by the edge of a garment at the neck.

necromancy *n.* art of predicting things by communicating with the dead. □ **necromancer** *n.*

necrosis *n.* death of bone or tissue. □ **necrotic** *adj.*

nectar *n.* **1** sweet fluid from plants, collected by bees. **2** any delicious drink.

nectarine *n.* smooth-skinned variety of peach.

née /nay/ *adj.* (before a married woman's maiden name) born.

need *n.* **1** requirement. **2** circumstances requiring action. **3** crisis, emergency. **4** poverty. ● *v.* be in need of, require. □ **need to** be obliged to.
■ *n.* **1** demand, necessity, requirement, want. **3** crisis, difficulty, distress, emergency, exigency, trouble. **4** destitution, indigence, penury, poverty. ● *v.* demand, require, want; be without, lack.

needful *adj.* necessary.

needle *n.* **1** small thin pointed piece of steel used in sewing. **2** thing shaped like this. **3** pointer of a compass or gauge. ● *v.* annoy, provoke.

needless *adj.* unnecessary. □ **needlessly** *adv.*
■ gratuitous, pointless, superfluous, uncalled-for, unnecessary, unwarranted.

needlework *n.* sewing or embroidery.

needy *adj.* (**-ier**, **-iest**) very poor.
■ destitute, impecunious, impoverished, indigent, necessitous, on the breadline, penniless, penurious, poor, poverty-stricken.

nefarious *adj.* wicked.

negate *v.* nullify, disprove. □ **negation** *n.*

negative *adj.* **1** expressing denial, refusal, or prohibition. **2** lacking positive attributes. **3** (of a quantity) less than zero. **4** (of a battery terminal) through which electric current leaves. ● *n.* **1** negative statement or word. **2** negative quality or quantity. **3** photograph with lights and shades or colours reversed, from which positive pictures can be obtained. □ **negatively** *adv.*
■ *adj.* **1** anti-, contradictory, contrary, opposing. **2** apathetic, defeatist, pessimistic, unenthusiastic, uninterested, unresponsive.

neglect *v.* **1** fail to care for or do. **2** forget the need to. **3** pay no attention to.

● *n.* neglecting, being neglected. □ **neglectful** *adj.*

■ *v.* **2** fail, forget, omit. **3** disregard, ignore, overlook, pay no attention to. ● *n.* dereliction, laxity, negligence.

negligee /néglizhay/ *n.* woman's light dressing gown.

negligence *n.* lack of proper care or attention. □ **negligent** *adj.*, **negligently** *adv.*

■ □ **negligent** careless, heedless, inattentive, neglectful, remiss, thoughtless, unmindful, unthinking.

negligible *adj.* too small to be worth taking into account.

■ inconsequential, insignificant, minor, petty, slight, small, trifling, trivial, unimportant.

negotiate *v.* **1** hold a discussion so as to reach agreement. **2** arrange by such discussion. **3** get past (an obstacle) successfully. □ **negotiation** *n.*, **negotiator** *n.*

■ **1** bargain, haggle; debate, parley, speak, talk. **2** arrange, bring about, engineer, get, obtain, organize, pull off, work out.

Negress *n.* female Negro.

Negro *n.* (*pl.* **-oes**) member of the black-skinned race that originated in Africa.

neigh *n.* horse's long high-pitched cry. ● *v.* make this cry.

neighbour *n.* person living next door or nearby.

neighbourhood *n.* district, vicinity. □ **neighbourhood watch** systematic vigilance by residents to deter crime in their area.

■ area, district, environs, locality, quarter, region, vicinity.

neighbouring *adj.* living or situated nearby.

neighbourly *adj.* kind and friendly. □ **neighbourliness** *n.*

■ affable, agreeable, amiable, considerate, cordial, friendly, helpful, kind, kindly, obliging, sociable, well-disposed.

neither *adj.*, *pron.*, & *adv.* not either.

nemesis /némmisiss/ *n.* inevitable retribution.

neo- *pref.* new.

neolithic *adj.* of the later part of the Stone Age.

neologism *n.* new word.

neon *n.* inert gas used in illuminated signs.

nephew *n.* one's brother's or sister's son.

nephritis *n.* inflammation of the kidneys.

nepotism *n.* favouritism shown to relatives in appointing them to jobs. □ **nepotistic** *adj.*

nerve *n.* **1** fibre carrying impulses of sensation or movement between the brain and a part of the body. **2** courage. **3** (*colloq.*) impudence. **4** (*pl.*) nervousness, effect of mental stress. ● *v.* give courage to. □ **get on a person's nerves** irritate a person.

■ *n.* **2** boldness, bravery, courage, daring, fearlessness, fortitude, *colloq.* grit, *colloq.* guts, intrepidity, mettle, pluck, spirit, valour. **3** cheek, effrontery, gall, impertinence, impudence, insolence, presumption, temerity. **4** (**nerves**) anxiety, *colloq.* the jitters, nervousness, tension, worry.

nervous *adj.* **1** of the nerves. **2** easily alarmed. **3** slightly afraid, anxious. □ **nervously** *adv.*, **nervousness** *n.*

■ **2** edgy, excitable, jumpy, highly-strung, nervy, *colloq.* uptight. **3** agitated, anxious, apprehensive, edgy, fearful, fidgety, frightened, *colloq.* in a tizzy, *colloq.* jittery, jumpy, keyed up, on tenterhooks, restless, scared, troubled, uneasy, worried.

nervy *adj.* nervous.

nest *n.* **1** structure or place in which a bird lays eggs and shelters its young. **2** breeding place, lair. **3** snug place, shelter. **4** set of articles (esp. tables) designed to fit inside each other. ● *v.* make or have a nest. □ **nest egg** money saved for future use.

nestle *v.* **1** settle oneself comfortably. **2** lie sheltered.

nestling *n.* bird too young to leave the nest.

net[1] *n.* **1** openwork material of thread, cord, or wire etc. **2** piece of this used for a particular purpose. ● *v.* (**netted**) **1** place nets in or on. **2** catch in a net.

■ *n.* **1** mesh, netting, openwork, web, webbing. **2** dragnet, fishing net, seine, trawl. ● *v.* **2** capture, catch, ensnare, snare, trap.

net[2] *adj.* **1** remaining after all deductions. **2** (of weight) not including wrappings etc. ● *v.* (**netted**) obtain or yield as net profit.

netball *n.* game in which a ball has to be thrown into a high net.

nether *adj.* lower.

netting *n.* netted fabric.

nettle *n.* wild plant with leaves that sting when touched. ● *v.* irritate, provoke.

□ **nettle-rash** *n.* skin eruption like nettle stings.

network *n.* **1** arrangement with intersecting lines. **2** complex system. **3** group of interconnected people or things.

neural *adj.* of nerves.

neuralgia *n.* sharp pain along a nerve. □ **neuralgic** *adj.*

neuritis *n.* inflammation of nerve(s).

neurology *n.* study of nerve systems. □ **neurological** *adj.*, **neurologist** *n.*

neurosis *n.* (*pl.* **-oses**) mental disorder producing depression or abnormal behaviour.

neurotic *adj.* **1** of or caused by a neurosis. **2** subject to abnormal anxieties or obsessive behaviour. ● *n.* neurotic person. □ **neurotically** *adv.*

neuter *adj.* **1** neither masculine nor feminine. **2** without male or female parts. ● *v.* castrate, spay.

neutral *adj.* **1** not supporting either side in a conflict. **2** without distinctive or positive characteristics. ● *n.* **1** neutral person, country, or colour. **2** neutral gear. □ **neutral gear** position of gear mechanism in which the engine is disconnected from driven parts. **neutrally** *adv.*, **neutrality** *n.*

■ *adj.* **1** non-belligerent, non-combatant; disinterested, impartial, unbiased, unprejudiced.

neutralize *v.* make ineffective. □ **neutralization** *n.*

■ cancel out, counteract, counterbalance, invalidate, negate, offset, undo.

neutrino *n.* (*pl.* **-os**) particle with zero electric charge and (probably) zero mass.

neutron *n.* nuclear particle with no electric charge. □ **neutron bomb** nuclear bomb that kills people but does little damage to buildings etc.

never *adv.* **1** at no time, on no occasion. **2** not. **3** (*colloq.*) surely not. □ **never mind** do not worry.

nevermore *adv.* at no future time.

nevertheless *adv.* in spite of that.

■ anyhow, anyway, despite that, however, in spite of that, notwithstanding, still, yet.

new *adj.* **1** not existing before, recently made, discovered, experienced, etc. **2** not worn or used. **3** different from the previous one. **4** additional. **5** unfamiliar, unaccustomed. **6** modern. ● *adv.* newly, recently. □ **new moon** moon seen as a crescent. **New Testament** part of the Bible concerned with Christ and his teaching. **New Year's Day** 1 Jan.

■ **1** brand-new, fresh, recent; different, innovative, novel, original. **2** in mint condition, pristine, unused, unworn, virgin. **4** additional, extra, fresh, further, more, supplementary. **5** different, strange, unaccustomed, unfamiliar, unusual. **6** avant-garde, contemporary, latest, modern, newfangled, present-day, *colloq.* trendy, up to date.

newcomer *n.* one who has arrived recently.

■ alien, colonist, immigrant, outsider, settler, stranger.

newel *n.* **1** top or bottom post of the handrail of a stair. **2** central pillar of a winding stair.

newfangled *adj.* objectionably new in method or style.

newly *adv.* recently, freshly. □ **newly-wed** *adj.* & *n.* recently married (person).

news *n.* **1** new or interesting information about recent events. **2** (**the news**) broadcast report of this. □ **newsy** *adj.*

■ **1** facts, information, intelligence, word; gossip, hearsay, *colloq.* low-down, rumour, talk.

newsagent *n.* shopkeeper who sells newspapers.

newscaster *n.* newsreader.

newsflash *n.* brief news item.

newsletter *n.* informal printed report containing news of interest to members of a club etc.

newspaper *n.* **1** printed daily or weekly publication containing news reports. **2** sheets of paper forming this.

■ **1** broadsheet, daily, gazette, journal, paper, publication, *derog.* rag, tabloid, weekly.

newsprint *n.* type of paper on which newspapers are printed.

newsreader *n.* person who reads broadcast news reports.

newsworthy *adj.* worth reporting as news.

newt *n.* small lizard-like amphibious creature.

next *adj.* nearest in position or time etc. ● *adv.* **1** in the next place or degree. **2** on the next occasion. ● *n.* next person or thing. □ **next door** in the next house or room. **next of kin** one's closest relative.

■ *adj.* adjacent, bordering, closest, contiguous, nearest, neighbouring; following, subsequent, succeeding.

nexus n. (pl. **-uses**) connected group or series.

nib n. metal point of a pen.

nibble v. take small quick or gentle bites (at). ● n. **1** small quick bite. **2** snack. □ **nibbler** n.

nice adj. **1** pleasant, satisfactory. **2** fine, subtle. **3** fastidious. □ **nicely** adv., **niceness** n.

■ **1** agreeable, affable, amiable, amicable, charming, cordial, courteous, friendly, genial, good-natured, kind, kindly, likeable, pleasant, polite; delightful, enjoyable, good, colloq. lovely, pleasing, pleasurable, satisfactory. **2** fine, precise, subtle. **3** dainty, fastidious, finicky, fussy, particular, colloq. pernickety.

nicety n. **1** precision. **2** detail. □ **to a nicety** exactly.

■ **1** accuracy, exactness, precision. **2** detail, nuance, subtlety.

niche n. **1** shallow recess esp. in a wall. **2** suitable position in life or employment.

■ **1** alcove, cubby hole, nook, recess. **2** place, position, slot.

nick n. small cut or notch. ● v. **1** make a nick in. **2** (sl.) steal. **3** (sl.) arrest. □ **in good nick** (colloq.) in good condition. **in the nick of time** only just in time.

nickel n. **1** hard silvery-white metal. **2** (US) 5-cent piece.

nickname n. name given humorously to a person or thing. ● v. give as a nickname.

nicotine n. poisonous substance found in tobacco.

niece n. one's brother's or sister's daughter.

niggardly adj. stingy. □ **niggard** n.

niggle v. fuss over details.

nigh adv. & prep. near.

night n. **1** dark hours between sunset and sunrise. **2** nightfall. □ **night-life** n. entertainment available at night. **night school** instruction provided in the evening.

nightcap n. (alcoholic) drink taken just before going to bed.

nightclub n. club providing entertainment etc. at night.

nightdress n. woman's or child's loose garment for sleeping in.

nightfall n. onset of night.

nightgown n. nightdress.

nightie n. (colloq.) nightdress.

nightingale n. small thrush, male of which sings melodiously.

nightjar n. night-flying bird with a harsh cry.

nightly adj. & adv. (happening) at night or every night.

nightmare n. **1** frightening dream. **2** (colloq.) unpleasant experience. □ **nightmarish** adj.

nightshade n. plant with poisonous berries.

nightshirt n. man's or boy's long shirt for sleeping in.

nihilism n. rejection of all religious and moral principles. □ **nihilist** n., **nihilistic** adj.

nil n. nothing.

nimble adj. able to move quickly. □ **nimbly** adv.

■ agile, fleet, graceful, lissom, lithe, lively, colloq. nippy, quick, sprightly, spry, swift.

nincompoop n. foolish person.

nine adj. & n. one more than eight. □ **ninth** adj. & n.

ninepins n. game of skittles played with nine objects.

nineteen adj. & n. one more than eighteen. □ **nineteenth** adj. & n.

ninety adj. & n. nine times ten. □ **ninetieth** adj. & n.

ninny n. foolish person.

nip¹ v. (**nipped**) **1** pinch or squeeze sharply. **2** bite quickly with the front teeth. **3** (sl.) go quickly. ● n. **1** sharp pinch, squeeze, or bite. **2** biting coldness.

nip² n. small drink of spirits.

■ dram, finger, colloq. shot, sl. snifter, tot.

nipple n. **1** small projection at the centre of a breast. **2** similar protuberance. **3** teat of a feeding bottle.

nippy adj. (**-ier**, **-iest**) (colloq.) **1** nimble, quick. **2** bitingly cold.

nirvana n. (in Buddhism and Hinduism) state of perfect bliss achieved by the soul.

nit n. egg of a louse or similar parasite. □ **nit-picking** n. & adj. (colloq.) petty fault-finding.

nitrate n. substance formed from nitric acid, esp. used as a fertilizer.

nitric acid corrosive acid containing nitrogen.

nitrogen n. gas forming about four-fifths of the atmosphere.

nitroglycerine n. explosive yellow liquid.

nitrous oxide gas used as an anaesthetic.

nitty-gritty n. (sl.) basic facts or realities of a matter.

nitwit n. (colloq.) stupid person.

no adj. **1** not any. **2** not a. ● adv. **1** (used as a denial or refusal of something). **2** not at all. ● n. (pl. **noes**) negative reply, vote against a proposal. □ **no-go area** area to which entry is forbidden or restricted. **no man's land** area not controlled by anyone, esp. between opposing armies. **no one** no person, nobody.

No. abbr. number.

nobble v. (sl.) **1** seize. **2** tamper with or influence dishonestly.

nobility n. **1** nobleness of character or of rank. **2** titled people.

■ **1** dignity, excellence, grandeur, greatness, honesty, integrity, magnanimity, probity, rectitude. **2** aristocracy, peerage, colloq. upper crust.

noble adj. **1** aristocratic. **2** of excellent character, not mean or petty. **3** impressive in appearance. ● n. member of the nobility. □ **nobly** adv., **nobleness** n.

■ adj. **1** aristocratic, blue-blooded, titled, upper class, colloq. upper crust. **2** decent, generous, good, honest, honourable, magnanimous, moral, principled, righteous, upright, virtuous. **3** grand, imposing, impressive, magnificent, majestic, splendid, stately. ● n. aristocrat, lady, lord, nobleman, noblewoman, peer, peeress.

nobleman, **noblewoman** ns. member of the nobility.

nobody pron. no person. ● n. person of no importance.

nocturnal adj. of, happening in, or active in the night. □ **nocturnally** adv.

nod v. (**nodded**) **1** incline the head, indicate (agreement or casual greeting) thus. **2** let the head droop, be drowsy. **3** (of flowers etc.) bend and sway. ● n. nodding movement, esp. in agreement or greeting.

node n. **1** knob-like swelling. **2** point on a stem where a leaf or bud grows out. □ **nodal** adj.

nodule n. small rounded lump, small node. □ **nodular** adj.

noise n. sound, esp. loud, harsh, or undesired.

■ babel, cacophony, caterwauling, clamour, clangour, commotion, din, hubbub, hullabaloo, racket, row, rumpus, sound, thunder, thundering, tumult, uproar.

noisy adj. (**-ier, -iest**) making much noise. □ **noisily** adv.

■ blaring, booming, cacophonous, clamorous, deafening, discordant, dissonant, loud, piercing, raucous, shrill, thunderous; boisterous, obstreperous, riotous, rowdy, uproarious.

nomad n. **1** member of a tribe that roams seeking pasture for its animals. **2** wanderer. □ **nomadic** adj.

nom de plume writer's pseudonym.

nomenclature n. system of names, e.g. in a science.

nominal adj. **1** in name only. **2** (of a fee) very small. □ **nominal value** face value of a coin etc. **nominally** adv.

■ **1** in name only, self-styled, titular. **2** inconsiderable, insignificant, minimal, minor, minuscule, small, tiny, trifling, trivial, token.

nominate v. **1** propose as a candidate. **2** appoint to an office. **3** appoint a place or date. □ **nomination** n., **nominator** n.

■ **1** propose, put forward, recommend, submit, suggest. **2** appoint, choose, designate, name, select. **3** choose, name, select.

nominee n. person nominated.

non- pref. not.

nonagenarian n. person in his or her nineties.

nonchalant adj. calm and casual. □ **nonchalantly** adv., **nonchalance** n.

■ blasé, calm, casual, collected, composed, easygoing, happy-go-lucky, imperturbable, insouciant, offhand, phlegmatic, relaxed, unconcerned, colloq. unflappable, unperturbed.

noncommittal adj. not revealing one's opinion.

■ careful, colloq. cagey, cautious, circumspect, guarded, wary.

nonconformist n. **1** person not conforming to established practices. **2** (**Nonconformist**) member of a Protestant sect not conforming to Anglican practices.

■ **1** dissenter, dissident, iconoclast, individualist, maverick, rebel, renegade.

nondescript adj. lacking distinctive characteristics.

■ bland, characterless, colourless, drab, insipid, ordinary, unexceptional, uninteresting, unremarkable.

none pron. **1** not any. **2** no person(s). ● adv. not at all.

nonentity n. person of no importance.

non-event n. event that was expected to be important but proves disappointing.

non-existent *adj.* not existing.
■ fanciful, fictional, fictitious, illusory, imaginary, imagined, mythical, unreal.

nonplussed *adj.* completely perplexed.
■ astonished, astounded, baffled, bemused, bewildered, confounded, dumbfounded, *colloq.* flummoxed, mystified, perplexed, puzzled, taken aback.

nonsense *n.* **1** absurd or meaningless words or ideas. **2** foolish talk or behaviour. □ **nonsensical** *adj.*
■ **1** balderdash, *sl.* bilge, *sl.* boloney, bunkum, double Dutch, drivel, gibberish, *colloq.* gobbledegook, mumbo-jumbo, *colloq.* piffle, *sl.* poppycock, *sl.* rot, rubbish, *sl.* tripe, twaddle. **2** antics, buffoonery, clowning, foolishness, silliness. □ **nonsensical** absurd, asinine, crazy, foolish, idiotic, laughable, ludicrous, mad, preposterous, ridiculous, senseless, silly, stupid.

non sequitur conclusion that does not follow from the evidence given.

non-starter *n.* **1** horse entered for a race but not running in it. **2** person or idea etc. not worth considering for a purpose.

non-stop *adj.* & *adv.* **1** without ceasing. **2** (of a train etc.) not stopping at intermediate places.
■ *adj.* **1** ceaseless, constant, continual, endless, *colloq.* eternal, incessant, never-ending, persistent, unceasing, unending, unremitting. **2** direct, through.

noodles *n.pl.* pasta in narrow strips, used in soups etc.

nook *n.* **1** secluded place. **2** recess.

noon *n.* twelve o'clock in the day.

noose *n.* loop of rope etc. with a knot that tightens when pulled.

nor *conj.* & *adv.* and not.

norm *n.* standard or pattern that is typical.
■ custom, pattern, rule, standard.

normal *adj.* **1** conforming to what is standard or usual. **2** free from mental or emotional disorders. □ **normally** *adv.*, **normality** *n.*
■ **1** average, common, conventional, customary, natural, ordinary, regular, routine, run-of-the-mill, standard, typical, usual. **2** rational, sane, well-adjusted.

north *n.* **1** point or direction to the left of person facing east. **2** northern part.
● *adj.* **1** in the north. **2** (of wind) from the north. ● *adv.* towards the north. □ **north-east** *n.* point or direction mid-way between north and east. **north-easterly** *adj.* & *n.*, **north-eastern** *adj.* **north-west** *n.* point or direction midway between north and west. **north-westerly** *adj.* & *n.*, **north-western** *adj.*

northerly *adj.* towards or blowing from the north.

northern *adj.* of or in the north.

northerner *n.* native of the north.

northernmost *adj.* furthest north.

northward *adj.* towards the north. □ **northwards** *adv.*

Norwegian *adj.* & *n.* (native, language) of Norway.

Nos. *abbr.* numbers.

nose *n.* **1** organ at the front of the head, used in breathing and smelling. **2** sense of smell. **3** open end of a tube. **4** front end or projecting part. ● *v.* **1** detect or search by use of the sense of smell. **2** push one's nose against or into. **3** push one's way cautiously ahead.

nosebag *n.* bag of fodder for hanging on a horse's head.

nosedive *n.* steep downward plunge, esp. of an aeroplane. ● *v.* make this plunge.

nostalgia *n.* sentimental memory of or longing for things of the past. □ **nostalgic** *adj.*
■ □ **nostalgic** homesick, maudlin, sentimental, wistful.

nostril *n.* either of the two external openings in the nose.

nosy *adj.* (**-ier, -iest**) (*colloq.*) inquisitive.

not *adv.* expressing a negative or denial or refusal.

notable *adj.* **1** worthy of notice, remarkable. **2** eminent. ● *n.* eminent person. □ **notably** *adv.*
■ *adj.* **1** conspicuous, impressive, memorable, noteworthy, outstanding, pre-eminent, remarkable, singular, striking, unforgettable, unusual. **2** celebrated, distinguished, eminent, famed, famous, great, illustrious, important, prominent, well-known. ● *n.* celebrity, dignitary, luminary, personage, worthy.

notation *n.* system of signs or symbols representing numbers, quantities, musical notes, etc.

notch *n.* V-shaped cut or indentation. ● *v.* make notch(es) in. □ **notch up** score, achieve.

note *n.* **1** brief record written down to aid memory. **2** short or informal letter or message. **3** short written comment. **4** banknote. **5** eminence. **6** notice, attention. **7** musical tone of definite pitch. **8**

symbol representing the pitch and duration of a musical sound. **9** each of the keys on a piano etc. ● v. **1** notice, pay attention to. **2** write down.

■ n. **1** colloq. memo, memorandum, record, reminder. **2** card, letter, line, colloq. memo, memorandum, message, postcard. **3** annotation, comment, observation, remark. **4** banknote, US bill. **5** consequence, distinction, eminence, importance, prestige, renown, reputation, repute. **6** attention, heed, regard, notice, thought. ● v. **1** mark, notice, observe, pay attention to, perceive, register, see. **2** jot down, put down, record, register, write down.

notebook n. book with blank pages on which to write notes.

notecase n. wallet for banknotes.

noted adj. famous, well-known.

■ acclaimed, celebrated, distinguished, eminent, famed, famous, illustrious, prominent, renowned, well-known.

notelet n. small folded card etc. for a short informal letter.

notepad n. notebook.

notepaper n. paper for writing letters on.

noteworthy adj. worthy of notice, remarkable.

■ exceptional, extraordinary, important, impressive, memorable, notable, outstanding, remarkable, signal, significant, singular.

nothing n. **1** no thing, not anything. **2** no amount, nought. **3** non-existence. **4** person or thing of no importance. ● adv. not at all. □ **nothingness** n.

notice n. **1** attention, observation. **2** intimation, warning. **3** formal announcement of the termination of an agreement or employment. **4** written or printed information displayed. **5** review in a newspaper. ● v. perceive, observe. □ **take notice** show interest. **take notice of** pay attention to.

■ n. **1** attention, awareness, cognizance, consciousness, observation, perception. **2** intimation, notification, warning. **4** advertisement, bill, placard, poster, sign. **5** review, colloq. write-up. ● v. descry, detect, discern, make out, observe, perceive, see, colloq. spot.

noticeable adj. easily seen or noticed. □ **noticeably** adv.

■ apparent, clear, conspicuous, detectable, discernible, distinct, distinguishable,

evident, manifest, observable, obvious, palpable, perceptible, recognizable, visible.

notifiable adj. that must be notified.

notify v. **1** inform. **2** report, make known. □ **notification** n.

■ **1** advise, apprise, inform, tell, warn. **2** announce, declare, make known, report.

notion n. **1** concept, idea. **2** vague belief or understanding. **3** whim.

■ **1** concept, conception, idea, opinion, thought, view. **2** feeling, impression, inkling, suspicion. **3** caprice, fancy, vagary, whim.

notional adj. hypothetical, imaginary. □ **notionally** adv.

notorious adj. well-known, esp. unfavourably. □ **notoriously** adv., **notoriety** n.

■ disreputable, ill-famed, infamous.

notwithstanding prep. in spite of. ● adv. nevertheless.

nougat /nōōgaa/ n. chewy sweet.

nought n. **1** the figure 0. **2** nothing.

noun n. word used as the name of a person, place, or thing.

nourish v. **1** keep alive and well by food. **2** cherish (a feeling).

nourishment n. food.

■ food, sl. grub, nutriment, nutrition, sustenance.

nous /nowss/ n. (colloq.) common sense.

nova n. (pl. -ae) star that suddenly becomes much brighter for a short time.

novel n. book-length story. ● adj. of a new kind.

■ adj. different, fresh, innovative, new, original, unconventional, unfamiliar, unusual.

novelette n. short (esp. romantic) novel.

novelist n. writer of novels.

novelty n. **1** novel quality or thing. **2** small toy etc.

■ **1** freshness, newness, originality. **2** bauble, gewgaw, knick-knack, toy, trinket.

novice n. **1** inexperienced person. **2** probationary member of a religious order.

■ **1** apprentice, beginner, greenhorn, learner, probationer, trainee.

now adv. **1** at the present time. **2** immediately. **3** (with no reference to time) I wonder or am telling you. ● conj. as a consequence of or simultaneously with the fact that. ● n. the present time.

□ **now and again**, **now and then** occasionally.

■ *adv.* **1** at present, at the present time, at this moment; nowadays, today. **2** at once, immediately, instantly, right away, straight away, without delay.

nowadays *adv.* in present times.

nowhere *adv.* not anywhere.

noxious *adj.* unpleasant and harmful.

■ dangerous, foul, harmful, injurious, nasty, pernicious, poisonous, toxic, unhealthy.

nozzle *n.* vent or spout of a hosepipe etc.

nuance /nyōō-ONSS/ *n.* shade of meaning.

nub *n.* **1** central point or core of a matter or problem. **2** small lump.

■ **1** centre, core, crux, essence, gist, heart, kernel, pith, substance.

nubile *adj.* (of a woman) marriageable or sexually attractive. □ **nubility** *n.*

nuclear *adj.* **1** of a nucleus. **2** of the nuclei of atoms. **3** using energy released or absorbed during reactions in these.

nucleus *n.* (*pl.* **-lei**) **1** central part or thing round which others are collected. **2** central portion of an atom, seed, or cell.

nude *adj.* naked. ● *n.* nude figure in a picture etc. □ **nudity** *n.*

■ *adj.* bare, (stark) naked, unclothed, undressed.

nudge *v.* **1** poke gently with the elbow to attract attention. **2** push slightly or gradually. ● *n.* this movement.

■ *v.* **1** elbow, jog, poke, prod, push.

nudist *n.* person who advocates or practises going unclothed. □ **nudism** *n.*

nugget *n.* rough lump of gold or platinum found in the earth.

nuisance *n.* annoying person or thing.

■ bore, menace, pest; annoyance, bother, *colloq.* hassle, headache, inconvenience, irritation, trial.

null *adj.* (esp. **null and void**) having no legal force. □ **nullity** *n.*

nullify *v.* **1** make null. **2** neutralize the effect of. □ **nullification** *n.*

■ **1** annul, cancel, invalidate, repeal, rescind, revoke. **2** counteract, counterbalance, make ineffective, negate, neutralize, offset.

numb *adj.* deprived of power to feel. ● *v.* make numb. □ **numbness** *n.*

■ *adj.* anaesthetized, dead, deadened, numbed, insensible.

number *n.* **1** symbol or word indicating how many. **2** total. **3** quantity. **4** person

or thing having a place in a series, esp. single issue of magazine, item in a programme, etc. ● *v.* **1** include. **2** amount to. **3** assign a number or numbers to. □ **number one** (*colloq.*) oneself. **number plate** plate on a motor vehicle, bearing its registration number.

■ *n.* **1** digit, figure, integer, numeral. **2** aggregate, sum, total. **3** amount, quantity. **4** copy, edition, issue.

numberless *adj.* innumerable.

numeral *n.* written symbol of a number.

numerate *adj.* having a good basic understanding of mathematics. □ **numeracy** *n.*

numerator *n.* number above the line in a vulgar fraction.

numerical *adj.* of number(s). □ **numerically** *adv.*

numerous *adj.* great in number.

■ a lot of, countless, innumerable, lots of, many, myriad.

nun *n.* member of a female religious community.

nunnery *n.* residence of a community of nuns.

nuptial *adj.* of marriage or a wedding. ● *n.pl.* wedding ceremony.

nurse *n.* **1** person trained to look after sick or injured people. **2** person employed to take charge of young children. ● *v.* **1** work as a nurse, act as nurse (to). **2** feed at the breast or udder. **3** hold carefully. **4** give special care to. **5** harbour. □ **nursing home** privately run hospital or home for invalids.

■ *v.* **1** care for, look after, take care of, tend. **2** breastfeed, feed, suckle. **4** cherish, foster, nurture.

nursery *n.* **1** room(s) for young children. **2** place where plants are reared, esp. for sale. □ **nursery rhyme** traditional verse for children. **nursery school** school for children below normal school age. **nursery slopes** slopes suitable for beginners at skiing.

nurseryman *n.* person growing plants etc. at a nursery.

nurture *v.* **1** bring up. **2** nourish. **3** foster. ● *n.* nurturing.

■ *v.* **1** bring up, care for, look after, raise, rear. **2** feed, nourish. **3** cherish, foster, nurse.

nut *n.* **1** fruit with a hard shell round an edible kernel. **2** this kernel. **3** small threaded metal ring for use with a bolt. **4** (*sl.*) head.

nutcase n. (sl.) crazy person.

nuthatch n. small climbing bird.

nutmeg n. hard fragrant tropical seed ground or grated as spice.

nutria n. fur of the coypu.

nutrient adj. & n. nourishing (substance).

nutriment n. nourishing substance.

nutrition n. food, nourishment. □ **nutritional** adj.

nutritious adj. nourishing.

■ healthful, healthy, nourishing, wholesome.

nuts adj. (sl.) crazy.

nutshell n. hard shell of a nut. □ **in a nutshell** expressed very briefly.

nutty adj. (**-ier, -iest**) **1** full of nuts. **2** tasting like nuts. **3** (sl.) crazy.

nuzzle v. press or rub gently with the nose.

NW abbr. **1** north-west. **2** north-western.

nylon n. **1** very light strong synthetic fibre. **2** fabric made of this.

nymph n. **1** mythological semi-divine maiden. **2** young insect.

nymphomania n. excessive sexual desire in a woman. □ **nymphomaniac** n.

NZ abbr. New Zealand.

Oo

oaf *n.* (*pl.* **oafs**) awkward lout.

oak *n.* **1** deciduous forest tree bearing acorns. **2** its hard wood. □ **oak-apple** *n.* = **gall**³.

oar *n.* **1** pole with a flat blade used to propel a boat by its leverage against water. **2** rower.

oasis *n.* (*pl.* **oases**) fertile spot in a desert, with a spring or well.

oath *n.* **1** solemn promise. **2** swear word.
■ **1** pledge, promise, vow, word (of honour). **2** curse, expletive, imprecation, profanity, swear word.

oatmeal *n.* **1** ground oats. **2** greyish-fawn colour.

oats *n.* **1** hardy cereal plant. **2** its grain.

obdurate *adj.* stubborn. □ **obdurately** *adv.*, **obduracy** *n.*

obedient *adj.* doing what one is told to do. □ **obediently** *adv.*, **obedience** *n.*
■ amenable, biddable, compliant, docile, dutiful, law-abiding, meek, submissive, tractable.

obeisance *n.* bow or curtsy.

obelisk *n.* tall pillar set up as a monument.

obese *adj.* very fat. □ **obesity** *n.*
■ corpulent, fat, fleshy, gross, heavy, overweight.

obey *v.* do what is commanded (by).
■ abide by, comply (with), conform (to), defer (to), follow, knuckle under, observe, respect, submit (to), toe the line.

obfuscate *v.* **1** darken. **2** confuse, bewilder. □ **obfuscation** *n.*

obituary *n.* printed statement of person's death (esp. in a newspaper).

object *n.* /óbjikt/ **1** something solid that can be seen or touched. **2** person or thing to which an action or feeling is directed. **3** purpose, intention. **4** noun etc. acted upon by a verb or preposition. ● *v.* /əbjékt/ **1** express opposition, disapproval, or reluctance. **2** protest. □ **no object** not a limiting factor. **object lesson** practical illustration of a principle. **objector** *n.*
■ *n.* **1** article, entity, item, thing. **2** butt, destination, focus, quarry, target. **3** aim, ambition, end, goal, intent, intention, objective, purpose. ● *v.* complain, demur, disapprove, draw the line, protest, remonstrate, take exception.

objection *n.* **1** expression or feeling of disapproval or opposition. **2** reason for objecting.

objectionable *adj.* unpleasant. □ **objectionably** *adv.*
■ disagreeable, distasteful, *colloq.* horrible, horrid, loathsome, nasty, obnoxious, odious, offensive, repellent, unpleasant.

objective *adj.* **1** not influenced by personal feelings or opinions. **2** of the form of a word used when it is the object of a verb or preposition. ● *n.* object, purpose. □ **objectively** *adv.*, **objectivity** *n.*
■ *adj.* **1** detached, disinterested, dispassionate, equitable, fair, impartial, neutral, unbiased, unprejudiced. ● *n.* aim, ambition, aspiration, design, end, goal, intent, intention, object, purpose, target.

objet d'art /óbzhay daár/ (*pl.* **objets d'art**) small artistic object.

oblation *n.* offering made to God.

obligate *v.* oblige.

obligation *n.* **1** compelling power of a law, duty, etc. **2** burdensome task, duty.
■ **1** compulsion, constraint. **2** burden, duty, charge, responsibility, task.

obligatory *adj.* compulsory.
■ compulsory, essential, mandatory, necessary, required, requisite.

oblige *v.* **1** compel. **2** help or gratify by a small service.
■ **1** compel, constrain, force, make, obligate, require. **2** gratify, indulge, humour, please.

obliged *adj.* indebted.

obliging *adj.* polite and helpful. □ **obligingly** *adv.*
■ accommodating, agreeable, amenable, considerate, cooperative, courteous, friendly, helpful, kind, kindly, neighbourly, polite, pleasant, willing.

oblique *adj.* **1** slanting. **2** indirect. □ **obliquely** *adv.*, **obliqueness** *n.*
■ **1** diagonal, slanted, slanting, sloping. **2** circuitous, circumlocutory, evasive, indirect, roundabout.

obliterate *v.* blot out, destroy. □ **obliteration** *n.*
■ blot out, delete, erase, rub out, strike out; annihilate, destroy, eradicate, expunge, extirpate, wipe out.

oblivion *n.* **1** state of being forgotten. **2** state of being oblivious.

oblivious *adj.* unaware. □ **obliviously** *adv.*, **obliviousness** *n.*
■ heedless, insensible, unaware, unconscious, unmindful.

oblong *adj.* & *n.* (having) rectangular shape with length greater than breadth.

obloquy *n.* **1** verbal abuse. **2** disgrace.

obnoxious *adj.* very unpleasant. □ **obnoxiously** *adv.*, **obnoxiousness** *n.*
■ abhorrent, disgusting, hateful, *colloq.* horrible, horrid, loathsome, nasty, objectionable, odious, repellent, repulsive, repugnant, revolting, sickening, vile.

oboe *n.* woodwind instrument of treble pitch. □ **oboist** *n.*

obscene *adj.* indecent in a repulsive or offensive way. □ **obscenely** *adv.*, **obscenity** *n.*
■ blue, coarse, dirty, filthy, gross, improper, indecent, lewd, offensive, pornographic, rude, scabrous, smutty, vulgar.

obscure *adj.* **1** not easily understood. **2** not famous. **3** indistinct. ● *v.* make obscure, conceal. □ **obscurely** *adv.*, **obscurity** *n.*
■ *adj.* **1** abstruse, arcane, baffling, confusing, cryptic, enigmatic, esoteric, incomprehensible, mysterious, mystifying, perplexing, puzzling, recondite, unclear. **2** insignificant, minor, undistinguished, unknown, unimportant. **3** dim, faint, fuzzy, hazy, indistinct, nebulous, shadowy, vague. ● *v.* cloud, darken, dim, obfuscate, shade, shadow; cloak, conceal, cover, disguise, hide, mask, screen, shroud, veil.

obsequies *n.pl.* funeral rites.

obsequious *adj.* excessively respectful. □ **obsequiously** *adv.*, **obsequiousness** *n.*
■ cringing, fawning, flattering, grovelling, ingratiating, mealy-mouthed, servile, slavish, *colloq.* smarmy, sycophantic, toadying, unctuous.

observance *n.* keeping of a law, custom, or festival.

observant *adj.* quick at noticing. □ **observantly** *adv.*
■ alert, attentive, perceptive, sharp, shrewd, vigilant, watchful, *colloq.* wide awake.

observation *n.* **1** observing, being observed. **2** remark. □ **observational** *adj.*
■ **1** attention, notice; examination, inspection, scrutiny, surveillance. **2** comment, remark, statement, utterance.

observatory *n.* building for observation of stars or weather.

observe *v.* **1** perceive, watch carefully. **2** keep (a law etc.). **3** celebrate (a festival). **4** remark. □ **observer** *n.*
■ **1** detect, discern, notice, perceive, see; contemplate, examine, eye, inspect, look at, monitor, regard, scrutinize, study, view, watch. **2** abide by, comply with, follow, keep, obey, respect. **3** celebrate, commemorate, keep, solemnize. **4** comment, declare, mention, note, remark, say, state.

obsess *v.* occupy the thoughts of continually. □ **obsessive** *adj.*

obsession *n.* **1** state of being obsessed. **2** persistent idea. □ **obsessional** *adj.*

obsolescent *adj.* becoming obsolete. □ **obsolescence** *n.*

obsolete *adj.* antiquated, no longer used.
■ antediluvian, antiquated, archaic, dated, dead, old, old-fashioned, outdated, outmoded, out of date.

obstacle *n.* thing that obstructs progress.
■ bar, barrier, catch, hindrance, hitch, hurdle, impediment, obstruction, snag, stumbling block.

obstetrics *n.* branch of medicine and surgery dealing with childbirth. □ **obstetric** *adj.*, **obstetrician** *n.*

obstinate *adj.* not easily persuaded or influenced. □ **obstinately** *adv.*, **obstinacy** *n.*
■ adamant, *colloq.* bloody-minded, dogged, headstrong, inflexible, intractable, intransigent, obdurate, pigheaded, recalcitrant, self-willed, stiff-necked, stubborn, tenacious, unbending, uncooperative, unyielding, wilful.

obstreperous *adj.* unruly, noisy.
■ boisterous, disorderly, irrepressible, riotous, rowdy, uncontrollable, unruly, wild; clamorous, loud, noisy, raucous.

obstruct v. **1** block. **2** hinder movement or progress. □ **obstructive** adj.
■ **1** block (up), clog, stop (up). **2** baulk, block, check, hamper, handicap, hinder, hold up, impede, inhibit, interfere with, retard, slow down, thwart.

obstruction n. **1** act or instance of obstructing. **2** obstacle or blockage.
■ **2** bar, barrier, hindrance, impediment, hurdle, obstacle; blockage, bottleneck.

obtain v. **1** get, come into possession of. **2** be customary.
■ **1** acquire, come by, gain, get, pick up, procure, secure; buy, purchase. **2** apply, be customary, be relevant, exist, prevail.

obtrude v. force (ideas or oneself) upon others. □ **obtrusion** n.

obtrusive adj. obtruding oneself, unpleasantly noticeable. □ **obtrusively** adv., **obtrusiveness** n.

obtuse adj. **1** slow at understanding. **2** of blunt shape. **3** (of an angle) more than 90° but less than 180°. □ **obtusely** adv., **obtuseness** n.
■ **1** dense, colloq. dim, dull, colloq. dumb, slow, stupid, colloq. thick, unintelligent.

obverse n. side of a coin bearing a head or the principal design.

obviate v. make unnecessary.

obvious adj. easy to perceive or understand. □ **obviously** adv., **obviousness** n.
■ apparent, clear, conspicuous, distinct, evident, manifest, noticeable, open, overt, patent, perceptible, plain, prominent, self-evident, unmistakable, visible.

ocarina n. egg-shaped wind instrument.

occasion n. **1** time at which a particular event takes place. **2** special event. **3** opportunity. **4** need or cause. ● v. cause.
■ n. **2** colloq. affair, event, function, happening, occurrence, time. **3** chance, opening, opportunity, time. **4** cause, grounds, justification, need, reason. ● v. bring about, cause, effect, elicit, engender, evoke, generate, give rise to, prompt, provoke, result in.

occasional adj. **1** happening sometimes but not frequently. **2** for a special occasion. □ **occasionally** adv.
■ **1** infrequent, intermittent, irregular, odd, periodic, sporadic.

Occident /óksid'nt/ n. (**the Occident**) the West, the western world. □ **occidental** adj.

occlude v. stop up, obstruct.

occlusion n. upward movement of a mass of warm air caused by a cold front overtaking it.

occult adj. **1** secret. **2** supernatural.
■ **1** arcane, dark, esoteric, obscure, recondite, secret. **2** magic, mysterious, mystical, preternatural, supernatural.

occupant n. person occupying a place or dwelling. □ **occupancy** n.
■ householder, inhabitant, lessee, occupier, owner, resident, tenant.

occupation n. **1** occupying or being occupied. **2** pastime. **3** employment.
■ **1** occupancy, possession, tenancy, tenure; conquest, invasion, seizure, takeover. **2** activity, pastime, pursuit. **3** career, craft, employment, job, position, profession, situation, trade, work.

occupational adj. of or caused by one's employment. □ **occupational therapy** creative activities designed to assist recovery from certain illnesses.

occupy v. **1** dwell in. **2** take possession of (a place) by force. **3** fill (a space or time or position). **4** keep busy. □ **occupier** n.
■ **1** dwell in, inhabit, live in, reside in. **2** capture, conquer, garrison, invade, overrun, seize, take over, take possession of. **3** cover, extend over; fill, take up, use (up). **4** absorb, engage, engross, hold, involve, preoccupy.

occur v. (**occurred**) **1** come into being as an event or process. **2** exist. □ **occur to** come into the mind of.
■ **1** arise, befall, come about, crop up, happen, materialize, take place.

occurrence n. **1** act or instance of occurring. **2** incident, event.
■ **2** colloq. affair, event, happening, incident, phenomenon.

ocean n. sea surrounding the continents of the earth. □ **oceanic** adj.

oceanography n. study of the ocean.

ocelot n. **1** leopard-like animal of Central and S. America. **2** its fur.

ochre n. **1** type of clay used as pigment. **2** pale brownish-yellow.

o'clock adv. by the clock.

octagon n. geometric figure with eight sides. □ **octagonal** adj.

octahedron n. solid with eight sides. □ **octahedral** adj.

octane n. hydrocarbon occurring in petrol.

octave *n.* **1** note six whole tones above or below a given note. **2** interval or notes between these.

octet *n.* **1** group of eight voices or instruments. **2** music for these.

octogenarian *n.* person in his or her eighties.

octopus *n.* (*pl.* **-puses**) sea animal with eight tentacles.

ocular *adj.* of, for, or by the eyes.

oculist *n.* specialist in the treatment of the eye.

odd *adj.* **1** unusual. **2** occasional. **3** (of a number) not divisible by 2. **4** not part of a set. **5** exceeding a round number or amount. □ **oddly** *adv.*, **oddness** *n.*
■ **1** abnormal, anomalous, atypical, bizarre, curious, eccentric, exceptional, extraordinary, funny, out of the ordinary, outlandish, peculiar, quaint, queer, strange, uncharacteristic, uncommon, unconventional, unexpected, unusual, weird. **2** irregular, occasional, random, sporadic.

oddity *n.* **1** strangeness. **2** unusual person or thing.

oddment *n.* thing left over, isolated article.
■ (**oddments**) bits, fragments, leftovers, odds and ends, pieces, remnants, scraps, snippets.

odds *n.pl.* **1** probability. **2** ratio between amounts staked by parties to a bet. □ **at odds** in conflict with. **odds and ends** oddments. **odds-on** *adj.* with success more likely than failure.

ode *n.* type of poem addressed to a person or celebrating an event.

odious *adj.* hateful. □ **odiously** *adv.*, **odiousness** *n.*
■ abhorrent, abominable, foul, hateful, *colloq.* horrible, horrid, loathsome, nasty, obnoxious, repellent, repugnant, repulsive, revolting, unpleasant, vile.

odium *n.* widespread hatred or disgust.

odoriferous *adj.* diffusing (usu. pleasant) odours.

odour *n.* smell. □ **odorous** *adj.*
■ aroma, bouquet, fragrance, perfume, redolence, scent, smell; *sl.* pong, stench, stink.

odyssey *n.* (*pl.* **-eys**) long adventurous journey.

oedema /ideémə/ *n.* excess fluid in tissues, causing swelling.

oesophagus /eesóffəgəss/ *n.* gullet.

of *prep.* **1** belonging to. **2** from. **3** composed or made from. **4** concerning. **5** for, involving.

off *adv.* **1** away. **2** out of position, disconnected. **3** not operating, cancelled. **4** (of food) beginning to decay. ● *prep.* **1** away from. **2** below the normal standard of. ● *adj.* of the right-hand side of a horse, vehicle, or road. □ **off chance** remote possibility. **off colour** not in the best of health. **off-licence** *n.* **1** licence to sell alcohol for consumption away from the premises. **2** shop with this. **off-putting** *adj.* (*colloq.*) **1** disconcerting. **2** unpleasant. **off-white** *adj.* not quite pure white.

offal *n.* edible organs from an animal carcass.

offbeat *adj.* unconventional.
■ bizarre, eccentric, odd, outlandish, peculiar, queer, strange, unconventional, unusual, weird.

offence *n.* **1** illegal act, transgression. **2** feeling of annoyance or resentment. □ **take offence** feel upset or hurt.
■ **1** crime, fault, misdeed, misdemeanour, sin, transgression, wrong. **2** annoyance, resentment, umbrage.

offend *v.* **1** cause offence to, upset. **2** displease. **3** do wrong. □ **offender** *n.*
■ **1** affront, hurt, insult, upset, wound. **2** annoy, displease, gall, irritate, nettle, pique, *colloq.* rile. **3** sin, transgress. □ **offender** criminal, *colloq.* crook, culprit, lawbreaker, malefactor, miscreant, sinner, transgressor, wrongdoer.

offensive *adj.* **1** causing offence, insulting. **2** disgusting. **3** used in attacking. ● *n.* aggressive action. □ **offensively** *adv.*, **offensiveness** *n.*
■ *adj.* **1** discourteous, disrespectful, impolite, impudent, insolent, insulting, rude, uncivil. **2** disgusting, distasteful, foul, *colloq.* horrible, horrid, nasty, obnoxious, repellent, repugnant, repulsive, revolting, sickening, unsavoury, vile. ● *n.* assault, attack, charge, onslaught, strike.

offer *v.* (**offered**) **1** present for acceptance or refusal, or for consideration or use. **2** express readiness, show intention. **3** make available for sale. ● *n.* **1** expression of willingness to do, give, or pay something. **2** amount offered.
■ *v.* **1** proffer, tender; advance, propose, put forward, submit, suggest. **2** volunteer. ● *n.* bid, proposal, proposition, tender.

offering *n.* gift, contribution.

offhand *adj.* casual or curt in manner. ● *adv.* in an offhand way. □ **offhanded** *adj.*
■ *adj.* blasé, careless, casual, cavalier, insouciant, nonchalant, offhanded, unceremonious, unconcerned; abrupt, brusque, curt, perfunctory.

office *n.* **1** room or building used for clerical and similar work. **2** position of authority or trust.

officer *n.* **1** official. **2** person holding authority on a ship or in the armed services. **3** policeman or policewoman.

official *adj.* **1** of office or officials. **2** authorized. ● *n.* person holding office. □ **officially** *adv.*
■ *adj.* **1** bureaucratic; ceremonial, ceremonious, formal. **2** authorized, certified, documented, endorsed, lawful, legal, legitimate, licensed, proper, recognized, sanctioned, valid. ● *n.* appointee, bureaucrat, commissioner, functionary, officer.

officiate *v.* act in an official capacity, be in charge.

officious *adj.* asserting one's authority. □ **officiously** *adv.*
■ *colloq.* bossy, dictatorial, domineering, imperious, overbearing, *colloq.* pushy, self-important.

offload *v.* unload.

offset *v.* (**-set**, **-setting**) counterbalance, compensate for.
■ balance (out), cancel out, compensate for, counteract, counterbalance, make up for, neutralize, nullify.

offshoot *n.* **1** side shoot. **2** subsidiary product.

offside *adj.* & *adv.* in a position where one may not legally play the ball (in football etc.).

offspring *n.* (*pl.* **-spring**) **1** person's child, children, or descendant(s). **2** animal's young.
■ **1** child(ren), descendant(s), heir(s), progeny, issue, successor(s). **2** brood, young.

often *adv.* **1** many times, at short intervals. **2** in many instances.
■ commonly, frequently, habitually, ordinarily, regularly, repeatedly, usually.

ogle *v.* eye flirtatiously.

ogre *n.* **1** man-eating giant in fairy tales. **2** terrifying person.

oh *int.* exclamation of delight or pain, or used for emphasis.

ohm *n.* unit of electrical resistance.

oil *n.* **1** thick slippery liquid that will not dissolve in water. **2** petroleum, a form of this. **3** oil paint. ● *v.* lubricate or treat with oil. □ **oil paint** paint made by mixing pigment with oil. **oil painting** picture painted in this. **oily** *adj.*

oilfield *n.* area where oil is found in the ground.

oilskin *n.* **1** cloth waterproofed by treatment with oil etc. **2** (*pl.*) waterproof clothing made of this.

ointment *n.* healing or cosmetic preparation for the skin.
■ balm, cream, embrocation, emollient, lotion, salve, unguent.

OK *adj.* & *adv.* (also **okay**) (*colloq.*) all right.

okapi *n.* (*pl.* **-is**) giraffe-like animal of Central Africa.

okra *n.* African plant with seed pods used as food.

old *adj.* **1** having lived, existed, or been known etc. for a long time. **2** of specified age. **3** shabby from age or wear. **4** former. **5** not recent or modern. □ **old age** later part of life. **old-fashioned** *adj.* no longer fashionable. **Old Testament** part of the Bible dealing with pre-Christian times. **old wives' tale** traditional but foolish belief.
■ **1** aged, ageing, ancient, elderly, getting on, hoary, senescent; long-standing, time-honoured, well-established; bygone, former. **3** crumbling, dilapidated, ramshackle, tumbledown; ragged, shabby, tattered, tatty, threadbare, worn. **4** erstwhile, ex-, former, previous, prior, recent, sometime. **5** ancient, antediluvian, antiquated, antique, dated, obsolete, old-fashioned, outdated, outmoded, out of date.

oleaginous *adj.* **1** producing oil. **2** oily.

oleander *n.* flowering shrub of Mediterranean regions.

olfactory *adj.* concerned with smelling.

oligarch *n.* member of an oligarchy.

oligarchy *n.* **1** government by a small group. **2** country governed in this way. □ **oligarchic** *adj.*

olive *n.* **1** small oval fruit from which an oil (**olive oil**) is obtained. **2** tree bearing this. **3** greenish colour. ● *adj.* **1** of this colour. **2** (of the complexion) yellowish-brown. □ **olive branch** gesture of peace.

ombudsman *n.* official appointed to investigate complaints against public authorities.

omega *n.* last letter of the Greek alphabet, = o.

omelette *n.* dish of beaten eggs cooked in a frying pan.

omen *n.* event regarded as a prophetic sign.
■ augury, portent, presage, sign.

ominous *adj.* seeming as if trouble is imminent. □ **ominously** *adv.*, **ominousness** *n.*
■ inauspicious, menacing, sinister, threatening, unfavourable, unpropitious.

omit *v.* (**omitted**) **1** leave out, not include. **2** neglect (to do something). □ **omission** *n.*
■ **1** disregard, drop, exclude, leave out, pass over, *colloq.* skip. **2** fail, forget, neglect, overlook.

omnibus *n.* **1** bus. **2** volume containing several novels etc.

omnipotent *adj.* having unlimited power. □ **omnipotence** *n.*

omnipresent *adj.* present everywhere. □ **omnipresence** *n.*

omniscient *adj.* knowing everything. □ **omniscience** *n.*

omnivorous *adj.* feeding on all kinds of food.

on *prep.* **1** supported by, attached to, covering. **2** close to. **3** towards. **4** (of time) exactly at, during. **5** in the state or process of. **6** concerning. **7** added to. ● *adv.* **1** so as to be on or covering something. **2** further forward, towards something. **3** with continued movement or action. **4** operating, taking place. □ **be** or **keep on at** (*colloq.*) nag. **on and off** from time to time.

once *adv.* **1** on one occasion or for one time only. **2** formerly. ● *conj.* as soon as. ● *n.* one time or occasion. □ **at once 1** immediately. **2** simultaneously. (**every**) **once in a while** occasionally. **once-over** *n.* (*colloq.*) rapid inspection. **once upon a time** at some vague time in the past.

oncology *n.* study of tumours.

oncoming *adj.* approaching.

one *adj.* single, individual, forming a unity. ● *n.* **1** smallest whole number. **2** single thing or person. ● *pron.* **1** person. **2** any person (esp. used by a speaker or writer of himself as representing people in general). □ **one another** each other. **one day** at some unspecified date. **one-sided** *adj.* unfair, prejudiced. **one-way street** street where traffic is permitted to move in one direction only.

onerous *adj.* needing much effort, burdensome.
■ arduous, burdensome, demanding, difficult, exacting, gruelling, hard, laborious, strenuous, taxing, tough, trying.

oneself *pron.* emphatic and reflexive form of *one*.

ongoing *adj.* continuing, in progress.

onion *n.* vegetable with a bulb that has a strong taste and smell.

onlooker *n.* spectator.
■ bystander, eyewitness, looker-on, observer, passer-by, spectator, viewer, watcher, witness.

only *adj.* **1** existing alone of its or their kind, sole. ● *adv.* **1** without anything or anyone else. **2** no longer ago than. ● *conj.* but then. □ **only too** extremely.
■ *adj.* lone, single, sole, solitary. ● *adv.* **1** exclusively, just, solely; merely, purely, simply.

onomatopoeia /ónnəmattəpeéə/ *n.* formation of words that imitate the sound of what they stand for. □ **onomatopoeic** *adj.*

onset *n.* **1** beginning. **2** attack.
■ **1** beginning, commencement, inception, start. **2** assault, attack, charge, onslaught, raid, sally, sortie, strike.

onslaught *n.* fierce attack.

onus *n.* duty or responsibility.
■ burden, charge, duty, load, obligation, responsibility, weight.

onward *adv.* & *adj.* **1** with an advancing motion. **2** further on. □ **onwards** *adv.*

onyx *n.* stone like marble.

oodles *n.pl.* (*colloq.*) very great amount.

oolite /óəlīt/ *n.* type of limestone.

ooze *v.* **1** trickle or flow out slowly. **2** exude. ● *n.* wet mud. □ **oozy** *adj.*
■ *v.* **1** drain, drip, flow, leak, trickle, seep. **2** exude, secrete.

opacity *n.* being opaque.

opal *n.* iridescent quartz-like stone. □ **opaline** *adj.*

opalescent *adj.* iridescent like an opal. □ **opalescence** *n.*

opaque *adj.* **1** not clear. **2** unintelligible. □ **opaqueness** *n.*
■ **1** clouded, cloudy, dark, muddy, murky, turbid. **2** baffling, enigmatic, incomprehensible, mystifying, obscure, perplexing, puzzling, unclear, unfathomable, unintelligible.

open *adj.* **1** not closed, locked, or blocked. **2** not covered, confined, or sealed. **3** unfolded. **4** frank. **5** undisguised. **6** not yet decided. ● *v.* **1** make or become open or more open. **2** begin, establish. ◻ **in the open air** not in a house or building etc. **open-ended** *adj.* with no fixed limit. **open-handed** *adj.* giving generously. **open house** hospitality to all comers. **open letter** one addressed to a person by name but printed in a newspaper. **open-plan** *adj.* without partition walls or fences. **open secret** one known to so many people that it is no longer secret. **open to 1** willing to receive. **2** likely to suffer from or be affected by. **openness** *n.*

■ *adj.* ● *v.* **1** ajar, unbolted, unclosed, unfastened, unlatched, unlocked; clear, passable, unblocked, unobstructed. **2** bare, exposed, unprotected; unenclosed, unfenced; uncovered, unsealed, unwrapped. **3** spread (out), unfolded, unfurled, unrolled. **4** candid, communicative, direct, forthright, frank, honest, outspoken, straightforward. **5** blatant, evident, manifest, obvious, patent, unconcealed, undisguised. **6** pending, undecided, unresolved, unsettled. ● *v.* **1** unbolt, unfasten, unlatch, unlock; undo, untie, unwrap; spread (out), unfold, unfurl, unroll. **2** begin, commence, get under way, inaugurate, initiate, launch, start; establish, set up. ◻ **open-handed** bountiful, free, generous, lavish, liberal, munificent, philanthropic.

opencast *adj.* (of mining) on the surface of the ground.

opener *n.* device for opening tins or bottles etc.

opening *n.* **1** gap, place where a thing opens. **2** beginning. **3** opportunity.

■ **1** aperture, breach, chink, cleft, cranny, crevice, fissure, gap, hole, orifice, slot, vent. **2** beginning, commencement, inauguration, initiation, launch, outset, start. **3** break, chance, occasion, opportunity.

openly *adv.* publicly, frankly.

openwork *n.* pattern with intervening spaces in metal, leather, lace, etc.

opera *n.* play(s) in which words are sung to music. ◻ **opera-glasses** *n.pl.* small binoculars.

operable *adj.* **1** able to be operated. **2** suitable for treatment by surgery.

operate *v.* **1** be in action. **2** control (a machine etc.). **3** produce an effect. **4** perform an operation.

■ **1** function, go, run, perform, work. **2** control, handle, manage, manipulate, use, work.

operatic *adj.* of or like opera.

operation *n.* **1** action, working. **2** military manoeuvre. **3** a surgical treatment.

■ **1** action, function, functioning, performance, running, working; control, handling, manipulation. **2** action, campaign, exercise, manoeuvre.

operational *adj.* **1** of or used in operations. **2** able or ready to function.

■ **2** functional, functioning, going, in use, in working order, operative, running, working.

operative *adj.* **1** working, functioning. **2** of surgical operations. ● *n.* worker, esp. in a factory.

operator *n.* person operating a machine, esp. connecting lines in a telephone exchange.

operetta *n.* short or light opera.

ophidian *adj.* & *n.* (member) of the snake family.

ophthalmic *adj.* of or for the eyes.

ophthalmology *n.* study of the eye. ◻ **ophthalmologist** *n.*

ophthalmoscope *n.* instrument for examining the eye.

opiate *n.* sedative containing opium.

opine *v.* express or hold as an opinion.

opinion *n.* **1** belief or judgement held without actual proof. **2** what one thinks on a particular point. ◻ **be of the opinion that** believe or think that.

■ belief, conviction, feeling, judgement, idea, impression, notion, point of view, sentiment, theory, thought, view, viewpoint.

opinionated *adj.* holding strong opinions obstinately.

■ doctrinaire, dogmatic, inflexible, obdurate, obstinate, pigheaded, stubborn.

opium *n.* narcotic drug made from the juice of certain poppies.

opossum *n.* small furry marsupial.

opponent *n.* one who opposes another.

■ adversary, antagonist, enemy, foe, rival.

opportune *adj.* **1** (of time) favourable. **2** well-timed.

■ **1** advantageous, auspicious, favourable, fortunate, good, happy, propitious. **2** appropriate, convenient, seasonable, suitable, timely, well-timed.

opportunist *n.* person who grasps opportunities. ▫ **opportunism** *n.*, **opportunistic** *adj.*

opportunity *n.* circumstances suitable for a particular purpose.
■ break, chance, occasion, opening, time.

oppose *v.* 1 argue or fight against. 2 place opposite. 3 place in opposition or contrast.
■ 1 attack, combat, contest, counter, defy, fight (against), resist, stand up to, take a stand against; argue against, challenge, dispute, object to, protest against.

opposite *adj.* 1 facing, on the further side. 2 as different as possible from. ● *n.* opposite thing or person. ● *adv.* & *prep.* in an opposite position or direction (to).
■ *adj.* 2 antithetical, conflicting, contradictory, contrary, contrasting, different, differing, opposing. ● *n.* antithesis, contrary, converse, reverse.

opposition *n.* 1 antagonism, resistance. 2 placing or being placed opposite. 3 people opposing something.
■ 1 antagonism, antipathy, hostility, objection, resistance. 2 adversaries, competition, competitors, enemies, opponents, rivals.

oppress *v.* 1 govern or treat harshly. 2 weigh down with cares. ▫ **oppression** *n.*, **oppressor** *n.*
■ 1 abuse, grind down, maltreat, persecute, ride roughshod over, tyrannize. 2 afflict, burden, overload, trouble, weigh down. ▫ **oppression** abuse, cruelty, maltreatment, persecution, torture, tyranny.

oppressive *adj.* 1 harsh or cruel. 2 (of weather) sultry and tiring. ▫ **oppressively** *adv.*, **oppressiveness** *n.*
■ 1 brutal, cruel, despotic, harsh, repressive, severe, tyrannical, unjust. 2 close, muggy, stifling, stuffy, suffocating, sultry.

opprobrious *adj.* abusive.

opprobrium *n.* great disgrace from shameful conduct.

opt *v.* 1 **opt for** make a choice. 2 **opt out** choose not to participate.
■ 1 choose, decide on, go for, pick, plump for, select.

optic *adj.* of the eye or sight.

optical *adj.* 1 of or aiding sight. 2 visual. ▫ **optically** *adv.*

optician *n.* maker or seller of spectacles.

optics *n.* study of sight and of light as its medium.

optimism *n.* tendency to take a hopeful view of things. ▫ **optimist** *n.*, **optimistic** *adj.*, **optimistically** *adv.*
■ ▫ **optimistic** bright, buoyant, cheerful, confident, hopeful, sanguine, *colloq.* upbeat.

optimum *adj.* & *n.* best or most favourable (conditions etc.).

option *n.* 1 thing that is or may be chosen. 2 freedom to choose. 3 right to buy or sell a thing within a limited time.

optional *adj.* not compulsory. ▫ **optionally** *adv.*
■ discretionary, elective, non-compulsory, voluntary.

opulent *adj.* 1 wealthy. 2 luxurious. ▫ **opulently** *adv.*, **opulence** *n.*
■ 1 affluent, moneyed, prosperous, rich, wealthy, *colloq.* well-heeled, well-off, well-to-do. 2 luxurious, magnificent, palatial, plush, plushy, splendid, sumptuous.

or *conj.* 1 as an alternative. 2 because if not. 3 also known as.

oracle *n.* person or thing giving wise guidance. ▫ **oracular** *adj.*
■ prophet, prophetess, seer, sibyl, soothsayer.

oral *adj.* 1 spoken not written. 2 of the mouth, taken by mouth. ● *n.* spoken exam. ▫ **orally** *adv.*

orange *n.* 1 round juicy citrus fruit with reddish-yellow peel. 2 this colour. ● *adj.* reddish-yellow.

orangeade *n.* orange-flavoured soft drink.

orang-utan *n.* large ape of Borneo and Sumatra.

oration *n.* long speech, esp. of a ceremonial kind.

orator *n.* maker of a formal speech. 2 skilful speaker.

oratorio *n.* (*pl.* **-os**) musical composition usu. with a biblical theme.

oratory *n.* 1 art of public speaking. 2 eloquent speech. ▫ **oratorical** *adj.*

orb *n.* sphere, globe.

orbit *n.* 1 curved path of a planet, satellite, or spacecraft round another. 2 sphere of influence. ● *v.* (**orbited**) move in an orbit (round).
■ *n.* 1 circuit, course, path, revolution, track. ● *v.* circle, go round, revolve round.

orbital *adj.* 1 of orbits. 2 (of a road) round the outside of a city.

orchard *n.* piece of land planted with fruit trees.

orchestra *n.* large group of people playing various musical instruments. □ **orchestral** *adj.*

orchestrate *v.* 1 compose or arrange (music) for an orchestra. 2 coordinate. □ **orchestration** *n.*

orchid *n.* showy often irregularly shaped flower.

ordain *v.* 1 appoint ceremonially to the Christian ministry. 2 destine. 3 decree authoritatively.

ordeal *n.* difficult experience.

■ affliction, hardship, *colloq.* nightmare, trial, tribulation, trouble.

order *n.* 1 way things are placed in relation to each other. 2 condition in which every part etc. is in its right place. 3 state of obedience to law, authority, etc. 4 authoritative direction or instruction. 5 request to supply goods etc., things supplied. 6 rank. 7 kind, quality. 8 group of plants or animals classified as similar. 9 group of people living under religious rules. ● *v.* 1 arrange in order. 2 command. 3 give an order for (goods etc.). □ **in order to** or **that** with the purpose of or intention that. **out of order** 1 not working properly. 2 not in proper sequence.

■ *n.* 1 arrangement, classification, codification, disposition, grouping, form, sequence, shape, structure, system, systematization. 2 harmony, neatness, orderliness, organization, pattern, regularity, symmetry, system, tidiness. 3 calm, peace, peacefulness, quiet, serenity, tranquillity. 4 command, decree, dictate, direction, directive, edict, instruction, ordinance; injunction, warrant, writ. 5 instruction, request, requisition. 6 class, degree, grade, level, position, rank, station, status. 7 kind, nature, quality, sort, type, variety. ● *v.* 1 arrange, categorize, classify, codify, lay out, put in order, regulate, sort (out), systematize. 2 command, direct, instruct, require, tell. 3 request, requisition; book, reserve. □ **out of order** 1 broken, faulty, inoperative, not in working order, not working.

orderly *adj.* 1 methodically arranged, tidy. 2 not unruly. ● *n.* 1 soldier assisting an officer. 2 hospital attendant. □ **orderliness** *n.*

■ *adj.* 1 methodical, neat, organized, shipshape, tidy, systematic, well-

organized. 2 disciplined, law-abiding, peaceable, peaceful, well-behaved.

ordinal *n.* (in full **ordinal number**) number defining position in a series (*first, second*, etc.).

ordinance *n.* decree.

ordinary *adj.* usual, not exceptional. □ **out of the ordinary** unusual. **ordinarily** *adv.*

■ accustomed, common, customary, everyday, expected, familiar, habitual, normal, regular, routine, standard, traditional, typical, usual; boring, commonplace, humdrum, mediocre, pedestrian, prosaic, run-of-the-mill, undistinguished, unexceptional, uninspired, unremarkable; modest, plain, simple, unpretentious, workaday.

ordination *n.* ordaining.

ordnance *n.* military materials. □ **Ordnance Survey** official survey of the UK producing detailed maps.

ordure *n.* dung.

ore *n.* solid rock or mineral from which metal is obtained.

organ *n.* 1 musical instrument with pipes supplied with wind by bellows and sounded by keys. 2 distinct part with a specific function in an animal or plant body. 3 medium of communication, esp. a newspaper.

organic *adj.* 1 of bodily organ(s). 2 of or formed from living things. 3 organized as a system. 4 using no artificial fertilizers or pesticides. □ **organically** *adv.*

organism *n.* a living being, individual animal or plant.

organist *n.* person who plays the organ.

organization *n.* 1 organizing. 2 organized system or group of people. □ **organizational** *adj.*

■ 1 coordination, organizing, structuring; categorization, classification, codification. 2 arrangement, composition, configuration, constitution, design, form, order, pattern, shape, structure, system; body, coalition, confederation, consortium, federation, group, institution, league, society, syndicate; business, company, concern, corporation, firm.

organize *v.* 1 arrange systematically. 2 initiate. 3 make arrangements for. □ **organizer** *n.*

■ 1 arrange, catalogue, categorize, classify, codify, order, sort (out), systematize. 2 establish, form, found, initiate, institute, set up, start. **3** deal with, do, handle, look after, see to, take care of.

orgasm n. climax of sexual excitement.

orgy n. **1** wild revelry. **2** unrestrained activity. □ **orgiastic** adj.

Orient n. **(the Orient)** the East, the eastern world.

orient v. place or determine the position of (a thing) with regard to points of the compass. □ **orient oneself 1** get one's bearings. **2** become accustomed to a new situation. **orientation** n.

oriental adj. of the Orient. ● n. **(Oriental)** native of the Orient.

orientate v. orient.

orienteering n. sport of finding one's way across country by map and compass.

orifice n. opening of a cavity etc.

origin n. **1** point, source, or cause from which a thing begins its existence. **2** (often pl.) ancestry.
■ **1** base, basis, provenance, root, source; beginning, cradle, dawn, dawning, genesis, inception, start. **2 (origins)** ancestry, descent, extraction, genealogy, lineage, pedigree, parentage.

original adj. **1** existing from the first, earliest. **2** being the first form of something. **3** inventive, creative. ● n. first form, thing from which another is copied. □ **originally** adv., **originality** n.
■ adj. **1** earliest, first, initial, primary; aboriginal, indigenous, native. **2** archetypal, prototypical. **3** creative, fresh, imaginative, ingenious, innovative, inventive, novel, unusual. ● n. archetype, master, model, pattern, prototype, source.

originate v. bring or come into being. □ **origination** n., **originator** n.
■ create, design, establish, found, inaugurate, initiate, institute, introduce, invent, launch, pioneer, set up, start; arise, begin, derive, develop, grow, proceed, spring, stem.

oriole n. bird with black and yellow plumage.

ormolu n. **1** gold-coloured alloy of copper. **2** things made of this.

ornament n. **1** decorative object or detail. **2** decoration. ● v. decorate with ornament(s), beautify. □ **ornamentation** n.
■ n. **1** bauble, gewgaw, knick-knack, trinket. **2** adornment, decoration, embellishment, ornamentation, trimming. ● v. adorn,

beautify, deck, decorate, embellish, embroider, garnish, trim.

ornamental adj. serving as an ornament. □ **ornamentally** adv.

ornate adj. elaborately ornamented. □ **ornately** adv.
■ baroque, elaborate, fancy, florid, fussy, ostentatious, rococo, showy.

ornithology n. study of birds. □ **ornithological** adj., **ornithologist** n.

orphan n. child whose parents are dead. ● v. make (a child) an orphan.

orphanage n. institution where orphans are cared for.

orrisroot n. fragrant iris root.

orthodontics n. correction of irregularities in teeth. □ **orthodontic** adj., **orthodontist** n.

orthodox adj. of or holding conventional or currently accepted beliefs, esp. in religion. □ **Orthodox Church** Eastern or Greek Church. **orthodoxy** n.
■ conservative, conventional, established, prevailing, traditional.

orthopaedics /orthapeédiks/ n. surgical correction of deformities in bones or muscles. □ **orthopaedic** adj., **orthopaedist** n.

oryx n. large African antelope.

oscillate v. **1** move to and fro. **2** vary. □ **oscillation** n.

oscilloscope n. device for recording oscillations.

osier n. **1** willow with flexible twigs. **2** twig of this.

osmosis n. diffusion of fluid through a porous partition into another fluid. □ **osmotic** adj.

osprey n. (pl. **-eys**) large bird preying on fish in inland waters.

osseous adj. like bone, bony.

ossify v. **1** turn into bone, harden. **2** make or become rigid and unprogressive. □ **ossification** n.

ostensible adj. apparent but not necessarily real. □ **ostensibly** adv.
■ alleged, apparent, outward, pretended, professed, purported, supposed.

ostentation n. showy display intended to impress people. □ **ostentatious** adj.
■ □ **ostentatious** elaborate, extravagant, flamboyant, colloq. flash, flashy, gaudy, loud, showy.

osteopath n. practitioner who treats certain diseases and abnormalities by manipulating bones and muscles. □ **osteopathic** adj., **osteopathy** n.

ostracize v. refuse to associate with.
□ **ostracism** n.
■ avoid, boycott, cold-shoulder, cut, shun, snub.

ostrich n. large swift-running African bird, unable to fly.

other adj. **1** alternative, additional. **2** being the remaining one of a set of two or more. **3** not the same. ● n. & pron. the other person or thing. ● adv. otherwise. □ **the other day** or **week** a few days or weeks ago.

otherwise adv. **1** in a different way. **2** in other respects. **3** in different circumstances.

otter n. fish-eating water animal with thick brown fur.

ottoman n. storage box with a padded top.

ought v.aux. expressing duty, rightness, advisability, or strong probability.

ounce n. unit of weight, one-sixteenth of a pound (about 28 grams).

our adj., **ours** poss.pron. belonging to us.

ourselves pron. emphatic and reflexive form of we and us.

oust v. drive out, eject.
■ depose, dismiss, drive out, eject, expel, force out, colloq. kick out, push out, remove, throw out, colloq. turf out.

out adv. **1** away from or not in a place, not at home. **2** not burning. **3** in error. **4** not possible. **5** unconscious. **6** into the open, so as to be heard or seen. **7** (of a secret) revealed. **8** (of a flower) blooming. ● prep. out of. ● n. way of escape. □ **be out** to be intending to. **out and out** thorough. **out of 1** from within or among. **2** without a supply of. **out of doors** in the open air. **out of the way 1** no longer an obstacle. **2** remote.
■ adv. **1** absent, away, elsewhere. **2** doused, extinguished, quenched, unlit. **4** impossible, impracticable, out of the question, unfeasible, unworkable. **5** comatose, insensible, knocked out, unconscious. □ **out and out** absolute, complete, downright, outright, perfect, sheer, thorough, total, unmitigated, unqualified, utter.

out- pref. more than, so as to exceed.

outboard adj. (of a motor) attached to the outside of a boat.

outbreak n. breaking out of anger, war, disease, etc.

outbuilding n. outhouse.

outburst n. explosion of feeling.
■ eruption, explosion, fit, outbreak, paroxysm, spasm.

outcast n. person driven out of a group or by society.

outclass v. surpass in quality.

outcome n. result of an event.
■ consequence, effect, result, upshot.

outcrop n. part of an underlying layer of rock that projects on the surface of the ground.

outcry n. **1** loud cry. **2** strong protest
■ clamour, commotion, hue and cry, hullabaloo, protest, protestation, uproar.

outdistance v. leave (a competitor) behind completely.

outdo v. (**-did, -done**) be or do better than.
■ beat, cap, eclipse, exceed, excel, outclass, outshine, outstrip, overshadow, surpass, top, transcend.

outdoor adj. of or for use in the open air.
□ **outdoors** adv.

outer adj. **1** further from the centre or inside. **2** exterior, external.

outermost adv. furthest outward.

outface v. disconcert by staring or by a confident manner.

outfit n. set of clothes or equipment.
■ costume, ensemble, get-up, colloq. rig-out, suit, turn-out; clothes, clothing, dress, garb, colloq. togs; apparatus, equipment, gear, kit, paraphernalia.

outfitter n. supplier of equipment or men's clothing.

outflank v. get round the flank of (an enemy).

outflow n. **1** outward flow. **2** what flows out.

outgoing adj. **1** retiring from office. **2** sociable.
■ **1** departing, ex-, former, past, retiring. **2** approachable, communicative, expansive, friendly, genial, gregarious, sociable, unreserved.

outgoings n.pl. expenditure.

outgrow v. (**-grew, -grown**) **1** grow faster than. **2** grow too large for. **3** leave behind (childish habit etc.).

outgrowth n. something which grows out of another thing.

outhouse n. shed, barn, etc.

outing n. pleasure trip.
■ excursion, expedition, jaunt, spin, tour, trip.

outlandish *adj.* looking or sounding strange or foreign.

■ bizarre, curious, eccentric, exotic, extraordinary, odd, offbeat, peculiar, queer, strange, unfamiliar, unusual, weird.

outlast *v.* last longer than.

outlaw *n.* **1** (*old use*) person deprived of the law's protection. **2** fugitive from the law. ● *v.* **1** make (a person) an outlaw. **2** declare illegal.

■ *n.* **2** bandit, brigand, criminal, desperado, fugitive, pirate, robber. ● *v.* **2** ban, bar, disallow, forbid, prohibit, proscribe.

outlay *n.* expenditure.

■ cost, disbursement, expenditure, expense, spending.

outlet *n.* **1** way out. **2** means for giving vent to energies or feelings. **3** distributor for goods.

outline *n.* **1** line(s) showing a thing's shape or boundary. **2** summary. ● *v.* **1** draw or describe in outline. **2** mark the outline of.

■ *n.* **1** contour, profile, silhouette. **2** abstract, digest, précis, résumé, summary, synopsis. ● *v.* define, delineate, draft, sketch, trace.

outlook *n.* **1** view, prospect. **2** mental attitude. **3** future prospect.

■ **1** aspect, prospect, view, vista. **2** attitude, opinion, perspective, point of view, standpoint, view, viewpoint. **3** forecast, prospect.

outlying *adj.* remote.

■ distant, far-away, far-off, outermost, out of the way, remote.

outmoded *adj.* no longer fashionable or accepted.

outnumber *v.* exceed in number.

outpace *v.* go faster than.

out-patient *n.* person visiting a hospital for treatment but not remaining resident there.

outpost *n.* outlying settlement or detachment of troops.

output *n.* amount of electrical power etc. produced. ● *v.* (**-put** or **-putted**) (of a computer) supply (results etc.).

outrage *n.* **1** act that shocks public opinion. **2** (act of) great violence or cruelty. ● *v.* shock and anger greatly.

■ *n.* **1** disgrace, scandal. **2** atrocity, barbarism, brutality, cruelty, enormity, evil, savagery, violation, violence. ● *v.* anger, appal, disgust, enrage, horrify, incense, infuriate, madden, scandalize, shock.

outrageous *adj.* greatly exceeding what is moderate or reasonable. □ **outrageously** *adv.*

■ excessive, exorbitant, extortionate, immoderate, inordinate, unjustifiable, unreasonable; appalling, disgraceful, dreadful, egregious, monstrous, preposterous, scandalous, shameful, shocking.

outrider *n.* mounted attendant or motor cyclist riding as guard.

outrigger *n.* **1** stabilizing strip of wood fixed outside and parallel to a canoe. **2** canoe with this.

outright *adv.* **1** completely. **2** not gradually. **3** frankly. ● *adj.* thorough, complete.

■ *adv.* **1** absolutely, altogether, completely, entirely, totally, utterly, wholly. **2** at once, immediately, instantaneously, instantly, straight away. **3** candidly, directly, frankly, honestly, openly, plainly. ● *adj.* absolute, complete, downright, out and out, thorough, total, unmitigated, unqualified, utter.

outrun *v.* (**-ran, -run, -running**) run faster or further than.

outset *n.* beginning.

outshine *v.* surpass in ability.

outside *n.* outer side, surface, or part. ● *adj.* of or from the outside. ● *adv.* on, at, or to the outside. ● *prep.* **1** on, at, or to the outside of. **2** other than.

■ *n.* case, exterior, façade, face, facing, front, shell, skin, surface. ● *adj.* exterior, external, outer; outdoor. ● *adv.* out, outdoors, out of doors.

outsider *n.* **1** non-member of a group. **2** horse etc. thought to have no chance in a contest.

■ **1** alien, foreigner, newcomer, stranger; gatecrasher, interloper, intruder, trespasser.

outsize *adj.* much larger than average.

outskirts *n.pl.* outer districts.

■ borders, edge, fringes, outlying districts, periphery, suburbs.

outsmart *v.* outwit.

outspoken *adj.* very frank.

■ blunt, candid, direct, explicit, forthright, frank, honest, open, plain, straightforward.

outstanding *adj.* **1** exceptionally good. **2** not yet paid or settled. □ **outstandingly** *adv.*

■ **1** excellent, exceptional, first-class, first-rate, magnificent, marvellous, memorable, notable, noteworthy, remarkable, splendid, superb, superior, unforgettable, wonderful; celebrated, distinguished, eminent, famous, important, prominent, renowned. **2** due, owed, owing, payable, unpaid, unsettled.

outstrip *v.* (**-stripped**) **1** run faster or further than. **2** surpass.
■ **1** outdistance, outpace, outrun, overtake. **2** beat, better, cap, exceed, outclass, outdo, outshine, overshadow, surpass, top.

outvote *v.* defeat by a majority of votes.

outward *adj.* on or to the outside. ● *adv.* outwards. □ **outwardly** *adv.*, **outwards** *adv.*
■ *adj.* exterior, external, outer, outside; apparent, discernible, evident, manifest, observable, obvious, perceptible, visible.

outweigh *v.* be of greater weight or importance than.

outwit *v.* (**-witted**) defeat by one's craftiness.
■ deceive, dupe, fool, get the better of, hoodwink, outsmart, trick.

ouzel /ōōz'l/ *n.* small bird of the thrush family.

ouzo /ōōzō/ *n.* Greek aniseed-flavoured spirit.

ova *see* **ovum**.

oval *n.* & *adj.* (of) rounded symmetrical shape longer than it is broad.

ovary *n.* **1** organ producing egg cells. **2** that part of a pistil from which fruit is formed. □ **ovarian** *adj.*

ovation *n.* enthusiastic applause.

oven *n.* enclosed chamber in which to cook food.

over *prep.* **1** in or to a position higher than. **2** throughout, during. **3** more than. **4** above and across. ● *adv.* **1** outwards and downwards from the brink or an upright position etc. **2** from one side or end etc. to the other. **3** across a space or distance. **4** besides. **5** with repetition. **6** at an end.

over- *pref.* **1** above. **2** excessively.

overall *n.* **1** protective outer garment. **2** (*pl.*) one-piece garment of this kind covering the body and legs. ● *adj.* total, taking all aspects into account. ● *adv.* taken as a whole.

overarm *adj.* & *adv.* with the arm brought forward and down from above shoulder level.

overawe *v.* overcome with awe.

overbalance *v.* **1** lose balance and fall. **2** cause to do this.

overbearing *adj.* domineering.
■ authoritarian, autocratic, *colloq.* bossy, bullying, dictatorial, domineering, high-handed, imperious, officious, peremptory, tyrannical.

overboard *adv.* from a ship into the water. □ **go overboard** (*colloq.*) show extreme enthusiasm.

overcast *adj.* covered with cloud.
■ clouded, cloudy, dark, dreary, dull, gloomy, grey, leaden, moonless, murky, sombre, starless, sunless.

overcharge *v.* charge too much.

overcoat *n.* warm outdoor coat.

overcome *v.* **1** win a victory over. **2** succeed in subduing or dealing with. **3** make helpless.
■ **1** beat, conquer, defeat, *colloq.* lick, overpower, overthrow, overwhelm, prevail over, subdue, triumph over, trounce, vanquish. **2** conquer, get over, get the better of, master, surmount.

overdo *v.* (**-did**, **-done**) **1** do too much. **2** cook too much.

overdose *n.* too large a dose. ● *v.* **1** give an overdose to. **2** take an overdose.

overdraft *n.* **1** overdrawing of a bank account. **2** amount of this.

overdraw *v.* (**-drew**, **-drawn**) draw more from (a bank account) than the amount credited.

overdrive *n.* mechanism providing an extra gear above top gear.

overdue *adj.* not paid or arrived etc. by the due time.
■ outstanding, owed, owing, unpaid; belated, late, tardy, unpunctual.

overestimate *v.* form too high an estimate of.

overflow *v.* **1** flow over the edge or limits (of). **2** be very abundant. ● *n.* **1** what overflows. **2** outlet for excess liquid.

overgrown *adj.* **1** grown too large. **2** covered with weeds etc.

overhang *v.* project or hang over. ● *n.* fact or amount of overhanging.

overhaul *v.* **1** examine and repair. **2** overtake. ● *n.* examination and repair.
■ *v.* **1** mend, recondition, renovate, repair, service.

overhead *adj.* & *adv.* **1** above the level of one's head. **2** in the sky.

overheads *n.pl.* expenses involved in running a business etc.

overhear *v.* (**-heard**) hear accidentally or without the speaker's knowledge.

overjoyed *adj.* filled with great joy.
- delighted, ecstatic, elated, euphoric, happy, joyful, jubilant, rapturous, thrilled.

overland *adj. & adv.* (travelling) by land.
□ **overlander** *n.*

overlap *v.* (**-lapped**) **1** extend beyond the edge of. **2** coincide partially. ● *n.* **1** overlapping. **2** part or amount that overlaps.

overleaf *adv.* on the other side of a leaf of a book etc.

overload *v.* put too great a load on or in. ● *n.* load that is too great.

overlook *v.* **1** fail to observe or consider. **2** condone (an offence etc.). **3** have a view over.
- **1** discount, disregard, ignore, miss, neglect, omit, pass over. **2** condone, excuse, forgive, make allowances for, pardon.

overman *v.* (**-manned**) provide with too many people as workmen or crew.

overnight *adv. & adj.* during a night.

overpass *n.* road crossing another by means of a bridge.

overpower *v.* overcome by greater strength or numbers.
- beat, conquer, crush, defeat, master, overcome, overwhelm, quash, quell, rout, subjugate, triumph over, trounce, vanquish.

overpowering *adj.* (of heat or feelings) extremely intense.
- compelling, intense, irresistible, overwhelming, powerful, strong.

overrate *v.* have too high an opinion of.

overreach *v.* **overreach oneself** fail through being too ambitious.

override *v.* (**-rode, -ridden**) **1** overrule. **2** prevail over. **3** intervene and make ineffective.

overrule *v.* set aside (a decision etc.) by using one's authority.

overrun *v.* (**-ran, -run, -running**) **1** spread over. **2** conquer (territory) by force. **3** exceed (a limit).
- **1** infest, spread over, swarm over. **2** conquer, defeat, invade, occupy, overwhelm, storm, take over, take possession of.

overseas *adj. & adv.* across or beyond the sea, abroad.

oversee *v.* (**-saw, -seen**) superintend.
□ **overseer** *n.*
- be in charge of, control, direct, manage, run, superintend, supervise.

oversew *v.* (**-sewn**) sew (edges) together so that each stitch lies over the edges.

overshadow *v.* **1** cast a shadow over. **2** cause to seem unimportant in comparison.
- **2** dominate, dwarf, eclipse, outshine, upstage.

overshoot *v.* (**-shot**) pass beyond (a target or limit etc.).

oversight *n.* **1** supervision. **2** unintentional omission or mistake.
- **1** control, direction, management, superintendence, supervision, surveillance. **2** *colloq.* boob, error, fault, lapse, mistake, omission, slip, *colloq.* slip-up.

overspill *n.* **1** what spills over. **2** surplus population leaving one area for another.

overstay *v.* **overstay one's welcome** stay so long that one is no longer welcome.

overstep *v.* (**-stepped**) go beyond (a limit).

overt *adj.* done or shown openly.
□ **overtly** *adv.*
- apparent, clear, conspicuous, evident, manifest, observable, obvious, open, patent, plain, unconcealed, undisguised, visible.

overtake *v.* (**-took, -taken**) **1** pass (a moving person or thing). **2** (of misfortune etc.) come suddenly upon.
- **1** outstrip, outdistance, overhaul, pass.

overthrow *v.* (**-threw, -thrown**) cause the downfall of. ● *n.* downfall, defeat.
- *v.* conquer, defeat, depose, oust, overcome, overpower, overwhelm, rout, unseat. ● *n.* collapse, conquest, defeat, destruction, downfall, fall, ousting, suppression.

overtime *adv.* in addition to regular working hours. ● *n.* **1** time worked in this way. **2** payment for this.

overtone *n.* additional quality or implication.
- hint, implication, indication, intimation, suggestion, undertone.

overture *n.* **1** orchestral composition forming a prelude to a performance. **2** (*pl.*) initial approach or proposal.

overturn *v.* **1** (cause to) turn over. **2** abolish.
- **1** capsize, keel over, turn over, turn turtle, turn upside down; knock over, upend, upset. **2** abolish, annul, cancel, invalidate, nullify, override, overrule, rescind, repeal, reverse, revoke.

overview *n.* general survey.

overwhelm v. **1** bury beneath a huge mass. **2** overcome completely. **3** make helpless with emotion. ☐ **overwhelming** adj.

■ **1** bury, deluge, engulf, flood, inundate, submerge, swamp. **2** conquer, crush, defeat, destroy, overcome, overpower, quash, subdue, trounce, vanquish. **3** astonish, astound, bowl over, dumbfound, overcome, shock, stagger, stun, take aback.

overwrought adj. in a state of nervous agitation.

■ agitated, distraught, edgy, frantic, colloq. in a state, colloq. in a tizzy, jumpy, keyed up, nervous, tense, colloq. uptight, worked up.

oviduct n. tube through which ova pass from the ovary.

oviparous adj. egg-laying.

ovoid adj. egg-shaped, oval.

ovulate v. produce or discharge an egg cell from an ovary. ☐ **ovulation** n.

ovule n. germ cell of a plant.

ovum n. (pl. **ova**) egg cell, reproductive cell produced by a female.

owe v. **1** be under an obligation to pay or repay. **2** be indebted to a person or thing for.

owing adj. owed and not yet paid. ☐ **owing to 1** caused by. **2** because of.

■ due, outstanding, owed, payable, unpaid.

owl n. bird of prey usu. flying at night. ☐ **owlish** adj.

own adj. belonging to oneself or itself. ● v. **1** have as one's own. **2** acknowledge as true or belonging to one. ☐ **of one's own** belonging to oneself. **on one's own 1** alone. **2** independently. **own up** confess. **owner** n., **ownership** n.

■ adj. individual, particular, personal, private. ● v. **1** be in possession of, have, hold, possess. **2** accept, acknowledge, admit, concede, confess, grant, recognize. ☐ **owner** holder, keeper, possessor, proprietor.

ox n. (pl. **oxen**) **1** animal of or related to the kind kept as domestic cattle. **2** fully grown bullock.

oxidation n. process of combining with oxygen.

oxide n. compound of oxygen and one other element.

oxidize v. **1** combine with oxygen. **2** coat with an oxide. **3** make or become rusty. ☐ **oxidization** n.

oxyacetylene adj. using a mixture of oxygen and acetylene, esp. in cutting or welding metals.

oxygen n. colourless gas existing in air.

oyster n. edible shellfish.

oz. abbr. ounce(s).

ozone n. **1** form of oxygen. **2** protective layer of this in the stratosphere.

Pp

pa *n.* (*colloq.*) father.

pace *n.* **1** single step in walking or running. **2** rate of progress. ● *v.* **1** walk steadily or to and fro. **2** measure by pacing. **3** set the pace for.
■ *n.* **1** footstep, step, stride. **2** rate, speed, velocity. ● *v.* **1** march, stride, walk.

pacemaker *n.* **1** person who sets the pace for another. **2** device regulating heart contractions.

pachyderm /pákkiderm/ *n.* large thick-skinned mammal such as the elephant. □ **pachydermatous** *adj.*

pacific *adj.* making or loving peace. □ **pacifically** *adv.*

pacifist *n.* person totally opposed to war. □ **pacifism** *n.*

pacify *v.* **1** calm and soothe. **2** establish peace in. □ **pacification** *n.*
■ **1** appease, calm (down), conciliate, mollify, placate, quiet, quieten, soothe.

pack *n.* **1** collection of things wrapped or tied for carrying or selling. **2** set of playing cards. **3** group of hounds or wolves. ● *v.* **1** put into or fill a container. **2** press or crowd together, fill (a space) thus. **3** cover or protect with something pressed tightly. □ **pack off** send away. **send packing** dismiss abruptly.
■ *n.* **1** bale, bundle, package, packet, parcel. ● *v.* **1** fill; bundle, cram, jam, ram, squeeze, stuff. **2** cram, crowd, jam, squash, squeeze. **3** package, wrap (up).

package *n.* **1** parcel. **2** box etc. in which goods are packed. **3** package deal. ● *v.* put together in a package. □ **package deal** set of proposals offered or accepted as a whole. **package holiday** one with a fixed inclusive price.

packet *n.* **1** small package. **2** (*colloq.*) large sum of money.

pact *n.* agreement, treaty.
■ agreement, arrangement, bargain, compact, contract, covenant, deal, entente, settlement, treaty, understanding.

pad *n.* **1** piece of padding. **2** set of sheets of paper fastened together at one edge. **3** soft fleshy part under an animal's paw. **4** flat surface for use by helicopters or for launching rockets. ● *v.* (**padded**) **1** put

padding on or into. **2** walk softly or steadily. □ **pad out** fill out (a book, speech, etc.).
■ *n.* **1** bolster, cushion, pillow; wad. **2** jotter, notebook, notepad. ● *v.* **1** cushion, fill, stuff, wad. □ **pad out** amplify, augment, expand, fill out, lengthen, protract, spin out.

padding *n.* soft material used to protect against jarring, add bulk, absorb fluid, etc.

paddle¹ *n.* short oar with broad blade(s). ● *v.* **1** propel by use of paddle(s). **2** row gently.

paddle² *v.* walk with bare feet in shallow water for pleasure.

paddock *n.* **1** small field where horses are kept. **2** enclosure for horses at a racecourse.

padlock *n.* detachable lock with a U-shaped bar secured through the object fastened. ● *v.* fasten with a padlock.

padre /paádri/ *n.* chaplain in the army etc.

paean /péean/ *n.* song of triumph.

paediatrics /péediátriks/ *n.* study of children's diseases. □ **paediatric** *adj.*, **paediatrician** *n.*

paella /pī-élla/ *n.* Spanish dish of rice, saffron, seafood, etc.

pagan *adj. & n.* heathen.

page¹ *n.* **1** sheet of paper in a book etc. **2** one side of this.

page² *n.* boy attendant of a bride. ● *v.* summon by an announcement, messenger, or pager.

pageant *n.* public show or procession, esp. with people in costume. □ **pageantry** *n.*
■ display, extravaganza, parade, procession, show, spectacle, tableau, tattoo. □ **pageantry** magnificence, pomp, showiness, splendour.

pager *n.* bleeping device for summoning the wearer.

pagoda *n.* temple or sacred tower in China, India, etc.

paid *see* **pay. put paid to** end (hopes or prospects etc.).

pail *n.* bucket.

pain *n.* **1** bodily suffering caused by injury, illness, etc. **2** mental suffering. **3** (*pl.*) careful effort. ● *v.* cause pain to.
■ *n.* **1** ache, aching, cramp, discomfort, hurt, pang, smarting, soreness, tenderness, twinge. **2** affliction, agony, anguish, distress, grief, heartache, misery, suffering, torment, torture, woe. **3** (**pains**) effort, exertion, labour, trouble. ● *v.* distress, grieve, hurt, sadden, trouble, wound.

painful *adj.* **1** causing or suffering pain. **2** laborious. □ **painfully** *adv.*
■ **1** aching, achy, agonizing, excruciating, raw, sensitive, smarting, sore, stinging, tender, throbbing; distressing, grievous, harrowing, heartbreaking, traumatic, upsetting. **2** arduous, demanding, exacting, laborious, onerous.

painless *adj.* not causing pain. □ **painlessly** *adv.*

painstaking *adj.* very careful.
■ assiduous, careful, conscientious, diligent, meticulous, scrupulous, sedulous, thorough.

paint *n.* **1** colouring matter for applying in liquid form to a surface. **2** (*pl.*) tubes or cakes of paint. ● *v.* **1** coat with paint. **2** portray by using paint(s) or in words. **3** apply (liquid) to.

painter[1] *n.* person who paints as artist or decorator.

painter[2] *n.* rope attached to a boat's bow for tying it up.

painting *n.* painted picture.
■ fresco, landscape, mural, oil painting, picture, portrait, still life, seascape, water colour.

pair *n.* **1** set of two things or people, couple. **2** article consisting of two parts. **3** other member of a pair. ● *v.* arrange or be arranged in pair(s).
■ *n.* **1** brace; couple, duo, set of two, twosome. ● *v.* join, match (up), put together, team up, twin.

pal *n.* (*colloq.*) friend.

palace *n.* **1** official residence of a sovereign, archbishop, or bishop. **2** splendid mansion.
■ **2** castle, chateau, mansion, stately home.

palaeography /pálliógrafi/ *n.* study of ancient writing and inscriptions. □ **palaeographer** *n.*

palaeolithic /pállió-/ *adj.* of the early part of the Stone Age.

palaeontology /pálli-/ *n.* study of life in the geological past. □ **palaeontologist** *n.*

palatable *adj.* pleasant to the taste or mind.
■ appetizing, savoury, tasty; acceptable, agreeable, pleasant, pleasing, satisfactory.

palate *n.* **1** roof of the mouth. **2** sense of taste.

palatial /paláysh'l/ *adj.* of or like a palace, splendid.
■ de luxe, grand, luxurious, magnificent, opulent, *colloq.* posh, plush, splendid, sumptuous.

palaver *n.* (*colloq.*) fuss.

pale[1] *adj.* **1** (of face) having less colour than normal. **2** (of colour or light) faint. ● *v.* turn pale. □ **palely** *adv.*, **paleness** *n.*
■ *adj.* **1** anaemic, ashen, ashy, colourless, pallid, pasty, peaky, wan, washed out, white. **2** faded, light, pastel; dim, faint, weak. ● *v.* blanch, fade, whiten.

pale[2] *n.* **beyond the pale** outside the bounds of acceptable behaviour.

Palestinian *adj.* & *n.* (native) of Palestine.

palette *n.* board on which an artist mixes colours. □ **palette-knife** *n.* blade with a handle, used for spreading paint or for smoothing soft substances in cookery.

paling *n.* railing(s).

pall[1] /pawl/ *n.* **1** cloth spread over a coffin. **2** heavy dark covering. ● *v.* become uninteresting.

pallbearer *n.* person helping to carry or walking beside the coffin at a funeral.

pallet[1] *n.* **1** straw mattress. **2** makeshift bed.

pallet[2] *n.* tray or platform for goods being lifted or stored.

palliasse *n.* straw mattress.

palliate *v.* **1** alleviate. **2** partially excuse. □ **palliative** *adj.*

pallid *adj.* pale, esp. from illness. □ **pallidness** *n.*, **pallor** *n.*
■ anaemic, ashen, ashy, ghastly, pale, pasty, peaky, wan, washed out, white.

pally *adj.* (*colloq.*) friendly.

palm *n.* **1** inner surface of the hand. **2** part of a glove covering this. **3** tree of warm and tropical climates, with large leaves and no branches. ● *v.* conceal in one's hand. □ **palm off** get (a thing) accepted fraudulently.

palmist *n.* person who tells people's fortunes or characters from lines in their palms. □ **palmistry** *n.*

palomino *n.* (*pl.* **-os**) golden or cream-coloured horse.

palpable *adj.* **1** able to be touched or felt. **2** obvious. □ **palpably** *adv.*, **palpability** *n.*

■ **1** solid, tangible, touchable. **2** apparent, blatant, clear, evident, manifest, obvious, patent, plain, unmistakable.

palpate *v.* examine medically by touch. □ **palpation** *n.*

palpitate *v.* **1** throb rapidly. **2** quiver with fear or excitement. □ **palpitation** *n.*

■ **1** flutter, pound, pulsate, pulse, throb. **2** quake, quaver, quiver, shake, tremble.

palsy *n.* paralysis, esp. with involuntary tremors. □ **palsied** *adj.*

paltry *adj.* (**-ier**, **-iest**) worthless. □ **paltriness** *n.*

■ base, contemptible, despicable, low, mean, miserable, sorry, worthless, wretched.

pampas *n.* vast grassy plains in S. America. □ **pampas-grass** *n.* large ornamental grass.

pamper *v.* treat very indulgently.

■ coddle, indulge, mollycoddle, spoil.

pamphlet *n.* small unbound booklet. □ **pamphleteer** *n.*

pan¹ *n.* **1** metal or earthenware vessel with a flat base, used in cooking. **2** similar vessel. ● *v.* (**panned**) **1** wash (gravel) in a pan in searching for gold. **2** (*colloq.*) criticize severely. □ **pan out** turn out (well). **panful** *n.*

pan² *v.* (**panned**) turn horizontally in filming.

pan- *pref.* all-, whole.

panacea /pánnəséeə/ *n.* remedy for all diseases or troubles.

panache *n.* confident stylish manner.

panama *n.* straw hat.

panatella *n.* thin cigar.

pancake *n.* thin round cake of fried batter.

panchromatic *adj.* sensitive to all visible colours.

pancreas *n.* gland near the stomach, discharging insulin into the blood. □ **pancreatic** *adj.*

panda *n.* **1** bear-like black and white animal native to China and Tibet. **2** racoon-like animal of India.

pandemic *adj.* (of a disease) widespread.

pandemonium *n.* uproar.

■ bedlam, chaos, confusion, disorder, havoc, tumult, turmoil, uproar.

pander *v.* **pander to** gratify by satisfying a taste or weakness.

■ cater to, fulfil, gratify, humour, indulge, satisfy.

pane *n.* sheet of glass in a window or door.

panegyric *n.* piece of written or spoken praise.

panel *n.* **1** distinct usu. rectangular section. **2** strip of board etc. forming this. **3** group assembled to discuss or decide something. **4** list of jurors, jury. ● *v.* (**panelled**) cover or decorate with panels.

panelling *n.* **1** series of wooden panels in a wall. **2** wood used for making panels.

panellist *n.* member of a panel.

pang *n.* sudden sharp pain.

pangolin *n.* scaly anteater.

panic *n.* sudden strong fear. ● *v.* (**panicked**) affect or be affected with panic. □ **panic-stricken** *adj.*, **panicky** *adj.*

■ *n.* alarm, anxiety, apprehension, consternation, dismay, dread, fear, fright, horror, terror, trepidation. ● *v.* alarm, frighten, scare, terrify, unnerve. □ **panic-stricken** afraid, agitated, alarmed, beside oneself, fearful, frightened, horrified, *colloq.* in a flap, *colloq.* in a tizzy, nervous, panicky, petrified, scared, terrified, unnerved.

pannier *n.* **1** large basket carried by a donkey etc. **2** bag fitted on a motor cycle or bicycle.

panoply *n.* splendid array.

panorama *n.* view of a wide area or set of events. □ **panoramic** *adj.*

■ □ **panoramic** comprehensive, extensive, far-reaching, overall, sweeping, wide, wide-ranging.

pansy *n.* garden flower of violet family with broad petals.

pant *v.* **1** breathe with short quick breaths. **2** utter breathlessly.

■ **1** blow, gasp, heave, huff, puff, wheeze.

pantechnicon *n.* large van for transporting furniture.

pantheism *n.* doctrine that God is in everything. □ **pantheist** *n.*, **pantheistic** *adj.*

panther *n.* leopard.

panties *n.pl.* (*colloq.*) short knickers.

pantile *n.* curved roof tile.

pantograph *n.* device for copying a plan etc. on any scale.

pantomime *n.* Christmas play based on a fairy tale.

pantry *n.* **1** room for storing china, glass, etc. **2** larder.

pants *n.pl.* **1** (*US*) trousers. **2** underpants. **3** knickers.

pap *n.* **1** soft food suitable for infants or invalids. **2** pulp.

papacy *n.* position or authority of the pope.

papal *adj.* of the pope or papacy.

papaya *n.* = pawpaw.

paper *n.* **1** substance manufactured in thin sheets from wood fibre, rags, etc., used for writing on, wrapping things, etc. **2** newspaper. **3** set of exam questions. **4** document. **5** dissertation. ● *v.* cover (walls etc.) with wallpaper.
■ *n.* **2** broadsheet, daily, gazette, journal, newspaper, organ, periodical, publication, *derog.* rag, tabloid, weekly. **4** certificate, deed, document, form. **5** article, dissertation, essay, report, study, thesis, treatise.

paperback *adj.* & *n.* (book) bound in flexible paper binding.

paperweight *n.* small heavy object to hold loose papers down.

papier mâché /páppay máshay/ moulded paper pulp used for making small objects.

papoose *n.* young N. American Indian child.

paprika *n.* red pepper.

papyrus *n.* **1** reed-like water plant from which the ancient Egyptians made a kind of paper. **2** this paper. **3** (*pl.* **-ri**) manuscript written on this.

par *n.* **1** average or normal amount or condition etc. **2** equal footing.

parable *n.* story told to illustrate a moral or spiritual truth.

paracetamol *n.* drug that relieves pain and reduces fever.

parachute *n.* device used to slow the descent of a person or object dropping from a great height. ● *v.* descend or drop by parachute. □ **parachutist** *n.*

parade *n.* **1** formal assembly of troops. **2** procession. **3** ostentatious display. **4** public square or promenade. ● *v.* **1** assemble for parade. **2** march or walk with display. **3** make a display of.
■ *n.* **2** cavalcade, march, procession. **3** display, exhibition, show, spectacle. **3** esplanade, mall, promenade, walk, way. ● *v.* **2** file, march, walk. **3** display, exhibit, flaunt, show off.

paradigm /párrədīm/ *n.* example, model.

paradise *n.* **1** heaven. **2** delightful place or state.
■ **2** heaven, Utopia; bliss, delight, ecstasy, happiness, joy, rapture.

paradox *n.* statement that seems self-contradictory but contains a truth.
□ **paradoxical** *adj.*, **paradoxically** *adv.*

paraffin *n.* oil from petroleum or shale, used as fuel.

paragon *n.* apparently perfect person or thing.
■ archetype, epitome, exemplar, ideal, model, pattern, quintessence.

paragraph *n.* one or more sentences on a single theme, beginning on a new line. ● *v.* arrange in paragraphs.

parakeet *n.* small parrot.

parallax *n.* apparent difference in an object's position when viewed from different points.

parallel *adj.* **1** (of lines or planes) going continuously at the same distance from each other. **2** similar, corresponding. ● *n.* **1** person or thing analogous to another. **2** line of latitude. **3** analogy. ● *v.* (**paralleled**) **1** be parallel to. **2** compare. □ **parallelism** *n.*
■ *adj.* **2** analogous, comparable, corresponding, equivalent, like, matching, similar. ● *n.* **1** analogue, counterpart, equal, equivalent, match. **3** analogy, correlation, correspondence, equivalence, likeness, similarity. ● *v.* **1** be analogous to, be comparable with, be similar to, correspond to match, resemble. **2** compare, equate, juxtapose, liken.

parallelogram *n.* four-sided geometric figure with its opposite sides parallel to each other.

paralyse *v.* **1** affect with paralysis. **2** render powerless.
■ **2** cripple, disable, incapacitate; bring to a standstill, halt, immobilize.

paralysis *n.* loss of power of movement.
□ **paralytic** *adj.* & *n.*

paramedic *n.* skilled person working in support of medical staff.

parameter *n.* variable quantity or quality that restricts what it characterizes.

paramilitary *adj.* organized like a military force.

paramount *adj.* most important.
■ cardinal, chief, foremost, main, pre-eminent, primary, prime, supreme, uppermost.

paranoia *n.* **1** mental disorder in which a person has delusions of grandeur or persecution. **2** abnormal tendency to mistrust others. □ **paranoid** adj. & n.

parapet n. low wall along the edge of a balcony or bridge.

paraphernalia n. numerous belongings or pieces of equipment.

■ accessories, accoutrements, apparatus, belongings, sl. clobber, effects, equipment, gear, kit, possessions, property, stuff, tackle, things, trappings.

paraphrase v. express in other words. ● n. rewording in this way.

paraplegia n. paralysis of the legs and part or all of the trunk. □ **paraplegic** adj. & n.

parapsychology n. study of mental perceptions that seem outside normal abilities.

paraquat n. extremely poisonous weedkiller.

parasite n. **1** animal or plant living on or in another. **2** person living off another or others and giving no useful return. □ **parasitic** adj.

parasol n. light umbrella used to give shade from the sun.

parboil v. partly cook by boiling.

parcel n. **1** thing(s) wrapped for carrying or post. **2** piece of land. ● v. (**parcelled**) **1** wrap as a parcel. **2** divide into portions.

parch v. make or become hot and dry.

parched adj. **1** hot and dry. **2** (colloq.) thirsty.

■ **1** arid, dehydrated, desiccated, dried out or up, dry, scorched.

parchment n. **1** writing material made from animal skins. **2** paper resembling this.

pardon n. forgiveness. ● v. (**pardoned**) forgive. □ **pardonable** adj., **pardonably** adv.

■ n. absolution, amnesty, exoneration, forgiveness, reprieve. ● v. absolve, condone, excuse, exonerate, forgive, let off, overlook, reprieve.

pare v. **1** trim the edges of. **2** peel. **3** reduce little by little.

parent n. **1** father or mother. **2** source from which other things are derived. □ **parental** adj., **parenthood** n.

parentage n. ancestry.

■ ancestry, birth, descent, extraction, family, line, lineage, origins, pedigree, stock.

parenthesis n. (pl. **-theses**) **1** word, phrase, or sentence inserted into a passage. **2** brackets (like these) placed round this. □ **parenthetic** adj.

pariah /pəríə/ n. outcast.

parietal bone each of a pair of bones forming part of the skull.

paring n. piece pared off.

parish n. **1** area with its own church and clergyman. **2** local government district.

parishioner n. inhabitant of a parish.

Parisian adj. & n. (native) of Paris.

parity n. equality.

park n. **1** public garden or recreation ground. **2** enclosed land of a country house. **3** parking area. ● v. place and leave (esp. a vehicle) temporarily.

parka n. thick jacket with a hood.

parlance n. phraseology.

parley n. (pl. **-eys**) discussion, esp. between enemies, to settle a dispute. ● v. (**parleyed**) hold a parley.

parliament n. assembly that makes a country's laws. □ **parliamentary** adj.

■ congress, diet, house, legislative assembly, legislature.

Parmesan n. hard Italian cheese.

parochial adj. **1** of a church parish. **2** interested in a limited area only. □ **parochially** adv., **parochialism** n.

■ **2** insular, limited, narrow-minded, provincial, restricted, small-minded.

parody n. comic or grotesque imitation. ● v. make a parody of.

■ n. burlesque, caricature, lampoon, mockery, satire, colloq. spoof, take-off. ● v. burlesque, caricature, lampoon, mimic, mock, satirize, send up, take off.

parole n. release of a prisoner before the end of his or her sentence on promise of good behaviour. ● v. release in this way.

paroxysm n. fit (of pain, rage, coughing etc.).

■ attack, convulsion, eruption, explosion, fit, outbreak, outburst, spasm.

parquet /paárki/ n. flooring of wooden blocks arranged in a pattern.

parricide n. killing or killer of own parent. □ **parricidal** adj.

parrot n. **1** tropical bird with a short hooked bill. **2** unintelligent imitator. ● v. (**parroted**) repeat mechanically.

parry v. **1** ward off (a blow). **2** evade (a question) skilfully.

■ **1** avert, deflect, fend off, stave off, turn aside, ward off. **2** avoid, circumvent, dodge, elude, evade, sidestep.

parsec n. unit of distance used in astronomy, about 3.25 light years.

parsimonious adj. stingy, very sparing. □ **parsimoniously** adv., **parsimony** n.
■ cheese-paring, close, mean, miserly, near, niggardly, penny-pinching, stingy, colloq. tight, tight-fisted.

parsley n. herb with crinkled green leaves.

parsnip n. vegetable with a large yellowish tapering root.

parson n. (colloq.) clergyman. □ **parson's nose** fatty lump on the rump of a cooked fowl.

parsonage n. rectory, vicarage.

part n. **1** some but not all. **2** distinct portion. **3** component. **4** portion allotted. **5** character assigned to an actor in a play etc. **6** (usu. pl.) region, district. ● adv. partly. ● v. separate, divide. □ **in good part** without taking offence. **part of speech** word's grammatical class (noun, verb, adjective, etc.). **part-time** adj. for or during only part of the working week. **part with** give up possession of.
■ n. **2** bit, division, piece, portion, section, segment; chapter, episode, instalment. **3** component, constituent, element, ingredient, unit. **4** allotment, percentage, quota, ration, share. **5** character, role. **6** area, district, neighbourhood, quarter, region. ● v. divide, separate, split (up). □ **part with** forgo, give up, relinquish, sacrifice, surrender.

partake v. (**-took, -taken**) **1** participate. **2** take a portion, esp. of food. □ **partaker** n.

partial adj. **1** favouring one side or person, biased. **2** not complete or total. □ **be partial to** have a strong liking for. **partially** adv.
■ **1** biased, discriminatory, one-sided, partisan, prejudiced, unfair. **2** fragmentary, incomplete. □ **be partial to** be fond of, be keen on, enjoy, have a soft spot for, have a weakness for, like, love.

partiality n. **1** bias, favouritism. **2** strong liking.
■ **1** bias, favouritism, partisanship, prejudice. **2** fondness, inclination, liking, love, penchant, predilection, preference, soft spot, taste, weakness.

participate v. have a share, take part in something. □ **participation** n., **participant** n.

participle n. word formed from a verb, as a **past participle** (e.g. burnt, frightened), **present participle** (e.g. burning, frightening). □ **participial** adj.

particle n. **1** very small portion of matter. **2** minor part of speech.
■ **1** atom, bit, crumb, fragment, iota, jot, molecule, morsel, piece, scrap, shred, sliver, speck, spot.

particoloured adj. coloured partly in one colour, partly in another.

particular adj. **1** relating to one person or thing and not others. **2** fastidious. ● n. **1** detail. **2** (pl.) points of information. □ **in particular** specifically. **particularly** adv.
■ adj. **1** certain, distinct, individual, single, specific. **2** colloq. choosy, fastidious, finicky, fussy, nice, colloq. pernickety. ● n. **1** detail, element, item, specific. **2** (particulars) details, facts, information, colloq. low-down.

parting n. **1** leave-taking. **2** line from which hair is combed in different directions.

partisan n. **1** strong supporter. **2** guerrilla. ● adj. **1** of partisans. **2** biased. □ **partisanship** n.
■ n. **1** champion, devotee, enthusiast, fan, fanatic, follower, supporter. ● adj. **2** biased, bigoted, one-sided, partial, prejudiced.

partition n. **1** division into parts. **2** structure dividing a room or space, thin wall. ● v. divide into parts or by a partition.

partly adv. partially.

partner n. **1** person sharing with another or others in an activity. **2** each of a pair. **3** husband or wife or member of an unmarried couple. ● v. **1** be the partner of. **2** put together as partners.
■ n. **1** accomplice, ally, associate, colleague, collaborator, comrade, confederate. **3** consort, husband, spouse, wife; boyfriend, girlfriend.

partnership n. **1** being a partner or partners. **2** joint business.
■ **1** alliance, association, collaboration, cooperation, union. **2** business, company, firm, practice.

partridge n. plump brown game bird.

parturition n. **1** process of giving birth to young. **2** childbirth.

party n. **1** social gathering. **2** group travelling or working as a unit. **3** group with common aims, esp. in politics. **4** one side in an agreement or dispute. □ **party line** set policy of a political party. **party wall** wall common to two buildings or rooms.

■ **1** ball, celebration, do, function, gathering, *colloq.* get-together, jamboree, reception. **2** band, body company, crew, gang, group, squad, team, troop. **3** faction, movement, side. **4** defendant, disputant, litigant, plaintiff.

paschal /pásk'l/ *adj.* **1** of the Passover. **2** of Easter.

pass *v.* (**passed**) **1** move onward or past. **2** go or send to another person or place. **3** elapse. **4** happen. **5** occupy (time). **6** allow (a bill in Parliament) to proceed. **7** examine and declare satisfactory. **8** achieve the required standard in a test. **9** go beyond. **10** (in a game) refuse one's turn. **11** discharge from the body as excreta. ● *n.* **1** passing, movement made with the hands or thing held. **2** permit to enter or leave. **3** gap in mountains, allowing passage to the other side. □ **make a pass at** (*colloq.*) make sexual advances to. **pass away** die. **pass on** transmit to the next person in a series. **pass out** become unconscious. **pass over** disregard. **pass up** (*colloq.*) refuse to accept.

■ *v.* **1** go, move, proceed, progress, travel; get ahead of, get past, overtake. **3** elapse, go by, slip by *or* away. **4** befall, come about, happen, occur, take place. **5** employ, fill, kill, occupy, spend, use, while away. **6** accept, agree to, allow, authorize, endorse, sanction. **8** be successful (in), get through, succeed (in). **9** exceed, go beyond, outdo, surpass, transcend. ● *n.* **2** permit, ticket. **3** canyon, defile, gap, gorge, passage, ravine. □ **pass away** *sl.* croak, die, expire, perish, *sl.* snuff it. **pass out** black out, collapse, faint, keel over. **pass over** disregard, ignore, overlook, pay no attention to, *colloq.* skip. **pass up** decline, refuse, reject, turn down.

passable *adj.* **1** able to be traversed. **2** just satisfactory.

■ **1** clear, navigable, open. **2** acceptable, adequate, all right, average, fair, *colloq.* OK, satisfactory, tolerable.

passage *n.* **1** passing. **2** right to pass or be a passenger. **3** way through, esp. with a wall on each side. **4** journey by sea. **5** section of a literary or musical work. **6** tube-like structure in the body. □ **passageway** *n.*

■ **1** course, passing, progress, transit. **3** corridor, hall, passageway; road, route, thoroughfare, way. **4** crossing, journey,

voyage, trip. **5** citation, excerpt, extract, part, quotation, section, selection; canto, stanza, verse.

passbook *n.* book recording a customer's deposits and withdrawals from a bank etc.

passenger *n.* **1** person (other than the driver, pilot, or crew) travelling in a vehicle, train, ship, or aircraft. **2** ineffective member of a team.

passer-by *n.* (*pl.* **passers-by**) person who happens to be going past.

passion *n.* **1** strong emotion. **2** sexual love. **3** (object arousing) great enthusiasm. **4** (**the Passion**) sufferings of Christ in his last days.

■ **1** ardour, emotion, fervency, fervour, fire, heat, intensity, vehemence, warmth, zeal. **2** desire, infatuation, love, lust. **3** craze, fad, mania, obsession; eagerness, enthusiasm, fascination, keenness.

passionate *adj.* full of passion, intense. □ **passionately** *adv.*

■ ardent, avid, burning, eager, emotional, enthusiastic, excited, fervent, fervid, fiery, impassioned, intense, vehement, zealous; amorous, lustful.

passive *adj.* **1** acted upon and not active. **2** not resisting, submissive. **3** showing no interest, initiative, or forceful qualities. □ **passively** *adv.*, **passivity** *n.*

■ **2** complaisant, compliant, docile, malleable, meek, submissive, tame, tractable, unresisting, yielding. **3** apathetic, impassive, inactive, inert, lifeless, listless, phlegmatic, quiescent, unresponsive.

Passover *n.* Jewish festival commemorating the escape of Jews from slavery in Egypt.

passport *n.* official document for use by a person travelling abroad.

password *n.* secret word(s), knowledge of which distinguishes friend from enemy.

past *adj.* belonging to the time before the present, gone by. ● *n.* **1** (**the past**) past time or events. **2** person's past life. ● *prep.* & *adv.* beyond. □ **past master** expert.

■ *adj.* last, recent; erstwhile, ex-, former, previous, prior; done, finished, over. ● *n.* **1** (**the past**) days gone by, days of yore, former times, yesterday. **2** background, career, history, life.

pasta *n.* **1** dried dough produced in various shapes. **2** cooked dish made with this.

paste n. **1** moist mixture. **2** adhesive. **3** edible doughy substance. **4** glass-like substance used in imitation gems. ● v. **1** fasten or coat with paste. **2** (sl.) thrash.

pasteboard n. cardboard.

pastel n. **1** chalk-like crayon. **2** drawing made with this. **3** light delicate shade of colour.

pasteurize v. sterilize by heating. □ **pasteurization** n.

pastille n. **1** small flavoured sweet for sucking. **2** lozenge.

pastime n. something done to pass time pleasantly.

■ amusement, entertainment, hobby, interest, leisure activity, recreation, sport.

pastor n. clergyman in charge of a church or congregation.

pastoral adj. **1** of country life. **2** of or appropriate to a pastor.

■ **1** bucolic, country, rural, rustic. **2** clerical, ecclesiastical, ministerial, priestly.

pastry n. **1** dough made of flour, fat, and water. **2** (item of) food made with this.

pasturage n. pasture land.

pasture n. grassy land suitable for grazing cattle. ● v. put (animals) to pasture, graze.

pasty[1] /pásti/ n. pastry with sweet or savoury filling, baked without a dish.

pasty[2] /páysti/ adj. (**-ier, -iest**) **1** of or like paste. **2** pallid.

pat v. (**patted**) tap gently with an open hand. ● n. **1** patting movement. **2** small mass of a soft substance. ● adv. & adj. known and ready.

patch n. **1** piece put on, esp. in mending. **2** distinct area or period. **3** piece of ground. ● v. **1** put patch(es) on. **2** piece (things) together. □ **not a patch on** (colloq.) not nearly as good as. **patch up 1** repair. **2** settle (a quarrel etc.).

■ n. **2** area, region, section; period, spell, time. **3** lot, parcel, piece, plot. **patch up 1** darn, fix, mend, repair. **2** heal, put right, resolve, settle.

patchwork n. **1** needlework in which small pieces of cloth are joined decoratively. **2** thing made of assorted pieces.

patchy adj. (**-ier, -iest**) existing in patches. **2** uneven in quality. □ **patchily** adv., **patchiness** n.

pâté /páttay/ n. paste of meat etc.

patella n. (pl. **-ae**) kneecap.

patent adj. **1** obvious. **2** patented. ● v. obtain or hold a patent for. ● n. **1** official right to be the sole maker or user of an

invention or process. **2** invention etc. protected by this. □ **patent leather** leather with glossy varnished surface. **patently** adv.

■ adj. **1** apparent, clear, evident, manifest, obvious, plain, unmistakable.

patentee n. holder of a patent.

paternal adj. **1** of a father. **2** fatherly. **3** related through one's father. □ **paternally** adv.

■ **2** fatherly, fond, indulgent, kindly, loving, solicitous.

paternalism n. policy of making kindly provision for people's needs but giving them no responsibility. □ **paternalistic** adj.

paternity n. fatherhood.

path n. **1** way by which people pass on foot. **2** line along which a person or thing moves. **3** course of action.

■ **1** bridle path, footpath, track, trail, walk. **2** circuit, course, orbit, route, track, trajectory. **3** approach, avenue, course of action, method, procedure, strategy.

pathetic adj. **1** arousing pity or sadness. **2** (colloq.) miserably inadequate. □ **pathetically** adv.

■ **1** emotional, emotive, heartbreaking, moving, piteous, pitiable, pitiful, poignant, sad, touching.

pathogenic adj. causing disease.

pathology n. study of disease. □ **pathological** adj., **pathologist** n.

pathos n. pathetic quality.

patience n. **1** calm endurance. **2** card game for one player.

■ **1** calmness, composure, endurance, equanimity, forbearance, fortitude, imperturbability, self-control, serenity, stoicism, tolerance.

patient adj. showing patience. ● n. person treated by a doctor or dentist etc. □ **patiently** adv.

■ adj. calm, composed, even-tempered, forbearing, long-suffering, serene, stoical, tolerant, uncomplaining.

patina n. sheen on a surface produced by age or use.

patio n. (pl. **-os**) paved courtyard.

patois /pátwaa/ n. dialect.

patriarch n. **1** male head of a family or tribe. **2** bishop of high rank in certain Churches. □ **patriarchal** adj., **patriarchate** n.

patriarchy n. social organization in which a male is head of the family.

patricide n. killing or killer of own father. □ **patricidal** adj.

patrimony n. heritage.

patriot n. person devoted to and ready to defend his or her country. □ **patriotic** adj., **patriotism** n.

patrol v. (**patrolled**) walk or travel regularly through (an area or building) to see that all is well. ● n. 1 patrolling. 2 person(s) patrolling.

> ■ v. defend, guard, keep guard over, police, protect. ● n. 1 beat, rounds. 2 guard, sentinel, sentry, watchman.

patron /páytrən/ n. 1 person giving influential or financial support to a cause. 2 regular customer. □ **patron saint** saint regarded as a protector.

> ■ 1 backer, benefactor, champion, friend, sponsor, supporter. 2 client, customer, colloq. regular.

patronage n. 1 patron's support. 2 patronizing behaviour.

patronize v. 1 treat in a condescending way. 2 be a regular customer of. 3 act as patron to.

> ■ 1 condescend to, talk down to. 2 be a customer of, frequent, shop at. 3 assist, back, help, finance, fund, sponsor, support.

patronymic n. name derived from that of a father or ancestor.

patter¹ n. sound of quick light taps or steps. ● v. (of rain etc.) make this sound.

patter² n. rapid glib speech.

pattern n. 1 decorative design. 2 model, design, or instructions showing how a thing is to be made. 3 sample of cloth etc. 4 excellent example. 5 regular manner in which things occur. □ **patterned** adj.

> ■ 1 design, motif. 2 blueprint, design, model, plan, stencil, template. 3 sample, specimen, swatch. 4 archetype, exemplar, ideal, model, paradigm, paragon, standard. 5 consistency, order, regularity, sequence, system.

patty n. small pie or pasty.

paucity n. smallness of quantity.

paunch n. protruding stomach.

pauper n. very poor person.

pause n. temporary stop. ● v. make a pause.

> ■ n. break, breather, delay, gap, hesitation, hiatus, interlude, intermission, interruption, interval, lull, respite, rest, stop. ● v. delay, halt, hesitate, rest, stop, take a break, wait.

pave v. cover (a street etc.) with a hard durable surface.

pavement n. paved path at the side of a road.

pavilion n. 1 building on a sports ground for players or spectators. 2 ornamental building.

pavlova n. meringue cake containing cream and fruit.

paw n. foot of an animal that has claws. ● v. 1 strike with a paw. 2 scrape (the ground) with a hoof. 3 (colloq.) touch with the hands.

pawl n. lever with a catch that engages with the notches of a ratchet.

pawn¹ n. 1 chessman of the smallest size and value. 2 person whose actions are controlled by others.

pawn² v. deposit with a pawnbroker as security for money borrowed.

pawnbroker n. person licensed to lend money on the security of personal property deposited.

pawnshop n. pawnbroker's premises.

pawpaw n. 1 fruit of a palm-like tropical tree. 2 this tree.

pay v. (**paid**) 1 give (money) in return for goods or services. 2 give what is owed. 3 give (attention, respect, etc.). 4 be profitable or worthwhile. 5 reward or punish. ● n. wages. □ **pay for 1** hand over money for. 2 bear the cost of. 3 suffer or be punished for. **pay off 1** pay (a debt) in full. 2 discharge (an employee). 3 yield good results. **pay-off** n. 1 (sl.) payment. 2 reward, retribution. 3 climax.

> ■ v. 1 disburse, expend, lay out, spend, colloq. stump up; remunerate, settle up with. 2 discharge, honour, pay off, recompense, refund, reimburse, repay, settle, square. 3 bestow, give, pass on. 4 avail, benefit, help, profit; be advantageous or profitable or worthwhile, pay off. 5 avenge oneself on, get revenge on, punish. ● n. emolument, income, remuneration, salary, stipend, wage(s).

payable adj. which must or may be paid.

> ■ due, outstanding, owed, owing, unpaid.

payee n. person to whom money is paid or is to be paid.

payload n. aircraft's or rocket's total load.

payment n. 1 act or instance of paying. 2 money etc. paid.

> ■ 1 compensation, remuneration, settlement. 2 instalment, premium, remittance.

payola n. bribery offered for dishonest use of influence to promote a commercial product.

payroll n. list of a firm's employees receiving regular pay.

pea n. **1** plant bearing seeds in pods. **2** its round seed used as a vegetable. □ **pea-green** adj. & n. bright green.

peace n. **1** calm, quiet. **2** freedom from or cessation of war.

> ■ **1** calm, calmness, peacefulness, quiet, repose, serenity, stillness, tranquillity. **2** accord, concord, harmony; armistice, ceasefire, truce.

peaceable adj. **1** fond of peace, not quarrelsome. **2** peaceful.

> ■ **1** amicable, cooperative, easygoing, friendly, genial, good-natured, inoffensive, mild, pacific, peace-loving.

peaceful adj. characterized by or not infringing peace. □ **peacefully** adv., **peacefulness** n.

> ■ calm, gentle, peaceable, placid, quiet, restful, serene, tranquil; law-abiding, orderly, well-behaved.

peacemaker n. person who brings about peace.

> ■ arbitrator, conciliator, intermediary, mediator.

peach n. **1** round juicy fruit with a rough stone. **2** tree bearing this. **3** its yellowish-pink colour.

peacock n. male bird with splendid plumage and a long fan-like tail.

peafowl n. peacock or peahen.

peahen n. female peafowl.

peak n. **1** pointed top, esp. of a mountain. **2** projecting part of the edge of a cap. **3** point of highest value or intensity etc. □ **peaked** adj.

> ■ **1** crest, pinnacle, summit, top. **2** brim, visor. **3** acme, apex, climax, culmination, height, high point, top, zenith.

peaky adj. (**-ier**, **-iest**) looking drawn and sickly.

peal n. **1** sound of ringing bell(s). **2** set of bells with different notes. **3** loud burst of thunder or laughter. ● v. sound in a peal.

> ■ n. **1** chime, ring, ringing, tinkling, toll, tolling. **2** carillon, chime. **3** clap, crash, roar, rumble. ● v. chime, ring, toll; crash, roar, rumble, thunder.

peanut n. **1** plant bearing underground pods with two edible seeds. **2** this seed. **3** (pl.) very trivial sum of money.

pear n. **1** rounded fruit tapering towards the stalk. **2** tree bearing this.

pearl n. **1** round usu. white gem formed inside the shell of certain oysters. □ **pearly** adj.

peasant n. person working on the land.

peasantry n. peasants collectively.

peat n. decomposed vegetable matter from bogs etc., used in horticulture or as fuel. □ **peaty** adj.

pebble n. small smooth round stone. □ **pebbly** adj.

pecan n. **1** smooth pinkish-brown nut. **2** tree bearing this.

peck v. **1** strike, nip, or pick up with the beak. **2** kiss hastily. ● n. pecking movement.

peckish adj. (colloq.) hungry.

pectin n. substance found in fruits that makes jam set.

pectoral adj. of, in, or on the chest or breast. ● n. pectoral fin or muscle.

peculiar adj. **1** strange, eccentric. **2** distinctive, special. □ **peculiar to** belonging exclusively to one person, place, or thing. **peculiarly** adv.

> ■ **1** abnormal, anomalous, bizarre, curious, different, eccentric, extraordinary, funny, odd, offbeat, outlandish, out of the ordinary, queer, strange, unconventional, unusual, weird. **2** characteristic, distinctive, distinguishing, idiosyncratic, individual, special, typical, unique.

peculiarity n. **1** idiosyncrasy. **2** characteristic. **3** being peculiar.

> ■ **1** eccentricity, idiosyncrasy, kink, oddity, quirk. **2** attribute, characteristic, feature, property, quality, trait.

pecuniary adj. of or in money.

pedagogue n. (derog.) person who teaches pedantically.

pedal n. lever operated by the foot. ● v. (**pedalled**) **1** work the pedal(s) of. **2** operate by pedals.

pedant n. person who insists on strict adherence to literal meaning or formal rules. □ **pedantic** adj., **pedantry** n.

peddle v. sell (goods) as a pedlar.

pedestal n. base supporting a column or statue etc.

pedestrian n. person walking, esp. in a street. ● adj. **1** of or for pedestrians. **2** dull.

> ■ adj. **2** banal, boring, commonplace, dull, humdrum, mundane, ordinary, prosaic, run-of-the-mill, tedious, unimaginative, uninspired, uninteresting.

pedicure *n.* care or treatment of the feet and toenails.

pedigree *n.* line or list of (esp. distinguished) ancestors. ● *adj.* (of an animal) of recorded and pure breeding.

> ■ *n.* ancestry, birth, blood, descent, extraction, family, genealogy, lineage, parentage, stock.

pediment *n.* triangular part crowning the front of a building.

pedlar *n.* person who sells small articles from door to door.

pedometer *n.* device for estimating the distance travelled on foot.

peduncle *n.* stalk of a flower etc.

pee (*colloq.*) *v.* urinate. ● *n.* urine.

peek *v.* & *n.* peep, glance.

peel *n.* skin of certain fruits and vegetables etc. ● *v.* **1** remove the peel of. **2** strip off. **3** come off in strips or layers, lose skin or bark etc. thus. □ **peelings** *n.pl.*

peep *v.* **1** look furtively or through a narrow opening. **2** come slowly into view. ● *n.* brief or surreptitious look. □ **peep-hole** *n.* small hole to peep through. **peeping Tom** furtive voyeur.

> ■ *v.* **1** glance, look quickly, peek, squint.

peer[1] *v.* look searchingly or with difficulty or effort.

peer[2] *n.* **1** duke, marquess, earl, viscount, or baron. **2** one who is the equal of another in rank or merit etc.

peerage *n.* **1** peers as a group. **2** rank of peer or peeress.

peeress *n.* **1** a female peer. **2** a peer's wife.

peerless *adj.* unequalled.

> ■ incomparable, inimitable, matchless, superb, superlative, supreme, unequalled, unique, unparalleled, unrivalled, unsurpassed.

peeved *adj.* (*colloq.*) annoyed.

peevish *adj.* irritable. □ **peevishly** *adv.*, **peevishness** *n.*

> ■ bad-tempered, cantankerous, crabby, crotchety, fractious, grumpy, irascible, irritable, pettish, petulant, prickly, querulous, snappy, testy, touchy, waspish.

peewit *n.* lapwing.

peg *n.* **1** wooden or metal pin or stake. **2** clip for holding clothes on a washing-line. ● *v.* (**pegged**) **1** fix or mark by means of peg(s). **2** keep (wages or prices) at a fixed level. □ **off the peg** (of clothes) ready-made.

pejorative *adj.* derogatory.

peke *n.* Pekingese dog.

Pekingese *n.* dog of a breed with short legs, flat face, and silky hair.

pelargonium *n.* plant with showy flowers.

pelican *n.* waterbird with a pouch in its long bill for storing fish. □ **pelican crossing** pedestrian crossing with lights operated by pedestrians.

pellagra *n.* deficiency disease causing cracking of the skin.

pellet *n.* **1** small round mass of a substance. **2** small shot.

pell-mell *adv.* **1** headlong, recklessly. **2** in disorder.

pellucid *adj.* very clear.

pelmet *n.* ornamental strip above a window etc.

pelt[1] *n.* an animal skin.

pelt[2] *v.* **1** throw missiles at. **2** run fast. □ **at full pelt** as fast as possible.

> ■ **1** bombard, pepper, shower. **2** career, dash, hare, hurtle, race, run, rush, speed, sprint, tear, whiz, zoom.

pelvis *n.* framework of bones round the body below the waist. □ **pelvic** *adj.*

pen[1] *n.* small fenced enclosure, esp. for animals. ● *v.* (**penned**) shut in or as if in a pen.

> ■ *n.* coop, US corral, enclosure, fold, hutch, pound, sty. ● *v.* confine, coop up, corral, enclose, shut in or up.

pen[2] *n.* device with a metal point for writing with ink. ● *v.* (**penned**) write (a letter etc.). □ **penfriend** *n.* friend with whom a person corresponds without meeting. **pen-name** *n.* author's pseudonym.

penal *adj.* of or involving punishment.

penalize *v.* **1** inflict a penalty on. **2** put at a disadvantage.

penalty *n.* punishment for breaking a law or rule.

> ■ punishment, sentence; fine, forfeit.

penance *n.* act performed as an expression of penitence.

> ■ atonement, reparation.

pence *see* **penny.**

penchant /pónsHon/ *n.* liking.

> ■ fondness, liking, love, partiality, predilection, preference, proclivity, soft spot, taste, weakness.

pencil *n.* instrument containing graphite, used for drawing or writing. ● *v.* (**pencilled**) write, draw, or mark with a pencil.

pendant *n.* ornament hung from a chain round the neck.

pendent *adj.* hanging.

pending *adj.* waiting to be decided or settled. ● *prep.* **1** during. **2** until.

pendulous *adj.* hanging loosely.

pendulum *n.* **1** weight hung from a cord and swinging freely. **2** rod with a weighted end that regulates a clock's movement.

penetrate *v.* **1** make a way into or through, pierce. **2** see into or through. □ **penetrable** *adj.*, **penetrability** *n.*, **penetration** *n.*

■ **1** enter, go into, make one's way through; bore into, perforate, pierce, prick, puncture.

penetrating *adj.* **1** showing great insight. **2** (of sound) piercing.

■ **1** acute, astute, clever, discerning, incisive, intelligent, keen, perceptive, percipient, perspicacious, sharp, shrewd. **2** loud, piercing, shrill.

penguin *n.* flightless seabird of Antarctic regions.

penicillin *n.* antibiotic obtained from mould fungi.

peninsula *n.* piece of land almost surrounded by water. □ **peninsular** *adj.*

penis *n.* organ by which a male mammal copulates and urinates.

penitent *adj.* feeling or showing regret that one has done wrong. ● *n.* penitent person. □ **penitently** *adv.*, **penitence** *n.*

■ *adj.* apologetic, ashamed, conscience-stricken, contrite, regretful, remorseful, repentant, rueful, sorry.

penitential *adj.* of penitence or penance.

pennant *n.* long tapering flag.

penniless *adj.* destitute.

pennon *n.* flag, esp. a long triangular or forked one.

penny *n.* (*pl.* **pennies** for separate coins, **pence** for a sum of money) **1** British bronze coin worth one-hundredth of £1. **2** former coin worth one-twelfth of a shilling. □ **penny-pinching** *adj.* niggardly.

pension *n.* income paid by the government, an ex-employer, or a private fund to a person who is retired, disabled, etc. ● *v.* pay a pension to. □ **pension off** dismiss with a pension.

pensionable *adj.* entitled or (of a job) entitling one to a pension.

pensioner *n.* person who receives a pension.

pensive *adj.* deep in thought. □ **pensively** *adv.*, **pensiveness** *n.*

■ contemplative, meditative, reflective, ruminative, thoughtful.

pentagon *n.* geometric figure with five sides. □ **pentagonal** *adj.*

pentagram *n.* five-pointed star.

pentathlon *n.* athletic contest involving five events.

Pentecost *n.* **1** Jewish harvest festival, 50 days after second day of Passover. **2** Whit Sunday.

penthouse *n.* flat on the roof of a tall building.

penultimate *adj.* last but one.

penumbra *n.* (*pl.* **-ae**) area of partial shadow.

penury *n.* poverty. □ **penurious** *adj.*

■ destitution, indigence, need, pennilessness, poverty. □ **penurious** destitute, impecunious, impoverished, indigent, necessitous, needy, penniless, poor, poverty-stricken.

peony *n.* plant with large round red, pink, or white flowers.

people *n.pl.* **1** persons in general. **2** (**the people**) citizens of a country. **3** (as *sing.*) persons composing a race or nation. **4** parents or other relatives. ● *v.* fill with people, populate.

■ *n.* **1** human beings, individuals, persons. **2** (**the people**) the *hoi polloi*, the masses, the populace, the (general) public. **3** folk, nation, race, tribe. **4** family, kin, kinsfolk, kith and kin, parents, relations, relatives.

pep *n.* vigour. ● *v.* (**pepped**) **pep up** fill with vigour. □ **pep talk** talk urging great effort.

pepper *n.* **1** hot-tasting seasoning powder made from the dried berries of certain plants. **2** capsicum. ● *v.* **1** sprinkle with pepper. **2** pelt. **3** sprinkle. □ **peppery** *adj.*

peppercorn *n.* dried black berry from which pepper is made. □ **peppercorn rent** very low rent.

peppermint *n.* **1** a kind of mint with strong fragrant oil. **2** this oil. **3** sweet flavoured with this.

pepsin *n.* enzyme in gastric juice.

peptic *adj.* of digestion.

per *prep.* **1** for each. **2** in accordance with. **3** by means of. □ **per annum** for each year. **per capita** for each person. **per cent** in or for every hundred.

perambulate *v.* walk through or round (an area). □ **perambulation** *n.*

perceive v. **1** become aware of by one of the senses. **2** apprehend, understand.
■ **1** catch sight of, descry, detect, discern, distinguish, espy, glimpse, make out, notice, observe, see, *colloq.* spot. **2** appreciate, apprehend, comprehend, grasp, realize, recognize, see, sense, understand.

percentage n. **1** rate or proportion per hundred. **2** proportion, part.

perceptible adj. able to be perceived. □ **perceptibly** adv., **perceptibility** n.
■ apparent, clear, detectable, discernible, distinguishable, evident, manifest, noticeable, observable, obvious, palpable, patent, perceivable, recognizable, unmistakable, visible.

perception n. perceiving, ability to perceive.
■ apprehension, consciousness, grasp, realization, recognition, understanding; feeling, insight, intuition, sense, sensitivity.

perceptive adj. showing insight and understanding. □ **perceptively** adv., **perceptiveness** n.
■ acute, astute, discerning, discriminating, intelligent, penetrating, percipient, perspicacious, quick, sensitive, sharp, shrewd.

perch[1] n. **1** bird's resting place, rod etc. for this. **2** high seat. ● v. rest or place on or as if on a perch.

perch[2] n. (pl. **perch**) edible freshwater fish with spiny fins.

percipient adj. perceptive. □ **percipience** n.

percolate v. **1** filter, esp. through small holes. **2** prepare in a percolator. □ **percolation** n.

percolator n. coffee pot in which boiling water is circulated repeatedly through ground coffee held in a perforated drum.

percussion n. playing of a musical instrument by striking it with a stick etc. □ **percussive** adj.

perdition n. eternal damnation.

peregrine n. a kind of falcon.

peremptory adj. imperious. □ **peremptorily** adv.
■ *colloq.* bossy, domineering, high-handed, imperious, overbearing.

perennial adj. **1** lasting a long time. **2** constantly recurring. **3** (of plants) living for several years. ● n. perennial plant. □ **perennially** adv.

perfect adj. /pérfikt/ **1** complete, entire. **2** faultless. **3** exact. ● v. /perfékt/ make perfect. □ **perfectly** adv., **perfection** n.
■ adj. **1** complete, entire, intact, undamaged, whole; absolute, out and out, outright, thorough, total, unmitigated, utter. **2** exemplary, excellent, faultless, flawless, ideal, incomparable, inimitable, matchless, peerless, superb, superlative, supreme, wonderful. **3** accurate, correct, exact, faithful, precise. ● v. improve, polish, refine.

perfectionism n. uncompromising pursuit of perfection. □ **perfectionist** n.

perfidious adj. treacherous, disloyal. □ **perfidy** n.

perforate v. make hole(s) through. □ **perforation** n.
■ bore through, penetrate, pierce, prick, puncture.

perform v. **1** carry into effect. **2** go through (a play, ceremony, etc.). **3** function. **4** act, sing, esp. in public. □ **performer** n., **performance** n.
■ **1** accomplish, achieve, bring off, carry out, complete, discharge, do, effect, execute, fulfil. **3** function, go, operate, run, work.

perfume n. **1** sweet smell. **2** fragrant liquid for applying to the body. ● v. give a sweet smell to.
■ n. **1** aroma, bouquet, fragrance, scent, smell. **2** eau-de-Cologne, scent, toilet water.

perfumery n. perfumes.

perfunctory adj. done or doing things without much care or interest. □ **perfunctorily** adv.
■ brief, careless, casual, cursory, desultory, hasty, hurried, offhand, quick, rapid, sketchy, superficial.

pergola n. arch of trellis-work with climbing plants trained over it.

perhaps adv. it may be, possibly.

pericardium n. membranous sac enclosing the heart.

perigee n. point nearest to the earth in the moon's orbit.

peril n. serious danger.
■ danger, jeopardy, risk, threat.

perilous adj. full of risk, dangerous. □ **perilously** adv.
■ dangerous, hazardous, risky, unsafe.

perimeter n. **1** outer edge of an area. **2** length of this.

period *n.* **1** length or portion of time. **2** occurrence of menstruation. **3** sentence. **4** full stop in punctuation. ● *adj.* characteristic of a past age.
■ *n.* **1** duration, interval, patch, spell, stretch, term, time, while; age, epoch, era.

periodic *adj.* happening at esp. regular intervals. □ **periodicity** *n.*
■ cyclical, periodical, recurrent, regular, repeated.

periodical *adj.* periodic. ● *n.* magazine etc. published at regular intervals. □ **periodically** *adv.*
■ *n.* journal, magazine, monthly, newspaper, organ, paper, publication, quarterly, weekly.

peripatetic *adj.* going from place to place.

peripheral *adj.* **1** of or on the periphery. **2** of minor but not central importance to something.
■ **1** external, outer, outside. **2** incidental, inessential, marginal, minor, secondary, unimportant.

periphery *n.* **1** boundary, edge. **2** outer or surrounding area.
■ **1** border, boundary, edge, fringe, margin, perimeter.

periscope *n.* tube with mirror(s) by which a person in a submarine etc. can see things above.

perish *v.* **1** suffer destruction, die. **2** rot.
■ **1** be killed, die, expire, lose one's life. **2** decay, decompose, deteriorate, rot.

perishable *adj.* liable to decay or go bad in a short time.

perishing *adj.* (*colloq.*) very cold.

peritoneum *n.* membrane lining the abdominal cavity.

peritonitis *n.* inflammation of the peritoneum.

periwinkle[1] *n.* trailing plant with blue or white flowers.

periwinkle[2] *n.* winkle.

perjure *v.* **perjure oneself** lie under oath.

perjury *n.* deliberate giving of false evidence while under oath.

perk[1] *v.* **perk up 1** cheer up. **2** brighten or smarten up.

perk[2] *n.* (*colloq.*) perquisite.

perky *adj.* (**-ier, -iest**) lively and cheerful.
■ animated, *colloq.* bouncy, bright, bubbly, buoyant, cheerful, chirpy, energetic, jaunty, lively, spirited, vivacious.

perm[1] *n.* permanent artificial wave in the hair. ● *v.* give a perm to.

perm[2] *n.* permutation. ● *v.* make a permutation of.

permafrost *n.* permanently frozen subsoil in polar regions.

permanent *adj.* lasting indefinitely. □ **permanently** *adv.*, **permanence** *n.*
■ abiding, enduring, everlasting, immutable, indestructible, invariable, lasting, long-lasting, perennial, perpetual, unchangeable, unchanging, undying, unending.

permeable *adj.* able to be permeated by fluids etc. □ **permeability** *n.*

permeate *v.* pass or flow into every part of. □ **permeation** *n.*
■ pervade, saturate, seep through, soak through, spread through.

permissible *adj.* allowable.
■ acceptable, allowable, allowed, lawful, legal, legitimate, *colloq.* OK, permitted, sanctioned.

permission *n.* consent or authorization to do something.
■ approbation, approval, assent, authorization, consent, dispensation, leave, licence, sanction.

permissive *adj.* tolerant, liberal. □ **permissiveness** *n.*
■ broad-minded, easygoing, indulgent, lax, lenient, liberal, tolerant.

permit *v.* /parmit/ (**permitted**) **1** give consent to, authorize. **2** make possible. ● *n.* /pérmit/ written permission, esp. for entry to a place.
■ *v.* **1** accept, agree to, allow, authorize, consent to, let, license, sanction, tolerate. **2** allow, enable, entitle. ● *n.* licence, pass, warrant.

permutation *n.* variation in the order of a set of things.

pernicious *adj.* harmful.

pernickety *adj.* (*colloq.*) fastidious.

peroration *n.* concluding part of a speech.

peroxide *n.* compound of hydrogen used to bleach hair. ● *v.* bleach with this.

perpendicular *adj.* **1** at an angle of 90° to a line or surface. **2** upright, vertical. ● *n.* perpendicular line or direction.

perpetrate *v.* commit (a crime), be guilty of (a blunder). □ **perpetration** *n.*, **perpetrator** *n.*

perpetual *adj.* **1** lasting. **2** not ceasing. □ **perpetually** *adv.*
■ **1** enduring, eternal, everlasting, lasting, never-ending, perennial, permanent, un-

dying, unending. **2** ceaseless, constant, continual, continuous, incessant, non-stop, persistent, unceasing, uninterrupted, unremitting.

perpetuate v. preserve from being forgotten or from going out of use. □ **perpetuation** n.

perpetuity n. **in perpetuity** for ever.

perplex v. bewilder, puzzle. □ **perplexity** n.

■ baffle, colloq. bamboozle, bemuse, bewilder, confound, confuse, disconcert, floor, colloq. flummox, mystify, puzzle, colloq. stump, colloq. throw.

perquisite n. profit or privilege given in addition to wages.

perry n. drink resembling cider, made from fermented pears.

persecute v. **1** treat with hostility because of race or religion. **2** harass. □ **persecution** n., **persecutor** n.

■ **1** abuse, ill-treat, mistreat, oppress, torment, torture, victimize, tyrannize. **2** annoy, badger, bother, harass, harry, colloq. hassle, hound, pester, colloq. plague.

persevere v. continue in spite of difficulties. □ **perseverance** n.

■ carry on, continue, keep going, persist, colloq. soldier on.

persimmon n. **1** edible orange plum-like fruit. **2** tree bearing this.

persist v. **1** continue firmly or obstinately. **2** continue to exist.

■ **1** be persistent, carry on, keep going, persevere, colloq. soldier on. **2** continue, endure, keep on, last, remain, survive.

persistent adj. **1** continuing obstinately, persisting. **2** constantly repeated. □ **persistence** n., **persistently** adv.

■ **1** determined, dogged, indefatigable, insistent, obstinate, persevering, pertinacious, resolute, stubborn, tenacious, unflagging. **2** constant, continual, continuous, incessant, interminable, non-stop, perpetual, unceasing, unending, unremitting.

person n. **1** individual human being. **2** one's body. **3** (in grammar) one of the three classes of personal pronouns and verb forms, referring to the person(s) speaking, spoken to, or spoken of. □ **in person** physically present.

■ **1** creature, human (being), individual, soul.

persona n. (pl. **-ae**) personality as perceived by others.

personable adj. attractive in appearance or manner.

personage n. person, esp. an important one.

personal adj. **1** of one's own. **2** of or involving a person's private life. **3** referring to a person. **4** done in person. □ **personally** adv.

■ **1** individual, particular, peculiar, unique. **2** confidential, intimate, private, secret.

personality n. **1** person's distinctive character. **2** well-known person.

■ **1** character, disposition, make-up, nature, persona, temperament. **2** celebrity, luminary, personage, star.

personalize v. identify as belonging to a particular person. □ **personalization** n.

personify v. **1** represent in human form or as having human characteristics. **2** embody in one's behaviour. □ **personification** n.

■ **2** embody, epitomize, exemplify, represent, symbolize, typify.

personnel n. employees, staff.

perspective n. **1** art of drawing so as to give an effect of solidity and relative position. **2** point of view. □ **in perspective 1** according to the rules of perspective. **2** not distorting a thing's relative importance.

■ **2** angle, outlook, point of view, standpoint, view, viewpoint.

perspicacious adj. showing great insight. □ **perspicaciously** adv., **perspicacity** n.

perspire v. sweat. □ **perspiration** n.

persuade v. cause (a person) to believe or do something by reasoning. □ **persuader** n.

■ coax, convince, get round, induce, inveigle, prevail on, prompt, sway, talk into, wheedle into, win over.

persuasion n. **1** persuading. **2** persuasiveness. **3** religious belief or sect.

persuasive adj. able or trying to persuade people. □ **persuasively** adv., **persuasiveness** n.

■ cogent, convincing, compelling, effective, forceful, influential, weighty.

pert adj. **1** cheeky. **2** lively. □ **pertly** adv., **pertness** n.

pertain v. **pertain to 1** be relevant to. **2** belong to as a part.

■ **1** affect, apply to, be relevant to, concern, have a bearing on, refer to, relate to.

pertinacious *adj.* persistent and determined. □ **pertinaciously** *adv.*, **pertinacity** *n.*

pertinent *adj.* relevant. □ **pertinently** *adv.*, **pertinence** *n.*

■ applicable, appropriate, apposite, fitting, germane, relevant, suitable, to the point.

perturb *v.* disturb greatly, make uneasy. □ **perturbation** *n.*

■ agitate, disconcert, distress, disturb, fluster, make anxious *or* uneasy, ruffle, trouble, unsettle, upset, worry.

peruse /pərōoz/ *v.* read carefully. □ **perusal** *n.*

■ examine, inspect, pore over, read, scan, scrutinize, study.

pervade *v.* spread throughout (a thing). □ **pervasive** *adj.*

■ fill, permeate, spread through, suffuse.

perverse *adj.* obstinately doing something different from what is reasonable or required. □ **perversely** *adv.*, **perversity** *n.*

■ awkward, contrary, *colloq.* cussed, difficult, obstinate, refractory, self-willed, stubborn, uncooperative, wayward, wilful.

pervert *v.* /pərvért/ **1** turn (a thing) aside from its proper use. **2** lead astray, corrupt. ● *n.* /pérvert/ perverted person. □ **perversion** *n.*

■ **1** distort, falsify, misapply, misconstrue, misrepresent, twist. **2** corrupt, deprave, lead astray, warp.

pervious *adj.* **1** permeable. **2** penetrable.

peseta *n.* unit of money in Spain.

peso *n.* (*pl.* **-os**) unit of money in several S. American countries.

pessimism *n.* tendency to take a gloomy view of things. □ **pessimist** *n.*, **pessimistic** *adj.*

■ cynicism, defeatism, despair, despondency, gloom, hopelessness. □ **pessimistic** cynical, despairing, despondent, gloomy, hopeless, negative.

pest *n.* **1** troublesome person or thing. **2** insect or animal harmful to plants, stored food, etc.

■ **1** annoyance, bother, irritant, menace, nuisance, trial.

pester *v.* annoy continually, esp. with requests or questions.

■ annoy, badger, bother, harass, harry, *colloq.* hassle, nag, persecute, *colloq.* plague, torment, worry.

pesticide *n.* substance used to destroy harmful insects etc.

pestilence *n.* deadly epidemic disease. □ **pestilential** *adj.*

pestle /péss'l/ *n.* instrument for pounding things to powder.

pet *n.* **1** tame animal treated with affection. **2** darling, favourite. ● *adj.* **1** kept as a pet. **2** favourite. ● *v.* (**petted**) **1** treat as a pet. **2** fondle. □ **pet name** name used affectionately.

■ *adj.* **1** domesticated, tame. **2** cherished, favoured, favourite, preferred, prized, special, treasured. ● *v.* **1** indulge, mollycoddle, pamper, spoil. **2** caress, fondle, pat, stroke.

petal *n.* one of the coloured outer parts of a flower head.

petite *adj.* of small dainty build.

petition *n.* **1** request, supplication. **2** formal written request, esp. one signed by many people. ● *v.* make a petition to.

■ *n.* **1** appeal, application, entreaty, plea, request, supplication. ● *v.* appeal to, ask, beg, beseech, entreat, plead with, solicit, supplicate.

petrel *n.* a kind of seabird.

petrify *v.* **1** turn or be turned into stone. **2** paralyse with fear or astonishment. □ **petrifaction** *n.*

■ **2** frighten, horrify, numb, paralyse, scare, terrify.

petrochemical *n.* substance obtained from petroleum or gas.

petrol *n.* inflammable liquid made from petroleum used as fuel in motor vehicles etc.

petroleum *n.* mineral oil found underground, refined for use as fuel or in dry-cleaning etc.

petticoat *n.* dress-length undergarment worn hanging from the shoulders or waist beneath a dress or skirt.

pettifogging *adj.* **1** trivial. **2** quibbling about petty details.

pettish *adj.* peevish, irritable.

petty *adj.* (**-ier**, **-iest**) **1** unimportant. **2** minor, on a small scale. **3** small-minded. □ **petty cash** money kept by an office etc. for small payments. **pettily** *adv.*, **pettiness** *n.*

■ **1** inconsequential, inessential, insignificant, minor, negligible, pettifogging, small, trifling, trivial, unimportant. **3** mean, small-minded, ungenerous.

petulant *adj.* peevish. ◻ **petulantly** *adv.*, **petulance** *n.*

■ bad-tempered, crabby, cross, crotchety, fractious, irritable, peevish, pettish, querulous, snappy, testy, touchy, waspish.

petunia *n.* garden plant with funnel-shaped flowers.

pew *n.* **1** long bench-like seat in a church. **2** (*colloq.*) seat.

pewter *n.* grey alloy of tin with lead or other metal.

phalanx *n.* compact mass esp. of people.

phallus *n.* (image of) the penis. ◻ **phallic** *adj.*

phantom *n.* ghost.

Pharaoh /fáirō/ *n.* title of the kings of ancient Egypt.

pharmaceutical *adj.* of or engaged in pharmacy.

pharmacist *n.* person skilled in pharmacy.

pharmacology *n.* study of the action of drugs. ◻ **pharmacological** *adj.*, **pharmacologist** *n.*

pharmacopoeia /fáamakapeea/ *n.* list or stock of drugs.

pharmacy *n.* **1** preparation and dispensing of medicinal drugs. **2** pharmacist's shop, dispensary.

pharynx *n.* cavity behind the nose and throat. ◻ **pharyngeal** *adj.*

phase *n.* stage of change or development. ● *v.* carry out in stages. ◻ **phase in** or **out** bring gradually into or out of use.

pheasant *n.* game bird with bright feathers.

phenomenal *adj.* extraordinary, remarkable.

■ amazing, astonishing, exceptional, extraordinary, fabulous, marvellous, miraculous, outstanding, prodigious, remarkable, sensational, singular, staggering, uncommon, unparalleled, unprecedented, wonderful.

phenomenon *n.* (*pl.* **-ena**) **1** fact, occurrence, or change perceived by the senses or the mind. **2** remarkable person or thing.

■ **1** experience, event, fact, happening, occurrence. **2** marvel, miracle, prodigy, sensation, wonder.

phial *n.* small bottle.

philander *v.* (of a man) flirt. ◻ **philanderer** *n.*

philanthropy *n.* love of humankind, esp. shown in benevolent acts. ◻ **philanthropist** *n.*, **philanthropic** *adj.*

■ ◻ **philanthropic** altruistic, beneficent, benevolent, charitable, generous, humanitarian, kind, magnanimous, public-spirited, unselfish.

philately *n.* stamp-collecting. ◻ **philatelic** *adj.*, **philatelist** *n.*

philistine *adj.* & *n.* uncultured (person).

philology *n.* study of languages. ◻ **philologist** *n.*, **philological** *adj.*

philosopher *n.* **1** person skilled in philosophy. **2** philosophical person.

philosophical *adj.* **1** of philosophy. **2** bearing misfortune calmly. ◻ **philosophically** *adv.*

■ **2** calm, cool, even-tempered, equable, imperturbable, patient, placid, serene, stoical, tranquil, unperturbed.

philosophize *v.* **1** theorize. **2** moralize.

philosophy *n.* **1** system or study of the basic truths and principles of the universe, life, and morals, and of human understanding of these. **2** person's principles.

■ **2** beliefs, convictions, ideas, ideology, principles, tenets, values.

philtre *n.* magic potion.

phlegm /flem/ *n.* bronchial mucus ejected by coughing.

phlegmatic *adj.* **1** not easily excited or agitated. **2** sluggish, apathetic. ◻ **phlegmatically** *adv.*

■ **1** calm, collected, composed, cool, impassive, imperturbable, placid, serene, tranquil, *colloq.* unflappable. **2** apathetic, indifferent, lethargic, listless, sluggish, stolid, unresponsive.

phlox *n.* plant bearing a cluster of red, purple, or white flowers.

phobia *n.* abnormal fear or great dislike. ◻ **phobic** *adj.* & *n.*

■ abhorrence, aversion, detestation, dread, fear, hatred, horror, loathing, terror.

phoenix /féeniks/ *n.* mythical Arabian bird said to burn itself and rise again from its ashes.

phone *n.* & *v.* (*colloq.*) telephone. ◻ **phone book** telephone directory. **phone-in** *n.* broadcast programme in which listeners participate by telephone.

phonetic *adj.* **1** of or representing speech sounds. **2** (of spelling) corresponding to pronunciation. ◻ **phonetically** *adv.*

phonetics *n.* study or representation of speech sounds. ◻ **phonetician** *n.*

phoney (*colloq.*) *adj.* (**-ier, -iest**) sham.
● *n.* phoney person or thing.

phosphate *n.* fertilizer containing phosphorus.

phosphorescent *adj.* luminous.
□ **phosphorescence** *n.*

phosphorus *n.* **1** non-metallic chemical element. **2** wax-like form of this appearing luminous in the dark.

photo *n.* (*pl.* **-os**) photograph. □ **photo finish** close finish where the winner is decided by a photograph.

photocopy *n.* photographed copy of a document. ● *v.* make a photocopy of. □ **photocopier** *n.*

photoelectric cell electronic device emitting an electric current when light falls on it.

photogenic *adj.* looking attractive in photographs.

photograph *n.* picture formed by the chemical action of light or other radiation on sensitive material. ● *v.* take a photograph of. □ **photographer** *n.*, **photography** *n.*, **photographic** *adj.*

photosynthesis *n.* process by which green plants use sunlight to convert carbon dioxide and water into complex substances.

phrase *n.* **1** group of words forming a unit. **2** unit in a melody. ● *v.* **1** express in words. **2** divide (music) into phrases. □ **phrasal** *adj.*

phraseology *n.* the way something is worded.

phylum *n.* (*pl.* **phyla**) major division of the plant or animal kingdom.

physical *adj.* **1** of the body. **2** of matter or the laws of nature. **3** of physics. □ **physical geography** study of earth's natural features. **physically** *adv.*

■ **1** bodily, corporal. **2** actual, concrete, corporeal, material, palpable, real, solid, tangible; carnal, earthly, worldly.

physician *n.* doctor, esp. one specializing in medicine as distinct from surgery.

physics *n.* study of the properties and interactions of matter and energy. □ **physicist** *n.*

physiognomy /fizziónnəmi/ *n.* features of a person's face.

physiology *n.* study of the bodily functions of living organisms. □ **physiological** *adj.*, **physiologist** *n.*

physiotherapy *n.* treatment of an injury etc. by massage and exercises. □ **physiotherapist** *n.*

physique *n.* bodily structure and muscular development.

■ body, build, figure, form, frame, shape.

pi *n.* Greek letter π used as a symbol for the ratio of a circle's circumference to its diameter (about 3.14).

pianist *n.* person who plays the piano.

piano *n.* (*pl.* **-os**) keyboard instrument with metal strings struck by hammers.

pianoforte *n.* piano.

piazza /piátsə/ *n.* public square or market place.

picador *n.* mounted bullfighter with a lance.

picaresque *adj.* (of fiction) dealing with the adventures of rogues.

piccalilli *n.* pickle of chopped vegetables and hot spices.

piccolo *n.* (*pl.* **-os**) small flute.

pick[1] *n.* **1** pickaxe. **2** plectrum.

pick[2] *v.* **1** select. **2** use a pointed instrument or the fingers or beak etc. to make (a hole) in or remove bits from (a thing). **3** detach (flower or fruit) from the plant bearing it. ● *n.* **1** picking. **2** selection. **3** best part. □ **pick a lock** open it with a tool other than a key. **pick a quarrel** provoke one deliberately. **pick holes in** find fault with. **pick off 1** pluck off. **2** shoot or destroy one by one. **pick on 1** nag, find fault with. **2** select. **pick out 1** select. **2** discern. **pick up 1** lift or take up. **2** call for and take away. **3** acquire by chance or without effort. **4** succeed in seeing or hearing by use of apparatus. **5** recover health, improve. **6** gather (speed). **7** become acquainted with casually. **pick-up** *n.* **1** small open motor truck. **2** stylus-holder in a record player.

■ *v.* **1** choose, decide on, elect, go for, opt for, pick on or out, plump for, select, single out. **3** collect, gather, harvest, pluck. ● *n.* **2** choice, option, selection. **3** best part, cream, flower. □ **pick on 1** carp at, criticize, *colloq.* get at, find fault with, nag. **pick out 2** discern, distinguish, identify, make out, perceive, recognize, see, *colloq.* spot. **pick up 3** acquire, come by, gain, get, find, obtain. **5** be on the mend, get better, improve, make progress, rally, recover.

pickaxe *n.* tool with sharp-pointed iron crossbar for breaking up ground etc.

picket *n.* **1** person(s) stationed at a workplace to dissuade others from entering during a strike. **2** party of sentries. **3** pointed stake set in the ground.

● *v.* (**picketed**) **1** form a picket on (a workplace). **2** enclose with stakes.

pickings *n.pl.* odd gains or perquisites.

pickle *n.* **1** vegetables preserved in vinegar or brine. **2** this liquid. **3** (*colloq.*) plight, mess. ● *v.* preserve in pickle.

pickpocket *n.* thief who steals from people's pockets.

picnic *n.* informal outdoor meal. ● *v.* (**picnicked**) take part in a picnic. □ **picnicker** *n.*

pictograph *n.* pictorial symbol used as a form of writing.

pictorial *adj.* **1** of, in, or like a picture or pictures. **2** illustrated. □ **pictorially** *adv.*

picture *n.* **1** representation of person(s) or object(s) etc. made by painting, drawing, or photography etc. **2** beautiful thing. **3** mental image. **4** description. **5** cinema film. ● *v.* **1** depict. **2** imagine.

■ *n.* **1** drawing, illustration, painting, portrait, print, representation, sketch; photo, photograph, shot, snap, snapshot. **3** idea, image, impression, notion. **4** description, portrait, portrayal, representation. **5** film, motion picture, *US colloq.* movie. ● *v.* **1** depict, draw, illustrate, paint, portray, represent. **2** envisage, fancy, imagine, visualize.

picturesque *adj.* **1** forming a pleasant scene. **2** (of words or description) very expressive.

■ **1** beautiful, charming, delightful, idyllic, lovely, pleasing, scenic. **2** colourful, graphic, vivid.

pidgin *n.* simplified language, esp. used between speakers of different languages.

pie *n.* baked dish of meat, fish, or fruit covered with pastry or other crust. □ **pie chart** diagram representing quantities as sectors of a circle.

piebald *adj.* with irregular patches of white and black.

piece *n.* **1** part, portion. **2** thing regarded as a unit. **3** musical, literary, or artistic composition. **4** small object used in board games. ● *v.* make by putting pieces together. □ **of a piece 1** of the same kind. **2** consistent. **piece-work** *n.* work paid according to the quantity done.

■ *n.* **1** part, portion, section, segment; bit, block, chip, chunk, crumb, fragment, lump, particle, scrap, shard, shred, slice, sliver, wedge. **2** component, constituent, element, unit. **3** article, composition, essay, poem, story, work.

piecemeal *adj.* & *adv.* done piece by piece, part at a time.

pied *adj.* particoloured.

pied-à-terre /pýaydaatáir/ *n.* (*pl.* **pieds-à-terre**) small dwelling for occasional use.

pier *n.* **1** structure built out into the sea. **2** pillar supporting an arch or bridge.

pierce *v.* **1** go into or through like a sharp-pointed instrument. **2** make (a hole) in.

■ **1** impale, lance, penetrate, puncture, skewer, spear, transfix. **2** bore into, drill into, perforate.

piercing *adj.* **1** (of cold or wind etc.) penetrating sharply. **2** (of sound) shrilly audible.

■ **1** biting, bitter, chilling, cold, freezing, icy, keen. **2** harsh, high-pitched, loud, shrill, penetrating, strident.

piety *n.* piousness.

■ devoutness, holiness, piousness, sanctity; sanctimoniousness, self-righteousness.

piffle *n.* (*colloq.*) nonsense.

pig *n.* **1** animal with short legs, cloven hooves, and a blunt snout. **2** (*colloq.*) greedy or unpleasant person. □ **pig-iron** *n.* crude iron from a smelting-furnace.

pigeon *n.* **1** bird of the dove family. **2** (*colloq.*) person's business or responsibility.

pigeon-hole *n.* small compartment in a desk or cabinet. ● *v.* **1** put away for future consideration or indefinitely. **2** classify.

piggery *n.* **1** pig farm. **2** pigsty.

piggy *adj.* like a pig. □ **piggyback** *adv.* & *n.* (ride) on a person's back or on top of a larger object. **piggy bank** money box shaped like a pig.

pigheaded *adj.* obstinate.

piglet *n.* young pig.

pigment *n.* colouring matter.

pigsty *n.* pen for pigs.

pigtail *n.* long hair worn in a plait at the back of the head.

pike *n.* **1** spear with long wooden shaft. **2** (*pl.* **pike**) large voracious freshwater fish.

pilaff *n.* = **pilau**.

pilaster *n.* rectangular usu. ornamental column.

pilau *n.* oriental dish of rice with meat, spices, etc.

pilchard *n.* small sea fish related to the herring.

pile¹ n. **1** a number of things lying one upon another. **2** (*colloq.*) large amount. **3** large imposing building. ● v. heap, stack, load. □ **pile up** accumulate. **pile-up** n. collision of several vehicles.

    ■ n. **1** accumulation, collection, heap, mass, mound, mountain, stack. ● v. heap (up), load (up), stack (up). □ **pile up** accumulate, amass, collect, hoard, stockpile. **pile-up** accident, collision, crash, smash.

pile² n. heavy beam driven vertically into ground as a support for a building or bridge.

pile³ n. cut or uncut loops on the surface of fabric.

pile⁴ n. haemorrhoid.

pilfer v. steal (small items or in small quantities). □ **pilferer** n.

    ■ filch, lift, misappropriate, *sl.* nick, *sl.* pinch, purloin, *colloq.* snaffle, steal, take, thieve.

pilgrim n. person who travels to a sacred place as an act of religious devotion. □ **pilgrimage** n.

pill n. **1** small ball or piece of medicinal substance for swallowing whole. **2** (**the pill**) contraceptive pill.

    ■ **1** capsule, lozenge, pastille, tablet.

pillage n. & v. plunder.

pillar n. vertical structure used as a support or ornament.

    ■ column, pilaster, pile, pole, post, stanchion, support, upright.

pillion n. saddle for a passenger behind the driver of a motor cycle. □ **ride pillion** ride on this.

pillory n. wooden frame in which offenders were locked and exposed to public abuse. ● v. ridicule publicly.

pillow n. cushion used (esp. in bed) for supporting the head. ● v. rest on or as if on a pillow.

pilot n. **1** person who operates an aircraft's flying-controls. **2** person qualified to steer ships into or out of a harbour. **3** guide. ● v. (**piloted**) **1** act as pilot of. **2** guide. □ **pilot-light** n. **1** small burning jet of gas which lights a larger burner. **2** electric indicator light.

    ■ n. **2** helmsman, navigator, steersman. **3** conductor, guide, leader. ● v. **1** fly, drive, navigate, sail, steer. **2** conduct, direct, guide, lead, shepherd, steer.

pimento n. (*pl.* **-os**) **1** allspice. **2** sweet pepper.

pimp n. man who solicits clients for a prostitute or brothel.

pimple n. small inflamed spot on the skin. □ **pimply** adj.

pin n. **1** short pointed piece of metal usu. with a round broadened head, used for fastening things together. **2** peg or stake of wood or metal. ● v. (**pinned**) **1** fasten with pin(s). **2** transfix. **3** hold down and make unable to move. **4** attach, fix. □ **pin down 1** establish clearly. **2** bind by a promise. **pins and needles** tingling sensation. **pin-up** n. (*colloq.*) picture of an attractive or famous person.

    ■ n. **2** bolt, dowel, nail, peg, spike, tack. ● v. **1** clip, fasten, secure, staple, tack. **2** impale, skewer, spike, transfix. **3** hold, pinion. **4** affix, attach, fix, stick.

pinafore n. apron. □ **pinafore dress** sleeveless dress worn over a blouse or jumper.

pincers n. **1** tool with pivoted jaws for gripping and pulling things. **2** claw-like part of a lobster etc.

pinch v. **1** squeeze between two surfaces, esp. between finger and thumb. **2** (*sl.*) steal. ● n. **1** pinching. **2** stress of circumstances. **3** small amount. □ **at a pinch** if really necessary.

pine¹ n. **1** evergreen tree with needleshaped leaves. **2** its wood.

pine² v. **1** waste away with grief etc. **2** feel an intense longing.

pineapple n. **1** large juicy tropical fruit. **2** plant bearing this.

ping n. short sharp ringing sound. ● v. make this sound.

ping-pong n. table tennis.

pinion¹ n. bird's wing. ● v. restrain by holding or binding the arms or legs.

pinion² n. small cogwheel.

pink¹ adj. pale red. ● n. **1** pink colour. **2** garden plant with fragrant flowers. □ **in the pink** (*colloq.*) in very good health. **pinkish** adj.

pink² v. **1** pierce slightly. **2** cut a zigzag edge on (fabric).

pink³ v. (of an engine) make slight explosive sounds when running imperfectly.

pinnacle n. **1** pointed ornament on a roof. **2** peak. **3** highest point.

    ■ **2** crest, crown, peak, summit, tip, top. **3** acme, apex, climax, culmination, height, highest point, peak, top, zenith.

pinpoint v. locate precisely.

pinstripe n. very narrow stripe in cloth fabric. □ **pinstriped** adj.

pint n. measure for liquids, one-eighth of a gallon (0.568 litre).

pioneer *n.* person who is one of the first to explore a new region or subject. ● *v.* 1 initiate, originate. 2 act as a pioneer.

pious *adj.* 1 devout in religion. 2 sanctimonious. □ **piously** *adv.*, **piousness** *n.*
■ 1 devout, faithful, God-fearing, good, holy, religious, reverent, saintly, virtuous. 2 goody-goody, hypocritical, sanctimonious, self-righteous.

pip¹ *n.* small seed in fruit.

pip² *n.* star showing rank on an army officer's uniform.

pip³ *v.* (**pipped**) (*colloq.*) defeat by a small margin.

pip⁴ *n.* short high-pitched sound.

pipe *n.* 1 tube through which something can flow. 2 wind instrument. 3 (*pl.*) bagpipes. 4 narrow tube with a bowl at one end for smoking tobacco. ● *v.* 1 convey through pipe(s). 2 play (music) on pipe(s). 3 utter in a shrill voice. □ **pipe down** (*colloq.*) be quiet. **pipedream** *n.* fanciful hope or scheme.

pipeline *n.* 1 long pipe for conveying oil etc. across country. 2 channel of supply or information. □ **in the pipeline** on the way, in preparation.

piper *n.* player of pipe(s).

pipette *n.* slender tube for transferring or measuring small amounts of liquid.

pipit *n.* small bird resembling a lark.

pippin *n.* a kind of apple.

piquant *adj.* pleasantly sharp in taste or smell. □ **piquancy** *n.*
■ pungent, savoury, sharp, spicy, tangy, tasty.

pique /peek/ *v.* hurt the pride of. ● *n.* feeling of hurt pride.

piquet /peekay/ *n.* card game for two players.

piranha /piraana/ *n.* fierce S. American freshwater fish.

pirate *n.* 1 person on a ship who robs another ship at sea or raids a coast. 2 one who infringes copyright or business rights, or broadcasts without due authorization. ● *v.* reproduce (a book etc.) without due authorization. □ **piratical** *adj.*, **piracy** *n.*

pirouette *n.* & *v.* spin on the toe in dancing.

pistachio /pistaashiō/ *n.* (*pl.* **-os**) a kind of nut.

piste *n.* ski run.

pistil *n.* seed-producing part of a flower.

pistol *n.* small gun.

piston *n.* sliding disc or cylinder inside a tube, esp. as part of an engine or pump.

pit *n.* 1 hole in the ground. 2 coal mine. 3 sunken area. 4 place where racing cars are refuelled etc. during a race. ● *v.* (**pitted**) 1 make pits or depressions in. 2 match or set in competition.
■ *n.* 1 cavity, chasm, crater, hole, trough. 2 coal mine, excavation, mine, quarry, working. 3 dent, depression, hollow, indentation.

pitch¹ *n.* dark tarry substance. □ **pitch-black**, **-dark** *adjs.*

pitch² *v.* 1 throw. 2 erect (a tent or camp). 3 express in a particular style or at a particular level. 4 fall heavily. 5 (of a ship) plunge forward and back alternately. ● *n.* 1 process of pitching. 2 steepness. 3 intensity. 4 degree of highness or lowness of a music note or voice. 5 place where a street trader or performer is stationed. 6 playing field. □ **pitched battle** one fought from prepared positions. **pitch in** (*colloq.*) set to work vigorously.
■ *v.* 1 cast, *colloq.* chuck, fling, hurl, launch, lob, *colloq.* sling, throw, toss. 2 erect, put up. 4 fall (headlong), plummet, plunge, topple, tumble. 5 heel, list, lurch, rock, roll, toss. ● *n.* 2 angle, inclination, slant, slope, steepness, tilt. 3 degree, height, intensity, level. 4 intonation, modulation, timbre, tone. 6 field, ground, playing field.

pitchblende *n.* mineral ore (uranium oxide) yielding radium.

pitcher¹ *n.* baseball player who delivers the ball to the batter.

pitcher² *n.* large jug.

pitchfork *n.* long-handled fork for lifting and tossing hay.

piteous *adj.* deserving or arousing pity. □ **piteously** *adv.*
■ distressing, heartbreaking, moving, pathetic, pitiable, pitiful, plaintive, poignant, sad.

pitfall *n.* unsuspected danger or difficulty.
■ danger, hazard, peril; catch, difficulty, snag.

pith *n.* 1 spongy tissue in stems or fruits. 2 essential part.
■ 2 core, crux, essence, gist, heart, kernel, nub, substance.

pithy *adj.* (**-ier**, **-iest**) brief and full of meaning. □ **pithily** *adv.*
■ 2 brief, compact, concise, laconic, succinct, terse.

pitiful *adj.* deserving or arousing pity or contempt. □ **pitifully** *adv.*
■ distressing, heartbreaking, moving, pathetic, piteous, pitiable, plaintive, poignant, sad, wretched; contemptible, miserable, *colloq.* pathetic, poor, sorry.

pitta *n.* a kind of flat bread.

pittance *n.* very small allowance of money.

pituitary gland gland at the base of the brain which influences bodily growth and functions.

pity *n.* **1** feeling of sorrow for another's suffering. **2** cause for regret. ● *v.* feel pity for. □ **take pity on** pity and try to help.
■ *n.* **1** compassion, sorrow, sympathy. **2** shame. ● *v.* feel sorry for, have compassion for, sympathize with, take pity on.

pivot *n.* central point or shaft on which a thing turns or swings. ● *v.* (**pivoted**) turn on a pivot. □ **pivotal** *adj.*

pixie *n.* a kind of fairy.

pizza *n.* layer of dough baked with a savoury topping.

pizzicato *adv.* by plucking the strings of a violin etc. instead of using the bow.

placard *n.* poster or similar notice. ● *v.* put up placards on.

placate *v.* conciliate. □ **placation** *n.*, **placatory** *adj.*
■ appease, calm (down), conciliate, mollify, pacify, soothe.

place *n.* **1** particular part of space or of an area etc. **2** particular town, district, building, etc. **3** position. **4** duty appropriate to one's rank. ● *v.* **1** put into a particular place, arrange. **2** locate. **3** identify. **4** put or give (an order for goods etc.). □ **be placed** (in a race) be among the first three. **out of place 1** in the wrong place. **2** unsuitable.
■ *n.* **1** area, location, point, position, scene, setting, site, spot. **2** area, district, locality, neighbourhood, quarter, region; city, hamlet, town, village. **3** grade, rank, standing, station, *status;* job, position, post, situation; niche, slot. **4** concern, duty, function, job, responsibility, role, task. ● *v.* **1** arrange, deposit, dispose, dump, lay, position, park, put, rest, set (out), *colloq.* stick. **2** locate, position, site, situate. **3** identify, recognize, remember.

placebo /pləséebō/ *n.* (*pl.* **-os**) harmless substance given as medicine, esp. to humour a patient.

placement *n.* placing.

placenta *n.* (*pl.* **-ae**) organ in the womb that nourishes the foetus. □ **placental** *adj.*

placid *adj.* calm, not easily upset. □ **placidly** *adv.*, **placidity** *n.*
■ calm, collected, composed, cool, easygoing, equable, even-tempered, gentle, imperturbable, mild, peaceful, phlegmatic, tranquil, *colloq.* unflappable.

plagiarize /pláyjərīz/ *v.* take and use (another's writings etc.) as one's own. □ **plagiarism** *n.*, **plagiarist** *n.*

plague *n.* **1** deadly contagious disease. **2** infestation. ● *v.* (*colloq.*) annoy, pester.
■ *n.* **1** epidemic, pestilence. ● *v.* annoy, badger, bother, harass, harry, *colloq.* hassle, hound, nag, persecute, pester, torment, worry.

plaice *n.* (*pl.* **plaice**) marine flatfish.

plaid /plad/ *n.* **1** long piece of woollen cloth worn as part of Highland costume. **2** tartan pattern.

plain *adj.* **1** unmistakable, easy to see, hear, or understand. **2** not elaborate. **3** candid. **4** ordinary, without affectation. **5** not good-looking. ● *adv.* plainly. ● *n.* large area of level country. □ **plain clothes** civilian clothes, not a uniform. **plain sailing** easy course of action. **plainly** *adv.*, **plainness** *n.*
■ *adj.* **1** apparent, clear, evident, manifest, obvious, patent, transparent, unmistakable; comprehensible, intelligible, lucid, simple, uncomplicated, understandable. **2** austere, bare, basic, simple, spartan, stark, unadorned, undecorated, unembellished, unostentatious. **3** blunt, candid, direct, forthright, frank, honest, open, outspoken, straightforward. **4** homely, modest, ordinary, simple, unassuming, unpretentious, unsophisticated, workaday. **5** *US* homely, ugly, unattractive, unprepossessing. ● *n.* grassland, pampas, prairie, savannah, steppe, tundra.

plaintiff *n.* person that brings an action in a court of law.

plaintive *adj.* sounding sad. □ **plaintively** *adv.*
■ doleful, melancholy, mournful, pathetic, piteous, pitiful, plangent, sad, sorrowful, woeful.

plait /plat/ *v.* weave (three or more strands) into one rope-like length. ● *n.* something plaited.

plan *n.* **1** diagram showing the relative position of parts of a building or town etc. **2** method thought out in advance. **3**

intention. ● v. (**planned**) 1 intend. 2 make a plan (of). □ **planner** n.

■ n. 1 blueprint, chart, design, diagram, drawing, layout, map. 2 method, procedure, scheme, strategy, system, tactic. 3 aim, ambition, design, end, intent, intention, purpose. ● v. 1 aim, contemplate, design, intend, mean, propose, purpose. 2 design, lay out, map out.

plane[1] n. tall spreading tree with broad leaves.

plane[2] n. 1 level surface. 2 level of thought or development. 3 aeroplane. ● adj. level.

■ n. 2 level, stratum. 3 aeroplane, aircraft, airliner, jet. ● adj. even, flat, horizontal, level.

plane[3] n. tool for smoothing wood by paring shavings from it. ● v. smooth or pare with this.

planet n. large body in space that revolves round the sun. □ **planetary** adj.

planetarium n. room with a domed ceiling on which lights are projected to show the positions of the stars and planets.

plangent adj. resonant, loud and mournful.

plank n. long flat piece of timber.

plankton n. minute life-forms floating in the sea, rivers, etc.

plant n. 1 living organism with neither the power of movement nor special organs of digestion. 2 factory. 3 its machinery. ● v. 1 place in soil for growing. 2 place in position.

plantain[1] n. herb whose seed is used as birdseed.

plantain[2] n. 1 tropical banana-like fruit. 2 tree bearing this.

plantation n. 1 area planted with trees or cultivated plants. 2 estate on which cotton, tobacco, or tea etc. is cultivated.

plaque n. 1 commemorative plate fixed on a wall. 2 film forming on teeth and gums.

plasma n. 1 colourless fluid part of blood. 2 a kind of gas. □ **plasmic** adj.

plaster n. 1 mixture of lime, sand, and water etc. used for coating walls. 2 sticking plaster. ● v. 1 cover with plaster. 2 coat, daub. □ **plaster of Paris** white paste made from gypsum. **plasterer** n.

plastic adj. 1 able to be moulded. 2 made of plastic. ● n. synthetic substance moulded to a permanent shape. □ **plastic**

surgery repair or restoration of lost or damaged etc. tissue. **plasticity** n.

■ adj. 1 ductile, flexible, malleable, pliable, pliant, soft.

Plasticine n. [P.] plastic substance used for modelling.

plate n. 1 almost flat usu. circular utensil for holding food. 2 articles of gold, silver, or other metal. 3 flat thin sheet of metal, glass, or other material. 4 illustration on special paper in a book. 5 (colloq.) denture. ● v. cover or coat with metal. □ **plate glass** thick glass for windows etc. **plateful** n.

plateau n. (pl. **-eaux**) 1 area of level high ground. 2 steady state following an increase.

platform n. raised level surface or area, esp. from which a speaker addresses an audience.

■ dais, podium, rostrum, stage.

platinum n. silver-white metal that does not tarnish. □ **platinum blonde** woman with very light blonde hair.

platitude n. commonplace remark. □ **platitudinous** adj.

■ banality, colloq. chestnut, cliché, truism. □ **platitudinous** banal, commonplace, colloq. corny, hackneyed, stale, trite, unimaginative, unoriginal.

platonic adj. involving affection but not sexual love.

platoon n. subdivision of a military company.

platter n. large plate for food.

platypus n. (pl. **-puses**) Australian aquatic egg-laying mammal with a duck-like beak.

plaudits n.pl. applause, expression of approval.

plausible adj. 1 seeming probable. 2 persuasive but deceptive. □ **plausibly** adv., **plausibility** n.

■ 1 believable, conceivable, convincing, credible, feasible, likely, possible, probable, reasonable, tenable.

play v. 1 occupy oneself in (a game) or in other recreational activity. 2 compete against in a game. 3 move (a piece, a ball, etc.) in a game. 4 act the part of. 5 perform on (a musical instrument). 6 cause (a radio, recording, etc.) to produce sound. 7 move lightly, allow (light or water) to fall on something. ● n. 1 playing. 2 activity, operation. 3 literary work for stage or broadcast performance. 4 freedom of movement, space for this.

□ **play at** perform in a half-hearted way. **play down** minimize the importance of. **play for time** seek to gain time by delaying. **play-pen** n. portable enclosure for a young child to play in. **play safe** not take risks. **play the game** behave honourably. **play up** cause trouble, be unruly. **player** n.

■ v. **1** amuse oneself, enjoy oneself, frolic, have fun, sport. **2** compete against, contend with, pit oneself against, take on. **4** act, perform, take the role or part of. ● n. **1** amusement, fun, horseplay, merrymaking, recreation, skylarking, sport. **2** action, activity, exercise, operation, working. **3** comedy, drama, farce, tragedy. **4** flexibility, freedom, give, leeway, margin, movement, room, space. □ **play down** belittle, diminish, make light of, minimize. **play for time** delay, hesitate, procrastinate, stall, temporize.

playboy n. pleasure-loving usu. rich man.

playful adj. **1** full of fun. **2** done in fun, not serious. □ **playfully** adv., **playfulness** n.

■ **1** frisky, fun-loving, high-spirited, lively, mischievous, skittish, sportive. **2** humorous, jocular, teasing, tongue-in-cheek.

playgroup n. group of preschool children who play regularly together under supervision.

playhouse n. theatre.

playing card one of a pack or set of (usu. 52) pieces of pasteboard used in card games.

playing field field used for outdoor games.

playmate n. child's companion in play.

playwright n. writer of plays.

plea n. **1** defendant's answer to a charge in a law court. **2** appeal, entreaty. **3** excuse.

■ **2** appeal, cry, entreaty, request, supplication. **3** excuse, explanation, justification, reason.

plead v. **1** give as one's plea. **2** put forward (a case) in a law court. **3** put forward as an excuse. □ **plead with** make an earnest appeal to.

■ □ **plead with** appeal to, beg, beseech, entreat, implore, petition, request, supplicate.

pleasant adj. **1** pleasing. **2** having an agreeable manner. □ **pleasantly** adv.

■ **1** agreeable, delightful, enjoyable, entertaining, colloq. lovely, nice, pleasing,

pleasurable, satisfying. **2** affable, agreeable, amiable, charming, congenial, engaging, friendly, genial, good-natured, likeable, nice, warm, winning.

pleasantry n. friendly or humorous remark.

please v. **1** give pleasure to. **2** think fit. ● adv. polite word of request. □ **please oneself** do as one chooses.

■ v. **1** amuse, appeal to, content, delight, divert, entertain, gladden, gratify, humour, satisfy. **2** choose, desire, like, think fit, want, wish.

pleased adj. feeling or showing pleasure or satisfaction.

■ contented, delighted, glad, gratified, happy, overjoyed, satisfied, thrilled.

pleasurable adj. causing pleasure, pleasant. □ **pleasurably** adv.

pleasure n. **1** feeling of satisfaction or joy. **2** source of this.

■ **1** contentment, delight, enjoyment, gratification, happiness, joy, satisfaction. **2** delight, joy, treat.

pleat n. flat fold of cloth. ● v. make a pleat or pleats in.

plebiscite /plébbisit/ n. referendum.

plectrum n. small piece of metal, bone, or ivory for plucking the strings of a musical instrument.

pledge n. **1** thing deposited as a guarantee (e.g. that a debt will be paid). **2** token of something. **3** solemn promise. ● v. **1** deposit as a pledge. **2** promise solemnly.

■ n. **1** bond, collateral, guarantee, security, surety. **2** mark, sign, symbol, token. **3** bond, guarantee, oath, promise, undertaking, vow, word (of honour). ● v. **1** deposit, pawn. **2** promise, swear, undertake, vow.

plenary /pléenəri/ adj. **1** entire. **2** attended by all members.

plenipotentiary adj. & n. (envoy) with full powers to take action.

plenitude n. **1** abundance. **2** completeness.

plentiful adj. existing in large amounts. □ **plentifully** adv.

■ abundant, ample, bountiful, copious, generous, lavish, liberal, plenteous, profuse, rich.

plenty n. enough and more. ● adv. (colloq.) quite, fully. □ **plenteous** adj.

■ n. a lot, heaps, colloq. loads, lots, masses, colloq. oodles, colloq. piles, quantities, colloq. stacks.

plethora n. over-abundance.

pleurisy *n.* inflammation of the membrane round the lungs.

pliable *adj.* flexible. □ **pliability** *n.*
■ bendable, ductile, elastic, flexible, malleable, plastic, pliant, whippy.

pliant *adj.* pliable. □ **pliancy** *n.*

pliers *n.pl.* pincers with flat surfaces for gripping things.

plight *n.* predicament.

plimsoll *n.* canvas sports shoe.

Plimsoll line mark on a ship's side showing the legal water level when loaded.

plinth *n.* slab forming the base of a column or statue etc.

plod *v.* (**plodded**) **1** walk doggedly, trudge. **2** work slowly but steadily. □ **plodder** *n.*
■ **1** clump, lumber, stomp, tramp, trudge. **2** labour, *colloq.* plug, slave, slog, toil, work.

plonk *n.* (*colloq.*) cheap or inferior wine.

plop *n. & v.* (**plopped**) sound like something small dropping into water with no splash.

plot *n.* **1** small piece of land. **2** story in a play, novel, or film. **3** conspiracy, secret plan. ●*v.* (**plotted**) **1** make a map or chart of, mark on this. **2** plan secretly. □ **plotter** *n.*
■ *n.* **1** lot, parcel, patch, piece. **2** scenario, story. **3** conspiracy, intrigue, machination, scheme, stratagem. ●*v.* **1** chart, draw, map (out), plan; indicate, mark. **2** conspire, intrigue, scheme.

plough /plow/ *n.* implement for cutting furrows in soil and turning it up. ●*v.* **1** cut or turn up (soil etc.) with a plough. **2** make one's way laboriously. □ **ploughman** *n.*

plover *n.* a wading bird.

ploy *n.* cunning manoeuvre.
■ dodge, manoeuvre, ruse, stratagem, tactic, trick.

pluck *v.* **1** pick or pull out or away. **2** strip (a bird) of its feathers. ●*n.* **1** plucking movement. **2** courage.
■ *v.* **1** pick; grab, snatch, tear, *colloq.* yank. ●*n.* **2** boldness, bravery, courage, *colloq.* grit, *colloq.* guts, intrepidity, mettle, nerve, spirit.

plucky *adj.* (**-ier, -iest**) brave.
■ bold, brave, courageous, fearless, game, *colloq.* gutsy, intrepid, mettlesome, spirited, valiant, valorous.

plug *n.* **1** thing fitting into and stopping or filling a hole or cavity. **2** device of this kind for making an electrical connection. ●*v.* (**plugged**) **1** put a plug into. **2** (*colloq.*) work diligently. **3** (*colloq.*) advertise by frequent recommendation. □ **plug in** connect electrically by putting a plug into a socket.

plum *n.* **1** fruit with sweet pulp round a pointed stone. **2** tree bearing this. **3** reddish-purple. **4** something desirable, the best.

plumage *n.* bird's feathers.

plumb /plum/ *n.* lead weight hung on a cord (**plumb line**), used for testing depths or verticality. ●*adv.* **1** exactly. **2** (*US*) completely. ●*v.* **1** measure or test with a plumb line. **2** reach (depths). **3** get to the bottom of. **4** work or fit (things) as a plumber.

plumber /plúmmər/ *n.* person who fits and repairs plumbing.

plumbing /plúmming/ *n.* system of water pipes and drainage pipes etc. in a building.

plume *n.* **1** feather, esp. as an ornament. **2** thing(s) resembling this. □ **plumed** *adj.*

plummet *v.* (**plummeted**) fall steeply, plunge.

plump[1] *adj.* having a full rounded shape. ●*v.* make or become plump. □ **plumpness** *n.*
■ *adj.* buxom, chubby, fat, podgy, pudgy, roly-poly, rotund, stout, tubby.

plump[2] *v.* plunge abruptly. □ **plump for** choose, decide on.

plunder *v.* rob. ●*n.* **1** plundering. **2** goods etc. acquired by this.
■ *v.* despoil, loot, pillage, ransack, rifle (through), rob, sack. ●*n.* **1** depredation, looting, pillage, ransacking, robbery. **2** booty, loot, spoils, *sl.* swag.

plunge *v.* **1** thrust or go forcefully into something. **2** go down suddenly. ●*n.* plunging, dive.
■ *v.* **1** drive, push, stick, thrust. **2** descend, drop, fall (headlong), nosedive, pitch, plummet. ●*n.* descent, dive, drop, fall, nosedive.

plunger *n.* thing that works with a plunging movement.

plural *n.* form of a noun or verb used in referring to more than one person or thing. ●*adj.* **1** of this form. **2** of more than one. □ **plurality** *n.*

plus *prep.* **1** with the addition of. **2** above zero. ●*adj.* **1** more than zero. **2** more than the amount indicated. ●*n.* **1** the sign +. **2** advantage.

plush n. cloth with a long soft nap. ● adj.
1 made of plush. **2** luxurious.
■ adj. **2** de luxe, lavish, lush, luxurious,
opulent, palatial, colloq. posh, plushy,
sumptuous.

plushy adj. (**-ier, -iest**) luxurious.

plutocrat n. wealthy and influential
person. □ **plutocracy** n., **plutocratic** adj.

plutonium n. radioactive metallic element.

pluvial adj. of or caused by rain.

ply¹ n. **1** thickness or layer of wood or
cloth etc. **2** plywood.

ply² v. **1** use or wield (a tool etc.). **2** work
(at a trade). **3** keep offering or supplying.
4 (of a vehicle etc.) go to and fro.

plywood n. board made by gluing layers
with the grain crosswise.

p.m. abbr. (Latin post meridiem) after
noon.

pneumatic /nyoomáttik/ adj. filled with
or operated by compressed air.

pneumonia /nyoomóniə/ n. inflammation of the lungs.

poach v. **1** cook (an egg without its shell)
in or over boiling water. **2** simmer in a
small amount of liquid. **3** take (game or
fish) illegally. **4** trespass, encroach.
□ **poacher** n.

pocket n. **1** small bag-like part in or on a
garment. **2** one's resources of money. **3**
pouch-like compartment. **4** isolated
group or area. ● adj. suitable for carrying in one's pocket. ● v. **1** put into one's
pocket. **2** appropriate. □ **in** or **out of
pocket** having made a profit or loss.
pocket money **1** money for small personal expenses. **2** money allowed to
children. **pocketful** n.

pock-marked adj. marked by scars or
pits.

pod n. long narrow seed case.

podgy adj. (**-ier, -iest**) short and fat.
□ **podginess** n.

podium n. (pl. **-ia**) **1** projecting base. **2**
rostrum.

poem n. literary composition in verse.
■ lyric, ode, rhyme, sonnet, verse.

poet n. writer of poems.

poetic adj. (also **poetical**) of or like
poetry. □ **poetically** adv.

poetry n. **1** poems. **2** poet's work. **3**
beautiful and graceful quality.

pogo stick stilt-like toy with a spring,
for jumping about on.

pogrom n. organized massacre.

poignant adj. arousing sympathy, deeply
moving. □ **poignantly** adv., **poignancy** n.
■ affecting, emotional, emotive, moving,
pathetic, piteous, pitiable, pitiful, sad,
touching, upsetting.

poinsettia n. plant with large scarlet
bracts.

point n. **1** tapered or sharp end, tip. **2**
promontory. **3** particular place, moment,
or stage. **4** unit of measurement or
scoring. **5** item, detail. **6** characteristic. **7**
sense, purpose. **8** advantage or value. **9**
significant or essential thing. **10** electrical socket. **11** movable rail for directing a train from one line to another. ● v.
1 aim, direct (a finger or weapon etc.). **2**
have a certain direction. **3** fill in (joints
of brickwork) with mortar or cement.
□ **on the point of** on the verge of (an action). **point-blank** adj. **1** aimed or fired at
very close range. **2** (of a remark) direct.
adv. in a point-blank manner. **point-duty**
n. that of a policeman stationed to regulate traffic. **point of view** way of looking
at a matter. **point out** draw attention to.
point to indicate. **point up** emphasize. **to
the point** relevant(ly).
■ n. **1** prong, spike, tine; apex, end, tip. **2**
cape, headland, peninsula, promontory. **3**
location, place, situation, site, spot; instant,
juncture, moment, stage, time. **5** aspect,
detail, element, facet, item, matter, particular, respect. **6** attribute, characteristic,
feature, property, quality, trait. **7** aim, end,
goal, intention, object, objective, purpose;
drift, gist, meaning, sense, significance. **8**
advantage, benefit, use, value. **9** crux,
essence, heart, sl. nitty-gritty, nub, substance. ● v. **1** aim, direct, level, train. **2**
face, look. □ **point of view** angle, outlook,
perspective, standpoint, view, viewpoint.
point up accent, accentuate, emphasize,
highlight, spotlight, stress, underline. **to
the point** applicable, apposite, germane,
pertinent, relevant.

pointed adj. **1** tapering to a point. **2** (of a
remark or manner) emphasized, clearly
aimed at a person or thing. □ **pointedly**
adv.

pointer n. **1** thing that points to something. **2** dog that points towards game
which it scents.

pointless adj. having no purpose or meaning. □ **pointlessly** adv., **pointlessness** n.

■ empty, fruitless, futile, hollow, meaningless, purposeless, senseless, useless, vain, worthless.

poise n. 1 balance. 2 dignified self-assured manner.

■ 1 balance, equilibrium, equipoise. 2 aplomb, calmness, composure, control, sl. cool, dignity, equanimity, self-assurance, self-possession, serenity.

poison n. substance that can destroy life or harm health. ● v. 1 give poison to. 2 put poison on or in. 3 corrupt, fill with prejudice. □ **poison-pen letter** malicious unsigned letter. **poisoner** n., **poisonous** adj.

■ n. toxin, venom. ● v. 2 adulterate, contaminate, defile, pollute, taint. 3 corrupt, deprave, pervert, warp. □ **poisonous** deadly, lethal, noxious, toxic, venomous; evil, harmful, malevolent, malign, malignant, pernicious.

poke v. 1 thrust with the end of a finger or stick etc. 2 thrust forward. ● n. poking movement. □ **poke about** search casually, pry. **poke fun at** ridicule.

■ v. 1 dig, jab, prod, push, stab, stick, thrust. □ **poke fun at** chaff, deride, gibe at, jeer at, laugh at, make fun of, mock, sl. rag, colloq. rib, ridicule, taunt, tease.

poker¹ n. stiff metal rod for stirring up a fire.

poker² n. gambling card game. □ **pokerface** n. one that does not reveal thoughts or feelings.

poky adj. (-ier, -iest) small and cramped. □ **pokiness** n.

polar adj. 1 of or near the North or South Pole. 2 of a pole of a magnet. □ **polar bear** white bear of Arctic regions.

polarize v. 1 confine similar vibrations of (light waves) to one direction. 2 give magnetic poles to. 3 set at opposite extremes of opinion. □ **polarization** n.

Pole n. Polish person.

pole¹ n. long rod or post. ● v. push along by using a pole. □ **pole position** most favourable starting position in a motor race.

■ n. mast, post, rod, shaft, spar, staff, stanchion, stick, upright.

pole² n. 1 north (**North Pole**) or south (**South Pole**) end of earth's axis. 2 one of the opposite ends of a magnet or terminals of an electric cell or battery.

□ **pole star** star near the North Pole in the sky.

polecat n. 1 small animal of the weasel family. 2 (US) skunk.

polemic n. verbal attack on a belief or opinion. □ **polemical** adj.

police n. civil force responsible for keeping public order. ● v. control or provide with police. □ **police state** country where political police supervise and control citizens' activities. **policeman** n., **policewoman** n.

policy¹ n. course or general plan of action.

■ approach, course, line, method, plan, procedure, programme, scheme, strategy, system, tactic.

policy² n. insurance contract.

polio n. (colloq.) poliomyelitis.

poliomyelitis n. infectious disease causing temporary or permanent paralysis.

Polish adj. & n. (language) of Poland.

polish v. 1 make smooth and glossy by rubbing. 2 refine, perfect. ● n. 1 glossiness. 2 polishing, substance used for this. 3 elegance. □ **polish off** finish off. **polisher** n.

■ v. 1 buff, burnish, gloss, shine, wax. 2 improve, perfect, refine. ● n. 1 gloss, glossiness, lustre, sheen, shine. 3 elegance, refinement, sophistication, urbanity. □ **polish off** consume, devour, eat up, finish off, gobble (up), wolf (down).

polished adj. (of manner or performance) elegant, perfected.

■ civilized, cultivated, elegant, polite, refined, sophisticated, suave, urbane; accomplished, faultless, flawless, impeccable, masterly, perfect.

polite adj. 1 having good manners, courteous. 2 refined. □ **politely** adv., **politeness** n.

■ 1 civil, courteous, diplomatic, respectful, tactful, well-mannered. 2 civilized, elegant, genteel, refined.

political adj. 1 of or involving politics. 2 of the way a country is governed. □ **politically** adv.

politician n. person engaged in politics.

politics n. 1 science and art of government. 2 political affairs or life. 3 (pl.) political principles.

polka n. lively dance for couples. □ **polka dots** round evenly spaced dots on fabric.

poll n. 1 votes at an election. 2 place for this. 3 estimate of public opinion made by questioning people. ● *v.* **1** receive as votes. **2** cut off the horns of (cattle) or the top of (a tree etc.). □ **poll tax** tax levied on every adult.

pollard *v.* poll (a tree) to produce a close head of young branches. ● *n.* **1** pollarded tree. **2** hornless animal.

pollen *n.* fertilizing powder from the anthers of flowers.

pollinate *v.* fertilize with pollen. □ **pollination** *n.*

pollute *v.* make dirty or impure. □ **pollution** *n.*, **pollutant** *n.*

> ■ contaminate, defile, dirty, foul, poison, soil, sully, taint.

polo *n.* game like hockey played by teams on horseback. □ **polo-neck** *n.* high turned-over collar.

polonaise *n.* slow processional dance.

poltergeist *n.* spirit that throws things about noisily.

polyandry *n.* system of having more than one husband at a time.

polyanthus *n.* (*pl.* **-thuses** or **-thus**) cultivated primrose.

polychrome *adj.* multicoloured. □ **polychromatic** *adj.*

polyester *n.* synthetic resin or fibre.

polygamy *n.* system of having more than one wife at a time. □ **polygamist** *n.*, **polygamous** *adj.*

polyglot *adj.* & *n.* (person) knowing or using several languages.

polygon *n.* geometric figure with many sides. □ **polygonal** *adj.*

polyhedron *n.* (*pl.* **-dra**) solid with many sides. □ **polyhedral** *adj.*

polymath *n.* person with knowledge of many subjects.

polymer *n.* compound whose molecule is formed from a large number of simple molecules.

polymerize *v.* combine into a polymer. □ **polymerization** *n.*

polyp *n.* **1** simple organism with a tube-shaped body. **2** abnormal growth projecting from mucous membrane.

polyphony *n.* combination of melodies. □ **polyphonal** *adj.*

polystyrene *n.* a kind of plastic.

polytheism *n.* belief in or worship of more than one god. □ **polytheist** *n.*, **polytheistic** *adj.*

polythene *n.* tough light plastic.

polyunsaturated *adj.* (of fat) not associated with the formation of cholesterol in the blood.

polyurethane *n.* synthetic resin or plastic.

pomander *n.* ball of mixed sweet-smelling substances.

pomegranate *n.* **1** tropical fruit with many seeds. **2** tree bearing this.

Pomeranian *n.* dog of a small silky-haired breed.

pommel /púmm'l/ *n.* **1** knob on the hilt of a sword. **2** upward projection on a saddle.

pomp *n.* splendid display, splendour.

> ■ glory, grandeur, magnificence, majesty, pageantry, splendour.

pom-pom *n.* decorative tuft or ball.

pompous *adj.* self-important, affectedly grand. □ **pompously** *adv.*, **pomposity** *n.*

> ■ arrogant, conceited, haughty, hoity-toity, pretentious, proud, self-important, *colloq.* stuck-up, *colloq.* uppity, vain; bombastic, flowery, grandiloquent, turgid.

poncho *n.* (*pl.* **-os**) type of cloak made like a blanket with a hole for the head.

pond *n.* small area of still water.

ponder *v.* **1** be deep in thought. **2** think over.

> ■ brood (over), cogitate, consider, contemplate, deliberate (over), meditate (on), mull over, muse (over), reflect (on), ruminate (on), think (over).

ponderous *adj.* **1** heavy, unwieldy. **2** dull, laboured. □ **ponderously** *adv.*

> ■ **1** cumbersome, heavy, hefty, unwieldy, weighty. **2** dull, laboured, strained, stodgy, tedious, turgid.

pong *n.* & *v.* (*sl.*) stink.

pontiff *n.* **1** bishop. **2** pope.

pontificate *v.* speak in a pompously dogmatic way.

pontoon[1] *n.* **1** flat-bottomed boat. **2** floating platform. □ **pontoon bridge** temporary bridge supported on pontoons.

pontoon[2] *n.* a kind of card game.

pony *n.* horse of any small breed. □ **pony-tail** *n.* long hair drawn back and tied to hang down.

poodle *n.* dog with thick curly hair.

pooh *int.* exclamation of contempt. □ **pooh-pooh** *v.* express contempt for.

pool[1] *n.* **1** small area of still water. **2** puddle. **3** swimming pool.

pool[2] *n.* **1** shared fund or supply. **2** game resembling snooker. **3** (*pl.*) football pools. ● *v.* put into a common fund or supply.

poop *n.* **1** ship's stern. **2** raised deck at the stern.

poor *adj.* **1** having little money or means. **2** not abundant. **3** not very good. **4** pitiful.

■ **1** *colloq.* broke, destitute, hard-up, impecunious, impoverished, Indigent, needy, penniless, penurious, poverty-stricken, *sl.* skint. **2** inadequate, insufficient, meagre, *sl.* measly, scant, scanty, skimpy, sparse. **3** bad, incompetent, inferior, *colloq.* lousy, mediocre, second-rate, shoddy, slipshod, substandard, unacceptable, unprofessional, unsatisfactory. **4** hapless, luckless, pitiable, pitiful, unfortunate, unlucky, wretched.

poorly *adv.* in a poor way, badly. ● *adj.* unwell.

pop[1] *n.* **1** small explosive sound. **2** fizzy drink. ● *v.* (**popped**) **1** make or cause to make a pop. **2** put, come, or go quickly.

pop[2] *adj.* in a popular modern style. ● *n.* pop record or music.

popcorn *n.* maize heated to burst and form puffy balls.

pope *n.* head of the RC Church.

poplar *n.* tall slender tree.

poplin *n.* plain woven fabric.

poppadam *n.* large thin crisp savoury Indian biscuit.

poppy *n.* plant with showy flowers and milky juice.

poppycock *n.* (*sl.*) nonsense.

populace *n.* the general public.

popular *adj.* **1** liked, enjoyed, or used etc. by many people. **2** of, for, or prevalent among the general public. □ **popularly** *adv.*, **popularity** *n.*

■ **1** favoured, favourite, well-liked; fashionable, in, in fashion, in vogue. **2** common, current, general, prevailing, prevalent, widespread.

popularize *v.* **1** make generally liked. **2** present in a popular non-technical form.

populate *v.* **1** form the population of. **2** fill with a population.

■ **1** dwell in, inhabit, live in, occupy, reside in. **2** colonize, people, settle.

population *n.* inhabitants of an area.

populous *adj.* thickly populated.

porcelain *n.* fine china.

porch *n.* roofed shelter over the entrance of a building.

porcine *adj.* of or like a pig.

porcupine *n.* animal covered with protective spines.

pore[1] *n.* tiny opening in a surface through which fluids may pass.

pore[2] *v.* **pore over** study closely.

■ examine, go over, inspect, peruse, read, scrutinize, study.

pork *n.* unsalted pig-meat.

porn *n.* (*colloq.*) pornography.

pornography *n.* writings or pictures intended to stimulate erotic feelings by portraying sexual activity. □ **pornographer** *n.*, **pornographic** *adj.*

porous *adj.* permeable by fluid or air. □ **porosity** *n.*

porphyry *n.* rock containing mineral crystals.

porpoise *n.* small whale with a blunt rounded snout.

porridge *n.* food made by boiling oatmeal etc. to a thick paste.

port[1] *n.* harbour. **2** town with this.

port[2] *n.* **1** opening in a ship's side. **2** porthole.

port[3] *n.* left-hand side of a ship or aircraft.

port[4] *n.* strong sweet wine.

portable *adj.* able to be carried. □ **portability** *n.*

portal *n.* door or entrance, esp. an imposing one.

portcullis *n.* vertical grating that slides down in grooves to block the gateway to a castle.

portend *v.* foreshadow.

■ augur, bode, foreshadow, indicate, presage.

portent *n.* omen, significant sign. □ **portentous** *adj.*

■ augury, indication, omen, presage, sign, warning.

porter[1] *n.* doorkeeper of a large building.

porter[2] *n.* person employed to carry luggage or goods.

portfolio *n.* (*pl.* **-os**) **1** case for loose sheets of paper. **2** set of investments.

porthole *n.* window in the side of a ship or aircraft.

portico *n.* (*pl.* **-oes**) columns supporting a roof to form a porch or similar structure.

portion *n.* **1** part, share. **2** amount of food for one person. ● *v.* divide into portions.

■ *n.* **1** allocation, allowance, *colloq.* cut, part, percentage, quota, ration, share. **2** helping, piece, serving, slice.

portly *adj.* (**-ier, -iest**) corpulent, stout. □ **portliness** *n.*

portrait *n.* **1** picture of a person or animal. **2** description.

■ **1** drawing, image, likeness, painting, picture, representation, sketch. **2** characterization, description, portrayal, profile.

portray *v.* **1** make a picture of. **2** describe. **3** represent in a play etc. □ **portrayal** *n.*

■ **1** delineate, depict, draw, paint, picture, represent, show. **2** characterize, depict, describe, paint, represent. **3** act, play, represent, take the part *or* role of.

Portuguese *adj.* & *n.* (native, language) of Portugal.

pose *v.* **1** put into or take a particular attitude. **2** put forward, present (a problem etc.). ● *n.* **1** attitude in which someone is posed. **2** pretence. □ **pose as** pretend to be.

■ *v.* **1** arrange, place, position; model, sit. **2** ask, present, put forward, raise, submit. ● *n.* **1** attitude, position, posture, stance. **2** act, affectation, façade, pretence, show. □ **pose as** be disguised as, imitate, impersonate, masquerade as, pretend to be.

poser *n.* **1** puzzling problem. **2** poseur.

poseur *n.* person who behaves affectedly.

posh *adj.* (*colloq.*) very smart, luxurious.

position *n.* **1** place occupied by or intended for a person or thing. **2** posture. **3** situation. **4** status. **5** job. ● *v.* place. □ **positional** *adj.*

■ *n.* **1** locality, location, place, setting, site, situation, spot, whereabouts. **2** attitude, pose, posture, stance. **3** circumstances, condition, situation, state. **4** grade, place, rank, standing, station, status. **5** appointment, job, place, post, situation. ● *v.* arrange, dispose, lay, locate, place, pose, put, set, settle, site, situate.

positive *adj.* **1** definite, explicit. **2** convinced. **3** constructive, favourable. **4** (of a quantity) greater than zero. **5** (of a battery terminal) through which electric current enters. **6** (of a photograph) with lights, shades, or colours as in the subject, not reversed. ● *n.* positive quality, quantity, or photograph. □ **positively** *adv.*, **positiveness** *n.*

■ *adj.* **1** categorical, certain, clear, conclusive, convincing, decisive, definite, explicit, firm, incontestable, indisputable, undeniable, unequivocal, unquestionable. **2** certain, confident, convinced, satisfied, sure. **3** constructive, helpful, productive, useful, valuable; complimentary, enthusiastic, favourable, good, supportive.

positron *n.* particle with a positive electric charge.

posse /póssi/ *n.* **1** group of law-enforcers. **2** strong force or company.

possess *v.* **1** own. **2** have as a quality etc. **3** dominate the mind of. □ **possessor** *n.*

■ **1** be in possession of, be the owner of, enjoy, have, own. **3** control, dominate, haunt, obsess, preoccupy.

possession *n.* **1** possessing. **2** thing possessed. □ **take possession of** become the possessor of.

■ **1** ownership, proprietorship, tenure. **2** (**possessions**) belongings, chattels, effects, goods, property, things.

possessive *adj.* **1** desiring to possess things. **2** jealous and domineering. □ **possessiveness** *n.*

possible *adj.* capable of existing, happening, being done, etc. □ **possibly** *adv.*, **possibility** *n.*

■ believable, conceivable, credible, feasible, imaginable, likely, plausible, tenable; achievable, attainable, practicable, viable.

possum *n.* (*colloq.*) opossum. □ **play possum** pretend to be unaware.

post[1] *n.* piece of timber, metal, etc. set upright to support or mark something. ● *v.* display (a notice etc.), announce thus.

■ *n.* column, picket, pile, pillar, pole, shaft, stake, stanchion, strut, upright.

post[2] *n.* **1** place of duty. **2** outpost of soldiers. **3** trading station. **4** job. ● *v.* place, station.

■ *n.* **4** appointment, job, place, position, situation.

post[3] *n.* **1** official conveyance of letters etc. **2** the letters etc. conveyed. ● *v.* send by post. □ **keep me posted** keep me informed. **postbox** *n.* box into which letters are put for sending by post. **posthaste** *adv.* with great haste. **post office** building or room where postal business is carried on.

post- *pref.* after.

postage *n.* charge for sending something by post.

postal *adj.* of or by post.

postcard *n.* card for sending messages by post without an envelope.

postcode *n.* group of letters and figures in a postal address to assist sorting.

poster *n.* large picture or notice announcing or advertising something.

poste restante /pōst restónt/ post office department where letters are kept until called for.

posterior *adj.* situated behind or at the back. ● *n.* buttocks.

posterity *n.* future generations.

postern *n.* small back or side entrance to a fortress etc.

posthumous *adj.* **1** (of a child) born after its father's death. **2** published or awarded after a person's death. □ **posthumously** *adv.*

postman *n.* person who delivers or collects letters etc.

postmark *n.* official mark stamped on something sent by post, giving place and date of marking. ● *v.* mark with this.

postmaster, postmistress *ns.* person in charge of certain post offices.

post-mortem *adj.* & *n.* (examination) made after death.

postnatal *adj.* after childbirth.

postpone *v.* keep (an event etc.) from occurring until a later time. □ **postponement** *n.*
■ adjourn, defer, delay, put off, shelve, suspend.

postprandial *adj.* after lunch or dinner.

postscript *n.* additional paragraph at the end of a letter etc.

postulate *v.* assume to be true, esp. as a basis for reasoning. □ **postulation** *n.*

posture *n.* **1** attitude of the body. **2** way in which a person stands, walks, etc. ● *v.* assume a posture, esp. for effect.
■ *n.* **1** attitude, pose, position, stance. **2** bearing, carriage, deportment.

posy *n.* small bunch of flowers.

pot *n.* vessel for holding liquids or solids, or for cooking in. ● *v.* (**potted**) **1** put into a pot. **2** send (a ball in billiards etc.) into a pocket. □ **go to pot** (*colloq.*) deteriorate.

pot-belly *n.* protuberant belly. **pot-boiler** *n.* literary or artistic work produced merely to make a living. **potluck** *n.* whatever is available for a meal. **pot-roast** *n.* piece of meat cooked slowly in a covered dish. *v.* cook in this way. **pot-shot** *n.* shot aimed casually.

potable *adj.* drinkable.

potash *n.* potassium carbonate.

potassium *n.* soft silvery-white metallic element.

potation *n.* **1** drinking. **2** a drink.

potato *n.* (*pl.* -oes) **1** plant with starchy tubers that are used as food. **2** one of these tubers.

potent *adj.* **1** powerful, strong. **2** cogent. □ **potency** *n.*
■ **1** forceful, influential, mighty, powerful, strong, vigorous. **2** compelling, cogent, convincing, effective, forceful, persuasive.

potentate *n.* monarch, ruler.

potential *adj.* & *n.* (ability etc.) capable of being developed or used. □ **potentially** *adv.*, **potentiality** *n.*
■ *adj.* budding, developing, dormant, future, latent, possible, undeveloped, unrealized. ● *n.* capability, capacity, possibility, promise.

pothole *n.* **1** hole formed underground by the action of water. **2** hole in a road surface.

potholing *n.* caving. □ **potholer** *n.*

potion *n.* liquid for drinking as a medicine or drug.
■ brew, concoction, draught, elixir, philtre, potation, tonic.

pot-pourri /pōpoŏri/ *n.* **1** scented mixture of dried petals and spices. **2** medley.

potsherd *n.* broken piece of earthenware.

potted *see* **pot**. *adj.* **1** preserved in a pot. **2** abridged.

potter[1] *n.* maker of pottery.

potter[2] *v.* work on trivial tasks in a leisurely way.

pottery *n.* **1** vessels and other objects made of baked clay. **2** potter's work or workshop.

potty[1] *adj.* (-ier, -iest) (*sl.*) **1** trivial. **2** crazy.

potty[2] *n.* (*colloq.*) child's chamber pot.

pouch *n.* small bag or bag-like formation.

pouffe *n.* padded stool.

poulterer *n.* dealer in poultry.

poultice *n.* moist usu. hot dressing applied to inflammation. ● *v.* put a poultice on.

poultry *n.* domestic fowls.

pounce *v.* swoop down and grasp or attack. ● *n.* pouncing movement.

pound[1] *n.* **1** unit of weight equal to 16 oz. (454 g). **2** unit of money in the UK and certain other countries.

pound[2] *n.* enclosure where stray animals, or vehicles officially removed, are kept until claimed.

pound[3] *v.* **1** beat or crush with heavy strokes. **2** walk or run heavily. **3** (of the heart) beat heavily.
■ **1** beat, crush, grind, mash, pulverize; batter, belabour, bludgeon, *sl.* clobber, cudgel, pummel, thump, *sl.* wallop. **2**

poundage | prank

clump, stomp, tramp, trudge. **3** palpitate, pulsate, pulse, throb.

poundage *n.* charge or commission per £ or per pound weight.

pour *v.* **1** flow, cause to flow. **2** rain heavily. **3** send out freely.
■ **1** cascade, course, flood, flow, gush, run, spout, spurt, stream. **2** bucket, rain, teem.

pout *v.* **1** push out one's lips. **2** (of lips) be pushed out. ● *n.* pouting expression.

poverty *n.* **1** state of being poor. **2** scarcity, lack. **3** inferiority. □ **poverty-stricken** very poor.
■ **1** destitution, indigence, necessity, need, penniless, penury, want. **2** dearth, deficiency, insufficiency, lack, meagreness, paucity, scarcity, shortage, want. **3** inferiority, meanness, poorness.

powder *n.* **1** mass of fine dry particles. **2** medicine or cosmetic in this form. **3** gunpowder. ● *v.* **1** cover with powder. **2** reduce to powder. □ **powdery** *adj.*

power *n.* **1** ability to do something. **2** vigour, strength. **3** control, influence, authority. **4** influential person or country etc. **5** product of a number multiplied by itself a given number of times. **6** mechanical or electrical energy. **7** electricity supply. ● *v.* supply with (esp. motive) power. □ **power station** building where electricity is generated for distribution.
■ *n.* **1** ability, capability, capacity, potential. **2** brawn, dynamism, energy, force, forcefulness, might, muscle, potency, strength, vigour. **3** ascendancy, authority, command, control, dominance, dominion, mastery, rule, sovereignty; *colloq.* clout, influence, pull, sway, weight.

powerful *adj.* having great power or influence. □ **powerfully** *adv.*
■ dynamic, mighty, muscular, potent, robust, strapping, strong, sturdy, vigorous; authoritative, cogent, compelling, effective, forceful, persuasive, weighty; important, impressive, influential.

powerless *adj.* without power to take action, wholly unable.
■ defenceless, feeble, helpless, impotent, incapable, incapacitated, ineffective, ineffectual, unable, weak.

practicable *adj.* able to be done. □ **practicability** *n.*
■ achievable, feasible, possible, viable, workable.

practical *adj.* **1** involving activity as distinct from study or theory. **2** suitable for use. **3** good at doing and making things. **4** sensible and realistic. **5** virtual. □ **practical joke** trick played on a person. **practicality** *n.*
■ **1** empirical. **2** functional, serviceable, usable, useful, utilitarian. **4** businesslike, down-to-earth, efficient, hard-headed, pragmatic, realistic, sensible.

practically *adv.* **1** in a practical way. **2** virtually, almost.

practice *n.* **1** action as opposed to theory. **2** custom. **3** repeated exercise to improve skill. **4** doctor's or lawyer's business. □ **put into practice** apply (an idea, method, etc.).
■ **1** action, enactment, execution, operation; actuality, effect, fact, reality. **2** convention, custom, habit, routine, tradition, usage, way. **3** drill, exercise, rehearsal, training.

practise *v.* **1** do something repeatedly or habitually. **2** (of a doctor or lawyer) perform professional work.

practised *adj.* expert.
■ able, accomplished, adept, capable, experienced, expert, masterly, proficient, qualified, skilful, skilled, talented.

practitioner *n.* professional worker, esp. in medicine.

pragmatic *adj.* treating things from a practical point of view. □ **pragmatically** *adv.*, **pragmatism** *n.*, **pragmatist** *n.*

prairie *n.* large treeless area of grassland, esp. in N. America.

praise *v.* **1** express approval or admiration of. **2** honour (God) in words. ● *n.* act or instance of praising.
■ *v.* **1** acclaim, applaud, commend, compliment, congratulate, eulogize, extol, honour, laud, pay tribute to. **2** exalt, glorify, worship. ● *n.* acclaim, approbation, approval, applause, commendation, compliments, congratulations, glory, plaudits, tribute; exaltation, glorification, worship.

praiseworthy *adj.* deserving praise. □ **praiseworthiness** *n.*
■ admirable, commendable, creditable, deserving, exemplary, laudable, meritorious, worthy.

pram *n.* four-wheeled carriage for a baby.

prance *v.* move springily.
■ bound, caper, cavort, frisk, jump, leap, skip, spring.

prank *n.* piece of mischief.

prankster n. person playing pranks.

prattle v. chatter in a childish or inconsequential way. ● n. childish chatter.

prawn n. edible shellfish like a large shrimp.

pray v. **1** say prayers. **2** entreat.

■ **2** appeal to, ask, beg, beseech, entreat, implore, importune, petition, plead with, solicit, supplicate.

prayer n. **1** solemn request or thanksgiving to God. **2** set form of words used in this. **3** act of praying. **4** entreaty.

■ **4** appeal, entreaty, petition, plea, request, supplication.

pre- pref. **1** before. **2** beforehand.

preach v. **1** deliver a sermon. **2** expound (the Gospel etc.). **3** advocate. **4** give moral advice. □ **preacher** n.

■ **2** expound, proclaim, teach. **3** advocate, recommend, urge. **4** moralize, pontificate, sermonize.

preamble n. preliminary statement, introductory section.

prearrange v. arrange beforehand. □ **prearrangement** n.

precarious adj. unsafe, not secure. □ **precariously** adv., **precariousness** n.

■ chancy, dangerous, sl. dicey, hazardous, insecure, perilous, risky, shaky, treacherous, uncertain, unpredictable, unreliable, unsafe, unsure.

precaution n. something done in advance to avoid a risk. □ **precautionary** adj.

precede v. come or go before in time or order etc.

precedence n. priority.

precedent n. previous case serving as an example to be followed.

precept n. rule for action or conduct.

■ command, dictate, direction, directive, guideline, instruction, law, principle, rule.

precession n. change by which equinoxes occur earlier in each sidereal year.

precinct n. **1** enclosed area, esp. round a cathedral. **2** area closed to traffic in a town. **3** (pl.) environs.

precious adj. **1** of great value. **2** beloved. **3** affectedly refined. □ **precious stone** small valuable piece of mineral.

■ **1** costly, expensive, invaluable, priceless, valuable. **2** adored, beloved, cherished, dear, dearest, loved, prized, treasured. **3** affected, pretentious, twee.

precipice n. very steep or vertical face of a cliff or rock.

precipitate v. /prisippitayt/ **1** throw headlong. **2** cause to happen suddenly or soon. **3** cause (a substance) to be deposited. **4** condense (vapour). ● n. /prisippitat/ **1** substance deposited from a solution. **2** moisture condensed from vapour. ● adj. /prisippitat/ hasty, rash. □ **precipitately** adv., **precipitation** n.

■ v. **1** cast, catapult, fling, hurl, launch, propel, throw. **2** accelerate, advance, bring about, expedite, facilitate, further, hasten, quicken, speed (up), trigger. ● adj. abrupt, fast, hasty, headlong, hurried, rapid, speedy, sudden, swift; foolhardy, harebrained, hotheaded, impetuous, impulsive, incautious, injudicious, rash, reckless.

precipitous adj. very steep.

précis /práysee/ n. (pl. **précis**) summary. ● v. make a précis of.

precise adj. **1** exact. **2** correct and clearly stated. **3** punctilious, scrupulous. □ **precisely** adv., **precision** n.

■ **1** exact, particular, very. **2** accurate, correct, error-free, exact, faithful, perfect, true, unerring. **3** careful, conscientious, meticulous, particular, punctilious, scrupulous.

preclude v. **1** prevent. **2** make impossible.

■ **1** bar, debar, exclude, impede, inhibit, obstruct, prevent, prohibit, stop. **2** forestall, obviate, remove, rule out.

precocious adj. having developed earlier than is usual. □ **precociously** adv.

precognition n. foreknowledge, esp. supernatural.

preconceived adj. (of an idea) formed beforehand. □ **preconception** n.

precondition n. condition to be fulfilled beforehand.

precursor n. forerunner.

predatory /préddatəri/ adj. preying on others. □ **predator** n. predatory animal.

predecease v. die earlier than (another person).

predecessor n. **1** former holder of an office or position. **2** ancestor.

■ **1** antecedent, forerunner, precursor. **2** ancestor, antecedent, forebear, forefather.

predicament n. difficult situation.

■ difficulty, dilemma, fix, colloq. hole, colloq. jam, mess, colloq. pickle, plight, quandary, scrape.

predicate n. the part of a sentence that says something about the subject (e.g. 'is short' in life is short). □ **predicative** adj.

predict v. foretell. □ **prediction** n., **predictive** adj., **predictor** n.

■ augur, forecast, foresee, foretell, presage, prognosticate, prophesy.

predictable adj. able to be predicted.

predilection n. special liking.

predispose v. **1** influence in advance. **2** render liable or inclined. □ **predisposition** n.

predominate v. **1** be most numerous or powerful. **2** exert control. □ **predominant** adj., **predominantly** adv., **predominance** n.

■ **1** be prevalent, dominate, preponderate, prevail. **2** control, dominate, have the upper hand, rule. □ **predominant** dominant, preponderant, preponderating, prevailing, prevalent; chief, controlling, leading, main, ruling, supreme.

pre-eminent adj. **1** excelling others, outstanding. **2** leading, principal. □ **pre-eminently** adv., **pre-eminence** n.

■ **1** distinguished, eminent, excellent, important, inimitable, matchless, outstanding, peerless, superb, supreme, unequalled, unsurpassed. **2** chief, first, foremost, leading, main, paramount, primary, principal.

pre-empt v. **1** forestall. **2** take (a thing) before anyone else can do so. □ **pre-emption** n., **pre-emptive** adj.

preen v. smooth (feathers) with the beak. □ **preen oneself 1** groom oneself. **2** show self-satisfaction.

prefabricate v. manufacture in sections for assembly on a site. □ **prefabrication** n.

preface n. introductory statement. ● v. **1** introduce with a preface. **2** lead up to (an event).

■ n. foreword, introduction, preamble, prologue. ● v. **1** begin, introduce, open, prefix, start.

prefect n. **1** senior pupil authorized to maintain discipline in a school. **2** administrative official in certain countries. □ **prefecture** n.

prefer v. (**preferred**) **1** choose as more desirable, like better. **2** put forward (an accusation).

preferable adj. more desirable. □ **preferably** adv.

preference n. **1** preferring or being preferred. **2** thing preferred. **3** prior right. **4** favouring.

■ **1** inclination, leaning, liking, partiality, predilection, proclivity. **2** favourite. **4** favour, favouritism, preferential treatment, priority.

preferential adj. of or involving preference. □ **preferentially** adv.

■ advantageous, better, favourable, privileged, special, superior.

preferment n. promotion.

prefigure v. foreshadow.

prefix n. (pl. **-ixes**) word or syllable placed in front of a word to change its meaning. ● v. add as a prefix or introduction.

pregnant adj. **1** having a child or young developing in the womb. **2** full of meaning. □ **pregnancy** n.

prehensile adj. able to grasp things. □ **prehensility** n.

prehistoric adj. of the period before written records were made. □ **prehistorically** adv.

■ ancient, antediluvian, earliest, early, primal, primeval, primitive, primordial.

prejudge v. form a judgement on before knowing all the facts. □ **prejudgement** n.

prejudice n. **1** unreasoning opinion or dislike. **2** harm to rights. ● v. **1** cause to have a prejudice. **2** cause harm to. □ **prejudiced** adj.

■ n. **1** bias, bigotry, chauvinism, discrimination, favouritism, partisanship, racialism, racism, sexism. **2** damage, detriment, harm, injury. ● v. **1** bias, colour, influence, poison, sway. **2** damage, harm, injure, mar, ruin, spoil. □ **prejudiced** biased, bigoted, intolerant, one-sided, partial, partisan, unfair.

prejudicial adj. harmful to rights or interests. □ **prejudicially** adv.

■ damaging, deleterious, detrimental, disadvantageous, harmful, hurtful, injurious, unfavourable.

prelate n. clergyman of high rank. □ **prelacy** n.

preliminary adj. & n. (action or event etc.) preceding and preparing for a main action or event.

■ adj. initial, introductory, opening, preceding, preparatory. ● n. beginning, introduction, opening, prelude, preparation.

prelude n. **1** action or event leading up to another. **2** introductory part of a poem etc.

■ **2** introduction, overture, preamble, preface, prologue.

premarital adj. before marriage.

premature *adj.* coming or done before the usual or proper time. □ **prematurely** *adv.*

■ early, ill-timed, too soon, unseasonable, untimely.

premedication *n.* medication in preparation for an operation.

premeditated *adj.* planned beforehand. □ **premeditation** *n.*

■ calculated, conscious, deliberate, intended, intentional, planned, preconceived, wilful.

premenstrual *adj.* of the time immediately before menstruation.

premier *adj.* first in importance, order, or time. ● *n.* prime minister. □ **premiership** *n.*

première /prémmiair/ *n.* first public performance.

premises *n.pl.* house or other building and its grounds.

premiss *n.* statement on which reasoning is based.

■ assumption, hypothesis, postulate, presupposition, proposition, supposition, thesis.

premium *n.* **1** amount or instalment paid for an insurance policy. **2** extra sum of money. □ **at a premium 1** above the nominal or usual price. **2** scarce and in demand.

premonition *n.* presentiment. □ **premonitory** *adj.*

■ feeling, foreboding, hunch, intuition, presage, presentiment, suspicion.

prenatal *adj.* **1** before birth. **2** before childbirth. □ **prenatally** *adv.*

preoccupied *adj.* mentally engrossed.

■ absorbed, engrossed, immersed, rapt, wrapped up.

preoccupy *v.* dominate the mind of. □ **preoccupation** *n.*

preparation *n.* **1** preparing or being prepared. **2** (often *pl.*) thing done to make ready. **3** substance prepared for use.

■ **1** groundwork, organization, planning; education, instruction, teaching, training, tuition. **2** (**preparations**) arrangements, measures, plans. **3** compound, concoction, mixture, product.

preparatory *adj.* preparing for something. ● *adv.* in a preparatory way.

prepare *v.* make or get ready. □ **be prepared** be disposed or willing.

■ arrange, get *or* make ready, make provisions, organize, put in order; lay, set; cook, get, make; brief, coach, groom, prime, train; adapt, equip, fit (out), modify.

preponderate *v.* be greater in number or intensity etc. □ **preponderant** *adj.*, **preponderance** *n.*

preposition *n.* word used with a noun or pronoun to show position, time, or means (e.g. *at* home, *by* train). □ **prepositional** *adj.*

prepossessing *adj.* attractive.

preposterous *adj.* absurd, outrageous. □ **preposterously** *adv.*

■ absurd, farcical, foolish, laughable, ludicrous, nonsensical, outrageous, ridiculous, risible, senseless, stupid.

prepuce *n.* foreskin.

prerequisite *adj.* & *n.* (thing) required before something can happen.

■ *n.* condition, essential, *colloq.* must, necessity, precondition, proviso, requirement, requisite, stipulation.

prerogative *n.* right or privilege belonging to a person or group.

presage *n.* **1** omen. **2** presentiment. ● *v.* **1** portend. **2** foresee.

Presbyterian *adj.* & *n.* (member) of a Church governed by elders of equal rank. □ **Presbyterianism** *n.*

prescribe *v.* **1** advise the use of (a medicine etc.). **2** dictate as a course of action or rule to be followed.

■ **2** decree, dictate, ordain, order, require, stipulate.

prescription *n.* **1** prescribing. **2** doctor's written instructions for the preparation and use of a medicine.

prescriptive *adj.* prescribing.

presence *n.* **1** being present. **2** person's bearing. **3** person or thing that is or seems present. □ **presence of mind** ability to act sensibly in a crisis.

■ **1** attendance, company, fellowship, society; existence. **2** air, bearing, demeanour, manner. **3** ghost, spectre, spirit, wraith.

present[1] /prézz'nt/ *adj.* **1** being in the place in question. **2** existing or being dealt with now. ● *n.* present time, time now passing. □ **at present** now. **for the present** temporarily.

■ *adj.* **1** here, in attendance, there. **2** contemporary, current, existing, existent.

present² n. /prézz'nt/ gift. ● v. /prizént/
1 give as a gift or award. **2** introduce. **3**
bring to the public. □ **presenter** n.
■ n. donation, gift, offering. ● v. **1** award,
bestow, confer, give, grant, hand over. **2**
introduce, make known. **3** offer, proffer, put
forward, submit, tender; display, exhibit,
mount, put on, stage.

presentable adj. fit to be presented, of
good appearance. □ **presentably** adv.

presentation n. **1** presenting or being
presented. **2** thing presented. **3** exhibition or theatrical performance.
■ **1** bestowal, donation, giving. **2** award,
donation, gift, offering, present. **3** performance, production, show, showing,
staging.

presentiment n. vague expectation,
foreboding.
■ feeling, foreboding, hunch, intuition,
premonition, presage.

presently adv. **1** soon. **2** (Sc. & US) now.

preservation n. preserving.

preservative adj. preserving. ● n. substance that preserves perishable food.

preserve v. **1** keep safe, unchanged, or in
existence. **2** treat (food) to prevent decay.
● n. **1** interests etc. regarded as one
person's domain. **2** (also pl.) jam.
■ v. **1** defend, guard, keep safe, protect,
safeguard, shelter, shield; conserve, keep
up, maintain, perpetuate, retain, sustain,
uphold. **2** cure, freeze, pickle, salt, smoke.
● n. **1** domain, field, province, realm,
sphere. **2** conserve, jam, jelly.

preside v. be president or chairman.
□ **preside over** be in a position of authority over.
■ □ **preside over** administrate, be in
charge of, control, direct, handle, lead,
manage, oversee, run, supervise.

president n. **1** head of an institution or
club. **2** head of a republic. □ **presidency**
n., **presidential** adj.

press¹ v. **1** apply weight or force against.
2 squeeze. **3** flatten, smooth (esp.
clothes). **4** urge. **5** throng closely. ● n. **1**
process of pressing. **2** instrument for
pressing something. **3** (**the press**)
newspapers and periodicals, people involved in producing these. □ **be pressed
for** have barely enough of. **press conference** interview before a number of
reporters. **press cutting** report etc. cut
from a newspaper. **press-stud** n. small
fastener with two parts that engage when
pressed together. **press-up** n. exercise of

pressing on the hands to raise the trunk
while prone.
■ v. **1** depress, push down. **2** compress,
crush, squeeze. **3** flatten, iron, smooth. **4**
beg, entreat, exhort, implore, pressure,
pressurize, urge. **5** crowd, flock, gather,
mill, swarm, throng. ● n. **3** (**the press**) the
media, the papers; journalists, reporters.

press² v. bring into use as a makeshift.
□ **press-gang** v. force into service.

pressing adj. urgent.
■ critical, important, serious, urgent, vital.

pressure n. **1** exertion of force against a
thing. **2** this force. **3** compelling or oppressive influence. ● v. pressurize (a
person). □ **pressure cooker** pan for
cooking things quickly by steam under
pressure. **pressure group** group seeking
to exert influence by concerted action.
■ n. **1,2** compression, force, power,
strength, tension. **3** coercion, compulsion,
constraint, force, inducement, influence,
persuasion. ● v. coerce, compel, constrain, dragoon, force, press, pressurize.

pressurize v. **1** try to compel into an action. **2** maintain a constant atmospheric
pressure (in a compartment).

prestige n. respect resulting from good
reputation or achievements.
■ cachet, distinction, eminence, esteem,
kudos, reputation, respect, standing, stature, status.

prestigious adj. having or giving prestige.
■ acclaimed, celebrated, distinguished,
eminent, esteemed, estimable, illustrious,
influential, notable, noteworthy, pre-
eminent, renowned, reputable, respected.

presumably adv. it may be presumed.

presume v. **1** suppose to be true. **2** be
presumptuous. □ **presumption** n.
■ **1** assume, imagine, infer, presuppose,
suppose, surmise, take for granted. **2** dare,
have the effrontery, venture.

presumptuous adj. unduly confident,
arrogant. □ **presumptuously** adv.
■ arrogant, audacious, bold, brazen,
cheeky, forward, impertinent, impudent,
insolent, over-confident, presuming.

presuppose v. **1** assume beforehand. **2**
assume the prior existence of. □ **presupposition** n.

pretence *n.* **1** pretending. **2** false show of intentions or motives, pretext. **3** claim (e.g. to merit or knowledge).
■ **1** fabrication, fiction, invention, make-believe, pretending. **2** blind, cloak, cover, façade, front, mask, semblance, veneer; affectation, masquerade, pose, show; excuse, pretext.

pretend *v.* **1** imagine to oneself in play. **2** claim or assert falsely. □ **pretender** *n.*
■ **1** fantasize, make believe. **2** affect, counterfeit, fake, feign, simulate.

pretension *n.* **1** asserting of a claim. **2** pretentiousness.

pretentious *adj.* **1** claiming great merit or importance. **2** ostentatious. □ **pretentiously** *adv.*, **pretentiousness** *n.*
■ **1** haughty, hoity-toity, lofty, pompous, self-important, snobbish, *colloq.* stuck-up, *colloq.* uppity. **2** grandiose, ostentatious, showy; bombastic, flowery, grandiloquent, turgid.

preternatural *adj.* beyond what is natural. □ **preternaturally** *adv.*

pretext *n.* reason put forward to conceal one's true reason.
■ blind, excuse, pretence.

pretty *adj.* (**-ier**, **-iest**) attractive in a delicate way. ● *adv.* fairly, moderately. □ **prettily** *adv.*, **prettiness** *n.*
■ *adj.* appealing, attractive, *Sc.* bonny, comely, *colloq.* cute, good-looking, lovely.

pretzel *n.* salted biscuit.

prevail *v.* **1** be victorious. **2** be the more usual or predominant. □ **prevail on** persuade.
■ **1** gain victory, succeed, triumph, win. **2** be prevalent *or* widespread, dominate, predominate, preponderate, reign. □ **prevail on** convince, get, induce, persuade, sway, talk into, win over.

prevalent *adj.* existing generally, widespread. □ **prevalence** *n.*
■ common, current, general, pervasive, popular, predominant, prevailing, widespread.

prevaricate *v.* speak evasively. □ **prevarication** *n.*
■ be evasive, equivocate, evade the issue, hedge, quibble.

prevent *v.* stop or hinder, make impossible. □ **prevention** *n.*, **preventable** *adj.*
■ baulk, block, curb, foil, forestall, frustrate, halt, hamper, hinder, impede, inhibit, obstruct, preclude, prohibit, stop, thwart.

preventative *adj.* & *n.* preventive.

preventive *adj.* & *n.* (thing) preventing something.

previous *adj.* coming before in time or order. □ **previously** *adv.*
■ earlier, erstwhile, former, past, prior, sometime; aforesaid, antecedent, foregoing, preceding.

prey *n.* **1** animal hunted or killed by another for food. **2** victim. ● *v.* **prey on 1** seek or take as prey. **2** cause worry to. □ **bird of prey** one that kills and eats animals.
■ *n.* **1** quarry. **2** quarry, target, victim. ● *v.* **1** eat, feed on, live off. **2** burden, haunt, oppress, torment, trouble, weigh on, worry.

price *n.* **1** amount of money for which a thing is bought or sold. **2** what must be given or done etc. to achieve something. ● *v.* fix, find, or estimate the price of.
■ *n.* **1** amount, charge, cost, expense, fee, outlay; value, worth. **2** cost, sacrifice. ● *v.* cost, evaluate, rate, value.

priceless *adj.* **1** invaluable. **2** (*colloq.*) very amusing or absurd.
■ **1** beyond price, costly, expensive, invaluable, precious, valuable.

prick *v.* **1** pierce slightly. **2** feel a pricking sensation. ● *n.* **1** act of pricking. **2** sensation of being pricked. □ **prick up one's ears 1** (of a dog etc.) erect the ears. **2** listen alertly.
■ *v.* **1** penetrate, perforate, pierce, puncture. **2** prickle, smart, sting, tingle.

prickle *n.* **1** small thorn or spine. **2** pricking sensation. ● *v.* feel or cause a pricking sensation.
■ *n.* **1** barb, bristle, needle, spike, spine, thorn. **2** itchiness, prick, sting, tingle, tingling. ● *v.* itch, smart, sting, tingle; prick.

prickly *adj.* (**-ier**, **-iest**) **1** having prickles. **2** irritable, touchy.
■ **1** barbed, bristly, spiky, spiny, thistly, thorny. **2** cantankerous, fractious, irascible, irritable, peevish, pettish, petulant, short-tempered, snappy, testy, touchy, waspish.

pride *n.* **1** feeling of pleasure or satisfaction about one's actions, qualities, or possessions. **2** source of this. **3** sense of dignity. **4** unduly high opinion of oneself. **5** group (of lions). ● *v.* **pride oneself on** be proud of. □ **pride of place** most prominent position. **take pride in** be proud of.
■ *n.* **2** boast, darling, delight, gem, jewel, joy, treasure. **3** dignity, self-esteem, self-

respect. **4** arrogance, conceit, egotism, self-admiration, self-love, self-importance, self-satisfaction, smugness, vainglory, vanity. ● v. be proud of, glory in, preen oneself on, revel in, take pride in.

priest n. **1** member of the clergy. **2** official of a non-Christian religion. □ **priesthood** n., **priestly** adj.
■ **1** clergyman, clergywoman, cleric, divine, ecclesiastic, minister, padre, reverend, vicar.

priestess n. female priest of a non-Christian religion.

prig n. self-righteous person. □ **priggish** adj., **priggishness** n.
■ □ priggish goody-goody, prim, prissy, prudish, puritanical, self-righteous, straitlaced.

prim adj. (**primmer, primmest**) **1** formal and precise. **2** prudish. □ **primly** adv., **primness** n.
■ **1** formal, precise, proper, punctilious, starchy, stiff. **2** priggish, prissy, prudish, puritanical, strait-laced, colloq. stuffy.

prima adj. **prima ballerina** chief ballerina. **prima donna** chief female singer in opera.

primal adj. **1** primitive, primeval. **2** fundamental.

primary adj. first in time, order, or importance. ● n. primary thing. □ **primary colour** one not made by mixing others, i.e. (for light) red, green, violet, or (for paint) red, blue, yellow. **primary school** one for children below the age of 11. **primarily** adv.
■ adj. earliest, initial, original; basic, cardinal, central, chief, first, foremost, fundamental, leading, main, major, paramount, pre-eminent, prime, principal.

primate n. **1** archbishop. **2** member of the highly developed order of animals that includes humans, apes, and monkeys.

prime¹ adj. **1** chief. **2** first-rate. **3** fundamental. ● n. state of greatest perfection. □ **prime minister** leader of a government. **prime number** number that can be divided exactly only by itself and one.
■ adj. **1** chief, foremost, leading, main, major, paramount, primary, principal. **2** choice, excellent, exceptional, finest, first-class, first-rate, outstanding, select, superior, colloq. tiptop. **3** basic, essential, fundamental, original.

prime² v. **1** prepare for use or action. **2** provide with information in preparation for something.
■ **1** get ready, prepare. **2** educate, instruct, teach, train, tutor; apprise, brief, inform.

primer n. **1** substance used to prime a surface for painting. **2** elementary textbook.

primeval adj. of the earliest times of the world.

primitive adj. **1** at an early stage of civilization. **2** simple, crude.
■ **1** ancient, antediluvian, early, prehistoric, primal, primeval, primordial. **2** basic, crude, rough, rude, rudimentary, simple.

primogeniture n. system by which an eldest son inherits all his parents' property.

primordial adj. primeval.

primrose n. **1** pale yellow spring flower. **2** its colour.

primula n. perennial plant of a kind that includes the primrose.

prince n. **1** male member of a royal family. **2** sovereign's son or grandson. **3** the greatest or best.

princely adj. **1** like a prince. **2** splendid, generous.

princess n. **1** female member of a royal family. **2** sovereign's daughter or granddaughter. **3** prince's wife.

principal adj. first in rank or importance. ● n. **1** head of certain schools or colleges. **2** person with highest authority or playing the leading part. **3** capital sum as distinct from interest or income.
■ adj. chief, first, foremost, key, leading, main, major, paramount, pre-eminent, primary, prime. ● n. **1** head, headmaster, headmistress. **2** colloq. boss, chief, director, head, manager, manageress, president, ruler; lead, star. **3** capital, funds, resources.

principality n. country ruled by a prince.

principally adv. mainly.
■ chiefly, especially, for the most part, largely, mainly, mostly, on the whole, particularly, predominantly, primarily.

principle n. **1** general truth used as a basis of reasoning or action. **2** (often pl.) personal rule of conduct. **3** scientific law shown or used in the working of something. □ **in principle** as regards the main elements. **on principle** because of one's moral beliefs.

■ **1** axiom, canon, doctrine, fundamental, law, precept, rule, tenet, truth. **2** conscience, honesty, honour, integrity, morality, probity; **(principles)** beliefs, ethics, morals, philosophy, values.

principled *adj.* based on or having (esp. praiseworthy) principles of behaviour.

■ ethical, honest, honourable, just, moral, noble, righteous, upright, virtuous.

print *v.* **1** press (a mark) on a surface, impress (a surface etc.) in this way. **2** produce by applying inked type to paper. **3** write with unjoined letters. **4** produce a positive picture from (a photographic negative). ● *n.* **1** mark left by pressing. **2** printed lettering or words. **3** printed design, picture, or fabric. □ **printed circuit** electric circuit with lines of conducting material printed on a flat sheet.

■ *v.* **1** impress, imprint, stamp. ● *n.* **1** fingerprint, footprint, impression, imprint, indentation, mark. **2** lettering, text, type. **3** design, pattern; illustration, lithograph, picture.

printer *n.* person who prints books or newspapers etc.

printout *n.* computer output in printed form.

prior[1] *adj.* coming before in time, order, or importance.

■ earlier, foregoing, former, previous.

prior[2] *n.* monk who is head of a religious community, or one ranking next below an abbot.

prioress *n.* female prior.

prioritize *v.* treat as a priority.

priority *n.* **1** right to be first. **2** thing that should be treated as most important.

■ **1** precedence, preference; importance, pre-eminence, seniority, superiority.

priory *n.* monastery or nunnery governed by a prior or prioress.

prise *v.* force out or open by leverage.

prism *n.* **1** solid geometric shape with ends that are equal and parallel. **2** transparent object of this shape with refracting surfaces.

prismatic *adj.* **1** of or like a prism. **2** (of colours) rainbow-like.

prison *n.* place of captivity, esp. a building to which people are consigned while awaiting trial or for punishment.

■ gaol, *sl.* glasshouse, jail, lock-up, reformatory.

prisoner *n.* **1** person kept in prison. **2** (in full **prisoner of war**) person captured in war. **3** person in confinement.

■ **1** convict, inmate, internee. **2** captive, hostage.

prissy *adj.* (**-ier, -iest**) prim. □ **prissily** *adv.*, **prissiness** *n.*

pristine *adj.* in its original and unspoilt condition.

privacy *n.* being private.

■ isolation, seclusion, solitude.

private *adj.* **1** belonging to a person or group, not public. **2** confidential. **3** secluded. **4** not provided by the state. ● *n.* soldier of the lowest rank. □ **in private** privately. **privately** *adv.*

■ *adj.* **1** individual, particular, personal. **2** clandestine, confidential, hush-hush, intimate, off the record, personal, secret. **3** isolated, quiet, remote, secluded, sequestered.

privation *n.* lack of comforts or necessities.

■ deprivation, destitution, hardship, necessity, need, penury, poverty, want.

privatize *v.* transfer from state to private ownership. □ **privatization** *n.*

privet *n.* bushy evergreen shrub used for hedges.

privilege *n.* **1** right, advantage, or immunity belonging to a person etc. **2** special benefit or honour. □ **privileged** *adj.*

■ **1** advantage, prerogative, right; dispensation, exemption, freedom, immunity. **2** honour, pleasure.

prize[1] *n.* **1** award for victory or superiority. **2** thing that can be won. ● *adj.* **1** winning a prize. **2** excellent. ● *v.* value highly.

■ *n.* **1** award, cup, medal, trophy; reward. ● *adj.* **2** choice, excellent, first-class, first-rate, select. ● *v.* cherish, hold dear, set store by, treasure, value.

prize[2] *v.* = **prise.**

pro[1] *n.* (*pl.* **-os**) (*colloq.*) professional.

pro[2] *n.* **pros and cons** arguments for and against something.

pro- *pref.* in favour of.

probable *adj.* likely to happen or be true. □ **probably** *adv.*, **probability** *n.*

■ believable, conceivable, credible, feasible, likely, plausible, possible, tenable.

probate *n.* **1** official process of proving that a will is valid. **2** certified copy of a will.

probation *n.* **1** testing of behaviour or abilities. **2** system whereby certain offenders are supervised by an official (**probation officer**) instead of being imprisoned. ◻ **probationary** *adj.*

probationer *n.* person undergoing a probationary period.

probe *n.* **1** blunt surgical instrument for exploring a wound. **2** unmanned exploratory spacecraft. **3** investigation. ● *v.* **1** explore with a probe. **2** investigate.
■ *n.* **3** examination, exploration, inquiry, investigation, scrutiny, study. ● *v.* **2** examine, explore, inquire into, investigate, look into, research, scrutinize, study.

probity *n.* honesty.

problem *n.* **1** something difficult to deal with or understand. **2** thing to be solved or dealt with.
■ **1** complication, difficulty, headache, trouble. **2** conundrum, enigma, riddle, poser, puzzle.

problematic *adj.* (also **problematical**) **1** difficult. **2** questionable.
■ **1** awkward, complicated, delicate, difficult, knotty, ticklish, tricky. **2** debatable, disputable, doubtful, questionable.

proboscis *n.* **1** long flexible snout. **2** insect's elongated mouthpart used for sucking things.

procedure *n.* **1** way of conducting business or performing a task. **2** series of actions. ◻ **procedural** *adj.*
■ approach, course of action, method, plan of action, policy, process, strategy, system; *colloq.* drill, practice, routine.

proceed *v.* **1** go forward or onward. **2** continue. **3** start a lawsuit. **4** originate.
■ **1** advance, go, make one's way, progress. **2** carry on, continue, go on. **4** arise, come, derive, develop, issue, originate, result, spring, start, stem.

proceedings *n.pl.* **1** what takes place. **2** published report of a conference etc. **3** lawsuit.

proceeds *n.pl.* profit from a sale or performance etc.
■ gate, income, profit(s), return(s), take, takings.

process *n.* **1** series of operations used in making something. **2** procedure. **3** series of changes or events. ● *v.* subject to a process.
■ *n.* **2** approach, course of action, method, procedure, system. **3** course, progress.

procession *n.* number of people, vehicles, or boats etc. going along in an orderly line.
■ cavalcade, cortège, line, march, motorcade, parade.

processor *n.* machine that processes things.

proclaim *v.* announce publicly. ◻ **proclamation** *n.*
■ advertise, announce, blazon, broadcast, declare, make known, promulgate, pronounce, trumpet. ◻ **proclamation** announcement, declaration, promulgation, pronouncement.

proclivity *n.* tendency.

procrastinate *v.* postpone action. ◻ **procrastination** *n.*
■ be dilatory, delay, *colloq.* dilly-dally, play for time, stall, temporize.

procreate *v.* produce (offspring). ◻ **procreation** *n.*

procure *v.* **1** obtain by care or effort, acquire. **2** act as procurer. ◻ **procurement** *n.*
■ **1** acquire, come by, get, land, obtain, pick up, secure; buy, purchase.

procurer *n.* person who obtains women for prostitution.

prod *v.* (**prodded**) **1** poke. **2** stimulate to action. ● *n.* **1** prodding action. **2** stimulus. **3** instrument for prodding things.
■ *v.* **1** dig, elbow, jab, nudge, poke. **2** move, motivate, prompt, provoke, rouse, spur, stimulate, stir, urge. ● *n.* **1** dig, jab, nudge, poke. **2** goad, spur, stimulus.

prodigal *adj.* wasteful, extravagant. ◻ **prodigally** *adv.*, **prodigality** *n.*
■ extravagant, improvident, profligate, spendthrift, wasteful.

prodigious *adj.* **1** amazing. **2** enormous. ◻ **prodigiously** *adv.*
■ **1** amazing, astonishing, astounding, extraordinary, incredible, marvellous, phenomenal, remarkable, sensational, staggering, startling, wonderful. **2** colossal, enormous, huge, large, massive, tremendous, vast.

prodigy *n.* **1** person with exceptional qualities or abilities. **2** wonderful thing.
■ **1** genius, wizard, *colloq.* whiz-kid. **2** marvel, miracle, phenomenon, sensation, wonder.

produce *v.* /prədyō͞os/ **1** bring forward for inspection. **2** bring (a performance etc.) before the public. **3** bring into ex-

istence, cause. **4** manufacture. ● *n.*
/pródyooss/ amount or thing(s) produced. □ **producer** *n.*, **production** *n.*

> ■ *v.* **1** bring forward, offer, present, show.
> **2** present, put on, stage. **3** bring about,
> cause, generate, give rise to, initiate, oc-
> casion, result in. **4** fabricate, make, manu-
> facture. ● *n.* commodities, goods, prod-
> ucts, staples.

product *n.* **1** thing produced. **2** number
obtained by multiplying.

> ■ **1** artefact, commodity; (**products**)
> goods, merchandise, produce, wares.

productive *adj.* **1** producing things, esp.
in large quantities. **2** useful.

> ■ **1** fecund, fertile, fruitful, prolific, rich.
> **2** constructive, helpful, useful, valuable,
> worthwhile.

productivity *n.* efficiency in industrial
production.

profane *adj.* **1** secular. **2** irreverent,
blasphemous. ● *v.* treat irreverently.
□ **profanely** *adv.*, **profanity** *n.*, **profana-
tion** *n.*

> ■ *adj.* **1** lay, non-religious, secular. **2**
> blasphemous, disrespectful, impious, ir-
> reverent, sacrilegious.

profess *v.* **1** claim (a quality etc.). **2** declare. **3** affirm faith in (a religion).

> ■ **1** claim, pretend. **2** affirm, assert, de-
> clare, maintain, state.

professed *adj.* **1** alleged. **2** self-
acknowledged. □ **professedly** *adv.*

profession *n.* **1** occupation requiring
advanced learning. **2** people engaged in
this. **3** declaration.

> ■ **1** calling, employment, field, line (of
> work), occupation, trade, vocation. **3** af-
> firmation, announcement, assertion,
> avowal, declaration, statement.

professional *adj.* **1** belonging to a profession. **2** skilful, worthy of a professional. **3** doing something for payment,
not as a pastime. ● *n.* professional
worker or player. □ **professionalism** *n.*,
professionally *adv.*

> ■ *adj.* **2** experienced, expert, masterly,
> practised, proficient, skilful, skilled,
> trained; businesslike, efficient, thorough.
> ● *n.* adept, expert, master, *colloq.* pro,
> specialist.

professor *n.* university teacher of the
highest rank. □ **professorial** *adj.*

proffer *v.* & *n.* offer.

proficient *adj.* expert, skilled. □ **proficiently** *adv.*, **proficiency** *n.*

> ■ able, accomplished, adept, capable,
> competent, experienced, expert, practised,
> professional, skilful, skilled, trained.

profile *n.* **1** side view, esp. of the face. **2**
short account of a person's character or
career.

profit *n.* **1** advantage, benefit. **2** money
gained. ● *v.* (**profited**) be beneficial to.
□ **profit from** obtain an advantage or
benefit.

> ■ *n.* **1** advantage, avail, benefit, good, in-
> terest, use, usefulness, value. **2** gain,
> proceeds, return. ● *v.* aid, avail, be ad-
> vantageous or beneficial to, benefit, help,
> serve. □ **profit from** capitalize on, cash in
> on, exploit, make use of, take advantage
> of, utilize.

profitable *adj.* bringing profit. □ **profit-
ably** *adv.*, **profitability** *n.*

> ■ gainful, lucrative, remunerative, reward-
> ing, well-paid; advantageous, beneficial,
> helpful, productive, useful, valuable,
> worthwhile.

profiteer *v.* make or seek excessive
profits. ● *n.* person who makes excessive
profits.

profiterole *n.* small hollow cake of choux
pastry with filling.

profligate *adj.* **1** wasteful, extravagant. **2**
dissolute. ● *n.* profligate person. □ **profligacy** *n.*

> ■ *adj.* **1** extravagant, improvident, prod-
> igal, spendthrift, wasteful. **2** corrupt, de-
> bauched, degenerate, depraved, dissi-
> pated, dissolute, immoral, unprincipled,
> wanton.

profound *adj.* **1** intense. **2** showing or
needing great insight. □ **profoundly** *adv.*,
profundity *n.*

> ■ **1** acute, deep, extreme, heartfelt, in-
> tense, keen, overpowering, overwhelming.
> **2** erudite, intellectual, learned, sagacious,
> scholarly; abstruse, arcane, esoteric, rec-
> ondite.

profuse *adj.* **1** lavish. **2** plentiful. □ **profusely** *adv.*, **profusion** *n.*

> ■ **1** bountiful, generous, lavish, liberal,
> unsparing, unstinting. **2** abundant, ample,
> copious, luxuriant, plenteous, plentiful,
> prolific, rich.

progenitor *n.* ancestor.
progeny *n.* offspring.
progesterone *n.* sex hormone that
maintains pregnancy.

prognosis n. (pl. **-oses**) forecast, esp. of the course of a disease. □ **prognostic** adj.

prognosticate v. forecast. □ **prognostication** n.

program n. 1 (US) = programme. 2 series of coded instructions for a computer. ● v. (**programmed**) instruct (a computer) by means of this. □ **programmer** n.

programme n. 1 plan of action. 2 list of items in an entertainment. 3 broadcast performance.

> ■ 1 agenda, plan of action, schedule. 3 broadcast, production, show.

progress n. /prógress/ 1 forward movement. 2 development. ● v. /prəgréss/ 1 make progress. 2 develop. □ **in progress** taking place. **progression** n.

> ■ n. 1 advancement, headway, progression. 2 advance, development, evolution, expansion, growth, improvement. ● v. 1 advance, forge ahead, make headway, make one's way, proceed. 2 advance, develop, evolve, expand, get better, grow, improve.

progressive adj. 1 favouring progress or reform. 2 (of a disease) gradually increasing in its effect. □ **progressively** adv.

prohibit v. 1 forbid. 2 prevent. □ **prohibition** n.

> ■ 1 ban, bar, debar, disallow, forbid, outlaw, proscribe, veto. 2 block, hamper, hinder, impede, inhibit, obstruct, preclude, prevent, rule out, stop.

prohibitive adj. 1 prohibiting. 2 (of prices etc.) extremely high.

project v. /prəjékt/ 1 extend outwards. 2 cast, throw. 3 estimate. 4 plan. ● n. /prójekt/ 1 plan, undertaking. 2 task involving research.

> ■ v. 1 beetle (out), bulge (out), jut (out), overhang, protrude, stick out. 2 cast, colloq. chuck, fling, hurl, launch, lob, propel, throw, toss. 3 calculate, estimate, forecast, predict. 4 contemplate, plan, propose. ● v. 1 idea, plan, proposal, scheme; assignment, enterprise, undertaking, venture.

projectile n. missile.

projection n. 1 process of projecting something. 2 thing projecting from a surface. 3 estimate of future situations based on a study of present ones.

> ■ 2 bulge, ledge, outcrop, overhang, protrusion, protuberance, spur. 3 estimate, forecast, prediction.

projectionist n. person who operates a projector.

projector n. apparatus for projecting images on to a screen.

proletariat n. working-class people. □ **proletarian** adj. & n.

proliferate v. reproduce rapidly, multiply. □ **proliferation** n.

> ■ burgeon, grow, increase, multiply, mushroom, snowball.

prolific adj. 1 abundantly productive. 2 copious.

> ■ 1 fecund, fertile, fruitful, productive. 2 abundant, copious, plenteous, plentiful, profuse.

prologue n. introduction to a poem or play etc.

prolong v. lengthen in extent or duration. □ **prolongation** n.

> ■ draw out, extend, lengthen, protract, spin out, stretch out.

prolonged adj. continuing for a long time.

prom n. (colloq.) 1 promenade. 2 promenade concert.

promenade n. paved public walk (esp. along a sea front). □ **promenade concert** one where part of the audience is not seated and can move about.

prominent adj. 1 projecting. 2 conspicuous. 3 well-known. □ **prominence** n.

> ■ 1 jutting, projecting, protruding, protuberant. 2 conspicuous, discernible, evident, noticeable, obvious, pronounced, recognizable, striking. 3 acclaimed, celebrated, distinguished, eminent, famed, famous, illustrious, notable, noted, renowned, well-known.

promiscuous adj. 1 having sexual relations with many people. 2 indiscriminate. □ **promiscuously** adv., **promiscuity** n.

promise n. 1 declaration that one will give or do a certain thing. 2 indication of future results. ● v. 1 make (a person) a promise, esp. to do or give (a thing). 2 seem likely, produce expectation of.

> ■ n. 1 assurance, bond, guarantee, oath, pledge, undertaking, vow, word (of honour). 2 ability, aptitude, capability, potential. ● v. 1 give one's word, guarantee, pledge, swear, undertake, vow. 2 augur, bespeak, betoken, foretell, indicate, presage.

promising *adj.* likely to turn out well or produce good results.

  ■ auspicious, bright, encouraging, favourable, hopeful, optimistic, propitious, rosy.

promontory *n.* high land jutting out into the sea or a lake.

promote *v.* 1 raise to a higher rank or office. 2 help the progress of. 3 publicize in order to sell. □ **promotion** *n.*, **promotional** *adj.*, **promoter** *n.*

  ■ 1 elevate, raise, upgrade. 2 advance, aid, assist, boost, encourage, forward, foster, further, help, support. 3 advertise, *colloq.* plug, publicize.

prompt *adj.* 1 done without delay. 2 ready, willing. ● *adv.* punctually. ● *v.* 1 incite. 2 supply (an actor or speaker) with forgotten words or with a suggestion. □ **promptly** *adv.*, **promptness** *n.*

  ■ *adj.* 1 fast, immediate, instantaneous, punctual, quick, rapid, speedy, swift, unhesitating. 2 eager, keen, quick, ready, willing. ● *v.* 1 egg on, encourage, incite, induce, make, motivate, move, prod, provoke, spur, urge.

prompter *n.* person stationed off stage to prompt actors.

promulgate *v.* make known to the public. □ **promulgation** *n.*

prone *adj.* 1 lying face downwards. 2 likely to do or suffer something.

  ■ 1 prostrate, reclining, recumbent. 2 apt, disposed, given, inclined, liable, predisposed; subject, susceptible.

prong *n.* each of the pointed parts of a fork. □ **pronged** *adj.*

pronoun *n.* word used as a substitute for a noun (e.g. *I, me, who, which*). □ **pronominal** *adj.*

pronounce *v.* 1 utter distinctly or in a certain way. 2 declare. □ **pronunciation** *n.*

  ■ 1 articulate, enunciate, say, utter, vocalize, voice. 2 announce, assert, declare, proclaim.

pronounced *adj.* noticeable.

  ■ clear, conspicuous, decided, definite, distinct, marked, noticeable, plain, prominent, recognizable, striking, unmistakable.

pronouncement *n.* declaration.

proof *n.* 1 evidence that something is true or exists. 2 demonstration or act of proving. 3 copy of printed matter for correction. ● *adj.* able to resist penetration or damage. ● *v.* make (fabric) proof against something (e.g. water).

  ■ *n.* 1 data, documentation, evidence, facts. 2 authentication, confirmation, corroboration, substantiation, validation, verification.

proofread *v.* read and correct (printed proofs). □ **proofreader** *n.*

prop¹ *n.* support to prevent something from falling, sagging, or failing. ● *v.* (**propped**) support (as) with a prop. □ **prop up** prevent from falling.

  ■ *n.* brace, buttress, mainstay, pier, post, support, upright. □ **prop up** bolster, brace, buttress, hold up, shore up, support.

prop² *n.* (*colloq.*) a stage property.

prop³ *n.* (*colloq.*) propeller.

propaganda *n.* publicity intended to persuade or convince people.

propagate *v.* 1 breed or reproduce from parent stock. 2 spread (news etc.). 3 transmit. □ **propagation** *n.*

  ■ 1 breed, multiply, procreate, reproduce. 2 broadcast, circulate, disseminate, make known, promulgate, publicize, spread.

propane *n.* hydrocarbon fuel gas.

propel *v.* (**propelled**) push forward or onward.

  ■ drive, impel, move, push *or* thrust forward.

propellant *n.* thing that propels something. □ **propellent** *adj.*

propeller *n.* revolving device with blades, for propelling a ship or aircraft.

propensity *n.* 1 tendency. 2 inclination.

proper *adj.* 1 suitable. 2 correct. 3 conforming to social conventions. 4 (*colloq.*) thorough. □ **proper name** *or* **noun** name of an individual person or thing.

  ■ 1 apposite, apt, appropriate, fit, fitting, right, suitable. 2 accepted, accurate, correct, established, orthodox, precise, right, true. 3 correct, decent, decorous, genteel, gentlemanly, ladylike, respectable, seemly. 4 absolute, complete, perfect, out and out, thorough, utter.

property *n.* 1 thing(s) owned. 2 real estate, land. 3 movable object used in a play etc. 4 quality, characteristic.

  ■ 1 assets, belongings, effects, possessions, things. 4 attribute, characteristic, feature, hallmark, quality, trait.

prophecy n. **1** power of prophesying. **2** statement prophesying something.

■ **1** augury, divination, fortune-telling, second sight, soothsaying. **2** forecast, prediction, prognostication.

prophesy v. foretell.

■ augur, forecast, foresee, foretell, predict, presage, prognosticate.

prophet, prophetess ns. **1** person who predicts. **2** teacher or interpreter of divine will.

■ **1** clairvoyant, fortune-teller, oracle, seer, sibyl, soothsayer.

prophetic adj. prophesying.

prophylactic adj. & n. (medicine or action etc.) preventing disease or misfortune. □ **prophylaxis** n.

propinquity n. nearness.

propitiate /prəpIshIayt/ v. appease. □ **propitiation** n., **propitiatory** adj.

propitious /prəpIshəss/ adj. auspicious, favourable.

■ advantageous, auspicious, bright, favourable, fortunate, happy, lucky, promising, providential, rosy.

proponent n. person putting forward a proposal.

proportion n. **1** fraction or share of a whole. **2** ratio. **3** correct or pleasing relation between things or parts of a thing. **4** (pl.) dimensions. □ **proportional** adj., **proportionally** adv.

■ **1** colloq. cut, division, part, percentage, portion, quota, ration, share. **2** ratio, relationship. **3** arrangement, balance, harmony, symmetry. **4** (proportions) dimensions, extent, magnitude, measurements, size.

proportionate adj. in due proportion. □ **proportionately** adv.

proposal n. **1** proposing of something. **2** thing proposed. **3** offer of marriage.

■ **1** bid, motion, offer, overture, proposition, recommendation, suggestion, tender.

propose v. **1** put forward for consideration. **2** intend. **3** nominate. **4** make a proposal of marriage. □ **proposer** n.

■ **1** advance, propound, put forward, recommend, submit, suggest, table. **2** aim, have in mind, intend, mean, plan, purpose. **3** nominate, put forward, recommend, suggest.

proposition n. **1** statement. **2** proposal, scheme proposed. **3** (colloq.) undertaking. ● v. (colloq.) put a proposal to.

propound v. put forward for consideration.

proprietary adj. **1** made and sold by a particular firm, usu. under a patent. **2** of an owner or ownership.

proprietor n. owner of a business. □ **proprietorial** adj.

propriety n. correctness of behaviour.

■ correctness, courtesy, decency, decorum, gentility, politeness, refinement, respectability, seemliness.

propulsion n. process of propelling or being propelled.

pro rata proportional(ly).

prosaic adj. ordinary, unimaginative. □ **prosaically** adv.

■ banal, boring, commonplace, dry, dull, flat, humdrum, lifeless, monotonous, mundane, ordinary, pedestrian, run-of-the-mill, tedious, unimaginative, uninspired, uninspiring.

proscribe v. forbid by law.

prose n. written or spoken language not in verse form.

prosecute v. **1** take legal proceedings against (a person) for a crime. **2** carry on, conduct. □ **prosecution** n., **prosecutor** n.

■ **1** arraign, bring to trial, charge, indict, sue. **2** carry on, conduct, perform, practise, pursue.

proselyte n. recent convert to a religion.

proselytize v. seek to convert.

prospect n. /próspekt/ **1** (often pl.) expectation, esp. of success in a career etc. **2** view. ● v. /prəspékt/ explore in search of something. □ **prospector** n.

■ n. **1** chance, expectation, hope, likelihood, possibility, probability. **2** panorama, scene, sight, view, vista.

prospective adj. expected to be or to occur, future or possible.

prospectus n. document giving details of a school, business, etc.

prosper v. be successful, thrive.

■ do well, flourish, grow, make good, succeed, thrive.

prosperous adj. financially successful. □ **prosperity** n.

■ affluent, moneyed, rich, wealthy, colloq. well-heeled, well-off, well-to-do.

prostate gland gland round the neck of the bladder in males.

prosthesis n. (pl. -theses) artificial limb or similar appliance. □ **prosthetic** adj.

prostitute *n.* woman who engages in sexual intercourse for payment. ● *v.* **1** make a prostitute of. **2** put (talent etc.) to an unworthy use. □ **prostitution** *n.*

prostrate *adj.* /próstrayt/ **1** face downwards. **2** lying horizontally. **3** exhausted, overcome. ● *v.* /prostráyt/ cause to be prostrate. □ **prostration** *n.*

■ *adj.* **2** prone, recumbent, stretched out. **3** drained, exhausted, fatigued, tired, wearied, worn-out; crushed, helpless, impotent, overcome, overpowered, overwhelmed, powerless. ● *v.* fell, floor, knock down; exhaust, fatigue, *sl.* knacker, tire (out), wear out, weary; crush, overcome, overpower, overwhelm.

protagonist *n.* **1** chief person in a drama, story, etc. **2** supporter.

protean *adj.* **1** variable. **2** versatile.

protect *v.* keep from harm or injury. □ **protector** *n.*

■ conserve, defend, guard, keep (safe), preserve, safeguard, shelter, shield.

protection *n.* **1** protecting, being protected. **2** defence.

■ **1** care, charge, custody, guardianship, safe-keeping. **2** defence, safeguard, screen, shelter, shield; safety, security.

protectionism *n.* policy of protecting home industries by tariffs etc. □ **protectionist** *n.*

protective *adj.* protecting, giving protection. □ **protectively** *adv.*

protectorate *n.* country that is under the official protection and partial control of a stronger one.

protégé /próttizhay/ *n.* (*fem.* **protégée**) person under the protection or patronage of another.

protein *n.* organic compound forming an essential part of humans' and animals' food.

protest *n.* /prótest/ statement or action indicating disapproval. ● *v.* /pratést/ **1** express disapproval. **2** declare firmly.

■ *n.* complaint, demur, expostulation, *colloq.* gripe, *colloq.* grouse, grumble, objection, outcry, protestation, remonstrance. ● *v.* **1** complain, demur, expostulate, *colloq.* gripe, *colloq.* grouse, grumble, *colloq.* kick up, make a fuss, object, remonstrate. **2** affirm, assert, declare, maintain, profess.

Protestant *n.* member of one of the western Churches that are separated from the RC Church. □ **Protestantism** *n.*

protestation *n.* firm declaration.

protocol *n.* **1** etiquette applying to rank or status. **2** draft of a treaty.

proton *n.* particle of matter with a positive electric charge.

protoplasm *n.* contents of a living cell.

prototype *n.* original example from which others are developed. □ **prototypical** *adj.*

protozoon /prótazó-on/ *n.* (*pl.* **-zoa**) one-celled microscopic animal. □ **protozoan** *adj.* & *n.*

protract *v.* prolong in duration. □ **protraction** *n.*

protractor *n.* instrument for measuring angles.

protrude *v.* project, stick out. □ **protrusion** *n.*, **protrusive** *adj.*

■ bulge, extend, jut (out), project, stick out. □ **protrusion** bulge, bump, excrescence, knob, lump, outgrowth, projection, protuberance, swelling, tumescence.

protuberant *adj.* bulging out. □ **protuberance** *n.*

■ bulbous, bulging, jutting, projecting, prominent, protruding, protrusive.

proud *adj.* **1** feeling greatly honoured or pleased. **2** haughty, arrogant. **3** imposing. **4** slightly projecting. □ **proudly** *adv.*

■ **1** contented, delighted, elated, gratified, honoured, pleased, satisfied. **2** arrogant, boastful, conceited, haughty, hoity-toity, self-important, self-satisfied, smug, *colloq.* snooty, *colloq.* stuck-up, supercilious, superior, vain, vainglorious. **3** grand, imposing, impressive, magnificent, majestic, splendid, stately.

prove *v.* **1** give or be proof of. **2** be found to be.

■ **1** authenticate, back up, confirm, corroborate, demonstrate, establish, show, substantiate, support, validate, verify.

proven *adj.* proved.

provenance *n.* place of origin.

proverb *n.* short well-known saying.

■ aphorism, maxim, saw, saying.

proverbial *adj.* **1** of or mentioned in a proverb. **2** well-known.

provide *v.* **1** supply, make available. **2** make preparations. □ **provide for** supply with the necessities of life. **provider** *n.*

■ **1** equip, furnish, lay on, provision, supply; afford, give, offer, present. **2** cater, get ready, make provision(s), prepare. □ **provide for** care for, keep, look after, support, take care of.

provided *conj.* on condition (that).

providence *n.* **1** being provident. **2** God's or nature's protection.

provident *adj.* showing wise forethought for future needs.
- canny, judicious, prudent, sagacious, sage, shrewd, wise; economical, frugal, thrifty.

providential *adj.* happening very luckily. □ **providentially** *adv.*
- fortunate, happy, lucky, opportune, timely.

providing *conj.* = **provided**.

province *n.* **1** administrative division of a country. **2** area of learning or responsibility. **3** (*pl.*) all parts of a country outside its capital city.
- **1** area, county, district, region, state, territory, zone. **2** area, concern, domain, field, *colloq.* pigeon, preserve, responsibility, sphere.

provincial *adj.* **1** of a province or provinces. **2** having limited interests and narrow-minded views. ● *n.* inhabitant of province(s).
- *adj.* **1** local, regional. **2** insular, limited, narrow-minded, parochial, small-minded, unsophisticated.

provision *n.* **1** process of providing things. **2** stipulation in a treaty or contract etc. **3** (*pl.*) supply of food and drink.
- **1** providing, supply, supplying. **2** condition, proviso, requirement, stipulation. **3** (**provisions**) comestibles, eatables, food, foodstuffs, stores, supplies, viands.

provisional *adj.* arranged temporarily. □ **provisionally** *adv.*
- interim, stopgap, temporary.

proviso /prəvízō/ *n.* (*pl.* **-os**) stipulation. □ **provisory** *adj.*

provoke *v.* **1** annoy, irritate. **2** rouse to action. **3** produce as a reaction. □ **provocation** *n.*, **provocative** *adj.*
- **1** anger, annoy, exasperate, gall, get on one's nerves, incense, infuriate, irk, irritate, madden, needle, nettle, pique, *colloq.* rile, vex. **2** drive, induce, motivate, move, prompt, rouse, spur (on), stimulate, stir. **3** cause, engender, give rise to, lead to, occasion, produce; excite, foment, incite, instigate, kindle.

prow *n.* projecting front part of a ship or boat.

prowess *n.* great ability or daring.
- ability, adroitness, aptitude, capability, dexterity, expertise, know-how, proficiency, skill, skilfulness; boldness, bravery, courage, daring, fearlessness, gallantry, intrepidity, mettle, pluck, valour.

prowl *v.* go about stealthily. ● *n.* prowling. □ **prowler** *n.*
- *v.* creep, lurk, skulk, slink, sneak, steal.

proximate *adj.* nearest.

proximity *n.* nearness.

proxy *n.* **1** person authorized to represent or act for another. **2** use of such a person.

prude *n.* person who is extremely correct and proper, one who is easily shocked. □ **prudery** *n.*

prudent *adj.* acting with or showing care and foresight. □ **prudently** *adv.*, **prudence** *n.*
- careful, canny, cautious, circumspect, sagacious, sensible, shrewd, wise; diplomatic, discreet, tactful.

prudish *adj.* showing prudery. □ **prudishly** *adv.*, **prudishness** *n.*
- goody-goody, priggish, prim, prissy, puritanical, strait-laced, *colloq.* stuffy.

prune¹ *n.* dried plum.

prune² *v.* **1** trim by cutting away dead or unwanted parts. **2** reduce.

prurient *adj.* having or encouraging excessive interest in sexual matters. □ **prurience** *n.*

pry *v.* inquire or peer impertinently (often furtively).
- be nosy, interfere, intrude, meddle, poke about, *colloq.* snoop.

psalm /saam/ *n.* sacred song.

psalmist /sáam-/ *n.* writer of psalms.

psalter /sáwl-/ *n.* copy of the Book of Psalms in the Old Testament.

psephology /sef-/ *n.* study of voting etc. □ **psephologist** *n.*

pseudo- /syōōdō/ *pref.* false.

pseudonym /syōō-/ *n.* fictitious name, esp. used by an author.

psoriasis /sərīəsis/ *n.* skin disease causing scaly red patches.

psyche /síki/ *n.* **1** soul, self. **2** mind.

psychiatry /sī-/ *n.* study and treatment of mental illness. □ **psychiatric** *adj.*, **psychiatrist** *n.*

psychic /síkik/ *adj.* **1** of the soul or mind. **2** of or having apparently supernatural powers. ● *n.* person with such powers.

psychoanalyse /sí-/ *v.* treat by psychoanalysis. □ **psychoanalyst** *n.*

psychoanalysis /sí-/ *n.* method of examining and treating mental conditions by investigating the interaction of conscious and unconscious elements.

psychology /sī-/ n. **1** study of the mind. **2** mental characteristics. □ **psychological** adj., **psychologist** n.

psychopath /sī-/ n. person suffering from a severe mental disorder sometimes resulting in antisocial or violent behaviour. □ **psychopathic** adj.

psychosis /sī-/ n. (pl. **-oses**) severe mental disorder involving a person's whole personality. □ **psychotic** adj. & n.

psychosomatic /sī-/ adj. (of illness) caused or aggravated by mental stress.

psychotherapy /sī-/ n. treatment of mental disorders by the use of psychological methods. □ **psychotherapist** n.

ptarmigan /taármigən/ n. bird of the grouse family.

pterodactyl /térrədáktil/ n. extinct reptile with wings.

ptomaine /tṓmayn/ n. (toxic) compound found in putrefying matter.

pub n. (colloq.) public house.

puberty n. stage in life at which a person's reproductive organs become able to function.

pubic adj. of the abdomen at the lower front part of the pelvis.

public adj. **1** of or for people in general. **2** done or existing openly. ● n. members of a community in general. □ **public house** place selling alcoholic drinks for consumption on the premises. **public school 1** secondary school for fee-paying pupils. **2** (in Scotland, USA, etc.) school run by public authorities. **public-spirited** adj. ready to do things for the community. **publicly** adv.
  ■ adj. **1** collective, common, communal, general, national, popular, universal. **2** conspicuous, known, manifest, obvious, open, overt, visible. ● n. citizens, community, nation, people, populace, population; hoi polloi, masses, proletariat, rank and file.

publican n. keeper of a public house.

publication n. **1** publishing. **2** published book, newspaper, etc.
  ■ **2** book, booklet, brochure, journal, leaflet, magazine, newsletter, newspaper, pamphlet, paper, periodical.

publicity n. **1** public attention directed upon a person or thing. **2** process of attracting this.

publicize v. bring to the attention of the public. □ **publicist** n.
  ■ advertise, plug, promote; air, announce, broadcast, circulate, make public, promulgate.

publish v. **1** issue copies of (a book etc.) to the public. **2** make generally known. □ **publisher** n.
  ■ **1** bring out, issue. **2** advertise, announce, broadcast, circulate, give out, make known or public, proclaim, promulgate, publicize, release, spread.

puce adj. & n. brownish-purple.

puck n. hard rubber disc used in ice hockey.

pucker v. & n. wrinkle.
  ■ v. crease, crinkle, furrow, purse, ruck, screw up, wrinkle.

pudding n. **1** baked, boiled, or steamed dish made of or enclosed in a mixture of flour and other ingredients. **2** sweet course of a meal. **3** a kind of sausage.

puddle n. small pool of rainwater or of liquid on a surface.

pudenda n.pl. genitals.

puerile adj. childish. □ **puerility** n.
  ■ babyish, childish, immature, infantile, juvenile.

puerperal adj. of or resulting from childbirth.

puff n. **1** short light blowing of breath, wind, smoke, etc. **2** soft pad for applying powder to the skin. **3** piece of advertising. ● v. **1** send (air etc.) or come out in puffs. **2** breathe hard, pant. **3** swell. □ **puffball** n. globular fungus. **puff pastry** very light flaky pastry.
  ■ n. blast, breath, gust, waft, whiff; colloq. drag, draw, pull. ● v. **1** blow (out), breathe (out), exhale. **2** blow, gasp, heave, huff, pant, wheeze. **3** balloon, distend, expand, inflate, swell.

puffin n. seabird with a short striped bill.

puffy adj. (**-ier**, **-iest**) puffed out, swollen. □ **puffiness** n.

pug n. dog of a small breed with a flat nose and wrinkled face.

pugilist /pyōōjilist/ n. professional boxer. □ **pugilism** n.

pugnacious adj. eager to fight, aggressive. □ **pugnaciously** adv., **pugnacity** n.
  ■ aggressive, antagonistic, argumentative, bellicose, belligerent, combative, contentious, disputatious, hostile, quarrelsome, unfriendly.

puke v. & n. (sl.) vomit.

pull v. **1** exert force upon (a thing) so as to move it towards the source of the force. **2** remove by pulling. **3** exert a pulling or driving force. **4** attract. ● n. **1** act of pulling. **2** force exerted by this. **3** means of exerting influence. **4** deep drink. **5** draw at a pipe etc. □ **pull in** move towards the side of the road or into a stopping place. **pull off** succeed in doing or achieving. **pull out** withdraw. **2** move away from the side of a road or a stopping place. **pull through** come or bring successfully through an illness or difficulty. **pull up** stop.

■ v. **1** jerk, pluck, tug, tweak, wrench, *colloq.* yank; drag, draw, haul, heave, lug, tow, trail. **2** extract, remove, take out. **4** attract, bring in, draw. ● n. **1** jerk, tug, tweak, wrench, *colloq.* yank. **2** appeal, attractiveness, magnetism, seductiveness. **3** authority, *colloq.* clout, influence, leverage, weight. **4** draught, drink, gulp, swallow. **5** *sl.* drag, draw, puff. □ **pull off** accomplish, bring off, carry out, do, manage, succeed in. **pull through** get better, improve, recover, survive.

pullet n. young hen.

pulley n. (pl. **-eys**) wheel over which a rope etc. passes, used in lifting things.

pullover n. knitted garment put on over the head.

pulmonary adj. of the lungs.

pulp n. fleshy part of fruit etc. ● v. reduce to pulp. □ **pulpy** adj.

pulpit n. raised enclosed platform from which a preacher speaks.

pulsar n. cosmic source of pulses of radiation.

pulsate v. expand and contract rhythmically. □ **pulsation** n.

■ beat, palpitate, pound, pulse, throb.

pulse[1] n. **1** rhythmical throbbing of arteries as blood is propelled along them, esp. as felt in the wrists or temples etc. **2** single beat, throb, or vibration. ● v. pulsate.

pulse[2] n. edible seed of beans, peas, lentils, etc.

pulverize v. **1** crush into powder. **2** become powder. **3** defeat thoroughly. □ **pulverization** n.

puma n. large brown American animal of the cat family.

pumice n. (in full **pumice-stone**) solidified lava used for scouring or polishing.

pummel v. (**pummelled**) strike repeatedly esp. with the fists.

pump n. machine for moving liquid, gas, or air. ● v. **1** use a pump. **2** cause (air, gas, water, etc.) to move (as) with a pump. **3** move vigorously up and down. **4** question persistently.

pumpkin n. large round orange-coloured fruit of a vine.

pun n. humorous use of a word to suggest another that sounds the same. □ **punning** adj. & n.

punch[1] v. **1** strike with the fist. **2** cut (a hole etc.) with a device. ● n. **1** blow with the fist. **2** device for cutting holes or impressing a design. □ **punch-drunk** adj. stupefied by repeated blows. **punchline** n. words giving the climax of a joke.

punch[2] n. drink made of wine or spirits mixed with fruit juices etc. □ **punch-bowl** n.

punctilious adj. **1** very careful about details. **2** conscientious. □ **punctiliously** adv., **punctiliousness** n.

punctual adj. arriving or doing things at the appointed time. □ **punctually** adv., **punctuality** n.

■ □ **punctually** in good time, on the dot, on time, promptly, sharp.

punctuate v. **1** insert the appropriate marks in written material to separate sentences etc. **2** interrupt at intervals. □ **punctuation** n.

puncture n. small hole made by something sharp, esp. in a tyre. ● v. **1** make a puncture in. **2** suffer a puncture.

pundit n. learned expert.

pungent adj. having a strong sharp taste or smell. □ **pungently** adv., **pungency** n.

■ hot, peppery, piquant, sharp, spicy, strong, tangy.

punish v. **1** cause (an offender) to suffer for his or her offence. **2** inflict a penalty for. **3** treat roughly. □ **punishment** n.

■ **1** castigate, chasten, chastise, discipline, penalize. **3** abuse, damage, harm, maltreat, mistreat.

punitive adj. inflicting or intended to inflict punishment.

punk n. **1** (sl.) worthless person. **2** (devotee of) punk rock. □ **punk rock** deliberately outrageous type of rock music.

punnet n. small basket or similar container for fruit etc.

punt[1] n. shallow flat-bottomed boat with broad square ends. ● v. **1** propel (a punt) by thrusting with a pole against the bottom of a river. **2** travel in a punt.

punt² v. kick (a dropped football) before it touches the ground. ● n. this kick.

punter n. 1 person who gambles. 2 (colloq.) customer.

puny adj. (-ier, -iest) 1 undersized. 2 feeble. □ **puniness** n.

■ **1** diminutive, little, minute, small, tiny, undersized. **2** feeble, frail, sickly, weak.

pup n. 1 young dog. 2 young wolf, rat, or seal. ● v. (**pupped**) give birth to pup(s).

pupa n. (pl. **-ae**) chrysalis.

pupil n. 1 person who is taught by another. 2 opening in the centre of the iris of the eye.

puppet n. 1 a kind of doll made to move as an entertainment. 2 person controlled by another. □ **puppetry** n.

■ **1** marionette. **2** cat's-paw, pawn, stooge, tool.

puppy n. young dog.

purchase v. buy. ● n. 1 buying. 2 thing bought. 3 firm hold to pull or raise something, leverage. □ **purchaser** n.

■ v. acquire, buy, get, obtain, pay for, procure. ● n. **1** acquisition, buying, purchasing. **2** acquisition, buy. **3** foothold, footing, grasp, grip, hold, leverage, toehold.

purdah n. screening of Muslim or Hindu women from strangers.

pure adj. 1 not mixed with any other substances. 2 mere, nothing but. 3 innocent. 4 chaste, not morally corrupt. 5 (of mathematics or sciences) dealing with theory, not with practical applications.

■ **1** unadulterated, unalloyed, uncontaminated, unmixed, unpolluted; solid, sterling. **2** absolute, complete, downright, mere, nothing but, out and out, outright, sheer, unmitigated, utter. **3** blameless, guiltless, innocent. **4** chaste, undefiled, unsullied, virgin, virginal; ethical, good, honest, honourable, incorruptible, moral, righteous, sinless, virtuous.

purée n. pulped fruit or vegetables etc. ● v. make into purée.

purely adv. 1 in a pure way. 2 entirely. 3 only.

purgative adj. strongly laxative. ● n. purgative substance.

purgatory n. place or state of suffering, esp. in which souls undergo purification. □ **purgatorial** adj.

purge v. 1 clear the bowels of by a purgative. 2 rid of undesirable people or things. ● n. process of purging.

purify v. make pure. □ **purification** n., **purifier** n.

■ clarify, clean, cleanse, decontaminate, disinfect, refine.

purist n. stickler for correctness. □ **purism** n.

puritan n. person who is strict in morals and regards certain pleasures as sinful. □ **puritanical** adj.

■ □ **puritanical** ascetic, austere, narrowminded, priggish, prim, prissy, prudish, strait-laced, colloq. stuffy.

purity n. pure state or condition.

■ cleanliness, cleanness, pureness; chastity, virtuousness, virginity; honesty, innocence, integrity, rectitude, sinlessness, virtue.

purl n. a kind of knitting stitch. ● v. produce this stitch (in).

purloin v. steal.

purple adj. & n. (of) a colour made by mixing red and blue. □ **purplish** adj.

purport n. /púrport/ meaning. ● v. /perpórt/ **1** have as its apparent meaning. **2** be intended to seem. □ **purportedly** adv.

purpose n. 1 intended result of effort. 2 intention to act, determination. 3 reason for which something is done or made. ● v. intend. □ **on purpose** by intention. **purpose-built** adj. built for a particular purpose.

■ n. **1** aim, end, goal, intent, intention, object, objective, plan, target. **2** determination, doggedness, drive, firmness, perseverance, purposefulness, resoluteness, resolution, resolve, single-mindedness, tenacity. **3** function, use. ● v. aim, design, have in mind, mean, intend, plan, propose. □ **on purpose** deliberately, intentionally, knowingly, purposely, purposefully, wilfully.

purposeful adj. having or showing purpose, intentional. □ **purposefully** adv.

■ deliberate, intended, intentional, planned, wilful; determined, dogged, resolute, resolved, steadfast, strong-willed, tenacious, unfaltering, unwavering.

purposely adv. on purpose.

purr n. 1 low vibrant sound that a cat makes when pleased. 2 similar sound. ● v. make this sound.

purse n. 1 small pouch for carrying money. 2 (US) handbag. 3 money, funds. ● v. pucker (one's lips).

purser n. ship's officer in charge of accounts.

pursuance *n.* performance (of duties etc.).

pursue *v.* 1 follow or chase. 2 continue. 3 proceed along. 4 engage in. □ **pursuer** *n.*
■ 1 chase, dog, go *or* run after, hunt, shadow, stalk, *colloq.* tail, track, trail. 2 carry on with, continue (with), persevere in, persist in, proceed with. 3 follow, keep to. 4 engage in, practise, prosecute.

pursuit *n.* 1 act or instance of pursuing. 2 activity to which one gives time or effort.
■ 1 chase, chasing, hunt, stalking, tracking, trailing. 2 activity, hobby, interest, occupation, pastime.

purulent *adj.* of or containing pus. □ **purulence** *n.*

purvey *v.* supply (articles of food) as a trader. □ **purveyor** *n.*

pus *n.* thick yellowish matter produced from infected tissue.

push *v.* 1 move away by exerting force. 2 press. 3 make one's way by pushing. 4 make demands on the abilities or tolerance of. 5 urge or impel. 6 (*colloq.*) sell (drugs) illegally. ● *n.* 1 act or force of pushing. 2 vigorous effort. □ **push off** (*sl.*) go away. **pusher** *n.*
■ *v.* 1 drive, propel, ram, shove, thrust. 2 depress, press. 3 elbow, force, jostle, shoulder, shove, thrust. 5 encourage, induce, motivate, move, persuade, press, pressurize, prod, prompt, spur, stimulate, urge; coerce, compel, dragoon, drive, force, impel.

pushchair *n.* folding chair on wheels, in which a child can be pushed along.

pushy *adj.* (**-ier**, **-iest**) (*colloq.*) self-assertive, determined to get on. □ **pushiness** *n.*

pusillanimous *adj.* cowardly. □ **pusillanimity** *n.*

puss *n.* cat.

pussy *n.* cat. □ **pussy willow** willow with furry catkins.

pussyfoot *v.* 1 move stealthily. 2 act cautiously.

pustule *n.* pimple, blister. □ **pustular** *adj.*

put *v.* (**put**, **putting**) 1 cause to be in a certain place, position, state, or relationship. 2 express, phrase. 3 throw (the shot or weight) as an athletic exercise. ● *n.* throw of the shot or weight. □ **put across** or **over** make understood. **put by** save for future use. **put down** 1 suppress. 2 snub, disparage. 3 have (an animal) killed. 4 record in writing. **put**

forward suggest, present for discussion. **put off** 1 postpone. 2 dissuade. 3 disconcert, offend. **put out** 1 disconcert or annoy. 2 inconvenience. 3 extinguish. 4 dislocate. **put up** 1 construct, build. 2 raise the price of. 3 provide (money etc.). 4 give temporary accommodation to. **put-up job** scheme concocted fraudulently. **put upon** (*colloq.*) unfairly burdened. **put up with** endure, tolerate.
■ *v.* 1 deposit, dump, lay, park, place, position, rest, set, *colloq.* shove, situate, station, *colloq.* stick; assign, attach, attribute, impute, pin. 2 couch, express, phrase, say, word. □ **put across** communicate, convey, explain, get across, make clear, make understood. **put by** hoard, lay up, *colloq.* salt away, save, set aside, stockpile, store. **put down** 1 crush, overthrow, quash, quell, stamp out, suppress. 2 ignore, slight, snub; belittle, criticize, deprecate, disparage, run down. 4 jot down, note (down), record, register, write down. **put forward** advance, move, offer, present, proffer, propose, propound, recommend, submit, suggest. **put off** 1 defer, delay, postpone, shelve. 2 discourage, dissuade, deter. 3 disconcert, disturb, fluster, perturb, *colloq.* throw, upset; disgust, offend, repel, revolt. **put out** 1 discomfit, disconcert, dismay, *colloq.* throw; annoy, gall, irritate, exasperate, irk, offend, vex. 2 bother, discommode, disturb, impose on, inconvenience, trouble. 3 blow out, douse, extinguish, quench, snuff out; switch off, turn off. **put up** 1 build, construct, erect, set up. 2 increase, raise. 3 contribute, donate, give, furnish, provide, supply. 4 accommodate, billet, lodge, house, quarter. **put up with** accept, bear, brook, endure, live with, stand (for), *colloq.* stick, stomach, swallow, suffer, tolerate.

putative *adj.* reputed, supposed.

putrefy *v.* rot. □ **putrefaction** *n.*
■ decay, decompose, go bad, go off, moulder, rot.

putrescent *adj.* rotting. □ **putrescence** *n.*

putrid *adj.* 1 rotten. 2 foul-smelling.
■ 1 bad, decayed, decaying, decomposed, decomposing, mouldy, putrescent, rotten, rotting. 2 fetid, foul-smelling, rank, stinking.

putt *v.* strike (a golf ball) gently to make it roll along the ground. ● *n.* this stroke. □ **putter** *n.* club used for this.

putty *n.* soft paste that sets hard, used for fixing glass in frames, filling up holes, etc.

puzzle *n.* **1** difficult question or problem. **2** problem or toy designed to test ingenuity etc. ● *v.* disconcert mentally, confound. □ **puzzle over** think deeply about. **puzzlement** *n.*

■ *n.* **1** enigma, mystery, problem. **2** conundrum, poser, riddle. ● *v.* baffle, bemuse, bewilder, confound, confuse, *colloq.* flummox, mystify, nonplus, perplex, *colloq.* stump. □ **puzzle over** consider, contemplate, meditate on, mull over, ponder, reflect on, think about.

pygmy *n.* **1** member of a dwarf people of equatorial Africa. **2** very small person or thing.

pyjamas *n.pl.* loose jacket and trousers esp. for sleeping in.

pylon *n.* lattice-work tower used for carrying electricity cables.

pyorrhoea /pírée@/ *n.* discharge of pus, esp. from tooth-sockets.

pyramid *n.* structure with triangular sloping sides that meet at the top. □ **pyramidal** *adj.*

pyre *n.* pile of wood etc. for burning a dead body.

pyrethrum *n.* **1** a kind of chrysanthemum. **2** insecticide made from its dried flowers.

pyrites /pīríteez/ *n.* mineral sulphide of (copper and) iron.

pyromaniac *n.* person with an uncontrollable impulse to set things on fire.

pyrotechnics *n.pl.* firework display. □ **pyrotechnic** *adj.*

Pyrrhic victory /pírrik/ one gained at too great a cost.

python *n.* large snake that crushes its prey.

Qq

quack¹ *n.* duck's harsh cry. ● *v.* make this sound.

quack² *n.* person who falsely claims to have medical skill.

quad *n.* (*colloq.*) 1 quadrangle. 2 quadruplet.

quadrangle *n.* four-sided courtyard enclosed by buildings.

quadrant *n.* 1 one-quarter of a circle or of its circumference. 2 graduated instrument for taking angular measurements.

quadraphonic *adj. & n.* (sound reproduction) using four transmission channels.

quadratic *adj. & n.* (equation) involving the second and no higher power of an unknown quantity or variable.

quadrilateral *n.* geometric figure with four sides.

quadrille *n.* square dance.

quadruped *n.* four-footed animal.

quadruple *adj.* 1 having four parts or members. 2 four times as much as. ● *v.* increase by four times its amount.

quadruplet *n.* one of four children born at one birth.

quaff *v.* drink in large draughts.

quagmire *n.* bog, marsh.

quail¹ *n.* bird related to the partridge.

quail² *v.* flinch, show fear.
  ■ blench, cower, cringe, flinch, recoil, shrink back, shy away.

quaint *adj.* odd in a pleasing way. □ **quaintly** *adv.*, **quaintness** *n.*
  ■ charming, curious, *colloq.* cute, droll, fanciful, *colloq.* sweet, twee, unusual, whimsical.

quake *v.* shake or tremble, esp. with fear.
  ■ quaver, quiver, shake, shiver, shudder, tremble.

qualification *n.* 1 qualifying. 2 thing that qualifies.

qualify *v.* 1 make or become competent, eligible, or legally entitled to do something. 2 limit the meaning of. □ **qualifier** *n.*
  ■ 1 equip, fit, make eligible, prepare; enable, entitle, permit. 2 limit, modify, restrict.

qualitative *adj.* of or concerned with quality.

quality *n.* 1 (degree of) excellence. 2 characteristic, something that is special in a person or thing.
  ■ 1 calibre, grade, order, standard; distinction, excellence, merit, pre-eminence, superiority. 2 attribute, characteristic, feature, point, property, trait.

qualm /kwaam/ *n.* misgiving, pang of conscience.
  ■ compunction, doubt, misgiving, regret, reservation, scruple, second thought.

quandary *n.* state of perplexity, difficult situation.
  ■ difficulty, dilemma, fix, *colloq.* pickle, plight, predicament.

quango *n.* (*pl.* **-os**) administrative group with members appointed by the government.

quantify *v.* express as a quantity. □ **quantifiable** *adj.*

quantitative *adj.* of or concerned with quantity.

quantity *n.* 1 amount or number of things. 2 ability to be measured. 3 (*pl.*) large amounts. □ **quantity surveyor** person who measures and prices building work.
  ■ 1 amount, extent, measure, volume, weight; number, sum, total.

quantum *n.* **quantum theory** theory of physics based on the assumption that energy exists in indivisible units.

quarantine *n.* isolation imposed on those who have been exposed to an infection which they could spread. ● *v.* put into quarantine.

quark *n.* component of elementary particles.

quarrel *n.* angry disagreement. ● *v.* (**quarrelled**) engage in a quarrel.
  ■ *n.* altercation, argument, *colloq.* bust-up, disagreement, dispute, fight, row, *colloq.* scrap, squabble, tiff, wrangle. ● *v.* argue, bicker, disagree, dispute, fall out, fight, row, *colloq.* scrap, spar, squabble, wrangle.

quarrelsome *adj.* liable to quarrel.
■ antagonistic, argumentative, belligerent, contentious, disagreeable, disputatious, irascible, irritable, pugnacious, truculent.

quarry[1] *n.* **1** intended prey or victim. **2** object of pursuit.
■ prey, victim; object, prize, target.

quarry[2] *n.* open excavation from which stone etc. is obtained. ● *v.* obtain from a quarry.

quart *n.* quarter of a gallon, two pints (1.137 litres).

quarter *n.* **1** one of four equal parts. **2** this amount. **3** (*US & Canada*) (coin worth) 25 cents. **4** fourth part of a year. **5** point of time 15 minutes before or after every hour. **6** direction, district. **7** mercy towards an opponent. **8** (*pl.*) lodgings, accommodation. ● *v.* **1** divide into quarters. **2** put into lodgings. □ **quarter-final** *n.* contest preceding a semifinal.
■ *n.* **6** direction; area, district, locality, neighbourhood, region, sector, territory, zone. **7** clemency, compassion, forgiveness, mercifulness, mercy, pity. **8** (**quarters**) accommodation, digs, dwelling, habitation, lodging(s), residence, rooms; barracks, billet. ● *v.* **2** accommodate, billet, board, house, lodge, put up.

quarterdeck *n.* part of a ship's upper deck nearest the stern.

quarterly *adj. & adv.* (produced or occurring) once in every quarter of a year. ● *n.* quarterly periodical.

quartermaster *n.* **1** regimental officer in charge of stores etc. **2** naval petty officer in charge of steering and signals.

quartet *n.* **1** group of four instruments or voices. **2** music for these.

quartz *n.* a kind of hard mineral. □ **quartz clock** one operated by electric vibrations of a quartz crystal.

quasar *n.* star-like object that is the source of intense electromagnetic radiation.

quash *v.* **1** annul. **2** suppress.
■ **1** annul, cancel, declare null and void, invalidate, nullify, overthrow, overturn, rescind, revoke, void. **2** crush, overcome, overwhelm, put an end to, put down, quell, squash, stamp out, subdue, suppress.

quasi- *pref.* seeming to be but not really so.

quatrain *n.* stanza of four lines.

quaver *v.* **1** tremble, vibrate. **2** speak or utter in a trembling voice. ● *n.* **1** trembling sound. **2** note in music, half a crotchet.
■ *v.* **1** quiver, shake, shiver, shudder, tremble, vibrate.

quay /kee/ *n.* landing place built for ships to load or unload alongside. □ **quayside** *n.*

queasy *adj.* **1** nauseous. **2** squeamish. □ **queasiness** *n.*
■ **1** bilious, ill, nauseous, off colour, queer, sick. **2** fastidious, squeamish.

queen *n.* **1** female ruler of a country by right of birth. **2** king's wife. **3** woman or thing regarded as supreme in some way. **4** piece in chess. **5** playing card bearing a picture of a queen. **6** fertile female of bee or ant etc. □ **queen mother** dowager queen who is the reigning sovereign's mother. **queenly** *adj.*

queer *adj.* **1** strange, odd, eccentric. **2** slightly ill or faint. **3** (*derog.*) homosexual. ● *n.* (*derog.*) homosexual. ● *v.* spoil.
■ *adj.* **1** abnormal, anomalous, atypical, bizarre, eccentric, extraordinary, funny, kinky, odd, offbeat, outlandish, peculiar, quaint, strange, uncanny, unconventional, unorthodox, unusual, weird. **2** groggy, ill, off colour, poorly, queasy, sick, under the weather, unwell; dizzy, faint, light-headed.

quell *v.* suppress.
■ crush, overcome, overpower, put down, quash, squash, stamp out, subdue, suppress.

quench *v.* **1** extinguish (a fire or flame). **2** satisfy (one's thirst) by drinking something.
■ **1** douse, extinguish, put out, snuff out. **2** satisfy, slake.

quern *n.* hand-mill for grinding corn or pepper.

querulous *adj.* complaining peevishly. □ **querulously** *adv.*

query *n.* **1** question. **2** question mark. ● *v.* ask a question or express doubt about.
■ *n.* **1** enquiry, question. ● *v.* ask, enquire; challenge, contest, dispute, doubt, question.

quest *n.* seeking, search.

question *n.* **1** sentence requesting information. **2** matter for discussion or solution. **3** doubt. ● *v.* ask or raise question(s) about. □ **in question** being discussed or disputed. **no question of** no possibility of. **out of the question** completely impracticable. **question mark** punctuation mark (?) placed after a question.

■ *n.* **1** enquiry, query. **2** concern, issue, matter, point; difficulty, problem. ● *v.* ask, catechize, examine, grill, interrogate, pump, quiz; challenge, contest, dispute, doubt, query. □ **out of the question** absurd, impossible, impracticable, inconceivable, preposterous, ridiculous, unthinkable.

questionable *adj.* open to doubt.

■ ambiguous, debatable, disputable, doubtful, dubious, problematic(al), uncertain.

questionnaire *n.* list of questions seeking information.

queue /kyōō/ *n.* line of people waiting for something. ● *v.* (**queuing**) wait in a queue.

quibble *n.* **1** petty objection. **2** evasion. ● *v.* **1** make petty objections. **2** be evasive.

■ *v.* **1** cavil, *colloq.* nit-pick. **2** be evasive, equivocate, evade the issue, hedge, prevaricate.

quiche /keesh/ *n.* savoury flan.

quick *adj.* **1** taking only a short time. **2** able to learn or think quickly. **3** (of temper) easily roused. ● *n.* sensitive flesh below the nails. □ **quickly** *adv.*

■ **1** expeditious, fast, fleet, *colloq.* nippy, rapid, speedy, swift; immediate, instantaneous, prompt; brief, cursory, hasty, hurried, perfunctory, precipitate, sudden, summary. **2** able, astute, bright, clever, intelligent, perceptive, perspicacious, sharp, shrewd, smart. **3** excitable, impatient, irritable, short, testy, touchy.

quicken *v.* make or become quicker or livelier.

■ accelerate, expedite, hasten, hurry, rush, speed up; animate, arouse, enliven, excite, galvanize, invigorate, kindle, rouse, stimulate, vivify.

quicklime *n.* = **lime**[1].

quicksand *n.* area of loose wet deep sand into which heavy objects will sink.

quicksilver *n.* mercury.

quid *n.* (*pl.* **quid**) (*sl.*) £1.

quid pro quo thing given in return.

quiescent *adj.* inactive, quiet. □ **quiescence** *n.*

quiet *adj.* **1** with little or no sound, silent. **2** free from disturbance or vigorous activity. **3** gentle, tranquil. ● *n.* quietness. ● *v.* quieten. □ **on the quiet** unob-

trusively, secretly. **quietly** *adv.*, **quietness** *n.*

■ *adj.* **1** hushed, noiseless, quiescent, silent, soundless; reserved, taciturn, uncommunicative. **2** calm, motionless, still, unmoving; peaceful, secluded, sleepy. **3** calm, gentle, peaceable, peaceful, placid, serene, tranquil. ● *n.* calm, calmness, hush, peace, quietness, serenity, silence, still, stillness, tranquillity.

quieten *v.* make or become quiet.

■ hush, quiet, *colloq.* shush, *colloq.* shut up, silence; calm, lull, pacify, settle, soothe, tranquillize.

quiff *n.* upright tuft of hair.

quill *n.* **1** large wing or tail feather. **2** pen made from this. **3** each of a porcupine's spines.

quilt *n.* padded bed-covering. ● *v.* line with padding and fix with lines of stitching.

quin *n.* (*colloq.*) quintuplet.

quince *n.* **1** hard yellowish fruit. **2** tree bearing this.

quinine *n.* bitter-tasting drug.

quinsy *n.* abscess on a tonsil.

quintessence *n.* **1** essence. **2** perfect example of a quality. □ **quintessential** *adj.*, **quintessentially** *adv.*

■ **1** core, essence, heart. **2** embodiment, epitome, exemplar, ideal, incarnation, model, personification.

quintet *n.* **1** group of five instruments or voices. **2** music for these.

quintuple *adj.* **1** having five parts or members. **2** five times as much as. ● *v.* increase by five times its amount.

quintuplet *n.* one of five children born at one birth.

quip *n.* witty or sarcastic remark. ● *v.* (**quipped**) utter as a quip.

quire *n.* twenty-five or twenty-four sheets of writing paper.

quirk *n.* **1** a peculiarity of behaviour. **2** trick of fate.

■ **1** characteristic, eccentricity, foible, idiosyncrasy, kink, oddity, peculiarity, vagary.

quisling *n.* traitor who collaborates with occupying forces.

quit *v.* (**quitted**) **1** leave. **2** abandon. **3** (*US*) cease.

■ **1** depart from, go away from, flee, leave, move out of, vacate. **2** abandon, forsake, give up, relinquish. **3** cease, desist from, discontinue, refrain from, stop.

quite *adv.* **1** completely. **2** somewhat. **3** (as an answer) I agree.

■ **1** absolutely, altogether, completely, entirely, fully, perfectly, thoroughly, totally, utterly, wholly. **2** fairly, moderately, pretty, rather, relatively, somewhat.

quits *adj.* on even terms after retaliation or repayment.

quiver[1] *n.* case for holding arrows.

quiver[2] *v.* shake or vibrate with a slight rapid motion. ● *n.* quivering movement or sound.

■ *v.* quaver, shake, shiver, shudder, tremble, vibrate, wobble.

quixotic *adj.* romantically chivalrous. □ **quixotically** *adv.*

quiz *n.* (*pl.* **quizzes**) series of questions testing knowledge, esp. as an entertainment. ● *v.* (**quizzed**) interrogate.

■ *v.* ask, examine, grill, interrogate, pump, question.

quizzical *adj.* done in a questioning way, esp. humorously. □ **quizzically** *adv.*

quoit /koyt/ *n.* ring thrown to encircle a peg in the game of **quoits**.

quorate *adj.* having a quorum present.

quorum *n.* minimum number of people that must be present to constitute a valid meeting.

quota *n.* **1** fixed share. **2** number of goods, people, etc. permitted or stipulated.

■ **1** allocation, allotment, allowance, *colloq.* cut, part, percentage, portion, ration, share.

quotable *adj.* worth quoting.

quotation *n.* **1** quoting. **2** passage or price quoted. □ **quotation marks** punctuation marks (' ' or " ") enclosing words quoted.

quote *v.* **1** repeat words from a book or speech. **2** mention in support of a statement. **3** state the price of, estimate.

■ **2** allude to, cite, instance, mention, refer to.

quotidian *adj.* daily.

quotient /kwôsh'nt/ *n.* result of a division sum.

rabbi n. (pl. **-is**) religious leader of a Jewish congregation.

rabbinical adj. of rabbis or Jewish doctrines or law.

rabbit n. burrowing animal with long ears and a short furry tail.

rabble n. disorderly crowd.
■ crowd, herd, horde, mob, swarm, throng.

rabid adj. **1** furious, fanatical. **2** affected with rabies.

rabies n. contagious fatal virus disease esp. of dogs.

race¹ n. **1** contest of speed. **2** (pl.) series of races for horses or dogs. ● v. **1** compete in a race (with). **2** move or operate at full or excessive speed. □ **racer** n.
■ n. **1** competition, contest. ● v. **1** compete (against), contend. **2** dash, fly, hare, hasten, hurry, run, rush, shoot, speed, sprint, tear, whiz, zip, zoom.

race² n. **1** large group of people with common ancestry and inherited physical characteristics. **2** genus, species, breed, or variety of animals or plants.
■ **1** ethnic group, folk, nation, people. **2** breed, genus, species, strain, variety.

racecourse n. ground where horse races are run.

racetrack n. **1** racecourse. **2** track for motor racing.

raceme n. flower cluster with flowers attached by short stalks along a central stem.

racial adj. of or based on race. □ **racially** adv.

racialism n. racism. □ **racialist** adj. & n.

racism n. **1** belief in the superiority of a particular race. **2** antagonism towards other races. □ **racist** adj. & n.

rack¹ n. **1** framework for keeping or placing things on. **2** bar with teeth that engage with those of a wheel. **3** instrument of torture on which people were tied and stretched. ● v. inflict great torment on. □ **rack one's brains** think hard about a problem.

rack² n. **rack and ruin** destruction.

racket¹ n. stringed bat used in tennis and similar games.

racket² n. **1** din, noisy fuss. **2** (sl.) fraudulent business or scheme.
■ **1** clamour, commotion, din, disturbance, fuss, hubbub, hue and cry, hullabaloo, noise, outcry, row, rumpus, to-do, uproar.

racketeer n. person who operates a fraudulent business etc. □ **racketeering** n.

raconteur n. person who is good at telling anecdotes.

racoon n. small arboreal mammal of N. America.

racy adj. (**-ier**, **-iest**) spirited and vigorous in style. □ **racily** adv.

radar n. system for detecting objects by means of radio waves.

radial adj. **1** of rays or radii. **2** having spokes or lines etc. that radiate from a central point. **3** (in full **radial-ply**) (of a tyre) having the fabric layers parallel and the tread strengthened. ● n. radial-ply tyre. □ **radially** adv.

radiant adj. **1** emitting rays of light or heat. **2** emitted in rays. **3** looking very bright and happy. □ **radiantly** adv., **radiance** n.
■ **1** beaming, blazing, bright, gleaming, glittering, glowing, incandescent, luminous, shimmering, shining, sparkling. **3** ecstatic, elated, happy, joyful, overjoyed, rapturous.

radiate v. **1** spread outwards from a central point. **2** send or be sent out in rays.
■ **1** fan out, spread out. **2** emanate, emit, give off, send out.

radiation n. **1** process of radiating. **2** sending out of rays and atomic particles characteristic of radioactive substances. **3** these rays and particles.

radiator n. **1** apparatus that radiates heat, esp. a metal case through which steam or hot water circulates. **2** engine-cooling apparatus.

radical adj. **1** fundamental. **2** drastic, thorough. **3** holding extremist views. ● n. person desiring radical reforms or holding radical views. □ **radically** adv.
■ **1** basic, elemental, essential, fundamental, inherent. **2** complete, comprehensive, drastic, far-reaching, sweeping,

thorough. **3** extreme, extremist, militant, revolutionary.

radicle *n.* embryo root.

radio *n.* (*pl.* **-os**) **1** process of sending and receiving messages etc. by electromagnetic waves. **2** transmitter or receiver for this. **3** sound broadcasting, station for this. ● *v.* transmit or communicate by radio.

radioactive *adj.* emitting radiation caused by decay of atomic nuclei. □ **radioactivity** *n.*

radiography *n.* production of X-ray photographs. □ **radiographer** *n.*

radiology *n.* study of X-rays and similar radiation. □ **radiological** *adj.*, **radiologist** *n.*

radiotherapy *n.* treatment of disease by X-rays or similar radiation. □ **radiotherapist** *n.*

radish *n.* plant with a crisp hot-tasting root that is eaten raw.

radium *n.* radioactive metal obtained from pitchblende.

radius *n.* (*pl.* **-dii**) **1** straight line from the centre to the circumference of a circle or sphere. **2** its length. **3** distance from a centre. **4** thicker long bone of the forearm.

raffia *n.* strips of fibre from the leaves of a kind of palm tree.

raffish *adj.* looking vulgarly flashy or rakish. □ **raffishness** *n.*

raffle *n.* lottery with an object as the prize. ● *v.* offer as the prize in a raffle.

raft *n.* flat floating structure of timber etc., used as a boat.

rafter *n.* one of the sloping beams forming the framework of a roof.

rag¹ *n.* **1** torn or worn piece of cloth. **2** (*derog.*) newspaper. **3** (*pl.*) old and torn clothes.

rag² *v.* (**ragged**) (*sl.*) tease. ● *n.* students' carnival in aid of charity.

ragamuffin *n.* person in ragged dirty clothes.

rage *n.* violent anger. ● *v.* **1** show violent anger. **2** (of a storm or battle) continue furiously. □ **all the rage** very popular.

■ *n.* anger, fury, ire, wrath. ● *v.* **1** boil, fulminate, fume, rail, rant, rave, seethe, storm.

ragged *adj.* **1** torn, frayed. **2** wearing torn clothes. **3** jagged.

■ **1** frayed, ripped, tattered, tatty, threadbare, torn, worn. **2** *colloq.* scruffy, shabby,

unkempt. **3** craggy, irregular, jagged, rough, serrated, uneven.

raglan *n.* type of sleeve joined to a garment by sloping seams.

ragout /raɡoō/ *n.* stew of meat and vegetables.

raid *n.* **1** brief attack to destroy or seize something. **2** surprise visit by police etc. to arrest suspected people or seize illicit goods. ● *v.* make a raid on. □ **raider** *n.*

■ *n.* **1** attack, charge, foray, incursion, invasion, onset, onslaught, sally, sortie. ● *v.* attack, invade, rush, storm; loot, pillage, plunder, ransack, sack.

rail¹ *n.* **1** horizontal bar. **2** any of the lines of metal bars on which trains or trams run. **3** railway(s).

rail² *v.* utter angry reproaches.

railing *n.* fence of rails supported on upright metal bars.

railroad *n.* (*US*) railway. ● *v.* force into hasty action.

railway *n.* **1** set of rails on which trains run. **2** system of transport using these.

rain *n.* **1** atmospheric moisture falling as drops. **2** a fall of this. **3** shower of things. ● *v.* send down or fall as or like rain.

■ *v.* bucket, drizzle, pour (down), spit, teem; lavish, shower.

rainbow *n.* arch of colours formed in rain or spray by the sun's rays.

raincoat *n.* rain-resistant coat.

raindrop *n.* single drop of rain.

rainfall *n.* total amount of rain falling in a given time.

rainforest *n.* dense wet tropical forest.

rainwater *n.* water that has fallen as rain.

rainy *adj.* (**-ier**, **-iest**) in or on which much rain falls.

raise *v.* **1** bring to or towards a higher level or an upright position. **2** increase the amount, value, or strength of. **3** cause to be heard or considered. **4** breed, grow. **5** bring up (a child). **6** collect, manage to obtain. ● *n.* (*US*) rise in salary. □ **raising agent** substance that makes bread etc. swell in cooking.

■ *v.* **1** elevate, haul up, hoist, lift (up), pull up; up-end. **2** increase, put up; amplify, augment, heighten, intensify, step up; boost, buoy up, lift, uplift. **3** bring up, broach, introduce, mention, put forward, suggest. **4** breed, rear; cultivate, farm, grow, propagate. **5** bring up, nurture, rear; educate. **6** collect, gather together, levy.

raisin *n.* dried grape.

raison d'être /ráysoɴ détrə/ reason for or purpose of a thing's existence.

rake¹ n. 1 tool with prongs for gathering of leaves etc. or smoothing loose soil. 2 implement used similarly. ● v. 1 gather or smooth with a rake. 2 search. 3 direct (gunfire etc.) along. □ rake-off n. (colloq.) share of profits. rake up revive (unwelcome) memory of.

rake² n. backward slope of an object. ● v. set at a sloping angle.

rake³ n. dissolute man. □ rakish adj. 1 like a rake. 2 jaunty.

rally v. 1 bring or come (back) together for a united effort. 2 revive, recover strength. ● n. 1 act of rallying, recovery. 2 series of strokes in tennis etc. 3 mass meeting. 4 driving competition over public roads.

■ v. 1 assemble, come or get together, convene, congregate; group; bring or call together, gather, marshal, mobilize, round up, summon; reassemble, regroup. 2 get better, improve, pick up, recuperate, revive. ● n. 1 improvement, recovery, recuperation, revival. 3 assembly, convention, gathering, meeting.

ram n. 1 uncastrated male sheep. 2 striking or plunging device. ● v. (rammed) strike or push heavily, crash against.

■ v. bump, butt, collide with, crash against or into, hit, run into, strike; cram, force, jam, pack, push, squeeze, stuff, thrust, wedge.

Ramadan n. ninth month of the Muslim year, when Muslims fast during daylight hours.

ramble n. walk taken for pleasure. ● v. 1 take a ramble, wander. 2 talk or write disconnectedly. □ rambler n.

■ n. amble, constitutional, saunter, stroll, walk. ● v. 1 amble, meander, perambulate, range, rove, saunter, stroll, walk, wander. 2 digress, maunder, wander.

ramify v. 1 form branches or subdivisions. 2 become complex. □ ramification n.

ramp n. slope joining two levels.

rampage v. /rampáyj/ behave or race about violently. ● n. /rámpayj/ violent behaviour. □ on the rampage rampaging.

rampant adj. flourishing excessively, unrestrained.

■ exuberant, flourishing, luxuriant, rank, profuse; rife, uncontrollable, unrestrained, widespread.

rampart n. broad-topped defensive wall or bank of earth.

ramshackle adj. tumbledown, rickety.

■ crumbling, decrepit, derelict, dilapidated, rickety, ruined, shaky, tumbledown.

ran see run.

ranch n. 1 cattle-breeding establishment in N. America. 2 farm where certain other animals are bred. ● v. farm on a ranch. □ rancher n.

rancid adj. smelling or tasting like stale fat. □ rancidity n.

rancour n. bitter feeling or ill will. □ rancorous adj.

■ acrimony, animosity, animus, antipathy, bitterness, enmity, hate, hatred, hostility, ill will, malevolence, malice, resentfulness, resentment, spite, spitefulness, venom, vindictiveness.

rand n. unit of money in S. African countries.

random adj. done or made etc. at random. □ at random without a particular aim or purpose.

■ accidental, arbitrary, casual, chance, fortuitous, haphazard, hit-or-miss, indiscriminate, unplanned, unsystematic.

randy adj. (-ier, -iest) lustful.

rang see ring².

range n. 1 series representing variety or choice. 2 limits between which something operates or varies. 3 distance a thing can travel or be effective. 4 line or row, esp. of mountains, etc. 5 large open area for grazing or hunting. 6 place with targets for shooting practice. ● v. 1 arrange in row(s) etc. 2 extend. 3 vary between limits. 4 go about a place. □ rangefinder n. device for calculating the distance to a target etc.

■ n. 1 assortment, choice, kind, selection, sort, variety. 2 ambit, area, compass, distance, extent, gamut, limit, reach, scope, span, sphere. 4 chain, line, row, series, string. ● v. 1 align, arrange, array, dispose, line up, order, rank. 2 extend, go, reach, stretch. 3 fluctuate, vary. 4 roam, rove, travel over, traverse, wander.

rangy adj. (-ier, -iest) tall and slim.

rank¹ n. 1 line of people or things. 2 place in a scale of quality or value etc. 3 high social position. 4 (pl.) ordinary soldiers, not officers. ● *v.* **1** arrange in a rank. **2** assign a rank to. **3** have a certain rank. □ **the rank and file** the ordinary people of an organization.

■ *n.* **1** column, file, line, row, string, tier. **2** grade, level, place, position, standing, status. ● *v.* **1** align, arrange, array, dispose, line up, order, range. **2** categorize, class, classify, grade, rate.

rank² *adj.* **1** growing too thickly and coarsely. **2** full of weeds. **3** foul-smelling. **4** complete and utter, unmistakable.

■ **1** abundant, dense, exuberant, flourishing, prolific, profuse. **3** fetid, foul-smelling, putrid, rancid, reeking, smelly, stinking. **4** blatant, complete, downright, flagrant, gross, out and out, sheer, unmistakable, unmitigated, utter.

rankle *v.* cause lasting resentment.

ransack *v.* **1** search thoroughly. **2** pillage.

■ **1** go through, rifle or rummage through, scour, search. **2** despoil, loot, pillage, plunder, raid, rob, sack.

ransom *n.* price demanded or paid for the release of a captive. ● *v.* demand or pay ransom for.

rant *v.* make a violent speech.

rap *n.* **1** quick sharp blow. **2** knocking sound. **3** monologue recited to music. **4** rock music with spoken words. **5** (*sl.*) blame, punishment. ● *v.* (**rapped**) **1** strike sharply. **2** knock. **3** (*sl.*) reprimand.

rapacious *adj.* grasping, violently greedy. □ **rapacity** *n.*

■ acquisitive, avaricious, covetous, grasping, greedy.

rape¹ *v.* have sexual intercourse with (esp. a woman) without consent. ● *n.* this act or crime.

rape² *n.* plant grown as fodder and for its seeds, which yield oil.

rapid *adj.* quick, swift. ● *n.pl.* swift current where a river bed slopes steeply. □ **rapidly** *adv.*, **rapidity** *n.*

■ *adj.* brisk, expeditious, express, fast, fleet, prompt, quick, speedy, swift; hasty, hurried, precipitate, sudden.

rapier *n.* thin light sword.

rapist *n.* person who commits rape.

rapport /rapór/ *n.* harmonious understanding relationship.

■ affinity, empathy, sympathy, understanding.

rapt *adj.* very intent and absorbed, enraptured. □ **raptly** *adv.*

■ absorbed, captivated, engrossed, enraptured, enthralled, fascinated, intent, spellbound.

rapture *n.* intense delight. □ **rapturous** *adj.*

■ bliss, delight, ecstasy, elation, euphoria, joy, joyfulness.

rare¹ *adj.* **1** very uncommon. **2** exceptionally good. **3** of low density. □ **rarely** *adv.*, **rareness** *n.*

■ **1** atypical, exceptional, extraordinary, out of the ordinary, uncommon, unfamiliar, unusual; infrequent, scarce. **2** excellent, exquisite, incomparable, matchless, outstanding, peerless, superlative, unparalleled.

rare² *adj.* (of meat) underdone.

rarebit *n.* see **Welsh rabbit**.

rarefied *adj.* (of air) of low density, thin. □ **rarefaction** *n.*

rarity *n.* **1** rareness. **2** rare thing.

rascal *n.* dishonest or mischievous person. □ **rascally** *adj.*

■ devil, imp, knave, mischief-maker, rogue, scallywag, scamp, scoundrel, wretch.

rash¹ *n.* eruption of spots or patches on the skin.

rash² *adj.* acting or done without due consideration of the risks. □ **rashly** *adv.*, **rashness** *n.*

■ foolhardy, hare-brained, hasty, hotheaded, ill-advised, ill-considered, impetuous, imprudent, impulsive, incautious, injudicious, madcap, precipitate, reckless, thoughtless, unthinking, unwise, wild.

rasher *n.* slice of bacon or ham.

rasp *n.* **1** coarse file. **2** grating sound. ● *v.* **1** scrape with a rasp. **2** utter with or make a grating sound.

raspberry *n.* **1** edible red berry. **2** plant bearing this. **3** (*sl.*) vulgar sound of disapproval.

rat *n.* **1** rodent like a large mouse. **2** scoundrel, treacherous deserter. ● *v.* (**ratted**) **rat on** desert or betray. □ **rat race** fiercely competitive struggle for success.

ratchet *n.* bar or wheel with notches in which a pawl engages to prevent backward movement.

rate *n.* **1** numerical proportion between two sets of things, esp. as the basis of calculating amount or value. **2** charge, cost, or value. **3** rapidity. ● *v.* **1** estimate the worth or value of. **2** consider, regard as. **3** deserve. □ **at any rate 1** no matter what happens. **2** at least.

■ *n.* **1** proportion, scale. **2** charge, cost, fee, price, tariff. **3** gait, pace, speed, tempo, velocity. ● *v.* **1** appraise, assess, calculate, estimate, evaluate, gauge, judge; class, grade, place, rank. **2** consider, count, deem, reckon, regard as. **3** be entitled to, be worthy of, deserve, merit.

rather *adv.* **1** slightly. **2** more exactly. **3** by preference. **4** emphatically yes.

■ **1** fairly, moderately, pretty, quite, slightly, somewhat. **3** preferably, sooner.

ratify *v.* confirm or accept (an agreement etc.) formally. □ **ratification** *n.*

■ agree to, accept, approve, back, confirm, endorse, sanction, support, uphold; sign.

rating *n.* **1** level at which a thing is rated. **2** non-commissioned sailor.

ratio *n.* (*pl.* **-os**) relationship between two amounts, reckoned as the number of times one contains the other.

ratiocinate *v.* reason logically. □ **ratiocination** *n.*

ration *n.* fixed allowance of food etc. ● *v.* limit to a ration.

■ *n.* allocation, allowance, lot, measure, percentage, portion, quota, share. ● *v.* confine, control, limit, restrict.

rational *adj.* **1** able to reason. **2** sane. **3** based on reasoning. □ **rationally** *adv.*, **rationality** *n.*

■ **1** discriminating, enlightened, intelligent, level-headed, reasonable, sensible, wise. **2** lucid, normal, of sound mind, sane, well-balanced. **3** logical, reasoned.

rationale /rashəna′l/ *n.* **1** fundamental reason. **2** logical basis.

rationalism *n.* treating reason as the basis of belief and knowledge. □ **rationalist** *n.*, **rationalistic** *adj.*

rationalize *v.* **1** invent a rational explanation for. **2** make more efficient by reorganizing. □ **rationalization** *n.*

■ **1** account for, excuse, explain, justify. **2** reorganize, streamline.

rattan *n.* palm with jointed stems.

rattle *v.* **1** (cause to) make a rapid series of short hard sounds. **2** (*colloq.*) make nervous. ● *n.* **1** rattling sound. **2** device for making this. □ **rattle off** utter rapidly.

■ *v.* **1** clank, clatter, clink, jangle, shake. **2** discomfit, disconcert, disturb, fluster, perturb, put off, shake, *colloq.* throw, unnerve.

rattlesnake *n.* poisonous American snake with a rattling tail.

raucous *adj.* loud and harsh. □ **raucously** *adv.*

■ discordant, dissonant, grating, harsh, jarring, loud, noisy, rasping, shrill, strident.

raunchy *adj.* (**-ier**, **-iest**) sexually provocative.

ravage *v.* do great damage to. ● *n.pl.* damages.

■ *v.* destroy, devastate, lay waste, ruin, wreak havoc on, wreck.

rave *v.* talk wildly or furiously. □ **rave about** or **over** be rapturously enthusiastic about.

ravel *v.* (**ravelled**) tangle.

raven *n.* black bird with a hoarse cry. ● *adj.* (of hair) glossy black.

ravenous *adj.* very hungry. □ **ravenously** *adv.*

■ famished, hungry, starved, starving.

ravine /rəveen′/ *n.* deep narrow gorge.

raving *adj.* completely (mad).

ravioli *n.* small square pasta cases with a savoury filling.

ravish *v.* **1** rape. **2** enrapture.

raw *adj.* **1** not cooked. **2** not yet processed. **3** stripped of skin, sensitive because of this. **4** (of weather) damp and chilly. □ **raw deal** unfair treatment.

■ **2** crude, natural, unprocessed, unrefined, untreated. **3** exposed, open; painful, sensitive, sore, tender. **4** bitter, chill, chilly, cold, damp, freezing, icy, *colloq.* nippy.

rawhide *n.* untanned leather.

ray[1] *n.* **1** single line or narrow beam of light. **2** radiating line.

■ **1** beam, gleam, shaft, streak.

ray[2] *n.* large marine flatfish.

rayon *n.* synthetic fibre or fabric, made from cellulose.

raze *v.* tear down (a building).

razor *n.* sharp-edged instrument for shaving.

razzmatazz *n.* **1** excitement. **2** extravagant publicity etc.

RC *abbr.* Roman Catholic.

re *prep.* concerning.

re- *pref.* **1** again. **2** back again.

reach *v.* **1** extend, go as far as. **2** arrive at. **3** establish communication with. **4** achieve, attain. ● *n.* **1** distance over which a person or thing can reach. **2** section of a river. □ **reach for** or **out**

stretch out a hand in order to touch or take something.

■ *v.* extend, go, run, stretch. **2** arrive at, come to, gain, get as far as, get to, hit, make. **3** contact, get in touch with. ● *v.* **1** accomplish, achieve, attain, make. ● *n.* **1** ambit, compass, extent, range, scope. □ **reach out** extend, hold out, outstretch, stretch out.

react *v.* undergo a reaction. □ **reactive** *adj.*

reaction *n.* **1** response to a stimulus or act or situation etc. **2** chemical change produced by substances acting upon each other. **3** occurrence of one condition after a period of the opposite.

reactionary *adj. & n.* (person) opposed to progress and reform.

reactor *n.* apparatus for the production of nuclear energy.

read *v.* (**read**) **1** understand the meaning of (written or printed words or symbols). **2** reproduce (such words etc.) mentally or vocally. **3** study or discover by reading. **4** interpret mentally. **5** have a certain wording. **6** (of an instrument) indicate as a measurement. ● *n.* (*colloq.*) session of reading.

■ *v.* **2** peruse, pore over, study; recite. **4** construe, interpret, understand.

readable *adj.* **1** pleasant to read. **2** legible. □ **readably** *adv.*

■ **1** absorbing, enjoyable, entertaining, interesting, stimulating. **2** comprehensible, decipherable, intelligible, legible.

reader *n.* **1** person who reads. **2** senior lecturer at a university. **3** device producing a readable image from a microfilm etc.

readership *n.* readers of a newspaper etc.

readily *adv.* **1** willingly. **2** easily.

■ **1** eagerly, gladly, happily, willingly. **2** easily, effortlessly.

readiness *n.* being ready.

ready *adj.* (**-ier, -iest**) **1** fit or available for action or use. **2** willing, inclined. **3** quick. ● *adv.* beforehand. □ **ready to** about to.

■ *adj.* **1** equipped, fit, prepared, primed, set. **2** eager, game, glad, happy, keen, pleased, willing; apt, disposed, given, inclined, likely, prone. **3** prompt, quick, rapid, speedy, swift; bright, clever, intelligent, keen, perceptive, sharp. □ **ready to** about to, in danger of, on the point of, on the verge of.

reagent *n.* substance used to produce a chemical reaction.

real *adj.* **1** existing as a thing or occurring as a fact. **2** genuine. □ **real estate** immovable assets, i.e. buildings, land.

■ **1** actual, existent, unimaginary; concrete, material, palpable, physical, tangible. **2** authentic, bona fide, genuine, legitimate, proper, true, verifiable, veritable; earnest, heartfelt, honest, sincere, unaffected, unfeigned.

realism *n.* representing or viewing things as they are in reality. □ **realist** *n.*

realistic *adj.* **1** showing realism. **2** practical. □ **realistically** *adv.*

■ **1** graphic, lifelike, naturalistic, vivid; factual. **2** businesslike, down-to-earth, hard-headed, practical, pragmatic, rational, reasonable, sensible.

reality *n.* **1** quality of being real. **2** something real and not imaginary.

realize *v.* **1** be or become aware of. **2** understand clearly. **3** fulfil (a hope or plan). □ **realization** *n.*

■ **1** appreciate, be aware of, be conscious of, know. **2** *colloq.* catch on to, comprehend, *colloq.* cotton on to, grasp, perceive, recognize, see, *colloq.* twig, understand. **3** accomplish, achieve, bring about, fulfil.

really *adv.* **1** in fact. **2** thoroughly. **3** I assure you, I protest.

realm *n.* **1** kingdom. **2** field of activity or interest.

■ **1** domain, empire, kingdom, principality. **2** area, domain, field, province, sphere.

ream *n.* **1** 500 sheets of paper. **2** (*pl.*) large quantity of writing.

reap *v.* **1** cut (grain etc.) as harvest. **2** receive as the consequence of actions. □ **reaper** *n.*

■ **1** collect, garner, gather, harvest. **2** acquire, gain, get, obtain, receive, secure.

rear¹ *n.* back part. ● *adj.* situated at the rear. □ **bring up the rear** be last. **rear admiral** naval officer next below vice admiral.

■ *n.* back, end, hind part, tail; stern.

rear² *v.* **1** bring up (children). **2** breed and look after (animals). **3** cultivate (crops). **4** (of a horse etc.) raise itself on its hind legs.

■ **1** bring up, nurture, raise; educate. **2** breed, care for, keep, look after, raise. **3** cultivate, farm, grow, propagate, raise.

rearguard *n.* troops protecting an army's rear.

rearm v. arm again. □ **rearmament** n.

rearrange v. arrange in a different way.
□ **rearrangement** n.

rearward adj., adv., & n. (towards or at)
the rear. □ **rearwards** adv.

reason n. **1** motive, cause, justification. **2**
ability to think and draw conclusions. **3**
sanity. **4** good sense or judgement. ● v.
use one's ability to think and draw conclusions. □ **reason with** try to persuade
by argument.
  ■ n. **1** cause, motivation, motive; defence,
  excuse, explanation, ground(s), justification. **2** intellect, intelligence, mind. **3** mind,
  sanity, senses. **4** common sense, judgement, perspicacity, sense, wisdom, wit.
  □ **reason with** argue with, persuade,
  plead with, prevail on.

reasonable adj. **1** ready to use or listen
to reason. **2** in accordance with reason,
logical. **3** moderate, not expensive.
□ **reasonably** adv.
  ■ **1** intelligent, judicious, logical, rational,
  sane, sensible, wise. **2** justifiable, logical,
  reasoned, sensible, tenable, valid, well-
  thought-out. **3** affordable, inexpensive, low,
  moderate, modest.

reassure v. restore confidence to. □ **reassurance** n.
  ■ buoy up, cheer up, comfort, encourage,
  hearten, put at ease.

rebate n. partial refund.

rebel n. /rébb'l/ person who fights
against or refuses allegiance to established government or conventions. ● v.
/ribél/ (**rebelled**) act as a rebel. □ **rebellion** n., **rebellious** adj.
  ■ n. insurgent, insurrectionist, mutineer,
  revolutionary; dissident, nonconformist,
  recusant. ● v. mutiny, revolt, rise (up).
  □ **rebellion** insurgency, insurrection, mutiny, revolt, revolution, uprising. **rebellious**
  defiant, insubordinate, insurgent, mutinous, revolutionary, seditious.

rebound v. /ribównd/ spring back after
impact. ● n. /reébownd/ act of re-
bounding. □ **on the rebound** while still
reacting to a disappointment etc.

rebuff v. & n. snub.
  ■ v. brush off, cut, ignore, put down, reject,
  slight, snub, spurn.

rebuild v. (**rebuilt**) build again after destruction.

rebuke v. reprove. ● n. reproof.
  ■ v. admonish, colloq. bawl out, berate,
  carpet, castigate, censure, chastise, chide,
  sl. rap, reprehend, reprimand, reproach,

reprove, scold, take to task, colloq. tell off,
colloq. tick off, upbraid. ● n. admonition,
castigation, dressing down, lecture, reprimand, reproof, scolding.

rebus n. representation of a word by
pictures etc. suggesting its parts.

rebut v. (**rebutted**) disprove. □ **rebuttal**
n.

recalcitrant adj. obstinately disobedient.
□ **recalcitrance** n.
  ■ contrary, defiant, disobedient, headstrong, intractable, obstinate, perverse, refractory, unmanageable, unruly, wayward,
  wilful.

recall v. **1** summon to return. **2** remember. ● n. recalling, being recalled.

recant v. withdraw and reject (one's
former statement or belief). □ **recanta-
tion** n.

recap (colloq.) v. (**recapped**) recapitulate.
● n. recapitulation.

recapitulate v. state again briefly.
□ **recapitulation** n.

recapture v. **1** capture again. **2** experience again. ● n. recapturing.

recede v. **1** go back. **2** become more distant.
  ■ **1** ebb, go or move back, retreat, subside.

receipt /riseét/ n. **1** act of receiving. **2**
written acknowledgement that some-
thing has been received or money paid.

receive v. **1** acquire, accept, or take in. **2**
experience, be treated with. **3** greet on
arrival.
  ■ **1** accept, acquire, be given, come by,
  gain, get, obtain, take. **2** be subjected to,
  endure, experience, meet with, suffer, undergo. **3** greet, meet, welcome.

receiver n. **1** person or thing that receives something. **2** one who deals in
stolen goods. **3** official who handles the
affairs of a bankrupt person or firm. **4**
apparatus that receives electrical signals
and converts them into sound or a picture. **5** earpiece of a telephone.

recent adj. happening or established in a
time shortly before the present. □ **recently** adv.
  ■ current, fresh, modern, new, up to date.

receptacle n. thing for holding what is
put into it.
  ■ container, holder, repository; bag, box,
  can, case, casket, chest, tin, vessel.

reception n. **1** act, process, or way of
receiving. **2** assembly held to receive

guests. **3** place where clients etc. are received on arrival.

receptionist *n.* person employed to receive and direct clients etc.

receptive *adj.* quick to receive ideas. □ **receptiveness** *n.*, **receptivity** *n.*

■ astute, bright, intelligent, perceptive, quick, sharp; amenable, impressionable, open, responsive, sensitive.

recess *n.* **1** space set back from the line of a wall or room etc. **2** temporary cessation from work. ● *v.* make a recess in or of.

■ *n.* **1** alcove, bay, hollow, niche, nook. **2** break, breather, interlude, intermission, interval, pause, respite, rest; holiday, vacation.

recession *n.* **1** receding from a point or level. **2** temporary decline in economic activity.

■ **2** depression, economic decline, slump.

recessive *adj.* tending to recede.

recidivist *n.* person who persistently relapses into crime. □ **recidivism** *n.*

recipe /réssipi/ *n.* **1** directions for preparing a dish. **2** way of achieving something.

recipient *n.* person who receives something.

reciprocal *adj.* mutual. □ **reciprocally** *adv.*, **reciprocity** *n.*

reciprocate *v.* **1** return (affection etc.). **2** give in return. **3** (of a machine part) move backwards and forwards. □ **reciprocation** *n.*

recital *n.* **1** reciting. **2** long account of events. **3** musical entertainment.

■ **1** description, narration, reading, recitation, recounting, relation. **2** account, narrative, report, story. **3** concert, performance.

recitation *n.* **1** reciting. **2** thing recited.

recite *v.* **1** repeat aloud from memory. **2** state (facts) in order.

■ **1** declaim, quote, read aloud *or* out, repeat. **2** detail, enumerate, itemize, list, rattle off, reel off.

reckless *adj.* wildly impulsive. □ **recklessly** *adv.*, **recklessness** *n.*

■ careless, daredevil, foolhardy, foolish, hare-brained, hasty, headlong, heedless, hotheaded, ill-advised, ill-considered, imprudent, impulsive, incautious, injudicious, irresponsible, madcap, precipitate, rash, thoughtless, unwise, wild.

reckon *v.* **1** count up. **2** have as one's opinion. **3** rely. □ **reckon with** take into account.

■ **1** add up, calculate, compute, count up, total, *colloq.* tot up. **2** assume, believe, be of the opinion, imagine, presume, suppose, think; consider, deem, judge, rate, regard. **3** bank, count, depend, rely. □ **reckon with** allow for, anticipate, consider, expect, foresee, take into account *or* consideration.

reclaim *v.* **1** take action to recover possession of. **2** make (waste land) usable. □ **reclamation** *n.*

recline *v.* lean (one's body), lie down.

■ lean back, lie (down), loll, lounge, sprawl, stretch out.

recluse *n.* person who avoids social life.

recognition *n.* recognizing.

recognizance *n.* **1** pledge made to a law court or magistrate. **2** surety for this.

recognize *v.* **1** identify as already known. **2** acknowledge as genuine, valid, or worthy. **3** realize or discover the nature of. □ **recognizable** *adj.*

■ **1** identify, know (again), place, recall, recollect, remember. **2** acknowledge, accept, admit, allow, concede, grant, own. **3** appreciate, be aware *or* conscious of, discover, perceive, realize, see, understand.

recoil *v.* **1** spring back. **2** shrink back in fear or disgust. ● *n.* act of recoiling.

■ *v.* **1** jump *or* spring back, shy away, start. **2** blench, flinch, quail, shrink back.

recollect *v.* remember, call to mind. □ **recollection** *n.*

recommend *v.* **1** advise. **2** suggest as suitable for employment or use etc.; speak favourably of. **3** (of qualities etc.) make desirable. □ **recommendation** *n.*

■ **1** advise, advocate, counsel, exhort, suggest, urge. **2** nominate, propose, put forward, suggest; commend, endorse, vouch for. □ **recommendation** advice, advocacy, counsel; proposal, suggestion; commendation, endorsement.

recompense *v.* repay, compensate. ● *n.* repayment.

reconcile *v.* **1** make friendly after an estrangement. **2** settle (quarrel) etc. **3** make compatible. □ **reconcile oneself to** accept something unwelcome, unpleasant, etc. **reconciliation** *n.*

■ **1** bring together, reunite, unite. **2** mend, patch up, put right, resolve, settle, sort out. □ **reconcile oneself to** accept, adjust to, come to terms with, get used to, habituate oneself to, resign oneself to.

recondite *adj.* obscure, dealing with an obscure subject.

■ abstruse, arcane, cryptic, dark, deep, esoteric, incomprehensible, obscure, profound, unfathomable.

recondition *v.* overhaul, repair.

reconnaissance *n.* preliminary survey, esp. exploration of an area for military purposes.

reconnoitre *v.* (**reconnoitring**) make a reconnaissance (of).

■ *sl.* case, examine, explore, inspect, investigate, scout (out), scrutinize, survey.

reconsider *v.* consider again, esp. for a possible change of decision. □ **reconsideration** *n.*

reconstitute *v.* **1** reconstruct. **2** restore to its original form. □ **reconstitution** *n.*

reconstruct *v.* construct or enact again. □ **reconstruction** *n.*

record *v.* /rɪkórd/ **1** set down in writing or other permanent form. **2** preserve (sound) on a disc or magnetic tape for later reproduction. **3** (of a measuring instrument) indicate, register. ● *n.* /rékkord/ **1** information set down in writing etc. **2** document bearing this. **3** disc bearing recorded sound. **4** facts known about a person's past. **5** best performance or most remarkable event etc. of its kind. ● *adj.* /rékkord/ best or most extreme hitherto recorded. □ **off the record** not for publication.

■ *v.* **1** catalogue, chronicle, enter, log, note or put or set or write down, put in writing, register. **3** display, indicate, read, register, show. ● *n.* **2** annals, archive(s), chronicle, diary, document, file, journal, log, minutes, report. **3** album, compact disc, disc, single. **4** background, career, history, life, past. □ **off the record** confidential, private, secret, unofficial.

recorder *n.* **1** person or thing that records. **2** a kind of flute.

recount *v.* narrate, tell in detail.

■ describe, narrate, recount, report, tell.

re-count *v.* count again. ● *n.* second or subsequent counting.

recoup *v.* **1** reimburse or compensate for a loss. **2** recover or regain (a loss).

recourse *n.* source of help to which one may turn. □ **have recourse to** turn to for help.

recover *v.* **1** regain possession or control of. **2** return to health. □ **recovery** *n.*

■ **1** get or win back, recapture, reclaim, recoup, regain, repossess, retake, retrieve; rescue, salvage, save. **2** be on the mend, convalesce, get better or well, improve, pick up, rally, recuperate, revive. □ **recovery** recapture, reclamation, repossession, retrieval; rescue, salvage; convalescence, improvement, recuperation.

recreation *n.* **1** pastime. **2** relaxation. □ **recreational** *adj.*

■ **1** hobby, interest, pastime. **2** amusement, diversion, enjoyment, entertainment, fun, play, sport.

recriminate *v.* make angry accusations in retaliation. □ **recrimination** *n.*, **recriminatory** *adj.*

recruit *n.* **1** newly enlisted member of the armed forces. **2** new member of a society or organization. ● *v.* **1** form by enlisting recruits. **2** enlist as a recruit. □ **recruitment** *n.*

■ *n.* **1** conscript. **2** apprentice, initiate, trainee. ● *v.* **1** form, mobilize, raise. **2** engage, enlist, enrol, take on.

rectal *adj.* of the rectum.

rectangle *n.* geometric figure with four straight sides and four right angles. □ **rectangular** *adj.*

rectify *v.* **1** put right. **2** purify, refine. **3** convert to direct current. □ **rectification** *n.*

■ **1** ameliorate, amend, better, correct, emend, fix, improve, mend, put or set right, remedy, repair, right.

rectilinear *adj.* bounded by straight lines.

rectitude *n.* correctness of behaviour or procedure.

■ correctness, decency, honesty, honour, integrity, morality, principle, probity, propriety, respectability, righteousness, virtue.

rector *n.* **1** clergyman in charge of a parish. **2** head of certain colleges and universities.

rectory *n.* house of a rector.

rectum *n.* last section of the intestine, between colon and anus.

recumbent *adj.* lying down.

■ lying down, prone, prostrate, reclining, supine.

recuperate *v.* recover (health, strength, or losses). □ **recuperation** *n.*, **recuperative** *adj.*

recur v. (**recurred**) happen again or repeatedly.

recurrent adj. recurring. □ **recurrence** n.

■ frequent, periodic, persistent, recurring, regular, repeated.

recusant n. person who refuses to submit or comply.

recycle v. convert (waste material) for reuse.

red adj. (**redder, reddest**) **1** of or like the colour of blood. **2** (of hair) reddish-brown. **3** Communist. ● n. **1** red colour or thing. **2** Communist. □ **in the red** with a debit balance. **red carpet** privileged treatment for an important visitor. **red-handed** adj. in the act of crime. **red herring** misleading clue or diversion. **red-hot** adj. **1** glowing red from heat. **2** (of news) completely new. **red-letter day** day of a very joyful occurrence. **red light 1** signal to stop. **2** danger signal. **red tape** excessive formalities in official transactions. **reddish** adj., **redness** n.

redbrick adj. (of universities) founded in the 19th century or later.

redcurrant n. **1** small edible red berry. **2** bush bearing this.

redden v. make or become red.

■ blush, colour, flush, go red.

redeem v. **1** buy back. **2** convert (tokens etc.) into goods or cash. **3** reclaim. **4** free from sin. **5** make up for (faults). □ **redemption** n., **redemptive** adj.

redeploy v. send to a new place or task. □ **redeployment** n.

redhead n. person with red hair.

redirect v. direct or send to another place. □ **redirection** n.

redolent adj. **1** smelling strongly. **2** reminiscent. □ **redolence** n.

■ **1** aromatic, odoriferous, odorous, perfumed, scented, sweet-smelling. **2** evocative, reminiscent, suggestive.

redouble v. increase or intensify.

redoubtable adj. formidable.

redress v. set right. ● n. reparation.

■ v. correct, put right, rectify, remedy. ● n. compensation, recompense, reparation, restitution.

reduce v. **1** make or become smaller or less. **2** make lower in rank. **3** slim. **4** convert into a simpler or more general form. □ **reduce to** bring into a specified state. **reduction** n., **reducible** adj.

■ **1** abridge, curtail, cut, shorten; abate, decrease, diminish, lessen; ease, moder-

ate, mitigate, tone down. **2** degrade, demote, downgrade. □ **reduce to** bring to, drive to, force to.

redundant adj. **1** superfluous. **2** no longer needed at work. □ **redundancy** n.

■ **1** inessential, superfluous, unnecessary. **2** jobless, out of work, unemployed.

redwood n. **1** very tall evergreen Californian tree. **2** its wood.

re-echo v. **1** echo. **2** echo repeatedly. **3** resound.

reed n. **1** water or marsh plant with tall hollow stems. **2** its stem. **3** vibrating part of certain wind instruments.

reedy adj. (of the voice) having a thin high tone. □ **reediness** n.

reef n. **1** ridge of rock or sand etc. reaching to or near the surface of water. **2** part of a sail that can be drawn in when there is a high wind. ● v. shorten (a sail). □ **reef-knot** n. symmetrical double knot.

reefer n. thick double-breasted jacket.

reek n. strong usu. unpleasant smell. ● v. smell strongly.

reel n. **1** cylinder on which something is wound. **2** lively Scottish or folk dance. ● v. **1** wind on or off a reel. **2** stagger. □ **reel off** recite rapidly.

■ v. **1** coil, turn, twine, twist, wind. **2** lurch, stagger, stumble, sway.

refectory n. dining room of a monastery or college etc.

refer v. (**referred**) **refer to 1** mention. **2** direct to an authority or specialist. **3** turn to for information. **4** be relevant to.

■ **1** allude to, bring up, mention, speak of, touch on. **2** direct to, pass on to, send to. **3** check, look at, study; ask, consult, speak to. **4** apply to, concern, pertain to, relate to.

referee n. **1** umpire, esp. in football and boxing. **2** person to whom disputes are referred for decision. **3** person willing to testify to the character or ability of one applying for a job. ● v. (**refereed**) act as referee (for).

■ n. **1, 2** arbitrator, judge, umpire.

reference n. **1** act of referring. **2** mention. **3** testimonial. **4** person willing to testify to another's character, ability, etc. **5** source of information. □ **in** or **with reference to** in connection with, about. **reference book** book providing information. **reference library** one containing books that can be consulted but not taken away.

■ **2** allusion, mention. **3** endorsement, recommendation, testimonial.

referendum n. (pl. **-ums**) referring of a question to the people for decision by a general vote.

referral n. referring.

refill v. /reefíl/ fill again. ● n. /reefíl/ **1** second or later filling. **2** material used for this.

refine v. **1** remove impurities or defects from. **2** make elegant or cultured. □ **refined** adj.

■ **1** cleanse, decontaminate, purify. **2** civilize, cultivate, improve, perfect, polish.

refinement n. **1** refining. **2** elegance of behaviour. **3** improvement added.

■ **1** development, enhancement, improvement, perfection; cleansing, purification, refining. **2** breeding, culture, elegance, gentility, polish, sophistication, urbanity. **3** addition, alteration, improvement, modification.

refinery n. establishment where crude substances are refined.

reflate v. restore (a financial system) after deflation. □ **reflation** n., **reflationary** adj.

reflect v. **1** throw back (light, heat, or sound). **2** show an image of. **3** have as a cause or source. **4** think deeply. **5** bring (credit or discredit). □ **reflection** n.

■ **2** mirror. **3** demonstrate, exemplify, exhibit, illustrate, point to, reveal, show. **4** brood, cogitate, deliberate, meditate, muse, ponder, ruminate, think.

reflective adj. **1** reflecting. **2** thoughtful.

■ **2** contemplative, meditative, pensive, ruminative, thoughtful.

reflector n. thing that reflects light or heat.

reflex n. reflex action. □ **reflex action** involuntary or instinctive movement in response to a stimulus. **reflex angle** angle of more than 180°.

reflexive adj. & n. (word or form) showing that the action of the verb is performed on its subject (e.g. he washed himself).

reflux n. flowing back.

reform v. **1** improve by removing faults. **2** (cause to) give up bad behaviour. ● n. reforming. □ **reformation** n., **reformer** n.

■ v. **1** ameliorate, amend, better, correct, emend, improve, make better, put right,

rectify, revise. **2** go straight, mend one's ways.

reformatory adj. reforming. ● n. institution to which offenders are sent to be reformed.

refract v. bend (a ray of light) where it enters water or glass etc. obliquely. □ **refraction** n., **refractor** n., **refractive** adj.

refractory adj. **1** resisting control or discipline. **2** resistant to treatment or heat.

refrain¹ n. **1** recurring lines of a song. **2** music for these.

refrain² v. **refrain from** keep oneself from doing something.

■ abstain from, avoid, eschew, forbear from; cease, desist from, discontinue, US quit, stop.

refresh v. **1** restore the vigour of by food, drink, or rest. **2** stimulate (a person's memory).

■ **1** fortify, invigorate, pep up, perk up, restore, revive.

refreshing adj. **1** restoring vigour, cooling. **2** welcome and interesting because of its novelty. □ **refreshingly** adv.

■ **1** enlivening, fortifying, invigorating, restorative, reviving, stimulating; bracing, cool, crisp.

refreshment n. **1** process of refreshing. **2** (pl.) food and drink.

■ **2** (**refreshments**) drinks, eatables, food, sl. grub, nibbles, snacks.

refrigerate v. make extremely cold, esp. in order to preserve. □ **refrigerant** n., **refrigeration** n.

refrigerator n. cabinet or room in which food is stored at a very low temperature.

refuge n. shelter from pursuit or danger.

■ asylum, haven, hiding place, retreat, sanctuary, shelter.

refugee n. person who has left home and seeks refuge (e.g. from war or persecution) elsewhere.

refund v. /rifúnd/ pay back. ● n. /réefund/ repayment, money refunded.

■ v. pay back, reimburse, repay.

refurbish v. brighten up, redecorate. □ **refurbishment** n.

■ decorate, do up, redecorate, renovate, revamp.

refuse[1] /rifyooz/ v. say or show that one is unwilling to accept or do (what is asked or required). □ **refusal** n.
∎ decline, *colloq.* pass up, turn down; deny, deprive of, withhold.

refuse[2] /réfyoos/ n. waste material.
∎ debris, dross, garbage, litter, rubbish, trash, waste.

refute v. prove falsity or error of. □ **refutation** n.
∎ *colloq.* debunk, discredit, disprove, prove wrong.

regain v. **1** obtain again after loss. **2** reach again.

regal adj. like or fit for a monarch. □ **regally** adv., **regality** n.
∎ dignified, kingly, majestic, noble, princely, queenly, royal.

regale v. feed or entertain well.

regalia n.pl. emblems of royalty or rank.

regard v. **1** look steadily at. **2** consider to be. ∎ n. **1** attention, care. **2** respect. **3** (pl.) kindly greetings conveyed in a message. □ **as regards, with regard to** regarding.
∎ v. **1** *poetic* behold, contemplate, gaze at, look at, observe, survey, view. **2** consider, judge, perceive, think of, view. ∎ n. **1** attention, care, concern, heed, notice, thought. **2** consideration, deference, esteem, honour, respect, reverence. **3** (regards) best wishes, compliments, greetings, salutations.

regarding prep. with reference to.

regardless adv. without paying attention. □ **regardless of** despite.

regatta n. boat or yacht races organized as a sporting event.

regency n. **1** rule by a regent. **2** period of this.

regenerate v. give new life or vigour to. □ **regeneration** n., **regenerative** adj.

regent n. person appointed to rule while the monarch is a child, ill, or absent.

reggae n. W. Indian style of music, with a strong beat.

regicide n. killing or killer of a king. □ **regicidal** adj.

regime /rayzheem/ n. method or system of government.

regimen n. **1** prescribed course of treatment etc. **2** way of life.

regiment n. **1** permanent unit of an army. **2** large array or number of things. ∎ v. organize rigidly. □ **regimentation** n.

regimental adj. of an army regiment.

region n. **1** part of a surface, space, or body. **2** administrative division of a country. □ **in the region of** approximately. **regional** adj.
∎ **2** area, district, division, locality, part, province, quarter, sector, territory, zone.

register n. **1** official list. **2** range of a voice or musical instrument. ∎ v. **1** enter in a register. **2** record esp. in writing. **3** notice and remember. **4** indicate. **5** make an impression. □ **register office** place where records of births, marriages, and deaths are kept and civil marriages are performed. **registration** n.
∎ n. **1** catalogue, directory, inventory, list, record, roll. **2** check in. ∎ v. **1** enter, note or put down; log, note, record, write down. **2** mark, note, notice, take note of. **4** indicate, measure, record; display, exhibit, express, show.

registrar n. **1** official responsible for keeping written records. **2** hospital doctor ranking just below specialist.

registry n. **1** registration. **2** place where written records are kept. □ **registry office** register office.

regress v. relapse to an earlier or more primitive state. □ **regression** n., **regressive** adj.

regret n. feeling of sorrow about a loss, or of annoyance or repentance. ∎ v. (regretted) feel regret about. □ **regretful** adj., **regretfully** adv.
∎ n. compunction, contrition, guilt, penitence, remorse, repentance, sadness, sorrow; (regrets) qualms, second thoughts. ∎ v. bemoan, be sorry about, feel remorse for, lament, rue.

regrettable adj. that is to be regretted. □ **regrettably** adv.
∎ awful, deplorable, dreadful, lamentable, sad, terrible, unfortunate.

regular adj. **1** acting, occurring, or done in a uniform manner or at a fixed time or interval. **2** conforming to a rule or habit. **3** even, symmetrical. **4** forming a country's permanent armed forces. ∎ n. **1** regular soldier etc. **2** (colloq.) regular customer etc. □ **regularly** adv., **regularity** n.
∎ adj. **1** even, rhythmical, steady, uniform; fixed, ordered, orderly, systematic. **2** accustomed, customary, habitual, normal, ordinary, routine, standard, traditional, usual; correct, legal, official, proper. **3** even, symmetrical, well-proportioned.

regularize v. make regular, lawful, or correct. □ **regularization** n.

regulate v. 1 control by rules. 2 adjust to work correctly or according to one's requirements. □ **regulator** n.
■ 1 administer, control, direct, govern, manage, monitor. 2 adjust, control, modify, modulate.

regulation n. 1 process of regulating. 2 rule.
■ 1 control, management; adjustment, modulation. 2 decree, directive, edict, law, order, rule, statute.

regurgitate v. 1 bring (swallowed food) up again to the mouth. 2 reproduce (information etc.). □ **regurgitation** n.

rehabilitate v. restore to a normal life or good condition. □ **rehabilitation** n.

rehash v. /reehásh/ put (old material) into a new form. ● n. /reehash/ 1 rehashing. 2 thing made of rehashed material.

rehearse v. practise beforehand. □ **rehearsal** n.

rehouse v. provide with new accommodation.

reign n. (period of) sovereignty or rule. ● v. 1 rule as king or queen. 2 prevail.
■ v. 1 govern, rule. 2 be prevalent, hold sway, predominate, prevail.

reimburse v. repay (a person), refund. □ **reimbursement** n.
■ pay back, refund, repay.

rein n. (also pl.) 1 long strap fastened to a bridle, used to guide or check a horse. 2 means of control. ● v. check or control with reins.

reincarnation n. rebirth of the soul in another body after death of the first. □ **reincarnate** v.

reindeer n. (pl. **reindeer**) deer of Arctic regions, with large antlers.

reinforce v. strengthen with additional people, material, or quantity. □ **reinforcement** n.
■ bolster, buttress, fortify, shore up, strengthen, support.

reinstate v. restore to a previous position. □ **reinstatement** n.

reiterate v. say or do again or repeatedly. □ **reiteration** n.

reject v. /rijékt/ 1 refuse to accept. 2 rebuff. ● n. /reejekt/ person or thing rejected. □ **rejection** n.
■ v. 1 decline, refuse, say no to, turn down, veto; discount, dismiss, disregard; discard, scrap, throw away. 2 brush off, rebuff, shun, snub, spurn.

rejoice v. feel or show great joy.
■ be happy or delighted, celebrate, exult, glory.

rejoin v. 1 retort. 2 join again.

rejoinder n. answer, retort.
■ answer, reply, response, retort.

rejuvenate v. restore youthful appearance or vigour to. □ **rejuvenation** n., **rejuvenator** n.

relapse v. fall back (into worse state after improvement). ● n. relapsing.
■ v. backslide, decline, deteriorate, lapse, regress, retrogress.

relate v. 1 narrate. 2 establish a relation between. □ **relate to 1** have a connection with. 2 feel sympathetic to.
■ 1 describe, narrate, recite, recount, tell. 2 associate, connect, link, tie. □ **relate to 1** apply to, be relevant to, concern, have a bearing on, pertain to, refer to. 2 empathize with, identify with, sympathize with, understand.

related adj. having a common descent or origin.

relation n. 1 similarity connecting people or things. 2 relative. 3 narrating. 4 (pl.) dealings with others. □ **in relation to** with reference to.
■ 1 association, connection, correspondence, interconnection, link, relationship, tie.

relationship n. 1 state of being related. 2 connection, relation. 3 emotional (esp. sexual) association between two people.
■ 3 affair, liaison, love affair, romance.

relative adj. considered in relation to something else. ● n. person related to another by descent or marriage. □ **relatively** adv.
■ n. (**relatives**) family, flesh and blood, folk, kindred, kinsfolk, kith and kin, relations.

relativity n. 1 being relative. 2 Einstein's theory of the universe, showing that all motion is relative and treating time as a fourth dimension related to space.

relax v. 1 make or become less tight, tense, or strict. 2 rest from work, indulge in recreation. □ **relaxation** n.
■ 1 loosen, release, slacken; calm down, unbend, colloq. unwind; moderate, modify, soften, temper, tone down. □ **relaxation** amusement, entertainment, fun, pleasure, recreation, rest.

relaxed adj. not worried or tense.
∎ calm, carefree, cool, easygoing, happy-go-lucky, insouciant, nonchalant, peaceful, serene, tranquil.

relay n. /réelay/ **1** fresh set of workers relieving others. **2** relay race. **3** relayed message or transmission. **4** device relaying things or activating an electrical circuit. ● v. /rilày/ (**relayed**) receive and pass on or retransmit. □ **relay race** race between teams in which each person in turn covers a part of the total distance.

release v. **1** set free. **2** remove from a fixed position. **3** make (information, a film or recording) available to the public. ● n. **1** releasing. **2** handle or catch etc. that unfastens something. **3** record, film, etc. released.
∎ v. **1** discharge, free, let go, liberate, loose, set free. **3** broadcast, circulate, disseminate, issue, make public, publish.

relegate v. consign to a less important position or group. □ **relegation** n.
∎ degrade, demote, downgrade.

relent v. become less severe or more lenient. □ **relentless** adj., **relentlessly** adv.
∎ capitulate, give way, melt, soften, yield.

relevant adj. related to the matter in hand. □ **relevance** n.
∎ applicable, apposite, appropriate, germane, pertinent, to the point.

reliable adj. able to be relied on. □ **reliably** adv., **reliability** n.
∎ dependable, infallible, safe, trusted, trustworthy, unfailing; honest, reputable, responsible.

reliance n. trust, confidence. □ **reliant** adj.

relic n. **1** thing that survives from earlier times. **2** (pl.) remains.

relief n. **1** ease given by reduction or removal of pain or anxiety etc. **2** thing that breaks up monotony. **3** assistance to those in need. **4** person replacing one who is on duty. **5** carving etc. in which the design projects from a surface. **6** similar effect given by colour or shading. □ **relief road** road by which traffic can avoid a congested area.
∎ **1** abatement, alleviation, easing; comfort, consolation, solace. **3** aid, assistance, charity, help, support.

relieve v. **1** give or bring relief to. **2** release from a task or duty. □ **relieve oneself** urinate or defecate.
∎ **1** alleviate, diminish, ease, lessen, moderate, reduce, soothe.

religion n. **1** belief in and worship of a superhuman controlling power. **2** system of this. **3** influence compared to religious faith.
∎ **2** belief, creed, faith; denomination, sect.

religious adj. **1** of religion. **2** devout, pious. **3** very conscientious. □ **religiously** adv.
∎ **2** devout, God-fearing, holy, pious. **3** conscientious, meticulous, painstaking, scrupulous.

relinquish v. give up, cease from. □ **relinquishment** n.
∎ abandon, cede, concede, forfeit, give up, surrender, waive, yield.

reliquary n. receptacle for relic(s) of a holy person.

relish n. **1** great enjoyment of something. **2** appetizing flavour, thing giving this. ● v. enjoy greatly.
∎ n. **1** delight, eagerness, enjoyment, enthusiasm, gusto, joy, pleasure, zest. ● v. appreciate, delight in, enjoy, love, revel in, take pleasure in.

relocate v. move to a different place. □ **relocation** n.

reluctant adj. unwilling, grudging one's consent. □ **reluctantly** adv., **reluctance** n.
∎ disinclined, hesitant, loath, unwilling.

rely v. **rely on** trust confidently, depend on for help etc.
∎ bank on, be sure of, count on, depend on, have faith in, trust.

remain v. **1** stay. **2** be left or left behind. **3** continue in the same condition.
∎ **3** carry on as, continue to be, go on as, keep, stay.

remainder n. **1** remaining people, things, or part. **2** quantity left after subtraction or division. ● v. dispose of unsold copies of (a book) at a reduced price.
∎ n. **1** excess, residue, rest, surplus. **2** balance, difference.

remains n.pl. **1** what remains, surviving parts. **2** dead body.
∎ **1** debris, fragments, leavings, leftovers, remnants, scraps. **2** body, cadaver, corpse, sl. stiff.

remand v. send back (a prisoner) into custody while further evidence is sought. □ **on remand** remanded.

remark n. spoken or written comment. ● v. **1** make a remark, say. **2** notice.
■ n. comment, observation, statement, utterance. ● v. **1** comment, declare, mention, note, observe, say. **2** note, notice, observe, perceive.

remarkable adj. worth noticing, unusual. □ **remarkably** adv.
■ amazing, astonishing, exceptional, extraordinary, impressive, incredible, marvellous, outstanding, singular, uncommon, unusual, wonderful.

remedy n. thing that cures or relieves a disease or puts right a matter. ● v. be a remedy for, put right. □ **remedial** adj.
■ n. cure, medicine, therapy, treatment. ● v. correct, cure, fix, heal, make good, put right, rectify, repair.

remember v. keep in one's mind and recall at will. □ **remembrance** n.
■ recall, recollect; reminisce.

remind v. cause to remember.

reminder n. thing that reminds someone, letter sent as this.
■ cue; keepsake, memento, souvenir.

reminisce v. think or talk about past events.

reminiscence n. **1** reminiscing. **2** (usu. pl.) account of what one remembers.

reminiscent adj. having characteristics that remind one (of something).
■ evocative, redolent, suggestive.

remiss adj. negligent.
■ careless, heedless, inattentive, lax, negligent, slack, thoughtless.

remission n. **1** remitting of a debt or penalty. **2** reduction of force or intensity.

remit v. /rimit/ (**remitted**) **1** cancel (a debt or punishment). **2** make or become less intense. **3** send (money etc.). **4** refer (a matter for decision) to an authority. ● n. /réemit/ terms of reference.

remittance n. **1** sending of money. **2** money sent.

remnant n. **1** small remaining quantity. **2** surviving trace.
■ **1** (**remnants**) debris, fragments, leftovers, remains, scraps. **2** relic, trace, vestige.

remonstrate v. make a protest. □ **remonstrance** n.
■ complain, expostulate, colloq. kick up, make a fuss, protest.

remorse n. deep regret for one's wrongdoing. □ **remorseful** adj., **remorsefully** adv.
■ contrition, guilt, penitence, regret, repentance, self-reproach.

remorseless adj. without compassion. □ **remorselessly** adv.
■ callous, cruel, hard-hearted, merciless, pitiless, ruthless.

remote adj. **1** far away in place or time, not close. **2** slight. □ **remotely** adv., **remoteness** n.
■ **1** distant, far-away, far-off, outlying; isolated, lonely, out of the way. **2** faint, slight.

remove v. **1** take off or away. **2** dismiss from office. **3** get rid of. ● n. degree of remoteness or difference. □ **removable** adj., **remover** n., **removal** n.
■ v. **1** doff, take off; detach, disconnect, separate, undo, unfasten; move, take away. **2** discharge, dismiss, fire, colloq. sack. **3** eliminate, eradicate, get rid of, root out; delete, efface, erase, rub out, wipe out.

remunerate v. pay or reward for services. □ **remuneration** n.
■ □ **remuneration** emolument, fee, pay, payment, salary, wages.

remunerative adj. giving good remuneration, profitable.
■ gainful, lucrative, profitable.

Renaissance n. **1** revival of art and learning in Europe in the 14th–16th centuries. **2** (**renaissance**) any similar revival.

renal adj. of the kidneys.

rend v. (**rent**) tear.

render v. **1** give, esp. in return. **2** cause to become. **3** perform. **4** submit (a bill etc.). **5** translate. **6** melt down (fat).

rendezvous /róndivōō/ n. (pl. -**vous**) prearranged meeting or meeting place. ● v. meet at a rendezvous.
■ n. appointment, assignation, colloq. date, meeting; venue.

rendition n. way something is rendered or performed.

renegade n. person who deserts from a group or cause etc.

renege /rináyg/ v. fail to keep a promise or agreement.

renew v. **1** revive. **2** replace. **3** resume. **4** repeat. □ **renewal** n.
■ **1** refresh, reinvigorate, restore, revive. **2** replace; refill, replenish. **3** restart, resume, return to, take up. **4** reiterate, repeat, restate.

rennet n. substance used to curdle milk in making cheese.

renounce v. **1** give up formally. **2** reject. □ **renouncement** n.
■ **1** forgo, give up, relinquish, surrender. **2** deny, disown, reject, repudiate, spurn.

renovate v. repair, restore to good condition. □ **renovation** n., **renovator** n.
■ decorate, do up, modernize, overhaul, redecorate, refurbish, repair, revamp.

renown n. fame. □ **renowned** adj.
■ celebrity, distinction, eminence, fame, glory, note, prominence. □ **renowned** celebrated, distinguished, eminent, famous, illustrious, noted, well-known.

rent[1] see rend. n. torn place.

rent[2] n. periodical payment for use of land, rooms, machinery, etc. ● v. pay or receive rent for.
■ v. hire (out), lease (out), let (out); charter.

rental n. **1** rent. **2** renting.

renunciation n. renouncing.

rep[1] n. (colloq.) business firm's travelling representative.

rep[2] n. (colloq.) repertory.

repair v. **1** put into good condition after damage or wear. **2** make amends for. ● n. **1** process of repairing. **2** repaired place. **3** condition for use. □ **repairer** n.
■ v. **1** fix, mend, overhaul, patch up, put right, renovate, restore, service. ● n. **3** condition, form, shape, working order.

reparation n. **1** making amends. **2** compensation.

repartee n. **1** witty reply. **2** exchange of witty remarks.

repast n. (formal) a meal.

repatriate v. send or bring back (a person) to his or her own country. □ **repatriation** n.

repay v. (**repaid**) pay back. □ **repayment** n., **repayable** adj.
■ pay back, recompense, refund, reimburse, settle up with.

repeal v. withdraw (a law) officially. ● n. repealing of a law.
■ v. abolish, abrogate, annul, cancel, rescind, revoke.

repeat v. **1** say, do, produce, or occur again. **2** tell (a thing told to oneself) to another person. ● n. **1** repeating. **2** thing repeated. □ **repeatedly** adv.
■ v. **1** colloq. recap, recapitulate, reiterate, restate, say again; echo; duplicate, reproduce; recur.

repel v. (**repelled**) **1** drive away. **2** be impossible for (a substance) to penetrate. **3** be repulsive to. □ **repellent** adj. & n.
■ **1** drive back, fend or fight or stave or ward off, repulse. **3** disgust, revolt, sicken.

repent v. feel regret about (what one has done or failed to do). □ **repentance** n., **repentant** adj.

repercussion n. **1** indirect effect or reaction. **2** recoil.
■ **1** consequence, effect, outcome, result, upshot.

repertoire /réppartwaar/ n. stock of songs, plays, etc., that a person or company is prepared to perform.

repertory n. **1** repertoire. **2** theatrical performances of various plays for short periods by one company (**repertory company**).

repetition n. **1** repeating. **2** instance of this. □ **repetitious** adj., **repetitive** adj.

repine v. fret, be discontented.

replace v. **1** put back in its place. **2** take the place of. **3** be or find a substitute for. □ **replacement** n.
■ **1** put back, return. **2** follow, succeed, supersede, supplant, take the place of.

replay v. /reepláy/ play again. ● n. /réeplay/ replaying.

replenish v. **1** refill. **2** renew (a supply etc.). □ **replenishment** n.

replete adj. **1** well-fed. **2** filled or well-supplied. □ **repletion** n.
■ **1** full, sated, satiated, well-fed.

replica n. exact copy.

replicate v. make a replica of. □ **replication** n.

reply v. & n. answer.
■ v. answer, rejoin, respond, retort. ● n. answer, rejoinder, response, retort, riposte.

report v. **1** give an account of. **2** tell as news. **3** make a formal complaint about. **4** present oneself on arrival. ● n. **1** spoken or written account. **2** written statement about a pupil's work etc. **3** rumour. **4** explosive sound.
■ v. **1** describe, give an account of, recount, relate, tell of. **2** announce, broadcast. ● n. **1** account, description, record,

statement; article, bulletin, feature, item, piece, story. **4** bang, blast, boom, explosion, shot.

reporter *n.* person employed to report news etc. for publication or broadcasting.
■ correspondent, hack, journalist.

repose *n.* **1** rest, sleep. **2** tranquillity. ● *v.* rest, lie.
■ *n.* **1** inactivity, peace, relaxation, rest; sleep, slumber. **2** calm, peace, quiet, stillness, tranquillity.

repository *n.* storage place.

repossess *v.* take back something for which payments have not been made. □ **repossession** *n.*

reprehend *v.* rebuke.

reprehensible *adj.* deserving rebuke. □ **reprehensibly** *adv.*
■ blameworthy, disgraceful, deplorable, indefensible, inexcusable, shameful, unforgivable.

represent *v.* **1** be an example or embodiment of. **2** show in a picture or play etc. **3** describe or declare (to be). **4** act on behalf of. □ **representation** *n.*
■ **1** embody, epitomize, exemplify, stand for, symbolize, typify. **2** depict, portray, show.

representative *adj.* typical of a group or class. ● *n.* **1** person's or firm's agent. **2** person chosen to represent others.
■ *adj.* characteristic, illustrative, typical. ● *n.* **1** agent, *colloq.* rep, salesman, saleswoman. **2** agent, delegate, emissary, envoy, spokesperson.

repress *v.* suppress, keep (emotions) from finding an outlet. □ **repression** *n.*, **repressive** *adj.*
■ contain, control, hold back, restrain, stifle, suppress.

reprieve *n.* **1** postponement or cancellation of punishment (esp. death sentence). **2** respite. ● *v.* give a reprieve to.

reprimand *v. & n.* rebuke.
■ *v.* berate, chastise, chide, rebuke, reproach, scold, take to task, *colloq.* tell off, *colloq.* tick off, upbraid.

reprint *v.* /reeprint/ print again. ● *n.* /reeprint/ book reprinted.

reprisal *n.* act of retaliation.

reproach *v.* express disapproval to (a person) for a fault or offence. ● *n.* **1** act or instance of reproaching. **2** (cause of)

discredit. □ **reproachful** *adj.*, **reproachfully** *adv.*
■ *v.* admonish, blame, castigate, censure, criticize, rebuke, reprehend, reprimand, reprove, take to task, upbraid.

reprobate *n.* immoral or unprincipled person.

reproduce *v.* **1** produce again. **2** produce a copy of. **3** produce further members of the same species. □ **reproduction** *n.*, **reproductive** *adj.*
■ **1,2** copy, duplicate, replicate. **3** breed, multiply, procreate.

reproof *n.* expression of condemnation for a fault or offence.
■ admonition, castigation, censure, condemnation, criticism, reproach.

reprove *v.* give a reproof to.

reptile *n.* member of the class of cold-blooded animals with a backbone and rough or scaly skin. □ **reptilian** *adj. & n.*

republic *n.* country in which the supreme power is held by the people or their representatives.

republican *adj.* of or advocating a republic. ● *n.* person advocating republican government.

repudiate *v.* reject or disown utterly, deny. □ **repudiation** *n.*
■ deny, disown, reject, renounce.

repugnant *adj.* distasteful, repulsive. □ **repugnance** *n.*

repulse *v.* **1** drive back (an attacking force). **2** reject, rebuff. ● *n.* **1** driving back. **2** rebuff.
■ *v.* **1** drive back, fend *or* fight *or* stave *or* ward off, repel.

repulsion *n.* **1** repelling. **2** strong feeling of distaste, revulsion.

repulsive *adj.* **1** arousing disgust. **2** able to repel. □ **repulsively** *adv.*, **repulsiveness** *n.*
■ **1** abhorrent, disgusting, distasteful, foul, hateful, horrible, loathsome, nasty, obnoxious, odious, offensive, repellent, repugnant, revolting, sickening, unpleasant, unsavoury, vile.

reputable *adj.* having a good reputation, respected.

reputation *n.* what is generally believed about a person or thing.

repute *n.* reputation.

reputed *adj.* said or thought to be. □ **reputedly** *adv.*
■ alleged, believed, considered, rumoured, supposed, thought.

request *n.* 1 asking for something. 2 thing asked for. ● *v.* make a request (for or of).

■ *n.* appeal, application, call, demand, entreaty, petition, plea. ● *v.* apply for, ask for, beg, beseech, demand, entreat, plead for, solicit.

requiem /rékwi-em/ *n.* 1 special mass for the repose of the soul(s) of the dead. 2 music for this.

require *v.* 1 need, depend on for success etc. 2 order, oblige. □ **requirement** *n.*

■ 1 demand, entail, necessitate, need; be short of, lack, want. 2 command, compel, force, instruct, make, oblige, order; demand, insist (on).

requisite *adj.* required, necessary. ● *n.* thing needed.

requisition *n.* formal written demand, order laying claim to use of property or materials. ● *v.* demand or order by this.

■ *v.* demand, order, request; appropriate, commandeer, confiscate, expropriate, seize, take possession of.

requite *v.* make a return for.

resale *n.* sale to another person of something one has bought.

rescind *v.* repeal or cancel.

rescue *v.* save from danger or capture etc. ● *n.* rescuing. □ **rescuer** *n.*

■ *v.* deliver, free, liberate, release, set free; salvage, save.

research *n.* study and investigation, esp. to discover new facts. ● *v.* perform research (into). □ **researcher** *n.*

■ *v.* analyse, examine, inquire into, look into, investigate, probe, study.

resemble *v.* be like. □ **resemblance** *n.*

■ be similar to, correspond to, look like, take after.

resent *v.* feel displeased and indignant about. □ **resentment** *n.*, **resentful** *adj.*, **resentfully** *adv.*

□ □ **resentful** angry, annoyed, bitter, displeased, grudging, envious, jealous, indignant, irritated, *colloq.* peeved.

reservation *n.* 1 reserving. 2 reserved accommodation etc. 3 doubt. 4 land set aside, esp. for occupation by American Indians.

■ 1,2 booking. 3 doubt, misgiving, qualm, scruple; hesitation, reluctance.

reserve *v.* 1 put aside for future or special use. 2 order or set aside for a particular person. 3 retain, esp. a power.

● *n.* 1 thing(s) reserved, extra stock available. 2 tendency to avoid showing feelings or friendliness. 3 (also *pl.*) forces outside the regular armed services. 4 land set aside for special use, esp. as habitat. 5 substitute player in team games. 6 lowest acceptable price for an item to be auctioned. □ **in reserve** unused, available.

■ *v.* 1 conserve, keep back, preserve, retain, save, set aside. 2 book, order; save. ● *n.* 1 cache, fund, hoard, stock, stockpile, store, supply. 2 caution, self-control, self-restraint; quietness, reticence, shyness, taciturnity. □ **in reserve** available, on hand, *colloq.* on tap, ready.

reserved *adj.* (of a person) showing reserve of manner.

■ aloof, cool, distant, formal, reticent, standoffish, taciturn, uncommunicative, unforthcoming, unresponsive, unsociable, withdrawn.

reservist *n.* member of a reserve force.

reservoir /rézzərvwaar/ *n.* 1 natural or artificial lake that is a source or store of water to a town etc. 2 container for a supply of fluid.

reshuffle *v.* interchange, reorganize. ● *n.* reshuffling.

reside *v.* dwell permanently.

residence *n.* 1 residing. 2 one's dwelling. □ **in residence** living or working in a specified place.

■ 2 abode, domicile, dwelling, home, house, lodging, quarters.

resident *adj.* residing, in residence. ● *n.* 1 permanent inhabitant. 2 (at a hotel) person staying overnight.

residential *adj.* 1 containing dwellings. 2 of or based on residence.

residual *adj.* left over as a residue. □ **residually** *adv.*

residue *n.* what is left over.

■ excess, remainder, rest, surplus; dregs, lees, remains.

resign *v.* give up (one's job, claim, etc.). □ **resign oneself to** accept (a situation etc.) reluctantly. **resignation** *n.*

■ □ **resign oneself to** accept, accommodate oneself to, come to terms with, face up to, reconcile oneself to.

resigned *adj.* having resigned oneself. □ **resignedly** *adv.*

resilient *adj.* 1 springy. 2 readily recovering from shock etc. □ **resiliently** *adv.*, **resilience** *n.*

resin n. **1** sticky substance from plants and certain trees. **2** similar substance made synthetically, used in plastics. □ **resinous** adj.

resist v. **1** oppose strongly or forcibly. **2** withstand the action or effect of. **3** abstain from (pleasure etc.). □ **resistance** n., **resistant** adj., **resistible** adj.
■ **1** combat, fight (against), oppose, strive or struggle against. **2** block, check, curb, hinder, impede, stem, stop, thwart; be proof against, withstand. **3** decline, forgo, colloq. pass up, refuse, turn down.

resistivity n. resistance to the passage of electric current.

resistor n. device having resistance to the passage of electric current.

resolute adj. showing great determination. □ **resolutely** adv., **resoluteness** n.
■ adamant, decided, determined, dogged, firm, purposeful, resolved, steadfast, unshakeable, unswerving, unwavering.

resolution n. **1** firm intention. **2** great determination, resolve. **3** formal statement of a committee's opinion. **4** resolving.

resolve v. **1** decide firmly. **2** solve or settle (a problem or doubts). **3** separate into constituent parts. ● n. great determination.
■ v. **1** decide, determine, make up one's mind. **2** settle, solve, sort out. ● n. determination, doggedness, firmness, perseverance, persistence, purpose, resoluteness, resolution, steadfastness, will-power.

resonant adj. **1** resounding, echoing. **2** reinforcing sound, esp. by vibration. □ **resonance** n.

resonate v. produce or show resonance. □ **resonator** n.

resort v. resort to adopt as an expedient. ● n. **1** expedient. **2** popular holiday place.

resound v. **1** fill a place or be filled with sound. **2** echo.
■ boom, echo, resonate, reverberate, ring.

resource n. **1** something to which one can turn for help. **2** ingenuity. **3** (pl.) available assets.
■ **3** (**resources**) assets, capital, cash, finances, funds, means, money, wealth, colloq. wherewithal.

resourceful adj. clever at finding ways of doing things. □ **resourcefully** adv., **resourcefulness** n.

respect n. **1** admiration or esteem. **2** consideration **3** particular aspect. **4** (pl.) polite greetings. ● v. **1** feel or show respect for. **2** agree to recognize. □ **with respect to** about, concerning. **respectful** adj., **respectfully** adv.
■ n. **1** admiration, esteem, regard. **2** civility, consideration, courtesy, deference, politeness, reverence; attention, care, concern, heed, regard, thought. **3** aspect, characteristic, detail, feature, particular, point, quality. **4** (**respects**) best wishes, compliments, greetings, regards, salutations. ● v. **1** admire, esteem, have a high opinion of, honour, look up to, revere, think highly of, value. **2** fulfil, honour, keep. □ **with respect to** about, apropos, as regards, concerning, re, regarding, with reference to, with regard to.

respectable adj. **1** worthy of respect. **2** considerable. □ **respectably** adv., **respectability** n.
■ **1** decent, estimable, honourable, respected, upright, worthy; decorous, genteel, proper, seemly. **2** appreciable, considerable, large, significant, sizeable, substantial.

respective adj. belonging to each as an individual. □ **respectively** adv.

respiration n. breathing.

respirator n. **1** device worn over the nose and mouth to purify air before it is inhaled. **2** device for giving artificial respiration.

respiratory adj. of respiration.

respire v. breathe.

respite n. **1** interval of rest or relief. **2** permitted delay.
■ **1** break, breather, interlude, intermission, interval, pause, rest.

resplendent adj. brilliant with colour or decorations. □ **resplendently** adv.

respond v. **1** answer. **2** react.
■ **1** answer, rejoin, reply, retort.

respondent n. defendant in a lawsuit, esp. in a divorce case.

response n. **1** answer. **2** act, feeling, or movement caused by a stimulus etc.
■ **1** answer, rejoinder, reply, retort, riposte.

responsibility n. **1** being responsible. **2** thing for which one is responsible.
■ **1** accountability, liability. **2** burden, charge, duty, job, role, task.

responsible adj. **1** liable to be blamed for loss or failure etc. **2** being the cause of or to blame for. **3** reliable, trustworthy. **4** involving important duties. □ **responsibly** adv.

■ **1** accountable, answerable, liable. **2** at fault, culpable, guilty, in the wrong, to blame. **3** dependable, honest, reliable, reputable, sensible, trustworthy.

responsive adj. **1** responding well to an influence. **2** sympathetic. □ **responsiveness** n.

rest¹ v. **1** be still or asleep. **2** (cause or allow to) cease from tiring activity. **3** place or be placed for support. **4** rely. **5** (of a matter) be left without further discussion. ● n. **1** (period of) inactivity or sleep. **2** prop or support for an object.

■ v. **1** doze, repose, sleep, slumber, snooze. **2** relax, slow down, take a break, colloq. unwind. **3** lay, place, prop, put; be supported, lean, lie. ● n. **1** break, breather, interlude, intermission, lull, pause, respite; ease, relaxation, repose; doze, nap, siesta, sleep, snooze.

rest² v. remain in a specified state. ● n. the remaining part, the others.

■ n. balance, difference, remainder, residue, surplus; leftovers, remains, remnants.

restaurant n. place where meals can be bought and eaten.

restaurateur n. restaurant-keeper.

restful adj. giving rest, relaxing. □ **restfully** adv., **restfulness** n.

■ calm, peaceful, quiet, relaxing, serene, tranquil.

restitution n. **1** restoring of a thing to its proper owner or original state. **2** compensation.

■ **2** amends, compensation, indemnification, recompense, redress, reparation.

restive adj. restless, impatient. □ **restively** adv., **restiveness** n.

restless adj. unable to rest or be still. □ **restlessly** adv., **restlessness** n.

■ agitated, edgy, fidgety, fretful, ill at ease, colloq. jittery, jumpy, nervous, restive, uneasy.

restoration n. **1** restoring. **2** restored thing.

restorative adj. restoring health or strength. ● n. restorative food, medicine, or treatment.

restore v. **1** bring back to its original state (e.g. by repairing), or to good health or vigour. **2** put back in a former position. □ **restorer** n.

■ **1** do up, rebuild, refurbish, renew, renovate, repair; cure, heal, make better; fortify, invigorate, refresh, revive.

restrain v. **1** hold back from movement or action. **2** keep under control. □ **restraint** n.

■ **1** check, control, curb, hinder, hold back, impede, prevent, stop. **2** contain, control, hold back, repress, stifle, suppress.

restrict v. put a limit on, subject to limitations. □ **restriction** n., **restrictive** adj.

■ bound, circumscribe, confine, delimit, limit.

result n. **1** product of an activity, operation, or calculation. **2** score, marks, or name of the winner in a sports event or competition. ● v. occur or have as a result.

■ n. **1** consequence, effect, outcome, repercussion, upshot. ● v. come about, develop, emerge, happen, occur.

resultant adj. occurring as a result.

resume v. **1** get or take again. **2** begin again after stopping. □ **resumption** n.

résumé /rézyoomay/ n. summary.

resurface v. **1** put a new surface on. **2** return to the surface.

resurgence n. revival after destruction or disappearance. □ **resurgent** adj.

resurrect v. bring back into use.

resurrection n. **1** rising from the dead. **2** revival after disuse.

resuscitate v. revive. □ **resuscitation** n.

retail n. selling of goods to the public. ● adj. & adv. in the retail trade. ● v. sell or be sold in the retail trade. □ **retailer** n.

retain v. **1** keep, esp. in one's possession or in use. **2** keep in mind.

■ **1** keep, preserve, reserve, save.

retainer n. fee paid to retain services.

retaliate v. repay an injury or insult etc. by inflicting one in return. □ **retaliation** n., **retaliatory** adj.

retard v. cause delay to. □ **retardation** n.

■ delay, hold up, set back, slow down; hamper, hinder, impede.

retarded adj. backward in mental or physical development.

retch v. strain one's throat as if vomiting.

retention n. retaining.

retentive adj. able to retain things.

rethink v. (**rethought**) reconsider, plan again and differently.

reticent adj. not revealing one's thoughts. □ **reticence** n.

■ diffident, quiet, reserved, retiring, secretive, shy, silent, taciturn, uncommunicative, unforthcoming.

retina n. (pl. **-as**) membrane at the back of the eyeball, sensitive to light.

retinue n. attendants accompanying an important person.

■ attendants, entourage, escort, suite, train.

retire v. 1 give up one's regular work because of age. 2 cause (an employee) to do this. 3 withdraw, retreat. 4 go to bed. □ **retirement** n.

■ 2 pension off. 3 depart, go (away), leave, move away, retreat, withdraw.

retiring adj. shy, avoiding society.

■ bashful, diffident, meek, self-effacing, shy, timid, unassuming.

retort[1] v. make (as) a witty or angry reply. ● n. reply of this kind.

■ n. answer, reaction, rejoinder, reply, response, riposte.

retort[2] n. 1 vessel with a bent neck, used in distilling. 2 vessel used in making gas or steel.

retouch v. touch up (a picture or photograph).

retrace v. go back over or repeat (a route).

retract v. withdraw. □ **retraction** n., **retractor** n., **retractable** adj.

■ draw back, pull back; cancel, deny, disavow, disclaim, recant, revoke, take back, withdraw.

retractile adj. retractable.

retreat v. withdraw, esp. after defeat or when faced with difficulty. ● n. 1 retreating, withdrawal. 2 military signal for this. 3 place of shelter or seclusion.

■ v. decamp, flee, move back, pull out, retire, withdraw. ● n. 1 flight, retirement, withdrawal. 3 asylum, haven, refuge, sanctuary, shelter.

retrench v. reduce expenses. □ **retrenchment** n.

retrial n. trial of a lawsuit or defendant again.

retribution n. punishment for crime or evil.

■ retaliation, revenge, vengeance; punishment.

retrieve v. 1 regain possession of. 2 bring back. 3 set right (an error etc.). □ **retrieval** n.

■ 1 get back, reclaim, recover, redeem, regain, repossess. 2 bring back, fetch, get.

retriever n. dog of a breed used to retrieve game.

retroactive adj. operating retrospectively. □ **retroactively** adv.

retrograde adj. 1 going backwards. 2 reverting to an inferior state.

retrogress v. 1 move backwards. 2 deteriorate. □ **retrogression** n., **retrogressive** adj.

retrospect n. **in retrospect** when one looks back on a past event.

retrospective adj. 1 looking back on the past. 2 (of a law etc.) applying to the past as well as the future. □ **retrospectively** adv.

retroverted adj. turned backwards. □ **retroversion** n.

retry v. (**-tried**) try (a lawsuit or defendant) again.

return v. 1 come or go back. 2 bring, give, put, or send back. ● n. 1 returning. 2 profit. 3 return ticket. 4 return match. 5 formal report submitted by order. □ **return match** second match between the same opponents. **return ticket** ticket for a journey to a place and back again.

■ v. come back, reappear; go or turn back; recur, reoccur. 2 bring back, put back, replace, restore; give back, refund, reimburse, repay. ● n. 1 reappearance, recurrence, re-emergence, renewal; replacement, restoration. 2 income, profit, revenue, yield.

reunion n. gathering of people who were formerly associated.

reunite v. bring or come together again.

rev (colloq.) n. revolution of an engine. ● v. (**revved**) 1 cause (an engine) to run quickly. 2 (of an engine) revolve.

Rev. abbr. Reverend.

revalue v. put a new (esp. higher) value on. □ **revaluation** n.

revamp v. renovate, give a new appearance to.

reveal v. 1 make visible by uncovering. 2 make known.

■ 1 display, expose, lay bare, show, uncover, unveil. 2 disclose, divulge, give away, sl. let on, make known.

reveille /riválli/ n. military waking-signal.

revel v. (**revelled**) make merry. ● n. (usu. pl.) lively festivities, merrymaking. □ **revel in** take great delight in. **reveller** n., **revelry** n.

■ v. celebrate, make merry. ● n. (**revels**) celebrations, festivity, fun, jollification, merrymaking, revelry. □ **revel in** delight in, enjoy, glory in, relish, savour, take pleasure in, wallow in.

revelation n. **1** revealing. **2** (surprising) thing revealed.

■ **2** admission, confession, declaration, disclosure, leak.

revenge n. **1** injury inflicted in return for what one has suffered. **2** opportunity to defeat a victorious opponent. ● v. avenge.

■ n. **1** reprisal, retaliation, retribution, vengeance.

revenue n. **1** income esp. from taxes etc. **2** department collecting this.

reverberate v. echo, resound. □ **reverberation** n.

revere v. feel deep respect or religious veneration for.

■ admire, esteem, have a high opinion of, honour, idolize, look up to, respect, venerate, worship.

reverence n. feeling of awe and respect or veneration.

■ admiration, awe, esteem, honour, respect, veneration.

reverend adj. **1** deserving to be treated with respect. **2** (**Reverend**) title of a member of the clergy.

reverent adj. feeling or showing reverence. □ **reverently** adv.

reverie n. daydream.

revers /rivéer/ n. (pl. **revers**) turned-back front edge at the neck of a jacket or bodice.

reverse adj. **1** opposite in character or order. **2** upside down. ● v. **1** turn the other way round, upside down, or inside out. **2** convert to the opposite. **3** annul (a decree etc.). **4** move backwards or in the opposite direction. ● n. **1** reverse or opposite side or effect. **2** piece of misfortune. **3** reverse motion or gear. □ **reversal** n., **reversible** adj.

■ adj. **1** contrary, converse, inverse, opposite. ● v. **1** invert, overturn, turn over or upside down; change, exchange, interchange, transpose. **3** annul, cancel, negate, nullify, override, overturn, rescind,

revoke. ● n. **1** antithesis, contrary, converse, opposite.

revert v. **1** return to a former condition or habit. **2** return to a subject in talk etc. **3** (of property etc.) pass to another holder when its present holder relinquishes it. □ **reversion** n.

review n. **1** general survey of events or a subject. **2** reconsideration. **3** critical report of a book or play etc. **4** ceremonial inspection of troops etc. ● v. make or write a review of. □ **reviewer** n.

■ n. **1** analysis, assessment, examination, study, survey. **2** reappraisal, reassessment, reconsideration, re-examination, rethinking. **3** commentary, criticism, notice, colloq. write-up. ● v. analyse, assess, comment on, consider, evaluate, judge, look at, study, survey; reassess, reconsider.

revile v. criticize angrily in abusive language.

revise v. **1** re-examine and alter or correct. **2** study again (work already learnt) in preparation for an exam. □ **reviser** n., **revision** n., **revisory** adj.

■ **1** alter, amend, change, correct, edit, emend, modify, update.

revivalist n. person who seeks to promote religious fervour. □ **revivalism** n., **revivalistic** adj.

revive v. come or bring back to life, consciousness, or vigour, or into use. □ **revival** n.

■ awake, come to, wake up; resuscitate, revive; invigorate, perk up, refresh, restore; re-establish, renew, resurrect.

revoke v. withdraw (a decree or licence etc.). □ **revocable** adj., **revocation** n.

■ annul, cancel, declare null and void, invalidate, nullify, quash, repeal, rescind, withdraw.

revolt v. **1** take part in a rebellion. **2** cause strong disgust in. ● n. **1** act or state of rebelling. **2** sense of disgust.

■ v. **1** mutiny, rebel, rise (up). **2** appal, disgust, horrify, offend, repel, shock, sicken. ● n. **1** coup, insurrection, mutiny, rebellion, revolution, uprising.

revolting adj. **1** in revolt. **2** causing disgust.

■ **2** abhorrent, disgusting, dreadful, execrable, hateful, loathsome, objectionable, obnoxious, odious, offensive, repellent, repulsive, unpleasant, vile.

revolution n. **1** revolving, single complete orbit or rotation. **2** complete change of method or conditions. **3** substitution of a new system of government, esp. by force.
■ **1** rotation, spin, turn, twirl; circuit, lap, orbit. **2** change, reorganization, transformation, upheaval.

revolutionary adj. **1** involving a great change. **2** of political revolution. ● n. person who begins or supports a political revolution.
■ adj. **1** innovative, new, novel, original; avant-garde, progressive.

revolutionize v. alter completely.

revolve v. **1** turn round. **2** move in an orbit.
■ circle, gyrate, loop, orbit, rotate, spin, spiral, turn, twirl, whirl.

revolver n. a kind of pistol.

revue n. entertainment consisting of a series of items.

revulsion n. **1** strong disgust. **2** sudden violent change of feeling.
■ **1** abhorrence, antipathy, detestation, disgust, hatred, loathing, odium, repugnance.

reward n. something given or received in return for a service or merit. ● v. give a reward to.

rewire v. renew the electrical wiring of.

rhapsodize v. talk or write about something ecstatically.

rhapsody n. **1** ecstatic statement. **2** romantic musical composition. □ **rhapsodic** adj.

rheostat n. device for varying the resistance to electric current.

rhesus n. small Indian monkey used in biological experiments. □ **rhesus factor** substance usu. present in human blood (**rhesus-positive** having this; **rhesus-negative** not having it).

rhetoric n. **1** art of using words impressively. **2** impressive language.

rhetorical adj. expressed so as to sound impressive. □ **rhetorical question** one used for dramatic effect, not seeking an answer. **rhetorically** adv.

rheumatic adj. of or affected with rheumatism. □ **rheumaticky** adj.

rheumatism n. disease causing pain in the joints, muscles, or fibrous tissue.

rheumatoid adj. having the character of rheumatism.

rhinestone n. imitation diamond.

rhino n. (pl. **rhino** or **-os**) (colloq.) rhinoceros.

rhinoceros n. (pl. **-oses**) large thick-skinned animal with one horn or two horns on its nose.

rhizome n. root-like stem producing roots and shoots.

rhododendron n. evergreen shrub with clusters of flowers.

rhomboid adj. like a rhombus. ● n. rhomboid figure.

rhombus n. quadrilateral with opposite sides and angles equal (and not right angles).

rhubarb n. plant with red leaf-stalks that are used like fruit.

rhyme n. **1** similarity of sound between words or syllables. **2** word providing a rhyme to another. **3** poem with line-endings that rhyme. ● v. form a rhyme.

rhythm n. pattern produced by emphasis and duration of notes in music or of syllables in words, or by regular movements or events. □ **rhythmic** adj., **rhythmical** adj., **rhythmically** adv.
■ accent, beat, cadence, lilt, measure, metre, tempo, time.

rib n. **1** one of the curved bones round the chest. **2** structural part resembling this. **3** pattern of raised lines in knitting. ● v. (**ribbed**) **1** knit as rib. **2** (colloq.) tease.

ribald adj. irreverent, coarsely humorous. □ **ribaldry** n.

riband n. ribbon.

ribbon n. **1** narrow band of silky material. **2** strip resembling this.

ribonucleic acid substance controlling protein synthesis in cells.

rice n. **1** cereal plant grown in marshes in hot countries, with seeds used as food. **2** these seeds.

rich adj. **1** having much wealth. **2** splendid, costly, valuable. **3** abundant. **4** fertile. **5** (of colour, sound, or smell) pleasantly deep and strong. **6** containing a large proportion of something (e.g. fat, fuel). □ **richness** n.
■ **1** affluent, moneyed, opulent, prosperous, wealthy, colloq. well-heeled, well-off, well-to-do. **2** gorgeous, luxurious, magnificent, palatial, splendid, sumptuous; costly, expensive, precious, priceless, valuable. **3** abundant, ample, bountiful, copious, plentiful, profuse. **4** fecund, fertile, fruitful, productive, prolific. **5** deep, dark, intense, strong; full, low, mellow, resonant, sonorous; aromatic, fragrant.

riches *n.pl.* wealth.

■ affluence, money, opulence, prosperity, wealth.

richly *adv.* **1** in a rich way. **2** fully, thoroughly.

rick[1] *n.* built stack of hay etc.

rick[2] *n.* slight sprain or strain. ● *v.* sprain or strain slightly.

rickety *adj.* shaky, insecure.

■ flimsy, insubstantial, ramshackle, shaky, tumbledown.

rickshaw *n.* two-wheeled hooded vehicle used in the Far East, drawn by one or more people.

ricochet /rikkəshay/ *n.* & *v.* (**ricocheted**) rebound from a surface after striking it with a glancing blow.

rid *v.* (**rid, ridding**) free from something unpleasant or unwanted. □ **get rid of** cause to go away or free oneself of.

■ □ **get rid of** discard, dispense with, dispose of, *sl.* ditch, do away with, jettison, throw away; destroy, eliminate, eradicate, remove.

ridden *see* ride. *adj.* full of.

riddle[1] *n.* **1** question etc. designed to test ingenuity, esp. for amusement. **2** something puzzling or mysterious.

■ **1** conundrum, poser, problem, puzzle. **2** enigma, mystery.

riddle[2] *n.* coarse sieve. ● *v.* **1** pass through a riddle. **2** permeate thoroughly.

ride *v.* (**rode, ridden**) **1** sit on and be carried by (a horse or bicycle etc.). **2** travel in a vehicle. **3** float (on). ● *n.* **1** spell of riding. **2** journey in a vehicle. **3** track for riding.

■ *n.* **2** drive, excursion, jaunt, journey, outing, run, spin, trip.

rider *n.* **1** one who rides a horse etc. **2** additional statement.

ridge *n.* **1** narrow raised strip. **2** line where two upward slopes meet. **3** elongated region of high barometric pressure.

ridicule *n.* making or being made to seem ridiculous. ● *v.* subject to ridicule, make fun of.

■ *n.* derision, mockery, taunting. ● *v.* deride, gibe (at), jeer at, laugh at, make fun of, mock, poke fun at, scoff at, taunt.

ridiculous *adj.* deserving to be laughed at, unreasonable. □ **ridiculously** *adv.*

■ absurd, daft, foolish, idiotic, insane, laughable, ludicrous, mad, nonsensical, preposterous, risible, silly, stupid, unreasonable.

rife *adj.* occurring frequently, widespread. □ **rife with** full of.

riff *n.* short repeated phrase in jazz etc.

riffle *v.* flick through (pages etc.).

riff-raff *n.* disreputable people.

rifle *n.* a gun with a long rifled barrel. ● *v.* **1** search and rob. **2** cut spiral grooves in (a gun barrel).

rift *n.* **1** cleft in earth or rock. **2** crack, split. **3** breach in friendly relations. □ **rift-valley** *n.* steep-sided valley formed by subsidence.

■ **1,2** cleft, crack, crevasse, crevice, fissure, split. **3** breach, break, estrangement, rupture, split.

rig[1] *v.* (**rigged**) **1** provide with clothes or equipment. **2** fit (a ship) with spars, ropes, etc. **3** set up, esp. in a makeshift way. ● *n.* **1** way a ship's masts and sails etc. are arranged. **2** apparatus for drilling an oil well etc. □ **rig-out** *n.* (*colloq.*) outfit.

rig[2] *v.* (**rigged**) manage or control fraudulently.

rigging *n.* ropes etc. used to support a ship's masts and sails.

right *adj.* **1** morally good. **2** proper. **3** correct, true. **4** in a good condition. **5** of or on the east side of a person facing north. ● *n.* **1** what is just. **2** something one is entitled to. **3** right hand, foot, or side. **4** people supporting more conservative policies than others in their group. ● *v.* **1** set right. **2** restore to a correct or upright position. ● *adv.* **1** directly. **2** exactly, correctly. **3** completely. **4** on or towards the right-hand side. □ **in the right** having truth or justice on one's side. **right angle** angle of 90°.

right away immediately. **right-hand man, woman** indispensable assistant.

right-handed *adj.* using the right hand.

right of way 1 right to pass over another's land. **2** path subject to this. **3** right to proceed while another vehicle must wait. **rightly** *adv.*

■ *adj.* **1** ethical, fair, good, honest, honourable, just, moral, proper, righteous. **2** apposite, appropriate, correct, fitting, proper, suitable. **3** accurate, correct, exact, precise, true. ● *n.* **1** equity, fairness, honesty, justice, morality, rightfulness, truth, virtue. **2** entitlement, freedom, liberty, licence, prerogative, privilege. ● *v.* **1** amend, correct, cure, fix, put right, rectify, remedy, repair. ● *adv.* **1** directly, immediately, straight. **2** exactly, just, precisely; accurately, correctly, properly, well.

□ **right away** at once, immediately, instantly, now, straight away, without delay.

righteous /ríchəss/ adj. 1 doing what is morally right, making a show of this. 2 morally justifiable. □ **righteously** adv., **righteousness** n.

rightful adj. proper, legal. □ **rightfully** adv., **rightfulness** n.

■ correct, lawful, legal, legitimate, proper, true.

rigid adj. 1 stiff. 2 strict, inflexible. □ **rigidly** adv., **rigidity** n.

■ 1 firm, hard, inflexible, stiff, strong, unbendable. 2 harsh, inflexible, intransigent, strict, unyielding.

rigmarole n. 1 long statement. 2 complicated procedure.

rigor mortis n. stiffening of the body after death.

rigorous adj. 1 strict, severe. 2 exact, accurate. □ **rigorously** adv., **rigorousness** n.

rigour n. 1 strictness, severity. 2 harsh conditions.

rile v. (colloq.) annoy.

rim n. edge or border of something more or less circular. □ **rimmed** adj.

rind n. tough outer layer on fruit, cheese, bacon, etc.

ring[1] n. 1 outline of a circle. 2 circular metal band usu. worn on a finger. 3 enclosure where a performance or activity takes place. 4 group of people acting together dishonestly. ● v. 1 put a ring on or round. 2 surround.

■ n. 1 circle, disc, round. ● v. 2 bound, circle, encircle, encompass, surround.

ring[2] v. (rang, rung) 1 give out a loud clear resonant sound. 2 cause (a bell) to do this. 3 signal by ringing. 4 telephone. 5 be filled with sound. ● n. 1 act or sound of ringing. 2 specified tone or feeling of a statement etc. 3 (colloq.) telephone call. □ **ring off** end a telephone call. **ring the changes** vary things. **ring up** make a telephone call.

■ v. 1 chime, peal, toll. 4 call, colloq. phone, ring up, telephone. 5 echo, resonate, resound, reverberate.

ringleader n. person who leads others in wrongdoing or riot etc.

ringlet n. long curly lock of hair.

ringside n. area beside a boxing ring. □ **ringside seat** position from which one has a clear view of the scene of action.

ringworm n. skin disease producing round scaly patches.

rink n. skating-rink.

rinse v. 1 wash lightly. 2 wash out soap etc. from. ● n. 1 process of rinsing. 2 solution for tinting or conditioning hair.

riot n. 1 wild disturbance by a crowd of people. 2 profuse display. 3 (colloq.) very amusing person or thing. ● v. take part in a riot. □ **run riot 1** behave in an unruly way. **2** grow in an uncontrolled way.

■ n. affray, disturbance, fracas, fray, tumult, uproar.

riotous adj. disorderly, unruly. □ **riotously** adv.

■ boisterous, disorderly, noisy, rowdy, tumultuous, uncontrollable, unruly, uproarious, wild.

rip v. (ripped) 1 tear apart. 2 make (a hole) by ripping. 3 become torn. 4 rush along. ● n. 1 act of ripping. 2 torn place. □ **rip-cord** n. cord for pulling to release a parachute. **rip off** (colloq.) 1 defraud. 2 steal. **rip-off** n. **ripper** n.

■ v. 1 pull apart, rend, split, tear. ● n. 2 hole, rent, split, tear.

ripe adj. 1 ready to be gathered and used. 2 (of age) advanced. 3 ready. □ **ripeness** n.

ripen v. make or become ripe.

riposte /ripóst/ n. quick counterstroke or retort. ● v. deliver a riposte.

ripple n. 1 small wave(s). 2 gentle sound that rises and falls. ● v. form ripples (in).

rise v. (rose, risen) 1 come, go, or extend upwards. 2 get up from lying or sitting, get out of bed. 3 increase, become higher. 4 rebel. 5 have its origin or source. ● n. 1 act or amount of rising, increase. 2 upward slope. 3 increase in wages. □ **give rise to** cause.

■ v. 1 arise, ascend, climb, come or go up, mount, soar; fly. 2 arise, get to one's feet, get up, stand up. 3 climb, escalate, increase, go up, rocket, shoot up. ● n. 1 ascent, climb; growth, escalation, increase, jump; gain, improvement, surge. 2 gradient, hill, incline, slope. □ **give rise to** bring about, cause, create, engender, lead to, occasion, produce, result in.

risible adj. ridiculous. □ **risibly** adv., **risibility** n.

risk n. 1 possibility of meeting danger or suffering harm. 2 person or thing representing a source of risk. ● v. 1 expose to the chance of injury or loss. **2** accept the risk of.

> ■ *n*. **1** chance, hazard, threat; danger, peril. ● *v*. **1** endanger, hazard, imperil, jeopardize; chance, venture.

risky *adj*. (**-ier, -iest**) full of risk. □ **riskily** *adv*., **riskiness** *n*.

risotto *n*. (*pl*. **-os**) savoury rice dish.

risqué /riskáy/ *adj*. slightly indecent.

rissole *n*. fried cake of minced meat.

rite *n*. ritual.

ritual *n*. series of actions used in a religious or other ceremony. ● *adj*. of or done as a ritual. □ **ritually** *adv*., **ritualistic** *adj*., **ritualism** *n*.

rival *n*. person or thing that competes with or can equal another. ● *v*. (**rivalled**) **1** be a rival of. **2** seem as good as. □ **rivalry** *n*.

> ■ *n*. adversary, antagonist, challenger, competitor, contender, opponent. ● *v*. **2** be on a par with, compare with, equal, match, measure up to.

river *n*. **1** large natural stream of water. **2** great flow.

rivet *n*. bolt for holding pieces of metal together, with its end pressed down to form a head when in place. ● *v*. (**riveted**) **1** fasten with a rivet. **2** attract and hold (the attention of).

> ■ *v*. **2** captivate, engross, enthral, entrance, fascinate, grip, hold spellbound, transfix.

rivulet *n*. small stream.

RNA *abbr*. ribonucleic acid.

roach *n*. (*pl*. **roach**) small freshwater fish of the carp family.

road *n*. **1** prepared track along which people and vehicles may travel. **2** way of reaching something. □ **on the road** travelling. **road-hog** *n*. reckless or inconsiderate driver. **road-metal** *n*. broken stone for making the foundation of a road or railway.

> ■ **1** avenue, boulevard, carriageway, highway, motorway, roadway, street, thoroughfare.

roadway *n*. road, esp. as distinct from a footpath beside it.

roadworks *n.pl*. construction or repair of roads.

roadworthy *adj*. (of a vehicle) fit to be used on a road. □ **roadworthiness** *n*.

roam *v*. & *n*. wander.

> ■ *v*. drift, range, rove, wander.

roan *n*. horse with a dark coat sprinkled with white hairs.

roar *n*. **1** long deep sound like that made by a lion. **2** loud laughter. ● *v*. **1** give a roar. **2** express in this way.

> ■ *v*. **2** bark, bawl, bellow, cry, shout, thunder, yell.

roaring *adj*. **1** noisy. **2** briskly active.

roast *v*. cook or be cooked by exposure to open heat or in an oven. ● *n*. roast joint of meat.

rob *v*. (**robbed**) **1** steal from. **2** deprive. □ **robber** *n*., **robbery** *n*.

> ■ **1** burgle, loot, pillage, plunder, raid, ransack, rifle; hold up, mug. □ **robber** burglar, housebreaker, intruder, mugger, thief.

robe *n*. long loose esp. ceremonial garment. ● *v*. dress in a robe.

robin *n*. brown red-breasted bird.

robot *n*. **1** machine resembling and acting like a person. **2** piece of apparatus operated by remote control. □ **robotic** *adj*.

robotics *n*. study of robots and their design, operation, etc.

robust *adj*. strong, vigorous. □ **robustly** *adv*., **robustness** *n*.

> ■ durable, hard-wearing, strong, sturdy, tough; brawny, burly, fit, hale, healthy, muscular, powerful, strapping, vigorous.

rock¹ *n*. **1** hard part of earth's crust, below the soil. **2** mass of this, large stone. **3** hard sugar sweet made in sticks. □ **on the rocks** (of a drink) served with ice cubes. **rock-bottom** *adj*. very low. **rock-cake** *n*. small cake with a rough surface.

> ■ **2** crag, tor, outcrop; boulder, stone.

rock² *v*. **1** move to and fro while supported. **2** disturb greatly by shock. ● *n*. **1** rocking movement. **2** a kind of modern music with a strong beat. □ **rock and roll** rock music with elements of blues.

> ■ *v*. **1** sway, teeter, totter, wobble; lurch, pitch, roll, shake, toss.

rocker *n*. **1** thing that rocks. **2** pivoting switch.

rockery *n*. collection of rough stones with soil between them on which small plants are grown.

rocket *n*. **1** firework that shoots into the air when ignited and then explodes. **2** structure that flies by expelling burning gases. ● *v*. (**rocketed**) move rapidly upwards or away.

rocketry *n*. science or practice of rocket propulsion.

rocky¹ *adj*. (**-ier, -iest**) of, like, or full of rocks. □ **rockiness** *n*.

rocky[2] adj. (-ier, -iest) (colloq.) unsteady.
□ **rockily** adv., **rockiness** n.

rococo adj. & n. (of or in) an ornate style of decoration in Europe in the 18th century.

rod n. **1** slender straight round stick or metal bar. **2** fishing rod.

rode see **ride**.

rodent n. animal with strong front teeth for gnawing things.

rodeo n. (pl. **-os**) competition or exhibition of cowboys' skill.

roe[1] n. **1** mass of eggs in a female fish's ovary (**hard roe**). **2** male fish's milt (**soft roe**).

roe[2] n. (pl. **roe** or **roes**) a kind of small deer.

roentgen /ˈrʌntgən/ n. unit of ionizing radiation.

roger int. (in signalling) message received and understood.

rogue n. **1** dishonest, unprincipled, or mischievous person. **2** wild animal living apart from the herd. □ **roguery** n.
■ **1** blackguard, cheat, colloq. crook, knave, malefactor, miscreant, rascal, ruffian, scoundrel, trickster, villain, wretch.

roguish adj. mischievous, playful.
□ **roguishly** adv.
■ **1** character, part. **2** duty, function, job, responsibility, task.

roll v. **1** move (on a surface) on wheels or by turning over and over. **2** turn on an axis or over and over. **3** form into a cylindrical or spherical shape. **4** flatten with a roller. **5** move or pass steadily. **6** rock from side to side. **7** undulate. ● n. **1** act of rolling. **2** cylinder of flexible material turned over and over upon itself. **3** official list or register. **4** long deep sound. **5** undulation. **6** small individual loaf of bread. □ **be rolling (in money)** (colloq.) be wealthy. **roll-call** n. calling of a list of names to check that all are present. **rolled gold** thin coating of gold on another metal. **rolling-pin** n. roller for flattening dough. **rolling-stock** n. railway engines and carriages, wagons, etc. **rolling stone** person who does not settle in one place.
■ v. **1,2** trundle, wheel; revolve, rotate, spin, turn. **5** glide, go, move, pass. **6** heel, list, lurch, pitch, toss. ● n. **1** revolution, rotation, spin, turn. **3** directory, index, in-

ventory, list, record, register, roster. **4** boom, reverberation, roar, rumble.

roller n. **1** cylinder rolled over things to flatten or spread them, or on which something is wound. **2** long swelling wave. □ **roller coaster** switchback at a fair etc. **roller skate** (see **skate**[2]).

rollicking adj. full of boisterous high spirits.

roly-poly n. pudding of suet pastry spread with jam, rolled up, and boiled. ● adj. plump, podgy.

Roman adj. & n. **1** (native, inhabitant) of Rome or of the ancient Roman republic or empire. **2** Roman Catholic. □ **Roman Catholic** (member) of the Church that acknowledges the Pope as its head. **Roman numerals** letters representing numbers (I = 1, V = 5, etc.).

roman n. plain upright type.

romance n. **1** love story, love affair resembling this. **2** imaginative story or literature. **3** romantic situation, event, or atmosphere. **4** picturesque exaggeration. ● v. distort the truth or invent imaginatively. □ **Romance languages** those descended from Latin.
■ n. **1** affair, intrigue, liaison, relationship. **2** epic, fantasy, legend, melodrama, saga, tale. **3** exoticism, glamour, mystery.

Romanesque adj. & n. (of or in) a style of art and architecture in Europe about 1050–1200.

romantic adj. **1** appealing to the emotions by its imaginative, heroic, or picturesque quality. **2** involving a love affair. ● n. romantic person. □ **romantically** adv.
■ adj. **1** fairy-tale, fanciful, idealized, idyllic, imaginary; exotic, glamorous, picturesque.

romanticism n. romantic style.

romanticize v. **1** make romantic. **2** indulge in romance.

Romany adj. & n. **1** gypsy. **2** (of) the gypsy language.

romp v. **1** play about in a lively way. **2** (colloq.) go along easily. ● n. spell of romping.

rondeau n. short poem with the opening words used as a refrain.

rondo n. (pl. **-os**) piece of music with a recurring theme.

roof n. (pl. **roofs**) upper covering of a building, car, cavity, etc. ● v. **1** cover with a roof. **2** be the roof of. □ **roofer** n.

rook[1] n. bird of the crow family.

rook² n. chess piece with a top shaped like battlements.

rookery n. colony of rooks.

room n. **1** space that is or could be occupied. **2** enclosed part of a building. **3** scope.
■ **1** area, capacity, space. **3** leeway, latitude, margin, scope.

roomy adj. (**-ier, -iest**) having plenty of space.
■ big, capacious, commodious, large, sizeable, spacious.

roost n. place where birds perch or rest. ● v. perch, esp. for sleep.

root¹ n. **1** part of a plant that grows into the earth and absorbs water and nourishment from the soil. **2** embedded part of hair, tooth, etc. **3** source, basis. **4** number in relation to another which it produces when multiplied by itself a specified number of times. **5** (pl.) emotional attachment to a place. ● v. **1** (cause to) take root. **2** cause to stand fixed and unmoving. □ **root out** or **up 1** drag or dig up by the roots. **2** get rid of. **take root 1** send down roots. **2** become established. **rootless** adj.
■ n. **1** radicle, rhizome, tuber. **3** base, basis, cause, fount, origin, source. □ **root out 1** destroy, do away with, eliminate, eradicate, get rid of, remove, stamp out.

root² v. **1** (of an animal) turn up ground with the snout or beak in search of food. **2** rummage, extract.

rope n. strong thick cord. ● v. **1** fasten or secure with rope. **2** fence off with rope(s). □ **know** or **show the ropes** know or show the procedure. **rope in** persuade to take part in.

rosary n. **1** set series of prayers. **2** string of beads for keeping count in this.

rose¹ n. **1** ornamental usu. fragrant flower. **2** bush or shrub bearing this. **3** deep pink colour.

rose² see **rise**.

rosé /rózay/ n. light pink wine.

rosemary n. shrub with fragrant leaves used to flavour food.

rosette n. round badge or ornament made of ribbons.

rosewood n. dark fragrant wood used for making furniture.

rosin n. a kind of resin.

roster n. & v. list showing people's turns of duty etc.

rostrum n. (pl. **-tra**) platform for one person.

rosy adj. (**-ier, -iest**) **1** deep pink. **2** promising, hopeful.
■ **2** auspicious, bright, encouraging, favourable, hopeful, optimistic, promising.

rot v. (**rotted**) **1** lose its original form by chemical action caused by bacteria or fungi etc. **2** cause to do this. **3** perish through lack of use. ● n. **1** rotting, rottenness. **2** (sl.) nonsense.
■ v. **1** decay, decompose, fester, go bad, go off, moulder, putrefy, spoil. ● n. **1** decay, decomposition, mould, putrefaction.

rota n. list of duties to be done or people to do them in turn.
■ list, roster, schedule.

rotary adj. acting by rotating.

rotate v. **1** revolve. **2** arrange or occur or deal with in a recurrent series. □ **rotation** n., **rotatory** adj.
■ **1** circle, go round, revolve, roll, spin, turn round.

rote n. **by rote 1** by memory without thought of the meaning. **2** by a fixed procedure.

rotor n. rotating part.

rotten adj. **1** rotted, breaking easily from age or use. **2** worthless, unpleasant. □ **rottenness** n.
■ **1** bad, decayed, decomposing, mouldy, off, putrescent, putrid.

Rottweiler n. dog of a large black and tan breed.

rotund adj. rounded, plump. □ **rotundity** n.
■ chubby, dumpy, fat, plump, podgy, pudgy, roly-poly, tubby.

rotunda n. circular domed building or hall.

rouble n. unit of money in Russia.

rouge n. reddish cosmetic colouring for the cheeks. ● v. colour with rouge.

rough adj. **1** having an uneven or irregular surface. **2** not gentle or careful, violent. **3** (of weather) stormy. **4** harsh in sound, taste, etc. **5** incomplete. **6** approximate. **7** unpleasant, severe. **8** lacking comfort, finish, etc. ● adv. in a rough way. ● n. **1** rough thing, person, or state. **2** rough ground. ● v. make rough. □ **rough-and-ready** adj. rough but effective. **rough-and-tumble** n. haphazard struggle. **rough diamond** person of good nature but lacking polished manners. **rough it** do without ordinary comforts.

rough out plan or sketch roughly. **roughly** adv., **roughness** n.

■ adj. **1** bumpy, coarse, irregular, pitted, rocky, stony, uneven. **2** cruel, hard, harsh, severe, violent; disorderly, rowdy, tumultuous, uproarious, wild; blunt, brusque, ill-mannered, impolite, rude, uncouth, ungracious. **3** blustery, squally, stormy, tempestuous. **4** gruff, guttural, harsh, hoarse, husky, rasping, throaty. **5** incomplete, rudimentary, sketchy, uncompleted, unfinished. **6** approximate, estimated, general, imprecise, inexact, vague. **7** arduous, demanding, difficult, severe, tough, unpleasant. **8** basic, crude, primitive, rude, rudimentary, spartan.

roughage n. dietary fibre.

roughen v. make or become rough.

roughshod adj. **ride roughshod over** treat inconsiderately.

roulette n. gambling game played with a small ball on a revolving disc.

round adj. curved, circular, spherical, or cylindrical. ● n. **1** round object. **2** circular or recurring course, route, or series. **3** song for two or more voices that start at different times. **4** shot from a firearm, ammunition for this. **5** one section of a competition. ● prep. **1** so as to circle or enclose. **2** to or on the other side of. **3** in the area near a place. **4** in or to many parts of. ● adv. **1** in a circle or curve. **2** so as to face in a different direction. **3** from one person, place, etc. to another. **4** to a person's house etc. **5** by a circuitous route. **6** measuring or marking the edge of. ● v. **1** make or become round. **2** express (a number) approximately. **3** travel round (corner etc.). □ **in the round** with all sides visible. **round about** **1** nearby. **2** approximately. **round of applause** outburst of clapping. **round off** complete. **round robin** statement signed by a number of people. **round the clock** continuously through day and night. **round trip** **1** circular tour. **2** outward and return journey. **round up** gather into one place. **round-up** n. **roundness** n.

■ n. **1** circle, disc, ring; ball, globe, orb, sphere. **2** circuit, lap, orbit; course, cycle, series, sequence. ● prep. **1** about, around, encircling, enclosing. **3** about, around, in the vicinity of, near. □ **round off** close, complete, crown, end, finish. **round up** assemble, collect, gather, marshal.

roundabout n. **1** revolving platform at a funfair, with model horses etc. to ride on. **2** road junction with a circular island round which traffic has to pass in one direction. ● adj. indirect.

■ adj. circuitous, indirect, tortuous; circumlocutory, oblique.

roundel n. **1** small disc. **2** rondeau.

rounders n. team game played with bat and ball, in which players have to run round a circuit. □ **rounder** n. unit of scoring in this.

roundly adv. **1** thoroughly, severely. **2** in a rounded shape.

roundworm n. parasitic worm with a rounded body.

rouse v. **1** wake. **2** cause to become active or excited.

■ **1** arouse, awaken, wake up, waken. **2** arouse, excite, fire, galvanize, invigorate, move, stimulate, stir.

rousing adj. vigorous, stirring.

rout n. **1** utter defeat. **2** disorderly retreat. ● v. **1** defeat completely. **2** put to flight.

■ v. **1** beat, conquer, crush, defeat, get the better of, colloq. lick, overwhelm, prevail over, thrash, triumph over, trounce, vanquish.

route n. course or way from starting point to finishing point. □ **route march** training-march for troops.

■ course, direction, itinerary, journey, path, road, track, way.

routine n. **1** standard procedure. **2** set sequence of movements. ● adj. **1** in accordance with routine. **2** unvarying, mechanical. □ **routinely** adv.

■ n. **1** custom, colloq. drill, form, procedure, way. ● adj. **1** commonplace, everyday, normal, ordinary, regular, usual. **2** dull, humdrum, mechanical, mundane, run-of-the-mill, tedious, uninteresting, unvarying.

roux /roo/ n. mixture of fat and flour used in sauces.

rove v. wander. □ **rover** n.

row[1] /rō/ n. people or things in a line.

row[2] /rō/ v. **1** propel (a boat) by using oars. **2** carry in a boat that one rows. ● n. spell of rowing. □ **rowboat**, **rowing boat** ns.

row[3] /row/ n. **1** loud noise. **2** quarrel, angry argument. ● v. quarrel, argue angrily.

■ n. **1** din, clamour, commotion, hubbub, noise, racket, rumpus, uproar. **2** altercation, argument, disagreement, dispute, fight, quarrel, colloq. scrap, squabble, tiff, wrangle. ● v. argue, bicker, disagree, dispute, fight, quarrel, *colloq.* scrap, spar, squabble, wrangle.

rowan *n.* tree bearing hanging clusters of red berries.

rowdy *adj.* (**-ier, -iest**) noisy and disorderly. ● *n.* rowdy person. □ **rowdily** *adv.*, **rowdiness** *n.*

■ *adj.* boisterous, disorderly, noisy, obstreperous, unruly, uproarious, wild.

rowlock /róllək/ *n.* device on the side of a boat securing and forming a fulcrum for an oar.

royal *adj.* **1** of or suited to a king or queen. **2** of the family or in the service or under the patronage of royalty. **3** splendid, of great size. ● *n.* (*colloq.*) member of a royal family. □ **royal blue** bright blue. **royally** *adv.*

■ *adj.* **1** imperial, kingly, majestic, noble, princely, queenly, regal.

royalist *n.* person supporting or advocating monarchy.

royalty *n.* **1** being royal. **2** royal person(s). **3** payment to an author etc. for each copy or performance of his or her work, or to a patentee for use of his or her patent.

RSVP *abbr.* (French *répondez s'il vous plaît*) please reply.

rub *v.* (**rubbed**) **1** press against a surface and slide to and fro. **2** polish, clean, dry, or make sore etc. by rubbing. ● *n.* act or process of rubbing. □ **rub it in** emphasize or remind a person constantly of an unpleasant fact. **rub out** erase with a rubber.

■ *v.* **2** buff, burnish, polish, shine, wipe; scour, scrub; chafe, gall, scrape, scratch.

rubber *n.* **1** tough elastic substance made from the juice of certain plants or synthetically. **2** piece of this for rubbing out pencil or ink marks, eraser. **3** device for rubbing things. □ **rubber-stamp** *v.* approve automatically without consideration. **rubbery** *adj.*

rubberize *v.* treat or coat with rubber.

rubbish *n.* **1** waste or worthless material. **2** nonsense.

■ **1** debris, garbage, junk, litter, refuse, scrap, trash, waste. **2** balderdash, *sl.* bilge, *sl.* boloney, bunkum, double Dutch, drivel, gibberish, *colloq.* gobbledegook, mumbojumbo, nonsense, *sl.* poppycock, *sl.* rot, twaddle.

rubble *n.* waste or rough fragments of stone or brick etc.

rubella *n.* German measles.

rubric *n.* words put as a heading or note of explanation.

ruby *n.* **1** red gem. **2** deep red colour. ● *adj.* deep red.

ruche /rōōsh/ *n.* fabric gathered as trimming. ● *v.* gather thus.

ruck *v.* & *n.* crease, wrinkle.

rucksack *n.* capacious bag carried on the back in hiking etc.

ructions *n.pl.* (*colloq.*) protests and noisy arguments, a row.

rudder *n.* flat piece hinged to the stern of a boat or aircraft, used for steering.

ruddy *adj.* (**-ier, -iest**) reddish. □ **ruddily** *adv.*, **ruddiness** *n.*

rude *adj.* **1** impolite, showing no respect. **2** primitive, roughly made. **3** indecent. □ **rudely** *adv.*, **rudeness** *n.*

■ **1** bad-mannered, discourteous, disrespectful, ill-mannered, impertinent, impolite, impudent, insolent, offensive, uncivil, uncouth, ungracious. **2** crude, primitive, rough, rudimentary, simple.

rudiment *n.* **1** rudimentary part. **2** (*pl.*) elementary principles.

■ **2** (**rudiments**) basics, elements, essentials, first principles, foundations, fundamentals, *sl.* nitty-gritty.

rudimentary *adj.* **1** basic, elementary. **2** incompletely developed.

■ **1** basic, elementary, fundamental, introductory, primary. **2** basic, crude, primitive, rude; imperfect, incomplete.

rue[1] *n.* shrub with bitter leaves.

rue[2] *v.* repent, regret.

rueful *adj.* showing or feeling good-humoured regret. □ **ruefully** *adv.*

ruff *n.* **1** pleated frill worn round the neck. **2** projecting or coloured ring of feathers or fur round a bird's or animal's neck. **3** bird of the sandpiper family.

ruffian *n.* violent lawless person.

■ hooligan, lout, rogue, thug, tough, vandal, *sl.* yob.

ruffle *v.* **1** disturb the calmness or smoothness (of). **2** annoy. ● *n.* gathered frill.

■ *v.* **1** dishevel, disorder, mess (up), rumple, tousle. **2** anger, annoy, displease, irritate, perturb, *colloq.* rile, upset.

rufous *adj.* reddish-brown.

rug *n.* **1** floor-mat. **2** thick woollen wrap or coverlet.

Rugby *n.* (in full **Rugby football**) game played with an oval ball which may be kicked or carried.

rugged adj. **1** rough, uneven, rocky. **2** sturdy, robust, tough. □ **ruggedly** adv., **ruggedness** n.

rugger n. (colloq.) Rugby football.

ruin n. **1** destruction. **2** loss of one's fortune or prospects. **3** broken remains. **4** cause of ruin. ● v. **1** cause ruin to. **2** reduce to ruins. □ **ruination** n.

■ n. **1** destruction, devastation, ruination. **2** collapse, downfall, end, failure. ● v. **1** blight, dash, destroy, end, put an end to, shatter, undo, wreck; damage, mar, spoil. **2** destroy, devastate, lay waste to, obliterate, ravage, raze, wreck.

ruinous adj. **1** bringing ruin. **2** in ruins, ruined. □ **ruinously** adv.

rule n. **1** statement of what can or should be done in certain circumstances or in a game. **2** governing, control. **3** dominant custom. **4** ruler used by carpenters etc. ● v. **1** govern, keep under control. **2** give an authoritative decision. **3** draw (a line) using a ruler. □ **as a rule** usually. **rule of thumb** rough practical method of procedure. **rule out** exclude.

■ n. **1** decree, directive, edict, law, order, ordinance, regulation, ruling. **2** administration, authority, command, control, dominion, government, jurisdiction, leadership, management, sovereignty, sway. **3** convention, custom, norm, practice, tradition. ● v. **1** be in charge of, command, control, dominate, govern, hold sway over, reign over. **2** decide, decree, dictate, find, judge, pronounce. □ **as a rule** generally, in general, mostly, normally, on the whole, ordinarily, usually. **rule out** ban, bar, forbid, exclude, preclude, prohibit, proscribe, veto.

ruler n. **1** person who rules. **2** straight strip used in measuring or for drawing straight lines.

■ **1** chief, chieftain, commander, head, king, leader, monarch, queen, sovereign.

ruling n. authoritative decision.

rum[1] n. alcoholic spirit distilled from sugar cane or molasses.

rum[2] adj. (colloq.) strange, odd.

rumba n. ballroom dance of Cuban origin.

rumble[1] v. make a low continuous sound. ● n. rumbling sound.

rumble[2] v. (sl.) detect the true character of.

rumbustious adj. (colloq.) boisterous, uproarious.

ruminant n. animal that chews the cud. ● adj. ruminating.

ruminate v. **1** chew the cud. **2** meditate, ponder. □ **rumination** n., **ruminative** adj.

■ **2** cogitate, deliberate, meditate, muse, ponder, reflect, think.

rummage v. & n. search by disarranging things. □ **rummage sale** jumble sale.

rummy n. card game played usually with two packs.

rumour n. information spread by talking but not certainly true. □ **be rumoured** be spread as a rumour.

■ gossip, hearsay, talk, tittle-tattle.

rump n. **1** buttocks. **2** bird's back near the tail.

rumple v. make or become crumpled.

■ crease, crinkle, crumple, crush, dishevel, tousle, wrinkle.

rumpus n. uproar, angry dispute.

■ commotion, din, disturbance, fracas, fray, furore, fuss, hullabaloo, colloq. kerfuffle, racket, row, stir, to-do, tumult, uproar.

run v. (**ran**, **run**, **running**) **1** move with quick steps and with always at least one foot off the ground. **2** go smoothly or swiftly. **3** spread, flow, exude liquid. **4** function. **5** manage, organize. **6** extend. **7** travel or convey from one point to another. **8** compete in a race. **9** be current or valid. **10** own and use (a vehicle etc.). ● n. **1** spell of running. **2** trip or journey. **3** continuous stretch or sequence. **4** enclosure where domestic animals can range. **5** ladder in fabric. **6** point scored in cricket or baseball. **7** permission to make unrestricted use of something. □ **in** or **out of the running** with a good or with no chance of winning. **in the long run** in the end, over a long period. **on the run** fleeing. **run across** happen to meet or find. **run a risk** take a risk. **run a temperature** be feverish. **run away** flee. **run down 1** reduce the numbers of. **2** knock down with a vehicle. **3** speak of in a slighting way. **4** discover after searching. **be run down** be weak or exhausted. **run-down** n. detailed analysis. **run into 1** collide with. **2** happen to meet. **run-of-the-mill** adj. ordinary. **run out** become used up. **run out of** have used up (one's stock). **run over** knock down or crush with a vehicle. **run up** allow (a bill) to mount. **run-up** *n.* period leading up to an event.

■ *v.* **1,2** jog, lope, sprint, trot; bolt, dart, hare, hurry, race, rush, speed, tear, zoom. **3** course, flood, flow, gush, pour, stream; seep, trickle. **4** be in working order, function, go, operate, work. **5** administer, control, direct, manage, organize, supervise. **6** extend, go, lead, reach, stretch. **7** convey, drive, take, transport. ● *n.* **2** drive, excursion, jaunt, journey, ride, spin, trip. **3** period, session, spell, stint, stretch. □ **run away** bolt, decamp, *sl.* do a bunk, escape, flee, fly, make off, *colloq.* skedaddle, take to one's heels. **run down 3** criticize, denigrate, deprecate, disparage, *sl.* knock, malign. **run-of-the-mill** average, commonplace, everyday, normal, ordinary, standard, unexceptional, usual.

rune *n.* letter of an early Germanic alphabet. □ **runic** *adj.*

rung¹ *n.* crosspiece of a ladder etc.

rung² see **ring²**.

runner *n.* **1** person or animal that runs. **2** messenger. **3** creeping stem that roots. **4** groove, strip, or roller etc. for a thing to move on. **5** long narrow strip of carpet or ornamental cloth. □ **runner-up** *n.* one who finishes second in a competition.

runny *adj.* semi-liquid, tending to flow or exude fluid.

runt *n.* undersized person or animal.

runway *n.* surface on which aircraft may take off and land.

rupee *n.* unit of money in India, Pakistan, etc.

rupture *n.* **1** breaking, breach. **2** abdominal hernia. ● *v.* **1** burst, break. **2** cause hernia in.

■ *n.* **1** breach, break, estrangement, rift, split; crack, fissure, fracture.

rural *adj.* of, in, or like the country.

ruse *n.* deception, trick.

■ deception, device, ploy, stratagem, trick, wile.

rush¹ *n.* marsh plant with a slender pithy stem.

rush² *v.* **1** go or convey with great speed. **2** act hastily. **3** force into hasty action. **4** attack with a sudden assault. ● *n.* **1** rushing, instance of this. **2** period of great activity. □ **rush hour** one of the times of day when traffic is busiest.

■ *v.* **1,2** hasten, hurry, make haste; dart, dash, fly, race, scoot, speed, tear, whiz, zoom.

rusk *n.* a kind of biscuit.

russet *adj.* soft reddish-brown. ● *n.* **1** russet colour. **2** a kind of apple with a rough skin.

rust *n.* brownish corrosive coating formed on iron exposed to moisture. ● *adj.* reddish-brown. ● *v.* make or become rusty. □ **rustproof** *adj. & v.*

rustic *adj.* **1** of or like country life or people. **2** made of rough timber or untrimmed branches. □ **rusticity** *n.*

rustle *v.* **1** (cause to) make a sound like paper being crumpled. **2** (*US*) steal (horses or cattle). ● *n.* rustling sound. □ **rustler** *n.*

rusty *adj.* (**-ier, -iest**) **1** affected with rust. **2** rust-coloured. **3** having lost quality by lack of use. □ **rustiness** *n.*

rut¹ *n.* **1** deep track made by wheels. **2** habitual usu. dull course of life.

rut² *n.* periodic sexual excitement of a male deer, goat, etc. ● *v.* (**rutted**) be affected with this.

ruthless *adj.* having no pity. □ **ruthlessly** *adv.*, **ruthlessness** *n.*

■ cruel, hard-hearted, harsh, heartless, inhuman, merciless, pitiless, remorseless, unfeeling, unforgiving, unsympathetic.

rye *n.* **1** a kind of cereal. **2** whisky made from rye.

Ss

S. *abbr.* **1** south. **2** southern.

sabbath *n.* day of worship and rest from work (Saturday for Jews, Sunday for Christians).

sabbatical *n.* leave granted at intervals to a university professor etc. for study and travel.

sable *n.* **1** small Arctic mammal with dark fur. **2** its fur. ● *adj.* black.

sabotage *n.* wilful damage to machinery or materials, or disruption of work. ● *v.* commit sabotage on. □ **saboteur** *n.*

sabre *n.* curved sword.

sac *n.* bag-like part in an animal or plant.

saccharin *n.* very sweet substance used instead of sugar.

saccharine *adj.* intensely and unpleasantly sweet.

sachet /sáshay/ *n.* small bag or sealed pack.

sack¹ *n.* **1** large bag of strong coarse fabric. **2** (**the sack**) (*colloq.*) dismissal from one's employment. ● *v.* (*colloq.*) dismiss. □ **sackful** *n.*

sack² *v.* plunder (a captured town). ● *n.* this act or process.

> ■ *v.* loot, pillage, plunder, raid, ransack.

sackcloth *n.* (also **sacking**) coarse fabric for making sacks.

sacral /sáykrəl/ *adj.* of the sacrum.

sacrament *n.* any of the symbolic Christian religious ceremonies. □ **sacramental** *adj.*

sacred *adj.* **1** holy. **2** dedicated (to a person or purpose). **3** connected with religion. **4** sacrosanct. □ **sacred cow** idea etc. which its supporters will not allow to be criticized.

> ■ **1** blessed, holy, sanctified.

sacrifice *n.* **1** slaughter of a victim or presenting of a gift to win a god's favour. **2** this victim or gift. **3** giving up of a valued thing for the sake of something else. **4** thing given up, loss entailed. ● *v.* offer, kill, or give up as a sacrifice. □ **sacrificial** *adj.*

> ■ *v.* immolate; forgo, give up, relinquish, renounce, surrender.

sacrilege *n.* disrespect to a sacred thing. □ **sacrilegious** *adj.*

sacrosanct *adj.* reverenced or respected and not to be harmed.

sacrum /sáykrəm/ *n.* bone at the base of the spine.

sad *adj.* (**sadder, saddest**) **1** showing or causing sorrow. **2** regrettable. □ **sadly** *adv.*, **sadness** *n.*

> ■ **1** crestfallen, dejected, depressed, despondent, dispirited, downcast, downhearted, glum, heartbroken, melancholy, miserable, sorrowful, unhappy, woebegone, wretched; bleak, depressing, disheartening, dismal, gloomy, sombre. **2** awful, deplorable, lamentable, regrettable, terrible, unfortunate.

sadden *v.* make or become sad.

saddle *n.* **1** seat for a rider. **2** joint of meat consisting of the two loins. ● *v.* **1** put a saddle on (an animal). **2** burden with a task.

saddler *n.* person who makes or deals in saddles and harness.

sadism *n.* (sexual) pleasure from inflicting or watching cruelty. □ **sadist** *n.*, **sadistic** *adj.*, **sadistically** *adv.*

safari *n.* expedition to hunt or observe wild animals. □ **safari park** park where exotic wild animals are kept in the open for visitors to see.

safe *adj.* **1** free from risk or danger. **2** secure. **3** reliable. ● *adv.* safely. ● *n.* strong lockable cupboard for valuables. □ **safe conduct** immunity from arrest or harm. **safe deposit** building containing safes and strongrooms for hire. **safely** *adv.*

> ■ *adj.* **1** harmless, innocuous; unharmed, unhurt, uninjured, unscathed. **2** impenetrable, impregnable, secure. **3** reliable, secure, sound, sure.

safeguard *n.* means of protection. ● *v.* protect.

> ■ *v.* conserve, defend, guard, keep (safe), maintain, preserve, protect, save.

safety *n.* being safe, freedom from risk or danger. □ **safety pin** brooch-like pin with a guard protecting and securing the point. **safety-valve** *n.* **1** valve that opens automatically to relieve excessive pressure in a steam boiler. **2** harmless outlet for emotion.

saffron *n.* **1** orange-coloured stigmas of a crocus, used to colour and flavour food. **2** colour of these.

sag *v.* (**sagged**) droop or curve down in the middle under weight or pressure. ● *n.* sagging.
■ *v.* bend, dip, droop, hang (down), sink, slump.

saga *n.* long story.

sagacious *adj.* wise. □ **sagaciously** *adv.*, **sagacity** *n.*
■ astute, discerning, intelligent, judicious, perceptive, perspicacious, prudent, sage, sensible, shrewd, wise.

sage¹ *n.* herb with fragrant grey-green leaves.

sage² *adj.* wise. ● *n.* old and wise man. □ **sagely** *adv.*

sago *n.* starchy pith of the sago palm, used in puddings.

said *see* **say**.

sail *n.* **1** piece of fabric spread to catch the wind and drive a boat along. **2** journey by boat. **3** arm of a windmill. ● *v.* **1** travel by water. **2** start on a voyage. **3** control (a boat). **4** move smoothly.
■ *v.* **3** navigate, pilot, steer. **4** float, glide, slide, sweep.

sailboard *n.* board with a mast and sail, used in windsurfing. □ **sailboarder** *n.*, **sailboarding** *n.*

sailcloth *n.* **1** canvas for sails. **2** canvas-like dress material.

sailor *n.* member of a ship's crew. □ **bad** or **good sailor** person liable or not liable to seasickness.
■ **1** boatman, mariner, old salt, sea dog, seafarer, seaman.

saint *n.* **1** holy person, esp. one venerated by the RC or Orthodox Church. **2** very good, patient, or unselfish person. □ **sainthood** *n.*, **saintly** *adj.*, **saintliness** *n.*
■ □ **saintly** devout, God-fearing, holy, pious, religious, reverent, righteous, virtuous.

sake¹ *n.* **for the sake of** in order to please or honour (a person) or to get or keep (a thing).

sake² /ˈsaːki/ *n.* Japanese fermented liquor made from rice.

salacious *adj.* lewd, erotic. □ **salaciously** *adv.*, **salaciousness** *n.*, **salacity** *n.*

salad *n.* cold dish of (usu. raw) vegetables etc.

salamander *n.* lizard-like animal.

salami *n.* strongly flavoured sausage, eaten cold.

salaried *adj.* receiving a salary.

salary *n.* fixed regular payment to an employee.

sale *n.* **1** selling, exchange of a commodity for money. **2** event at which goods are sold. **3** disposal of stock at reduced prices. □ **for** or **on sale** offered for purchase.

saleable *adj.* fit to be sold, likely to find a purchaser.

salesman, saleswoman, salesperson *ns.* one employed to sell goods.

salesmanship *n.* skill at selling.

salient *adj.* projecting, most noticeable. ● *n.* projecting part.

saline *adj.* salty, containing salt(s). □ **salinity** *n.*

saliva *n.* colourless liquid that forms in the mouth.

salivary *adj.* of or producing saliva.

salivate *v.* produce saliva. □ **salivation** *n.*

sallow¹ *adj.* (of the complexion) yellowish.

sallow² *n.* low-growing willow.

sally *n.* **1** sudden swift attack. **2** lively or witty remark. ● *v.* **sally forth 1** rush out in attack. **2** set out on a journey.
■ *n.* **1** assault, attack, charge, foray, incursion, onslaught, raid, sortie.

salmon /ˈsammən/ *n.* (*pl.* **salmon**) **1** large fish with pinkish flesh. **2** salmon-pink. □ **salmon-pink** *adj.* & *n.* yellowish-pink.

salmonella *n.* bacterium causing food poisoning.

salon *n.* **1** elegant room for receiving guests. **2** place where a hairdresser, couturier, etc. receives clients.

saloon *n.* **1** public room, esp. on board ship. **2** saloon car. □ **saloon car** car with body closed off from luggage area.

salsify *n.* plant with a long fleshy root used as a vegetable.

salt *n.* **1** sodium chloride used to season and preserve food. **2** chemical compound of a metal and an acid. **3** (*pl.*) substance resembling salt in form, esp. a laxative. ● *adj.* **1** tasting of salt. ● *v.* **1** season with salt. **2** preserve in salt. □ **old salt** experienced sailor. **salt away** (*colloq.*) put aside for the future. **salt-cellar** *n.* small container for salt used at meals. **salt marsh** marsh flooded by the sea at high tide. **take with a grain** or **pinch of salt** regard sceptic-

ally. **worth one's salt** competent. **salty**
adj., **saltiness** *n.*

salting *n.* salt marsh.

saltpetre *n.* salty white powder used in
gunpowder, in medicine, and in preserving meat.

salubrious *adj.* health-giving.
- ■ beneficial, healthful, healthy, salutary,
wholesome.

saluki *n.* (*pl.* **-is**) tall swift silky-coated
dog.

salutary *adj.* producing a beneficial or
wholesome effect.

salutation *n.* **1** word(s) or gesture of
greeting. **2** expression of respect.

salute *n.* gesture of respect or greeting.
● *v.* make a salute to.
- ■ *v.* address, greet, hail; acclaim, extol,
honour, pay tribute to, praise.

salvage *n.* **1** rescue of a ship or its cargo
from loss at sea, or of property from fire
etc. **2** saving and use of waste material. **3**
items saved in this way. ● *v.* save from
loss or for use as salvage.
- ■ *v.* recover, rescue, retrieve, save.

salvation *n.* saving, esp. from the consequences of sin.

salve *n.* **1** soothing ointment. **2** thing
that soothes. ● *v.* soothe (conscience
etc.).

salver *n.* small tray.

salvo *n.* (*pl.* **-oes**) **1** simultaneous firing of
guns. **2** round of applause.

sal volatile /sál voláttili/ solution of
ammonium carbonate used as a remedy
for faintness.

samba *n.* ballroom dance of Brazilian
origin.

same *adj.* **1** being of one kind, not
changed or different. **2** previously mentioned. ● *pron.* the same person or thing.
□ **sameness** *n.*
- ■ *adj.* **1** identical, selfsame, very; unchanging, unvarying.

samphire *n.* plant with edible leaves,
growing by the sea.

sample *n.* **1** small part showing the
quality of the whole. **2** specimen. ● *v.*
test by taking a sample or getting an
experience of.
- ■ *n.* **1** example, illustration, specimen. ● *v.*
experience, taste, test, try.

sampler *n.* piece of embroidery worked
in various stitches to show one's skill.

sanatorium *n.* (*pl.* **-ums**) **1** establishment
for treating chronic diseases or conval-

escents. **2** room for sick people in a
school.

sanctify *v.* make holy or sacred. □ **sanc-**
tification *n.*

sanctimonious *adj.* making a show of
righteousness or piety. □ **sanctimoni-**
ously *adv.*, **sanctimoniousness** *n.*

sanction *n.* **1** permission, approval. **2**
penalty imposed on a country or organization. ● *v.* give sanction to, authorize.
- ■ *n.* **1** agreement, approbation, approval,
assent, authorization, blessing, consent,
go-ahead, permission. ● *v.* agree to, allow,
approve (of), assent to, authorize, consent
to, endorse, give the go-ahead for, *colloq.*
give the green light to, permit.

sanctity *n.* sacredness, holiness.

sanctuary *n.* **1** sacred place. **2** place
where birds or wild animals are protected. **3** refuge.
- ■ **2** conservation area, reserve. **3** asylum,
haven, refuge, retreat, shelter.

sanctum *n.* **1** holy place. **2** person's
private room.

sand *n.* **1** very fine loose fragments of
crushed rock. **2** (*pl.*) expanse of sand,
sandbank. ● *v.* **1** sprinkle with sand. **2**
smooth with sandpaper.

sandal *n.* light shoe with straps.

sandalwood *n.* a kind of scented wood.

sandbag *n.* bag filled with sand, used to
protect a wall or building. ● *v.* (**sand-**
bagged) protect with sandbags.

sandbank *n.* underwater deposit of sand.

sandblast *v.* treat with a jet of sand
driven by compressed air or steam.

sandcastle *n.* structure of sand, usu.
made by a child.

sandpaper *n.* paper with a coating of
sand or other abrasive substance, used
for smoothing surfaces. ● *v.* smooth with
this.

sandstone *n.* rock formed of compressed
sand.

sandstorm *n.* desert storm of wind with
blown sand.

sandwich *n.* **1** two or more slices of
bread with a layer of filling between. **2**
thing arranged like this. ● *v.* put between two others.

sandy *adj.* (**-ier**, **-iest**) **1** like sand. **2**
covered with sand. **3** yellowish-red.

sane *adj.* **1** having a sound mind. **2** rational. □ **sanely** *adv.*
- ■ **1** lucid, normal, of sound mind, rational,
right-minded.

sang *see* **sing**.

sangria n. Spanish drink of red wine, lemonade, and fruit.

sanguinary adj. **1** full of bloodshed. **2** bloodthirsty.

sanguine adj. optimistic.
■ cheerful, confident, full of hope, hopeful, optimistic, colloq. upbeat.

sanitary adj. **1** of hygiene or sanitation. **2** hygienic.
■ **2** aseptic, clean, disinfected, germ-free, hygienic, sterile.

sanitation n. arrangements to protect public health, esp. drainage and disposal of sewage.

sanitize v. make sanitary.

sanity n. condition of being sane.

sank see **sink**.

sap n. **1** vital liquid in plants. **2** (sl.) foolish person. ● v. (**sapped**) exhaust gradually. □ **sappy** adj.
■ v. debilitate, drain, enervate, exhaust, weaken, wear out.

sapling n. young tree.

sapphire n. **1** blue precious stone. **2** its colour. ● adj. bright blue.

saprophyte n. fungus or related plant living on decayed matter. □ **saprophytic** adj.

sarcasm n. ironically scornful remark(s). □ **sarcastic** adj., **sarcastically** adv.
■ □ sarcastic biting, bitter, caustic, cutting, mordant, sardonic, scathing, sharp, spiteful, stinging.

sarcophagus n. (pl. **-gi**) stone coffin.

sardine n. young pilchard or similar small fish.

sardonic adj. humorous in a grim or sarcastic way. □ **sardonically** adv.

sargasso n. seaweed with berry-like air-vessels.

sari n. (pl. **-is**) length of cloth draped round the body, worn by Hindu women.

sarong n. strip of cloth worn tucked round the body.

sarsen n. sandstone boulder.

sartorial adj. **1** of tailoring. **2** of men's clothing.

sash[1] n. strip of cloth worn round the waist or over one shoulder.

sash[2] n. frame holding a pane of a window and sliding up and down in grooves.

sat see **sit**.

satanic adj. **1** of or like Satan. **2** devilish, hellish.

Satanism n. worship of Satan.

satchel n. bag for school books, hung over the shoulder(s).

sate v. satiate.

sateen n. closely woven cotton fabric resembling satin.

satellite n. **1** heavenly or artificial body revolving round a planet. **2** country that is subservient to another. □ **satellite dish** dish-shaped aerial for receiving broadcasts transmitted by satellite.

satiate /sáyshiayt/ v. satisfy fully, glut. □ **satiation** n.
■ glut, gorge, overfill, overindulge, sate, satisfy, surfeit.

satiety /sətí-iti/ n. condition of being satiated.

satin n. silky material that is glossy on one side. ● adj. smooth as satin. □ **satiny** adj.

satire n. **1** use of ridicule, irony, or sarcasm. **2** novel or play etc. that ridicules something. □ **satirical** adj., **satirically** adv.
■ **1** caricature, irony, parody, ridicule. **2** burlesque, lampoon, parody, colloq. spoof, take-off.

satirize v. attack or describe with satire. □ **satirist** n.
■ burlesque, caricature, lampoon, make fun of, parody, ridicule, send up, take off.

satisfactory adj. satisfying, adequate. □ **satisfactorily** adv.
■ acceptable, adequate, all right, fair, good enough, colloq. OK, passable, tolerable.

satisfy v. **1** meet the expectations or wishes of. **2** meet (an appetite or want). **3** rid (a person) of an appetite or want. **4** make pleased or contented. **5** convince. □ **satisfaction** n.
■ **1** answer, comply with, fulfil, meet. **2** quench, sate, satiate, slake. **3** gratify, indulge, pander to. **4** appease, content, mollify, pacify, placate, please. **5** convince, persuade.

satsuma n. a kind of tangerine.

saturate v. **1** make thoroughly wet. **2** cause to absorb or accept as much as possible. □ **saturation** n.

saturnine adj. having a gloomy temperament or appearance.

satyr /sáttər/ n. woodland god in classical mythology, with a goat's ears, tail, and legs.

sauce n. **1** liquid preparation added to food to give flavour or richness. **2** (sl.) impudence.

saucepan n. metal cooking pot with a long handle.

saucer n. **1** curved dish on which a cup stands. **2** thing shaped like this.

saucy adj. (**-ier, -iest**) impudent. □ **saucily** adv.

> ■ cheeky, disrespectful, forward, impertinent, impudent, irreverent, pert, rude.

sauerkraut /sówərkrowt/ n. chopped pickled cabbage.

sauna n. Finnish-style steam bath.

saunter v. & n. stroll.

> ■ v. amble, stroll, walk, wander.

saurian adj. of or like a lizard.

sausage n. minced seasoned meat in a tubular case of thin skin.

savage adj. **1** fierce, cruel. **2** wild, primitive. ● n. savage person. ● v. maul savagely. □ **savagely** adv., **savagery** n.

> ■ adj. **1** barbaric, bestial, bloodthirsty, brutal, cruel, ferocious, fierce, merciless, ruthless, vicious, violent. **2** primitive, uncivilized, untamed, wild.

savannah n. grassy plain in hot regions.

save v. **1** rescue. **2** protect. **3** avoid wasting. **4** keep for future use, put aside money in this way. **5** prevent the scoring of (a goal etc.). ● n. act of saving in football etc. □ **saver** n.

> ■ v. **1** deliver, release, rescue; recover, retrieve, salvage. **2** conserve, keep (safe), preserve, protect, safeguard. **3** accumulate, collect, garner, hoard, keep back, lay up, put by, reserve, colloq. salt away, set aside, stockpile, store up; economize.

saveloy n. highly seasoned sausage.

savings n.pl. money put aside for future use.

saviour n. person who rescues people from harm or danger.

savory n. spicy herb.

savour n. **1** flavour. **2** smell. ● v. appreciate, enjoy.

> ■ n. **1** flavour, tang, taste. ● v. appreciate, delight in, enjoy, luxuriate in, relish, revel in, take pleasure in.

savoury adj. **1** having an appetizing taste or smell. **2** salty or piquant, not sweet. ● n. savoury dish, esp. at the end of a meal.

savoy n. a kind of cabbage.

saw[1] see **see**[1].

saw[2] n. cutting tool with a zigzag edge. ● v. (**sawed, sawn**) **1** cut with a saw. **2** make a to-and-fro movement.

saw[3] n. old saying, maxim.

sawdust n. powdery fragments of wood, made in sawing timber.

sawfish n. large sea fish with a jagged blade-like snout.

sawmill n. mill where timber is cut into planks etc.

sawn see **saw**[2].

sax n. (colloq.) saxophone.

saxe blue adj. & n. greyish-blue.

saxifrage n. a kind of rock plant.

saxophone n. brass wind instrument with finger-operated keys. □ **saxophonist** n.

say v. (**said**) **1** utter. **2** express in words, state. **3** give as an opinion. **4** suppose as a possibility etc. ● n. **1** opportunity to express view. **2** power to decide.

> ■ v. **1** articulate, pronounce, speak, utter, voice. **2** communicate, express, put into words, verbalize; affirm, announce, assert, comment, declare, mention, observe, remark, state. **3** conjecture, estimate, guess, imagine, judge. ● n. **2** authority, colloq. clout, influence, power, voice, weight.

saying n. well-known phrase or proverb.

> ■ aphorism, axiom, expression, idiom, maxim, motto, phrase, proverb, saw.

scab n. **1** crust forming over a sore. **2** skin disease or plant disease causing similar roughness. **3** (colloq., derog.) blackleg. □ **scabby** adj.

scabbard n. sheath of a sword etc.

scabies n. contagious skin disease causing itching.

scabious n. herbaceous plant with clustered flowers.

scabrous adj. **1** rough-surfaced. **2** indecent.

scaffold n. **1** platform for the execution of criminals. **2** scaffolding.

scaffolding n. temporary structure of poles, planks, etc. for building work.

scald v. **1** injure with hot liquid or steam. **2** cleanse with boiling water. ● n. injury by scalding.

scale[1] n. **1** each of the overlapping plates of horny membrane protecting the skin of many fish and reptiles. **2** thing resembling this. **3** incrustation caused by hard water or forming on teeth. ● v. **1** remove scale(s) from. **2** come off in scales. □ **scaly** adj.

scale[2] n. **1** pan of a balance. **2** (pl.) instrument for weighing things.

scale[3] n. **1** ordered series of units or qualities etc. for measuring or classifying things. **2** relationship between actual size and the size on a map or plan. **3**

fixed series of notes in a system of music. **4** relative size or extent. ● *v.* climb.

■ *n.* **2** proportion, ratio. ● *v.* ascend, clamber up, climb, go up, mount.

scallop *n.* **1** shellfish with hinged fan-shaped shells. **2** one shell of this. **3** (*pl.*) semicircular curves as an ornamental edging. □ **scalloped** *adj.*

scallywag *n.* rascal.

scalp *n.* skin of the head excluding the face. ● *v.* cut the scalp from.

scalpel *n.* surgeon's or painter's small straight knife.

scamp *n.* rascal.

scamper *v.* run hastily or in play. ● *n.* scampering run.

■ *v.* dash, hasten, hurry, rush, scoot, scramble, scurry, scuttle.

scampi *n.pl.* large prawns.

scan *v.* (**scanned**) **1** look at all parts of intently or quickly. **2** pass a radar or electronic beam over. **3** (of verse) have a regular rhythm. ● *n.* scanning. □ **scanner** *n.*

■ *v.* **1** examine, inspect, peruse, scrutinize, study, survey; flick *or* leaf *or* skim through, glance at.

scandal 1 something disgraceful. **2** malicious gossip. □ **scandalous** *adj.*, **scandalously** *adv.*

■ *n.* **1** disgrace, outrage, shame, sin. **2** dirt, gossip, rumour, tittle-tattle. □ **scandalous** deplorable, disgraceful, monstrous, outrageous, shameful, shocking, sinful, terrible, wicked.

scandalize *v.* shock, outrage.

■ appal, horrify, outrage, shock.

scandalmonger *n.* person who invents or spreads scandal.

Scandinavian *adj.* & *n.* (native) of Scandinavia.

scansion *n.* scanning of verse.

scant *adj.* not or barely enough.

scanty *adj.* (**-ier, -iest**) **1** small in amount or extent. **2** barely enough. □ **scantily** *adv.*, **scantiness** *n.*

■ insufficient, limited, meagre, minimal, scant, scarce, sparse.

scapegoat *n.* person bearing the blame due to others.

scapula *n.* (*pl.* **-lae**) shoulder blade. □ **scapular** *adj.*

scar *n.* mark where a wound has healed. ● *v.* (**scarred**) **1** mark with a scar. **2** form scar(s).

■ *n.* cicatrice. ● *v.* **1** blemish, disfigure, mar, mark.

scarab *n.* sacred beetle of ancient Egypt.

scarce *adj.* not enough to supply a demand, rare.

scarcely *adv.* **1** only just, almost not. **2** not, surely not.

■ **1** barely, hardly, (only) just.

scarcity *n.* lack or shortage.

■ dearth, deficiency, insufficiency, lack, need, paucity, shortage, want.

scare *v.* **1** frighten. **2** be frightened. ● *n.* sudden fright.

■ *v.* **1** alarm, dismay, frighten, intimidate, panic, petrify, *colloq.* put the wind up, shock, startle, terrify. ● *n.* fright, shock, start, turn.

scarecrow *n.* figure dressed in old clothes and set up to scare birds away from crops.

scaremonger *n.* alarmist. □ **scaremongering** *n.*

scarf *n.* (*pl.* **scarves**) piece or strip of material worn round the neck or over the head.

scarify *v.* **1** make slight cuts in. **2** criticize harshly.

scarlet *adj.* & *n.* brilliant red. □ **scarlet fever** infectious fever producing a scarlet rash.

scarp *n.* steep slope on a hillside.

scary *adj.* (**-ier, -iest**) (*colloq.*) frightening.

scathing *adj.* (of criticism) very severe.

■ biting, bitter, caustic, cutting, mordant, savage, scornful, sharp, stinging, vitriolic.

scatter *v.* **1** throw or put here and there. **2** go or send in different directions. ● *n.* small scattered amount.

■ *v.* **1** distribute, litter, spread, sprinkle, strew.

scatterbrain *n.* forgetful person. □ **scatterbrained** *adj.*

■ ■ **scatterbrained** absent-minded, careless, disorganized, forgetful, *colloq.* scatty.

scatty *adj.* (**-ier, -iest**) (*colloq.*) lacking concentration.

scavenge *v.* **1** search for (usable objects) among rubbish etc. **2** (of animals) search for decaying flesh as food. □ **scavenger** *n.*

scenario n. (pl. **-os**) **1** script or summary of a film or play. **2** imagined sequence of events.

scene n. **1** place of an event. **2** display of temper or emotion. **3** view of a place. **4** incident. **5** piece of continuous action in a play or film. **6** stage scenery. **7** (sl.) area of activity. □ **behind the scenes** hidden from view.

■ **1** location, place, setting, site. **2** commotion, disturbance, fuss, tantrum, to-do. **3** landscape, panorama, prospect, view, vista.

scenery n. **1** general (esp. picturesque) appearance of a landscape. **2** structures used on a theatre stage to represent the scene of action.

scenic adj. picturesque.

scent n. **1** pleasant smell. **2** liquid perfume. **3** animal's trail perceptible to a hound's sense of smell. ● v. **1** discover by smell. **2** suspect the presence or existence of. **3** apply scent to, make fragrant.

■ n. **1** aroma, bouquet, fragrance, perfume, redolence. **2** eau-de-Cologne, perfume, toilet water.

sceptic /sképtik/ n. sceptical person.

sceptical /sképtik'l/ adj. unwilling to believe things. □ **sceptically** adv., **scepticism** n.

■ cynical, distrustful, doubtful, dubious, incredulous, mistrustful, unconvinced.

sceptre n. ornamental rod carried as a symbol of sovereignty.

schedule n. programme or timetable of events. ● v. appoint in a schedule.

■ n. plan, programme, timetable. ● v. arrange, fix, organize, plan, programme, time.

schematic adj. in the form of a diagram. □ **schematically** adv.

schematize v. put into schematic form. □ **schematization** n.

scheme n. plan of work or action. ● v. make plans, plot. □ **schemer** n.

■ n. plan, programme, strategy; game, plot, ploy, sl. racket, ruse. ● v. conspire, intrigue, plan, plot.

scheming adj. cunning, deceitful.

■ artful, crafty, cunning, deceitful, devious, sly, treacherous, tricky, underhand, wily.

scherzo /skáirtsō/ n. (pl. **-os**) lively piece of music.

schism /síss'm/ n. division into opposing groups through difference in belief or opinion. □ **schismatic** adj. & n.

schist /shist/ n. rock with components in layers.

schizoid adj. like or suffering from schizophrenia. ● n. schizoid person.

schizophrenia n. mental disorder in which a person is unable to act or reason rationally. □ **schizophrenic** adj. & n.

scholar n. **1** learned person. **2** pupil. **3** holder of a scholarship. □ **scholarly** adj.

■ **1** academic, highbrow, intellectual, thinker. □ **scholarly** academic, erudite, highbrow, intellectual, learned, scholastic.

scholarship n. **1** grant of money towards education. **2** scholars' methods and achievements.

scholastic adj. **1** of schools or education. **2** academic.

school[1] n. shoal of fish or whales.

school[2] n. **1** institution for educating children or giving instruction. **2** group of artists etc. following the same principles. ● v. train, discipline. □ **schoolboy** n., **schoolchild** n., **schoolgirl** n.

■ v. coach, drill, educate, instruct, teach, train, tutor.

schoolteacher n. teacher in a school.

schooner n. **1** a kind of sailing ship. **2** measure for sherry etc.

science n. branch of knowledge requiring systematic study and method, esp. dealing with substances, life, and natural laws. □ **scientific** adj., **scientifically** adv.

scientist n. expert in science(s).

scimitar n. short curved sword.

scintillating adj. lively, witty.

scion /síən/ n. **1** shoot, esp. cut for grafting. **2** descendant.

scissors n.pl. cutting instrument with two pivoted blades.

sclerosis n. abnormal hardening of tissue.

scoff[1] v. speak contemptuously.

■ gibe, jeer, laugh, mock, sneer.

scoff[2] v. (colloq.) eat quickly.

scold v. rebuke (esp. a child). □ **scolding** n.

■ berate, chide, rebuke, reprimand, reprove, colloq. tell off, colloq. tick off, upbraid.

sconce n. ornamental bracket on a wall, holding a light.

scone /skon, skōn/ n. soft flat cake eaten buttered.

scoop n. **1** deep shovel-like tool. **2** a kind of ladle. **3** piece of news published by one newspaper before its rivals. ● v. **1**

lift or hollow with (or as if with) a scoop. **2** forestall with a news scoop.

scoot v. run, dart.

scooter n. **1** child's toy vehicle with a footboard and long steering-handle. **2** lightweight motor cycle.

scope n. **1** range of a subject etc. **2** opportunity.

■ **1** area, breadth, compass, extent, range, sphere. **2** freedom, latitude, leeway, opportunity, room, space.

scorch v. burn or become burnt on the surface.

scorching adj. extremely hot.

score n. **1** number of points gained in a game or competition. **2** set of twenty. **3** line or mark cut into something. **4** written or printed music. **5** music for a film or play. ● v. **1** gain (points etc.) in a game or competition. **2** keep a record of the score. **3** cut a line or mark into. **4** achieve (an advantage). **5** write or compose as a musical score. □ **score out** cross out. **scorer** n.

■ n. **1** tally, total. ● v. **1** notch up, win. **3** cut, incise, mark, nick, notch, scratch.

scorn n. strong contempt. ● v. **1** feel or show scorn for. **2** reject with scorn. □ **scornful** adj., **scornfully** adv., **scornfulness** n.

■ n. contempt, derision, disdain. ● v. **1** be contemptuous of, deride, despise, disdain, look down on, mock, ridicule, sneer at.

scorpion n. small animal of the spider group with lobster-like claws and a sting in its long tail.

Scot n. native of Scotland.

Scotch adj. Scottish. ● n. Scotch whisky.

scotch v. put an end to (a rumour).

scot-free adj. **1** unharmed, not punished. **2** free of charge.

Scots adj. Scottish. ● n. Scottish form of the English language. □ **Scotsman** n., **Scotswoman** n.

Scottish adj. of Scotland or its people.

scoundrel n. dishonest or unprincipled person.

■ blackguard, good-for-nothing, knave, rascal, rat, rogue, scallywag, scamp, villain, wretch.

scour[1] v. **1** cleanse by rubbing. **2** clear out (a channel etc.) by flowing water. ● n. scouring. □ **scourer** n.

scour[2] v. search thoroughly.

scourge /skurj/ n. **1** whip. **2** great affliction. ● v. **1** flog. **2** afflict greatly.

■ n. **2** affliction, bane, blight, curse, misfortune, torment.

scout n. person sent to gather information, esp. about enemy movements etc. ● v. **1** act as scout. **2** search.

scowl n. sullen or angry frown. ● v. make a scowl.

■ v. frown, glare, glower, grimace.

scrabble v. scratch or search busily with hands, paws, etc.

scraggy adj. (**-ier**, **-iest**) lean and bony. □ **scragginess** n.

scram v. (**scrammed**) (colloq.) go away.

scramble v. **1** clamber. **2** move hastily or awkwardly. **3** mix indiscriminately. **4** cook (eggs) by heating and stirring. **5** make (a transmission) unintelligible except by means of a special receiver. **6** (of aircraft or crew) hurry to take off quickly. ● n. **1** scrambling walk or movement. **2** eager struggle. **3** motor cycle race over rough ground. □ **scrambler** n.

■ v. **1** clamber, climb. **2** dash, hurry, race, rush, scurry; blunder, flounder, struggle, stumble. **3** confuse, jumble, mix up, muddle. ● n. **2** race, rush, scrimmage, scrum, scuffle, struggle, tussle.

scrap[1] n. **1** fragment. **2** waste material. **3** discarded metal suitable for reprocessing. ● v. (**scrapped**) discard as useless.

■ v. **1** bit, fragment, piece, remnant, shred, snippet. **2** debris, junk, rubbish, waste. ● v. discard, dispose of, sl. ditch, dump, get rid of, jettison, throw away.

scrap[2] n. & v. (**scrapped**) (colloq.) fight, quarrel.

scrapbook n. book in which to keep newspaper cuttings etc.

scrape v. **1** clean, smooth, or damage by passing a hard edge across a surface. **2** pass (an edge) across in this way. **3** make the sound of scraping. **4** get along or through etc. with difficulty. **5** be very economical. ● n. **1** scraping movement or sound. **2** scraped place. **3** awkward situation. □ **scraper** n.

■ v. **1** bark, chafe, graze, scratch. ● n. **2** abrasion, graze, scratch. **3** difficulty, fix, colloq. jam, mess, colloq. pickle, predicament.

scrappy adj. (**-ier**, **-iest**) made up of scraps or disconnected elements.

scratch v. **1** scrape with the fingernails. **2** damage or wound superficially, esp.

with sharp object. **3** withdraw from a race or competition. ● n. **1** mark, wound, or sound made by scratching. **2** spell of scratching. ● adj. collected from what is available. □ **from scratch** from the very beginning or with no preparation. **up to scratch** up to the required standard. **scratchy** adj.

■ n. **1** abrasion, cut, graze, mark, nick, scrape. □ **up to scratch** adequate, competent, good enough, satisfactory.

scratchings n.pl. crisp residue of pork fat left after rendering lard.

scrawl n. **1** bad handwriting. **2** something written in this. ● v. write in a scrawl, scribble.

scrawny adj. (**-ier, -iest**) scraggy.

■ bony, emaciated, gaunt, lean, scraggy, skeletal, skinny, thin.

scream v. make a long piercing cry or sound. ● n. **1** screaming cry or sound. **2** (sl.) extremely amusing person or thing.

■ v. cry, howl, screech, shriek, squeal, wail, yowl.

scree n. mass of loose stones on a mountain side.

screech n. harsh high-pitched scream or sound. ● v. make or utter with a screech.

screed n. **1** tiresomely long letter etc. **2** thin layer of cement.

screen n. **1** structure used to conceal, protect, or divide something. **2** windscreen. **3** blank surface on which pictures, cinema films, or television transmissions etc. are projected. ● v. **1** shelter, conceal. **2** show (images etc.) on a screen. **3** examine for the presence or absence of a disease or quality etc.

■ n. **1** barrier, divider, partition; protection, shelter, shield. ● v. **1** camouflage, conceal, cover (up), disguise, hide, mask, protect, shelter, shield, veil.

screw n. **1** metal pin with a spiral ridge round its length, fastened by turning. **2** thing twisted to tighten or press something. **3** propeller. **4** act of screwing. ● v. **1** fasten or tighten with screw(s). **2** turn (a screw). **3** twist, become twisted. **4** oppress, extort. □ **screw up 1** summon up (one's courage etc.). **2** (sl.) bungle.

screwdriver n. tool for turning screws.

scribble v. **1** write hurriedly or carelessly. **2** make meaningless marks. ● n. something scribbled.

scribe n. **1** person who (before the invention of printing) made copies of writings. **2** (in New Testament times) professional religious scholar.

scrimmage n. confused struggle. ● v. engage in this.

scrimp v. skimp.

script n. **1** handwriting. **2** style of printed characters resembling this. **3** text of a play, film, or broadcast talk.

scripture n. **1** sacred writings. **2** (**the Scriptures**) those of the Christians or the Jews. □ **scriptural** adj.

scroll n. **1** roll of paper or parchment. **2** ornamental design in this shape. ● v. move (a display on a VDU screen) up or down as the screen is filled.

scrotum n. (pl. **-ta**) pouch of skin enclosing the testicles.

scrounge v. obtain by cadging. □ **scrounger** n.

■ beg, borrow, cadge, sponge.

scrub[1] n. **1** vegetation consisting of stunted trees and shrubs. **2** land covered with this.

scrub[2] v. (**scrubbed**) **1** rub hard esp. with something coarse or bristly. **2** (colloq.) cancel. ● n. process of scrubbing.

■ v. **1** clean, rub, scour.

scruff n. back of the neck.

scruffy adj. (**-ier, -iest**) (colloq.) shabby and untidy. □ **scruffily** adv., **scruffiness** n.

scrum n. **1** scrummage. **2** confused struggle.

scrummage n. grouping of forwards in Rugby football to struggle for possession of the ball by pushing.

scrumptious adj. (colloq.) delicious.

scrunch v. & n. crunch.

scruple n. doubt about doing something produced by one's conscience. ● v. hesitate because of scruples.

■ n. compunction, doubt, hesitation, misgiving, qualm, reservation.

scrupulous adj. very conscientious or careful. □ **scrupulously** adv., **scrupulousness** n.

■ careful, conscientious, meticulous, painstaking, precise, punctilious, thorough.

scrutinize v. make a scrutiny of.

■ examine, go over, inspect, look into, peruse, study; contemplate, look at, observe, regard, survey.

scrutiny n. careful look or examination.

scuba n. an aqualung (acronym from self-contained underwater breathing apparatus). □ **scuba-diving** n.

scud v. (**scudded**) move along fast and smoothly.

scuff v. **1** scrape or drag (one's feet) in walking. **2** mark or scrape by doing this.

scuffle n. confused struggle or fight. ● v. take part in a scuffle.

■ n. brawl, fight, colloq. scrap, scrimmage, struggle, tussle.

scull n. **1** one of a pair of small oars. **2** oar used to propel a boat from the stern. ● v. row with scull(s).

sculpt v. sculpture.

sculptor n. maker of sculptures.

sculpture n. **1** art of carving or modelling. **2** work made in this way. ● v. **1** represent in or decorate with sculpture. **2** be a sculptor. □ **sculptural** adj.

■ n. **2** bust, figure, statue, statuette. ● v. **1** carve, chisel, fashion, hew, model, sculpt.

scum n. **1** layer of impurities or froth etc. on the surface of a liquid. **2** worthless person(s).

scupper n. opening in a ship's side to drain water from the deck. ● v. **1** sink (a ship) deliberately. **2** (sl.) ruin.

scurf n. **1** flakes of dry skin, esp. from the scalp. **2** similar scaly matter. □ **scurfy** adj.

scurrilous adj. grossly or obscenely abusive. □ **scurrilously** adv., **scurrility** n.

■ abusive, defamatory, derogatory, disparaging, insulting, opprobrious, offensive, slanderous, vituperative.

scurry v. run hurriedly, scamper. ● n. scurrying, rush.

■ v. dart, dash, hasten, hurry, race, run, rush, scamper, scoot, scramble, scuttle.

scurvy n. disease caused by lack of vitamin C in the diet.

scuttle¹ n. box or bucket for holding coal in a room.

scuttle² v. sink (a ship) by letting in water.

scuttle³ v. & n. scurry.

scythe /sīth/ n. implement with a curved blade on a long handle, for cutting long grass or grain.

SE abbr. **1** south-east. **2** south-eastern.

sea n. **1** expanse of salt water surrounding the continents. **2** section of this. **3** large inland lake. **4** waves of the sea. **5** vast expanse. **6** perplexed. □ **at sea 1** in a ship on the sea. **2** perplexed. **sea dog** old sailor. **sea-green** adj. & n. bluish-green. **sea horse** small fish with a horse-like head. **sea level** level corresponding to the mean level of the sea's surface. **sea lion** large

seal. **sea urchin** sea animal with a round spiky shell.

seaboard n. coast.

seafarer n. seafaring person.

seafaring adj. & n. working or travelling on the sea.

seafood n. fish or shellfish from the sea eaten as food.

seagoing adj. for sea voyages.

seagull n. gull.

seal¹ n. amphibious sea animal with thick fur or bristles.

seal² n. **1** engraved piece of metal used to stamp a design. **2** its impression. **3** action etc. serving to confirm or guarantee something. **4** paper sticker. **5** thing used to close an opening very tightly. ● v. **1** stick down. **2** close or coat so as to prevent penetration. **3** settle, decide. □ **seal off** prevent access to (an area).

sealant n. substance for coating a surface to seal it.

sealskin n. seal's skin or fur used as a clothing material.

seam n. **1** line where two edges join. **2** layer of coal etc. in the ground. ● v. join by a seam. □ **seamless** adj.

seaman n. **1** sailor. **2** person skilled in seafaring. □ **seamanship** n.

seamstress n. woman who sews.

seance /sáyonss/ n. spiritualist meeting.

seaplane n. aircraft designed to take off from and land on water.

sear v. scorch, burn.

search v. look, feel, or go over (a person or place etc.) in order to find something. ● n. process of searching. □ **searcher** n.

■ v. comb, hunt or rummage through, ransack, scour; sl. frisk. ● n. hunt, pursuit, quest.

searching adj. thorough.

searchlight n. **1** outdoor lamp with a powerful beam. **2** its beam.

seascape n. picture or view of the sea.

seasick adj. made sick by a ship's motion. □ **seasickness** n.

seaside n. coast, esp. as a place for holidays.

season n. **1** section of the year associated with a type of weather. **2** time when something takes place or is plentiful. ● v. **1** give extra flavour to (food). **2** dry or treat until ready for use. □ **season ticket** ticket valid for any number of journeys or performances in a specified period.

seasonable adj. **1** suitable for the season. **2** timely. □ **seasonably** adv.

seasonal *adj.* **1** of a season or seasons. **2** varying with the seasons. □ **seasonally** *adv.*

seasoned *adj.* experienced.

seasoning *n.* substance used to season food.

■ condiments, flavouring, spice.

seat *n.* **1** thing made or used for sitting on. **2** buttocks, part of a garment covering these. **3** place where something is based. **4** country mansion. **5** place as member of a committee or parliament etc. ● *v.* **1** cause to sit. **2** have seats for. □ **be seated** sit down. **seat belt** strap securing a person to a seat in a vehicle or aircraft.

■ *n.* **1** chair, *colloq.* pew, place. **3** base, centre, cradle, focus, heart, hub. ● *v.* **2** accommodate, have room for, hold.

seaward *adj.* & *adv.* towards the sea. □ **seawards** *adv.*

seaweed *n.* any plant that grows in the sea.

seaworthy *adj.* (of ships) fit for a sea voyage. □ **seaworthiness** *n.*

sebaceous *adj.* secreting an oily or greasy substance.

secateurs *n.pl.* clippers for pruning plants.

secede *v.* withdraw from membership. □ **secession** *n.*

seclude *v.* keep (a person) apart from others. □ **seclusion** *n.*

secluded *adj.* hidden from view, very quiet.

■ isolated, lonely, private, quiet, remote, sequestered.

second[1] /sékkənd/ *adj.* **1** next after the first. **2** additional. ● *n.* **1** second thing, class, etc. **2** sixtieth part of a minute of time or (in measuring angles) degree. **3** short time. **4** (*pl.*) goods of an inferior quality. ● *v.* state one's support of (a proposal) formally. □ **second-best** *adj.* **1** next to the best in quality. **2** inferior. **second-class** *adj.* & *adv.* next or inferior to first-class in quality etc. **second cousin** (*see* cousin). **second-hand** *adj.* bought after use by a previous owner. **second nature** habit or characteristic that has become automatic. **second-rate** *adj.* inferior in quality. **second sight** supposed power to foresee future events. **second thought(s)** revised opinion. **second wind** renewed capacity for effort.

■ *adj.* **1** following, next, subsequent. **2** additional, extra, further, other, supple-

mentary. ● *n.* **3** bit, instant, minute, moment, split second, *colloq.* tick, while. ● *v.* approve, back, endorse, support. □ **second-rate** bad, inferior, poor, second-best, second-class, shoddy, substandard, tawdry.

second[2] /sikónd/ *v.* transfer temporarily to another job or department. □ **secondment** *n.*

secondary *adj.* coming after or derived from what is primary. ● *n.* secondary thing. □ **secondary colours** those obtained by mixing two primary colours. **secondary education, secondary school** that for children who have received primary education. **secondarily** *adv.*

■ *adj.* additional, ancillary, extra, minor, non-essential, peripheral, subordinate, subsidiary.

secondly *adv.* furthermore.

secret *adj.* kept from the knowledge of most people. ● *n.* **1** something secret. **2** mystery. □ **in secret** secretly. **secretly** *adv.*, **secrecy** *n.*

■ *adj.* concealed, hidden; clandestine, covert, furtive, surreptitious, undercover; classified, confidential, hush-hush, private; arcane, cryptic, mysterious.

secretariat *n.* administrative office or department.

secretary *n.* **1** person employed to deal with correspondence and routine office work. **2** official in charge of an organization's correspondence. **3** ambassador's or government minister's chief assistant. □ **Secretary-General** *n.* principal administrative officer. **secretarial** *adj.*

secrete *v.* **1** put into a place of concealment. **2** produce by secretion. □ **secretor** *n.*

■ **1** cache, conceal, hide, *colloq.* stash away. **2** discharge, emit, exude, ooze, produce.

secretion *n.* **1** process of secreting. **2** production of a substance within the body. **3** this substance.

secretive *adj.* making a secret of things. □ **secretively** *adv.*, **secretiveness** *n.*

■ close, reserved, reticent, silent, taciturn, uncommunicative, unforthcoming; conspiratorial, furtive, mysterious.

secretory *adj.* of physiological secretion.

sect *n.* group with beliefs that differ from those generally accepted.

■ cult, denomination, faith, order, persuasion, religion.

sectarian *adj.* **1** of a sect or sects. **2** narrow-mindedly promoting the interests of one's sect.

section *n.* **1** distinct part. **2** subdivision. **3** cross-section. ● *v.* divide into sections.
■ *n.* **1** part, portion, segment; stage. **2** branch, department, division, sector, subdivision.

sectional *adj.* **1** of a section or sections. **2** made in sections.

sector *n.* **1** part of an area. **2** branch of an activity. **3** section of a circular area between two lines drawn from centre to circumference.
■ **1** area, district, part, quarter, region, territory, zone.

secular *adj.* of worldly (not religious or spiritual) matters.
■ earthly, material, mundane, temporal, worldly; lay.

secure *adj.* **1** safe. **2** certain not to move or fail. ● *v.* **1** make secure. **2** fasten securely. **3** obtain. □ **securely** *adv.*
■ *adj.* **1** impregnable, inviolable, invulnerable, protected, safe; bolted, closed, fastened, locked, shut. **2** attached, fast, fastened, fixed; assured, certain, reliable, safe, sound, sure. ● *v.* **1** defend, guard, make or keep safe, protect, safeguard. **2** bolt, close, fasten, lock, shut. **3** acquire, come by, gain, get, obtain, procure, win.

security *n.* **1** safety, confidence. **2** safety or precaution against espionage, theft, or other danger. **3** thing serving as a pledge. **4** certificate showing ownership of financial stocks etc.
■ **1** protection, safety, shelter; assurance, certainty, confidence, conviction.

sedate[1] *adj.* calm and dignified. □ **sedately** *adv.*, **sedateness** *n.*
■ calm, collected, composed, cool, decorous, dignified, imperturbable, placid, serene, staid, tranquil, unruffled.

sedate[2] *v.* treat with sedatives. □ **sedation** *n.*

sedative *adj.* having a calming effect. ● *n.* sedative drug.
■ *n.* barbiturate, narcotic, opiate, tranquillizer.

sedentary *adj.* **1** seated. **2** (of work) done while sitting.

sedge *n.* grass-like plant(s) growing in marshes or by water.

sediment *n.* particles of solid matter in a liquid or deposited by water or wind. □ **sedimentary** *adj.*, **sedimentation** *n.*
■ deposit, dregs, grounds, lees, precipitate, residue, silt.

sedition *n.* words or actions inciting rebellion. □ **seditious** *adj.*, **seditiously** *adv.*
■ □ **seditious** insurgent, mutinous, rebellious, revolutionary, riotous, subversive.

seduce *v.* entice into sexual activity or wrongdoing. □ **seducer** *n.*, **seduction** *n.*, **seductive** *adj.*, **seductiveness** *n.*
■ □ **seductive** attractive, desirable, erotic, sexy, voluptuous; alluring, captivating, enticing, irresistible, tempting.

sedulous *adj.* diligent and persevering. □ **sedulously** *adv.*

see[1] *v.* (**saw**, **seen**) **1** perceive with the eye(s) or mind. **2** understand. **3** find out. **4** consider. **5** escort. **6** make sure. **7** interview, visit. **8** meet socially. **9** watch. **10** experience. □ **see to** attend to. **seeing that** in view of the fact that.
■ **1** catch sight of, descry, discern, distinguish, espy, make out, note, notice, observe, perceive, *colloq.* spot; envisage, foresee, foretell, imagine. **2** appreciate, comprehend, *colloq.* get, grasp, know, realize, understand. **3** ascertain, determine, discover, find out. **4** consider, deliberate, reflect, think. **5** accompany, escort, take. **6** ensure, make sure, mind. □ **see to** arrange, attend to, deal with, do, organize, prepare, sort out, take care of.

see[2] *n.* district of a bishop or archbishop.

seed *n.* **1** plant's fertilized ovule. **2** semen, milt. **3** origin. ● *v.* **1** produce seed. **2** sprinkle with seeds. **3** remove seeds from. □ **go** or **run to seed 1** cease flowering as seed develops. **2** become shabby or less efficient. **seedless** *adj.*

seedling *n.* very young plant growing from a seed.

seedy *adj.* (**-ier**, **-iest**) looking shabby and disreputable.
■ dilapidated, disreputable, shabby, sleazy, squalid.

seek *v.* (**sought**) **1** try to find or obtain. **2** try (to do something).
■ **1** hunt for, look for, search for, try to find. **2** aim, attempt, endeavour, strive, try.

seem *v.* appear to be or exist or be true. □ **seemingly** *adv.*
■ appear, feel, give an impression of, look, strike one as.

seemly adj. (**-ier, -iest**) in good taste, decorous. □ **seemliness** n.
■ decent, decorous, dignified, genteel, proper, respectable.

seen see **see**[1].

seep v. ooze slowly out or through. □ **seepage** n.

seer n. prophet.

seersucker n. fabric woven with a puckered surface.

see-saw n. **1** a long board balanced on a central support so that children sitting on each end can ride up and down alternately. **2** constantly repeated up-and-down change. ● v. **1** make this movement or change. **2** vacillate.
■ v. **2** alternate, change, fluctuate, oscillate, swing, vacillate, vary.

seethe v. **1** bubble as if boiling. **2** be very angry.

segment n. **1** part cut off or marked off or separable from others. **2** part of a circle or sphere cut off by a straight line or plane. □ **segmented** adj.
■ **1** division, fragment, part, piece, portion, section.

segregate v. put apart from others. □ **segregation** n.

seine /sayn/ n. large fishing net that hangs from floats.

seismic /ˈsīzmik/ adj. of earthquake(s).

seismograph n. instrument for recording earthquakes.

seismology n. study of earthquakes. □ **seismological** adj., **seismologist** n.

seize v. **1** take hold of forcibly or suddenly. **2** take possession of by force or legal right. **3** affect suddenly. □ **seize on** make use of eagerly. **seize up** become stuck through overheating.
■ **1** clasp, clutch, grab, grasp, snatch, take hold of. **2** annex, capture, conquer, occupy, take possession of; appropriate, commandeer, confiscate, take; abduct, carry off, kidnap; apprehend, arrest.

seizure n. **1** seizing. **2** sudden violent attack of an illness.
■ **2** attack, fit, paroxysm, spasm, colloq. turn.

seldom adv. rarely, infrequently.

select v. pick out as best or most suitable. ● adj. **1** carefully chosen. **2** exclusive. □ **selector** n.
■ v. choose, decide on, go for, opt for, pick, plump for, single out; name, nomin-

ate. ● adj. **1** choice, exceptional, finest, first-class, first-rate, prime, superior.

selection n. **1** selecting. **2** thing(s) selected. **3** things from which to choose.
■ **2** choice, option; excerpt, extract, passage. **3** assortment, collection, range, variety.

selective adj. chosen or choosing carefully. □ **selectively** adv., **selectivity** n.
■ colloq. choosy, discerning, discriminating, fastidious, fussy, particular, colloq. pernickety.

self n. (pl. **selves**) **1** person as an individual. **2** person's special nature. **3** one's own advantage or interests.

self- pref. of, to, or done by oneself or itself. □ **self-assertive** adj. assertive in promoting oneself, one's claims, etc. **self-assured** adj. self-confident. **self-centred** adj. thinking chiefly of oneself. **self-confident** adj. having confidence in oneself. **self-conscious** adj. shy, embarrassed. **self-contained** adj. complete in itself, having all the necessary facilities. **self-controlled** adj. able to control one's behaviour. **self-denial** n. deliberately going without things one would like to have. **self-determination** n. **1** free will. **2** nation's own choice of its form of government or allegiance etc. **self-evident** adj. clear without proof. **self-governing** adj. governing itself or oneself. **self-interest** n. one's own advantage. **self-made** adj. successful or rich by one's own efforts. **self-possessed** adj. calm and dignified. **self-respect** n. proper regard for oneself and one's own dignity and principles etc. **self-righteous** adj. smugly sure of one's own righteousness. **self-satisfied** adj. smugly pleased with oneself. **self-seeking** adj. & n. seeking to promote one's own interests rather than those of others. **self-service** adj. at which customers help themselves and pay a cashier for goods taken. **self-styled** adj. using a name or description one has adopted without right. **self-sufficient** adj. capable of supplying one's own needs. **self-willed** adj. obstinately doing what one wishes.
■ □ **self-centred** egocentric, egotistical, narcissistic, selfish. **self-conscious** awkward, diffident, embarrassed, ill at ease, shy, uncomfortable. **self-evident** clear, evident, incontrovertible, manifest, patent, plain, unmistakable. **self-possessed** calm, collected, composed,

controlled, dignified, even-tempered, imperturbable, placid, self-controlled, serene, tranquil, *colloq.* unflappable, unperturbed. **self-righteous** complacent, goody-goody, pious, priggish, sanctimonious, self-satisfied, smug. **self-willed** determined, headstrong, intractable, intransigent, obstinate, pigheaded, stubborn, uncontrollable, unruly, wilful.

selfish *adj.* thinking only about one's own needs or wishes. □ **selfishly** *adv.*, **selfishness** *n.*

■ egocentric, egotistical, inconsiderate, self-centred, self-seeking, thoughtless.

selfless *adj.* unselfish. □ **selflessly** *adv.*

■ altruistic, considerate, thoughtful, unselfish.

selfsame *adj.* the very same.

sell *v.* (**sold**) **1** exchange (goods etc.) for money. **2** keep (goods) for sale. **3** promote sales of. **4** (of goods) be sold. **5** have a specified price. **6** persuade into accepting (an idea etc.). ●*n.* manner of selling. □ **sell off** dispose of by selling, esp. at a reduced price. **sell out 1** dispose of all one's stock etc. by selling. **2** betray. **sell up** sell one's business or business. **seller** *n.*

■ *v.* **1** *sl.* flog, vend. **2** carry, have in stock, keep, stock; deal in, handle, market, retail, trade in, traffic in. **3** advertise, market, *colloq.* plug, promote.

Sellotape *n.* [P.] adhesive usu. transparent tape.

selvedge *n.* (also **selvage**) edge of cloth woven to prevent fraying.

semantic *adj.* of meaning in language. □ **semantically** *adv.*

semantics *n.* study of meaning.

semaphore *n.* **1** system of signalling with the arms. **2** signalling device with mechanical arms.

semblance *n.* **1** outward appearance, show. **2** resemblance.

■ **1** air, appearance, aspect, exterior, façade, front, guise, look, manner, mask, show, veneer.

semen *n.* sperm-bearing fluid produced by male animals.

semi- *pref.* **1** half. **2** partly.

semibreve *n.* note in music, equal to two minims.

semicircle *n.* half of a circle. □ **semicircular** *adj.*

semicolon *n.* punctuation mark (;).

semiconductor *n.* substance that conducts electricity in certain conditions.

semi-detached *adj.* (of a house) joined to another on one side.

semifinal *n.* match or round preceding the final. □ **semifinalist** *n.*

seminal *adj.* **1** of seed or semen. **2** giving rise to new developments. □ **seminally** *adv.*

seminar *n.* small class for discussion and research.

seminary *n.* training college for priests or rabbis.

semiprecious *adj.* (of a gem) less valuable than a precious stone.

semiquaver *n.* note in music, equal to half a quaver.

Semite *n.* member of the group of races that includes Jews and Arabs. □ **Semitic** *adj.*

semitone *n.* half a tone in music.

semolina *n.* hard grains of wheat used for puddings.

senate *n.* **1** upper house of certain parliaments. **2** governing body of certain universities.

senator *n.* member of a senate.

send *v.* (**sent**) **1** order or cause to go to a certain destination. **2** send a message. **3** cause to move, go, or become. □ **send for** order to come or be brought. **send-off** *n.* friendly demonstration of goodwill at a person's departure. **send up** ridicule by imitating.

■ **1** communicate, consign, convey, dispatch, forward, mail, post, ship, transmit; broadcast, radio, telegraph. **3** discharge, launch, project, propel, shoot, throw. □ **send up** caricature, lampoon, make fun of, parody, ridicule, satirize, take off.

senescent *adj.* growing old. □ **senescence** *n.*

senile *adj.* weak in body or mind because of old age. □ **senility** *n.*

senior *adj.* **1** older. **2** higher in rank or authority. **3** for older children. ●*n.* **1** senior person. **2** member of a senior school. □ **senior citizen** elderly person, pensioner. **seniority** *n.*

senna *n.* dried pods or leaves of a tropical tree, used as a laxative.

sensation *n.* **1** feeling produced by stimulation of a sense organ or of the mind. **2** excited interest. **3** person or thing producing this.

■ **1** awareness, consciousness, feeling, impression, perception, sense. **2** commotion, furore, stir. **3** hit, success, *sl.* wow.

sensational adj. causing great excitement or admiration. □ **sensationally** adv.

■ amazing, astonishing, astounding, breathtaking, exciting, incredible, phenomenal, remarkable, spectacular, staggering, thrilling; colloq. fantastic, marvellous, colloq. stunning, superb, wonderful.

sensationalism n. use of or interest in sensational matters. □ **sensationalist** n.

sense n. **1** any of the special powers (sight, hearing, smell, taste, touch) by which a living thing becomes aware of the external world. **2** ability to perceive a thing, consciousness. **3** practical wisdom. **4** meaning. **5** purpose. **6** (pl.) sanity. ● v. perceive by sense(s) or by a mental impression. □ **make sense 1** have a meaning. **2** be a sensible idea. **make sense of** find a meaning in.

■ n. **1** faculty. **2** awareness, consciousness, feeling, impression, perception, sensation. **3** brain(s), common sense, intellect, intelligence, colloq. nous, understanding, wisdom, wit. **4** drift, gist, import, meaning, purport. ● v. become aware of, detect, discern, divine, feel, perceive, realize, suspect.

senseless adj. **1** foolish. **2** unconscious.

■ **1** absurd, crazy, daft, fatuous, foolish, idiotic, ludicrous, meaningless, nonsensical, pointless, ridiculous, silly, stupid.

sensibility n. sensitiveness.

sensible adj. **1** having or showing good sense. **2** aware. □ **sensibly** adv.

■ **1** down-to-earth, intelligent, judicious, level-headed, logical, prudent, rational, realistic, sagacious, shrewd, wise.

sensitive adj. **1** easily hurt or damaged. **2** showing sympathetic understanding. **3** easily hurt or offended. **4** requiring tact. □ **sensitively** adv., **sensitivity** n.

■ **1** delicate, tender. **2** perceptive, sympathetic, understanding. **3** emotional, highly-strung, temperamental, touchy. **4** awkward, delicate, difficult, colloq. sticky, ticklish.

sensitize v. make sensitive. □ **sensitization** n., **sensitizer** n.

sensor n. device that responds to a certain stimulus.

sensory adj. **1** of the senses. **2** receiving and transmitting sensations.

sensual adj. **1** gratifying to the body. **2** indulging oneself with physical pleas-

ures. □ **sensualism** n., **sensually** adv., **sensuality** n.

■ **1** carnal, erotic, sexual. **2** hedonistic, pleasure-loving, sybaritic, voluptuous.

sensuous adj. affecting the senses pleasantly. □ **sensuously** adv., **sensuousness** n.

sent see **send**.

sentence n. **1** series of words making a single complete statement. **2** punishment awarded by a law court. ● v. declare sentence on.

sententious adj. dull and moralizing. □ **sententiously** adv., **sententiousness** n.

sentient adj. capable of perceiving and feeling things. □ **sentiently** adv., **sentience** n.

sentiment n. **1** mental feeling, opinion. **2** sentimentality.

■ **1** belief, feeling, opinion, thought, view. **2** sentimentalism, sentimentality.

sentimental adj. full of romantic or nostalgic feeling. □ **sentimentalism** n., **sentimentally** adv., **sentimentality** n.

■ emotional, maudlin, mawkish, mushy, nostalgic, romantic, colloq. soppy.

sentinel n. sentry.

sentry n. soldier posted to keep watch and guard something.

■ guard, lookout, sentinel, watchman.

sepal n. each of the leaf-like parts forming a calyx.

separable adj. able to be separated. □ **separability** n.

separate adj. /sépərət/ not joined or united with others. ● v. /sépərayt/ **1** divide. **2** set, move, or keep apart. **3** cease to live together as a married couple. □ **separately** adv., **separation** n., **separator** n.

■ adj. detached, disconnected, separated, unattached; different, disparate, distinct, individual, other, unrelated. ● v. **1** detach, disconnect, divide, partition, sever, uncouple; branch, diverge, fork, split, subdivide. **2** classify, sort; disband, disperse; keep apart, isolate, segregate. **3** part, split (up).

separatist n. person who favours separation from a larger (esp. political) unit. □ **separatism** n.

sepia n. **1** brown colouring matter. **2** rich reddish-brown.

sepsis n. septic condition.

septet n. **1** group of seven instruments or voices. **2** music for these.

septic *adj.* infected with harmful micro-organisms. □ **septic tank** tank in which sewage is liquefied by bacterial activity.

septicaemia /séptiseémiə/ *n.* blood poisoning.

septuagenarian *n.* person in his or her seventies.

sepulchre /séppəlkər/ *n.* tomb.

sequel *n.* 1 what follows, esp. as a result. 2 novel or film etc. continuing the story of an earlier one.

sequence *n.* 1 following of one thing after another. 2 set of things belonging next to each other in a particular order. 3 section dealing with one topic in a film.
■ 1,2 chain, course, cycle, order, pattern, series, set, string, succession, train.

sequential *adj.* forming a sequence. □ **sequentially** *adv.*

sequester *v.* 1 seclude. 2 confiscate.

sequestrate *v.* confiscate. □ **sequestration** *n.*
■ appropriate, commandeer, confiscate, expropriate, remove, seize, sequester, take away.

sequin *n.* circular spangle. □ **sequinned** *adj.*

sequoia /sikwóyə/ *n.* Californian tree growing to a great height.

seraglio /seraáliō/ *n.* (*pl.* **-os**) harem of a Muslim palace.

seraph *n.* (*pl.* **-im**) member of the highest order of angels. □ **seraphic** *adj.*

serenade *n.* music played by a lover to his lady. ● *v.* perform a serenade to.

serendipity *n.* making of pleasant discoveries by accident.

serene *adj.* calm and cheerful. □ **serenely** *adv.*, **serenity** *n.*
■ calm, collected, composed, peaceful, placid, relaxed, self-controlled, self-possessed, tranquil, unperturbed, unruffled, untroubled.

serf *n.* 1 medieval farm labourer forced to work for his landowner. 2 oppressed labourer. □ **serfdom** *n.*

serge *n.* strong twilled fabric.

sergeant /saárjənt/ *n.* 1 non-commissioned army officer ranking just above corporal. 2 police officer ranking just below inspector.

serial *n.* story presented in a series of instalments. ● *adj.* of or forming a series. □ **serially** *adv.*

serialize *v.* produce as a serial. □ **serialization** *n.*

series *n.* (*pl.* **series**) number of things of the same kind, or related to each other, occurring or arranged or produced in order.
■ chain, line, progression, row, sequence, set, string, succession, train.

serious *adj.* 1 solemn. 2 sincere. 3 important. 4 not slight. □ **seriously** *adv.*, **seriousness** *n.*
■ 1 grave, earnest, humourless, sober, solemn, sombre, stern, unsmiling. 2 earnest, honest, sincere. 3 crucial, grave, important, major, momentous, pressing, significant, urgent, weighty. 4 acute, critical, grave, life-threatening; awful, bad, desperate, dire, dreadful, severe, terrible.

sermon *n.* talk on a religious or moral subject, esp. during a religious service.

sermonize *v.* give a long moralizing talk. □ **sermonizer** *n.*

serpent *n.* large snake.

serpentine *adj.* twisting like a snake.

serrated *adj.* having a series of small projections. □ **serration** *n.*

serried /sérrid/ *adj.* arranged in a close series.

serum *n.* (*pl.* **sera**) 1 fluid left when blood has clotted, esp. used for inoculation. 2 watery fluid in animal tissue. □ **serous** *adj.*

servant *n.* person employed to do domestic work in a household or as an attendant.

serve *v.* 1 perform or provide services for. 2 be employed (in the army etc.). 3 be suitable (for). 4 present (food etc.) for others to consume. 5 (of food) be enough for. 6 attend to (customers). 7 set the ball in play at tennis etc. 8 deliver (a legal writ etc.) to (a person). ● *n.* service in tennis etc. □ **server** *n.*
■ *v.* 3 answer, be acceptable *or* suitable, do, fulfil, meet, satisfy, suffice; act, function. 4 dish up, present; wait on.

service *n.* 1 assistance, use. 2 working for an employer. 3 maintenance and repair of machinery. 4 religious ceremony or meeting. 5 department of people employed by a public organization. 6 system that performs work for customers or supplies public needs. 7 set of dishes etc. for serving a meal. 8 act of serving in tennis etc. 9 game in which one serves. 10 (*pl.*) armed forces. ● *v.* 1 maintain and repair (machinery). 2 supply with service(s). 3 pay the interest on (a loan). □ **service area** area beside a motorway where petrol and refreshments etc. are available. **service flat** flat where domestic service is provided. **service road** road giving access to houses etc. but not for use by through traffic. **service station** garage selling petrol etc.

■ *n.* **1** aid, assistance, help, support; advantage, benefit, use, utility. **3** maintenance, overhaul, repair, servicing. **4** ceremonial, ceremony, rite, ritual.

serviceable *adj.* **1** useful, usable. **2** hard-wearing.

■ **1** functional, practical, useful, utilitarian; operative, usable.

serviceman, servicewoman *ns.* member of the armed services.

serviette *n.* table napkin.

servile *adj.* **1** of or like a slave. **2** excessively submissive. □ **servilely** *adv.*, **servility** *n.*

■ **2** deferential, fawning, flattering, grovelling, obsequious, submissive, subservient, sycophantic, unctuous.

serving *n.* quantity of food served to one person.

servitude *n.* condition of being forced to work for others.

servo- *pref.* power-assisted.

sesame /séssami/ *n.* **1** tropical plant with seeds that yield oil or are used as food. **2** its seeds.

session *n.* **1** meeting(s) for discussing or deciding something. **2** period spent in an activity. **3** academic year in certain universities.

■ **2** bout, period, run, spell, stint, time.

set¹ *v.* (**set**, **setting**) **1** put, place, or fix in position or readiness. **2** make or become hard or firm. **3** fix or appoint (a date etc.). **4** assign as something to be done. **5** put into a specified state, cause to do something. **6** represent a story, play, etc. as happening in a certain time or place. **7** be brought towards or below the horizon by earth's movement. ● *n.* **1** way a thing sets or is set. **2** scenery or stage for a play or film. **3** = **sett**. ● *adj.* **1** fixed, determined. **2** ready. □ **be set on** be determined about. **set about 1** begin (a task). **2** attack. **set back 1** halt or slow the progress of. **2** (*colloq.*) cost (a person) a specified amount. **set-back** *n.* setting back of progress. **set eyes on** catch sight of. **set fire to** cause to burn. **set forth** set off. **set in** become established. **set off 1** begin a journey. **2** cause to begin. **3** cause to explode. **4** improve the ap-

pearance of by contrast. **set out 1** exhibit. **2** begin a journey. **3** declare. **set piece** formal or elaborate construction. **set sail** begin a voyage. **set square** right-angled triangular drawing instrument. **set up** establish, build. **set-up** *n.* structure of an organization.

■ *v.* **1** deposit, lay, place, pose, position, put, situate, stand, *colloq.* stick; arrange, prepare; adjust, correct, regulate. **2** clot, coagulate, congeal, harden, *colloq.* jell, solidify, thicken. **3** appoint, arrange, decide, designate, determine, establish, fix, name, ordain, schedule, settle, specify. ● *adj.* **1** arranged, determined, established, fixed, prescribed; accustomed, customary, normal, regular, standard, usual. **2** prepared, ready. **set about 1** begin, buckle down to, embark on, start, tackle. **2** assail, assault, attack, beat up, *sl.* go for, *colloq.* lay into. **set back 1** delay, hold up, retard, slow up *or* down. **set-back** difficulty, hindrance, hitch, hold-up, problem, snag. **set fire to** fire, ignite, kindle, light, set alight, set on fire. **set off 1** be on one's way, depart, go, leave, *sl.* push off, sally forth, set forth, set out. **2** initiate, prompt, stimulate, trigger. **3** blow up, detonate, explode, touch off. **set out 1** arrange, display, exhibit, lay out, spread out. **set up** create, establish, found, institute, organize, start; assemble, build, construct, erect, put together *or* up.

set² *n.* **1** people or things grouped as similar or forming a unit. **2** games forming part of a match in tennis etc. **3** radio or television receiver.

■ **1** circle, clique, coterie, faction, gang; assortment, batch, collection, group, lot, series.

sett *n.* badger's burrow.

settee *n.* sofa.

setter *n.* **1** person or thing that sets. **2** dog of a long-haired breed.

setting *n.* **1** way or place in which a thing is set. **2** surroundings, environment. **3** cutlery etc. for one person.

■ **1** location, place, position, situation, spot. **2** environment, habitat, milieu, surroundings.

settle¹ *n.* wooden seat with a high back and arms.

settle² *v.* **1** make or become comfortably positioned. **2** make one's home. **3** occupy (a previously unoccupied area). **4** make or become calm or orderly. **5** arrange or agree finally or satisfactorily, deal with.

6 come to rest. **7** sink, subside. **8** pay (a bill etc.). **9** bestow legally. □ **settle on** choose, decide on. **settle up** pay what is owing. **settler** n.

■ **2** set up home, take up residence. **3** colonize, people, populate. **4** calm, lull, pacify, quiet, quieten; become quiet, quieten down. **5** arrange, choose, decide on, determine, establish, finalize, fix, select, set; patch up, put right, reconcile, resolve; organize, put in order, sort out, straighten out. **6** alight, come to rest, land.

settlement n. **1** settling. **2** agreement or arrangement. **3** amount or property settled legally on a person. **4** place occupied by settlers.

■ **2** agreement, arrangement, bargain, contract, deal, pact, understanding.

seven adj. & n. one more than six. □ **seventh** adj. & n.

seventeen adj. & n. one more than sixteen. □ **seventeenth** adj. & n.

seventy adj. & n. seven times ten. □ **seventieth** adj. & n.

sever v. cut or break off. □ **severance** n.

■ break off, cut off, disconnect, split off, sunder.

several adj. a few, more than two but not many. ● pron. several people or things.

severe adj. **1** strict, harsh. **2** extreme, intense. **3** serious, critical. **4** plain in style. □ **severely** adv., **severity** n.

■ **1** draconian, harsh, rigorous, stiff, strict, tough; austere, dour, grim, forbidding, stern, stony. **2** acute, bitter, extreme, fierce, harsh, intense, keen, sharp, violent. **3** critical, dangerous, grave, perilous, serious.

sew /sō/ v. (**sewed**, **sewn** or **sewed**) **1** fasten by passing thread through material, using a threaded needle or an awl etc. **2** make or fasten (a thing) by sewing. □ **sewing** n.

■ baste, darn, hem, stitch, tack.

sewage /sōō-ij/ n. liquid waste drained from houses etc. for disposal.

sewer[1] /sōər/ n. one who sews.

sewer[2] /sōōər/ n. drain for carrying sewage.

sewerage n. system of sewers.

sewn see **sew**.

sex n. **1** either of the two main groups (*male* and *female*) into which living things are placed according to their reproductive functions. **2** fact of belonging to one of these. **3** sexual feelings or impulses. **4** sexual intercourse. ● v. judge the sex of.

sexagenarian n. person in his or her sixties.

sexism n. prejudice or discrimination against people (esp. women) because of their sex. □ **sexist** adj. & n.

sexless adj. **1** lacking sex, neuter. **2** not involving sexual feelings.

sextant n. instrument for finding one's position by measuring the height of the sun etc.

sextet n. **1** group of six instruments or voices. **2** music for these.

sexton n. official in charge of a church and churchyard.

sextuplet n. one of six children born at one birth.

sexual adj. **1** of sex or the sexes. **2** (of reproduction) occurring by fusion of male and female cells. □ **sexual intercourse** insertion of the penis into the vagina. **sexually** adv., **sexuality** n.

sexy adj. (**-ier**, **-iest**) sexually attractive or stimulating. □ **sexily** adv., **sexiness** n.

■ arousing, desirable, erotic, seductive, sensual, voluptuous.

shabby adj. (**-ier**, **-iest**) **1** dilapidated, worn. **2** poorly dressed. **3** unfair, dishonourable. □ **shabbily** adv., **shabbiness** n.

■ **1** dilapidated, in disrepair, ramshackle, seedy, squalid; frayed, ragged, colloq. scruffy, tattered, tatty, threadbare, worn. **3** contemptible, despicable, dishonourable, mean, shameful, unfair.

shack n. roughly built hut.

■ cabin, hovel, hut, shanty.

shackle n. one of a pair of metal rings joined by a chain, for fastening a prisoner's wrists or ankles. ● v. **1** put shackles on. **2** impede, restrict.

shade n. **1** comparative darkness, place sheltered from the sun. **2** screen or cover used to block or moderate light. **3** small amount. **4** degree or depth of colour. **5** differing variety. ● v. **1** block the rays of. **2** give shade to. **3** darken (parts of a drawing etc.). **4** pass gradually into another colour or variety.

■ n. **2** awning, blind, cover, curtain, screen. **3** hint, suggestion, tinge, touch, trace. **4** hue, tinge, tint, tone. ● v. **1, 2** cover, protect, screen, shield.

shadow n. **1** shade. **2** patch of this where a body blocks light rays. **3** person's inseparable companion. **4** slight trace. **5**

gloom. ● v. 1 cast shadow over. 2 follow and watch secretly. □ **shadow-boxing** n. boxing against an imaginary opponent. **shadower** n., **shadowy** adj.

■ v. 2 follow, pursue, stalk, colloq. tail, trail.

shady adj. (-ier, -iest) 1 giving or situated in shade. 2 disreputable, not completely honest. □ **shadily** adv., **shadiness** n.

shaft n. 1 arrow, spear. 2 long slender straight part of a thing. 3 long bar or axle. 4 vertical or sloping passage or opening.

shag n. 1 shaggy mass. 2 strong coarse tobacco. 3 cormorant.

shaggy adj. (-ier, -iest) 1 having long rough hair or fibre. 2 (of hair etc.) rough and thick. □ **shaggy-dog story** lengthy anecdote. **shagginess** n.

shagreen n. 1 untanned granulated leather. 2 sharkskin.

shake v. (**shook, shaken**) 1 move quickly up and down or to and fro, tremble, vibrate. 2 shock. 3 make less firm. 4 (of the voice) become uneven. 5 (colloq.) shake hands. ● n. shaking, being shaken. □ **shake hands** clasp right hands in greeting, parting, or agreement. **shake up** 1 mix by shaking. 2 rouse from lethargy, shock. **shake-up** n. upheaval, reorganization.

■ v. 1 agitate; rock, sway, swing; quiver, shiver, tremble, vibrate. 2 disconcert, distress, disturb, fluster, perturb, ruffle, shock, trouble, unsettle, upset.

shaky adj. (-ier, -iest) 1 shaking, unsteady. 2 unreliable. □ **shakily** adv., **shakiness** n.

■ 1 flimsy, insubstantial, rickety, unstable, unsteady; shaking, trembling, wobbly. 2 tenuous, uncertain, unreliable, weak.

shale n. slate-like stone. □ **shaly** adj.

shall v.aux. used with I and we to express future tense, and with other words in promises or statements of obligation.

shallot n. onion-like plant.

shallow adj. 1 of little depth. 2 superficial. ● n. shallow place. □ **shallowness** n.

sham n. 1 pretence. 2 person or thing that is not genuine. ● adj. pretended, not genuine. ● v. (**shammed**) pretend (to be).

■ adj. affected, artificial, bogus, fake, false, feigned, fraudulent, insincere, colloq. phoney, simulated. ● v. fake, feign, pretend, simulate.

shamble v. & n. walk or run in a shuffling or lazy way.

shambles n. scene or condition of great bloodshed or disorder.

shame n. 1 painful mental feeling aroused by something dishonourable or ridiculous. 2 ability to feel this. 3 something regrettable. 4 person or thing causing shame. ● v. 1 bring shame on, make ashamed. 2 compel by arousing shame. □ **shameful** adj., **shamefully** adv., **shameless** adj., **shamelessly** adv.

■ n. 1 chagrin, embarrassment, humiliation, mortification; discredit, disgrace, dishonour, disrepute, ignominy, obloquy, opprobrium. 3 pity. ● v. 1 embarrass, humiliate, mortify; discredit, disgrace, dishonour.

shamefaced adj. showing shame.

■ abashed, ashamed, chastened, embarrassed, mortified.

shammy n. chamois leather.

shampoo n. 1 liquid used to wash hair. 2 preparation for cleaning upholstery etc. 3 process of shampooing. ● v. wash or clean with shampoo.

shamrock n. clover-like plant.

shandy n. mixed drink of beer and ginger beer or lemonade.

shank n. 1 leg, esp. from knee to ankle. 2 thing's shaft or stem.

shantung n. soft Chinese silk.

shanty[1] n. shack. □ **shanty town** area with makeshift housing.

shanty[2] n. sailors' traditional song.

shape n. 1 area or form with a definite outline. 2 form, condition. 3 orderly arrangement. ● v. 1 give shape to. 2 influence. □ **shapeless** adj.

■ n. 1 configuration, contour, figure, form, outline, profile, silhouette. 2 appearance, guise, form; condition, health, state. ● v. 1 create, fashion, form, make, model, mould. 2 affect, control, determine, govern, influence.

shapely adj. (-ier, -iest) having a pleasant shape. □ **shapeliness** n.

shard n. broken piece of pottery.

share n. 1 part or amount of something divided between several people. 2 one of the equal parts forming a business company's capital and entitling the holder to a proportion of the profits. ● v. give, have, or use a share (of), divide.

□ **share-out** n. division into shares.
shareholder n., **sharer** n.

■ n. **1** allocation, colloq. cut, part, percentage, portion, quota, ration. ● v. apportion, distribute, divide, split.

shark n. **1** large voracious sea fish. **2** (colloq.) extortioner, swindler.

sharkskin n. fabric with a slightly lustrous textured weave.

sharp adj. **1** having a fine edge or point capable of cutting. **2** severe, harsh. **3** mentally alert. **4** abrupt, not gradual. **5** pungent. **6** well-defined. **7** unscrupulous. **8** above the correct pitch in music. ● adv. **1** punctually. **2** suddenly. **3** at a sharp angle. ● n. (sign indicating) music note raised by a semitone. □ **sharp practice** barely honest dealing. **sharply** adv., **sharpness** n.

■ adj. **1** keen, pointed, sharpened. **2** acute, intense, severe, strong, violent; bitter, cutting, harsh, hurtful, scathing. **3** astute, bright, clever, intelligent, perceptive, shrewd, smart. **4** abrupt, sheer, steep, sudden. **5** piquant, pungent, tangy, tart. **6** clear, distinct, vivid, well-defined.

sharpen v. make or become sharp or sharper. □ **sharpener** n.

■ grind, hone, whet.

sharpshooter n. marksman.

shatter v. **1** break violently into small pieces. **2** destroy utterly. **3** severely upset.

■ **1** break, shiver, smash, splinter. **2** dash, destroy, put an end to, ruin, spoil, wreck. **3** crush, devastate, overwhelm.

shave v. **1** scrape (growing hair) off the skin. **2** clear (the chin etc.) of hair in this way. **3** cut thin slices from. **4** graze gently in passing. ● n. shaving. □ **shaver** n.

shaven adj. shaved.

shaving n. thin strip of wood etc. shaved off.

shawl n. large piece of soft fabric worn round the shoulders or wrapped round a baby.

she pron. female (or thing personified as female) previously mentioned. ● n. female animal.

sheaf n. (pl. **sheaves**) **1** bundle of papers. **2** tied bundle of cornstalks.

shear v. (**shorn** or **sheared**) cut or trim with shears or other sharp device. □ **shearer** n.

shears n.pl. large cutting instrument shaped like scissors.

sheath /sheeth/ n. close-fitting cover, esp. for a blade or tool.

sheathe /sheeth/ v. **1** put into a case. **2** encase in a covering.

shed[1] n. building for storing things, or for use as a workshop.

shed[2] v. (**shed, shedding**) **1** lose by a natural falling off. **2** take off. **3** allow to fall or flow.

sheen n. gloss, lustre.

sheep n. (pl. **sheep**) grass-eating animal with a thick fleecy coat.

sheepdog n. dog trained to guard and herd sheep.

sheepish adj. bashful, embarrassed. □ **sheepishly** adv., **sheepishness** n.

sheepskin n. sheep's skin with the fleece on.

sheer[1] adj. **1** pure, not mixed or qualified. **2** very steep. **3** (of fabric) diaphanous. ● adv. directly, straight up or down. □ **sheerly** adv., **sheerness** n.

■ **1** absolute, complete, downright, out and out, pure, unmitigated, utter. **2** abrupt, precipitous, sharp, steep. **3** diaphanous, flimsy, thin, transparent.

sheer[2] v. swerve from a course.

sheet n. **1** piece of cotton used in pairs as inner bedclothes. **2** large thin piece of glass, metal, paper, etc. **3** expanse of water, flame, etc. **4** rope securing the lower corner of a sail. □ **sheet anchor 1** large anchor for emergency use. **2** thing on which one relies.

sheikh /shayk/ n. Arab ruler. □ **sheikhdom** n. his territory.

shekel n. **1** unit of money in Israel. **2** (pl., colloq.) money, riches.

shelf n. (pl. **shelves**) **1** board or slab fastened horizontally for things to be placed on. **2** thing resembling this, ledge. □ **shelf-life** n. time for which a stored thing remains usable.

shell n. **1** hard outer covering of eggs, nut kernels, and of animals such as snails and tortoises. **2** firm framework or covering. **3** metal case filled with explosive, for firing from a large gun. ● v. **1** remove the shell(s) of. **2** fire explosive shells at. □ **shell-shock** n. nervous breakdown from exposure to battle conditions.

shellac n. resinous substance used in varnish. ● v. (**shellacked**) coat with this.

shellfish n. water animal that has a shell.

shelter n. **1** structure that shields against danger, wind, rain, etc. **2** refuge.

3 shielded condition. ● v. **1** provide with shelter. **2** find or take shelter.

■ n. **2** haven, refuge, sanctuary. **3** cover, protection, safety, security. ● v. **1** conceal, guard, harbour, hide, protect, screen, shield.

shelve v. **1** put aside, esp. temporarily. **2** slope.

■ **1** defer, hold in abeyance, postpone, put off.

shelving n. **1** shelves. **2** material for these.

shepherd n. person who tends sheep. ● v. guide (people). □ **shepherd's pie** pie of minced meat topped with mashed potato.

■ v. conduct, escort, guide, herd, steer, usher.

sherbet n. **1** fizzy sweet drink. **2** powder from which this is made.

sheriff n. **1** Crown's chief executive officer in a county. **2** chief judge of a district in Scotland. **3** (US) chief law-enforcing officer of a county.

Sherpa n. member of a Himalayan people of Nepal and Tibet.

sherry n. strong wine orig. from southern Spain.

shibboleth n. old slogan or principle still considered essential by some members of a party.

shield n. **1** piece of armour carried on the arm to protect the body. **2** trophy in the form of this. **3** thing giving protection. ● v. protect, screen.

■ n. **3** defence, protection, safeguard. ● v. defend, guard, protect, screen, shelter.

shift v. **1** change or move from one position to another. **2** remove. **3** (sl.) move quickly. ● n. **1** change of place or form etc. **2** set of workers who start work when another set finishes. **3** time for which they work.

■ v. **1** budge, change position, move; carry, transfer. ● n. **1** alteration, change, movement, swing, switch, transfer.

shiftless adj. lazy and inefficient.

shifty adj. (-ier, -iest) seeming untrustworthy.

Shiite /shee-It/ n. & adj. (member) of a Muslim sect opposed to the Sunni.

shilly-shally v. be unable to make up one's mind firmly.

shimmer v. & n. (shine with) a soft quivering light.

shin n. **1** front of the leg below the knee. **2** lower foreleg. ● v. (**shinned**) **shin up** climb.

shindig n. (colloq.) din, brawl.

shine v. (**shone**) **1** give out or reflect light, be bright. **2** cause to shine. **3** excel. **4** (**shined**) polish. ● n. **1** brightness. **2** high polish.

■ v. **1** beam, blaze, gleam, glint, glisten, glitter, glow, shimmer, sparkle, twinkle. **4** buff, burnish, polish. ● n. **2** gleam, gloss, lustre, patina, polish, sheen.

shingle[1] n. wooden roof tile.

shingle[2] n. **1** small rounded pebbles. **2** stretch of these, esp. on a shore. □ **shingly** adj.

shingles n. disease with a rash of small blisters.

Shinto n. Japanese religion revering ancestors and nature-spirits. □ **Shintoism** n.

shiny adj. (-ier, -iest) shining, glossy. □ **shininess** n.

ship n. large sea-going vessel. ● v. (**shipped**) **1** put or take on board a ship. **2** transport. □ **shipper** n.

■ n. boat, craft, vessel. ● v. **2** carry, convey, ferry, transport.

shipmate n. fellow member of a ship's crew.

shipment n. **1** shipping of goods. **2** consignment shipped.

shipping n. ships collectively.

shipshape adv. & adj. in good order, tidy.

shipwreck n. destruction of a ship by storm or striking rock etc. □ **shipwrecked** adj.

shipyard n. establishment where ships are built.

shire n. county. □ **shire-horse** n. horse of a heavy powerful breed.

shirk v. avoid (duty or work etc.) selfishly. □ **shirker** n.

■ avoid, dodge, duck, evade, get out of.

shirt n. lightweight garment for the upper part of the body.

shirty adj. (colloq.) annoyed.

shiver[1] v. tremble slightly esp. with cold or fear. ● n. shivering movement. □ **shivery** adj.

■ v. quake, quiver, shake, shudder, tremble.

shiver[2] v. shatter.

shoal[1] n. great number of fish swimming together. ● v. form shoals.

shoal² *n.* **1** shallow place. **2** underwater sandbank.

shock¹ *n.* **1** effect of a violent impact or shake. **2** sudden violent effect on the mind or emotions. **3** acute weakness caused by injury, pain, or mental shock. **4** effect of a sudden discharge of electricity through the body. ● *v.* astonish, horrify, outrage.

■ *n.* **2** blow, bombshell, jolt, surprise; fright, scare, start, *colloq.* turn. ● *v.* astonish, astound, dismay, dumbfound, shake, shatter, stagger, stun, take aback; alarm, appal, devastate, horrify, outrage, revolt, scandalize, sicken, upset.

shock² *n.* bushy mass of hair.

shocker *n.* (*colloq.*) shocking person or thing.

shocking *adj.* **1** causing great indignation, disgust, etc. **2** (*colloq.*) very bad.

■ **1** appalling, deplorable, disgusting, disgraceful, dreadful, horrible, horrifying, monstrous, outrageous, revolting, scandalous, shameful, sickening.

shod *see* shoe.

shoddy *adj.* (**-ier**, **-iest**) of poor quality. □ **shoddily** *adv.*, **shoddiness** *n.*

■ inferior, poor, second-rate, substandard, tawdry, trashy.

shoe *n.* **1** outer covering for a person's foot. **2** horseshoe. **3** part of a brake that presses against a wheel. ● *v.* (**shod**, **shoeing**) fit with a shoe or shoes. □ **shoe-tree** *n.* shaped block for keeping a shoe in shape.

shoehorn *n.* curved implement for easing one's heel into a shoe.

shoelace *n.* a cord for lacing up shoes.

shoestring *n.* **1** shoelace. **2** (*colloq.*) barely adequate amount of capital.

shone *see* shine.

shoo *int.* sound uttered to frighten animals away. ● *v.* (**shooed**) drive away by this.

shook *see* shake.

shoot *v.* (**shot**) **1** fire (a gun etc., or a missile). **2** kill or wound with a missile from a gun etc. **3** hunt with a gun for sport. **4** send out or move swiftly. **5** (of a plant) put forth buds or shoots. **6** take a shot at goal. **7** photograph, film. ● *n.* young branch or new growth of a plant. □ **shooting star** small meteor seen to move quickly. **shooting stick** walking stick with a small folding seat in the

handle. **shoot up 1** rise suddenly. **2** grow rapidly. **shooter** *n.*

■ *v.* **1** fire, open fire; launch. **4** dart, dash, fly, hurry, race, rush, speed, tear, zoom. **5** germinate, grow, sprout. ● *n.* offshoot, scion, sprout. □ **shoot up 1** escalate, go up, increase, rocket.

shop *n.* **1** building or room where goods or services are sold to the public. **2** workshop. **3** one's own work as a subject of conversation. ● *v.* (**shopped**) **1** go into a shop or shops to buy things. **2** (*sl.*) inform against. □ **shop around** look for the best bargain. **shop-floor** *n.* workers as distinct from management or senior union officials. **shop-soiled** *adj.* soiled from being on display in a shop. **shop steward** trade union official elected by fellow workers as their spokesperson.

shoplifter *n.* person who steals goods that are displayed in a shop. □ **shoplifting** *n.*

shopper *n.* **1** person who shops. **2** bag for holding shopping.

shopping *n.* **1** buying goods in shops. **2** goods bought.

shore¹ *n.* land along the edge of a sea or lake.

■ beach, coast, littoral, seashore, seaside, strand.

shore² *v.* prop or support with a length of timber.

shorn *see* shear.

short *adj.* **1** measuring little from end to end in space or time, or from head to foot. **2** (having) insufficient. **3** concise, brief. **4** curt. **5** (of pastry) crisp and easily crumbled. ● *adv.* abruptly. ● *n.* **1** (*colloq.*) drink of spirits. **2** short circuit. **3** (*pl.*) trousers that do not reach the knee. ● *v.* (*colloq.*) short-circuit. □ **short-change** *v.* cheat, esp. by giving insufficient change. **short circuit** fault in an electrical circuit when current flows by a shorter route than the normal one. **short-circuit** *v.* **1** cause a short circuit in. **2** bypass. **short cut** quicker route or method. **short-handed** *adj.* having insufficient workers. **short-list** *v.* put on a short list from which a final choice will be made. **short-sighted** *adj.* **1** able to see clearly only what is close. **2** lacking foresight. **short ton** (*see* ton) short ton. **short wave** radio wave of frequency greater than 3 MHz.

■ *adj.* **1** diminutive, little, slight, small; brief, ephemeral, fleeting, fugitive, transient, transitory. **2** deficient, lacking, wanting; inadequate, insufficient, low, scant, scanty, unplentiful. **3** brief, concise, laconic, pithy, succinct, terse. **4** abrupt, blunt, brusque, curt, rude, terse.

shortage *n.* lack, insufficiency.
■ dearth, deficiency, insufficiency, lack, paucity, scarcity, want.

shortbread *n.* rich sweet biscuit.

shortcake *n.* shortbread.

shortcoming *n.* failure to reach a required standard, fault.
■ defect, failing, fault, flaw, imperfection, weakness, weak spot.

shorten *v.* make or become shorter.
■ abbreviate, abridge, cut, edit, truncate; curtail, cut down, decrease, reduce.

shortfall *n.* deficit.

shorthand *n.* method of writing rapidly with special symbols.

shortly *adv.* **1** after a short time. **2** in a few words. **3** curtly.

shot *see* **shoot**. *n.* **1** firing of a gun etc. **2** sound of this. **3** person of specified skill in shooting. **4** missile(s) for a cannon or gun etc. **5** attempt. **6** photograph. **7** heavy ball thrown as a sport. **8** attempt to hit something or reach a target. **9** stroke in certain ball games. **10** injection. **11** (*colloq.*) dram of spirits. □ **like a shot** (*colloq.*) without hesitation.
■ **2** bang, blast, crack, report. **5** attempt, go, *colloq.* stab, try. **6** photo, snap, snapshot.

shotgun *n.* gun for firing small shot at close range.

should *v.aux.* used to express duty or obligation, possible or expected future event, or (with *I* and *we*) a polite statement or a conditional or indefinite clause.

shoulder *n.* **1** part of the body where the arm or foreleg is attached. ● *v.* **1** animal's upper foreleg as a joint of meat. ● *v.* **1** push with one's shoulder. **2** take (blame or responsibility) on oneself. □ **shoulder blade** large flat bone of the shoulder.

shout *n.* loud cry or utterance. ● *v.* **1** utter a shout. **2** call loudly. □ **shout down** silence by shouting.
■ *v.* bawl, bellow, call, cry, roar, scream, thunder, yell.

shove *n.* rough push. ● *v.* **1** push roughly. **2** (*colloq.*) put.

shovel *n.* **1** spade-like tool for scooping earth etc. **2** mechanical scoop. ● *v.*

(**shovelled**) **1** shift or clear with or as if with a shovel. **2** scoop roughly.

shoveller *n.* duck with a broad shovel-like beak.

show *v.* (**showed**, **shown**) **1** allow or cause to be seen, offer for inspection or viewing. **2** demonstrate, point out, prove. **3** conduct. **4** present an image of. **5** cause to understand. **6** be able to be seen. ● *n.* **1** display. **2** public exhibition or performance. **3** outward appearance. □ **show business** entertainment profession. **show off 1** display well or proudly or ostentatiously. **2** try to impress people. **show of hands** raising of hands in voting. **show-piece** *n.* excellent specimen used for exhibition. **show up 1** make or be clearly visible. **2** reveal (a fault etc.). **3** (*colloq.*) arrive.
■ *v.* **1** display, exhibit, present. **2** demonstrate, display, evince, indicate, manifest; expose, lay bare, reveal, uncover; confirm, establish, illustrate, point out, prove, verify. **3** accompany, conduct, escort, guide, lead, usher. **4** depict, illustrate, portray, represent. ● *n.* **1** array, display, exhibition, spectacle. **2** exhibition, exposition, fair; musical, performance, play, production. **3** appearance, pretence, semblance, veneer. □ **show off 1** display, flaunt, parade.

showdown *n.* confrontation that settles an argument.

shower *n.* **1** brief fall of rain or snow, stones, etc. **2** sudden influx of letters or gifts etc. **3** device or cabinet in which water is sprayed on a person's body. **4** wash in this. ● *v.* **1** send or come in a shower. **2** take a shower. □ **showery** *adj.*
■ *v.* hail, pelt, pour, rain; bestow, heap, lavish.

showerproof *adj.* (of fabric) able to keep out slight rain. ● *v.* make showerproof.

showjumping *n.* competitive sport of riding horses to jump over obstacles. □ **showjumper** *n.*

showman *n.* **1** proprietor of a circus etc. **2** person skilled at presenting entertainment, goods, etc. □ **showmanship** *n.*

shown *see* **show**.

showroom *n.* room where goods are displayed for inspection.

showy *adj.* (**-ier**, **-iest**) making a good display, brilliant, gaudy. □ **showily** *adv.*, **showiness** *n.*
■ baroque, fancy, flamboyant, flashy, florid, gaudy, ornate, ostentatious, rococo.

shrank *see* **shrink**.

shrapnel *n.* pieces of metal scattered from an exploding bomb.

shred *n.* **1** small strip torn or cut from something. **2** small amount. ● *v.* (**shredded**) tear or cut into shreds. □ **shredder** *n.*

■ *n.* **1** bit, fragment, piece, scrap. **2** bit, iota, jot, speck, trace.

shrew *n.* small mouse-like animal.

shrewd *adj.* showing sound judgement, clever. □ **shrewdly** *adv.*, **shrewdness** *n.*

■ acute, astute, canny, clever, intelligent, perceptive, perspicacious, sharp, smart, wise.

shriek *n.* shrill cry or scream. ● *v.* utter (with) a shriek.

■ *v.* cry, scream, screech, shout, squeal.

shrike *n.* bird with a strong hooked beak.

shrill *adj.* piercing and high-pitched in sound. □ **shrilly** *adv.*, **shrillness** *n.*

■ high-pitched, penetrating, piercing, piping, squeaky.

shrimp *n.* **1** small edible shellfish. **2** (*colloq.*) very small person.

shrine *n.* sacred or revered place.

shrink *v.* (**shrank, shrunk**) **1** make or become smaller. **2** draw back to avoid something. ● *n.* (*sl.*) psychiatrist.

shrinkage *n.* **1** shrinking of textile fabric. **2** loss by theft or wastage.

shrivel *v.* (**shrivelled**) shrink and wrinkle from great heat or cold or lack of moisture.

shroud *n.* **1** cloth wrapping a dead body for burial. **2** thing that conceals. **3** one of the ropes supporting a ship's mast. ● *v.* **1** wrap in a shroud. **2** conceal.

shrub *n.* woody plant smaller than a tree. □ **shrubby** *adj.*

shrubbery *n.* area planted with shrubs.

shrug *v.* (**shrugged**) raise (one's shoulders) as a gesture of indifference, doubt, or helplessness. ● *n.* this movement.

shrunk *see* **shrink**.

shrunken *adj.* having shrunk.

shudder *v.* shiver or shake violently. ● *n.* this movement.

■ *v.* quake, quiver, shake, shiver, tremble.

shuffle *v.* **1** walk without lifting one's feet clear of the ground. **2** rearrange, jumble. ● *n.* **1** shuffling movement or walk. **2** rearrangement.

■ *v.* **2** disarrange, jumble, mix (up), muddle, rearrange.

shun *v.* (**shunned**) avoid.

■ avoid, give a wide berth to, keep away from, steer clear of.

shunt *v.* **1** move (a train) to a side track. **2** divert.

shush *int.* & *v.* (*colloq.*) hush.

shut *v.* (**shut, shutting**) **1** move (a door or window etc.) into position to block an opening. **2** be moved in this way. **3** (make a business etc.) close for trade. **4** bring or fold parts of (a thing) together. **5** trap or exclude by shutting something. □ **shut down** stop or cease working or business. **shut-down** *n.* this process. **shut-eye** *n.* (*colloq.*) sleep. **shut up 1** shut securely. **2** (*colloq.*) stop or cease talking or making a noise.

■ **1** bolt, close, fasten, latch, lock, secure, shut up.

shutter *n.* **1** screen that can be closed over a window. **2** device that opens and closes the aperture of a camera. □ **shuttered** *adj.*

shuttle *n.* **1** device carrying the weft-thread in weaving. **2** vehicle used in a shuttle service. **3** spacecraft for repeated use. ● *v.* move, travel, or send to and fro. □ **shuttle service** transport service making frequent journeys to and fro.

shuttlecock *n.* small cone-shaped feathered object struck to and fro in badminton.

shy[1] *adj.* timid and lacking self-confidence. ● *v.* jump or move suddenly in alarm. □ **shyly** *adv.*, **shyness** *n.*

■ *adj.* bashful, diffident, inhibited, introverted, reserved, reticent, self-conscious, self-effacing, timid, withdrawn.

shy[2] *v.* & *n.* throw.

SI *abbr.* Système International, the international metric system.

Siamese *adj.* of Siam, former name of Thailand. □ **Siamese cat** cat with pale fur and darker face, paws, and tail. **Siamese twins** twins whose bodies are joined at birth.

sibling *n.* brother or sister.

sibyl *n.* pagan prophetess.

sic *adv.* used or spelt in the way quoted.

Sicilian *adj.* & *n.* (native) of Sicily.

sick *adj.* **1** unwell. **2** vomiting, likely to vomit. **3** disgusted. **4** finding amusement in misfortune or morbid subjects

■ **1** ailing, ill, in bad health, indisposed, infirm, not well, off colour, poorly, sickly, under the weather, unwell. **2** ill, nauseous, queasy.

sicken v. **1** become ill. **2** disgust. □ **be sickening for** be in the first stages of (a disease).

■ **2** appal, disgust, outrage, repel, repulse, revolt, shock.

sickle n. curved blade used for cutting corn etc.

sickly adj. (**-ier, -iest**) **1** unhealthy. **2** causing sickness. **3** faint, pale. □ **sickliness** n.

■ **1** delicate, feeble, frail, infirm, peaky, unhealthy, weak.

sickness n. **1** illness. **2** vomiting.

■ **1** bad health, ill health, infirmity; ailment, complaint, condition, disease, disorder, indisposition.

side n. **1** surface of an object, esp. one that is not the top, bottom, front, back, or end. **2** bounding line of a plane or solid figure. **3** either of the two halves into which something is divided. **4** either of the two surfaces of something flat and thin. **5** region next to or farther from a person or thing. **6** part near an edge. **7** aspect of a problem etc. **8** one of two opposing groups or teams etc. **9** slope of a hill. ● adj. **1** at or on the side. **2** subordinate. ● v. join forces (with a person) in a dispute. □ **on the side 1** as a sideline. **2** as a surreptitious activity. **side by side** close together. **side effect** secondary (usu. bad) effect. **side-saddle** n. saddle on which a woman rider sits with both legs on the same side of the horse. adv. sitting in this way.

■ n. **2** facet, plane, surface. **6** border, boundary, brink, edge, margin, perimeter, rim, verge. **7** aspect, element, facet, feature. **8** faction, movement, party; squad, team.

sideboard n. **1** piece of dining-room furniture with drawers and cupboards for china etc. **2** (pl., colloq.) sideburns.

sideburns n.pl. short whiskers on the cheek.

sidelight n. **1** incidental information. **2** either of two small lights on the front of a vehicle.

sideline n. **1** thing done in addition to one's main activity. **2** (pl.) lines bounding the sides of a football pitch etc., places for spectators. **3** (pl.) position etc. apart from the main action.

sidelong adj. & adv. sideways.

sidereal /sɪˈdɪəriəl/ adj. of or measured by the stars.

sideshow n. small show forming part of a large one.

sidestep v. (**-stepped**) **1** avoid by stepping sideways. **2** evade.

■ avoid, circumvent, dodge, duck, evade, steer clear of.

sidetrack v. divert.

■ deflect, distract, divert, turn aside.

sidewalk n. (US) pavement.

sideways adv. & adj. **1** to or from one side. **2** with one side forward.

siding n. short track by the side of a railway, used in shunting.

sidle v. advance in a timid, furtive, or cringing way.

siege n. surrounding and blockading of a place by armed forces, in order to capture it.

sienna n. **1** a kind of clay used as a pigment. **2** its colour of reddish- or yellowish-brown.

sierra n. chain of mountains with jagged peaks, esp. in Spain or Spanish America.

siesta n. afternoon nap or rest, esp. in hot countries.

sieve /sɪv/ n. utensil with a mesh through which liquids or fine particles can pass. ● v. put through a sieve.

sift v. **1** sieve. **2** examine carefully and select or analyse.

sigh n. long deep breath given out audibly in sadness, tiredness, relief, etc. ● v. give or express with a sigh.

sight n. **1** ability to see. **2** seeing, being seen. **3** thing seen or worth seeing. **4** unsightly thing. **5** device looked through to aim or observe with a gun or telescope etc. ● v. **1** get a sight of. **2** aim or observe with a gunsight etc. □ **at** or **on sight** as soon as seen. **catch sight of** see suddenly or for a moment. **sight-read** v. play or sing (music) without preliminary study of the score.

■ n. **1** eyesight, vision. **2** glimpse, look, view. **3** display, scene, spectacle; marvel, rarity, wonder. **4** eyesore, fright. □ **catch sight** descry, discern, espy, glimpse, notice, observe, perceive, see, colloq. spot, spy.

sightless adj. blind.

sightseeing n. visiting places of interest. □ **sightseer** n.

■ □ **sightseer** holiday-maker, tourist, traveller, tripper, visitor.

sign n. **1** mark or symbol used to represent something. **2** thing perceived that suggests the existence of something. **3**

board, notice, etc. displayed. **4** action or gesture conveying information etc. **5** any of the twelve divisions of the zodiac. ● *v.* **1** make a sign. **2** write (one's name) on a document. **3** convey or engage or acknowledge by this.

■ *n.* **1** emblem, insignia, logo, mark, symbol, trade mark. **2** clue, hint, indication, manifestation, mark, proof, suggestion, token, trace; augury, omen, portent, presage, warning. **3** notice, placard, poster. **4** gesticulation, gesture, motion, signal.

signal *n.* **1** sign or gesture giving information or a command. **2** object placed to give notice or warning. **3** event which causes immediate activity. **4** sequence of electrical impulses or radio waves transmitted or received. ● *v.* (**signalled**) **1** make a signal or signals. **2** communicate with or announce thus. ● *adj.* noteworthy. □ **signal-box** *n.* small railway building with signalling apparatus. **signally** *adv.*

■ *n.* **1** cue, gesticulation, gesture, motion, movement, sign. ● *v.* **1** beckon, gesticulate, gesture, indicate, motion, wave.

signalman *n.* person responsible for operating railway signals.

signatory *n.* one of the parties who sign an agreement.

signature *n.* **1** person's name or initials written when signing something. **2** indication of key or tempo at the beginning of a musical score. □ **signature tune** tune used to announce a particular performer or programme.

signet ring finger ring with an engraved design.

significance *n.* **1** meaning. **2** importance. □ **significant** *adj.*, **significantly** *adv.*

■ **1** essence, gist, meaning, purport, sense, signification. **2** consequence, import, importance, moment, relevance, value, weight.

signification *n.* meaning.

signify *v.* **1** be a sign or symbol of. **2** have as a meaning. **3** make known. **4** matter.

■ **1** betoken, denote, indicate, represent, stand for, symbolize. **2** connote, denote, indicate, mean. **3** communicate, convey, express, make known. **4** be important, count, matter.

signpost *n.* post showing the direction of certain places.

Sikh /seek/ *n.* member of an Indian religion believing in one God. □ **Sikhism** *n.*

silage *n.* green fodder stored and fermented in a silo.

silence *n.* absence of sound or of speaking. ● *v.* make silent.

■ *n.* hush, peace, quiet, stillness; reticence, taciturnity. ● *v.* hush, quiet, quieten, *colloq.* shush, *colloq.* shut up.

silencer *n.* device for reducing sound.

silent *adj.* without sound, not speaking. □ **silently** *adv.*

■ hushed, noiseless, quiescent, soundless; *colloq.* mum, mute, quiet, tongue-tied.

silhouette /siloo-ét/ *n.* dark shadow or outline seen against a light background. ● *v.* show as a silhouette.

■ *n.* contour, form, outline, profile, shadow, shape.

silica *n.* compound of silicon occurring as quartz and in sandstone etc. □ **siliceous** *adj.*

silicate *n.* compound of silicon.

silicon *n.* chemical substance found in the earth's crust in its compound forms. □ **silicon chip** silicon microchip.

silicone *n.* organic compound of silicon, used in paint, varnish, and lubricants.

silicosis *n.* lung disease caused by inhaling dust that contains silica.

silk *n.* **1** fine strong soft fibre produced by silkworms. **2** thread or cloth made from it or resembling this. □ **silky** *adj.*

silken *adj.* like silk.

silkworm *n.* caterpillar which spins its cocoon of silk.

sill *n.* strip of stone, wood, or metal at the base of a doorway or window opening.

silly *adj.* (-**ier**, -**iest**) **1** lacking good sense, foolish, unwise. **2** feeble-minded. □ **silliness** *n.*

■ **1** absurd, asinine, *sl.* batty, crazy, daft, foolish, idiotic, illogical, imbecilic, inane, irrational, laughable, ludicrous, mad, nonsensical, *sl.* potty, preposterous, ridiculous, risible, senseless, stupid, unreasonable, unwise, witless; babyish, childish, frivolous, giddy, immature, infantile, juvenile, puerile.

silo *n.* (*pl.* -**os**) **1** pit or airtight structure for holding silage. **2** pit or tower for storing grain, cement, or radioactive waste. **3** underground place where a missile is kept ready for firing.

silt *n.* sediment deposited by water in a channel or harbour etc. ● *v.* block or become blocked with silt.

silver *n.* **1** white precious metal. **2** articles made of this. **3** coins made of an alloy resembling it. **4** household cutlery. **5** colour of silver. ● *adj.* made of or coloured like silver. □ **silver jubilee, wedding** 25th anniversary.

silverfish *n.* small wingless insect with a fish-like body.

silverside *n.* joint of beef cut from the haunch, below topside.

silvery *adj.* **1** like silver. **2** having a clear gentle ringing sound.

simian *adj.* monkey-like, ape-like. ● *n.* monkey, ape.

similar *adj.* resembling but not the same, alike. □ **similarly** *adv.*, **similarity** *n.*
■ akin, alike, analogous, comparable, equivalent, like.

simile /simmili/ *n.* figure of speech in which one thing is compared to another.

similitude *n.* similarity.

simmer *v.* **1** boil very gently. **2** be in a state of barely suppressed anger or excitement. □ **simmer down** become less excited.

simper *v.* smile in an affected way. ● *n.* affected smile.

simple *adj.* **1** not difficult. **2** not showy or elaborate, plain. **3** foolish, inexperienced. **4** of one element or kind. □ **simply** *adv.*, **simplicity** *n.*
■ **1** basic, easy, effortless, elementary, straightforward, uncomplicated, understandable. **2** austere, basic, plain, spartan, unadorned, unostentatious, unpretentious; homely, modest, ordinary.

simpleton *n.* foolish person.

simplify *v.* make simple, make easy to do or understand. □ **simplification** *n.*

simplistic *adj.* over-simplified. □ **simplistically** *adv.*

simulate *v.* **1** pretend. **2** imitate the form or condition of. □ **simulation** *n.*, **simulator** *n.*
■ **1** affect, fake, feign, pretend, sham. **2** imitate, replicate, reproduce.

simultaneous *adj.* occurring at the same time. □ **simultaneously** *adv.*, **simultaneity** *n.*
■ □ **simultaneously** at once, at the same time, in unison, together.

sin *n.* **1** breaking of a religious or moral law. **2** act which does this. ● *v.* (**sinned**) commit a sin.
■ *n.* **1** corruption, depravity, evil, immorality, iniquity, misconduct, wickedness, wrongdoing, vice. **2** crime, fault, misdeed, misdemeanour, offence, transgression, wrong. ● *v.* do wrong, err, offend, transgress.

since *prep.* **1** after. **2** from (a specified time) until now, within that period. ● *conj.* **1** from the time that. **2** because. ● *adv.* since that time or event.

sincere *adj.* without pretence or deceit. □ **sincerely** *adv.*, **sincerity** *n.*
■ candid, earnest, frank, honest, genuine, heartfelt, real, straightforward, true, truthful, unfeigned, wholehearted.

sine *n.* ratio of the length of one side of a right-angled triangle to the hypotenuse.

sinecure *n.* position of profit with no work attached.

sinew *n.* **1** tough fibrous tissue joining muscle to bone, tendon. **2** (*pl.*) muscles, strength. □ **sinewy** *adj.*

sinful *adj.* full of sin, wicked. □ **sinfully** *adv.*, **sinfulness** *n.*
■ bad, corrupt, depraved, evil, immoral, iniquitous, vile, wicked.

sing *v.* (**sang, sung**) **1** make musical sounds with the voice. **2** perform (a song). **3** make a humming sound. □ **singer** *n.*

singe /sinj/ *v.* (**singeing**) **1** burn slightly. **2** burn the ends or edges of. ● *n.* slight burn.

single *adj.* **1** one only, not double or multiple. **2** designed for one person or thing. **3** unmarried. **4** (of a ticket) valid for an outward journey only. ● *n.* **1** one person or thing. **2** room etc. for one person. **3** single ticket. **4** pop record with one piece of music on each side. **5** (usu. *pl.*) game with one player on each side. ● *v.* **single out** choose or distinguish from others. □ **single figures** numbers from 1 to 9. **single-handed** *adj.* & *adv.* without help. **single-minded** *adj.* with one's mind set on a single purpose. **single parent** person bringing up a child or children without a partner. **singly** *adv.*
■ *adj.* **1** distinct, individual, particular, separate; lone, sole, solitary. ● *v.* choose, decide on, go for, opt for, pick, select. □ **single-minded** determined, dogged, persevering, resolute, tireless, unwavering.

singlet n. sleeveless vest.

singsong adj. with a monotonous rise and fall of the voice. ● n. 1 singsong manner. 2 informal singing by a group of people.

singular n. form of a noun or verb used in referring to one person or thing. ● adj. 1 of this form. 2 uncommon, extraordinary. □ **singularly** adv., **singularity** n.

■ adj. 2 exceptional, extraordinary, outstanding, rare, remarkable, uncommon, unparalleled, unusual; bizarre, curious, eccentric, odd, peculiar, strange.

sinister adj. 1 suggestive of evil. 2 involving wickedness.

■ 1 dark, forbidding, menacing, ominous, threatening. 2 criminal, evil, nefarious, wicked.

sink v. (**sank**, **sunk**) 1 fall or come gradually downwards. 2 make or become submerged. 3 lose strength or value. 4 dig. 5 send (ball) into a pocket at billiards or hole at golf etc. 6 invest (money). ● n. fixed basin with a drainage pipe. □ **sink in** become understood. **sinking fund** money set aside regularly for repayment of a debt etc.

■ v. 1 descend, droop, drop, fall, go down, sag, slump. 2 founder, go under, submerge; scupper, scuttle. 3 decline, degenerate, deteriorate, fade, languish, weaken, worsen; decrease, dwindle. 4 bore, dig, drill, excavate.

sinker n. weight used to sink a fishing line etc.

sinner n. person who sins.

■ evildoer, offender, malefactor, miscreant, reprobate, transgressor, wrongdoer.

sinuous adj. curving, undulating.

sinus /sínass/ n. (pl. -**uses**) cavity in bone or tissue, esp. that connecting with the nostrils.

sip v. (**sipped**) drink in small mouthfuls. ● n. amount sipped.

siphon n. 1 bent pipe or tube used for transferring liquid by utilizing atmospheric pressure. 2 bottle from which soda water etc. is forced out by pressure of gas. ● v. 1 flow or draw out through a siphon. 2 take from a source.

sir n. 1 polite form of address to a man. 2 (**Sir**) title of a knight or baronet.

sire n. animal's male parent. ● v. be the father of.

siren n. 1 device that makes a loud prolonged sound as a signal. 2 dangerously fascinating woman.

sirloin n. upper (best) part of loin of beef.

sirocco n. (pl. -**os**) hot wind that reaches Italy from Africa.

sisal /sísl/ n. fibre made from a tropical plant.

sissy n. weak or timid person. ● adj. characteristic of a sissy.

sister n. 1 daughter of the same parents as another person. 2 woman who is a fellow member of a group or Church etc. 3 nun. 4 senior female nurse. □ **sister-in-law** n. (pl. **sisters-in-law**) 1 husband's or wife's sister. 2 brother's wife. **sisterly** adj.

sisterhood n. 1 relationship of sisters. 2 order of nuns. 3 group of women with common aims.

sit v. (**sat**, **sitting**) 1 take or be in a position with the body resting on the buttocks. 2 cause to sit. 3 pose for a portrait. 4 perch. 5 (of animals) rest with legs bent and body on the ground. 6 (of birds) remain on the nest to hatch eggs. 7 be situated. 8 be a candidate (for). 9 (of a committee etc.) hold a session.

sitar n. guitar-like Indian musical instrument.

sitcom n. (colloq.) situation comedy.

site n. place where something is, was, or is to be located. ● v. locate, provide with a site.

■ n. location, place, position, spot. ● v. locate, place, position, put, situate.

sitter n. 1 person sitting. 2 babysitter.

sitting see **sit**. n. 1 time during which a person or assembly etc. sits. 2 clutch of eggs. □ **sitting room** room in which to sit and relax. **sitting tenant** one already in occupation.

situate v. place or put in a certain position. □ **be situated** be in a certain position.

■ locate, place, position, put, site.

situation n. 1 place (with its surroundings) occupied by something. 2 set of circumstances. 3 position of employment. □ **situation comedy** broadcast comedy involving the same characters in a series of episodes. **situational** adj.

■ 1 location, position, setting, site, spot. 2 case, circumstances, state of affairs. 3 appointment, job, place, position, post.

six adj. & n. one more than five.

sixteen *adj* & *n*. one more than fifteen. □ **sixteenth** *adj*. & *n*.

sixth *adj*. & *n*. next after fifth. □ **sixth sense** supposed intuitive faculty. **sixthly** *adv*.

sixty *adj*. & *n*. six times ten. □ **sixtieth** *adj*. & *n*.

size¹ *n*. **1** relative bigness, extent. **2** one of a series of standard measurements in which things are made and sold. ● *v*. group according to size. □ **size up 1** estimate the size of. **2** (*colloq*.) form a judgement of.

■ *n*. **1** area, dimensions, expanse, extent, magnitude, measurements, proportions. □ **size up 2** appraise, assess, evaluate, judge, weigh up.

size² *n*. gluey solution used to glaze paper or stiffen textiles etc. ● *v*. treat with size.

sizeable *adj*. fairly large.

sizzle *v*. make a hissing sound like that of frying.

skate¹ *n*. (*pl*. **skate**) edible marine flatfish.

skate² *n*. boot with a blade or (**roller skate**) wheels attached, for gliding over ice or a hard surface. ● *v*. move on skates. □ **skate over** have only a passing reference to. **skater** *n*.

skateboard *n*. small board with wheels for riding on while standing. ● *v*. ride on a skateboard.

skedaddle *v*. (*colloq*.) run away.

skein /skayn/ *n*. **1** loosely coiled bundle of yarn. **2** flock of wild geese etc. in flight.

skeletal *adj*. of or like a skeleton.

skeleton *n*. **1** hard supporting structure of an animal body. **2** any supporting structure, framework. □ **skeleton service, staff** one reduced to a minimum. **skeleton key** key made so as to fit many locks.

sketch *n*. **1** rough drawing or painting. **2** brief account. **3** short usu. comic play. ● *v*. make a sketch or sketches (of).

■ *n*. **1** draft, outline, rough. ● *v*. draft, draw, outline, rough out.

sketchy *adj*. (**-ier**, **-iest**) rough and not detailed or substantial. □ **sketchily** *adv*., **sketchiness** *n*.

■ cursory, incomplete, patchy, perfunctory, rough, superficial.

skew *adj*. slanting, askew. ● *v*. **1** make skew. **2** turn or twist round.

skewbald *adj*. (of an animal) with irregular patches of white and another colour.

skewer *n*. pin to hold meat or pieces of food together while cooking. ● *v*. pierce with a skewer.

ski *n*. (*pl*. **-is**) one of a pair of long narrow strips of wood etc. fixed under the feet for travelling over snow. ● *v*. (**ski'd**, **skiing**) travel on skis. □ **skier** *n*.

skid *v*. (**skidded**) (of a vehicle) slide uncontrollably. ● *n*. skidding movement. □ **skid-pan** *n*. surface used for practising control of skidding vehicles.

skiff *n*. small light rowing boat.

skilful *adj*. having or showing great skill. □ **skilfully** *adv*.

■ able, accomplished, adept, adroit, capable, competent, deft, dexterous, expert, handy, masterly, practised, proficient, skilled, talented.

skill *n*. ability to do something well. □ **skilled** *adj*.

■ ability, aptitude, competence, expertise, know-how, proficiency, prowess, talent, workmanship.

skim *v*. (**skimmed**) **1** take (matter) from the surface of (liquid). **2** glide. **3** read quickly. □ **skimmed milk** milk with the cream removed.

skimp *v*. supply or use rather less than what is necessary.

skimpy *adj*. (**-ier**, **-iest**) scanty. □ **skimpily** *adv*., **skimpiness** *n*.

skin *n*. **1** outer covering of the human or other animal body. **2** material made from animal skin. **3** complexion. **4** outer layer. **5** skin-like film on liquid. ● *v*. (**skinned**) strip skin from. □ **skin diving** sport of swimming under water with flippers and breathing apparatus.

■ *n*. **1** epidermis. **2** fleece, hide, pelt. **3** coating, covering, film; peel rind, shell. ● *v*. bark, graze, scrape; flay, strip.

skinflint *n*. miserly person.

skinny *adj*. (**-ier**, **-iest**) very thin.

■ bony, emaciated, gaunt, scraggy, scrawny, thin.

skint *adj*. (*sl*.) with no money left.

skip¹ *v*. (**skipped**) **1** move lightly, esp. taking two steps with each foot in turn. **2** jump with a skipping rope. **3** (*colloq*.) omit. **4** (*colloq*.) go away hastily or secretly. ● *n*. skipping movement.

■ *v*. **1** bound, caper, cavort, frisk, gambol, leap, prance, spring. **3** disregard, leave out, omit, overlook, pass over.

skip² *n*. large container for builders' rubbish etc.

skipper *n*. & *v*. captain.

skipping rope rope turned over the head and under the feet while jumping.

skirmish n. minor fight or conflict. ● v. take part in a skirmish.

■ n. brawl, conflict, fight, fray, *colloq.* scrap, struggle, tussle.

skirt n. 1 woman's garment hanging from the waist. 2 this part of a garment. 3 similar part. 4 cut of beef from the lower flank. ● v. go or be along the edge of.

skirting (board) n. narrow board round the bottom of the wall of a room.

skit n. short parody.

skittish adj. frisky.

skittle n. one of the wooden pins set up to be bowled down with a ball in the game of **skittles**.

skua n. large seagull.

skulduggery n. (*colloq.*) trickery.

skulk v. loiter stealthily.

skull n. 1 bony framework of the head. 2 representation of this.

skullcap n. small cap with no peak.

skunk n. 1 black bushy-tailed American animal able to spray an evil-smelling liquid. 2 (*sl.*) contemptible person.

sky n. region of the clouds or upper air. □ **sky-blue** adj. & n. bright clear blue.

skydiving n. parachuting in which the parachute is not opened until the last moment.

skylark n. lark that soars while singing. ● v. play mischievously.

skylight n. window set in the line of a roof or ceiling.

skyscraper n. very tall building.

slab n. broad flat piece of something solid.

slack adj. 1 not tight. 2 negligent. 3 not busy. ● n. slack part. ● v. 1 slacken. 2 be lazy about work. □ **slackness** n.

■ adj. limp, loose. 2 careless, inattentive, lax, negligent, remiss.

slacken v. make or become slack.

slacks n.pl. casual trousers.

slag n. solid waste left when metal has been smelted. ● v. (**slagged**) (*sl.*) criticize, insult. □ **slag-heap** n. mound of waste matter.

slain see **slay**.

slake v. 1 satisfy (thirst). 2 combine (lime) with water.

slalom n. 1 ski race down a zigzag course. 2 obstacle race in canoes etc.

slam v. (**slammed**) 1 shut forcefully and noisily. 2 put or hit forcefully. 3 (*sl.*) criticize severely. ● n. slamming noise.

slander n. 1 false statement uttered maliciously that damages a person's reputation. 2 crime of uttering this. ● v. utter slander about. □ **slanderer** n., **slanderous** adj.

■ n. calumny, defamation, denigration, obloquy, vilification. ● v. calumniate, defame, insult, libel, malign, traduce, vilify.

slang n. words or phrases or particular meanings of these used very informally for vividness or novelty. □ **slangy** adj.

slant v. 1 slope. 2 present (news etc.) from a particular point of view. ● n. 1 slope. 2 way news etc. is slanted, bias. □ **slantwise** adv.

■ v. 1 bank, incline, lean, list, slope, tilt. 2 bias, colour, distort, misrepresent, twist. ● n. 1 inclination, incline, gradient, pitch, slope, tilt. 2 angle, bias, perspective, viewpoint.

slap v. (**slapped**) 1 strike with the open hand or with something flat. 2 place forcefully or carelessly. ● n. slapping blow. ● adv. with a slap, directly. □ **slap-happy** adj. (*colloq.*) cheerfully casual. **slap-up** adj. (*colloq.*) lavish.

slapdash adj. hasty and careless.

■ careless, hasty, hurried, slipshod, sloppy.

slapstick n. boisterous comedy.

slash v. 1 gash. 2 make a sweeping stroke. 3 strike in this way. 4 reduce drastically. ● n. slashing stroke or cut.

■ v. 1,3 cut, gash, knife, lacerate, slit. ● n. diagonal, line, stroke.

slat n. narrow strip of wood, metal, etc.

slate n. 1 rock that splits easily into flat blue-grey plates. 2 piece of this used as roofing-material or (formerly) for writing on. ● v. 1 cover with slates. 2 (*colloq.*) criticize severely.

slaughter v. 1 kill (animals) for food. 2 kill ruthlessly or in great numbers. ● n. this process.

■ v. 2 butcher, exterminate, kill, massacre, murder, put to death, slay. ● n. carnage, bloodshed, butchery, genocide, killing, massacre.

slaughterhouse n. place where animals are killed for food.

Slav n. & n. (member) of any of the peoples of Europe who speak a Slavonic language.

slave n. 1 person who is owned by and must work for another. 2 victim of or to a dominating influence. 3 drudge. ● v.

work very hard. □ **slave-driver** n. hard taskmaster.

slaver v. have saliva flowing from the mouth.

slavery n. **1** existence or condition of slaves. **2** very hard work.

■ **1** bondage, captivity, servitude.

slavish adj. excessively submissive or imitative. □ **slavishly** adv.

■ fawning, obsequious, servile, submissive, sycophantic; unimaginative, unoriginal.

Slavonic adj. & n. (of) the group of languages including Russian and Polish.

slay v. (**slew, slain**) kill.

sleazy adj. (**-ier, -iest**) dirty, disreputable. □ **sleaziness** n.

sledge n. cart with runners instead of wheels, used on snow. ● v. travel or convey in a sledge.

sledgehammer n. large heavy hammer.

sleek adj. **1** smooth and glossy. **2** looking well fed and thriving. □ **sleekness** n.

sleep n. **1** natural condition of rest with unconsciousness and relaxation of muscles. **2** spell of this. ● v. (**slept**) **1** be or spend (time) in a state of sleep. **2** provide with sleeping accommodation.

■ n. **2** catnap, doze, nap, rest, siesta, snooze. ● v. **1** doze, repose, rest, slumber, snooze.

sleeper n. **1** one who sleeps. **2** beam on which the rails of a railway rest. **3** railway coach fitted for sleeping in. **4** ring worn in a pierced ear to keep the hole from closing.

sleeping bag padded bag for sleeping in.

sleepwalk v. walk about while asleep. □ **sleepwalker** n.

sleepy adj. (**-ier, -iest**) **1** feeling a desire to sleep. **2** quiet. □ **sleepily** adv., **sleepiness** n.

■ **1** drowsy, somnolent, tired. **2** peaceful, quiet, tranquil.

sleet n. hail or snow and rain falling simultaneously. ● v. fall as sleet. □ **sleety** adj.

sleeve n. **1** part of a garment covering the arm. **2** tube-like cover. **3** cover for a record. □ **up one's sleeve** concealed but available.

sleigh /slay/ n. sledge, esp. drawn by horses.

sleight of hand /slīt/ skill in using the hands to perform conjuring tricks etc.

slender adj. **1** slim and graceful. **2** small in amount. □ **slenderness** n.

■ **1** slim, svelte, thin, willowy. **2** little, meagre, scanty, slight, slim, small.

slept see **sleep**.

sleuth /slooth/ n. detective.

slew[1] v. turn or swing round.

slew[2] see **slay**.

slice n. **1** thin flat piece (or a wedge) cut off an item of food. **2** portion. **3** implement for lifting or serving food. **4** slicing stroke. ● v. **1** cut, esp. into slices. **2** strike (a ball) so that it spins away obliquely. □ **slicer** n.

■ n. **1** bit, helping, piece, portion, serving, slab, wedge. **2** part, portion, share.

slick adj. **1** skilful, efficient. **2** smooth. ● n. patch of oil on the sea. ● v. make sleek.

slide v. (**slid**) **1** (cause to) move along a smooth surface touching it always with the same part. **2** move or pass smoothly. ● n. **1** act of sliding. **2** smooth slope or surface for sliding. **3** sliding part. **4** piece of glass for holding an object under a microscope. **5** picture for projecting onto a screen. **6** hinged clip for holding hair in place. □ **sliding scale** scale of fees or taxes etc. that varies according to the variation of some standard.

■ v. glide, skid, skim, slip, slither.

slight adj. **1** not much, not great, not thorough. **2** slender, small. ● v. treat disrespectfully, ignore. ● n. act of slighting. □ **slightly** adv., **slightness** n.

■ adj. **1** inconsequential, insignificant, minimal, minor, negligible, small, trifling; faint, remote, slim, small. **2** diminutive, petite, slender, slim, small, thin. ● v. affront, insult, offend; ignore, rebuff, scorn, snub, spurn. ● n. affront, insult, slur, snub.

slim adj. (**slimmer, slimmest**) **1** of small girth or thickness. **2** small, slight, insufficient. ● v. (**slimmed**) make (oneself) slimmer by dieting, exercise, etc. □ **slimmer** n., **slimness** n.

■ adj. **1** lean, skinny, slender, slight, thin.

slime n. unpleasant thick slippery liquid substance. □ **slimy** adj., **slimily** adv., **sliminess** n.

sling n. **1** strap or bandage etc. looped round an object to support or lift it. **2** looped strap used to throw a stone etc. ● v. (**slung**) **1** suspend, lift, or hurl with a sling. **2** (colloq.) throw.

slink v. (**slunk**) move in a stealthy or shamefaced way.

■ creep, skulk, sneak, steal.

slinky adj. smooth and sinuous.

slip[1] v. (**slipped**) 1 slide accidentally. 2 lose one's balance thus. 3 go or put smoothly. 4 escape hold or capture. ● n. 1 act of slipping. 2 casual mistake. 3 petticoat. 4 liquid containing clay for coating pottery. □ **give a person the slip** escape from or avoid him or her. **slip by** (of time) pass rapidly. **slipped disc** disc of cartilage between vertebrae that has become displaced and causes pain. **slip-road** n. road for entering or leaving a motorway. **slip up** (colloq.) make a mistake. **slip-up** n.

■ v. 1 glide, skid, slide, slither. 2 fall, stumble, trip, tumble. ● n. 2 blunder, colloq. boob, error, gaffe, mistake, oversight, colloq. slip-up.

slip[2] n. small piece of paper.

slipper n. light loose shoe for indoor wear.

slippery adj. 1 smooth or wet and difficult to hold or causing slipping. 2 (of a person) not trustworthy. □ **slipperiness** n.

slipshod adj. done or doing things carelessly.

■ careless, disorganized, haphazard, slapdash, sloppy.

slipstream n. current of air driven backward as something is propelled forward.

slipway n. sloping structure on which boats are landed or ships built or repaired.

slit n. narrow straight cut or opening. ● v. (**slit**, **slitting**) 1 cut a slit in. 2 cut into strips.

■ n. aperture, cleft, crack, cut, fissure, opening, split, vent.

slither v. slide unsteadily.

sliver n. small thin strip.

slobber v. slaver, dribble.

sloe n. 1 blackthorn. 2 its small dark plum-like fruit.

slog v. (**slogged**) 1 hit hard. 2 work or walk hard and steadily. ● n. 1 hard hit. 2 spell of hard steady work or walking.

slogan n. word or phrase adopted as a motto or in advertising.

sloop n. small ship with one mast.

slop v. (**slopped**) spill, splash. ● n. 1 unappetizing liquid. 2 slopped liquid. 3 (pl.) liquid refuse.

slope v. lie or put at an angle from the horizontal or vertical. ● n. 1 sloping surface. 2 amount by which a thing slopes.

■ v. bank, lean, slant, tilt, tip. ● n. angle, gradient, inclination, incline, pitch, slant, tilt.

sloppy adj. (**-ier**, **-iest**) 1 wet, slushy. 2 slipshod. 3 weakly sentimental. □ **sloppily** adv., **sloppiness** n.

slosh v. 1 (colloq.) splash, pour clumsily. 2 (sl.) hit. ● n. 1 (colloq.) splashing sound. 2 (sl.) blow.

sloshed adj. (sl.) drunk.

slot n. 1 narrow opening into or through which something is to be put. 2 position in a series or scheme. ● v. (**slotted**) 1 make slot(s) in. 2 put or fit into a slot. □ **slot machine** machine operated by inserting a coin into a slot.

■ n. 1 channel, cleft, groove, notch, slit. 2 niche, position, space, spot.

sloth /slōth/ n. 1 laziness. 2 slow-moving S. American animal.

slothful adj. lazy. □ **slothfully** adv.

■ idle, indolent, inert, lazy, lethargic, slow, sluggish, torpid.

slouch v. stand, sit, or move in a lazy awkward way. ● n. slouching movement or posture.

slough[1] /slow/ n. swamp, marsh.

slough[2] /sluf/ v. 1 shed (skin). 2 be shed in this way.

slovenly adj. careless and untidy. □ **slovenliness** n.

■ careless, messy, sloppy, unmethodical, untidy.

slow adj. 1 not quick or fast. 2 showing an earlier time than the correct one. 3 stupid. ● adv. slowly. ● v. reduce the speed (of). □ **slowly** adv., **slowness** n.

■ adj. 1 easy, dilatory, gentle, gradual, leisurely, sluggish, steady, unhurried. ● v. brake, decelerate; delay, hinder, hold up, impede, retard, set back.

slowcoach n. person who is slow in his or her actions or work.

slow-worm n. legless lizard.

sludge n. thick mud.

slug[1] n. 1 small slimy animal like a snail without a shell. 2 small lump of metal. 3 bullet.

slug[2] v. (**slugged**) (US) hit hard.

sluggard n. slow or lazy person.

sluggish adj. slow-moving, not lively. □ **sluggishly** adv., **sluggishness** n.
■ inactive, indolent, languid, lethargic, listless, slow, torpid.

sluice /slooss/ n. 1 sliding gate controlling a flow of water. 2 this water. 3 channel carrying off water.

slum n. squalid house or district

slumber v. & n. sleep.

slump n. sudden great fall in prices or demand. ● v. 1 undergo a slump. 2 sit or fall limply.
■ n. crash, depression, economic decline, recession. ● v. 1 decline, drop, fall, nose-dive, plummet, plunge. 2 collapse, drop, fall, flop.

slung see sling.

slunk see slink.

slur v. (slurred) 1 utter with each letter or sound running into the next. 2 pass lightly over (a fact). ● n. 1 slurred sound. 2 curved line marking notes to be slurred in music. 3 discredit.

slurp v. & n. (make) a noisy sucking sound.

slurry n. thin semi-liquid cement, mud, manure, etc.

slush n. 1 partly melted snow on the ground. 2 silly sentimental talk or writing. □ **slushy** adj.

slut n. slovenly or promiscuous woman. □ **sluttish** adj.

sly adj. 1 unpleasantly cunning and secret. 2 mischievous and knowing. □ **on the sly** secretly. **slyly** adv., **slyness** n.
■ 1 artful, crafty, cunning, deceitful, devious, scheming, tricky, underhand, wily.

smack¹ n. 1 slap. 2 loud kiss. ● v. 1 slap, hit hard. 2 close and part (lips) noisily.

smack² n. & v. (have) a slight flavour or trace.

smack³ n. single-masted boat.

small adj. 1 not large or great. 2 unimportant. 3 petty. ● n. 1 narrowest part (of the back). 2 (pl., colloq.) underwear. ● adv. in a small way. □ **small hours** period soon after midnight. **small-minded** adj. narrow or selfish in outlook. **small talk** social conversation on unimportant subjects. **small-time** adj. unimportant. **smallness** n.
■ adj. 1 diminutive, little, miniature, petite, slight, colloq. teeny, tiny, Sc. wee; humble, modest, unpretentious. 2 inconsequential, insignificant, negligible, slight, trifling, trivial, unimportant. □ **small-minded** insular,

narrow-minded, parochial; mean, petty, selfish, ungenerous.

smallholding n. small farm. □ **smallholder** n.

smallpox n. disease with pustules that often leave bad scars.

smarmy adj. (-ier, -iest) (colloq.) ingratiating, obsequious. □ **smarmily** adv., **smarminess** n.

smart adj. 1 neat and elegant. 2 clever. 3 fashionable. 4 brisk. ● v. & n. (feel) a stinging pain. □ **smartly** adv., **smartness** n.
■ adj. 1 dapper, elegant, neat, sl. snazzy, spruce, trim, well-groomed, well-turned-out. 2 able, brainy, bright, clever, gifted, intelligent, quick, sharp. 3 chic, elegant, fashionable, colloq. posh, stylish, colloq. swish. 4 brisk, energetic, lively, quick, vigorous.

smarten v. make or become smarter.

smash v. 1 break noisily into pieces. 2 strike forcefully. 3 crash. 4 ruin. ● n. 1 act or sound of smashing. 2 collision.
■ v. 1 break, shatter, shiver, splinter. ● n. 2 accident, collision, crash, pile-up.

smashing adj. (colloq.) excellent.

smattering n. slight knowledge.

smear v. 1 spread with a greasy or dirty substance. 2 try to damage the reputation of. ● n. 1 mark made by smearing. 2 slander. □ **smeary** adj.
■ v. 1 dirty, smudge, soil, stain, streak. 2 blacken, calumniate, defame, malign, slander, sully, tarnish, vilify.

smell n. 1 ability to perceive things with the sense organs of the nose. 2 quality perceived in this way. 3 unpleasant quality of this kind. 4 act of smelling. ● v. (smelt or smelled) 1 perceive the smell of. 2 give off a smell. □ **smelly** adj.
■ n. 2 aroma, bouquet, fragrance, perfume, redolence, savour, scent. 3 odour, sl. pong, reek, stench, stink. □ **smelly** fetid, foul-smelling, putrid, rancid, rank, reeking, stinking.

smelt¹ see smell.

smelt² v. 1 heat and melt (ore) to extract metal. 2 obtain (metal) thus.

smelt³ n. small fish related to the salmon.

smile n. facial expression indicating pleasure or amusement, with lips stretched and their ends upturned. ● v. 1 give a smile. 2 look favourably.

smirch v. & n. discredit.

smirk n. self-satisfied smile. ● v. give a smirk.

smite v. (**smote, smitten**) (*old use*) **1** hit hard. **2** affect suddenly.

smith n. **1** person who makes things in metal. **2** blacksmith.

smithereens n.pl. small fragments.

smithy n. blacksmith's workshop.

smitten see **smite**.

smock n. loose overall.

smog n. dense smoky fog.

smoke n. **1** visible vapour given off by a burning substance. **2** spell of smoking tobacco. **3** (*sl.*) cigarette, cigar. ● v. **1** give out smoke or steam. **2** preserve with smoke. **3** draw smoke from (a cigarette, cigar, or pipe) into the mouth. **4** do this as a habit. □ **smoky** adj.

smokeless adj. with little or no smoke.

smoker n. person who smokes tobacco as a habit.

smokescreen n. thing intended to disguise or conceal activities.

smooth adj. **1** having an even surface with no projections. **2** moving evenly without bumping. **3** free from difficulties or problems. **4** polite but perhaps insincere. **5** not harsh in sound or taste. ● v. make smooth. □ **smoothly** adv., **smoothness** n.

■ adj. **1** even, flat, level, plane; glossy, satiny, shiny, silken, silky, sleek. **2** easy, effortless, steady. **3** glib, slick, suave, urbane.

smote see **smite**.

smother v. **1** suffocate, stifle. **2** cover thickly. **3** suppress.

■ **1** asphyxiate, stifle, suffocate. **2** cover, heap, pile. **3** hide, muffle, repress, stifle, suppress.

smoulder v. **1** burn slowly with smoke but no flame. **2** burn inwardly with concealed anger etc.

smudge n. dirty or blurred mark. ● v. **1** make a smudge on or with. **2** become smudged. **3** blur. □ **smudgy** adj., **smudginess** n.

■ n. blot, blotch, mark, smear, splodge, splotch, spot.

smug adj. (**smugger, smuggest**) self-satisfied. □ **smugly** adv., **smugness** n.

■ complacent, self-righteous, self-satisfied.

smuggle v. **1** convey secretly. **2** bring (goods) illegally into or out of a country, esp. without paying customs duties. □ **smuggler** n.

smut n. **1** small flake of soot. **2** small black mark. **3** indecent talk, pictures, or stories. □ **smutty** adj.

snack n. small or casual meal. □ **snack bar** place where snacks are sold.

snaffle n. horse's bit without a curb. ● v. (*colloq.*) take for oneself.

snag n. **1** unexpected drawback. **2** jagged projection. **3** tear caused by this. ● v. (**snagged**) catch or tear on a snag.

■ n. **1** catch, complication, difficulty, hitch, problem, set-back, stumbling block.

snail n. soft-bodied animal with a shell. □ **snail's pace** very slow pace.

snake n. reptile with a long narrow body and no legs. ● v. move in a winding course. □ **snaky** adj.

■ v. bend, curve, meander, turn, twist, wind, zigzag.

snakeskin n. leather made from snakes' skins.

snap v. (**snapped**) **1** (cause to) make a sharp cracking sound. **2** break suddenly. **3** speak with sudden irritation. **4** bite at suddenly. **5** move smartly. **6** take a snapshot of. ● n. **1** act or sound of snapping. **2** snapshot. **3** small crisp biscuit. ● adj. done without forethought. □ **snap up** take eagerly.

snapdragon n. plant with flowers that have a mouth-like opening.

snapper n. any of several edible sea fish.

snappy adj. (**-ier, -iest**) **1** irritable. **2** brisk. **3** neat and elegant. □ **snappily** adv., **snappiness** n.

snapshot n. photograph taken informally or casually.

snare n. trap, usu. with a noose. ● v. trap in a snare.

■ v. capture, catch, ensnare, trap.

snarl v. **1** growl angrily with teeth bared. **2** speak or utter in a bad-tempered way. **3** become entangled. ● n. **1** act or sound of snarling. **2** tangle.

snarl-up n. **1** traffic jam. **2** muddle.

snatch v. **1** seize quickly or eagerly. **2** steal, kidnap. ● n. **1** act of snatching. **2** short or brief part.

■ v. **1** clasp, clutch, grab, grasp, seize, take hold of. **2** *sl.* nab, make off with, seize, steal, take; abduct, capture, carry off, kidnap.

snazzy adj. (**-ier, -iest**) (*sl.*) stylish.

sneak v. **1** go, convey, or (*sl.*) steal furtively. **2** (*sl.*) tell tales. ● n. (*sl.*) tell-tale.

■ v. **1** creep, pussyfoot, sidle, slink, steal, tiptoe.

sneaking *adj.* persistent but not openly acknowledged.

sneer *n.* scornful expression or remark. ● *v.* show contempt by a sneer.

■ *v.* be scornful, jeer, mock, scoff.

sneeze *n.* sudden audible involuntary expulsion of air through the nose. ● *v.* give a sneeze.

snicker *v. & n.* snigger.

snide *adj.* sneering slyly.

sniff *v.* **1** draw air audibly through the nose. **2** draw in as one breathes. **3** try the smell of. ● *n.* act or sound of sniffing. □ **sniffer** *n.*

sniffle *v.* sniff slightly or repeatedly. ● *n.* this act or sound.

snifter *n.* (*sl.*) small drink of alcoholic liquor.

snigger *v. & n.* (give) a sly giggle.

■ *v.* giggle, laugh, snicker, titter.

snip *v.* (**snipped**) cut with scissors or shears in small quick strokes. ● *n.* **1** act or sound of snipping. **2** (*sl.*) bargain.

snipe *n.* (*pl.* **snipe**) wading bird with a long straight bill. ● *v.* **1** fire shots from a hiding place. **2** make sly critical remarks. □ **sniper** *n.*

snippet *n.* small piece.

snivel *v.* (**snivelled**) cry in a miserable whining way.

■ cry, grizzle, weep, whimper, whine, *colloq.* whinge.

snob *n.* person with an exaggerated respect for social position, wealth, or certain tastes and who despises those he or she considers inferior. □ **snobbery** *n.*, **snobbish** *adj.*

■ □ **snobbish** condescending, hoity-toity, pretentious, *colloq.* snooty, *colloq.* stuck-up, supercilious, superior, *colloq.* uppity.

snooker *n.* game played on a baize-covered table with 15 red and 6 other coloured balls.

snoop *v.* (*colloq.*) pry. □ **snooper** *n.*

snooty *adj.* (*colloq.*) haughty and contemptuous. □ **snootily** *adv.*

snooze *n. & v.* nap.

snore *n.* snorting or grunting sound made during sleep. ● *v.* make such sounds. □ **snorer** *n.*

snorkel *n.* tube by which an underwater swimmer can breathe. ● *v.* (**snorkelled**) swim with a snorkel.

snort *n.* sound made by forcing breath through the nose, esp. in indignation.

● *v.* **1** make a snort. **2** (*sl.*) inhale (a powdered drug).

snout *n.* animal's long projecting nose or nose and jaws.

snow *n.* **1** frozen atmospheric vapour falling to earth in white flakes. **2** fall or layer of snow. ● *v.* fall as or like snow. □ **snowed under** **1** overwhelmed with work etc. **2** covered with snow. **snowstorm** *n.* **snowy** *adj.*

snowball *n.* snow pressed into a compact mass for throwing. ● *v.* increase in size or intensity.

snowdrift *n.* mass of snow piled up by the wind.

snowdrop *n.* plant with white flowers blooming in spring.

snowman *n.* figure made of snow.

snowplough *n.* device for clearing roads of snow.

snub[1] *v.* (**snubbed**) treat (a person) contemptuously with sharp words or a lack of politeness. ● *n.* treatment of this kind.

■ *v.* cold-shoulder, cut, ignore, put down, rebuff, reject, slight, spurn.

snub[2] *adj.* (of the nose) short and stumpy. □ **snub-nosed** *adj.*

snuff[1] *n.* powdered tobacco for sniffing up the nostrils.

snuff[2] *v.* put out (a candle). □ **snuff it** (*sl.*) die.

snuffle *v.* breathe with a noisy sniff. ● *n.* snuffling sound.

snug *adj.* (**snugger**, **snuggest**) **1** cosy. **2** close-fitting. □ **snugly** *adv.*

■ **1** comfortable, cosy, homely, warm, welcoming.

snuggle *v.* nestle, cuddle.

so *adv. & conj.* **1** to the extent or in the manner or with the result indicated. **2** very. **3** for that reason. **4** also. □ **so-and-so** *n.* **1** person or thing that need not be named. **2** (*colloq.*) disliked person. **so-called** *adj.* called (wrongly) by that name. **so that** in order that.

soak *v.* **1** make or become thoroughly wet. **2** (of liquid) penetrate. **3** absorb. ● *n.* **1** soaking. **2** (*sl.*) heavy drinker.

■ *v.* **1** drench, saturate, wet; douse, immerse, souse, steep, submerge. **2** penetrate, permeate.

soap *n.* **1** substance used in washing things, made of fat or oil and an alkali. **2** (*colloq.*) soap opera. ● *v.* apply soap to. □ **soap opera** television or radio serial dealing with domestic issues.

soapstone *n.* steatite.

soapsuds *n.pl.* froth of soapy water.

soapy *adj.* **1** of or like soap. **2** containing or smeared with soap. **3** unctuous. □ **soapiness** *n.*

soar *v.* rise high, esp. in flight.

■ ascend, fly, rise, wing; escalate, increase, rocket, shoot up.

sob *n.* uneven drawing of breath when weeping or gasping. ● *v.* (**sobbed**) weep, breathe, or utter with sobs.

■ *v.* bawl, blubber, cry, howl, wail, weep, whimper.

sober *adj.* **1** not drunk. **2** serious. **3** (of colour) not bright. ● *v.* make or become sober. □ **soberly** *adv.*, **sobriety** *n.*

■ *adj.* **2** dignified, earnest, grave, restrained, sedate, self-controlled, serious, solemn, staid, steady, temperate.

soccer *n.* football played with a spherical ball not to be handled in play except by the goalkeeper.

sociable *adj.* **1** fond of company. **2** characterized by friendly companionship. □ **sociably** *adv.*, **sociability** *n.*

■ affable, companionable, congenial, convivial, friendly, genial, gregarious, outgoing, social.

social *adj.* **1** living in a community. **2** of society or its organization. **3** sociable. ● *n.* social gathering. □ **social security** state assistance for those who lack economic security. **social services** welfare services provided by the state. **social worker** person trained to help people with social problems. **socially** *adv.*

socialism *n.* political and economic theory that resources, industries, and transport should be owned and managed by the state. □ **socialist** *n.*, **socialistic** *adj.*

socialite *n.* person prominent in fashionable society.

socialize *v.* behave sociably.

society *n.* **1** organized community. **2** system of living in this. **3** people of the higher social classes. **4** mixing with other people. **5** group organized for a common purpose.

■ **1** civilization, community, culture. **4** companionship, company, fellowship. **5** alliance, association, circle, club, group, guild, organization, union.

sociology *n.* study of human society or of social problems. □ **sociological** *adj.*, **sociologist** *n.*

sock¹ *n.* **1** knitted covering for the foot. **2** loose insole.

sock² (*colloq.*) *v.* hit forcefully. ● *n.* forceful blow.

socket *n.* hollow into which something fits. □ **socketed** *adj.*

sod *n.* **1** turf. **2** a piece of this.

soda *n.* **1** compound of sodium. **2** soda water. □ **soda water** water made fizzy by being charged with carbon dioxide under pressure.

sodden *adj.* made very wet.

sodium *n.* soft silver-white metallic element.

sofa *n.* long upholstered seat with a back and raised ends.

soft *adj.* **1** not hard, firm, or rough. **2** not loud or bright. **3** gentle. **4** (too) sympathetic and kind. **5** weak, foolish. **6** (of drinks) non-alcoholic. **7** (of drugs) not highly addictive. □ **soft fruit** small stoneless fruit. **soft option** easy alternative. **soft-pedal** *v.* refrain from emphasizing. **soft spot** feeling of affection. **softly** *adv.*, **softness** *n.*

■ **1** ductile, flexible, malleable, plastic, pliant; fleecy, fluffy, furry, silky, smooth, velvety. **2** hushed, low, muffled, muted, quiet, subdued; light, pale, pastel. **3** gentle, light, mild, moderate, pleasant. **4** easygoing, indulgent, lax, lenient, liberal, permissive. □ **soft spot** affection, fondness, liking, love, partiality, penchant, predilection, weakness.

soften *v.* make or become soft or softer. □ **softener** *n.*

■ alleviate, assuage, cushion, diminish, ease, lessen, mitigate, moderate, reduce, temper; deaden, muffle, mute, tone down; appease, mollify, pacify, placate.

software *n.* computer programs or tapes containing these.

softwood *n.* soft wood of coniferous trees.

soggy *adj.* (**-ier, -iest**) sodden, moist and heavy. □ **sogginess** *n.*

soil¹ *n.* **1** loose earth. **2** ground as territory.

■ **1** dirt, earth, ground, loam.

soil² *v.* make or become dirty.

■ dirty, foul, muddy, stain.

sojourn *n.* temporary stay. ● *v.* stay temporarily.

solace *v. & n.* comfort in distress.

■ *n.* comfort, consolation, relief, support.

solar *adj.* **1** of or from the sun. **2** reckoned by the sun. □ **solar cell** device converting solar radiation into electricity. **solar plexus 1** network of nerves at the pit of the stomach. **2** this area. **solar system** sun with the planets etc. that revolve round it.

sold *see* sell.

solder *n.* soft alloy used to cement metal parts together. ● *v.* join with solder. □ **soldering iron** tool for melting and applying solder.

soldier *n.* member of an army. ● *v.* serve as a soldier. □ **soldier on** (*colloq.*) persevere doggedly. **soldierly** *adj.*

sole¹ *n.* **1** under-surface of a foot. **2** part of a shoe etc. covering this. ● *v.* put a sole on.

sole² *n.* edible flatfish.

sole³ *adj.* **1** one and only. **2** belonging exclusively to one person or group. □ **solely** *adv.*
■ **1** lone, only, single, solitary.

solemn *adj.* **1** not smiling or cheerful. **2** formal and dignified. □ **solemnly** *adv.*, **solemnity** *n.*
■ **1** earnest, grave, serious, sober, sombre, unsmiling. **2** august, ceremonial, ceremonious, dignified, formal, ritual, stately.

solemnize *v.* **1** celebrate (a festival etc.). **2** perform with formal rites. □ **solemnization** *n.*

solenoid *n.* coil of wire magnetized by electric current.

sol-fa *n.* system of syllables (*doh, ray, me,* etc.) representing the notes of a musical scale.

solicit *v.* seek to obtain by asking (for). □ **solicitation** *n.*
■ appeal for, ask for, beg, beseech, entreat, importune, petition, request.

solicitor *n.* lawyer who advises clients and instructs barristers.

solicitous *adj.* anxious about a person's welfare or comfort. □ **solicitously** *adv.*, **solicitude** *n.*

solid *adj.* **1** keeping its shape, firm, not liquid or gas. **2** without holes or spaces. **3** of the same substance throughout. **4** three-dimensional. **5** strong. **6** sound and reliable. **7** continuous. ● *n.* solid substance or body or food. □ **solidly** *adv.*, **solidity** *n.*
■ **1** firm, hard, rigid. **2** compact, dense. **3** pure, sterling. **5** firm, robust, stable, strong, sturdy. **6** dependable, reliable, sound, stalwart, staunch, steadfast; cogent, convincing, persuasive, valid. **7** continuous, unbroken, undivided, uninterrupted.

solidarity *n.* unity resulting from common aims or interests etc.

solidify *v.* make or become solid. □ **solidification** *n.*
■ clot, coagulate, congeal, harden, *colloq.* jell, set.

soliloquize *v.* utter a soliloquy.

soliloquy *n.* speech made aloud to oneself.

solitaire *n.* **1** gem set by itself. **2** game for one person played on a board with pegs.

solitary *adj.* **1** single. **2** not frequented. **3** lonely. ● *n.* recluse.
■ *adj.* **1** lone, single, sole. **2** desolate, isolated, lonely, out of the way, remote, secluded, unfrequented. **3** forlorn, friendless, lonely, lonesome.

solitude *n.* being solitary.

solo *n.* (*pl.* **-os**) **1** music for a single performer. **2** unaccompanied performance etc. ● *adj.* & *adv.* unaccompanied, alone.

soloist *n.* performer of a solo.

solstice *n.* either of the times (about 21 June and 22 Dec.) or points reached when the sun is furthest from the equator.

soluble *adj.* **1** able to be dissolved. **2** able to be solved. □ **solubility** *n.*

solution *n.* **1** process of solving a problem etc. **2** answer found. **3** liquid containing something dissolved. **4** process of dissolving.

solve *v.* find the answer to. □ **solvable** *adj.*
■ crack, decipher, figure out, resolve, sort out, work out.

solvent *adj.* **1** having enough money to pay one's debts etc. **2** able to dissolve another substance. ● *n.* liquid used for dissolving something. □ **solvency** *n.*

sombre *adj.* dark, gloomy.
■ black, dark, murky, overcast; dismal, gloomy, lugubrious, melancholy, morose, sad, serious, solemn.

sombrero *n.* (*pl.* **-os**) man's hat with a very wide brim.

some *adj.* **1** unspecified quantity or number of. **2** unknown, unnamed. **3** considerable quantity. **4** approximately. ● *pron.* some people or things.

somebody *n.* & *pron.* **1** unspecified person. **2** person of importance.

somehow *adv.* in an unspecified or unexplained manner.

someone *n.* & *pron.* somebody.

somersault n. & v. leap or roll turning one's body upside down and over.

something n. & pron. **1** unspecified thing or extent. **2** important or praiseworthy thing. □ **something like** approximately.

sometime adj. former. ● adv. at some unspecified time.

sometimes adv. at some times but not all the time.
■ from time to time, now and again, now and then, occasionally, once in a while, periodically.

somewhat adv. to some extent.
■ fairly, moderately, pretty, quite, rather, relatively, to some extent.

somewhere adv. at, in, or to an unspecified place.

somnambulist n. sleepwalker. □ **somnambulism** n.

somnolent adj. **1** sleepy. **2** inducing sleep. □ **somnolence** n.

son n. male in relation to his parents. □ **son-in-law** n. (pl. **sons-in-law**) daughter's husband.

sonar n. device for detecting objects under water by reflection of sound waves.

sonata n. musical composition for one instrument or two, usu. in several movements.

song n. **1** music for singing. **2** singing. □ **going for a song** (colloq.) being sold very cheaply.

songbird n. bird with a musical cry.

songster n. **1** singer. **2** songbird.

sonic adj. of sound waves.

sonnet n. type of poem of 14 lines.

sonorous adj. resonant. □ **sonorously** adv., **sonority** n.
■ deep, full, loud, resonant, resounding, rich.

soon adv. **1** in a short time. **2** early. **3** readily. □ **as soon as 1** at the moment that. **2** as early as. **sooner or later** at some time, eventually.
■ **1** old use anon, before long, by and by, directly, in a minute or moment, in the near future, presently, shortly. **2** early, fast, quickly, speedily. **3** gladly, happily, readily, willingly.

soot n. black powdery substance in smoke. □ **sooty** adj.

soothe v. **1** calm. **2** ease (pain etc.). □ **soothing** adj.
■ **1** appease, calm, lull, mollify, pacify, placate, quieten, settle. **2** allay, alleviate, ease, lessen, palliate, reduce, relieve.

soothsayer n. prophet.

sop n. concession to pacify a troublesome person. ● v. (**sopped**) soak up (liquid).

sophisticated adj. **1** cultured and refined. **2** complicated, elaborate. □ **sophistication** n.
■ **1** cultured, discriminating, elegant, polished, refined, suave, urbane. **2** complex, complicated, elaborate, intricate.

sophistry n. (also **sophism**) clever but perhaps misleading reasoning. □ **sophist** n.

soporific adj. tending to cause sleep. ● n. soporific drug etc.

sopping adj. very wet, drenched.

soppy adj. (**-ier**, **-iest**) (colloq.) sentimental in a sickly way.

soprano n. (pl. **-os**) highest female or boy's singing voice.

sorbet /sórbay/ n. flavoured water ice.

sorcerer n. magician. □ **sorcery** n.
■ enchanter, enchantress, magician, witch, wizard.

sordid adj. **1** dirty, squalid. **2** (of motives etc.) not honourable. □ **sordidly** adv., **sordidness** n.
■ **1** dirty, filthy, foul, seedy, sleazy, squalid. **2** base, corrupt, despicable, dishonourable, ignoble, mean, shameful, vile.

sore adj. **1** causing or suffering pain from injury or disease. **2** hurt and angry. ● n. **1** sore place. **2** source of distress or annoyance. □ **soreness** n.
■ adj. **1** inflamed, painful, raw, tender. **2** aggrieved, angry, annoyed, irked, irritated, colloq. peeved, upset, vexed.

sorely adv. very much, severely.

sorghum n. tropical cereal plant.

sorrel¹ n. sharp-tasting herb.

sorrel² adj. reddish-brown.

sorrow n. **1** mental suffering caused by loss or disappointment etc. **2** thing causing this. ● v. feel sorrow, grieve. □ **sorrowful** adj., **sorrowfully** adv.
■ n. **1** anguish, despair, distress, grief, heartache, misery, sadness, unhappiness, woe. **2** affliction, trial, tribulation, trouble, woe, worry. ● v. grieve, lament, mourn.

sorry adj. (**-ier**, **-iest**) **1** feeling pity, regret, or sympathy. **2** wretched.
■ **1** apologetic, conscience-stricken, contrite, penitent, regretful, remorseful, repentant, rueful; distressed, sad, sorrowful, unhappy. **2** miserable, pathetic, pitiful, wretched.

sort n. particular kind or variety. ● v. arrange systematically. □ **sort out 1** select from a group. **2** resolve. **3** disentangle, put into order.

■ n. brand, class, kind, make, type, variety; breed, genus, species. ● v. arrange, categorize, classify, group, order, organize, sort out, systematize. □ **sort out 1** choose, decide on, pick, select, single out. **2** fix, put right, resolve, settle, solve.

sortie n. **1** sally by troops from a besieged place. **2** flight of an aircraft on a military operation.

SOS n. **1** international code-signal of distress. **2** urgent appeal for help.

sot n. habitual drunkard.

soufflé n. light dish made with beaten egg white.

sough /sow, suf/ n. & v. (make) a moaning or whispering sound as of wind in trees.

sought see seek.

soul n. **1** person's spiritual or immortal element. **2** mental, moral, or emotional nature. **3** personification. **4** person. **5** (also **soul music**) type of black American music.

■ **1,2** psyche, spirit. **3** embodiment, epitome, essence, personification, quintessence. **4** human being, individual, mortal, person.

soulful adj. showing deep feeling, emotional. □ **soulfully** adv.

soulless adj. **1** lacking sensitivity or noble qualities. **2** dull.

sound¹ n. **1** vibrations of air detectable by the ear. **2** thing that can be heard. **3** mental impression produced by a piece of news, description, etc. ● v. **1** produce or cause to produce sound. **2** seem when heard. **3** utter, pronounce. □ **sound barrier** high resistance of air to objects moving at speeds near that of sound. **sound off** (colloq.) express one's opinions loudly.

■ v. **1** resonate, resound, reverberate, ring; blow, play. **2** appear, give the impression of, seem, strike one as.

sound² adj. **1** not diseased or damaged. **2** financially secure. **3** correct, wellfounded. **4** thorough. □ **soundly** adv., **soundness** n.

■ **1** fit, hale, healthy, undiseased, uninjured; intact, undamaged, unscathed, whole. **2** good, reliable, safe, secure. **3** correct, judicious, sensible, valid, wellfounded, wise.

sound³ v. **1** test the depth of (a river or sea etc.). **2** examine with a probe.

sound⁴ n. strait.

sounding board board to reflect sound or increase resonance.

soundproof adj. impervious to sound. ● v. make soundproof.

soup n. liquid food made from meat or vegetables etc. ● v. **soup up** (colloq.) increase the power of (an engine etc.). □ **soup-kitchen** n. place supplying free soup to the needy. **soupy** adj.

sour adj. **1** tasting sharp. **2** not fresh, tasting or smelling stale. **3** bad-tempered. ● v. make or become sour. □ **sourly** adv., **sourness** n.

■ adj. **1** acid, sharp, tart, vinegary. **2** bad, curdled, off, rancid, spoiled. **3** bad-tempered, bitter, churlish, crabby, crusty, embittered, jaundiced, surly.

source n. **1** place from which something comes or is obtained. **2** person or book etc. supplying information. **3** river's starting point.

■ **1** cause, origin, root, start.

sourpuss n. (colloq.) bad-tempered person.

souse v. **1** steep in pickle. **2** drench.

south n. **1** point or direction to the right of a person facing east. **2** southern part. ● adj. **1** in the south. **2** (of wind) from the south. ● adv. towards the south. □ **south-east** n. point or direction midway between south and east. **south-easterly** adj. & n., **south-eastern** adj. **south-west** n. point or direction midway between south and west. **south-westerly** adj. & n., **south-western** adj.

southerly adj. towards or blowing from the south.

southern adj. of or in the south.

southerner n. native of the south.

southernmost adj. furthest south.

southpaw n. (colloq.) left-handed person.

southward adj. towards the south. □ **southwards** adv.

souvenir n. thing serving as a reminder of an incident or place visited.

■ keepsake, memento, reminder, token.

sou'wester n. waterproof hat with a broad flap at the back.

sovereign n. king or queen who is the supreme ruler of a country. ● adj. **1** supreme. **2** (of a state) independent. □ **sovereignty** n.

■ n. emperor, empress, king, monarch, potentate, queen, ruler. ● adj. **1** absolute, royal, supreme. **2** autonomous, free, independent, self-governing.

sow[1] /sō/ v. (**sowed**, **sown** or **sowed**) **1** plant or scatter (seed) for growth. **2** plant seed in. **3** implant (ideas etc.). □ **sower** n.

sow[2] /sow/ n. adult female pig.

soy n. soya bean.

soya n. plant from whose seed (**soya bean**) an edible oil and flour are obtained.

sozzled adj. (colloq.) drunk.

spa n. place with a therapeutic mineral spring.

space n. **1** continuous expanse in which things exist and move. **2** portion of this. **3** empty area or extent. **4** universe beyond earth's atmosphere. **5** interval. ● v. arrange with spaces between.
   ■ n. **1** area, expanse, extent. **2** gap, interval, opening. **3** area, capacity, room. **5** duration, hiatus, interval, lapse, period, time, while.

spacecraft n. (pl. **-craft**) vehicle for travelling in outer space.

spaceship n. spacecraft.

spacious adj. providing much space, roomy. □ **spaciousness** n.
   ■ capacious, extensive, large, roomy, sizeable.

spade[1] n. tool for digging, with a broad metal blade on a handle.

spade[2] n. playing card of the suit marked with black figures shaped like an inverted heart with a small stem.

spadework n. hard preparatory work.

spaghetti n. pasta in long thin strands.

span n. **1** extent from end to end. **2** part between the uprights of a bridge etc. ● v. (**spanned**) extend across.
   ■ n. **1** extent, reach, sweep; duration, interval, period, stretch, time. ● v. bridge, cross, pass over, traverse.

spangle n. small piece of glittering material ornamenting a dress etc. ● v. cover with spangles or sparkling objects.

Spaniard n. native of Spain.

spaniel n. a kind of dog with drooping ears and a silky coat.

Spanish adj. & n. (language) of Spain.

spank v. slap on the buttocks.

spanner n. tool for gripping and turning the nut on a screw etc.

spar[1] n. strong pole used as a ship's mast, yard, or boom.

spar[2] v. (**sparred**) **1** box, esp. for practice. **2** quarrel, argue.

spare v. **1** refrain from hurting or harming, not inflict. **2** afford to give. **3** use with restraint. ● adj. **1** additional to what is usually needed or used, kept in reserve. **2** thin. ● n. extra thing kept in reserve. □ **to spare** additional to what is needed.
   ■ v. **1** let off, pardon, reprieve; protect, save. **2** afford, do without, give up, manage without, part with, relinquish. ● adj. **1** additional, auxiliary, extra, other, supplementary.

sparing adj. economical, not generous or wasteful.
   ■ careful, economical, frugal, prudent, thrifty.

spark n. **1** fiery particle. **2** flash of light produced by an electrical discharge. **3** particle (of energy, genius, etc.). ● v. give off spark(s). □ **spark(ing) plug** device for making a spark in an internal-combustion engine.

sparkle v. **1** shine with flashes of light. **2** be lively or witty. **3** (of wine etc.) effervesce. ● n. sparkling light.
   ■ v. **1** blaze, flash, flicker, gleam, glint, glitter, glow, shimmer, shine, twinkle, wink.

sparkler n. sparking firework.

sparrow n. small brownish-grey bird.

sparrowhawk n. small hawk.

sparse adj. thinly scattered. □ **sparsely** adv., **sparseness** n.

spartan adj. (of conditions) simple and sometimes harsh.

spasm n. **1** strong involuntary contraction of a muscle. **2** sudden brief spell of activity or emotion etc.
   ■ **1** convulsion, paroxysm.

spasmodic adj. of or occurring in spasms. □ **spasmodically** adv.
   ■ fitful, intermittent, irregular, occasional, periodic, sporadic, uneven.

spastic adj. affected by cerebral palsy which causes jerky, involuntary movements. ● n. person with this condition. □ **spasticity** n.

spat[1] see **spit**[1].

spat[2] n. short gaiter.

spate n. sudden flood.

spatial adj. of or existing in space. □ **spatially** adv.

spatter v. scatter or fall in small drops (on). ● n. **1** splash(es). **2** sound of spattering.
   ■ v. shower, splash, splatter, spray.

spatula *n.* broad-bladed implement used esp. by artists and in cookery.

spawn *n.* eggs of fish, frogs, etc. ● *v.* 1 deposit spawn. 2 generate.

spay *v.* sterilize (a female animal) by removing the ovaries.

speak *v.* (**spoke, spoken**) 1 utter (words) in an ordinary voice. 2 converse. 3 express by speaking. 4 know (a language).

■ 1 enunciate, pronounce, say, state, utter, vocalize, voice. 2 chat, communicate, converse, talk. 3 communicate, express, make known, verbalize.

speaker *n.* 1 person who speaks, esp. in public. 2 loudspeaker.

spear *n.* 1 weapon for hurling, with a long shaft and pointed tip. 2 pointed stem. ● *v.* pierce with or as if with a spear.

spearhead *n.* foremost part of an advancing force. ● *v.* be the spearhead of.

spearmint *n.* a kind of mint.

spec *n.* **on spec** (*colloq.*) as a speculation.

special *adj.* 1 distinctive, specific. 2 for a particular purpose. 3 exceptional. □ **specially** *adv.*

■ 1 characteristic, distinctive, individual, particular, peculiar, specific, unique. 2 exclusive, specialized. 3 exceptional, extraordinary, rare, remarkable, singular, uncommon, unusual; especial, extra, particular.

specialist *n.* expert in a particular branch of a subject.

■ authority, connoisseur, expert, professional.

speciality *n.* special quality, product, or activity.

specialize *v.* 1 be or become a specialist. 2 adapt for a particular purpose. □ **specialization** *n.*

species *n.* (*pl.* **species**) group of similar animals or plants which can interbreed.

specific *adj.* 1 particular. 2 exact, not vague. ● *n.* specific aspect. □ **specifically** *adv.*

■ *adj.* 1 distinctive, individual, particular, peculiar, unique. 2 clear, definite, exact, precise, unambiguous, unequivocal.

specification *n.* 1 specifying. 2 details describing a thing to be made or done.

specify *v.* 1 mention definitely. 2 include in specifications.

■ designate, detail, enumerate, indicate, itemize, list, spell out, state, stipulate; determine, establish, fix, settle.

specimen *n.* part or individual taken as an example or for examination or testing.

■ example, illustration, instance, model, representation, sample.

specious *adj.* seeming good or sound but lacking real merit. □ **speciously** *adv.*

speck *n.* small spot or particle.

■ bit, dot, fleck, particle, pinch, spot.

speckle *n.* small spot, esp. as a natural marking. □ **speckled** *adj.*

spectacle *n.* 1 lavish public show. 2 impressive sight. 3 ridiculous sight. 4 (*pl.*) pair of lenses set in a frame, worn to assist sight.

■ 1 ceremony, display, pageant, parade, performance, show, sight, spectacular.

spectacular *adj.* impressive. ● *n.* spectacular performance or production. □ **spectacularly** *adv.*

■ *adj.* breathtaking, dramatic, exciting, impressive, sensational, *colloq.* stunning, thrilling.

spectator *n.* person who watches a show, game, or incident.

spectral *adj.* 1 of or like a spectre. 2 of the spectrum.

spectre *n.* 1 ghost. 2 haunting fear.

spectrum *n.* (*pl.* **-tra**) 1 bands of colour or sound forming a series according to their wavelengths. 2 entire range of ideas etc.

speculate *v.* 1 form opinions by guessing. 2 buy in the hope of making a profit. □ **speculation** *n.*, **speculator** *n.*, **speculative** *adj.*

■ 1 cogitate, conjecture, meditate, muse, ponder, reflect, ruminate, theorize, think, wonder.

speculum *n.* medical instrument for looking into bodily cavities.

sped *see* **speed**.

speech *n.* 1 act, power, or manner of speaking. 2 spoken communication, esp. to an audience. 3 language, dialect.

■ 1 diction, elocution, enunciation, pronunciation. 2 address, discourse, lecture, oration, talk; monologue, soliloquy. 3 dialect, jargon, language, parlance, slang.

speechless *adj.* unable to speak because of great emotion.

speed *n.* 1 rate of time at which something moves or operates. 2 rapidity. ● *v.* 1 (**sped**) move, pass, or send quickly. 2

(speeded) travel at an illegal speed. □ **speed up** accelerate.
■ *n.* **1** pace, rate, tempo, velocity. **2** haste, promptness, rapidity, swiftness. ● *v.* **1** dash, fly, race, rush, shoot, tear, zoom. □ **speed up** accelerate, go faster, pick up speed; expedite, hasten, hurry, precipitate, quicken.

speedboat *n.* fast motor boat.

speedometer *n.* device in a vehicle, showing its speed.

speedway *n.* **1** arena for motor cycle racing. **2** (*US*) road for fast traffic.

speedy *adj.* (**-ier, -iest**) rapid. □ **speedily** *adv.,* **speediness** *n.*
■ expeditious, fast, prompt, quick, rapid, snappy, swift.

spell[1] *n.* **1** words supposed to have magic power. **2** their influence. **3** fascination.
■ **1** charm, incantation.

spell[2] *v.* (**spelt**) **1** give in correct order the letters that form (a word). **2** produce as a result. □ **spell out** state explicitly. **speller** *n.*

spell[3] *n.* period of time, weather, or activity.
■ bout, interval, patch, period, session, stint, time.

spellbound *adj.* entranced.

spelt *see* **spell**[2].

spend *v.* (**spent**) **1** pay out (money) in buying something. **2** pass (time etc.). **3** use up. □ **spender** *n.*
■ **1** disburse, expend, lay out, pay. **2** fill, kill, occupy, pass, use, while away. **3** consume, exhaust, expend, go through, use up.

spendthrift *n.* wasteful spender.

spent *see* **spend**.

sperm *n.* (*pl.* **sperms** or **sperm**) **1** male reproductive cell. **2** semen. □ **sperm whale** large whale.

spermatozoon /spérmətōzō-on/ *n.* (*pl.* **-zoa**) fertilizing cell of a male organism.

spermicidal *adj.* killing sperm.

spew *v.* **1** vomit. **2** cast out in a stream.

sphagnum *n.* moss growing on bogs.

sphere *n.* **1** perfectly round solid geometric figure or object. **2** field of action or influence etc.
■ **1** ball, globe, orb, round. **2** area, domain, field, preserve, province, speciality, subject, territory.

spherical *adj.* shaped like a sphere.

sphincter *n.* ring of muscle controlling an opening in the body.

sphinx *n.* **1** ancient Egyptian statue with a lion's body and human or ram's head. **2** enigmatic person.

spice *n.* **1** flavouring substance with a strong taste or smell. **2** thing that adds zest. ● *v.* flavour with spice. □ **spicy** *adj.*

spider *n.* small animal with a segmented body and eight legs. □ **spidery** *adj.*

spigot *n.* plug stopping the vent-hole of a cask or controlling the flow of a tap.

spike *n.* **1** pointed thing. **2** pointed piece of metal. ● *v.* **1** put spikes on. **2** pierce or fasten with a spike. **3** (*colloq.*) add alcohol to (drink). □ **spiky** *adj.*
■ *n.* **2** barb, nail, pin, point, prong, skewer, spine, spit, stake, tine.

spill[1] *n.* thin strip of wood or paper for transferring flame.

spill[2] *v.* (**spilt**) **1** cause or allow to run over the edge of a container. **2** become spilt. ● *n.* **1** spilling or being spilt. **2** fall. □ **spillage** *n.*

spin *v.* (**spun, spinning**) **1** turn rapidly on its axis. **2** draw out and twist into threads. **3** make (yarn etc.) thus. ● *n.* **1** spinning movement. **2** short drive for pleasure. □ **spin-off** *n.* incidental benefit. **spin out** prolong.
■ *v.* **1** circle, go round, gyrate, revolve, rotate, turn round, twirl. ● *n.* **1** revolution, rotation, turn, twirl. **2** drive, excursion, jaunt, outing, ride, run, trip. □ **spin out** draw out, extend, prolong, protract, stretch out.

spinach *n.* vegetable with dark-green leaves.

spinal *adj.* of the spine.

spindle *n.* **1** rod on which thread is wound in spinning. **2** revolving pin or axis.

spindly *adj.* long or tall and thin.

spindrift *n.* sea spray.

spine *n.* **1** backbone. **2** needle-like projection. **3** part of a book where the pages are hinged. □ **spine-chilling** terrifying.

spineless *adj.* lacking determination.

spinet *n.* small harpsichord.

spinnaker *n.* large extra sail on a racing yacht.

spinneret *n.* thread-producing organ in a spider, silkworm, etc.

spinney *n.* (*pl.* **-eys**) thicket.

spinster *n.* unmarried woman.

spiny *adj.* full of spines, prickly.

spiral *adj.* forming a continuous curve round a central point or axis. ● *n.* **1** spiral line or thing. **2** continuous increase or decrease in two or more quantities alternately. ● v. (**spiralled**) move in a spiral course. □ **spirally** adv.

■ n. **1** coil, convolution, corkscrew, curl, helix, whirl, whorl. ● v. coil, curl, snake, twist, wind.

spire n. tall pointed structure esp. on a church tower.

spirit n. **1** mind or animating principle as distinct from body. **2** soul. **3** ghost. **4** person's nature. **5** liveliness, boldness. **6** state of mind or mood. **7** real meaning. **8** distilled extract. **9** (pl.) person's feeling of cheerfulness or depression. **10** (pl.) strong distilled alcoholic drink. ● v. carry off swiftly and mysteriously. □ **spirit level** device used to test horizontality.

■ n. **3** apparition, ghost, phantom, spectre, colloq. spook, wraith. **4** character, disposition, nature, temper, temperament. **5** energy, life, liveliness, vitality, vivacity; boldness, courage, colloq. guts, mettle, pluck, valour. **6** atmosphere, mood, morale. **7** essence, meaning, purport, sense, tenor.

spirited adj. lively, bold. □ **spiritedly** adv.

■ bold, brave, courageous, energetic, enthusiastic, lively, sprightly, vigorous, vivacious.

spiritual adj. **1** of the human spirit or soul. **2** of the Church or religion. ● n. religious folk song of black Americans. □ **spiritually** adv., **spirituality** n.

spiritualism n. attempted communication with spirits of the dead. □ **spiritualist** n., **spiritualistic** adj.

spirituous adj. strongly alcoholic.

spit¹ v. (**spat** or **spit**, **spitting**) **1** eject from the mouth. **2** eject saliva. **3** (of rain) fall lightly. ● n. **1** spittle. **2** act of spitting.

spit² n. **1** spike holding meat while it is roasted. **2** strip of land projecting into the sea.

spite n. ill will, malice. ● v. hurt or annoy from spite. □ **in spite of** not being prevented by. **spiteful** adj., **spitefully** adv.

■ n. animosity, bitterness, ill will, malevolence, malice, rancour, resentment, spitefulness, venom. ● v. annoy, irritate, upset, vex. □ **in spite of** despite, notwithstanding, regardless of. **spiteful** colloq. bitchy, hurtful, malevolent, malicious, mean, nasty, unkind, venomous, vindictive.

spitfire n. fiery-tempered person.

spittle n. saliva.

splash v. **1** cause (liquid) to fly about in drops. **2** move or fall or wet with such drops. **3** decorate with irregular patches of colour etc. **4** display in large print. **5** spend (money) freely. ● n. **1** act, mark, or sound of splashing. **2** patch of colour or light. **3** striking display. □ **splashy** adj.

■ v. **1,2** colloq. slosh, spatter, splatter, spray, spring.

splatter v. & n. splash, spatter.

splay v. **1** spread apart. **2** slant outwards or inwards. ● adj. splayed.

spleen n. abdominal organ regulating the proper condition of the blood. □ **splenic** adj.

splendid adj. **1** brilliant, very impressive. **2** excellent. □ **splendidly** adv.

■ **1** beautiful, brilliant, dazzling, fine, glorious, gorgeous, grand, impressive, luxurious, magnificent, resplendent, spectacular, sumptuous, superb. **2** excellent, first-rate, first-rate, marvellous, outstanding, colloq. super, colloq. terrific, tremendous, wonderful.

splendour n. splendid appearance.

splenetic adj. bad-tempered.

splice v. join by interweaving or overlapping the ends.

splint n. rigid framework preventing a limb etc. from movement, e.g. while a broken bone heals. ● v. secure with a splint.

splinter n. thin sharp piece of broken wood etc. ● v. break into splinters. □ **splinter group** small group that has broken away from a larger one.

split v. (**split**, **splitting**) **1** break or come apart, esp. lengthwise. **2** divide, share. ● n. **1** splitting (up). **2** split thing or place. **3** (pl.) acrobatic position with legs stretched fully apart. □ **split second** very brief moment. **split up** end a relationship.

■ v. **1** break, cleave, crack, fracture, rupture, separate. **2** apportion, distribute, divide, halve, share; bifurcate, branch, fork. ● n. **2** break, cleft, crack, cranny, crevice, fissure, fracture, rift, rupture, slit. □ **split up** divorce, part, separate.

splodge v. & n. splotch.

splotch v. & n. splash, blotch.

■ n. blot, blotch, mark, smudge, splash, splodge, spot.

splurge n. ostentatious display, esp. of wealth. ● v. make a splurge, spend money freely.

splutter v. **1** make a rapid series of spitting sounds. **2** speak or utter incoherently. ● n. spluttering sound.

spoil v. (**spoilt** or **spoiled**) **1** make useless or unsatisfactory. **2** harm the character of (a person) by being indulgent. **3** become unfit for use. ● n. (also pl.) plunder.

■ v. **1** damage, disfigure, harm, impair, mar; destroy, mess up, queer, ruin, wreck. **2** coddle, indulge, mollycoddle, pamper. **3** decompose, go bad, go off, moulder, rot. ● n. (**spoils**) booty, loot, plunder, sl. swag.

spoilsport n. person who spoils others' enjoyment.

spoke¹ n. any of the bars connecting the hub to the rim of a wheel.

spoke², **spoken** see **speak**.

spokesperson n. person who speaks on behalf of a group.

spoliation n. pillaging.

sponge n. **1** water animal with a porous structure. **2** its skeleton, or a similar substance, esp. used for washing, cleaning, or padding. **3** sponge cake. ● v. **1** wipe or wash with a sponge. **2** live off the generosity of others. □ **sponge cake**, **pudding** one with a light open texture. **spongeable** adj., **spongy** adj.

sponger n. person who sponges on others.

sponsor n. **1** person who gives to charity in return for another's activity. **2** godparent. **3** one who provides funds for a broadcast, sporting event, etc. ● v. act as sponsor for. □ **sponsorship** n.

■ n. **3** backer, patron, supporter. ● v. back, finance, fund, subsidize, support, underwrite.

spontaneous adj. **1** acting, done, or occurring without external cause. **2** instinctive. □ **spontaneously** adv., **spontaneity** n.

■ **2** automatic, impulsive, instinctive, involuntary, reflex, unconscious.

spoof n. (colloq.) hoax, parody.

spook n. (colloq.) ghost. □ **spooky** adj.

spool n. reel on which something is wound. ● v. wind on a spool.

spoon n. **1** utensil with a rounded bowl and a handle, used for eating, serving, or stirring food. **2** amount it contains. ● v. take with a spoon. □ **spoonful** n.

spoonfeed v. (**-fed**) **1** feed from a spoon. **2** give excessive help to.

spoor n. track or scent left by an animal.

sporadic adj. occurring here and there or now and again. □ **sporadically** adv.

■ fitful, intermittent, occasional, periodic, spasmodic.

spore n. one of the tiny reproductive cells of fungi, ferns, etc.

sporran n. pouch worn hanging in front of a kilt.

sport n. **1** athletic (esp. outdoor) activity. **2** game(s), pastime(s). **3** (colloq.) sportsmanlike person. ● v. **1** play, amuse oneself. **2** wear. □ **sports car** open low-built fast car. **sports jacket** man's jacket for informal wear.

■ n. **2** activity, game, pastime.

sporting adj. **1** of or interested in sport. **2** like a sportsman. □ **sporting chance** reasonable chance of success.

sportive adj. playful. □ **sportively** adv., **sportiveness** n.

sportsman, **sportswoman** ns. **1** person engaging in sport. **2** fair and generous person. □ **sportsmanlike** adj., **sportsmanship** n.

spot n. **1** round mark or stain. **2** pimple. **3** place. **4** small amount. **5** drop. **6** spotlight. ● v. (**spotted**) **1** mark with a spot or spots. **2** (colloq.) notice. **3** rain slightly. **4** watch for and take note of. □ **on the spot 1** without delay or change of place. **2** (colloq.) compelled to take action or justify oneself. **spot check** random check. **spotter** n.

■ n. **1** blot, blotch, dot, fleck, mark, patch, smudge, speck, speckle, splodge, splotch, stain. **2** blackhead, pimple, pustule. **3** location, locality, place, position, setting, site, situation, venue. **4** bit, dash, jot, morsel, piece, pinch, scrap, touch, trace. **5** bead, blob, drip, drop, droplet, globule. ● v. **1** blot, fleck, mark, smudge, spatter, splash, stain. **2** catch sight of, descry, discern, glimpse, make out, notice, observe, see, spy.

spotless adj. free from stain or blemish. □ **spotlessly** adv., **spotlessness** n.

■ clean, immaculate, unstained, untarnished; faultless, flawless, impeccable, pure, unblemished, unsullied, untainted.

spotlight n. lamp or its beam directed on a small area. ● v. (**-lit** or **-lighted**) **1** direct a spotlight on. **2** draw attention to.

spotty adj. marked with spots.

spouse n. husband or wife.

spout n. **1** projecting tube through which liquid is poured or conveyed. **2** jet of liquid. ● v. **1** come or send out forcefully as a jet of liquid. **2** utter or speak lengthily.

> ■ *v.* **1** flow, gush, pour, shoot, spew, spurt, squirt, stream; discharge, disgorge, eject, emit. **2** declaim, expatiate, pontificate, ramble on, rant, talk.

sprain *v.* injure by wrenching violently. ● *n.* this injury

sprang *see* **spring**.

sprat *n.* small herring-like fish

sprawl *v.* **1** sit, lie, or fall with arms and legs spread loosely. **2** spread untidily. ● *n.* sprawling attitude or arrangement.

spray[1] *n.* **1** branch with its leaves and flowers. **2** bunch of cut flowers. **3** ornament in similar form.

spray[2] *n.* **1** liquid dispersed in very small drops. **2** liquid for spraying. **3** device for spraying liquid. ● *v.* **1** come or send out as spray. **2** wet with liquid thus. □ **spray-gun** *n.* device for spraying paint etc. **sprayer** *n.*

> ■ *n.* **1** mist, spindrift; sprinkle, sprinkling. **3** aerosol, atomizer, sprayer, spray-gun, sprinkler. ● *v.* **1** gush, spout, spurt. **2** shower, spatter, sprinkle, water.

spread *v.* (**spread**) **1** open out. **2** become longer or wider. **3** apply as a layer. **4** make or become widely known, felt, etc. **5** distribute, become distributed. ● *n.* **1** spreading. **2** (*colloq.*) lavish meal. **3** thing's range. **4** paste for spreading on bread. □ **spread-eagled** *adj.* with arms and legs spread.

> ■ *v.* **1** fan out, lay out, open out, unfold, unfurl, unroll. **2** broaden, enlarge, expand, extend, grow, increase, mushroom, proliferate, spread, widen. **3** apply, cover, paint, plaster, rub, smear. **4** air, announce, broadcast, circulate, disseminate, make known *or* public, pronounce, promulgate, publicize, publish. **5** distribute, scatter, sow, strew. ● *n.* **1** broadening, enlargement, expansion, extension, growth, increase, proliferation, widening; broadcasting, circulation, dissemination, promulgation. **2** banquet, feast, meal, *formal* repast. **3** extent, range, reach, scope, span, sweep.

spreadsheet *n.* computer program for manipulating esp. tabulated numerical data.

spree *n.* (*colloq.*) lively outing.

sprig *n.* twig, shoot.

sprightly *adj.* (**-ier**, **-iest**) lively, full of energy. □ **sprightliness** *n.*

> ■ active, animated, brisk, energetic, frisky, full of life, jaunty, lively, perky, spirited, spry, vigorous, vivacious.

spring *v.* (**sprang**, **sprung**) **1** jump, move rapidly. **2** issue, arise. **3** produce or cause to operate suddenly. ● *n.* **1** act of springing, jump. **2** device that reverts to its original position after being compressed, tightened, or stretched. **3** elasticity. **4** place where water or oil flows naturally from the ground. **5** season between winter and summer. □ **spring-clean** *v.* clean (one's home etc.) thoroughly. **spring tide** tide when there is the largest rise and fall of water.

> ■ *v.* **1** bounce, bound, dart, jump, leap, skip, vault. **2** arise, begin, derive, descend, issue, originate, proceed, start, stem. ● *n.* **1** bounce, bound, jump, leap, skip, vault. **3** bounce, elasticity, flexibility, resilience, springiness. **4** fountain, geyser, spa.

springboard *n.* flexible board for leaping or diving from.

springbok *n.* S. African gazelle.

springtime *n.* season of spring.

springy *adj.* (**-ier**, **-iest**) able to spring back easily after being squeezed, tightened, or stretched. □ **springiness** *n.*

> ■ elastic, flexible, pliable, resilient, stretchy, whippy.

sprinkle *v.* scatter or fall in drops or particles on (a surface). ● *n.* light shower. □ **sprinkler** *n.*

> ■ *v.* dust, dredge, powder, scatter, spray, strew.

sprinkling *n.* small sparse number or amount.

sprint *v.* & *n.* run or swim etc. at full speed. □ **sprinter** *n.*

sprite *n.* elf, fairy, or goblin.

sprocket *n.* projection engaging with links on a chain etc.

sprout *v.* **1** begin to grow or appear. **2** put forth. ● *n.* **1** plant's shoot. **2** Brussels sprout.

> ■ *v.* **1** bud, germinate; develop, grow, shoot up, spring up. **2** grow, put forth.

spruce[1] *adj.* neat, smart. ● *v.* smarten. □ **sprucely** *adv.*, **spruceness** *n.*

> ■ *n.* dapper, neat, smart, tidy, trim, well-groomed, well-turned-out. ● *v.* neaten, smarten, straighten, tidy, *colloq.* titivate.

spruce[2] *n.* a kind of fir.

sprung *see* **spring**.

spry *adj.* lively, sprightly. □ **spryly** *adv.*, **spryness** *n.*

spud *n.* **1** narrow spade. **2** (*sl.*) potato.

spume *n.* froth.

spun *see* **spin**.

spur *n.* **1** pricking-device worn on a rider's heel. **2** stimulus, incentive. **3** projection. ● *v.* (**spurred**) **1** urge on (a horse) with one's spurs. **2** incite, stimulate. □ **on the spur of the moment** on impulse.

■ *n.* **2** goad, impetus, incentive, incitement, inducement, prod, provocation, stimulation, stimulus. ● *v.* **2** drive, egg on, encourage, goad, incite, inspire, motivate, prod, prompt, provoke, stimulate, urge.

spurious *adj.* not genuine or authentic. □ **spuriously** *adv.*

■ artificial, bogus, counterfeit, fake, false, feigned, forged, fraudulent, imitation, mock, *colloq.* phoney, sham, simulated.

spurn *v.* reject contemptuously.

■ brush off, cold-shoulder, rebuff, reject, repulse, scorn, snub.

spurt *v.* **1** (cause to) gush out in a jet or stream. **2** increase speed suddenly. ● *n.* **1** sudden gush. **2** short sudden effort or increase in speed.

sputter *v. & n.* splutter.

sputum *n.* expectorated matter.

spy *n.* person who secretly watches or gathers information. ● *v.* **1** catch sight of. **2** be a spy. □ **spy on** watch secretly.

■ *v.* **1** catch sight of, descry, discern, espy, glimpse, make out, see, *colloq.* spot. □ **spy on** follow, keep under observation or surveillance, observe, shadow, *colloq.* tail, watch.

sq. *abbr.* square.

squabble *v.* quarrel pettily or noisily. ● *n.* quarrel of this kind.

squad *n.* small group working or being trained together.

squadron *n.* **1** division of a cavalry unit or of an airforce. **2** detachment of warships.

squalid *adj.* **1** dirty and unpleasant. **2** morally degrading. □ **squalidly** *adv.*, **squalor** *n.*

■ **1** *sl.* crummy, dirty, disgusting, filthy, foul, grimy, grubby, insanitary, seedy, sleazy, sordid, unpleasant. **2** degrading, dishonourable, shameful, sordid.

squall *n.* sudden storm or wind. □ **squally** *adj.*

squander *v.* spend wastefully.

■ dissipate, fritter away, misspend, splurge, waste.

square *n.* **1** geometric figure with four equal sides and four right angles. **2** area or object shaped like this. **3** product of a number multiplied by itself. ● *adj.* **1** of square shape. **2** right-angled. **3** of or using units expressing the measure of an area. **4** properly arranged. **5** equal, not owed or owing anything. **6** fair and honest. **7** direct. ● *adv.* squarely, directly. ● *v.* **1** make right-angled. **2** mark with squares. **3** place evenly. **4** multiply by itself. **5** settle (an account etc.). **6** make or be consistent. **7** (*colloq.*) bribe. □ **square dance** dance in which four couples face inwards from four sides. **square meal** substantial meal. **square root** number of which a given number is the square. **square up to 1** face in a fighting attitude. **2** face resolutely. **squarely** *adv.*

■ *n.* **2** piazza, *colloq.* quad, quadrangle. ● *adj.* **4** arranged, in order, organized, settled, straight, straightened out. **5** equal, even, level, level-pegging, on a par; quits. **6** above-board, decent, equitable, ethical, fair, honest, just, on the level, straightforward, upright. ● *v.* **5** discharge, pay, settle (up). **6** make consistent, reconcile; agree, be consistent, correspond, match, tally.

squash *v.* **1** crush, squeeze or become squeezed flat or into pulp. **2** crowd. **3** suppress. **4** silence with a crushing reply. ● *n.* **1** crowd of people squashed together. **2** fruit-flavoured soft drink. **3** (also **squash rackets**) game played with rackets and a small ball in a closed court. □ **squashy** *adj.*

■ *v.* **1** compress, crush, flatten, mash, pulp, squeeze. **2** cram, crowd, jam, pack, squeeze. **3** crush, put an end to, put down, quash, quell, stamp out, suppress.

squat *v.* (**squatted**) **1** sit on one's heels. **2** (*colloq.*) sit. **3** be a squatter. ● *n.* **1** squatting posture. **2** place occupied by squatters. ● *adj.* dumpy.

squatter *n.* person who takes unauthorized possession of unoccupied premises.

squawk *n.* loud harsh cry. ● *v.* make or utter with a squawk.

squeak *n.* short high-pitched cry or sound. ● *v.* make or utter with a squeak. □ **narrow squeak** narrow escape. **squeaky** *adj.*

squeal n. long shrill cry or sound. ● v. **1** make or utter with a squeal. **2** (sl.) become an informer.

squeamish adj. **1** easily nauseated or disgusted. **2** excessively fastidious. □ **squeamishly** adv., **squeamishness** n.
■ **1** fastidious, queasy. **2** dainty, fastidious, finicky, fussy, particular, colloq. pernickety.

squeeze v. **1** exert pressure on. **2** extract moisture in this way. **3** force into or through, force one's way, crowd. **4** obtain (money etc.) by extortion. **5** bring pressure to bear on. ● n. **1** squeezing. **2** affectionate clasp or hug. **3** small quantity produced by squeezing. **4** crowd, crush. **5** restrictions on borrowing.
■ v. **1** compress, constrict, crush, nip, pinch, press, squash, wring. **2** express, extract. **3** cram, crowd, force, jam, pack, ram, squash, stuff, wedge. **4** bleed, extort, screw, wrest. **5** lean on, pressure, pressurize. ● n. **2** clasp, cuddle, embrace, hug. **3** bit, dash, drop, spot, touch.

squelch v. & n. sound like someone treading in thick mud.

squib n. small exploding firework.

squid n. sea creature with ten arms round its mouth.

squiggle n. short curly line. □ **squiggly** adj.

squint v. **1** have the eyes turned in different directions. **2** look sideways or through a small opening. ● n. **1** squinting condition. **2** sideways glance.

squire n. country gentleman, esp. landowner.

squirm v. **1** wriggle. **2** feel embarrassment. ● n. wriggle.
■ v. **1** fidget, twist, wiggle, wriggle, writhe. **2** be embarrassed or uncomfortable, writhe.

squirrel n. small tree-climbing animal with a bushy tail.

squirt v. **1** send out (liquid) or be sent out in a jet. **2** wet in this way. ● n. jet of liquid.

squish v. & n. (move with) a soft squelching sound. □ **squishy** adj.

St abbr. Saint.

St. abbr. Street.

stab v. (**stabbed**) **1** pierce or wound with something pointed. **2** aim a blow with such a weapon. ● n. **1** act or result of stabbing. **2** sharply painful sensation. **3** (colloq.) attempt.
■ v. **1** gore, impale, knife, lance, skewer, spear, spike, transfix. **2** jab, lunge, poke, thrust.

stabilize v. make or become stable. □ **stabilization** n., **stabilizer** n.

stable[1] adj. firmly fixed or established, not easily shaken or destroyed. □ **stably** adv., **stability** n.
■ anchored, fast, firm, fixed, immovable, moored, secure, steady; enduring, established, lasting, solid, steadfast, strong, unchanging, unwavering.

stable[2] n. **1** building in which horses are kept. **2** establishment for training racehorses. **3** horses, people, etc. from the same establishment. ● v. put or keep in a stable.

staccato adj. & adv. in a sharp disconnected manner.

stack n. **1** orderly pile or heap. **2** (colloq.) large quantity. **3** tall chimney. **4** storage section of a library. ● v. **1** arrange in a stack or stacks. **2** arrange (cards) secretly for cheating. **3** cause (aircraft) to fly at different levels while waiting to land.
■ n. **1** accumulation, collection, heap, mass, mound, mountain, pile, stockpile. **2** (stacks) a lot, colloq. heaps, colloq. loads, lots, colloq. piles, plenty, quantities. ● v. **1** accumulate, amass, collect, gather, heap, pile (up).

stadium n. sports ground with tiered seats for spectators.

staff n. **1** stick used as a weapon, support, or symbol of authority. **2** the people employed by an organization. **3** (pl. **staves**) set of five horizontal lines on which music is written. ● v. provide with a staff of people.
■ n. **1** baton, cane, club, crook, mace, pike, pole, rod, sceptre, standard, stave, stick, truncheon. **2** employees, personnel, workforce.

stag n. fully grown male deer. □ **stag beetle** beetle with branched projecting mouthparts. **stag-night** n. all-male party for a man about to marry.

stage n. **1** raised floor or platform. **2** one on which plays etc. are performed. **3** (**the stage**) theatrical profession. **4** division of or point reached in a process or journey. ● v. **1** present on the stage. **2** arrange and carry out. □ **go on the stage** become an actor or actress. **stage fright**

nervousness on facing an audience. **stage whisper** one meant to be overheard.

■ *n.* **1** dais, platform, podium, rostrum. **4** juncture, period, phase, point, step; lap, leg, part, section. ● *v.* **1** mount, present, produce, put on. **2** arrange, engineer, orchestrate, organize.

stagger *v.* **1** move or go unsteadily. **2** shock deeply. **3** arrange so as not to coincide exactly. ● *n.* staggering movement.

■ *v.* **1** dodder, falter, lurch, reel, stumble, sway, teeter, totter, wobble. **2** amaze, astonish, astound, dumbfound, *colloq.* flabbergast, overwhelm, shake, shock, startle, stun, stupefy, surprise, take aback.

staggering *adj.* astonishing.

stagnant *adj.* **1** not flowing, still and stale. **2** inactive, sluggish. □ **stagnancy** *n.*

■ **1** motionless, still, unmoving; contaminated, dirty, foul, polluted, stale. **2** inactive, quiet, sluggish, static, torpid.

stagnate *v.* be or become stagnant. □ **stagnation** *n.*

■ decline, degenerate, deteriorate, *colloq.* go to pot, spoil, vegetate.

staid *adj.* steady and serious.

■ quiet, restrained, sedate, serious, sober, solemn, steady.

stain *v.* **1** be or become discoloured. **2** blemish. **3** colour with a penetrating pigment. ● *n.* **1** mark caused by staining. **2** blemish. **3** substance for staining things.

■ *v.* **1** blotch, discolour, mark, smudge, soil, spot, tinge. **2** blemish, blot, mar, sully, taint, tarnish. **3** colour, dye, paint. ● *n.* **1** blot, blotch, discoloration, mark, smudge, spot, splodge, splotch. **2** blemish, blot, taint. **3** colour, colourant, dye, paint, pigment, tint.

stainless *adj.* free from stains. □ **stainless steel** steel alloy not liable to rust or tarnish.

stair *n.* **1** one of a set of fixed indoor steps. **2** (*pl.*) such a set.

staircase *n.* stairs and their supporting structure.

stairway *n.* staircase.

stake *n.* **1** pointed stick or post for driving into the ground. **2** money etc. wagered. **3** share or interest in an enterprise etc. ● *v.* **1** fasten, support, or mark with a stake or stakes. **2** wager.

□ **at stake** being risked. **stake a claim** claim a right to something. **stake out** place under surveillance. **stake-out** *n.*

■ *n.* **1** picket, pole, post, stave, stick, upright. **2** ante, bet, wager. **3** concern, interest, investment, share. ● *v.* **1** fasten, hitch, lash, leash, picket, secure, tether, tie (up). **2** bet, gamble, wager; chance, hazard, risk, venture.

stalactite *n.* deposit of calcium carbonate hanging like an icicle.

stalagmite *n.* deposit of calcium carbonate standing like a pillar.

stale *adj.* **1** not fresh. **2** unpleasant or uninteresting from lack of freshness. **3** spoilt by too much practice. ● *v.* make or become stale. □ **staleness** *n.*

■ *adj.* **1** limp, mouldy, musty, old, sour, spoiled, wilted, withered; close, fusty, stuffy. **2** banal, clichéd, *colloq.* corny, hackneyed, platitudinous, stereotyped, trite, unoriginal.

stalemate *n.* **1** drawn position in chess. **2** drawn contest. **3** deadlock. ● *v.* bring to such a state.

stalk[1] *n.* stem or similar supporting part.

stalk[2] *v.* **1** walk in a stately or haughty manner. **2** track or pursue stealthily. □ **stalker** *n.*

■ **1** flounce, march, stride, strut, walk. **2** follow, hunt, pursue, shadow, *colloq.* tail, track, trail.

stall *n.* **1** stable, shelter for cows. **2** compartment in this. **3** ground floor seat in a theatre. **4** booth or stand where goods are displayed for sale. **5** stalling of an aircraft. ● *v.* **1** place or keep in a stall. **2** (of an engine) stop suddenly through lack of power. **3** (of an aircraft) begin to drop because the speed is too low. **4** cause to stall. **5** play for time when being questioned.

■ *n.* **1** byre, cowshed, shed, stable. **4** booth, cubicle, kiosk, stand. ● *v.* **5** delay, hesitate, hedge, play for time, prevaricate, stonewall, temporize.

stallion *n.* uncastrated male horse.

stalwart *adj.* **1** strong, sturdy. **2** dependable and loyal. ● *n.* stalwart person.

■ *adj.* **1** hale, hardy, healthy, hearty, lusty, muscular, robust, stout, strapping, strong, tough, vigorous. **2** dependable, faithful, firm, loyal, reliable, staunch, steadfast, true, unswerving, unwavering.

stamen *n.* pollen-bearing part of a flower.

stamina *n.* ability to withstand long physical or mental strain.

stammer *v.* speak with involuntary pauses or repetitions of a syllable. ● *n.* this act or tendency.

stamp *v.* 1 bring (one's foot) down heavily on the ground. 2 flatten or crush in this way. 3 walk with heavy steps. 4 press so as to cut or leave a mark or pattern. 5 fix a postage stamp to. 6 give a specified character to. ● *n.* 1 act or sound of stamping. 2 instrument for stamping a mark etc., this mark. 3 small adhesive label for affixing to an envelope or document to show the amount paid as postage or a fee etc. 4 characteristic quality. □ **stamping ground** usual haunt.

stamp out destroy, suppress by force.
■ *v.* 2 crush, flatten, press, squash, tramp, trample. 3 clump, stomp, tramp. 4 emboss, engrave, impress, imprint, mark, print. 6 brand, categorize, characterize, designate, label, mark. ● *n.* 4 characteristic(s), hallmark, mark, quality. □ **stamp out** crush, destroy, eliminate, put an end to, put down, quash, quell, repress, squash, suppress, wipe out.

stampede *n.* sudden rush of animals or people. ● *v.* (cause to) take part in a stampede.

stance *n.* manner of standing.
■ attitude, pose, position, posture, stand.

stanch *v.* stop or slow down the flow of (blood) from a wound.

stanchion *n.* upright post or support.

stand *v.* (**stood**) 1 have, take, or keep a stationary upright position. 2 be situated. 3 place, set upright. 4 stay firm or valid. 5 offer oneself for election. 6 endure. 7 provide at one's own expense. ● *n.* 1 stationary condition. 2 position or attitude taken up. 3 resistance to attack. 4 rack, pedestal. 5 raised structure with seats at a sports ground etc. 6 stall for goods. □ **stand a chance** have a chance of success. **stand by 1** look on without interfering. 2 stand ready for action. 3 support in a difficulty. 4 keep to (a promise etc.). **stand-by** *adj. & n.* (person or thing) available as a substitute. **stand down** withdraw. **stand for 1** represent. 2 (*colloq.*) tolerate. **stand in** deputize. **stand-in** *n.* deputy, substitute. **stand one's ground** not yield. **stand to reason** be logical. **stand up 1** come to or place in a standing position. 2 be valid. 3 (*colloq.*) fail to keep an appointment with. **stand up for** speak in defence of. **stand up to 1**

resist courageously. 2 be resistant to (wear, use, etc.).
■ *v.* 1 arise, get to one's feet, get up, rise, stand up. 3 place, position, prop, put, rest, set. 4 apply, hold, obtain, prevail, remain in force *or* valid. 6 abide, accept, allow, bear, brook, endure, put up with, *colloq.* stick, stomach, *colloq.* stand for, take, tolerate; experience, undergo, suffer, survive, weather, withstand. 7 buy, treat to. ● *n.* 4 frame, rack, rest; pedestal, plinth; easel, tripod. 6 booth, kiosk, stall. □ **stand by 3** back, be loyal to, defend, stand up for, *colloq.* stick up for, support, take the side of, uphold. 4 abide by, adhere to, stick to. **stand for 1** betoken, denote, indicate, mean, represent, signify, symbolize. **stand-in** deputy, locum, replacement, substitute, surrogate, understudy. **stand up to 1** brave, challenge, confront, face (up to), resist.

standard *n.* 1 thing serving as a basis, example, or principle to which others (should) conform, or by which others are judged. 2 average quality. 3 required level of quality or proficiency. 4 distinctive flag. ● *adj.* 1 serving as or conforming to a standard. 2 of normal or usual quality. □ **standard lamp** household lamp set on a tall support.
■ *n.* 1 benchmark, criterion, gauge, measure, touchstone; yardstick; archetype, exemplar, model, paradigm, pattern, type; guideline, precept, principle. 3 grade, level, rating. 4 banner, ensign, flag, pennant, pennon. ● *adj.* 2 average, conventional, customary, normal, ordinary, regular, stock, usual.

standardize *v.* cause to conform to a standard. □ **standardization** *n.*

standing *n.* 1 status. 2 duration.
■ 1 footing, place, position, rank, station, status; eminence, prominence, reputation, repute.

standoffish *adj.* cold or distant in manner.
■ aloof, cold, cool, distant, frosty, reserved, unapproachable, unfriendly, unsociable, withdrawn.

standpipe *n.* vertical pipe for fluid to rise in, esp. for attachment to a water main.

standpoint *n.* point of view.
■ angle, attitude, opinion, outlook, perspective, point of view, view, viewpoint.

standstill n. stoppage, inability to proceed.

■ halt, stop, stoppage; deadlock, impasse, stalemate.

stank see **stink**.

stanza n. verse of poetry.

staphylococcus n. (pl. -ci) pus-producing bacterium. □ **staphylococcal** adj.

staple[1] n. U-shaped piece of wire for fastening papers together, fixing netting to a post, etc. ● v. secure with staple(s). □ **stapler** n.

staple[2] adj. & n. principal or standard (food or product etc.).

star n. 1 heavenly body appearing as a point of light. 2 asterisk. 3 star-shaped mark indicating a category of excellence. 4 famous actor or performer etc. ● v. (**starred**) 1 put an asterisk beside (an item). 2 present or perform as a star actor.

■ n. 1 comet, lodestar, nova, pole star, shooting star. 2 asterisk, pentagram. 4 celebrity, luminary, personality.

starboard n. right-hand side of a ship or aircraft.

starch n. 1 white carbohydrate. 2 preparation for stiffening fabrics. 3 stiffness of manner. ● v. stiffen with starch. □ **starchy** adj.

stardom n. being a star actor etc.

stare v. gaze fixedly, esp. in surprise, horror, etc. ● n. staring gaze.

■ v. gape, colloq. gawp, gaze, glare, goggle.

starfish n. star-shaped sea creature.

stark n. 1 desolate, bare. 2 sharply evident. 3 downright. ● adv. completely. □ **starkly** adv., **starkness** n.

■ adj. 1 austere, bare, barren, bleak, cheerless, desolate, dreary, empty, grim. 2 clear, conspicuous, evident, obvious, overt, patent, plain, unmistakable. 3 absolute, complete, downright, out and out, outright, perfect, pure, sheer, thorough, total, unmitigated, utter.

starling n. noisy bird with glossy black speckled feathers.

starry adj. 1 full of stars. 2 starlike. □ **starry-eyed** adj. (colloq.) enthusiastic but impractical.

start v. 1 begin, cause to begin. 2 (cause to) begin operating. 3 begin a journey. 4 make a sudden movement, esp. from pain or surprise. ● n. 1 beginning. 2 place where a race etc. starts. 3 advantage gained or allowed in starting. 4 sudden movement of pain or surprise. □ **starter** n.

■ v. 1 begin, commence, embark on, get going, get under way, open, set about, set in motion; establish, found, inaugurate, initiate, institute, launch, originate, pioneer, set up. 2 activate, crank up, switch on, turn on. 3 depart, go, leave, move off, set off or out. 4 blench, draw back, flinch, jump, recoil, shrink back. ● n. 1 beginning, commencement, dawn, dawning, foundation, founding, genesis, inauguration, inception, initiation, institution, kick-off, launch, onset, opening, origin, outset, threshold. 3 advantage, lead. 4 jump, jolt, twitch.

startle v. shock, surprise.

■ alarm, astonish, catch unawares, frighten, jolt, scare, shock, surprise, take aback.

starve v. 1 die or suffer acutely from lack of food. 2 cause to do this. 3 force by starvation. 4 (colloq.) feel very hungry. □ **starvation** n.

stash v. (colloq.) 1 conceal in a safe place. 2 hoard.

state n. 1 mode of being, with regard to characteristics or circumstances. 2 (colloq.) excited or agitated condition of mind. 3 grand imposing style. 4 (often **State**) political community under one government or forming part of a federation. 5 civil government. ● adj. 1 of or involving the state. 2 ceremonial. ● v. 1 express in words. 2 specify.

■ n. 1 circumstance(s), condition(s), position, situation; form, order, repair, shape, trim. 2 colloq. flap, panic, colloq. stew, colloq. tizzy. 3 glory, grandeur, magnificence, pomp, splendour. 4 commonwealth, country, land, nation, realm, republic. ● adj. 1 federal, governmental, national. 2 ceremonial, dignified, formal, majestic, regal, royal, stately. ● v. 1 affirm, announce, assert, communicate, declare, express, maintain, make known, proclaim, profess, say, utter, voice. 2 define, designate, fix, set, specify.

stateless adj. not a citizen or subject of any country.

stately adj. (-ier, -iest) dignified, grand. □ **stately home** large historic house, esp. one open to the public. **stateliness** n.

■ august, ceremonial, dignified, grand, formal, impressive, majestic, noble, regal, solemn.

statement n. **1** process of stating. **2** thing stated. **3** formal account of facts. **4** written report of a financial account.

　■ **1,2** affirmation, allegation, announcement, assertion, declaration, proclamation, profession, utterance. **3** account, affidavit, deposition, report, testimony.

stateroom n. **1** room used on ceremonial occasions. **2** private cabin on a passenger ship.

statesman, stateswoman ns. experienced and respected politician. □ **statesmanship** n.

static adj. **1** of force acting by weight without motion. **2** stationary, not moving. ● n. **1** electrical disturbances in the air, causing interference in telecommunications. **2** (also **static electricity**) electricity present in a body, not flowing as current.

　■ adj. **2** immobile, immovable, inert, invariable, motionless, stagnant, stationary, still, unchanging, unmoving, unvarying.

station n. **1** place where a person or thing stands or is stationed. **2** place where a public service or specialized activity is based. **3** broadcasting channel. **4** stopping place on a public transport route. **5** status. ● v. put at or in a certain place for a purpose. □ **station wagon** (US) estate car.

　■ n. **1** location, place, position, post, site, situation, spot; base, centre, headquarters. **4** US depot, terminal, terminus; stop. **5** level, position, rank, standing, status. ● v. locate, place, position, post, put, set, site, situate, stand.

stationary adj. **1** not moving. **2** not movable.

stationer n. dealer in stationery.

stationery n. writing paper, envelopes, labels, etc.

statistic n. **1** item of information expressed in numbers. **2** (pl.) science of collecting and interpreting numerical information. □ **statistical** adj., **statistically** adv.

statistician n. expert in statistics.

statue n. sculptured, cast, or moulded figure.

　■ bust, colossus, figure, figurine, image, likeness, model, representation, sculpture, statuette.

statuesque adj. like a statue, esp. in dignity or beauty.

statuette n. small statue.

stature n. **1** bodily height. **2** greatness gained by ability or achievement.

status n. (pl. **-uses**) **1** person's position or rank in relation to others. **2** high rank or prestige. □ **status quo** existing previous state of affairs.

　■ **1** footing, level, place, position, rank, standing, station. **2** eminence, importance, pre-eminence, prestige, prominence, reputation, repute, stature.

statute n. law passed by Parliament or a similar body.

statutory adj. fixed, done, or required by statute.

staunch adj. firm in opinion or loyalty. □ **staunchly** adv.

　■ constant, dependable, faithful, firm, loyal, reliable, stalwart, steadfast, steady, true, trusted, trustworthy, trusty, unswerving, unwavering.

stave n. **1** one of the strips of wood forming the side of a cask or tub. **2** staff in music. ● v. (**stove** or **staved**) dent, break a hole in. □ **stave off** (**staved**) ward off.

stay v. **1** continue in the same place or state. **2** dwell temporarily. **3** postpone. **4** show endurance. ● n. **1** period of staying. **2** postponement. □ **stay the course** be able to reach the end of it. **staying power** endurance.

　■ v. **1** hang about, linger, loiter, remain, stop, wait; continue, keep. **2** sojourn, visit; dwell, live, lodge. **3** defer, delay, postpone, put off, suspend. **4** endure, last. ● n. **1** sojourn, visit. **2** deferral, delay, postponement, suspension.

stead n. **in a person's** or **thing's stead** as a substitute. **stand in good stead** be useful to.

steadfast adj. firm and not changing or yielding. □ **steadfastly** adv.

　■ constant, dependable, devoted, faithful, firm, loyal, stalwart, staunch, steady, true, unswerving, unwavering; determined, indefatigable, persevering, resolute, resolved, single-minded, tireless, unflagging.

steady adj. (**-ier, -iest**) **1** not shaking. **2** regular, uniform. **3** dependable, not excitable. **4** constant, persistent. ● adv. steadily. ● v. make or become steady. □ **steadily** adv., **steadiness** n.

　■ adj. **1** balanced, fast, firm, poised, secure, settled, stable. **2** consistent, constant, even, invariable, regular, uniform, unchanging, unvarying. **3** dependable, imperturbable, level-headed, reliable, sedate, sensible, serious, sober, staid, temperate, *colloq.* unflappable. **4** ceaseless, constant, continual, continuous, endless, incessant, never-ending, non-stop, perpetual, persistent, unbroken, unceasing, unremitting. ● *v.* balance, secure, stabilize; calm, compose, control, settle.

steak *n.* slice of meat (esp. beef) or fish, usu. grilled or fried.

steal *v.* (**stole, stolen**) **1** take dishonestly. **2** move stealthily. ● *n.* (*colloq.*) bargain, easy task. □ **steal the show** outshine other performers.
■ *v.* **1** appropriate, embezzle, filch, *sl.* knock off, lift, make off with, misappropriate, *sl.* nick, pilfer, *sl.* pinch, pocket, purloin, *colloq.* snaffle, *colloq.* swipe, thieve, *sl.* whip; copy, pirate, plagiarize. **2** creep, pussyfoot, sidle, slink, sneak, tiptoe.

stealth *n.* secrecy, secret behaviour.

stealthy *adj.* (**-ier, -iest**) done or moving with stealth. □ **stealthily** *adv.*, **stealthiness** *n.*
■ clandestine, covert, furtive, secret, surreptitious, undercover.

steam *n.* **1** gas into which water is changed by boiling. **2** this as motive power. **3** energy, power. ● *v.* **1** give out steam. **2** cook or treat by steam. **3** move by the power of steam. **4** cover or become covered with steam. □ **steam engine** engine or locomotive driven by steam. **steamy** *adj.*

steamer *n.* **1** steam-driven ship. **2** container in which things are cooked or heated by steam.

steamroller *n.* heavy engine with a large roller, used in road-making.

steatite /stéeətīt/ *n.* greyish talc that feels smooth and soapy.

steel *n.* **1** strong alloy of iron and carbon. **2** steel rod for sharpening knives. ● *v.* make resolute. □ **steel wool** fine shavings of steel used as an abrasive. **steely** *adj.*, **steeliness** *n.*

steep[1] *v.* soak or bathe in liquid.
■ bathe, douse, drench, immerse, saturate, soak, souse, submerge, wet; marinade.

steep[2] *adj.* **1** sloping sharply not gradually. **2** (*colloq.*, of price) unreasonably high. □ **steeply** *adv.*, **steepness** *n.*
■ **1** abrupt, precipitous, sharp, sheer. **2** dear, excessive, exorbitant, extortionate, high, stiff, unreasonable.

steeple *n.* tall tower with a spire, rising above a church roof.

steeplechase *n.* race for horses or athletes with fences to jump.

steeplejack *n.* repairer of tall chimneys etc.

steer[1] *n.* bullock.

steer[2] *v.* direct the course of, guide by mechanism. □ **steer clear of** avoid.
■ direct, guide, navigate, pilot. □ **steer clear of** avoid, circumvent, dodge, give a wide berth to, keep away from, shun.

steersman *n.* person who steers a ship.

stellar *adj.* of a star or stars.

stem[1] *n.* **1** supporting usu. cylindrical part, esp. of a plant. **2** main usu. unchanging part of a noun or verb. ● *v.* (**stemmed**) **stem from** have as its source.

stem[2] *v.* (**stemmed**) **1** restrain the flow of. **2** dam.

stench *n.* foul smell.

stencil *n.* **1** sheet of card etc. with a cut-out design, painted over to reproduce this on the surface below. **2** design reproduced thus. ● *v.* (**stencilled**) produce or ornament by this.

stenographer *n.* shorthand writer.

stentorian *adj.* (of a voice) extremely loud.

step *v.* (**stepped**) **1** lift and set down a foot or alternate feet. **2** move a short distance thus. **3** progress. ● *n.* **1** movement of a foot and leg in stepping. **2** distance covered thus. **3** short distance. **4** pattern of steps in dancing. **5** one of a series of actions. **6** level surface for placing the foot on in climbing. **7** stage in a scale. **8** (*pl.*) stepladder. □ **in step** stepping in time with others. **2** conforming. **mind** or **watch one's step** take care. **step by step** gradually. **step in 1** intervene. **2** enter. **step up** increase.
■ *v.* **1** pace, stride, tread, walk. ● *n.* **1,2** footstep, pace, stride. **5** action, initiative, measure, move. **6** rung, stair, tread; (**steps**) staircase, stairs, stairway. **7** level, stage. □ **step up** augment, escalate, increase, intensify, raise, redouble, strengthen.

step- *pref.* related by re-marriage of a parent, as **stepfather**, **stepmother**, **stepson**, etc.

stepladder *n.* short ladder with a supporting framework.

steppe *n.* grassy plain, esp. in south-east Europe and Siberia.

stepping-stone *n.* **1** raised stone for stepping on in crossing a stream etc. **2** means of progress.

stereo n. (pl. **-os**) **1** stereophonic sound or record player etc. **2** stereoscopic effect.

stereophonic adj. using two transmission channels so as to give the effect of naturally distributed sound.

stereoscopic adj. giving a three-dimensional effect.

stereotype n. standardized conventional idea or character etc. ● v. standardize, cause to conform to a type.

sterile adj. **1** barren. **2** free from micro-organisms. □ **sterility** n.

■ **1** arid, barren, infertile, unfruitful, unproductive. **2** antiseptic, aseptic, clean, disinfected, germ-free, sanitary, sterilized.

sterilize v. **1** make sterile. **2** deprive of the power of reproduction. □ **sterilization** n., **sterilizer** n.

■ **1** clean, cleanse, disinfect, fumigate, pasteurize, purify.

sterling n. British money. ● adj. **1** of standard purity. **2** excellent.

stern[1] adj. not kind or cheerful. □ **sternly** adv., **sternness** n.

■ austere, dour, forbidding, grave, grim, serious, solemn, sombre, stony, unsmiling; hard, harsh, rigorous, severe, strict, stringent, tough.

stern[2] n. rear of a ship or aircraft.

sternum n. breastbone.

steroid n. any of a group of organic compounds that includes certain hormones.

stertorous adj. making a snoring or rasping sound.

stethoscope n. instrument for listening to heart, lungs, etc.

stetson n. hat with a wide brim and high crown.

stevedore n. docker.

stew v. **1** cook by simmering in a closed vessel. **2** (colloq.) swelter. ● n. **1** dish made by stewing. **2** (colloq.) state of great anxiety.

steward n. **1** person employed to manage an estate etc. **2** passengers' attendant on a ship, aircraft, or train. **3** official at a race meeting or show etc. □ **stewardess** n. female steward on a ship etc.

stick[1] n. **1** thin piece of wood. **2** thing shaped like this for use as a support, weapon, etc. **3** implement used to propel the ball in hockey, polo, etc. **4** (colloq.) criticism.

■ **1** branch, stalk, switch, twig. **2** crook, pole, rod, staff, stake, wand; cane, walking stick; baton, club, cudgel, truncheon.

stick[2] v. (**stuck**) **1** thrust (a thing) into something. **2** (colloq.) put. **3** fix or be fixed by glue or suction etc. **4** jam. **5** (colloq.) remain in a specified place. **6** (colloq.) endure. □ **stick-in-the-mud** n. person who will not adopt new ideas etc. **stick out 1** stand above the surrounding surface. **2** be conspicuous. **stick to 1** remain faithful to. **2** keep to (a subject or position etc.). **stick together** (colloq.) remain united. **stick to one's guns** not yield. **stick up for** (colloq.) stand up for.

■ **1** dig, jab, plunge, poke, push, thrust. **2** deposit, dump, park, place, put, set, colloq. shove. **3** affix, attach, cement, fasten, fix, glue, gum, paste, solder. **4** jam, lodge, wedge. **5** linger, remain, stay. **6** abide, bear, endure, put up with, stand, stomach, take, tolerate. □ **stick-in-the-mud** conservative, fogey, sl. fuddy-duddy. **stick out 1** beetle (out), bulge (out), jut (out), poke out, project, protrude. **stick up for** defend, stand by, stand up for, support, take the side of.

sticker n. adhesive label or sign.

sticking plaster adhesive fabric for covering small cuts.

stickleback n. small fish with sharp spines on its back.

stickler n. **stickler for** person who insists on something.

sticky adj. (**-ier, -iest**) **1** sticking to what is touched. **2** humid. **3** (colloq.) difficult, unpleasant. □ **stickily** adv., **stickiness** n.

■ **1** adhesive, gummed; gluey, glutinous, colloq. gooey, gummy, tacky, viscid, viscous. **2** clammy, close, damp, humid, muggy, oppressive, steamy, sultry.

stiff adj. **1** not bending or moving easily. **2** difficult. **3** formal in manner. **4** (of wind) blowing briskly. **5** (of a drink etc.) strong. **6** (of a penalty or price) severe. ● n. (sl.) corpse. □ **stiff-necked** adj. **1** obstinate. **2** haughty. **stiffly** adv., **stiffness** n.

■ adj. **1** brittle, firm, hard, inelastic, inflexible, rigid, stiffened, unyielding; stretched, taut, tense. **2** arduous, challenging, difficult, exhausting, fatiguing, hard, laborious, onerous, tiring, tough. **3** chilly, cool, distant, formal, prim, standoffish, starchy, unfriendly. **4** brisk, forceful, fresh, gusty, strong, vigorous. **5** alcoholic, potent, powerful, strong. **6** drastic, harsh, punitive, severe, strict, stringent, tough; excessive, exorbitant, extortionate, high, colloq. steep, unreasonable.

stiffen v. make or become stiff. □ **stiffener** n.
∎ clot, coagulate, congeal, harden, set, solidify, thicken; strengthen, tauten, tighten.

stifle v. **1** feel or cause to feel unable to breathe. **2** suppress.
∎ **1** asphyxiate, choke, smother, suffocate. **2** curb, hold back, muffle, repress, restrain, silence, suppress, withhold; crush, destroy, quash, quell, stamp out.

stigma n. (pl. **-as**) **1** shame, disgrace. **2** part of a pistil.
∎ blot, discredit, disgrace, dishonour, shame, slur, smirch, taint.

stigmatize v. describe as unworthy or disgraceful.

stile n. steps or bars for people to climb over a fence.

stiletto n. (pl. **-os**) dagger with a narrow blade. □ **stiletto heel** long tapering heel of a shoe.

still¹ adj. **1** with little or no motion or sound. **2** (of drinks) not fizzy. ● n. **1** silence and calm. **2** photograph taken from a cinema film. ● adv. **1** without moving. **2** then or now as before. **3** nevertheless. **4** in a greater amount or degree. □ **still life** picture of inanimate objects. **stillness** n.
∎ adj. **1** calm, immobile, inactive, inert, motionless, peaceful, placid, quiescent, serene, static, stationary, stock-still, tranquil, undisturbed, unmoving; noiseless, quiet, silent, soundless. ● n. **1** calm, calmness, hush, quiet, peace, peacefulness, quietness, serenity, stillness, tranquillity.

still² n. distilling apparatus.

stillborn adj. born dead.

stilted adj. stiffly formal.

stilts n.pl. **1** pair of poles with footrests for walking at a distance above the ground. **2** piles or posts supporting a building.

stimulant adj. stimulating. ● n. stimulating drug or drink.

stimulate v. **1** make more active. **2** apply a stimulus to. □ **stimulation** n., **stimulator** n., **stimulative** adj.
∎ animate, arouse, encourage, excite, fire, galvanize, goad, inflame, inspire, kindle, prompt, provoke, rouse, spur, stir up, whet, whip up.

stimulus n. (pl. **-li**) something that rouses a person or thing to activity or energy.
∎ encouragement, goad, impetus, incentive, incitement, inducement, inspiration, prod, spur.

sting n. **1** sharp wounding part or organ of an insect or plant etc. **2** wound made thus. **3** its infliction. **4** sharp bodily or mental pain. ● v. (**stung**) **1** wound or affect with a sting. **2** feel or cause sharp pain. **3** (sl.) overcharge, extort money from.

stingy adj. (**-ier**, **-iest**) spending, giving, or given grudgingly or in small amounts. □ **stingily** adv., **stinginess** n.
∎ cheese-paring, close, mean, miserly, niggardly, parsimonious, penny-pinching, colloq. tight, tight-fisted.

stink n. **1** offensive smell. **2** (colloq.) row or fuss. ● v. (**stank** or **stunk**) **1** give off a stink. **2** (colloq.) seem very unpleasant or dishonest.

stinker n. (sl.) **1** very objectionable person. **2** very difficult task.

stinking adj. **1** that stinks. **2** (sl.) very objectionable.

stint v. restrict to a small allowance. ● n. allotted amount of work.

stipend /stipend/ n. salary.

stipendiary adj. receiving a stipend.

stipple v. paint, draw, or engrave in small dots. ● n. this process or effect.

stipulate v. demand or insist (on) as part of an agreement. □ **stipulation** n.
∎ demand, insist on, prescribe, require, specify. □ **stipulation** condition, demand, prerequisite, proviso, requirement, requisite, specification.

stir v. (**stirred**) **1** move. **2** mix (a substance) by moving a spoon etc. round in it. **3** stimulate, excite. ● n. **1** act or process of stirring. **2** commotion, excitement. □ **stir up** **1** mix thoroughly. **2** incite. **3** arouse, stimulate.
∎ v. **1** disturb, move, ruffle, rustle; budge, shift. **2** beat, blend, mix, stir up, whip, whisk. **3** animate, arouse, excite, galvanize, kindle, inspire, quicken, rouse, stimulate. ● n. **2** ado, bustle, commotion, disturbance, excitement, flurry, fuss, hullabaloo, hubbub, colloq. kerfuffle, to-do.

stirrup n. support for a rider's foot, hanging from the saddle.

stitch n. **1** single movement of a thread in and out of fabric in sewing, or of a needle or hook in knitting or crochet. **2** loop made thus. **3** method of making a stitch. **4** sudden pain in the side. ● v. **1** sew. **2** join or close with stitches. □ **in stitches** (*colloq.*) laughing uncontrollably.

stoat n. animal of the weasel family.

stock n. **1** amount of something available. **2** livestock. **3** lineage. **4** business company's capital, portion of this held by an investor. **5** standing or status. **6** liquid made by stewing bones, meat, fish, or vegetables. **7** plant with fragrant flowers. **8** plant into which a graft is inserted. **9** handle of a rifle. **10** cravat. **11** (*pl.*) framework on which a ship rests during construction. **12** (*pl.*) wooden frame with holes for a seated person's legs, used like the pillory. ● adj. **1** stocked and regularly available. **2** commonly used, hackneyed. ● v. **1** keep in stock. **2** provide with a supply. □ **in stock** available immediately for sale.
stock-car n. car used in racing where deliberate bumping is allowed. **stock exchange** stock market. **stock-in-trade** n. all the requisites for carrying on a trade or business. **stock market 1** institution for buying and selling stocks and shares. **2** transactions of this. **stock-still** adj. motionless. **stocktaking** n. making an inventory of stock.

■ n. **1** accumulation, cache, hoard, quantity, reserve, stockpile, store, supply; commodities, goods, merchandise, wares. **2** animals, cattle, fatstock, livestock. **3** ancestry, blood, descent, family, line, lineage, origins, parentage, pedigree. **4** assets, capital, funds. **5** reputation, standing, status. ● adj. **1** ordinary, regular, standard. **2** banal, clichéd, commonplace, conventional, *colloq.* corny, customary, hackneyed, predictable, routine, set, standard, stereotyped, trite, unimaginative, unoriginal, usual. ● v. **1** carry, handle, have, keep, sell. **2** equip, furnish, provide, supply.

stockade n. protective fence.

stockbroker n. person who buys and sells shares for clients.

stockinet n. fine machine-knitted fabric used for underwear etc.

stocking n. close-fitting covering for the foot and leg.

stockist n. firm that stocks certain goods.

stockpile n. accumulated stock of goods etc. kept in reserve. ● v. accumulate a stockpile of.

stocky adj. (-ier, -iest) short and solidly built. □ **stockily** adv.

■ beefy, burly, chunky, dumpy, sturdy, thickset.

stodge n. (*colloq.*) stodgy food.

stodgy adj. (-ier, -iest) **1** (of food) heavy and filling. **2** dull.

stoic /stṓ-ik/ n. stoical person.

stoical adj. calm and uncomplaining. □ **stoically** adv., **stoicism** n.

■ calm, forbearing, impassive, imperturbable, long-suffering, patient, philosophical, phlegmatic, resigned, stolid, uncomplaining, *colloq.* unflappable.

stoke v. tend and put fuel on (a fire etc.). □ **stoker** n.

stole[1] n. woman's wide scarf-like garment.

stole[2], **stolen** see **steal**.

stolid adj. not excitable. □ **stolidly** adv., **stolidity** n.

stomach n. **1** internal organ in which the first part of digestion occurs. **2** abdomen. **3** appetite, inclination. ● v. endure, tolerate.

■ n. **2** abdomen, belly, insides, *colloq.* tummy; paunch, pot-belly. **3** appetite, hunger, inclination, liking, relish, taste. ● v. abide, accept, bear, brook, endure, put up with, stand, *colloq.* stick, swallow, take, tolerate.

stomp v. tread heavily.

stone n. **1** piece of rock. **2** stones or rock as a substance or material. **3** gem. **4** hard substance formed in the bladder or kidney etc. **5** hard case round the kernel of certain fruits. **6** (*pl.* **stone**) unit of weight, 14 lb. ● adj. made of stone. ● v. **1** pelt with stones. **2** remove stones from (fruit). □ **Stone Age** prehistoric period when weapons and tools were made of stone.

stonemason n. person who shapes stone or builds in stone.

stonewall v. give noncommittal replies.

stoneware n. heavy kind of pottery.

stony adj. (-ier, -iest) **1** full of stones. **2** unfeeling, unresponsive. □ **stonily** adv.

■ **1** gravelly, pebbly, rocky, shingly. **2** callous, cold, hard, hard-hearted, heartless, merciless, pitiless, uncaring, unfeeling, unresponsive.

stood see **stand**.

stooge n. **1** comedian's assistant. **2** person whose actions are controlled by another.

stool n. **1** movable seat without arms or raised back. **2** footstool. **3** (pl.) faeces. □ **stool-pigeon** n. decoy, esp. to trap a criminal.

stoop v. **1** bend forwards and down. **2** condescend. **3** descend to (something shameful). ● n. stooping posture.

■ v. **1** bend, bow, duck, lean. **2,3** condescend, deign, demean oneself, descend, lower oneself, sink.

stop v. (**stopped**) **1** put an end to movement, progress, or operation (of). **2** discontinue (an action etc.). **3** effectively hinder or prevent. **4** come to an end. **5** cease from motion etc. **6** not permit or supply as usual. **7** close by plugging or obstructing. ● n. **1** stopping, being stopped. **2** place where a train or bus etc. stops regularly. **3** thing that stops or regulates motion. **4** row of organ pipes providing tones of one quality, knob etc. controlling these. □ **stop press** late news inserted in a newspaper after printing has begun.

■ v. **1** bring to a halt, bring to an end, put an end to, terminate, wind up. **2** cease, conclude, desist from, discontinue, end, finish, give up, colloq. knock off, colloq. lay off, refrain from, US quit. **3** bar, frustrate, hamper, hinder, impede, prevent, restrain, thwart; arrest, check, stanch, stem; intercept, waylay. **4** be over, come to an end, draw to a close, end, finish, fizzle out. **5** come to a halt or standstill, draw up, halt, pause, pull up. **6** discontinue, interrupt, suspend, withhold. **7** block, clog, fill, jam, obstruct, plug, seal, stuff. ● n. **1** cessation, close, conclusion, end, finish, halt, standstill, stoppage, termination. **2** depot, station, terminal, terminus.

stopcock n. valve regulating the flow in a pipe etc.

stopgap n. temporary substitute.

stoppage n. **1** stopping. **2** obstruction.

stopper n. plug for closing a bottle etc.

stopwatch n. watch that can be instantly started and stopped.

storage n. **1** storing. **2** space for this.

store n. **1** supply of something available for use. **2** large shop. **3** storehouse. ● v. **1** collect and keep for future use. **2** deposit in a warehouse. □ **in store 1** being stored. **2** destined to happen. **set store by** value greatly.

■ n. **1** accumulation, cache, collection, hoard, mine, quantity, reserve, reservoir, stock, stockpile, supply. **2** department store, hypermarket, shop, supermarket. **3** depository, repository, storehouse, warehouse. ● v. **1** accumulate, amass, hoard, collect, lay up, keep, put by, colloq. salt away, colloq. stash (away), stockpile.

storehouse n. place where things are stored.

storeroom n. room used for storing things.

storey n. (pl. **-eys**) each horizontal section of a building.

stork n. large wading bird.

storm n. **1** disturbance of the atmosphere with strong winds and usu. rain or snow. **2** shower (of missiles etc.). **3** outbreak (of anger or abuse etc.). ● v. **1** rage, be violent. **2** attack or capture suddenly. □ **stormy** adj.

■ n. **1** squall, tempest; cyclone, hurricane, mistral, tornado, typhoon, whirlwind; cloudburst, downpour, thunderstorm; blizzard, snowstorm. **2** barrage, bombardment, hail, shower, torrent, volley. **3** eruption, explosion, outbreak, outburst. ● v. **1** bluster, explode, fume, rage, rant, rave, roar, thunder. **2** assault, attack, charge, raid, rush; capture, overrun, take. □ **stormy** blustery, choppy, gusty, rough, squally, tempestuous, thundery, wild, windy.

story n. account of real or imaginary events.

■ n. account, anecdote, narrative, tale, colloq. yarn; allegory, epic, fable, fairy story or tale, folk-tale, legend, myth, parable, romance, saga; article, composition, piece; detective story, mystery, thriller, colloq. whodunit.

stout adj. **1** thick and strong. **2** fat. **3** brave and resolute. ● n. strong dark beer. □ **stoutly** adv., **stoutness** n.

■ adj. **1** solid, strong, sturdy, thick. **2** bulky, burly, corpulent, fat, overweight, plump, portly, rotund, stocky, tubby. **3** bold, brave, courageous, dauntless, fearless, gallant, intrepid, plucky, resolute, valiant, valorous; determined, firm, resolute, staunch, steadfast.

stove[1] n. **1** apparatus containing an oven. **2** closed apparatus used for heating rooms etc.

stove[2] see **stave**.

stow v. place in a receptacle for storage. □ **stow away** conceal oneself as a stowaway.

stowaway n. person who hides on a ship etc. so as to travel free of charge.

straddle v. 1 sit or stand (across) with legs wide apart. 2 stand or place (things) in a line across.

strafe v. attack with gunfire.

straggle v. 1 grow or spread untidily. 2 trail behind others in a march, race, etc. □ **straggler** n., **straggly** adj.

straight adj. 1 extending or moving in one direction, not curved or bent. 2 correctly or tidily arranged, level. 3 in unbroken succession. 4 honest, frank. 5 without additions. ● adv. 1 in a straight line. 2 in the right direction. 3 without delay. 4 frankly. ● n. straight part. □ **go straight** live honestly after being a criminal. **straight away** without delay. **straight face** not smiling. **straight fight** contest between only two candidates. **straight off** (colloq.) immediately. **straightness** n.

■ adj. 1 direct, linear, unbending, undeviating, unswerving. 2 in order, neat, orderly, organized, shipshape, tidy; even, flat, level, horizontal; erect, perpendicular, upright, vertical. 3 consecutive, successive, unbroken. 4 candid, direct, forthright, frank, honest, straightforward; decent, equitable, fair, honourable, just, colloq. on the level, trustworthy, upright. 5 neat, pure, unadulterated, undiluted, unmixed. □ **straight away** at once, directly, immediately, instantly, post-haste, right away, colloq. straight off, without delay.

straighten v. make or become straight.

■ unbend, uncurl, unravel, untwist; arrange, neaten, put in order, tidy (up).

straightforward adj. 1 honest, frank. 2 without complications. □ **straightforwardly** adv.

■ 1 candid, direct, forthright, frank, honest, plain, straight, truthful. 2 easy, elementary, simple, uncomplicated.

strain[1] n. 1 lineage. 2 variety or breed of animals etc. 3 slight or inherited tendency.

strain[2] v. 1 make taut. 2 injure by excessive stretching or over-exertion. 3 make an intense effort (with). 4 sieve to separate solids from liquid. ● n. 1 straining, force exerted thus. 2 injury or exhaustion caused by straining. 3 severe demand on strength or resources. 4 part of a tune or piece of music. □ **strainer** n.

■ v. 1 stretch, tauten, tense, tighten. 2 damage, hurt, injure, rick, sprain, twist, wrench; overburden, overtax, push, stretch, tax, try. 3 exert oneself, labour, strive, struggle. 4 filter, riddle, sieve, sift. ● n. 1 force, pressure, stress, tension. 2 injury, rick, sprain, twist, wrench. 3 burden(s), demand(s), pressure, stress. 4 air, melody, tune.

strained adj. (of manner etc.) tense, not natural or relaxed.

■ artificial, awkward, forced, laboured, stiff, tense, unnatural.

strait n. 1 (also pl.) narrow stretch of water connecting two seas. 2 (pl.) difficult state of affairs. □ **strait-jacket** n. strong garment put round a violent person to restrain their arms. **strait-laced** adj. puritanical.

straitened adj. (of conditions) poverty-stricken.

strand[1] n. 1 single thread. 2 each of those twisted to form a cable or yarn etc. 3 lock of hair.

■ 1 fibre, filament, thread. 3 lock, tress, wisp.

strand[2] n. shore. ● v. 1 run aground. 2 leave in difficulties.

strange adj. 1 unusual, odd. 2 unfamiliar, alien. 3 unaccustomed. □ **strangely** adv., **strangeness** n.

■ 1 abnormal, atypical, bizarre, curious, eccentric, exceptional, extraordinary, funny, inexplicable, kinky, mysterious, odd, offbeat, outlandish, out of the ordinary, peculiar, quaint, queer, singular, surprising, unaccountable, uncanny, uncommon, unheard-of, unnatural, unusual, weird. 2 alien, exotic, foreign, unfamiliar. 3 unaccustomed, unused.

stranger n. person new to a place, company, etc.

■ alien, foreigner, newcomer, outsider, visitor.

strangle v. 1 kill or be killed by squeezing the throat. 2 restrict the growth or utterance of. □ **strangler** n.

■ 1 choke, garrotte, throttle. 2 curb, gag, repress, restrict, stifle, suppress.

stranglehold n. strangling grip.

strangulation n. strangling.

strap n. strip of leather or other flexible material for holding things together or in place, or supporting something. ● v. (strapped) secure with strap(s). □ **strapped for** (colloq.) short of.

strapping adj. tall and robust.

strata see stratum.

stratagem n. cunning plan or scheme.
■ artifice, device, dodge, manoeuvre, plan, plot, ploy, ruse, scheme, subterfuge, tactic, trick, wile.

strategic adj. **1** of strategy. **2** (of weapons) very long-range. □ **strategically** adv.

strategist n. expert in strategy.

strategy n. **1** planning and directing of a campaign or war. **2** plan, policy.
■ **2** blueprint, plan, policy, programme, scheme.

stratify v. arrange in strata. □ **stratification** n.

stratosphere n. layer of the atmosphere about 10–60 km above the earth's surface.

stratum n. (pl. **strata**) one of a series of layers or levels.

straw n. **1** dry cut stalks of corn etc. **2** single piece of this. **3** thin tube for sucking liquid through. □ **straw poll** unofficial poll as a test of general feeling.

strawberry n. soft juicy edible red fruit with yellow seeds on the surface. □ **strawberry mark** red birthmark.

stray v. **1** leave one's group or proper place aimlessly, wander. **2** deviate from a subject. ● adj. **1** having strayed. **2** isolated, occasional. ● n. stray animal.
■ v. **1** drift, go astray, meander, range, roam, rove, straggle, wander. **2** deviate, digress, get off the subject, get sidetracked, go off at a tangent, ramble, wander. ● adj. **1** homeless, lost, strayed, vagrant, wandering. **2** accidental, chance, haphazard, isolated, lone, occasional, odd, random.

streak n. **1** thin line or band of a colour or substance different from its surroundings. **2** element, strain. **3** spell, series. ● v. **1** mark with streaks. **2** move very rapidly. **3** (colloq.) run naked in a public place. □ **streaker** n., **streaky** adj.
■ n. **1** band, bar, line, mark, striation, strip, stripe. **2** element, strain, trace. **3** patch, period, run, series, spell, stretch. ● v. **1** line, mark, stripe. **2** dart, dash, flash, fly, hurtle, race, run, rush, scoot, shoot, speed, sprint, tear, whiz, zip, zoom.

stream n. **1** small river. **2** flow of liquid, things, or people. **3** direction of this. **4** section into which schoolchildren of the same level of ability are placed. ● v. **1** flow. **2** run with liquid. **3** float or wave at full length. **4** arrange (schoolchildren) in streams. □ **on stream** in active operation or production.
■ n. **1** beck, brook, Sc. burn, US creek, river, rivulet, tributary, watercourse. **2** cascade, current, deluge, flood, flow, gush, outpouring, rush, spate, spurt, surge, torrent. ● v. **1** course, flow, glide, run, slide; cascade, flood, gush, pour, shoot, spill, spout, spurt, surge. **3** blow, flap, float, flutter, waft, wave.

streamer n. **1** long narrow flag. **2** strip of ribbon or paper etc. attached at one or both ends.

streamline v. **1** give a smooth even shape that offers least resistance to movement through water or air. **2** make more efficient by simplifying.

street n. public road in a town or village lined with buildings. □ **street credibility** familiarity with a fashionable urban subculture.
■ avenue, boulevard, byway, crescent, cul-de-sac, lane, road, thoroughfare.

strength n. **1** quality of being strong. **2** its intensity. **3** advantageous skill or quality. **4** total number of people making up a group. □ **on the strength of** relying on as a basis or support.
■ **1** brawn, durability, endurance, force, might, mightiness, muscle, power, resilience, robustness, sinews, stamina, sturdiness, toughness, vigour; courage, firmness, fortitude, colloq. grit, colloq. guts, nerve, perseverance, pertinacity, resoluteness, resolution, tenacity, will-power; concentration, intensity, potency; cogency, efficacy, persuasiveness, weight. **3** advantage, asset, strong point, virtue.

strengthen v. make or become stronger.
■ bolster, brace, buttress, fortify, reinforce, shore up, toughen; heighten, increase, intensify, step up; boost, encourage, hearten, invigorate, rejuvenate, restore, revive; back up, confirm, corroborate, substantiate, support.

strenuous adj. making or requiring great effort. □ **strenuously** adv., **strenuousness** n.
■ active, determined, dogged, energetic, indefatigable, tenacious, tireless, unflagging, vigorous, zealous; arduous, demanding, difficult, hard, exhausting, gruelling, laborious, taxing, tiring, toilsome, tough.

streptococcus n. (pl. **-ci**) bacterium causing serious infections.

stress *n.* **1** emphasis. **2** extra force used on a sound in speech or music. **3** pressure or tension exerted on an object **4** physical or mental strain. ● *v.* lay stress on.

■ *n.* **1** emphasis, importance, weight. **2** accent, accentuation, emphasis. **3** pressure, strain, tension. **4** anxiety, distress, pressure, strain, tension, trauma, worry. ● *v.* accent, accentuate, dwell on, emphasize, feature, highlight, point up, spotlight, underline.

stretch *v.* **1** pull out tightly or to a greater extent. **2** be able or tend to become stretched. **3** be continuous. **4** thrust out one's limbs. **5** strain. **6** exaggerate. ● *n.* **1** stretching. **2** ability to be stretched. **3** continuous expanse or period. ● *adj.* able to be stretched. □ **stretch a point** agree to something not normally allowed. **stretch out 1** extend (a limb etc.). **2** prolong. **3** relax by lying at full length. **stretchy** *adj.*

■ *v.* **1** draw *or* pull out, elongate, lengthen, widen; make taut, tense, tighten. **3** extend, range, reach, spread. **5** overburden, overtax, push, strain, tax. **6** exaggerate, overstate. ● *n.* **3** area, expanse, extent, range, reach, spread, sweep, tract; period, run, spell, stint. □ **stretch out 1** extend, hold out, outstretch, reach out. **2** draw out, extend, lengthen, prolong, protract, spin out. **3** lie (down), lounge, recline, sprawl.

stretcher *n.* framework for carrying a sick or injured person in a lying position.

strew *v.* (**strewed**, **strewn** *or* **strewed**) **1** scatter over a surface. **2** cover with scattered things.

striation *n.* each of a series of lines or grooves.

stricken *adj.* afflicted by an illness, shock, or grief.

strict *adj.* **1** precisely limited or defined. **2** without exception, complete. **3** requiring complete obedience or exactitude. □ **strictly** *adv.*, **strictness** *n.*

■ **1** accurate, exact, literal, precise, rigid. **2** absolute, complete, perfect, total, utter. **3** authoritarian, hard, harsh, inflexible, rigorous, severe, stern, stringent, tough, uncompromising.

stricture *n.* **1** severe criticism. **2** abnormal constriction.

stride *v.* (**strode**, **stridden**) walk with long steps. ● *n.* **1** single long step. **2**

manner of striding. **3** (usu. in *pl.*) progress.

strident *adj.* loud and harsh. □ **stridently** *adv.*, **stridency** *n.*

■ discordant, grating, harsh, jarring, loud, noisy, rasping, raucous, screeching, shrill, unmelodious, unmusical.

strife *n.* quarrelling, conflict.

■ animosity, antagonism, arguing, bickering, conflict, disagreement, discord, disharmony, dissension, enmity, friction, hostility, ill will, quarrelling, squabbling.

strike *v.* (**struck**) **1** hit. **2** come or bring sharply into contact with. **3** attack suddenly. **4** (of a disease) afflict. **5** ignite (a match) by friction. **6** agree on (a bargain). **7** indicate (the hour) or be indicated by a sound. **8** find (oil etc.) by drilling. **9** occur to the mind, produce a mental impression on. **10** take down (a flag or tent etc.). **11** stop work in protest. **12** assume (an attitude) dramatically. ● *n.* **1** act or instance of striking. **2** attack. **3** workers' refusal to work as a protest. □ **on strike** taking part in an industrial strike. **strike home** deal an effective blow. **strike out** cross out. **strike up 1** begin playing or singing. **2** start (a friendship etc.) casually.

■ *v.* **1** bash, *sl.* belt, *sl.* biff, *sl.* clobber, clout, cuff, hit, punch, rap, slap, smack, *old use* smite, spank, thump, thwack, *sl.* wallop, *colloq.* whack; batter, beat, hammer, pound. **2** bang into, bump into, collide with, crash into, dash against, hit, knock, run into. **3** assault, attack, storm. **4** affect, afflict, attack, hit. **5** ignite, light. **6** agree (on), conclude, make, reach, settle (on). **7** chime, sound. **9** come to, dawn on, occur to. **10** let down, lower, take down; dismantle. **11** go on strike, stop work, walk out. **12** affect, assume, display. ● *n.* **1** assault, attack, blitz, incursion, invasion, offensive, onslaught, raid, sortie. □ **strike out** blot out, cross out, delete, erase, obliterate, rub out, score out.

strikebound *adj.* immobilized by a workers' strike.

striker *n.* **1** person or thing that strikes. **2** worker who is on strike. **3** footballer whose main function is to try to score goals.

striking *adj.* **1** sure to be noticed. **2** impressive. □ **strikingly** *adv.*

■ **1** conspicuous, marked, noticeable, salient, prominent, unmistakable. **2** imposing, impressive, magnificent, marvellous, outstanding, remarkable, splendid, stunning, superb, wonderful.

string n. 1 narrow cord. 2 stretched piece of catgut or wire etc. in a musical instrument, vibrated to produce tones. 3 set of things strung together. 4 series of people or things. 5 (pl.) conditions insisted upon. 6 (pl.) stringed instruments in an orchestra etc. ● v. (**strung**) 1 fit or fasten with string(s). 2 thread on a string. □ **pull strings** use one's influence. **string along** (colloq.) 1 deceive. 2 go along (with). **string out** spread out on a line. **string up** 1 hang up on string. 2 kill by hanging. 3 make tense.
■ n. 1 cord, thread, twine; lace, thong, tie; lead, leash. 4 chain, column, concatenation, file, line, procession, queue, row, sequence, series, succession, train.

stringent adj. strict, with firm restrictions. □ **stringently** adv., **stringency** n.

stringy adj. 1 like string. 2 fibrous, tough.

strip[1] v. (**stripped**) 1 remove (clothes, coverings, or parts etc.). 2 pull or tear away (from). 3 undress. 4 deprive, e.g. of property or titles. □ **stripper** n.
■ 1 unclothe, undress; excoriate, flay, peel, skin; defoliate; dismantle, take apart, take to pieces. 2 peel off, remove, take off. 3 disrobe, get undressed, remove or take off one's clothes, undress (oneself). 4 deprive, dispossess, divest.

strip[2] n. long narrow piece or area. □ **comic strip, strip cartoon** sequence of cartoons. **strip light** tubular fluorescent lamp.
■ band, bar, belt, ribbon, sliver, stripe, swath.

stripe n. 1 long narrow band on a surface, differing in colour or texture from its surroundings. 2 chevron on a sleeve, indicating rank. □ **striped** adj., **stripy** adj.
■ 1 band, bar, line, streak, striation, strip.

stripling n. a youth.

striptease n. entertainment in which a performer gradually undresses.

strive v. (**strove, striven**) 1 make great efforts. 2 struggle or contend.
■ 1 attempt, endeavour, exert oneself, make an effort, seek, strain, struggle, take pains, try, work. 2 battle, compete, contend, fight, struggle.

strobe n. (colloq.) stroboscope.

stroboscope n. apparatus for producing a rapidly flashing bright light. □ **stroboscopic** adj.

strode see **stride**.

stroke[1] n. 1 act of striking something. 2 single movement, action, or effort. 3 particular sequence of movements (e.g. in swimming). 4 mark made by a movement of a pen or paintbrush etc. 5 sound made by a clock striking. 6 sudden loss of ability to feel and move, caused by rupture or blockage of the brain artery.
■ 1 blow, hit, knock, rap, slap, smack, colloq. swipe, tap, thump, thwack, sl. wallop, colloq. whack.

stroke[2] v. pass the hand gently along the surface of. ● n. act of stroking.
■ v. caress, fondle, pat, pet.

stroll v. & n. walk in a leisurely way. □ **stroller** n.
■ v. & n. amble, meander, saunter, ramble, walk, wander.

strong adj. 1 capable of exerting or resisting great power. 2 powerful in numbers, resources, etc. 3 (of emotions, opinons, etc.) firmly held. 4 forceful or powerful in effect. 5 having a great effect on the senses, intense. 6 concentrated, containing much alcohol. 7 having a specified number of members. ● adv. strongly. □ **strong language** forcible language, swearing. **strong-minded** adj. determined. **strongly** adv.
■ adj. 1 durable, hard-wearing, indestructible, solid, stout, sturdy, substantial, tough, unbreakable; brawny, burly, hardy, husky, lusty, mighty, muscular, powerful, resilient, robust, sinewy, stalwart, strapping, vigorous, wiry; fit, hale, healthy, well. 2 formidable, great, mighty, powerful, redoubtable. 3 decided, definite, deep, earnest, fervent, fierce, firm, heartfelt, intense, keen, passionate, profound, unshakeable, unwavering, vehement. 4 forceful, influential, powerful, vigorous; cogent, compelling, convincing, persuasive, potent, weighty. 5 bright, dazzling, glaring, intense, vivid; acrid, piquant, pungent, sharp, spicy. 6 concentrated, undiluted; alcoholic, stiff.

stronghold n. 1 fortified place. 2 centre of support for a cause.

strongroom n. room designed for safe storage of valuables.

strontium *n.* silver-white metallic element. □ **strontium 90** its radioactive isotope.

strove *see* **strive**.

struck *see* **strike**.

structure *n.* **1** constructed unit. **2** way a thing is constructed, organized, etc. □ **structural** *adj.*, **structurally** *adv.*
■ **1** building, construction, edifice. **2** arrangement, composition, configuration, construction, design, form, formation, make-up, organization, shape.

struggle *v.* **1** make vigorous efforts to get free. **2** make great efforts under difficulties. **3** fight strenuously. **4** make one's way with difficulty. ● *n.* **1** act or spell of struggling. **2** vigorous effort. □ **struggle along** or **on** manage to survive in spite of difficulties.
■ *v.* **1,2** attempt, endeavour, exert oneself, labour, strain, strive, toil, try, wrestle. **3** battle, contend, fight, grapple, wrestle; scuffle, tussle. **4** flounder, scramble, toil. ● *n.* **1** battle, competition, contest, fight, scrimmage, scuffle, tussle. **2** effort, endeavour, exertion, travail.

strum *v.* (**strummed**) play unskilfully or monotonously on (a musical instrument). ● *n.* sound made by strumming.

strung *see* **string**.

strut *n.* **1** bar of wood or metal supporting something. **2** strutting walk. ● *v.* (**strutted**) walk in a pompous self-satisfied way.

strychnine /strikneen/ *n.* bitter highly poisonous substance.

stub *n.* **1** short stump. **2** counterfoil of a cheque or receipt etc. ● *v.* (**stubbed**) strike (one's toe) against a hard object. □ **stub out** extinguish (a cigarette) by pressure.

stubble *n.* **1** cut stalks of corn left in the ground after harvest. **2** short stiff hair, esp. on an unshaven face. □ **stubbly** *adj.*

stubborn *adj.* obstinate. □ **stubbornly** *adv.*, **stubbornness** *n.*
■ adamant, *colloq.* bloody-minded, headstrong, inflexible, intractable, intransigent, obdurate, obstinate, persistent, pertinacious, pigheaded, recalcitrant, refractory, self-willed, stiff-necked, uncompromising, uncooperative, unyielding, wilful.

stubby *adj.* (**-ier, -iest**) short and thick. □ **stubbiness** *n.*

stucco *n.* plaster or cement for coating walls or moulding into decorations. □ **stuccoed** *adj.*

stuck *see* **stick²**. *adj.* unable to move. □ **stuck-up** *adj.* (*colloq.*) **1** conceited. **2** snobbish.

stud¹ *n.* **1** projecting nail-head or similar knob on a surface. **2** device for fastening e.g. a detachable shirt-collar. ● *v.* (**studded**) **1** decorate with studs or precious stones. **2** strengthen with studs.

stud² *n.* **1** horses kept for breeding. **2** place keeping these.

student *n.* person engaged in studying something, esp. at a college or university.
■ fresher, undergraduate; pupil, scholar, schoolboy, schoolchild, schoolgirl; apprentice, trainee.

studied *adj.* deliberate and artificial.
■ affected, calculated, conscious, contrived, feigned, forced, intentional, purposeful, wilful.

studio *n.* (*pl.* **-os**) **1** workroom of a painter, photographer, etc. **2** place for making films, recordings, or broadcasts. □ **studio flat** one-room flat with a kitchen and bathroom.

studious *adj.* **1** spending much time in study. **2** deliberate and careful. □ **studiously** *adv.*, **studiousness** *n.*
■ **1** academic, bookish, scholarly. **2** assiduous, careful, deliberate, diligent, industrious, meticulous, painstaking, sedulous, thorough.

study *n.* **1** process of acquiring information etc., esp. from books. **2** work presenting the results of studying. **3** investigation of a subject. **4** musical composition designed to develop a player's skill. **5** preliminary drawing. **6** room used for studying. ● *v.* **1** give one's attention to acquiring knowledge of (a subject). **2** examine attentively.
■ *n.* **1** cramming, learning, reading, research, *colloq.* swotting, work. **2** dissertation, essay, paper, thesis. **3** analysis, examination, exploration, investigation, review, survey. **5** drawing, sketch. **6** den, library. ● *v.* **1** learn (about), read; cram, revise, *colloq.* swot. **2** analyse, examine, explore, go over, inquire into, inspect, investigate, look into, monitor, observe, scrutinize, survey; look at, peruse, pore over, read, scan.

stuff *n.* **1** material. **2** unnamed things, belongings, subjects, etc. ● *v.* **1** pack tightly. **2** force or cram (a thing). **3** eat greedily.

■ *n.* **1** fabric, material, matter, substance. **2** articles, objects, things; accessories, accoutrements, belongings, *sl.* clobber, effects, equipment, gear, kit, paraphernalia, possessions, property, tackle, trappings. ● *v.* **1** fill, pack, pad. **2** cram, force, jam, press, ram, shove, squash, squeeze, thrust, wedge. **3** gobble, gorge, overeat, scoff.

stuffing *n.* **1** padding used to fill something. **2** mixture put inside poultry etc., before cooking.

stuffy *adj.* (-ier, -iest) **1** lacking fresh air or ventilation. **2** dull. **3** (*colloq.*) prim, narrow-minded. □ **stuffily** *adv.*, **stuffiness** *n.*

■ **1** airless, close, frowzy, fuggy, fusty, oppressive, stale, stifling, suffocating, unventilated. **2** boring, dreary, dull, tedious, uninteresting. **3** conventional, *sl.* fuddy-duddy, narrow-minded, old-fashioned, priggish, prim, prudish, strait-laced.

stultify *v.* impair, make ineffective. □ **stultification** *n.*

stumble *v.* **1** trip and lose one's balance. **2** walk with frequent stumbles. **3** make mistakes in speaking etc. ● *n.* act of stumbling. □ **stumbling block** obstacle, difficulty.

■ *v.* **1** fall, lose one's balance, slip, trip. **2** falter, lurch, stagger, teeter, totter. **3** blunder, falter, stammer, stutter. □ **stumbling block** bar, barrier, hindrance, hurdle, impediment, obstacle, obstruction; catch, difficulty, drawback, hitch, snag.

stump *n.* **1** base of a tree left in the ground when the rest has gone. **2** similar remnant of something cut, broken, or worn down. **3** one of the uprights of a wicket in cricket. ● *v.* **1** walk stiffly or noisily. **2** (*colloq.*) baffle. □ **stump up** (*colloq.*) pay over (money required).

stumpy *adj.* (-ier, -iest) short and thick. □ **stumpiness** *n.*

stun *v.* (**stunned**) **1** knock senseless. **2** astound.

■ **1** daze, knock out, stupefy. **2** amaze, astonish, astound, bowl over, dumbfound, *colloq.* flabbergast, overcome, overwhelm, shock, stagger, stupefy, transfix.

stung see **sting**.

stunk see **stink**.

stunner *n.* (*colloq.*) stunning person or thing.

stunning *adj.* (*colloq.*) very impressive or attractive. □ **stunningly** *adv.*

stunt[1] *v.* hinder the growth or development of.

■ hamper, hinder, impede, inhibit, retard, slow (down).

stunt[2] *n.* something unusual or difficult done as a performance.

stupefy *v.* **1** dull the wits or senses of. **2** stun. □ **stupefaction** *n.*

stupendous *adj.* **1** amazing. **2** exceedingly great. □ **stupendously** *adv.*

■ **1** amazing, astonishing, astounding, breathtaking, extraordinary, marvellous, miraculous, phenomenal, remarkable, staggering, wonderful. **2** colossal, enormous, gigantic, huge, immense, massive, prodigious.

stupid *adj.* **1** not clever or intelligent. **2** showing lack of good judgement. **3** in a stupor. □ **stupidly** *adv.*, **stupidity** *n.*

■ **1** bovine, brainless, dense, *colloq.* dim, doltish, dopey, dull, *colloq.* dumb, foolish, obtuse, *colloq.* thick, unintelligent, witless. **2** absurd, asinine, *sl.* barmy, *sl.* batty, *colloq.* crack-brained, crazy, daft, fatuous, foolhardy, foolish, hare-brained, idiotic, ill-advised, imprudent, inane, insane, laughable, ludicrous, lunatic, mad, mindless, nonsensical, ridiculous, risible, senseless, silly, unthinking, unwise, wild. **3** dazed, insensible, stunned, stupefied, unconscious.

stupor *n.* dazed almost unconscious condition.

sturdy *adj.* (-ier, -iest) **1** strongly built, hardy, **2** vigorous and determined. □ **sturdily** *adv.*, **sturdiness** *n.*

■ **1** durable, solid, sound, strong, stout, substantial, tough, well-made; brawny, burly, hardy, husky, muscular, powerful, robust, stocky, strapping. **2** determined, firm, resolute, stalwart, staunch, steadfast, unswerving, unwavering, vigorous.

sturgeon *n.* (*pl.* **sturgeon**) large shark-like fish yielding caviare.

stutter *v.* & *n.* stammer.

sty[1] *n.* pigsty.

sty[2] *n.* inflamed swelling on the edge of the eyelid.

style *n.* **1** manner of writing, speaking, or doing something. **2** design. **3** elegance. **4** fashion in dress etc. ● *v.* design, shape, or arrange, esp. fashionably. □ **in style** elegantly, luxuriously.

■ *n.* **1** approach, manner, method, technique, way; phraseology, wording. **2** cut, design, genre, kind, make, manner, sort, type, variety. **3** chic, elegance, panache, polish, sophistication, stylishness, taste, tastefulness.. **4** craze, fad, fashion, mode, trend, vogue. ● *v.* arrange, cut, design, make, shape, tailor.

stylish *adj.* fashionable, elegant. □ **stylishly** *adv.,* **stylishness** *n.*
■ chic, dapper, dressy, elegant, fashionable, modish, smart, snappy, *sl.* snazzy, *colloq.* trendy.

stylist *n.* **1** person who has a good style. **2** person who styles things.

stylistic *adj.* of literary or artistic style. □ **stylistically** *adv.*

stylized *adj.* painted, drawn, etc. in a conventional style.

stylus *n.* (*pl.* **-uses** or **-li**) needle-like device for cutting or following a groove in a record.

stymie *v.* (**stymieing**) thwart.

styptic *adj.* checking bleeding by causing blood vessels to contract.

suave /swaav/ *adj.* smooth-mannered, polite, sophisticated. □ **suavely** *adv.,* **suavity** *n.*
■ charming, courteous, civilized, cultivated, debonair, gracious, polished, polite, smooth-mannered, sophisticated, urbane.

sub *n.* (*colloq.*) **1** submarine. **2** subscription. **3** substitute.

sub- *pref.* **1** under. **2** subordinate.

subaltern *n.* army officer below the rank of captain.

subatomic *adj.* **1** smaller than an atom. **2** occurring in an atom.

subcommittee *n.* committee formed from some members of a main committee.

subconscious *adj.* & *n.* (of) our own mental activities of which we are not aware. □ **subconsciously** *adv.*
■ *adj.* hidden, latent, repressed, subliminal, suppressed, unconscious; instinctive, intuitive.

subcontinent *n.* large land mass forming part of a continent.

subcontract *v.* give or accept a contract to carry out all or part of another contract. □ **subcontractor** *n.*

subculture *n.* culture within a larger one.

subcutaneous *adj.* under the skin.

subdivide *v.* divide (a part) into smaller parts. □ **subdivision** *n.*

subdue *v.* **1** bring under control. **2** make quieter or less intense.
■ **1** conquer, control, crush, defeat, gain the upper hand over, get the better of, master, overpower, put down, quash, quell, repress, subjugate, suppress, tame, triumph over, vanquish. **2** moderate, mute, quieten, soften, temper, tone down.

subhuman *adj.* **1** less than human. **2** not fully human.

subject¹ /súbjikt/ *adj.* not politically independent. ● *n.* **1** person subject to a particular political rule or ruler. **2** person or thing being discussed or studied. **3** word(s) in a sentence that name who or what does the action of the verb. □ **subject-matter** *n.* matter treated in a book or speech etc. **subject to 1** conditional on. **2** liable or exposed to. **subjection** *n.*
■ *n.* **1** citizen, national. **2** guinea-pig, patient; subject-matter, topic; area, course of study, discipline, field. □ **subject to 1** conditional on, contingent on, dependent on. **2** at the mercy of, exposed to, liable to, open to, prone to, susceptible to, vulnerable to.

subject² /səbjékt/ *v.* subjugate. □ **subject to** cause to undergo.

subjective *adj.* dependent on personal taste or views etc. □ **subjectively** *adv.*
■ idiosyncratic, individual, personal; biased, partial, prejudiced.

subjugate *v.* conquer, bring into subjection. □ **subjugation** *n.*
■ conquer, crush, enslave, master, overpower, quash, subdue, subject, suppress, vanquish.

sublet *v.* (**sublet, subletting**) let (rooms etc. that one holds by lease) to a tenant.

sublimate *v.* divert the energy of (an emotion or impulse) into a culturally higher activity. □ **sublimation** *n.*

sublime *adj.* of the most admirable kind, causing awe and reverence. □ **sublimely** *adv.,* **sublimity** *n.*
■ awe-inspiring, exalted, glorious, great, lofty, magnificent, majestic, noble, splendid, transcendent.

subliminal *adj.* below the level of conscious awareness.

sub-machine-gun *n.* lightweight machine-gun held in the hand.

submarine *adj.* under the surface of the sea. ● *n.* vessel that can operate under water.

submerge v. **1** put or go below the surface of water or other liquid. **2** flood. □ **submersion** n.

■ **1** dip, douse, dunk, immerse, soak, steep; descend, dive, plummet, plunge, sink. **2** bury, deluge, drown, engulf, flood, inundate, overwhelm, swamp.

submersible adj. able to submerge. ● n. submersible craft.

submission n. **1** submitting. **2** thing submitted. **3** obedience.

■ **1** acquiescence, capitulation, concession, giving in, surrender, yielding. **2** application, presentation, proposal, proposition, suggestion, tender. **3** compliance, deference, docility, meekness, obedience, passivity, submissiveness, timidity, tractability.

submissive adj. humble, obedient. □ **submissively** adv., **submissiveness** n.

■ acquiescent, amenable, biddable, compliant, deferential, docile, humble, malleable, meek, obedient, passive, timid, tractable, unassertive, yielding; ingratiating, obsequious, servile, slavish, subservient, sycophantic.

submit v. (**submitted**) **1** yield to authority or control, surrender. **2** present for consideration. □ **submit to** subject to a process.

■ **1** bow, capitulate, cave in, give in or up or way, knuckle under, succumb, surrender, throw in the towel, yield; accede, agree, comply, concede, consent. **2** advance, offer, present, proffer, propose, put forward; hand or send in.

subordinate adj. /səbórdinət/ of lesser importance or rank. ● n. /səbórdinət/ person working under another's authority. ● v. /səbórdinayt/ make or treat as subordinate. □ **subordination** n.

■ adj. minor, secondary, subsidiary; inferior, junior, lesser, lower. ● n. aide, assistant, junior; inferior, derog. minion, servant, underling.

suborn v. induce by bribery to commit perjury or other crime.

subpoena /səbpeena/ n. writ ordering a person to appear in a law court. ● v. (**subpoenaed**) serve a subpoena on.

subscribe v. **subscribe to 1** pay (a specified sum) for membership of an organization or receipt of a publication. **2** agree with an opinion etc. □ **subscriber** n.

subscription n. **1** sum of money contributed. **2** membership fee. **3** process of subscribing.

subsequent adj. occurring after. □ **subsequently** adv.

■ ensuing, following, future, later, next, succeeding, successive; consequent, resultant, resulting.

subservient adj. **1** subordinate. **2** servile. □ **subserviently** adv., **subservience** n.

■ **1** secondary, subordinate, subsidiary. **2** fawning, ingratiating, obsequious, servile, colloq. smarmy, submissive, sycophantic, toadying, unctuous.

subside v. **1** become less intense. **2** (of water) sink to a lower or normal level. **3** (of ground) cave in. □ **subsidence** n.

■ **1** abate, calm (down), decrease, die (down), diminish, dwindle, ebb, lessen, colloq. let up, moderate, wane. **2** drop, go down, recede, sink. **3** cave in, collapse, give way.

subsidiary adj. **1** of secondary importance. **2** (of a business company) controlled by another. ● n. subsidiary thing.

■ adj. **1** ancillary, auxiliary, lesser, minor, secondary, subordinate.

subsidize v. pay a subsidy to or for. □ **subsidization** n.

■ back, finance, fund, invest in, sponsor, support, underwrite.

subsidy n. money given to support an industry etc. or to keep prices down.

subsist v. keep oneself alive, exist. □ **subsistence** n.

subsoil n. soil lying immediately below the surface layer.

subsonic adj. of or flying at speeds less than that of sound.

substance n. **1** particular kind of matter with more or less uniform properties. **2** essence of something spoken or written. **3** reality, solidity.

■ **1** material, matter, stuff. **2** core, essence, gist, heart, nub, pith, quintessence; import, meaning, point, purport, significance, signification. **3** actuality, concreteness, corporeality, reality, solidity.

substantial adj. **1** of solid material or structure. **2** of considerable amount, intensity, or validity. **3** wealthy. **4** in essentials. □ **substantially** adv.

■ **1** durable, solid, sound, strong, stout, sturdy, well-built. **2** ample, big, considerable, generous, handsome, large, respectable, sizeable; important, material, significant, valuable, worthwhile. **3** affluent, moneyed, prosperous, rich, successful, wealthy.

substantiate *v.* support with evidence. □ **substantiation** *n.*

■ attest, authenticate, back up, confirm, corroborate, prove, support, validate, verify.

substitute *n.* person or thing that acts or serves in place of another. ● *v.* **substitute for** act or cause to act as a substitute. □ **substitution** *n.*

■ *n.* alternative, deputy, locum, proxy, relief, replacement, reserve, stand-by, stand-in, surrogate, understudy. ● *v.* deputize for, fill in for, relieve, stand in for, take the place of; exchange for, replace with.

substructure *n.* underlying or supporting structure.

subsume *v.* bring or include under a particular classification.

subtenant *n.* person to whom a room etc. is sublet.

subterfuge *n.* trick used to avoid blame or defeat etc.

■ artifice, device, dodge, manoeuvre, ploy, ruse, scheme, stratagem, trick, wile.

subterranean *adj.* underground.

subtitle *n.* **1** subordinate title. **2** caption on a cinema film. ● *v.* provide with subtitle(s).

subtle /sútt'l/ *adj.* **1** hard to detect or describe. **2** making fine distinctions. **3** ingenious. □ **subtly** *adv.*, **subtlety** *n.*

■ **1** delicate, elusive, faint, slight, understated; fine, nice. **2** acute, astute, discerning, discriminating, perceptive, sensitive, shrewd. **3** clever, cunning, ingenious, sophisticated.

subtotal *n.* total of part of a group of figures.

subtract *v.* remove (a part, quantity, or number) from a greater one. □ **subtraction** *n.*

subtropical *adj.* of regions bordering on the tropics.

suburb *n.* residential area outside the central part of a town. □ **suburban** *adj.*, **suburbanite** *n.*

suburbia *n.* suburbs and their inhabitants.

subvention *n.* subsidy.

subvert *v.* destroy the authority of (a political system etc.). □ **subversion** *n.*, **subversive** *adj.*

■ destroy, overthrow, overturn, ruin, sabotage, undermine, wreck.

subway *n.* **1** underground passage. **2** (*US*) underground railway.

succeed *v.* **1** be successful. **2** take the place previously filled by. **3** come next in order.

■ **1** *colloq.* arrive, be a success, be successful, do well, flourish, get on, make good, make it, make the grade, prevail, prosper, thrive; be effective, *colloq.* do the trick, work. **2** follow, replace, supplant, take over from, take the place of.

success *n.* **1** favourable outcome. **2** attainment of one's aims, or of wealth, fame, etc. **3** successful person or thing.

successful *adj.* having success. □ **successfully** *adv.*

■ triumphant, victorious, winning; celebrated, eminent, famed, famous, renowned, well-known; fruitful, lucrative, moneymaking, profitable, remunerative; affluent, flourishing, prosperous, rich, thriving, wealthy, well-to-do.

succession *n.* **1** following in order. **2** series of people or things following each other. **3** succeeding to a throne or other position. □ **in succession** one after another.

■ **1,2** chain, course, cycle, line, order, progression, round, run, sequence, series, string. □ **in succession** consecutively, in a row, in turn, one after another, *colloq.* on the trot, successively.

successive *adj.* following in succession. □ **successively** *adv.*

successor *n.* person who succeeds another.

succinct /səksíngkt/ *adj.* brief, concise. □ **succinctly** *adv.*

■ brief, compact, concise, condensed, pithy, short, terse.

succour *v.* & *n.* help.

succulent *adj.* **1** juicy. **2** (of plants) having thick fleshy leaves. ● *n.* succulent plant. □ **succulence** *n.*

succumb *v.* give way to something overpowering.

■ bow, capitulate, give in, give way, submit, surrender, yield.

such *adj.* **1** of the same or that kind or degree. **2** so great or intense. ● *pron.*

that. □ **such-and-such** adj. particular but not now specified.

suchlike adj. of the same kind.

suck v. **1** draw (liquid or air etc.) into the mouth. **2** draw liquid from in this way. ● n. act or process of sucking. □ **suck in** absorb, involve (a person). **suck up to** (colloq.) treat sycophantically.

sucker n. **1** organ or device that can adhere to a surface by suction. **2** (sl.) person who is easily deceived.

suckle v. feed at the breast.

suckling n. unweaned child or animal.

sucrose n. sugar.

suction n. **1** sucking. **2** production of a partial vacuum so that external atmospheric pressure forces fluid etc. into the vacant space or causes adhesion.

sudden adj. happening or done quickly or without warning. □ **suddenly** adv., **suddenness** n.
■ surprising, unannounced, unanticipated, unexpected, unforeseen; abrupt, hurried, immediate, meteoric, quick, rapid, swift; hasty, impetuous, impulsive, precipitate, rash, snap. □ **suddenly** in a flash, in an instant, in a trice, instantly; abruptly, quickly, rapidly, speedily, swiftly; all of a sudden, out of the blue, unexpectedly, without warning.

suds n.pl. soapsuds.

sue v. (**suing**) take legal proceedings against.

suede /swayd/ n. leather with a velvety nap on one side.

suet n. hard fat round an animal's kidneys, used in cooking.

suffer v. **1** feel pain, discomfort, grief, etc. **2** undergo or be subjected to (pain, loss, damage, etc.). **3** tolerate. □ **suffering** n.
■ **1** agonize, be in pain or distress, hurt. **2** endure, experience, feel, go through, sustain, undergo. **3** abide, bear, endure, put up with, stand, stomach, take, tolerate. □ **suffering** agony, anguish, distress, grief, hardship, misery, pain, sorrow, torment, torture, tribulation, unhappiness, woe

sufferance n. **on sufferance** tolerated but only grudgingly.

suffice v. be enough (for).
■ answer, be enough or sufficient, do, serve.

sufficient adj. enough. □ **sufficiently** adv., **sufficiency** n.
■ adequate, ample, enough.

suffix n. (pl. **-ixes**) letter(s) added at the end of a word to make another word.

suffocate v. **1** kill by stopping the breathing. **2** cause discomfort to by making breathing difficult. **3** be suffocated. □ **suffocation** n.
■ **1** asphyxiate, choke, smother, stifle.

suffrage n. right to vote in political elections.

suffuse v. spread throughout or over. □ **suffusion** n.
■ cover, flood, permeate, pervade, saturate, spread through or over.

sugar n. sweet crystalline substance obtained from the juices of various plants. □ **sugar beet** white beet from which sugar is obtained. **sugar cane** tall tropical plant from which sugar is obtained.

sugary adj.

suggest v. **1** bring to mind. **2** propose (theory, plan, etc.).
■ **1** call to mind, evoke; hint (at), imply, indicate, insinuate, intimate. **2** advance, move, present, propound, propose, put forward, recommend; advise, counsel, urge.

suggestible adj. easily influenced. □ **suggestibility** n.

suggestion n. **1** suggesting. **2** thing suggested. **3** slight trace.
■ **2** piece of advice, proposal, proposition, recommendation, tip; implication, insinuation, intimation. **3** hint, shade, suspicion, tinge, touch, trace.

suggestive adj. **1** conveying a suggestion. **2** suggesting something indecent. □ **suggestively** adv.

suicidal adj. **1** of or involving suicide. **2** liable to commit suicide. □ **suicidally** adv.

suicide n. **1** intentional killing of oneself. **2** person who commits suicide. **3** act destructive to one's own interests. □ **commit suicide** kill oneself intentionally.

suit /sōot/ n. **1** set of clothing, esp. jacket and trousers or skirt. **2** any of the four sets into which a pack of cards is divided. **3** lawsuit. ● v. **1** make or be suitable or convenient for. **2** give a pleasing appearance upon.
■ n. **1** ensemble, outfit. **3** action, case, cause, lawsuit, proceedings. ● v. **1** accommodate, adapt, adjust, fit, make suitable, tailor; be acceptable (to), be suitable or convenient (for), please, satisfy; agree with. **2** become, befit, look good on.

suitable *adj.* right for the purpose or occasion. □ **suitably** *adv.*, **suitability** *n.*
  ■ apposite, appropriate, apt, becoming, befitting, fit, fitting, proper, right, seemly; acceptable, convenient, opportune, satisfactory; eligible, qualified.

suitcase *n.* rectangular case for carrying clothes.

suite /sweet/ *n.* **1** set of rooms or furniture. **2** retinue. **3** set of musical pieces.

sulk *v.* be sullen because of resentment or bad temper. ● *n.* (also **the sulks**) fit of sulking. □ **sulky** *adj.*, **sulkily** *adv.*

sullen *adj.* **1** gloomy and unresponsive. **2** dark and dismal. □ **sullenly** *adv.*, **sullenness** *n.*
  ■ **1** bad-tempered, brooding, gloomy, grumpy, ill-humoured, moody, morose, resentful, sulking, sulky, uncommunicative, unresponsive. **2** dark, dismal, gloomy, leaden, murky, sombre.

sully *v.* stain, blemish.

sulphate *n.* salt of sulphuric acid.

sulphide *n.* compound of sulphur and an element or radical.

sulphite *n.* salt of sulphurous acid.

sulphur *n.* pale yellow non-metallic element. □ **sulphurous** *adj.*

sulphuric acid strong corrosive acid.

sultan *n.* Muslim sovereign.

sultana *n.* **1** seedless raisin. **2** sultan's wife, mother, or daughter.

sultanate *n.* sultan's territory.

sultry *adj.* (**-ier**, **-iest**) **1** hot and humid. **2** (of a woman) passionate and sensual. □ **sultriness** *n.*
  ■ **1** close, hot, humid, muggy, oppressive, steamy, sticky, stifling, suffocating, sweltering.

sum *n.* **1** total. **2** amount of money. **3** problem in arithmetic. □ **sum total** total. **sum up 1** give the total of. **2** summarize. **3** form an opinion of.
  ■ **1** aggregate, sum total, total, whole. **2** amount, quantity. □ **sum up 1** add up, calculate, reckon, total, *colloq.* tot up. **2** encapsulate, *colloq.* recap, recapitulate, summarize. **3** assess, evaluate, form an opinion of, *colloq.* size up.

summarize *v.* make or be a summary of. □ **summarization** *n.*
  ■ abridge, condense, encapsulate, give a résumé *or* synopsis of, outline, précis, *colloq.* recap, recapitulate, sum up.

summary *n.* statement giving the main points of something. ● *adj.* brief, without details or formalities. □ **summarily** *adv.*
  ■ *n.* abridgement, abstract, digest, encapsulation, outline, précis, *colloq.* recap, recapitulation, résumé, synopsis. ● *adj.* abrupt, brief, hasty, hurried, perfunctory, quick, rapid, short, sudden.

summation *n.* **1** adding up. **2** summarizing.

summer *n.* warmest season of the year. □ **summer house** small building in a garden giving shade in summer. **summertime** *n.* summer. **summer time** period from March to October when clocks are advanced one hour. **summery** *adj.*

summit *n.* **1** highest point. **2** top of a mountain. **3** conference between heads of states.
  ■ **1** acme, climax, culmination, height, peak, pinnacle, zenith. **2** apex, crest, crown, peak, tip, top.

summon *v.* **1** send for (a person). **2** order to appear in a law court. **3** call together. □ **summon up** gather together (courage etc.).
  ■ **1** call upon, send for. **2** subpoena, summons. **3** assemble, call, convene, convoke, gather together, rally.

summons *n.* **1** command summoning a person. **2** written order to appear in a law court. ● *v.* serve with a summons.

sump *n.* **1** reservoir of oil in a petrol engine. **2** hole or low area into which liquid drains.

sumptuous *adj.* splendid and costly-looking. □ **sumptuously** *adv.*, **sumptuousness** *n.*
  ■ de luxe, gorgeous, luxurious, magnificent, opulent, palatial, plush, plushy, rich, splendid.

sun *n.* **1** star around which the earth travels. **2** light or warmth from this. **3** any fixed star. ● *v.* (**sunned**) expose to the sun.

sunbathe *v.* expose one's body to the sun. □ **sunbather** *n.*

sunbeam *n.* ray of sun.

sunburn *n.* inflammation from exposure to sun. □ **sunburnt** *adj.*

sundae /súnday/ *n.* dish of ice cream and fruit, nuts, syrup, etc.

Sunday school school for religious instruction of Christian children, held on Sundays.

sunder *v.* break or tear apart.

sundial *n.* device that shows the time by means of a shadow on a scaled dial.

sundown *n.* sunset.

sundry *adj.* various. ● *n.pl.* (**sundries**) various small items. □ **all and sundry** everyone.

■ *adj.* assorted, different, diverse, miscellaneous, mixed, various.

sunflower *n.* tall plant with large yellow flowers.

sung *see* **sing.**

sunk *see* **sink.**

sunken *adj.* lying below the level of the surrounding surface.

Sunni *n.* & *adj.* (*pl.* **Sunni** or **-is**) (person) belonging to a Muslim sect opposed to Shiites.

sunny *adj.* (**-ier, -iest**) **1** full of sunshine. **2** cheerful. □ **sunnily** *adv.*

■ **1** bright, clear, cloudless, fine, sunlit, sunshiny. **2** bright, bubbly, buoyant, cheerful, cheery, gay, happy, light-hearted, merry.

sunrise *n.* rising of the sun.

sunset *n.* **1** setting of the sun. **2** coloured sky associated with this.

sunshade *n.* **1** parasol. **2** awning.

sunshine *n.* direct sunlight. □ **sunshiny** *adj.*

sunspot *n.* **1** dark patch observed on the sun's surface. **2** (*colloq.*) place with a sunny climate.

sunstroke *n.* illness caused by too much exposure to sun.

super *adj.* (*colloq.*) excellent.

superb *adj.* of the most impressive or splendid kind. □ **superbly** *adv.*

■ *colloq.* divine, excellent, exceptional, exquisite, *colloq.* fabulous, *colloq.* fantastic, fine, first-class, first-rate, glorious, gorgeous, *colloq.* great, *colloq.* heavenly, impressive, magnificent, marvellous, outstanding, peerless, sensational, *colloq.* smashing, splendid, stupendous, *colloq.* super, superlative, *colloq.* wonderful.

supercharge *v.* increase the power of (an engine) by a device that forces extra air or fuel into it. □ **supercharger** *n.*

supercilious *adj.* haughty and superior. □ **superciliously** *adv.*, **superciliousness** *n.*

■ arrogant, condescending, contemptuous, disdainful, haughty, hoity-toity, lofty, patronizing, scornful, snobbish, *colloq.* snooty, *colloq.* stuck-up, superior.

superficial *adj.* **1** of or on the surface, not deep or penetrating. **2** having no

depth of character. □ **superficially** *adv.*, **superficiality** *n.*

■ **1** exterior, external, outside, surface; cursory, hasty, hurried, perfunctory, quick, rapid, swift. **2** frivolous, shallow, trivial.

superfluous *adj.* more than is required. □ **superfluously** *adv.*, **superfluity** *n.*

■ excess, excessive, extra, redundant, surplus, unnecessary, unneeded; gratuitous, needless.

superhuman *adj.* exceeeding ordinary human capacity or power.

superimpose *v.* place on top of something else. □ **superimposition** *n.*

superintend *v.* supervise. □ **superintendence** *n.*

superintendent *n.* **1** supervisor. **2** police officer next above inspector.

superior *adj.* **1** higher in position or rank. **2** above average in quality etc. **3** showing that one feels wiser or better etc. than others. ● *n.* person or thing of higher rank, ability, or quality. □ **superiority** *n.*

■ *adj.* **1** higher, higher-ranking, senior. **2** better, choice, *colloq.* classier, excellent, exceptional, first-class, first-rate, outstanding, select, superlative, supreme. **3** condescending, disdainful, haughty, hoity-toity, lofty, patronizing, *colloq.* snooty, *colloq.* stuck-up, supercilious.

superlative *adj.* **1** of the highest quality. **2** of the grammatical form expressing 'most'. ● *n.* superlative form.

■ *adj.* **1** exceptional, first-class, first-rate, incomparable, matchless, outstanding, peerless, perfect, superb, supreme, unequalled, unparalleled, unrivalled, unsurpassed.

superman *n.* man of superhuman powers.

supermarket *n.* large self-service shop.

supernatural *adj.* of or involving a power above the forces of nature. □ **supernaturally** *adv.*

■ magical, mysterious, mystic(al), occult, preternatural, psychic, uncanny, unearthly, unnatural, weird; ghostly, spectral.

supernumerary *adj.* & *n.* extra.

superpower *n.* extremely powerful nation.

superscript *adj.* written or printed above.

supersede *v.* take the place of.

■ displace, replace, succeed, supplant, take over from.

supersonic adj. of or flying at speeds greater than that of sound. □ **supersonically** adv.

superstition n. **1** belief in magical and similar influences. **2** idea or practice based on this. **3** widely held but wrong idea. □ **superstitious** adj.

superstore n. supermarket.

superstructure n. structure that rests on something else.

supervene v. occur as an interruption or a change. □ **supervention** n.

supervise v. direct and inspect. □ **supervision** n., **supervisor** n., **supervisory** adj.

■ be in charge of, control, direct, handle, head, manage, oversee, run, superintend, watch (over). □ **supervisor** colloq. boss, chief, director, foreman, colloq. gaffer, head, manager, overseer, superintendent, superior.

supine /soopin/ adj. **1** lying face upwards. **2** indolent.

supper n. evening meal, last meal of the day.

supplant v. oust and take the place of. □ **supplanter** n.

■ displace, eject, oust, remove, replace, supersede, take the place of, unseat.

supple adj. bending easily. □ **supply** adv., **suppleness** n.

■ bendable, flexible, pliable, pliant, whippy; athletic, graceful, lissom, lithe, willowy.

supplement n. thing added as an extra part. ● v. provide or be a supplement to.

■ n. addition, adjunct; extra, surcharge; addendum, appendix, codicil, insert, postscript, rider. ● v. add to, augment, increase, top up.

supplementary adj. serving as a supplement.

■ accessory, added, additional, ancillary, extra, further.

suppliant /súpliənt/ n. & adj. (person) asking humbly for something.

supplicate v. make a humble petition to or for. □ **supplication** n.

supply v. **1** give or provide with, make available. **2** satisfy (a need). ● n. **1** supplying. **2** stock, amount provided or available.

■ v. **1** afford, contribute, donate, give, furnish, present, provide; equip, fix up, kit out, provision. **2** fulfil, meet, satisfy. ● n. **1** providing, provision, supplying. **2** cache,

fund, hoard, reserve, reservoir, stock, stockpile, store.

support v. **1** bear the weight of. **2** keep from falling, sinking, or failing. **3** provide for. **4** help by one's approval or sympathy, or by giving money. **5** give corroboration to. **6** speak in favour of. **7** be a regular customer or a fan of. ● n. **1** act or instance of supporting. **2** person or thing that supports. □ **supporter** n., **supportive** adj.

■ v. **1** bear, carry, hold (up), sustain, take. **2** bolster, brace, buttress, fortify, prop (up), reinforce, shore up, strengthen. **3** keep, look after, maintain, provide for, take care of. **4** aid, assist, buoy up, encourage, fortify, help, sustain; back (up), champion, stand by, stand up for, colloq. stick up for, uphold; finance, sponsor, subsidize, underwrite. **5** authenticate, back up, confirm, corroborate, endorse, ratify, substantiate, validate, verify. **6** advocate, recommend, second, speak in favour of. ● n. **1** aid, assistance, backing, encouragement, fortification, help, succour. **2** beam, brace, buttress, column, foundation, frame, guy, joist, pillar, post, prop, stanchion, strut, substructure, truss; keep, maintenance, subsistence, upkeep; finances, funding; comfort, mainstay, tower of strength. □ **supporter** adherent, admirer, advocate, assistant, backer, benefactor, champion, defender, devotee, enthusiast, helper, fan, follower, patron, promoter, sponsor, upholder. **supportive** caring, encouraging, helpful, sympathetic, understanding.

suppose v. **1** be inclined to think. **2** assume to be true. **3** consider as a proposal. □ **be supposed** be expected or required.

■ **1** believe, conjecture, fancy, guess, imagine, reckon, think. **2** assume, presuppose, presume, surmise, take for granted. **3** postulate, theorize.

supposedly adv. according to supposition.

supposition n. **1** process of supposing. **2** what is supposed.

■ **1** assumption, inference, postulation. **2** assumption, belief, conjecture, hypothesis, guess, inference, surmise, theory.

suppository n. solid medicinal substance placed in the rectum or vagina and left to melt.

suppress v. **1** put an end to the activity or existence of. **2** keep from being seen, heard, known, etc. □ **suppression** n., **suppressor** n.

■ **1** colloq. crack down on, crush, extinguish, overcome, overpower, put an end to, put down, quash, quell, squash, stamp out, subdue. **2** contain, control, curb, repress, restrain, silence, smother, stifle, strangle, withhold; conceal, cover up, hide, keep secret; censor.

suppurate v. form pus, fester. □ **suppuration** n.

supra- pref. above, over.

supreme adj. highest in authority, rank, or quality. □ **supremely** adv., **supremacy** n.

■ chief, first, foremost, greatest, highest, principal, sovereign, top, topmost, uppermost; best, incomparable, inimitable, matchless, outstanding, peerless, perfect, superlative, unequalled, unparalleled, unsurpassed.

supremo n. (pl. **-os**) supreme leader.

surcharge n. additional charge. ● v. make a surcharge on or to.

sure adj. **1** without doubt or uncertainty. **2** reliable, unfailing. ● adv. (colloq.) certainly. □ **make sure** act so as to be certain. **sure-footed** adj. never slipping or stumbling. **sureness** n.

■ adj. **1** assured, certain, confident, convinced, definite, positive. **2** accurate, dependable, foolproof, infallible, reliable, unerring, unfailing; inescapable, inevitable, unavoidable.

surely adv. **1** in a sure manner. **2** (used for emphasis) that must be right. **3** (as an answer) certainly.

surety n. **1** guarantee. **2** guarantor of a person's promise.

surf n. foam of breaking waves. ● v. engage in surfing.

surface n. **1** outside or outward appearance of something. **2** any side of an object. **3** top of a liquid or of the ground. ● adj. of or on the surface. ● v. **1** put a specified surface on. **2** come or bring to the surface. **3** become visible or known.

■ n. **1** façade, face, exterior, outside, top. **2** face, side. **3** meniscus. ● adj. exterior, external, outside, outward, superficial. ● v. **1** coat, top; concrete, pave, tarmac. **2,3** appear, come to light, come up, crop up, emerge, materialize.

surfboard n. narrow board for riding over surf.

surfeit /súrfit/ n. too much, esp. of food or drink. ● v. **1** overfeed. **2** satiate.

■ n. excess, glut, over-abundance, superfluity, surplus. ● v. **1** gorge, overfeed, stuff. **2** glut, sate, satiate.

surfing n. sport of riding on a surfboard.

surge v. move forward in or like waves. ● n. **1** surging movement. **2** sudden occurrence or increase.

■ v. billow, eddy, heave, roll, swell; flow, gush, pour, rush, stream. ● n. **1** billowing, eddying, heaving, rolling, swell; gush, flood, rush, stream. **2** increase, rise, upsurge.

surgeon n. doctor qualified to perform surgical operations.

surgery n. **1** treatment by cutting or manipulation of affected parts of the body. **2** place where or times when a doctor or dentist or an MP etc. is available for consultation. □ **surgical** adj., **surgically** adv.

surly adj. (**-ier, -iest**) bad-tempered and unfriendly. □ **surliness** n.

■ bad-tempered, cantankerous, churlish, crabby, cross, crotchety, crusty, disagreeable, grumpy, ill-tempered, irascible, irritable, rude, sour, splenetic, sulky, sullen, testy, unpleasant, unfriendly.

surmise n. conjecture. ● v. infer doubtfully.

■ v. assume, conclude, conjecture, deduce, fancy, feel, gather, guess, imagine, infer, presume, speculate, suppose, suspect, understand.

surmount v. overcome (a difficulty or an obstacle). □ **surmountable** adj.

surname n. family name.

surpass v. outdo, be better than.

■ beat, better, cap, eclipse, exceed, excel, outclass, outdo, outshine, outstrip, overshadow, top, transcend.

surplus n. amount left over after what is needed has been used.

■ excess, glut, superfluity, surfeit; balance, leftovers, remainder, residue, rest.

surprise n. **1** emotion aroused by something sudden or unexpected. **2** thing causing this. ● v. **1** cause to feel surprise. **2** come upon or attack unexpectedly. □ **take by surprise** affect with surprise.

■ n. **1** astonishment, incredulity, shock, stupefaction, wonder. **2** blow, bombshell, eye-opener, jolt, shock, colloq. shocker. ● v. **1** amaze, astonish, astound, bowl over, dumbfound, *colloq.* flabbergast, shock, stagger, startle, stun, stupefy, take aback, take by surprise. **2** ambush, pounce on, swoop on; catch napping, catch red-handed, catch unawares.

surrealism *n.* style of art and literature seeking to express what is in the subconscious mind. □ **surrealist** *n.*, **surrealistic** *adj.*

surrender *v.* **1** hand over, give into another's power or control, esp. under compulsion. **2** give oneself up. ● *n.* surrendering.
■ *v.* **1** cede, concede, forgo, forsake, give up, hand over, let go (of), part with, relinquish, renounce, yield. **2** admit defeat, bow, capitulate, cave in, give oneself up, submit, throw in the towel.

surreptitious *adj.* acting or done stealthily. □ **surreptitiously** *adv.*
■ clandestine, covert, furtive, secret, sly, stealthy, underhand.

surrogate *n.* deputy. □ **surrogate mother** woman who bears a child on behalf of another. **surrogacy** *n.*

surround *v.* come, place, or be all round, encircle. ● *n.* border.
■ *v.* circle, encircle, enclose, encompass, envelop, girdle, hedge in, hem in, ring; beset, besiege.

surroundings *n.pl.* things or conditions around a person or place.
■ background, conditions, element, environment, habitat, milieu, setting.

surveillance *n.* close observation.

survey *v.* /sərváy/ **1** look at and take a general view of. **2** examine the condition of (a building). **3** determine the area and features of (a piece of land). **4** investigate the behaviour, opinions, etc. of (a group of people). ● *n.* /súrvay/ **1** general view or consideration. **2** report produced by surveying.
■ *v.* **1** contemplate, examine, inspect, look at, observe, scan, scrutinize, view; appraise, assess, consider, evaluate, investigate, review, look into, study. **3** map out, measure, plot; explore, reconnoitre. **4** canvass, interview, question. ● *n.* **1** appraisal, assessment, consideration, contemplation, evaluation, examination, inspection, investigation, review, scrutiny, study.

surveyor *n.* person who surveys land or buildings, esp. professionally.

survival *n.* **1** surviving. **2** relic.

survive *v.* **1** continue to live or exist. **2** remain alive or in existence after. **3** remain alive in spite of (a danger, accident, etc.). □ **survivor** *n.*
■ **1** continue, endure, exist, keep going, last, live (on), remain, persist, subsist; pull through; cope, get by, make do, manage, struggle along *or* on. **2** outlast, outlive. **3** live through, stand, weather, withstand.

susceptible *adj.* impressionable. □ **susceptible to** likely to be affected by. **susceptibility** *n.*
■ credulous, gullible, impressionable, naive, suggestible.

sushi *n.* Japanese dish of flavoured balls of cold rice usu. garnished with fish.

suspect *v.* /səspékt/ **1** feel that something may exist or be true. **2** mistrust. **3** feel to be guilty but have no proof. ● *n.* /súspekt/ person suspected of a crime etc. ● *adj.* /súspekt/ suspected, open to suspicion.
■ *v.* **1** be inclined to think, believe, guess, fancy, feel, have a feeling, imagine, sense, suppose, think. **2** be suspicious of, disbelieve, distrust, doubt, have doubts *or* misgivings about, mistrust. ● *adj.* doubtful, dubious, fishy, questionable, shady, suspicious.

suspend *v.* **1** hang up. **2** keep from falling or sinking in air or liquid. **3** stop temporarily. **4** debar temporarily from a position, privilege, etc.
■ **1** hang (up), sling. **3** adjourn, defer, delay, hold in abeyance, interrupt, postpone, shelve.

suspender *n.* attachment to hold up a sock or stocking by its top.

suspense *n.* anxious uncertainty while awaiting an event etc.
■ anxiety, anxiousness, apprehension, excitement, expectation, expectancy, nervousness, tension, uncertainty.

suspension *n.* **1** suspending. **2** means by which a vehicle is supported on its axles. □ **suspension bridge** bridge suspended from cables that pass over supports at each end.

suspicion *n.* **1** suspecting. **2** unconfirmed belief. **3** mistrust. **4** slight trace.
■ **2** belief, feeling, guess, hunch, idea, impression, inkling, notion, premonition, presentiment. **3** distrust, doubt, misgiving, mistrust, scepticism, uncertainty, wariness.

4 hint, shade, suggestion, tinge, touch, trace.

suspicious *adj.* feeling or causing suspicion. □ **suspiciously** *adv.*

■ disbelieving, distrustful, doubtful, incredulous, mistrustful, sceptical, wary; dubious, fishy, shady, shifty, suspect.

sustain *v.* 1 support. 2 keep alive. 3 keep (a sound or effort) going continuously. 4 undergo. 5 endure. 6 uphold the validity of.

■ 1 bear, carry, hold, support, take. 2 feed, keep (alive), maintain, nourish. 3 continue, keep going, keep up, maintain. 4 be subjected to, experience, suffer, undergo. 5 endure, stand, tolerate, weather, withstand. 6 ratify, support, uphold, validate.

sustenance *n.* food, nourishment.

■ comestibles, eatables, food, foodstuffs, *sl.* grub, nourishment, nutriment, provisions, viands.

suture /sōochər/ *n.* 1 surgical stitching of a wound. 2 stitch or thread used in this. ● *v.* stitch (a wound).

svelte *adj.* slender and graceful.

SW *abbr.* 1 south-west. 2 south-western.

swab *n.* 1 mop or pad for cleansing, drying, or absorbing things. 2 specimen of a secretion taken with this. ● *v.* (**swabbed**) cleanse with a swab.

swaddle *v.* swathe in wraps or warm garments.

swag *n.* (*sl.*) loot.

swagger *v.* walk or behave self-importantly. ● *n.* this gait or manner.

■ *v.* parade, strut; boast, brag, show off, *colloq.* swank.

Swahili *n.* Bantu language widely used in E. Africa.

swallow¹ *v.* 1 cause or allow to go down one's throat. 2 work throat muscles in doing this. 3 take in and engulf or absorb. 4 accept. ● *n.* 1 act of swallowing. 2 amount swallowed.

■ *v.* 1 consume, devour, eat, ingest; bolt, gobble, guzzle, scoff, wolf; *colloq.* down, drink, gulp, imbibe, quaff, swill. 3 absorb, assimilate, consume, engulf, envelop. 4 accept, believe, credit, fall for.

swallow² *n.* small migratory bird with a forked tail.

swam see **swim**.

swamp *n.* marsh. ● *v.* 1 flood, drench or submerge in water. 2 overwhelm with numbers or quantity. □ **swampy** *adj.*

■ *n.* bog, fen, marsh, mire, morass, quagmire, slough. ● *v.* 1 deluge, flood, immerse, inundate, submerge; drench, soak. 2 deluge, engulf, flood, inundate, overload, overwhelm, snow under.

swan *n.* large usu. white waterbird with a long slender neck.

swank (*colloq.*) *n.* 1 boastful person or behaviour. 2 ostentation. ● *v.* behave with swank.

swansong *n.* person's last performance or achievement etc.

swap *n.* & *v.* (**swapped**) exchange.

swarm¹ *n.* large cluster of people, insects, etc. ● *v.* move in a swarm. □ **swarm with** be crowded or infested with.

■ *n.* army, drove, flock, herd, horde, host, mass, multitude, pack, throng. ● *v.* crowd, flock, pour, stream, surge, throng. □ **swarm with** abound in, be full of, be infested with, be overrun with, teem with.

swarm² *v.* **swarm up** climb by gripping with arms and legs.

swarthy *adj.* (**-ier, -iest**) having a dark complexion.

swashbuckling *adj.* & *n.* swaggering boldly. □ **swashbuckler** *n.*

swastika *n.* symbol formed by a cross with ends bent at right angles.

swat *v.* (**swatted**) hit hard with something flat. □ **swatter** *n.*

swatch *n.* sample(s) of cloth etc.

swath /swawth/ *n.* (*pl.* **swaths**) strip cut in one sweep or passage by a scythe or mowing-machine.

swathe *v.* wrap with layers of coverings.

■ bandage, envelop, muffle (up), shroud, swaddle, wrap.

sway *v.* 1 (cause to) lean unsteadily from side to side. 2 influence the opinions of. 3 waver in one's opinion. ● *n.* 1 swaying movement. 2 rule or control.

■ *n.* 1 bend, lean, move to and fro *or* from side to side, roll, swing; lurch, reel, rock, totter, wobble. 2 convince, influence, persuade, prevail on, talk into, win over; incline, move, swing. 3 fluctuate, oscillate, vacillate, waver. ● *n.* 2 authority, command, control, dominion, influence, jurisdiction, leadership, mastery, power, sovereignty.

swear *v.* (**swore, sworn**) 1 state or promise on oath. 2 state emphatically. 3

use a swear word. □ **swear by** have great confidence in. **swear word** profane or indecent word.

■ **1** give one's word, pledge, promise, undertake, vow. **2** assert, avow, declare, insist, testify. **3** blaspheme, curse, *colloq.* cuss, utter profanities. □ **swear by** believe in, count on, have confidence *or* faith in, rely on, trust (in).

sweat *n.* **1** moisture given off by the body through the pores. **2** state of sweating. **3** moisture forming in drops on a surface. ● *v.* **1** exude sweat or as sweat. **2** be in a state of great anxiety. **3** work long and hard. □ **sweat-band** *n.* band of material worn to absorb or wipe away sweat. **sweated labour** labour of workers with poor pay and conditions. **sweaty** *adj.*

sweater *n.* jumper, pullover.

sweatshirt *n.* cotton sweater with sleeves.

sweatshop *n.* place employing sweated labour.

Swede *n.* native of Sweden.

swede *n.* large variety of turnip.

Swedish *adj. & n.* (language) of Sweden.

sweep *v.* (**swept**) **1** clear away with a broom or brush. **2** clean or clear (a surface) thus. **3** go smoothly and swiftly or majestically. **4** extend in a continuous line. ● *n.* **1** sweeping movement or line. **2** act of sweeping. **3** range or scope. **4** chimney sweep. **5** sweepstake. □ **sweep the board** win all the prizes.

sweeping *adj.* **1** wide in range or effect. **2** taking no account of particular cases.

■ **1** broad, comprehensive, exhaustive, extensive, general, radical, thorough, universal, wholesale, wide-ranging. **2** broad, generalized, inexact, oversimplified.

sweepstake *n.* form of gambling in which the money staked is divided among those who have drawn numbered tickets for the winners.

sweet *adj.* **1** tasting as if containing sugar. **2** fragrant. **3** melodious. **4** pleasant. **5** (*colloq.*) charming. ● *n.* **1** small shaped piece of sweet substance. **2** sweet dish forming one course of a meal. **3** beloved person. □ **sweet pea** climbing plant with fragrant flowers. **sweet tooth** liking for sweet things. **sweetly** *adv.*, **sweetness** *n.*

■ *adj.* **1** honeyed, sugared, sugary, sweetened, syrupy. **2** aromatic, balmy, fragrant, perfumed, scented. **3** dulcet, euphonious, harmonious, melodious, mu-

sical, silvery, tuneful. **4** agreeable, amiable, considerate, easygoing, friendly, genial, kind, nice, pleasant, thoughtful, warm. **5** appealing, attractive, charming, *colloq.* cute, endearing, lovable, winning, winsome. ● *n.* **1** (**sweets**) *US* candy, confectionery. **2** dessert, pudding.

sweetbread *n.* animal's thymus gland or pancreas used as food.

sweeten *v.* make or become sweet or sweeter.

sweetener *n.* **1** thing that sweetens. **2** (*colloq.*) bribe.

sweetheart *n.* either of a pair of people in love with each other.

swell *v.* (**swelled**, **swollen** or **swelled**) **1** (cause to) become larger from pressure within. **2** make or become greater in amount or intensity. ● *n.* **1** act or state of swelling. **2** heaving of the sea. **3** a crescendo. **4** (*colloq.*) fashionable or stylish person.

■ *v.* **1** balloon, billow, blow up, bulge, dilate, inflate, puff up *or* out. **2** escalate, expand, grow, increase, mount, multiply, mushroom, rise, snowball; heighten, intensify, raise, step up. ● *n.* **1** enlargement, escalation, expansion, growth, increase, rise. **2** billowing, heaving, rolling, surging.

swelling *n.* abnormally swollen place, esp. on the body.

■ bulge, bump, distension, excrescence, lump, node, nodule, protrusion, protuberance, tumescence, tumour; abscess, blister, boil, carbuncle, pustule, spot.

swelter *v.* be uncomfortably hot.

swept *see* **sweep.**

swerve *v.* turn aside from a straight course. ● *n.* swerving movement or direction.

■ *v.* change direction, deviate, diverge, sheer off, skew, swing, turn (aside), veer.

swift *adj.* quick, rapid. ● *n.* swift-flying long-winged bird. □ **swiftly** *adv.*, **swiftness** *n.*

■ *adj.* brisk, fast, fleet, *colloq.* nippy, quick, rapid, speedy; meteoric, sudden; immediate, instant, prompt.

swill *v.* **1** wash, rinse. **2** (of water) pour. **3** drink greedily. ● *n.* **1** rinse. **2** sloppy food fed to pigs.

swim *v.* (**swam**, **swum**) **1** travel through water by movements of the body. **2** be covered with liquid. **3** seem to be whirling or waving. **4** be dizzy. ● *n.* act or period of swimming. □ **swimming bath,**

pool artificial pool for swimming in. **swimmer** n.

swimmingly adv. with easy unobstructed progress.

swindle v. cheat in a business transaction. ● n. piece of swindling. □ **swindler** n.

■ v. bilk, cheat, sl. con, deceive, defraud, colloq. do down, double-cross, colloq. fiddle, fleece, hoodwink, colloq. rip off, sting, trick. ● n. sl. con, confidence trick, colloq. fiddle, fraud, colloq. rip-off, scam, trick.

swine n. 1 (pl. **swine**) pig. 2 (colloq.) (pl. **swine** or -**s**) hated person or thing.

swing v. (**swung**) 1 move to and fro while supported. 2 turn in a curve. 3 (cause to) change from one mood or opinion to another. ● n. 1 act, movement, or extent of swinging. 2 hanging seat for swinging in. 3 jazz with the time of the melody varied. □ **in full swing** with activity at its greatest. **swing-bridge** n. bridge that can be swung aside for ships to pass. **swing-wing** n. aircraft wing that can be moved to slant backwards. **swinger** n.

■ v. 1 dangle, move to and fro or back and forth, oscillate, rock, sway. 2 spin, turn, veer, wheel. 3 change, fluctuate, oscillate, see-saw; incline, move, sway. ● n. 1 fluctuation, oscillation; change, movement, shift, switch, variation.

swingeing adj. 1 forcible. 2 huge in amount or scope.

swipe (colloq.) v. 1 hit with a swinging blow. 2 snatch, steal. ● n. swinging blow.

swirl v. & n. whirl, flow with a whirling movement.

swish v. move with a hissing sound. ● n. swishing sound. ● adj. (colloq.) smart, fashionable.

Swiss adj. & n. (native) of Switzerland. □ **Swiss roll** thin flat sponge cake spread with jam etc. and rolled up.

switch n. 1 device operated to turn electric current on or off. 2 flexible stick or rod, whip. 3 tress of hair tied at one end. 4 shift in opinion or method etc. ● v. 1 (cause to) change, esp. suddenly. 2 reverse the positions of, exchange. □ **switch on** or **off** turn (an electrical device) on or off.

■ n. 4 alteration, change, reversal, shift, U-turn. ● v. 1 change, divert, shift, redirect, transfer. 2 change, exchange, reverse, substitute, swap, transpose.

switchback n. 1 railway used for amusement at a fair etc., with alternate steep ascents and descents. 2 road with similar slopes.

switchboard n. panel of switches for making telephone connections or operating electric circuits.

swivel n. link or pivot enabling one part to revolve without turning another. ● v. (**swivelled**) turn on or as if on a swivel.

swollen see **swell**.

swoop v. 1 make a sudden downward rush. 2 attack suddenly. ● n. swooping movement or attack.

swop v. & n. = **swap**.

sword /sord/ n. weapon with a long blade and a hilt. □ **swordsman** n.

■ claymore, cutlass, rapier, sabre, scimitar.

swordfish n. sea fish with a long sword-like upper jaw.

swore see **swear**.

sworn see **swear**. adj. open and determined, esp. in enmity.

swot (colloq.) v. (**swotted**) study hard. ● n. person who studies hard.

swum see **swim**.

swung see **swing**.

sybarite n. person who is excessively fond of comfort and luxury. □ **sybaritic** adj.

sycamore n. large tree of the maple family.

sycophant n. person who tries to win favour by flattery. □ **sycophantic** adj.

■ □ **sycophantic** fawning, flattering, ingratiating, obsequious, servile, slavish, colloq. smarmy, subservient, toadying, unctuous.

syllable n. unit of sound in a word. □ **syllabic** adj.

syllabub n. dish of whipped cream flavoured with wine.

syllabus n. (pl. -**buses**) statement of the subjects to be covered by a course of study.

sylph n. slender girl or woman.

symbiosis n. (pl. -**oses**) relationship of different organisms living in close association. □ **symbiotic** adj.

symbol n. 1 thing regarded as suggesting something. 2 mark or sign with a special meaning.

■ 1 emblem, figure, metaphor, representation, sign, token. 2 badge, emblem, insignia, hallmark, logo, mark, trade mark; character, pictograph.

symbolic *adj.* (also **symbolical**) of, using, or used as a symbol. □ **symbolically** *adv.*
■ allegorical, emblematic, figurative, metaphorical, representative.

symbolism *n.* use of symbols to express things. □ **symbolist** *n.*

symbolize *v.* **1** be a symbol of. **2** represent by means of a symbol.
■ **1** betoken, connote, denote, epitomize, exemplify, express, indicate, mean, represent, stand for, typify.

symmetry *n.* state of having parts that correspond in size, shape, and position on either side of a dividing line or round a centre. □ **symmetrical** *adj.*, **symmetrically** *adv.*

sympathetic *adj.* **1** feeling, showing, or resulting from sympathy. **2** likeable. □ **sympathetically** *adv.*
■ **1** caring, compassionate, concerned, considerate, kind, kind-hearted, kindly, solicitous, supportive, understanding; like-minded. **2** agreeable, companionable, congenial, friendly, likeable, nice, pleasant.

sympathize *v.* **sympathize with** feel or express sympathy for. □ **sympathizer** *n.*
■ commiserate with, condole with, feel sorry for; empathize with, identify with, relate to, understand.

sympathy *n.* **1** ability to share the feelings of others. **2** (*sing.* or *pl.*) feeling or expression of sorrow or pity. **3** liking for each other.
■ **1** empathy, fellow-feeling. **2** commiseration, compassion, concern, pity, solicitousness, solicitude; condolences. **3** affinity, compatibility, harmony, liking, rapport.

symphony *n.* long elaborate musical composition for a full orchestra. □ **symphonic** *adj.*

symposium *n.* (*pl.* **-ia**) meeting for discussing a particular subject.

symptom *n.* sign of the existence of a condition.

symptomatic *adj.* serving as a symptom.

synagogue *n.* building for public Jewish worship.

synchromesh *n.* device that makes gear wheels revolve at the same speed.

synchronize *v.* **1** (cause to) occur or operate at the same time. **2** cause (clocks etc.) to show the same time. □ **synchronization** *n.*

synchronous *adj.* occurring or existing at the same time.

syncopate *v.* change the beats or accents in (music). □ **syncopation** *n.*

syndicate *n.* /sindikət/ association of people or firms to carry out a business undertaking. ● *v.* /sindikayt/ **1** combine into a syndicate. **2** arrange publication in many newspapers etc. simultaneously. □ **syndication** *n.*
■ *n.* alliance, association, bloc, cartel, combine, confederation, consortium, group, league, trust, union.

syndrome *n.* combination of signs, symptoms, etc. characteristic of a specified condition.

synonym *n.* word or phrase meaning the same as another in the same language. □ **synonymous** *adj.*

synopsis *n.* (*pl.* **-opses**) summary, brief general survey.

syntax *n.* grammatical arrangement of words. □ **syntactic** *adj.*

synthesis *n.* (*pl.* **-theses**) **1** process or result of combining. **2** artificial production of a substance that occurs naturally.

synthesize *v.* make by synthesis.

synthesizer *n.* electronic musical instrument able to produce a great variety of sounds.

synthetic *adj.* made by synthesis. ● *n.* synthetic substance or fabric. □ **synthetically** *adv.*

syphilis *n.* a venereal disease. □ **syphilitic** *adj.*

syringe *n.* device for drawing and injecting liquid. ● *v.* wash out or spray with a syringe.

syrup *n.* **1** thick sweet liquid. **2** water sweetened with sugar. □ **syrupy** *adj.*

system *n.* **1** set of connected things that form a whole or work together. **2** animal body as a whole. **3** (**the system**) traditional practices, methods, and rules existing in a society, institution, etc. **4** method of classification, notation, or measurement. **5** orderliness.
■ **1** arrangement, network, organization, set-up, structure. **4** approach, method, practice, procedure, process, scheme, technique, way. **5** method, order, orderliness.

systematic *adj.* methodical. □ **system-atically** *adv.*

■ businesslike, efficient, methodical, orderly, organized, planned, systematized, well-organized.

systematize *v.* arrange according to a carefully organized system. □ **system-atization** *n.*

systemic *adj.* of or affecting the body as a whole.

tab *n.* small projecting flap or strip. □ **keep tabs on** (*colloq.*) keep under observation.

tabard *n.* short sleeveless tunic-like garment.

tabby *n.* cat with grey or brown fur and dark stripes.

table *n.* **1** piece of furniture with a flat top supported on one or more legs. **2** list of facts or figures arranged in columns. ● *v.* submit (a motion or report) for discussion. □ **at table** taking a meal. **table tennis** game played with bats and a light hollow ball on a table.

■ *n.* **2** chart, graph, index, inventory, list.

tableau /táblō/ *n.* (*pl.* **-eaux**) silent motionless group arranged to represent a scene.

table d'hôte /taáb'l dốt/ (meal) served at a fixed inclusive price.

tableland *n.* plateau of land.

tablespoon *n.* **1** large spoon for serving food. **2** amount held by this. □ **tablespoonful** *n.*

tablet *n.* **1** slab bearing an inscription etc. **2** measured amount of a drug compressed into a solid form.

■ **2** capsule, lozenge, pill.

tabloid *n.* small-sized newspaper, often sensational in style.

taboo *n.* ban or prohibition made by religion or social custom. ● *adj.* prohibited by a taboo.

tabular *adj.* arranged in tables.

tabulate *v.* arrange in tabular form. □ **tabulation** *n.*

tachograph *n.* device in a motor vehicle to record speed and travel time.

tacit *adj.* implied or understood without being put into words. □ **tacitly** *adv.*

■ implicit, implied, silent, undeclared, unspoken.

taciturn *adj.* saying very little. □ **taciturnity** *n.*

■ quiet, reserved, reticent, uncommunicative, unforthcoming, untalkative.

tack¹ *n.* **1** small broad-headed nail. **2** course of action or policy. **3** long temporary stitch. **4** sailing ship's oblique course. ● *v.* **1** nail with tack(s). **2** stitch with tacks. **3** sail a zigzag course. □ **tack on** add as an extra thing.

■ *n.* **1** drawing-pin, nail, pin. **2** approach, course, direction, line, method, policy, procedure, way. ● *v.* **1** nail, pin. **2** baste, sew, stitch. □ **tack on** add (on), append, attach, tag on.

tack² *n.* harness, saddles, etc.

tackle *n.* **1** equipment for a task or sport. **2** set of ropes and pulleys for lifting etc. **3** act of tackling in football etc. ● *v.* **1** try to deal with or overcome (an opponent or problem etc.). **2** intercept (an opponent who has the ball in football etc.).

■ *n.* **1** accoutrements, apparatus, *sl.* clobber, equipment, gear, paraphernalia, tools. ● *v.* **1** address (oneself to), apply oneself to, face up to, have a go at, take on.

tacky *adj.* (of paint etc.) sticky, not quite dry. □ **tackiness** *n.*

tact *n.* skill in avoiding offence or in winning goodwill. □ **tactful** *adj.*, **tactless** *adj.*

■ consideration, delicacy, diplomacy, discretion, finesse, politeness, sensitivity, thoughtfulness. □ **tactful** considerate, delicate, diplomatic, discreet, judicious, polite, sensitive, thoughtful. **tactless** blunt, clumsy, gauche, hurtful, impolite, impolitic, inappropriate, inconsiderate, indelicate, indiscreet, insensitive, thoughtless, undiplomatic.

tactic *n.* **1** (usu. *pl.*) plan or means of achieving something, skilful device(s). **2** (*pl.*) the skilful arrangement and use of military forces to win a battle.

■ **1** device, manoeuvre, plan, ploy, ruse, scheme, stratagem; (**tactics**) policy, strategy.

tactical *adj.* **1** of tactics. **2** (of weapons) for use in a battle or at close quarters. □ **tactically** *adv.*

tactician *n.* expert in tactics.

tactile *adj.* of or using the sense of touch. □ **tactility** *n.*

tadpole *n.* larva of a frog or toad etc. at the stage when it has gills and a tail.

taffeta *n.* shiny silk-like fabric.

tag *n.* **1** label. **2** much-used phrase or quotation. **3** metal point on a shoelace etc. ● *v.* **(tagged)** label. □ **tag on** attach, add.

tail *n.* **1** animal's hindmost part, esp. when extending beyond its body. **2** rear, hanging, or inferior part. **3** (*colloq.*) person tailing another. **4** (*pl.*) reverse of a coin, turned upwards after being tossed. ● *v.* (*colloq.*) follow closely. □ **tail-end** *n.* very last part. **tail-light** *n.* light at the back of a motor vehicle or train etc. **tail off 1** gradually diminish. **2** end inconclusively.

tailback *n.* queue of traffic extending back from an obstruction.

tailboard *n.* hinged or removable back of a lorry etc.

tailcoat *n.* man's coat with the skirt tapering and divided at the back.

tailgate *n.* rear door in a motor vehicle.

tailor *n.* maker of men's clothes, esp. to order. ● *v.* **1** make (clothes) as a tailor. **2** make or adapt for a special purpose. □ **tailor-made** *adj.*

tailplane *n.* horizontal part of an aeroplane's tail.

tailspin *n.* aircraft's spinning dive.

taint *n.* trace of decay, infection, or other bad quality. ● *v.* affect with a taint.
■ *n.* blemish, blot, flaw, mark, stain. ● *v.* blemish, blot, damage, harm, smear, stain, sully, tarnish.

take *v.* **(took, taken) 1** get possession of. **2** capture. **3** make use of. **4** cause to come or go with one. **5** carry. **6** remove. **7** accept, endure. **8** study or teach (a subject). **9** need. **10** make a photograph (of). ● *n.* **1** amount taken or caught. **2** instance of photographing a scene for a cinema film. □ **be taken by** or **with** find attractive. **be taken ill** become ill. **take after** resemble (a parent etc.). **take-away** *n.* & *adj.* **1** (cooked meal) bought at a restaurant etc. for eating elsewhere. **2** (place) selling this. **take back** withdraw (a statement). **take in 1** deceive, cheat. **2** include. **3** make (a garment etc.) smaller. **4** understand. **take off 1** remove (clothing etc.). **2** mimic humorously. **3** become airborne. **take-off** *n.* **1** humorous mimicry. **2** process of becoming airborne. **take on 1** undertake. **2** engage (an employee). **3** accept as an opponent. **4** acquire. **take oneself off** depart. **take one's time** not hurry. **take out** remove. **take over** take control of. **takeover** *n.* **take part** share in an activity. **take**

place occur. **take sides** support one side or another. **take to 1** develop a liking or ability for. **2** adopt as a habit or custom. **3** go to as a refuge. **take up 1** take as a hobby or cause. **2** occupy (time or space). **3** resume. **4** accept (an offer). **5** interrupt or question (a speaker). **take up with** begin to associate with. **taker** *n.*
■ *v.* **1** acquire, get (hold of), lay one's hands on, obtain, pick up, procure; grab, grasp, grip, seize, snatch. **2** abduct, apprehend, arrest, capture, catch, kidnap, seize, take prisoner. **3** book, engage, hire, rent, reserve; travel by, use; buy, subscribe to. **4** accompany, conduct, escort, go with, guide, lead. **5** contain, hold, support; bring, carry, convey, transport. **6** appropriate, *sl.* nick, *sl.* pinch, pocket, purloin, remove, *colloq.* snaffle, steal. **7** abide, accept, bear, brook, cope with, endure, put up with, stand, *colloq.* stick, stomach, tolerate, withstand. **8** learn, read, study; teach. **9** demand, necessitate, need, require. □ **take in 1** cheat, *sl.* con, deceive, dupe, fool, hoodwink, mislead, trick. **2** comprise, cover, encompass, include, incorporate. **take off 1** doff, remove, strip off. **2** caricature, imitate, mimic, parody, satirize, send up.

taking *adj.* attractive, captivating. ● *n.pl.* money taken in business.

talc *n.* **1** a kind of smooth mineral. **2** talcum powder.

talcum *n.* talc. □ **talcum powder** talc powdered and usu. perfumed for use on the skin.

tale *n.* **1** narrative, story. **2** report spread by gossip.
■ **1** account, anecdote, narration, narrative, story, *colloq.* yarn; fable, legend, saga.

talent *n.* special ability.
■ ability, aptitude, bent, flair, genius, gift, knack.

talented *adj.* having talent.
■ able, accomplished, adept, bright, capable, clever, gifted, good, proficient, skilful, skilled.

talisman *n.* (*pl.* **-mans**) object supposed to bring good luck.
■ amulet, charm, mascot.

talk *v.* **1** convey or exchange ideas by spoken words. **2** use (a specified language) in talking. ● *n.* **1** talking, conversation. **2** style of speech. **3** informal lecture. **4** rumour. □ **talk down to** speak condescendingly to. **talk into** persuade by talking. **talk out of** dissuade by talking. **talk over** discuss. **talking-to** n. reproof. **talker** n.

■ v. **1** chat, chatter, converse, colloq. natter, speak. ● n. **1** chat, conversation, dialogue, discourse, discussion, colloq. natter, tête-à-tête. **2** dialect, jargon, language, speech. **3** address, discourse, lecture, speech. **4** gossip, hearsay, rumour, tittle-tattle. □ **talk over** confer about, consider, debate, deliberate about or over, discuss.

talkative adj. fond of talking.

■ chatty, garrulous, loquacious, voluble.

tall adj. of great or specified height. □ **tall order** difficult task. **tall story** (colloq.) one that is hard to believe. **tallness** n.

■ big, giant, high, lofty, towering.

tallboy n. tall chest of drawers.

tallow n. animal fat used to make candles, lubricants, etc.

tally n. total of a debt or score. ● v. correspond.

■ n. score, sum, total. ● n. accord, agree, coincide, correspond, match, square.

Talmud n. body of Jewish law and tradition. □ **Talmudic** adj.

talon n. bird's large claw.

tambourine n. percussion instrument with jingling discs.

tame adj. **1** (of animals) domesticated, not wild or shy. **2** docile. **3** not exciting. ● v. make tame or manageable. □ **tamely** adv., **tameness** n.

■ adj. **1** domesticated, house-trained. **2** compliant, docile, gentle, meek, mild, obedient, submissive, tractable. **3** bland, boring, dreary, dull, humdrum, mundane, unexciting, uninteresting. ● v. domesticate, train; calm, control, master, subdue.

Tamil n. member or language of a people of southern India and Sri Lanka.

tamp v. pack down tightly.

tamper v. **tamper with** meddle or interfere with.

tampon n. plug of absorbent material inserted into the body.

tan v. (**tanned**) **1** convert (hide) into leather. **2** make or become brown by exposure to sun. **3** (sl.) thrash. ● n. **1** yellowish-brown. **2** brown colour in suntanned skin. ● adj. yellowish-brown.

tandem n. bicycle for two people one behind another. ● adv. one behind another. □ **in tandem** arranged in this way.

tandoor n. Indian etc. clay oven.

tandoori n. food cooked in a tandoor.

tang n. strong taste, flavour, or smell. □ **tangy** adj.

■ flavour, piquancy, savour, sharpness, taste.

tangent n. straight line that touches the outside of a curve without intersecting it. □ **go off at a tangent** diverge suddenly from a line of thought etc. **tangential** adj.

tangerine n. **1** a kind of small orange. **2** its colour.

tangible adj. **1** able to be perceived by touch. **2** clear and definite, real. □ **tangibly** adv., **tangibility** n.

■ concrete, definite, material, palpable, physical, real.

tangle v. twist into a confused mass, entangle. ● n. tangled mass or condition. □ **tangle with** become involved in conflict with.

tango n. (pl. **-os**) ballroom dance with gliding steps. ● v. dance a tango.

tank n. **1** large container for liquid or gas. **2** armoured fighting vehicle moving on Caterpillar tracks.

tankard n. large one-handled usu. metal drinking vessel.

tanker n. ship, aircraft, or vehicle for carrying liquid in bulk.

tanner n. person who tans hides.

tannery n. place where hides are tanned into leather.

tannic acid tannin.

tannin n. substance used in tanning and dyeing.

tantalize v. torment by the sight of something desired but kept out of reach or withheld.

■ frustrate, provoke, taunt, tease, tempt, torment.

tantamount adj. equivalent.

■ comparable, equal, equivalent.

tantra n. any of a class of Hindu or Buddhist mystical or magical writings.

tantrum n. outburst of bad temper.

tap¹ n. **1** tubular plug with a device for allowing liquid to flow through. **2** connection for tapping a telephone. ● v. (**tapped**) **1** obtain supplies etc. or information from. **2** fit a listening device in (a telephone circuit). **3** fit a tap into. **4** draw off through a tap or incision. □ **on tap** (colloq.) available for use. **tap root** plant's chief root.

tap² v. (**tapped**) knock gently. ● n. **1** light blow. **2** sound of this. □ **tap-dance** n.

dance in which the feet tap an elaborate rhythm.

■ *n. & v.* hit, knock, pat, rap.

tape *n.* **1** narrow strip of material for tying, fastening, or labelling things. **2** tape recording. **3** magnetic tape. **4** tape-measure. ● *v.* **1** record on magnetic tape. **2** tie or fasten with tape. □ **have a thing taped** (*colloq.*) understand fully. **tape-measure** strip of tape etc. marked for measuring length. **tape recorder** apparatus for recording and reproducing sounds on magnetic tape. **tape recording** recording made on magnetic tape.

taper *n.* **1** thin candle. **2** narrowing. ● *v.* make or become gradually narrower. □ **taper off** diminish.

tapestry *n.* textile fabric woven or embroidered ornamentally.

tapeworm *n.* tape-like worm living as a parasite in intestines.

tapioca *n.* starchy foodstuff prepared from cassava.

tapir /táypeer/ *n.* small pig-like animal with a long snout.

tappet *n.* projection used in machinery to tap against something.

tar *n.* **1** thick dark liquid distilled from coal etc. **2** similar substance formed by burning tobacco. ● *v.* (**tarred**) coat with tar.

tarantella *n.* rapid whirling dance.

tarantula *n.* large black hairy spider.

tardy *adj.* (**-ier**, **-iest**) **1** slow. **2** late. □ **tardily** *adv.*, **tardiness** *n.*

■ **1** dilatory, slow, sluggish. **2** belated, delayed, late, overdue, unpunctual.

tare[1] *n.* a kind of vetch.

tare[2] *n.* allowance for the weight of the container or vehicle weighed with the goods it holds.

target *n.* **1** object or mark to be hit in shooting etc. **2** object of criticism. **3** objective. ● *v.* (**targeted**) aim at (as) a target.

■ *n.* **2** butt, object, victim. **3** aim, ambition, end, goal, object, objective.

tariff *n.* **1** list of fixed charges. **2** duty to be paid.

■ **1** charges, price-list. **2** duty, excise, levy, tax, toll.

Tarmac *n.* **1** [P.] broken stone or slag mixed with tar. **2** (**tarmac**) area surfaced with this. □ **tarmacked** *adj.*

tarnish *v.* **1** (cause to) lose lustre. **2** blemish (a reputation). ● *n.* **1** loss of lustre. **2** blemish.

■ *v.* **1** discolour, dull, stain. **2** blemish, damage, disgrace, mar, spoil, stain, sully, taint.

tarot /tárrō/ *n.* pack of 78 cards mainly used for fortune-telling.

tarpaulin *n.* waterproof canvas.

tarragon *n.* aromatic herb.

tarsus *n.* (*pl.* **-si**) set of small bones forming the ankle.

tart[1] *adj.* acid in taste or manner. □ **tartly** *adv.*, **tartness** *n.*

■ acid, sharp, sour, tangy, vinegary; astringent, biting, caustic, cutting, harsh, mordant.

tart[2] *n.* **1** pie or pastry flan with sweet filling. **2** (*sl.*) prostitute. ● *v.* **tart up** (*colloq.*) dress gaudily, smarten up.

tartan *n.* **1** pattern (orig. of a Scottish clan) with coloured stripes crossing at right angles. **2** cloth with this.

Tartar *n.* **1** member of a group of Central Asian peoples. **2** bad-tempered or difficult person.

tartar *n.* **1** hard deposit forming on teeth. **2** deposit formed by fermentation in a wine cask.

tartare sauce sauce of mayonnaise, chopped gherkins, etc.

tartlet *n.* small tart.

task *n.* piece of work to be done. □ **take to task** rebuke. **task force** group organized for a special task.

■ assignment, business, charge, chore, duty, errand, job, piece of work, responsibility. □ **take to task** berate, chastise, chide, criticize, rebuke, reprimand, reproach, scold, *colloq.* tell off, *colloq.* tick off, upbraid.

taskmaster *n.* person who imposes a task, esp. regularly or severely.

tassel *n.* ornamental bunch of hanging threads. □ **tasselled** *adj.*

taste *n.* **1** sensation caused in the tongue by things placed upon it. **2** ability to perceive this. **3** small quantity (of food or drink). **4** liking. **5** ability to perceive what is beautiful or fitting. **6** slight experience. ● *v.* **1** discover or test the flavour of. **2** have a certain flavour. **3** experience.

■ *n.* **1** flavour, savour. **3** bit, dash, drop, hint, pinch, *colloq.* spot, touch; morsel, nibble, titbit; nip, sip. **4** appetite, desire, fancy, fondness, liking, partiality, penchant, preference. **5** discernment, discrimination, judgement, refinement, style.

tasteful *adj.* showing good taste. □ **tastefully** *adv.*, **tastefulness** *n.*
■ aesthetic, artistic, attractive, charming, elegant, graceful, stylish; decorous, proper, seemly.

tasteless *adj.* **1** having no flavour. **2** showing poor taste. □ **tastelessly** *adv.*, **tastelessness** *n.*
■ **1** bland, flavourless, insipid, vapid, watery. **2** flashy, garish, gaudy, loud, tawdry.

tasty *adj.* (**-ier**, **-iest**) having a strong flavour, appetizing.
■ appetizing, delicious, luscious, savoury, *colloq.* scrumptious, *colloq.* yummy.

tat *n.* (*colloq.*) tatty thing(s).

tattered *adj.* ragged.
■ ragged, ripped, shabby, tatty, threadbare, torn, worn-out.

tatters *n.pl.* torn pieces.

tattle *v.* chatter idly, reveal information thus ● *n.* idle chatter.
■ *v.* chatter, gossip, *colloq.* natter, prattle, talk; blab, *sl.* squeal, tittle-tattle. ● *n.* chatter, gossip, small talk, talk.

tattoo¹ *n.* **1** military display or pageant. **2** tapping sound.

tattoo² *v.* **1** mark (skin) by puncturing it and inserting pigments. **2** make (a pattern) thus. ● *n.* tattooed pattern.

tatty *adj.* (**-ier**, **-iest**) **1** ragged, shabby and untidy. **2** tawdry. □ **tattily** *adv.*, **tattiness** *n.*
■ **1** old, ragged, *colloq.* scruffy, shabby, tattered, threadbare, untidy, worn-out.

taught *see* **teach**.

taunt *v.* jeer at provocatively. ● *n.* taunting remark.
■ *v.* gibe at, goad, jeer at, make fun of, mock, tease, torment. ● *n.* barb, dig, gibe, jeer.

taut *adj.* stretched tightly.
■ firm, rigid, stiff, stretched, tense, tight.

tauten *v.* make or become taut.

tautology *n.* repetition of the same thing in different words. □ **tautological** *adj.*, **tautologous** *adj.*

tavern *n.* (*old use*) inn, pub.

tawdry *adj.* (**-ier**, **-iest**) showy but without real value.
■ flashy, garish, gaudy, loud, showy, tasteless, tatty.

tawny *adj.* orange-brown.

tax *n.* **1** money to be paid to a government. **2** thing that makes a heavy demand. ● *v.* **1** impose a tax on. **2** make heavy demands on. □ **taxation** *n.*, **taxable** *adj.*
■ *n.* **1** customs, duty, excise, levy, tariff. **2** burden, demand, drain, pressure, strain. ● *v.* **2** burden, overload, strain, stretch.

taxi *n.* (*pl.* **-is**) car with driver which may be hired. ● *v.* (**taxied**, **taxiing**) (of an aircraft) move along ground under its own power. □ **taxi-cab** *n.* taxi.

taxidermy *n.* process of preparing, stuffing, and mounting the skins of animals in lifelike form. □ **taxidermist** *n.*

taxonomy *n.* classification of organisms. □ **taxonomical** *adj.*, **taxonomist** *n.*

taxpayer *n.* person who pays tax.

tea *n.* **1** dried leaves of a tropical evergreen shrub. **2** hot drink made by infusing these (or other substances) in boiling water. **3** afternoon or evening meal at which tea is drunk. □ **tea bag** small porous bag holding tea for infusion. **tea chest** wooden box in which tea is exported. **tea cloth** tea towel. **tea leaf** leaf of tea, esp. after infusion. **tea rose** rose with scent like tea. **tea towel** towel for drying washed crockery etc.

teacake *n.* bun for serving toasted and buttered.

teach *v.* (**taught**) impart information or skill to (a person) or about (a subject). □ **teachable** *adj.*, **teacher** *n.*
■ coach, drill, educate, instruct, school, train, tutor. □ **teacher** coach, instructor, lecturer, schoolmaster, schoolmistress, professor, trainer, tutor.

teak *n.* hard durable wood.

teal *n.* (*pl.* **teal**) a kind of duck.

team *n.* **1** set of players. **2** set of people or animals working together. ● *v.* **team up** combine into a team or set.
■ *n.* **1** side, squad. **2** band, corps, crew, gang, group, pair. ● *v.* combine, gang up, join together, link up, unify, unite.

teamwork *n.* combined effort, cooperation.

teapot *n.* vessel with a spout, in which tea is made.

tear¹ /tair/ *v.* (**tore**, **torn**) **1** pull apart or away or to pieces. **2** make (a hole etc.) thus. **3** become torn. **4** move or travel hurriedly. ● *n.* hole etc. torn.
■ *v.* **1** pull apart, rend, rip. **4** bolt, bound, dart, dash, fly, hasten, hurry, race, run,

rush, scoot, shoot, speed, sprint, zoom.
● *n.* hole, rent, rip, split.

tear² /teer/ *n.* drop of liquid forming in
and falling from the eye. □ **in tears** with
tears flowing. **tear gas** gas causing severe irritation of the eyes.

tearaway *n.* unruly young person.

tearful *adj.* shedding or ready to shed
tears. □ **tearfully** *adv.*

tease *v.* **1** try to provoke in a playful or
unkind way. **2** pick into separate
strands. ● *n.* person fond of teasing
others.

■ *v.* **1** bait, chaff, goad, make fun of, provoke, *sl.* rag, *colloq.* rib, taunt, torment.

teasel *n.* plant with bristly heads.

teaset *n.* set of cups and plates etc. for
serving tea.

teashop *n.* shop where tea is served to
the public.

teaspoon *n.* **1** small spoon for stirring
tea etc. **2** amount held by this. □ **tea-
spoonful** *n.*

teat *n.* **1** nipple on a breast or udder. **2**
rubber nipple for sucking milk from a
bottle.

technical *adj.* **1** of the mechanical arts
and applied sciences. **2** using technical
terms. **3** of a particular subject or craft
etc. **4** in a strict legal sense. □ **technically** *adv.*, **technicality** *n.*

technician *n.* **1** expert in the techniques
of a subject or craft. **2** skilled mechanic.

technique *n.* method of performing or
doing something.

■ art, artistry, craft, craftsmanship, expertise, knack, skill; approach, manner,
method, mode, style, system, way.

technocracy *n.* rule by technical ex-
perts. □ **technocrat** *n.*

technology *n.* **1** study of mechanical
arts and applied sciences. **2** these subjects. **3** their application in industry etc.
□ **technological** *adj.*, **technologically**
adv., **technologist** *n.*

teddy bear toy bear.

tedious *adj.* tiresome because of length,
slowness, or dullness. □ **tediously** *adv.*,
tediousness *n.*, **tedium** *n.*

■ boring, deadly, dreary, dull, flat, humdrum, interminable, long-winded, monotonous, repetitive, tiresome, uninspiring,
uninteresting, wearisome.

tee *n.* **1** cleared space from which a golf
ball is driven at the start of play. **2** small
heap of sand or piece of wood for sup-

porting this ball. ● *v.* **(teed) tee off** make
the first stroke in golf.

teem¹ *v.* be present in large numbers.
□ **teem with** be full of.

■ □ **teem with** abound in, be abundant in,
be full of, be overflowing with, swarm with.

teem² *v.* (of water or rain) pour.

teenager *n.* person in his or her teens.

teens *n.pl.* years of age from 13 to 19.
□ **teenage** *adj.*, **teenaged** *adj.*

teeny *adj.* (**-ier**, **-iest**) (*colloq.*) tiny.

tee shirt = **T-shirt**.

teeter *v.* stand or move unsteadily.

■ rock, sway, totter, wobble.

teeth *see* **tooth**.

teethe *v.* (of a baby) have its first teeth
appear through the gums. □ **teething
troubles** problems in the early stages of
an enterprise.

teetotal *adj.* abstaining completely from
alcohol. □ **teetotaller** *n.*, **teetotalism** *n.*

telecommunication *n.* **1** communication by telephone, radio, etc. **2** (*pl.*)
technology for this.

telegram *n.* message sent by telegraph.

telegraph *n.* system or apparatus for
sending messages, esp. by electrical
impulses along wires. ● *v.* communicate
in this way.

telegraphist *n.* person employed in
telegraphy.

telegraphy *n.* communication by telegraph. □ **telegraphic** *adj.*, **telegraphic-
ally** *adv.*

telemeter *n.* apparatus for recording and
transmitting the readings of an instrument at a distance. □ **telemetry** *n.*

telepathy *n.* communication between
minds other than by the senses. □ **tele-
pathic** *adj.*, **telepathist** *n.*

telephone *n.* device for transmitting
speech by wire or radio. ● *v.* send (a
message) to (a person) by telephone.
□ **telephonic** *adj.*, **telephonically** *adv.*,
telephony *n.*

telephonist *n.* operator of a telephone
switchboard.

telephoto lens lens producing a large
image of a distant object for photography.

teleprinter *n.* telegraph instrument for
sending and receiving typewritten messages.

telesales *n.pl.* selling by telephone.

telescope *n.* optical instrument for
making distant objects appear larger.
● *v.* **1** make or become shorter by sliding
each section inside the next. **2** compress

or become compressed forcibly. □ **tele-scopic** adj., **telescopically** adv.

teletext n. service transmitting written information to subscribers' television screens.

televise v. transmit by television.

television n. **1** system for reproducing on a screen a view of scenes etc. by radio transmission. **2** televised programmes. **3** (in full **television set**) apparatus for receiving these. □ **televisual** adj.

telex n. system of telegraphy using teleprinters and public transmission lines. ● v. send (a message) to (a person) by telex.

tell v. (**told**) **1** make known in words. **2** give information to. **3** reveal a secret. **4** predict. **5** distinguish. **6** direct, order. **7** produce an effect. □ **tell apart** distinguish between. **tell off** (colloq.) reprimand. **tell-tale** n. person who tells tales. **tell tales** reveal secrets.

■ **1** narrate, recount, relate. **2** announce, communicate, declare, disclose, divulge, impart, make known, say, state, utter. **3** blab, sl. squeal, tattle. **4** forecast, foresee, foretell, predict. **5** differentiate, distinguish. **6** bid, command, direct, instruct, order. □ **tell off** colloq. bawl out, berate, chastise, chide, rebuke, reprimand, reproach, scold, take to task, colloq. tick off, upbraid.

teller n. **1** narrator. **2** person appointed to count votes. **3** bank cashier.

telling adj. having a noticeable effect.
■ considerable, marked, noticeable, significant, striking.

telly n. (colloq.) television.

temerity n. **1** impudence. **2** rashness.

temp n. (colloq.) temporary employee.

temper n. **1** mental disposition, mood. **2** fit of anger. **3** calmness under provocation. ● v. **1** bring (metal or clay) to the required hardness or consistency. **2** moderate the effects of.

■ n. **1** character, disposition, make-up, nature, personality, temperament; frame of mind, humour, mood. **2** fury, rage, tantrum. **3** calm, calmness, composure, sl. cool, equanimity, self-control. ● v. **1** anneal, harden, strengthen, toughen. **2** assuage, cushion, moderate, modify, soften, tone down.

tempera n. method of painting using colours mixed with egg.

temperament n. person's nature and character.
■ character, disposition, make-up, nature, personality, temper

temperamental adj. **1** of or relating to temperament. **2** excitable or moody. □ **temperamentally** adv.
■ **2** changeable, emotional, excitable, highly-strung, mercurial, moody, sensitive, touchy, volatile.

temperance n. **1** self-restraint. **2** total abstinence from alcohol.

temperate adj. **1** self-restrained, avoiding excess. **2** (of climate) without extremes. □ **temperately** adv.
■ **1** disciplined, equable, even-tempered, moderate, restrained, self-controlled, sensible.

temperature n. **1** degree of heat or cold. **2** body temperature above normal.

tempest n. violent storm.

tempestuous adj. stormy.
■ stormy, turbulent, wild.

template n. pattern or gauge, esp. for cutting shapes.

temple[1] n. building dedicated to the presence or service of god(s).

temple[2] n. flat part between forehead and ear.

tempo n. (pl. **-os** or **-i**) **1** time, speed, or rhythm of a piece of music. **2** speed, pace.
■ **1** beat, cadence, measure, metre, rhythm, stress, tempo, time. **2** pace, rate, speed.

temporal adj. **1** earthly. **2** of or denoting time. **3** of the temple(s) of the head.
■ **1** earthly, human, material, mortal, physical, secular, worldly.

temporary adj. lasting for a limited time. □ **temporarily** adv.
■ interim, makeshift, provisional.

temporize v. avoid committing oneself in order to gain time.

tempt v. **1** persuade or try to persuade by the prospect of pleasure or advantage. **2** arouse a desire in. □ **temptation** n., **tempter** n., **temptress** n.
■ **1** coax, entice, inveigle, persuade, woo. **2** allure, attract, captivate, lure, seduce. □ **temptation** allure, appeal, attractiveness, charm, fascination, pull, seductiveness.

ten adj. & n. one more than nine.

tenable *adj.* able to be defended or held. □ **tenability** *n.*
■ arguable, defensible, justifiable, plausible, reasonable, supportable, viable, workable.

tenacious *adj.* holding or sticking firmly. □ **tenaciously** *adv.*, **tenacity** *n.*
■ determined, dogged, persistent, pertinacious, resolute, single-minded, steadfast, unswerving.

tenancy *n.* use of land or a building etc. as a tenant.

tenant *n.* person who rents land or a building etc. from a landlord.

tench *n.* (*pl.* **tench**) fish of the carp family.

tend¹ *v.* take care of.
■ care for, look after, mind, minister to, see to, take care of.

tend² *v.* have a specified tendency.

tendency *n.* **1** way a person or thing is likely to be or behave. **2** thing's direction.
■ **1** bent, inclination, leaning, predisposition, proclivity, propensity, susceptibility, trend.

tendentious *adj.* biased, not impartial. □ **tendentiously** *adv.*

tender¹ *adj.* **1** not tough or hard. **2** delicate. **3** painful when touched. **4** compassionate. **5** loving, gentle. □ **tenderly** *adv.*, **tenderness** *n.*
■ **2** delicate, fragile, sensitive, weak. **3** painful, raw, sensitive, sore. **4** compassionate, kind, soft-hearted, sympathetic. **5** affectionate, caring, fond, loving, warm; delicate, gentle, light, soft.

tender² *v.* **1** offer formally. **2** make a tender for. ● *n.* formal offer to supply goods or carry out work at a stated price. □ **legal tender** currency that must be accepted in payment.
■ *v.* **1** offer, proffer, submit. ● *n.* bid, offer, quotation.

tender³ *n.* **1** vessel or vehicle conveying goods or passengers to and from a larger one. **2** truck attached to a steam locomotive and carrying fuel and water etc.

tendon *n.* strip of strong tissue connecting a muscle to a bone etc.

tendril *n.* **1** thread-like part by which a climbing plant clings. **2** slender curl of hair etc.

tenement *n.* large house let in portions to tenants.

tenet *n.* firm belief or principle.
■ axiom, belief, canon, conviction, creed, doctrine, maxim, precept, principle, theory.

tenfold *adj.* & *adv.* ten times as much or as many.

tennis *n.* ball game played with rackets over a net, with a soft ball on an open court (**lawn tennis**) or with a hard ball in a walled court (**real tennis**).

tenon *n.* projection shaped to fit into a mortise.

tenor *n.* **1** general meaning. **2** highest ordinary male singing voice. ● *adj.* of tenor pitch.

tense¹ *n.* any of the forms of a verb that indicate the time of the action.

tense² *adj.* **1** stretched tightly. **2** nervous, anxious. ● *v.* make or become tense. □ **tensely** *adv.*, **tenseness** *n.*
■ *adj.* **1** firm, rigid, stiff, stretched, taut, tight. **2** agitated, anxious, concerned, edgy, fretful, *colloq.* jittery, jumpy, keyed up, nervous, on tenterhooks, uneasy, *colloq.* uptight, worried; *colloq.* fraught, stressful, worrying.

tensile *adj.* **1** of tension. **2** capable of being stretched.

tension *n.* **1** stretching. **2** tenseness, esp. of feelings. **3** effect produced by forces pulling against each other. **4** electromotive force.
■ **1** force, pressure, pull, strain, stress, tightness. **2** anxiety, apprehension, nervousness, strain, stress, suspense, tenseness.

tent *n.* portable shelter or dwelling made of canvas etc.

tentacle *n.* slender flexible part of certain animals, used for feeling or grasping things.

tentative *adj.* **1** hesitant. **2** done as a trial. □ **tentatively** *adv.*
■ **1** cautious, hesitant, uncertain, unsure. **2** experimental, exploratory, provisional.

tenterhooks *n.pl.* **on tenterhooks** in suspense because of uncertainty.

tenth *adj.* & *n.* next after ninth. □ **tenthly** *adv.*

tenuous *adj.* **1** very slight. **2** very thin. □ **tenuousness** *n.*
■ **1** doubtful, dubious, flimsy, insubstantial, shaky, slight, weak.

tenure *n.* holding of office or of land or accommodation etc.

tepee /téepee/ *n.* conical tent used by N. American Indians.

tepid *adj.* lukewarm.

tequila *n.* Mexican liquor made from the sap of an agave plant.

tercentenary *n.* 300th anniversary.

term *n.* **1** fixed or limited period. **2** word or phrase. **3** (*pl.*) conditions offered or accepted. **4** (*pl.*) relations between people. **5** period of weeks during which a school etc. is open or in which a law court holds sessions. **6** each quantity or expression in a mathematical series or ratio etc. □ **come to terms with** reconcile oneself to (a difficulty etc.).
■ **1** duration, period, span, spell, stretch, time. **2** denomination, designation, name, phrase, title, word. **3** (**terms**) conditions, prerequisites, provisions, provisos, requirements, stipulations. □ **come to terms with** accept, face up to, reconcile oneself to, resign oneself to.

termagant *n.* bullying woman.

terminal *adj.* **1** of or forming an end. **2** of or undergoing the last stage of a fatal disease. ● *n.* **1** point of input or output to a computer etc. **2** terminus. **3** building where air passengers arrive and depart. **4** point of connection in an electric circuit. □ **terminally** *adv.*

terminate *v.* end. □ **termination** *n.*
■ bring to an end, conclude, discontinue, end, finish, halt, put an end to, stop, wind up. □ **termination** cessation, close, conclusion, discontinuation, ending.

terminology *n.* technical terms of a subject. □ **terminological** *adj.*

terminus *n.* (*pl.* **-ni**) **1** end. **2** last stopping place on a rail or bus route.

termite *n.* small insect that is very destructive to timber.

tern *n.* seabird with long wings.

terrace *n.* **1** raised level place. **2** paved area beside a house. **3** row of houses joined by party walls.

terracotta *n.* **1** brownish-red unglazed pottery. **2** its colour.

terra firma dry land, the ground.

terrain *n.* land with regard to its natural features.
■ country, ground, land, territory.

terrapin *n.* freshwater tortoise.

terrestrial *adj.* **1** of the earth. **2** of or living on land.

terrible *adj.* **1** appalling, distressing. **2** very bad. □ **terribly** *adv.*
■ **1** appalling, awful, bad, dire, disastrous, distressing, dreadful, fearful, frightful, ghastly, grave, horrible, serious, severe. **2** hopeless, incompetent, inept, inexpert, unskilful.

terrier *n.* small active dog.

terrific *adj.* **1** (*colloq.*) huge, excellent. **2** causing terror. □ **terrifically** *adv.*

terrify *v.* fill with terror.
■ alarm, dismay, frighten, horrify, petrify, scare, terrorize.

terrine *n.* **1** pâté or similar food. **2** earthenware dish for this.

territorial *adj.* of territory. □ **Territorial Army** a volunteer reserve force.

territory *n.* **1** land under the control of a person, state, etc. **2** sphere of action or thought.
■ **1** area, district, dominion, land, province, region, sector, zone.

terror *n.* **1** extreme fear. **2** terrifying person or thing. **3** (*colloq.*) troublesome person or thing.
■ **1** alarm, dread, fear, fright, horror, panic, trepidation.

terrorism *n.* use of violence and intimidation. □ **terrorist** *n.*

terrorize *v.* **1** fill with terror. **2** coerce by terrorism.
■ **1** frighten, petrify, scare, terrify. **2** browbeat, bully, coerce, cow, intimidate, threaten.

terry *n.* looped cotton fabric used for towels etc.

terse *adj.* **1** concise. **2** curt. □ **tersely** *adv.*, **terseness** *n.*
■ **1** brief, concise, laconic, pithy, short, succinct, to the point. **2** abrupt, blunt, brusque, curt, short.

tertiary /térshəri/ *adj.* next after secondary.

tessellated *adj.* resembling mosaic.

test *n.* **1** something done to discover a person's or thing's qualities or abilities etc. **2** examination (esp. in a school) on a limited subject. **3** test match. ● *v.* subject to a test. □ **test match** one of a series of international cricket or Rugby football matches. **test-tube** *n.* tube of thin glass with one end closed, used in laboratories. **tester** *n.*
■ *n.* **1** appraisal, assessment, check, evaluation, examination, trial. **2** exam, examination. ● *v.* appraise, assess, check, evaluate, examine, screen, try (out).

testament *n.* **1** a will. **2** written statement of beliefs. **3** (**Testament**) main division of the Christian Bible.

testate *adj.* having left a valid will at death. □ **testacy** *n.*

testator *n.* person who has made a will.

testes *see* **testis.**

testicle *n.* male organ that secretes sperm-bearing fluid.

testify *v.* 1 give evidence. 2 be evidence of.
■ 1 affirm, assert, attest, avow, declare, state, swear.

testimonial *n.* 1 formal statement testifying to character, abilities, etc. 2 gift showing appreciation.

testimony *n.* 1 declaration (esp. under oath). 2 supporting evidence.
■ 1 attestation, declaration, deposition, evidence, statement, submission.

testis *n.* (*pl.* **testes**) testicle.

testosterone *n.* male sex hormone.

testy *adj.* irritable. □ **testily** *adv.*
■ bad-tempered, crabby, cross, crotchety, disagreeable, fractious, grumpy, irritable, peevish, petulant, prickly, quarrelsome, snappy, splenetic, surly.

tetanus *n.* bacterial disease causing painful muscular spasms.

tête-à-tête /táytaatáyt/ *n.* private conversation, esp. between two people.
● *adj. & adv.* together in private.

tether *n.* rope etc. fastening an animal so that it can graze. ● *v.* fasten with a tether. □ **at the end of one's tether** having reached the limit of one's endurance.

tetrahedron *n.* (*pl.* **-dra**) solid with four sides.

Teutonic *adj.* of Germanic peoples or their languages.

text *n.* 1 main body of a book as distinct from illustrations etc. 2 sentence from Scripture used as the subject of a sermon. □ **textual** *adj.*

textbook *n.* book of information for use in studying a subject.

textile *n.* woven or machine-knitted fabric. ● *adj.* of textiles.
■ *n. & adj.* cloth, fabric, material.

texture *n.* way a fabric etc. feels to the touch. □ **textural** *adj.*

textured *adj.* having a noticeable texture.

than *conj.* used to introduce the second element in a comparison.

thank *v.* express gratitude to. □ **thank you** polite expression of thanks. **thanks** *n.pl.* 1 expressions of thanks. 2 (*colloq.*) thank you.

thankful *adj.* feeling or expressing gratitude. □ **thankfully** *adv.*
■ appreciative, beholden, grateful, indebted, obliged.

thankless *adj.* not likely to win thanks. □ **thanklessness** *n.*

thanksgiving *n.* expression of gratitude, esp. to God.

that *adj. & pron.* (*pl.* **those**) 1 the (person or thing) referred to. 2 further or less obvious (one) of two. ● *adv.* to such an extent. ● *rel.pron.* used to introduce a defining clause. ● *conj.* introducing a dependent clause.

thatch *n.* roof made of straw or reeds etc. ● *v.* roof with thatch. □ **thatcher** *n.*

thaw *v.* 1 make or become unfrozen. 2 become less cool or less formal in manner. ● *n.* thawing, weather that thaws ice etc.

the *adj.* applied to a noun standing for a specific person or thing, or one or all of a kind, or used to emphasize excellence or importance. 2 (of prices) per.

theatre *n.* 1 place for the performance of plays etc. 2 plays and acting. 3 lecture hall with seats in tiers. 4 room where surgical operations are performed.
■ 2 acting, drama, show business, the stage.

theatrical *adj.* 1 of or for the theatre. 2 exaggerated for effect. ● *n.pl.* theatrical (esp. amateur) performances. □ **theatrically** *adv.*, **theatricality** *n.*
■ *adj.* 1 dramatic, histrionic, stage. 2 affected, camp, exaggerated, *sl.* hammed, histrionic, overacted, overdone.

thee *pron.* (*old use*) objective case of *thou.*

theft *n.* stealing.
■ burglary, embezzlement, misappropriation, pilfering, robbery, shoplifting, stealing, thievery, thieving.

their *adj.*, **theirs** *poss.pron.* belonging to them.

theism /thée-iz'm/ *n.* belief that the universe was created by a god. □ **theist** *n.*, **theistic** *adj.*

them *pron.* objective case of *they.*

theme *n.* 1 subject being discussed. 2 melody which is repeated. □ **theme park** park with amusements organized round one theme. **thematic** *adj.*
■ 1 subject, subject-matter, text, thesis, topic.

themselves *pron.* emphatic and reflexive form of *they* and *them.*

then *adv.* **1** at that time. **2** next, and also. **3** in that case. ● *adj.* & *n.* (of) that time.

thence *adv.* from that place or source.

thenceforth *adv.* from then on.

theocracy *n.* form of government by a divine being or by priests. □ **theocratic** *adj.*

theodolite *n.* surveying instrument for measuring angles.

theology *n.* study or system of religion. □ **theological** *adj.*, **theologian** *n.*

theorem *n.* mathematical statement to be proved by reasoning.

theoretical *adj.* based on theory only. □ **theoretically** *adv.*
■ hypothetical, putative, speculative, unproven.

theorist *n.* person who theorizes.

theorize *v.* form theories.
■ conjecture, guess, speculate.

theory *n.* **1** set of ideas formulated to explain something. **2** opinion, supposition. **3** statement of the principles of a subject.
■ **2** conjecture, hypothesis, idea, opinion, supposition, thesis, view.

theosophy *n.* system of philosophy that aims at direct intuitive knowledge of God. □ **theosophical** *adj.*

therapeutic /thérrəpyóotik/ *adj.* of or for the cure of disease. □ **therapeutically** *adv.*
■ beneficial, healing, health-giving, medicinal, restorative.

therapist *n.* specialist in therapy.

therapy *n.* medical or healing treatment.

there *adv.* **1** in, at, or to that place. **2** at that point. **3** in that matter. ● *n.* that place. ● *int.* exclamation of satisfaction or consolation.

thereabouts *adv.* near there.

thereafter *adv.* after that.

thereby *adv.* by that means.

therefore *adv.* for that reason.
■ as a result, consequently, for that reason, hence, so, thus.

therein *adv.* in that place.

thereof *adv.* of that.

thereto *adv.* to that.

thereupon *adv.* in consequence of that, because of that.

thermal *adj.* of or using heat. ● *n.* rising current of hot air.

thermodynamics *n.* science of the relationship between heat and other forms of energy.

thermometer *n.* instrument for measuring heat.

thermonuclear *adj.* of or using nuclear reactions that occur only at very high temperatures.

Thermos *n.* [P.] vacuum flask.

thermostat *n.* device that regulates temperature automatically. □ **thermostatic** *adj.*, **thermostatically** *adv.*

thesaurus *n.* (*pl.* **-ri**) dictionary of synonyms.

these *see* **this**.

thesis *n.* (*pl.* **theses**) **1** theory put forward and supported by reasoning. **2** lengthy essay submitted for a university degree.
■ **1** argument, case, contention, premiss, proposition, theory. **2** dissertation, essay, paper.

they *pron.* people or things mentioned or unspecified.

thick *adj.* **1** of great or specified distance between opposite surfaces. **2** densely covered or filled. **3** fairly stiff in consistency. **4** (*colloq.*) stupid. **5** (*colloq.*) intimate. ● *adv.* thickly. ● *n.* busiest part. □ **thick-skinned** *adj.* not sensitive to criticism or snubs. **thickly** *adv.*, **thickness** *n.*
■ *adj.* **1** broad, wide. **2** chock-a-block, crowded, dense, full, impenetrable, packed. **3** clotted, gelatinous, glutinous, viscid, viscous. ● *n.* centre, core, heart.

thicken *v.* make or become thicker.
■ clot, coagulate, congeal, *colloq.* jell, set, solidify, stiffen.

thicket *n.* close group of shrubs and small trees etc.
■ coppice, copse, covert, grove, spinney.

thickset *adj.* **1** set or growing close together. **2** stocky, burly.

thief *n.* (*pl.* **thieves**) one who steals. □ **thievish** *adj.*, **thievery** *n.*
■ burglar, housebreaker, pickpocket, robber, shoplifter.

thieve *v.* steal, be a thief.
■ filch, lift, misappropriate, *sl.* nick, pilfer, *sl.* pinch, pocket, purloin, *colloq.* rip off, steal, *colloq.* swipe.

thigh *n.* upper part of the leg, between hip and knee.

thimble *n.* hard cap worn to protect the end of the finger in sewing.

thin *adj.* (**thinner, thinnest**) **1** not thick. **2** lean, not plump. **3** not plentiful. **4** lacking substance, weak. ● *adv.* thinly. ● *v.*

(**thinned**) make or become thinner. □ **thinly** adv., **thinness** n.

■ adj. **1** fine, narrow, slender; delicate, diaphanous, filmy, fine, gauzy. **2** lean, scraggy, scrawny, skinny, slender, slight, slim, spindly. **3** inadequate, insufficient, meagre, scanty, scarce, sparse. **4** insubstantial, feeble, flimsy, lame, tenuous; watery, weak.

thine adj. & poss.pron. (old use) belonging to thee.

thing n. **1** any unspecified object or item. **2** any fact, event, quality, action, etc. **3** (pl.) belongings, utensils, circumstances.

■ **1** article, item, object, whatnot. **2** detail, fact, piece of information; event, happening, incident, occurrence; characteristic, feature, quality; act, action, deed. **3** (**things**) belongings, sl. clobber, effects, goods, possessions, property; apparatus, equipment, gear, tools, utensils; circumstances, conditions, matters.

think v. (**thought**) **1** exercise the mind, form ideas. **2** form or have as an idea or opinion. ● n. (colloq.) act of thinking. □ **think about** or **of** consider. **think better of it** change one's mind after thought. **think-tank** n. group providing ideas and advice on national or commercial problems. **think up** (colloq.) devise. **thinker** n.

■ v. **2** cogitate, contemplate, deliberate, meditate, muse, ponder, reflect, ruminate. **2** believe, consider, deem, imagine, judge, reckon, regard (as), suppose. □ **think about** consider, contemplate, have in mind, intend, propose.

third adj. next after second. ● n. **1** third thing, class, etc. **2** one of three equal parts. □ **third party** another person etc. besides the two principals. **third-rate** adj. very inferior in quality. **Third World** developing countries of Asia, Africa, and Latin America. **thirdly** adv.

thirst n. **1** feeling caused by a desire to drink. **2** strong desire. ● v. feel a thirst. □ **thirst for** have a strong desire for. **thirsty** adj., **thirstily** adv.

■ n. **2** appetite, craving, desire, hankering, hunger, itch, longing, yearning, colloq. yen. □ **thirst for** crave, desire, hanker after, hunger for, long for, lust after, want, wish for, yearn for.

thirteen adj. & n. one more than twelve. □ **thirteenth** adj. & n.

thirty adj. & n. three times ten. □ **thirtieth** adj. & n.

this adj. & pron. (pl. **these**) the (person or thing) near, present, or mentioned.

thistle n. prickly plant. □ **thistledown** n. very light fluff on thistle seeds. **thistly** adj.

thong n. strip of leather used as a fastening or lash etc.

thorax n. part of the body between head or neck and abdomen. □ **thoracic** adj.

thorn n. **1** small sharp pointed projection on a plant. **2** thorn-bearing tree or shrub. □ **thorny** adj.

■ **1** prickle, spine. **2** bramble, brier. □ **thorny** prickly, scratchy, sharp, spiky, spiny.

thorough adj. **1** complete in every way. **2** done with great care. **3** absolute. □ **thoroughly** adv., **thoroughness** n.

■ **1** complete, comprehensive, detailed, exhaustive, extensive, far-reaching, full, sweeping, wide-ranging. **2** assiduous, careful, methodical, meticulous, painstaking, scrupulous. **3** absolute, complete, downright, out and out, perfect, pure, sheer, total, unmitigated, utter.

thoroughbred n. & adj. (horse etc.) bred of pure or pedigree stock.

thoroughfare n. public way open at both ends.

those see **that**.

thou pron. (old use) you.

though conj. in spite of the fact that, even supposing. ● adv. (colloq.) however.

thought see **think**. n. **1** process, power, or way of thinking. **2** idea etc. produced by thinking. **3** intention. **4** consideration.

■ **1** intelligence, reason, reasoning; cogitation, consideration, contemplation, meditation, reflection, rumination. **2** US brainstorm, brainwave, idea. **3** design, expectation, intention, hope, plan. **4** attention, concern, consideration, regard, solicitude, thoughtfulness.

thoughtful adj. **1** thinking deeply. **2** thought out carefully. **3** considerate. □ **thoughtfully** adv., **thoughtfulness** n.

■ **1** contemplative, introspective, meditative, pensive, reflective. **2** intelligent, reasoned. **3** caring, considerate, helpful, kind, neighbourly, solicitous, unselfish.

thoughtless adj. **1** careless. **2** inconsiderate. □ **thoughtlessly** adv., **thoughtlessness** n.

■ **1** careless, heedless, inattentive, negligent, remiss, unthinking. **2** impolite, inconsiderate, insensitive, rude, tactless, undiplomatic.

thousand *adj.* & *n.* ten hundred. □ **thousandth** *adj.* & *n.*

thrash *v.* **1** beat, esp. with a stick or whip. **2** defeat thoroughly. **3** thresh. **4** make flailing movements. □ **thrash out** discuss thoroughly.

■ **1** bash, batter, beat, *sl.* clobber, flog, hit, lash, *colloq.* lay into, strike, thwack, *sl.* wallop, *colloq.* whack, whip. **2** beat, conquer, crush, defeat, destroy, get the better of, *colloq.* lick, overcome, overpower, rout, subdue, triumph over, trounce, vanquish.

thread *n.* **1** thin length of spun cotton or wool etc. **2** thing compared to this. **3** spiral ridge of a screw. ● *v.* **1** pass a thread through. **2** pass (a strip or thread etc.) through or round something. **3** make (one's way) through a crowd etc.
■ *n.* **1** fibre, filament, (piece of) yarn, strand.

threadbare *adj.* **1** with nap worn and threads visible. **2** shabbily dressed.
■ **1** ragged, shabby, tattered, tatty, worn-out. **2** *colloq.* scruffy, shabby, tatty, untidy.

threadworm *n.* small thread-like parasitic worm.

threat *n.* **1** expression of intention to punish, hurt, or harm. **2** person or thing thought likely to bring harm or danger.
■ **1** intimidation, menace, warning. **2** danger, hazard, peril, risk.

threaten *v.* make or be a threat (to).
■ browbeat, bully, intimidate, menace, terrorize; endanger, imperil, jeopardize, put in jeopardy.

three *adj.* & *n.* one more than two. □ **three-dimensional** *adj.* having or appearing to have length, breadth, and depth.

threefold *adj.* & *adv.* three times as much or as many.

threesome *n.* group of three people.

thresh *v.* **1** beat out (grain) from husks of corn. **2** make flailing movements.

threshold *n.* **1** piece of wood or stone forming the bottom of a doorway. **2** point of entry. **3** beginning.
■ **2** doorway, entrance. **3** beginning, commencement, dawn, outset, start, verge.

threw *see* **throw**.

thrice *adv.* (*old use*) three times.

thrift *n.* **1** economical management of resources. **2** plant with pink flowers. □ **thrifty** *adj.*
■ **1** economy, frugality, husbandry, parsimony, prudence. □ **thrifty** careful, economical, frugal, parsimonious, provident, prudent, sparing.

thrill *n.* wave of feeling or excitement. ● *v.* feel or cause to feel a thrill.
■ *n.* buzz, *colloq.* kick. ● *v.* delight, excite, stimulate, stir, titillate.

thriller *n.* exciting story or play etc., esp. involving crime.

thrive *v.* (**throve** or **thrived**, **thrived** or **thriven**) **1** grow or develop well. **2** prosper.
■ **1** blossom, burgeon, develop, flourish, grow. **2** boom, do well, flourish, prosper, succeed.

throat *n.* **1** front of the neck. **2** passage from mouth to oesophagus or lungs. **3** narrow passage.

throaty *adj.* uttered deep in the throat, hoarse. □ **throatily** *adv.*
■ deep, gruff, guttural, hoarse, husky.

throb *v.* (**throbbed**) **1** (of the heart or pulse) beat with more than usual force. **2** vibrate or sound with a persistent rhythm. ● *n.* throbbing beat or sound.
■ *v.* **1** beat, palpitate, pound, pulsate, pulse. **2** beat, vibrate.

throes *n.pl.* severe pangs of pain. □ **in the throes of** struggling with the task of.

thrombosis *n.* formation of a clot of blood in a blood vessel or organ of the body.

throne *n.* **1** ceremonial seat for a monarch, bishop, etc. **2** sovereign power.

throng *n.* crowded mass of people. ● *v.* **1** move or press in a throng. **2** fill with a throng.
■ *n.* crowd, crush, drove, flock, gathering, herd, horde, host, mob, multitude, pack, swarm. ● *v.* **1** assemble, collect, congregate, crowd, flock, gather, herd, mass, press, swarm.

throttle *n.* **1** valve controlling the flow of fuel or steam etc. to an engine. **2** lever controlling this. ● *v.* strangle. □ **throttle back** or **down** reduce an engine's speed by means of the throttle.

through *prep.* & *adv.* **1** from end to end or side to side (of), entering at one point and coming out at another. **2** from beginning to end (of). **3** by the agency, means, or fault of. **4** so as to have finished, so as to have passed (an exam). **5** so as to be connected by telephone (to). ● *adj.* **1** going through. **2** passing without stopping.

throughout *prep.* & *adv.* right through, from end to end (of).

throughput *n.* amount of material processed.

throve *see* **thrive**.

throw *v.* (**threw**, **thrown**) **1** send with some force through the air. **2** cause to fall. **3** (*colloq.*) disconcert. **4** put (clothes etc.) on or off hastily. **5** shape (pottery) on a wheel. **6** cause to be in a certain state. **7** operate (a switch or lever). **8** have (a fit or tantrum). **9** (*colloq.*) give (a party). ● *n.* **1** act of throwing. **2** distance something is thrown. □ **throw away 1** part with as useless or unwanted. **2** fail to make use of. **throw-away** *adj.* to be thrown away after use. **throw in the towel** admit defeat or failure. **throw out 1** discard. **2** reject. **throw up 1** bring to notice. **2** resign from. **3** vomit. **4** raise, erect. **thrower** *n.*

■ *v.* **1** *sl.* bung, cast, *colloq.* chuck, fling, *colloq.* heave, hurl, lob, pitch, shy, *colloq.* sling, toss. **3** confound, confuse, discomfit, disconcert, floor, *colloq.* flummox, fluster, *colloq.* rattle, *colloq.* stump, unnerve. □ **throw away 1** discard, dispose of, *sl.* ditch, dump, get rid of, jettison, scrap, throw out, toss out. **2** fritter away, squander, waste.

thrush¹ *n.* kind of songbird.

thrush² *n.* fungal infection of the mouth, throat, or vagina.

thrust *v.* (**thrust**) **1** push forcibly. **2** make a forward stroke with a sword etc. ● *n.* thrusting movement or force.

■ *v.* **1** drive, force, push, ram, shove. **2** lunge, plunge, stab.

thud *n.* dull low sound like that of a blow. ● *v.* (**thudded**) make or fall with a thud.

thug *n.* vicious ruffian. □ **thuggish** *adj.*, **thuggery** *n.*

■ hoodlum, hooligan, lout, ruffian, tough, *sl.* yob.

thumb *n.* short thick finger set apart from the other four. ● *v.* **1** touch or turn (pages etc.) with the thumbs. **2** request (a lift) by signalling with one's thumb. □ **under the thumb of** completely under the influence of.

thump *v.* strike or knock heavily (esp. with the fist), thud. ● *n.* **1** heavy blow. **2** sound of thumping.

■ *v.* bash, beat, *sl.* clobber, clout, hit, pound, punch, strike, thwack, *sl.* wallop, *colloq.* whack.

thunder *n.* **1** loud noise that accompanies lightning. **2** similar sound. ● *v.* **1** sound with or like thunder. **2** utter loudly. **3** make a forceful attack in words. □ **steal a person's thunder** forestall him or her. **thundery** *adj.*

■ *v.* **1** boom, resonate, resound, reverberate, roar, rumble. **2** bawl, bellow, roar, shout, yell.

thunderbolt *n.* **1** imaginary missile thought of as sent to earth with a lightning flash. **2** startling formidable event or statement.

thunderclap *n.* clap of thunder.

thunderous *adj.* like thunder.

■ booming, deafening, loud, noisy, roaring.

thunderstorm *n.* storm accompanied by thunder.

thunderstruck *adj.* amazed.

thus *adv.* **1** in this way. **2** as a result of this. **3** to this extent.

thwack *v.* strike with a heavy blow. ● *n.* this blow or sound.

thwart *v.* prevent from doing what is intended or from being accomplished. ● *n.* oarsman's bench across a boat.

■ *v.* baulk, foil, frustrate, hinder, impede, *sl.* scupper, stop, stymie.

thy *adj.* (*old use*) belonging to thee.

thyme /tīm/ *n.* herb with fragrant leaves.

thymus *n.* ductless gland near the base of the neck.

thyroid gland large ductless gland in the neck.

thyself *pron.* (*old use*) emphatic and reflexive form of *thou* and *thee*.

tiara *n.* woman's jewelled semi-circular headdress.

tibia *n.* (*pl.* **-ae**) shin-bone.

tic *n.* involuntary muscular twitch.

tick¹ *n.* **1** regular clicking sound, esp. made by a clock or watch. **2** (*colloq.*) moment. **3** small mark placed against an item in a list etc., esp. to show that it is correct. ● *v.* **1** (of a clock etc.) make a series of ticks. **2** mark with a tick. □ **tick off** (*colloq.*) reprimand. **tick over** (of an engine) idle. **tick-tack** *n.* semaphore signalling by racecourse bookmakers.

tick² *n.* parasitic insect.

tick³ *n.* (*colloq.*) financial credit.

ticket *n.* **1** marked piece of card or paper entitling the holder to a certain right (e.g. to travel by train etc.). **2** certificate of qualification as a ship's master or pilot etc. **3** label. **4** notification of a traffic offence. **5** list of candidates for office. **6** (**the ticket**) (*colloq.*) the correct or desirable thing. ● *v.* (**ticketed**) put a ticket on.

tickle *v.* **1** touch or stroke lightly so as to cause a slight tingling sensation. **2** feel this sensation. **3** amuse, please. ● *n.* act or sensation of tickling.

ticklish *adj.* **1** sensitive to tickling. **2** (of a problem) requiring careful handling.

■ **2** awkward, delicate, difficult, sensitive, *colloq.* sticky, tricky.

tidal *adj.* of or affected by tides.

tiddler *n.* (*colloq.*) small fish, esp. stickleback or minnow.

tiddly *adj.* (*colloq.*) slightly drunk.

tiddly-winks *n.pl.* game of flicking small counters (**tiddly-winks**) into a receptacle.

tide *n.* **1** sea's regular rise and fall. **2** trend of feeling or events etc. □ **tide over** help temporarily.

tidings *n.pl.* news.

tidy *adj.* (**-ier, -iest**) neat and orderly. ● *v.* make tidy. □ **tidily** *adv.*, **tidiness** *n.*

■ *adj.* neat, orderly, shipshape, smart, spruce, straight, trim. ● *v.* arrange, neaten, put in order, smarten (up), sort (out), spruce (up), straighten.

tie *v.* (**tying**) **1** attach or fasten with cord etc. **2** form into a knot or bow. **3** connect. **4** make the same score as another competitor. **5** restrict, limit. ● *n.* **1** cord etc. used for tying something. **2** thing that unites or restricts. **3** equality of score between competitors. **4** sports match between two of a set of teams or players. **5** strip of material worn below the collar and knotted at the front of the neck. □ **tie-break** *n.* means of deciding the winner when competitors have tied. **tie-clip, -pin** *ns.* ornamental clip or pin for holding a necktie in place. **tie in** link or (of information etc.) be connected with something else. **tie up 1** fasten with cord etc. **2** make (money etc.) not readily available for use. **3** occupy fully. **tie-up** *n.* connection, link.

■ *v.* **1** bind, fasten, hitch, lash, make fast, moor, rope, secure, tether. **2** knot. **3** associate, connect, link. **4** be even *or* level, be neck and neck, draw, finish equal. **5** confine, curb, limit, restrain, restrict. ● *n.* **1** band, cord, ligature, string. **2** association, bond, connection, link, relationship. **3** draw, stalemate.

tied *adj.* **1** (of a pub) bound to supply only one brewer's beer. **2** (of a house) for

occupation only by a person working for its owner.

tier /*teer*/ *n.* any of a series of rows or ranks or units of a structure placed one above the other.

■ level, line, rank, row, storey.

tiff *n.* petty quarrel.

■ altercation, argument, disagreement, quarrel, row, *colloq.* scrap, squabble.

tiger *n.* large striped animal of the cat family. □ **tiger lily** orange lily with dark spots.

tight *adj.* **1** held or fastened firmly, fitting closely. **2** tense, not slack. **3** (*colloq.*) stingy. **4** (*colloq.*) drunk. **5** (of money etc.) severely restricted. ● *adv.* tightly. □ **tight corner** difficult situation. **tight-fisted** *adj.* stingy. **tightly** *adv.*, **tightness** *n.*

■ *adj.* **1** fast, firm, fixed, secure; close-fitting. **2** firm, rigid, stiff, stretched, taut, tense.

tighten *v.* make or become tighter.

tightrope *n.* tightly stretched rope on which acrobats perform.

tights *n.pl.* garment covering the legs and lower part of the body.

tigress *n.* female tiger.

tile *n.* thin slab of baked clay etc. for roofing, paving, etc. ● *v.* cover with tiles.

till[1] *v.* prepare and use (land) for growing crops. □ **tillage** *n.*

■ cultivate, farm, plough, work.

till[2] *prep. & conj.* up to (a specified time).

till[3] *n.* receptacle for money in a shop etc.

tiller *n.* bar by which a rudder is turned.

tilt *v.* move into a sloping position. ● *n.* sloping position. □ **at full tilt** at full speed or force.

■ *v.* angle, careen, heel over, incline, lean, list, slant, slope.

tilth *n.* **1** tillage. **2** tilled soil.

timber *n.* **1** wood prepared for use in building or carpentry. **2** trees suitable for this. **3** wooden beam used in constructing a house or ship.

■ **1** beams, lumber, planks, wood.

timbered *adj.* **1** constructed of timber or with a timber framework. **2** (of land) wooded.

timbre /*támbər*/ *n.* characteristic quality of the sound of a voice or instrument.

time *n.* **1** all the years of the past, present, and future. **2** portion or point of this. **3** occasion, instance. **4** rhythm in music. **5** (*pl.*) contemporary circumstances. **6** (*pl.*, in multiplication or comparison) taken a number of times. ● *v*. **1** choose the time for. **2** measure the time taken by. □ **behind the times** out of date. **for the time being** until another arrangement is made. **from time to time** at intervals. **in time 1** not late. **2** eventually. **on time** punctual(ly). **time-and-motion** *adj*. concerned with measuring the efficiency of effort. **time bomb** bomb that can be set to explode after an interval. **time-honoured** *adj*. respected because of antiquity, traditional. **time-lag** *n*. interval between two connected events. **time-share** *n*. share in a property that allows use by several joint owners at agreed different times. **time switch** one operating automatically at a set time. **time zone** region (between parallels of longitude) where a common standard time is used.

■ *n*. **2** age, day(s), epoch, era, period; interval, period, spell, stretch; hour, instant, juncture, moment, point. **3** chance, occasion, opportunity; instance, occurrence. **4** beat, measure, rhythm, stress, tempo. **5** (**times**) circumstances, conditions, things. □ **behind the times** antiquated, old, old-fashioned, outdated, outmoded, out of date. **time-honoured** accepted, conventional, customary, established, habitual, traditional, usual.

timeless *adj*. not affected by the passage of time. □ **timelessness** *n*.

■ ageless, eternal, everlasting, immortal, immutable, unchangeable, unchanging, undying.

timely *adj*. occurring at just the right time. □ **timeliness** *n*.

■ convenient, opportune, seasonable, well-timed.

timepiece *n*. clock or watch.

timetable *n*. list showing the times at which certain events take place.

timid *adj*. easily alarmed, shy. □ **timidly** *adv*., **timidity** *n*.

■ bashful, coy, diffident, faint-hearted, fearful, frightened, meek, mousy, retiring, self-conscious, scared, shy, timorous, unassuming.

timorous *adj*. timid. □ **timorously** *adv*., **timorousness** *n*.

timpani *n.pl.* kettledrums. □ **timpanist** *n*.

tin *n*. **1** silvery-white metal. **2** metal box or other container, one in which food is sealed for preservation. ● *v*. (**tinned**) **1** coat with tin. **2** seal (food) into a tin.

tincture *n*. **1** solution of a medicinal substance in alcohol. **2** slight tinge.

tinder *n*. any dry substance that catches fire easily.

tine *n*. prong or point of a fork, harrow, or antler.

tinge *v*. (**tingeing**) **1** colour slightly. **2** give a slight trace of an element or quality to. ● *n*. slight colouring or trace.

tingle *v*. have a slight pricking or stinging sensation. ● *n*. this sensation.

tinker *n*. **1** travelling mender of pots and pans. **2** (*colloq*.) mischievous person or animal. ● *v*. work at something casually trying to repair or improve it.

tinkle *n*. series of short light ringing sounds. ● *v*. make or cause to make a tinkle.

tinsel *n*. glittering decorative metallic strips or threads.

tint *n*. variety or slight trace of a colour. ● *v*. colour slightly.

■ *n*. colour, hue, shade, tincture, tinge, tone. ● *v*. colour, tinge.

tiny *adj*. (**-ier, -iest**) very small.

■ diminutive, little, miniature, minuscule, minute, small, *colloq*. teeny, *colloq*. wee.

tip[1] *n*. end, esp. of something small or tapering. ● *v*. (**tipped**) provide with a tip.

■ *n*. cap, end, head, point.

tip[2] *v*. (**tipped**) **1** tilt, topple. **2** discharge (a thing's contents) by tilting. **3** name as a likely winner. **4** make a small present of money to, esp. in acknowledgement of services. ● *n*. **1** small money present. **2** useful piece of advice. **3** place where rubbish etc. is tipped. □ **tip off** give a warning or hint to. **tip-off** *n*. such a warning etc. **tipper** *n*.

■ *v*. **1** incline, lean, list, slant, slope, tilt; knock over, overturn, topple (over), upend, upset. ● *n*. **1** gratuity. **2** piece of advice, recommendation, suggestion, tip-off. **3** dump, rubbish heap. □ **tip off** advise, alert, caution, forewarn, notify, warn.

tipple *v*. drink (wine or spirits etc.) repeatedly. ● *n*. (*colloq*.) alcoholic or other drink.

tipster *n*. person who gives tips about racehorses etc.

tipsy *adj*. slightly drunk.

tiptoe *v*. (**tiptoeing**) walk very quietly or carefully.

tiptop *adj*. (*colloq*.) first-rate.

tirade *n*. long angry piece of criticism or denunciation.

tire v. make or become tired.
■ drain, exhaust, fatigue, *sl.* knacker, wear out, weary.

tired adj. feeling a desire to sleep or rest. □ **tired of** having had enough of.
■ all in, dead beat, drained, exhausted, *colloq.* fagged, fatigued, *sl.* knackered, weary, *colloq.* whacked, worn-out.

tireless adj. not tiring easily. □ **tirelessly** adv., **tirelessness** n.
■ energetic, hard-working, indefatigable, industrious, tenacious, unflagging, untiring, vigorous.

tiresome adj. **1** annoying. **2** tedious.
■ **1** annoying, bothersome, exasperating, *colloq.* infernal, infuriating, irksome, irritating, maddening, trying, vexatious. **2** boring, deadly, dreary, dull, tedious, uninteresting, wearisome.

tissue n. **1** substance forming an animal or plant body. **2** tissue-paper. **3** piece of soft absorbent paper used as a handkerchief etc. □ **tissue-paper** n. thin soft paper used for packing things.

tit n. any of several small birds.

titanic adj. gigantic.
■ colossal, enormous, gargantuan, giant, gigantic, huge, immense, mammoth, massive, monumental, vast.

titanium n. dark-grey metal.

titbit n. choice bit of food or item of information.
■ delicacy, *colloq.* goody, treat.

tithe n. one-tenth of income or produce formerly paid to the Church.

titillate v. excite or stimulate pleasantly. □ **titillation** n.

titivate v. (*colloq.*) smarten up, put finishing touches to. □ **titivation** n.

title n. **1** name of a book, poem, or picture etc. **2** word denoting rank or office, or used in speaking of or to the holder. **3** championship in sport. **4** legal right to ownership of property. □ **title-deed** n. legal document proving a person's title to a property. **title role** part in a play etc. from which the title is taken.

titled adj. having a title of nobility.

titmouse n. (*pl.* **-mice**) = **tit**.

titter n. high-pitched giggle. ● v. give a titter.
■ n. & v. giggle, laugh, snicker, snigger.

tittle-tattle v. & n. gossip.
■ n. gossip, hearsay, rumour, talk.

titular adj. **1** of a title. **2** having the title of ruler etc. but no real authority.

tizzy n. (*colloq.*) state of nervous agitation or confusion.

TNT abbr. trinitrotoluene, a powerful explosive.

to prep. **1** towards. **2** as far as. **3** as compared with, in respect of. **4** for (a person or thing to hold or possess or be affected by. **5** (with a verb) forming an infinitive, or expressing purpose or consequence etc.; used alone when the infinitive is understood. ● adv. **1** to a closed position. **2** into a state of consciousness or activity. □ **to and fro** backwards and forwards. **to-do** n. fuss.

toad n. frog-like animal living chiefly on land. □ **toad-in-the-hole** n. sausages baked in batter.

toadflax n. wild plant with yellow or purple flowers.

toadstool n. fungus (usu. poisonous) with a round top on a stalk.

toady n. sycophant. ● v. behave sycophantically.

toast n. **1** toasted bread. **2** person or thing in whose honour a company is requested to drink. **3** this request or instance of drinking. ● v. **1** brown by heating. **2** express good wishes to by drinking.

toaster n. electrical device for toasting bread.

tobacco n. **1** plant with leaves that are used for smoking or snuff. **2** its prepared leaves.

tobacconist n. shopkeeper who sells cigarettes etc.

toboggan n. small sledge used for sliding downhill. ● v. ride on a toboggan.

toby jug mug or jug in the form of a seated old man.

tocsin n. **1** bell rung as an alarm signal. **2** signal of disaster.

today adv. & n. **1** (on) this present day. **2** (at) the present time.

toddle v. (of a young child) walk with short unsteady steps.

toddler n. child who has only recently learnt to walk.

toddy n. sweetened drink of spirits and hot water.

toe n. **1** any of the divisions (five in humans) of the front part of the foot. **2** part of a shoe or stocking covering the toes. ● v. touch with the toe(s). □ **on one's toes** alert or eager. **toe-hold** n. slight foothold. **toe the line** conform, obey orders.

toff *n.* (*sl.*) distinguished or well-dressed person.

toffee *n.* sweet made with heated butter and sugar. □ **toffee-apple** *n.* toffee-coated apple on a stick.

tog *n.* **1** unit for measuring the warmth of duvets. **2** (*pl.*, *colloq.*) clothes. ●*v.* (**togged**) **tog out** or **up** (*colloq.*) dress.

toga *n.* loose outer garment worn by men in ancient Rome.

together *adv.* **1** simultaneously. **2** in or into company or conjunction. **3** towards each other.

■ **1** at once, at the same time, in unison, simultaneously.

toggle *n.* **1** short piece of wood etc. passed through a loop as a fastening device. **2** switch that turns a function on and off alternately.

toil *v.* work or move laboriously. ●*n.* **1** laborious work. **2** (*pl.*) net, snare. □ **toilsome** *adj.*

■ *v.* drudge, exert oneself, labour, slave (away), slog (away), work. ●*n.* **1** donkey work, drudgery, *colloq.* fag, *sl.* graft, grind, labour, slog, travail, work.

toilet *n.* **1** lavatory. **2** process of dressing and grooming oneself. □ **toilet water** light perfume.

toiletries *n.pl.* articles used in washing and grooming oneself.

token *n.* **1** sign, symbol. **2** keepsake. **3** voucher that can be exchanged for goods. **4** disc used as money in a slot machine etc. ●*adj.* **1** symbolic. **2** perfunctory.

■ *n.* **1** badge, mark, sign, symbol. **2** keepsake, memento, reminder, souvenir. **3** coupon, voucher. **4** counter, disc. ●*adj.* **1** emblematic, symbolic. **2** nominal, perfunctory, slight, superficial.

tokenism *n.* granting of minimal concessions.

told *see* **tell**. **all told** counting everything or everyone.

tolerable *adj.* **1** endurable. **2** passable. □ **tolerably** *adv.*

■ **1** acceptable, bearable, endurable, supportable. **2** adequate, average, fair, mediocre, *colloq.* OK, passable, satisfactory.

tolerance *n.* **1** willingness to tolerate. **2** permitted variation. □ **tolerant** *adj.*, **tolerantly** *adv.*

■ **1** broad-mindedness, charity, forbearance, indulgence, lenience, patience, understanding. **2** allowance, play, variation. □ **tolerant** broad-minded, charitable, forbearing, indulgent, lenient, liberal, patient, permissive, understanding, unprejudiced.

tolerate *v.* **1** permit without protest or interference. **2** endure. □ **toleration** *n.*

■ **1** accept, allow, consent to, permit, sanction, *colloq.* stand for. **2** abide, bear, brook, endure, live with, put up with, stand, *colloq.* stick, stomach, take.

toll¹ *n.* **1** tax paid for the use of a public road etc. **2** loss or damage caused by a disaster etc. □ **toll-gate** *n.* barrier preventing passage until a toll is paid.

toll² *v.* ring with slow strokes, esp. to mark a death. ●*n.* stroke of a tolling bell.

tom *n.* (in full **tom-cat**) male cat.

tomahawk *n.* light axe used by N. American Indians.

tomato *n.* (*pl.* **-oes**) red fruit used as a vegetable.

tomb *n.* grave or other place of burial.

■ crypt, grave, mausoleum, sepulchre, vault.

tombola *n.* lottery resembling bingo.

tomboy *n.* girl who enjoys rough and noisy activities.

tombstone *n.* memorial stone set up over a grave.

tome *n.* large book.

tomorrow *adv.* & *n.* **1** (on) the day after today. **2** (in) the near future.

tom-tom *n.* drum beaten with the hands.

ton *n.* **1** measure of weight, either 2240 lb (**long ton**) or 2000 lb (**short ton**) or 1000 kg (**metric ton**). **2** unit of volume in shipping.

tone *n.* **1** musical or vocal sound, esp. with reference to its pitch, quality, and strength. **2** full interval between one note and the next in an octave. **3** shade of colour. **4** general character. **5** proper firmness of muscles etc. ●*v.* **1** give tone to. **2** harmonize in colour. □ **tone-deaf** *adj.* unable to perceive differences of musical pitch. **tone down** make less intense. **tonal** *adj.*, **tonally** *adv.*, **tonality** *n.*

■ *n.* **1** note, sound; inflection, modulation, pitch, quality, timbre. **3** colour, hue, shade, tincture, tinge, tint. **4** atmosphere, character, feeling, mood, spirit. □ **tone down** moderate, modify, reduce, soften, temper.

toneless *adj.* without positive tone, not expressive. □ **tonelessly** *adv.*

tongs *n.pl.* instrument with two arms used for grasping things.

tongue *n.* **1** muscular organ in the mouth, used in tasting and speaking. **2**

tongue of an ox etc. as food. **3** language. **4** projecting strip. **5** tapering jet of flame. □ **tongue-tied** adj. too shy to speak. **tongue-twister** n. sequence of words difficult to pronounce quickly and correctly. **tongue-in-cheek** adj. with sly sarcasm.

tonic n. **1** medicine etc. with an invigorating effect. **2** keynote in music. **3** tonic water. ● adj. invigorating. □ **tonic sol-fa** (see **sol-fa**). **tonic water** mineral water, esp. flavoured with quinine.

■ n. **1** restorative, stimulant. ● adj. fortifying, invigorating, refreshing, restorative, reviving, stimulating, strengthening.

tonight adv. & n. (on) the present or approaching evening or night.

tonnage n. **1** ship's carrying capacity expressed in tons. **2** charge per ton for carrying cargo.

tonne n. metric ton, 1000 kg.

tonsil n. either of two small organs near the root of the tongue.

tonsillitis n. inflammation of the tonsils.

tonsure n. **1** shaving the top or all of the head as a religious symbol. **2** this shaven area. □ **tonsured** adj.

too adv. **1** to a greater extent than is desirable. **2** also. **3** (colloq.) very.

■ **1** excessively, overly, unduly. **2** additionally, also, as well, besides, furthermore, in addition.

took see **take**.

tool n. **1** thing used for working on something. **2** person used by another for his or her own purposes. ● v. **1** shape or ornament with a tool. **2** equip with tools.

■ n. **1** appliance, implement, instrument, utensil. **2** cat's-paw, dupe, pawn, puppet, stooge.

toot n. short sound produced by a horn or whistle etc. ● v. make or cause to make a toot.

tooth n. (pl. **teeth**) **1** each of the white bony structures in the jaws, used in biting and chewing. **2** tooth-like part or projection. □ **toothed** adj.

toothpaste n. paste for cleaning the teeth.

toothpick n. small pointed instrument for removing bits of food from between the teeth.

toothy adj. having many or large teeth.

top[1] n. **1** highest point or part or position. **2** thing forming the upper part or covering. **3** upper surface. **4** utmost degree or intensity. **5** garment for the up-

per part of the body. ● adj. highest in position or rank etc. ● v. (**topped**) **1** provide or be a top for. **2** be higher or better than. **3** add as a final thing. **4** reach the top of. □ **on top of** in addition to. **top dog** (colloq.) master, victor. **top dress** apply fertilizer on the top of (soil). **top hat** man's tall hat worn with formal dress. **top-heavy** adj. heavy at the top and liable to fall over. **top-notch** adj. (colloq.) first-rate. **top secret** of utmost secrecy. **top up 1** complete (an amount). **2** fill up (something half empty).

■ n. **1** apex, crest, crown, head, peak, pinnacle, point, summit, tip, vertex; acme, climax, culmination, height, zenith. **2** cap, cover, covering, lid. ● adj. highest, topmost, uppermost; best, finest, first, foremost, greatest, leading, pre-eminent, supreme. ● v. **2** beat, better, cap, exceed, outdo, outstrip, surpass, transcend. **3** decorate, garnish.

top[2] n. toy that spins on its point when set in motion.

topaz n. semiprecious stone of various colours, esp. yellow.

topcoat n. **1** overcoat. **2** final coat of paint etc.

topiary adj. & n. (of) the art of clipping shrubs etc. into ornamental shapes.

topic n. subject of a discussion or written work.

■ issue, subject, text, theme.

topical adj. having reference to current events. □ **topically** adv., **topicality** n.

topknot n. tuft, crest, or bow etc. on top of the head.

topless adj. leaving or having the breasts bare.

topmost adj. highest.

topography n. local geography, position of the rivers, roads, buildings, etc., of a place or district. □ **topographical** adj.

topper n. (colloq.) top hat.

topple v. **1** be unsteady and fall. **2** cause to do this.

■ **1** fall, keel over, overbalance, tumble. **2** knock over, overturn, up-end, upset.

topside n. beef from the upper part of the haunch.

topsoil n. top layer of the soil.

topsy-turvy adv. & adj. **1** upside down. **2** in or into great disorder.

■ adj. chaotic, disordered, disorderly, disorganized, higgledy-piggledy, jumbled, messy, untidy.

tor n. hill or rocky peak.

torch *n.* **1** small hand-held electric lamp. **2** burning piece of wood etc. carried as a light. □ **torchlight** *n.*

tore *see* **tear**[1].

toreador *n.* fighter (esp. on horseback) in a bullfight.

torment *n.* /tórment/ **1** severe suffering. **2** cause of this. ● *v.* /tormént/ **1** subject to torment. **2** tease, annoy. □ **tormentor** *n.*

■ *n.* **1** agony, anguish, distress, misery, pain, suffering, torture. **2** affliction, bane, blight, bother, curse, nuisance, scourge. ● *v.* **1** afflict, bedevil, distress, rack, trouble; abuse, ill-treat, maltreat, mistreat, torture. **2** bait, chaff, goad, make fun of, provoke, *sl.* rag, tease, taunt; *colloq.* aggravate, annoy, bother, *sl.* bug, drive mad, infuriate, madden, nettle, pester, *colloq.* rile.

torn *see* **tear**[1].

tornado *n.* (*pl.* **-oes**) violent destructive whirlwind.

torpedo *n.* (*pl.* **-oes**) explosive underwater missile. ● *v.* attack or destroy with a torpedo.

torpid *adj.* sluggish and inactive. □ **torpidly** *adv.*, **torpidity** *n.*

■ apathetic, inactive, languid, lethargic, listless, slow, sluggish.

torpor *n.* sluggish condition.

■ apathy, inactivity, indolence, inertia, languor, lassitude, lethargy, listlessness, sluggishness.

torque *n.* force that produces rotation.

torrent *n.* **1** rushing stream or flow. **2** downpour. □ **torrential** *adj.*

torrid *adj.* intensely hot.

torsion *n.* twisting, spiral twist.

torso *n.* (*pl.* **-os**) trunk of the human body.

tort *n.* any private or civil wrong (other than breach of contract) for which damages can be claimed.

tortoise *n.* slow-moving reptile with a hard shell.

tortoiseshell *n.* mottled yellowish-brown shell of certain turtles, used for making combs etc. □ **tortoiseshell cat** one with mottled colouring.

tortuous *adj.* full of twists and turns. □ **tortuously** *adv.*

■ circuitous, convoluted, curved, meandering, serpentine, twisting, winding, zigzag.

torture *n.* **1** severe pain. **2** infliction of this as a punishment or means of coer-

cion. ● *v.* inflict torture upon. □ **torturer** *n.*

■ *n.* **1** agony, anguish, pain, suffering, torment.

toss *v.* **1** throw lightly. **2** throw up (a coin) to settle a question by the way it falls. **3** roll about from side to side. **4** coat (food) by gently shaking it in dressing etc. ● *n.* tossing. □ **toss off 1** drink rapidly. **2** compose rapidly.

toss-up *n.* **1** tossing of a coin. **2** even chance.

■ *v.* **1** *sl.* bung, cast, *colloq.* chuck, pitch, *colloq.* sling, throw. **2** flick, flip. **3** pitch, rock, roll.

tot[1] *n.* **1** small child. **2** small quantity of spirits.

tot[2] *v.* (**totted**) **tot up** (*colloq.*) add up.

total *adj.* **1** including everything or everyone. **2** complete. ● *n.* total amount. ● *v.* (**totalled**) **1** reckon the total of. **2** amount to. □ **totally** *adv.*, **totality** *n.*

■ *adj.* **1** complete, entire, full, gross, overall, whole. **2** absolute, complete, out and out, perfect, pure, thorough, unmitigated, unqualified, utter. ● *n.* amount, sum. ● *v.* **1** add (up), count (up), reckon, sum up, *colloq.* tot up. **2** add up to, amount to, come to, equal, make.

totalitarian *adj.* of a regime in which no rival parties or loyalties are permitted. □ **totalitarianism** *n.*

totalizator *n.* device that automatically registers bets, so that the total amount can be divided among the winners.

tote[1] *n.* (*sl.*) totalizator.

tote[2] *v.* (*US*) carry. □ **tote bag** large capacious bag.

totem *n.* tribal emblem among N. American Indians. □ **totem-pole** *n.* pole carved or painted with totems.

totter *v.* walk or rock unsteadily. ● *n.* tottering walk or movement. □ **tottery** *adj.*

■ *v.* dodder, rock, stagger, sway, teeter, wobble.

toucan *n.* tropical American bird with an immense beak.

touch *v.* **1** be, come, or bring into contact. **2** feel or stroke. **3** press or strike lightly. **4** reach. **5** match. **6** rouse sympathy in. **7** (*sl.*) persuade to give or lend money. ● *n.* **1** act, fact, or manner of touching. **2** ability to perceive things through touching them. **3** style of workmanship. **4** slight trace. **5** detail. □ **in touch** in communication. **touch-**

and-go *adj.* uncertain as regards result.

touch down 1 touch the ball on the ground behind the goal line in Rugby football. **2** (of an aircraft) land. **touchdown** *n.* side limit of a football field. **touch off 1** cause to explode. **2** start (a process). **touch on** mention briefly. **touch up** improve by making small additions.

■ *v.* **1** abut, be against, border on, brush against. **2** feel, finger, handle; caress, fondle, stroke. **3** brush, graze, knock, tap. **4** attain, make, reach, rise to. **5** be in the same league as, be on a par with, compare with, equal, match, rival. **6** affect, move. ● *n.* **1** brush, caress; knock, pat, tap. **2** feeling, sensation. **3** manner, method, style, technique. **4** bit, dash, hint, jot, piece, pinch, speck, spot, suggestion, trace. □ **touch on** allude to, bring up, broach, mention, raise, refer to, speak of.

touché /tōōsháy/ *int.* acknowledgement of a hit in fencing, or of a valid criticism.

touching *adj.* moving, pathetic. ● *prep.* concerning.

■ *adj.* emotional, emotive, moving, pathetic, poignant, stirring. ● *prep.* about, apropos, concerning, re, regarding, with respect to.

touchstone *n.* standard or criterion.

■ benchmark, criterion, measure, norm, standard, yardstick.

touchy *adj.* (**-ier, -iest**) easily offended. □ **touchiness** *n.*

■ highly-strung, moody, sensitive, temperamental, volatile.

tough *adj.* **1** hard to break, cut, or chew. **2** hardy. **3** unyielding. **4** difficult. **5** (*colloq.*, of luck) hard. ● *n.* rough violent person. □ **toughness** *n.*

■ *adj.* **1** durable, hard-wearing, long-lasting, stout, strong, sturdy; chewy, fibrous, gristly, hard, leathery, stringy. **2** hardy, robust, stalwart, strong, sturdy. **3** adamant, hard, harsh, inflexible, severe, stern, strict, unyielding. **4** arduous, challenging, demanding, difficult, exacting, onerous, taxing; baffling, knotty, perplexing, puzzling.

toughen *v.* make or become tough or tougher.

toupee /tōōpay/ *n.* small wig.

tour *n.* journey through a place, visiting things of interest or giving performances. ● *v.* make a tour (of). □ **on tour** touring.

■ *n.* excursion, expedition, jaunt, journey, outing, trip.

tour de force feat of strength or skill.

tourism *n.* organized touring or other services for tourists.

tourist *n.* person travelling or visiting a place for recreation.

■ holiday-maker, sightseer, traveller, tripper, visitor, voyager.

tournament *n.* contest of skill involving a series of matches.

tousle *v.* make (hair etc.) untidy by ruffling.

tout *v.* pester people to buy. ● *n.* **1** person who touts. **2** person who sells tickets for popular events at high prices.

tow[1] *n.* coarse fibres of flax etc.

tow[2] *v.* pull along behind one. ● *n.* act of towing. □ **tow-path** *n.* path beside a canal or river, orig. for horses towing barges.

■ *v.* drag, draw, haul, lug, pull, trail, tug.

toward *prep.* towards.

towards *prep.* **1** in the direction of. **2** in relation to. **3** as a contribution to. **4** near.

towel *n.* absorbent cloth for drying oneself or wiping things dry. ● *v.* (**towelled**) rub with a towel.

towelling *n.* fabric for towels.

tower *n.* tall structure, esp. as part of a church or castle etc. ● *v.* be very tall. □ **tower block** tall building with many storeys. **tower of strength** source of strong reliable support.

town *n.* **1** collection of buildings (larger than a village). **2** its inhabitants. **3** central business and shopping area. □ **go to town** (*colloq.*) do something lavishly or with enthusiasm. **town hall** building containing local government offices etc. **townsman** *n.*, **townswoman** *n.*

■ **1** borough, city, conurbation, metropolis, municipality.

township *n.* **1** small town. **2** (*S. Afr.*) urban area formerly set aside for black people.

toxaemia /tokséemiə/ *n.* **1** blood poisoning. **2** abnormally high blood pressure in pregnancy.

toxic *adj.* **1** of or caused by poison. **2** poisonous. □ **toxicity** *n.*

■ **2** dangerous, deadly, harmful, lethal, noxious, poisonous.

toxicology n. study of poisons. □ **toxicologist** n.

toxin n. poisonous substance, esp. formed in the body.

toy n. **1** thing to play with. **2** (attrib., of a dog) of a diminutive variety. ● v. **toy with 1** handle idly. **2** deal with (a thing) without seriousness. □ **toy boy** (colloq.) woman's much younger male lover.

trace¹ n. **1** track or mark left behind. **2** sign of what has existed or occurred. **3** very small quantity. ● v. **1** follow or discover by observing marks or other evidence. **2** outline. **3** copy by using tracing-paper or carbon paper. □ **trace element** one required only in minute amounts. **traceable** adj., **tracer** n.

■ n. **1** footprint, mark, print, track, trail. **2** clue, evidence, hint, indication, mark, sign, vestige. **3** bit, dash, drop, hint, jot, pinch, speck, spot, suggestion, touch. ● v. **1** detect, discover, find, unearth; follow, pursue, shadow, stalk, colloq. tail, track, trail. **2** delineate, map out, outline, sketch (out).

trace² n. each of the two side-straps by which a horse draws a vehicle. □ **kick over the traces** become insubordinate.

tracery n. **1** openwork pattern in stone. **2** lacelike pattern.

trachea /trəkeeə/ n. windpipe.

tracheotomy n. surgical opening into the trachea.

tracing n. copy of a map or drawing etc. made by tracing it. □ **tracing-paper** n. transparent paper used in this.

track n. **1** mark(s) left by a moving person or thing. **2** course. **3** path, rough road. **4** railway line. **5** particular section on a record or recording tape. **6** continuous band round the wheels of a tractor etc. ● v. follow the track of. □ **keep** or **lose track of** keep or fail to keep oneself informed about. **track down** find by tracking. **track suit** loose warm suit worn for exercising etc. **tracker** n.

■ n. **1** footprint, mark, print, spoor, trace, trail. **2** course, racecourse, racetrack. **3** bridle path, footpath, path, route, trail. **4** line, rails, railway. ● v. follow, pursue, shadow, stalk, colloq. tail, trace, trail. □ **track down** detect, dig up, discover, ferret out, find, locate, trace, turn up, uncover, unearth.

tract¹ n. **1** stretch of land. **2** system of connected parts of the body, along which something passes.

tract² n. pamphlet with a short essay, esp. on a religious subject.

tractable adj. easy to deal with or control. □ **tractability** n.

■ amenable, biddable, compliant, docile, manageable, yielding.

traction n. **1** pulling. **2** grip of wheels on the ground. **3** use of weights etc. to exert a steady pull on an injured limb etc.

tractor n. powerful motor vehicle for pulling heavy equipment.

trade n. **1** exchange of goods for money or other goods. **2** business or customers of a particular kind. **3** skilled job. ● v. **1** engage in trade, buy and sell. **2** exchange (goods) in trading. □ **trade in** give in (a used article) as partial payment for a new one. **trade-in** n. **trade mark** company's registered emblem or name etc. used to identify its goods. **trade off** exchange as a compromise. **trade union** (pl. **trade unions**) organized association of employees formed to further their common interests. **trade-unionist** n. member of a trade union. **trade wind** constant wind blowing towards the equator. **trader** n.

■ n. **1** barter, business, buying and selling, commerce, dealings, traffic. **2** business, clientele, custom, customers, patrons, shoppers. **3** business, calling, career, craft, job, line, profession, vocation, work. ● v. **1** buy and sell, do business, have dealings, traffic. **2** barter, change, exchange, interchange, swap, switch.

tradesman n. **1** craftsman. **2** shopkeeper. **3** person who delivers goods to private houses.

■ **1** artisan, craftsman. **2** dealer, merchant, retailer, shopkeeper, trader.

tradition n. **1** belief or custom handed down from one generation to another. **2** long-established procedure. □ **traditional** adj., **traditionally** adv.

■ **1** convention, custom, habit, institution, practice, usage, way; belief, folklore, lore. □ **traditional** conventional, customary, established, habitual, normal, regular, routine, time-honoured, usual.

traditionalist n. person who upholds traditional beliefs etc. □ **traditionalism** n.

traduce v. slander. □ **traducement** n.

traffic n. **1** vehicles, ships, or aircraft moving along a route. **2** trading. ● v. (**trafficked**) trade. □ **traffic warden** official who controls the movement and parking of road vehicles. **trafficker** n.

tragedian *n.* **1** writer of tragedies. **2** actor in tragedy.

tragedienne *n.* actress in tragedy.

tragedy *n.* **1** event causing great sadness. **2** serious drama with unhappy events or a sad ending.
■ **1** calamity, cataclysm, catastrophe, disaster, misfortune.

tragic *adj.* **1** causing great sadness. **2** of or in tragedy. □ **tragically** *adv.*
■ **1** appalling, awful, calamitous, catastrophic, disastrous, dreadful, fatal, fearful, horrible, terrible.

tragicomedy *n.* drama of mixed tragic and comic events.

trail *v.* **1** drag behind, esp. on the ground. **2** hang loosely. **3** lag, straggle. **4** track. **5** move wearily. ● *n.* **1** thing that trails. **2** track, trace. **3** beaten path. **4** line of people or things following something.
■ *v.* **1** drag, pull, tow. **2** dangle, hang. **3** dawdle, lag behind, linger, loiter, straggle. **4** follow, pursue, shadow, stalk, *colloq.* tail, trace, track. ● *n.* **2** footprints, marks, prints, spoor, tracks, traces. **3** footpath, path, route, track.

trailer *n.* **1** truck etc. designed to be hauled by a vehicle. **2** short extract from a film etc., shown in advance to advertise it.

train *n.* **1** railway engine with linked carriages or trucks. **2** retinue. **3** sequence of things. **4** part of a long robe that trails behind the wearer. ● *v.* **1** bring or come to a desired standard of efficiency or condition or behaviour etc. by instruction and practice. **2** aim (a gun etc.). **3** cause (a plant) to grow in the required direction. □ **in train** in preparation.
■ *n.* **2** entourage, escort, retinue, suite. **3** chain, line, sequence, series, string, succession. ● *v.* **1** coach, discipline, drill, educate, instruct, school, teach, tutor; exercise, practise, work out.

trainee *n.* person being trained.

trainer *n.* **1** person who trains horses or athletes etc. **2** (*pl.*) soft sports or running shoes.

traipse *v.* (*colloq.*) trudge.

trait *n.* characteristic.
■ attribute, characteristic, feature, idiosyncrasy, peculiarity, property, quality, quirk.

traitor *n.* person who behaves disloyally, esp. to his or her country. □ **traitorous** *adj.*

trajectory *n.* path of a projectile.

tram *n.* public passenger vehicle running on rails laid in the road.

tramcar *n.* tram.

tramlines *n.pl.* **1** rails on which a tram runs. **2** (*colloq.*) pair of parallel sidelines in tennis etc.

trammel *v.* (**trammelled**) hamper, restrain.

tramp *v.* **1** walk heavily. **2** go on foot across (an area). **3** trample. ● *n.* **1** sound of heavy footsteps. **2** long walk. **3** vagrant. **4** (*sl.*) promiscuous woman.
■ *v.* **1** clump, plod, stamp, stomp, *colloq.* traipse, trudge. **2** hike, march, slog, trek, trudge, walk. ● *n.* **2** hike, march, slog, trek, trudge, walk. **3** *US sl.* bum, down-and-out, vagabond, vagrant.

trample *v.* tread repeatedly, crush or harm by treading.
■ stamp, step, tramp, tread; crush, flatten, press, squash.

trampoline *n.* sheet attached by springs to a frame, used for jumping on in acrobatic leaps, ● *v.* use a trampoline.

trance *n.* sleep-like or dreamy state.

tranquil *adj.* calm and undisturbed. □ **tranquilly** *adv.*, **tranquillity** *n.*
■ calm, peaceful, placid, quiet, relaxed, serene, still, untroubled.

tranquillize *v.* make calm.
■ sedate; calm, pacify, quiet, quieten, soothe.

tranquillizer *n.* drug used to relieve anxiety and tension.

transact *v.* perform or carry out (business etc.). □ **transaction** *n.*

transatlantic *adj.* **1** on or from the other side of the Atlantic. **2** crossing the Atlantic.

transcend *v.* **1** go beyond the range of (experience, belief, etc.). **2** surpass. □ **transcendent** *adj.*, **transcendence** *n.*
■ **2** exceed, excel, outdo, outshine, outstrip, surpass, top.

transcendental *adj.* **1** transcendent. **2** abstract, obscure, visionary.

transcontinental *adj.* crossing or extending across a continent.

transcribe *v.* **1** copy in writing. **2** produce in written form. **3** arrange (music) for a different instrument etc. □ **transcription** *n.*

transcript *n.* written copy.

transducer *n.* device that receives waves or other variations from one system and conveys related ones to another.

transept n. part lying at right angles to the nave in a church.

transfer v. /tránsfér/ (**transferred**) convey from one place, person, or application to another. ● n. /tránsfer/ **1** transferring. **2** document transferring property or a right. **3** design for transferring from one surface to another. □ **transference** n., **transferable** adj.
> ■ v. carry, convey, move, remove, send, shift, transport; hand over, make over, pass on.

transfigure v. make nobler or more beautiful in appearance. □ **transfiguration** n.

transfix v. **1** pierce through, impale. **2** make motionless with fear or astonishment.
> ■ **2** freeze, paralyse, stun; captivate, enthral, fascinate, hold spellbound, hypnotize, mesmerize, rivet.

transform v. **1** change greatly in appearance or character. **2** change the voltage of (electric current). □ **transformation** n., **transformer** n.
> ■ **1** alter, change, convert, metamorphose, revolutionize, transfigure, transmute. □ **transformation** alteration, change, conversion, metamorphosis, transfiguration, transmutation.

transfuse v. **1** give a transfusion of or to. **2** permeate, imbue.

transfusion n. injection of blood or other fluid into a blood vessel.

transgress v. break (a rule or law). □ **transgression** n., **transgressor** n.
> ■ break, contravene, defy, disobey, flout, infringe, violate. □ **transgression** error, fault, misdeed, misdemeanour, offence, sin, wrongdoing, violation.

transient adj. passing away quickly. □ **transience** n.
> ■ brief, ephemeral, fleeting, fugitive, momentary, short, temporary, transitory.

transistor n. **1** very small semiconductor device which controls the flow of an electric current. **2** portable radio set using transistors. □ **transistorized** adj.

transit n. process of going or conveying across, over, or through.

transition n. process of changing from one state or style etc. to another. □ **transitional** adj.
> ■ alteration, change, conversion, development, evolution, metamorphosis, shift, transformation.

transitory adj. brief, fleeting.

translate v. **1** express in another language or other words. **2** be able to be translated. **3** transfer. □ **translation** n., **translator** n.

transliterate v. convert to the letters of another alphabet. □ **transliteration** n.

translucent adj. allowing light to pass through but not transparent. □ **translucence** n.

transmigrate v. (of the soul) pass into another body after a person's death. □ **transmigration** n.

transmission n. **1** transmitting. **2** broadcast. **3** gear transmitting power from engine to axle.

transmit v. (**transmitted**) **1** pass on from one person, place, or time to another. **2** send out (a signal or programme etc.) by cable or radio waves. □ **transmissible** adj., **transmitter** n.
> ■ **1** convey, deliver, relay, send, transfer; communicate, pass on, spread. **2** broadcast, relay.

transmute v. change in form or substance. □ **transmutation** n.

transom n. **1** horizontal bar across the top of a door or window. **2** fanlight.

transparency n. **1** being transparent. **2** photographic slide.

transparent adj. **1** able to be seen through. **2** easily understood. □ **transparently** adv.
> ■ **1** clear, crystalline, limpid, pellucid, translucent. **2** apparent, clear, evident, manifest, obvious, plain, unmistakable.

transpire v. **1** become known. **2** (of plants) give off (vapour) from leaves etc. □ **transpiration** n.
> ■ **1** become known, be revealed, come to light, emerge, turn out.

transplant v. /tranzplaánt/ **1** plant elsewhere. **2** transfer (living tissue). ● n. /tránzplaant/ **1** transplanting of tissue. **2** thing transplanted. □ **transplantation** n.

transport v. /tranzpórt/ convey from one place to another. ● n. /tránzport/ **1** process of transporting. **2** means of conveyance. **3** (pl.) condition of strong emotion. □ **transportation** n., **transporter** n.
> ■ v. bear, carry, sl. cart, convey, ferry, haul, move, send, ship. ● n. **1** carriage, conveyance, haulage, moving, shipping, shipment.

transpose v. **1** cause (two or more things) to change places. **2** change the

position of. **3** put (music) into a different key. □ **transposition** n.
■ 1 exchange, interchange, rearrange, reverse, swap, switch.

transsexual n. & adj. (person) having the physical characteristics of one sex and psychological characteristics of the other. □ **transsexualism** n.

transuranic adj. having atoms heavier than those of uranium.

transverse adj. crosswise.

transvestism n. dressing in clothing of the opposite sex. □ **transvestite** n.

trap n. **1** device for capturing an animal. **2** scheme for tricking or catching a person. **3** trapdoor. **4** compartment from which a dog is released in racing. **5** curved section of a pipe holding liquid to prevent gases from coming upwards. **6** two-wheeled horse-drawn carriage. **7** (sl.) mouth. ● v. (**trapped**) catch in or by means of a trap.
■ n. **1** snare. **2** device, ploy, ruse, stratagem, trick, wile. ● v. capture, catch, ensnare, net, snare; deceive, dupe, fool, trick; confine, imprison.

trapdoor n. door in a floor, ceiling, or roof.

trapeze n. a kind of swing on which acrobatics are performed.

trapezium n. **1** quadrilateral with only two opposite sides parallel. **2** (US) trapezoid.

trapezoid n. **1** quadrilateral with no sides parallel. **2** (US) trapezium.

trapper n. person who traps animals, esp. for furs.

trappings n.pl. accessories.
■ accessories, accoutrements, apparatus, equipment, finery, gear, paraphernalia, trimmings.

trash n. worthless stuff. □ **trashy** adj.

trauma n. **1** wound, injury. **2** emotional shock producing a lasting effect. □ **traumatic** adj.
■ □ **traumatic** distressing, disturbing, harrowing, painful, shocking, upsetting.

travail n. & v. labour.

travel v. (**travelled**) **1** go from one place to another. **2** journey along or through. ● n. travelling, esp. abroad. □ **traveller** n.
■ v. **1** go, journey, take a trip, tour, voyage. ● n. globe-trotting, touring, tourism. □ **traveller** globe-trotter, holiday-maker, sightseer, tourist, voyager.

traverse v. travel, lie, or extend across. ● n. **1** thing that lies across another. **2** lateral movement. □ **traversal** n.
■ v. range, rove, travel, wander; bridge, cross, pass over, span.

travesty n. absurd or inferior imitation. ● v. make or be a travesty of.

trawl n. large wide-mouthed fishing net. ● v. fish with a trawl.

trawler n. boat used in trawling.

tray n. **1** board with a rim for dishes etc. **2** shallow box for papers etc.

treacherous adj. **1** showing treachery. **2** not to be relied on, dangerous. □ **treacherously** adv.
■ 1 disloyal, false, perfidious, traitorous, treasonous. **2** dangerous, hazardous, perilous, precarious, unreliable, unsafe.

treachery n. **1** betrayal of a person or cause. **2** act of disloyalty.
■ 1 betrayal, disloyalty, faithlessness, perfidy, treason.

treacle n. thick sticky liquid produced when sugar is refined. □ **treacly** adj.

tread v. (**trod, trodden**) **1** walk, step. **2** walk on, press or crush with the feet. ● n. **1** manner or sound of walking. **2** horizontal surface of a stair. **3** part of a tyre that touches the ground. □ **tread water** keep upright in water by making treading movements.
■ v. **1** go, step, walk. **2** crush, flatten, press, squash, stamp on, step on, tramp on, trample.

treadle n. lever worked by the foot to drive a wheel.

treadmill n. **1** mill-wheel formerly turned by people treading on steps round its edge. **2** tiring monotonous routine work.

treason n. treachery towards one's country. □ **treasonous** adj.

treasonable adj. involving treason.

treasure n. **1** collection of precious metals or gems. **2** highly valued object or person. ● v. **1** value highly. **2** store as precious. □ **treasure trove** treasure of unknown ownership, found hidden.
■ n. **1** fortune, riches, valuables, wealth. **2** darling, delight, gem, jewel, joy. ● v. **1** cherish, hold dear, prize, value.

treasurer n. person in charge of the funds of an institution.

treasury n. **1** place where treasure is kept. **2** department managing a country's revenue.

treat v. **1** act or behave towards or deal with in a specified way. **2** give medical treatment to. **3** buy something for (a person) in order to give pleasure. **4** subject to a chemical or other process. ● n. something special that gives pleasure.
■ v. **1** deal with, handle, manage; consider, regard, view. **2** dose, medicate, minister to, tend. **3** entertain, pay for, stand, take out. ● n. gift, present; delicacy, *colloq.* goody, luxury, titbit.

treatise n. written work dealing with one subject.
■ dissertation, essay, paper.

treatment n. **1** manner of dealing with a person or thing. **2** something done to relieve illness etc.
■ **1** care, handling, management. **2** healing, therapy; cure, remedy.

treaty n. formal agreement made, esp. between countries.
■ agreement, compact, entente, pact, settlement.

treble adj. **1** three times as much or as many. **2** (of a voice) high-pitched, soprano. ● n. **1** treble quantity or thing. **2** treble voice, person with this. □ **trebly** adv.

tree n. perennial plant with a single thick woody stem.

trefoil n. **1** plant with three leaflets (e.g. clover). **2** thing shaped like this.

trek n. long arduous journey. ● v. (**trekked**) make a trek.
■ n. & v. hike, march, slog, tramp, trudge, walk.

trellis n. light framework of crossing strips of wood etc.

tremble v. **1** shake, quiver. **2** feel very anxious. ● n. trembling movement. □ **trembly** adj.
■ v. **1** quake, quaver, quiver, shake, shiver, shudder.

tremendous adj. **1** immense. **2** (*colloq.*) excellent. □ **tremendously** adv.
■ **1** big, colossal, enormous, gigantic, huge, immense, large, massive, vast.

tremor n. **1** slight trembling movement. **2** thrill of fear etc.

tremulous adj. trembling, quivering. □ **tremulously** adv.

trench n. deep ditch. □ **trench coat** belted double-breasted raincoat.

trenchant adj. (of comments etc.) strong and effective.
■ effective, incisive, keen, penetrating, pointed.

trend n. **1** general tendency. **2** fashion. □ **trend-setter** n. person who leads the way in fashion etc.
■ **1** bent, bias, inclination, leaning, tendency. **2** craze, fad, fashion, mode, style, vogue.

trendy adj. (**-ier, -iest**) (*colloq.*) following the latest fashion. □ **trendily** adv., **trendiness** n.

trepidation n. fear, anxiety.

trespass v. **1** enter land or property unlawfully. **2** intrude. ● n. act of trespassing. □ **trespasser** n.

tress n. lock of hair.

trestle n. one of a set of supports on which a board is rested to form a table. □ **trestle-table** n.

trews n.pl. close-fitting usu. tartan trousers.

tri- pref. three times, triple.

triad n. **1** group of three. **2** Chinese usu. criminal secret society.

trial n. **1** examination in a law court by a judge. **2** process of testing qualities or performance. **3** trying person or thing. □ **on trial** undergoing a trial.
■ **1** case, hearing, lawsuit, proceedings. **2** check, *colloq.* dry run, dummy run, test, try-out. **3** bane, bother, nuisance, pest, worry; affliction, difficulty, hardship, misfortune, ordeal, tribulation, trouble.

triangle n. **1** geometric figure with three sides and three angles. **2** triangular steel rod used as a percussion instrument.

triangular adj. **1** shaped like a triangle. **2** involving three people.

triangulation n. measurement or mapping of an area by means of a network of triangles.

tribe n. related group of families living as a community. □ **tribal** adj., **tribesman** n.

tribulation n. great affliction.

tribunal n. board of officials appointed to adjudicate on a particular problem.

tributary n. & adj. (stream) flowing into a larger stream or a lake.

tribute n. **1** something said or done as a mark of respect. **2** payment that one country or ruler was formerly obliged to pay to another.
■ **1** accolade, commendation, compliment, honour, praise.

trice n. **in a trice** in an instant.

trichology *n.* study of hair and its diseases. □ **trichologist** *n.*

trick *n.* **1** something done to deceive or outwit someone. **2** technique, knack. **3** mannerism. **4** mischievous act. ● *v.* deceive or persuade by a trick. □ **do the trick** (*colloq.*) achieve what is required.

■ *n.* **1** artifice, *sl.* con, deceit, deception, device, ploy, ruse, stratagem, subterfuge, trap, wile. **2** art, knack, skill, technique. **3** characteristic, idiosyncrasy, mannerism, peculiarity, quirk, trait. **4** gag, hoax, (practical) joke, prank. ● *v.* cheat, *sl.* con, deceive, double-cross, dupe, fool, hoodwink, mislead, pull the wool over someone's eyes, swindle, take in.

trickery *n.* use of tricks, deception.

■ artfulness, chicanery, deceit, deception, double-dealing, duplicity, fraud, guile, hocus-pocus, *colloq.* jiggery-pokery, *colloq.* skulduggery.

trickle *v.* **1** (cause to) flow in a thin stream. **2** come or go gradually. ● *n.* trickling flow.

■ *v.* **1** dribble, drip, drop, flow, leak, ooze, seep.

tricky *adj.* (**-ier**, **-iest**) **1** crafty, deceitful. **2** requiring careful handling. □ **trickiness** *n.*

■ **1** artful, crafty, cunning, deceitful, devious, dishonest, double-dealing, duplicitous, guileful, scheming, shifty, slippery, sly, wily. **2** awkward, delicate, difficult, sensitive, ticklish.

tricolour *n.* flag with three colours in stripes.

tricycle *n.* three-wheeled pedal-driven vehicle. □ **tricyclist** *n.*

trident *n.* three-pronged spear.

triennial *adj.* **1** happening every third year. **2** lasting three years.

trier *n.* person who tries hard.

trifle *n.* **1** thing of only slight value or importance. **2** very small amount. **3** sweet dish of sponge cake and jelly etc. topped with custard and cream. ● *v.* **trifle with** treat frivolously.

trifling *adj.* trivial.

■ *sl.* footling, frivolous, inconsequential, insignificant, minor, petty, trivial, unimportant.

trigger *n.* lever for releasing a spring, esp. to fire a gun. ● *v.* (also **trigger off**) set in action, cause. □ **trigger-happy** *adj.* apt to shoot on slight provocation.

trigonometry *n.* branch of mathematics dealing with the relationship of sides and angles of triangles etc.

trike *n.* (*colloq.*) tricycle.

trilateral *adj.* having three sides or three participants.

trilby *n.* man's soft felt hat.

trill *n.* vibrating sound, esp. in music or singing. ● *v.* sound or sing with a trill.

trillion *n.* **1** a million million million. **2** a million million.

trilobite *n.* a kind of fossil crustacean.

trilogy *n.* group of three related books, plays, etc.

trim *adj.* (**trimmer**, **trimmest**) neat and orderly. ● *v.* (**trimmed**) **1** reduce or neaten by cutting. **2** ornament. **3** make (a boat or aircraft) evenly balanced by distributing its load. ● *n.* **1** ornamentation. **2** colour or type of upholstery etc. in a car. **3** trimming of hair etc.

■ *adj.* neat, orderly, shipshape, smart, spruce, straight, tidy. ● *v.* **1** bob, clip, crop, cut, dock, lop, pare, prune, shear, snip. **2** adorn, beautify, deck, decorate, dress, embellish, garnish, ornament. ● *n.* **1** adornment, decoration, embellishment, ornamentation.

trimaran *n.* vessel like a catamaran, with three hulls.

trimming *n.* **1** thing added as a decoration. **2** (*pl.*) pieces cut off when something is trimmed.

trinity *n.* **1** group of three. **2** (**the Trinity**) the three members of the Christian deity (Father, Son, Holy Spirit) as constituting one God.

trinket *n.* small fancy article or piece of jewellery.

trio *n.* (*pl.* **-os**) **1** group or set of three. **2** music for three instruments or voices.

trip *v.* (**tripped**) **1** go lightly and quickly. **2** (cause to) catch one's foot and lose balance. **3** (cause to) make a blunder. **4** release (a switch etc.) so as to operate a mechanism. ● *n.* **1** journey or excursion, esp. for pleasure. **2** stumble. **3** (*colloq.*) visionary experience caused by a drug. **4** device for tripping a mechanism.

■ *v.* **1** caper, cavort, dance, frisk, frolic, gambol, skip. **2** fall, slip, stumble, tumble. ● *n.* **1** drive, excursion, expedition, jaunt, journey, outing, tour.

tripartite *adj.* consisting of three parts.

tripe *n.* **1** stomach of an ox etc. as food. **2** (*sl.*) nonsense.

triple *adj.* **1** having three parts or members. **2** three times as much or as many. ● *v.* increase by three times its amount.

triplet *n.* **1** one of three children born at one birth. **2** set of three.

triplex *adj.* triple, threefold.

triplicate *adj.* & *n.* existing in three examples. □ **in triplicate** as three identical copies.

tripod *n.* three-legged stand.

tripper *n.* person who goes on a pleasure trip.

triptych /tríptik/ *n.* picture or carving with three panels fixed or hinged side by side.

trite *adj.* hackneyed.
■ banal, clichéd, *colloq.* corny, hackneyed, platitudinous, stale, unimaginative, unoriginal.

triumph *n.* **1** fact of being successful or victorious. **2** great success. **3** joy at this. ● *v.* be successful or victorious, rejoice at this. □ **triumphant** *adj.*, **triumphantly** *adv.*
■ *n.* **2** conquest, success, victory, win. **3** elation, exultation, joy, jubilation, rejoicing. ● *v.* be victorious, prevail, succeed, win. □ **triumphant** conquering, successful, victorious, winning.

triumphal *adj.* celebrating or commemorating a triumph.

triumvirate *n.* government or control by a board of three.

trivet *n.* metal stand for a kettle or hot dish etc.

trivia *n.pl.* trivial things.

trivial *adj.* of only small value or importance. □ **trivially** *adv.*, **triviality** *n.*
■ *sl.* footling, frivolous, inconsequential, insignificant, minor, petty, trifling, unimportant.

trod, trodden *see* **tread**.

troglodyte *n.* cave dweller.

troll *n.* giant or dwarf in Scandinavian mythology.

trolley *n.* (*pl.* **-eys**) **1** platform on wheels for transporting goods. **2** small cart. **3** small table on wheels.

trollop *n.* promiscuous or slovenly woman.

trombone *n.* large brass wind instrument with a sliding tube.

troop *n.* **1** company of people or animals. **2** cavalry or artillery unit. ● *v.* go as a troop or in great numbers.
■ *n.* band, company, crowd, drove, flock, gang, group, herd, horde, throng. ● *v.* file, march, walk.

trooper *n.* **1** soldier in a cavalry or armoured unit. **2** (*US*) member of a state police force.

trophy *n.* **1** memento of any success. **2** object awarded as a prize.
■ **1** keepsake, memento, reminder, souvenir, token. **2** award, cup, medal, prize.

tropic *n.* **1** line of latitude 23° 27' north or south of the equator. **2** (*pl.*) region between these, with a hot climate. □ **tropical** *adj.*

troposphere *n.* layer of the atmosphere between the earth's surface and the stratosphere.

trot *n.* **1** running action of a horse etc. **2** moderate running pace. ● *v.* (**trotted**) go or cause to go at a trot. □ **on the trot** (*colloq.*) **1** continually busy. **2** in succession. **trot out** (*colloq.*) produce, repeat.

troth *n.* promise, fidelity.

trotter *n.* animal's foot as food.

troubadour *n.* medieval romantic poet.

trouble *n.* **1** difficulty, distress, misfortune. **2** cause of this. **3** conflict. **4** illness. **5** exertion. ● *v.* **1** cause trouble to. **2** make or worried. **3** exert oneself.
■ *n.* **1** anxiety, concern, difficulty, distress, *colloq.* hassle, inconvenience, misfortune, unpleasantness, woe, worry. **2** bother, inconvenience, irritation, nuisance, pest. **3** conflict, discord, disorder, disturbance, fighting, strife, turmoil, unrest, violence. **4** disease, illness, sickness; ache, pain. **5** bother, care, effort, exertion, pains. ● *v.* **1** annoy, bother, harass, *colloq.* hassle, nag, pester, *colloq.* plague, torment, vex; discommode, impose on, inconvenience, put out. **2** agitate, alarm, disquiet, perturb, unsettle, upset, worry. **3** be concerned, bother, care, concern oneself, exert oneself, take pains.

troubleshooter *n.* person employed to deal with faults or problems.

troublesome *adj.* causing trouble, annoying.
■ awkward, burdensome, difficult, inconvenient, annoying, bothersome, irksome, irritating, tiresome, vexatious, vexing, worrying.

trough *n.* **1** long open receptacle, esp. for animals' food or water. **2** channel or hollow like this. **3** region of low atmospheric pressure.

trounce v. defeat heavily.

■ beat, conquer, defeat, *colloq.* lick, overwhelm, thrash, vanquish.

troupe /troop/ n. company of actors or other performers.

trouper n. **1** member of a troupe. **2** staunch colleague.

trousers n.pl. two-legged outer garment reaching from the waist usu. to the ankles.

trousseau /trōossō/ n. (pl. -eaux) bride's collection of clothing etc. for her marriage.

trout n. (pl. **trout**) freshwater fish related to the salmon.

trowel n. **1** small garden tool for digging. **2** similar tool for spreading mortar etc.

troy weight system of weights used for precious metals.

truant n. pupil who stays away from school without permission. □ **play truant** stay away as a truant. **truancy** n.

truce n. agreement to cease hostilities temporarily.

■ armistice, ceasefire, peace.

truck n. **1** open container on wheels for transporting loads. **2** open railway wagon. **3** lorry.

trucker n. lorry driver.

truculent adj. defiant and aggressive. □ **truculently** adv. **truculence** n.

■ aggressive, antagonistic, bad-tempered, belligerent, defiant, ill-tempered, quarrelsome, surly.

trudge v. walk laboriously. ● n. laborious walk.

■ v. plod, slog, *colloq.* traipse, tramp, trek.

true adj. **1** in accordance with fact, genuine. **2** exact, accurate. **3** loyal, faithful. ● adv. truly, accurately.

■ adj. **1** authentic, bona fide, genuine, legitimate, real, rightful, veritable; accurate, correct, factual, faithful, literal, truthful, veracious. **2** accurate, correct, exact, precise, proper. **3** constant, dependable, devoted, faithful, firm, loyal, staunch, steadfast, trusted, trustworthy.

truffle n. **1** rich-flavoured underground fungus valued as a delicacy. **2** soft chocolate sweet.

truism n. self-evident or hackneyed statement.

truly adv. **1** truthfully. **2** genuinely. **3** faithfully.

trump n. **1** playing card of a suit temporarily ranking above others. **2** (*colloq.*) person who behaves in a helpful or useful way. ● v. **trump up** invent fraudulently. □ **turn up trumps** (*colloq.*) be successful or helpful.

trumpet n. **1** metal wind instrument with a flared mouth. **2** thing shaped like this. ● v. (**trumpeted**) **1** proclaim loudly. **2** (of an elephant) make a loud sound with its trunk. □ **trumpeter** n.

truncate v. shorten by cutting off the end. □ **truncation** n.

truncheon n. short thick stick carried as a weapon.

trundle v. roll along, move along heavily on wheels.

trunk n. **1** tree's main stem. **2** body apart from head and limbs. **3** large box with a hinged lid, for transporting or storing clothes etc. **4** elephant's long flexible nose. **5** (*US*) boot of a car. **6** (pl.) shorts for swimming etc. □ **trunk road** important main road.

■ **1** bole, stem. **2** torso. **3** box, chest, coffer, crate, tea chest.

truss n. **1** framework supporting a roof etc. **2** device worn to support a hernia. ● v. tie up securely.

trust n. **1** firm belief in the reliability, truth, or strength etc. of a person or thing. **2** confident expectation. **3** responsibility, care. **4** association of business firms, formed to defeat competition. **5** property legally entrusted to someone. ● v. **1** have or place trust in. **2** entrust. **3** hope earnestly. □ **in trust** held as a trust. **on trust** accepted without investigation. **trustful** adj., **trustfully** adv.

■ n. **1** belief, certainty, confidence, credence, faith, reliance. **2** belief, conviction, expectation. **3** care, charge, custody, guardianship, keeping, protection. **4** cartel, corporation, group, syndicate. ● v. **1** bank on, believe in, be sure of, count on, depend on, have faith in, rely on. **2** commit, consign, delegate, entrust, give, hand over.

trustee n. **1** person who administers property held as a trust. **2** one of a group managing the business affairs of an institution.

trustworthy adj. worthy of trust.

■ dependable, faithful, honest, loyal, principled, reliable, responsible, steady, true, trusty.

trusty adj. trustworthy.

truth *n.* **1** quality of being true. **2** something that is true.
■ **1** accuracy, correctness, genuineness, truthfulness, veracity. **2** actuality, fact(s), reality.

truthful *adj.* **1** habitually telling the truth. **2** true. □ **truthfully** *adv.*, **truthfulness** *n.*
■ **1** candid, frank, honest, reliable, sincere, veracious. **2** accurate, correct, factual, true, veracious.

try *v.* **1** attempt. **2** test, esp. by use. **3** be a strain on. **4** hold a trial of. ● *n.* **1** attempt. **2** touchdown in Rugby football, entitling the player's side to a kick at goal. □ **try on** put (a garment) on to see if it fits. **try out** test by use. **try-out** *n.*
■ *v.* **1** attempt, endeavour, essay, have a go, make an effort, seek, strive, venture. **2** appraise, assess, evaluate, test, sample. **3** strain, tax. **4** adjudge, adjudicate, judge. ● *n.* **1** attempt, bid, effort, endeavour, go, shot, *colloq.* stab.

trying *adj.* **1** annoying. **2** difficult.
■ **1** annoying, bothersome, exasperating, infuriating, irksome, irritating, maddening, tiresome, vexatious. **2** demanding, difficult, hard, stressful, taxing, tiring, tough.

tsar /zaar/ *n.* title of the former emperor of Russia.

tsetse *n.* African fly that transmits disease by its bite.

T-shirt *n.* short-sleeved casual cotton top.

T-square *n.* large T-shaped ruler used in technical drawing.

tub *n.* open usu. round container.

tuba *n.* large low-pitched brass wind instrument.

tubby *adj.* (**-ier, -iest**) short and fat. □ **tubbiness** *n.*
■ chubby, dumpy, plump, podgy, portly, pudgy, roly-poly, rotund.

tube *n.* **1** long hollow cylinder. **2** thing shaped like this. **3** cathode-ray tube.

tuber *n.* short thick rounded root or underground stem from which shoots will grow.

tubercle *n.* small rounded swelling.

tubercular *adj.* of or affected with tuberculosis.

tuberculosis *n.* infectious wasting disease, esp. affecting lungs.

tuberous *adj.* **1** of or like a tuber. **2** bearing tubers.

tubing *n.* **1** tubes. **2** a length of tube.

tubular *adj.* tube-shaped.

tuck *n.* flat fold stitched in a garment etc. ● *v.* **1** put into or under something so as to be concealed or held in place. **2** cover or put away compactly. □ **tuck in** (*colloq.*) eat heartily. **tuck shop** shop selling sweets etc. to schoolchildren.

tuft *n.* bunch of threads, grass, or hair etc. held or growing together at the base. □ **tufted** *adj.*
■ bunch, clump, knot.

tug *v.* (**tugged**) **1** pull vigorously. **2** tow. ● *n.* **1** vigorous pull. **2** small powerful boat for towing others. □ **tug of war** contest of strength in which two teams pull opposite ways on a rope.
■ *v.* **1** jerk, pull, tweak, *colloq.* yank. **2** haul, pull, tow.

tuition *n.* teaching or instruction, esp. of an individual or small group.
■ education, instruction, schooling, teaching, tutelage.

tulip *n.* garden plant with a cup-shaped flower. □ **tulip-tree** *n.* tree with tulip-like flowers.

tulle /työol/ *n.* fine silky net fabric.

tumble *v.* **1** (cause to) fall. **2** roll, push, or move in a disorderly way. **3** perform somersaults etc. **4** rumple. ● *n.* **1** fall. **2** untidy state. □ **tumble-drier** *n.* machine for drying washing in a heated rotating drum. **tumble to** (*colloq.*) grasp the meaning of.
■ *v.* **1** collapse, *sl.* come a cropper, drop, fall, overbalance, stumble, topple (over). **4** disarrange, disorder, mess (up), ruffle, rumple, tousle. ● *n.* **1** cropper, fall, spill, stumble. **2** clutter, disorder, jumble, mess, muddle.

tumbledown *adj.* dilapidated.
■ decrepit, derelict, dilapidated, ramshackle, rickety, ruined.

tumbler *n.* **1** drinking glass with no handle or foot. **2** pivoted piece in a lock etc. **3** acrobat.

tumescent *adj.* swelling. □ **tumescence** *n.*

tummy *n.* (*colloq.*) stomach.

tumour *n.* abnormal mass of new tissue growing in or on the body.

tumult *n.* **1** uproar. **2** conflict of emotions. □ **tumultuous** *adj.*
■ **1** commotion, disorder, disturbance, fracas, pandemonium, rumpus, turmoil, unrest, uproar. **2** confusion, turmoil, upheaval. □ **tumultuous** boisterous, disor-

derly, excited, riotous, rowdy, *colloq.* rumbustious, turbulent, unruly, uproarious.

tun *n.* 1 large cask. 2 fermenting-vat.

tuna *n.* (*pl.* **tuna**) 1 tunny. 2 its flesh as food.

tundra *n.* vast level Arctic regions with permafrost.

tune *n.* melody. ● *v.* 1 put (a musical instrument) in tune. 2 set (a radio) to the desired wavelength. 3 adjust (an engine) to run smoothly. □ **in tune** 1 playing or singing at the correct musical pitch. 2 harmonious. **out of tune** not in tune. **tune up** bring musical instruments to the correct or uniform pitch.

■ *n.* air, melody, motif, song, strain, theme.

tuneful *adj.* melodious.

■ dulcet, euphonious, harmonious, mellifluous, melodious, musical, sweet-sounding.

tungsten *n.* heavy grey metal.

tunic *n.* 1 close-fitting jacket worn as part of a uniform. 2 loose garment reaching to the knees.

tunnel *n.* underground passage. ● *v.* (**tunnelled**) make a tunnel (through), make (one's way) in this manner.

■ *v.* bore, burrow, dig, excavate.

tunny *n.* large edible sea fish.

turban *n.* 1 Muslim or Sikh man's headdress of cloth wound round the head. 2 woman's hat resembling this.

turbid *adj.* 1 (of liquids) muddy, not clear. 2 disordered. □ **turbidity** *n.*

turbine *n.* machine or motor driven by a wheel that is turned by a flow of water or gas.

turbo- *pref.* 1 using a turbine. 2 driven by such engines.

turbot *n.* large flat edible sea fish.

turbulent *adj.* 1 in a state of commotion or unrest. 2 moving unevenly. □ **turbulently** *adv.,* **turbulence** *n.*

■ 1 confused, disorderly, restless, riotous, tumultuous, wild.

tureen *n.* deep covered dish from which soup is served.

turf *n.* (*pl.* **turfs** or **turves**) 1 short grass and the soil just below it. 2 piece of this. 3 (**the turf**) horse racing. ● *v.* lay (ground) with turf. □ **turf accountant** bookmaker. **turf out** (*colloq.*) throw out.

turgid *adj.* 1 swollen and not flexible. 2 (of language) pompous. □ **turgidly** *adv.,* **turgidity** *n.*

■ 2 bombastic, flowery, grandiloquent, pompous, pretentious.

Turk *n.* native of Turkey.

turkey *n.* (*pl.* **-eys**) 1 large bird reared for its flesh. 2 this as food.

Turkish *adj.* & *n.* (language) of Turkey. □ **Turkish bath** hot air or steam bath followed by massage etc. **Turkish delight** sweet consisting of flavoured gelatine coated in powdered sugar.

turmeric *n.* bright yellow spice from the root of an Asian plant.

turmoil *n.* state of great disturbance or confusion.

■ chaos, confusion, disorder, havoc, mayhem, pandemonium, tumult, unrest, uproar.

turn *v.* 1 move round a point or axis. 2 take or give a new direction (to). 3 aim. 4 invert, reverse. 5 pass (a certain hour or age). 6 change in form or appearance etc. 7 make or become sour. 8 give an elegant form to. 9 shape in a lathe. ● *n.* 1 process of turning. 2 change of direction or condition etc. 3 bend in a road. 4 service of a specified kind. 5 opportunity or obligation coming in succession. 6 short performance in an entertainment. 7 (*colloq.*) attack of illness, momentary nervous shock. □ **in turn** in succession. **out of turn** 1 before or after one's proper turn. 2 indiscreetly, presumptuously. **to a turn** so as to be cooked perfectly. **turn against** make or become hostile to. **turn down** 1 reject. 2 fold down. 3 reduce the volume or flow of. **turn in** 1 hand in. 2 (*colloq.*) go to bed. **turn off** 1 stop the operation of. 2 (*colloq.*) cause to lose interest. **turn on** 1 start the operation of. 2 (*colloq.*) excite sexually. **turn out** 1 expel. 2 turn off (a light etc.). 3 equip, dress. 4 produce by work. 5 appear. 6 prove to be the case eventually. 7 empty and search or clean. **turn-out** *n.* 1 number of people attending a gathering. 2 outfit. 3 process of turning out a room etc. **turn the tables** reverse a situation and put oneself in a superior position. **turn up** 1 discover. 2 be found. 3 make one's appearance. 4 increase the volume or flow of. **turn-up** *n.* turned-up part, esp. at the lower end of a trouser leg.

■ *v.* 1 circle, gyrate, orbit, revolve, roll, rotate, spin, swivel, whirl. 2 bear, head, move, swerve, swing, veer, wheel; bend, curve, meander, snake, twist, wind. **3** aim, direct, point, train. **6** adapt, alter, change, modify, refashion, remodel, reshape, transform; become, get. **7** curdle, go bad, go off, sour, spoil. **8** construct, create, fashion, form. ● *n.* **1** revolution, rotation, spin, twirl, whirl. **2** alteration, change, shift; direction, drift, trend. **3** bend, corner, curve, turning, twist. **4** act, deed, service. **5** chance, go, opportunity. **6** act, performance, routine. **7** attack, seizure; fright, scare, shock, start, surprise. □ **turn down 1** decline, refuse, reject, *colloq.* pass up. **turn out 1** eject, evict, expel, *colloq.* kick out, oust, throw out, *colloq.* turf out. **2** extinguish, switch off, turn off. **turn up 1** come across, dig up, discover, find, uncover, unearth. **2** appear, come to light. **3** appear, arrive, put in an appearance, *colloq.* show up.

turncoat *n.* person who changes his or her principles.

turner *n.* person who works with a lathe.

turning *n.* place where one road meets another, forming a corner. □ **turning point** point at which a decisive change takes place.

turnip *n.* (plant with) a round white root used as a vegetable.

turnover *n.* **1** pasty. **2** amount of money taken in a business. **3** rate of replacement.

turnstile *n.* revolving barrier for admitting people one at a time.

turntable *n.* circular revolving platform.

turpentine *n.* oil used for thinning paint and as a solvent.

turpitude *n.* wickedness.

turps *n.* (*colloq.*) turpentine.

turquoise *n.* **1** blue-green precious stone. **2** its colour.

turret *n.* small tower-like structure. □ **turreted** *adj.*

turtle *n.* sea creature like a tortoise. □ **turn turtle** capsize. **turtle-dove** *n.* wild dove noted for its soft cooing. **turtle-neck** *n.* high round close-fitting neckline.

tusk *n.* long pointed tooth outside the mouth of certain animals.

tussle *v.* & *n.* struggle, conflict.
 ■ *n.* conflict, fight, *colloq.* scrap, scuffle, skirmish, struggle.

tussock *n.* tuft or clump of grass.

tutelage *n.* **1** guardianship. **2** tuition.

tutor *n.* private or university teacher. ● *v.* act as tutor (to).
 ■ *n.* lecturer, professor, teacher. ● *v.* coach, educate, instruct, school, teach, train.

tutorial *adj.* of a tutor. ● *n.* student's session with a tutor.

tut-tut *int.* exclamation of annoyance, impatience, or rebuke.

tutu *n.* dancer's short skirt made of layers of frills.

tuxedo /tukseédō/ *n.* (*pl.* **-os**) (*US*) dinner jacket.

twaddle *n.* nonsense.

twang *n.* **1** sharp ringing sound like that made by a tense wire when plucked. **2** nasal intonation. ● *v.* make or cause to make a twang.

tweak *v.* & *n.* (pinch, twist, or pull with) a sharp jerk.

twee *adj.* affectedly dainty or quaint.

tweed *n.* **1** thick woollen fabric. **2** (*pl.*) clothes made of tweed. □ **tweedy** *adj.*

tweet *n.* & *v.* chirp.

tweeter *n.* loudspeaker for reproducing high-frequency signals.

tweezers *n.pl.* small pincers for handling very small things.

twelve *adj.* & *n.* one more than eleven. □ **twelfth** *adj.* & *n.*

twenty *adj.* & *n.* twice ten. □ **twentieth** *adj.* & *n.*

twerp *n.* (*sl.*) stupid or objectionable person.

twice *adv.* **1** two times. **2** in double amount or degree.

twiddle *v.* twist idly about. ● *n.* act of twiddling. □ **twiddle one's thumbs** have nothing to do.

twig[1] *n.* small shoot issuing from a branch or stem.

twig[2] *v.* (**twigged**) (*colloq.*) realize, grasp the meaning of.

twilight *n.* **1** light from the sky after sunset. **2** period of this.
 ■ **2** dusk, evening, gloaming, sundown, sunset.

twill *n.* fabric woven so that parallel diagonal lines are produced. □ **twilled** *adj.*

twin *n.* **1** one of two children or animals born at one birth. **2** one of a pair that are exactly alike. ● *adj.* being a twin or twins. ● *v.* (**twinned**) combine as a pair. □ **twin towns** two towns that establish special social and cultural links.

twine *n.* strong thread or string. ● *v.* twist, wind.

　　■ *n.* cord, string, thread. ● *v.* braid, coil, entwine, plait, twist, wind.

twinge *n.* slight or brief pang.

twinkle *v.* shine with a light that flickers rapidly. ● *n.* twinkling light.

　　■ *v.* glint, glisten, glitter, shimmer, shine, sparkle.

twirl *v.* twist lightly or rapidly. ● *n.* **1** twirling movement. **2** twirled mark. □ **twirly** *adj.*

　　■ *v.* gyrate, pirouette, revolve, rotate, spin, turn, twist, whirl.

twist *v.* **1** wind (strands etc.) round each other, esp. to form a single cord. **2** make by doing this. **3** bend, turn. **4** contort, wrench. **5** distort. **6** wriggle. ● *n.* **1** process of twisting. **2** thing formed by twisting. **3** bend, turn. **4** unexpected development etc.

　　■ *v.* **1,2** braid, coil, entwine, plait, twine, weave, wind. **3** bend, curve, meander, snake, wind, zigzag. **4** contort, distort, screw up; rick, sprain, wrench. **5** distort, falsify, garble, misrepresent, pervert, slant. **6** squirm, wiggle, worm, wriggle, writhe. ● *n.* **2** braid, plait; coil, curl, helix, spiral, whorl. **3** bend, corner, curve, turn, zigzag.

twit *n.* (*sl.*) foolish person.

twitch *v.* **1** quiver or contract spasmodically. **2** pull with a light jerk. ● *n.* twitching movement.

twitter *v.* **1** make light chirping sounds. **2** talk rapidly in an anxious or nervous way. ● *n.* twittering.

　　■ *v.* **1** cheep, chirp, tweet, warble.

two *adj.* & *n.* one more than one. □ **be in two minds** be undecided. **two-dimensional** *adj.* having or appearing to have length and breadth but no depth. **two-faced** *adj.* insincere, deceitful.

　　■ □ **two-faced** deceitful, double-dealing, duplicitous, hypocritical, insincere, untrustworthy.

twofold *adj.* & *adv.* twice as much or as many.

twosome *n.* group of two people.

tycoon *n.* magnate.

tying *see* **tie**.

tympanum *n.* (*pl.* **-na**) **1** eardrum. **2** space between the lintel and the arch above a door.

type *n.* **1** kind, class. **2** typical example or instance. **3** set of characters used in printing. **4** (*colloq.*) person of specified character. ● *v.* **1** write with a typewriter. **2** classify according to type.

　　■ *n.* **1** category, class, genre, genus, group, kind, make, order, set, sort, species, variety. **2** archetype, epitome, exemplar, model, paradigm. **3** lettering, fount.

typecast *v.* cast (an actor) repeatedly in similar roles.

typesetter *n.* person or machine that sets type for printing.

typescript *n.* typewritten document.

typewriter *n.* machine for producing print-like characters on paper, by pressing keys.

typhoid *n.* **typhoid fever** serious infectious feverish disease.

typhoon *n.* violent hurricane.

typhus *n.* infectious feverish disease transmitted by parasites.

typical *adj.* having the distinctive qualities of a particular type of person or thing. □ **typically** *adv.*

　　■ characteristic, classic, representative, standard; average, conventional, normal, ordinary; regular, usual.

typify *v.* be a representative specimen of.

　　■ characterize, epitomize, exemplify, illustrate, personify, represent, symbolize.

typist *n.* person who types.

typography *n.* art or style of printing. □ **typographical** *adj.*

tyrannize *v.* rule as or like a tyrant.

　　■ browbeat, bully, domineer over, intimidate, oppress, subjugate, terrorize, torment.

tyranny *n.* **1** government by a tyrant. **2** tyrannical use of power. □ **tyrannical** *adj.*, **tyrannically** *adv.*

　　■ **1** authoritarianism, autocracy, despotism, dictatorship, totalitarianism. □ **tyrannical** authoritarian, autocratic, despotic, dictatorial, domineering, imperious, overbearing.

tyrant *n.* ruler or other person who uses power in a harsh or oppressive way.

　　■ autocrat, despot, dictator; bully, martinet, slave-driver.

tyre *n.* covering round the rim of a wheel to absorb shocks.

Uu

ubiquitous *adj.* found everywhere. □ **ubiquity** *n.*

udder *n.* bag-like milk-producing organ of a cow, goat, etc.

ugly *adj.* (**-ier, -iest**) **1** unpleasant to look at or hear. **2** threatening, hostile. □ **ugliness** *n.*
■ **1** grotesque, hideous, *US* homely, plain, unattractive, unsightly, unprepossessing. **2** hostile, menacing, nasty, ominous, sinister, threatening, unpleasant.

UHF *abbr.* ultra-high frequency.

UK *abbr.* United Kingdom.

ukulele /yŏŏkəláyli/ *n.* small four-stringed guitar.

ulcer *n.* open sore. □ **ulcerous** *adj.*

ulcerated *adj.* affected with ulcer(s). □ **ulceration** *n.*

ulna *n.* (*pl.* **-ae**) thinner long bone of the forearm. □ **ulnar** *adj.*

ulterior *adj.* beyond what is obvious or admitted.
■ concealed, covert, hidden, secret, undisclosed.

ultimate *adj.* **1** last, final. **2** fundamental. □ **ultimately** *adv.*
■ **1** closing, concluding, eventual, final, last, terminating. **2** basic, elemental, essential, fundamental, primary, underlying.

ultimatum *n.* (*pl.* **-ums**) final demand, with a threat of hostile action if this is rejected.

ultra- *pref.* **1** beyond. **2** extremely.

ultra-high *adj.* (of frequency) between 300 and 3000 MHz.

ultramarine *adj. & n.* deep bright blue.

ultrasonic *adj.* above the range of normal human hearing.

ultrasound *n.* ultrasonic waves.

ultraviolet *adj.* of or using radiation with a wavelength shorter than that of visible light rays.

ululate *v.* howl, wail. □ **ululation** *n.*

umber *n.* natural brownish colouring matter.

umbilical *adj.* of the navel. □ **umbilical cord** flexible tube connecting the placenta to the navel of a foetus.

umbra *n.* (*pl.* **-ae**) area of total shadow cast by the moon or earth in an eclipse.

umbrage *n.* offence taken.

umbrella *n.* circle of fabric on a folding framework of spokes attached to a central stick, used as protection against rain.

umpire *n.* person appointed to supervise a game or contest etc. and see that rules are observed. ● *v.* act as umpire in.
■ *n.* arbitrator, judge, referee.

umpteen *adj.* (*sl.*) very many. □ **umpteenth** *adj.*

UN *abbr.* United Nations.

un- *pref.* **1** not. **2** reversing the action indicated by a verb, e.g. *unlock*. (The number of words with this prefix is almost unlimited and many of those whose meaning is obvious are not listed below.)

unaccountable *adj.* **1** unable to be explained. **2** not having to account for one's actions etc. □ **unaccountably** *adv.*
■ **1** incomprehensible, inexplicable, mysterious, odd, strange.

unadulterated *adj.* pure, complete.

unalloyed *adj.* pure.

unanimous *adj.* **1** all agreeing. **2** agreed by all. □ **unanimously** *adv.*, **unanimity** *n.*

unarmed *adj.* without weapons.

unassuming *adj.* not arrogant.

unavoidable *adj.* unable to be avoided. □ **unavoidably** *adv.*
■ certain, ineluctable, inescapable, inevitable.

unawares *adv.* **1** unexpectedly. **2** without noticing.
■ **1** abruptly, by surprise, off (one's) guard, suddenly, unexpectedly. **2** by accident *or* mistake, inadvertently, unconsciously, unintentionally, unwittingly.

unbalanced *adj.* **1** not balanced. **2** mentally unsound. **3** biased.

unbeknown *adj.* unknown.

unbend *v.* (**unbent**) **1** change from a bent position. **2** become relaxed or affable.

unbending *adj.* inflexible, refusing to alter one's demands.

unbidden *adj.* not commanded or invited.

unbounded *adj.* without limits.
■ boundless, endless, infinite, limitless, unlimited.

unbridled *adj.* unrestrained.

unburden v. **unburden oneself** reveal one's thoughts and feelings.

uncalled-for adj. given or done impertinently or unjustifiably.

uncanny adj. (**-ier, -iest**) **1** strange and rather frightening. **2** extraordinary. □ **uncannily** adv.
■ **1** eerie, frightening, ghostly, mysterious, *colloq.* spooky, strange, unearthly, weird. **2** astonishing, extraordinary, incredible, remarkable.

unceremonious adj. without proper formality or dignity.

uncertain adj. **1** not known or not knowing certainly. **2** not to be depended on. □ **uncertainly** adv., **uncertainty** n.
■ **1** ambiguous, indefinite, questionable, touch-and-go, undetermined, unforeseeable; ambivalent, doubtful, dubious, indecisive, in two minds, irresolute, undecided, unsure, vague. **2** changeable, unpredictable, unreliable, unsettled, variable.

uncle n. brother or brother-in-law of one's father or mother.

unclean adj. **1** not clean. **2** ritually impure.

uncommon adj. unusual.

uncompromising adj. not allowing or not seeking compromise, inflexible.
■ dogged, inflexible, intransigent, resolute, stubborn, unyielding.

unconcern n. lack of concern.

unconditional adj. not subject to conditions. □ **unconditionally** adv.
■ absolute, complete, full, total, unequivocal, unqualified.

unconscionable adj. **1** unscrupulous. **2** contrary to what one's conscience feels is right.

unconscious adj. **1** not conscious. **2** not aware. **3** done without conscious intention. □ **unconsciously** adv., **unconsciousness** n.
■ **1** comatose, insensible, knocked out, out. **2** heedless, oblivious, unaware. **3** inadvertent, instinctive, involuntary, subconscious, unintentional, unpremeditated, unthinking.

unconsidered adj. disregarded.

uncork v. pull the cork from.

uncouple v. disconnect (things joined by a coupling).

uncouth adj. uncultured, rough.

uncover v. **1** remove a covering from. **2** reveal, expose.
■ **2** disclose, discover, expose, lay bare, make known, reveal, unmask, unveil.

unction n. **1** anointing with oil, esp. as a religious rite. **2** excessive politeness.

unctuous adj. **1** unpleasantly flattering. **2** greasy. □ **unctuously** adv., **unctuousness** n.
■ **1** fawning, flattering, obsequious, servile, *colloq.* smarmy, sycophantic.

undeniable adj. undoubtedly true. □ **undeniably** adv.

under prep. **1** in or to a position or rank etc. lower than. **2** less than. **3** governed or controlled by. **4** subjected to. **5** in accordance with. **6** known or classified as. ● adv. **1** in or to a lower position or subordinate condition. **2** in or into a state of unconsciousness. **3** below a certain quantity, rank, age, etc. □ **under age 1** not old enough, esp. for some legal right. **2** not yet of adult status. **under way** making progress.

under- *pref.* **1** below. **2** lower, subordinate. **3** insufficiently.

underarm adj. & adv. **1** in the armpit. **2** with the hand brought forwards and upwards.

undercarriage n. **1** aircraft's landing wheels and their supports. **2** supporting framework of a vehicle.

underclass n. social class below mainstream society.

undercliff n. terrace or lower cliff formed by a landslip.

underclothes n.pl. (also **underclothing**) underwear.

undercoat n. layer of paint used under a finishing coat.

undercover adj. done or doing things secretly.

undercurrent n. **1** current flowing below a surface. **2** underlying feeling, influence, etc.
■ **1** undertow. **2** atmosphere, feeling, overtone, sense, suggestion, undertone.

undercut v. (**undercut**) **1** cut away the part below. **2** sell or work for a lower price than.

underdog n. person etc. in an inferior or subordinate position.

underdone adj. not thoroughly cooked.

underestimate v. & n. (make) too low an estimate (of).
■ v. belittle, minimize, set little store by, underrate, undervalue.

underfelt *n.* felt for laying under a carpet.

underfoot *adv.* **1** on the ground. **2** under one's feet.

undergo *v.* (**-went**, **-gone**) experience, endure.

■ bear, be subjected to, endure, experience, go *or* live through, put up with, stand, suffer, weather, withstand.

undergraduate *n.* person studying for a first degree.

underground *adj.* **1** under the surface of the ground. **2** secret. ● *n.* underground railway.

■ *adj.* **1** buried, subterranean. **2** clandestine, covert, secret, undercover. ● *n.* US subway.

undergrowth *n.* thick growth of shrubs and bushes under trees.

underhand *adj.* **1** secret, sly. **2** underarm.

■ **1** clandestine, covert, cunning, devious, dishonest, furtive, secret, sly, surreptitious.

underlay *n.* material laid under another as a support.

underlie *v.* (**-lay**, **-lain**, **-lying**) be the basis of. □ **underlying** *adj.*

underline *v.* **1** draw a line under. **2** emphasize.

■ **2** accentuate, draw attention to, emphasize, highlight, point up, stress.

underling *n.* subordinate.

undermanned *adj.* having too few staff or crew etc.

undermine *v.* **1** weaken gradually. **2** weaken the foundations of.

■ **1** damage, debilitate, harm, ruin, spoil, subvert, weaken, wreck.

underneath *prep.* & *adv.* below or on the inside of (a thing).

underpants *n.pl.* undergarment for the lower part of the torso.

underpass *n.* road passing under another.

■ subway, tunnel.

underpin *v.* (**-pinned**) support, strengthen from beneath.

underprivileged *adj.* not having the normal standard of living or rights in a community.

underrate *v.* underestimate.

underseal *v.* coat the lower surface of (a vehicle) with a protective layer. ● *n.* this coating.

undersell *v.* (**-sold**) sell at a lower price than.

undershoot *v.* (**-shot**) land short of (a runway etc.).

undersigned *adj.* who has or have signed this document.

underskirt *n.* petticoat.

understand *v.* (**-stood**) **1** see the meaning or importance of. **2** be sympathetically aware of the character or nature of. **3** infer, take as implied. □ **understandable** *adj.*

■ **1** apprehend, *colloq.* catch on to, comprehend, *colloq.* cotton on to, fathom, follow, *colloq.* get, grasp, make out, perceive, realize, recognize, see, take in, *colloq.* twig. **2** accept, appreciate, empathize with, sympathize with. **3** assume, conclude, deduce, gather, infer, presume, suppose, surmise.

understanding *adj.* showing insight or sympathy. ● *n.* **1** ability to understand. **2** judgement of a situation. **3** sympathetic insight. **4** agreement. **5** thing agreed.

■ *adj.* compassionate, considerate, kind, sensitive, supportive, sympathetic, thoughtful. ● *n.* **1** brain(s), intellect, intelligence, mind, sense. **2** interpretation, judgement, opinion, perception, view. **3** compassion, empathy, feeling, insight, sensitivity, sympathy. **4** accord, agreement, concord, harmony. **5** agreement, arrangement, bargain, compact, contract, deal, pact, settlement.

understate *v.* **1** express in restrained terms. **2** represent as less than it really is. □ **understatement** *n.*

understudy *n.* actor ready to take another's role when required. ● *v.* be an understudy for.

undertake *v.* (**-took**, **-taken**) agree or promise (to do something).

■ agree, consent, guarantee, pledge, promise, swear, vow.

undertaker *n.* one whose business is to organize funerals.

undertaking *n.* **1** work etc. undertaken. **2** promise, guarantee.

■ **1** endeavour, enterprise, job, project, task, venture. **2** agreement, commitment, guarantee, pledge, promise, vow.

undertone *n.* underlying quality or feeling.

■ atmosphere, feeling, overtone, sense, suggestion, undercurrent.

undertow *n.* undercurrent moving in the opposite direction to the surface current.

underwear *n.* garments worn under indoor clothing.

■ lingerie, *colloq.* smalls, underclothes, *colloq.* undies.

underwent *see* **undergo**.

underworld *n.* **1** (in mythology) abode of spirits of the dead, under the earth. **2** part of society habitually involved in crime.

underwrite *v.* (-wrote, -written) **1** accept liability under (an insurance policy). **2** undertake to finance. □ **underwriter** *n.*

undesirable *adj.* not desirable, objectionable. □ **undesirably** *adv.*

■ disagreeable, objectionable, obnoxious, offensive, repugnant, unacceptable, unpleasant.

undies *n.pl.* (*colloq.*) women's underwear.

undo *v.* (-did, -done) **1** unfasten. **2** annul, cancel. **3** ruin.

■ **1** loosen, open, unfasten, untie; unbolt, unlock; uncover, unwrap. **2** annul, cancel, nullify, reverse. **3** destroy, ruin, spoil, wreck.

undone *adj.* **1** unfastened. **2** not done.

undoubted *adj.* not disputed. □ **undoubtedly** *adv.*

undress *v.* take clothes off.

undue *adj.* excessive. □ **unduly** *adv.*

■ excessive, extreme, immoderate, unjustifiable, unreasonable.

undulate *v.* have or cause to have a wavy movement or appearance. □ **undulation** *n.*

undying *adj.* everlasting.

■ endless, eternal, everlasting, immortal, perpetual, unending.

unearth *v.* **1** uncover or bring out from the ground. **2** find by searching.

■ **1** dig up, disinter, excavate, exhume, uncover. **2** come across, discover, find, turn up, uncover.

unearthly *adj.* **1** not of this earth. **2** mysterious and frightening. **3** (*colloq.*) very early. ˙

■ **1** celestial, heavenly. **2** preternatural, supernatural; creepy, eerie, frightening, ghostly, mysterious, *colloq.* scary, *colloq.* spooky, strange, uncanny, weird.

uneasy *adj.* disturbed or uncomfortable in body or mind. □ **uneasily** *adv.*, **uneasiness** *n.*

■ anxious, apprehensive, disturbed, ill at ease, nervous, restive, restless, tense, troubled, worried.

uneatable *adj.* not fit to be eaten.

uneconomic *adj.* not profitable.

unemployable *adj.* not fit for paid employment.

unemployed *adj.* **1** without a paid job. **2** not in use. □ **unemployment** *n.*

■ **1** jobless, laid off, *colloq.* on the dole, out of work. **2** idle, inactive, unused.

unequivocal *adj.* clear, unambiguous. □ **unequivocally** *adv.*

■ categorical, clear, direct, explicit, plain, unambiguous, unmistakable.

unerring *adj.* making no mistake.

uneven *adj.* **1** not level. **2** of variable quality. □ **unevenly** *adv.*, **unevenness** *n.*

■ **1** bumpy, rough; lopsided, unbalanced, unequal. **2** erratic, inconsistent, patchy, variable.

unexceptionable *adj.* with which no fault can be found.

unfailing *adj.* **1** constant. **2** reliable.

unfair *adj.* not impartial, not in accordance with justice. □ **unfairly** *adv.*, **unfairness** *n.*

■ biased, bigoted, inequitable, one-sided, prejudiced, unjust.

unfaithful *adj.* **1** not loyal. **2** having committed adultery. □ **unfaithfully** *adv.*, **unfaithfulness** *n.*

■ **1** disloyal, faithless, false, fickle, inconstant, perfidious, unreliable.

unfeeling *adj.* lacking sensitivity, callous. □ **unfeelingly** *adv.*

■ callous, hard, hard-hearted, harsh, heartless, insensitive, ruthless, unkind, unsympathetic.

unfit *adj.* **1** unsuitable. **2** not in perfect physical condition. ● *v.* (**unfitted**) make unsuitable.

unflappable *adj.* (*colloq.*) remaining calm in a crisis.

unfold *v.* **1** open, spread out. **2** become known.

■ **1** open, spread (out), stretch out, uncoil, unfurl, unwind.

unforgettable *adj.* impossible to forget. □ **unforgettably** *adv.*

unfortunate *adj.* **1** having bad luck. **2** regrettable. □ **unfortunately** *adv.*

■ **1** hapless, luckless, poor, unlucky, wretched. **2** deplorable, lamentable, regrettable.

unfounded *adj.* with no basis.

■ baseless, groundless, unjustified, unproven, unsupported, unwarranted.

unfrock v. dismiss (a priest) from the priesthood.

unfurl v. unroll, spread out.

ungainly adj. awkward-looking, not graceful. □ **ungainliness** n.
■ awkward, clumsy, gauche, gawky, maladroit, ungraceful.

ungodly adj. **1** impious, wicked. **2** (colloq.) outrageous.

ungovernable adj. uncontrollable.

ungracious adj. not courteous or kindly. □ **ungraciously** adv.
■ churlish, discourteous, gauche, ill-mannered, impolite, rude, uncivil, unkind.

unguarded adj. **1** not guarded. **2** incautious.
■ **2** careless, ill-considered, imprudent, incautious, indiscreet, thoughtless, unthinking, unwise.

unguent /únggwənt/ n. ointment, lubricant.

ungulate adj. & n. hoofed (animal).

unhappy adj. (-ier, -iest) **1** not happy, sad. **2** unfortunate. **3** unsuitable. □ **unhappily** adv., **unhappiness** n.
■ **1** blue, crestfallen, dejected, depressed, despondent, disconsolate, dispirited, downcast, downhearted, fed up, forlorn, glum, heavy-hearted, in low spirits, in the doldrums, melancholy, miserable, sad, sorrowful, woebegone. **2** hapless, luckless, unfortunate, unlucky. **3** inappropriate, infelicitous, unfortunate, unsuitable.

unhealthy adj. (-ier, -iest) **1** not healthy. **2** harmful to health. □ **unhealthily** adv.
■ **1** ailing, ill, indisposed, poorly, sick, sickly, unwell. **2** insalubrious, insanitary, unhygienic, unwholesome.

unheard-of adj. unprecedented.

unhinge v. cause to become mentally unbalanced.

unholy adj. (-ier, -iest) **1** wicked, irreverent. **2** (colloq.) very great.

unicorn n. mythical horse-like animal with one straight horn.

uniform n. distinctive clothing worn by members of the same organization etc. ● adj. always the same. □ **uniformly** adv., **uniformity** n.
■ adj. consistent, constant, even, regular, unchanging, unvarying.

unify v. unite. □ **unification** n.

unilateral adj. done by or affecting one person or group etc. and not another. □ **unilaterally** adv.

unimpeachable adj. completely trustworthy.

uninviting adj. unattractive, repellent.
■ disagreeable, offensive, colloq. off-putting, repellent, repulsive, unappealing, unappetizing, unattractive, unpleasant, unsavoury.

union n. **1** uniting, being united. **2** a whole formed by uniting parts. **3** trade union (see trade). □ **Union Jack** national flag of the UK.
■ **1** amalgamation, coalition, combination, fusion, merger, synthesis, unification. **2** alliance, association, coalition, confederation, consortium, federation, partnership, syndicate.

unionist n. **1** member of a trade union. **2** supporter of trade unions. **3** one who favours union.

unionize v. organize into or cause to join a union. □ **unionization** n.

unique adj. **1** being the only one of its kind. **2** unequalled. □ **uniquely** adv.
■ **2** incomparable, inimitable, matchless, peerless, unequalled, unparalleled.

unisex adj. designed in a style suitable for people of either sex.

unison n. **in unison 1** all together. **2** sounding or singing together.
■ at once, at the same time, simultaneously, together.

unit n. **1** individual thing, person, or group, esp. as part of a complex whole. **2** fixed quantity used as a standard of measurement. □ **unit trust** investment company paying dividends based on the average return from the various securities which they hold.
■ **1** component, constituent, element, item, part, piece.

unitary adj. of a unit or units.

unite v. **1** join together, make or become one. **2** act together, cooperate.
■ **1** amalgamate, coalesce, combine, integrate, join, merge, synthesize. **2** ally, cooperate, join forces, team up.

unity n. **1** state of being one or a unit. **2** agreement. **3** complex whole.
■ **2** accord, agreement, concord, consensus, harmony, solidarity, unanimity.

universal adj. of, for, or done by all. □ **universally** adv.
■ common, general, global, widespread, worldwide.

universe *n.* all existing things, including the earth and its creatures and all the heavenly bodies.

university *n.* educational institution for advanced learning.

unkempt *adj.* untidy, neglected.
■ dishevelled, messy, *colloq.* scruffy, untidy.

unkind *adj.* harsh, hurtful. □ **unkindly** *adv.*, **unkindness** *n.*
■ callous, cruel, hard, hard-hearted, heartless, hurtful, inconsiderate, insensitive, malicious, mean, nasty, spiteful, thoughtless, uncaring, uncharitable, unfeeling, unsympathetic.

unknown *adj.* not known. ● *n.* unknown person, thing, or place.

unleaded *adj.* (of petrol etc.) without added lead.

unleash *v.* release, let loose.

unless *conj.* except when, except on condition that.

unlettered *adj.* illiterate.

unlike *adj.* not like. ● *prep.* differently from.

unlikely *adj.* not likely to happen or be true or be successful.
■ doubtful, dubious, far-fetched, implausible, improbable.

unlisted *adj.* not included in a (published) list.

unload *v.* **1** remove a load or cargo (from). **2** get rid of. **3** remove the ammunition from (a gun).

unlock *v.* **1** release the lock of. **2** release by unlocking.

unlooked-for *adj.* unexpected.

unmanned *adj.* operated without a crew.

unmask *v.* **1** remove a mask (from). **2** expose the true character of.

unmentionable *adj.* not fit to be spoken of.

unmistakable *adj.* clear, obvious, plain. □ **unmistakably** *adv.*
■ clear, incontrovertible, indisputable, manifest, obvious, patent, plain, undeniable.

unmitigated *adj.* not modified, absolute.
■ absolute, complete, downright, out and out, perfect, pure, sheer, thorough, total, unadulterated, unqualified, utter.

unmoved *adj.* not moved, not persuaded, not affected by emotion.

unnatural *adj.* different from what is normal or expected, not natural. □ **unnaturally** *adv.*
■ abnormal, bizarre, extraordinary, odd, outlandish, peculiar, strange, uncanny, uncharacteristic, unusual, weird; affected, artificial, false, feigned, forced, insincere, *colloq.* phoney, studied.

unnecessary *adj.* **1** not necessary. **2** more than is necessary. □ **unnecessarily** *adv.*
■ **1** dispensable, expendable, inessential, needless, unneeded. **2** excessive, superfluous, undue.

unnerve *v.* deprive of confidence.
■ discomfit, disconcert, dismay, disturb, fluster, perturb, *colloq.* rattle, ruffle, shake, *colloq.* throw, unsettle, upset.

unnumbered *adj.* **1** not marked with a number. **2** countless.

unobtrusive *adj.* not making oneself or itself noticed. □ **unobtrusively** *adv.*
■ discreet, inconspicuous, low-key, unassuming, unpretentious.

unpack *v.* **1** open and remove the contents of (a suitcase etc.). **2** take out from its packaging.

unparalleled *adj.* never yet equalled.
■ incomparable, inimitable, matchless, peerless, unequalled, unique, unmatched, unprecedented, unrivalled, unsurpassed.

unpick *v.* undo the stitching of.

unplaced *adj.* not placed as one of the first three in a race etc.

unpleasant *adj.* not pleasant. □ **unpleasantly** *adv.*, **unpleasantness** *n.*
■ *colloq.* beastly, disagreeable, distasteful, *colloq.* horrible, horrid, nasty, objectionable, offensive, repellent, unsavoury.

unpopular *adj.* not popular, disliked. □ **unpopularity** *n.*

unprecedented *adj.* having no precedent, unparalleled.

unprepared *adj.* **1** not prepared beforehand. **2** not ready or not equipped to do something.

unpretentious *adj.* not pretentious, not showy or pompous.
■ humble, modest, plain, unassuming, unostentatious.

unprincipled *adj.* without good moral principles, unscrupulous.

unprintable *adj.* too indecent or libellous etc. to be printed.

unprofessional adj. contrary to the standards of behaviour for members of a profession. □ **unprofessionally** adv.

unqualified adj. **1** not qualified. **2** unmitigated.

unquestionable adj. too clear to be doubted. □ **unquestionably** adv.

■ certain, incontestable, incontrovertible, indubitable, irrefutable, undeniable, undisputed, undoubted, unmistakable.

unravel v. (**unravelled**) **1** disentangle. **2** undo (knitted fabric). **3** become unravelled.

unreasonable adj. **1** not reasonable. **2** excessive. □ **unreasonably** adv.

■ **1** absurd, foolish, illogical, irrational, ludicrous, preposterous, ridiculous. **2** excessive, exorbitant, extravagant, immoderate, inordinate, outrageous, unjustifiable.

unrelieved adj. monotonously uniform.

unremitting adj. incessant.

unrequited adj. (of love) not returned.

unreservedly adv. without reservation, completely.

unrest n. disturbance, turmoil.

■ disquiet, disturbance, strife, trouble, turbulence, turmoil.

unrivalled adj. having no equal.

unroll v. open after being rolled.

unruly adj. not easy to control, disorderly. □ **unruliness** n.

■ disobedient, disorderly, insubordinate, mutinous, obstreperous, rebellious, recalcitrant, riotous, rowdy, uncontrollable, undisciplined, ungovernable, unmanageable, wayward, wild.

unsaid adj. not spoken or expressed.

unsavoury adj. **1** disagreeable to the taste or smell. **2** morally offensive.

■ **1** unappetizing, unpalatable. **2** disgusting, distasteful, nasty, objectionable, offensive, repugnant, repulsive, revolting.

unscathed adj. without suffering any injury.

■ safe, intact, unharmed, unhurt, uninjured.

unscramble v. **1** sort out. **2** make (a scrambled transmission) intelligible.

unscrew v. **1** loosen (a screw etc.). **2** unfasten by removing screw(s).

unscripted adj. without a prepared script.

unscrupulous adj. not prevented by scruples of conscience.

■ amoral, corrupt, colloq. crooked, dishonest, immoral, unethical, unprincipled.

unseat v. **1** dislodge (a rider). **2** remove from a parliamentary seat.

unselfish adj. considering others' needs before one's own. □ **unselfishly** adv., **unselfishness** n.

■ altruistic, charitable, considerate, generous, kind, selfless, thoughtful.

unsettle v. make uneasy, disturb.

■ agitate, discomfit, disquiet, disturb, perturb, colloq. rattle, ruffle, shake, colloq. throw, unnerve, upset, worry.

unsettled adj. (of weather) changeable.

unshakeable adj. firm.

unsightly adj. not pleasant to look at, ugly. □ **unsightliness** n.

■ hideous, plain, ugly, unattractive, unlovely, unprepossessing.

unskilled adj. not having or needing skill or special training.

unsocial adj. **1** not sociable. **2** not conforming to normal social practices.

unsolicited adj. not requested.

unsophisticated adj. simple and natural or naive.

■ artless, callow, childlike, green, inexperienced, ingenuous, innocent, naive, natural, simple, unworldly.

unsound adj. not sound or strong. □ **of unsound mind** insane.

unsparing adj. giving lavishly.

■ generous, lavish, liberal, munificent, open-handed.

unspeakable adj. too bad to be described in words.

unstable adj. **1** not stable. **2** likely to change suddenly.

■ **2** capricious, changeable, unpredictable, unreliable, volatile.

unstuck adj. detached after being stuck on or together. □ **come unstuck** (colloq.) suffer disaster, fail.

unstudied adj. natural in manner.

unsullied adj. not sullied, pure.

unswerving adj. **1** not turning aside. **2** unchanging.

■ **2** constant, firm, steadfast, unchanging, unwavering.

unthinkable adj. too bad or too unlikely to be thought about.

unthinking adj. **1** thoughtless. **2** inadvertent.

■ **1** careless, inconsiderate, rude, tactless, thoughtless. **2** inadvertent, involuntary, unintentional.

untidy *adj.* (**-ier, -iest**) not tidy. □ **untidily** *adv.*, **untidiness** *n.*

■ chaotic, disordered, disorderly, disorganized, higgledy-piggledy, messy, topsy-turvy; dishevelled, *colloq.* scruffy, unkempt.

untie *v.* **1** unfasten. **2** release from being tied up.

■ **1** loose, loosen, open, undo, unfasten. **2** free, release, unchain, unfetter, unleash.

until *prep.* & *conj.* = **till²**.

untimely *adj.* **1** inopportune. **2** premature.

■ **1** ill-timed, inappropriate, inconvenient, inopportune, unseasonable, unsuitable. **2** early, premature.

untold *adj.* **1** not told. **2** too much or too many to be counted.

■ **2** countless, innumerable, many, numerous, *sl.* umpteen; immeasurable, incalculable, unlimited.

untouchable *adj.* that may not be touched. ● *n.* member of the lowest Hindu social group.

untoward *adj.* unexpected and inconvenient.

untruth *n.* **1** untrue statement, lie. **2** lack of truth. □ **untruthful** *adj.*, **untruthfully** *adv.*

■ **1** fabrication, falsehood, fib, lie, *sl.* whopper.

unusual *adj.* **1** not usual. **2** remarkable, rare. □ **unusually** *adv.*

■ **1** abnormal, atypical, bizarre, curious, different, odd, out of the ordinary, peculiar, strange, surprising, uncommon, unconventional, unexpected. **2** exceptional, extraordinary, rare, remarkable, singular.

unutterable *adj.* beyond description. □ **unutterably** *adv.*

unvarnished *adj.* **1** not varnished. **2** plain, straightforward.

unveil *v.* **1** remove a veil (from). **2** remove concealing drapery from. **3** disclose, make publicly known.

■ **3** disclose, divulge, expose, lay bare, make known, reveal, uncover, unmask.

unversed *adj.* **unversed in** not experienced in.

unwarranted *adj.* unjustified.

■ indefensible, inexcusable, uncalled-for, unjustified.

unwell *adj.* not in good health.

■ ailing, ill, indisposed, off-colour, poorly, sick, sickly, under the weather, unhealthy.

unwieldy *adj.* awkward to move or control because of its size, shape, etc. □ **unwieldiness** *n.*

■ awkward, bulky, clumsy, cumbersome, unmanageable.

unwind *v.* (**unwound**) **1** draw out or become drawn out from being wound. **2** (*colloq.*) relax.

unwise *adj.* not wise, foolish. □ **unwisely** *adv.*

■ foolhardy, foolish, ill-advised, ill-judged, imprudent, incautious, misguided, rash, reckless, senseless, short-sighted, silly, stupid.

unwitting *adj.* **1** unaware. **2** unintentional. □ **unwittingly** *adv.*

unwonted *adj.* not customary, not usual. □ **unwontedly** *adv.*

unworldly *adj.* **1** spiritual. **2** naive. □ **unworldliness** *n.*

unworthy *adj.* of little or no value. □ **unworthy of** unsuitable to the character of (a person or thing).

■ inferior, mediocre, second-rate, substandard. □ **unworthy of** below, beneath, inappropriate to, inconsistent with, unbecoming to, unsuitable for.

unwritten *adj.* **1** not written down. **2** based on custom not statute.

up *adv.* **1** to, in, or at a higher place or state etc. **2** to a vertical position. **3** completed or completely. **4** as far as a stated place, time, or amount. **5** out of bed. **6** (*colloq.*) amiss, happening. ● *prep.* **1** upwards along or through or into. **2** at a higher part of. ● *adj.* **1** directed upwards. **2** travelling towards a central place. ● *v.* (**upped**) (*colloq.*) **1** raise. **2** get up (and do something). □ **time is up** time is finished. **up in** (*colloq.*) knowledgeable about. **ups and downs** alternate good and bad fortune. **up to 1** occupied with, doing. **2** required as a duty or obligation from. **3** capable of.

upbeat *n.* unaccented beat. ● *adj.* (*colloq.*) optimistic, cheerful.

upbraid *v.* reproach.

■ admonish, berate, chastise, chide, criticize, rebuke, reprimand, reproach, reprove, scold, take to task, *colloq.* tell off.

upbringing *n.* training and education during childhood.

update *v.* bring up to date.

up-end *v.* set or rise up on end.

upgrade *v.* raise to higher grade.

upheaval n. **1** sudden heaving upwards. **2** violent disturbance.
■ **2** chaos, confusion, disorder, disruption, disturbance, havoc, turmoil.

uphill adj. & adv. going or sloping upwards.

uphold v. (**upheld**) support.
■ defend, maintain, preserve, protect, stand by, support, sustain.

upholster v. put fabric covering, padding, etc. on (furniture).

upholstery n. **1** upholstering. **2** material used in this.

upkeep n. **1** keeping (a thing) in good condition and repair. **2** cost of this.
■ **1** maintenance. **2** expenses, overheads, running costs.

upland n. & adj. (of) higher or inland parts of a country.

uplift v. raise. ● n. **1** being raised. **2** mentally elevating influence.

upon prep. on.

upper adj. higher in place, position, or rank. ● n. part of a shoe above the sole.
□ **upper case** capital letters. **upper class** highest class of society. **upper crust** (colloq.) aristocracy. **upper hand** dominance.
■ adj. higher, superior. □ **upper class** aristocracy, elite, nobility, colloq. upper crust. **upper hand** advantage, authority, command, control, dominance, power, superiority, sway.

uppermost adj. & adv. in, on, or to the top or most prominent position.
■ adj. highest, top, topmost; first, foremost, most important, paramount, preeminent, principal.

uppity adj. (colloq.) having too high an opinion of oneself.

upright adj. **1** in a vertical position. **2** honest or honourable. ● n. vertical part or support.
■ adj. **1** erect, perpendicular, straight, upstanding, vertical. **2** decent, ethical, good, honest, honourable, incorruptible, law-abiding, moral, principled, righteous, virtuous. ● n. column, pillar, pole, post, stanchion.

uprising n. rebellion.
■ coup d'état, insurrection, mutiny, rebellion, revolt, revolution.

uproar n. outburst of noise and excitement or anger.
■ clamour, commotion, din, fracas, hubbub, hullabaloo, noise, pandemonium, racket, rumpus, tumult.

uproarious adj. noisy, with loud laughter. □ **uproariously** adv.
■ clamorous, deafening, noisy, riotous, rowdy, tumultuous, wild.

uproot v. **1** pull out of the ground together with its roots. **2** force to leave an established place.

upset v. /úpsét/ (**upset**, **upsetting**) **1** overturn. **2** disrupt. **3** disturb the temper, composure, or digestion of. ● n. /úpset/ upsetting, being upset.
■ v. **1** knock over, overturn, tip over, topple, turn up-end, upturn. **2** disrupt, disturb, mess up, ruin, spoil, thwart, wreck. **3** annoy, dismay, distress, disturb, grieve, hurt, offend, pain, perturb, put out, trouble, unsettle, worry.

upshot n. outcome.
■ conclusion, consequence, effect, outcome, repercussion, result.

upside down **1** with the upper part underneath. **2** in great disorder.

upstage adv. & adj. nearer the back of a theatre stage. ● v. divert attention from, outshine.

upstairs adv. & adj. to or on a higher floor.

upstanding adj. **1** strong and healthy. **2** standing up.

upstart n. person newly risen to a high position, esp. one who behaves arrogantly.

upstream adj. & adv. in the direction from which a stream flows.

upsurge n. upward surge, rise.

upswing n. upward movement or trend.

uptake n. **quick on the uptake** (colloq.) quick to understand.

uptight adj. (colloq.) nervously tense or angry.

upturn v. /úptúrn/ turn up or upwards or upside down. ● n. /úptúrn/ **1** upheaval. **2** upward trend, improvement.

upward adj. moving or leading up.

upwards adv. towards a higher place etc.

uranium n. heavy grey metal used as a source of nuclear energy.

urban adj. of a city or town.

urbane *adj.* having smooth manners. □ **urbanely** *adv.*, **urbanity** *n.*

■ charming, civilized, courteous, cultivated, debonair, gracious, polished, sophisticated, suave, well-mannered.

urbanize *v.* change (a place) into an urban area. □ **urbanization** *n.*

urchin *n.* mischievous child.

Urdu *n.* language related to Hindi.

ureter /yooreetar/ *n.* duct from the kidney to the bladder.

urethra /yooreethra/ *n.* duct carrying urine from the body.

urge *v.* 1 impel, drive forcibly. 2 encourage or entreat earnestly or persistently. 3 advocate emphatically. ● *n.* feeling or desire urging a person to do something.

■ *v.* 1 drive, force, hasten, hustle, impel, push; egg on, goad, incite, prod, prompt, spur. 2 beg, beseech, encourage, entreat, exhort, implore, plead with, press. 3 advise, advocate, counsel, recommend. ● *n.* craving, desire, longing, yearning, *colloq.* yen.

urgent *adj.* needing or calling for immediate attention or action. □ **urgently** *adv.*, **urgency** *n.*

■ acute, critical, desperate, imperative, important, necessary, pressing, serious, vital.

urinal *n.* receptacle or structure for receiving urine.

urinate *v.* discharge urine from the body. □ **urination** *n.*

urine *n.* waste liquid which collects in the bladder and is discharged from the body. □ **urinary** *adj.*

urn *n.* 1 a kind of vase, esp. for a cremated person's ashes. 2 large metal container with a tap, for keeping water etc. hot.

ursine *adj.* of or like a bear.

us *pron.* objective case of *we.*

US, USA *abbrs.* United States (of America).

usable *adj.* able or fit to be used.

usage *n.* 1 manner of using or treating something. 2 customary practice.

■ 1 handling, management, treatment, use. 2 convention, custom, habit, practice, tradition.

use *v.* /yooz/ 1 cause to act or to serve for a purpose. 2 treat. 3 exploit selfishly. ● *n.* /yooss/ 1 using, being used. 2 power of using. 3 purpose for which a thing is used.

■ *v.* 1 employ, exercise, make use of, utilize. 2 act or behave towards, treat. 3 abuse, capitalize on, cash in on, exploit, make use of, misuse, profit from, take advantage of. ● *n.* 1 application, employment, usage, utilization. 2 function, power. 3 advantage, benefit, gain, good, profit, service; object, point, purpose.

used /yoozd/ *adj.* second-hand. □ **used to** /yoosst/ *v.* was accustomed to (do). *adj.* familiar with by practice or habit.

useful *adj.* 1 fit for a practical purpose. 2 able to produce good results. □ **usefully** *adv.*, **usefulness** *n.*

■ 1 convenient, functional, handy, helpful, practical, serviceable, utilitarian. 2 advantageous, beneficial, constructive, fruitful, productive, salutary, valuable, worthwhile.

useless *adj.* not usable, not useful. □ **uselessly** *adv.*, **uselessness** *n.*

■ fruitless, futile, impractical, ineffective, ineffectual, pointless, purposeless, unproductive, vain.

user *n.* one who uses something. □ **user-friendly** *adj.* easy for a user to understand and operate.

usher *n.* person who shows people to their seats in a public hall etc. ● *v.* lead, escort.

■ *v.* accompany, conduct, escort, guide, lead, shepherd.

usherette *n.* woman who ushers people to seats in a cinema etc.

usual *adj.* such as happens or is done or used etc. in many or most instances. □ **usually** *adv.*

■ accustomed, common, conventional, customary, established, everyday, familiar, habitual, normal, ordinary, regular, routine, set, standard, traditional, typical. □ **usually** as a rule, customarily, for the most part, generally, in general, mainly, mostly, normally.

usurp *v.* take (power, position, or right) wrongfully or by force. □ **usurpation** *n.*, **usurper** *n.*

usury *n.* lending of money at excessively high rates of interest. □ **usurer** *n.*

utensil *n.* instrument or container, esp. for domestic use.

■ appliance, implement, instrument, tool.

uterus *n.* womb. □ **uterine** *adj.*

utilitarian *adj.* useful rather than decorative or luxurious.
| ▪ functional, practical, serviceable, useful.

utilitarianism *n.* theory that actions are justified if they benefit the majority.

utility *n.* **1** usefulness. **2** useful thing. ● *adj.* severely practical.

utilize *v.* use, find a use for. □ **utilization** *n.*

utmost *adj.* & *n.* furthest, greatest, or extreme (point or degree etc.).

Utopia *n.* imaginary place or state where all is perfect. □ **Utopian** *adj.*

utter[1] *adj.* complete, absolute. □ **utterly** *adv.*

▪ absolute, complete, downright, out and out, outright, pure, sheer, thorough, total, unmitigated, unqualified.

utter[2] *v.* **1** make (a sound or words) with the mouth or voice. **2** speak. □ **utterance** *n.*

▪ **1** emit, give. **2** articulate, express, pronounce, speak, voice.

uttermost *adj.* & *n.* = **utmost**.

U-turn *n.* **1** driving of a vehicle in a U-shaped course to reverse its direction. **2** reversal of policy or opinion.

uvula /yōōvyoolar/ *n.* small fleshy projection hanging at the back of the throat. □ **uvular** *adj.*

uxorious *adj.* excessively fond of one's wife.

V *abbr.* volt(s).

vac *n.* (*colloq.*) vacation.

vacancy *n.* **1** state of being vacant. **2** vacant place, post, etc.

vacant *adj.* **1** unoccupied. **2** showing no interest. □ **vacantly** *adv.*
  ■ **1** empty, free, uninhabited, unoccupied. **2** blank, emotionless, expressionless, vacuous.

vacate *v.* cease to occupy.
  ■ abandon, desert, evacuate, leave, quit, withdraw from.

vacation *n.* **1** interval between terms in universities and law courts. **2** (*US*) holiday. **3** vacating of a place etc.

vaccinate *v.* inoculate with a vaccine. □ **vaccination** *n.*

vaccine /vákseen/ *n.* preparation that gives immunity from an infection.

vacillate *v.* keep changing one's mind. □ **vacillation** *n.*

vacuous *adj.* **1** inane. **2** expressionless, vacant. □ **vacuously** *adv.*, **vacuity** *n.*
  ■ **1** foolish, inane, senseless, silly, stupid, unintelligent.

vacuum *n.* (*pl.* **-cua** or **-cuums**) space from which air has been removed. ● *v.* (*colloq.*) clean with a vacuum cleaner. □ **vacuum cleaner** electrical apparatus that takes up dust by suction. **vacuum flask** container for keeping liquids hot or cold. **vacuum-packed** *adj.* sealed after removal of air.

vagabond *n.* wanderer or vagrant
  ■ gypsy, rolling stone, rover, tramp, vagrant, wanderer, wayfarer.

vagary *n.* capricious act or idea, fluctuation.
  ■ caprice, fancy, quirk, whim.

vagina *n.* passage leading from the vulva to the womb. □ **vaginal** *adj.*

vagrant *n.* person without a settled home. □ **vagrancy** *n.*

vague *adj.* **1** not clearly explained or perceived. **2** (of a person or mind) inexact in thought, expression, etc. □ **vaguely** *adv.*, **vagueness** *n.*
  ■ **1** ambiguous, generalized, hazy, imprecise, unclear, woolly; amorphous, blurred, dim, faint, fuzzy, indistinct, obscure, neb-

ulous, shadowy, shapeless. **2** hesitant, uncertain, undecided, unsure; absent-minded, dreamy.

vain *adj.* **1** conceited. **2** useless, futile. □ **in vain** uselessly. **vainly** *adv.*
  ■ **1** cocky, conceited, egotistical, haughty, narcissistic, proud, self-important, *colloq.* stuck-up, vainglorious. **2** fruitless, futile, unsuccessful, useless.

vainglory *n.* great vanity. □ **vainglorious** *adj.*

valance *n.* short curtain or hanging frill.

vale *n.* valley.

valediction *n.* farewell. □ **valedictory** *adj.*

valency *n.* (also **valence**) combining power of an atom as compared with that of the hydrogen atom.

valentine *n.* **1** person to whom one sends a romantic greetings card on St Valentine's Day (14 Feb.). **2** this card.

valet *n.* man's personal attendant. ● *v.* (**valeted**) act as valet to.

valetudinarian *n.* person of poor health or unduly anxious about health.

valiant *adj.* brave. □ **valiantly** *adv.*
  ■ bold, brave, courageous, daring, fearless, heroic, indomitable, intrepid, plucky, spirited, valorous.

valid *adj.* **1** having legal force, usable. **2** logical. □ **validity** *n.*
  ■ **2** logical, rational, reasonable, sound, well-founded.

validate *v.* make valid, confirm. □ **validation** *n.*

valley *n.* (*pl.* **-eys**) low area between hills.
  ■ coomb, dale, dingle, glen, vale.

valour *n.* bravery. □ **valorous** *adj.*
  ■ boldness, bravery, courage, daring, fearlessness, fortitude, *colloq.* guts, nerve, spirit.

valuable *adj.* of great value or worth. ● *n.pl.* valuable things.
  ■ *adj.* expensive, invaluable, precious, priceless, treasured; advantageous, beneficial, helpful, useful, worthwhile.

valuation *n.* estimation or estimate of a thing's worth.

value *n.* **1** amount of money or other commodity etc. considered equivalent to something else. **2** usefulness, importance. **3** (*pl.*) moral principles. ● *v.* **1** estimate the value of. **2** consider to be of great worth. ◻ **value added tax** tax on the amount by which a thing's value has been increased at each stage of its production. **value judgement** subjective estimate of quality etc.

■ *n.* **1** cost, price, worth. **2** advantage, benefit, importance, merit, usefulness. **3** (values) ethics, morals, philosophy, principles. ● *v.* **1** assess, estimate, evaluate, price. **2** appreciate, prize, rate highly, respect, treasure.

valuer *n.* person who estimates values professionally.

valve *n.* **1** device controlling flow through a pipe. **2** structure allowing blood to flow in one direction only. **3** each half of the hinged shell of an oyster etc. ◻ **valvular** *adj.*

vamoose *v.* (*US sl.*) depart hurriedly.

vamp *n.* upper front part of a boot or shoe. ● *v.* improvise (esp. a musical accompaniment).

vampire *n.* ghost or reanimated body supposed to suck blood.

van¹ *n.* **1** covered vehicle for transporting goods etc. **2** railway carriage for luggage or goods.

van² *n.* vanguard, forefront.

vandal *n.* person who damages things wilfully. ◻ **vandalism** *n.*

■ hoodlum, hooligan, lout, ruffian, *sl.* yob.

vandalize *v.* damage wilfully.

vanguard *n.* foremost part of an advancing army etc.

vanilla *n.* a kind of flavouring, esp. obtained from the pods of a tropical orchid.

vanish *v.* disappear completely.

■ become invisible, disappear, dissolve, evaporate, fade (away), melt (away).

vanity *n.* **1** conceit. **2** futility. ◻ **vanity case** woman's small case for carrying cosmetics etc.

■ **1** conceit, egotism, haughtiness, narcissism, pride, self-admiration, self-love, vainglory. **2** futility, pointlessness, uselessness, worthlessness.

vanquish *v.* conquer.

■ beat, conquer, defeat, get the better of, *colloq.* lick, overcome, subjugate, thrash, triumph over.

vantage *n.* advantage (esp. as a score in tennis). ◻ **vantage point** position giving a good view.

vapid *adj.* insipid, uninteresting. ◻ **vapidly** *adv.*, **vapidity** *n.*

■ bland, dull, insipid, unexciting, uninteresting, wishy-washy.

vaporize *v.* convert or be converted into vapour. ◻ **vaporization** *n.*

vapour *n.* moisture suspended in air, into which certain liquids or solids are converted by heating. ◻ **vaporous** *adj.*

variable *adj.* varying. ● *n.* thing that varies. ◻ **variability** *n.*

■ *adj.* changeable, erratic, fluctuating, inconsistent, inconstant, mutable, protean, uncertain, unpredictable, unstable, varying.

variance *n.* **at variance** disagreeing.

variant *adj.* differing. ● *n.* variant form or spelling etc.

variation *n.* **1** varying, extent of this. **2** variant. **3** repetition of a melody in a different form.

■ **1** alteration, change, difference, modification; choice, diversity, variety.

varicose *adj.* (of veins) permanently swollen.

varied *adj.* of different sorts.

■ assorted, diverse, heterogeneous, miscellaneous, mixed.

variegated *adj.* having irregular patches of colours. ◻ **variegation** *n.*

variety *n.* **1** quality of not being the same. **2** quantity of different things. **3** sort or kind. **4** entertainment with a series of short performances.

■ **1** contrast, difference, diversity, heterogeneity, variation. **2** array, assortment, collection, miscellany, mixture, multiplicity, number, range, selection. **3** brand, category, class, genre, group, kind, make, sort, species, type.

various *adj.* **1** of several kinds. **2** several. ◻ **variously** *adv.*

■ **1** assorted, different, diverse, miscellaneous, varying. **2** many, numerous, several, sundry.

varnish *n.* liquid that dries to form a shiny transparent coating. ● *v.* coat with varnish.

vary *v.* make, be, or become different.

■ adjust, alter, change, modify; deviate, differ, diverge; alternate, fluctuate, shift, swing.

vascular *adj.* of vessels or ducts for conveying blood or sap.

vase *n.* decorative jar, esp. for holding cut flowers.

vasectomy *n.* surgical removal of part of the ducts that carry semen from the testicles, esp. as a method of birth control.

vassal *n.* humble subordinate.

vast *adj.* very great in area or size.
□ **vastly** *adv.*, **vastness** *n.*
■ colossal, elephantine, enormous, extensive, gigantic, great, huge, immense, large, mammoth, massive, monumental, prodigious, tremendous.

VAT *abbr.* value added tax.

vat *n.* large tank for liquids.

vault[1] *n.* **1** arched roof. **2** cellar used as a storage place. **3** burial chamber.
□ **vaulted** *adj.*

vault[2] *v. & n.* jump, esp. with the help of the hands or a pole.

vaunt *v. & n.* boast.

VDU *abbr.* visual display unit.

veal *n.* calf's flesh as food.

vector *n.* **1** thing (e.g. velocity) that has both magnitude and direction. **2** carrier of disease.

veer *v.* change direction.

vegan /veegan/ *n.* person who eats no meat or animal products.

vegetable *n.* plant grown for food. ● *adj.* of or from plants.

vegetarian *n.* person who eats no meat or fish. □ **vegetarianism** *n.*

vegetate *v.* live an uneventful life.

vegetation *n.* plants collectively.

vehement *adj.* showing strong feeling.
□ **vehemently** *adv.*, **vehemence** *n.*
■ ardent, eager, enthusiastic, fervent, impassioned, intense, keen, passionate, zealous.

vehicle *n.* **1** conveyance for transporting passengers or goods on land or in space. **2** means by which something is expressed or displayed. □ **vehicular** *adj.*

veil *n.* piece of fine net or other fabric worn to protect or conceal the face. ● *v.* cover with or as if with a veil.
■ *v.* camouflage, cloak, conceal, cover, hide, mask, shroud.

vein *n.* **1** any of the blood vessels conveying blood towards the heart. **2** a similar structure in an insect's wing etc. **3** narrow layer in rock etc. **4** mood.
□ **veined** *adj.*
■ **3** lode, seam, stratum. **4** humour, mood, spirit, temper.

vellum *n.* **1** fine parchment. **2** smooth writing paper.

velocity *n.* speed.
■ celerity, quickness, rapidity, speed, swiftness.

velour /vəloor/ *n.* heavy plush-like fabric.

velvet *n.* woven fabric with thick short pile on one side. □ **velvet glove** outward gentleness concealing inflexibility. **velvety** *adj.*

velveteen *n.* cotton velvet.

venal *adj.* **1** able to be bribed. **2** involving bribery. □ **venality** *n.*

vend *v.* sell, offer for sale.

vendetta *n.* feud.
■ conflict, dispute, feud, quarrel.

vending machine slot machine selling small articles.

vendor *n.* seller.

veneer *n.* **1** thin covering layer of fine wood. **2** superficial show of a quality.
● *v.* cover with a veneer.
■ *n.* **2** appearance, façade, guise, mask, semblance, show.

venerate *v.* respect deeply, esp. because of great age. □ **veneration** *n.*, **venerable** *adj.*
■ admire, esteem, honour, look up to, respect, revere, worship.

venereal *adj.* (of infections) contracted by sexual intercourse with an infected person.

Venetian *adj. & n.* (native) of Venice.
□ **Venetian blind** window blind of adjustable horizontal slats.

vengeance *n.* punishment inflicted for a wrong. □ **with a vengeance** in an extreme degree.
■ retaliation, retribution, revenge.

vengeful *adj.* seeking vengeance.

venial *adj.* (of a sin) pardonable, not serious. □ **veniality** *n.*

venison *n.* deer's flesh as food.

venom *n.* **1** poisonous fluid of snakes etc. **2** bitter feeling or language. □ **venomous** *adj.*
■ **1** poison, toxin. **2** animosity, bitterness, enmity, hate, hatred, hostility, ill will, malevolence, malice, rancour, spite.

vent[1] *n.* slit at the lower edge of the back or side of a coat.

vent² *n.* opening allowing gas or liquid to pass through. ● *v.* give vent to. □ **give vent to** give an outlet to (feelings).
■ *n.* aperture, hole, opening, outlet; chimney, duct, flue, funnel. □ **give vent to** air, articulate, express, release, voice.

ventilate *v.* cause air to circulate freely in. □ **ventilation** *n.*
■ aerate, air, freshen.

ventilator *n.* device for ventilating a room etc.

ventral *adj.* of or on the abdomen.

ventricle *n.* cavity, esp. in the heart or brain. □ **ventricular** *adj.*

ventriloquism *n.* skill of speaking without moving the lips. □ **ventriloquist** *n.*

venture *n.* undertaking that involves risk. ● *v.* **1** dare. **2** dare to go or say. □ **venturesome** *adj.*
■ *n.* endeavour, enterprise, gamble, undertaking. ● *v.* **1** dare, endeavour, presume, try. **2** chance, hazard, risk.

venue *n.* appointed place for a meeting etc.

veracious *adj.* **1** truthful. **2** true. □ **veraciously** *adv.*, **veracity** *n.*
■ **1** candid, frank, honest, sincere, truthful. **2** accurate, correct, factual, true, truthful.

veranda *n.* roofed terrace.

verb *n.* word indicating action or occurrence or being.

verbal *adj.* **1** of or in words. **2** spoken. **3** of a verb. □ **verbally** *adv.*

verbalize *v.* **1** express in words. **2** be verbose. □ **verbalization** *n.*

verbatim /verbáytim/ *adv.* & *adj.* in exactly the same words.

verbiage *n.* excessive number of words.

verbose *adj.* using more words than are needed. □ **verbosely** *adv.*, **verbosity** *n.*
■ long-winded, wordy.

verdant *adj.* (of grass etc.) green.

verdict *n.* **1** decision reached by a jury. **2** decision or opinion reached after testing something.
■ conclusion, decision, finding, judgement, opinion, ruling.

verdigris *n.* green deposit forming on copper or brass.

verdure *n.* green vegetation.

verge¹ *n.* **1** extreme edge. **2** grass edging of a road etc. □ **on the verge of** very near to.
■ **1** border, brim, brink, edge, lip, rim, side.

verge² *v.* **verge on** border on.

verger *n.* church caretaker.

verify *v.* check the truth or correctness of. □ **verification** *n.*
■ authenticate, check, confirm, corroborate, make sure of, prove, substantiate, validate.

verisimilitude *n.* appearance of being true.

veritable *adj.* real, rightly named.
■ actual, authentic, genuine, proper, real, true.

vermicelli *n.* pasta made in slender threads.

vermiform *adj.* worm-like in shape.

vermilion *adj.* & *n.* bright red.

vermin *n.* (*pl.* **vermin**) animal or insect regarded as a pest.

verminous *adj.* infested with vermin.

vermouth *n.* wine flavoured with herbs.

vernacular *n.* ordinary language of a country or district.

vernal *adj.* of or occurring in spring.

veronica *n.* a kind of flowering herb or shrub.

verruca /verōōkə/ *n.* (*pl.* **-ae**) wart, esp. on the foot.

versatile *adj.* able to do or be used for many different things. □ **versatility** *n.*
■ adaptable, flexible, resourceful; handy, multi-purpose.

verse *n.* **1** metrical (not prose) composition. **2** group of lines forming a unit in a poem or hymn. **3** numbered division of a Bible chapter.

versed *adj.* **versed in** experienced in.

versify *v.* **1** express in verse. **2** compose verse. □ **versification** *n.*

version *n.* **1** particular account of a matter. **2** special or variant form. **3** translation.
■ **1** account, description, report, story. **2** design, form, kind, model, style, type, variant.

versus *prep.* against.

vertebra *n.* (*pl.* **-brae**) segment of the backbone. □ **vertebral** *adj.*

vertebrate *n.* & *adj.* (animal) having a backbone.

vertex *n.* (*pl.* **-tices**) highest point of a hill etc., apex.
■ apex, crest, crown, peak, pinnacle, point, summit, top.

vertical *adj.* perpendicular to the horizontal, upright. ● *n.* vertical line or position. □ **vertically** *adv.*
■ *adj.* erect, on end, perpendicular, upright.

vertigo *n.* dizziness.
■ dizziness, giddiness, light-headedness.

verve *n.* enthusiasm, vigour.
■ animation, *colloq.* bounce, dynamism, élan, enthusiasm, gusto, life, liveliness, pep, spirit, vigour, *colloq.* vim, vitality, vivacity, zeal, zest, zip.

very *adv.* in a high degree, extremely. ● *adj.* **1** actual, truly such. **2** mere. □ **very best, worst, etc.** absolute best, worst, etc. **very high frequency** frequency in the range 30-300 MHz. **very well** expression of consent.
■ *adv.* especially, exceedingly, exceptionally, extremely, greatly, highly, most, particularly, really, thoroughly, totally, truly, unusually, utterly. ● *adj.* **1** actual, exact, precise; same, selfsame.

vesicle *n.* **1** sac, esp. containing liquid. **2** blister.

vessel *n.* **1** receptacle, esp. for liquid. **2** boat, ship. **3** tube-like structure conveying blood or other fluid in the body of an animal or plant.
■ **1** container, receptacle. **2** craft, boat, ship.

vest *n.* **1** undergarment covering the trunk. **2** (*US*) waistcoat. ● *v.* confer or furnish with (power) as a firm or legal right. □ **vested interest** advantageous right held by a person or group.

vestibule *n.* **1** entrance hall. **2** porch.

vestige *n.* **1** small remaining bit. **2** very small amount. □ **vestigial** *adj.*, **vestigially** *adv.*
■ **1** evidence, mark, sign, suggestion, trace. **2** fragment, iota, particle, scrap, shred, speck; hint, suggestion, suspicion.

vestment *n.* ceremonial garment, esp. of clergy or a church choir.

vet (*colloq.*) *n.* veterinary surgeon. ● *v.* (**vetted**) examine critically for faults etc.

vetch *n.* plant of the pea family used as fodder for cattle.

veteran *n.* person with long experience, esp. in the armed forces.

veterinarian *n.* veterinary surgeon.

veterinary *adj.* of or for the treatment of diseases and disorders of animals. □ **veterinary surgeon** person skilled in such treatment.

veto *n.* (*pl.* **-oes**) **1** rejection of something proposed. **2** right to make this. ● *v.* reject by a veto.
■ *n.* **1** ban, embargo, interdict, prohibition. ● *v.* ban, disallow, forbid, outlaw, prevent, prohibit, proscribe, quash, reject, stop, turn down.

vex *v.* annoy. □ **vexed question** problem that is much discussed. **vexation** *n.*, **vexatious** *adj.*
■ *colloq.* aggravate, anger, annoy, drive mad, enrage, exasperate, gall, incense, infuriate, irk, irritate, madden, *colloq.* rile.

VHF *abbr.* very high frequency.

via *prep.* by way of, through.

viable *adj.* **1** practicable. **2** capable of living or surviving. □ **viability** *n.*
■ **1** feasible, possible, practicable, practical, workable.

viaduct *n.* long bridge over a valley.

vial *n.* small bottle.

viands *n.pl.* articles of food.

vibrant *adj.* **1** vibrating, resonant. **2** thrilling with energy.
■ **2** alive, animated, dynamic, energetic, lively, spirited, vivacious.

vibraphone *n.* percussion instrument like a xylophone but with a vibrating effect.

vibrate *v.* **1** move rapidly and continuously to and fro. **2** sound with rapid slight variation of pitch. □ **vibrator** *n.*, **vibratory** *adj.*
■ **1** oscillate, pulsate, pulse, quiver, shake, throb, tremble.

vibration *n.* **1** vibrating. **2** (*pl.*) atmosphere etc. felt intuitively.

vicar *n.* member of the clergy in charge of a parish.

vicarage *n.* house of a vicar.

vicarious *adj.* **1** experienced indirectly. **2** acting or done etc. for another. □ **vicariously** *adv.*

vice[1] *n.* **1** great wickedness. **2** criminal and immoral practices.
■ corruption, degeneracy, depravity, evil, immorality, iniquity, sin, turpitude, venality, viciousness, villainy, wickedness, wrongdoing.

vice[2] *n.* instrument with two jaws for holding things firmly.

vice- *pref.* **1** substitute or deputy for. **2** next in rank to.

vice-chancellor *n.* chief administrator of a university.

viceroy *n.* person governing a colony etc. as the sovereign's representative. □ **viceregal** *adj.*

vice versa with terms the other way round.

vicinity *n.* surrounding district. □ **in the vicinity (of)** near.

■ area, district, environs, locality, neighbourhood, precincts, region.

vicious *adj.* 1 bad-tempered, spiteful. 2 violent and dangerous. □ **vicious circle** bad situation producing effects that intensify its original cause. **viciously** *adv.*

■ 1 bad-tempered, *colloq.* bitchy, bitter, malicious, malignant, mean, nasty, spiteful, venomous, vitriolic. 2 aggressive, barbaric, brutal, cruel, dangerous, ferocious, fierce, savage, violent.

vicissitude *n.* change of circumstances or luck.

victim *n.* 1 person injured, killed, or made to suffer. 2 creature sacrificed to a god etc.

■ 1 martyr; casualty, fatality.

victimize *v.* single out to suffer ill-treatment. □ **victimization** *n.*

victor *n.* winner.

■ champion, conqueror, winner.

Victorian *n.* & *adj.* (person) of the reign of Queen Victoria (1837-1901).

victorious *adj.* having gained victory.

■ conquering, successful, triumphant, winning.

victory *n.* success achieved by gaining mastery over opponent(s) or having the highest score.

vicuña /vikyōōna/ *n.* 1 S. American animal related to the llama. 2 soft cloth made from its wool.

video *n.* (*pl.* **-os**) 1 recording or broadcasting of pictures. 2 apparatus for this. 3 videotape. ● *v.* make a video of. □ *v.* record on this.

videotape *n.* magnetic tape suitable for recording television pictures and sound. ● *v.* record on this.

videotex *n.* (also **videotext**) electronic information system, esp. teletext or viewdata.

vie *v.* (**vying**) carry on a rivalry, compete.

■ compete, contend, contest, strive, struggle.

view *n.* 1 range of vision. 2 what is seen. 3 mental attitude, opinion. ● *v.* 1 look at. 2 consider. 3 watch television. □ **in view of** considering. **on view** displayed for

inspection. **with a view to** with the hope or intention of. **viewer** *n.*

■ *n.* 1 sight, vision. 2 aspect, outlook, panorama, prospect, scene, vista. 3 attitude, belief, conviction, feeling, opinion, point of view, standpoint, viewpoint. ● *v.* 1 *poetic* behold, contemplate, gaze at, look at, observe, regard, survey, watch. 2 consider, deem, judge, regard, think of.

viewdata *n.* news and information service from a computer source to which a television screen is connected by a telephone link.

viewfinder *n.* device on a camera showing the extent of the area being photographed.

viewpoint *n.* point of view.

vigil *n.* period of staying awake to keep watch or pray.

vigilant *adj.* watchful. □ **vigilantly** *adv.*, **vigilance** *n.*

■ alert, attentive, awake, careful, circumspect, heedful, observant, on one's guard, on one's toes, on the lookout, wary, watchful, *colloq.* wide awake.

vigilante /víjilánti/ *n.* member of a self-appointed group trying to prevent crime etc.

vignette /veenyét/ *n.* short written description.

vigour *n.* active physical or mental strength, forcefulness. □ **vigorous** *adj.*, **vigorously** *adv.*

■ animation, drive, dynamism, energy, enthusiasm, force, gusto, liveliness, power, spirit, strength, verve, *colloq.* vim, zeal, zest.

Viking *n.* ancient Scandinavian trader and pirate.

vile *adj.* 1 extremely disgusting. 2 wicked. □ **vilely** *adv.*, **vileness** *n.*

■ 1 disgusting, distasteful, foul, loathsome, nasty, objectionable, obnoxious, offensive, repellent, repugnant, repulsive, sickening. 2 bad, base, contemptible, corrupt, degenerate, depraved, immoral, iniquitous, sinful, villainous, wicked.

vilify *v.* say evil things about. □ **vilification** *n.*, **vilifier** *n.*

■ abuse, calumniate, defame, insult, libel, malign, run down, slander.

villa *n.* 1 holiday home, esp. abroad. 2 house in a suburban district.

village *n.* group of houses etc. in a country district. □ **villager** *n.*

villain *n.* wicked person. □ **villainous** *adj.*, **villainy** *n.*

■ blackguard, criminal, *colloq.* crook, evildoer, malefactor, miscreant, rogue, scoundrel, wretch, wrongdoer.

vim *n.* (*colloq.*) vigour.

vinaigrette *n.* salad dressing of oil and vinegar.

vindicate *v.* **1** clear of blame. **2** justify. □ **vindication** *n.*

■ **1** absolve, acquit, clear, exonerate. **2** justify, prove, support.

vindictive *adj.* showing a desire for vengeance. □ **vindictively** *adv.*, **vindictiveness** *n.*

■ avenging, revengeful, vengeful; malicious, spiteful, unforgiving.

vine *n.* climbing plant whose fruit is the grape.

vinegar *n.* sour liquid made from wine, malt, etc., by fermentation. □ **vinegary** *adj.*

vineyard *n.* plantation of vines for winemaking.

vintage *n.* **1** wine from a season's grapes, esp. when of high quality. **2** date of origin or existence. ● *adj.* of high quality, esp. from a past period.

vintner *n.* wine-merchant.

vinyl /vĩnil/ *n.* a kind of plastic.

viola[1] /viólə/ *n.* instrument like a violin but of lower pitch.

viola[2] /vĩələ/ *n.* plant of the genus to which violets belong.

violate *v.* **1** break (an oath or treaty etc.). **2** treat (a sacred place) irreverently. **3** disturb. **4** rape. □ **violation** *n.*, **violator** *n.*

■ **1** break, contravene, disobey, disregard, flout, infringe, transgress. **2** desecrate, profane.

violent *adj.* **1** involving great force or intensity. **2** using excessive physical force. □ **violently** *adv.*, **violence** *n.*

■ **1** acute, extreme, forceful, furious, intense, mighty, powerful, severe, strong, uncontrollable, vehement, wild. **2** barbaric, brutal, cruel, ferocious, fierce, savage, vicious.

violet *n.* **1** small plant, often with purple flowers. **2** bluish-purple colour. ● *adj.* bluish-purple.

violin *n.* musical instrument with four strings of treble pitch, played with a bow. □ **violinist** *n.*

violoncello /vĩələnchéllō/ *n.* (*pl.* **-os**) cello.

viper *n.* small poisonous snake.

virago *n.* (*pl.* **-os**) aggressive woman.

viral /vĩrəl/ *adj.* of a virus.

virgin *n.* **1** person who has never had sexual intercourse. **2** (**the Virgin**) Mary, mother of Christ. ● *adj.* **1** virginal. **2** not yet used. □ **virginal** *adj.*, **virginity** *n.*

virile *adj.* having masculine strength or procreative power. □ **virility** *n.*

virology *n.* study of viruses. □ **virologist** *n.*

virtual *adj.* being so in effect though not in name. □ **virtually** *adv.*

■ □ **virtually** all but, almost, as good as, more or less, nearly, practically.

virtue *n.* **1** moral excellence, goodness. **2** chastity. **3** good characteristic. □ **by** or **in virtue of** because of.

■ **1** decency, goodness, honesty, honour, integrity, morality, probity, righteousness. **2** chastity, innocence, purity, virginity. **3** asset, good point, strength.

virtuoso *n.* (*pl.* **-si**) expert performer. □ **virtuosity** *n.*

■ expert, genius, maestro, master, wizard.

virtuous *adj.* morally good. □ **virtuously** *adv.*

■ decent, good, honest, honourable, moral, noble, principled, respectable, righteous, upright; chaste, innocent, pure, virginal.

virulent *adj.* **1** (of poison or disease) extremely strong or violent. **2** bitterly hostile. □ **virulently** *adv.*, **virulence** *n.*

■ **1** dangerous, deadly, harmful, life-threatening. **2** acrimonious, bitter, hostile, malicious, malignant, nasty, spiteful, venomous, vicious, vitriolic.

virus *n.* (*pl.* **-uses**) **1** minute organism able to cause disease. **2** (*colloq.*) such a disease. **3** destructive code hidden in a computer program.

visa *n.* official mark on a passport, permitting the holder to enter a specified country.

visage *n.* person's face.

vis-à-vis /véezaavée/ *adv.* & *prep.* **1** with regard to. **2** as compared with.

viscera /vĩssərə/ *n.pl.* internal organs of the body. □ **visceral** *adj.*

viscid /vĩssid/ *adj.* viscous.

viscose *n.* **1** viscous cellulose. **2** fabric made from this.

viscount /vĩkownt/ *n.* nobleman ranking between earl and baron.

viscountess *n.* **1** woman with the rank of viscount. **2** viscount's wife or widow.

viscous *adj.* thick and gluey. □ **viscosity** *n.*

visibility *n.* **1** state of being visible. **2** range of vision or clarity.

visible *adj.* able to be seen or noticed. □ **visibly** *adv.*
 ■ apparent, conspicuous, discernible, evident, manifest, obvious, noticeable, perceivable, perceptible, plain.

vision *n.* **1** ability to see, sight. **2** thing seen in the imagination or a dream. **3** foresight. **4** person of unusual beauty.
 ■ **1** eyesight, sight. **2** dream, fantasy; apparition, chimera, ghost, hallucination, mirage, phantom, spectre. **3** foresight, imagination.

visionary *adj.* **1** fanciful. **2** not practical. ● *n.* person with visionary ideas.
 ■ *adj.* **1** fanciful, idealistic, romantic, unrealistic. ● *n.* dreamer, idealist, romantic.

visit *v.* **1** go or come to see. **2** stay temporarily with or at. ● *n.* act of visiting. □ **visitor** *n.*
 ■ *v.* **1** call on, drop in on, look up, pay a visit to. ● *n.* call, sojourn, stay. □ **visitor** caller, guest.

visitation *n.* **1** official visit. **2** trouble regarded as divine punishment.

visor /vízar/ *n.* **1** movable front part of a helmet, covering the face. **2** shading device at the top of a vehicle's windscreen.

vista *n.* extensive view, esp. seen through a long opening.

visual *adj.* of or used in seeing. □ **visual display unit** device displaying a computer output or input on a screen. **visually** *adv.*

visualize *v.* form a mental picture of. □ **visualization** *n.*
 ■ conceive of, envisage, imagine, picture, think of.

vital *adj.* **1** essential to life. **2** essential to a thing's existence or success. **3** full of vitality. ● *n.pl.* vital organs of the body. □ **vital statistics** those relating to population figures. **2** (*colloq.*) measurements of a woman's bust, waist, and hips. **vitally** *adv.*
 ■ *adj.* **1,2** critical, crucial, essential, fundamental, imperative, indispensable, key, necessary. **3** alive, animated, energetic, lively, spirited, vibrant, vivacious.

vitality *n.* liveliness, persistent energy.
 ■ animation, *colloq.* bounce, dynamism, élan, energy, go, gusto, life, liveliness, pep, spirit, verve, vigour, *colloq.* vim, vivacity, zeal, zest, zip.

vitamin *n.* any of the organic substances present in food and essential to nutrition.

vitaminize *v.* add vitamins to.

vitiate /vishiayt/ *v.* make imperfect or ineffective.
 ■ harm, impair, mar, ruin, spoil.

viticulture *n.* vine-growing.

vitreous *adj.* having a glass-like texture or finish.

vitrify *v.* change into a glassy substance. □ **vitrifaction** *n.*

vitriol *n.* **1** sulphuric acid. **2** caustic speech. □ **vitriolic** *adj.*
 ■ □ **vitriolic** bitter, caustic, cruel, hostile, hurtful, malicious, savage, scathing, vicious, virulent.

vituperate *v.* criticize abusively. □ **vituperation** *n.*, **vituperative** *adj.*

vivacious *adj.* lively, high-spirited. □ **vivaciously** *adv.*, **vivacity** *n.*
 ■ animated, bubbly, cheerful, ebullient, energetic, exuberant, high-spirited, lively, perky, spirited, sprightly, spry.

vivarium *n.* (*pl.* **-ia**) place for keeping living animals etc. in natural conditions.

vivid *adj.* **1** bright and strong. **2** clear. **3** (of imagination) lively. □ **vividly** *adv.*, **vividness** *n.*
 ■ **1** bright, brilliant, colourful, intense, strong. **2** clear, detailed, graphic, realistic. **3** active, creative, fertile, inventive, lively, prolific.

vivify *v.* put life into.

viviparous *adj.* bringing forth young alive, not egg-laying.

vivisection *n.* performance of experiments on living animals.

vixen *n.* female fox.

viz. *adv.* namely.

vocabulary *n.* **1** list of words with their meanings. **2** words known or used by a person or group.

vocal *adj.* of, for, or uttered by the voice. ● *n.* piece of sung music. □ **vocally** *adv.*

vocalist *n.* singer.

vocalize *v.* utter. □ **vocalization** *n.*

vocation *n.* **1** strong desire or feeling of fitness for a certain career. **2** trade, profession. □ **vocational** *adj.*
 ■ **1** calling. **2** business, career, employment, job, line, occupation, profession, trade, work.

vociferate v. say loudly, shout. □ **vociferation** n.
■ bawl, bellow, roar, scream, shout, thunder, yell.

vociferous adj. making a great outcry. □ **vociferously** adv.
■ clamorous, insistent, loud, noisy, obstreperous.

vodka n. alcoholic spirit distilled chiefly from rye.

vogue n. current fashion. □ **in vogue** in fashion.
■ craze, fad, fashion, mode, trend. □ **in vogue** chic, fashionable, in, in fashion, *colloq.* trendy.

voice n. **1** sounds formed in the larynx and uttered by the mouth. **2** expressed opinion. **3** right to express an opinion. ● v. express, vocalize. □ **voice-over** n. narration in a film etc. without a picture of the speaker.
■ n. **2** belief, feeling, opinion, view. **3** say, vote. ● v. air, articulate, communicate, declare, enunciate, give vent to, make known, put into words, state, utter, verbalize.

void adj. **1** empty. **2** not valid. ● n. empty space, emptiness. ● v. **1** make void. **2** excrete.
■ adj. **1** empty, unfilled, unoccupied, vacant. **2** invalid, null and void. ● n. emptiness, vacuum. ● v. **1** annul, cancel, invalidate, nullify, quash.

voile n. very thin dress fabric.

volatile adj. **1** evaporating rapidly. **2** changing quickly in mood. □ **volatility** n.
■ **2** capricious, changeable, emotional, fickle, inconstant, mercurial, moody, temperamental, unpredictable, unstable.

vol-au-vent /vóllōvon/ n. puff pastry case with a savoury filling.

volcano n. (pl. **-oes**) mountain with a vent through which lava is expelled. □ **volcanic** adj.

vole n. small rodent.

volition n. use of one's own will in making a decision etc.
■ choice, choosing, discretion, (free) will, preference.

volley n. (pl. **-eys**) **1** simultaneous discharge of missiles etc. **2** outburst of questions or other words. **3** return of the ball in tennis etc. before it touches the ground. ● v. send in a volley.
■ n. **1** barrage, bombardment, cannonade, salvo. **2** hail, shower, storm, stream, torrent.

volleyball n. game for two teams of six people sending a large ball by hand over a net.

volt n. unit of electromotive force.

voltage n. electromotive force expressed in volts.

volte-face /vóltfaass/ n. complete change of attitude to something.

voluble adj. speaking or spoken with a great flow of words. □ **volubly** adv., **volubility** n.
■ chatty, garrulous, loquacious, talkative; fluent, glib.

volume n. **1** book. **2** amount of space occupied or contained. **3** amount. **4** strength of sound.
■ **1** book, tome. **2** bulk, capacity, content, mass, size. **3** amount, quantity, sum total.

voluminous adj. **1** having great volume, bulky. **2** prolific.
■ **1** ample, big, bulky, capacious, enormous, great, large, roomy, spacious, substantial.

voluntary adj. **1** done, given, or acting by choice. **2** working or done without payment. **3** maintained by voluntary contributions. □ **voluntarily** adv.
■ **1** discretionary, elective, optional. **2** unpaid.

volunteer n. **1** person who offers to do something. **2** one who enrols voluntarily for military service. ● v. **1** undertake or offer voluntarily. **2** be a volunteer.

voluptuary n. person fond of luxury etc.

voluptuous adj. **1** full of or fond of sensual pleasures. **2** having a full attractive figure. □ **voluptuously** adv., **voluptuousness** n.
■ **1** hedonistic, pleasure-loving, sensual, sensuous, sybaritic. **2** attractive, *colloq.* curvaceous, desirable, seductive, sexy, shapely.

vomit v. (**vomited**) eject (matter) from the stomach through the mouth. ● n. vomited matter.

voodoo n. form of religion based on witchcraft. □ **voodooism** n.

voracious *adj.* **1** greedy. **2** insatiable. □ **voraciously** *adv.*, **voracity** *n.*
■ **1** gluttonous, greedy, *colloq.* gutsy, insatiable, ravenous. **2** ardent, avid, eager, enthusiastic, insatiable, passionate.

vortex *n.* (*pl.* **-exes** or **-ices**) **1** whirlpool. **2** whirlwind.

vote *n.* **1** formal expression of one's opinion or choice on a matter under discussion. **2** choice etc. expressed thus. **3** right to vote. ● *v.* give or decide by a vote. □ **vote for** choose by a vote. **voter** *n.*
■ *n.* **1** ballot, election, plebiscite, poll, referendum. **2** choice, preference, selection. **3** franchise, suffrage. □ **vote for** choose, elect, pick, opt for, select.

votive *adj.* given to fulfil a vow.

vouch *v.* **vouch for** guarantee the accuracy or reliability etc. of.
■ answer for, attest to, bear witness to, certify, confirm, guarantee.

voucher *n.* **1** document exchangeable for certain goods or services. **2** a kind of receipt.

vow *n.* solemn promise, esp. to a deity or saint. ● *v.* make a vow.
■ *n.* oath, pledge, promise. ● *v.* pledge, promise, swear, undertake.

vowel *n.* **1** speech sound made without audible stopping of the breath. **2** letter(s) representing this.

voyage *n.* journey made by water or in space. ● *v.* make a voyage. □ **voyager** *n.*
■ *n.* cruise, journey, passage, trip. ● *v.* cruise, journey, sail, travel.

voyeur /vwaayör/ *n.* person who gets sexual pleasure from watching others having sex or undressing.

vulcanite *n.* hard black vulcanized rubber.

vulcanize *v.* strengthen (rubber) by treating with sulphur. □ **vulcanization** *n.*

vulgar *adj.* lacking refinement or good taste. □ **vulgar fraction** one represented by numbers above and below a line. **vulgarly** *adv.*, **vulgarity** *n.*
■ boorish, coarse, ill-mannered, uncouth; cheap, flashy, garish, gaudy, tasteless, tawdry; crude, indecent, indelicate, obscene, rude, unseemly.

vulgarian *n.* vulgar (esp. rich) person.

vulgarism *n.* vulgar word(s) etc.

vulnerable *adj.* able to be hurt or injured. □ **vulnerability** *n.*
■ defenceless, exposed, unguarded, unprotected, weak.

vulture *n.* large carrion-eating bird of prey.

vulva *n.* external parts of the female genital organs.

vying *see* **vie**.

W. *abbr.* **1** west. **2** western.

wad *n.* **1** pad of soft material. **2** bunch of papers or banknotes. ● *v.* (**wadded**) pad.

wadding *n.* padding.

waddle *v. & n.* walk with short steps and a swaying movement.

wade *v.* walk through water or mud. □ **wade through** proceed slowly and laboriously through (work etc.).

wader *n.* **1** long-legged waterbird. **2** (*pl.*) high waterproof boots.

wafer *n.* **1** thin light biscuit. **2** small thin slice. □ **wafery** *adj.*

waffle¹ (*colloq.*) *n.* vague wordy talk or writing. ● *v.* talk or write waffle.

waffle² *n.* small cake of batter cooked in a **waffle-iron**.

waft *v.* carry or travel lightly through air or over water. ● *n.* wafted odour.
■ *v.* blow, drift, float, glide.

wag *v.* (**wagged**) shake briskly to and fro. ● *n.* **1** wagging movement. **2** humorous person.

wage¹ *v.* engage in (war).

wage² *n.* (also **wages**) employee's regular pay.
■ emolument, pay, remuneration, salary, stipend.

wager *n. & v.* bet.
■ *n.* bet, *colloq.* flutter, gamble, stake. ● *v.* bet, gamble, risk, stake, venture.

waggle *v. & n.* wag.

wagon *n.* (also **waggon**) **1** four-wheeled goods vehicle pulled by horses or oxen. **2** open railway truck.

wagtail *n.* small bird with a long tail that wags up and down.

waif *n.* homeless child.

wail *v. & n.* **1** (utter) a long sad cry. **2** lament.
■ *v.* **1** cry, howl, lament, sob, weep.

wainscot *n.* (also **wainscoting**) wooden panelling in a room.

waist *n.* **1** part of the human body between ribs and hips. **2** narrow middle part.

waistcoat *n.* close-fitting waist-length sleeveless jacket.

waistline *n.* outline or size of the waist.

wait *v.* **1** defer an action or departure until a specified time or event occurs. **2** be postponed. **3** act as waiter or waitress. ● *n.* act or period of waiting. □ **wait on** hand food and drink to (people) at a meal.
■ *v.* **1** *sl.* hang on, linger, pause, remain, stay. **2** be deferred, be postponed, be put off. ● *n.* delay, hold-up, interval, pause.

waiter, waitress *ns.* person employed to wait on customers in a restaurant etc.

waive *v.* refrain from using or insisting on. □ **waiver** *n.*
■ forgo, give up, relinquish, renounce; disregard, overlook.

wake¹ *v.* (**woke** or **waked**, **woken** or **waked**) **1** cease or cause to cease sleeping. **2** evoke. ● *n.* (*Ir.*) **1** watch by a corpse before burial. **2** attendant lamentations and merrymaking. □ **wake up 1** wake. **2** make or become alert.
■ *v.* **1** awake, awaken, rouse, waken, wake up. **2** arouse, evoke, stir up. ● *n.* **1** vigil. □ **wake up 2** animate, enliven, galvanize, rouse, stimulate, stir.

wake² *n.* track left on water's surface by a ship etc. □ **in the wake of 1** behind. **2** following.

wakeful *adj.* **1** unable to sleep. **2** sleepless. □ **wakefulness** *n.*

waken *v.* wake.

walk *v.* **1** progress by setting down one foot and then lifting the other(s) in turn. **2** travel (over) in this way. **3** accompany in walking. ● *n.* **1** journey on foot. **2** manner or style of walking. **3** place or route for walking. □ **walk of life** occupation. **walk out 1** depart suddenly and angrily. **2** go on strike. **walk-out** *n.* **walk out on** desert. **walkover** *n.* easy victory.
■ *v.* **1** amble, hike, march, pace, pad, perambulate, plod, ramble, saunter, stalk, step, stride, stroll, strut, trudge. **3** accompany, escort, take. ● *n.* **1** amble, constitutional, hike, perambulation, ramble, saunter, stroll. **2** gait. **3** footpath, lane, path, route, track, trail; beat, circuit, route. □ **walk out on** abandon, desert, forsake, leave.

walkabout *n.* informal stroll among a crowd by royalty etc.

walkie-talkie *n.* small portable radio transmitter and receiver.

walking stick stick carried or used as a support when walking.

wall *n.* **1** continuous upright structure forming one side of a building, room, or area. **2** thing like this in form or function. ● *v.* surround or enclose with a wall.
■ *n.* **2** barrier, fence, partition, screen; impediment, obstacle.

wallaby *n.* small species of kangaroo.

wallet *n.* small folding case for banknotes or documents.

wallflower *n.* garden plant with fragrant flowers.

wallop (*sl.*) *v.* (**walloped**) thrash, hit hard. ● *n.* heavy blow.

wallow *v.* roll in mud or water etc. ● *n.* act of wallowing. □ **wallow in** take unrestrained pleasure in.
■ □ **wallow in** bask in, delight in, glory in, indulge (oneself) in, luxuriate in, revel in, savour.

wallpaper *n.* paper for covering the interior walls of rooms.

wally *n.* (*sl.*) stupid person.

walnut *n.* **1** nut containing a wrinkled edible kernel. **2** tree bearing this. **3** its wood.

walrus *n.* large seal-like Arctic animal with long tusks.

waltz *n.* **1** ballroom dance. **2** music for this. ● *v.* **1** dance a waltz. **2** (*colloq.*) move gaily or casually.

wan *adj.* pallid. □ **wanly** *adv.*
■ anaemic, ashen, colourless, pale, pallid, pasty, peaky, washed out, white.

wand *n.* slender rod, esp. associated with the working of magic.

wander *v.* **1** go from place to place aimlessly. **2** stray from a path etc. **3** digress. ● *n.* act of wandering. □ **wanderer** *n.*
■ *v.* **1** drift, meander, *colloq.* mooch, ramble, range, roam, rove, stray. **3** deviate, digress, drift, go off at a tangent, ramble. ● *n.* amble, ramble, saunter, stroll.

wanderlust *n.* strong desire to travel.

wane *v.* **1** decrease in vigour or importance. **2** (of the moon) show a decreasing bright area after being full. □ **on the wane** waning.
■ **1** abate, decline, decrease, diminish, dwindle, ebb, fall, lessen, subside, weaken.

wangle *v.* (*colloq.*) contrive to obtain (a favour etc.).

want *v.* **1** desire. **2** need. **3** lack. **4** be without. ● *n.* **1** desire. **2** need. **3** lack.
■ *v.* **1** crave, desire, fancy, hanker after, *colloq.* have a yen for, wish for. **2** need, require. **3** be deficient in, be short of, lack. ● *n.* **1** craving, desire, fancy, hankering, wish, *colloq.* yen. **2** need, poverty. **3** dearth, deficiency, insufficiency, lack, need, scarcity, shortage.

wanted *adj.* (of a suspected criminal) sought by the police.

wanting *adj.* lacking, deficient.
■ deficient, disappointing, imperfect, inadequate, insufficient, lacking, unsatisfactory.

wanton *adj.* **1** random, arbitrary. **2** licentious.
■ **1** arbitrary, gratuitous, indiscriminate, motiveless, random, senseless, unjustified, unnecessary, unprovoked. **2** dissolute, immoral, licentious, profligate, promiscuous.

wapiti /wóppiti/ *n.* large N. American deer.

war *n.* **1** (a period of) fighting (esp. between countries). **2** open hostility. **3** organized campaign of action. ● *v.* (**warred**) make war. □ **at war** engaged in a war.
■ *n.* **1** battle, combat, conflict, fighting, hostilities, warfare. **3** battle, campaign, crusade, drive, fight, struggle. ● *v.* do battle, fight, strive, struggle, wage war.

warble *v.* sing, esp. with a gentle trilling note. ● *n.* warbling sound.

ward *n.* **1** room with beds for patients in a hospital. **2** division of a city or town, electing a councillor to represent it. **3** person (esp. a child) under the care of a guardian or law court. ● *v.* **ward off** keep away, repel.
■ *n.* **2** district, division, quarter, sector, zone. **3** charge, dependant, protégé. ● *v.* fend off, fight off, forestall, hold at bay, keep away, repel, stave off.

warden *n.* **1** official with supervisory duties. **2** churchwarden.

warder *n.* prison officer.

wardrobe *n.* **1** large cupboard for storing clothes. **2** stock of clothes.

ware *n.* **1** manufactured goods of the kind specified. **2** (*pl.*) articles offered for sale.

■ **2** (**wares**) commodities, goods, merchandise, stock.

warehouse *n.* building for storing goods or furniture.

warfare *n.* making war, fighting.

warhead *n.* explosive head of a missile.

warlike *adj.* **1** fond of making war, aggressive. **2** of or for war.

■ **1** aggressive, bellicose, belligerent, combative, militaristic, pugnacious. **2** martial, military.

warm *adj.* **1** moderately hot. **2** providing warmth. **3** enthusiastic, hearty. **4** kindly and affectionate. ● *v.* make or become warm. □ **warm-blooded** *adj.* having blood that remains warm permanently. **warm to** become cordial towards (a person) or more animated about (a task). **warm up 1** warm. **2** reheat. **3** prepare for exercise etc. by practice beforehand. **4** make or become more lively. **warmly** *adv.*, **warmness** *n.*

■ *adj.* **1** balmy; lukewarm, tepid. **3** ardent, eager, earnest, enthusiastic, hearty, sincere, wholehearted. **4** affable, amiable, cheerful, cordial, friendly, genial, hospitable, kindly, pleasant; affectionate, caring, loving, tender.

warmonger *n.* person who seeks to bring about war.

warmth *n.* warmness.

warn *v.* **1** inform about a present or future danger or difficulty etc. **2** advise about action in this. □ **warn off** tell (a person) to keep away or to avoid (a thing).

■ alert, apprise, forewarn, inform, notify, tip off; advise, caution, counsel.

warning *n.* thing that serves to warn a person.

■ notification, tip-off; advice, caution, counsel, augury, indication, omen, portent, sign, signal.

warp *v.* **1** make or become bent by uneven shrinkage or expansion. **2** pervert. ● *n.* **1** warped condition. **2** lengthwise threads in a loom.

warrant *n.* **1** thing that authorizes an action etc. **2** written authorization. ● *v.* **1** justify. **2** guarantee.

■ *n.* **1** authorization, certification, permission, sanction; guarantee, warranty. **2** licence, permit, writ. ● *v.* **1** excuse, justify. **2** answer for, attest to, certify, guarantee, vouch for.

warranty *n.* guarantee.

warren *n.* **1** series of burrows where rabbits live. **2** labyrinthine building or district.

warrior *n.* person who fights in a battle.

wart *n.* small hard abnormal growth. □ **warthog** *n.* African wild pig with wartlike growths on its face. **warty** *adj.*

wary *adj.* (**-ier, -iest**) cautious, on one's guard. □ **warily** *adv.*, **wariness** *n.*

■ apprehensive, careful, cautious, chary, circumspect, heedful, on one's guard, prudent, vigilant, watchful.

wash *v.* **1** cleanse with water or other liquid. **2** wash oneself or clothes etc. **3** be washable. **4** flow past, against, or over. **5** carry by flowing. **6** coat thinly with paint. **7** (*colloq.*, of reasoning) be valid or credible. ● *n.* **1** process of washing or being washed. **2** clothes etc. to be washed. **3** disturbed water or air behind a moving ship or aircraft etc. **4** thin coating of paint. □ **washed out 1** pallid. **2** faded. **washed up** (*sl.*) defeated, having failed. **wash one's hands of** refuse to take responsibility for. **wash out 1** make (a sport) impossible by heavy rainfall. **2** (*colloq.*) cancel. **wash-out** *n.* (*colloq.*) complete failure. **wash up 1** wash (dishes etc.) after use. **2** cast up on the shore. **washable** *adj.*

■ *v.* **1** clean, cleanse, mop, scour, scrub, shampoo, sponge, wipe. **2** bath, shower; launder. ● *n.* **1** ablutions, bath, shampoo, shower; scour, scrub, wipe. **3** backwash, wake. □ **washed out 1** ashen, colourless, pale, pallid, pasty, peaky, wan, white. **wash-out** disaster, failure, fiasco, *sl.* flop.

washbasin *n.* bowl for washing one's hands and face.

washer *n.* ring of rubber or metal etc. placed between two surfaces to give tightness.

washing *n.* clothes etc. to be washed. □ **washing-up** *n.* **1** dishes etc. for washing after use. **2** process of washing these.

washroom *n.* (*US*) room with a lavatory.

wasp *n.* stinging insect with a black and yellow striped body.

waspish *adj.* irritable. □ **waspishly** *adv.*

■ bad-tempered, crabby, crotchety, grumpy, irritable, peevish, snappy, splenetic, surly, testy.

wastage n. 1 loss or diminution by waste. 2 loss of employees by retirement or resignation.

waste v. 1 use or be used extravagantly or without adequate result. 2 fail to use. 3 make or become gradually weaker. ● adj. 1 thrown away because not wanted. 2 (of land) unfit for use. ● n. 1 act or instance of wasting. 2 waste material or food etc. 3 waste land. 4 waste pipe. □ **waste pipe** pipe carrying off used or superfluous water or steam.

■ v. 1 dissipate, fritter away, misuse, squander. 2 lose, miss. 3 debilitate, disable, enervate, enfeeble, weaken; atrophy, wither. ● adj. 1 superfluous, unused, unwanted, useless, worthless. 2 barren, desert, uncultivated, unproductive. ● n. 1 dissipation, misuse; extravagance, improvidence, prodigality, profligacy, wastefulness. 2 debris, dross, garbage, litter, refuse, rubbish, trash.

wasteful adj. extravagant. □ **wastefully** adv., **wastefulness** n.

■ extravagant, improvident, lavish, overindulgent, prodigal, profligate, spendthrift, thriftless, uneconomical.

waster n. 1 wasteful person. 2 good-for-nothing person.

watch v. 1 keep under observation. 2 be in an alert state. 3 pay attention to. 4 exercise protective care. ● n. 1 act of watching, constant observation or attention. 2 sailor's period of duty, people on duty in this. 3 small portable device indicating the time. □ **on the watch** waiting alertly. **watch out** be on one's guard. **watch-tower** n. tower from which observation can be kept. **watcher** n.

■ v. 1 contemplate, eye, gaze at, look at, observe, regard, view. 2 be one one's guard, be on the watch or lookout, look out. 3 note, observe, pay attention to, take heed of. 4 look after, mind, supervise, take care of, tend. ● n. 1 lookout; observation, surveillance.

watchdog n. 1 dog kept to guard property. 2 guardian of people's rights etc.

watchful adj. watching closely. □ **watchfully** adv., **watchfulness** n.

■ alert, attentive, heedful, observant, on one's toes, on the lookout, wary, colloq. wide awake.

watchmaker n. person who makes or repairs watches.

watchman n. man employed to guard a building etc.

watchword n. word or phrase expressing a group's principles.

water n. 1 colourless odourless tasteless liquid that is a compound of hydrogen and oxygen. 2 this as supplied for domestic use. 3 lake, sea. 4 watery secretion, urine. 5 level of the tide. ● v. 1 sprinkle, supply, or dilute with water. 2 secrete tears or saliva. □ **by water** in a boat etc. **water-bed** n. mattress of rubber etc. filled with water. **water-biscuit** n. thin unsweetened biscuit. **water-butt** n. barrel used to catch rainwater. **water-cannon** n. device giving a powerful jet of water to dispel a crowd etc. **water-closet** n. lavatory flushed by water. **water colour** 1 artists' paint mixed with water (not oil). 2 painting done with this. **water down** 1 dilute. 2 make less forceful. **water ice** frozen flavoured water. **water lily** plant with broad floating leaves. **water main** main pipe in a water supply system. **water-meadow** n. meadow that is flooded periodically by a stream. **water melon** melon with red pulp and watery juice. **water-mill** n. mill worked by a waterwheel. **water-pistol** n. toy pistol that shoots a jet of water. **water polo** ball game played by teams of swimmers. **water-power** n. power obtained from flowing or falling water. **water-rat** n. small rodent living beside a lake or stream. **water-skiing** n. sport of skimming over water on flat boards while towed by a motor boat. **water-table** n. level below which the ground is saturated with water. **water-wings** n.pl. floats worn on the shoulders by a person learning to swim.

■ v. 1 damp, dampen, douse, drench, flood, hose, irrigate, moisten, saturate, soak, splash, spray, sprinkle, wet. 2 run, stream. □ **water down** 1 dilute, weaken. 2 moderate, modify, soften, tone down.

watercourse n. 1 stream or artificial waterway. 2 its channel.

watercress n. a kind of cress that grows in streams and ponds.

waterfall n. stream that falls from a height.

■ cascade, cataract, falls.

waterfront n. part of a town that borders on a river, lake, or sea.

watering-can n. container with a spout for watering plants.

watering place 1 pool where animals drink. 2 spa, seaside resort.

waterline *n.* line along which the surface of water touches a ship's side.

waterlogged *adj.* saturated with water.

watermark *n.* manufacturer's design in paper, visible when the paper is held against light.

waterproof *adj.* unable to be penetrated by water. ● *n.* waterproof garment. ● *v.* make waterproof.

watershed *n.* **1** line of high land separating two river systems. **2** turning point in the course of events.

waterspout *n.* column of water between sea and cloud, formed by a whirlwind.

watertight *adj.* **1** made or fastened so that water cannot get in or out. **2** impossible to disprove.

waterway *n.* navigable channel.

waterwheel *n.* wheel turned by water to drive machinery.

waterworks *n.* establishment with machinery etc. for supplying water to a district.

watery *adj.* **1** of or like water. **2** containing too much water. **3** (of colour) pale. ▫ **wateriness** *n.*
■ **1** aqueous. **2** diluted, runny, thin, watered down, weak.

watt *n.* unit of electric power.

wattage *n.* amount of electric power, expressed in watts.

wattle[1] *n.* interwoven sticks used as material for fences, walls, etc.

wattle[2] *n.* fold of skin hanging from the neck of a turkey etc.

wave *n.* **1** moving ridge of water. **2** wave-like curve(s), e.g. in hair. **3** temporary increase of an influence or condition. **4** act of waving. **5** advancing group. **6** wave-like motion by which heat, light, sound, or electricity etc. is spread. **7** single curve in this. ● *v.* **1** move loosely to and fro or up and down. **2** move (one's arm etc.) thus as a signal. **3** give or have a wavy course or appearance.
■ *n.* **1** billow, breaker, ripple, roller, wavelet, white horse. **2** curl, kink. **3** surge, swell, upsurge. **4** gesticulation, gesture, sign, signal. ● *v.* **1** billow, flap, flutter, ripple, undulate. **2** gesticulate, gesture, sign, signal.

waveband *n.* range of wavelengths.

wavelength *n.* distance between corresponding points in a sound wave or electromagnetic wave.

wavelet *n.* small wave.

waver *v.* **1** be or become unsteady. **2** show hesitation or uncertainty. ▫ **waverer** *n.*
■ **1** rock, shake, sway, teeter, wobble. **2** be in two minds, be uncertain, dither, shilly-shally, vacillate.

wavy *adj.* (**-ier**, **-iest**) full of wave-like curves.

wax[1] *n.* **1** beeswax. **2** any of various similar soft substances. **3** polish containing this. ● *v.* coat, polish, or treat with wax. ▫ **waxy** *adj.*

wax[2] *v.* **1** increase in vigour or importance. **2** (of the moon) show an increasing bright area until becoming full.

waxwing *n.* small bird with red tips on some of its wing-feathers.

waxwork *n.* wax model, esp. of a person.

way *n.* **1** path, road, street, etc. **2** route, direction. **3** space free of obstacles so that people etc. can pass. **4** progress. **5** aspect. **6** method, style, manner. **7** manner of behaving, idiosyncrasy. **8** chosen or desired course of action. **9** distance in space or time. ● *adv.* (*colloq.*) far. ▫ **by the way** incidentally, as an irrelevant comment. **by way of 1** by going through. **2** serving as. **in a way** to a limited extent, in some respects. **in the way** forming an obstacle or hindrance. **on one's way** in the process of travelling or approaching. **on the way 1** on one's way. **2** (of a baby) conceived but not yet born. **way of life** normal pattern of life of a person or group.
■ *n.* **1** path, road, street, thoroughfare, track. **2** course, direction, route. **4** headway, progress. **5** aspect, detail, feature, particular, point, respect. **6** approach, course of action, method, procedure, technique; fashion, manner, mode, style. **7** character, disposition, nature, personality, temperament; habit, idiosyncrasy, mannerism, peculiarity.

wayfarer *n.* traveller.

waylay *v.* (**-laid**) lie in wait for.

wayside *n.* side of a road or path.

wayward *adj.* childishly self-willed, capricious. ▫ **waywardness** *n.*
■ capricious, difficult, disobedient, headstrong, perverse, refractory, self-willed, uncooperative, wilful.

we *pron.* **1** used by a person referring to himself or herself and another or others. **2** used instead of 'I' in newspaper editorials and by a royal person in formal proclamations.

weak *adj.* **1** lacking strength, power, or resolution. **2** not convincing. **3** much diluted. □ **weak-kneed** *adj.* lacking determination. **weakly** *adv.*

■ **1** debilitated, delicate, enervated, exhausted, feeble, frail, groggy, incapacitated, infirm, sickly, worn-out; defenceless, helpless, powerless, vulnerable; cowardly, impotent, ineffectual, irresolute, namby-pamby, powerless, pusillanimous, spineless, unassertive, weak-kneed. **2** feeble, flimsy, hollow, insubstantial, lame, poor, unconvincing. **3** diluted, thin, watery.

weaken *v.* make or become weaker.

■ debilitate, diminish, enervate, enfeeble, exhaust, lessen, lower, reduce, sap, undermine, vitiate; dilute, water down; abate, ebb, decline, dwindle, fade, flag, subside, wane.

weakling *n.* feeble person or animal.

weakness *n.* **1** state of being weak. **2** weak point, fault. **3** self-indulgent liking.

■ **1** debility, feebleness, fragility, frailty, infirmity, vulnerability; impotence, powerlessness, timidity. **2** Achilles heel, defect, deficiency, failing, fault, flaw, foible, imperfection, shortcoming. **3** appetite, fondness, liking, partiality, penchant, predilection, soft spot, taste.

weal *n.* ridge raised on flesh esp. by the stroke of a rod or whip.

wealth *n.* **1** money and valuable possessions. **2** possession of these. **3** great quantity.

■ **1** assets, money, riches. **2** affluence, opulence, prosperity. **3** abundance, profusion.

wealthy *adj.* (**-ier, -iest**) having wealth, rich. □ **wealthiness** *n.*

■ affluent, moneyed, prosperous, rich, *colloq.* well-heeled, well off, well-to-do.

wean *v.* **1** accustom (a baby) to take food other than milk. **2** cause to give up something gradually.

weapon *n.* **1** thing designed or used for inflicting harm or damage. **2** means of coercing someone.

wear *v.* (**wore, worn**) **1** have on the body as clothing or ornament. **2** damage or become damaged by prolonged use. **3** endure continued use. ● *n.* **1** wearing, being worn. **2** clothing. **3** capacity to endure being used. □ **wear down** overcome (opposition etc.) by persistence. **wear off** pass off gradually. **wear out 1** use or be used until no longer usable. **2**

tire or become tired out. **wearer** *n.*, **wearable** *adj.*

■ *v.* **1** be dressed *or* clothed in, sport. **2** damage, erode, fray, rub away, wash away. **3** endure, last, survive. ● *n.* **2** apparel, attire, clothes, clothing, dress, garb. ● **wear off** decrease, diminish, fade, subside, wane. **wear out 2** drain, exhaust, fatigue, *sl.* knacker, tire, weary.

wearisome *adj.* tedious.

■ boring, dreary, monotonous, tedious, tiresome, uninteresting.

weary *adj.* (**-ier, -iest**) **1** very tired. **2** tiring. ● *v.* make or become weary. □ **wearily** *adv.*, **weariness** *n.*

■ *adj.* **1** all in, dead beat, drained, exhausted, *colloq.* fagged, fatigued, *sl.* knackered, tired, *colloq.* whacked, worn-out.

weasel *n.* small ferocious reddish-brown flesh-eating mammal.

weather *n.* state of the atmosphere with reference to sunshine, rain, wind, etc. ● *v.* **1** (cause to) be changed by exposure to the weather. **2** come safely through (a storm). □ **under the weather** feeling unwell or depressed. **weather-beaten** *adj.* bronzed or worn by exposure to weather. **weather vane** weathercock.

■ *v.* **2** endure, live through, survive, withstand. □ **under the weather** ailing, ill, indisposed, infirm, not well, off colour, poorly, sick, unwell; depressed, dispirited.

weatherboard *n.* sloping board for keeping out rain.

weathercock *n.* revolving pointer to show the direction of the wind.

weave[1] *v.* (**wove, woven**) **1** make (fabric etc.) by passing crosswise threads or strips under and over lengthwise ones. **2** form (thread etc.) into fabric thus. **3** compose (a story etc.). ● *n.* style or pattern of weaving.

weave[2] *v.* move in an intricate course to avoid obstacles.

weaver *n.* **1** person who weaves. **2** tropical bird that builds an intricately woven nest.

web *n.* **1** network of fine strands made by a spider etc. **2** skin filling the spaces between the toes of ducks, frogs, etc. □ **web-footed** *adj.* having toes joined by web.

webbing *n.* strong band(s) of woven fabric used in upholstery.

wed v. (**wedded**) **1** marry. **2** unite.
■ **1** get married, espouse, marry. **2** ally, combine, join, unite.

wedding n. marriage ceremony and festivities.
■ marriage, nuptials.

wedge n. piece of solid substance thick at one end and tapering to a thin edge at the other. ● v. **1** force apart or fix firmly with a wedge. **2** crowd tightly.
■ v. **2** cram, crowd, jam, pack, ram, squeeze, stuff.

wedlock n. married state.

wee adj. **1** (Sc.) little. **2** (colloq.) tiny.

weed n. **1** wild plant growing where it is not wanted. **2** thin weak-looking person. ● v. **1** uproot and remove weeds (from). □ **weed out** remove as inferior or undesirable. **weedy** adj.

week n. **1** period of seven successive days, esp. from Monday to Sunday or Sunday to Saturday. **2** the weekdays of this. **3** working period during a week.

weekday n. day other than Sunday and usu. Saturday.

weekend n. Saturday and Sunday.

weekly adj. & adv. (produced or occurring) once a week. ● n. weekly periodical.

weep v. (**wept**) **1** shed (tears). **2** shed or ooze (moisture) in drops. ● n. spell of weeping. **weeper** n., **weepy** adj.
■ v. **1** bawl, sl. blub, blubber, cry, grizzle, lament, shed tears, snivel, sob, wail, whimper.

weeping adj. (of a tree) having drooping branches.

weevil n. small beetle that feeds on grain, nuts, tree-bark, etc.

weft n. crosswise threads in weaving.

weigh v. **1** measure the weight of. **2** have a specified weight. **3** consider the relative importance of. **4** have influence. □ **weigh anchor** raise the anchor and start a voyage. **weigh down 1** bring or keep down by its weight. **2** depress, oppress. **weigh up** make a person worry. **weigh up** form an estimate of.
■ **3** assess, consider, contemplate, estimate, evaluate, gauge, judge, mull over, ponder, weigh up. **4** be important, carry weight, count, matter. □ **weigh down 2** burden, depress, oppress, strain, trouble, worry.

weighbridge n. weighing machine with a plate set in a road etc. for weighing vehicles.

weight n. **1** object's mass numerically expressed using a recognized scale of units, heaviness. **2** unit or system of units used thus. **3** piece of metal of known weight used in weighing. **4** heavy object. **5** burden. **6** influence. ● v. **1** attach a weight to. **2** hold down with a weight. □ **weightless** adj.
■ n. **5** burden, cross, load, millstone, onus. **6** authority, colloq. clout, influence, power; consequence, importance, significance, value.

weighting n. extra pay given in special cases.

weighty adj. (**-ier, -iest**) **1** heavy. **2** important. **3** influential.
■ **1** heavy, hefty, massive, ponderous. **2** consequential, important, momentous, serious, significant. **3** authoritative, cogent, convincing, forceful, influential, persuasive, powerful.

weir n. **1** small dam built so that some of a stream's water flows over it. **2** waterfall formed thus.

weird adj. uncanny, bizarre. □ **weirdly** adv., **weirdness** n.
■ bizarre, curious, freakish, odd, outlandish, peculiar, colloq. spooky, strange, uncanny.

welcome adj. **1** received with pleasure. **2** freely permitted. ● int. greeting expressing pleasure or reception. ● n. kindly greeting or reception. ● v. receive with a welcome.
■ adj. **1** agreeable, gratifying, pleasant, pleasing. ● n. greeting, reception. ● v. greet, hail, meet, receive.

weld v. **1** unite or fuse (pieces of metal) by heating or pressure. **2** unite into a whole. ● n. welded joint. □ **welder** n.

welfare n. **1** well-being. **2** practical care for the health, safety, etc. of a particular group. □ **welfare state** country with highly developed social services.
■ **1** benefit, good, happiness, health, well-being.

well[1] n. **1** shaft sunk to obtain water or oil etc. **2** enclosed shaft-like space. ● v. rise or spring.
■ v. flow, rise, spring, surge.

well[2] adv. (**better, best**) **1** in a satisfactory way. **2** with distinction or talent. **3** thoroughly, carefully. **4** favourably, kindly. **5** probably. **6** to a considerable extent. ● adj. **1** in good health. **2** satisfactory. ● int. expressing surprise, relief, or resignation etc., or said when one is hesitating. □ **as well 1** in addition. **2** desirable, reasonably. **as well as** in addition to. **well-adjusted** *adj.* mentally and emotionally stable. **well-appointed** *adj.* well-equipped. **well-being** *n.* good health, happiness, and prosperity. **well-disposed** *adj.* having kindly or favourable feelings. **well-founded** *adj.* based on good evidence. **well-heeled** *adj.* (*colloq.*) wealthy. **well-meaning, -meant** *adjs.* acting or done with good intentions. **well off 1** in a fortunate situation. **2** rich. **well-read** *adj.* having read much literature. **well-spoken** *adj.* speaking in a polite and correct way. **well-to-do** *adj.* prosperous.

■ *adv.* **1** correctly, nicely, properly, satisfactorily. **2** ably, competently, expertly, proficiently, skilfully. **3** carefully, exhaustively, thoroughly. **4** approvingly, favourably, highly, warmly; considerately, hospitably, kindly, thoughtfully. ● *adj.* **1** fit, hale, healthy, in good health, *colloq.* in the pink, strong, thriving. **2** all right, fine, good, in order, *colloq.* OK, satisfactory. □ **as well 1** additionally, also, besides, furthermore, in addition, moreover, too. **well off 1** blessed, fortunate, lucky. **2** affluent, moneyed, prosperous, rich, wealthy, *colloq.* well-heeled, well-to-do.

wellington *n.* boot of rubber or other waterproof material.

well-nigh *adv.* almost.

Welsh *adj.* & *n.* (language) of Wales. □ **Welsh rabbit** or **rarebit** melted cheese on toast. **Welshman** *n.*, **Welshwoman** *n.*

welsh *v.* **1** avoid paying one's debts. **2** break an agreement.

welt *n.* **1** leather rim attaching the top of a boot or shoe to the sole. **2** ribbed or strengthened border of a knitted garment. **3** weal. ● *v.* **1** provide with a welt. **2** raise weals on, thrash.

welter *n.* **1** turmoil. **2** disorderly mixture.

■ **1** chaos, confusion, disorder, turmoil. **2** jumble, hotchpotch, mess, muddle, tangle.

wen *n.* benign tumour on the skin.

wend *v.* **wend one's way** go.

went *see* **go**.

wept *see* **weep**.

werewolf /ˈweərwo͝olf/ *n.* (*pl.* **-wolves**) (in myths) person who at times turns into a wolf.

west *n.* **1** point on the horizon where the sun sets. **2** direction in which this lies. **3** western part. ● *adj.* **1** in the west. **2** (of wind) from the west. ● *adv.* towards the west. □ **go west** (*sl.*) be destroyed, lost, or killed.

westerly *adj.* towards or blowing from the west.

western *adj.* of or in the west. ● *n.* film or novel about cowboys in western N. America.

westerner *n.* native or inhabitant of the west.

westernize *v.* make (an oriental country etc.) more like a western one in ideas and institutions. □ **westernization** *n.*

westernmost *adj.* furthest west.

westward *adj.* towards the west. □ **westwards** *adv.*

wet *adj.* (**wetter, wettest**) **1** soaked or covered with water or other liquid. **2** rainy. **3** not dry. **4** (*colloq.*) lacking vitality. ● *v.* (**wetted**) make wet. ● *n.* **1** moisture, water. **2** wet weather. □ **wet blanket** gloomy person. **wet-nurse** *n.* woman employed to suckle another's child. *v.* **1** act as wet-nurse to. **2** coddle as if helpless. **wetsuit** *n.* porous garment worn by a skin diver etc. **wetly** *adv.*, **wetness** *n.*

■ *adj.* **1** damp, drenched, dripping, moist, soaked, sodden, soggy, sopping, waterlogged, watery; clammy, dank, humid. **2** rainy, showery. **3** sticky, tacky. ● *v.* damp, dampen, douse, drench, moisten, saturate, soak, spray, sprinkle, water.

wether *n.* castrated ram.

whack *v.* & *n.* (*colloq.*) hit. □ **do one's whack** (*sl.*) do one's share.

whacked *adj.* (*colloq.*) tired out.

whale *n.* very large sea mammal.

whalebone *n.* horny substance from the upper jaw of whales, formerly used as stiffening.

whaler *n.* **1** whaling ship. **2** seaman hunting whales.

whaling *n.* hunting whales.

wham *int.* & *n.* sound of a forcible impact.

wharf *n.* (*pl.* **wharfs**) landing-stage where ships load and unload.

what *adj.* **1** asking for a statement of amount, number, or kind. **2** how great or remarkable. **3** the or any that. ● *pron.* **1** what thing(s). **2** what did you say? ● *adv.* to what extent or degree. ● *int.* exclamation of surprise. □ **what for?** why?

whatever *adj.* of any kind or number. ● *pron.* **1** anything or everything. **2** no matter what.

whatnot *n.* something trivial or indefinite.

whatsoever adj. & pron. whatever.

wheat n. **1** grain from which flour is made. **2** plant producing this.

wheatear n. a kind of small bird.

wheaten adj. made from wheat.

wheedle v. coax.

■ cajole, charm, coax, entice, inveigle, persuade.

wheel n. **1** disc or circular frame that revolves on a shaft passing through its centre. **2** wheel-like motion. ● v. **1** push or pull (a cart or bicycle etc.) along. **2** turn. **3** move in circles or curves. □ **at the wheel 1** driving a vehicle, directing a ship. **2** in control of affairs. **wheel and deal** engage in scheming to exert influence. **wheel-clamp** v. fix a clamp on (an illegally parked car etc.).

■ v. **2** spin, swing, swivel, turn, veer, whirl. **3** circle, gyrate.

wheelbarrow n. open container for moving small loads, with a wheel at one end.

wheelbase n. distance between a vehicle's front and rear axles.

wheelchair n. chair on wheels for a person who cannot walk.

wheeze v. breathe with a hoarse whistling sound. ● n. this sound. □ **wheezy** adj.

whelk n. spiral-shelled mollusc.

whelp n. young dog, puppy. ● v. give birth to (puppies).

when adv. **1** at what time, on what occasion. **2** at which time. ● conj. **1** at the time that. **2** whenever. **3** as soon as. **4** although. ● pron. what or which time.

whence adv. & conj. **1** from where. **2** from which.

whenever conj. & adv. **1** at whatever time. **2** every time that.

where adv. & conj. **1** at or in which place or circumstances. **2** in what respect. **3** from what place or source. **4** to what place. ● pron. what place.

whereabouts adv. in or near what place. ● n. a person's or thing's approximate location.

whereas adv. **1** since it is the fact that. **2** but in contrast.

whereby adv. by which.

whereupon adv. after which, and then.

wherever adv. at or to whatever place.

wherewithal n. (colloq.) (money etc.) needed for a purpose.

wherry n. **1** light rowing boat. **2** large light barge.

whet v. (**whetted**) **1** sharpen by rubbing against a stone etc. **2** stimulate (appetite or interest).

■ **1** hone, sharpen. **2** arouse, awaken, excite, fire, kindle, stimulate, stir.

whether conj. introducing an alternative possibility.

whetstone n. shaped hard stone used for sharpening tools.

whey n. watery liquid left when milk forms curds.

which adj. & pron. **1** what particular one(s) of a set. **2** and that. ● rel.pron. thing or animal referred to.

whichever adj. & pron. any which, that or those which.

whiff n. puff of air or odour etc.

■ breath, puff, scent, waft.

while n. **1** period of time. **2** time spent in doing something. ● conj. **1** during the time that, as long as. **2** although. ● v. **while away** pass (time) in a leisurely or interesting way.

whilst conj. while.

whim n. sudden fancy.

■ caprice, fancy, impulse, notion, vagary.

whimper v. make feeble crying sounds. ● n. whimpering sound.

■ v. cry, grizzle, sniffle, snivel.

whimsical adj. **1** impulsive and playful. **2** fanciful, quaint. □ **whimsically** adv., **whimsicality** n.

■ **1** capricious, impulsive, mischievous, playful. **2** curious, fanciful, fantastic, odd, quaint, unusual.

whine v. **1** make a long high complaining cry or a similar shrill sound. **2** complain or utter with a whine. ● n. whining sound or complaint. □ **whiner** n.

whinge v. (colloq.) whine, complain.

whinny n. gentle or joyful neigh. ● v. utter a whinny.

whip n. **1** cord or strip of leather on a handle, used for striking a person or animal. **2** food made with whipped cream etc. ● v. (**whipped**) **1** strike or urge on with a whip. **2** beat into a froth. **3** move or take suddenly. **4** (sl.) steal. □ **have the whip hand** have control. **whip-round** n. appeal for contributions from a group. **whip up** incite.

■ n. **1** lash, scourge, thong. ● v. **1** beat, flagellate, flay, flog, lash, scourge, thrash. **2** beat, stir, whisk. **3** dart, dash, fly, hurry, race, run, rush, scamper, scoot, scurry; jerk, pull, snatch, whisk, colloq. yank.

□ **whip up** arouse, excite, incite, kindle, rouse, stir up, work up.

whipcord n. **1** cord of tightly twisted strands. **2** twilled fabric with prominent ridges.

whiplash n. **1** lash of a whip. **2** jerk.

whippet n. small dog resembling a greyhound, used for racing.

whipping-boy n. scapegoat.

whippy adj. flexible, springy.

whirl v. **1** swing or spin round and round. **2** convey or go rapidly in a vehicle. ● n. **1** whirling movement. **2** confused state. **3** bustling activity.

■ v. **1** circle, gyrate, revolve, rotate, spin, swirl, turn, twirl. ● n. **1** pirouette, spin, swirl, turn, twirl.

whirlpool n. current of water whirling in a circle.

■ eddy, vortex.

whirlwind n. mass of air whirling rapidly about a central point.

■ cyclone, hurricane, tornado, typhoon.

whirr n. continuous buzzing or vibrating sound. ● v. make this sound.

■ n. & v. buzz, drone, hum, murmur, purr.

whisk v. **1** convey or go rapidly. **2** brush away lightly. **3** beat into a froth. ● n. **1** whisking movement. **2** instrument for beating eggs etc. **3** bunch of bristles etc. for brushing or flicking things.

■ v. **1** dart, dash, hasten, hurry, rush, scurry, jerk, pull, snatch, whip, colloq. yank. **2** brush, sweep. **3** beat, stir, whip.

whisker n. **1** long hair-like bristle near the mouth of a cat etc. **2** (pl.) hair growing on a man's cheek. □ **whiskered** adj., **whiskery** adj.

whiskey n. Irish whisky.

whisky n. spirit distilled from malted grain (esp. barley).

whisper v. **1** speak or utter softly, not using the vocal cords. ● n. **1** whispering sound or speech or remark. **2** rumour.

whist n. card game usu. for two pairs of players.

whistle n. **1** shrill sound made by blowing through a narrow opening between the lips. **2** similar sound. **3** instrument for producing this. ● v. **1** make this sound. **2** signal or produce (a tune) in this way. □ **whistler** n.

Whit adj. of or close to **Whit Sunday**, seventh Sunday after Easter.

white adj. **1** of the colour of milk or fresh snow. **2** having a light-coloured skin. **3** pale from illness or fear etc. ● n. **1** white colour or thing. **2** transparent substance round egg yolk. **3** member of a light-skinned race. □ **white ant** termite. **white-collar** adj. (of worker or work) non-manual, clerical. **white elephant** useless possession. **white hope** person expected to achieve much. **white horses** white-crested waves on sea. **white-hot** adj. (of metal) glowing white after heating. **white lie** harmless lie. **white sale** sale of household linen. **white spirit** light petroleum used as a solvent. **white wine** wine of yellow colour. **whiteness** n., **whitish** adj.

■ adj. **1** chalky, ivory, milky, snowy; silver. **3** anaemic, ashen, pale, pallid, pasty, wan.

whitebait n. (pl. **whitebait**) small silvery-white fish.

whiten v. make or become white or whiter.

■ blanch, bleach, fade, lighten.

whitewash n. **1** liquid containing quicklime or powdered chalk, used for painting walls or ceilings etc. **2** means of glossing over mistakes. ● v. **1** paint with whitewash. **2** gloss over mistakes in.

■ v. **2** camouflage, conceal, cover (up), disguise, gloss over, hide.

whither adv. (old use) to what place.

whiting n. (pl. **whiting**) small edible sea fish.

whitlow n. small abscess under or affecting a nail.

Whitsun n. Whit Sunday and the days close to it. □ **Whitsuntide** n.

whittle v. trim (wood) by cutting thin slices from the surface. □ **whittle down** reduce by removing various amounts.

whiz v. (**whizzed**) **1** make a sound like something moving at great speed through air. **2** move very quickly. ● n. **1** whizzing sound. □ **whiz-kid** n. (colloq.) brilliant or successful young person.

who pron. **1** what or which person(s)? **2** the particular person(s).

whodunit n. (colloq.) detective or mystery story or play etc.

whoever pron. any or every person who, no matter who.

whole adj. **1** with no part removed or left out. **2** not injured or broken. ● n. **1** full amount, all parts or members. **2** complete system made up of parts. □ **on the whole** considering everything.

wholehearted adj. without doubts or reservations. **whole number** number consisting of one or more units with no fractions.

■ adj. **1** complete, entire, full, total. **2** undamaged, unharmed, unhurt, uninjured, unscathed; complete, entire, intact, unabridged, uncut. □ **wholehearted** ardent, earnest, fervent, genuine, hearty, sincere, true; complete, heartfelt, unconditional, unqualified, unreserved.

wholemeal adj. made from the whole grain of wheat etc.

wholesale n. selling of goods in large quantities to be retailed by others. ● adj. & adv. **1** in the wholesale trade. **2** on a large scale. □ **wholesaler** n.

wholesome adj. good for health or well-being.

■ healthful, healthy, nourishing, nutritious, salubrious.

wholly adv. entirely.

■ absolutely, completely, entirely, fully, quite, thoroughly, totally.

whom pron. objective case of who.

whoop v. utter a loud cry of excitement. ● n. this cry.

■ v. cheer, cry, shout, shriek, yell.

whooping cough infectious disease esp. of children, with a violent convulsive cough.

whopper n. (sl.) **1** something very large. **2** great lie.

whore n. prostitute.

whorl n. **1** one turn of a spiral. **2** circle of ridges in a fingerprint. **3** ring of leaves or petals.

whose pron. **1** of whom. **2** of which.

whosoever pron. whoever.

why adv. **1** for what reason or purpose? **2** on account of which. ● int. exclamation of surprised discovery or recognition.

wick n. length of thread in a candle or lamp etc., by which the flame is kept supplied with melted grease or fuel.

wicked adj. **1** given to or involving immorality. **2** playfully malicious. **3** (colloq.) very bad. □ **wickedly** adv., **wickedness** n.

■ **1** amoral, bad, base, corrupt, criminal, degenerate, depraved, evil, heinous, immoral, iniquitous, nefarious, scandalous, shameful, sinful, vile, villainous, wrong. **2** devilish, mischievous, naughty, sly, roguish.

wicker n. osiers or thin canes interwoven to make furniture or baskets etc. □ **wickerwork** n.

wicket n. **1** set of three stumps and two bails used in cricket. **2** part of a cricket ground between or near the two wickets.

wide adj. **1** measuring much from side to side. **2** having a specified width. **3** extending far. **4** fully opened. **5** far from the target. ● adv. widely. □ **wide awake 1** fully awake. **2** (colloq.) alert. **widely** adv., **wideness** n.

■ adj. **1** broad, extensive, large, spacious, vast. **3** broad, comprehensive, extensive, sweeping, wide-ranging, widespread.

widen v. make or become wider.

■ broaden, enlarge, expand, increase; dilate, distend.

widespread adj. found or distributed over a wide area.

■ common, extensive, general, prevalent, sweeping.

widgeon n. wild duck.

widow n. woman whose husband has died and who has not remarried. □ **widowhood** n.

widowed adj. made a widow or widower.

widower n. man whose wife has died and who has not remarried.

width n. **1** distance from side to side. **2** wideness. **3** piece of material of full width.

wield v. **1** hold and use (a tool etc.) with the hands. **2** have and use (power).

■ **1** employ, ply, use; brandish, flourish, wave. **2** exercise, exert.

wife n. (pl. **wives**) married woman in relation to her husband. □ **wifely** adj.

wig n. artificial covering of hair worn on the head.

wiggle v. move repeatedly from side to side. ● n. act of wiggling.

wigwam n. N. American Indian's conical tent.

wild adj. **1** not domesticated, tame, or cultivated. **2** not civilized. **3** disorderly. **4** stormy. **5** full of strong unrestrained feeling. **6** extremely foolish. **7** random. ● adv. in a wild manner. ● n. (usu. pl.) desolate uninhabited place. □ **wild-goose chase** useless quest. **wildly** adv., **wildness** n.

■ adj. **1** feral, undomesticated, untamed; natural, uncultivated. **2** primitive, savage, uncivilized. **3** chaotic, disorderly, riotous, rowdy, uncontrollable, uncontrolled, undisciplined, unmanageable, unrestrained, unruly, uproarious, tumultuous. **4** stormy, tempestuous, turbulent. **5** excited, feverish, frantic, frenzied, hysterical; *colloq.* crazy, enthusiastic, mad, passionate. **6** absurd, crazy, foolhardy, foolish, ill-advised, impractical, imprudent, silly. **7** arbitrary, haphazard, random.

wildcat *adj.* **1** reckless. **2** (of strikes) sudden and unofficial.

wildebeest *n.* gnu.

wilderness *n.* wild uncultivated area.

wildfire *n.* **spread like wildfire** spread very fast.

wildfowl *n.* birds hunted as game.

wildlife *n.* wild animals and plants.

wile *n.* piece of trickery.
■ artifice, device, ploy, stratagem, subterfuge, trap, trick.

wilful *adj.* **1** intentional, not accidental. **2** self-willed. □ **wilfully** *adv.*, **wilfulness** *n.*
■ **1** conscious, deliberate, intentional, premeditated. **2** headstrong, obdurate, obstinate, pigheaded, recalcitrant, refractory, self-willed, stubborn, unyielding.

will[1] *v.aux.* used with *I* and *we* to express promises or obligations, and with other words to express a future tense.

will[2] *n.* **1** mental faculty by which a person decides upon and controls his or her actions. **2** determination. **3** desire. **4** person's attitude in wishing good or bad to others. **5** written directions made by a person for disposal of their property after their death. ● *v.* **1** try to cause by will-power. **2** intend unconditionally. **3** bequeath by a will. □ **at will** whenever one pleases. **will-power** *n.* control exercised by one's will.
■ *n.* **2** determination, drive, purpose, resolution, resolve, will-power. **3** desire, wish. **4** attitude, disposition, feeling(s). **5** testament. ● *v.* **1** compel, force, make. **2** command, desire, intend, ordain, order, require, want, wish. **3** bequeath, hand down, leave, make over, pass on.

willing *adj.* **1** desiring to do what is required, not objecting. **2** given or done readily. □ **willingly** *adv.*, **willingness** *n.*
■ **1** acquiescent, agreeable, amenable, complaisant, compliant, eager, enthusiastic, game, pleased, prepared, ready.

will-o'-the-wisp *n.* **1** phosphorescent light seen on marshy ground. **2** hope or aim that can never be fulfilled.

willow *n.* **1** tree or shrub with flexible branches. **2** its wood.

willowy *adj.* **1** full of willows. **2** slender and supple.
■ **2** flexible, lissom, lithe, slender, slim, supple, svelte.

willy-nilly *adv.* whether one desires it or not.

wilt *v.* **1** lose freshness, droop. **2** lose one's energy.
■ **1** droop, wither. **2** flag, grow tired, languish, tire, weaken.

wily /wīli/ *adj.* **(-ier, -iest)** full of wiles, cunning. □ **wiliness** *n.*
■ artful, canny, clever, crafty, cunning, deceitful, designing, devious, guileful, machiavellian, scheming, shrewd, sly.

wimp *n.* (*sl.*) feeble or ineffective person.

win *v.* **(won, winning) 1** be victorious (in). **2** obtain as the result of a contest etc., or by effort. ● *n.* victory, esp. in a game. □ **win over** gain the favour or support of.
■ *v.* **1** be victorious, come *or* finish first, prevail, succeed, triumph. **2** achieve, attain, carry off, earn, gain, get, obtain, receive, secure. ● *n.* conquest, success, triumph, victory. □ **win over** charm, get round, influence, persuade, sway.

wince *v.* make a slight movement from pain or embarrassment etc. ● *n.* this movement.
■ *v.* blench, cringe, flinch.

winceyette *n.* cotton fabric with a soft downy surface.

winch *n.* machine for hoisting or pulling things by a cable that winds round a revolving drum. ● *v.* hoist or pull with a winch.

wind[1] /wind/ *n.* **1** current of air. **2** gas in the stomach or intestines. **3** useless or boastful talk. **4** breath as needed in exertion or speech etc. **5** orchestra's wind instruments. ● *v.* cause to be out of breath. □ **get wind of** hear a hint or rumour of. **in the wind** happening or about to happen. **put the wind up** (*colloq.*) frighten. **take the wind out of a person's sails** frustrate a person by anticipating him or her. **wind-break** *n.* screen shielding something from the wind. **wind-chill** *n.* cooling effect of the wind. **wind instrument** musical instrument sounded by a current of air, esp. by the player's breath. **wind-sock** *n.* canvas cylinder flown at an airfield to show the direction of the wind. **wind-tunnel** *n.*

enclosed tunnel in which winds can be created for testing things.

■ *n.* **1** breeze, draught, gust, *poetic* zephyr. **3** bluster, boasting, claptrap, *colloq.* gas, *colloq.* hot air.

wind² /wīnd/ *v.* (**wound**) **1** move or go in a curving or spiral course. **2** wrap closely around something or round upon itself. **3** move by turning a windlass or handle etc. **4** wind up (a clock etc.). □ **wind up 1** set or keep (a clock etc.) going by tightening its spring. **2** bring or come to an end. **3** settle the affairs of and close (a business company). **winder** *n.*

■ **1** bend, curve, meander, snake, turn, twist, zigzag. **2** enfold, envelop, wrap; coil, reel, turn, twine, twist. □ **wind up 2** bring to an end, close, conclude, end, finish, terminate. **3** dissolve, liquidate.

windbag *n.* (*colloq.*) person who talks lengthily.

windfall *n.* **1** fruit blown off a tree by the wind. **2** unexpected gain, esp. a sum of money.

windlass *n.* winch-like device using a rope or chain that winds round a horizontal roller.

windmill *n.* mill worked by the action of wind on projecting parts that radiate from a shaft.

window *n.* **1** opening in a wall etc. to admit light and often air, usu. filled with glass. **2** this glass. **3** space for display of goods behind the window of a shop. □ **window-box** *n.* trough fixed outside a window, for growing flowers etc. **window-dressing** *n.* **1** arranging a display of goods in a shop window. **2** presentation of facts so as to give a favourable impression. **window-shopping** *n.* looking at displayed goods without buying.

windpipe *n.* air passage from the throat to the bronchial tubes.

windscreen *n.* glass in the window at the front of a vehicle.

windsurfing *n.* sport of surfing on a board to which a sail is fixed.

windswept *adj.* exposed to strong winds.

windward *adj.* situated in the direction from which the wind blows. ● *n.* this side or region.

wine *n.* **1** fermented grape-juice as an alcoholic drink. **2** fermented drink made from other fruits or plants. **3** dark red. ● *v.* **1** drink wine. **2** entertain with wine. □ **wine bar** bar or small restaurant serving wine as the main drink.

wing *n.* **1** each of a pair of projecting parts by which a bird or insect etc. is able to fly. **2** wing-like part of an aircraft. **3** projecting part. **4** bodywork above the wheel of a car. **5** either end of a battle array. **6** player at either end of the forward line in football or hockey etc., side part of playing area in these games. **7** extreme section of a political party. **8** (*pl.*) sides of a theatre stage. ● *v.* **1** fly, travel by wings. **2** wound slightly in the wing or arm. □ **on the wing** flying. **take wing** fly away. **under one's wing** under one's protection. **wing-collar** *n.* high stiff collar with turned-down corners.

winged *adj.* having wings.

winger *n.* wing player in football etc.

wink *v.* **1** blink one eye as a signal. **2** shine with a light that flashes or twinkles. ● *n.* act of winking.

■ *v.* **2** flash, glint, glitter, shine, sparkle, twinkle.

winker *n.* flashing indicator.

winkle *n.* edible sea snail. ● *v.* **winkle out** extract, prise out.

winner *n.* **1** person or thing that wins. **2** something successful.

■ **1** champion, conqueror, victor.

winning *adj.* charming, attractive. ● *n.pl.* money won. □ **winning post** post marking the end of a race.

■ *adj.* appealing, attractive, captivating, charming, delightful, enchanting, endearing, engaging, pleasing, winsome.

winnow *v.* fan or toss (grain) to free it of chaff.

winsome *adj.* charming.

winter *n.* coldest season of the year. ● *v.* spend the winter. □ **wintry** *adj.*

winy *adj.* wine-flavoured.

wipe *v.* **1** clean, dry, or remove by rubbing. **2** spread thinly on a surface. ● *n.* act of wiping. □ **wipe out** destroy completely.

■ □ **wipe out** annihilate, destroy, eliminate, eradicate, exterminate, get rid of, obliterate, stamp out.

wiper *n.* device that automatically wipes rain etc. from a windscreen.

wire *n.* **1** strand of metal. **2** length of this used for fencing, conducting electric current, etc. ● *v.* provide, fasten, or strengthen with wire(s). □ **wire-haired** *adj.* having stiff wiry hair.

wireworm *n.* destructive larva of a beetle.

wiring n. system of electric wires in a building, vehicle, etc.

wiry adj. (-ier, -iest) 1 like wire. 2 lean but strong. □ **wiriness** n.

wisdom n. 1 being wise, soundness of judgement. 2 wise sayings. □ **wisdom tooth** hindmost molar tooth, not usu. cut before the age of 20.

■ 1 astuteness, discernment, insight, intelligence, judgement, perspicacity, sagacity, sense, shrewdness, understanding.

wise adj. 1 showing soundness of judgement. 2 having knowledge. □ **wisely** adv.

■ 1 astute, discerning, intelligent, perspicacious, sagacious, sage, shrewd; advisable, judicious, prudent, sensible. 2 erudite, intelligent, knowledgeable, learned, well-educated, well-read.

wiseacre n. person who pretends to have great wisdom.

wisecrack (colloq.) n. witty remark. ● v. make a wisecrack.

wish n. 1 desire, request, or aspiration. 2 expression of this. ● v. 1 have or express as a wish. 2 express one's hopes for. 3 (colloq.) foist.

■ n. 1 aspiration, craving, desire, fancy, hankering, longing, need, request, want, yearning, colloq. yen.

wishbone n. forked bone between a bird's neck and breast.

wishful adj. desiring. □ **wishful thinking** belief founded on wishes not facts.

wishy-washy adj. weak in colour, character, etc.

■ bland, insipid, vapid; feeble, ineffectual, namby-pamby, spineless, weak-kneed, colloq. wet.

wisp n. 1 small separate bunch. 2 small streak of smoke etc. ● **wispy** adj., **wispiness** n.

wisteria n. climbing shrub with hanging clusters of flowers.

wistful adj. full of sad or vague longing. □ **wistfully** adv., **wistfulness** n.

■ forlorn, melancholy, mournful, pensive, sad, sorrowful.

wit n. 1 amusing ingenuity in expressing words or ideas. 2 person who has this. 3 intelligence. □ **at one's wits' end** worried and not knowing what to do.

■ 1 drollery, humour, wittiness. 2 comedian, comedienne, comic, wag. 3 brains, intelligence, colloq. nous, sense, understanding, wisdom.

witch n. 1 person (esp. a woman) who practises witchcraft. 2 bewitching woman. □ **witch-doctor** n. tribal magician. **witch hazel** 1 N. American shrub. 2 astringent lotion made from its bark. **witch-hunt** n. persecution of people thought to hold unorthodox or unpopular views.

■ 1 enchantress, sorceress.

witchcraft n. practice of magic.

■ enchantment, magic, necromancy, sorcery, wizardry.

with prep. 1 in the company of, among. 2 having, characterized by. 3 by means of. 4 of the same opinion as. 5 at the same time as. 6 because of. 7 under the conditions of. 8 by addition or possession of. 9 in regard to, towards.

withdraw v. (withdrew, withdrawn) 1 take back or away. 2 remove (deposited money) from a bank etc. 3 cancel (a statement). 4 go away from a place or from company. □ **withdrawal** n.

■ 1 draw back, pull back, retract; extract, remove, take out. 3 annul, nullify, rescind, retract, revoke, take back. 4 depart, leave, retire, retreat.

withdrawn adj. (of a person) unsociable.

■ aloof, distant, introverted, reserved, standoffish, unfriendly, unsociable.

wither v. 1 shrivel, lose freshness or vitality. 2 subdue by scorn.

■ 1 droop, shrivel, wilt.

withhold v. (withheld) 1 refuse to give. 2 restrain.

■ 1 deny, deprive of, refuse. 2 control, curb, hold back, repress, restrain, suppress.

within prep. 1 inside. 2 not beyond the limit or scope of. 3 in a time no longer than. ● adv. inside.

without prep. 1 not having. 2 in the absence of. 3 with no action of. ● adv. outside.

withstand v. (withstood) endure successfully.

■ bear, brave, cope with, endure, handle, stand, colloq. stick, survive, take, tolerate, weather.

withy n. tough flexible shoot, esp. of willow.

witless adj. foolish.

witness n. 1 person who sees or hears something. 2 one who gives evidence in a law court. 3 one who confirms another's signature. 4 thing that serves as

evidence. ● *v.* be a witness of. ▫ **bear witness to** attest the truth of.
  ■ *n.* **1** bystander, eyewitness, observer, onlooker, spectator. ● *v.* observe, see, watch. ● **bear witness to** attest (to), confirm, prove, show, testify (to).

witticism *n.* witty remark.

witty *adj.* (**-ier, -iest**) full of wit. ▫ **wittily** *adv.*, **wittiness** *n.*
  ■ amusing, comical, droll, funny, humorous, scintillating, sparkling.

wives *see* **wife**.

wizard *n.* **1** male witch, magician. **2** person with amazing abilities. ▫ **wizardry** *n.*
  ■ **1** enchanter, magician, sorcerer. **2** expert, genius, maestro, master, mastermind, virtuoso, *colloq.* whiz-kid.

wizened /wizz'nd/ *adj.* full of wrinkles, shrivelled with age.

woad *n.* **1** blue dye obtained from a plant. **2** this plant.

wobble *v.* **1** stand or move unsteadily. **2** quiver. ● *n.* **1** wobbling movement. **2** quiver. ▫ **wobbly** *adj.*
  ■ *v.* **1** dodder, rock, sway, teeter, totter, waver. **2** quaver, quiver, shake, tremble.

wodge *n.* (*colloq.*) chunk, wedge.

woe *n.* **1** sorrow, distress. **2** trouble causing this, misfortune. ▫ **woeful** *adj.*, **woefully** *adv.*
  ■ **1** anguish, distress, grief, heartache, misery, sadness, sorrow, suffering, unhappiness. **2** affliction, calamity, hardship, misfortune, problem, trial, tribulation, trouble.

woebegone *adj.* looking unhappy.
  ■ crestfallen, dejected, disconsolate, dispirited, doleful, downhearted, forlorn, gloomy, glum, melancholy, miserable, sad, sorrowful, unhappy.

wok *n.* bowl-shaped frying pan used esp. in Chinese cookery.

woke, woken *see* **wake**[1].

wold *n.* (esp. in *pl.*) area of open upland country.

wolf *n.* (*pl.* **wolves**) **1** wild animal of the dog family. **2** (*sl.*) aggressive male flirt. ● *v.* eat quickly and greedily. ▫ **cry wolf** raise false alarms. **wolf-whistle** *n.* man's admiring whistle at an attractive woman. **wolfish** *adj.*

wolfram *n.* tungsten (ore).

wolverine *n.* N. American animal of the weasel family.

woman *n.* (*pl.* **women**) **1** adult female person. **2** women in general.

womanhood *n.* state of being a woman.

womanize *v.* (of a man) be promiscuous. ▫ **womanizer** *n.*

womankind *n.* women in general.

womanly *adj.* having qualities considered characteristic of a woman. ▫ **womanliness** *n.*

womb *n.* hollow organ in female mammals in which the young develop before birth.

wombat *n.* small bear-like Australian animal.

women *see* **woman**.

womenfolk *n.* **1** women in general. **2** women of one's family.

won *see* **win**.

wonder *n.* **1** feeling of surprise and admiration, curiosity, or bewilderment. **2** remarkable thing. ● *v.* **1** feel wonder or surprise. **2** be curious to know.
  ■ *n.* **1** admiration, amazement, astonishment, awe, curiosity, fascination, surprise, wonderment. **2** curiosity, marvel, miracle, phenomenon, prodigy, spectacle. ● *v.* **1** be amazed *or* awed, marvel. **2** conjecture, meditate, muse, ponder, speculate, think.

wonderful *adj.* very good or remarkable. ▫ **wonderfully** *adv.*
  ■ *colloq.* fabulous, *colloq.* fantastic, *colloq.* great, *colloq.* smashing, splendid, *colloq.* super, *colloq.* terrific, *colloq.* tremendous, amazing, astounding, excellent, extraordinary, first-class, incredible, magnificent, marvellous, outstanding, remarkable, superb.

wonderland *n.* place full of wonderful things.

wonderment *n.* feeling of wonder.

wont *adj.* accustomed. ● *n.* custom, habit.

woo *v.* **1** court. **2** try to achieve, obtain, or coax.

wood *n.* **1** tough fibrous substance of a tree. **2** this cut for use. **3** (also *pl.*) trees growing fairly densely over an area of ground. ▫ **out of the wood(s)** clear of danger or difficulty.
  ■ **2** lumber, timber. **3** coppice, copse, forest, grove, spinney, thicket, woodland.

woodbine *n.* wild honeysuckle.

woodcock *n.* a kind of game bird.

woodcut *n.* **1** engraving made on wood. **2** picture made from this.

wooded *adj.* covered with trees.

wooden *adj.* **1** made of wood. **2** expressionless. ▫ **woodenly** *adv.*

woodland *n.* wooded country.

woodlouse *n.* (*pl.* **-lice**) small crustacean with many legs, living in decaying wood etc.

woodpecker *n.* bird that taps tree trunks to find insects.

woodpigeon *n.* a kind of large pigeon.

woodwind *n.* wind instruments originally made of wood.

woodwork *n.* **1** art or practice of making things from wood. **2** wooden things or fittings.

woodworm *n.* larva of a kind of beetle that bores in wood.

woody *adj.* **1** like or consisting of wood. **2** full of woods.

woof *n.* dog's gruff bark. ● *v.* make this sound.

woofer *n.* loudspeaker for reproducing low-frequency signals.

wool *n.* **1** soft hair from sheep or goats etc. **2** yarn or fabric made from this. □ **pull the wool over someone's eyes** deceive him or her.

woollen *adj.* made of wool. ● *n.pl.* woollen cloth or clothing.

woolly *adj.* (**-ier, -iest**) **1** covered with wool. **2** like wool, woollen. **3** vague. ● *n.* (*colloq.*) woollen garment. □ **woolliness** *n.*

word *n.* **1** sound(s) expressing a meaning independently and forming a basic element of speech. **2** this represented by letters or symbols. **3** thing said. **4** talk. **5** message, news. **6** promise or assurance. **7** command. ● *v.* express in words. □ **word of mouth** spoken (not written) words. **word-perfect** *adj.* having memorized every word perfectly. **word processor** computer programmed for storing, correcting, and printing out text entered from a keyboard.

■ *n.* **3** comment, declaration, expression, observation, remark, statement, utterance. **4** chat, conversation, discussion, talk, tête-à-tête. **5** information, intelligence, news; bulletin, communiqué, message, report. **6** assurance, guarantee, oath, pledge, promise, undertaking, vow. **7** command, direction, order, signal. ● *v.* couch, express, phrase, put.

wording *n.* form of words used.

wordy *adj.* verbose.

wore *see* **wear**.

work *n.* **1** use of bodily or mental power in order to do or make something. **2** task to be undertaken. **3** thing done or produced by work. **4** things made of certain

materials or with certain tools. **5** literary or musical composition. **6** employment. **7** (*pl.*, usu. treated as *sing.*) factory. **8** (*pl.*) operations of building etc. **9** (*pl.*) operative parts of a machine. **10** (usu. *pl.*) defensive structure. ● *v.* **1** perform work. **2** make efforts. **3** be employed. **4** operate, esp. effectively. **5** bring about, accomplish. **6** shape, knead, or hammer etc. into a desired form or consistency. **7** make (a way) or pass gradually by effort. **8** become (loose etc.) through repeated stress or pressure. **9** be in motion. **10** ferment. **11** (**the works**) (*sl.*) all that is available. □ **work off** get rid of by activity. **work out 1** find or solve by calculation. **2** plan the details of. **3** have a specified result. **4** take exercise. **work to rule** cause delay by over-strict observance of rules, as a form of protest. **work up 1** bring gradually to a more developed state. **2** excite progressively. **3** advance (to a climax).

■ *n.* **1** donkey work, drudgery, effort, exertion, *sl.* graft, grind, industry, labour, slog, toil, travail. **5** composition, piece. **6** employment, occupation, profession, trade. ● *v.* **1** beaver (away), drudge, exert oneself, *sl.* graft, labour, *colloq.* plug (away), slave (away), slog (away), toil. **2** exert oneself, make an effort, strive. **4** be in working order, function, go, operate, run; be effective, succeed. **5** accomplish, achieve, bring about, cause, create, effect, produce. □ **work out 1** calculate, figure out, solve. **2** develop, devise, draw up, formulate, plan, prepare, put together. **3** go, pan out, turn out. **4** exercise, train.

workable *adj.* able to be done or used successfully.

■ feasible, practicable, practical, viable.

workaday *adj.* ordinary, everyday, practical.

worker *n.* **1** person who works. **2** member of the working class. **3** neuter bee or ant that does the work of the hive or colony.

workforce *n.* workers engaged or available, number of these.

workhouse *n.* former public institution where people unable to support themselves were housed.

working *adj.* engaged in work. ● *n.* excavation(s) made in mining, tunnelling, etc. □ **in working order** (esp. of a machine) able to function properly. **working class** class of people who are employed for wages, esp. in manual or industrial work. **working knowledge** knowledge adequate to work with.

workman n. man employed to do manual labour.

workmanlike adj. showing practical skill.

workmanship n. skill in working or in a thing produced.
■ art, artistry, craftsmanship, skill, skilfulness.

workout n. session of physical exercising.

workshop n. room or building in which manual work or manufacture etc. is carried on.

workstation n. **1** computer terminal and keyboard. **2** desk with this. **3** location of a stage in a manufacturing process.

world n. **1** the earth. **2** all that concerns or all who belong to a specified class, time, or sphere of activity. **3** all that exists. **4** very great amount.
■ **1** earth, globe. **2** community, domain, field, realm, sphere; age, epoch, era, period, time. **3** cosmos, universe.

worldly adj. of or concerned with earthly life or material gains, not spiritual. □ **worldliness** n.
■ carnal, earthly, human, material, mortal, mundane, physical, secular, temporal.

worldwide adj. extending through the whole world.
■ global, universal, world.

worm n. **1** animal with a long soft body and no backbone or limbs. **2** (pl.) internal parasites. **3** insignificant or contemptible person. **4** spiral part of a screw. ● v. **1** make one's way with twisting movements. **2** insinuate oneself. **3** obtain by crafty persistence. **4** rid of parasitic worms. □ **worm-cast** n. pile of earth cast up by an earthworm. **wormy** adj.

wormeaten adj. full of holes made by insect larvae.

wormwood n. woody plant with a bitter flavour.

worn see WEAR. adj. **1** damaged or altered by use or wear. **2** looking exhausted. □ **worn-out** adj.
■ **1** old, ragged, colloq. scruffy, shabby, tattered, tatty, threadbare. **2** drawn, haggard.

worried adj. feeling or showing worry.
■ anxious, apprehensive, fearful, fretful, nervous, tense, troubled, uneasy, colloq. uptight.

worry v. **1** give way to anxiety. **2** make anxious. **3** be troublesome to. **4** seize with the teeth and shake or pull about. ● n. **1** worried state, mental uneasiness. **2** thing causing this. □ **worrier** n.
■ v. **1** agonize, brood, fret. **2** concern, disquiet, distress, disturb, trouble, unnerve, unsettle. **3** annoy, bother, harass, colloq. hassle, nag, pester, trouble. ● n. **1** anxiety, apprehension, concern, disquiet, distress, nervousness, unease, uneasiness. **2** bother, burden, care, concern, headache, problem, trouble.

worse adj. & adv. **1** more bad, more badly, more evil or ill. **2** less good. ● n. something worse.

worsen v. make or become worse.
■ aggravate, exacerbate, make worse; decline, degenerate, deteriorate, get worse.

worship n. **1** reverence and respect paid to a deity. **2** adoration of or devotion to a person or thing. ● v. (**worshipped**) **1** honour as a deity. **2** idolize, treat with adoration. **3** take part in an act of worship. □ **worshipper** n.
■ n. **1** glorification, homage, respect, reverence, veneration. **2** adoration, devotion, idolization, love. ● v. **1** glorify, honour, praise, pray to, revere, venerate. **2** adore, idolize, love.

worst adj. & adv. most bad, most badly, least good. ● n. worst part, feature, event, etc. ● v. defeat. □ **get the worst of** be defeated in.
■ v. beat, conquer, defeat, get the better of, overcome, rout, subdue, trounce, vanquish.

worsted /wõostid/ n. smooth woollen yarn or fabric.

worth adj. **1** having a specified value. **2** deserving. **3** possessing as wealth. ● n. **1** value, merit, usefulness. **2** amount that a specified sum will buy. □ **for all one is worth** (colloq.) with all one's energy. **worth while** or **worth one's while** worth the time or effort needed.
■ n. **1** advantage, benefit, good, importance, merit, usefulness, value.

worthless adj. without merit or value. □ **worthlessness** n.
■ meaningless, paltry, valueless; fruitless, futile, pointless, vain; cheap, tawdry, trashy.

worthwhile *adj.* worth while.

■ advantageous, beneficial, fruitful, gainful, good, helpful, profitable, useful, valuable.

worthy *adj.* (**-ier**, **-iest**) **1** having great merit. **2** deserving. ● *n.* worthy person. □ **worthily** *adv.*, **worthiness** *n.*

■ *adj.* **1** admirable, commendable, creditable, estimable, honourable, laudable, meritorious, praiseworthy. ● *n.* dignitary, luminary.

would *v.aux.* used in senses corresponding to *will*[1] in the past tense, conditional statements, questions, polite requests and statements, and to express probability or something that happens from time to time. □ **would-be** *adj.* desiring or pretending to be.

wound[1] /wŏŏnd/ *n.* **1** injury done to tissue by violence. **2** injury to feelings. ● *v.* inflict a wound upon.

■ *n.* **1** cut, injury, laceration, lesion, trauma. **2** affront, injury, insult, slight. ● *v.* harm, hurt, injure, maim; distress, grieve, offend, pain, upset.

wound[2] /wownd/ *see* **wind**[2].

wove, woven *see* **weave**[1].

wow *int.* exclamation of astonishment. ● *n.* (*sl.*) sensational success.

wrack *n.* a type of seaweed.

wraith *n.* ghost, spectral apparition of a living person.

■ apparition, ghost, phantom, spectre, spirit, *colloq.* spook.

wrangle *v.* argue or quarrel noisily. ● *n.* noisy argument.

■ *v.* argue, bicker, disagree, dispute, fall out, fight, quarrel, row, squabble. ● *n.* altercation, argument, disagreement, dispute, fight, quarrel, row, squabble, tiff.

wrap *v.* (**wrapped**) arrange (a soft or flexible covering) round (a person or thing). ● *n.* shawl. □ **be wrapped up in** have one's attention deeply occupied by.

■ *v.* enfold, envelop, shroud, swaddle, swathe. ● *n.* cape, cloak, mantle, shawl, stole.

wrapper *n.* cover of paper etc. wrapped round something.

wrapping *n.* material for wrapping things.

wrasse /rass/ *n.* brightly coloured sea fish.

wrath *n.* anger, indignation. □ **wrathful** *adj.*, **wrathfully** *adv.*

■ anger, annoyance, fury, indignation, ire, irritation, rage, vexation.

wreak *v.* inflict (vengeance etc.).

wreath /reeth/ *n.* (*pl.* **-ths**) flowers or leaves etc. fastened into a ring, used as a decoration or placed on a grave etc.

wreathe /reeth/ *v.* **1** encircle. **2** twist into a wreath. **3** wind, curve.

wreck *n.* **1** destruction, esp. of a ship by storms or accident. **2** ship that has suffered this. **3** something ruined or dilapidated. **4** person whose health or spirits have been destroyed. ● *v.* **1** cause the wreck of. **2** ruin. □ **wrecker** *n.*

■ *v.* **2** destroy, devastate, put paid to, ruin, shatter, spoil.

wreckage *n.* remains of something wrecked.

■ debris, flotsam, fragments, remains, rubble.

wren *n.* very small bird.

wrench *v.* **1** twist or pull violently round. **2** damage or pull by twisting. ● *n.* **1** violent twisting pull. **2** pain caused by parting. **3** adjustable spanner-like tool.

■ *v.* **1** jerk, pull, rip, tear, tug, twist, wrest, *colloq.* yank. **2** rick, sprain, twist.

wrest *v.* **1** wrench away. **2** obtain by force or effort.

wrestle *v.* **1** fight (esp. as a sport) by grappling and trying to throw an opponent to the ground. **2** struggle to deal with.

■ **2** battle, fight, grapple, struggle.

wretch *n.* **1** unfortunate or pitiable person. **2** rascal.

■ **2** blackguard, knave, rascal, rat, rogue, scallywag, scoundrel, villain.

wretched *adj.* **1** miserable, unhappy. **2** of bad quality. **3** contemptible. □ **wretchedly** *adv.*, **wretchedness** *n.*

■ **1** dejected, desolate, despondent, forlorn, melancholy, miserable, sad, sorrowful, unhappy, woebegone, woeful; pathetic, pitiful, sorry, unfortunate. **2** inferior, mean, miserable, poor, shabby, squalid. **3** contemptible, despicable, shameful, vile.

wriggle *v.* move with short twisting movements. ● *n.* wriggling movement.

■ *v.* fidget, squirm, twist, wiggle, worm, writhe.

wring *v.* (**wrung**) **1** twist and squeeze, esp. to remove liquid. **2** squeeze firmly or forcibly. **3** obtain with effort or difficulty.

wrinkle *n.* **1** crease in skin or other flexible surface. **2** (*colloq.*) useful hint or device. ● *v.* form wrinkles (in). ▢ **wrinkly** *adj.*

  ■ *n.* **1** crease, crinkle, fold, furrow, line, pucker.

wrist *n.* **1** joint connecting hand and forearm. **2** part of a garment covering this. ▢ **wrist-watch** *n.* watch worn on the wrist.

wristlet *n.* band or bracelet etc. worn round the wrist.

writ *n.* formal written authoritative command.

write *v.* (**wrote, written, writing**) **1** make letters or other symbols on a surface, esp. with a pen or pencil. **2** compose in written form, esp. for publication. **3** be an author. **4** write and send a letter. ▢ **write down** record in writing. **write off** recognize as lost. **write-off** *n.* something written off, esp. a vehicle too damaged to be worth repairing. **write up** write an account of. **write-up** *n.* (*colloq.*) published account of something, review.

  ■ **1** inscribe, scrawl, scribble. **2** compose, draft, pen. ▢ **write down** jot down, log, note, put down, record, register.

writer *n.* person who writes, author. ▢ **writer's cramp** cramp in the muscles of the hand.

  ■ author, columnist, dramatist, journalist, novelist, playwright, poet, scriptwriter.

writhe *v.* **1** twist one's body about, as in pain. **2** wriggle. **3** suffer because of embarrassment, squirm.

writing *n.* **1** handwriting. **2** literary work. ▢ **in writing** in written form. **writing paper** paper for writing (esp. letters) on.

written *see* **write.**

wrong *adj.* **1** incorrect, not true. **2** contrary to morality or law. **3** not what is required or desirable. **4** not in a satis-factory condition. ● *adv.* in a wrong manner or direction, mistakenly. ● *n.* **1** what is wrong, wrong action etc. **2** injustice. ● *v.* treat unjustly. ▢ **in the wrong** not having truth or justice on one's side. **wrongly** *adv.*, **wrongness** *n.*

  ■ *adj.* **1** erroneous, fallacious, false, inaccurate, incorrect, inexact, mistaken, untrue. **2** amoral, bad, evil, immoral, sinful, unethical, unconscionable, wicked; criminal, dishonest, illegal, illicit, unlawful. **3** improper, imprudent, inappropriate, incorrect, misguided, unacceptable, undesirable, unsuitable. **4** amiss, awry, defective, faulty, not working, out of order. ● *adv.* amiss, awry, badly, imperfectly, improperly, inappropriately, incorrectly, wrongly. ● *n.* **1** crime, misdeed, misdemeanour, offence, transgression; inequality, iniquity, unfairness, unjustness. **2** bad turn, injury, injustice. ● *v.* abuse, harm, ill-treat, injure, maltreat. ▢ **in the wrong** at fault, blameworthy, culpable, guilty, responsible.

wrongdoer *n.* person who acts illegally or immorally. ▢ **wrongdoing** *n.*

  ■ criminal, *colloq* crook, lawbreaker, malefactor, miscreant, offender, transgressor, villain.

wrongful *adj.* contrary to what is right or legal. ▢ **wrongfully** *adv.*

  ■ injurious, unfair, unjust, unjustified; illegal, unlawful.

wrote *see* **write.**

wrought /rawt/ *adj.* (of metals) shaped by hammering. ▢ **wrought iron** pure form of iron used for decorative work.

wrung *see* **wring.**

wry *adj.* **1** (of the face) contorted in disgust or disappointment. **2** (of humour) dry, mocking. ▢ **wryly** *adv.*, **wryness** *n.*

  ■ **1** contorted, distorted, twisted. **2** droll, dry, ironic, sarcastic, sardonic.

wych elm elm with broad leaves and spreading branches.

Xx

xenophobia /zénnəfóbiə/ *n.* strong dislike or distrust of foreigners.

Xmas *n.* (*colloq.*) Christmas.

X-ray *n.* photograph or examination made by a kind of electromagnetic radiation (**X-rays**) that can penetrate solids.

● *v.* photograph, examine, or treat by X-rays.

xylophone *n.* musical instrument with flat wooden bars struck with small hammers.

Yy

yacht /yot/ n. **1** light sailing vessel for racing. **2** larger vessel for private pleasure trips. ● v. race or cruise in a yacht. □ **yachtsman** n., **yachtswoman** n.

yak n. long-haired Asian ox.

yam n. **1** tropical climbing plant. **2** its edible tuber. **3** sweet potato.

yank (colloq.) v. pull sharply. ● n. sharp pull.

yap n. shrill bark. ● v. (**yapped**) bark shrilly.

yard¹ n. **1** measure of length, = 3 feet (0.9144 metre). **2** pole slung from a mast to support a sail.

yard² n. piece of enclosed ground, esp. attached to a building.

yardage n. length measured in yards.

yardstick n. standard of comparison.

■ benchmark, criterion, gauge, measure, standard, touchstone.

yarmulke /yaarmǝlkǝ/ n. skullcap worn by Jewish men.

yarn n. **1** any spun thread. **2** (colloq.) tale.

yarrow n. perennial plant with strong-smelling flowers.

yashmak n. veil worn by Muslim women in certain countries.

yaw v. (of a ship or aircraft) fail to hold a straight course. ● n. yawing.

yawl n. a kind of fishing boat or sailing boat.

yawn v. **1** open the mouth wide and draw in breath, as when sleepy or bored. **2** have a wide opening. ● n. act of yawning.

yaws n. tropical skin disease.

yd abbr. yard.

year n. **1** time taken by the earth to orbit the sun (about 365¼ days). **2** period from 1 Jan. to 31 Dec. inclusive. **3** consecutive period of twelve months. **4** (pl.) age.

yearling n. animal between 1 and 2 years old.

yearly adj. happening, published, or payable once a year. ● adv. annually.

yearn v. **yearn for** feel great longing for. □ **yearning** n.

■ crave, desire, hunger for, long for, pine for, thirst for, want, wish for.

yeast n. fungus used to cause fermentation in making beer and wine and as a raising agent.

yell v. & n. shout.

■ v. bawl, bellow, cry, roar, shout.

yellow adj. **1** of the colour of buttercups and ripe lemons. **2** (colloq.) cowardly. ● n. yellow colour or thing. ● v. turn yellow. □ **yellowish** adj.

yellowhammer n. bird of the finch family with a yellow head, neck, and breast.

yelp n. shrill yell or bark. ● v. utter a yelp.

yen¹ n. (pl. **yen**) unit of money in Japan.

yen² n. (colloq.) longing, yearning.

yes adv. & n. expression of agreement or consent, or of reply to a summons etc. □ **yes-man** n. weakly acquiescent person.

yesterday adv. & n. **1** (on) the day before today. **2** (in) the recent past.

yet adv. **1** up to this or that time, still. **2** besides. **3** eventually. **4** even. **5** nevertheless. ● conj. nevertheless, in spite of that.

yeti n. (pl. **-is**) large human-like or bear-like animal said to exist in the Himalayas.

yew n. **1** evergreen tree with dark needle-like leaves. **2** its wood.

Yiddish n. language used by Jews from eastern Europe.

yield v. **1** give as fruit, gain, or result. **2** surrender. **3** allow (victory, right of way, etc.) to another. **4** bend or break under pressure. ● n. amount yielded or produced.

■ v. **1** give, produce, supply; earn, generate, net, pay. **2** capitulate, cave in, concede, give in, submit, succumb, surrender, throw in the towel. **3** abandon, cede, give up, relinquish, surrender.

yielding adj. **1** submissive, compliant. **2** able to bend.

yippee int. exclamation of delight or excitement.

yob n. (sl.) lout, hooligan. □ **yobbish** adj.

yodel v. (**yodelled**) sing with a quickly alternating change of pitch. ● n. yodelling cry. □ **yodeller** n.

yoga n. Hindu system of meditation and self-control.

yoghurt *n.* food made of milk that has been thickened by the action of certain bacteria.

yoke *n.* **1** wooden crosspiece fastened over the necks of two oxen pulling a plough etc. **2** piece of wood shaped to fit a person's shoulders and hold a load slung from each end. **3** top part of a garment. **4** oppression. ● *v.* **1** harness with a yoke. **2** unite.

■ *v.* **2** connect, couple, join, link, tie, unite.

yokel *n.* country fellow, bumpkin.

yolk *n.* yellow inner part of an egg.

yonder *adj.* & *adv.* over there.

yonks *adv.* (*sl.*) a long time.

yore *n.* **of yore** long ago.

Yorkshire pudding baked batter pudding eaten with meat.

you *pron.* **1** person(s) addressed. **2** one, anyone, everyone.

young *adj.* **1** having lived or existed for only a short time. **2** youthful. **3** having little experience. ● *n.* offspring of animals.

■ *adj.* **1,2** immature, juvenile, youthful. **3** callow, green, immature, inexperienced, innocent, naive, unsophisticated. ● *n.* brood, litter, offspring, progeny.

youngster *n.* child.

■ adolescent, boy, child, girl, juvenile, *colloq.* kid, lad, *Sc. & N. Engl.* lass, minor, teenager, youth.

your *adj.*, **yours** *poss.pron.* belonging to you.

yourself *pron.* (*pl.* **yourselves**) emphatic and reflexive form of *you*.

youth *n.* (*pl.* **youths**) **1** state or period of being young. **2** young man. **3** young people. □ **youth club** club with leisure activities for young people. **youth hostel** hostel providing cheap accommodation for young travellers.

■ **1** adolescence, boyhood, childhood, girlhood, minority, puberty, teens. **3** adolescents, children, juveniles, *colloq.* kids, young people.

youthful *adj.* **1** young. **2** having the characteristics of youth. □ **youthfulness** *n.*

yowl *v.* & *n.* howl.

yucca *n.* tall plant with white flowers and spiky leaves.

yule *n.* (in full **yule-tide**) (*old use*) Christmas festival.

yummy *adj.* (*colloq.*) delicious.

yuppie *n.* (*colloq.*) young urban professional person.

Zz

zany *adj.* (**-ier, -iest**) crazily funny. ● *n.* zany person.

zeal *n.* enthusiasm, hearty and persistent effort.

■ ardour, eagerness, enthusiasm, fervour, gusto, passion, zest.

zealot /zéllət/ *n.* fanatic.

■ bigot, extremist, fanatic, maniac.

zealous /zélləss/ *adj.* full of zeal. □ **zealously** *adv.*

■ ardent, eager, earnest, energetic, enthusiastic, fervent, fervid, impassioned, keen, passionate.

zebra *n.* African horse-like animal with black and white stripes. □ **zebra crossing** striped pedestrian crossing.

Zen *n.* form of Buddhism.

zenith *n.* **1** the part of the sky that is directly overhead. **2** highest point.

■ **2** apex, climax, height, peak, pinnacle, summit, top.

zephyr *n.* (*poetic*) soft gentle wind.

zero *n.* (*pl.* **-os**) **1** nought, the figure 0. **2** nil. **3** point marked 0 on a graduated scale, temperature corresponding to this. □ **zero hour** hour at which something is timed to begin. **zero in on 1** aim at or for. **2** focus attention on.

■ **1,2** cipher, nil, nothing, nought. □ **zero in on 1** take aim at, target. **2** concentrate on, fix on, focus on.

zest *n.* **1** keen enjoyment or interest. **2** orange or lemon peel as flavouring. □ **zestful** *adj.*

■ **1** appetite, eagerness, enjoyment, enthusiasm, gusto, interest, relish, zeal.

zigzag *n.* line or course turning right and left alternately at sharp angles. ● *adj.* & *adv.* as or in a zigzag. ● *v.* (**zigzagged**) move in a zigzag.

zinc *n.* bluish-white metal.

zing (*colloq.*) *n.* vigour, zip. ● *v.* move swiftly or shrilly.

Zionism *n.* movement that campaigned for a Jewish homeland in Palestine. □ **Zionist** *n.*

zip *n.* **1** short sharp sound. **2** vigour, liveliness. **3** zip-fastener. ● *v.* (**zipped**) **1** fasten with a zip-fastener. **2** move with vigour or at high speed. □ **zip-fastener** *n.* fastening device with teeth that interlock when brought together by a sliding tab.

zipper *n.* zip-fastener.

zircon *n.* bluish-white gem cut from a translucent mineral.

zirconium *n.* grey metallic element.

zither *n.* stringed instrument played with the fingers.

zodiac *n.* (in astrology) band of the sky divided into twelve equal parts (**signs of the zodiac**) each named from a constellation. □ **zodiacal** *adj.*

zombie *n.* **1** (in voodoo) corpse said to have been revived by witchcraft. **2** (*colloq.*) person who seems to have no mind or will.

zone *n.* area with particular features, purpose, or use. ● *v.* divide into zones. □ **zonal** *adj.*

■ *n.* area, belt, district, quarter, region, sector.

zoo *n.* place where wild animals are kept for exhibition and study.

zoology *n.* study of animals. □ **zoological** *adj.*, **zoologist** *n.*

zoom *v.* **1** move quickly, esp. with a buzzing sound. **2** rise sharply. **3** (in photography) make a distant object appear gradually closer by means of a **zoom lens**.

■ **1** dart, dash, fly, race, rush, shoot, speed, streak, tear, whiz.

zucchini /zookeéni/ *n.* (*pl.* **-i** or **-is**) courgette.

Zulu *n.* member or language of a Bantu people of S. Africa.

zygote *n.* cell formed by the union of two gametes.

Reverse Dictionary Supplement

Compiled by
David Edmonds

A

aardvark *alternative term*: ant bear

Aaron's beard *alternative term*: rose of Sharon

abalone *alternative term*: ear shell

abandoned child *alternative term*: foundling

abandonment *abandonment of claim etc.*: waiver

abbreviation *adjectives*: acrologic, acrological

abele *alternative term*: white poplar

abominable snowman *alternative term*: yeti

about *combining forms*: circum-, peri-

about to happen imminent, impending

about-turn volte-face

above *combining forms*: epi-, super-, supra-, sur-, trans-

absence without permission □ French leave □ *child absent without permission from school etc.*: truant

absolute power or dictatorship autocracy, despotism, totalitarianism

absurdity □ *absurd misrepresentation*: travesty □ *seemingly absurd but in fact true statement*: paradox □ *demonstration of a statement's absurdity by developing it to its logical conclusion*: reductio ad absurdum

academic □ *academic conference*: colloquium □ *academic thesis etc.*: dissertation

accent *Irish accent*: brogue

accepted *generally accepted, believed, etc.*: received

accessory fruit *technical term*: pseudocarp

account book ledger

across *combining forms*: dia-, trans-

acting □ *combining form*: pro- □ *person acting for absent etc. doctor*: locum □ *person acting for absent etc. monarch*: regent

actor □ *sardonic term for actor*: Thespian □ *bad actor*: ham □ *actor who has prepared another actor's role, in order to replace him if necessary*: understudy □ *actor who performs in silence*: mime

acupuncture *technical term*: stylostixis

acupressure *Japanese acupressure therapy*: shiatsu

addition □ *addition to will etc.*: codicil □ *addition to a collection etc.*: accession

additional □ *combining form*: epi- □ *additional charge*: surcharge □ *additional clause to a parliamentary bill, jury's verdict, or other document*: rider

address □ *address used as a collecting-point for mail*: accommodation address □ *address for a letter to be left at a post office until called for*: poste restante □ *African polite form of address to a man*: bwana □ *Indian polite form of address to a man*: sahib □ *Turkish polite form of address to a man*: effendi

adjective □ *technical terms*: modifier, qualifier, determiner, attributive adjective, predicative adjective □ *abusive or disparaging adjective*: epithet

admiration *deserving admiration*: commendable, estimable, laudable, admirable, praiseworthy

admission □ *admission ritual to tribe etc.*: initiation □ *admission ceremony to university etc.*: matriculation □ *right of admission*: entrée, entry

adultery □ *man whose wife has committed adultery*: cuckold □ *person alleged in a divorce case to have committed adultery etc.*: respondent □ *person alleged in a divorce case to have committed adultery with the respondent*: co-respondent

advance *advance payment*: ante

adverb *technical term*: modifier, qualifier

advertisement □ *catchphrase used in an advertisement*: slogan □ *simple tune used in an advertisement*: jingle □ *large board to display advertisements*: hoarding □ *person who writes the text for advertisements*: copywriter □ *stick up unauthorized advertisements*: fly-post

adviser *influential but unofficial adviser(s) to a person in authority*: guru, kitchen cabinet

afraid of *combining form*: -phobe

after *combining forms*: epi-, post-

afterbrain *technical term*: myencephalon

afternoon □ *adjective*: postmeridian □ *afternoon sleep*: siesta □ *afternoon performance*: matinée

again *combining forms*: ana-, re-

against *combining forms*: anti-, contra-, counter-, ob-

agnail *alternative term*: hangnail

agreed □ *agreed by everyone*: unanimous □ *general agreement*: consensus

air □ *combining forms*: aero-, atmo-, pneum(o)- □ *adjective*: pneumatic

airship □ *technical term*: dirigible □ *German military airship used in First World War*: Zeppelin □ *cabin etc. suspended beneath an airship*: gondola

airsock *alternative term*: windsock

airtight *adjective*: hermetic

alcoholism □ *technical term*: dipsomania □ *delusions etc. caused by alcoholism*: delirium tremens

alfalfa *alternative term*: lucerne

all *combining forms*: omni-, pan-, panto-

allergy *medicine used to treat allergies*: antihistamine

alligator pear *alternative term*: avocado

all-in *alternative term*: freestyle

all-knowing *alternative term*: omniscient

all-powerful *alternative term*: omnipotent

all together *alternative terms*: en bloc, en masse

almond □ *adjective*: amygdalate □ *almond paste, used on cakes etc.*: marzipan □ *scald almonds to remove skin*: blanch □ *almond-shaped*: amygdaloid

alone *combining forms*: mon-, mono-, uni- □ *person who lives alone*: recluse

almost *combining form*: quasi-

alpine house chalet

altar □ *altar canopy*: baldacchino, ciborium □ *embroidered etc. hanging in front of altar*: frontal □ *sculpture etc. on wall behind altar*: reredos

altar boy *alternative terms*: acolyte, server

alternative energy *alternative term*: renewable energy

altitude sickness *alternative term*: mountain sickness

amenity bed *alternative term*: pay bed

American eagle *alternative term*: bald eagle

American Indian Amerindian, Native American, Red Indian

among *combining form*: inter-

among other things inter alia

amoretto *alternative term*: cherub, putto

ancient *combining forms*: archaeo-, palaeo-

angle □ *combining form*: -gon □ *instrument to measure or draw angles*: protractor, set square

aniline *technical term*: phenylamine

animal □ *combining forms*: theri-, zoo- □ *animals of a particular region*: fauna □ *animal used to pull carts, ploughs, etc.*: draught animal □ *animal used to carry loads*: beast of burden

ankh *alternative term*: crux ansata

ankle *ankle-covering, worn over shoe etc.*: gaiter, spat

ankle bones *technical terms*: astragalus, talus

annual ring *alternative term*: tree ring

anointing □ *ritual anointing for religious purposes*: unction □ *oil used for ritual anointing*: chrism

answer *witty answer that occurs to one after the opportunity to make it has gone*: esprit de l'escalier

ant □ *adjective*: formic □ *combining form*: myrmec(o)- □ *study of ants*: myrmecology

ant bear *alternative term*: aardvark

antidote *supposed antidote to all poisons*: mithridate

antique *alternative term*: object of virtu

antler □ *flat section of antler*: palm □ *prong of antler*: tine

anus □ *combining form*: proct(o)- □ *surgical construction of an artificial anus*: colostomy □ *muscle closing the anus*: sphincter

anvil *anvil in ear, technical term*: incus

apart *combining form*: dia-

ape *adjective*: simian

Aphrodite *Latin name*: Venus

appeal *litigant who appeals to a higher court*: appellant

appearance *combining form*: -phany

appendix □ *medical term*: vermiform appendix □ *surgical removal of appendix*: appendectomy

appetite *adjective*: orectic

appetizer □ *first course of a meal*: hors d'oeuvre, starter □ *small open sandwich etc. served as appetizer*: canapé □ *alcoholic drink taken before a meal as an appetizer*: aperitif

apple □ *apple brandy*: Calvados

□ *apple of one's eye*: cynosure

approved school *official term*: community home

aquilegia columbine

Arab □ *Arab sailing boat*: dhow □ *Arab covered market*: souk □ *Arab quarter in town*: kasbah □ *Arab prince etc.*: emir, sheik □ *Arab cloak*: burnous, djellaba □ *Arab headdress*: keffiyeh

archer *astrological term*: sagittarius

Ares *Latin name*: Mars

argument *adjective*: eristic

arm □ *adjective*: brachial □ *arm of octopus etc.*: tentacle

armed forces *adjective*: military

armpit □ *adjective*: axillary □ *technical term*: axilla

around *combining forms*: amph-, circum-, epi-, peri-

arrogance *arrogance leading to one's downfall*: hubris

arrow □ *arrow for crossbow*: bolt, quarrel □ *case for arrows*: quiver

art *vulgar or sentimental art*: kitsch

Artemis *Latin name*: Diana

artery *hardening of the arteries, technical term*: arteriosclerosis

artist □ *artist's studio*: atelier □ *artist's complete output*: corpus, oeuvre

ash □ *adjectives*: cinerary, cinerous □ *container for cremated ashes*: urn

assumed name alias

Athena *Latin name*: Minerva

athlete's foot *technical term*: tinea pedis

atom smasher *technical term*: accelerator

attack *medical combining form*: -lepsy

autumn crocus meadow saffron

away *combining forms*: ap-, apo-, ec-, ex-

B

baby □ *set of clothes etc for a new-born baby*: layette □ *discourage a baby from breast-feeding*: wean □ *apparatus providing special environment for a premature baby*: incubator □ *abandoned baby of unknown parentage*: foundling □ *baby secretly substituted for another*: changeling

Bacchus □ *Greek name*: Dionysus □ *female follower of Bacchus*: Maenad □ *staff carried by Bacchus' followers*: thyrsus

back □ *combining forms*: dors-, not- □ *adjective*: dorsal □ *lying on one's back*: supine □ *back of a leaf of paper*: verso

back again *combining forms*: ana-, re-, retr(o)-

backbone □ *adjectives*: spinal, myeloid □ *technical term*: spinal column □ *having a backbone*: vertebrate □ *having no backbone*: invertebrate □ *joint of meat containing a backbone*: chine

back country *alternative terms*: hinterland, outback

bacon-and-eggs *alternative term*: bird's-foot trefoil

bad *combining forms*: caco-, dys-, mal-, mis-

bad breath *technical term*: halitosis

badger's burrow sett

bagpipes □ *pipe on bagpipes on which the tune is played*: chanter □ *pipe on bagpipes used to produce a continuous bass note*: drone

balance □ *adjective*: equilibrious □ *noun*: equilibrium □ *astrological term*: libra

ball *adjective*: globular, spherical

ball and socket joint *technical term*: enarthrosis

ballerina *ballerina's short skirt*: tutu

bandage *bandage etc. bound tight to stop the flow of blood*: tourniquet

barber *adjective*: tonsorial

barking deer muntjac

barrel □ *person who makes barrels*: cooper □ *plank from which barrels are made*: stave □ *metal band compressing a barrel's staves*: hoop □ *open a barrel*: broach

basket □ *basket for picnic food or laundry*: hamper □ *basket for strawberries etc.*: punnet □ *basket for garden vegetables*: trug □ *basket on a bicycle or donkey*: pannier

bastardy *heraldic indication of bastardy*: bend sinister

bath □ *adjective*: balneal □ *hot bath with underwater jets*: jacuzzi™ □ *steam bath*: Turkish bath □ *hot-air bath*: sauna

battle *the ultimate battle, or one causing huge destruction*: Armageddon

beach *adjective*: littoral

beach flea *alternative term*: sandhopper

beads □ *large string of beads used in prayer*: rosary □ *small string of beads used in prayer*: chaplet

beam □ *beam supporting a ceiling etc.*: joist □ *beam supporting joists*: summer □ *beam above a window, door etc.*: lintel □ *horizontal beam dividing a window*: transom □ *vertical beam dividing a window*: mullion

bean *adjective*: leguminous

bean aphid *alternative term*: blackfly

bear *adjective*: ursine

bearer *combining forms*: -fer, -phore, -phorous

bearing *combining form*: -ferous

beast *adjective*: bestial, animal, feral

becoming *combining form*: -escent

bed □ *canvas bed suspended by cords at its ends*: hammock □ *Japanese* *quilted mattress used on the floor as a bed*: futon □ *canopy over a bed*: tester

bedsore *technical term*: decubitus ulcer

bee □ *adjective*: apian □ *female bee*: queen □ *male bee*: drone □ *group of beehives*: apiary

beekeeper *technical term*: apiarist

beetle □ *adjective*: coleopterous □ *sacred beetle of ancient Egypt*: scarab

before □ *combining forms*: ante-, fore-, pre- □ *feeling, when in a new situation, of having experienced it before*: déjà vu

beggar *adjective*: mendicant

begging the question *technical term*: petitio principii

beginning □ *combining form*: -escent □ *adjectives*: embryonic, incipient, inceptive, inchoate, nascent

behaviour *person's distinctive behaviour*: trait, quirk, mannerism, idiosyncrasy

being *combining form*: onto-

bell □ *bell rung to instruct people to return to their houses*: curfew □ *bell rung for the recitation of Roman Catholic prayers commemorating the Incarnation*: angelus □ *art of bell-ringing*: campanology □ *alarm bell*: tocsin

belladonna *alternative term*: deadly nightshade

bellflower *alternative term*: campanula

bell tower campanile

below □ *combining forms*: hypo-, infra-, sub- □ *below the threshold of consciousness*: subliminal

belt □ *belt worn by some army officers, with a strap over the shoulder*: Sam Browne □ *similar belt, carrying cartridges*: bandoleer □ *ornamental belt, worn with men's evening dress*: cummerbund □ *ornamental belt, won by champion boxer*: Lonsdale Belt

bench □ *long wooden bench with high*

back: settle □ *upholstered bench against wall in restaurant etc.*: banquette

bends *technical terms*: caisson disease, decompression sickness

beneath □ *combining forms*: hypo-, infra-, sub- □ *beneath one's dignity*: infra dig

beside *combining form*: para-

best *best of all*: crème de la crème

between *combining form*: inter-

beyond □ *combining forms*: hyper-, meta-, para-, super-, supra-, sur-, trans-, ultra- □ *beyond one's authority*: ultra vires □ *beyond what is necessary*: supererogatory, de trop

bicycle □ *bicycle for two riders, one seated behind the other*: tandem □ *bicycle with one wheel*: monocycle, unicycle □ *early bicycle with one very large and one small wheel*: penny-farthing

big toe *technical term*: hallux

big wheel *alternative term*: Ferris wheel

bile *combining form*: chole-

bilharzia *technical term*: schistosomiasis

billionth *combining form*: nano-

bindweed *alternative term*: convolvulus

biological classification *technical term*: taxonomy

bird □ *combining form*: ornith- □ *adjectives*: avian, ornithic □ *study of birds*: ornithology □ *mythical bird, said to burn itself every 500 years and rise again from the ashes*: phoenix

birth □ *combining form*: -genesis □ *adjective*: natal □ *giving birth by means of eggs*: oviparous □ *giving birth to live offspring*: viviparous □ *giving birth from eggs hatched within the body*: ovoviviparous

bishop □ *adjective*: episcopal □ *bishop's hat*: mitre □ *bishop's staff*: crosier □ *bishop's area of authority*: diocese, see □ *chief bishop*: primate

black □ *combining form*s: melan-, □ *black box in an aircraft, technical term*: flight recorder

blackcurrant syrup cassis

blackhead *technical term*: comedo

black hole □ *technical term in astronomy*: collapsar □ *boundary of black hole*: event horizon

black lung *technical terms*: pneumoconiosis, anthracosis

black magic □ diabolism, the occult □ *black magic as practised in Haiti*: voodoo □ *black magic as practised in the West Indies*: obeah

blackthorn *alternative term*: sloe

bladder □ *combining form*: cyst- □ *adjective*: vesical

blame □ *free from blame*: exculpate, exonerate □ *person made to bear the blame for another's wrongdoing*: scapegoat, whipping boy

bleeder *medical technical term*: haemophiliac

blind gut *technical term*: caecum

blind worm *alternative term*: slow-worm

blink *technical term*: nictitate

blood □ *combining form*s: haem-, haemat- □ *adjective*s: haemal, haematic, sanguineous □ *blood transfer*: transfusion □ *artificial purification of the blood*: haemodialysis

blood clot *combining form*: thromb(o)-

blood feud *alternative term*: vendetta

blood poisoning *technical term*: septicaemia, toxaemia

blood pressure □ *high blood pressure*: hypertension □ *low blood pressure*: hypotension □ *instrument for measuring blood pressure*: sphygmomanometer

blunder *social blunder*: gaffe, faux pas

blush *adjective*: erubescent

body □ *combining form*s: somat-, -some □ *adjective*: corporal □ *entertainer who twists his body into abnormal positions*: contortionist

bogbean *alternative term*: buckbean

bog myrtle *alternative term*: sweet gale

bomb □ *hand-thrown bomb*: grenade □ *crude hand-thrown petrol bomb*: Molotov cocktail □ *bomb containing jellied petrol*: napalm bomb

bone □ *combining form*: osteo- □ *adjective*s: osseous, osteal □ *person who manipulates bones to ease pain etc.*: osteopath □ *brittleness of bones in the old*: osteoporosis □ *bone-house in church etc.*: charnel house

book □ *combining form*: biblio- □ *account-book*: ledger □ *list of books*: bibliography

bookplate *alternative term*: ex-libris

borderland *borderland between England and Wales or Scotland*: marches

born □ *born in wedlock*: legitimate □ *born out of wedlock*: illegitimate, natural

both *combining form*s: ambi-, amphi-, bi-

bottle □ *unmarked bottle for serving wine or water*: carafe, decanter □ *large bottle for acids etc.*: carboy

bow □ *traditional Muslim bow of greeting*: salaam □ *former Chinese bow of greeting*: kowtow

bowls □ *large black ball used in bowls*: wood □ *small white ball used in bowls*: jack □ *French bowls*: boules, pétanque

brain □ *combining form*s: encephal-, cerebr(o)- □ *adjective*: cerebral □ *technical term*: encephalon

branch *adjective*: ramose

breast □ *combining form*: mast- □ *adjective*s: mammary, pectoral

□ *chemical polymer used in breast implants*: silicone □ *surgical removal of a breast*: mastectomy □ *surgical removal of a breast tumour*: lumpectomy

breastbone *technical term*: sternum

breastwork *alternative term*: parapet

breath *combining form*: spiro-

bridge □ *many-arched bridge carrying road or railway*: viaduct □ *many-arched bridge carrying river or canal*: aqueduct □ *raisable bridge in front of castle etc.*: drawbridge

bring □ *bring back to life*: resuscitate, reanimate, revivify □ *bring up (food etc.)*: regurgitate

bristle *adjective*: setaceous

broadcast *simultaneous broadcast of a programme on radio and television*: simulcast

bronze *combining form*: chalco-

brother □ *combining form*: fratr(i)- □ *adjective*: fraternal □ *murder of one's brother*: fratricide

brown coal *technical term*: lignite

brown lung *technical term*: byssinosis

brown owl *alternative term*: tawny owl

building □ *adjectives*: architectural, tectonic □ *sham building erected as a landscape decoration etc.*: folly

bulge *adjectives*: bulbous, tumescent

bull □ *adjective*: taurine □ *astrological term*: taurus

bundle *adjectives*: fascicular, fasciculate

burden *adjective*: onerous

burial *adjectives*: funerary, sepulchral

busy Lizzie *alternative term*: balsam

butter *clarified butter, used in Indian cuisine*: ghee

butterfly *butterfly expert*: lepidopterist

butterfly bush *alternative term*: buddleia

butterfly nut *alternative term*: wing nut

buttock *technical term*: natis (pl. nates)

buyer *let the buyer beware*: caveat emptor

buzzing *buzzing in the ears*: tinnitus

C

cabbage salad coleslaw

cable □ *cable for securing a ship to a pier*: hawser □ *cable for steadying a mast etc.*: guyrope

caisson disease *alternative terms*: decompression sickness, the bends

cake shop *alternative term*: patisserie

calamus *alternative term*: sweet flag

calceolaria *alternative term*: slipperwort

calf love *alternative term*: puppy love

call in or **up** invoke

Cambridge University □ *Cambridge college annual feast*: Commemoration □ *Cambridge college servant*: gyp □ *Cambridge first-degree examination or course*: tripos □ *person gaining first-class honours in the Cambridge mathematical tripos*: wrangler

camel □ *camel with one hump*: dromedary □ *camel with two humps*: Bactrian camel

camellia *alternative term*: japonica

camera □ *crosswise movement of a camera*: pan □ *move a camera towards or away from object*: track □ *bring an object into close or distant camera focus*: zoom

campanula *alternative term*: bell-flower

canal □ *path along side of a canal*: towpath □ *boat used on Venetian canals*: gondola □ *bridge to carry a canal over a valley, road, etc.*: aqueduct

cancer □ *combining form*: carcin- □ *technical term*: carcinoma □ *cancer treatment by drugs*: chemotherapy □ *cancer treatment by X-rays*: radiotherapy

cancerous *technical term*: carcinomatous, malignant

candlestick □ *candlestick attached to wall*: sconce □ *suspended multi-light candlestick*: chandelier □ *Jewish liturgical candlestick*: menorah

cane *cane carried by military officers*: swagger stick

cannibal *adjective*: anthropophagous

car □ *old and inefficient car*: banger, jalopy, rattletrap, tin lizzie □ *car that is modified to give high performance*: hot rod

carbohydrate *combining form*: -ose

career *summary of a person's career and education*: curriculum vitae

carnation *alternative term*: clove pink

carrying *combining forms*: -fer, -ferous, -phore, -phorous

cart *cart used in the French Revolution to convey condemned persons to the guillotine*: tumbril

Carthage *adjective*: Punic

cartilage *combining form*: chondr(o)-

case history *technical term*: anamnesis

cassava *alternative term*: manioc

cast off □ *cast off an old skin (of a snake etc.)*: slough □ *the skin so cast off*: slough □ *action of casting off a skin*: ecdysis

castrate □ *castrated man*: eunuch □ *castrated male singer in baroque opera or the papal chapel*: castrato □ *castrated cockerel*: capon □ *castrated stallion*: gelding □ *castrated ram*: wether

cat *adjective*: feline

Catherine wheel *alternative term*: pinwheel

cattle *adjective*: bovine

cauliflower ear *technical term*: aural hematoma

cause *adjective*: aetiological

causing *combining forms*: -genesis, -genous, -facient, -fic, -otic

cave *combining form*: speleo-

cell *combining forms*: -cyt-, cyto-, -cyte, -blast, -plast

cement □ *cement used between bricks*: pointing □ *cement used between tiles*: grout □ *cement used to cover a floor*: screed □ *cement used to cover a wall*: parget

centre *combining form*: mes-

ceremony □ *admission ceremony*: initiation □ *ceremony to make an award*: investiture □ *ceremony to place a person in office*: induction □ *ceremony to denote a turning-point in a person's life*: rite of passage □ *memorial ceremony*: commemoration

Ceres *Greek name*: Demeter

chalk *adjective*: calcareous

chamber *adjective*: cameral

chance *adjective*: fortuitous

change □ *combining forms*: -trop-, -tropic, tropo- □ *radical change*: quantum leap □ *change sides*: apostatize □ *change of the Eucharistic elements*: transubstantiation □ *person who changes his principles to suit the times*: trimmer, time-server

change of life *technical term*: menopause

charity *adjective*: eleemosynary

Charlemagne *adjectives*: Carolingian, Carlovingian

Charles I and II *adjective*: Caroline

cheek *adjectives*: buccal, malar

cheekbone *technical term*: zygomatic bone

cheese □ *adjective*: caseous □ *sprinkled with grated cheese and browned*: au gratin

chemical *combining forms*: chem-, chemi-, chemo-

cherry brandy *alternative term*: kirsch

cherub *technical terms in art*: amoretto, putto

chess □ *winning position in chess*: checkmate □ *draw in chess*: stalemate □ *opening tactic in chess*: gambit

chest □ *adjectives*: pectoral, thoracic □ *technical term*: thorax

chew *chew the cud, technical term*: ruminate

chicken pox *technical term*: varicella

chickpea □ *chickpea paste*: hummus □ *chickpea rissole*: felafel

child □ *combining form*: paedo-, paedi· □ *child under state guardianship*: ward of court □ *nursery for young children*: crèche

childbirth □ *technical terms*: confinement, parturition □ *adjective*: puerperal □ *medical care and study of those giving birth*: obstetrics □ *doctor providing such care, or person making such study*: obstetrician □ *nurse attending at childbirth*: midwife □ *matter discharged after childbirth*: afterbirth

Chinese □ *combining form*: Sino- □ *Chinese frying pan*: wok □ *Chinese game played with small tiles*: mah-jong □ *Chinese therapy by needles*: acupuncture □ *Chinese official*: mandarin □ *study of Chinese culture etc.*: Sinology □ *Chinese gooseberry*: kiwi fruit □ *Chinese ink*: Indian ink

choice □ *difficult choice*: dilemma □ *choice with no real alternatives*: Hobson's choice □ *choice made to allocate scarce resources*: triage

church □ *adjective*: ecclesiastical □ *church usher*: verger □ *churchwarden's assistant*: sidesman □ *church gravedigger etc.*: sexton □ *forms of church service*: liturgy □ *church assembly*: synod, convocation □ *church court*: consistory □ *church law*: canon □ *expel from a church*: excommunicate □ *grotesque stone figure on the outside of a church*: gargoyle □ *roofed gate in a churchyard, for cover when starting the burial service*: lich gate □ *a tenth of one's income given to the Church*: tithe

cider *strong and rough cider*: scrumpy

circle □ *combining form*: cycl- □ *imagined circle joining the earth's poles*: meridian □ *imagined circle round the earth equidistant from its poles*: equator □ *prehistoric circle of stones etc.*: henge

city □ *adjectives*: civic, urban □ *chief city*: metropolis □ *large city made by the fusion of several towns or cities*: megalopolis

classification □ *classification of plants and animals*: taxonomy □ *classification of plants and animals by genus and species*: Linnaean nomenclature, binomial nomenclature □ *classification according to rank*: hierarchy □ *classification according to shared ancestry*: cladistics

clay □ *clay used for pottery*: argil □ *clay used to make reddish pottery*: terracotta □ *thin clay used to decorate pottery*: slip □ *clay used for bricks and walls*: adobe □ *clay used as a filter*: fuller's earth

clerical collar *alternative term*: dog collar

climb *climb down a sheer cliff etc. using ropes*: abseil

clock □ *clock mechanism*: escapement □ *art or study of clock-making*: horology □ *precise clock*: chronometer

cloth □ *cloth-merchant*: mercer, draper □ *roll of cloth in a shop etc.*: bolt □ *cloth to cover a corpse*: shroud, winding sheet

clothes □ *adjective*: sartorial □ *clothes for a new baby*: layette □ *liturgical clothes*: vestments □ *clothes designer*: couturier

cloud *adjective*: nebulous

clove pink *alternative term*: carnation

club □ *adjectives*: clavate, claviform □ *Irish club*: shillelagh □ *Australian aborigine's club*: waddy □ *African club*: knobkerrie □ *veto someone's proposed membership of a club etc.*: blackball

coal miner's lung *technical terms*: pneumoconiosis, anthracosis

coast □ *adjective*: littoral □ *scenic coast road*: corniche

coat □ *coat with flour, sugar, etc.*: dredge □ *coat with plaster or cement*: render □ *coat with planks etc.*: clad

codes □ *study of codes*: cryptography, cryptology □ *deciphering of codes*: cryptanalysis

coffee □ *strong black coffee made under steam pressure*: espresso □ *coffee topped with frothed milk*: cappuccino □ *stimulant in coffee*: caffeine

coffin □ *stone coffin*: sarcophagus □ *stand for a coffin*: bier, catafalque □ *coffin-carrier*: pallbearer

coin □ *adjective*: nummary □ *face of a coin*: obverse □ *back of a coin*: reverse □ *ridges on a coin's edge*: milling □ *study of coins*: numismatics

cold □ *combining forms*: cryo-, psychro- □ *sleepy etc. state brought on by extreme cold*: hypothermia

cold sore *technical term*: herpes labialis

collarbone *technical term*: clavicle

collection □ *collection of writings etc.*: anthology, miscellany, omnibus □ *collection of miscellaneous items*: farrago, job lot

collective farm □ *collective farm in Israel*: kibbutz □ *collective farm in Russia*: kolkhoz

collector □ *collector of bygones*: antiquary □ *collector of beer mats*: tegestologist □ *collector of books*: bibliophile □ *collector of butterflies and moths*: lepidopterist □ *collector of coins and medals*: numismatist □ *collector of matchboxes*: phillumenist □ *collector of stamps*: philatelist

college □ *college dining room*: hall, refectory □ *college doorkeeper*: porter □ *college doorkeeper's room*: lodge □ *college principal's apartments*: lodgings □ *annual college feast*: gaudy, commemoration

colour □ *adjective*: chromatic □ *range of colours*: spectrum

columbine *alternative term*: aquilegia

combat □ *medieval mock combat between mounted knights*: joust □ *place for such combat*: lists □ *mock sea battle staged in a Roman arena*: naumachia

combatant *person who fought in a Roman arena to entertain*: gladiator

combination *combination of businesses*: conglomerate, consortium, syndicate, cartel

command *adjectives*: mandatory, preceptive

command economy *alternative term*: planned economy

comment *comment made in passing*: obiter dictum

common fraction *alternative term*: simple fraction

Common Market *official name*: European Community

common noun *technical term*: appellative

complaint □ *adjective*: querulous □ *government official investigating complaints*: ombudsman

complete *combining form*: hol(o)-

complex fraction *alternative term*: compound fraction

compliance *minimal compliance with a law etc.*: tokenism

compressed air *adjective*: pneumatic

conclusion □ *conclusion derived by logic*: deduction, inference □ *conclusion inferred from a limited number of instances*: generalization □ *conclusion wrongly inferred*: non sequitur

condition *combining forms*: -osis, -tude

connoisseur □ *connoisseur of food and drink*: gourmet, gastronome □ *connoisseur of antiques etc.*: virtuoso

conqueror *Spanish conqueror of South America*: conquistador

contact *spread by contact*: contagious

contain *combining form*: -fer-

container □ *container for fluids*: reservoir, cistern □ *sealed container for a measured amount of medicine etc.*: ampoule □ *container for molten metal*: crucible □ *container for wine or oil*: ampulla, cruse □ *container for tea*: caddy □ *container for petrol or water*: jerrycan □ *container for relics*: reliquary

continental quilt *alternative term*: duvet

contradiction *apparent contradiction used for rhetorical effect*: oxymoron

contrast *contrast of light and shade in a picture etc.*: chiaroscuro

cooked *lightly cooked*: al dente

cooking *adjective*: culinary

copper □ *combining forms*: chalc-, cupr- □ *adjectives*: cupric, cuprous

copy □ *copying the work of another and claiming it as one's own*: plagiarism, piracy □ *exact genetic copy*: clone

corn on the cob *alternative term*: maize

corpse □ *combining form*: necr- □ *corpse used for medical research*: cadaver □ *dissection of a corpse*: postmortem, autopsy □ *building etc. for storing corpses*: mortuary, morgue □ *deep-freezing of corpses*: cryonics □ *preservation of a corpse by injecting chemicals*: embalmment □ *destruction of a corpse by fire*: cremation □ *burial of a corpse*: interment □ *corpse revived by witchcraft*: zombie

correct *combining form*: ortho-

cot death *technical term*: sudden infant death syndrome

cottage pie *alternative term*: shepherd's pie

cough □ *technical term*: tussis □ *cough medicine*: expectorant

counterpoint *adjective*: contrapuntal

country *adjectives*: rural, pastoral

cowboy □ *South American cowboy*: gaucho □ *cowboy's leather overtrousers*: chaps

coyote *alternative term*: prairie wolf

crab *astrological term*: cancer

crane-fly *alternative term*: daddy-long-legs

criminal □ *criminal who betrays his fellows to the police* (Brit): grass □ *criminal intent, technical term*: mens rea

criticism *person etc. thought to be above criticism*: sacred cow

crow *adjective*: corvine

crown □ *crown worn by a nobleman*: coronet □ *crown worn by the pope*: tiara

crux ansata *alternative term*: ankh

cud-chewer *technical term*: ruminant

culture □ *person having no cultural interests*: philistine □ *study of primitive cultures*: ethnology

cup *Eucharistic cup*: chalice □ *cup used by Christ at the Last Supper*: Holy Grail

Cupid *Greek name*: Eros

curve *adjective*: sinuous

cut *combining forms*: -tom-, -tomy

D

daddy-long-legs *alternative term*: crane-fly

dancer *dancer's close-fitting garment covering the torso, and sometimes the arms and legs*: leotard

danger □ *hidden danger*: pitfall □ *danger inherent in a task etc.*: occupational hazard

dalton *alternative term*: atomic mass unit

daughter *adjective*: filial

dawn *adjective*: auroral

day □ *adjective*: diurnal □ *day in which hours of daylight and darkness are equal*: equinox □ *longest or shortest day*: solstice

day blindness *technical term*: hemeralopia

dayfly *alternative term*: mayfly

Day of Atonement *alternative term*: Yom Kippur

dead □ *service for the dead*: requiem □ *medical examination of a dead person*: post-mortem □ *medical examiner of dead person*: pathologist □ *published history of a dead person*: obituary □ *tomb-inscription*: epitaph □ *summon up the dead by magic*: necromancy

dead end □ *road with no exit at its far end*: cul-de-sac □ *deadlock in argument or discussion*: impasse, stalemate

deadly nightshade *alternative term*: belladonna

dean *adjective*: decanal

death □ *combining form*: mori-, necr-, -thanasia □ *adjectives*: fatal, lethal, mortal □ *causing death*: lethal, fatal, terminal □ *at the point of death*: moribund □ *death inflicted to relieve suffering*: euthanasia □ *death of body tissue*: necrosis, mortification, gangrene □ *stiffness of joints after death*: rigor mortis □ *magistrate investigating cause of person's death*: coroner □ *reminder of death's inevitability*: memento mori □ *after-death*: posthumous

decay □ *combining form*: sapr- □ *decay of teeth or bones*: caries □ *decayed organic matter in the soil*: humus

deceive *easily deceived*: credulous, gullible

decompose *able to be decomposed by bacteria*: biodegradable

decompression sickness *alternative terms*: caisson sickness, the bends

deep *combining form*: bath-

deer □ *adjective*: cervine □ *deer meat*: venison □ *deer's track*: slot

degree □ *degree awarded to a candidate who was ill at the time of the examination*: aegrotat □ *degree conferred when the graduate is elsewhere*: in absentia

delay □ *adjective*: dilatory □ *delay by non-cooperation*: stonewall □ *delay by lengthy speeches*: filibuster

delusion *delusions of being persecuted*: paranoia

Demeter *Latin name*: Ceres

dentist □ *dentist who corrects the position of teeth*: orthodontist □ *dentist's assistant who cleans teeth*: hygienist

descent □ *direct descent*: lineal □ *descent by a parallel line*: collateral □ *of the male line of descent*: patrilineal □ *of the female line of descent*: matrilineal

desire □ *adjective, technical term*: orectic □ *desire another's property*: covet

despair *despair at imagined lack of progress*: accidie

destruction □ *destruction from within*: sabotage □ *destruction of revered objects or ideas*: iconoclasm □ *malicious or purposeless destruction*: vandalism □ *total destruction*: holocaust

detail *subtle detail*: nicety, quibble, niggle, technicality, punctilio

devil □ *adjectives*: diabolic, diabolical □ *worship of the devil*: diabolism

dial □ *conventional watch etc. dial with moving hands*: analog □ *watch etc. dial with changing numerical display*: digital

Diana *Greek name*: Artemis

diaphragm *medical adjective*: phrenic

dictator □ *title of German dictator*: führer □ *title of Italian dictator*: duce □ *title of Spanish dictator*: caudillo □ *small group exercising dictatorial powers*: junta

dictionary □ *small dictionary at the back of a textbook etc.*: glossary, vocabulary □ *dictionary of places etc.*: gazetteer □ *dictionary of synonyms and antonyms*: thesaurus □ *dictionary in which the definition precedes the headword (as here)*: reverse dictionary □ *person who compiles dictionaries*: lexicographer

difference □ *subtle difference*: nuance □ *difference in brightness in a picture*: contrast

different □ *combining forms*: allo-, aniso-, heter-, vari- □ *of many different colours*: motley, pied, variegated □ *having a different content*: heterogeneous

difficult *combining form*: dys-

digestion *adjective*: peptic

dinner *adjective*: prandial

Dionysus □ *Latin name*: Bacchus □ *female follower of Dionysus*: Maenad □ *staff carried by Dionysus' followers*: thyrsus

disappointing *disappointing outcome*: anticlimax, bathos

discharge *combining forms*: -rrhoea, -rrhagia

discontinue *discontinue meetings of a parliament etc. without dissolution*: prorogue

discovery □ *method of discovery by trial and error*: heuristic □ *faculty of making fortunate discoveries*: serendipity

discuss □ *discuss publicly*: ventilate, air □ *avoid discussion*: fence, prevaricate

disease □ *combining forms*: nos(o)-, patho-, -pathy, -osis □ *temporary abatement of a disease*: remission □ *general outbreak of a disease*: epidemic □ *resumption of a disease*: recrudescence □ *study of disease*: pathology □ *group of symptoms indicating a particular disease*: syndrome □ *denoting a disease passed on by physical contact*: contagious □ *denoting a disease often or only found in a certain region or race*: endemic

diseased *combining forms*: dys-, -otic

dislike *person or thing particularly disliked*: bête noire

dismiss *dismiss with dishonour (from the armed forces etc.)*: cashier

disseminated sclerosis *alternative term*: multiple sclerosis

dissolution *combining forms*: lyso-, -lys-, -lysis

distance *combining form*: tel(e)-

distant *ultimately distant spot*: ultima Thule

distillation flask retort

distinction □ *subtle distinction*: nicety, nuance □ *over-subtle distinction*: hair-splitting, quibble

ditch *hidden ditch separating gardens from parkland*: ha-ha

diver □ *diver's compressed-air apparatus*: scuba, aqualung □ *diver's* *enclosed vessel for deep-sea observations*: bathyscaphe □ *painful condition suffered by diver after sudden reduction of pressure*: the bends, caisson disease, decompression sickness

divide *combining form*: -sect

divine *divine for water*: dowse

division □ *combining form*: schiz(o)- □ *division into opposing factions etc.*: polarization, schism

divorce □ *spouse initiating a divorce action*: applicant □ *spouse against whom a divorce action is brought*: respondent □ *person cited in a divorce action as having committed adultery with the partner being sued*: co-respondent □ *court's provisional divorce ruling*: decree nisi □ *court's final divorce ruling*: decree absolute □ *financial support to be given by a former spouse after divorce*: maintenance

doctor □ *doctor in charge of a particular branch of medicine at a hospital*: consultant □ *hospital doctor assisting a consultant*: registrar □ *junior hospital doctor*: houseman □ *family doctor*: general practitioner □ *replacement doctor*: locum

document □ *document containing a sworn statement*: affidavit □ *document recording a contract*: deed □ *document showing ownership of a property*: title deed □ *document recording the transfer of ownership of a property*: conveyance □ *document written entirely by its author*: holograph □ *document signed by its author*: autograph

doer *combining forms*: -tor, -tress, -trix

dog □ *adjective*: canine □ *female dog*: bitch □ *male dog*: dog □ *give birth to dogs*: whelp

dog collar *alternative term*: clerical collar

done *something done and unalterable*: fait accompli

doorman □ *doorman at an hotel or theatre etc.*: commissionaire □ *doorman at a block of flats*: concierge □ *doorman at a college etc.*: porter

downwards *combining form*: cata-

drawing □ *combining form*: -graphy □ *drawing of a machine etc. showing its parts as if separated by an explosion*: exploded view □ *drawing of a machine etc. with parts of its casing removed to show inner workings*: cutaway □ *drawing of a vertical aspect of a building*: elevation □ *drawing of a floor layout of a building*: plan

dream □ *combining form*: oneir(o)- □ *adjective*: oneiric

drift anchor *alternative term*: sea anchor

dripstone *alternative term*: hood mould

drug □ *combining forms*: pharmaco-, narco- □ *drug that sharpens the senses*: stimulant □ *drug that dulls the senses*: narcotic □ *drug producing hallucinations*: psychedelic, hallucinogenic □ *hormonal drug used by athletes to improve performance*: steroid □ *inject a drug directly into a vein*: mainline □ *cure of addiction by complete deprivation of drugs*: cold turkey □ *cure of addiction by progressive deprivation of drugs*: withdrawal

drum □ *pitched bowl-shaped drum*: timpano, kettledrum □ *drum with resonating strings along its underside*: snare drum □ *drum in Latin American band*: bongo □ *jazz drum beaten with the hands*: tom-tom □ *Indian drum*: tabla

dry *combining form*: xero-

dummy *jointed dummy used by artists*: lay figure

dung □ *combining form*: copro- □ *dung-eating, technical term*: coprophagous □ *dung of seabirds sold as a fertilizer*: guano

duty □ *adjective*: deontic □ *beyond the call of duty*: supererogatory

duvet *alternative term*: continental quilt

dwarf □ *dwarf bean*: French bean, kidney bean □ *dwarf plant or tree as cultivated in Japan*: bonsai

E

each other *adjectives*: mutual, reciprocal

eagle *adjective*: aquiline

eagle's nest *alternative term*: eyrie

ear □ *adjective*: aural □ *combining forms*: ot-, oto-

earache *technical term*: otalgia

eardrum *technical terms*: tympanic membrane, tympanum

ear, nose, and throat *technical term*: otorhinolaryngology

ear-shaped *adjective*: auriculate

ear shell *alternative term*: abalone

earth *adjectives*: terrestrial, telluric

earth *combining form*: geo-

earthquake *adjective*: seismic

earwax *technical term*: cerumen

east *adjective*: oriental

Easter *adjective*: Paschal

Easter cactus *alternative term*: Christmas cactus

East Germany *official title*: German Democratic Republic

eating □ *combining forms*: -phag-, -phagous, -vorous □ *eating all foods*: omnivorous □ *meat-eating*: carnivorous □ *plant-eating*: herbivorous □ *eating grasses and cereals*: graminivorous □ *fish-eating*: piscivorous □ *eating corpses*: necrophagous □ *eating dung*: coprophagous

ebonite *alternative term*: vulcanite

ecology *technical term*: bionomics

ecstatic speech *technical term*: glossolalia

eel-shaped *adjective*: anguilliform

efficiency *analysis of workplace efficiency*: operational research

egg *combining forms*: -oo-, -ovi-, -ovo-

egg-shaped *adjective*: oval, ovate, ovoid

eglantine *alternative term*: sweetbrier

Egyptian scripts demotic, hieratic

Egyptian tomb mastaba

eight *combining form*: octo-, octa-

eighty-year-old *alternative term*: octogenarian

election □ *election campaign*: hustings □ *study of voting at elections*: psephology

electric eye *alternative term*: photocell

electric □ *electric shock treatment*: electroconvulsive therapy □ *electric supply failure*: outage

electronic music keyboard moog synthesizer

elements *table of the chemical elements arranged by atomic number*: periodic table

elephant □ *elephant driver*: mahout □ *seat on elephant's back*: howdah

eleven *combining form*: hendeca-

elf □ *alternative term*: pixie □ *in Irish folklore*: leprechaun

emotion *adjective*: affective

emotional release *in response to a moving play, novel, etc.*: catharsis

emotional shock *technical term*: trauma

emperor □ *emperor of Germany*: Kaiser □ *emperor of Japan*: Mikado □ *emperor of Russia*: Tsar

end □ *combining forms*: □ *purpose*: tel-, tele- □ *tip*: acro-

end of the world *theological study of the end of the world*: eschatology

enemy *adjective*: inimical

English *combining form*: Anglo-

English-speaking *adjective*: anglophone

engraving *adjective*: glyptic

enlightenment *theological term in Buddhism or Hinduism*: nirvana

enteric fever *alternative term*: typhoid fever

entertain *adjective*: amusing, diverting

entire *combining forms*: pan-, panto-

environment *combining form*: eco-

enzyme *combining form*: -ase

equal *combining form*: equi-, iso-

equal in size *adjective*: coextensive, coterminous

equivalent return quid pro quo

Eros *Latin name*: Cupid

erosion *projecting wall or fence to limit sea's erosion of coast*: groyne

error in logic fallacy

escape *person who entertains audiences by demonstrating skill in escaping*: escapologist

escort □ *female escort for young woman*: chaperone, duenna □ *male escort for older woman*: gigolo

Eskimo *Eskimo ice-house*: igloo □ *Eskimo sledge-dog*: husky, malamute □ *Eskimo canoe*: kayak □ *Eskimo inhabitant of the islands off Alaska*: Aleut □ *Eskimo inhabitant of North America or Greenland*: Inuit

essential condition prerequisite, sine qua non

estimator *one who estimates the cost of a proposed building etc.*: quantity surveyor

estragon *alternative term*: tarragon

euphrasy *alternative term*: eyebright

evaporating rapidly *technical term*: volatile

event □ *important event*: milestone, landmark □ *possible sequence of events*: scenario

everyday speech *technical terms*: demotic, vernacular

everything *combining forms*: pan-, panto-

evidence *object shown in court as evidence*: exhibit

evil *averting evil*: apotropaic

evil spirit □ *spirit said to take female form to seduce a sleeping man*: succubus □ *spirit said to take male form to seduce a sleeping woman*: incubus □ *person posssessed by an evil spirit*: demoniac □ *drive out evil spirits*: exorcize

examination □ *combining forms*: -opsy, -scopy □ *examination of financial accounts*: audit □ *verbal examination*: oral, viva □ *supervisor of persons taking a written examination*: invigilator □ *medical examination of a corpse*: autopsy, post-mortem □ *medical examination of tissue from a living body*: biopsy □ *theological examination of heretic etc.*: inquisition □ *mental examination of one's thoughts etc.*: introspection

example □ *example to be imitated*: paradigm □ *example cited to justify similar action*: precedent □ *cite as an example*: adduce

exceeding *combining forms*: super-, ultra-

excessive *combining form*: hyper-

excrement □ *combining form*: copro-, scato- □ *eating excrement, technical term*: coprophagous □ *excrement of seabirds sold as a fertilizer*: guano

exempt from blame exonerate

existence *combining form*: onto-

existing situation status quo

expelling *combining form*: -fuge

experience □ *in handling tricky social or business situations etc.*: savoir faire □ *a short but unpleasant interview etc.*: mauvais quart d'heure

experimentation *on living animals*: vivisection

explanation □ *provisional explanation*: hypothesis □ *of a difficult word in a text etc.*: gloss

explosive □ *explosive material in a missile's warhead*: payload □ *explosive charge to propel a rocket etc.*: propellant □ *explosive situation*: powder keg, tinderbox

extermination *extermination of an entire nation or race*: genocide

external *combining form*: exo-

extra *combining form*: super-, ultra-

eye □ *adjectives*: ocular, ophthalmic □ *combining form*: ophthalmo- □ *medical specialist for vision problems*: oculist, optician, optometrist □ *an eye for an eye, legal concept*: lex talionis

eyeblack *alternative term*: mascara

eyebright *alternative term*: euphrasy

eyelash *technical term*: cilium

eyelid *adjective*: palpebral

eyeshadow *alternative term*: kohl

eye socket *technical term*: orbit

eyestrain *technical term*: asthenopia

eye tooth *technical term*: canine

F

face □ *combining form*: -hedron □ *with an unexpressive face*: deadpan, inscrutable, poker-faced

facing □ *combining forms*: -ward, -wards □ *lying facing downwards*: prone □ *lying facing upwards*: supine

fact *an unalterable fact*: fait accompli

false *combining form*: pseud(o)-

false fruit *technical term*: pseudocarp

family *narrowest family unit, consisting of a couple and their children only*: nuclear family

family tree *alternative terms*: genealogy, pedigree

fantasy □ *fantasy world*: Cockaigne, cloud-cuckoo-land, Utopia □ *person living in a fantasy world*: Walter Mitty

Far East *adjective*: oriental

far sight *technical terms*: hyperopia, hypermetropia, presbyopia

farming *adjective*: agr-

fast *combining form*: tach-

fat □ *combining forms*: lipo-, seb(o)-, steat(o)- □ *adjective*: sebaceous

fate □ *fate in Hindu and Buddhist thought*: karma □ *fate in Islamic thought*: kismet

father □ *combining form*: patr(i)- □ *adjective*: paternal □ *murder of one's father*: patricide

fault □ *fault-finding*: captious, carping, niggling □ *minor personal fault*: foible, peccadillo

faulty *combining form*: dys-

Faunus *Greek name*: Pan

favouritism *favouritism towards one's relatives*: nepotism

fear □ *combining form*: -phobia □ *fear of confined spaces*: claustrophobia □ *fear of foreigners*: xenophobia □ *fear of public places*: agoraphobia □ *fear of homosexuals*: homophobia □ *fear of heights*: acrophobia □ *fear of water*: hydrophobia

feast *adjective*: festal

Feast of Lights *alternative term*: Hannukkah

Feast of Tabernacles *alternative term*: Sukkoth

Feast of Weeks *alternative term*: Shavuoth

fee □ *initial fee paid to a barrister*: retainer □ *further fee paid to a barrister*: refresher □ *fee paid to cover expenses etc. of someone doing 'unpaid' work*: honorarium □ *percentage fee on sales made etc.*: commission □ *fee paid to an author etc. for copies sold or performances given*: royalty

feeding *combining forms*: troph-, -trophy

feelings □ *combining form*: -pathy □ *ability to share another's feelings*: empathy

female *combining forms*: gyno-, -gyn-, -ess, -tress, -trix

ferroconcrete *alternative term*: reinforced concrete

fever *technical term*: pyrexia

field *adjective*: campestral

film □ *combining form*: cine- □ *film expert or enthusiast*: cineaste

filtration *filtration process for blood of patient suffering kidney failure*: dialysis

final □ *final part of a speech*: peroration □ *final part of a play*: denouement, epilogue □ *final part of a piece of music*: coda

finger □ *combining form*: dactyl(o)- □ *adjective*: digital

fingerprint *technical term*: dactylogram

fire □ *combining form*: pyro- □ *fire for burning a corpse*: pyre □ *person starting fires for malicious purposes*: arsonist □ *mythical creature living in fire*: salamander

fireplace □ *grid at front of fireplace to keep in burning material*: fender □ *shelf along side of fireplace for kettle etc.*: hob □ *stand for kettle etc. at front of fireplace*: trivet □ *stand to support logs in a fireplace*: andiron, firedog □ *metal plate at the back of a fireplace*: reredos

first □ *combining forms*: proto-, ur- □ *first example*: prototype □ *first appearance of a performer*: debut □ *first performance*: premiere □ *first-year student at a university*: freshman

fish □ *combining forms*: ichthy(o)-, pisc- □ *adjective*: piscine □ *fish eggs*: spawn □ *fish sperm*: milt

fishes *astrological term*: pisces

fishing □ *adjective*: piscatorial □ *catch fish with one's hands*: guddle

five □ *combining forms*: pent-, quin-, quinque- □ *five-sided figure*: pentagon □ *five-pointed star*: pentagram □ *group of five*: pentad

flag *adjective*: vexillary

flat □ *top-floor flat*: penthouse □ *flat on two or more floors, with its own outside door*: maisonette □ *flat kept for occasional use*: pied-à-terre □ *large building divided into flats*: tenement

fleet □ *fleet of warships*: armada □ *fleet of merchant ships*: argosy □ *fleet of small ships*: flotilla

flesh □ *combining forms*: carn-, sarc(o)- □ *adjective*: carnal

float □ *float attached to side of a canoe etc*: outrigger □ *float supporting a bridge*: pontoon □ *float used to raise sunken ships*: caisson

flood □ *adjective*: diluvial □ *sudden flood*: flash flood □ *before the (biblical) Flood*: antediluvian

floor □ *floor of a building having principal reception rooms etc.*: piano nobile □ *floor set in a building between main floors*: mezzanine □ *floor of wood blocks*: parquet

flour *adjective*: farinaceous

flow *combining forms*: rheo-, -rrhoea, -rrhagia

flower □ *combining forms*: antho-, flor-, anthous □ *adjective*: floral □ *sweet liquid collected by bees from flowers*: nectar □ *fine dust collected by bees from flowers*: pollen □ *flower that keeps its colour when dried*: immortelle

fluid □ *body fluid in early medicine*: humour □ *body fluid surrounding embryo*: amniotic fluid □ *body fluid around joints*: sinovia

fodder □ *fodder of fermented grass etc.*: silage □ *tall fodder plant with yellow flowers*: rape

fond *combining forms*: phil(o)-, -phile

food □ *adjective*: alimentary □ *food for the gods*: ambrosia □ *food for pigs*: swill □ *food for horses*: tack □ *season-*

ing for food: condiment □ *food additive used in Chinese cuisine*: monosodium glutamate □ *shop selling foreign foods*: delicatessen □ *denoting food prepared in accordance with Jewish law*: kosher □ *denoting food unacceptable to Jewish law*: tref □ *food poisoning*: botulism, salmonellosis

fool's gold *technical term*: iron pyrites

foot □ *combining forms*: pedi-, -pod, -pode □ *wart growing on feet*: verruca □ *specialist treating hands and feet*: chiropodist

forehead *adjectives*: frontal

foreign □ *combining form*: xeno- □ *foreign girl who does domestic work in return for keep and English lessons*: au pair

foreskin □ *technical term*: prepuce □ *removal of the foreskin*: circumcision

forest *adjective*: sylvan

form *combining forms*: morpho-, -morphic

formal logic *alternative term*: symbolic logic

fortification □ *fortification of wooden stakes*: palisade, stockade □ *concrete fortification, with loopholes for guns etc.*: blockhouse □ *underground fortified shelter*: bunker

fortune telling □ *fortune telling from lines on the hand*: palmistry □ *fortune telling from the stars*: astrology □ *fortune telling from playing cards*: cartomancy □ *fortune telling from dreams*: oneiromancy □ *fortune telling by drawing lots*: sortilege

found object *alternative term*: objet trouvé

four □ *combining forms*: quadr-, tetr- □ *four children born at a birth*: quadruplets □ *four-legged animal*: quadruped □ *four-line verse stanza*: quatrain □ *four-track stereophonic sound*: quadraphony

fowl □ *adjective*: gallinaceous □ *cas-*

trated fowl: capon □ *fowl's edible offal*: giblets

fox □ *adjective*: vulpine □ *female fox*: vixen □ *male fox*: dog □ *fox's lair*: earth □ *fox's tail*: brush

fraction □ *number placed above the line in a fraction*: numerator □ *number placed below the line in a fraction*: denominator □ *fraction equal to less than one*: proper fraction □ *fraction equal to more than one*: improper fraction

France *combining forms*: Franco-, Gallo-

freeze *combining form*: cryo-

French bean *alternative terms*: dwarf bean, haricot, kidney bean

friction *combining form*: tribo-

frog *adjective*: batrachian

front □ *front of a building*: façade □ *front of an army*: vanguard □ *front of a leaf of paper*: recto

fruit *combining forms*: fruct-, -carp

fruit fly *alternative term*: drosophila

fruit sugar *technical term*: fructose

fungus □ *combining forms*: myco-, -mycete □ *edible fungus growing underground*: truffle

furnace □ *furnace for steel*: blast furnace □ *furnace for pottery*: kiln □ *furnace for rubbish*: incinerator

fusion bomb *alternative term*: thermonuclear bomb

gall *combining form*: chole-

gallery *exterior gallery on an upper floor*: loggia

game *game killed during a day's shoot etc.*: bag

gangrene *technical terms*: necrosis, mortification

garden □ *formal garden with paths between small beds etc.*: knot garden

□ *garden pavilion with view*: gazebo
□ *garden shelter*: alcove, arbour, bower
□ *ornamental hedge-clipping in a garden*: topiary

garlic □ *adjective*: alliaceous
□ *garlic mayonnaise*: aioli

gas □ *combining forms*: aero-, pneum(o)- □ *laboratory gas burner*: Bunsen burner □ *gas in the digestive tract*: flatulence □ *foul-smelling gas*: mephitis, effluvium □ *gas formerly thought to fill all space*: ether

gas mask *technical term*: respirator

gate □ *revolving gate*: turnstile □ *fortified gate*: barbican □ *back gate*: postern

gear □ *gear system causing the parts to revolve at the same speed before engagement*: synchromesh □ *system changing cycle gears by moving the chain*: derailleur

general assistant factotum

geranium *alternative term*: pelargonium

germ □ *technical term*: pathogen □ *blood protein counteracting germs*: antibody □ *germ provoking the production of antibodies*: antigen

German measles *technical term*: rubella

German shepherd dog *alternative term*: alsatian

germ warfare *alternative term*: biological warfare

ghost □ *ghostly double of a living person*: doppelgänger □ *ghost that throws things about*: poltergeist □ *ghostly emanation from a medium during a seance*: ectoplasm

gift of tongues *technical term*: glossolalia

give *person who gives*: donor

glandular fever *technical term*: infectious mononucleosis

Glasgow *adjective*: Glaswegian

glass □ *combining form*: vitr- □ *adjectives*: vitreous

glass fibre *alternative term*: optical fibre

glue-sniffing *technical term*: solvent abuse

gnu *alternative term*: wildebeest

goat □ *adjectives*: caprine, hircine □ *male goat*: billy goat □ *female goat*: nanny goat □ *fabric made from goat hair*: mohair □ *astrological term*: capricorn

god □ *combining form*: the- □ *adjective*: divine □ *belief in a single god*: monotheism □ *belief in many gods*: polytheism □ *belief that God is identical with the created universe*: pantheism □ *drink of the gods*: nectar □ *food of the gods*: ambrosia □ *blood of the gods*: ichor □ *woodland god*: satyr, faun □ *creator-god*: demiurge □ *god's appearance to men*: epiphany, theophany □ *of a god taking animal form*: zoomorphic □ *of a god taking human form*: anthropomorphic □ *belief that there can be no sure evidence of a god's existence*: agnosticism □ *belief that there is no god*: atheism

gold □ *combining forms*: auri-, chryso-, -chrys- □ *gold in bulk*: bullion □ *gold bar*: ingot □ *lump of natural gold*: nugget □ *search for natural gold*: prospect □ *stone said to turn base metals to gold*: philosopher's stone

goose *adjective*: anserine □ *group of geese*: gaggle □ *group of geese flying in formation*: skein

goose-flesh *technical term*: horripilation

government □ *combining forms*: -archy, -cracy, -nomy □ *moral authority given to a government by its election majority*: mandate □ *transfer of governmental power to regional authorities*: devolution □ *organization that is independent but government-sponsored*: quango

gradual □ *gradual development*: evolution □ *gradual absorption*: osmosis

grain □ *combining form*: grani- □ *grain-eating*: granivorous □ *grain fungus*: ergot □ *funnel for dispensing grain*: hopper □ *gather leftover grain from a harvest field*: glean □ *separate chaff from grain by the wind*: winnow □ *separate chaff from grain by beating*: thresh □ *storage tower or pit for threshed grain*: silo □ *storehouse for threshed grain*: granary

grammar □ *mistake in grammar*: solecism □ *mistake in grammar made by inappropriate application of a rule*: hypercorrection

grape □ *grape harvest*: vintage □ *fermenting grape juice*: must □ *remains of grapes after pressing*: marc

grandfather clock *alternative term*: longcase clock

grass □ *adjectives*: graminaceous, gramineous □ *grass-eating*: graminivorous □ *circle of darker grass in lawn etc.*: fairy ring □ *clump of grass dislodged by horse's hoof etc.*: divot □ *synthetic grass surface used on sports fields*: AstroTurf™

grassland □ *extensive grassland in Russia*: steppe □ *extensive grassland in North America*: prairie □ *extensive grassland in South America*: pampas □ *extensive grassland in warm regions*: savannah □ *extensive grassland in South Africa*: veldt

grave □ *adjective*: sepulchral □ *prehistoric grave mound*: barrow, tumulus

Greek □ *combining form*: Graeco-, Hellen- □ *adjective*: Hellenic □ *Greek restaurant*: taverna □ *Greek resin-flavoured wine*: retsina □ *Greek mandolin*: bouzouki □ *white skirt in Greek men's traditional dress*: fustanella □ *citadel of ancient Greek city*: acropolis

green □ *combining forms*: chlor(o)- □ *adjective*: verdant □ *green pepper*: capsicum □ *green pigment in plants*: chlorophyll □ *green crystallized crust forming on exposed copper, brass, etc.*: verdigris

groin *adjective*: inguinal

groove *adjective*: sulcate

group □ *group of people of equal social status*: peer group □ *group of people living together and sharing all property*: commune □ *group of people pressing a common interest*: lobby □ *group of actors etc.*: troupe □ *group of businesses*: consortium, syndicate, cartel

guard *adjective*: custodial

guardian *adjective*: tutelary

guide □ *moral guide*: mentor, guru □ *tourists' guide*: cicerone

guillotine □ *cart carrying prisoners to the guillotine*: tumbrel □ *woman knitting by the guillotine*: tricoteuse

guilt □ *produce arguments or evidence to lessen someone's guilt*: extenuate, mitigate □ *feeling of guilt*: compunction

guitar *small disc used to pluck a guitar's strings*: plectrum

gullet *technical term*: oesophagus

gum □ *technical term*: gingiva □ *gum disease caused by plaque, with bleeding etc.*: gingivitis

gunfire □ *simultaneous fire from all the guns on one side of a ship*: broadside □ *rapid burst of gunfire*: fusillade, volley

gunman *hidden gunman*: sniper

guru *Hindu guru*: maharishi

gut *adjective*: visceral

gypsy □ *gypsy person, or their language*: Romany □ *Romany word for 'man'*: rom □ *Romany word for a non-gypsy*: gorgio □ *Italian gypsy*: Zingaro □ *Hungarian gypsy*: tzigane □ *itinerant tinker or scrap-metal dealer*: didicoi

H

habit □ *strange habit*: eccentricity, idiosyncrasy, mannerism □ *of a person possessed by compulsive habits*: inveterate, pathological

hair □ *combining forms*: pil-, -trich- □ *adjective*: capillary □ *bristling of the hair in fear etc.*: goose-flesh □ *removal of unwanted hair*: depilation □ *having tightly curled hair*: ulotrichan □ *study of hair and its diseases*: trichology

hairdressing *adjective*: tonsorial

hair oil brilliantine, pomade, Macassar oil

half □ *combining forms*: demi-, hemi-, semi- □ *half-board*: demi-pension □ *half-line of verse*: hemistich

hallucination □ *producing or produced by hallucinations*: psychedelic □ *hallucinations etc. suffered by alcoholics*: delirium tremens

hammer □ *hammer used by auctioneers etc.*: gavel □ *diagnostic hammer used by doctors*: plexor □ *flat part of a hammer head, used for striking*: face □ *rounded or wedge-shaped part of a hammer head, opposite to the face*: peen □ *V-shaped device for removing nails, set opposite to the face*: claw □ *technical term for a bone in the ear*: malleus

hand □ *combining forms*: chiro-, manu- □ *adjective*: manual, palmate □ *able to use both hands equally well*: ambidextrous

hand over *hand over a person to a foreign power for trial etc.*: extradite

handle □ *handle of a sword or knife*: haft, hilt □ *handle of an axe or hammer*: helve □ *handle of a whip or fishing rod*: stock

handwriting *psychological study of handwriting*: graphology

hangnail *alternative term*: agnail

hard *combining form*: scler(o)-

hard coal *alternative term*: anthracite

hardening of the arteries *technical term*: arteriosclerosis

hare □ *adjective*: leporine □ *female hare*: doe □ *male hare*: buck □ *young hare*: leveret □ *hare-hunting*: coursing

haricot *alternative term*: French bean

hat □ *cowboy's hat*: stetson □ *Mexican hat*: sombrero □ *academic hat*: square, mortarboard, bonnet □ *soft cloth hat with brims at front and back, and earflaps that may be tied up*: deerstalker □ *hat of stiffened straw with a low flat crown*: boater □ *sailor's oilskin hat*: sou'wester

hate *combining forms*: mis-, -phobe, -phobia, -phobic

hatred □ *hatred of men*: misandry □ *hatred of women*: misogyny □ *hatred of people*: misanthropy

head *combining forms*: cephalo-, -cephal-, -capit-

headache *severe headache with nausea and impaired vision*: migraine

headband □ *Arab's headband*: agal □ *Jew's liturgical headband*: frontlet

health *person obsessed by his own health*: hypochondriac, valetudinarian

hearing □ *combining form*: audi- □ *adjectives*: acoustic, auditory

heart □ *combining form*: cardi- □ *adjective*: cardiac □ *heart specialist*: cardiologist

heart attack *technical term*: coronary thrombosis, myocardial infarction

heartbeat □ *electrically traced record of a heartbeat*: electrocardiogram □ *irregular heartbeat*: arrhythmia □ *abnormally slow heartbeat*: bradycardia □ *abnormally fast heartbeat*: tachycardia

heat □ *combining forms*: cal(o)-, therm(o)-, -thermy □ *adjectives*:

thermal, caloric □ *heat milk etc. to increase shelf-life*: pasteurize □ *heat spiced wine or ale*: mull

heating □ *underfloor heating system in Roman houses*: hypocaust □ *progressive heating of the earth's atmosphere due to breaches in ozone layer*: global warming, greenhouse effect

hedge-trimming *ornamental hedge-trimming*: topiary

hedgehog *adjective*: erinaceous

heel *combining form*: -calc-

heel bone *technical term*: calcaneus

height □ *combining forms*: acro-, alt-, hyps- □ *dizziness caused by heights etc.*: vertigo □ *fear of heights*: acrophobia □ *instrument measuring an aircraft's height*: altimeter

heir *adjective*: hereditary

Hermes □ *Latin name*: Mercury □ *Hermes' snake-twined staff*: caduceus

hermit □ *adjective*: eremitic □ *hermit living on the top of a pillar*: stylite

hiccup *technical term*: singultus

hidden □ *combining form*: crypt(o)- □ *hidden store*: cache, stash

higher *combining forms*: super-, supra-

Hindu □ *Hindu teacher*: guru, maharishi, pandit □ *Hindu ascetic*: fakir □ *Hindu state of blessedness*: nirvana □ *Hindu erotic classic*: Karma Sutra □ *Hindu seclusion of women*: purdah □ *Hindu widow's self-cremation*: suttee □ *Hindu meditation technique poupular in the West*: Transcendental Meditation

hip □ *hip bone*: innominate bone, coxa □ *hip joint*: coxa □ *hip socket for thigh bone*: acetabulum

hives *technical term*: urticaria

holy *combining forms*: hagi(o)-, hier(o)-

holy war □ *by Christians to recover the Holy Land*: crusade □ *by Muslims against infidels*: jihad

honey □ *alcoholic drink made from honey*: mead □ *sweetmeat made of honey and sesame flour*: halva □ *liquid collected by bees from flowers to make honey*: nectar

hook □ *hooked pole used to land large fish etc.*: gaff □ *hooked device on a rope thrown to gain purchase on the top of a wall etc.*: grappling iron, grapnel

hoop *hoop attached to a skirt to support it*: farthingale

hormone □ *hormone secreted when under stress*: adrenaline □ *hormone regulating blood sugar levels*: insulin □ *hormone used by athletes to improve performance*: steroid □ *hormone used to treat allergies and arthritis*: cortisone □ *hormone governing female secondary sexual characteristics*: oestrogen □ *hormones governing male secondary sexual characteristics*: androgen, testosterone

horn □ *combining form*: kerat(o)- □ *adjective*: corneous □ *horn of plenty*: cornucopia

horse □ *combining forms*: equi-, hippo- □ *adjective*: equine □ *small prehistoric horse*: eohippus □ *female horse*: mare □ *young female horse*: filly □ *castrated male horse*: gelding □ *uncastrated male horse*: stallion, entire horse □ *young male horse*: colt □ *thoroughbred horses*: bloodstock □ *wild American horse*: mustang, bronco □ *person who rides horses*: equestrian □ *person who shoes horses*: farrier □ *horse-slaughterer*: knacker

hospital *hospital for the terminally ill*: hospice

hot water □ *natural hot spring*: geyser □ *pan of hot water above which food may be cooked or kept warm*: bain-marie

house □ *Eskimo's house made of ice blocks*: igloo □ *Russian summer residence*: dacha □ *traditional wooden* *house in Switzerland*: chalet □ *traditional conical stone house of southern Italy*: trullo □ *children's play-house*: Wendy house

housemaid's knee *technical term*: prepatellar bursitis

huge *combining forms*: mega-, megalo-, macro-

human □ *combining form*: -anthrop(o)- □ *attribution of human form or behaviour to gods, animals, or inanimate objects*: anthropomorphism □ *assumption of human form by a god, concept, etc.*: embodiment, incarnation □ *attribution of human emotions etc. to inanimate objects*: pathetic fallacy

hundred *combining forms*: cent-, hecto-

Hungarian □ *Hungarian cavalryman*: hussar □ *Hungarian gypsy*: tzigane □ *Hungarian stew*: goulash □ *Hungarian person or his language*: Magyar

hunting □ *adjective*: venatic □ *animal etc. pursued by hunters*: quarry □ *time of year when hunting etc. is permitted*: open season □ *artificial scent used in sham hunts*: drag

husband □ *monarch's husband*: consort □ *husband of unfaithful wife*: cuckold □ *servility of a husband towards his wife*: uxoriousness □ *custom or state of having only one husband at a time*: monandry □ *custom or state of having several husbands at a time*: polyandry

hymn □ *hymn sung as the clergy etc. enter the church for a service*: introit □ *hymn sung during a procession*: processional □ *hymn sung as the clergy etc. leave the church after a service*: recessional □ *Lutheran hymn or its music*: chorale

I

ice □ *adjective*: glacial □ *river of ice*: glacier □ *floating sheet of ice*: floe □ *large floating block of ice*: iceberg □ *area of water crowded with floating blocks of ice*: pack ice □ *thin transparent layer of ice on road etc.*: black ice □ *drink poured over crushed ice*: frappé □ *water ice made from fruit etc.*: sorbet □ *Italian ice cream of various flavours with glacé fruits etc.*: cassata

identical □ *identical twins, technical term*: monozygotic twins □ *genetically identical organism*: clone

illegal □ *official's illegal use of powers or funds entrusted to him*: malversation □ *alcohol distilled illegally in Ireland*: poteen □ *alcohol distilled illegally in the USA*: moonshine

illegitimacy *heraldic indication of illegitimacy*: bar sinister

illness □ *feign illness to avoid work etc.*: malinger □ *denoting a physical illness that has a psychological cause*: psychosomatic □ *denoting an illness caused by medical intervention*: iatrogenic

illusion □ *illusion seen in a desert*: mirage □ *illusion seen on mountain peaks*: Brocken spectre □ *illusionist technique of mural painting*: trompe l'oeil

illustration □ *illustration at the front of a book*: frontispiece □ *illustration used to fill the page at the end of a chapter etc.*: tailpiece □ *illustration of a machine etc. showing the parts separated for clarity*: exploded view □ *illustration of a machine etc. showing its casing cut away*: cutaway

immature *immature works of an artist etc.*: juvenilia

immigrant *immigrant worker in Germany*: Gastarbeiter

immunity □ *immunity offered to previous offenders*: amnesty □ *immun-*

ity from local laws enjoyed by foreign diplomats: extraterritoriality

imprisonment □ *wartime imprisonment of enemy aliens*: internment □ *imprisonment with forced labour*: penal servitude □ *writ to assess the legality of someone's imprisonment*: habeas corpus

impurities *add impurities to food or drink*: adulterate

in *combining forms*: endo-, entro-, intra-, intro-

incidental *incidental remark in a legal judgement*: obiter dictum

income □ *person's income before taxes are deducted*: gross income □ *person's income after taxes have been deducted*: net income, disposable income □ *adequate income*: competence

inconsistency *statement containing two apparently inconsistent elements*: paradox, oxymoron

Indian □ *Indian ruler*: maharaja, raja, nawab, nizam □ *Indian soldier*: sepoy □ *Indian elephant-driver*: mahout □ *Indian fan*: punkah □ *Indian corn, alternative term*: maize □ *flight of steps leading down to a river in India*: ghat □ *Indian ink, alternative term*: Chinese ink

indigestion □ *technical term*: dyspepsia □ *bloated feeling resulting from indigestion*: flatulence

individual *combining form*: idio-

industrial disputes □ *use of a third party to negotiate a settlement*: conciliation □ *recourse to a third party who adjudicates a settlement*: arbitration

inferior *combining forms*: infra-, sub-

inflammation *medical combining form*: -itis

informer *criminal supplying information to the police*: stool-pigeon, nark, grass

inhabitant *original inhabitant*: aboriginal, autochthon

inscription *study of ancient inscriptions*: epigraphy

insect □ *combining form*: entomo- □ *study of insects*: entomology □ *insect in immature grub-like form*: larva □ *insect in inactive stage between larva and adult*: pupa, chrysalis □ *larva of certain insects which develops directly into the adult stage*: nymph □ *transformation of an insect between these stages*: metamorphosis □ *mature insect*: imago □ *insect's feeding tube*: proboscis □ *insect excrement*: frass □ *insect of greenfly or blackfly type, living on plant juices*: aphid

interest □ *interest paid on capital only*: simple interest □ *interest paid on capital and on accumulated interest of previous periods*: compound interest □ *lowest available rate of interest on a bank loan*: prime rate

interval □ *interval between two successive reigns etc.*: interregnum □ *music etc. performed in a theatre interval*: intermezzo, entr'acte

intestines □ *combining form*: enter(o)- □ *pig's intestines prepared as food*: chitterlings □ *pain in the intestines*: colic

into *combining form*: intro-

introductory *combining form*: fore-

invention *document granting an inventor sole right to the exploitation of his work*: patent

investment □ *list of investments made*: portfolio □ *certificate assuring ownership of investments*: securities □ *company holding a wide and changing share portfolio and inviting clients to invest in the whole*: unit trust □ *person living off dividends from investments etc.*: rentier

inward *combining form*: intro-

ion □ *ion having a negative charge*: anion □ *ion having a positive charge*: cation

Ireland □ *adjective*: Hibernian □ *Celtic language of Ireland*: Erse □ *citizen of Ireland, especially if an Erse-speaker*: Gael □ *area of Ireland where Erse is spoken*: Gaeltacht □ *citizen of Northern Ireland who wishes to retain political links with the UK*: Unionist, Loyalist □ *citizen of Ireland who seeks the political unification of the island*: Nationalist

Irish □ *Irish social gathering*: ceilidh □ *Irish accent*: brogue □ *Irish cudgel*: shillelagh □ *Irish police force*: Garda

iron □ *combining forms*: ferro-, ferri-, sider(o)- □ *adjectives*: ferrous □ *block of crude cast iron*: pig

irrigation □ *irrigation device of a bucket on a pole*: shadouf □ *irrigation device of buckets on a wheel*: Noria

island □ *adjective*: insular □ *island on a lake or river*: ait, holm, eyot □ *group of islands*: archipelago □ *low coral island*: cay, key

Israeli □ *Israeli nationalist*: Zionist □ *Israeli collective farm*: kibbutz □ *Isaeli smallholders' cooperative*: moshav

itch □ *technical term*: pruritus □ *itchy feeling as if of ants crawling over the skin*: formication

J

Jamaican *Jaimaican religion regarding Haile Selassie as God*: Rastafarianism

Japanese □ *Japanese emperor*: mikado □ *Japanese art of paper-folding*: origami □ *Japanese wrestling*: sumo □ *Japanese warrior*: samurai □ *ritual suicide required of dishonoured Japanese warrior etc.*: hara-kiri □ *Japanese art of self-defence*: judo, jujitsu, aikido □ *Japanese sport of fencing with wooden swords*: kendo □ *Japanese suicide pilot*: kamikaze □ *Japanese prostitute*: geisha □ *Japanese alcoholic drink made from rice*: sake □ *Japanese dwarf tree*: bonsai □ *Japanese puppet theatre*: bunraku □ *Japanese traditional theatre*: Noh □ *Japanese popular theatre*: kabuki □ *Japanese poem of 17 syllables*: haiku

japonica *alternative term*: camellia

jar *storage jar in classical times*: amphora

jaundice □ *technical term*: icterus □ *liver disease producing jaundice*: hepatitis

Java *Javan percussion orchestra*: gamelan

jaw □ *combining forms*: -gnath-, -gnathic □ *adjective*: gnathic □ *paralysis of the jaws*: lockjaw, trismus

jelly □ *jelly made from meat or fish stock*: aspic □ *dish served in aspic*: galantine

jester □ *jester's cap*: coxcomb □ *jester's baton*: bauble □ *jester's parti-coloured suit*: motley

Jew □ *combining form*: Judaeo- □ *food etc. that conforms to Jewish dietary regulations*: kosher □ *food etc. that does not conform to Jewish dietary regulations*: tref □ *Jewish unleavened bread*: matzo □ *Jewish seven-branched candlestick*: menorah □ *Orthodox Jew's skullcap*: yarmulke □ *Jewish girl's coming of age ceremony*: bat mitzvah □ *Jewish boy's coming of age ceremony*: bar mitzvah □ *language used by Jews of central and eastern Europe*: Yiddish □ *language used by some mediterranean Jews*: Ladino □ *Jewish quarter in a city*: ghetto □ *organized massacre of Jews in 19th-c. Russia etc.*: pogrom □ *Hitler's programme for the extermination of European Jews*: Holocaust □ *Jewish term for non-Jew*: goy

job *job in which no work is required*: sinecure

joint □ *combining forms*: arthr-, -arthr- □ *painful inflammation of the joints*: arthritis

judge □ *adjective*: judicial □ *judge's office for private hearings etc.*: chambers □ *judge's order for enforcement of a law etc.*: injunction □ *expert adviser who sits with a judge in technical cases*: assessor □ *attempt to corrupt a judge*: embracery

judo □ *judo teacher*: judoka □ *judo suit*: judogi □ *judo mat*: dojo

jump □ *sprung stick for making large jumps*: pogo stick □ *sheet stretched taut for jumping on*: trampoline

justice □ *system of justice where the judge or magistrate acts as prosecutor*: inquisitorial system □ *system of justice where the judge or magistrate adjudicates between prosecution and defence*: accusatorial system □ *out-of-court negotiations between prosecution and defence lawyers to secure a reduced charge in return for an admission of guilt*: plea bargaining

K

kidney □ *combining forms*: nephr-, ren-, -ren- □ *adjective*: renal, nephritic

kidney bean *alternative term*: dwarf bean, French bean

kidney machine *technical term*: haemodialyser

kidney stone *technical term*: renal calculus, renal concretion

kill □ *kill by beheading*: decapitate □ *kill by suffocation*: asphyxiate □ *kill selectively, to reduce a herd etc.*: cull □ *killing one's brother*: fratricide □ *killing one's father*: patricide □ *killing one's mother*: matricide □ *killing a parent or other near relative*: parricide □ *killing oneself*: suicide □ *killing a sovereign*: regicide □ *killing a whole race*: genocide □ *mercy killing*: euthanasia

killer *combining form*: -cide

king □ *adjectives*: royal, regal

□ *person who governs during a king's illness etc.*: regent □ *disease formerly thought to be cured by the sovereign's touch*: king's evil

kitchen □ *adjective*: culinary □ *kitchen on a ship or aircraft*: galley

kiwi *technical term*: apteryx

kiwi fruit *alternative term*: Chinese gooseberry

kneecap *technical term*: patella

knee-jerk *technical term*: patellar reflex

kidney vetch *alternative terms*: ladies' fingers, okra

knife *knife-maker*: cutler

knotwork *ornamental knotwork made with string*: macramé

knowledge □ *combining forms*: -gnosis, -nomy, -sophy □ *scholarly knowledge*: erudition □ *rote knowledge*: pedantry □ *shallow knowledge*: sciolism □ *instinctive knowledge*: intuition □ *social knowledge*: savoir-faire □ *knowledge before the event*: precognition □ *knowledge after the event*: hindsight □ *knowledge of many subjects*: polymathy □ *knowledge of everything*: omniscience

L

lake □ *adjective*: lacustrine □ *Scottish lake*: loch □ *Irish lake*: lough □ *mountain lake*: tarn □ *lake made by blocked-up loop of river*: oxbow lake □ *study of lakes*: limnology

ladies' fingers *alternative terms*: kidney vetch, okra

Lama □ *chief Lama of Tibet*: Dalai Lama □ *second Lama of Tibet*: Panchen Lama, Tashi Lama

lament □ *Irish lament*: keen □ *Scottish lament*: pibroch

land □ *adjective*: terrestrial □ *right of way over another's land*: easement □ *ownership of land or the land owned*:

domain □ *a government's right to take privately owned land into public use*: eminent domain □ *the taking of such land*: expropriation □ *land given for the support of a beneficed clergyman*: glebe □ *land in Holland etc. reclaimed from the sea*: polder □ *narrow strip of land projecting into water*: peninsula □ *narrow strip of land connecting two larger areas*: isthmus □ *narrow strip of land projecting into the holdings of others*: panhandle

language □ *combining forms*: lingu-, -glot □ *adjective*: linguistic □ *everyday language*: vernacular □ *simplified language, often drawn from several sources, used by foreign traders etc.*: pidgin, lingua franca □ *form of a native language that has been corrupted by colonists' speech*: creole □ *basic sound unit in a language*: phoneme □ *basic meaning unit in a language*: semanteme, sememe □ *basic word unit in a language*: morpheme □ *distinctive language of an individual*: idiolect □ *distinctive language of a region*: dialect □ *language as people actually use it*: parole □ *language as described in grammar books*: langue □ *study of language*: linguistics

large *combining forms*: macro-, maxi-, mega-, megalo-

laser *laser-produced three-dimensional image*: hologram

laughing jackass *alternative term*: kookaburra

law □ *adjective*: legal □ *redress of an injustice offered or gained by law*: remedy □ *required by law*: liable □ *academic study of law*: jurisprudence

lead *combining forms*: plumb-

leader □ *combining forms*: -agogue, -arch □ *nominal leader*: figurehead, front man, puppet

leaf □ *combining forms*: -foli-, -phyll- □ *adjectives*: foliaceous, foliate □ *leaves in general*: foliage □ *leaf-stalk*: petiole □ *strip of leaves*: defoliate

leap year □ *adjective*: bissextile □ *technical term*: intercalary year

learning □ *learning from a course in a book or computer*: programmed learning □ *learning through tapes played while asleep*: hypnopaedia □ *learning by controlled trial and error*: heuristic

lease □ *person granting a lease*: lessor □ *person taking a lease*: lessee

leather □ *leather formerly used for writing*: parchment □ *leather strap formerly used to punish Scottish schoolchildren*: tawse □ *impressed ornamentation on leather*: tooling

leave □ *leave to be absent from school*: exeat □ *leave taken without asking permission*: French leave

left □ *combining form*: laev(o)- □ *adjective*: sinistral □ *left-hand page in a book*: verso □ *left-handed person*: southpaw □ *left side of a ship as seen by one facing its prow*: port

leg □ *adjective*: crural □ *swollen vein on the leg*: varicose vein □ *metal support strapped to a broken etc. leg*: calliper

lemon *adjectives*: citric, citrous, citrine

lens □ *variable opening for a camera lens*: aperture □ *camera lens allowing rapid changes in magnification*: zoom lens □ *uneven focus of an eye due to a fault in the cornea or lense*: astigmatism

leprosy *technical term*: Hansen's disease

let *let the buyer beware*: caveat emptor

letter □ *adjective*: epistolary, literal □ *letter sent to all bishops by the Pope*: encyclical □ *letter which each recipient is asked to copy out and send to several others*: chain letter □ *letter sent by a woman breaking off a relationship*: Dear John □ *conventional letter of thanks for hospitality etc.*: Collins □ *opening greeting in a letter*: salutation □ *message added to a letter after the*

writer's *signature*: postscript □ *write out in the letters of a different alphabet*: transliterate

level □ *social level*: stratum, echelon □ *set level to each other, making a single flat surface*: flush □ *device with an air-bubble in liquid to show if surfaces are level*: spirit level

lice *infestation with lice*: pediculosis

lie □ *adjective*: mendacious □ *telling lies when under oath to speak the truth*: perjury □ *lie detector*: polygraph

life □ *combining form*: bio-, vit- □ *adjectives*: animate, vital □ *bodily processes that support life*: metabolism □ *study of living organisms*: physiology □ *long life*: longevity

lifeboat *ship's crane for a lifeboat*: davit

lift □ *lift for food in restaurant etc.*: dumb waiter □ *continuously moving lift with doorless compartments*: paternoster

light *combining forms*: lumin-, photo-, -phos-, -phot-

like *combining forms*: -esque, -oid, -ose

liker *combining forms*: phil(o)-, -phile

lilac *alternative term*: syringa

lime *combining form*: calci-

line □ *line of latitude*: parallel □ *line of longitude*: meridian

lion □ *adjective*: leonine □ *astrological term*: leo

lip □ *combining form*: labi(o)- □ *adjective*: labial

live □ *living on land*: terrestrial □ *living in or near water*: aquatic □ *living in the sea*: marine □ *able to live on land and in water*: amphibious

liver □ *combining form*: hepat- □ *adjective*: hepatic □ *inflammation of the liver, causing jaundice*: hepatitis □ *degeneration of the liver due to alcoholism or hepatitis*: cirrhosis

Liverpool *adjective*: Liverpudlian

lizard □ *combining forms*: sauro-, -saur, -saurus □ *adjective*: saurian □ *lizard that can change its colour for camouflage*: chameleon □ *mythical lizard said to live in fire*: salamander

loan translation *alternative term*: calque

locomotive *frame on the top of an electric locomotive that rises to the overhead wires*: pantograph

loin *adjective*: lumbar

logic □ *false step in reasoning*: fallacy, non sequitur, paralogism □ *deliberately misleading step in reasoning*: sophism □ *disproof of a proposition by demonstrating the absurdity of its consequences*: reductio ad absurdum □ *system of logical reasoning that moves from a general rule to a particular instance*: deduction □ *system of logical reasoning that derives a general rule from particular instances*: induction □ *logical proposition that is verified by the meanings of the words that make it*: analytic proposition □ *logical proposition that is verified by experience*: synthetic proposition

lockjaw *technical term*: trismus

long sight *technical terms*: hypermetropia, hyperopia, presbyopia

lorry □ *articulated lorry's skid into a V-shape*: jackknife □ *device recording a lorry driver's speeds and spells of driving*: tachograph □ *lorry's unladen weight*: tare □ *large covered lorry for furniture etc.*: pantechnicon

loudspeaker □ *loudspeaker for low-pitched sounds*: woofer □ *loudspeaker for high-pitched sounds*: tweeter

love □ *combining forms*: philo-, -phil-, -phile □ *adjectives*: amorous, amatory

loyalty *group loyalty*: esprit de corps

lucerne *alternative term*: alfalfa

luggage *rotating luggage delivery system at an airport etc.*: carousel

lung □ *combining form*: pneumo- □ *adjective*: pulmonary

lying □ *lying face-downwards*: prone □ *lying face-upwards*: supine

M

machine □ *adjective*: mechanical □ *person who behaves like a machine*: automaton □ *person opposed to the introduction of machines*: Luddite

mad cow disease *technical term*: bovine spongiform encephalitis

mad dog *disease caused by the bite of a mad dog*: rabies

made to order *technical term*: bespoke

Mafia □ *Neapolitan Mafia*: Camorra □ *US Mafia*: Cosa Nostra □ *leader of US Mafia*: capo, godfather

magic *object thought to have magic powers*: amulet, fetish, juju, talisman

magistrate *professional magistrate*: stipendiary magistrate

magnetism □ *destroy an object's magnetism*: degauss □ *personal magnetism*: charisma

maidenhead *medical term*: hymen

maize *alternative term*: Indian corn

making *combining forms*: -facient, -fic, -poiesis

malaria □ *drug that cures malaria*: quinine □ *type of mosquito that carries malaria*: anopheles

Malayan □ *Malayan village*: kampong □ *Malayan dagger*: kris □ *Malayan garment*: sarong

male □ *combining forms*: andro-, -andr- □ *aggressive maleness*: machismo □ *development of male characteristics in women*: virilism

mammal □ *mammal with incisor teeth*: rodent □ *mammal that chews the cud*: ruminant □ *thick-skinned mammal (e.g. rhinoceros)*: pachyderm

man □ *combining forms*: andro-, anthropo-, -andr-, -anthrop- □ *adjectives*: male, virile

Manchester *adjective*: Mancunian

mania □ *mania for drink*: dipsomania □ *mania for books*: bibliomania □ *mania for starting fires*: pyromania □ *mania for power or self-aggrandizement*: megalomania □ *manic obsession with a single idea*: monomania □ *mania for stealing*: kleptomania

manioc *alternative term*: cassava

manipulation □ *therapeutic manipulation of bones*: osteopathy □ *manipulation of electoral boundaries for party advantage*: gerrymandering

manners *code of good manners*: etiquette

manuscript □ *manuscript written by the author of the text it contains*: autograph □ *manuscript wholly written by the author of the text it contains*: holograph □ *manuscript with a text written over an earlier text*: palimpsest □ *sheepskin or goatskin prepared for use as a manuscript*: parchment □ *calfskin prepared for use as a manuscript*: vellum

Manx *Manx emblem of three legs*: triskelion

many *combining forms*: multi-, poly-, pluri-

marble *adjective*: marmoreal

marriage □ *combining form*: -gam- □ *adjectives*: conjugal, connubial, marital, matrimonial, nuptial □ *unsuccessful marriage*: misalliance □ *marriage with a social inferior*: mésalliance □ *marriage formalized by a legal ceremony only*: civil marriage □ *clothing etc. collected by a bride before her marriage*: trousseau, bottom drawer □ *property etc. brought by a bride to her marriage*: dowry □ *crime of being simultaneously married to several spouses*: bigamy □ *practice of being simultaneously married to several spouses*: polygamy □ *practice of having only one spouse at a time*: monogamy □ *practice of living together without being married*: cohabitation, common-law marriage

Mars *Greek name*: Ares

marsh □ *adjective*: paludal □ *marsh gas*: methane □ *moving light seen over marshes when the methane ignites*: will-o'-the-wisp, ignis fatuus

mask □ *mask to protect the eyes*: visor □ *mask to aid breathing*: respirator □ *mask with attached cloak*: domino

massage *massage treatment using fragrant oils*: aromatherapy

master *adjective*: magisterial

matchbox *collector of matchbox labels*: phillumenist

matter *combining form*: hyl-

mattress □ *mattress stuffed with straw*: pallet, palliasse □ *strong cloth used to cover mattresses, pillows, etc.*: ticking

meadow saffron *alternative term*: autumn crocus

meal □ *meal taken as breakfast and lunch*: brunch □ *self-service meal*: buffet □ *light meal*: tiffin, collation □ *restaurant meal with a fixed global price and offering few alternatives*: table d'hôte □ *restaurant meal chosen from a range of separately priced dishes*: à la carte

meaning □ *adjective*: semantic □ *general meaning of a text etc.*: burden, gist, gravamen □ *word having the same meaning as another*: synonym □ *word having the opposite meaning to another*: antonym

measles *technical term*: morbilli, rubella

measurement □ *combining forms*: -metr-, -metry □ *adjectives*: mensural, metrical

meat □ *cold cooked meats*: charcuterie □ *meat minced for stuffing*: forcemeat □ *seasoned smoked beef*: pastrami □ *German pork sausage*: bratwurst □ *Italian peppered pork and beef sausage*: pepperoni □ *Italian garlic sausage*: salami □ *spiced Italian pork sausage*: mortadella □ *Italian ham*:

prosciutto □ *meat cooked very rare*: au bleu □ *meat cooked rare*: saignant □ *medium-cooked meat*: à point □ *well-cooked meat*: bien cuit

medical examination *combining form*: -opsy

medical treatment □ *combining form*: -pathy □ *medical treatment of children*: paediatrics □ *medical treatment of old people*: geriatrics □ *medical treatment of women*: gynaecology □ *medical treatment of the skin*: dermatology □ *medical treatment of bones and muscles*: orthopaedics □ *medical treatment of the blood*: haematology □ *medical treatment of the nervous system*: neurology □ *medical treatment of mental diseases*: psychiatry □ *medical treatment by small doses of drugs that would induce the disease*: homoeopathy □ *medical treatment by drugs that resist the disease*: allopathy

medicine *combining form*: pharm(aco)-

meeting □ *meeting for academic discussion*: colloquium, seminar, symposium □ *meeting for church government*: synod, consistory □ *meeting of cardinals to elect a pope*: conclave □ *meeting of political delegates etc.*: congress, convention □ *mass meeting of supporters etc.*: rally □ *meeting of heads of state*: summit □ *minimum attendance required for a meeting to be valid*: quorum

membrane □ *membrane dividing the thorax from the abdomen*: diaphragm □ *membrane lining the abdomen*: peritoneum □ *membrane blocking a virgin's vagina*: hymen

memory □ *loss of memory*: amnesia, oblivion □ *formula etc. used to aid memorization or recall*: mnemonic

men □ *rule by men*: patriarchy □ *hatred of men*: misandry □ *party for men*: stag party

menstruation □ *first onset of menstruation at puberty*: menarche □ *men-*

strual blood: menses □ *painful or difficult menstruation*: dysmenorrhoea □ *abnormal absence of menstruation*: amenorrhoea □ *cessation of menstruation in middle age*: menopause

Mercury □ *Greek name*: Hermes □ *Mercury's snake-twined staff*: caduceus

mercy killing *technical term*: euthanasia

middle □ *combining forms*: medi-, mes- □ *adjectives*: medial, median □ *middle ear*: tympanum

military □ *swift and intense military attack*: blitzkrieg □ *military officer assisting a senior officer*: adjutant, aide-de-camp □ *military officers who plan a campaign*: general staff □ *long-term military plans*: strategy □ *short-term military plans*: tactics □ *provision of military manpower and supplies*: logistics □ *military stores and materials*: ordnance □ *military court*: court martial

milk □ *combining forms*: lact-, galact- □ *adjectives*: lactic, lacteal

million *combining form*: mega-

millionth *combining form*: micro-

mind *adjective*: mental

Minerva *Greek name*: Athena

mirror *adjective*: catoptric

misfortune *delight in the misfortunes of others*: schadenfreude

mix □ *mix to make uniform throughout*: homogenize □ *mix to create something different*: synthesize □ *mix socially with*: fraternize

mock orange *alternative term*: syringa

modification *modification to parliamentary bill or judicial verdict*: rider

moisture □ *combining form*: hygro- □ *full of moisture*: saturated, desiccated □ *void of moisture*: dehydrated

mole *technical term*: naevus

Monaco *adjective*: Monegasque

money □ *adjectives*: pecuniary, monetary, numismatic □ *money paid to ensure secrecy*: hush money □ *money paid as a political bribe*: slush money □ *money paid as consolation to a redundant etc. executive*: golden handshake, golden parachute □ *extra money paid to employees working in a high cost-of-living area*: weighting □ *dispose of money so as to conceal its illegal origins*: launder

mongolism *technical term*: Down's syndrome

monkey *adjective*: simian

moon □ *combining forms*: lun-, selen- □ *adjective*: lunar

mortgage □ *person granting a mortgage*: mortgagee □ *person taking out a mortgage*: mortgager

Moscow *adjective*: Muscovite

mosque □ *mosque tower*: minaret □ *person calling the faithful to prayer from a minaret*: muezzin □ *mosque's pulpit*: mimbar □ *niche in a mosque's wall facing Mecca*: mimbar

moss □ *combining form*: bryo- □ *study of mosses*: bryology

mother □ *combining form*: matri- □ *adjective*: maternal □ *murder of one's mother*: matricide

motion *adjective*: kinetic

mountain sickness *alternative term*: altitude sickness

mouse *adjective*: murine

mouth □ *combining forms*: or-, stomato-, -stom-, -stome □ *adjectives*: oral, buccal

much *combining forms*: multi-, poly-

muscle *muscle-building drug used by athletes etc.*: anabolic steroid

musician *street musician*: busker

Muslim □ *Muslim name for God*: Allah □ *Muslim scriptures*: Koran □ *Muslim month-long fast*: Ramadan □ *Muslim pilgrimage to Mecca*: haj □ *Muslim mystic*: dervish, sufi □ *Muslim who calls the faithful to prayer*: muezzin □ *Muslim religious* *leader*: ayatollah, imam, mullah □ *Muslim holy war*: jihad □ *Muslim prince*: emir □ *Muslim princess*: begum □ *Muslim judge*: cadi □ *Muslim chronological era*: Hegira □ *Muslim food regulations*: halal □ *Muslim term for forbidden foods*: haram □ *Muslim seclusion of women*: purdah □ *Muslim woman's veil*: yashmak □ *Muslim woman's overgarment*: chador

N

nail □ *adjective*: ungual □ *dead skin at the base of a nail*: cuticle □ *piece of torn skin beside a nail*: agnail □ *inflammation near a nail*: whitlow

name □ *combining forms*: onom-, nomin-, -nym □ *adjective*: onomastic □ *false name*: pseudonym, alias, nom de plume

Naples *adjective*: Neapolitan

Native American *alternative terms*: American Indian, Amerindian, Red Indian

navel □ *technical term*: umbilicus □ *adjective*: umbilical

navigation *navigation based on computation of position from speed and direction of travel*: dead reckoning

Nazi □ *official title*: National Socialist □ *Nazi emblem*: swastika □ *Nazi marching step*: goose step □ *Nazi secret police*: Gestapo □ *Nazi regional governor*: Gauleiter

neck □ *adjective*: jugular □ *fold of skin hanging from a bird's neck*: wattle □ *fold of skin hanging from the necks of cattle*: dewlap

Neptune *Greek name*: Poseidon

nerve □ *combining form*: neur(o)- □ *adjective*: neural

net □ *adjective*: retiform □ *woman's hairnet*: snood □ *Roman gladiator armed with net*: retiarius

nettle-rash *technical term*: urticaria

new □ *combining forms*: ana-, neo- □ *new thing*: innovation □ *new word*: neologism

newspaper □ *newspaper with large pages*: broadsheet □ *newspaper with small pages*: tabloid

night □ *combining forms*: noct-, nyct- □ *adjective*: nocturnal

night blindness *technical term*: nyctalopia

non-interference *government policy of non-interference*: laissez-faire

non-violence □ *Hindu and Buddhist principle of non-violence towards all living things*: ahimsa □ *non-violent resistance as a form of political protest*: civil disobedience □ *non-violent resistance as advocated by Gandhi in India*: satyagraha

north *adjective*: boreal

northern lights *technical term*: aurora borealis

nose □ *combining forms*: nas(o)-, -rhin(o)- □ *adjectives*: nasal, rhinal □ *hooked nose*: Roman nose □ *straight nose*: Grecian nose

nosebleed *technical term*: epistaxis

nostril □ *technical term*: naris (*plural* nares) □ *adjective*: narial

not *combining forms*: a-, an-, -dis-, un-

notebook *notebook containing a personal collection of literary quotations etc.*: commonplace book

noun *adjective*: nominal

novel □ *novel depicting real persons or events but with changed names*: roman à clef □ *novel depicting its hero's early life*: Bildungsroman □ *family novel, usually dealing with several generations*: roman-fleuve □ *novel presented as a series of letters*: epistolary novel

nuclear reactor □ *type of nuclear reactor producing more nuclear fuel than it consumes*: breeder □ *overheating and destruction of a nuclear reactor's core*: meltdown

number □ *number indicating quantity*: cardinal number □ *number indicating position in a sequence*: ordinal number □ *whole number*: integer □ *number system based on 10*: decimal system □ *number system based on 0 and 1*: binary system □ *number system based on 12*: duodecimal system

nut *combining forms*: nuci-

nutrition *combining forms*: troph-, -troph

nymph □ *tree nymph*: hamadryad □ *wood nymph*: dryad □ *mountain nymph*: oread □ *river nymph*: naiad □ *sea nymph*: nereid

O

oath □ *evidence given under oath*: deposition □ *written statement made under oath*: affidavit □ *solicitor entitled to administer oaths*: Commissioner for Oaths

offal □ *deer's offal*: umbles □ *fowl's offal*: giblets

official *government official investigating complaints against public bodies*: ombudsman

oil □ *combining form*: ole- □ *adjective*: oleaginous □ *sacramental oil*: chrism, unguent

okra *alternative terms*: kidney vetch, ladies' fingers

old *combining forms*: archaeo-, palaeo-

old age □ *combining form*: geront- □ *mental and physical decay characteristic of old age*: senility □ *study of old age*: geriatrics

old woman *adjective*: anile

one *combining forms*: mon(o)-, uni-

one and a half *combining form*: sesqui-

opera □ *word-book of an opera*: libretto □ *running translation of an opera displayed above the stage*: sur-

titles □ *famous female opera singer*: diva □ *person teaching opera singers in their music*: répétiteur

opposite □ *opposite side of the world*: antipodes □ *word having the opposite sense*: antonym

orbit □ *point in an orbit furthest from the earth, moon, sun*: apogee, apolune, aphelion □ *point in an orbit closest to the earth, moon, sun*: perigee, perilune, perihelion □ *orbit that keeps a satellite fixed over a terrestrial point*: geostationary orbit □ *star etc. round which a satellite orbits*: primary

order □ *order for supplies*: requisition □ *order for work to be undertaken*: commission □ *order sent from a higher to a lower court*: mandamus □ *order for a person to attend a court*: summons, subpoena □ *court order requiring a certain action to be performed or avoided*: writ, injunction

organization □ *organization sponsored but not controlled by government*: quango □ *detailed practical organization required to implement a plan*: logistics

origin □ *combining forms*: -genesis, -geny □ *geographical origin of a work of art*: provenance □ *study of the origins of words*: etymology □ *study of the origins of names*: onomastics

Orkneys *adjective*: Orcadian

ostrich *adjective*: struthious

other *combining form*: heter(o)-

otter *otter's lair*: holt, lodge

out *combining forms*: e-, ec-, ex-

ovary □ *combining form*: oophor- □ *immature ovum in the ovary*: oocyte □ *ovary cavity for the ovum*: follicle

over *combining forms*: hyper-, super-, supra-, sur-, trans-

overeating *compulsive overeating*: bulimia

Oxford University □ *Oxford University annual feast*: encaenia □ *Oxford University formal dress*:

subfusc □ *Oxford college annual feast*: gaudy □ *Oxford college servant*: scout

P

pain □ *combining forms*: alg-, -algia □ *pain that shoots along a nerve*: neuralgia □ *pain felt away from its real source*: referred pain

painting □ *painting on wet plaster*: fresco □ *painting on dry plaster*: secco □ *painting intended to give a deceptive three-dimensional view*: trompe l'oeil □ *painting in shades of grey to imitate sculpture, masonry, etc.*: grisaille □ *painting in shades of a single colour*: monochrome □ *small cracks on an old painting's surface*: craquelure □ *reappearance of traces of earlier painting*: pentimento

pair *combining form*: zyg-

pancake □ *French pancake*: crêpe □ *Russian pancake*: blini

paper □ *front side of a sheet of paper*: recto □ *reverse side of a sheet of paper*: verso □ *maker's emblem etc. in a sheet of paper*: watermark □ *quality of paper used for top copies*: bond □ *quality of paper used for carbon copies etc.*: bank □ *art of folding paper into decorative shapes*: origami

parachute □ *cord pulled by the parachuter to open a parachute*: ripcord □ *cord fixed to the aircraft to open a jumper's parachute*: static line □ *expanding part of a parachute that arrests and directs its movement*: canopy □ *ropes that hold and control a parachute's canopy*: shrouds □ *sort of parachute used to decelerate a landing aircraft*: drogue parachute

paralysis □ *combining form*: -plegia □ *paralysis from the neck down*: quadriplegia, tetraplegia □ *paralysis from the waist down*: paraplegia □ *paralysis of one side of the body*: hemiplegia □ *paralysis of a single limb*: monoplegia

parish *adjective*: parochial

parrot □ *adjective*: psittacine □ *pneumonia-like disease caught by humans from parrots*: psittacosis

part □ *combining forms*: mero-, -merous □ *composed of similar parts*: homogeneous □ *composed of dissimilar parts*: heterogeneous

Passover □ *adjective*: paschal □ *Jews' name for Passover*: Pesach □ *Passover ceremonies and feast*: Seder □ *Passover bread*: matzo

pastry □ *place where pastries are sold*: patisserie □ *soft light pastry for éclairs etc.*: choux pastry □ *light pastry used in sausage rolls etc.*: puff pastry □ *Greek pastry rolled into thin leaves*: filo pastry

patch □ *having black and white patches*: piebald □ *having patches of white and of some other colour (not black)*: skewbald

path □ *raised path used by models in a fashion show*: catwalk □ *raised path over land liable to flooding*: causeway □ *country path for walkers and horseriders*: bridlepath □ *path alongside a canal*: towpath

pause □ *pause for food, sleep, private discussion, etc. in a court or parliamentary session*: adjournment □ *pause for holidays in a parliamentary session*: recess □ *pause for holidays in a court session*: vacation □ *pause in the middle of a line of verse*: caesura

pay bed *technical term*: amenity bed

payment □ *divorced person's payment to former spouse*: maintenance □ *advance payment made for club membership, or for a series of performances, issues of a journal, etc.*: subscription □ *payment made for services not officially charged for*: honorarium □ *payment made in kind*: truck □ *initial payment made to a barrister*: retainer □ *subsequent payment made to a barrister in a long case*: refresher

peacock *adjective*: pavonine

Peking *currently preferred translit-eration*: Beijing

permission □ *permission to be absent from school*: exeat □ *ecclesiastical permission to publish a book*: imprimatur □ *absence without permission*: French leave

permit *customs permit for the temporary import of a motor vehicle*: carnet

petrol bomb □ *crude bomb made by filling a bottle with petrol*: Molotov cocktail □ *jellied petrol used in US incendiary bombs in Vietnam etc.*: napalm

picture □ *simplified picture used to represent a word in some ancient writing systems*: pictograph □ *picture puzzle in which a word is represented by pictures of objects whose names make its syllables*: rebus

pig □ *adjective*: porcine □ *pig's offal used as food*: chitterlings, haslet □ *pig's feet used as food*: trotters □ *smallest piglet in a litter*: runt

piles *technical term*: haemorrhoids

pillar □ *combining forms*: styl-, -stylar □ *prehistoric ring of pillars*: henge □ *classical pillar carved to resemble a man*: telamon □ *classical pillar carved to resemble a woman*: caryatid □ *early Christian saint living on the top of a pillar*: stylite □ *Amerindian carved pillar*: totem pole

pilot *Japanese suicide pilot*: kamikaze

pimento *alternative term*: pimiento

pinwheel *alternative term*: Catherine wheel

pipe □ *long-stemmed clay pipe*: churchwarden □ *Amerindian peace pipe*: calumet □ *oriental smoker's pipe in which the smoke is passed through water*: hookah, narghile

pitch *drop in pitch of a sound that passes the hearer and moves away*: Doppler effect

pith helmet *alternative term*: sola topi

pituitary gland *technical term*: hypophysis

pivot □ *pivot on a rudder*: pintle □ *pivot on a large gun*: trunnion

place □ *combining form*: top- □ *list of places*: gazetteer □ *'feel' of a place*: genius loci

plain □ *plain in Russia*: steppe □ *plain in South Africa*: veldt □ *grassy plain in warm countries*: savannah □ *Arctic plain*: tundra

planning □ *planning method that evaluates a complex set of alternatives*: critical path analysis □ *practical planning, especially of transport*: logistics □ *planning schedule*: PERT chart

plant □ *combining forms*: phyto-, -phyte □ *plant living for one year only*: annual □ *plant living for two years only*: biennial □ *plant living for three or more years*: perennial □ *use by green plants of sunlight energy*: photosynthesis

plant louse *technical term*: aphid

planned economy *alternative term*: command economy

plaster □ *decorative plasterwork*: pargeting □ *fine plaster for frescos etc.*: stucco □ *roughen a plaster surface to aid adhesion*: key □ *smooth a plaster surface*: float

plastic □ *sheet plastic used as glazing etc.*: Perspex™ □ *plastic-coated cloth used for tablecloths etc.*: American cloth □ *plastic lamination for kitchen work surfaces etc.*: Formica™ □ *plastic used for gramophone records etc.*: vinyl □ *plastic used in paints*: acrylic, vinyl □ *plastic used for packing*: expanded polystyrene

plastic surgery *technical term*: anaplasty

platform □ *platform for a gibbet etc.*: scaffold □ *platform for election speeches*: hustings

pleasure □ *pleasure-loving*: hedonistic □ *pleasure derived from the suffering of others*: Roman holiday

□ *pleasure gained from the contemplation of others' misfortunes*: schadenfreude

plug □ *plug for the vent of a cask*: spigot, spile □ *plug for the muzzle of a large gun*: tampion □ *plug for a cannon's touch-hole*: spike

poem □ *poem celebrating a marriage*: epithalamium, prothalamium □ *poem about rural life*: bucolic, eclogue, georgic □ *poem lamenting a person's death*: elegy, threnody □ *five-line nonsense poem*: limerick □ *Japanese three-line poem of 17 syllables*: haiku □ *poem constructed so that certain letters from each line form a name etc.*: acrostic

poet □ *successful poet at an Eisteddfod*: bard □ *French medieval poet*: troubadour, trouvère □ *Scandinavian medieval poet*: skald

Poseidon □ *Latin name*: Neptune □ *Poseidon's three-pronged spear*: trident

poison □ *combining forms*: toxi-, toxo- □ *poison produced by a fungus on peanuts*: aflatoxin □ *poison produced by a fungus on cereals*: ergot □ *poison drunk by Socrates*: hemlock □ *cure for a poison*: antitoxin, antivenin

pole *pole used to push a punt etc.*: quant

police □ *police van*: Black Maria □ *police kit for assembling a likeness of a wanted person*: identikit, photofit

policy □ *published policy statement*: manifesto □ *reversal of policy*: about-face, volte-face, U-turn

polio *technical terms*: poliomyelitis, infantile paralysis

politics □ *political agenda driven by practical needs rather than moral principles*: realpolitik □ *persistent dissemination of political propaganda via the media*: agitprop □ *discarded political system*: ancien régime □ *political opposition in a one-party state*: dissidence □ *splinter group within a political*

party: faction, caucus □ *political enthusiast*: activist, militant, Young Turk

poll □ *public poll on some issue of current concern*: plebiscite, referendum □ *officer who counts the votes cast in a poll*: scrutineer □ *officer administering a poll and announcing its result*: returning officer

pope □ *adjective*: papal □ *pope's triple crown*: tiara □ *pope's letter to the Church*: bull, brief, encyclical □ *pope's ambassador*: nuncio □ *clergyman acting as a pope's representative*: legate □ *pope's administrative staff*: curia □ *meeting of cardinals to elect a new pope*: conclave

population □ *combining form*: dem(o)- □ *study of population statistics*: demography

position *cross-legged position with the legs resting on opposite thighs*: lotus position

possession □ *useless possession*: white elephant □ *possession giving social prestige*: status symbol

post-mortem □ *technical term*: autopsy □ *doctor conducting post-mortem examination*: pathologist □ *magistrate conducting post-mortem judicial inquiry*: coroner

pouch □ *kangaroo's pouch*: marsupium □ *Scotsman's pouch*: sporran

power □ *combining form*: dynam(o)- □ *absolute power*: carte blanche □ *transfer of power from central to regional authorities*: devolution

prairie wolf *alternative term*: coyote

pregnancy □ *technical term*: cyesis □ *adjectives*: antenatal, prenatal □ *craving for strange foods during pregnancy*: pica □ *custom in some cultures of the husband's taking to his bed during the latter stages of a pregnancy*: couvade □ *spontaneous expulsion of the foetus early in pregnancy*: miscarriage □ *medically induced expulsion or destruction of an unviable foetus*: abortion □ *diag-*

nostic sampling of amniotic fluid during pregnancy: amniocentesis □ *toxic condition during pregnancy*: eclampsia □ *false pregnancy*: pseudocyesis

price □ *lowest price at which an auctioned item may be sold*: reserve price □ *raise a previously agreed price*: gazump

prickly heat *technical term*: miliaria

priest □ *adjective*: sacerdotal □ *priest's robes*: vestments □ *Roman Catholic priest's hat*: biretta □ *Anglican priest's house*: rectory, vicarage □ *Roman Catholic priest's house*: presbytery □ *Buddhist priest in China or Japan*: bonze □ *Orthodox priest in Greece*: pope, papas □ *Orthodox priest in Russia*: pope

principle □ *principle that if anything can go wrong it will*: Murphy's law, sod's law □ *principle that employees are always promoted beyond their abilities*: Peter principle □ *principle that work expands to fill the time available*: Parkinson's law

prison □ *Nazi prison camp*: stalag □ *Soviet labour prison*: gulag

prisoner *prisoner who has won privileges by good behaviour*: trusty

prize □ *prize given to near-winner*: consolation prize, proxime accessit □ *prize given to worst contestant*: booby prize, wooden spoon

problem □ *problem-solving by application of logic*: vertical thinking □ *problem-solving by a seemingly illogical thought process*: lateral thinking □ *problem-solving by random trial and error*: heuristic

producing *combining forms*: -facient, -fer, -fic, -gen, -genic, -genous

property □ *legal document transferring ownership of property*: conveyance □ *government's right to seize private property for state use*: eminent domain □ *seize property for the repay-*

ment of a debt: distrain, sequester □ *repossess a mortgaged property upon failure of payments*: foreclose

prophet □ *prophet of doom*: Jeremiah □ *prophet of doom who is ignored*: Cassandra

pulp □ *pulp of pressed grapes*: marc □ *pulp of pressed apples*: pomace

punishment □ *combining form*: pen(o)- □ *adjective*: penal □ *punishment seen as a deterrent to others*: exemplary punishment □ *punishment seen as society's revenge on the criminal*: retributive punishment □ *study of punishment*: penology

puppy love *alternative term*: calf love

purification *purification of the emotions through drama etc.*: catharsis

pus □ *combining form*: pyo- □ *adjective*: purulent

putto *alternative terms*: amoretto, cherub

queen *adjectives*: royal, regal

question □ *set of questions and answers used as a means of instruction*: catechism □ *question returned diplomat etc. about his misson*: debrief

quick □ *quick and efficient*: expeditious □ *quick and careless*: perfunctory

R

rabbit □ *female rabbit*: doe □ *male rabbit*: buck □ *very young rabbit*: kitten □ *disease fatal to rabbits*: myxomatosis

rabies *technical term*: hydrophobia

radioactivity □ *instrument for measuring radioactivity*: Geiger counter □ *atmospheric radioactivity after a nuclear explosion*: fallout

□ *radioactive substance whose passage though the body is monitored for diagnostic purposes*: tracer

rain □ *combining form*: pluvi(o)- □ *rain cloud*: nimbus □ *rainy season in India etc.*: monsoon □ *spraying chemicals into a cloud to produce rain*: seeding

rainbow *band of colours seen in the rainbow*: spectrum

rally *rally of Scouts and/or Guides*: jamboree

random *of music allowing for some random elements in its performance*: aleatoric

rapid *combining forms*: tach(o)-, tach(y)-

raven *adjective*: corvine

ray *adjective*: radial

read □ *inability to read due to ignorance*: illiteracy □ *inability to read due to brain damage*: alexia □ *difficulty with reading due to brain dysfunction*: dyslexia

reason *adjective*: rational

recent *combining form*: neo-

record □ *combining form*: -gram □ *set of records, papers, etc. on a particular topic*: dossier □ *record of a person's education and career*: curriculum vitae □ *record of a business meeting*: minutes □ *record of a learned society's meetings*: proceedings, transactions □ *collection of written etc. records*: archive

recorder *combining form*: -graph

recruitment □ *former services' recruitment unit, employing force and trickery*: pressgang □ *entice (esp. senior) employees away from other companies*: headhunt

rectum *combining form*: proct(o)-

red *combining forms*: erythr(o)-, rhod(o)-, rub(i)

Red Indian *alternative terms*: American Indian, Amerindian, Native American

refuse □ *refuse to do business with*: boycott □ *refuse to socialize with*: ostracize

registration plate *specially purchased vehicle registration plates that contain the owner's initials etc.*: vanity plates

reign □ *adjective*: regnal □ *period between two reigns*: interregnum

related □ *related by blood*: consanguineous □ *related through marriage or adoption*: affined □ *related through the paternal line*: agnate □ *related through the maternal line*: cognate □ *(of words) related by having a common source*: cognate □ *related at a distance of x generations*: x times removed

relative density *apparatus measuring a liquid's relative density*: hydrometer

religion □ *religious belief in the existence of a single god*: monotheism □ *religious belief in the existence of several gods*: polytheism □ *religious belief in counterbalanced forces of good and evil*: dualism □ *religious belief that God created the world but has had no further involvement with it*: deism □ *religious belief that God created the world and continues to be active in it*: theism □ *religious belief that God and the universe are identical*: pantheism

remote *remote area*: ultima Thule

renewable energy *alternative term*: alternative energy

rent □ *nominal rent*: peppercorn rent □ *excessive rent*: rack-rent □ *person living on rental income*: rentier

replacement □ *temporary replacement for doctor etc.*: locum □ *fertile woman replacing a would-be mother unable to bear children*: surrogate

report □ *government report with proposals for public discussion*: green paper □ *government report with proposals for legislation*: white paper

reproduction □ *combining forms*: gon-, -gen-, -genesis □ *reproducing by means of eggs*: oviparous □ *reproducing live offspring*: viviparous □ *reproducing by giving birth from eggs hatched within the body*: ovoviviparous

reptile *combining form*: herpet(o)-

retort *witty retort that comes to mind after the chance to make it has gone*: esprit de l'escalier

rhyme □ *rhyme between final stressed syllables*: masculine rhyme □ *rhyme between words with final unstressed syllables*: feminine rhyme □ *false rhyme between words that look but do not sound the same*: eye-rhyme □ *game of inventing successive lines of rhyming verse*: crambo

rib *adjective*: costal

riches *imaginary land of great riches*: eldorado

rickets *technical term*: rachitis

right □ *combining forms*: dextro- □ *correct, upright*: ortho- □ *right of way etc. enjoyed over another's property*: easement □ *right of way etc. that one must allow another over one's property*: servitude □ *right side of a ship as seen by one facing its prow*: starboard

ring □ *adjective*: annular □ *ring for the leash on a dog's collar*: terret □ *leather ring for Scout's neckerchief*: woggle □ *finger ring having a seal instead of a stone*: signet ring □ *plain ring worn in a pierced ear to prevent its healing*: sleeper □ *ring inserted in the lip*: labret □ *ring of muscle*: sphincter □ *ring of light round the sun or moon*: aureole, corona

ringing *persistent ringing sound heard in one or both ears*: tinnitus

ringworm *technical term*: tinea pedis

risk *risk inherent in a particular activity*: occupational hazard

ritual □ *admission ritual*: initiation □ *ritual marking a new stage in life*: rite

of passage □ *ritual pouring of liquid*: libation

river □ *adjectives*: fluvial, potamic, riverine □ *ice river*: glacier □ *small island in a river*: ait, eyot □ *horseshoe-shaped bend in a river's course*: oxbow □ *triangular area, with many streams, at a river's mouth*: delta □ *wide area of water at a river's mouth*: estuary □ *low dam in a river to regulate its flow*: weir □ *dry river bed*: wadi □ *high wave moving up a river at the spring tide*: bore, eagre

river bank *adjective*: riparian

road □ *scenic coast road*: corniche □ *road on which no stopping is permitted*: clearway □ *road with no exit*: cul-de-sac □ *rise in a road's surface towards the centre, to assist drainage*: camber □ *hump built across a road to limit speeds*: sleeping policeman

rock □ *combining forms*: litho-, petro-, -lith-, -lite □ *loose pieces of rock on a hillside*: scree

rocket □ *rocket's curving course*: trajectory □ *scaffold supporting a space rocket before take-off*: gantry

rod □ *rod said to indicate underground springs etc. by twitching*: dowsing rod □ *bundle of rods with an axe, carried before Roman magistrates*: fasces

root □ *combining forms*: rhiz-, -radic- □ *adjective*: radical

rope □ *adjective*: funicular □ *ship's heavy rope for mooring etc.*: hawser □ *secure a rope*: belay □ *interweave two ropes*: splice □ *bind a rope-end to prevent fraying*: whip □ *descend a rock face using a double rope coiled round the body*: abseil

rot *combining form*: sapr-

row *combining forms*: stich-, -stichous

rowing boat □ *support for rowing boat's oar*: rowlock □ *seat for oarsman*: thwart □ *rowing boat for a single oarsman*: scull □ *steersman in a rowing boat*: cox □ *oarsman next to the cox*: stroke

rule □ *combining forms*: -archy, -cracy □ *rules for social behaviour*: etiquette □ *procedural rules for diplomatic etc. occasions*: protocol □ *rules for the grammatical arrangement of words in a language*: syntax □ *rules of boxing*: Queensberry Rules

ruler □ *combining forms*: -arch, -crat □ *former chief magistrate at Genoa and Venice*: doge □ *Nazi ruler of Germany*: führer □ *former rulers in India*: nawab, nizam □ *former ruler of Iran*: shah □ *Islamic rulers*: ayatollah, caliph, emir □ *Fascist ruler of Italy*: duce □ *former Japanese rulers*: mikado, shogun □ *Ottoman rulers*: aga, bey, khedive, pasha, sultan □ *Spanish military dictator*: caudillo □ *former ruler of Tibet*: Dalai Lama □ *former ruler of Russia*: tsar □ *ruling group (often military officers) following a coup d'état*: junta

rumour □ *false, often malicious, rumour*: canard □ *source of rumours*: bush telegraph, grapevine

runic alphabet *technical term*: futhorc

running *combining form*: -dromous

rupture *technical term*: hernia

Russian □ *Russian script*: Cyrillic □ *old Russian woman*: babushka □ *set of Russian babushka dolls*: matrioshka □ *Russian cavalryman*: cossack □ *Russian country cottage*: dacha □ *Russian citadel*: kremlin □ *Russian guitar*: balalaika □ *Russian pancake*: blini □ *Russian beetroot soup*: bortsch □ *Russian beer*: kvass □ *Russian tea urn*: samovar

S

sacred *combining form*: hier(o)-

saddle *second saddle on a horse or motorcycle*: pillion

safety *safety switch in a locomotive cab that cuts the engine unless constantly depressed by the driver*: dead man's handle

sailor □ *ordinary sailor*: rating □ *sailor's canvas bed*: hammock □ *dried bread formerly eaten by sailors*: hard tack, ship's biscuit □ *punish a sailor by dragging him beneath the ship*: keelhaul

saint □ *combining form*: hagi(o)- □ *declare a person to be a saint*: canonize □ *person arguing for a saint's canonization*: postulator □ *person arguing against a saint's canonization*: devil's advocate

Saint Vitus' dance *technical term*: Sydenham's chorea

same □ *combining form*: taut(o)- □ *of the same age or time*: coetaneous, coeval, contemporary □ *of the same size*: commensurate □ *of the same extent or meaning*: coterminous □ *of the same shape*: congruent □ *having the same meaning*: synonymous

satellite *communications etc. satellite orbiting at a fixed position relative to the earth*: geostationary satellite, geosynchronous satellite

sausage □ *seasoned smoked sausage*: saveloy □ *small thin spicy sausage*: chipolata □ *German pork sausage*: bratwurst □ *Italian peppered pork and beef sausage*: pepperoni □ *Italian garlic sausage*: salami □ *spiced Italian pork sausage*: mortadella

saying □ *wise saying*: aphorism, epigram □ *trite saying*: platitude, cliché, bromide

scale □ *scale for wind velocities*: Beaufort scale □ *scale for earthquake intensities*: Richter scale □ *scale for child intelligence*: Binet–Simon scale □ *relating to a twelve-tone musical scale*: chromatic □ *relating to an eighttone musical scale*: diatonic

scales *astrological term*: libra

scaly *technical term*: squamose

scarlet fever *technical term*: scarlatina

scent *dried petals used for scent*: pot-pourri

scissors *tailor's serrated scissors*: pinking shears

scorpion *astrological term*: scorpio

screen □ *sliding screen in a Japanese house*: shoji □ *screen in an Indian house concealing women from view*: purdah

screw □ *screw with a cross-shaped slot*: Phillips screw □ *screw with a hexagonal slot*: Allen screw

scriptures □ *Islamic scriptures*: Koran □ *Sikh scriptures*: Granth □ *Hindu scriptures*: Veda □ *Buddhist scriptures*: Tripitaka □ *Zoroastrian scriptures*: Avesta

scurvy *adjective*: scorbutic

sea *adjectives*: marine, maritime

second *combining forms*: deut-, deutero-

secret societies □ *Sicilian secret criminal and political organization*: Mafia □ *Neapolitan branch of the Mafia*: Camorra □ *US branch of the Mafia*: Cosa Nostra □ *Chinese secret criminal gang*: Tong, Triad □ *US secret society promoting White supremacy*: Klu Klux Klan □ *international secret society with allegedly social purposes*: Freemasonry

security *security given for a loan*: collateral

seed *adjective*: seminal

seizure *seizure of a debtor's property*: distraint, sequestration

self □ *combining form*: aut(o)- □ *self-government*: autonomy, autarchy □ *self-sufficiency*: autarky

sell □ *selling by sending out unsolicited items and then demanding payment if they are not returned*: inertia selling □ *selling through a hierarchy of agents*: pyramid selling □ *sell goods by association (e.g. inscribed sweatshirts at a pop concert)*: merchandize □ *sell goods abroad at a giveaway price, to maintain their home price*: dump

seller □ *combining form*: -monger □ *person selling from door to door*: hawker, pedlar □ *person selling fruit etc. in a street market*: costermonger □ *person selling a specified type of goods*: chandler □ *former seller of quack medicines etc. at fairs*: mountebank

sentence □ *sentence containing every letter of the alphabet*: pangram □ *sentence that tails off uncompleted*: aposiopesis □ *prison sentence to be served only upon re-offending*: suspended sentence □ *reduction of a prison sentence for good behaviour*: remission

sentimentality *sentimentality in music or art*: kitsch, schmaltz

servant □ *military officer's servant*: batman □ *junior public-school boy who acts as servant to a senior boy*: fag □ *Cambridge college servant*: gyp □ *Oxford college servant*: scout □ *Indian servant operating a large ceiling fan*: punkah wallah

sesame □ *paste made from sesame seeds*: tahini □ *sweet made from sesame seeds*: halva

seven □ *combining forms*: hept(a)-, sept(i)- □ *adjective*: septenary

sexual activity *adjective*: venereal

shakes *technical term*: Parkinson's disease

shape *combining forms*: morph(o)-, -form, -morphic

share □ *list of an investor's shares*: portfolio □ *share-buying company selling to the public shares in its whole portfolio*: unit trust □ *offer shares for sale*: float □ *periodic payment made by a successful company to its shareholders*: dividend □ *shares offering a guaranteed dividend*: gilts □ *speculator who sells shares because he expects their price to fall*: bear □ *speculator who buys shares because he expects their price to rise*: bull □ *speculator who buys new share issues for a quick resale*: stag

sharp □ *combining form*: oxy- □ *sharpness of a picture*: definition □ *mental sharpness*: acuity

shed □ *shed feathers or fur*: moult □ *shed an outer skin or shell*: slough □ *shedding its leaves annually*: deciduous

sheep □ *adjective*: ovine □ *sheep's brain disease thought to cause BSE*: scrapie □ *castrated male sheep, leader of the flock*: bellwether

sheet *sheet for a corpse*: shroud

shell □ *combining forms*: concho-, -conch- □ *fragments of an exploding artillery shell*: shrapnel

shell-shock *technical term*: combat neurosis

shepherd *adjective*: bucolic

shepherd's pie *alternative term*: cottage pie

shield □ *shield bearing a coat of arms*: escutcheon □ *knob in the centre of a shield*: boss, umbo □ *Roman legionaries' roof of linked shields*: testudo

shin bone *technical term*: tibia

shingles *technical term*: herpes zoster

ship □ *adjective*: marine, maritime □ *line painted on a ship's side to show permitted submersion levels*: Plimsoll line □ *list of a ship's cargo*: bill of lading, manifest □ *dock worker employed to unload a ship*: stevedore □ *recovery of a wrecked or abandoned ship*: salvage □ *cargo thrown overboard from a ship to lighten it in a storm*: jetsam □ *cargo washed overboard from a ship*: flotsam □ *cargo thrown overboard from a ship but marked with buoys etc. for later recovery*: lagan □ *common room for a warship's senior officers*: wardroom □ *common room for a warship's junior officers*: gunroom

shock *shock that may cause lasting psychological harm*: trauma

shock treatment *technical term*: electroconvulsive therapy

shoot □ *shoot growing from a plant's roots etc.*: sucker □ *shoot prepared for planting or grafting*: scion, slip □ *climbing plant's shoot used to gain support*: tendril

shore *adjective*: littoral

short *combining form*: brach-

short-sightedness *technical term*: myopia

shoulder blade *technical term*: scapula

sickle *adjective*: falcate

sickly *sickly person*: valetudinarian

sided *combining forms*: -gon, -gonal

sight □ *combining form*: -scopy □ *adjective*: visual

signal □ *bell rung as an alarm*: tocsin □ *signalling system based on combinations of long and short flashes, marks, or sounds*: Morse □ *signalling system based on flags hand-held in various positions*: semaphore □ *signalling system used by bookmakers' assistants*: tick-tack

silence *Cistercian monk vowed to silence*: Trappist

silver *adjective*: argent-

simple fraction *alternative term*: common fraction

singer □ *range of notes a singer can sing*: compass, register □ *range within which the majority of notes in a song fall*: tessitura

single *combining forms*: mono-, uni-

sister □ *combining form*: soror(i)- □ *murder of a sister*: sororicide

situation *perplexing situation*: dilemma, predicament

six *combining forms*: hexa-, hexi-, sexa-, sexi-

sixth sense *perception by a 'sixth sense'*: extrasensory perception

skin □ *combining forms*: derm(o)-, dermat(o)- □ *technical term*: cutis, dermis □ *adjective*: cutaneous □ *beneath the skin*: hypodermic, subcutaneous □ *blemish on the skin*: naevus, macula, stigma □ *strip off the skin*: flay □ *shed a skin*: slough □ *shedding of a skin*: slough, ecdysis

skirt □ *ballet dancer's stiff short skirt*: tutu □ *short skirt as part of traditional Greek male dress*: fustanella □ *padding formerly worn under the rear of a skirt*: bustle □ *hoops formerly supporting a skirt*: farthingale

skull □ *combining forms*: cephal(o)-, -cephal- □ *technical term*: cranium □ *study of the size and shape of the skull as a supposed indicator of character and mental ability*: phrenology □ *bore a hole in the skull for surgical purposes*: trepan, trephine

skullcap □ *skullcap worn by some Roman Catholoic clergymen*: zucchetto □ *skullcap worn by male Orthodox Jews*: yarmulka

slave *adjective*: servile

sleep □ *combining forms*: hypn(o)-, narc(o)-, somni-, somno- □ *learning while asleep*: hypnopaedia □ *sleep with dreaming and eye movements*: paradoxical sleep, REM sleep □ *shallow sleep induced by surgical anaesthesia*: twilight sleep □ *sleep through the winter*: hibernate □ *sleep through the summer*: aestivate

sleeping sickness □ *technical term*: encephalitis lethargica, trypanosomiasis □ *African fly causing sleeping sickness*: tsetse

sleepwalking *technical terms*: somnambulism, noctambulism

slip of the tongue □ *technical term*: lapsus linguae □ *slip of the tongue thought to reveal the speaker's true thoughts*: Freudian slip

sloe *alternative term*: blackthorn

slope □ *combining forms*: clin-, -clin- □ *steep slope at the end of a plateau*: escarpment □ *slope of a stage etc.*: rake □ *slope of a road etc.*: gradient □ *skier's diagonal route across sloping ground*: traverse

slow □ *combining form*: brady- □ *Chinese system of slow exercises*: t'ai chi ch'uan

slum clearance *alternative term*: urban renewal

small □ *combining forms*: micro-, mini-, nano-, -cle, -ule □ *smallest possible*: marginal, minimal, minuscule □ *infinitely small*: infinitesimal □ *small amount*: soupçon, smidgen, vestige

smallpox *technical term*: variola

smell □ *adjectives*: □ *sense of smell*: olfactory □ *stink*: mephitic, hircine

smelling salts *technical term*: sal volatile

snake □ *adjective*: anguine □ *snake's poison*: venom □ *antidote to this*: serum, antivenin

snapdragon *alternative term*: antirrhinum

sneezing *technical term*: sternutation

soccer *technical term*: Association Football

social □ *socially correct*: comme il faut □ *social rules or custom*: etiquette □ *social blunder*: gaffe, faux pas □ *social skills*: savoir-faire □ *social climber*: arriviste, parvenu □ *social prestige*: cachet □ *gaining social status*: upwardly mobile □ *losing social status*: déclassé

society □ *person ostracized by society*: pariah □ *group thought to have a hidden but pervasive control of society*: the Establishment

solar system *mechanical model of the solar system*: orrery

sole of the foot *adjectives*: plantar, volar

solvent □ *universal solvent sought by alchemists*: alkahest □ *strong solvent attacking most substances*: aqua regia

son *adjective*: filial

song □ *improvised West Indian song on topical theme*: calypso □ *sailors'* *work song*: shanty □ *gondolier's song*: barcarole □ *Renaissance secular part-song*: madrigal □ *German art-song*: lied

soot *adjective*: fuliginous

sound □ *combining forms*: audi-, phon(o)-, -phony □ *adjectives*: acoustic, sonic □ *of sound recorded and reproduced via a single channel*: monophonic □ *of sound recorded and reproduced via several channels*: streophonic □ *of sound recorded and reproduced via two separate channels*: binaural □ *of sound recorded and reproduced via four separate channels*: quadraphonic □ *slow pitch-distortion of recorded sound*: wow □ *fast pitch-distortion of recorded sound*: flutter □ *name for the indefinite sound often made by English vowels*: schwa

south *adjectives*: austral, meridional

South Africa □ *South African barbecue*: braai □ *South African native club*: knobkerrie □ *South African native spear*: assegai □ *South African whip*: sjambok □ *South African cattle pound*: kraal □ *small town in South Africa*: dorp □ *South African wagon encampment*: laager □ *open bush in South Africa*: bundu □ *veranda in South Africa*: stoep □ *former South African policy of racial segregation*: apartheid

South American □ *South American cloak having a hole for the head*: poncho □ *South American cowboy*: gaucho

Soviet □ *Soviet party official*: commissar □ *Soviet secret police*: KGB □ *Soviet forced labour camp*: gulag □ *Soviet collective farm*: kolkhoz □ *Soviet worker who achieves exceptional output*: stakhanovite □ *underground publishing in Soviet Russia*: samizdat □ *Soviet youth organization*: Komsomol

speak *that cannot be spoken*: ineffable

specific gravity □ *technical term*: relative density □ *apparatus measuring a liquid's specific gravity*: hydrometer

spectacles □ *spectacles supported by a nose clip*: pince nez □ *single eyeglass*: monocle □ *pair of eyeglasses on a long handle*: lorgnette □ *spectacles with combined lenses to give near and far vision*: bifocals

speech □ *combining forms*: logo-, phono-, -log-, -phon(o)-, -logue, -phone, -phony □ *adjective*: oral □ *inability to express or understand speech due to brain damage*: aphasia □ *inability to express speech due to loss of voice*: aphonia

speed □ *combining form*: tach- □ *speed at which an object can defy gravity*: escape velocity □ *object's maximum possible air speed*: terminal velocity □ *instrument measuring a vehicle's speed*: speedometer □ *instrument measuring an engine's speed*: rev counter, tachometer □ *automatic regulator of an engine's speed*: governor □ *automatic recorder of a vehicle's speed*: tachograph

spelling *technical term*: orthography

spirit □ *combining forms*: pneumat- □ *spirit of the age*: zeitgeist □ *spirit of a place*: genius loci, numen

spiritualist □ *spiritualist thought to be able to contact the dead*: medium □ *spiritualist meeting for contact with the dead*: seance □ *substance said to exude from a spritualist medium during a trance*: ectoplasm □ *boards used for messages in a spiritualist seance*: ouija board, planchette □ *form of spiritualism practised by some Native Americans, Aleuts, etc.*: shamanism

split *combining form*: schiz(o)-

squint *technical term*: strabismus

squirrel *squirrel's nest*: drey

staff □ *bishop's staff*: crosier □ *monarch's staff*: sceptre □ *beadle's* *staff*: mace □ *verger's staff*: verge □ *Dionysus' staff*: thyrsus □ *Hermes' staff*: caduceus

stain *brownish stain on the paper of a book or engraving*: foxing

stained glass *lead strip holding pieces of stained glass*: came

stamp collecting *technical term*: philately

standard *standard used for comparison*: benchmark, control, yardstick

star □ *combining forms*: astr-, sider(o)- □ *adjectives*: astral, sidereal, stellar □ *cluster of stars*: asterism □ *exploding star*: nova □ *large cool star*: red giant □ *small cool star*: red dwarf □ *group of stars thought to form a particular figure*: constellation □ *star that is the brightest in its constellation*: alpha □ *measure of a star's brightness*: magnitude □ *building with a domed ceiling for displaying images of the stars*: planetarium

start □ *start a car from another car's battery*: jump-start □ *start a car by pushing it and then engaging the gears*: bump-start

state *combining forms*: -osis, -tude

statement *legal statement made under oath*: affidavit, deposition

steal □ *steal someone's ideas*: plagiarize □ *steal from money entrusted to one*: embezzle, peculate, defalcate □ *steal small items from the workplace*: pilfer □ *person who knowingly buys or stores stolen goods*: receiver □ *person who finds a buyer for stolen goods*: fence □ *compulsive urge to steal, regardless of need*: kleptomania

stirrup bone *technical term*: stapes

stomach □ *combining form*: gastr(o)- □ *adjective*: gastric

stomach-ache *technical term*: gastralgia

stone □ *combining forms*: lapid-, lith(o)-, petr(o)- □ *adjective*: lithic □ *large standing stone in a prehistoric monument*: megalith □ *prehistoric stone chamber tomb*: dolmen □ *stone coffin*: sarcophagus □ *person who shapes building stone or builds with it*: mason, stonemason □ *grotesque stone figure serving as rainwater spout*: gargoyle □ *stone believed by alchemists to turn base metals into gold*: philosophers' stone

store □ *secret store*: cache, stash □ *funnel-shaped store for coal, grain, etc.*: hopper

storm *still area at the centre of a storm*: eye

strangle *execute a criminal by strangling*: garrotte

stroke *technical term*: cerebral haemorrhage

study □ *combining form*: -logy □ *study of the universe*: cosmology □ *study of the stars*: astronomy □ *study of mankind*: anthropology □ *study of primitive cultures*: ethnology □ *study of statistics of births, deaths, and disease*: demography □ *study of language*: philology □ *study of living organisms*: physiology □ *study of the skin*: dermatology □ *study of diseases*: pathology □ *study of resistance to infection*: immunology □ *study of tumours*: oncology □ *study of poisons*: toxicology □ *study of voting at elections*: psephology □ *study of crime*: criminology □ *study of punishment*: penology □ *study of family trees*: genealogy □ *study of the soil*: pedology □ *study of mosses*: bryology □ *study of fossils*: palaeontology □ *study of earthquakes*: seismology □ *study of the weather*: meteorology □ *study of unidentified flying objects*: ufology

stuffing □ *stuffing dead animals*: taxidermy □ *stuffing made of chopped meat or vegetables*: forcemeat

substitute *fraudulently substituted*: supposititious

subtraction □ *number from which subtraction is to be made*: minuend □ *number to be subtracted*: subtrahend

sugar □ *combining forms*: glyc(o)-, sacchar- □ *adjective*: saccharine □ *hormone regulating the blood sugar level*: insulin □ *disease characterized by excess sugar in the blood and urine*: diabetes mellitus

sugar pea *alternative term*: mangetout

summer □ *adjective*: aestival □ *resumption of summer weather in the autumn*: Indian summer

summer house *raised summer house with a view*: gazebo, belvedere

sun □ *combining forms*: heli-, sol- □ *adjective*: solar □ *sun's highest point in the sky*: zenith □ *orbiting planet's furthest point from the sun*: aphelion □ *orbiting planet's nearest point to the sun*: perihelion

sunburn *technical term*: erythema solare

supporting *combining form*: pro-

surgical cutting *combining forms*: -tom-, -tome, -tomy

surgical opening *combining form*: -stomy

surgical removal *combining form*: -ectomy

surveyor □ *surveyor's rotating telescope for measuring angles*: theodolite □ *surveyor's incised mark in wall etc.*: benchmark □ *surveyor's striped sightpole*: ranging pole

survive *capable of surviving independently*: viable

suspicious *pathologically suspicious*: paranoid

sweat □ *technical term*: hidrosis □ *adjective*: hidrotic

sweating sickness *technical term*: miliary fever

sweet □ *excessively sweet*: cloying □ *sweet-voiced*: mellifluous

Swiss □ *Swiss state*: canton □ *Swiss breakfast food of cereals, dried fruit, and nuts*: muesli □ *Swiss mountaineers' style of song*: yodelling

symbol □ *identifying symbol used for a company, product, etc.*: logo, trade mark □ *symbol replacing a word*: logogram □ *system of symbols, each of which represents a syllable in a certain language*: syllabary □ *system of symbols, each of which represents a word in a certain language*: ideograms

symptom *set of symptoms whose joint presence indicates a particular disease*: syndrome

syringa *alternative terms*: lilac, mock orange

T

table □ *table of the elements arranged to group those of similar chemical structure*: periodic table □ *table giving the results of various mathematical calculations*: ready reckoner

tail □ *combining forms*: caud-, -urous □ *adjective*: caudal □ *fox's tail*: brush □ *rabbit or deer's tail*: scut

tailor *adjective*: sartorial

tar □ *tar used to preserve wood*: creosote □ *tar used on roofs and roads*: bitumen □ *tar mixed with gravel etc. for road-making*: asphalt

target □ *disk thrown up as a shooting target*: clay pigeon □ *revolving target in a medieval tiltyard*: quintain

tawny owl *alternative term*: brown owl

taxation □ *adjective*: fiscal □ *taxation of income*: direct taxation □ *taxation of expenditure*: indirect taxation □ *avoidance of tax liability by legal means*: tax avoidance □ *avoidance of tax liability by dishonest means*: tax evasion □ *former tax of 10% payable to the Church*: tithe □ *former tax levied upon every adult*: poll tax

teacher *teacher engaged to give a few lessons at each of several schools*: peripatetic

tear *adjective*: lachrymal

tear gas *alternative term*: CS gas

telephone □ *telephone link for a computer*: modem □ *direct emergency telephone line between heads of state*: hotline

temper *temper metal or glass by heating and cooling*: anneal

temperament □ *of a gloomy temperament*: saturnine □ *of a changeable temperament*: mercurial, volatile

temperature □ *temperature-controlled switch*: thermostat □ *cooling effect of the wind upon air temperature*: chill factor, wind-chill factor

ten *combining forms*: deca-, deci-

tent □ *Native American tent*: teepee, wigwam □ *large tent for flower shows etc.*: marquee □ *tent shrine used by the ancient Israelites*: tabernacle

territory *national policy of regaining former territories*: revanchism, irredentism

test *test of actors or musicians applying for work*: audition

thermometer □ *thermometer that plots the temperature on a revolving graph*: thermograph □ *thermometer for low temperatures*: cryometer □ *thermometer for high temperatures*: pyrometer □ *pair of thermometers that measure humidity*: psychrometer

thermonuclear bomb *alternative term*: fusion bomb

thigh bone *technical term*: femur

thing □ *thing as perceived by the senses*: phenomenon □ *thing as conceived by the mind*: noumenon

thinking □ *thinking in which problems are solved by logical deduction*: vertical thinking □ *thinking in which problems are solved by apparently illogical association of ideas*: lateral thinking

this side *combining form*: cis-

thoroughbred *thoroughbred horses*: bloodstock

thousand *combining forms*: kilo-, milli-

thousand million *combining form*: giga-

thousand millionth *combining form*: nano-

thousandth *combining form*: milli-

threat □ *threat made by a hostile military build-up*: sabre-rattling □ *constant threat of disaster*: sword of Damocles

three □ *combining forms*: ter-, tri- □ *adjectives*: ternary, treble, triple □ *occurring once in, or lasting for, three years*: triennial □ *Three Wise Men*: Magi □ *three in one*: triune □ *painting etc. covering three panels*: triptych □ *ancient ship with three banks of oars*: trireme □ *three-dimensional picture produced by lasers*: hologram

threshold *adjective*: liminal

ticket *person buying up tickets to resell at inflated prices*: tout

tide □ *tide that rises highest*: spring tide □ *tide that rises least*: neap tide □ *rising tide*: flood tide □ *falling tide*: ebb tide

tile □ *wooden exterior tile for roofs and walls*: shingle □ *curved interlocking roof tile*: pantile

time □ *combining forms*: chron(o)-, temp- □ *adjectives*: chronological, temporal □ *ticking device that helps musicians keep time*: metronome □ *law setting a time limit for initiating a prosecution*: statute of limitations

times over *combining form*: -fold

toast □ *thin crisp toast*: Melba toast □ *small piece of toast served on soup or a salad*: crouton

tomb □ *large and elaborate tomb*: mausoleum □ *inscription on a tomb*: epitaph

tongue □ *combining form*: gloss(o)- □ *adjectives*: glossal, lingual

tooth □ *combining forms*: dent-, odont-, -odont □ *adjective*: dental

□ *narrow tooth used to cut*: incisor
□ *broad tooth used to grind*: molar
□ *pointed tooth at front corner of mouth*:
canine □ *tooth emerging at the back of
the jaw during adulthood*: wisdom
tooth □ *tooth decay*: caries □ *bacterial
film on teeth*: plaque □ *hard yellowish
deposit forming on teeth*: tartar □ *alloy
used to fill teeth*: amalgam □ *teeth
present in a mouth*: dentition □ *toothed
wheel*: cog □ *toothed projection on a
wheel or cylinder*: sprocket

toothache *technical term*: odon-
talgia

touch *adjective*: tactile

tournament *tournament for
medieval knights*: joust

tower □ *stepped temple tower in
ancient Mesopotamia*: ziggurat
□ *ancient Scottish tower*: broch
□ *mosque tower*: minaret

trade *adjective*: mercantile
□ *trade restrictions imposed upon a
foreign country until it changes its policies*: sanctions

training *training mock-up of an aircraft's flight deck etc.*: simulator

transplant *drug given to prevent
rejection of a transplanted organ*:
immunosuppressor

treaty □ *formal acceptance of a
treaty*: accession □ *formal rejection of a
treaty*: denunciation □ *basic draft of a
treaty*: protocol

tree □ *combining forms*: arbor-,
dendro-, dendri-, silv(i)- □ *adjective*:
arboreal □ *type of tree that sheds its leaves
annually*: deciduous □ *type of tree that
retains its leaves*: evergreen □ *botanical
garden devoted to trees*: arboretum

tree ring *alternative term*: annual
ring

trellis □ *trellis along which the
branches of fruit trees are trained*:
espalier □ *trellis carrying climbing
plants over a garden path or arbour*:
pergola

trial and error *trial-and-error
method of solving problems*: heuristic

triangle □ *triangle with three equal
sides*: equilateral triangle □ *triangle
with two equal sides*: isosceles triangle
□ *triangle with unequal sides*: scalene
□ *longest side of a right-angled triangle*:
hypotenuse

tumour □ *combining forms*: onco-,
-cele, -oma □ *tumour that does not seriously threaten health*: benign
□ *tumour that spreads out of control
and returns after treatment*: malignant

tunnel *tunnel dug under an enemy's
defences*: sap

turn □ *combining forms*: trop-, -trop-,
-tropic □ *turn in office etc. assigned by
rote*: Buggins' turn □ *turn into stone*:
petrify □ *turn into bone*: ossify

turning □ *combining forms*: trop-,
-tropism, -tropy □ *turning force*: torque
□ *crucial turning point*: Rubicon,
watershed

twelve □ *combining form*: dodeca-
□ *adjectives*: duodecimal, duodenary
□ *twelve-tone musical system*: serial-
ism, dodecaphony

twenty *adjective*: vigesimal

twice □ *combining forms*: bi-, di-,
duo-, semi- □ *occurring twice a year*:
biannual, semi-annual

twilight *adjective*: crepuscular

twin □ *combining form*: zyg- □ *twin-
hulled boat*: catamaran

trust *adjective*: fiduciary

turpentine *adjective*: terebinthine

twins *astrological term*: gemini

two □ *combining forms*: ambi-, bi-,
di-, du(o)- □ *adjectives*: binary, double,
dual □ *cut in two*: bisect □ *having two
parts*: binary, dual □ *two-sided*: bilateral □ *living for, or occurring once
every, two years*: biennial □ *having two
chambers (of a parliament etc.)*: bicam-
eral □ *painting etc. covering two panels*:
diptych □ *two-faced*: duplicitous

U

unanimously *technical term*: nem. con.

unarmed combat *sports giving skill in unarmed combat*: martial arts

uncle *adjective*: avuncular

unconsciousness □ *long period of deep unconsciousness*: coma □ *state of unconsciousness with bodily rigidity*: catalepsy, catatonia

under *combining forms*: hypo-, infra-, sub-

underground □ *underground cemetery*: catacomb □ *underground railway in London*: tube □ *underground railway in Paris*: metro □ *underground railway in Rome*: metropolitana □ *underground railway in New York*: subway

undermine □ *undermine a fortification by tunnelling beneath it*: sap □ *undermine an organization by establishing agents within it*: infiltrate

understanding □ *sympathetic understanding*: empathy □ *informal diplomatic understanding negotiated between two nations*: ententecordiale

underwater □ *sealed underwater chamber for repair workers etc.*: caisson □ *underwater wall reaching to the surface to provide a dry area for repairs etc.*: coffer □ *divers' underwater vessel open at the bottom and filled with air*: diving bell □ *submarine-like vessel for deep underwater exploration*: bathyscaphe

unequal *combining form*: aniso-

unity *pursuit of unity between all Christian churches*: ecumenism

union □ *enforced union of Austria with Germany in 1938*: Anschluss □ *temporary union between political parties to form a government*: coalition □ *temporary union between business companies undertaking a large project*: consortium □ *secret union between firms to prevent competition*: cartel □ *secret union of purchasers at an auction etc. to force down prices*: ring

urinate *technical term*: micturate

urine □ *duct by which urine passes from the kidney to the bladder*: ureter □ *duct by which urine passes from the bladder to the kidney*: urethra □ *substance causing increased production of urine*: diuretic □ *tube inserted into the body for draining off urine*: catheter □ *horse and cattle urine*: stale

uterus □ *combining forms*: hyster(o)-, metr-, uter(o)- □ *surgical scraping of the uterus*: dilatation and curettage □ *vacuuming the uterus as a means of abortion*: vacuum aspiration □ *diagnostic sampling of fluid from a pregnant uterus*: amniocentesis □ *surgical removal of the uterus*: hysterectomy

V

V *V-shaped pattern*: chevron

vaccine *supplementary dose of vaccine*: booster

vagina □ *combining form*: colp- □ *membrane partially blocking the entrance of a virgin's vagina*: hymen □ *surgical cutting of the vagina to ease childbirth*: episiotomy

valley □ *valley in Scotland or Ireland*: glen □ *valley in Wales*: cwm □ *wooded valley*: dene

value *loss of value due to wear and tear*: depreciation

vegetarian *strict vegetarian who avoids all animal products*: vegan

vein □ *combining forms*: phleb(o)-, vene-, veni-, veno- □ *adjective*: venous □ *swollen vein in the legs*: varicose vein □ *in or into a vein*: intravenous □ *surgical opening of a vein*: phlebotomy, venesection

Venice □ *former ruler of Venice*: Doge □ *small Venetian passenger boat*: gondola □ *song of Venetian gondoliers*: barcarole □ *Venetian water bus*: vaporetto

Venus *Greek name*: Aphrodite

verse □ *metrical analysis of verse*: scansion □ *theory and practice of versification*: prosody □ *metrical unit in versification*: foot □ *central pause in a line of verse*: caesura

viceroy *adjective*: viceregal

vine □ *cultivation of vines*: viticulture □ *insect that destroys vines*: phylloxera

vinegar *adjective*: acetic

virgin *astrological term*: virgo

virgin birth *technical term*: parthenogenesis

voice □ *combining forms*: phon(o)-, -phone, -phony □ *adjective*: vocal

vote □ *chairman's vote to decide a tied poll*: casting vote □ *vote given to exclude a candidate*: blackball □ *person empowered to cast another's vote*: proxy □ *parliamentary vote*: division

voting □ *voting strategy aimed at defeating an otherwise strong candidate or party*: tactical voting □ *study of voting patterns etc.*: psephology

W

wagon *wagon for condemned prisoners in the French Revolution*: tumbril

wake *signal for waking in an army camp etc.*: reveille

walking *combining form*: -grade

walking stick □ *walking stick with a handle that makes a seat*: shooting stick □ *walking stick's metal tip*: ferrule

wall □ *adjectives*: □ *of a building*: mural □ *in the body*: parietal □ *building's wall of two layers with a gap between*: cavity wall □ *layer of cement etc. on a wall surface*: rendering □ *row of spikes or broken glass set on a wall's top*: cheval-de-frise □ *rounded bricks etc. at a wall's top*: coping □ *watertight wall dividing the interior of a ship etc.*: bulkhead □ *wall of a body cavity*: paries

wandering □ *wandering in search of trade*: itinerant □ *wandering in search of adventure*: errant

war □ *adjective*: martial □ *of a war waged without nuclear weapons*: conventional □ *person favouring recourse to war*: hawk □ *person avoiding recourse to war*: dove

wasp *adjective*: vespine

water □ *combining forms*: aqua-, aqui-, hydr- □ *adjectives*: aqueous, aquatic □ *operated by water*: hydraulic □ *temporary vertical water pipe with a tap*: standpipe

water-carrier *astrological term*: aquarius

water on the brain *technical term*: hydrocephalus

weakness □ *minor weakness of character etc.*: foible □ *weak spot*: Achilles' heel

wealth □ *wealth or its pursuit seen as a corrupting influence*: Mammon □ *source of wealth*: bonanza □ *fabulous place of great wealth*: eldorado

wear *gradual wearing down*: attrition, erosion

weather □ *low-pressure weather system*: cyclone □ *high-pressure weather system*: anticyclone □ *line on a weather map linking places with the same atmospheric pressure*: isobar □ *line on a weather map linking places with the same temperature*: isotherm □ *balloon-borne radio transmitter sending weather information*: radiosonde

weaving □ *threads running lengthways in weaving*: weft, woof □ *threads running crossways in weaving*: warp □ *cylinder holding a weaver's thread*: bobbin □ *double-ended bobbin used on a mechanical loom*: shuttle

week *adjective*: hebdomadal

well *well in which the water rises by natural pressure through a borehole*: artesian well

Welsh □ *adjectives*: Cambrian, Cymric □ *Welsh Nationalist Party*: Plaid Cymru □ *Welsh competition for poets and musicians*: eisteddfod □ *Welsh poetry sung in counterpoint to a traditional harp melody*: penillion

west *adjective*: occidental

West Indian □ *West Indian song improvised on a topical theme*: calypso □ *West Indian popular music with a strong secondary beat*: reggae □ *West Indian sorcery*: obeah, voodoo

whiplash injury *technical term*: hyperextension-hyperflexion injury

white □ *combining forms*: leuc(o)-, leuk(o)- □ *white-skinned person*: Caucasian □ *person or animal having white skin and hair due to a pigment defect*: albino

white ant *alternative term*: termite

white whale *alternative term*: beluga

whooping cough *technical term*: pertussis

widow □ *widow holding a title from her late husband*: dowager □ *estate etc. left a widow by her late husband's will*: jointure

wife *adjective*: uxorial

will □ *adjectives*: wish: volitional, voluntary □ *legal document*: testamentary □ *person making a will*: testator □ *person appointed to carry out the terms of a will*: executor □ *gift made in a will*: bequest, legacy □ *person receiving a gift from a will*: beneficiary □ *legal authentication of a will*: probate

wildebeest *alternative term*: gnu

wind □ *combining form*: anemo- □ *instrument for measuring wind speed*: anemometer □ *scale for wind velocities*: Beaufort scale □ *build-up of gas in the digestive tract causing the breaking of wind*: flatulence □ *humid southerly wind in southern Europe*: sirocco □ *cold northerly wind blowing down the Rhone*: mistral □ *warm southerly wind blowing off the Alps*: föhn

window □ *adjective*: fenestral □ *window made of vertically sliding glazed sections*: sash window □ *side-hinged window*: casement □ *small window over a door etc.*: fanlight □ *small diamond-shaped pane of window-glass*: quarry □ *ornamental stonework subdividing a window*: tracery □ *angled wall-opening for a window*: embrasure

windpipe *technical term*: trachea

wine □ *combining form*: vin- □ *adjective*: vinous □ *spice and warm wine*: mull □ *wine expert*: oenologist □ *wine merchant*: vintner □ *wine waiter*: sommelier □ *charge made for serving the customer's own wine at a restaurant*: corkage

wing □ *combining forms*: pter(o)-, -pter- □ *adjective*: alar

winter □ *adjectives*: hibernal, hiemal □ *sleep through the winter*: hibernate

wire *wires used to start a car from the battery of another*: jump leads

wisdom tooth *technical term*: third molar

witch □ *gathering of witches*: coven □ *witch's attendant spirit*: familiar □ *male witch*: warlock

without *combining forms*: a-, an-

witness □ *witness's evidence given in court*: testimony □ *sworn statement made by a witness out of court*: deposition □ *lying by a witness underoath*: perjury

wolf □ *adjective*: lupine □ *person who changes into a wolf*: lycanthrope, were-wolf

woman □ *combining forms*: gyn(o)-, gynaeco- □ *adjective*: feminine *woman with intellectual or literary pretensions*: bluestocking □ *arrogant and domineering woman*: prima donna □ *woman whose husband is often absent*: grass widow □ *party for women only*: hen party □ *hatred of women*: mysogyny

wood □ *combining forms*: ligno-, ligni-, xylo-, xyli- □ *wooden plate*: trencher □ *ornamental inlay of wood, ivory, etc.*: marquetry

womb *technical term*: uterus

word □ *combining forms*: lexi-, logo-, logi-, -log-, -nym □ *adjective*: verbal □ *study of the meaning of words*: semantics □ *study of the forms of words*: morphology

word-blindness *technical term*: alexia

work □ *combining form*: erg(o)- □ *belief that work has an intrinsic moral value*: work ethic □ *person addicted to work*: workaholic

works *complete works of an artist etc.*: oeuvre, corpus

worm □ *combining form*: vermi- □ *adjectives*: vermicular, vermiform

worship *combining form*: -latry

wrist □ *technical term*: carpus □ *adjective*: carpal

wrong *combining forms*: caco-, mal-, mis-

X-rays □ *study or use of X-rays*: radiography □ *X-ray of a section through the body*: tomography □ *X-ray of body tissue*: computerized axial tomography □ *treatment of cancer etc. by X-rays*: radiotherapy

youth *artistic creations of one's youth, often later suppressed as immature*: juvenilia

Z

zigzag *zigzag course taken by a vessel sailing into the wind*: tacking, traverse

zinc *coat a metal with zinc*: galvanize